USA TODAY BESTSELLING AUTHOR

KAREN TOMLINSON

Join Karen's newsletter :
HERE.

Follow Karen's Mighty Network Here: Karen Tomlinson's Shadow Sentinels.

BEGINNINGS

KAREN TOMLINSON

SHADOW SENTINELS

BEGINNINGS

For Judi.
Thank you!
***Your honesty, suggestions, and hard work have helped me make Ember and
Connor's story amazing! x***

FOREWORD

This series is adult paranormal romance. It contains graphic language, explicit sexual scenes and a hot alpha male shifter. (well, several when the series gets going!)

The heroine is not sweet and innocent and is kick-ass enough to bring this alpha to his knees.

If this sounds like your cup of tea hold onto your knickers and dive in!

This book is written by a UK author and has been extensively edited. As such, it contains some colloquial sayings and grammar, (Realise vs realize) English slang, dialect and other quirky sayings that have been intentionally included to make your reading experience unique.

If you still manage to find any of those pesky typos please email the author NOT AMAZON so that corrections can be made without upsetting sales. Just let me know your a reader so I don't think you are sending dodgy links;)

This is a four book series, so get comfy and get ready for the ride!

Many thanks dearest reader, for supporting me by reading! If you have time, please leave a review on Amazon, Goodreads and Bookbub. It really helps with visibility.

Now go and enjoy Ember and Connor! XX

email@karentomlinson.com

CHAPTER 1

mber

"HIT HARDER!" Authority laced Rawson's deep voice. His intense eyes narrowed, assessing how far he could push me.

Grunting, I breathed heavily through my nose, needing to stop and catch my breath, but I nodded, not willing to show any weakness to him—or anyone.

Cain Rawson was in his mid-thirties, lean, fit, and one tough son of a bitch alpha. He was the one who pulled me off the streets and offered me a safe place to stay. Yeah, he was officially my saviour—my *married* saviour. And that was cool with me. I mean, sure, he was *hot*; six feet three inches of ripped muscles, confidence, and when he wasn't being tough and bossy—kindness. But "hot" wasn't how I saw him. He was my lifeline, along with Lyss, his wife, who was one of the sweetest and most beautiful people, both inside and out, that I'd ever met.

"Now!" His grey eyes flashed.

I jumped, my heart banging in my chest. I gave him a dark scowl, but he just raised his brows. My arms shook, and my chest heaved, but I took a deep breath, curling my fingers inside the training gloves. Then, as instructed, I twisted my body and dropped my shoulder exactly as he had taught me and smashed my fist into the pad.

"Now front jab!"

I did.

"Reverse punch!"

I did.

Noisy breaths escaped from my mouth and nose, and sweat dripped down my face and neck, soaking my cropped sports top. I was no stranger to fighting or hard physical workouts. I loved them. But the training regimen Rawson had me doing, after my classes at the Supernatural Bureau's Academy ended, was exhausting. Not that I'd tell him. I would never tell a soul if I was struggling. No matter your age, if you showed weakness, you became prey. The vipers of this world struck when they thought you were down and vulnerable, and I had vowed, years ago, I would never be vulnerable again.

"Now, kick! Roundhouse. Go!"

The pain of my past drove me just as it always did. It kept me going every single day. It gave me purpose; to be the strongest, fastest and most vicious version of me that I could possibly be. Lifting my chin, I adjusted my body weight and turned on my standing foot. Lifting my knee high, I swung my leg. *Slam!* My instep connected with the pad. The force rocked Rawson's big arm sideways, even if it was only a couple of inches. Before I could even snap my strike back, he was ordering me into my next move.

"Spin. Back kick. Now, Ember!"

Sweet Jesus, he was relentless.

My kick landed, and I spun my head around, bringing my body and the other leg with it. Using the momentum, I smashed my heel into the pad with a solid whack, a grunt exploding from my lungs with the effort.

"Well, look at you. A regular firecracker now, aren't you?" drawled a deep voice from behind me.

My whole body instantly stiffened, going on alert. Gods, but I loved and hated that deep, smooth voice. I whirled around, my heart thumping even harder in my chest. Connor, another one of Rawson's strays, stood there grinning at me. He lounged against the training room door frame, looking sexy as sin. His bright blue eyes twinkled, wrinkling slightly at the corners. He was too near Rawson's age to be considered a foster son; still, Rawson had pulled him off the streets and given him a home and a purpose—one that I'd heard he was good at; really, really good at, to the point he now ran his own squad of agents. The fact he was a total asshat while he worked at being a top notch, undercover Supernatural Bureau of Investigation agent didn't matter to me— not anymore. Even so, my stomach lurched at the sight of him, and I was glad my cheeks were already flushed and sweaty. At least I had an excuse when they heated further under his way too intense gaze.

"Piss off!"

Connor might be beautiful and tie me in knots, but as soon as he opened his mouth, my hackles went up. He'd moved out of Rawson's a few years ago, and on the rare occasions I had seen him since, it was as if he always found me amusing in some way; like he found all my efforts to be independent and strong a joke.

"Arsehole," I mumbled under my breath. And he was. I had been an idiot to trust him—to rely on him in any way in the past. I had learned my lesson though...

"Hey! Language! No swearing in my house." Rawson tapped my temple with the focus pad.

I glared at him. "That wasn't swearing, that was name calling. Anyway, you let him swear." And I pointed at Connor with my gloved fist.

Both men laughed and exchanged a look. I just rolled my eyes at that typical show of male solidarity.

"Yeah, but only because I can't stop him opening that big mouth." Rawson flashed his perfect white teeth in a wide grin. "And once he does, which is a given, considering how much he likes the sound of his own voice, it means I can kick him out on his arse."

Connor's brows raised and his chin dipped. "Really. I'd like to see you try, *old man.*"

"Bro' there'd be no trying, and you'd be out fast enough to make even your thick head spin. Besides, I'm not old. I'm only thirty three, you shit."

I tried not to smile at Rawson's obvious disgruntlement, but just barely succeeded.

Connor just shook his head. He grinned, but kept quiet. It was true, it would be one hell of a fight, and I wasn't really sure who would win if it came to it. Rawson wasn't just any old alpha shifter; he was one of the SBI's top agents—and had at least twelve years experience to Connor's seven.

I suppose, technically, Connor was my foster brother. Rawson had been in his early twenties when he and Lyss had convinced Connor it would be safer to live with them than to live in London's back alleys and doorways. Like me, he had shadows in his past, ones that had shaped who he was now.

We were really close once...or so I'd thought.

It was hard for me to tear my attention away from him, even though he wasn't really a part of my life anymore, and I promised myself I wouldn't pine after him any longer. Connor was always good looking, but now he was a full grown man with broad shoulders, a slim waist and arms that made the girls in my training programme drool. Yep, he was hot as hell.

As a young girl, my hormones had gone into overdrive every time he was near. He was the first boy I'd ever spent time with, and I'd secretly worshipped the ground he walked on. I'd trained my skinny, undernourished body so hard, not just to keep up with him, but more to try and impress him. I'd even fooled myself into thinking I mattered to him. He used to come into my room when I screamed through my nightmares, my body burning up from the inside. He'd wake me, and even hold me until I stopped shaking.

I snarled at the memory and went back to hitting the pad. One, two. One, one, two. One, one, two—kick...

For years Connor had been my rock. I'd even been his when I'd sat with him when he whimpered in the darkness of the night. Neither of us discussed what demons haunted us, and by unspoken agreement, neither of us asked. We simply took care of each other. That's why it had hurt so much when I realised I'd become insignificant. The stronger and more gorgeous he became, the more popular he was; and the less time he had for me.

Eventually, I just learned to deal with my own nightmares.

Distancing myself from Connor was necessary for my own sanity. I was still a loner, just as I had always been. Girls at the academy drooled over Connor all of the time, and there was no way I could trust that any of them truly wanted my friendship. Letting Connor back into my heart, even a little bit, would be a mistake.

The whack of the pad upside my head threw me right back into the training room.

"Fuck!" I hissed, shaking my head.

"Well, concentrate then! And don't swear..."

"Yeah, swearing is very unattractive in girls," Connor said, his shoulders shaking as he chuckled.

I tried not to notice just how wide and toned those shoulders were under his form fitting black tee shirt.

"You still here, jackass? And I'm not a *girl*."

Connor ignored me. Instead, he crossed his large arms over his impressive pecs and clasped his chin between his forefinger and thumb, raising one brow. "Right, well, seems to me, girls, or women, or females, or whatever, have far more important uses for their mouths than swearing." He smirked and winked.

I rolled my eyes. "You're disgusting."

"Oh, I don't know. They don't seem to think so." He waggled his brows even more.

"Oh my gods, you are such an arrogant shit!" I snarled, then spun, smashing a punch into the pad Rawson still held.

Rawson lowered the pad. "Okay, that's enough for today." He pulled at the velcro on my gloves, undid them, and yanked them off. The stink of old sweat drifted up from the glove lining. "And I agree, he is an arrogant shit." He winked at me, and I smirked. "So? You gonna tell me why you're really here?" Rawson glanced at Connor, his eyes sharp and focused.

I looked back over my shoulder. Connor stared at Rawson, his face dark, his eyes missing the sparkle that had been there a moment ago. This wasn't a social call then, and he didn't want an audience.

I smiled sweetly, though it hurt to know he didn't trust me enough to talk in front of me. "If you ask me nicely, maybe I'll leave you two to whisper sweet nothings in each other's ears. Otherwise, I'm staying right here." And I crossed my arms over my chest and raised my chin. Being defiant to Connor was ingrained in my blood.

Rawson chuckled at the same time as Connor. Connor's face cleared and his azure eyes glinted, his mouth curling up at the corner.

"Someone's sure gonna have their hands full when you're ready to use that mouth for something other than swearing, Firecracker."

"Yeah? Well, it won't be you." For some reason I was really pissed off at his words. *Does he really still see me as an innocent little girl? Not that I care. But, still...* "And what makes you think I haven't already?" I smirked and batted my eyelashes, crossing my arms over my chest just under my boobs.

For a moment, there was silence. Connor's jaw tightened, and darkness seeped into his eyes.

I swallowed, hard. I'd never seen Connor's wolf, but I'd heard about it. An ebony creature, with the sort of power that could bring even the biggest wolves to their knees. And, damned if that's not what I could see glaring out from his eyes at me right now.

Thick, powerful waves of...something...washed over me. *I feel like I should kneel...* My wolf cowered down, trying to pull me with her...

Oh, no you don't!

I knew Connor was powerful, but I never realised he was a Prime! Though it made perfect sense that he would be an alpha that other alphas bowed to.

He uncrossed his arms from his chest, his biceps rippling with cut muscle. He inhaled deeply, his nostrils flaring. My heart skipped a few beats, and my stomach clenched. He was scent reading me. *Shit!* The blue from his eyes was swallowed whole by an obsidian gaze that burrowed into me, seeing my lie. "Because, Firecracker, I know you, and I can scent that you haven't touched another male, with your mouth or any other part of your body."

If I thought my face was hot before, it was blazing now. I was speechless. He might sense I was far more innocent than I pretended, but that didn't mean I was some shrinking violet, or that he knew me as well as he thought anymore. I didn't cower from anyone or anything—especially him. I survived from age six on the streets of London until Rawson took me in at twelve. And I did that by being smart, learning how to fight, and yeah, I've killed more than once, too. I also learned very early on never to show fear or the human and supernatural predators that lurked in the shadows would pounce. And Connor was a predator; a top-of-the-food-chain predator. Instead of cowering as he called me out, I straightened my spine, tilted my chin up, curled my upper lip and held his eyes.

The air pulsed around me, causing goosebumps to burst all over my bare skin. A wonderful spicy scent drifted up my nose and I inhaled, deeply. Gods, what was that? My heart raced and my belly clenched. A sudden wave of warmth, pooled at the apex of my thighs. For just a moment, as my wolf strained to break free, I forgot we weren't alone.

Connor tilted his head, and his eyes narrowed, his fingers tightening into fists as he swallowed hard.

A loud cough from behind made me jump, breaking the spell between us. I blinked rapidly. What the hell had just happened? At eighteen years old, I knew I was near what everyone else thought was my first shift—my *Primis*, but in truth, my first shift had come soon after my parents had been killed. I had done it alone, in the dark, screaming—and no matter how much my wolf wanted freedom, I sure as hell wasn't letting her out. Not again. At least, not yet.

Connor's muscles were tense as he watched me, the veins in his neck popping despite his relaxed posture against the door frame. Rawson coughed again, muttering something under his breath. All I could concentrate on was the darkness in Connor's eyes as it faded into a sea of blue until only obsidian flecks remained. Even when his eyes were that beautiful azure colour again, Connor's face remained dark, his jaw clenched.

The air between us burned with—something. I dropped my gaze, confusion halting my smart mouth. I had no idea what had just passed between us. For a few seconds, I just gathered my composure, feeling his gaze burn into me. Taking a breath, I plastered a scowl on my face, looked up—and did a double take.

Connor's full lips were pulled back in a grin, that self-assurance and cockiness back in place. "Like I said, Firecracker, a handful."

Emotions tumbled through me. Part of me wanted to deck him, part of me wanted to kiss him. Although, if he kept on laughing at me, I was going to kick him squarely in his junk. My gaze dropped to that part of his anatomy of their own accord. My body heated, like someone had lit a fire in my blood. What would it be like to touch him; to have him touch me, his fingers stroking... My cheeks flamed. Oh, Christ! I shouldn't be thinking about Connor like this! He was way out of my league, and way too experienced to bother with someone like me. Besides, I knew better than to trust him. He'd left me once, he'd leave me again.

His gaze met mine, and his pupils darkened again like someone had dropped ink into them. His intense, burning attention travelled down my sweat coated body, right over my cropped top and gym leggings which didn't hide much of my skinny frame. A low growl came from his throat. My blood heated at the pure desire in that sound. It set my mind ablaze, leaving my body achy and shaking, and my throat parched. *I need to touch him. He's the only one who can stop this thirst, this ache...* I swayed towards him, until a large, firm hand on my shoulder stopped me.

"Connor, that's enough!" Rawson snarled viciously, glaring at Connor. Connor stopped that deep resonant growl, and forced his attention away from me. He inhaled deeply, exhaled slowly, and then shrugged like it was no big deal.

Rawson shook his head, his hand dropping from my shoulder. With a grim look, he turned and stalked over to the training room cupboard, stuffing the fighting pads in a canvas sack so they could be stored away.

"Em! Hit the shower!" he yelled, his voice muffled from inside the cupboard. "I need to talk to Connor, alone."

I shrugged in acknowledgement. "Fine by me." I was still unsettled by the heady scent that lingered in my nostrils. I barged past Connor, heat from his arm searing my skin. My breath caught in my throat. That spicy scent hit me again and the urge to stop and touch him, to run my fingers over those arms to see if they felt as good as they looked, was almost overwhelming. My wolf whined, sniffing the air and pushing against my skin. Hands fisted, I clenched my jaw, then deliberately turned my head away and walked past him.

I paused on the stairs to try and regain some steadiness in my legs. "What the fuck was that?" I overheard Rawson snap just as the training room door slammed shut.

❧

"Argh!" I threw myself on my bed, covering my eyes with both of my fore-arms. Blood oozed into my mouth. *Damn!* I rolled my eyes. I'd bitten my bottom lip while stomping back to my room. Slapping my palms on my bed, my hand brushed a soft pink bunny that Lyss had bought me years ago. I smiled. Lyss was so sweet. When I first arrived in her home, and she said she wanted me to have some nice 'girly' things, I hated the thought of anyone buying me anything. It would leave me feeling indebted, and back then, I was determined I was going to run away before these people got the chance to hurt me or let me down. Secretly, I loved that someone cared enough to buy me a pink rabbit, even if it was hideous. It was now one of my favourite possessions. I picked it up and held it above me, looking into its shiny blue eyes. "He's such a dick."

"He won't answer," said an amused voice from my doorway.

I looked at Lyss and rolled my eyes. "I know."

She grinned. "But I agree with you."

I set Mr Bunny down onto the bed at my side. "You do?"

Lyss walked across my carpet, pink of course, and lowered herself to sit elegantly on my bed. I hid a scowl, envying her walk. It really wasn't fair, I decided, also noticing how tight her shirt was across her generous breasts. Some women had everything going for them. Lyss was tall and pretty, with full lips that looked like she'd been kissing Rawson for hours, which she probably had...ew! Where did that come from? She had cat-like green eyes and a figure that had curves and dips most women would sell their souls to possess.

"Of course. The bunny's always been a dick." She grinned at me and winked.

I snorted a laugh. "Mr Bunny's not the problem."

"I know, sweetness." She laid down beside me. Her blonde curly hair spilled over the bed and her delicate perfume tickled my nose. It was nice—a smell that I now equated with safety.

I ignored the 'sweetness' label. We both knew I was as far from sweet as you could get.

"Remember, Connor has been with us since he was a teenager, only a few years older than you were, and he's always been a handful. It was clear early on that he was a powerful alpha, and that he was almost too old to learn control. I even tried to persuade Cain to send him to the bureau for assessment."

I swallowed hard. An assessment by the SBI meant they would decide if a shifter was too dangerous to live in society—if they failed the assessment they were terminated.

"But my man didn't want to give up on him." Lyss smiled and cocked her head. "I'm glad he didn't. With Cain's help, Connor's managed to beat his anger issues, and controls his demons—most of the time. I know he's arrogant, but it's because he can be; he's good looking, successful, powerful, has a body to die for and can handle himself in almost any given situation. That, along with a heavy dose of self-confidence and Prime Alpha vibes is a heady combination for any girl whose hormones are awake and buzzing. But...yeah, he knows it and that makes him a bit of a dick. One day, maybe he'll get his heart broken and realise you can't treat people like shit—well, women anyway." She shrugged. "Or he'll meet someone who can see beyond that alpha male bullshit to the scared little boy, the one who fights attachments, who's reluctant to trust; remember, he's been abandoned in the past..."

I sighed and sat up. Rubbing my face, I wondered if Lyss knew that, with those last words, she was describing me. "I don't care." Connor wouldn't ever let anyone that close—certainly not me.

"Sure you don't." Lyss cocked a brow. "But *you* are already beautiful, far more than you realise. And dicks like him will be chasing you wherever you go. You'll be able to have your pick of dicks."

"Oh good gods!" I exclaimed, shaking my head. "I can't believe you just said that...*dicks will be chasing me?* That's just so wrong! I really don't want to be chased by dicks...like ever..." I pretended to shudder. "Great. Now I have an image of big phallus thingies chasing me up the street! Ah! It's going to give me nightmares, and it's your fault!" I laughed and shuddered while pushing away the sudden image of Connor's gaze running over my body.

Lyss fell into a fit of giggles. "Oh, your face! I knew that would cheer you up."

I held my palms up in surrender. "Yeah, well it worked. Consider me cheered up. You can go now. I'm going to hit the shower and try not to have nightmares about dicks chasing me." And, although I was trying for disgust, I giggled, again. It was true, Lyss always did manage to cheer me up, no matter what happened in my day.

CHAPTER 2

mber

"Hey!" I yelled.

My books and pencil case hit the floor, their contents spilling everywhere. Feet kicked my stuff down the corridor, their owners completely oblivious. I didn't normally carry such things around with me, now that I'd finished my exams. But today was when I cleaned out my locker and left this school to start the bureau's agent training programme full time. It was a five year intense programme of physical pain, advanced weapons training, placements, and fieldwork. I really wasn't looking forward to it. Working in a team, relying on others and having them rely on me was not my idea of fun, but there was another reason for going through with it...even if that other reason was a dick undercover SBI agent. Except people like these assholes who just sent my stuff flying onto the floor were also going in the training programme.

"What d'you do that for?" I was not in the mood for queen bitch today.

Shannon was one of those privileged, plastic, pretty girls with gorgeous hair and perfect teeth, who used too much makeup; but it wasn't her looks that made me want to smash my fist in her face; it was just...her. My fingers curled, and my teeth actually creaked, my jaw was clenched so tightly. I wanted to do it, I truly did. Only respect for Rawson and Lyss stopped me.

The breath I inhaled and then exhaled slowly calmed the storm in my belly. I would not embarrass them by getting kicked out of the agency training programme before it had even started. And that's what would happen if I attacked another student. I'd worked damn hard to hit top marks at this academy, and I wouldn't waste all that hard work on the likes of her.

Shannon's big brown eyes narrowed, and her head tilted. She was studying me. Her eyes glinted amber for a split second, her wolf shining through, right before she kicked one of my books into my face. A shifter's kick is far more powerful than any human's, and does far more damage.

A sharp pain stung beneath my right eye. I grunted. *Don't do it. Don't do it,* I repeated to myself, closing my eyes as I struggled to temper my anger while centering the heat that surged through me. Claws itched to burst from under my fingernails. Yeah, I was a shifter, but no one, and I mean no one, knew what the other spirit in my soul was—not even me. I forced her behind a wall in my soul, my own fear caging her. I might not know what she was, but I knew she was destructive, and dangerous, and I couldn't control her if she soared free. Right now, the lupine side of me strained to get to Shannon and rip her throat out. Squeezing my eyes shut, all I could think about was that I couldn't release my wolf. I'd planned on going through my fake *Primis* change alone. Mainly because it would be my second change, still painful, but not as slow or agonising as the first, and if anyone recognised it wasn't a true *Primis,* it would raise too many questions about why I'd changed into a wolf at such a young age.

"Aw, look, the runt is trying not to cry," Shannon taunted.

My eyes flew open. *Runt? Cry?* I don't cry. It was true though, even at eighteen I was still skinny, with no tits or arse. I grinned inside. But what I did have in spades was anger and a viciousness that I'd kept hidden all these years from everyone here.

The stupid girls that shadowed Shannon giggled at her words.

Maybe I'd punch their lights out, too...

"W-what?" I stuttered. As always, when my anger reared its ugly head, my blood heated to the point I could barely speak, my throat burning as if I might spew fire.

"You. You're an ugly, skinny reject that nobody wants." She leaned in closer, her eyes narrowing. "Even your foster parents didn't want you. I heard my dad say Rawson only hunted you down because he'd been ordered to bring you in. My dad wants you where the SBI can watch you. And he's Rawson's boss, so..." She shrugged her shoulders, but her eyes glinted looking me up and down and her top lip curled. "Why does my dad want you so badly? What makes you so special...? Oh yeah, and when Connor came round last night to fuck me...Oops..." She giggled and put her hand over her mouth, her eyes wide and innocent. The stupid girls behind her tittered again. "Oh well, the cat's out of the bag now, though I don't think even my father knows about our relationship. I guess he thought Connor fucking his eldest daughter, and then killing her, would be enough." A smirk curled her painted mouth. "Connor laughed at how pathetic you are with your crush on him, and how he likes to wind you up by flirting with you."

My face flamed. "I don't have a crush on that imbecile!" I swiped at the blood beneath my eye.

She leaned back, folding her arms under her ample chest.

"Oh, no? I've seen the way you look at him when he's in the training rooms with us; like you want to rip his clothes off and ride him like Ava always used to."

"Gods, you're disgusting. And how do you know what your sister and Connor did, anyway? Did you spy on them or something?"

Rather than be embarrassed, queen bitch just smirked and shrugged. "Maybe. Or maybe he showed me."

Pain lanced my heart. He wouldn't stoop so low, not when he could have any woman he wanted. Besides, I had no reason, or right, to be jealous over who Connor slept with or spent his time with. Except, I'd always thought of him as mine, especially when he could soothe my anxiety with a mere touch. He always convinced me everything was okay; that *I'd* be okay. And I always allowed myself to believe him, trusting him almost as much as I trusted Rawson and Lyss, which admittedly wasn't completely, but it was still trust. Except, I hardly saw him now, unless he was in the huge training halls at the academy. Or like last month, when he dropped in at home to see Rawson. He gave up on me a long time ago, and left me to fight through my demons alone. He left me.

I bent down to retrieve my stuff, totally over this conversation. My fingers curled around a pen and plucked it from the ground.

Shannon squatted down in front of me. Her little black miniskirt moved up her legs revealing her legs right up to her pink panties. I turned my head and glared at the floor. She really had no shame.

"Bet I can get him to fuck me tonight, too…"

I froze, but my blood didn't, it boiled. Fury slammed through me. Connor was better than her! Or was he? I broke out into a cold sweat at the thought that he might want Shannon.

"Mmm, all those hard, big muscles covering my body." She licked her lips and groaned, her eyes fluttering shut. "All those alpha vibes he has going on." She touched her panties between her legs. "The way his dick…"

"Enough!" Fire surged forth from her cage, heating my skin as my fist connected with Shannon's chin. Her teeth snapped together with a loud crack, and she was airborne. Blood spurted from between those pouty lips. Her stupid friends screamed, but none of them ran to help her. They just stood there—gaping.

I froze too, hoping I hadn't killed her. I knew my strength when my wolf was riled, even if no one else did. Crap! Now I was going to end up in one holy heap of trouble. It was my last bloody day, and she'd wrecked my chances at the bureau! Bitch!

Everyone around us stopped and stared. I could feel the weight of their attention. I forced Fire, as I called that inner raging spirit, away, and snarled at them all. It was always the way; when you were being picked on no one gave a shit, but if you fought back you were suddenly under a spotlight.

"Fight!" Someone shouted. A stampede of feet and shouts came our way.

I cocked my head and straightened, staring at my prey. The animal in me stirred at the smell of her blood. Fire watched from her cage, ready to jump to my aid, even as I did my best to keep her confined.

"What the hell is going on here!?" yelled one of the teachers. "Everyone stay exactly where you are!" A geeky looking man in his mid-twenties pushed through the crowd of teenagers. He lowered himself with surprising grace and ease, his knees bumping against the tiles. His eyes narrowed, and his lips pressed tightly together as he shook Shannon's shoulders. Queen bitch moaned, spitting blood when he shook her harder.

My attention zoned in on the burn on her jaw. Damn! How was I going to explain that one? The strength I could pass off as my wolf, but the burn? That was another thing entirely.

The geeky teacher took his glasses off and looked at me with wide brown eyes. "You!" He pointed at me.

I jumped.

"Get yourself to the head's office."

I didn't move. I couldn't.

"Right now!" he yelled.

It wasn't that I was being deliberately rude, I was just frozen, freaking out about how I was going to explain causing a burn. No shifters had that kind of supernatural power.

There was an odd pulse of energy. *That's weird.* I looked around, but no one else seemed to notice it.

"Everyone else, clear out! Get to class!" the teacher bellowed in a voice that didn't suit his geekiness at all.

A sigh exploded from me. I knew I'd just fucked myself out of going into the Bureau training programme. I grabbed my stuff from the floor, quickly picking up the stray pieces from my pencil case. Starting my walk of shame to the head's office, I pushed through the crowd of chattering teenagers and got the hell out of there.

Shannon wasn't lying when she said Rawson worked for her dad. Shannon's father was the head of the British branch of the SBI. I licked my dry lips. And I had just knocked her on her arse, probably ruining all her wonderful dental work.

My stomach turned, the lunch I'd just eaten like a brick in my belly. I tried to control my pounding heart and took some deep breaths. I'd not been in trouble for fighting in years...maybe that would go in my favour...

I hoped Rawson wouldn't be blamed for my behaviour. Doherty seemed to enjoy finding any reason to punish Rawson or Connor, especially if I was somehow involved. Oh gods, they might redeploy Rawson somewhere else, or sack him, or....

I was close to hyperventilating. Making myself breathe deeply was the only way to calm myself and to think sensibly. It was true the SBI was a large, powerful and world wide beast, but the British headquarters was in Kent, on the outskirts of London, and I reasoned it would be ridiculous to move an experienced agent because of an altercation at the academy.

The kids in the academy were children of bureau employees, and most were shifters, or they had some kind of supernatural heritage. We were all watched closely by the staff. When we reached our final year, as I have, they gave us a choice: go into a civilian training programme, where they ensured shifters were safe to live among human society, or try out for the agency training programme at the SBI.

It was hard to swallow my angry tears as I marched into the head's office. I really didn't want to get Rawson in trouble, but I'd allowed Shannon to goad me, and Doherty might take it out on Rawson. With a bored expression, the head's secretary pointed to an old, worn out chair. I sat and folded my arms over my books in my lap, stewing over what might happen next. It was at least ten minutes until the head mistress called me in.

I followed her rigid form through the half glass door and stopped in front of her desk.

Dressed in a mid-calf straight skirt and a tweed jacket, with her hair in a tight bun, the headmistress looked severe and proper. I itched to turn around and walk back out; after all, I didn't owe this school a thing, and this was my last day. Only the thought of Rawson's disappointment kept me from walking.

She looked at me coldly. "Sit."

I did. I sat quietly, not saying a word while the woman ranted at me. To be honest, it was almost too easy to switch off. She wasn't scary, no matter how she dressed. Seeing homeless tramps pulled apart by red eyed, shadowy figures; women hypnotised by glamoured fae and coerced into performing sexual acts; having to eat the remains of rotting animals to survive as a six-year-old, now *those* were scary. I shuddered. I'd seen death and killing and much, much, more in the years before Rawson had found me, but I'd also learned how to hide, how to make myself small and use the shadows to become invisible. I'd learned how to fight and even how to kill, all before my seventh birthday. Just like many kids who lived below the surface veneer of tall buildings, flashy cars, glamorous stores and chain coffee shops, I learned how to survive; not live, just stay alive. Most of the time I could hide that feral part of me away—but sometimes it reared its ugly head, and Shannon had really pushed my buttons. Her and Connor together? No way... I snarled, my skin prickling.

I was busy cracking my knuckles when the door creaked open and that heady woodsy scent I constantly dreamed about blasted my senses. My whole body went rigid and on alert. Connor!

"Ah, it's you. Where's Mr Rawson?" The head's voice softened taking the harshness away, if only slightly.

I looked up and then wished I hadn't.

Connor glared down at me, his eyes glinting.

I schooled my face into a blank mask, but found it hard to swallow against my dry mouth. He looked good—*really* good.

"Mrs Winter, I'm here on Rawson's request. He's out on assignment at the moment—as I'm sure Ember could have informed you..."

He shot another glower my way. I stared back, my stomach flipping. I'd forgotten Rawson had left this morning—and Lyss worked on Fridays.

Mrs Winter turned her gaze on me, at least it felt like it. I didn't bother looking at her. "No, she didn't tell me that. In fact, she hasn't spoken a word about the incident—nothing at all."

"Really?" Connor's eyes held a question and took on that intense stare he got when he was demanding an answer.

No way was I explaining I decked Shannon because I was jealous. I held his stare, my eyebrows dipping and my nostrils flaring. The weight of his power pressed down on me, pulling at my will, making me want to go to him, to wrap myself around him, nuzzle that strong neck and confess my darkest secret.

What the fuck...?

Now I snarled, and pushed back. Making my spine snap straight, I sat bolt upright and refused to bend to his will.

"That's interesting." A dark smirk curled his lips, one that promised he wouldn't let the matter drop.

I didn't know if he meant it was interesting that I hadn't explained why I'd lost my temper or that I'd just defied the pressure of his alpha compulsion.

"Yes, well, Ember is now an adult and as of the end of today is no longer a pupil at this school. I need to wait for word of the other girl's injuries. If she is badly hurt I will inform the head of the agent training programme and recommend that Ember is dismissed into the civil training programme, instead. They will assess her there for her ability to maintain control, especially considering her history of assault during her time at this school."

My gaze shot to her. I couldn't help it. My palms began to sweat, my heart racing, but I bit my lip, I'd only make this situation worse by protesting my innocence.

Connor tilted his head and his eyes narrowed on me.

Oh gods, he could hear my heart race, probably scent my heightened emotions, too.

The civil training programme was really a way to ascertain if shifters could enter into human society and manage to live there safely; if they couldn't control their shifts or anger and animal urges to hunt or kill, they were locked up...or destroyed.

A man walked in front of the window. I stiffened. The geeky teacher, Mr Blaze, I'd heard him called, glared at me through the window. The light reflected off his glasses making his eyes seem like they were glowing.

I swallowed. How could I have let Shannon get to me? Now I was going to have to grab my escape bag and run. There was no way I was letting them lock me up or put me down like a rabid dog. I shuffled, ready to bolt through the door.

"... furthermore, Mrs Winter, the past incidents were years ago when Ember first started here. She was protecting herself from bullies then—as I am sure she was doing today. Perhaps, for all your ability to run such an upstanding school, procedures on the proper way for the school to handle bullying should be revisited. And let's not forget, the older pupils here are about to go through their *Primis* and tempers can fray easily..."

My attention snapped to Connor. Trust him to deliver an insult wrapped so tidily you think you should thank him. Mrs Winter looked like she was sucking a lemon. Her glasses had fallen down the bridge of her nose and she was giving Connor a really terrifying glare. He'd been leaning forward, hands on the big, old desk, but now pulled himself up to his full six foot five inch glory. Power pulsed again.

I tilted my head, keeping my face neutral. Even I wanted to cower from the pure dominance he emitted.

Mrs Winter tried holding eye contact. To give her her due, she managed longer than most female wolf shifters would with Connor; Mr arrogant alpha shifter extraordinaire. She eventually caved, though.

I would have smirked, but my mouth was busy hanging open. Normally, he gave me as much of a verbal roasting as Rawson did.

".... and if *any* male is ever stupid enough to corner Ember and attempt to use his powers to hurt her again, if she doesn't rip his throat out, then I'll do it myself. Perhaps you ought to mention that in your report to the head of the agent training programme." A growl rippled up his throat, his wolf near the surface.

I stifled a gasp. When I was sixteen, a senior, who had just gone through his *Primis,* attacked me. He had cornered me, yanked my skirt up and torn my panties before I could even comprehend what he'd done.

My stomach churned, and I swallowed hard at the memory.

By the time I'd pulled myself together enough to fight off my attacker, his dick was out of his pants. It hadn't ended well for him, but I'd been the one hauled into this very same office to explain myself. Again, I'd remained silent until Rawson and Lyss had arrived. It wasn't until I'd shown Lyss my ripped undies, the bruises around my neck where he'd held me, and the scratches on my hips, that I'd been exonerated from any wrongdoing. Connor had never mentioned that day. I didn't even realise Rawson had told him, but it had obviously stuck in Connor's mind. Gods knew it was stuck in mine.

Mrs Winter pressed her lips together and nodded hurriedly. I even felt a bit sorry for the hard faced cow. Having one of your past pupils come back and throw their powerful alpha vibes in your face must be a bit disconcerting.

"Good. In fact, I'll even have a word with Mr Evans myself. He's the head of the agency programme, by the way—and a good friend." Connor stepped back, and the weighty pulse of alpha energy receded from the air.

Mrs Winter gave a little cough and pushed her glasses back up her nose.

I released a breath through my nose and rubbed at the goosebumps covering my arms. I hadn't truly appreciated how powerful Connor was until just that moment.

"Of course, Mr Maxwell..."

I almost barked a laugh at Connor's disgruntled face. He really didn't like being addressed so formally, though he had taken Lyss's maiden name not Rawson's surname to avoid confusion. He had never known his true surname.

The door opened and Mr Blaze walked in. He met Connor's gaze then immediately dropped his stare.

Yeah, no alpha vibes with this one. The geeky teacher stepped to the edge of the room, as far from Connor as possible.

"It seems Shannon is unhurt, and she can't seem to remember what happened to her." Mr Blaze shot a look at me.

What? Did he think I'd done something to wipe her memory? That magical pulse might have done it but it sure as hell didn't come from me.

Connor's brows dipped, but I didn't miss the smirk on his full lips before he hid it.

My mouth opened ready to blurt out the questions tumbling through my mind when Connor glared at me, so I snapped it shut. Black seeped into his blue eyes. His wolf. This time my chest tightened in response; those dark eyes were brimming with warning. Absentmindedly, I rubbed at my chest and looked away first. I couldn't help it. Connor was powerful by himself, but together, he and his wolf were an overwhelming force. And they were both pissed at me.

"I beg your pardon, Mr Blaze?" said Mrs Winter.

Mr Blaze wrung his hands and glanced at me through narrowed eyes.

"Shannon has no apparent injuries, and the girls who were with her seem to have forgotten what happened, too. In fact, I can't find anyone who witnessed the situation."

"Really?" Mrs Winter peered down her nose at me.

"I'm afraid so. I picked Shannon up off the floor and there was no sign of an injury on her. She said she was fine, so I sent her home. It's her last day anyway."

It was hard to keep the disbelief from my face, but I did.

Mrs Winter frowned then raised her hands. "Well then, you may go, Ember. It seems your trip was wasted, Mr Maxwell."

Mr Blaze turned to me and looked over his glasses. "I'm not sure what happened today, but I personally think it deserves a bit more investigation. I saw Shannon fly backwards and hit the ground, even if I didn't see how you did it." Mr Blaze flashed Connor a dark look.

Connor raised a brow looking totally unintimidated. He crossed his arms over his chest and took one step forward, then another. I raised my brows. The dweeby teacher actually stood his ground, though he couldn't prevent the bead of sweat that ran down his temple.

Connor grinned and reached out. He scooped it up with his forefinger, studied it, then grunted and wiped it on the shoulder of the other man's tweed jacket. "I'm sure you won't find a thing."

Mr Blaze grunted. "We'll see." He spun on his heel and left quickly, his footsteps fading away down the corridor.

"Let's go." Connor headed for the door.

I listened to him for once. This wasn't the time to be giving Connor shit; besides, I couldn't wait to get out of this school and never look back. Connor grunted a farewell at Mrs Winter, and he guided me out with a gentle, but firm hand on my lower back.

Outside was hot and humid, with dark thunder clouds gathering over the Kent countryside. Fat raindrops hit my skin. "Oh, for...!" I grunted, rolling my eyes. *Could this day get any worse?*

"Ember. Go to the car." Connor gave me a gentle push in the right direction.

I stiffened at the command in his voice and opened my mouth to tell him not to order me about. The warning on his face stopped me. Mr Blaze was just disappearing around the corner of the building. Connor's attention focused on him like prey. Fed up with this whole situation, I shouldered my rucksack, lowered my head and set off at a run for the car. Getting soaked was not on my list of 'fun things to do' for today.

"Ember? Haven't you forgotten something?"

I skidded to a halt and turned back. "What?" My brain was still trying to understand why Shannon had no injuries on her face. I smashed my fist into her chin and saw the blood as well as the burn on her skin. How could she not be injured, or her friends not remember what happened? It was bizarre. I remembered that energy pulse. Perhaps someone had fixed her face and her memory? I shook my head. The only people with supernatural abilities on school premises were the teachers, and they were mainly shifters, as far as I knew. No witches, wizards or mages were ever allowed on school grounds unaccompanied, and any pupil who had gone through their *Primis* was quickly moved into the programme chosen for them by the bureau.

"Keys?" Connor quirked a brow at me. His blue eyes glinted with flecks of anthracite, the remaining blue twinkling brightly.

I flushed. Great, even his wolf was laughing at me now. I stomped forward and snatched the keys from his finger. He turned away, ignoring my dramatics, and went after the geeky teacher with the stupid name. Trying not to think about what Connor was about to do to said geek, I got in the car, put my earbuds in and shut my eyes. Music was one escape that I loved. Tapping my foot and humming to myself, I almost managed to forget about Shannon.

The car door opened, blasting me with hot, damp air. The smell of rain on hot tarmac drifted into the car, along with Connor's spicy scent. I inhaled deeply unable to stop myself. My whole body instantly heated. My eyes snapped open, and my attention zoned in on his wet t-shirt, and how it clung to every cut of muscle on his chest and stomach. Jesus, I wanted to run my hands down that amazing body. My mouth dried out. It wasn't fair that he could affect me like this.

He reached in and gripped the steering wheel. Raindrops dripped down his corded forearm, falling on the denim covering his powerful thighs, which was already dark with moisture, outlining the strength in them. Heat unfurled low in my belly as my gaze honed in on what was between those thighs. Gods, I'd never been even remotely interested in sex with anyone—except Connor. I quickly closed my eyes again, trying to get myself back under control.

The whole goddamn car rocked when Connor dropped his bulk into the driver's seat of the Mercedes.

"Now, what really happened?" He twisted his body to face me.

Just to annoy him, I pulled an ear bud out, and kept an innocent look on my face. "Sorry? What did you say?"

His blue eyes narrowed. "Don't give me that bullshit. You heard me."

I shrugged even though his power pressed in on me, compelling me to tell him the truth. I tilted my head letting my red hair fall in a soft curtain which hid my face from him. No way was I telling him the truth.

"Did you lose control, Firecracker?" he said, more gently this time.

I shook my head. "Not really. I just...nevermind." I sighed, really not wanting to get into why I'd hit queen bitch.

"What happened, then? And how is Shannon not injured? I've seen your moves, and you can pack a punch when you want to." He chuckled.

It was a deep rich sound that gave me goosebumps. Irritatingly, I flushed at his compliment.

"I don't know."

"Did you hit her?"

Another shrug.

Another chuckle. "I'll take that as a yes. Why?"

I clamped my mouth shut. *"Bet I can get him to fuck me tonight too..."*

My heartrate spiked, and my hands heated in my lap. Smouldering. I hissed and lifted them off my legs before my clothes started to burn.

"Hey." Connor took my hands in his. "You only lose control like this when you're really upset or angry. It hasn't happened for years, right?"

"No." I pulled against his grip. My heart jumped, I could hurt him.

"Don't worry, Firecracker, you won't burn me. You can't."

I met his gaze. "Why can't I? I burn anyone or anything else I touch when Fire is riled." Only... I blinked, my eyebrows pulling down into a frown. I'd never burned Connor, even when I'd been really pissed off at him. I'd lost control of Fire only once before; not long after I'd started living with Rawson and Lyss. A nightmare of flames and pain had sucked me in. I swallowed and tried to shake the memory of that nightmare away. Connor had woken me. My skin had been burning up, my bedclothes and pajamas singed. He didn't even hesitate, just took my hands and led me to the shower. Flicking on the cold water, in nothing but PJ bottoms and me in a nightshirt, he stood in the stream with me, enduring the cold, and held me until he was blue—and I finally calmed down...

"You just won't." He smiled and released my right hand. Gently, he tucked a bit of hair behind my ear. That soft touch sent a delicious tremor through my whole body, but I kept my gaze fixed on our joined hands. His hand surrounding mine felt so good.

Silence settled between us. Connor was the only one who knew that my skin heated like hot coals when I got extremely emotional. After that night, he had vowed to keep my secret, and I had vowed never to tell anyone about his nightmares. I'd buried Fire deep in my soul, so that red hot flash of uncontrolled rage that had hit me today was very rare.

Connor's thumb brushed my knuckles, that gentle caress stealing my breath. The air in the car became thick with that deep musky smell I loved. I inhaled deeply and sighed, my body relaxing even as heat shot through me. I bit my lower lip and closed my eyes. It was the most heavenly scent I'd ever come across.

A low rumble escaped from Connor's chest.

At that resonant sound, my breath hitched, but I didn't dare look up. My reaction to the scent Connor was giving off was confusing, not to mention it sparked feelings that were useless. He could have any woman he wanted. No way was I going to fawn over him just so that he could reject me...

Connor released me and turned his hand palm up. "See? I'm fine." His voice was lower than usual, a deep baritone that sent another wave of heat coiling between my legs. I squeezed my thighs tightly together. What the hell was going on with me? I hadn't reacted like this with any other guy—ever. "You can't burn me, Firecracker. Now what did that spoiled princess do to make you lose your shit?"

Another gentle wave of power seeped into my skin, warming my flesh and bones. I swallowed hard. Between those alpha vibes, his touch and his voice, I couldn't think straight. I met his gaze with my own. "Stop that."

"Stop what?" He raised his brows in mock innocence, his dark eyes penetrating my soul.

"Hitting me with that alpha nonsense you use on everyone else."

His lips curled, baring his teeth in a feral smile. "I can't help it, Em, it's who I am. My wolf is always near the surface, just waiting to escape. I have to fight him all day, every day. And he's more of a handful than ever when I'm near you. Besides, you seem to like it—when you let yourself." His voice was a low purr now.

I dipped my head. Once again, my hair fell forward in a heavy curtain and hid my heated cheeks. Oh gods! Could he really tell how turned on I was right now?

He reached out and tucked my hair behind my ear again, letting his fingers brush through the silky strands. "I adore all this gorgeous red hair, but don't hide yourself from me with it."

I shivered at his touch, and my eyes fluttered closed, a small moan of pleasure escaping me.

A calloused finger touched the superficial cut under my eye. "Em...You still haven't answered my question." His voice was low, but that soothing purr was accompanied with another pulse of power; a big one that had me gasping.

My blood instantly overheated. So did my skin. Fire awoke from her slumber, her attention perking up at my reaction to this alpha's touch. She wanted to tangle with him, to pitch herself against him; to fight and to win. I snarled and forced her back. My wolf on the other hand wanted something very different; she wanted to submit, to let this alpha command her however he wanted.

This time I did yank my hand from his. No way was I letting that happen! But my wolf lurched inside me, snarling at the loss of his touch. She had no intention of listening to me.

"Okay! Fine! It was you! Queen bitch said she was going to get you to fuck her! Again!" I blurted the words, unable to bite them back. My skin heated all over, my face flaming red, and not with my power. I snapped my mouth shut, and closed my eyes. The soft leather seat creaked as I sank deeper. *Traitor!* I growled at my wolf. She'd forced those words from my mouth. She ignored me and merely curled up, totally content at succumbing to Connor's compulsion.

Silence.

I could still hear the music playing through my ear buds. With shaking fingers I put them back in their case, missing one. It fell into my lap. Connor plucked it up between his forefinger and thumb.

"Ember, you need to listen." He leaned close enough his body heat washed over me. With a precise movement, he placed the ear bud carefully back in the box. His warmth, and that spicy scent, bathed me head to toe.

I swallowed hard. Would he laugh at me? Or think me ridiculous for losing my temper over such a stupid thing? It wasn't as if there was, or ever had been anything more between us than a crush on my part.

His voice was gentle. "I have absolutely no interest in Shannon. She's a nasty piece of work. She's not worth one second of my time, and definitely not worth you worrying over. I haven't seen her for months—not since Ava...died."

"I don't care. It's none of my business who you fuck." It was so hard to hide my bitterness. His life, his friendship, and his attention was mine once, and I had adored it—I had adored *him*—but he'd left me behind... And yet, despite that, I couldn't stand thinking of him with anyone else. It was truly painful to imagine that gorgeous body worshipping another female, of his lips kissing another's, let alone Shannon's.

"Em...it's not that..." He sighed heavily and rubbed his hand over his face. "Listen, don't get in fights on my account. You need to stay under the radar. Especially while you're in the agent training programme. The bureau doesn't like uncontrolled shifters; don't get on the wrong side of them, especially Shannon's father. Doherty's got power, and he doesn't like Rawson—or me. I know Shannon is allocated to the same training group as you, so you steer clear of her. And no matter what she says, especially about me, you ignore her. Okay?"

I still couldn't look at him. Weariness leached all the energy from my limbs and I wanted this whole shit storm done with. It was a mistake letting Connor know he meant something to me. I sighed and looked out of the window, watching the rain hit the ground, bounce, then join the flow and rush away in a fast stream. Just like the rain, people fell into your life, but eventually everyone left, caught in the flow of an unavoidable destiny; there was no point in loving anyone.

Firm but gentle fingers grasped my chin. Connor turned me to face him. "Okay, Firecracker?" I gulped at the tenderness in his eyes and the softness of his voice.

"Okay," I whispered, unable to look away.

He stared at me, his wolf bleeding into his gaze. That heady scent seeped into the air around us and I trembled, my wolf's rumble resonating through me. Connor exhaled and his warm breath caressed my face. Instinctively, I inhaled as if his breath was a gift, especially for me. His attention settled on my mouth, and my heart stuttered. Energy crackled between us. My tongue reflexively licked a trail of moisture over my lips. A small snarl curled his lips, and before I could even consider what that meant, he groaned and slanted his lips over mine.

My world tilted on its axis. His kiss was earth-shattering; everything I thought it would be and more. His tongue pushed against my lips, demanding entry. I gladly opened and let him in. My mind exploded with sensation as his tongue tangled with mine, tasting me, taking all I was and ruining me for anyone else. Desire slammed through my flesh and bones, making me ache for more. I writhed on the seat, crossing my thighs to try and relieve the need that burned between my legs. I was on fire; his taste—his touch, only stoked the flames of my lust. I lost myself in that kiss, knowing he now owned me. He pulled back, and I whimpered. But the loss was only for a moment. His teeth nipped and pulled on the softness of my lower lip, then he ran his tongue gently over my swollen flesh easing it. I'd never experienced anything like it; sensation swamped me, everywhere.

I didn't want to be parted from him. The pain from his gentle nips sent jolts of pleasure shooting straight to the juncture between my thighs. When his lips sought mine again, I kissed him back, humming low in my throat. His scent filled my nose and curled around my heart, cementing itself there. His other hand thrust into my hair, and he wound the mass of red waves around his fist. He tugged it firmly and angled my head. I groaned with pleasure at the burst of commanding pressure on my scalp. My voice seemed to spur him on. His lips crushed against mine, our teeth clashing together. His grip tightened in my hair, and he controlled the angle of my head, tilting me and urging me forward so he could devour me.

Blood pounded in my ears and heat rushed to my core. The scent of my own arousal was sweet in the air, mixing with Connor's deep spicy smell. And, gods, but I loved it.

Connor pulled back, his hooded gaze searching. I fought against his hold on my hair, leaning forward enough to bite his swollen bottom lip. He yanked me closer and moaned my name against my lips, his voice strained. He kissed me brutally; pain and pleasure a powerful mixture. My spine arched towards him and, without thought, my hands lifted. I was done letting him take the lead. I needed to touch him, to be closer to him. I grabbed onto his shoulders, digging my fingers into the wet cotton of his t-shirt, attempting to reach the hard muscle beneath. A growl rumbled from his chest and his grip tightened further, sending electric jolts of pleasure across my scalp and down my neck.

Emboldened by his response, I moved one hand around his neck and speared my fingers into his soft hair. My wolf rumbled her approval and pushed closer to the surface. I was totally unprepared when she launched her spirit at Connor, determined to give herself to this alpha.

Connor jerked away. The loss of his touch was a physical stab in my chest. My wolf howled and my eyes flew open. I gasped, unable to control my breathing. My hands slapped against my chest, the pain so intense that my shoulders curved forward trying to stop the agony of his withdrawal.

Connor's chest rose and fell in deep rapid movements. It was some consolation to know he was as affected by me, and what my wolf had almost done, as I was. Slowly, I raised my gaze, my heart thudding against my ribs. His wolf stared back at me with eyes that were entirely black, burning with lust and feral need.

I pressed my lips together, not sure what to say. Spirit bonding was only supposed to happen between chosen mates, and even then it wasn't always possible. I blinked, slowly trying to control my labored breathing. I could still taste him on my tongue. I inhaled, needing more of that sensual scent of his. And I got it, mixed with the sweetness of my desire. Heat flooded me again as it dawned on me; that scent meant he was as turned on as I was.

"Damn, Ember..." He stared, rapidly shifting his gaze from one of my eyes to the other. He reached out and gently gripped my chin, his thumb brushing over my swollen bottom lip. His eyes flared with need again, and his throat bobbed. Abruptly, he dropped his hold and moved away. "Fuck!" He ran a shaking hand through his hair before he smacked the steering wheel. Closing his eyes, he curled his grip around it until his knuckles turned white. My stomach sank as he breathed deeply several times. He released the wheel and flicked the switch for the window. It became clear that he wanted the fresh air to erase any lingering scent of our mutual lust. My cheeks burned from something other than desire. He even wiped his hand on his jeans as if to erase the feel of my skin.

"I'm sorry, Em. I shouldn't have done that." He clenched his teeth. "Let's get you home. I have to get back to work."

I recoiled into my seat. He wanted to leave without even acknowledging what had just happened between us?

He pressed the start button and the engine roared to life.

"Buckle up." He didn't look at me. His jaw muscles bunched and his expression darkened.

I swallowed hard and did what he said, but my embarrassment quickly turned to anger. He didn't get to kiss me like that and then just ignore me.

"Aren't you going to say anything?" My question was pretty damned steady considering how I trembled inside and out.

Swearing, he flicked the automatic transmission into drive and roared out of the school driveway and onto the country lane. "No. But we will definitely talk about this later." His eyes flicked my way, a low growl to his tone.

"Fine." That was hard to believe, and even if he meant it, I prepared myself for his consolatory words of rejection.

"No, nothing about this situation is fucking fine, Firecracker. But it will be."

I didn't bother answering, I just stared out of the window as the Kent countryside whizzed by. No matter how much that kiss had turned us both on, it was obvious this sinfully gorgeous man, who had once been my best friend, regretted the hell out of kissing me. And even though I was nowhere near ready for a mate, being cast away was like being burned from the inside out. My wolf curled up inside me, whining pitifully. My eyes burned, and I blinked away tears. I didn't cry—ever, but it didn't stop the hurt eating at my heart like acid.

Fifteen minutes later we pulled into my road. Without uttering another word, Connor dropped me on the driveway outside Rawson's home and sped away. I refused to watch him drive off like some lovesick princess. Instead, I turned towards the door, my movements automatic. It was far easier to tell myself our kiss meant nothing than to admit what relationship I had left with Connor was ruined. Thankfully the house was empty. Hating how much I already wanted to see him later, I threw my clothes off, donned my training gear and headed to the gym.

onnor

"Fuck!" I roared at the top of my voice and hit the steering wheel with the heel of my hand. My heart still raced, Ember's taste lingering on my tongue. Kissing her had rocked my fucking world, but it didn't change the fact that I shouldn't have done it. Everything about her called to me, and in the confined space of my car, I didn't possess the strength to turn away; those pretty pink lips stole my self-control. Something about Ember had always drawn me in, and for years I resisted the temptation to pursue her. Today I just snapped. I succumbed to the red-hot rush of need that hit me. I hadn't even thought about reining in myself or my wolf. He snarled inside me, urging me to go back and take what was ours. "Settle down," I muttered, pushing my foot down on the accelerator in response.

I dreamed of Ember almost every night, and it had been worse when I lived under the same roof. At first my feelings had been protective, but by the time I hit my *Primis*, I'd had to leave. It was a game of self-control I knew I'd lose while learning to control the predator in my veins. She'd been too young then, and so had I. I swallowed. She wasn't now.

After what had happened in the training room a few weeks ago, I'd avoided Em, though my wolf had made it perfectly clear she was ours; our mate. He had tried to get to her that day. Her wildness and defiance had called to us both, and seeing her spirit and sensing her strength, when I had denied myself being anywhere near her for months, had snapped something in me. If Rawson hadn't been there, I couldn't in all honesty say I would have held back.

I'd had lovers, plenty of them, but no other woman had ever affected me the way Ember always had, and still did. Jesus! My need for her had become a painful ache in my soul. Perhaps it would be better for both of us if I distanced myself completely—just until my life was more...stable. There was something happening in the SBI that even I didn't understand and now was not a good time to tie my life to someone—not if I could be sent into a situation that might put my life—and hers—at risk. I wouldn't endanger Ember, ever. I ground my teeth. I'd always do what it took to keep her safe, and if that meant leaving, freeing her of my presence, then that's what I'd do.

I exhaled, my stomach churning. That woman had my heart in a vice, yet had no idea of the power she held over me.

The indicator clicked as I flicked it on. Turning the wheel I pulled onto the main drive up to the SBI headquarters. A huge metal gate blocked my way. I lowered my window and pulled up at the retinal scanner. The guard remained in his hut but I knew his weapon would be trained right at my head. Doppelgängers were rare, but the bureau was always vigilant, and SBI security was the best in the world. These guards would shoot first and ask questions later if they perceived any threat.

The scanner eased silently forward and I placed my face into the wrap around device. It was cold on my skin, but the bright light it used no longer bothered me. It beeped and slid smoothly away. Next was my hand. I placed it against the glass pad, waiting patiently while cold metal bands clicked into place, holding me immobile. I readied myself. Blood couldn't be forged, not when you didn't know where on your hand it was going to be taken from. This time it was the base of my thumb. I hissed at the sting. The next moment a soothing coolness negated the discomfort. A green light flickered up on the screen.

"Welcome, Agent Maxwell," said a female voice.

The bands released with a snap.

I pulled my arm in and waited. While my identity was verified, scanners had risen from the ground around my car. They finished their inspection and sank back into the tarmac.

"You may proceed," the disembodied voice told me.

I flicked the switch to bring the window up. It closed as the gates opened. I wasn't fooled though, I knew there were bollards underground all along the driveway that could shoot up at a moment's notice and prevent any moving object from getting further. I drove forward steadily.

In the corner of my eye, a dark shadow moved. It was a habit to scan the surrounding area for anything unusual. My instincts were not easily ignored, nor were my mission experiences from the past four years. I noted the position of all the guards just as I did everyday. I knew their formations, their shift times and what weapons they normally carried, and looked for anything unusual. Perhaps I wasn't supposed to know, but I'd put away some powerful people over the years and they, in turn, had powerful allies. Friends could turn on you at the drop of a hat. I swallowed and shook my head. I knew that all too well.

I drove towards the figure of a woman dressed in an agency issued uniform. Cold spread through my insides, my heart rate speeding up. She shouldn't be here! She turned and watched me drive by. Her shoulder length blonde hair shone, and her dead eyes followed me, accusation in their depths.

No! She isn't real! She isn't here! Shit!

Breath hissed from between my clenched teeth. I fought to control my heart rate even as sweat slicked my palms. *Damn it!* I'd triggered myself again. Unwilling to let my past get the upper hand, I stamped on the breaks, pulled the car over to the verge and concentrated on controlling my breathing.

I'd started to suffer from post traumatic stress six months ago when Ava, my sometimes lover, had stopped me from killing the man she truly loved— by throwing herself into the path of my bullet. Rawson and my men knew what had happened, so did Doherty; Ava was his oldest daughter after all, but no one outside that loop knew. I'd been sent for counselling and taken off field work. I was getting better at controlling my flashbacks; enough so that I'd been reinstated for active duty, but being near Ember shot my emotions to shit.

I closed my eyes and took a deliberate and slow breath then exhaled equally as slowly.

Ava's face and voice were vivid in my mind.

"You're fighting for the wrong side, Connor. Please, don't do this." I needed to let this bit of the scene play out, so I gripped the steering wheel. Goosebumps rose on my arms, and bile burned my throat. I knew what was coming, but was helpless to stop it. Nightmares you could learn to manage and control; memories, not so much. They were real, living things, and though some faded, I knew this one never would. In my mind, I held the gun out straight, pointing it at the chest of the man who had been my partner and my friend for years. Lance glared at me, hatred and disgust on his damaged face. My orders were to hunt him down and kill him—and I had.

My stomach threatened to expel its contents as the memory continued.

"You are working for the wrong side. If you do this, you side with them," Lance said.

"Don't do it, Connor. Please."

I looked at Ava's devastated face. "He's a traitor. He has betrayed everything we stand for. He's working with the fae for god's sake! To harm your father!"

I couldn't comprehend why she wanted to be with a man who had just tried to kill her father, not then and not now.

My past self squeezed the trigger just as Ava jumped in front of Lance, but it was too late. The gunshot resounded in my head, blocking out all coherent thought. My palms were slick with sweat and slipped off the steering wheel. I was barely aware as I struggled to breathe, a cold sweat breaking out over my body. *My fault! It was my fault!* A vice gripped my throat. Inside me my wolf howled, scratching at my insides wanting to be free, to soothe my troubled mind and aching heart. His distress was the only thing that pulled me out of my flashback. I focused on his darkness, on his strength, and got a waft of Ember's unique sweet and slightly smoky scent. It grounded me and I absorbed every bit of it, allowing it to calm my heart rate.

My eyes opened, I shook my hands out, ridding myself of the pins and needles that had come on with my rapid breathing. A few moments later, I started the car and drove onward towards the massive mansion house that was the UK's SBI headquarters.

My thoughts drifted to Ember. Leaving her alone like that was a piss poor way to handle what had happened. I just hadn't been prepared for her wolf to try and bond with mine like that. Merging spirits was something I'd only ever read about. No one in my circle of friends, or agency colleagues, had ever mentioned being that perfect a match with their mates. Had I accepted her wolf spirit right then, there would have been no stopping what happened next.

Heat swamped my body and things got uncomfortable in my jeans. I adjusted myself as best I could, gritting my teeth against the ache in my cock. Bonding our spirits would have meant us mating, right then and there in the car. It wasn't a choice, our wolves would have demanded it, and I couldn't have stopped it. I shook my head. I didn't give a shit who saw my naked arse, but Em deserved better than that. The truth was, she was better than me, and she sure as hell deserved a life before becoming anyone's mate. I knew my Firecracker had suffered in the past, but she was a survivor. I could only imagine the horrors she had endured as a child on the streets of London, open to the predators of the supernatural world. Her nightmares, like mine, were testament to those past horrors.

Despite that, despite her strength and the fire that lived in her soul, something told me she didn't realise what the consequences of mating and spirit bonding to an alpha were. She would be mine to call upon and to take, whenever and wherever I wished, helpless to stop the urge to submit to my demands. My brow furrowed. Though she had resisted my compulsion so far, in fact she revelled in defying me.

A groan bubbled up from my chest at the thought of having access to Ember's gorgeous, lithe body whenever I desired it. "Jesus, Connor, get a grip." I rolled my eyes, knowing I would never truly want to control Ember. Her beautiful wildness and unpredictability were what drew me to her like a moth to a flame. I grinned at the analogy. The inner spirit that gave her the ability to superheat her skin and burn the air was just an externalization of her own indomitable fire. Besides, she was far too stubborn to give me, or anyone else, total control or power over her, even if her wolf submitted to me.

The towers and chimneys of the old house came into view. I relaxed my grip on the steering wheel before I bent it out of shape, and forced Ember from my thoughts. I needed a clear mind for the meeting ahead of me.

The sun came out, reflecting off the glass and metal space-age training facility, which they had built beside the main house. I squinted against the brightness as I turned the car into a parking space facing the old house. The mansion itself was a sixteenth-century place of sandy stone-coloured construction with columns, windows and grand architecture that was as imposing as it was impressive. I both loved it and hated it as a symbol of the strength, wealth and power of the SBI. The bureau owned so many of these properties around the world. I had seen a few, but this one always blew me away with its history, and then made me cringe with the lack of taste shown by adding in such a modern building right next to it.

I climbed from the air conditioned interior, and buried thoughts of Ember deep in my mind. I wasn't Connor here; I was Agent Maxwell, and I had a job to do, one that I would not allow to hurt Ember.

Heat from the sun warmed my face. I inhaled deeply, enjoying the smell of the damp ground, sun and rain. I splashed through the puddles and made my way along a gravel pathway, around to the back of the house.

I followed the path, nodding to the gardeners and guards who watched my progress, some more openly than others. Topiary hedges and old, bent yew trees dulled the echo of my footsteps. Five minutes later, I approached the orangery.

The glass house was as beautiful as everything else about this estate. Long oval topped windows soaked up the sun, turning the inside into a tropical paradise. The door clicked open on my arrival, the cameras and lasers I'd activated on my approach announcing my arrival. Stepping inside was always a strange pleasure for me. Damp heat stole my breath, but I loved the smell of the plants and blossoms that bloomed inside. I inhaled deeply, the sweet scent of the flowers calming me. This was one of the most important meetings of my career and I needed to be in control, not thinking of Ember or Rawson and Lyss, or how this last interview might affect them.

Cameras tracked my every move as I prowled along the walkways. Guns loaded with silver bullets pointed right at me. They were attached to the camera casings, not to mention fixed separately to the roof, walls and even some of the plants.

I reached the stone steps at the back of the orangery and jogged up them.

"Place your hand on the control panel, Agent Maxwell."

I did. Again the titanium bands held me while a needle stabbed the tip of my fourth finger.

"You may enter."

The projection of the stone wall dematerialised and I watched a thick bomb resistant door swing open. Inside, four guards in full battle gear pointed the bureau's version of machine guns at me.

"Okay, sir, you know the drill."

My grin was predatory and challenging. I released a little power against these men. All wolf shifters and all below me.

"Easy…" one of them advised the others as a finger or two tightened around a trigger.

I smirked at the guard, holding his eyes as I stripped naked. To his credit he didn't bow under my stare. I would have kicked his arse if he did, and he knew it. These were my men—and they needed to do what they were trained to do, no matter the amount of power I wielded.

With my arms out at shoulder height I twisted giving them all a good look of my naked muscular body. Thank god my cock wasn't standing to attention anymore. Could have been awkward, I quietly chuckled. I hoped Ember never made it into the undercover programme and came down here. I wasn't sure how I'd handle the guards ordering her to strip and giving her the once over. My wolf growled showing me exactly what he would do.

"Captain," greeted Owen Brady, my second in command.

"Brady." I nodded and walked naked through the inner blast doors with my men at my back. Nakedness was something a shifter had to get used to. Nevertheless, I snarled as someone blocked my way into the changing room.

The blond haired female crossed her arms over her ample chest and looked at me over the top of her glasses.

I stopped short and glared down at her. We'd met before. The first set of interviews for the top-secret job I'd been asked to apply for were conducted through her. Even I hadn't been given any details, only that it was undercover, working alone and that it had no definite end date.

"You're late." Her bright red lips were stark against her pale skin, which was made more translucent by the deep blue pinstripe power suit she wore. "You should have been here over five minutes ago. The Overseer doesn't tolerate tardiness."

"You know, if you kept your mouth shut, you'd almost be able to give the illusion of being sexy." I plastered an arrogant smirk on my lips, deliberately stepping closer and observing her reaction.

She looked me up and down. Her attention lingered deliberately on what was between my legs, but her grey eyes remained like chips of ice despite the answering smirk on her lips. She gave a delicate cough and stepped back. She was a good actress, I'd give her that, but even taking a step back from my bulk didn't convince me that she was intimidated by me. No, this was a top caliber agent posing as a personal assistant to the European bureau's leader.

"Get dressed. I need to conclude this process. The Overseer wants to make a decision in the next hour, so you have very little time left to …" Her eyes drifted down again. "…impress them." Her gaze returned slowly to my face.

My brows twitched upward in response. It was tempting to ignore her, but this assignment would help get me away from Ember. And, as much as I hated to admit it, my Firecracker needed time to explore her adulthood without me getting all possessive over her. The only way I could manage that was to be far away when she took a lover. That hellacious thought had a cold sweat breaking out down my spine.

I grabbed the standard black t-shirt, boxers, socks and cargo trousers from the shelves, and dressed. Once I'd tied my black boots, I grabbed my weapon from my lockbox, stepped out of the changing room and followed the woman I knew only as Miss X down the corridor to the interview room. Owen shadowed me while the others went back to their posts at the orangery entrance.

Owen waited outside of the door, more to get his orders once I was done than to protect either Miss X or me. I nodded my thanks at my friend and closed the door.

An empty chair sat opposite Miss X. I folded my big body down into it and rested my hands on the large table that separated us. A tight smile stretched those ruby lips as she tapped on her earpiece.

All the way through this process, communication with her boss wasn't something I was party to. Even with my acute hearing the frequency was too low. Irritation simmered in my chest, but I kept my face utterly blank.

"Yes, sir, I understand," she said a moment later.

The hair on the back of my neck tickled. Her words were flat. Something was off. She'd always sounded crisp and coldly professional, but never so…unemotional.

"The Overseer would like to offer you the job."

I nodded, throwing out my wolf senses to listen for anything unusual. Nothing grabbed my attention. Except she gulped, and there was a slight sheen of sweat on her upper lip. My eyes narrowed on her throat. My wolf growled and intensified my senses. "So what happens now?" I asked in a measured voice, watching her and the door closely. Something was wrong, but I couldn't pinpoint what.

A pulse of energy, followed by a shockwave of air hit me from behind. To stop myself pitching forward onto my chest, I grabbed the table top. My chair was pushed right up against the table which was slowly being driven across the floor. Slamming my weight backwards against the force of the pulsation, I forced my body to straighten and tried to turn my head to see what the fuck was behind me. I felt a sudden sting in the side of my neck. As an alpha wolf shifter, and potential Prime, my reactions and strength were beyond most shifters, let alone any human, but it didn't matter. Whatever I'd been hit with rendered me instantly immobile. I could move my eyes, but not my body. Hell, I couldn't even blink.

Hard, powerful fingers grabbed my head and turned me back to face Miss X. I watched her stand and walk around the table, her heels clicking on the tiled floor. I sat, helpless inside the frozen biomechanical suit of my human body with my wolf thrashing to get out. She reached down and pulled my weapon from the holster on my hip.

"What happens now, Mr Maxwell is this…" she murmured in my ear, her lips brushing my skin.

My heart thrashed against my ribs while I watched her pluck my grip from the table, lift my arm, curl my hand around the weapon and place my finger on the trigger.

The cameras! Surely someone would see what was happening in here. Then I remembered and my stomach dropped. The lights were red. On the request of Miss X and her boss, the cameras had been switched off all week during these interviews. Whoever this Overseer was, they had a shit load of power.

I growled and yanked on my wolf. He snarled and fought to break free, tearing at me from the inside. It was impossible for him to pull free with my body poisoned and totally out of my control.

Miss X strode back to her original position and stared at me before she looked at whoever was behind me. I had no idea how they had got in this room, but this entire situation was beyond comprehension. My palms were slick with sweat, my heart pounding. I hated being out of control like this! Just like my flashback earlier came on its own, the dark, early memories of my childhood were coming through, where I'd been out of control, until I'd run. *That's right, son. Take the pain. It will make you into a real man; a leader… like me….* I shoved that dreaded voice back behind the wall in the deepest, darkest part of my mind, and fought the drug in my system.

A black gloved hand reached forward and curled around mine. It aimed the weapon. I bellowed and thrashed in the prison of my body. Breath rapidly hissed in and out of my nostrils.

Miss X stared at me with cold eyes. Her whole body went lax and her shoulders curled inwards. She lifted her chin and nodded at the person behind me.

And the person holding my hand pulled the trigger.

Miss X's head shot back, a hole appearing in her forehead, the back of her skull exploding out across the wall behind her.

"You'll get your orders soon," whispered a voice in my ear.

Another needle stung my neck and a moment later my limbs released. "No!" I bellowed. Her body hit the ground, but I was already moving, spinning and training that weapon on whoever was behind me. Nothing! There was no one there.

The door burst open and Owen lunged through, his weapon trained on my chest.

His gaze flicked to the remains of Miss X. "What the fuck, Captain!?"

Jesus. It was a mess. Bone and brain matter painted the wall. I had no idea what had just happened. She'd just offered me a fucking job for chistsakes! Now she was dead and I had *killed* her?!

"Captain, drop your weapon! Down on your knees. Right now." Owen's order was calm, but firm. I did what he said and dropped to my knees. His eyes narrowed on me. I locked my hands behind my head. Owen was my friend, but first and foremost, he was an agent. He was a trained killer, and he would pull the trigger without a moment's hesitation.

Keeping his weapon trained on me, he circled behind, clicked a handcuff around one wrist and yanked my hand down behind my back.

I hissed at the burn from the silver.

"Both hands. You know the procedure."

I complied and brought my other hand down. There was no point fighting. Even if I overpowered Owen, the building would be on lock down. If I ran, I'd be shot on sight or ripped to pieces by an army of shifters.

"What the hell happened in here, Connor? Jesus, man, I hope it was fucking worth it." He cuffed both of my hands behind my back.

"I have no fucking idea what just happened, man." And that was the truth. There was no explanation. In a state of shock, I waited for the inevitable rush of agents as Owen stood at my back, his weapon trained at my head. Miss X's glassy dead eyes stared at me. I swallowed. Blood and gore was nothing new, but that bullet hole in her forehead appeared obscene on her otherwise flaw-less face with its perfectly painted ruby red lips. I didn't want to look at her brain matter splattered over the wall, so I closed my eyes, centering on my wolf. My mind delved into his spirit and took solace in his strength. He couldn't rise to the fore, the silver stopped him, instead he centered his anger and memorised everything that had just happened. So much for being prepared for this final interview. Not in a million life times could I have antic-ipated what had just occurred.

The sound of booted feet charged down the corridor and soon guards surrounded us, all bearing arms and all pointed at Owen and me. Swallowing my pride, I dropped my gaze and kept it down on the tiled floor. Antagonising anyone right now was not a good idea.

The click of shoes, not boots, came from my right. Soon I was staring at a shiny pair of Salvator Ferrangamos. I hid my snarl. There was only one person in this building who wore such expensive attire—and I detested him, I always had, mainly because of his perverse interest in Ember. My wolf snarled in agreement.

"Well, well, Agent Maxwell. What an unfortunate position you find yourself in." Doherty, the director of the British SBI branch, had a slight Irish lilt to his voice, which instantly grated on my nerves. The man had always gunned for Rawson and me, especially after Em had come into our lives. He was always stopping me to ask about her, and he did it in such a fashion he always had my hackles up. It seemed the director had a hard on for her, the sick fuck. I'd always wanted to slam my fist in his superior face, but never so much as right now. On my knees in front of this prick was not where I ever wanted to be.

His soles slipped easily as he pivoted. "Agent Brady, put your weapon down and raise your hands."

That got my attention. I raised my head and twisted toward Owen.

"Sir?" Owen's heavy brow furrowed, almost as deeply as mine.

Doherty gave a snake's smile, his eyes cold and predatory. "Put. Your. Weapon. Down." He enunciated each word as if Owen were stupid.

Owen looked at me. I nodded. I had no idea what was going on here, but something told me Doherty had an agenda, and Owen and I were a large part of it. Slowly, Owen complied, placing his weapon on the ground. At a nod from Doherty, one of the other guards disarmed him completely.

"Down." Doherty inclined his head at the ground next to me. Devoid of all weapons, Owen dropped to his knees, his jaw tight. He met my eyes with fury and accusation.

I didn't blame him. It looked like I'd killed her. I wanted to tell him what had happened to Miss X, to explain that this truly hadn't been my doing, but right now I couldn't. Not that he would listen. He looked majorly pissed off as his wolf shone through his eyes.

Doherty stared down at us. The silence stretched, but both of us knew it was useless to plead our case or ask what the hell was going on. Doherty wouldn't tell us anything. It was in his eyes which gleamed with a twisted kind of triumph. He lifted his perfectly manicured hand and touched his ear.

"Did you get it?" Silence as someone obviously answered him. "That doesn't matter. Was any of it on camera? Good. No one else but Maxwell and the woman?" Silence. Doherty's eyes flicked to Owen. "Interesting," he murmured.

Owen's eyes narrowed when Doherty's attention settled on him.

A quick glance at the cameras told me they'd been switched back on. When had that happened?

"A black gloved hand? Standard issue?" Doherty's gaze dropped to Owen's hands. "No one in or out of this room other than them?" He tapped the ear piece and looked at the man who had disarmed Owen. "Agents Maxwell and Brady are under arrest for murder. You will take them to the holding cells. They are to be incarcerated until such time as a trial can be arranged."

"Sir!" One of the agents pointed at the body of Miss X.

Owen's wolf disappeared from his eyes and his gaze fixed on Miss X. "Holy shit! What the fuck is happening to her?"

In front of us, Miss X disintegrated into fine ash. The ash rose into the air and floated upward, disappearing into the ventilation duct as if it knew where it was going.

Grunts and exclamations of disbelief resounded behind me.

"You will disregard what you just saw," Doherty instructed the other men. His eyes were narrowed but his expression was controlled.

"What the hell is going on, Captain?" Owen uttered under his breath, meeting my eyes.

"I have no idea, man." I was totally out of my depth.

Neither of us fought as we were yanked to our feet and marched down through the corridors to the holding cells.

CHAPTER 4

mber

THE FULL MOON bathed Rawson's back garden in soft silvery light. Frost sparkled like a dusting of glitter over the hard ground making the shadows, which lurked by the large bushes and trees, seem malevolent. I shivered and rubbed my arms. Even in my thick toweling robe I was cold. My wolf tried to reassure me that I would be fine, that we would both be fine. *I know. I just wish he was here...*

"You okay, sweetness?" Lyss walked up behind me, her footsteps as light and delicate as she was.

I turned to face her. In this brilliant shaft of moonlight she looked stunningly beautiful, almost ethereal. She gave a small smile and kissed my forehead. "I'm sorry Rawson's not here," she said a frown creasing her brow, and then she added quietly, "or Connor."

I blinked and tried to return her smile even though my chest ached. It was a poor effort. My wolf was clamouring for release to run in this full moon and I couldn't hold her back. We both needed the release, and I craved for her to take over for a while, if only so I could lose myself to my feral side and detach my heart from the devastation of losing Connor. "Lyss, you don't have to apologise for Rawson." I just couldn't acknowledge Connor's name. My heart broke every time I thought of him. "I can manage this alone." I reassured her. After all, managing alone was how I always ended up. If Rawson or Connor had been here, they would have shifted and run with me. A wolf should never be alone in their *Primis*. If they couldn't control their wolf and it took charge, they needed an alpha, or their mate to force a shift back to human form.

Lyss nodded, but she bit her bottom lip.

Worrying wasn't an option I gave myself, even though I'd changed before, the last time had been when I was seven years old. A year after escaping the burning house my parents had died in, a man had attacked me in an ally. Surviving the attack was only possible because of my wolf. She had burst from my skin, helping me fight and bite my way out of death's clutches before Fire could react.

No one knew I'd completed my *Primis* so young. Even I had no idea how I'd done it.

I took a deep breath and released it slowly, trying to calm the butterflies in my stomach. This was going to hurt. My bones would break and reshape; every cell in my body would change. And whereas this would normally be done in a small pack with the support of an alpha and others, I would wander this beautiful night alone. I shoved my fear down deep. I had done this before, I could do it again.

I reached out and touched Lyss's hand. "It's alright. I'll be fine alone, Lyss. You go back inside where it's warm. I'll see you at dawn." I tried to sound reassuring but I was scared as hell; not of my wolf, I was well acquainted with my animal spirit, but I wanted to do this alone in case either of us regressed to that time in the alley and I went into survival or attack mode. My self-control since Connor left me on the drive way and never returned was stretched to breaking point.

My wolf whined.

I know you wouldn't hurt her, not on purpose. But I'd rather not chance it right now.

Lyss nodded and pulled me into a hug. I hugged her back, then gently pushed her away. My skin was getting itchy, and my heart was pounding in my ears as I answered the call of the moon. "Go. I'll be fine."

Lyss bit her bottom lip. "Are you sure? I really don't want you to go through this alone." Her eyes shone with tears. She lifted her hands and slapped them down on her thighs. "Ah, Rawson's being such a prick! He should be here with you. I'm going to kick his alpha arse when I see him again!" She crossed her arms tightly over her chest.

"Hey, it's not his fault. He's not handling Connor's disappearance well. Hell, neither am I, but...." I shrugged and raised my chin. "I'm a big girl, and I don't need a man *or* an alpha to help me do this. I can do it alone."

"I know you can, sweetness, but the point is, you shouldn't have to. Everyone needs support at some point in their life."

"It would be nice, but you're wrong, I don't need it. Like I said, I'm fine. Besides you'll be here when I return."

She gave me a watery smile.

It took me everything to return it, though I couldn't be angry with Rawson. Since Connor had disappeared, he'd become obsessed with finding out what happened. Rawson's slide into neglecting Lyss was sad to see. Lyss didn't complain outwardly, not for herself anyway, but she didn't laugh like she used to either, and she had lost some of her charismatic zest for life.

"I will." Lyss nodded, gave my forehead a swift kiss and walked back through the gate which led into the garden. She closed it and locked it. "I'll be here at dawn with food and a nice hot cup of tea!" she shouted.

"Thanks," I murmured and turned away. I had to do this alone. The only person I wanted with me was nowhere to be found. I'd not seen Connor again after our kiss. At first, I thought he was just avoiding me, but then we got the news that he'd disappeared from the SBI radar, too. I rubbed the familiar tightness from my chest and took a deep breath. Something about his disappearance stank. Rawson knew it and so did I. The difference was, he could do something to find Connor. Me? Not so much. I ground my teeth together, facing the dark country lane and the fields. Shadows closed in around me. I didn't mind. They always protected me from prying eyes and hid me from evil; now they would protect my wolf.

My wolf sent a pulse of reassurance, pushing to get through my body.

Fine. I'm coming! It's alright for you to say it won't be as bad this time. Even if it hurts half as much, it'll not be pleasant.

Another pulse. I swallowed. There were plenty of fields at the back of Rawson's home. His garden bordered the dark country lane, and on the far side were miles of countryside which led to the outskirts of London.

I shed my robe and slippers, letting the silvery moonlight bathe my naked body. Its power and influence shot through me, and energy filled my body. Howling filled my mind just as pain erupted through my limbs. Blood roared through my ears, my pulse racing while my bones simultaneously cracked and reshaped. I screamed as my internal organs restructured and hair pushed through my skin. Within seconds, the pain passed, and I lurched forward onto all four of my legs.

My wolf howled at being allowed to break free of my human body. Observing from inside her, I gave her control and sat back, determined to enjoy the ride. Seeing the world in a vivid expanse of sights, sounds and smells was extraordinary. With a grunt of joy, my wolf bounded across the road and into the fields beyond.

❧

I WRAPPED my damp robe around me, my frozen fingers slipping as I tried to tie the belt, and missed for the third time.

Lyss gently pushed my hand away. "Let me help."

I stretched my fingers then curled them into fists. In and out, then I shook my hands, willing the tremors and throbbing in my fingertips to disappear. It had proved harder to command my wolf to return to my human body than it had been to free her. Despite my frozen fingers and toes, my skin was on fire and my bones ached.

"It'll get easier, you know," Lyss said. It wasn't a question, more a soft reassurance.

I smiled and nodded, not sure if I was trying to convince her or me that I agreed. Last night, my wolf ran free for at least two hours, enjoying the thrill of chasing rabbits through the fields and revelling in the energy of the moon. Even my sadness over Connor was quenched for a while—until my wolf decided she needed some fun of a different kind. I realised her intent and tried to stop her, but it was no use, she didn't listen, even when I screamed from inside her.

In the shadows, she prowled around the fencing of Connor's modest home, but he was nothing if not security conscious. Her determination to get inside, nearer to the faint scent she recognised as her chosen mate, left a hole in my heart. Hours later, no matter how much I pleaded with her to stop, she shimmied on her belly, under the fencing and through the hollow she dug in the soil. It didn't matter that I reminded her he disappeared months ago, when she saw that Connor's house was dark and empty, she howled and howled and refused to leave.

I blinked tears from my eyes. I had cried so much since the SBI informed us that Connor had disappeared on assignment and was presumed dead. After our kiss, I longed to see him again. My head was certain that he wouldn't want me, that he would break me if I let him in, but my heart didn't care. With every day that passed, I'd still hoped he'd return and tell me he wanted me as much as our wolves wanted each other—until the day we knew he was gone and all our lives changed...

Lyss hissed and took hold of one of my hands. "Oh my god! What did she do?"

I stared in a detached fashion at my broken and bleeding nails. Until me and my wolf were used to shifting and fully in sync, it would take a few hours; but they would still heal. Not so much my heart.

"Oh, sweetie." Lyss's voice was soft. "She tried to find Connor, didn't she?"

I nodded, unable to stop the sob that shook its way free of my chest.

"I thought...I mean, I guessed a long time ago you were going to be something special to each other, but I didn't know your wolf..." her voice petered out. "...that your wolves were possible mates."

I'd never told her about what had happened between me and Connor, or how my wolf had tried to bond with his. It had seemed private at the time and now there was no point. "It's okay, Lyss, she's just having a hard time accepting he's gone." I forced the words out, my voice thick with emotion. My limbs shook and all I wanted was to curl into a ball and sleep. At least then the pain would go away for a while.

Lyss sighed. "Yeah, she's not the only one. Come on, let's get you inside. Then you can eat and go to bed for a few hours."

The November morning was frozen, the world sparkling with a glittering beauty I couldn't appreciate. I wrapped my arms around myself for warmth, my mind full of Connor. Lyss put her arm around my shoulders, and started guiding me through the back garden to the kitchen. We were about half way across the lawn when the back door burst open. We both hesitated and gaped at Rawson. He spent most of his time at the bureau now—or elsewhere. Neither of us knew where he was most of the time. He never told us, and we'd given up asking. He only came home once a week, if that, some weeks, and even then he was distant.

Lyss looked him up and down, her eyes flashing. He was a mess. He'd lost weight and obviously hadn't shaved for days. His hair was longer and unkempt, looking like he'd run his hand through it for hours. Even though we'd both agreed Connor's disappearance, or death, or whatever the bureau wanted to call it, was suspicious, I didn't know why Rawson was so obsessed by it to the point he'd neglect Lyss. But there was definitely something eating away at him. I narrowed my eyes. After last night, being included in whatever he was doing to uncover what happened to Connor was top of my list. I'd make Rawson tell me why he'd lost his shit. If Connor was dead, then both me and my wolf needed to know so that we could accept it, even if I would never really move on. I curled my bleeding fingers into fists, hissing at the fresh wave of pain.

Rawson strode to meet us, his gaze flicking warily from Lyss to me and back again.

It was impossible to miss the anger emanating from Lyss, even though she watched him carefully. My heart broke for them; they'd been so happy before Connor had died.

Rawson didn't meet Lyss's glare. Instead, he stopped a foot from us, staring down at the patio as if trying to find the right words to say. For an awkward moment we all stood in silence.

"I'm sorry I wasn't here." Rawson raised his head and looked at me.

I believed him, I really did, but it didn't matter. There was a gaping hole in my heart. All my emotions had poured from me last night, and now I was hollow, just like I'd been when the fire took my parents. I'd wanted to find Connor as much as my wolf, but his disappearance had also destroyed the people I cared about most. I swallowed hard. I was withdrawing from them, but that realisation didn't frighten me as much as it should have. Distancing myself seemed easier than waiting for their inevitable break up. I was realistic enough to know that either one of them—or both—could ask me to leave. I was an extra burden that they didn't need, and I was old enough to fend for myself now. My emergency bag was already packed; money, clothes, weapons, even a fucking photo of the three of them; they were more my family than my parents, who were just a faded memory now. I could leave at a moment's notice. My heart stuttered. I always assumed I would be okay with running when the time came. Only now I realised I didn't want to leave any of them.

"Why?" Lyss snapped at Rawson, her fingers digging into my skin. It wasn't worth pointing it out, not when I understood that her heart was hurting far worse than the physical pain she was inflicting on me. Yes, she'd lost Connor, but she'd also lost the man she loved even though he was standing in front of her. The worst of it was, neither of us knew why Rawson was so determined to discover what had happened, and he wouldn't elaborate; he just told us it was safer for us if we didn't know.

"I should have been here. I, well, Ember's my responsibility, too. It was her *Primis* and I missed it...I'm sorry..." he said, shoving his hands through his hair again.

"It's fine." Seeing them argue was worse than my aching bones, damaged skin or even the constant emptiness that dragged at me. They were alive and real—and my family. It was awful to see them in such pain.

"I meant why weren't you here? Not why are you sorry, you shit." Lyss's eyes flashed, her fingers releasing me.

Rawson's spine straightened at the challenge in her tone.

I swallowed hard, recognising that reaction. The contempt in his mate's voice called to him, commanding he respond...as an alpha, not some down and out excuse for the man he had become.

Rawson turned to me, his grey eyes now deep brown and stormy as his bear surfaced. "Em, go inside. Grab something to eat and get some rest. I'll be here when you get up." Fixing his attention back on Lyss, his voice growled up from his chest. "Right now. There's something I need to do."

Lyss went to walk past him but Rawson was having none of that. He grabbed her wrist. She slapped him with her free hand; a resounding slap that rang in the air. Electricity, lust and so many other emotions thickened the air between them. *Time for me to go.*

I held the sides of my robe together and hurried into the house, my freezing bare feet slapping on the stone path. I turned, but hesitated to close the door. Rawson had speared one hand into Lyss' tumbling blond hair and held her with the flat of his other hand in the curve of her lower back. His pelvis pushed against hers and he leaned close to her ear. His lips moved and though I couldn't hear his words, even with my shifter hearing, I could see the desperation in his face. Lyss pushed against his chest and shook her head. Rawson's expression darkened and his lips moved again.

Lyss hissed something up at him. Maybe I couldn't hear, but when he tilted his head, I could read Rawson's reply on his lips.

Because I love you. More than anything in this world.

Her face crumpled and she pounded his solid chest with a fist. He held her and leaned his forehead against hers, whispering more words. Lyss stared at him then grabbed the back of his head and yanked him down. Their mouths met in a passionate kiss that left me both hot all over and even more hollow. I was the worst kind of voyeur, watching them, but I couldn't tear my eyes away. Their passion was mesmerizing. Rawson pulled back and rested his forehead against hers again. They spoke a few more words before he kissed her—tenderly this time—and thoroughly.

I swallowed my tears hoping this meant they could work on their issues. Then I sighed, a few hot kisses, even some steamy make up sex couldn't always fix a relationship. I turned away, closed the door, flung open a cupboard and pulled out a loaf of bread. My stomach growled as I dropped a couple of slices in the toaster.

The door swung open and Rawson barged in. Both him and Lyss remained silent as he led her upstairs to the third floor of the house and into their own space. I breathed through the heavy sense of power Rawson left behind, not to mention the sultry scent of their lust. I hung my head trying to ignore my aching loneliness. The house was silent other than the click of the timer on the toaster. I cocked my head. There was no noise of sex, make up or otherwise, or even yelling from upstairs. Maybe they were talking; gods knew they needed to.

The toast pinged up, making me jump. I dropped it onto a plate and carefully buttered it. Taking a seat on a bar stool I attempted to eat, but Connor's face wouldn't leave my mind, the sensation of his lips on mine was as raw as if it had only been yesterday that he'd kissed me. I pushed my plate across the granite breakfast bar and stared out of the window into the garden. My wolf curled up tighter into the small ball of energy that was her heartbroken soul.

Trying the toast again, just to get rid of the nausea in my gut, didn't help a bit. Even the cup of coffee I'd made did nothing to make the toast slide down my gullet. Both were now cold, the toast like chewing rubber. I gave up and dropped it down onto my plate, wrinkling my nose. With a grunt, I pushed my stool back and threw my wasted food in the bin.

Brewing more coffee only took a moment. I grabbed my earbuds and phone and headed to my room, exhaustion weighing my limbs down. I had forgotten how hard shifting was. Outside my window, the countryside melted into the distant London skyline as a low early morning mist swathed the fields like a blanket.

The coffee burned my throat, but warmed me inside. I closed my eyes and listened to the steady beat of music from my earbuds, really needing to lift myself out of this funk. Connor wasn't going to suddenly return; I knew that. I'd stayed in the training programme and attended the SBI because it had seemed a good way to stay close to Connor—or at least something that had meant a lot to him—but conforming to all of its rules and regulations wasn't my thing. I hated not being able to smash queen bitch's face in every time a derogatory remark fell from her poisonous mouth, or tell one of my instructors to go fuck themselves when they put me down for not trying hard enough in their eyes. I wanted—no, I needed—more from my life. I needed the freedom to be me, to make my own choices and find my strengths, not just be told about my weaknesses.

Perhaps it was time to pay a visit to Somnelaire. The Bogwart fae was my main source of income, and my planned escape route, he had been since I'd moved in here. No one else knew about my connection to him and that was the way it would stay. He was a remnant from my time on the streets. A disgusting lowlife from the land of Faerie who had always taken advantage of my need for money, but who had also looked out for me for reasons I couldn't fathom. Once Rawson had taken me in, I had stayed in touch with the faerie. After all, life was an unpredictable bitch, so it paid to be prepared. Somnelaire gave me low level delivery jobs anytime I asked, and always paid me; not much, but it was still money, and I had saved all my money from those jobs for years, just in case...

There was a bang from upstairs and a loud grunt. I smiled, glad I had my music on. Turning it up to drown them out, I hoped whatever was going on up there was make up and not break up sex. When I'd finished my coffee, I shed my robe, put my earbuds away and headed into the shower to scrub the dirt from my skin and blood from my nails. I winced at the sting, but they were already healing, thanks to my wolf and my shifter abilities.

Dressed in a comforting pair of soft pajamas, I put my earbuds back in, snuggled under my covers and closed my eyes. For Lyss and Rawson I'd stay, but if Rawson wouldn't include me in whatever he was up to, then I'd find out what had happened to Connor by myself. I'd even stay at the SBI if it meant I could use their technology and equipment in my search. I just wasn't ready to admit defeat and accept him as dead. Not yet.

CHAPTER 5

mber

I GRABBED MY BAG, my hand shaking. The bus stopped and I jumped off, running as soon as my feet hit the ground. Our house blazed brightly, every window lit up from within. Around the outside blue lights flashed, illuminating the darkness with that ominous glow that meant pain and trouble.

Police were everywhere, their cars and at least one riot van were parked haphazardly across the roads. I swallowed, my heart thumping wildly when I noticed four black range rovers with the SBI emblem on the side. The monstrous cars were blocking the driveway. Either to stop people getting in— or perhaps to stop someone or something from getting out?

My stomach lurched. Was it Connor? Had they found him? Since Rawson had promised Lyss he'd drop his search for Connor about two months ago, he'd been home more and was so attentive, it had become almost irritating. I suspected he hadn't really stopped his search for Connor, but whatever he did, he did it discreetly. The day of my *Primis*, Doherty had given him a warning. Apparently, it wasn't acceptable to use SBI resources or their technical support and weapons for personal use.

I'd tried to stay out of trouble, too, and behaved during my training, though being submissive and toeing the line grated on my last nerve most of the time. I always ensured I did slightly worse than Shannon in my assessments just to keep her off my back. In turn, she ignored me. It seemed

Connor not being around had made me insignificant to her. I was, by all accounts, invisible. Not that I gave a shit about Shannon or the programme, not really. Out of the limelight and in the shadows was where I was happiest. At home, I trained alone or went for long runs as my wolf. Lyss had gone back to work as a counsellor, so I spent most of my time either alone or working for Som.

That's where I'd been tonight. It had been too early to run back from the outskirts of London as my wolf. I hadn't wanted to be seen, so the bus was my only option.

I ran up to the first policeman who stood guard.

"What's going on!?"

"Nothing to concern yourself with, Miss. Run along home, now."

I frowned at the kindly yet condescending way he spoke.

"I live here. I need to get in!"

"Really?" He looked me up and down, his gaze eventually resting on my face. "Well, okay then, you just wait right here with me…" His fingers snaked out and clamped hold of my arm as he made eye contact with another policeman, who nodded and walked hurriedly up the drive and towards the house.

I yanked my arm out of his grasp and sprinted over to the nearest SBI agent.

"No one's getting in here," this one told me. "But if you live here, Director Doherty will want to speak to you. Stay right there."

My stomach sank. Something was very wrong. If they'd found Connor the human police wouldn't be here; it was something else; something bad enough to have both the SBI and the police involved.

My instincts yelled at me to get the hell out of there. I grunted in reply to the agent, but as soon as he turned away and opened his mouth to shout something to the agent guarding the front door, I ran.

No fucking way was I waiting for Shannon's crazy-assed dad to grab me. The guy was just plain creepy. I sprinted down the drive, back out into the street and kept going straight before darting left. Thankfully the moon was waning and not even a sliver of light was visible. Light-footed and quick, I sprinted along the pitch black lane. I could hear loud shouts and the echo of booted feet. My heart pounded as I leaped off the road and ran through the fields next to the lane. These agents were shifters, they would scent me just as I could smell their wolves, and there was no way I'd lead them straight to the bushes behind Rawson's, so I jumped into a small stream. Cold water splashed up my legs, soaking my jeans and helping cover my scent. Ignoring the freezing cold, I dashed up the opposite bank, ran a few steps, doubled back and grabbed an overhead branch. With a grunt of effort, I flung myself back into the water as far upstream as possible. Not pausing for a second, I ran through the water until I reached a small bridge. I peered above and along the lane, careful not to make any sudden moves. There were no headlights or shadows of looming vehicles parked in the nearby darkness. In a smooth move, I pulled myself up onto the road. Expanding my lungs as much as possible, I tried to recover my breath. Staying on the verge and in the shadows, I ran back down towards the bushes at the back of my home. My heart thundered and my throat was raw, but I didn't stop. Fear for Rawson and Lyss drove me on. Only a short way off, my footsteps slowed. I halted and cocked my head, listening carefully. I could hear male voices coming from the garden but none in the lane. I guessed they knew how vigilant Rawson was about his security. Almost as careful as Connor...

I inched forward, ensuring the lane was still clear. Quietly, I scurried across the road and bent down onto my haunches, ignoring where my wet jeans had chaffed my thighs. Sharp sticks and thorns scratched my exposed skin as I edged my way through the spiky bushes that I'd painstakingly created a path in. I stopped and took a few quiet, deep breaths. I couldn't creep past any guards when I was breathing like a steam train. Thanks to all the running I'd done recently, I was fit, and soon got my breathing under some control, though my heart still raced.

If there was such a security presence at the front of the house, the back would be no different, especially now that I'd been seen and had bolted from their grasp. Thankfully, none of these people knew about the little tunnel I'd created for myself. Over the years, I'd dug down under Rawson's security fence, careful not to upset his systems. This was my emergency way in and out of this house. I used it to sneak in and out of the house when Lyss and Rawson thought I was in bed. I often visited Som, or if he had no work for me, I prowled the London streets, watching and waiting for a chance to strike against those who preyed upon the vulnerable. Supernatural or human, it made no difference to me.

I crawled past the dead rats that I'd placed in strategic positions. No agents would pick up my scent over the rot of those things. I smirked as I peered out from the base of the bushes, using the shadows to hide me. All the SBI personnel were steering clear of this area. I had to agree, the stench was repulsive, so it was good that Lyss and Rawson hardly ever spent time in their garden, or my tunnel being discovered was inevitable.

Light from the kitchen door and window fell on the nearest pair of agents and my breath hitched. They weren't ordinary agents; the agents that the rest of the world saw on the news. No, these carried special issue automatic multi-function handguns, exclusive to the special ops division Connor had worked in. Their huge bodies were decked in armour, their faces completely covered. Thank god they didn't have night vision equipment. I sent a short prayer of thanks to the mother wolf while I studied their weapons. They had stun capability and tranquilliser settings as well as bullets.

A shudder rippled down my spine.

After rubbing the stink of the rotting rat flesh over my shirt sleeves and wet jeans, I pressed my lips together, gagging, and continued to crawl through the bushes that marked the border of Rawson's home. There was a small vent next to the wall of the house just in front of the base of the bushes. I'd found it not long after I'd moved in. No one else seemed to know it was there, not even Connor.

It was quiet and pitch black around this side of the house. I tugged on my wolf, begging for her help. Gladly she gifted me some of her power. My eyesight sharpened and my nails grew, along with my teeth.

Enough, I commanded and my shift halted. I had learned many things since my last shift. Full and partial shifting on demand being two of the most useful.

Right now, my heightened senses and extra strength were what I needed. I crawled from beneath the bush and hooked my fingers under the hatch where I'd bent the metal settings it rested on. I lifted the metal, careful not to make any noise. I was well practiced at sneaking in this way. Head first, I dropped into the space. Twisting my body to close the hatch was awkward but I managed it. Ignoring the discomfort, I wriggled on my belly alongside the pipe work. When I got beneath the training room storage cupboard I stopped. Voices reached me. My blood froze, my heart thundering.

There was the thud of fist against flesh. Bile surged up my throat.

"You're an evil bastard." Rawson's voice gurgled and he panted, clearly in pain.

There was another thud, followed by a grunt.

I inhaled—and almost threw up. The stench of blood and other fluids hit my sensitive nose. I swallowed a cry, bile rushing up my throat. I knew that underlying sweet scent. I didn't want to see what lay up there but knew I needed to. I pushed up the air grate which was set in the floor and shimmied out from my hiding place. I didn't replace it. If I needed to leave quickly, that was my only way out.

I breathed slowly hoping my scent and the stench of dead rats would be covered by the blood and other smells. Careful to remain quiet, I shuffled forward and squatted near the door.

"Oh, we're all evil to some degree, but I guess it depends on your point of view. Take you for instance; a strong and powerful alpha who has gone mad with grief. You, Rawson, are going to show all those fucking human sheep out there just how evil an upstanding member of the shifter community can become. And I am going to be their fucking saviour by locking you up," Doherty said, brushing an imaginary speck of dust from his shoulder.

A low growl rumbled from Rawson's chest. "That's my *wife! My mate!* Let me. Go to. Her!" He panted hard, blood running from his ravaged lips.

My breath caught in my throat. Rawson was struggling to even talk. He was wounded badly, and not just his face.

Doherty's cold laugh coated my insides with ice.

I peeped through the slats of wood which made up the door, trying my best to get a better look. I didn't care if it was Doherty, I needed to get Rawson out of there.

Doherty had his back to me but I'd know him anywhere; his silver grey hair, his tall slim frame, and even if I couldn't see his face I could hear his Irish accent, and the familiar coldness to his voice.

"Oh, but you just killed her, Rawson. There is no going back now."

"Killed her!" Rawson's eyes were so swollen they were almost shut, but I could see their wildness, and they grew darker by the second, his bear fighting to take control. "I didn't kill her! I love her more than my own fucking life! She's my life mate."

He tried to crawl on his hands and knees to what remained of Lyss; of the sweet natured, beautiful woman who had cared for me and loved me for years. Tears obstructed my vision and my heart tore apart so viciously, I had to shove the back of my hand against my mouth to stifle my sobs.

Rawson roared over and over, cursing Doherty with everything he had.

I couldn't imagine what seeing Lyss's torn and broken body was like for the kind man who had saved me from the clutches of London's underworld. This whole situation was fucked up! They'd been close again recently, their love the only light in my otherwise dark days. Rawson had never talked to me about what he'd been doing, almost as if he'd thought better of it. Despite my vow to find out what had happened to Connor, I hadn't wanted to push him, not when he and Lyss had been working things out.

I bit my hand trying not to cry out as Rawson threw himself toward Lyss. Tears ran down my cheeks when I saw the true state of his face. His mouth was cut and bruised, and his nose was broken, dripping blood down his shirt. And he crawled. I had *never* seen Rawson lower himself physically to anyone before, not even Doherty.

Doherty snorted, his body shifting and I almost vomited on the spot. The only thing I could do to stop myself was bite my hand harder. The pain I inflicted upon myself was nothing compared to the agony inside my soul.

Lyss was literally in pieces. Ripped apart by something frenzied and wild. Rawson tried his best to get to her, sobbing for his mate. Tears ran down his swollen and bruised cheeks, mixing with blood and saliva before they dripped onto the floor.

Doherty prowled around Rawson before he smiled and brought his foot back. He landed a vicious kick in Rawson's ribs. Rawson grunted and fell onto his belly. Doherty kicked him again and again. Each time Rawson pushed back up, his eyes on the ruins of Lyss's face. I wanted to scream at the man who had saved me to save himself, to fight like he should. Bone cracked, and he fell face-first into the blood of his mate.

My blood chilled. He didn't care that he was going to die, he just wanted to get to Lyss before he did.

"Let! Me! Touch! My! Wife!" He panted hoarsely.

Doherty laughed. "Oh, you won't be touching her again—ever. No, where you're going the only people you'll get to touch are the guards when they force you on your knees to do whatever they want you to."

Bile burned my throat. I had no idea what had happened here, but I knew Rawson hadn't killed Lyss.

Doherty kneeled next to Rawson's ruined body. My blood froze when he growled, "You're mine now, Rawson. I *own* you." He stood and spoke to someone else.

I shrank back. I hadn't even seen the other man in the room. His movements were predatory and powerful. He had to be a supernatural to move so fluidly for such a big man. His head was covered in a mask and helmet, and his body armour was the same as the other agents. Only his eyes showed. Minutely, his head moved, and I was sure he stared right at me before he turned his glowing red gaze to Doherty, then leaned his bulk back against the wall—watching.

The director peered down at Rawson again. "It's time to prove you're not as invincible as you believe, Rawson." He huffed a humorless laugh. "If you hadn't interfered in Connor's disappearance or my life, then none of this would have happened." He shrugged. "But you did, even after my warning, so this…" He grabbed Rawson's bloodied head and forced him to look into Lyss's dead eyes. "…is on you. *You* killed her." He released his grip before slamming Rawson's head into the floor.

Doherty stood, his face twisting as he wiped Rawson's blood off his hands with a pristine white handkerchief. "The police have no authority when a shifter loses control and kills others." He fixed the red eyed man with a challenging stare. "This man is out of control and is a danger to society. Imprison him with the others. You know where."

"No!" Rawson's voice was little more than a harsh whisper. "You'll. Not get. Away. With this."

Doherty shrugged. "I will. I always do."

"You evil fuck!" Rawson spat blood from his mouth onto Doherty's shoes.

The red eyed man unfurled his body in one smooth move and studied Rawson. Rawson didn't look away. No, his eyes turned deep brown, fury burning in them.

Doherty cocked his head and grinned. "Oh, I am. You have no idea how evil, but you are going to find out. This?" He gestured to Lyss's mutilated body. "This is nothing. I am going to break you; or rather my partner is, with the help of our friend here."

Rawson roared and lunged, his form shifting from man to beast. The bear leapt for Doherty but red eyes burst into action. They crashed together in a storm of claws, teeth and power. I willed Rawson to win. His claws swiped at the agent who moved quicker than my eyes could track. One moment the agent was locked in the bear's claws, the next he was behind Rawson. Rawson's bear flew across the room like he weighed nothing. Rawson's head slammed into the wall, his huge body landing with a thud and a grunt of pain.

I swallowed my gasp. Whatever this man was, he had just flung a huge alpha bear away like he was swatting a fly. I needed to leave. I knew it, but couldn't seem to move.

Rawson forced himself up and charged again. His eyes were wild. His roar rocked the foundations of the house, vibrating through the floor and walls, right before he barrelled through the red eyed man, sending him flying this time. Doherty yelled, his eyes wide. He tried to spin out of the murderous bear's way but Rawson was quicker. He swiped his claws, catching Doherty's face. Doherty fell, screaming and clutching his severed flesh.

Red eyes flipped to his feet and pressed on the mask which covered his mouth. I swallowed hard. There must be a microphone embedded in it.

My heart sank as he called for reinforcements. I knew I should run, but I couldn't. Instead, I grabbed the door handle. It was suicide to go out there but I needed to help the man who had taken me in and given me everything. I swallowed the ache in my throat. He was my family.

Rawson inhaled. He growled and glared at the cupboard. His eyes narrowed on me and he shook his big furry head. He turned towards red eyes who now had his weapon trained at Rawson.

There was a slight *pop, pop, pop.*

Rawson spun, his claws slipping on the laminate floor. He opened his massive jaw and bellowed, staggering forward, but it wasn't to get to red eyes. No, he knew what they'd shot into him. His last conscious moments, he wanted to spend with Lyss. Her soul wasn't there anymore, but it didn't matter. Rawson limped towards her remains and laid down against his beloved mate, placing his huge head next to hers.

He released the most pained, mournful sound I'd ever heard. Tears blurred my vision. He glanced at me just before his eyes dropped shut and the door burst open.

SBI agents piled in, their weapons held steady and pointed at the bear.

Holding in my sobs, I forced myself to crawl back into the vent and headed away from my family. Halfway to the exit, I grabbed the bag I'd stowed for emergencies. I had all the money Rawson and Lyss had given me over the years, and the cash I'd earned from Som's jobs. I'd spent very little. I hadn't bought clothes because Rawson and Lyss had always bought them for me. I didn't wear makeup, and I only needed a few toiletries. I didn't have a passport but that didn't matter. I knew how to survive under the radar of the SBI. I grabbed the knives and sheaths I'd taken from Lyss's stash, then the weapons Rawson pretended he didn't know I had from where I'd stuck them to the pipes.

Like I said—prepared.

Voices echoed behind me.

"I can scent someone in here!" a voice yelled.

Shit! I stuffed everything in my bag, wriggling and crawling as quickly as I could through the duct. There was no time for being careful. I shoved the bag up through the hatch, not bothering to close it, and dove straight under the bushes. I could hear men swearing from inside the duct.

Hope you're stuck there forever. I could squeeze through because I was small, only five feet four inches and still skinny, but a grown-assed shifter? No way in hell were they going to fit. I scuttled along on my hands and knees right past the rats. Grimacing, I grabbed a rotting carcass and smeared it on my bag, jeans and jacket. It was better than being hunted down.

Dragging the bag behind me with my leg through the handle, I crawled back through the bushes. I reached the lane just as the back garden was illuminated. Glancing back over my shoulder was a big mistake. I didn't see the agents waiting in the lane. A hand reached into the bush and grabbed my hair. Pain burned across my scalp, but I had the presence of mind to kick the bag off my leg. I prayed that it would be missed in the darkness. I'd be back for it...

The hand wrapped in my bright red hair and dragged me, screeching, from the bushes.

"Shackle her quickly, before she shifts. Don't want an angry she-wolf on our hands."

Yeah, especially this one! I wasn't going down without a fight! My muscles tensed and I slammed my fist up into the SBI agent's groin. He let go of my hair as I'd hoped he would. I threw my weight down. Landing on my back, I swung my leg around the back of his and took his knees out. He fell forward with a yell. Taking my opportunity, I hammered my boot heel down on his head in an axe kick. He grunted, then laid still. I flicked up onto my feet only to feel a sting in the side of my neck. Instinctively my hand slapped to the source of the pain. Damn! The dart was lodged into my skin. I tugged at it but couldn't pull it out.

Out of the darkness the shape of a large man approached. Red eyes glinted at me.

"Oh shit..." I uttered and tried to run but my legs wouldn't respond. I looked down at my stupid unresponsive feet and cursed my own body. Confusion fogged my mind. I had to run. Why couldn't I? I lashed out at another figure I sensed standing to my right, calling on my wolf to help me. I missed him, my heart squeezing and a cold sweat breaking out on my forehead when my wolf thrashed to escape and couldn't. Fire perked to attention, sensing my plight. *Too late...* I told her. I blinked slowly as a blurred figure came to a halt in front of me where I swayed drunkenly.

"Now, now, Ember. Don't fight. I can't let you go, not after what you witnessed." Doherty held a cloth to his bleeding face. Inside, I smirked even though I knew the muscles of my face weren't responding. I hoped the wounds Rawson had inflicted got infected, and the evil fucker dropped dead. "Besides, I need you for another reason." His fingers brushed my face and he leaned in close enough his breath warmed my cheek. I flinched away, or I tried. He'd always had an unhealthy obsession with me—one I didn't understand. "You took something from me, Ember. I want it back. And I'll do whatever it takes to get it."

There was another sharp sting in my neck.

I hissed.

Doherty gave a truly terrifying smile. "Until I find what I need to retrieve her, I can use you for something else."

The world tilted as I began to fall.

I hit the tarmac but didn't feel a thing, not even when my head bounced on the road. My eyes closed no matter how much I tried to keep them open.

"Bring her," Doherty ordered, his voice muffled.

I was lifted, far more gently than I'd expected and shuffled until I was resting against a broad shoulder. The smell of burning and something dark that reminded me of Som, filled my nose. It wasn't unpleasant, but it was overpowering, making my heart pound as if subconsciously I knew I should be scared of this person. But running wasn't an option, and despite pushing against my body, my wolf couldn't break through. My head lolled sideways onto hard muscle when I lost all coherent thought and fell into the darkness.

CHAPTER 6

onnor

WATER DRIPPED. One. Two. Three...Pause...One. Two. Three...Pause. It was the same goddamn rhythm all day, every day. I peered at my expensive watch. At least the bloody thing still worked. My phone had been taken and smashed right after my arrest for Miss X's murder.

I marked off another day. It was one minute past midnight. That made it ninety two days since I'd been shoved in this stinking shit hole. Owen was down here, too. We talked every day, mostly about nothing but it helped keep us both sane. I had no idea what Doherty was up to, but it was clear we weren't getting any kind of trial, fair or otherwise.

We'd been bundled into the cells at the SBI and kept there for less than a day. In the middle of the night we'd been darted and left to fall into unconsciousness. When I woke up, I'd been incarcerated in this underground cell. I had no idea where we were. It wasn't somewhere I'd ever been before. The place was old, really old, almost like an old fort's underground prison. The floors were stone blocks, as were the walls, while the front of the cells were constructed of iron bars. It was freezing and stank of old piss, shit and mold.

My cold fingers explored the collar around my neck. The fucking thing was impregnated with silver, enough to leave superficial burns and keep my wolf from breaking free, but not enough to do any permanent damage.

"Owen?" My dry throat made it difficult to talk. Guards came once a day to push a bucket of water in through the barred door of each cell and throw us enough food to keep us alive. It depended on the guard as to how much water was in each bucket. Yesterday's bucket had only contained an inch of filthy water in the bottom. It wasn't fit to drink, and I was dehydrated, so dry, my tongue stuck to the roof of my mouth. I groaned as my stomach growled, and my wolf snarled, wanting to be free to hunt for food. The weaker I got, the weaker he became, too.

The water dripping in the background was torture to my fluid starved body.

"Yo, Brady!" I rasped.

Owen sighed. "What, man?"

"That's ninety two days we've been in this shit hole. Any ideas how to get out yet?"

"Nah, man. Like I said a hundred times before, this bit of our prison is shitty, but that door at the top of those steps would need a bomb to blow it open. And then we'd need weapons to take out whoever's up there. Why? You got some weapons shoved up that a-hole of yours that you just now decided to tell me about? In fact, how about you tell me how I ended up in this shit hole courtesy of you, you selfish shit! Seeing as you haven't given me *any* explanation yet...let alone the goddamn truth!" His voice rose to a bellow.

"Yeah, I got three machine guns shoved up my arse, you dick! And I just thought it'd be nice to chill down here for a while, you know, spend some quality time with you. I already told you, I have no fucking idea what happened! And I don't know why Doherty dragged you down here with me, either. So when are you going to stop being pissed at me about it?"

"Never, you fucker! Now shut up and let me get some sleep."

I didn't answer. Instead I went back to counting water drops while trying to ignore the moans from the poor fuckers who'd been brought down here last night. I'd counted the cells when the guards flicked the lights on, which was, usually, only when they brought another prisoner down. Otherwise, the only sliver of light in the place was from a small barred window near the top of the stone stairs which didn't illuminate much at all.

There were eight cells down here. Only the one directly opposite mine was empty. Once that was filled, I suspected we'd be moved elsewhere. My gut tightened. I was a trained agent, but I was utterly out of control here, and the alpha in me hated it.

My eyes had long since adjusted to the dark and I didn't falter as I stepped up to the cell bars and peered through. In the cell next to the empty one, a pair of luminous ice blue eyes regarded me. At first I'd been unnerved by the fae. The fae weren't supposed to be able to get into this world, not without the say so of their royal family—it seemed this one had broken the laws of both worlds and was paying for it. His unwavering attention had such a level of coldbloodedness and detachment that it scared even me. I knew a little about the fae, but the thing that stuck in my mind was that they were vicious and uncompromising warriors. They showed no mercy to their enemies. I wondered how this one got caught. It was hard to see his build clearly in the darkness, though he moved fluidly through the shadows of his cell.

"Evening, Walker." I grinned. He just stared at me, unblinking and ghostly. "Yeah, fuck you too, you creepy son of a bitch," I muttered, still grinning. Well, he'd been less than forthcoming about his name, and I needed to call him something. Besides, he looked so much like a white walker from Game of Thrones that it was a perfect name for him.

"Got any faerie magic you can use to get us out?" I knew he would remain silent. Maybe he didn't understand me, though I had to wonder if he could even speak.

"Hey, keep it down would ya? I'm trying to get my beauty sleep," Owen complained.

I snorted and grinned. "Jesus, you're going to have to sleep a lot then, Brady! You're one ugly assed mother fucker and sleep hasn't helped you so far!"

"With all due respect, sir...fuck off!" he growled back.

There were some answering yells to the same effect of shut up and let us sleep.

I swallowed against my dry throat and grinned at Walker, who blinked. "Ha!" I banged the bars. "That was a laugh, wasn't it? Or your version of one! I knew it! You're not totally dead, Walker, just a bit zombie-like."

He tilted his head and his ridiculously pretty, white hair fell to one side and over his shoulder, almost reaching down to his waist. His gaze slowly shifted from me to the steps that led up to the blast door. My whole body stiffened. Another prisoner; that was the only reason the guards came at night.

The locks on the door clattered and light flooded the stairwell. I winced, quickly looking away. Walker hissed and lifted his hand to shield his eyes, catching his fingers on the cell bars. His skin sizzled. He spat words I didn't understand and snatched his hand back. The scent of sweet, burned flesh permeated the air. Yeah, the bars were iron, a fae's worst nightmare.

"Watch yourself there, Walker. You might need to fight should I ever figure out how to get us out of here."

He blinked, and I was sure he nodded slightly before he stepped back from the bars.

Black booted feet jogged down the steps until I could see standard issue SBI cargo trousers. The guard flicked on the lights and there were shouts of discomfort from my fellow inmates. Walker hissed and stepped back into the shadows. None of us had seen sunlight since we'd been down here, and

Walker had already been staring at me when I woke up in my cell. He'd been here alone before any of us arrived.

"Settle down!" yelled a voice.

It was one I recognised. I called him Misery. That word epitomised everything about him. All the guards that brought new prisoners down here were careful not to use names, so, much as I had for Walker, I made up my own for them. Apparently, names had special power over a fae, and likewise they could control those who were stupid enough to offer their own name. I guess names were a bit of a gift and a lot of a curse to the fae.

Misery looked up the steps. "Bring them down."

I snarled as Perversion and Vice, two more of our regular guards, dragged a heavy looking male down the steps. His head lolled forward and he stank of blood and death. It clung to his skin and filled the air as they dragged him to the cell opposite mine. My blood froze. Under that blood and stink I knew that male's smell almost as well as I knew my own.

They threw Rawson's body onto the ground. A grunt escaped him but he didn't move.

"Fuck. Fuck. Fuck!" My fists curled and uncurled.

"Hmmm? What was that?" Vice narrowed his attention on me. I stared out through the bars, a snarl on my lips. I didn't need my wolf to challenge this piece of shit.

He sneered. "Oh, don't worry, wanker, we've got a surprise especially for you."

I held my breath. The mix of alcohol, cannabis, and his rotten teeth made it too vile to breathe in. Yeah, this one liked his booze and drugs. "Hey! Let's go get the girl!" He slapped Perversion on his back.

The other man swung his head my way, his slimy gaze running over me. Lust oozed from him, just like it did when he looked at any of the other alphas incarcerated down here. Yeah, this disgusting piece of shit liked being in a position of power over those who didn't like to submit. He got his rocks off tormenting and abusing the inmates. He hadn't quite got to me or Owen yet, other than a few strokes of my dick when he'd locked us up. I guessed my time might be up soon. I held his eyes and he smiled, licking his lips.

I'd bite the fucker's dick off or rip his throat out with my teeth if he came anywhere near me...

"Hey!" Vice smacked Perversion's bicep. "The girl?"

Rawson uttered a word, and I turned my attention to him, but he just lay on his side, blood running from his smashed face. He dragged his knees up into a foetal position as if he were in too much pain to do anything else.

I strained my ears.

"Lyss, Lyss, Lyss..."

My heart froze. Seeing him like this, beaten and broken, I knew what had to have happened.

There was a scuffle at the top of the stairs, and grunts filled the air.

"Hey!" There was the sound of slap. "Behave, or I'll ignore the boss's warning and punish you myself."

My fingers curled around the bars. Vice was a bastard and my stomach sank at the thought of him and his buddies dragging a woman down here. It couldn't be Lyss, could it? I prayed to the Mother Wolf that Perversion wasn't going to carry out his usual abuse. It would drive all the alphas in here mad, to hear another rape and not be able to stop it—me included. Maybe that was the point—more torture. Hearing Perversion's grunts as he forced himself on the drugged newbies made me sick to my soul.

I placed my cheek against the bars and peered up at the three sets of legs at the top. The woman was fighting hard, kicking out at her captors' knees. She managed to hook her foot behind Perversion's knee and must have slammed her head back. There was a resounding crack and grunt followed by a vicious curse.

"Bitch!" he roared and yanked the woman out of Vice's grasp. He shoved her, and she fell down the steps, bouncing off the walls. Red hair tumbled in a veil of fiery colour. There was the pop of bone followed by a high pitched scream.

My heart stuttered, and time stopped. That voice. That hair.

I gripped the iron bars, my muscles tensing as I tried to rip the iron apart to get to her. A vice gripped my chest. I couldn't breathe! "Ember!"

Walker stepped up to the bars, his ice blue gaze fixed on me, but I didn't care what he thought. I'd bare my soul for Ember. She shouldn't be here!

"Connor? What's wrong!" yelled Owen.

The cells were in an uproar, my pained roar awakening every alpha.

Perversion ran down the steps, followed closely by Vice. Blood ran from his broken nose and split lip.

"Don't you touch her!" I thumped the bars with my clenched fist, hard enough they bent.

Perversion grabbed Ember's stunning fiery hair and yanked her head back. He grinned at me, blood covering his teeth. "Hey, sweetheart, looks like the director was right. You're gonna be a hot bargaining chip with these dogs." He lifted her to her feet by her hair.

Ember clenched her jaw clearly in pain, but too stubborn to scream. Sheer fury burned in her eyes, a spark of flame igniting them. When she bent forward, I could see her shoulder was in an odd position. Gods, he'd dislocated it. My wolf snarled, clawing at my insides to get to her. There was no question she was in agony, with her wrists shackled behind her back. They'd put a silver collar around her neck as well. I smashed my fists against the cell bars again. They had caged her wolf just like mine.

I silently promised the gods above that Doherty and these men...everyone responsible for Ember's pain, would die in deep fucking agony.

"Ember?" I tried not to choke on my fury.

Her green eyes widened, tears lining her eyes, the expression on her face something I'd never forget.

"Connor?" she whispered, her voice breaking. She swallowed hard and deep furrows creased her brow. As if it was too painful to look at me, she dragged her gaze to Rawson instead.

Perversion chuckled. "Looks like you're in the doghouse, Maxwell. Did you fuck this one and leave her? She looks pissed at you." He sneered and swung her towards Rawson then back to me. Ember whimpered. I growled. That movement must have jarred her damaged shoulder, but she bit her lip. She'd never scream for him.

"Let's see. Who shall we put her with? Maybe the fae would like a taste. I hear they like to take the will of human females and use them as slaves. I wonder what he'd do with a shifter?" He licked his lips in anticipation. "I'd like to see him in action. Is your dick blue too?" Walker stared at Ember implacably before that cold gaze lifted to Perversion. Something feral flashed in Walker's eyes. Perversion quickly stepped back. It was apparent he wasn't sure he could take on this fae and win. "Nah, you're right." He grinned at Walker. "You're too important to let escape. I'll keep her with me." And with that, he swung her against the wall beside my cell and shoved his groin into hers. The pig was tall enough he needed to bend his knees for positioning. He licked up the side of her face. "Mmm, she tastes so good. I can see why she's driving you mad." He slid a look my way before he grunted, pulled his pelvis back, and slammed into her again.

"Finish what you're doing with the she-wolf, and get your arse back upstairs. I'm taking the car. Transfer is tonight, so I'll be back in an hour." Misery jogged up the steps.

Perversion didn't even react. He just kept looking at me the whole time he ground on Ember. My blood boiled. "I'll kill you." My growling rattled the bars of each cell, sending dust cascading from the roof. He grinned and bit her neck, pushing on her injured shoulder as he did.

Ember cried out then went lax, drooping in his arms.

I roared, my fingers curling around the bars. I strained, pulling at them, desperate to get to her. There was a cracking sound the harder I pulled.

"Fuck me, you really do want some of this don't you?" Perversion crooned, eyeing the bars with glee.

Vice stood with his arms crossed, watching. The fucker wasn't going to stop this anytime soon. Did he get off on watching rape, too? Occasionally the other guards stopped Perversion from going too far—but not always.

I forced myself to release the bars and prowled to the ones nearest to him. An icy void filled my chest. I knew precisely what it meant. If I had to break these walls down with my bare hands, he was gonna die. "You gonna stand for that, Firecracker?" I stared at her face, which he'd turned towards me. Her scrunched up eyes snapped open, and she glared at me, fire sparking in their emerald depths. "That's it." I willed her to fight.

Perversion pulled back and then thrust against her again. Ember waited until he pulled away, and shifted sideways. When he drove forward once more, she rammed her knee skillfully into his groin, then slammed her forehead into his face. Perversion yelped and sagged forward. With a yell, Ember rammed him with her good shoulder, hooking a foot behind his ankles and sending him toppling towards me. He fell at my feet, only the cell bars separating us. Without hesitation, I reached through and grabbed his neck. He was still stunned, but wouldn't be for long. Damn, it was good to get my hands around his throat. I squeezed, helpless to do anything to aid Ember other than stop this bastard ever touching her again. All the frustration and anger at what these men had done centered in my grip. I squeezed even harder, a guttural roar escaping my throat.

Walker watched unblinkingly.

Vice leaped forward, his hands outstretched to grab Ember, but she was quicker. She spun around him and landed a kick in his kidneys. An agonised cry escaped her. Her chest rose and fell hard, and her eyes watered as she gripped her injured shoulder.

"Firecracker!"

Vice twisted and caught her with a punch to her belly. She fell to her knees, coughing and spluttering. The next kick slammed into her chest, and she doubled over. For the first time in my life I froze. Her gasping breaths echoed through me and blood surged through my veins, roaring in my ears. It blinded me to anything but getting to her. My wolf snarled and ripped at my insides, caged by the silver collar. His howls fuelled my own wrath to the point where I snapped. My fingers clenched tighter around Perversion's throat. A wet sound bubbled from him as I ripped his flesh apart with my bare hands.

Vice prowled behind Ember staring right at me as he took out a knife. He moved up quietly, a grin on his face, and raised the knife. The heat in my blood turned to ice. "Don't you do it!"

Vice grinned wider and wound Ember's hair gently around his fist, forcing her head up and exposing the creamy length of her throat. Her eyes were closed, breath blowing from her nose and between her clenched teeth.

I shook Perversion's blood from my hand and rattled the bars again. "No!

You kill her, and I will destroy you!"

"What the fuck is happening!?" Owen roared. The other alphas were baying, demanding to know, too. Walker stared at me in that dead way of his. I ignored them all, my attention fixed on Ember. I'd failed her. And right now, I realised how much. She was mine; my mate and now I had to watch her die because I'd failed…

Vice pressed the blade to Ember's throat. Blood bloomed where he cut into her skin.

I swallowed, pain tearing at my heart.

Then her beautiful eyes opened. Flames.

I almost sobbed. I knew Ember was different; so did she. The silver collar had imprisoned her wolf, but Doherty had no idea about Ember's other gift. She was scared of it; I knew she was. She had no influence over it, and it only ever surfaced when her emotions were out of control. I had no idea what it was, but, right now I didn't care, not if it could help her escape this hell hole.

Her burning gaze held mine. But then the flames stuttered, and she blinked rapidly, shaking her head, her eyes gleaming with moisture.

"Use it. Save yourself and get out of here." I had no idea what damage her fire could bring down on us all, but I was willing to bet she would survive it. To me that was all that mattered.

Vice pushed the blade into Ember's neck. Her soft creamy skin split open, her blood spilling; enough that I was sure she would die. Her chest rose and fell rapidly. She stared directly at me, those flames reappearing.

"Do it!" I yelled.

She screamed, and yanked her arms from behind her back. She'd melted the cuffs. Her hands glowed like hot coals. She grabbed one of his wrists and pushed against his face with her other hand. Vice screamed and dropped the blade. It clattered to the ground. She twisted, opening the wound on her neck further, but it didn't seem to bother her. Vice's skin sizzled, the stench of burning flesh filling the air. She grabbed his clothes, and they ignited, flames licking over his body and setting his hair alight.

The sweet, metallic scent of Ember's blood was all I could smell. I rattled the bars, bellowing from the base of my lungs. My chest squeezed, an adrenaline surge lending me strength. Dust fell from the concrete surrounding the bars. Opposite me, Rawson raised his head, then shook it as if trying to clear his vision.

Ember shuffled away from Vice, who thrashed his arms and staggered about.

Ember felt her throat, where her blood still flowed. Her fingers turned slick and red, but her touch cauterised the wound enough that it stopped bleeding. She snarled and kicked the burning man to the ground. Agonised screams erupted from his mouth.

"That's right! Burn you fucker!" I yelled.

Ember's beautiful red hair swung over her shoulder as she twisted to her feet. She cocked her head and touched the silver collar until it glowed brightly. It fell away, melted by the heat. Reaching down, she picked up Vice's knife with her uninjured arm. "Nice blade," she commented coldly, and thrust it through the flames straight into his heart. "I really should have let you suffer, you evil fuck, but I need those keys." She knelt down and unclipped a glowing-hot bunch of keys from Vice's waistband. At the same time an alarm began to blare out in the building above. The smoke had drifted up through the open door.

"Shit." She ran to me. Blood had dripped down her neck soaking the collar of her vest top.

She tried to find a key that looked like it might fit my cell, but she was shaking and using one hand. They fell from her grip and clattered to the ground. "Sorry." Her eyes darted to mine. "My-my fire...she's gone."

"Hey." I reached through the bars and touched her cheek before she could kneel down to pick them up, then yanked my hand back when I noticed I was covered in blood. I wouldn't touch her with Perversion's blood contaminating my skin. "It's okay. You did amazing, Firecracker. Now let me help. Give me the keys." My eyes drifted to the cauterised wound on her neck. I swallowed hard, wanting badly to heal her. My wolf rumbled in agreement. "And use your wolf to heal your shoulder."

She swallowed and nodded, but I suspected she was too weak to heal herself. With her right hand she scooped the keys from the floor, trying to hide her wince. I took the keys, and within moments, I was free. Her emerald gaze searched my face as if she couldn't believe I was in front of her. "They told us you died." Her voice broke. I cursed Doherty for the pain he'd caused my family. Careful of her injuries, I pulled her into my arms. "No, Firecracker, I didn't," I whispered into her hair. "And even if I did, I'd somehow find my way back to you."

"Hey! That's nice and all, but get me the fuck out of here!" Owen roared.

I pulled back. She stared up at me, her face softening. Without any hesitation I kissed her. It was a mere brush of my lips over hers, but heat seared my chest. A strange energy sizzled over my skin, combining with my own, and stirred my wolf into a frenzy. A small whimper fell from her lips. I smiled as she leaned closer, her lips parted, and her eyes closed. I ignored the baying of my friend and kissed her again, deeper this time. She was my mate, she was alive and she was amazing; unlike anyone I'd ever met; a storm of fury and power just waiting to erupt. Heat seared through my chest. I wouldn't admit it out loud, but my eyes burned, my whole body shaking and my knees trembling as I held her in my arms.

"Hey!" yelled Owen again, banging his cell bars.

I released a heavy breath, staring at Ember's wide eyes and pale face when I pulled away. I couldn't resist dropping another kiss on her swollen lips. "Don't go anywhere," I whispered against her mouth. I turned away from her and unlocked Rawson's cell, then Owen's. I eyed the other cells, then looked back at Rawson's ruined body. He needed help. Fighting my urge to keep Ember by my side, I held the keys out to her. "I know you're hurt, but can you free them while we get Rawson up? I'll put your shoulder back in once they're out."

Without hesitation, she took the keys and nodded.

Owen helped me haul Rawson up. Once on his feet, he groaned, but pushed us away; swaying, though he managed to stay up right. How, I had no idea. His face was badly damaged and his eyes...Jesus... The bleak look in them was something I'd never forget.

"Can you walk?" I held back, keeping my distance out of respect for him. He was a strong alpha who would never admit to any weakness. I pressed my lips into a tight line. But it wasn't just his body that was broken; it was his mind and spirit, and until he healed I'd be his strength, even if he didn't want it.

His eyes shifted to the burned and ravaged corpses of his captors. His eyes darkened as his bear fought for release against the collar. I could see his skin burn beneath it. I narrowed my eyes studying his features. Rawson was normally objective and the strongest shifter I knew—as strong as me—but he had lost his soul mate, been beaten and imprisoned all in one night. He was not thinking straight. If he lost control, we were all at risk. And once we figured out how to get the collars off, an injured and grieving bear would not be easy to subdue, not even for so many alphas. He nodded and peered at me through his swollen eyes. "I can. And I want Doherty's blood, not any of yours." His nostrils flared and his gaze met mine as if he had read my thoughts.

The door at the top of the stairs swung shut with a loud slam. It clicked, locking us in.

Owen swung his head to the noise. "Damn! Those fire alarms have closed it."

Ember had worked her way down one side of the corridor, opening the cells, and then back up the other. Walker gave her his dead eyed stare and she halted in front of him. "I know what you are, and if you try and hurt anyone, especially Connor, I'll shove fire so far down your throat, there will be nothing but dust left."

Heat slammed through me, warming the coldest reaches of my heart as I grasped that she would protect me as fiercely as I would her. I didn't bother to hide the lust her words ignited inside me and fixed my heated stare on her face.

She soon noticed. "Stop looking at me like that."

I smirked.

Walker stepped out of his cell, giving the iron bars a wide berth. He prowled up to her, and even at only five feet four inches, my Firecracker didn't give an inch. The fae wasn't stacked with muscle like me, but moved with a beautiful grace that spoke of hidden power and speed. Maybe all fae moved like him. I didn't know. The only ones I'd ever seen before I'd been required to kill, which I generally did from a distance with a weapon that fired iron bullets.

Ember's eyes flashed with warning, but Walker just tilted his head. Then he did the damnedest thing—he bowed—low. Like some kind of ancient knight. "Thank you. I owe you a debt." He stood tall, and turned to me. "Both of you."

I swallowed hard and nodded. Fae did not put themselves in debt to others easily.

Walker's clothes were caked in grime and dirt, but it didn't hide how well made and expensive they were. He wore a heavily embroidered silk shirt, leather trousers and knee high boots. No weapons. By all accounts, he looked expensively dressed- as if he'd just stepped out of the pages of some historical romance novel—that was until you looked in his eyes and a predator stared back at you.

He moved his hand, and something in me went on alert. Jumping in front of Ember, I snarled into the fae's face. At six foot five, we seemed evenly matched. I still had that damn collar on, but my hands were weapons enough, as Perversion had found out. "Don't touch her."

Walker blinked but was otherwise totally unaffected by my protective reaction or the threat in my voice.

"I can heal your mate." He looked around my shoulder and down at Ember, who tutted and shoved me sideways.

"I'm not his mate."

She wasn't strong enough to push me out of the way, but I wasn't about to ignore her demand to move, nor would I ignore that statement.

Unable to stop myself, I curled my hands around her hips. "Not yet. But you will be."

Ember rolled her eyes but otherwise chose to ignore my statement. She couldn't hide the increase in her heart rate from me, though. I smirked and kept my eyes on her face, enjoying the flush that spread over her cheeks.

Walker peered down at her. "I will heal your shoulder, and my debt to you is no more," he said.

She nodded in agreement and pushed my hands away.

The fae put his blue-skinned hand on her shoulder. A strange, soft light emanated from his fingers. There was a *pop*, and Ember screeched.

I instantly tensed. "What did you do!?"

"I'm fine! I'm fine!" Ember grabbed my hand to prevent me from seizing his throat and ending him. It was then she swung her arm experimentally and smiled at Walker. "Thank you," she said.

"You healed her?" My voice shook, my gut tightening hard enough to be painful. Magic like that only existed between soul mates, at least in this world.

Walker merely grunted. "Now I owe only you." His voice was smooth and deep. Far deeper than I expected.

"Hey! Does anyone have any ideas? This door's not gonna budge," shouted one of the alphas, distracting me from my need to push this otherworldly male away from Ember. I exhaled and entwined my fingers with Ember's, wanting contact with her. I had no idea what was typical for fae magic, but the thought of this cold-eyed fae being a potential mate for Ember, and rival for me, had my blood boiling. She frowned and gently but firmly pulled her hand from my grasp. I let her go but positioned myself between her and Walker. "No, but come on down and let us up. Brady! You're the explosives expert. Go and have a look at it. There's electricity, silver, iron, and a whole load of other shit down here, including Perv's weapons. Let's see if you can do anything with it to get us out."

"If you wait, the guards will come," remarked Walker. He crossed his arms over his chest and watched us.

I glanced at him, so did Ember. His cold eyes studied the door and then me. "You got some magic there we can use?" Instinct told me he was holding something back, so I did nothing to hide my mistrust. "You appear to be high fae, which means you're powerful, so why didn't you escape?"

Owen glanced at me and stepped closer, recognising the suspicion in my tone.

Walker remained utterly unimpressed, his eyes like illuminated chips of ice. I didn't like that he had healed Ember, but I could smell a lie a mile off. I strained my ears to listen to his heart rate and breathing.

"I am not high fae, and like any other fae, the iron stops my magic from working. I need to be further away from it for longer before my magic will be strong enough to cause damage."

His heartrate didn't increase, neither did his breathing. He wasn't lying, but it didn't escape me his answers were deliberately vague.

"He's right." Rawson shuffled out of the shadows of his cell and spat a mouthful of blood on the ground.

I bit back my retort to Walker, watching Ember as she registered Rawson was awake.

She blinked and with a little cry, ran to him and flung her arms around him. "I'm so sorry about Lyss," she whispered brokenly into his chest.

I swallowed a growl at seeing her hold another man, even if it was

Rawson. It was damn hard. All my wolf wanted was to claim her; the need to do so burning deep in my gut. I wanted nothing more than to drag her into the nearest cell and do just that. But I shook off my selfish desires. She was right, she wasn't mine, and I was an insensitive bastard for even thinking of claiming her right now. And commanding her not to touch another person, especially one she loved, would only earn me a fist in my face or a boot in my nuts.

"What happened to Lyss?" I asked Rawson.

His throat bobbed. "I—can't..." He screwed his eyes up as if in pain.

"Then don't." I growled, my own throat aching at the thought of Lyss being gone. It was a fucking miracle Rawson was even functioning if Lyss was dead. I wasn't sure I'd be able to breathe if Ember died, let alone function. It was becoming impossible not to grab her and keep her close. I glanced at Vice's smoldering body. I wished I could bring him back, just so that I could kill the bastard again.

"No, don't," Ember whispered up at Rawson, agreeing with me. She kissed his cheek, tears trickling from her eyes. My stomach flipped at that sign of distress, when I knew she would rather bite her own finger off than cry. Lyss had been kind to me when no other person on this planet seemed to have a heart. Even Rawson had kicked my arse when I'd first come to live with him. I knew the pain Ember suffered, even if I couldn't express it the same way. Whoever had killed a kind-hearted soul like Lyss deserved to suffer an eternity in hell.

Ember spun away from Rawson. A look of determination crossed her face. I cocked my head, watching her through narrowed eyes. My Firecracker had a plan. Her boots clicked on the concrete as she strode to the stairwell, sidestepping the smoking embers of Vice's body. The whole place stunk of burning flesh.

She peered up at the three alphas at the top of the stairs. "Come out of the way, guys."

They hesitated, one eyed me warily, the other two gave her heated looks. I narrowed my eyes and rolled my shoulders, my fists curling so tightly, my fingernails scored my palms. Jealousy was not an emotion I was familiar with. I went after whatever woman I wanted with a single-minded purpose, and they never refused. But Ember was different. She was mine. My mate. Not theirs. And I hated that they even looked at her with interest, never mind the lust that burned in their eyes. *Bloody alphas!* "Now!" I curled my top lip back in a snarl. My wolf might be caged, but so were theirs. The difference between us? I was still capable of ripping them to shreds. The biggest of them eyed Perversion's corpse. His silver grey hair and eyes shone eerily when he looked back at me. "That's right." I grinned viciously. "Get away from her. Now."

The alpha narrowed his eyes, nodded and urged the others down the steps, past Ember. They stopped near me, and again I positioned myself between them and her. I inhaled and caught a scent vaguely like Walker's from the silver haired man.

Ember eyed me, then them. No question she was pissed that they had listened to me and not her. I shrugged. "Alpha," I reminded her, but it wasn't just that. It hadn't escaped my notice that all these other men were shifters, but not just any old shifters; they were all potential alphas, too.

Without another word, Ember ran up the steps.

I had an idea what she was doing. The only trouble was, if it worked, there was no knowing what was outside that door. "What's your name?" I asked the grey haired man.

"Stone," he answered coldly.

"Don't go near her, Stone. And make sure the others stay away from her."

His face remained blank and cold. "Why? Frightened she'd prefer them over you, alpha?"

It was interesting that he didn't include himself in that comment. "No. Sure, I'll still kill them if they look at her the wrong way." Yeah, I was not a nice guy around my mate and other alphas. "But see this guy here that she burned to a crisp?" He nodded. "It has more to do with the fact you'll end up like that if you upset *her*." I shrugged and stepped over to Perversion's body. Squatting, I pulled two guns from the holsters on his smoldering legs. One looked like some kind of tranq' gun. It was loaded with tiny darts that held a small phial of green liquid. My nostrils flared in recognition. Careful to avoid his scorched flesh, I searched his body and discovered one large knife and two smaller ones.

I peered up at Owen. "Here you take the gun. Check it still works. I'll take the knife. I'm better at close combat than you. Hey, Walker?"

Icy eyes looked at me. "You want this?" I waved the dart gun in the air.

He nodded once, walked over and took it.

"Still a man of few words, hmm?"

He just looked at me.

I grinned. The two smaller blades I handed to Stone. "We stay together up there," I said. No one argued. A pack stood a better chance of survival than a lone wolf. "You need help there, old man?" I asked Rawson, hiding my worry for him. Rawson shook his head and gestured for me to go ahead. I didn't like leaving him to stagger along behind, but neither could I stay and help him, not that he would accept it. Forcing my worry aside, I jogged up the steps. Getting Ember out was my priority right now.

Ember had her hands flat on the metal door, right over the locking mechanism. "Don't you come near me."

"You can't burn me, remember?" But my attention was on her hands, fascinated with the way heat pulsed from her skin.

"I know, but it doesn't mean I won't try, you bastard." Her eyes opened, and she turned her head to glare at me. They shone wetly, and my gut tightened. I hated to see those tears and know I was the cause. I'd fucked up when I'd left her after our kiss.

"You left me. Without so much as a word, you dumped me on the driveway, and then you just disappeared." She turned her face towards the door again, closing her eyes.

I swallowed, my heart squeezing, even my wolf hung his head. "I'm sorry, Firecracker, but it wasn't my fault..."

"I know. Not this time." Her voice was tight, and I didn't know if it was with the effort of summoning enough heat to melt the lock or if it was a far darker emotion. "It's just the way things are. People leave...My parents left me. And you? You left me years ago, well before you disappeared this time." She sighed, and removed her hands from the door, shaking them out. "It was Doherty who told us you were dead." Her statement was flat and unemotional.

Anger surged in my veins at the depth of the director's deceit.

"Rawson left me and Lyss after you disappeared. He spent hours, days and then weeks away from us trying to find the truth about what really happened."

My attention flicked down to Rawson. He leaned against the wall and stared at the floor. That man had given me a shot at a decent life, and it seemed he had lost his own trying to save me—again. Oh, I knew he wasn't dead, but he may as well be. He'd lost Lyss, and she was his whole life. Nausea rolled in my gut. Looking for me had cost him dearly. I owed him—big time. I also needed to know what devils he'd unearthed to make Doherty come down on him so hard. But right now it was Ember who needed me most. We had to get away from here, and she needed to know I wouldn't leave her again, that she could trust me.

Her gaze followed mine to rest on Rawson's damaged face. "And now he will leave again, especially with Lyss being gone. He will tear down the world to find those responsible for killing her. None of us can go home."

"He's not going to leave you, Ember, neither am I."

"You will," she said, her voice still flat, her eyes so distant I shuddered. "You'll help him bring Doherty down, and to do that you'll both have to leave. I have no idea why he was keeping you all here, but he can't be allowed to get away with it."

The other alphas watched us, their faces dark, their fists clenched, but I ignored them. Walker prowled to the bottom of the stairs.

I brushed her cheek with the back of my fingers. "Even if we have to leave, we'll always come back."

She sighed, and blinked slowly. "No, Connor, there are no guarantees you will, and even if you do, it doesn't mean you'll stay."

I had no idea what was going on in her head, or her heart, but it was clear she didn't trust me, and now wasn't the time for a deep conversation like this. I needed to get her and the others out of here.

She swallowed hard and looked away from me. "I can't do this," she whispered, studying her hands. She held them up, desperation in her voice.

My heart lurched, until I realised she was talking about her gift, not our possible relationship. "I can't make my fire work. It won't work. Why won't it work when I need it to?" she asked, her words were fast, her eyes wide.

"I don't know." I took hold of her hands, hoping to calm her. My lips pressed together. We needed her fire to get out of this door. If we waited for the guards to enter we would be at a massive disadvantage but... "Ember, it's okay, you've only ever been able to summon it when you're in an extreme state of emotion or are in mortal danger."

Wide eyed she stared up at me. "No." She shook her head. "It has to work. We have to get out!"

"Allow me." Walker didn't wait for my answer, he strode up the remaining stairs, stepped around Ember and me and up to the door. With a glowing finger, he traced runes over the lock. The words he whispered were soft and musical, drifting into my ears and echoing before drifting away. Each rune he drew burned with light then sank into the metal. And just like that, the door unlocked. Walker's white brows dipped. It was the first emotion I'd ever seen on his face.

"Didn't you do that?"

"I'm afraid not," he said and twisted away from the door just as it swung open.

I lunged for Ember's arm and pushed us sideways. We slammed into the wall just before bullets pinged against the door and the walls, sending bits of concrete into my back and shoulders. I nudged Ember further out of harm's way, keeping my body wrapped around her like a shield. Unless we could somehow get their weapons from them, we were fucked. I spun around, making sure my bulk still protected Ember. She touched my back as if she needed to reassure herself that I was there. I looked back at her. "Okay?" My gut squeezed at her ashen face.

She nodded, blinking rapidly.

Owen jogged up the steps, stopping with his back to the wall, gun at the ready. "Now what?"

Walker met my gaze. Pure predator stared out of his icy eyes. That predatory need to kill lurked in me, too; clamouring to escape, just like my wolf. The fae studied the gun in his hand then shoved it into his waistband. "Now, we wait for them to come closer," he answered before I could speak. "Then, we kill them." And he stretched his glowing fingers and cracked his neck.

CHAPTER 7

MY THROAT BURNED. I craved water or a drink of any kind. Calling on Fire like that depleted me of moisture, leaving me shaky. It had been the first time I'd ever used her gift deliberately. The only times it had appeared in the past was when I was dying, or I was out of emotional control. I took a deep breath, trying to process what I'd done. I'd killed a man. Shouldn't I feel guilt, or remorse or something? Leaning on the wall, I searched inside myself. Connor's scent filled my senses, his broad back blocking my view of the others and protecting me from flying bits of stone. Nope, there was nothing but relief at getting away from that evil man. And finding Connor? Jesus, I'd thought I was hallucinating when I'd heard his voice. I reached out, needing to make sure he was real. I rested my palm on the middle of his back. Hard muscle shifted beneath my touch.

He turned his head and peered down at me. "Okay?"

I nodded, though I was far from okay. All I wanted to do was wrap my arms around him and make sure he didn't disappear again. The silver collar around his neck glinted, stoking my fury. I blinked rapidly. Such a beautiful and powerful alpha should never be collared like a pet. A piece of stone hit the wall above my shoulder, the shard bouncing off and hitting me. I winced and my wolf snarled. Unlike all the alphas waiting to fight for their freedom, my wolf was free. They might want to rip their captors apart, but so did I; the difference was, I could. Connor's muscles shifted under my hand. My body heated at that contact, and something clicked into place inside me. I needed to know he was safe. And I'd break that bloody collar from his neck with my bare hands if I had to. I couldn't melt his collar right now. I'd shoved Fire back into her cage and even if she hadn't gone willingly, I couldn't risk burning his skin with molten metal.

While Walker, Connor and Owen decided what our next move was, I decided on mine. Behind the protection of Connor's broad back, I shed my clothes.

Walker was the first to notice me. His face didn't change but he cocked his head then looked back at Connor.

"Holy shit." Owen's mouth dropped open, before his gaze travelled over my nakedness.

I flushed but refused to cover myself. These other men were all shifters and should be used to getting naked. With a huff, I smirked. Just not in the middle of a prison break. Connor swiveled to face me, ducking a little when another barrage of bullets hit the wall and door. Owen stuck his gun out of the door and pulled the trigger blindly.

Connor's eyes met mine. He growled and stood in front of me. A snarl curled his lip, but he couldn't stop his gaze dropping to my toes and slowly rising. Heat banked in his gaze when his perusal paused on the juncture between my thighs before rising over my flat stomach to my breasts. He inhaled deeply, and I knew he was scenting me; my fear and the lust that shivered through me at the desire in his gaze.

"Move." My voice was more of a squeak than a demand.

"No fucking way." His eyes flashed, his fists clenched. "Put your clothes back on." The possessive growl in his voice had goosebumps exploding over my skin.

As much as I wanted to argue with the challenge in his tone, and wrap myself around that honed and magnificent body, now was not the time. I narrowed my eyes and bent down to pick up my bundled clothes. Instead of answering, I closed my eyes and called my fire to heat my hands, praying hard for her to answer. I needed to get Connor out of this place. My wolf heeded my desperation and faded into the recesses of my mind, giving Fire access. If I couldn't do this we were all going to die. A burst of heat rushed down my arms, and into my hands. The bundle of clothes burst into flame. I staggered back as Fire immediately receded into the depths of my soul. Pushing off the wall, I darted around Connor before I threw them through the doorway. Smoke rose, creating a screen.

"What the hell are you doing?" Connor yelled before his eyes widened and he shook his head at me. "Damn stubborn, clever woman." He glared at me, yanking his shirt off those impressive shoulders. I swallowed against my dry throat. His body was a work of art, all sculpted lines and hard muscle. I tried not to stare, more aware of my nakedness than ever. "Quick! Feed it!"

Walker yanked his silk shirt off and threw it on the pile. "Damn!" Owen hissed and threw his into the mix, before looking down at the others. "Shirts off, boys, now!"

They obliged and smoke soon filled the corridor.

Connor turned to peer out of the door. I didn't wait to see his face when he spun back and reached for me. If I looked in those beautiful sky blue eyes, I wouldn't want to leave his side. Instead, I let my wolf burst free. Mid change, I leaped from the doorway. Like me, she wanted to stay with her mate, but the urge to protect him was stronger. We needed to rip apart the people who had imprisoned him.

I darted through the smoke.

"Ember!" Connor's urgent shout was lost in the gun fire. Bullets hit the wall above my head. I lowered my body down and headed to the edge of the corridor, away from the line of sight to the door, then dipped down to my haunches trying to make myself an even smaller target. Low to the ground I slunk along. The stench of fear and sweat hit my nostrils. I lowered down more, almost on my belly, and watched shadowy figures inch forward, firing round after round of silver bullets through the smoke, at the doorway. Connor and the others wouldn't stand a chance of getting out. Once Owen's gun ran out of ammo that would be it.

I crept closer. Hatred hit me like a freight train. These men were dressed in SBI uniforms. I couldn't fathom why the SBI were locking up alphas and fae in underground cells, and taking away their ability to shift.

I snarled. Two agents came into view. Their attention remained on the door. They had no idea of the danger inching ever closer.

"Keep pushing, they can't have that much ammo left," one said.

My wolf was hungry for blood, so I released her. Within seconds she had latched onto the man's forearm, tearing at the joints of his armour until it came away. She sunk her teeth into his flesh and severed it away. He screamed, his fingers loosening on his weapon. Clamping her great jaws around the gun, she yanked it from his grasp. I took control and shifted back to human. The man's eyes widened at my naked form. Grinning evilly, I flipped the gun around, and shot him in his visor.

Shifting back to my wolf, I darted away from the next nearest agent. This time my wolf skidded to a halt near the wall and spun around. Without hesitation, she bent to her haunches, gathered her strength and leaped. Her front paws pushed his weapon down at the same time as she ripped at the armour around his neck. But this armour was meant to protect against wolves bigger than me, and though I knew where the vulnerabilities lay, I couldn't get through. A sharp pain stung my side. Instinctively, I jumped away. Snapping, I didn't give him a chance to raise his gun or throw the knife that he'd stabbed me with. I let my wolf's viciousness take over. She launched at the only other vulnerable area. His face. I detached myself as she ripped at his flesh, the metallic taste of hot blood hitting her throat. She revelled in it, the scent of her prey only making her more wild. The other alphas rushed forward. One went down, shot in the chest, but the others barrelled into the armed men with no fear. Not even the bullet wounds they sustained in their arms and legs stopped them. The alphas ripped the guns away from the agents, and killed them.

"Ember!" My wolf's attention snapped to the man who was our mate. She trotted up to him and rubbed against his legs. "We have to get out of here," Connor said, keeping his gun trained on the corridor. I put my nose down to the ground and followed the scent of the guard who'd brought me in, looking behind occasionally to make sure Connor was following.

"I got you covered, Firecracker." Owen and Walker jogged along behind Connor, the other alphas behind them. All of them were now armed thanks to the agents.

A locked door loomed before us. "Here!" Owen chucking an ID badge forward.

"That's no good." Connor, cursing loudly. "It's a blood lock."

Walker prowled up. Calmly, he held out a severed hand with part of its forearm attached.

Connor blinked and his brows dipped. He obviously wondered the same thing as me: how did Walker sever the man's hand? But right then it didn't matter. We needed to get out. Connor took the hand and slammed the palm on the pad. The metal bands clicked into place followed by the snap of a needle, and the door slid open. He glared at the cameras on the roof, aimed and shot them out. I ran forward, knowing we had to get to the next hatch before security had time to take this agent's blood profile out of the system. The next door opened and a storm of bullets rained forth.

Red hot agony slammed into my shoulder. My wolf went down. *Come on. Get back up. If you stay here we're both going to die,* I told her, trying to ignore the pain.

The sound of gunshots deafened me. Connor yelled, his scent mixed with the coppery smell of iron. *Blood.* He'd been hit again. My heart hammered against my ribs. I urged my wolf forward. She sprang up from the floor, and ignoring the bullets whizzing past her, and Connor's bellow, she ran, launching herself at the first agent. These men were not dressed in armour but in street clothes. My wolf sank further into a killing rage. I had no idea why these men were here, nor did I care. They'd locked up the only two people left in this world that I loved, and they'd pay for it. My wolf snarled her agreement and we melded our thoughts.

The first man we reached didn't stand a chance. I lunged and ripped out his throat while my momentum drove him backwards. He was dead before he hit the ground. I bounded to the next one and jumped on his back. My teeth embedded in the back of his neck, and I ripped at flesh and bone until his agonised screams stopped. Before I could release his neck and go for the next man in line a redhot pain lanced my back leg. I glanced at where a knife protruded. Whimpering, I limped a few steps before I was too dizzy to go further. I'd lost more blood than I thought from my other wound. My fur was coated and sticky. I whined and lay down, the blood loss and exhaustion catching up with me. I sank to my belly on the tiled floor.

"Ember!" Connor yelled. He skidded on his knees to my side, blood leaking from a wound in his arm. I whimpered and licked his wound. He stroked my fur. "Shh, I'm okay. Change back." But I couldn't. I was too weak. I gave him a gentle snarl. I just needed a minute.

"Okay, but the fighting is done, and I at least need you to get up before we open that door." Connor eased my body off the floor and helped me stand. I whined as pain flooded my lupine body. "Easy, I'll get us out, then I'll help you change back."

I peered at him. He was still kneeling, so I leaned forward and licked his cheek. His wolf might be locked behind that collar, but his power still crackled against my soul. It would be more than enough to assist my shift. His small smile warmed my heart, even though worry remained in his eyes. "You'll be fine, Firecracker. Owen! Grab that piece of shit." He stood tall and pointed at a dead agent, but his face remained tight as he studied my injuries and the handle of the small knife that protruded from my fur. "You sure you don't want me to carry you?"

I growled.

He laughed softly. "Thought not."

Owen grabbed the dead agent's arm and dragged him across the floor to the pad. Streaks of blood tracked after them, stark against the white floor.

"We'll find a way to stop the bleeding once we're out, but you can't shift with this in your flesh. Sorry, this is going to sting like a bitch." And before I realised his intentions, Connor pulled the small knife from my flesh. I snapped at the air between us. "Easy." Gently, he put his hand on my head. I allowed it, and even welcomed the soft pulse of power he sent into me. He smiled. "That's it, Firecracker, let me help."

The door popped open, air hissing from the seals.

Walker prowled up, taking in my injuries and blood loss. In my wolf form I could smell his unique scent. Like the freshest of winter mornings and the pureness of a glacial spring. "Let me try."

Connor narrowed his eyes, his jaw tightening. After a moment of hesitation, he nodded and removed his hand from my bleeding wound. Walker placed his own hand over my lacerated flesh. That same sense of cold and soothing swamped me though I jumped when his other hand rested over the bullet wound.

I whined, my body shaking.

"Steady, brave one, I will not harm you further."

There was a sharp pain when the bullet was forced out by my healing flesh. It bounced on the floor. My flesh blazed with pain that ebbed as it healed. Within moments the cold sensation of his magic receded. Walker removed his hands, stood up in one fluid motion, his muscles rippling, and wiped my blood on his trousers.

"Thank you," Connor said tightly, also uncoiling his powerful body.

I nudged my head against his legs, needing to touch him, and to reassure him I was stronger. He gently placed his palm on the top of my head. It was hard not to succumb to the comfort of that touch, but I was not given to letting my mate protect me. I could protect myself, so I nudged him away from me and yipped.

"Okay, Firecracker, I get it; you can look after yourself."

Tentatively I took a step, testing out my stride. There was very little pain. I peered up at Walker, noticing his strange blue eyes were ringed with green as he looked down at me, his face implacable. I bowed my head. He nodded back and walked out of the door behind the other alphas.

Connor growled. "Idiots. There could be all sorts of weapons out there."

I could hear the worry in his voice. He had taken on the role of their leader, and along with it, responsibility for their safety.

But nothing happened.

He slowly approached the exit and we both peered out. There were no gunshots, no shouts. I trotted through, Connor following close behind. Late evening sun hit my face, and the smell of damp undergrowth and pine needles surrounded us. There was a distant rush of traffic but it was clear we were in the countryside, definitely not at the SBI headquarters despite the agents and technology that was used in this place.

"Where the hell are we?" Connor asked.

Owen turned on the spot, his brows dipped. "Damned if I know. I don't recognise this place at all."

I limped to the edge of the clearing. The alphas had all stopped, some contemplated the forest, others the small dirt track that led across the fields. In the distance a dust cloud rose. The vehicles that approached from a gateway about a mile down the track dipped behind a gentle hill and disappeared before they reappeared.

As a unit the alphas looked back at Connor. Stone jogged back through the door and came back a moment later with more weapons. Tucking a spare in his belt, he held one out to one of the others. Connor checked his weapon.

"We need to run, but it can't be this easy to walk out of here and into that forest. Check your weapons. There will be wolves waiting. We stay together as a pack until we're out of this, until we know who locked us up and why; and we know how Doherty is involved. I suggest you stay away from your homes and families. I have somewhere we can all go." He turned to Walker, who had moved to one side and seemed to be chanting.

Walker swirled his hand in a huge circle and the air shifted. The blue stoned ring he wore on his right hand glowed.

I snarled. I knew what he was doing even if the others didn't. I'd seen Som work his magic on a portal before.

Connor shielded his eyes from the brightness. "What the hell is that?"

Walker turned to us a grim look on his stunning face. In the daylight, his skin took on an otherworldly, almost frosted, glow. "I have my own way home," he said and barked a sharp word.

A wave of energy hit us and a portal materialised. We all staggered back. Walker stepped into the swirling air. "Unfortunately, Connor, you cannot leave here. You have a job to do. But you and I will meet again." He looked at me. "As will we."

It was then I noticed the tranquilliser gun held loosely in his left hand. He raised it and shot Connor, then Owen and Stone before they had time to realise what was happening.

I howled and bounded forward, but he just stared at me. *I will kill him!* His throat bobbed before he disappeared into the portal and it collapsed.

Closer now, the engines of the Range Rovers roared, and tires skidded in the dirt.

I pushed my wolf aside and changed back to my human form, not caring one bit about my naked state or the alphas surrounding me. "Run!" I yelled at them. "Now!"

None of them did.

One of them turned to me, a tall man with dark brown hair and eyes. "No, we stay with our alpha." He glanced down at Connor. "He fought for us, just as you did. You should shift and run. He will suffer if he knows they caught you, too. They will use you against him."

"He's right," rasped Rawson who had caught up with us. He limped to my side. "You should go. Stay well away from Doherty, and don't try to find us. Next time, you'll stand no chance of escape."

I shook my head. "No, I can't leave you—or him…"

"Ember, you have to. Please. They took Lyss from me. I can't stand the thought of losing you, too. Please get out of here. Hide from the SBI, and don't ever come back."

I hugged Rawson, uncaring I was naked, before I dropped to my knees beside Connor. His eyes were furious, sweat beading on his forehead as he fought—and lost against the incapacitating serum. I wiped the beads of sweat away. He couldn't move but his eyes darted to the forest and then to the cars. "Run," he whispered.

Footsteps cracked through the forest to our right. Car doors slammed to our left. Right now, it seemed behind the entrance to the underground facility was the only way out.

I wrapped my arms around him and kissed his lips hard. My wolf howled.

Connor blinked furiously, a trapped frustrated rumble resounding in his chest.

"Ember! Get the fuck out of here. Now!" yelled Rawson, resting his big hands on his muscular thighs and panting hard.

Sobbing, I shifted. Without looking back, I ran into the dark shadows of the forest. Gun fire echoed through the trees. I forced my wolf not to howl, and even though my heart was breaking, I ran.

CHAPTER 8

mber

MY HEART HAMMERED against my ribs, and breath exploded from my lungs.
No matter how much I wanted to go back; I couldn't. There was no way I
could win against the shit storm of armed men that had descended on
Connor, and that knowledge was killing me. I wanted to be stronger, to be
enough to save him and Rawson, but I wasn't. I was leaving my mate to die.
Doherty wouldn't keep them alive, not now. They'd seen too much—and he
would hunt me down. I had to disappear from this life, and there was only
one place I could go.

Dusk fell and the forest became wreathed in shadows. I skidded to a halt,
listening hard over my panting breaths. A stick cracked, the sound like a
gunshot in the still forest. Carefully, I slunk along, low to the ground, my
wolf's steps light enough she didn't make a sound. Shadows swathed me, so,
just as I did when I was younger, I made myself smaller and faded into them.
Another faint crack of undergrowth. They were approaching slowly. Perhaps
they were waiting for me to run right into their trap.

A fallen tree lay nearby. It's rough and rotting bark was covered in moss
and surrounded by a messy carpet of pine needles. Several large phallus
shaped fungi grew near it. I could have cried. Its pungent stink would hide my
own scent from the shifters. I darted into the dip beneath the rotten tree
trunk, and, carefully missing the fungi, I hunkered down and waited.

My thirst raged, cobwebs tickled my nose, and little creatures crawled through my fur. Still, I didn't move. I inhaled deeply. Under the foul fungi stink, the scents of aftershave, sweat and shifter were unmistakable. The agents were moving, but going slowly, warily.

I cowered lower, willing them to pass me by. My muscles cramped and shook, and it took every bit of my self-control to regulate my breathing when all I wanted to do was leap out and rip apart the men who killed my family. Because of them, I had no one.

After the death of my parents, I had promised myself I would never love or rely on anyone again. Well, that promise was shot to shit. Now there was a new hole in my chest, and no matter how much I wanted to believe Connor was alive, those gunshots had told me all I needed to know. I swallowed the ache in my throat and pushed down my fear. I would survive, if only so I could hunt down Doherty and destroy him.

Hours passed, and I continued to remain quiet and still. The agents had inched forward and I tracked the shadows of wolves that stalked between them. I could hear their breathing and prayed the fungus and the smell of other animals in the forest would cover my own scent. Patiently they waited for any movement in the shadows, but I was good at this game; I'd played it a lot when I was a young girl. I'd survived by becoming invisible. So, I kept utterly still, ignoring the numbness in all four of my limbs. I knew if I moved, the pain from a surge of circulation would cripple me.

A sniff came from nearby, followed by a low throaty growl.

Damn it! Go away, go away. There was no way I could run, not now, my legs were useless.

The faint crackle of a radio reached my ears. Holding my breath, I watched the silhouette of a large wolf move past about ten feet away. He loped up to the shadow of a man who squatted beneath a pine tree.

"Yes, sir. Director says move out!" The shadow yelled into the darkness.

I released a slow breath, my head spinning. They started to walk away, making far more noise than necessary, so I used the commotion as cover and shook out my limbs. I gritted my teeth against the onslaught of pins and needles, then got back to making myself invisible.

I'd also played *this* game before. Evil liked to try and lure its victims in. If I stayed low and melted into the shadows, evil wouldn't even notice me.

The hollowness in my soul became a chasm. I lay there, empty and just waiting for daybreak. Finally the sun rose, warming the damp forest floor. My stomach growled, and my throat was so raw I could barely swallow. The sun scorched me. Panting away the heat from my body, I prayed for the patience of my enemies to run out before my body gave out from dehydration.

Sometime in the afternoon I heard distant voices. Shouts and yells. My eyes burned, and my body shook. There was another round of twigs cracking and the snap of bones; wolves shifting back into men. "Do one more quick sweep!" ordered a voice. But it was clear their enthusiasm had waned.

There were many fallen trees near mine. This was just another unremarkable one. I sent a silent prayer of thanks to anyone listening. Not only did this fungi leave a horrid stench, the wolves and men had left their scents all over the forest, hiding mine. No shifter would know my scent among these, especially if these agents weren't a pack and had no loyalty to or knowledge of each other.

The noise of the search eventually faded. Engines roared to life and then disappeared into the distance. I crawled out. Too weak to shift, and with no clothes to wear, I stayed in my wolf form. My internal fire flared, sensing the danger my body was in. Warmth eased along my bones, just enough to give me the strength to run. My gait was faltering and clumsy at first, but sticking to the shadows I was soon running with desperation and a heaviness in my soul that I knew would never leave me.

Rawson had been right. I could do nothing against Doherty and the agency. I was too weak and too alone. I had to let them go. My stomach churned and my chest ached, but I wouldn't allow such crippling guilt to paralyse me—not yet.

A LOW MENACING growl was the only warning before a dark shadow leapt at me. I couldn't tell what it was, but its solid bulk hit me from the side and sent me sprawling. A female wolf, with ice white fur and deep amber eyes circled me. Even in this dire situation I gasped at how beautiful she was; a dangerous and stunning creature. Those eyes settled on me and gleamed with predatory intent. She snarled—a challenge. My answering snarl wasn't as intimidating. My body was depleted of fluid and nutrients, and my limbs shook, but there was no way I was going down without a fight. Without hesitation, I attacked. In a nimble move she jumped sideways and her jaws clamped around my neck.

Her teeth cut into my flesh, pain lancing my throat. I thrashed and snapped my jaws, but the other wolf's teeth clamped down harder. Warmth saturated my fur. An artery. No matter how much I wanted to fight, my limbs became heavy. Blood poured from me. I was dying. The wolf shook me, deepening my wounds. My vision blurred until all I could see was the redness of my blood staining her white fur. Fire stirred, sensing my end was too near to stop it. She soothed me and held me in her fiery embrace as my wolf's heart ceased to beat. Within moments I was nothing but an ethereal form, standing and looking down at the body of my beautiful wolf. She was limp, lying flat on the ground, her fur stained bright red and her body in a pool of congealing dark blood.

It was one of the hardest things I'd ever done, to allow my beautiful wolf to be chewed apart by another. I wanted to scream and shout, but for me to be safe, my wolf had to end.

Something brushed against my leg. When I looked down, there was the spirit of my beautiful wolf, staring up at me. She licked my hand before she began to fade away.

Thank you for being with me. Go to the Mother Wolf now. I'll pray to her for your rebirth. Tears blurred my vision as she faded away.

Soon my attacker's gruesome task was complete. My wolf's head fell free of her body. The white wolf receded leaving a human woman in her place. Pressing my lips into a tight line, I latched onto the spirit of the white wolf, and pulled. I'd done this once before, but unlike last time, I was not a child and I would not permit this human to live.

I ripped her wolf away. The woman doubled over and screamed. I opened my soul and welcomed the beautiful white wolf in. Once she was mine, flames surged from my hands. Without remorse, I burned the screaming woman until there was nothing left but ash.

CHAPTER 9

onnor.

PAIN WOKE ME. It throbbed in my shoulder and arm, reminding me I'd been shot. I bit back a groan as I tried to control the agony and awaken my wolf enough to heal me. He didn't respond. Underneath me, the bed shook and vibrated. *Weird.* I twisted my head, and my face banged into something hard and cold. I grunted, lifting my hand to my forehead. My fingers connected with a large metallic structure. "What the hell?"

"Hey, man. Take it easy."

"Brady?"

"Yeah." He sounded weak.

I forced my eyes to open. My head ached from the brightness of the overhead lights. I blinked away the discomfort, attuning my hearing to that incessant drone.

"Engines. Why the fuck are there engines?" But Brady didn't answer. My brain was foggy and my thoughts were muddled. The last thing I remembered was watching the alphas form a protective line in front of me. Hell, even Rawson had staggered over to join them. It was no use, they were taken down by a single shot each, and then pumped full of darts. Doherty himself had taken great pleasure in slugging me right in the shoulder, his face twisted into a mask of fury—one that promised retribution and pain. I had no idea what was going on, but that bastard would pay.

I closed my eyes again. *Ember.* A pain stabbed through my heart. She'd gone. I could only hope she had run far and fast. The memory of her taste, of her mouth on mine as she cried her goodbye against my lips… I would carry that with me through whatever hell we were facing. I sent her a silent promise that no matter what happened, I would find her again. I emptied my mind and pushed the limited power I had into my flesh to begin its healing. I lay there, recovering, and listened to that droning. It dawned on me what it was.

I pushed myself up. "We're on a plane?" My throat was so dry, I only just managed to croak the words. I swallowed, trying to work some saliva into my mouth.

Owen lifted his head and opened his eyes. He was leaning with his back against the body of the plane, his face pallid, but I could see he'd healed his leg. "Yeah."

"You okay?"

"I've been better, but at least the fuckers used normal bullets, not silver." Sitting forward, he rested his forearms on his thighs.

I thought about it for a moment. "They wanted us to heal ourselves, but not until they were ready."

"It seems so."

Uncurling my bruised and stiff body, I sat up and took stock of where we were.

Metal surrounded us. Literally. We were in a metal cage that had been built into the body of the plane. The structure gleamed brightly, just as buffed silver would. It seemed we had swapped one cell for another. But, at least we were still breathing.

I noticed Stone watching us from the opposite side of the cage. His silver eyes were hard and glinted, his face a cold mask. I held his gaze, asserting my dominance. My wolf stirred. Stone merely nodded minutely and looked away. Next to him another male, with a broken nose, curled his lip and glared. I glared right back.

Owen followed my gaze. "Ah, shit." He rolled his head on his shoulders and cracked his knuckles. "And so it begins."

"It does." Perhaps I said that with too much relish. But there was no way anyone in this cage was going to be an alpha over me. I snarled, cracked my neck and clenched my fingers into fists. I was ready to do battle. Stone turned his head and watched. Something told me he had my back, after all, he had fought fearlessly back at the prison. The other guy held my gaze longer than I'd normally tolerate, but I gave him another ten seconds. *Three. Two. One.* I stood up, never once moving my stare from his. He snarled, but dropped his challenge. A growl rumbled through my chest causing some of the prisoners around me to shuffle away, their eyes wide, the stench of fear seeping from them.

I sat back down and deliberately didn't look at any of the others. Challenges would come from the males in this cage, but I wanted to study our captors more before I showed my strength.

On the other side of the silver bars, guards watched us. They carried weapons that looked even more space age than my own.

"They're well funded."

Owen took his time studying them, too. "Very. Look at their body armour. It's reinforced, and they have full face visors. Their helmets and gloves are sealed onto their uniforms, each plate overlapping the last. Even your Firecracker wouldn't be able to get her teeth through it to rip it away."

I breathed out and smiled. "True."

"Hey!" yelled one of the males to a huge man who marched past the cage. He stood at least six inches taller than the other guards, possibly my height. He turned.

I studied him closely. "Shit. What the fuck is he?"

Searing red eyes fixated on the male.

"Where're you taking us?" the male demanded.

Red eyes didn't answer, he merely cocked his head and then swiveled his gaze to me, almost as if he sensed my attention. A sense of recognition hit me. Of what, I had no idea. Did I know this man? I frowned and blinked and the connection between us broke.

"Hey! You ignorant asshole! Tell us what's going on!" yelled the male again.

Red eyes pulled his gaze from me and contemplated the shifter with no expression at all on his harsh features. The male reached out and grabbed the bars, and was immediately caught in a gruesome dance. His hair sizzled and caught fire, then the stench of burning flesh filled the cage. His mouth opened in a silent scream, his muscles contracting until his spine arched so far it looked like it might snap.

Still jerking, his burning corpse fell to the ground.

I screwed my nose up. "Jesus Christ."

Silence fell.

"Put him out." Red eyes didn't even look at the dead man again.

One of the guards grabbed a fire extinguisher and covered the corpse in white foam.

"I don't think JC is going to help us wherever they're taking us, Captain," Owen murmured.

I pulled my attention from the smoldering corpse. "No, probably not. Wherever we're going, it looks like we're expendable."

"It does." The skin between Owen's brows creased.

My expression mirrored his. "They shot us to stop us running, and drugged us to make us easier to transport. These damned collars will stop our shifts and dampen our abilities. And that?" I inclined my chin at the burning corpse. "Well, that was just a show of power."

Owen grunted in agreement, his attention on Red, his gaze predatory.

Red glanced at me before sauntering down the plane and in through the flight deck door.

Sitting against the rear wall of the cage, I studied my fellow prisoners. Some of the faces I recognised from our previous prison. Most of them I didn't. They were big guys, all of them. And all wearing silver collars. With their beasts caged, tempers would become frayed. I kept my attention on two big guys who circled the dead body. They moved with predatory gaits. Their eyes focused on each other, and challenging snarls curled their lips.

"Where's Rawson?" I asked Owen, unable to see him anywhere in the crowded cage. I blinked and my lips flattened into a tight line. Rawson was more than a benefactor, he was my friend and my brother, and I would always owe him. Exhaling slowly through my nose, I forced my worry away.

Owen's shoulders sagged. "I don't know, man. After they shot me, he attacked them. He took down two of those fuckers before he got shot. If he's not here, maybe they killed him."

My throat was so tight it was difficult to swallow. My fists curled, white hot anger simmering beneath my skin, but I managed to nod. "What about Ember? Did she get away?" All the prisoners in the cage were male. I held onto the belief she was strong enough and clever enough to escape. It would break me to know she hadn't. My wolf growled in agreement, ready to tear the world apart if any harm had come to her.

Owen tilted his head, his yellow eyes noting every move the big guys made. There was a gap around the circling pair now, and the atmosphere changed. Aggression poured off the two males. "I don't know. She ran into the woods. That's all I know." He turned and contemplated me, his big body leaning forward a little. "What's it like? To meet your mate?"

Images of Ember tumbled around my head. I swallowed, my body heating. I rubbed my face then dropped my hand to my chest, rubbing at the ache in my heart. "Absolutely terrifying," I admitted quietly.

Owen snorted and shook his head. "Bullshit. Nothing terrifies you."

"She does."

"Why? She's just a woman. A damn hot one, but still, just a woman."

"Nah, man, she's *the* woman. I've known her for so long she's a part of me. I tried to stay away from her...you know? While she was younger, but now..." I swallowed, thinking about the taste and softness of her lips against mine, her silky skin beneath my fingers. "Shit, she owns a part of my soul, she always has, and that makes me weak, because if it came to a choice between her life or anyone else's, even mine, she would always come first."

Owen shook his head a little. Hearing me admit the depth of my feelings for Ember had to be a shock to him. After all, I'd been totally dedicated to my role as an agent. An acrid taste coated my mouth as I thought of Ava and Lance. Maybe I'd once believed in the principles and integrity of the SBI, but no longer. Doherty had destroyed my loyalty the moment he went after the people I loved.

Before I could say anything else, my wolf pricked up his ears and snarled viciously. Waves of aggression and dominance hit me from every direction. I rolled my head and loosened my shoulders. "Here we go." A growl built, as I revelled in the change in atmosphere. I was spoiling for a fight. I'd lost my mate and ended up a prisoner, again. My fingers burned as I touched the collar around my neck. It might have taken my wolf's freedom but I was still a Prime, one of the most powerful alphas in existence. A snarl curled my top lip. And these weaker alphas were about to find out just what that meant. My wolf surfaced, pushing against the confines of the silver. We growled together as my vision changed.

"You ready to fight with me, Beta?" I stood, pulling on my wolf's power.

Owen's throat bobbed. The position I'd just bestowed on him spoke of total trust. He'd have to fight to keep it, just as I would have to fight to gain and defend my position as Prime. Dominance and violence crackled in the waves of my Prime power. His eyes hardened then he gave me a vicious grin. His gaze moved, fixing on the two males, who roared and barrelled into each other, colliding in a torrent of fists, teeth and blood. The air vibrated, aggression rolling through the cage. It fed the other males who watched, their bodies coiled and ready to strike. None of us could shift but this would still be a fight to the death.

"Always, alpha." Owen pushed himself up and stood by my side.

I forced all thoughts of soft skin and warm lips from my mind. If I wanted to get out of this mess and find Ember, I needed to survive. Inside my soul, my wolf bayed for blood. Every single, powerful male in this cage knew this fight had to happen. There could be only one alpha, one that all others feared, one who would rule them—or anarchy would reign, and we would kill each other off.

The guards observed us like they had seen this hundreds of times before. Warning bells went off in my mind and ice wound its way through my veins. They already knew we would fight each other to establish a pack hierarchy. I thrust that knowledge aside. I'd think about it later. Instead, I cracked my knuckles.

I snarled. "Good. Show no mercy, until they submit to me."

Owen grunted his agreement. We'd been here before; fighting side by side. The trust I'd gifted him was not unfounded. I knew with certainty he'd have my back. Together we bellowed a war cry at the top of our lungs. I released the power that simmered in my blood and bones; the force that merged my wolf and me together as one.

The fighting males separated, their bodies thrust apart by the force of my will.

Bloodied and sweaty, they turned to us, compelled to challenge the mightiest force in the cage.

Me.

Growls and roars rattled my ears. That sound of challenge and war, compounded with the coppery stink of blood, only fuelled my inner beast. I roared back, my wolf flooding my body with his power. As an agent, I had always subdued my wolf, having to dampen the predator in my soul. But here, it was kill or be killed.

I grinned viciously at the biggest male.

My wolf and I were utterly single minded in our purpose: kill all those who thought themselves our equal, and dominate the rest.

CHAPTER 10

Ember

THE PADS of my paws were sore, but still I ran. Breath rasped in my throat and escaped in clouds of mist into the icy air. I refused to think about everything that had happened until I reached my destination. It was enough just to stay alive.

I urged my wolf onward, stopping only to lap water from the first stream we came across. My new wolf spirit was unsure of me. She held her memories and emotions close and did not allow me access. As soon as her spirit had entered me I had sensed her relief at losing her last host. I wouldn't push her to tell me what had happened, but it wasn't hard to guess. The loss of my first wolf lay heavy inside me, but I didn't blame this beautiful white female. No, I blamed the human who had controlled her.

She sensed my urgency and didn't resist; instead she forged ahead through her exhaustion and went where I directed. I thanked her, knowing I would lose a battle of wills right now.

My thoughts went to Walker. That faerie bastard had deserted us. Not only that, I didn't understand why he'd darted Connor. I mean, he'd literally thrown him to the wolves. A snarl curled my mouth. I would find Walker, eventually—and rip him to shreds. Where I was going, there would be an opportunity to hunt in Faerie. It might take some time to get Som to trust me, but I would do it. If I couldn't get to the SBI or Doherty, I'd track

Walker. Even if it took years, I'd find him and make him pay for what he'd done.

I leaped over ditches and crossed fields, but exhaustion was setting in, allowing the ache of losing my family to consume me. When night fell, I allowed myself to stop at a stream. My wolf's chest heaved and she drank deeply. I let her rest, but once she'd regained her breath, I urged her onwards, avoiding any signs of human life. My despair would just have to wait.

With single minded purpose, I held to my direction and headed for Rawson's house. There would be agents observing the front and the lane, but I doubted they would be in the fields at the back. Still, I took my time approaching. The stunning white wolf that was now mine whined. Her anxiety filtered into me, so I sent a lick of reassurance down our bond. She shuddered, but kept going.

The smell of society; of cars and rubbish, cooking and sewage, assaulted my senses, but there was no sign or scent of other wolves.

My wolf inched forward on her belly, keeping low to the ground. Her bright white fur was thankfully covered in mud and, from the smell of it, cow shit. I grimaced. It had been my idea to roll in the mud before we reached the outskirts of the town. We reeked to high heaven, but it was far safer than standing out in the darkness.

A grey car was parked at the entrance of the lane, moonlight glinting off the paint. A shadow moved inside. I growled, sniffing the air. I knew all the cars that used these roads, and that car had never belonged to any of the agency families who lived here.

Once the clouds obscured the moon, I encouraged my wolf to dart forward. We dove beneath the bushes at the back of Rawson's home, *my* home. It was hard to ignore the pain at that thought. It was no longer *my* home. I would not return here again. My wolf clamped her teeth around the handle of the bag I'd left behind. The clouds moved away, leaving the lane bathed in soft silvery light. Ice sparkled on the ground and it was bright enough to cast shadows, so we waited beneath the bushes. Moments later the moon was gone again. She darted back across the road and into the fields. There were no shouts, no gunshots or growls.

Breathing heavily she ran along the familiar route I used to get to Som's, enduring her sore paws and fatigue while carrying the bag between her jaws.

Once the outskirts of the city came into view, I urged her to slow. The shadows were enough to hide us as we made our way through the emerging human world. Cars rushed along nearby roads, the noise scaring my new shifter spirit. This was a bad idea as even the suburbs of London didn't sleep, and I had to negotiate my way through the concrete jungle to my destination on the banks of the Thames. But this was the only place I could go.

I'd have to work for my keep at Som's, and I'd need to negotiate the terms of my employment, but if anyone could live under the SBI's radar it was Somnelaire. As a bogwart, Som was a lower caste fae. I frowned, Walker was definitely different from any of the fae I'd ever seen. Could he have been high fae, like Connor had suspected, even though he had said he wasn't? The location to the gates of Faerie was a closely guarded secret in the SBI. Other than Som's workers and the psychos that hunted prey in the shadows, Walker was the only fae I'd seen, and even I knew that trick he'd pulled with the portal was something special.

Som occasionally did business with the servants of the high fae. How they got into our world, I had no idea, but they did. And the fae, especially the rich ones, loved their drugs just the same as humans and shifters did; only opiates didn't do it for them, no, it was the Digitalis Purpurea plant, or plain old Foxglove that sent them into a drug induced haze. Highly toxic and deadly to humans, fae reacted differently. It was like heroin to them. There were entire underground markets for Digitalis leaves and dried flowers—anything the fae could get, in any form, was in demand, and Som provided the lot—with a little help from me as a mule and dealer when he needed it.

It was nearing dawn when I slowed to a walk. My wolf's muscles screamed and her whole body shook. The stench of rotten food and the sour smell of the Thames banks mixed with the smell of sewage and salt. My wolf balked, but I encouraged her to keep going.

Nearly there, brave one. It's best if I take control now. I know the way well. She whimpered, her legs shaking.

Soon, a painted green gate appeared. Bolting around the corner, I leaped onto the old wall that followed the edge of the Thames. Brown water surged below, full of shit and silt as the tide ebbed. I teetered on unsteady legs, the bag I carried in my jaws unbalancing me. I stopped and straightened, calming my wolf's anxious spirit, then inched along the wall. If we fell that would be it for her; not so much for me. Fire always stepped in to protect me if she sensed my end was near. It would still suck to drown in that swirling, brown mess though.

I took a breath and lowered my head. I'd done this balancing act many times before—and I could do it now—except I was shaking like a leaf and my wolf was new—and scared.

I sent a burst of warmth along her bones, trying to reassure her that we were in this together. The wind eddied around us as I took more careful steps. Slowly, we progressed along our treacherous route.

Som had no idea how I continually got into his compound. No matter how hard he looked, he'd never found my entrance—or at least that's what he said.

About twenty feet along the river wall the boundary to Som's compound appeared. The wall loomed twelve feet high and was topped with razor wire. I'd never attempted to go over it. Instead, I dropped down into a small space between the two walls. I shifted, and my wolf receded without hesitation. The shift was painful and far slower than usual. We were both drained and not yet familiar with each other, but I knew precisely how to twist my human body to fit into the confined space under the storage building. I pushed in through the hole in the wall I'd found as a child. I'd grown, but I still managed to squeeze through it. I crawled along on my belly, ignoring the pebbles and rough ground that scored my breasts and stomach, and scratched my limbs.

The space became tighter, but I didn't panic. Instead I pushed through, dragging the bag behind me with my foot through its handle. About seven feet further along it opened out into a two foot high foundation space under another storehouse. I tugged on the wolf who was becoming a part of me. She scrambled to do my bidding, fear of what I would ask of her filtering down our link. I swallowed my anger. The shifter who had been gifted this beautiful spirit had really done a number on her.

I will never harm you, I reassured her gently. She whined in acknowledgement and pushed through my skin. I encouraged her to clamp her teeth around my bag, ignoring my need to fall down and sleep. Skulking through the foundations, I used my nose to push at the loose grate under the steps of the store room. It swung in the center like a flap, just as it had always done. Cautiously, I waited in the shadows for a moment and sniffed the air. The compound was silent. There was the faint scent of the two guards who patrolled, but nothing unusual. I grabbed the handles of my bag in my teeth and darted out. It took only moments to reach the set of metal stairs that led up to a heavy wooden door.

Once I'd negotiated the steps, I raised up on my hind legs and scratched at the door. Flakes of red paint floated down and stuck in my fur. My shaking body wouldn't hold me up for long. My wolf's determination to do as I wished filtered into me. *We can do this.* I shook the paint off and lifted on my back legs again, scratching harder. The hinges on the door were loose and old so it banged loudly against my assault. Above me a camera blinked, it's red light like a tiny eye.

"All right! All right! I'm coming! Quit scratching my door!" Som's raspy voice was almost a comfort.

I watched the handle. It moved down and the door was pushed open. I launched myself inside.

Som staggered back. "Jeez, give me a chance to open it, girlie!"

I skidded to a halt, my claws slipping on the old wooden flooring.

Som's beady black eyes widened. "Yee gods! Where ya been, girlie? Ya stink like shit and death."

I snarled. Of course I did.

I changed back and stood as naked as the day I was born in front of Som.

Yeah, I was way past being embarrassed about my nakedness. Plenty of people had seen it now—and I didn't care.

Som raised his brows, but I knew he wasn't in the least bit interested in my human female form. Bogwarts didn't have sexual reproductive organs. They could not reproduce, they were a freak of nature said to be born from the womb of the Bogwart Queen herself, birthed into the mud and sludge in the darkest reaches of Orth, the dark realm of Faerie.

I didn't care where Som came from. All I knew was that I was safe with him; well, from sexual attention, anyway. I didn't trust him as far as I could throw him otherwise, and that wasn't far. He was about four feet tall and about the same in girth. His face was squashed and his teeth black. He wore an old, stained Queen T-shirt and trousers with braces to hold them up, and he reeked worse than I ever could, no matter what I'd rolled in.

He smoothed his wisp of greasy grey hair into his combover style and frowned at my naked body.

"Why d'ya stink of shit, blood and death, girlie?"

"I need a place to crash and work. Can you fix me up?" I sidestepped his question. Like most fae, Bogwarts could smell a lie a mile off. Som had told me the fae couldn't lie, or rather that the high fae couldn't, but it seemed many other castes were learning to—or at least learning to twist the truth very well. Thinking of Walker, I wondered if that stretched to betrayal, too. Perhaps that was why he hadn't said much. Not speaking had meant he didn't need to worry about lying.

Som rubbed his triple chin with his long spindly fingers. His attention narrowed in on my bag. "Depends how long you're going to commit for. And remember who you're dealing with."

I cocked my head, ready for this negotiation. My family was gone. I was on my own again. Even if I wanted to go back, or was stupid enough to go back to that holding prison, Connor and Rawson would be gone. I armoured my heart against the pain that squeezed it and concentrated on my future. If I was going to survive, I needed help, money and anonymity. And if I was going to find Walker, I needed access to Faerie. "Depends what you're offering." Striking a deal with a fae was binding. If I broke it, I'd belong to Som forever, and according to faerie law that would mean I'd have no rights whatsoever.

Som grinned, looking like the greedy fae he was. He could use me—earn money from me—and we both knew it. But I was using him just as much. "You sure you wanna do this, girlie?"

I swallowed and nodded.

"Fine. You can have a place to stay and I'll give you paid work—plenty of it. But you have to be my mule; my little digitalis dealer, with my own kind."

My mouth dried out. Not with fear, but with anticipation. "You want me to go through the gates? Into Faerie?"

Som grinned. "Sure do, buttercup. And you have to take an oath. A faerie oath to keep this quiet from the authorities. If you ever get caught—by either side—you cannot tell them who you work for. You cannot inform the authorities how you enter Faerie, nor who you get the merchandise from that you will sell. If you break this oath, you will belong to me until I am willing to dissolve my claim on you."

I wanted to laugh at that, but I didn't. That threat didn't hold anything over my head, not anymore. The only people who had ever given a shit about me were gone. Violently. Doherty was dangerous. He had an agenda that had nothing to do with the SBI and all I could do now was lay low and hope he forgot about me.

"Sure, Som. I'll be your Yellow. But you have to pay me fifty percent of the take from any deals there."

"Fifty!? No way!"

"Come on, Som, you can't go into Faerie. They'd sense you straight away. I can get through your gate because of what I am, and I know Blue does it. She can teach me. You know it's getting risky for your customers to send people here to pick up their stash. And the SBI is looking for illegal portals to Faerie, so unless you can send us and then close the gate after us, they'll track you down." I had no idea if that was true, but I needed to give Som a push to strike this deal with me.

Som continued to stroke his triple chins and he was silent for long enough to make my heart race.

I kept my face impassive.

"Fine, but ten percent."

I cocked an eyebrow. "Don't insult me, Som. I've known you too long, and I know how much I can earn you. Forty five."

"Yeah, but you're more desperate than I am." He inhaled. "I can smell it."

I cocked a brow at him. "Really? Like I can't survive on my own? You're not the only dealer I know, Som." I infused an edge of warning in my voice.

"Fine. Twenty percent."

Hands on my naked hips, I shook my head. "Come on now. Forty."

"Twenty five."

"Thirty five. And I'll use this to sweeten any deals in Faerie if our clients get awkward." I gestured to my body. I had no intention of prostituting myself, but Som didn't need to know that. Fae loved to lose themselves in human lovers. It was some kind of dominance or hormone thing—or something. I didn't care; I just knew that no fae was getting me. Any potential clients didn't need to know I wasn't totally human, and I knew Som would keep my mixed blood quiet.

Som glanced over my body. Once I would have died of shame, but not anymore. A whole pack of alphas had seen my naked body less than forty eight hours ago. I was strong, fit and had enough toned muscles, hidden strength and fighting ability not to be too worried about going to Faerie, especially if I got to work alongside Blue. She'd teach me all I'd need to know.

Som grunted. "Thirty percent. And that's only because I know I can trust you."

I almost laughed out loud. No one could trust me, not even I trusted me. Instead, I smiled and held out my hand. "Deal."

Som took it.

His skin was slimy and cold against mine. I tried not to balk.

"You sure, Yellow?" he said, using my new name.

"I'm sure, but I get to break the contract after two years if I'm still alive, not in prison, or just want to move on."

"Three years. But I think you'll want to stay, Yellow. After all, something tells me you ain't got that nice safe human haven anymore. Have ya?"

I just smiled. Som didn't know much about me other than I was a shifter and I'd been fostered by a lovely human family. Lies always helped with the fae. They thought humans were as bad at lying as they were. Besides the best lies were always based in truth, and I wasn't about to give Som any information about what had just happened, or who might be searching for me. He'd drop me like a hot coal and then I'd have nowhere to go.

I was about to pull my hand away when Som gripped me harder.

"Hold on, Yellow, I'm not done yet. Let's seal the deal, faerie style."

Pain zipped up my arm and into the simmering core of my magic. I hissed. I couldn't stop my other spirit reacting and heat burned through my blood. I closed my eyes, forcing Fire to retreat. Disgruntled at the surge of faerie magic, she curled back up, but not without spitting her displeasure at being bound to a magical contract.

"There." Som wheezed a laugh, his belly jiggling up and down. "Now, go get a shower and cover your skinny human ass with some clothes. You can bunk with Blue."

"Oh, I'm sure she'll love that." But I was already grabbing my bag.

Som chuckled. "I'm certain of it."

The Bogwart waddled away. Wincing, I inspected the thick dark tattoo that had been burned onto my hand and arm. It wasn't pretty. Thick vines and thorns twisted around my skin, drops of blood falling where they appeared to pierce my flesh.

I scowled and flexed my fingers. There was nothing to be done about it, so I made my way up the creaking stairs and threw open the door to Blue's room.

I dropped my bag with a thud and grinned at the woman lounging on the single bed. "Hi, roomie!" Her slim fingers didn't pause in their task of tossing and catching a small knife.

I didn't flinch when the knife whizzed past my ear, taking a few strands of my red hair with it before it thudded into the door frame.

"You've got to be kidding me." Blue's pencil perfect brows dipped, joining the scowl on her face.

I met her gaze. "Nope. I'm here to stay, bitch, so get used to it."

"Yay!" Blue squealed and vaulted off the bed. She ran across the small room, her bare feet slapping on the floor boards. It took some effort not to fall over when she slammed her much taller body into mine and wrapped me in a fierce hug.

I patted her back. "Well, okay then."

Blue pulled back. Her dyed cerulean hair was plaited down either side of her head and she wore her signature leather trousers and a blue vest top. Her deep brown eyes darkened. "So that's good and everything, but I know you, something bad happened if you're bunking here. Wanna talk about it?"

I sighed, my stomach tightening. The events of the last few days were too raw to tell even my one and only friend. "No, not yet. But I need to stay under the radar of everyone, even the underworld, so I struck a deal with Som." I shrugged even as her eyes narrowed. "I'm here for the foreseeable future."

"You are?" Blue contemplated me, her expression dark. "You haven't got yourself stuck in a faerie contract like me, have you? Not that I don't want you here—I do, I just don't want to think of you as imprisoned, like me. I mean it's so easy to make a mistake. Som owns me now. I don't want him to own you, too."

"Hey," I said jumping on the other small bed. "I'm here and I'm fine. Let's concentrate on that. I'll be his little digitalis dealer from now on, well, for the next three years anyway, so just call me Yellow."

"Okay." Blue sighed, but knew better than to push the subject. Then she grinned and reached under her bed. She straightened and dangled a bottle of vodka from her fingers. "Well then, *Yellow*, welcome to the beginning of your new life. Let's celebrate and hope whatever you're running from doesn't find you and bite you in the arse, and that you live long enough to see the end of your contract and get out of here."

I forced a smile on my face, my fingers closing around the bottle, then I took a long drink. The alcohol burned right into that hollow space inside my gut.

"That's it, bitch. Drink it down and forget your last life. You belong to Som now."

Once we'd drunk the lot and eaten a chicken sandwich Blue had conjured from the kitchen, I tipped my head back, closed my eyes and floated away on an alcohol-fuelled buzz. My bed and the room spun uncomfortably. Connor's vivid blue eyes as he told me to run were all I could see. The ache in my throat was unbearable, and tears burned behind my closed lids.

I wouldn't leave here even when my contract was finished. Where the hell else would I go?

I took a slow deep breath and gritted my teeth. It was fine. *I* was fine. This was just another beginning, one of several I'd survived in my life. Against my will, a stray tear escaped. Only there were no pink carpets, or fluffy bunny rabbits; no Lyss or Rawson, and definitely no Connor with this new start. I filed away my lovely memories of Lyss and Rawson, but reserved a special corner of my soul for the man who had stolen my heart. Another tear trailed down my cheek. I knew I would treasure those memories no matter what else happened in my life. But now I had to try and piece together the broken shards of my heart and soul, enough to survive this new life. And survive I would. Life was fluid, forever changing, and when it turned to shit again, I'd fight my way through the sludge and move on to my next new beginning.

EPILOGUE

onnor

SNOW SWIRLED in front of me making it difficult to see. I rubbed the crusted blood from under my nose and studied the unimpressive building on the far side of the tarmac landing strip. It looked unassuming and small, but that didn't mean a thing. My attention moved to the surrounding area. The whole place was covered in a white blanket of snow, the heavy flakes making it impossible to see clearly in the dark. Only the runway had been cleared and was illuminated. I squinted, pretty sure that trees edged the area of clear ground around the fenced compound. The double fence was too tall to jump, even for a shifter, and the thick posts told me it was fed with electric current.

I shuddered from the bone-deep cold and inhaled. Pine sap, snow and fresh air. No cloying exhaust emissions, or the stink of a nearby city. We were in the middle of nowhere.

I shivered. My shirt was a memory, burned by Ember in our escape attempt, and my naked chest stung from the vicious cold. With effort, I stood tall, trying not to curl into a ball to keep from freezing to death. My teeth chattered, so I clenched them together. This damn cold had no mercy; it slayed my skin and gripped my lungs, trying to rip them from my chest. On top of that, the silver collar burned, leaving blisters as my wolf tried to push through to save me. All he could do was howl and snarl against his forced imprisonment in my body.

Determined not to show any weakness, I squared my shoulders and moved my feet along the frozen airstrip. I had fought hard for the position I now held.

Prime. Alpha of alphas.

The other men filed out of the cage behind me. All alphas, and all now sworn to me.

Needles of ice whipped through the air, stinging my exposed skin and burning my lungs.

"Fuck me," wheezed Owen.

"Not today, man. I need to recover from kicking their arses first."

While we moved, I scanned our surroundings, looking through the night for any weakness in the security.

There was none.

Guards watched us from the platforms of observation towers, their weapons and spotlights trained directly on us. Shifters circled us. They were predators; their eyes honed in on us, their need for blood evident. Snarls and challenging growls sounded as they prowled closer. I curled my upper lip and snarled back, but held back the power that crackled through my veins.

I discovered something on the plane that I needed time to process. When I killed with my bare hands, I absorbed the power of that shifter's spirit. Why was a mystery to me. But for now it didn't matter why. Only the fact that killing made me stronger mattered.

I had no idea where we were or what was going on, but I did know we were being tested. The fight in the cage had been to see who would survive and emerge the strongest. I hadn't decided yet if it was good to be at the top, or bad. Whoever ran this operation only wanted the strongest shifters, and I had no doubt there were more people involved than Doherty. He was a weasel; a bastard of the first degree, sure, but he wasn't powerful enough to arrange all this.

All the prisoners who were incarcerated with me were strong, vicious and bloodthirsty. Even Walker had displayed his own brand of power. I wondered again why he had thrown me and the others to the wolves. I doubted he was working with the SBI, but it was clear he hadn't wanted me to escape either.

I shelved my thoughts about Walker's betrayal and grinned at a yellow-eyed tiger who prowled too close. I cracked my knuckles and rolled my head, ready to take it on. I'd rip its heart out if it attacked, even if I died doing it.

Footsteps and cursing came from behind as the other shifters were forced to move out of the plane and into the wind and snow. If they stumbled or resisted, they got a cattle prod as an incentive. The red eyed guard marched out. He didn't even need to speak, just point. Snarling, the tiger dropped back, its gaze fixed on me like I was its next meal. Once I was sure it wasn't going to pounce, my attention shifted to Red.

He stared directly at me. My eyeballs burned looking into those orbs of flame, but the fucker could go to hell; I'd not look away first. My wolf rumbled in agreement.

Red huffed and shook his head. "In there." He pointed toward the building.

I planted my feet and crossed my arms over my chest. I was prepared for some pain, and I wanted to see what happened if I pushed.

Red exhaled heavily through his nose. "Fine." He nodded to one of the guards.

Without hesitation, the guard turned to me. I tensed, prepared to take a hit from his weapon, which I'd already seen was set to stun. It would hurt like a bitch, but wouldn't kill me. He lifted it—and changed the setting. "What're you doing?" I asked, my eyes narrowed. Before I could blink, he turned the gun on Owen and pulled the trigger. Red's other guards simultaneously fired into the group of shifters who now saw me as their Prime. Bodies fell to the ground. I released a bellow, my heart pounding. I knew what they'd done. The little bullets were now wedged under my pack's flesh.

"Fry them," ordered Red.

They all started twitching and shaking, their cries of agony inciting my wolf's anger.

"You are their alpha. You behave, they stay safe. You disobey, your pack suffers."

I growled unable to hold my wolf back. He wanted blood. My neck swelled, my body straining, my wolf trying to push through. The silver collar burned away my skin. I hissed and forced him back, taking control of him, pushing him down away from the silver. He snarled and paced inside me, his need to rip apart the men who tortured his pack hard to deny.

I'd been played. These bastards needed an alpha to control a pack, but the pack would give them leverage against the alpha himself. It was inherent in an alpha to protect those who were his responsibility. And by fighting, winning and dominating these other trapped shifters, I'd put myself in the position of their Prime. I hadn't wanted it, but it was necessary to stop more bloodshed on the plane. I cursed. They had me exactly where they wanted me.

Red gave me an evil smile. "I see you've worked it out. Now, move."

As soon as I took my first few steps the others were released from the grip of the internal taser. I kept walking. They'd be safe—for now—so long as I complied.

Inside the building I was shoved off to one side.

"Take the rest to gen pop," Red said.

I was shackled and led down an empty corridor. Aluminium shone around me, fluorescent lights bright above. There were very few doors, and all of them had keypad locks at the side. Some had retinal scanners, and others blood locks. The inside of this building was a far cry from the ancient brick and metal structure on the outside, which was camouflage for what lay beneath it.

Red led the way down the corridor and into a lift. Four men piled in after us and I stood in the middle looking for any way out of this situation. For some reason, Miss X came to mind. I brushed off the memory of her body falling into ash and disappearing into the vents. Perhaps it was the clinical and impersonal nature of this lift? It was very like the room she'd been killed in. The lift pinged and there was no time to mull further on the nature of the woman's death. I glanced at the buttons. There were only four and none were marked.

I glanced at Red. "Don't tell me, you reserved the penthouse for me, only it's underground."

"Something like that."

I was shoved between my shoulder blades and had no option but to step out of the lift. The guards waited, their weapons trained on me, while Red took the lead. We marched down yet another sterile corridor, all the time monitored by cameras, and past more locked doors.

Red halted outside one and placed his hand on it. Then turned and looked up. I inhaled sharply as a drone floated silently down. Panels opened on its curved sides and guns dropped and locked in place. Another panel opened underneath and it spat out two mini drones.

Jesus! What the fuck is this place?

The momma 'bot scanned Red's face and body, then it scanned me. All the while the baby drones scanned the other guards. There was no doubt, if momma 'bot was unhappy with what it found, we were all dead.

Seemingly satisfied, the 'bot recalled its baby bots and returned to its place up near the ceiling. There was a metallic click, and the door in front of us opened. Red entered. I followed, still mind-fucked over what was going on here.

"Sit." Red indicated a metal chair in front of an aluminium topped table. There was nothing else in the room other than another momma 'bot. Its red light blinked like a tiny all seeing eye. I stared steadily at the lense, wondering if whoever was watching would be visiting me soon. It was time to find out what my role as Prime was in this place.

I sat with my hands shackled in my lap, my skin blistering from the silver. It burned like a son of a bitch, but I'd be damned if I'd let Red and his guys know how painful it was. I blinked and compartmentalised the agony, separating it from my mind. Something dark stirred inside me and took that pain, relishing its presence.

We sat and waited for what seemed like hours. This was a game I was used to, but these bastards didn't realise I could play this game for longer than them. After all, I had nothing but time now. I closed my eyes, though I didn't really doze off. My whole body tensed when the door behind me opened. Inhaling, I jolted upright. I knew that scent.

Doherty's footsteps were unhurried. He stopped in front of me, the table between us, and cocked his head. His dark blue suit was immaculate, his shoes polished, and despite the weather outside, he looked like he'd just stepped from the pages of a GQ magazine. His salt and pepper hair was slicked back and he was clean shaven. He smiled, baring his perfect, white teeth.

It was like coming face to face with a shark, one who had hidden his nature, but now had no problem showing its true self. Just to piss him off, I ignored him and turned my attention to the man by his side.

Red stiffened, his arms unfolding from his chest and his fingers curling slowly into fists as the man glanced at him before studying me.

Interesting.

Red's reaction was soon understandable. I wasn't scared of much, but this guy made me want to run for the hills. Pain and death swirled in his dark gaze, an air of utter coldness surrounding him.

My wolf snarled, unwilling to be cowed by this evil fuck, but I kept that snarl off my own lips, instinct telling me if I wanted to live through the next few minutes, I needed to be compliant.

"Hello, Agent Maxwell, it's so good to see you like this." He gestured at my shackles. "Especially after you ruined my holding cell and killed my men. How *did* you set my man on fire, when you and the other males were all behind bars?"

I settled back in my chair and stared right into his cold eyes. I ignored his question though my stomach clenched. Doherty couldn't have told him about Ember, and I wasn't going to enlighten anyone about her gift. Sliding my gaze back to Doherty, I studied him. "I knew you'd never really forgiven me for Ava's death. Is she the reason for all this?" I was genuinely curious about the answer, but the question also deflected their attention from Ember.

"Ava? No. Ava died because she fell in love with a traitor. You were just my tool to get rid of them both."

Somehow, I kept my face blank. He'd used me to kill his own daughter? My trust and belief in the SBI had been so unshakable I hadn't even considered that might be the case. Lance's face came to mind. He had pleaded with me to listen to him. I swallowed down the bile that hit my throat. How naive and blind I was.

"No, Connor, you're the strongest and most vicious alpha I know. That's why you're here. I need you to control the shifters in this prison. I don't know why you did it, but killing that bureau woman just gave me the excuse I needed to arrest you in front of the other guards. They all believe you stood trial and are serving a life sentence for murder. They are all sworn to secrecy. No one has questioned the circumstances of your 'death'; other than Rawson, who has been nothing but a pain in my arse, delving into things that aren't his concern." A vicious smile curled his lips. "But that's been dealt with."

I clenched my teeth and tried not to show my worry for Rawson. Doherty appeared to honestly believe I had killed Miss X. Instinct told me to keep my mouth shut even though I'd had absolutely nothing to do with her death. The murderer had materialised from a portal as quickly as Walker had disappeared through one when he'd shot me full of tranquilisers. I still had no idea why he had done it, or what the fae had to do with any of this, but I needed to live to find out. He had also only shot me, not Ember, for which I was eternally grateful. The only thing keeping me sane in all of this, was the thought that she had escaped.

"Why did you take Ember?" It was impossible to hide the anger in my voice. "She had nothing to do with Ava or Lance."

A shadow passed over Doherty's face, but he hid it quickly. He shrugged and glanced at Red. "I needed her to control you, but since you helped her escape I guess I'll have to use someone else. Your pack will be useful, but you do not have loyalties there...yet. Time will tell."

I had no intention of being around long enough to form strong pack bonds.

The door clicked open. Grunts and the sounds of a scuffle ensued from behind me. A familiar scent hit my nostrils and my whole body stiffened. *Rawson!*

I gripped my thighs, my knuckles turning white, my wolf baying for freedom. My brother was bloodied and beaten, his previous injuries compounded by fresh marks. His face was so swollen he could barely see through the slit of his eyes. One eye socket had been crushed and his cheekbone was misshapen. His torso was naked, deep slash marks on his skin. His blood dripped to the floor and he swayed.

Lifting his nose, he caught my scent. "Connor...?"

The female at his back shoved him hard and he fell to his knees, revealing the bag she clutched in her hands. It was heavy plastic and waterproof, but the smell coming from it...

I gagged, fisting my fingers so hard my nails cut my palms. *Oh god, no, no, no...!* My wolf howled and tried to break free. I shoved up from my chair and, head down, charged the female. She snarled and snatched the bag away. She needn't have bothered. With a flick of his fingers, the man behind Doherty froze me in mid air.

Doherty took two steps, which brought him right in front of me. "I always detested you, Maxwell. You are just a crazy son of a bitch, who has somehow landed more power than any shifter I know. By all accounts, you should have been exterminated. Do you know I sent Rawson to kill you all those years ago? But instead of ending you as the unstable killer that you are, he took pity on you. He saved you. Well, now he's paying for disobeying me, not just once but twice. He should have stayed out of your missing person's file, but he didn't. Now, neither of you will taste freedom ever again."

I thrashed against the invisible bonds that held me immobile. The female watched me, a slight smirk on her mouth. Her eyes flashed yellow.

The tiger. I'd kill her.

"Ah, ah. No, you won't," said the dark eyed man. *Could he read my mind?* "You belong to me now. If you harm any of my guards, or do anything that displeases me..." He looked at Rawson; for a split second the man's gaze was consumed with fire. Rawson began to choke, his face turning purple as if someone were strangling him. "He will suffer. Not die, unless I will it. But you must understand, there are worse things than death, and I am very adept at elongating someone's suffering—I can prolong it for an eternity if I wish."

My eyes were the only thing I could move. I blinked rapidly, my heart squeezing like a vice. My wolf snarled and growled inside me, tearing at my insides, fighting to escape the confines of my body.

The power that held me hostage shoved me back into my chair. My chest was bound by invisible ropes so that I could only just breathe, but Rawson was released. He slumped over his knees, gasping for air, blood gurgling in his airway. I wanted to help him, but knew I couldn't. My gaze went back to the bag. I knew what was inside. Pain cleaved my heart and I couldn't bear to look at it. My wolf howled, echoing in my mind until all other sounds were drowned out. His grief only amplified my own.

The female tiger slammed the heavy bag on the table in front of me.

I refused to lift my attention from the floor. I couldn't.

"Look at it, or your friend will suffer," the man's cold voice instructed.

I tried to distance myself, to pretend this wasn't real. It was a nightmare that I would wake up from. It had to be.

I raised my gaze.

Doherty reached for the bag.

I'll kill him! I'll kill them all!

Doherty smirked, his eyes glacial. All I wanted right then, was to rip his head off. "That's right, Maxwell. You have no reason to go back out into the world." He undid the ties and reached into the bag. "This is your world now. Carry out your responsibilities as Prime and you get to see Rawson alive, but every time you defy us, he will suffer, and so will your pack..."

My wolf snapped, his claws ripping through my chest, the silver collar burning me. I couldn't fight him, my attention was fixed on that bag, the scent of Ember's wolf filling my nostrils. And all my fight left me.

Doherty lifted the head of Ember's grey and white wolf from the bag. Her beautiful eyes, once full of fire, were dead and stared at me accusingly. Her mouth was agape and crusted in the blood of another. I didn't recognise that scent, but I would never forget it. *Ember's killer.*

My heart shattered, and I couldn't force air in or out of my lungs. The room started to spin. I slumped, blood running from the injuries my wolf had inflicted. He'd clawed from the inside of my body and lacerated the skin on my stomach. I watched my dark red blood trickle down between my legs and pool on the chair.

Maybe, if I died, the pain in my heart and soul would go away but I doubted it. This sorrow would follow me to hell and beyond. The roaring in my head became so loud, I could no longer think. Maybe the bastards in this room spoke, I didn't care, I was sucked into the empty void of my heart.

The female tiger yanked my head back and punched my jaw. I felt nothing. I just stared at the wolf's head, hoping my beautiful mate hadn't suffered. It didn't matter what they did to me now. Ember was gone. My stomach spasmed. She had died alone and frightened. Vomit rushed up my throat and, unable to move my head in the tiger's grasp, I spewed bile and saliva down my chin and chest, not bothered about spitting it away.

"Oh no, Connor, you do not get to give up on life, or I will take his soul and torture him. I will bring him back as an abomination..." said the man. Rawson was yanked up and slammed onto the table in front of me. "And all those you have just assumed responsibility for? They will suffer every hour of every day until you comply."

"This..." Doherty said, replacing the tiger's hand with his own and lifting my head to make me look at the wolf. "...is your doing. She could have been here with you. You could have had her, mated and fucked her as many times as you liked, but instead you chose to oppose me, and she died. Now we have both lost her..."

I frowned. Those words were wrong. *He'd lost her...*What the hell did that mean?

"You can save Rawson. He's your only family, the one who saved you. Now's the time to return the favour. Comply, and he and your pack will not pay for your weakness. You couldn't protect her, but what are you willing to do to protect him?"

I swallowed, trying to control my need to vomit again. Forcing myself, I looked into the eyes of my dead mate, and my soul shriveled. I couldn't imagine a world without Ember in it. My brain just couldn't contemplate it. My wolf growled. I was shutting down, and he knew it. I willingly granted him control, knowing he would not allow his pack to die, but Doherty was wrong about Rawson. Rawson might be my only family, but I couldn't bring myself to care that he was bleeding out in front of me, or that he might suffer —I couldn't bring myself to care about anything. Ember had been my light, my purpose, my whole life; now she was gone and I embraced the darkness.

There was no need to fight the shadows any longer. My wolf howled—and took control.

Please leave that super important review HERE

READ *WRECKED* NOW and find out what happens to Ember and how far into darkness Connor falls... Get your next fix of these characters HERE.

WRECKED

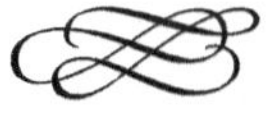

KAREN TOMLINSON

WRECKED

SHADOW SENTINELS

TO ALL MY NATIONAL HEALTH
SERVICE COLLEAGUES!

Especially those who looked after my dad.

You are all AMAZING!

To 2020, it feels like you were sent to break so many lives, and challenge the spirit of many others. If you have been affected in any way by grief, loss, or any other unwelcome change in your life, stay strong and know that you are not alone. Keep your will to fight!

I love this quote from Mahatma Gandhi:
"Strength does not come from physical capacity. It comes from an indomitable will"

Mourn for your lost loved ones, jobs, energy, life styles, freedoms and happiness, then kick 2020 in the arse and lift your chin (and your middle finger) and use that indomitable will. Do not let this year (or however long this pandemic lasts, to break you. XX

CHAPTER 1

mber

MY STRIKE WASN'T HARD. I had no stomach for hurting this spindly, strange-looking fae who cowered against the wall. This clearly wasn't the first time he'd been beaten. The male trembled like a leaf and tried to protect himself with his long thin upper arms.

With my wolf's strength to draw on, I could break him into pieces without thinking twice, but that wasn't my goal. My eyes narrowed on the tiny barbs my weapon had left in his skin. The spiked metal glinted in the dull light of the twin fae moons before they burrowed further into his turquoise skin.

I sighed and stood to my full height. Placing my hands on my hips, I stared down at him. This fae was just doing what his master had ordered. Like many of the lower castes in the Summer Kingdom, he had no power and was repeatedly beaten into submission. I could see the old bruises on his arms and neck. Whatever bastard owned this blue-skinned, yellow-eyed servant did not treat him well.

I narrowed my eyes on him. "Who's your master?"

He peered up at me. His throat bobbed. "I-I can't tell you, Yellow. He'll kill me and sell my family to the traders."

I flicked my dyed-blonde hair off my shoulder. Normally I plaited it so it was out of my way, but I didn't bother today. My lead on Walker, the fae who betrayed my family and me, had come to nothing again. I curled my fists and

121

took a deep breath. The disappointment meant mundane things like my hair were easily forgotten. My target watched me with wide eyes as I quickly braided the stuff out of my way. I had to agree, it did seem like a weird thing to do when I was supposed to be threatening him. I shrugged. My work involved a lot of fighting, and these days we often had to run from the fae authorities. It would just get in the way. I suppose I could cut it off, but Connor, the guy I grew up with and the only person whose opinion mattered to me, had loved it, so I wanted to keep it even if I did have to disguise its normally bright red colour.

"Fine. Get lost. But if I catch you sniffing around this place again, your boss won't get a chance to end you. I'll do it myself." I infused my voice with enough venom to make the threat believable. I hated the hierarchical system in Faerie. It was like going back to the middle ages on Earth.

"Whoa, Yell, you can't just let him go. He knows where our stash is, and if he knows, so does his master." Blue, who was my friend, and the most awesome, bad-assed bitch I could have as my partner, looked at me like I was crazy.

I yanked the tall, ridiculously thin fae up from the ground. He swayed a bit, a sickly sheen covering his skin as I straightened his clothes. I made a show of smoothing down his silk waistcoat. He obviously worked for one of the disgustingly rich high fae families.

"What's your name?" I asked, knowing full well he wouldn't give it to me. Names held too much power in this land. But Blue was right; we couldn't afford for him to go spreading word of where we hid our stash of digitalis. The petals, leaves and roots of the plant we knew as Foxglove were worth a fortune here in Faerie. Blue and I dealt in the sale and distribution of the plant. It was deadly to humans, but to the fae, it had opiate-like effects that they paid for handsomely.

We'd been dealing here for four years now, but rather than the authorities managing to catch us and shut us down, we just got more creative and always evaded them. It was a dangerous career choice, but definitely worth the risk to our lives. Though it was more than the riches, which I never really spent, that made me continue with this unlawful existence—it was the challenge and the fact I got to search for Walker. I loved evading the cunning and powerful fae royal families. We'd been dealing within the borders of the summer realm for about a year now. Rumour had it that it wasn't just the Summer King who was out for our blood but the High King of Faerie: the Winter King.

Fortunately, the threat of capture didn't matter to me. I had nothing beyond this life. No, I'd lost everyone I'd loved years ago, so there was nothing to hold me on Earth. I went back because we had to go there to resupply, but other than a good Chinese takeaway and perhaps an occasional McDonalds, there was nothing there I wanted. I did, however, have a reason to be in Faerie. I was still searching for Walker, and I always would, until either I caught him and ripped out his heart, or I reached the end of my days; which, courtesy of my mother's gift, would not be for a very very long time. My nostrils flared, my anger still as raw as it was the day Walker left me and the man I loved to the mercy of our enemy. Except they didn't have any mercy.

I tilted my head and contemplated the spindly fae. The last thing I needed was to free someone who could ruin our business here. When I was eighteen, I'd struck a deal with Somnelaire, the Bogwart fae who was our boss. I got thirty percent of the profits from our Faerie drug deals. But it was the chance to hunt for Walker that drove my success and gave me purpose. Our illegal portal between Earth and Faerie was nearby, and if that were found, we'd all be in deep shit. Som had no loyalty to anyone but himself. I didn't take offense; it was just the way fae like him were made. Nothing personal. If necessary, he would run to save himself and hang us out to dry. Both Blue and I knew it.

The spindly fae pressed his wide thin lips together, his eyes glowing eerily.

I contemplated the little device I held between my finger and thumb. My leather jacket creaked as I shrugged. "Fine." And I pressed the button.

The fae squealed, his body going rigid and jerking. His eyes rolled back in his head and spit dribbled down his chin. I kept my finger on the button long enough that when I released him, he fell to the ground, still twitching when I squatted next to him. I inhaled the sweet smell of summer grass and sunshine that surrounded us, and grinned, though I didn't really relish this side of my job.

Carefully, I brushed strands of silken hair from his sweating face and kept my voice hard. "I can keep doing this, you know. But if you give me your name, and your master's, oh, and definitely the name of the person who told you about our store, I won't press this itty bitty button anymore."

He pressed his mouth together and shook his head, looking so scared I felt sorry for him. The poor bugger was stuck between a rock and a hard place; me or his vicious master. I pressed the button again, I had to make a point; we had lingered here too long.

The stink of urine hit my sensitive nose and my wolf grumbled, her dislike of my harsh treatment of this creature a feeling I didn't relish—at all. She had been mistreated by her past host and I had promised never to disrespect her like that. I hadn't, but she still hated when I had to get violent. *Hush. This is necessary if you don't want me dead again. I might get reborn, but you would end up on your way back to the Mother Wolf.* She huffed her disapproval but settled, leaving me to do my job.

I took a breath but kept up my cool, drug dealer facade. "Just so you know, those little barbs in your skin can't be removed. They just burrow right on in, and if you try to dig them out or disturb them, they will release an overdose of digitalis serum and you'll die. Understand?"

He nodded, his eyes wide enough that black surrounded their solid yellow center.

"Good. Now what's your name? Come on, don't be shy. I promise I have no idea how to turn a name into any kind of faery magic."

He studied me, his wide eyes staring into mine. "Waib."

I smiled, but not necessarily in a friendly way. "Hi, Waib. Now, who's your master? And I know you can't lie, so let's make this less painful for us both. Just tell me and we can save a lot of time."

He blinked.

I looked at the egg sized device again while Waib turned an ugly shade of purple. Having spent the last four years of my life breaking the law in the land of Faerie, I knew this was his version of going pale. I made a show of lifting the device and pressing my thumb on the button that would bring those barbs to life again.

"A'nar Voltair!"

I tilted my head, sending my plait swinging over my shoulder. "Damn!" The Voltair caste were closely related to the Winter King, I was sure of it. A'nar meant *'youngest son of'*. It figured high fae like them would abuse their staff and force them to do their dirty work. And they were so extremely vocal about condemning drug use, even for good reasons like pain relief. It really shouldn't surprise me that they'd be so hypocritical as to send their staff out to buy those same drugs for their own use.

I held back a snarl. "Thank you, Waib. Now, who told you about this place? Your master is clearly very well off; a high fae of the royal bloodline. And seeing as our store and dealings are under the radar of the fae guard, even the Summer King, how did your master find out? We're miles from the Winter Kingdom."

Waib blinked and sat up. "My master told me about this place. He bid me to spy on you and try to steal a sample, but I don't know how he found out about your...er...store."

"Really? Well." I shoved a little packet in his pocket. "Tell him this is on the house, but if he or you, ever breathe a word of this location to anyone, I will take great pleasure in ripping your throats out. Do I make myself clear?" My voice was as cold as my glare, as I let my wolf show in my eyes.

Waib nodded, his fear a bitter scent up my nose.

"It's true, this servant knows nothing, it was an anonymous tip to my father. So you can stop torturing him now because you won't discover the answer," said a deep, commanding voice.

"Shit!"

"Damn!"

Blue and I both cursed together.

I flicked the switch on the barbs and poor Waib started to fit and thrash on the floor. It was not a pretty sight. I swallowed hard, knowing I had just made him our distraction. Looking down at him I mouthed, "I'm sorry."

"Let him go, drop your weapons and surrender to us. Do that, and I will let you live." The voice came from the shadows of the forest, colder this time. In fact, I could swear the temperature had dropped a few degrees. I shuddered.

Blue slapped her hand against the stone of the cliff. "No fucking chance." Instantly, a shield of energy slammed down in front of us, stretching from the mouth of the cave, which was our store, to a thicket of thorn bushes on the other side. "That'll only hold them for a few minutes, I'm afraid. Whoever that is, might let us live, but it won't be a pleasant existence." She pulled her weapon. "And I am not getting stuck in Faerie as a human slave."

A beautiful man stepped from the shadows. His blue, waist-length hair gleamed and his form-fitting armour moulded to his powerful, yet elegant body. My jaw dropped. He was gorgeous. He grinned like he'd heard Blue's words, though his startling pale green eyes were as cold as ice. He drew back his hand. Ice green magic swirled around his fist before he released it. Power exploded across the shield, erupting like a thunder crack as the two forms of energy connected. He directed a snarl right at Blue, before bombarding the shield again and again.

My faith in Blue's talents was normally unshakable; after all, my partner-in-crime was the cleverest person I had ever met. But right then, saying a prayer to the Mother Wolf to save our arses seemed like a good thing to do.

Blue's bobbed blue hair swung as she turned to face me. Behind her, more fae guards stepped from the shadows, all dressed in battle armour, and all carrying beautifully crafted bows. Fae weapons were infused with magic, but they were made all the more powerful by their own brand of technology. And these had to be royal guards, their expensive and elaborately etched armour a huge calling card.

My heart slammed against my ribs.

"Damn it! They're not summer fae. That armour isn't like any I've seen before, and we've been to every kingdom except Winter and the dark fae in the Orth Kingdom."

"Shit!" Blue's face blanched.

"We need to get to the portal. Now! That fae's magic is also far stronger than any other fae's I've ever seen. Come on!"

Blue glanced over her shoulder at the small army now approaching.

The fae commander stopped on the other side of the shield and fixed his gaze on Blue. His lips stretched into a cold smile. "You're mine, human."

Blue rolled her eyes and gave him the finger. "In your dreams, motherfucker."

Even in this dire situation, I had to laugh. She had the biggest balls of anyone I knew. "Yep! Let's go. He's got too much of a hard on for you to risk fighting it out."

Blue nodded and winked at him. "He surely does."

Keeping my weapon in my hand, I jumped over Waib's twitching body, knowing Blue would follow. We sprinted into the dark forest towards the stinking bog that Som had used as a landmark to form his portal.

There was a huge explosion behind us.

"Damn! That guy's already destroyed the shield. Jump!" Blue yelled.

Together we leapt into the swirling portal. My wolf growled as power tried to rip her spirit from me. Fire—my other spirit, the one that hibernated deep inside me, didn't like my wolf's distress, not one bit. My first wolf spirit had returned to the Mother Wolf when I was eighteen. Fire and I had sacrificed her to give me a chance to escape the people who had taken Connor. Now I housed a lovely white wolf, one I had taken from a murderer that very same day. Fire never liked travelling through the bridge between worlds. I sensed she couldn't tell whether my human body was dying each time I did it. I had to admit, leaping from Faerie to Earth, and vice versa, was painful enough that I could believe my soul was being ripped from my flesh. My lungs squeezed so tight I couldn't breathe, and an icy cold seeped into my bones, reaching so deep I was sure it was trying to freeze me from the inside out. With a yell, I battled the effects of the portal and fought to keep my wolf inside me. She whined and dug in her claws.

Blue watched me carefully. She was totally human and had no shifter power to control in the portal. The lack of duality made it as easy for humans as it was for fae to go through the portals.

The tarmac of Som's lockup loomed ahead. My feet slammed into the ground, but I had done this hundreds of times, as had Blue. We hit the ground running, and I held my weapon out steady. It was programmed to stun, the setting that had taken Waib down. With my thumb, I flicked it to kill and ignored my ebbing discomfort from the leap as I turned to face the portal.

If that fae showed his face, he'd get a bullet between his teeth—no matter how gorgeous he was. I doubted even a fae like him could move fast enough with his magic to stop it.

"No, Em! You go and find Som! I don't know where that slimy shit has gone, but something doesn't feel right. He's normally here by the time we get back, waiting to shut the gate down!"

Blue grabbed another gun from behind the storage crate where we hid extra weapons and stood with her feet apart, a weapon now in each hand, trained on the swirling vortex. Her stance was solid, and her expression fierce, ready to take down anything—or anyone who came through.

I didn't want to leave her, but she was right; Som was never absent. My eyes drifted to the storage building across the yard. Underneath it was our escape route.

"Fine! But if that fae is the next one through, you shoot him between the eyes and then run! You hear me? He's got an army at his back, and we don't." I grabbed another weapon.

Blue flicked her attention to me and nodded her agreement. "Go!"

I held one gun in each hand and ran up the rickety wooden steps of Som's place. My stomach clenched, but I forced myself not to look back at my friend. I knew deep down she wouldn't run; she was even more stubborn than me.

Not one for carelessness, I stopped and pressed my back against the wall. Slowly, I opened the door of Som's warehouse office. My senses sharpened. He never left it unlocked.

The stench of blood and bowel contents hit me first. I wrinkled my nose as my guts fizzed and bile splurged my throat. Grimacing, I swallowed the vile stuff back down and made my way inside. Carefully, I missed the squeaky floorboards and crept down the poorly lit corridor.

The stench of death grew stronger.

Something dark and evil slithered against my skin. I shuddered and peered back over my shoulder. Nothing but shadows. My wolf whined, urging me to run. She was right. If that smell was anything to go by, Som was already dead and I needed to get back to Blue. I cocked my head and listened with my shifter hearing. There was no sound of a fight and no gunshots from the yard. And Blue would fight—if she could. That thought spurred me on towards Som's office. If Som was dead, I needed to know so that I could grab my emergency bag from under the storehouse in the yard and get the hell out of here.

My heart thumped a fast, erratic rhythm, and my palms were sweating. The last time I had run for my life, I'd lost everyone I loved. But Som wasn't my family, he was just a Bogwart fae who had been banished from Faerie. He worked under the radar of just about everyone and could glamour better than any fae I'd ever seen. I'd worked with him since my parents died when I was six, and I had to survive in London's back streets. Surprisingly, he'd been the only one I could trust to hide me when my foster family had been betrayed by the very agency they'd all worked for. Doherty, the director of the Supernatural Bureau of Investigation in Britain, and the man I suspected had killed them, had always wanted something from me. I didn't hang around to find out what; instead I hid here.

I crept down the dull corridor, my footsteps near silent, my breathing controlled. A droplet of sweat ran from my hairline down my neck and spine. My wolf snarled, wanting me to let her out. I was sorely tempted to do just that, but I had a feeling being dexterous enough to use my weapons would be more useful than fangs and teeth.

The stink of death became overpowering. I froze and took slow and controlled breaths, just like I learned in my time as a trainee SBI agent. If Som was dead, his killer might still be here—which also meant the portal couldn't be closed.

Shit... That put Blue at more risk. The fae could come through and cause havoc in this world. And a portal open for longer than an hour would mean Doherty would be alerted. The SBI sensors would pick up the portal's energy surge, and he'd send a team here to close it.

Adrenaline coursed through my blood, sending my heart rate skyhigh. Blue and I needed to get out, right now. Fire uncoiled, sensing my anxiety. She pushed against the walls I'd locked her behind, but I ignored her, just as I had since the day I'd left Connor to die. Instead, I nudged my wolf forward just a little. She responded, and I gritted my teeth as my bones stretched, making my ears and claws grow. I stopped well short of a full shift, just needing her heightened senses, and though she grumbled at me, she complied.

I paused and strained my ears. Nothing. No sound. Just the wind shifting around the outside of the building. The hair on the back of my neck rose. It was eerie—and wrong. Som always had some kind of crazy heavy metal banging away in the background. He said he found it relaxing.

With the guns clutched in my clawed hands, I edged down the corridor. Taking a deep breath, I tensed my muscles and kicked open the door to his office. Instantly, I retched. Not even *my* stomach could ignore the blood and body fluids painting the floor and walls. In the moonlight that streamed through the small, dirty window, the bits of skin I could see appeared dark, like Som's. I had no idea if it really was the Bogwart or not, as Som's little gang of fae creatures all had blue, purple or grey skin when in their true form.

I spun in a circle, expecting some kind of enemy to still be there. It didn't help my nerves when the room appeared empty. *Something* had done this, something strong—and vicious. The office had been trashed. The metal filing cabinets were ripped open, huge jagged gashes torn through the sides. Whatever had done this didn't have the pure magic or knowledge to undo Som's fae charmed locks, so they had gone for the pure muscle method of getting in. Papers were strewn over the floor, covered in blood and other grim stuff.

I had no idea what the thieves were looking for, and I didn't want to know. Som's dealings were not legal—in any world. His glamour worked on humans to hide his drugs and magic, but not on shifters, SBI agents, or on other fae. Maybe that beautiful fae that had found us had actually found Som first.

"Blue..." I whispered, my heart racing. The floor was slick with congealed blood, and my boot sole slipped as I pivoted. There was no time to even blink as the shadows came to life. Red eyes burned through the darkness. My wolf snarled, and so did I. Recognition hit me. This thing had darted and drugged Rawson. Rawson had been a powerful alpha bear, yet it took him down in a heartbeat.

Run... urged my wolf. I roared through my surging memories, pushing down my fear.

Red eyes moved. His body was huge, almost too big to be human or even alpha shifter, but still he was quick.

Shit!

I couldn't see him clearly, so there was no way I could fight him and win. I knew that for sure because this bastard had caught me before, right after he'd caught Rawson. Reflexively, my forefingers squeezed on the triggers of the guns I swung in his direction. Bullets fired in quick succession. The force vibrated up my arm, but I held them steady; it wasn't the first time I'd fired my weapons.

I didn't wait to see what happened. I ran. I could shift into another form, but Blue couldn't—she was totally human. Even if she was one of the best and most cunning fighters I knew, she'd need my help.

I sprinted back down the corridor using my wolf's speed. It wasn't fast enough! Footsteps pounded behind me, getting closer. I burst out of the door and rammed straight through the banister rails into mid air. I twisted as I fell and fired up at red eyes. His body jerked as the silver bullets slammed into his flesh, and he toppled after me.

Dammit! There was no time to turn or shift to save myself. All I could do was force my body to relax and hope I bounced on the pile of rubbish that was always under the steps. I blinked once, then hit the mound of boxes. Pain slammed through me, but my bones didn't break.

Red eyes fell towards me, bellowing.

"Shit!" I rolled sideways, an arm outstretched. And fired.

There was a heavy thud, and the bellow cut off.

I pulled my wolf back, arched my spine, flipped to my feet then launched into a sprint towards Blue. My friend had her arms outstretched and her guns held steady, pointing towards the portal.

"Blue!" I yelled. "We gotta go!"

She didn't even turn her head.

My wolf growled, the sound echoing inside my skull.

"Blue! What the hell? Run! Now!"

Nothing. Not even a twitch. My blood ran cold. I reached her and skidded to a halt. Her face was like one of those freaky china dolls, utterly blank— almost translucent in the moonlight.

I froze and stared. "Blue?" My voice was barely more than a whisper. I had no idea what was going on, but it was bad—very, very bad.

Nothing.

She was totally and utterly frozen. My heart hammered against my ribs and my wolf howled. *Run! Run!* But I couldn't leave my friend. Her deep brown eyes suddenly flicked my way. She blinked rapidly and her pupils dilated. Desperate noises came from her throat.

"I can't!" I glanced back at red eyes who unfolded his body like a predator. Not shifter then; if he was, my bullets would have killed him. He straightened with powerful grace and precision and stalked towards me. Keeping my eyes on him, I curled my fingers into Blue's jacket and shook. But even shaking her hard had no effect. She blinked and blinked until a tear fell from her right eye, blazing a path over the soft pale skin of her cheek.

"Blue! Snap out of it! Whatever magic this is, fight it! I know you can!" I shook her again. Blue blinked even more rapidly. She was right, I had to go.

Gods damn it! It was happening again! I was going to have to run—alone. Only this time there was no Som for me to run to.

"Move!" I yelled at Blue, shaking her viciously.

"It's really no good," said a smooth voice; one I'd had nightmares about for years.

I yanked my hands back.

"Neither of you are going anywhere."

I spun and faced the man who had taken everyone I loved from me. Doherty was still as smooth looking as ever, dressed in an immaculate grey suit and shiny shoes. Grey peppered his hair, and there were more lines on his face, but his jawline was as hard and sharp as it ever was, as were his eyes. They glinted as he looked me up and down.

I swallowed hard, praying Som's glamour held. With my dyed blonde hair and altered appearance, perhaps he wouldn't recognise me.

Doherty frowned, but there was no recognition on his face. Hatred churned in my gut. This man had taken Connor from me. On instinct, and in a move I'd repeated over and over in my head, I raised my gun and pulled the trigger. There was a blur of movement in front of me. I didn't wait to see what it was, I launched into a sprint only to slam into a wall of muscle. I bounced back, the air knocked from my lungs. There'd been no one there; only space. A fist in my belly dropped me to my knees.

Coughing and spluttering, I raised my gun—only to freeze.

No!

Rawson loomed above me, his body stuck in Were form—a half-shift. His face was a grotesque mask of hair and teeth, but I'd know those eyes anywhere. They'd once held such kindness, such spirit. Now they were utterly empty, as if his deformed body was there, but his soul was gone.

Pain tore at my chest, tears burning my eyes. He wasn't here...he was dead. I'd grieved for him. I swallowed over and over. This couldn't be happening. My mind whirled with what this meant. Could Connor be alive, too?

Red eyes stood next to Doherty. He held his right arm out straight and opened his clenched palm. A bullet fell to the ground, pinging as it hit the concrete.

"Now, now, settle down. There is no escape for you. My men surround this place. Besides, you'll not be missed by anyone here and I need females. You've been sold to me," Doherty said.

I peered up at red eyes, unable to even look at Rawson. I didn't believe Doherty had a whole army here. He was working under the radar again, and I was his captive—only this time he didn't realise I was the girl who'd escaped his clutches four years ago.

"Our intel told us we were waiting for the murderer of the proprietor to resurface—and you did."

That got my attention. My head jerked, and I gave him my full attention. "What? I didn't kill anyone."

Doherty shrugged. "Well, someone killed those fae up there, and you seem like the best person to blame. Either way, if you try and run, not only will you die, so will your friend."

I swallowed my fear. I could possibly shift and rip red eyes a new one, I might even be quick enough to kill Doherty. But Rawson? He'd be faster than me, and he clearly had no control over his mind. If he was told to kill me, he would. And what about Blue? She was human—and she'd been bespelled; she couldn't run. My gaze slipped to her, and I ground my teeth.

"That's right. She *will* die." Doherty stepped aside, allowing me an unobstructed view of the portal. My stomach sank.

The beautiful fae glared back at me, no hint of softness in his face. "It's true, I can end you both for entering my world without permission. You are both mine now."

"Oh no, no, no, that's not the agreement, Prince B'nar. This one is mine. The crime of murder far outweighs trespass and drug dealing."

Prince! Shit! I looked at Blue, hoping he wouldn't take her. High fae were powerful, but those with royal blood were the most powerful, the most cunning and definitely the cruelest fae around. For someone like him, compelling her and controlling her body would be child's play.

The fae prince snarled at Doherty. Magic swirled around his arm, and he eyed the director with such coldness I prayed the man might drop dead from it.

B'nar looked at Blue, then back at me. I tried to hold that powerful gaze, but it was hard even for me. My wolf cowered from the weight of his power and dominance.

"In the interests of peace between our worlds, I will allow you to keep the dealer known as Yellow. This one... this Blue... comes with me. She will await trial, *at my pleasure*, for crimes against my people and the laws of Faerie."

It could have been my imagination, but I was sure Doherty's shoulders relaxed a little. Whichever fae prince this was, he was a threat to the director, maybe even our world.

The director gave a small nod towards me.

I glanced up at Rawson, searching for any sign of the man beneath, ready to plead for my life, but it wasn't him who moved. Red eyes raised a familiar looking dart gun. I didn't fight. There was no point. A dart pierced my neck. Pain instantly burned through my body, ripping through my cells. With a gasp I dropped to my knees and the ground tilted as I pitched sideways. My wolf howled and thrashed to get free, but she was imprisoned in my paralysed body. I watched through heavy lids as the tall fae snapped his fingers in front of Blue's face and she dropped to her knees. She must have completely lost control of her actions, but she managed to meet my gaze. We were both in a bad place, but we were fighters, so no matter what happened now, we would survive. I tried to let her see I would get out. "I'll find you," I whispered. Her swallow was answer enough.

The fae made a summoning gesture towards the portal, and two armoured fae stepped through. They grabbed Blue, hoisted her under her arms, and dragged her into the vortex.

The fae didn't even glance back at me. He merely stepped into the portal and disappeared, the portal closing behind him.

My breathing was quick and shallow as I stared impotently at the empty space. The only faerie, besides Som, I'd seen summon and disperse a portal had been Walker.

Strong hands gripped me and flipped me onto my back.

My vision blurred as my heart slowed, and my wolf became silent. Sensing my body shutting down, Fire flared through my blood; a defense mechanism as the prelude to death.

Red eyes squatted beside me, blocking my view of Doherty and Rawson.

"Don't." He shook his head, and his hand gripped mine, absorbing the heat from my body. Red flames flared in his eyes. "The drug will not kill you, and he doesn't recognise you. Keep her hidden, don't give him your secret, or your life will get far worse."

I gritted my teeth and tried to keep my eyes open. What did he mean *her*? Did he know what I was? "I can't. Stop."

"I know. That's why you need to sleep. It's safer for everyone, including you." There was another sharp sting and his harsh features faded into a blur. My eyes closed, my wolf howled from far away, and the flames faded from my blood.

CHAPTER 2

mber

MY HEAD JOLTED side to side and my chin bounced on my chest, sending shooting pains down my neck and spine. *Shit!* I snapped open my eyes and raised my head, then groaned. My head pounded like there was a hammer bashing the inside of my skull.

It had been the same last time I'd been darted by red eyes, or...maybe I'd just call him Red.

I blinked rapidly. I couldn't see where I was, but the sway and bounce of the seat underneath me told me this wasn't a cell but a moving vehicle.

Wanting to rub my eyes, I tried to raise my arm, only it didn't move. There was a harsh metallic sound when I tried again. *What the hell?* I peered down. My arms and torso were wreathed in silver chains, and my wrists were handcuffed together in my lap. I hissed as pain from my burned wrists along with the numbness in my backside all registered through the fog of my pounding head. I'd probably been in this upright position for a while.

I squeezed my eyes shut against the pounding in my skull, letting my nausea settle. The weight of another presence pressed against my awareness, so tentatively, I opened them again and slowly raised my head.

Red regarded me steadily.

I held his stare. "What're you looking at, dickhead?" Yeah, maybe my verbal attack didn't hold quite the force and venom I'd have liked. My voice

133

reverberated like a fog horn in my skull, but barely more than a rasp escaped my lips.

His eyes narrowed almost as if he was laughing at me, but he kept his face expressionless and merely lifted a finger to his lips, then nodded to where Rawson slumbered next to me. My eyes widened. The Were was held down by chains just like mine, only there were more of them. Was he that unpredictable?

"Piss off!" I snarled and yanked my body around rattling the chains. If I woke Rawson and wound him up enough, maybe he'd break his chains or cause enough of a diversion for me to escape mine. I eyed the back doors and sides of the van. Damn! No windows—anywhere. No matter, I'd find a way out somehow. Red had to have a key...

Red leaned back against the metal sides of the van and crossed his arms over his chest, watching me until I ran out of energy. Even the bumping of the prison van didn't phase him. He managed to look cool and in control even as I was being shaken around.

"I need to pee." I winced as another bump made my bladder scream.

He merely shrugged, leaned his head back and closed his eyes.

"Hey! Unless you want me to pee all over the floor, you need to let me out!"

Nothing. The bastard didn't even flinch.

"Let me out!" My bladder was so full, it hurt. I had no idea how long I'd been in this van, but the stench coming from my clothes told me I'd been here long enough to wet myself before, and for it to dry. My cheeks flamed.

I called on my wolf to help, but no matter how she fought, there was no breaking past the effects of the silver chains. I glared at my captor, praying to the devil himself to see this demon struck down.

A huff, which sounded suspiciously like a chuckle, came from Red, then he settled back down without even opening his eyes.

Surely he didn't read minds, did he?

I closed my eyes, concentrated on my breathing, and tried to ignore the fact that my bladder wanted to burst and my kidneys were ready to explode. I concentrated on not letting my pelvis relax even for a second, but every bump and turn in the road was torture. I didn't even care where I was going, only that I didn't want to piss my pants in front of Red.

A bang at the partition between us and the cab made me jump enough to let a little escape. I bit back a pained groan.

"Heads up! Nearly there!" shouted a disembodied voice.

Red opened his eyes and straightened. He inhaled and growled, his features twisting.

"Be grateful I haven't pissed all over your shoes—yet," I said sweetly.

He merely grunted and leaned forward. His bulk was intimidating this close, but I didn't shrink away; I wouldn't. There was a sting in my neck. I hissed. "Again?" The world went fuzzy, but I was aware when warmth ran down my legs.

There was a muttered curse.

"Serves you right." I smirked before I lost consciousness completely.

THIS TIME when I woke up it was to the sound of growling and banging. Once again, agony stabbed behind my eyes. I inhaled sharply, and gagged on the stench of stale urine, vomit, and yes, faeces. *Urgh!* I swallowed over and over unwilling to open my eyes, praying it wasn't me who'd made that awful stink. There was no burning when I moved my arms, so I figured I wasn't chained, although there was the weight of a silver collar hanging around my neck.

My wolf howled, delighted that I was waking up. *Whoa there, sweetie. Gently now. I'm a bit delicate. Just quiet down for a moment.* Her relief washed through me. *Yeah, I'm glad to be conscious again, too.*

Around me, male and female voices yelled. I cracked open my eyelids just enough to see—and did my level best not to react. *What the hell?* I was on the metal floor of a huge cage with curved sides. There were no windows, but there was the steady thrum of engines beneath the chaos of swearing, and snarled threats.

Three large men faced off against one another. Their wolf and feline scents mixed with the general nastiness of the scents encasing me. Around the small group, men and women yelled, egging the males on to fight. The atmosphere was volatile and burning with alpha aggression and violence. This was somewhere you didn't ever want to be, stuck in a cage full of shifters all vying for the ultimate position of power—to be alpha.

No one noticed that I was awake so I kept my position on the floor, but pushed myself backwards right up against the metal walls. Then I just studied my surroundings. Trying to make my five feet four inches as small and unnoticeable as possible, I curled my shoulders down and my legs in. I could hold my own against any of these shifters if I had to, but it was always wise to weigh both their strength and my situation first.

Beyond the thick metal bars of the cage, guards observed the matches. I couldn't see their faces because of the full face masks they wore, but their whole demeanour suggested they were disinterested, and would do absolutely nothing to intervene. All of them held weapons far outmatching anything I'd ever seen at Rawson's house, or that Blue had ever developed. All of them wore black armoured jumpsuits with no identifying marks. Only the fact that Red sat against the bulkhead at the far end of the space on the other side of this cage, told me this was all part of what had happened at Som's. I didn't know what the director was up to, but thinking about it sent ice skittering down my spine. I sure wasn't going to any supernatural court in Britain—I was on a bloody plane!

I lost my view of Red as the crowd on my side of the bars closed in on the antagonists. The wolves snarled and launched themselves at their enemy. The stink of pheromones and blood lust flooded the air. My wolf slammed against the power of the silver collar, my vision merging with hers. I winced. My skin burned as she tried to burst through and protect me, only to be forced back.

The crowd parted for a body to come flying through the air, its arm hanging on by a thread.

Jesus! The shift might be held back by the collars, but the viciousness of the predators in this cage was not.

I snarled as one of the large males leaped closer to me. He was obviously trying to get to the victim who was bleeding out all over the floor.

I honed my vision in on that male wolf and gripped the edge of the bench, ready to tear his heart out if he so much as looked my way. My heart rate spiked, but I took a deep breath and exhaled. Yes, I was at risk here, but my life was not in immediate danger. I could fight if I had to, I'd been trained by the best—Rawson and Connor—and I had not exactly played the prim and proper princess in Faerie these last years. Besides, it wasn't the others in this cage that I was most worried about, it was the guards, particularly Red. I didn't know what his deal was, or why we were here, but I had a feeling if I ended up being the most vicious fighter, I'd get special treatment and not necessarily of the good kind.

A second, smaller wolf pounced on the back of the feline shifter, digging its teeth into the back of the man's neck. He roared and shook, trying to dislodge his enemy. While he was distracted, a big male wolf, with shoulder length blonde hair and the golden sun-kissed look of a surfer, pounced. He clamped his large hands onto the feline's head, twisted and pulled. The metallic stench of blood flooded the air. The feline male hadn't stood a chance, not alone.

Christ! I cringed as the headless body fell to the ground. The large male threw the head over his shoulder. Right at me. *The fucker!* It thudded to the floor and bounced then came to a halt about two feet away. I deliberately didn't look at the gruesome trophy. I'd seen more death than I cared to admit of late —especially in Faerie—and I'd dealt out my fair share. Not saying my halo was still bright, or even still there, but I'd only ever killed in self-defense, or to save myself and Blue, never out of pure, predatory evil.

I grimaced as the fight continued. This many shifters in a confined space made fighting for the top position of alpha an inevitability. I lamented the loss of my weapons, but if all else failed, Fire would break free. Things would have to become critical for that to happen, though, like me being close to death, so

I kind of hoped it wouldn't be necessary. I'd managed once in the past to summon enough heat to help Connor escape a silver collar just like mine, but I hadn't been able to summon Fire at will since. It was as if my mind and body had locked her away and she had no choice but to stay in her cage.

The blood and aggression drew in the other shifters. They bayed for more blood—all except one, a large man who sat in the far corner of the cage, opposite me. His face was heavy, his jaw square and his nose flat and misshapen. Golden wavy hair fell to his shoulders in a tousled, greasy mess, and his clothes were ripped and dirty, making me wonder what had happened to him and how long he'd already been imprisoned.

His amber eyes watched the others carefully—coldly detached and predatory. I shuddered. Now, there was the predator to worry about amongst this lot, not the one who had just killed the feline male. Whatever this man's shifter spirit was, it was powerful and patient and totally in harmony with the man. He'd tamed it enough to do what I did—see through its eyes and use its senses and strength without fully shifting. Only the most harmonised shifters could manage that.

As though he could feel my gaze, he slid his attention to me. His eyes narrowed as the weight of his dominance pushed against me. That same shiver of power that Connor had always used to intimidate others, slid over my skin. I kept my face impassive, but did not lower my gaze. That would show weakness, and I was anything but weak. His eyes gleamed with something akin to respect. My stomach tightened as he contemplated me, then he returned his amber gaze back to the crowd. Watching. Waiting. Deciding when to pounce.

I gave a short sigh of relief and swallowed against my dry throat, unable to resist the urge to wipe my sweaty palms down my jeans. My skin prickled with awareness, so I scanned the cage. Red studied me coolly, almost as if he was wondering what I'd do next.

I dragged my gaze away from the cold hearted fucker. It was more important to be aware of what was happening in this cage.

Claws sliced and teeth ripped. Flesh and blood splattered the floor and walls. The overwhelming coppery scent of blood was a catalyst for the other shifters to take each other on. I pushed back against the bulkhead of the plane, hoping it would soon be decided who the alpha was, finally establishing a hierarchy. It didn't matter to me who won since not one of them here deserved my loyalty. I looked after myself. And bowing to an alpha wasn't going to happen—ever.

The guards continued to watch the struggle impassively. Red had closed his eyes again.

How could he sleep through this racket, with the stench of blood and death everywhere?

I kept my head down, attempting to look as non-threatening as possible. The amber-eyed male across from me remained still but alert, his body relaxed. It was a deceptive posture. Anyone with any sense would know he was ready to attack.

Red opened his glowing eyes and tilted his head. "Light them up."

The guard nearest the cage flicked a switch and I could have sworn lightning struck me. My whole body spasmed, my muscles turning to concrete, as my teeth snapped together. Mercifully, it finally stopped, and everyone fell to the ground. Groans and cries echoed around me. All the shifters had received the same jolt of energy from their collar. The male wolf roared, an inhuman sound of anger and challenge.

Red looked over. "Again."

This time as my muscles seized, Fire reared inside me, smashing through her confines in my soul. "No," I whispered, trying to keep her at bay. I couldn't let these guards see her. Here was not a good place for her to be released. There were far too many witnesses. I glared at him. *Evil fucker!*

His gaze turned to me. His body uncoiled and he leaned forward, elbows on his knees. His eyes were like something from an eighties vampire flick; they actually glowed. Through my eyes, Fire looked right back at him. He huffed, a smirk curling his mouth as he leaned back.

I had no idea what that meant, but it was clear he knew about Fire. That thought turned my blood cold. Why was he keeping it to himself?

"Cut it. That should keep 'em quiet while we land."

The electric pulse was shut off and the agony in my body receded. I lay there panting, my body exhausted and twitching. Perhaps this was karma for all the times I'd shot my enemies full of taser bullets. Waib's face came to mind. Bizarrely, I wondered if he was alright. He'd been terrified of his master. I just hoped Blue never came face to face with Waib or the rich asshole who owned him. I doubted that would end well. Then again, why in the hell would Blue ever meet Waib? She was a prisoner. I shuddered, my heart squeezing hard. There was no way I could have prevented her capture, but that didn't make me feel any better.

Worn out by the shocks, I drifted in semi-consciousness, only stirring when the plane tilted, and the engines changed pitch. We were landing.

CHAPTER 3

onnor

A WAVE of power bristled against my skin. I cocked my head as I internalised my anger. Standing behind me, my brothers growled as one, a resonant rumble that fed my own need for blood. I watched through my wolf's eyes, unconcerned that he was at the forefront running the show. For four years, my wolf and I worked as one to keep our pack together and alive. The other shifters in this hell hole were expendable, but my brothers were not.

The stench of burned flesh seeped into the air as the new recruits tried to shift. Even if they realised fighting the silver collars was pointless, most were unable to control the need. That compulsion to free their animal side would soon become as painful as the broken bones they were about to sustain if they didn't back down.

A blonde haired surfer dude snarled, his eyes cold and hard. He inclined his head at the row of cells behind him. "This is ours now. So are the women."

My eyes didn't even flicker to the woman who had wrapped her skinny arms around one of the newbies. It was a matter of survival. These women weren't fighters, so they saved themselves in whatever way they could. I didn't judge them, and I didn't care about them. So long as they kept out of my way, I left them alone.

My wolf snarled at the newcomer, who believed himself an alpha. Maybe he was, albeit a new one, but he would still bow to me—or he would die.

The first challenge came from the tall, ripped man in front of me. He kept eye contact as he lowered his head and snarled. My features twisted into a vicious snarl to mirror his, and I released a wave of power. All noise in the vast underground prison wing ceased, and a space opened around me, my brothers and the newbies. I glanced down at the body of the previous alpha. I didn't care that he was dead, the guy had been an arsehole, but, then again, so were most of the inmates in this place—including me. In fact, I was the worst of them.

My wolf growled at me and scraped his claws against my insides. He didn't care who died, so long as it wasn't our brothers.

"Owen."

My beta grunted an acknowledgment. My brothers, the men who had been with me from the beginning of this sick adventure, followed his lead. They prowled around this new pack, surrounding them, their wolves rolling across their eyes. No one stepped in to help the newbies. The north wing wolves who had just lost their alpha, shifted from foot to foot, moving away from us.

I gave a feral grin. There would be no mercy for these new recruits. If this newly self-made alpha didn't submit to me and ordered his new followers to fight, they would all die.

This prison was mine. In here, I was king. I kept the shifters in line.

I curled my lip as the cowards and weakest members of the group hunched their shoulders and dropped their eyes to the ground. It was easy to dominate them, but the alpha didn't budge, nor did five of the males around him. Instead, aggression rolled off them in spades.

I straightened to my full height and kept the predatory grin on my face, enjoying the knowledge that my wolf stared out from my eyes, right at the alpha. It would be a waste to kill him. He was just the kind of vicious shifter that would make a lot of money for the warden and Doherty.

So long as the alpha submitted to me, he could keep his new followers and take the north wing pack, too, if he wished. But if he challenged me, he *would* die, and I would send all of these shifters out into the general population. I should care about the hopeless existence of those in gen pop, but I didn't—nor did my wolf. He was a killer, an apex predator who didn't give a shit about anyone since the loss of his mate. And me? I preferred not to feel anything. My heart had withered along with Ember's life. I really didn't care about any of these strangers—at all.

The new alpha's cold blue eyes narrowed on me. His stance dropped to a defensive one, and his jaw jutted forward. Under his blonde curly mop, black bruises covered his face and torso, along with crusted blood. His injuries were recent, hours old at most. The eight men at his back all had similar wounds. The fight for supremacy on the plane had obviously been brutal, as it always was. The silver collars around our necks not only neutralised our ability to change but reduced all our other abilities as well. We retained our strength, vicious nature, and a portion of our healing abilities. They were about to discover just how much they missed their rapid healing once I was done with them.

I let my attention weigh upon each of the pack members who stood behind the new alpha. They had already fallen into a hierarchy. Behind them stood six more males; north wing members who had chosen to submit to this new alpha. I could see why, given their own alpha had been more of a sadistic dick than a strong leader, and had been so easily killed.

My wolf sought out those at the back of the pack. They were the weakest of the males, but by no means powerless. They soon dropped their gazes, though, unwilling to challenge me. I growled. I wanted them to capitulate, but I had no respect for them. They were weak willed and cruel, vermin that did not deserve respect.

My gaze roved over the dead bodies of the alpha and beta of the north wing pack. This new alpha was not to be underestimated. His blonde hair, blue eyes and surfer boy looks gave the appearance of charm, but underneath the veneer, he was definitely strong, fast and vicious. A killer.

A slow grin stretched my lips; just like me...

"Submit or die." I sent another wave of dominance surging over the males and the new alpha.

He didn't drop his gaze, merely stretched his lips over his teeth in a fierce challenge. Now my attention wasn't on them, his new pack rallied behind him, cracking their necks and curling their fists. Owen sank into an attack stance, one I could see without dropping the alpha's gaze. He and my brothers would stop the others getting to me as I subdued this arrogant wanker.

Owen had been my second in command for eight years at the SBI, so there had been no question in my mind about who would be my beta in this prison. And my other brothers were all alphas; all strong and powerful in their own right, and clever enough to know that I was the only one who had any chance of protecting them here through my role as Prime. I trusted them with my life, just as they trusted me. We had fought together for the last four years, and our loyalty to each other would never be questioned.

I toed the line with the warden and Doherty because of that loyalty. On the one occasion I had defied them, one of my brothers had died and Rawson, who they kept as insurance of my cooperation, had suffered humiliating torture. I pushed the images of that night away. I would never subject Rawson or my brothers to anything like that again, no matter how many others in this prison suffered for it.

The alpha cracked his knuckles, and the stench of burning filled the air as he instinctively tried to shift.

I raised my brows. "Hurts, doesn't it?" More blisters appeared around his neck where the collar touched him. "You have to learn to hold back your shift if you don't want that fucker to burn through your flesh and kill you."

Amber rolled over his eyes, his wolf fighting the effects of the silver. He panted, his chest heaving and sweat rolling down his face.

"Curb your frustration, boy. There are many other ways in here to vent it. But let me be completely clear. I am Alpha Prime, here. That means I'm *your* alpha. Submit to me, and I will let you live. Defy me, and I will kill you."

Together, my wolf and I threw our power forward making the males behind the alpha groan and stagger. The alpha's nostrils flared and sweat rolled down his temples, but still he fought my dominance.

"No!" he yelled, then charged.

I darted sideways and slammed my fist into his solar plexus, the blow precise and with enough power to break his sternum. He grunted and dropped to his knees, clutching his chest. Prowling behind him, I considered my options. Killing him would cause a void; an inconvenient one that would have to be filled. We needed to keep up with the training regime for all the packs, and I didn't have time for pack politics and petty power struggles. If I allowed him to live, he would have to stake his claim over and over for a few weeks, but it served my purpose to have an alpha in place to run the north wing and its pack.

Standing behind the male as he struggled to breathe, I let his anticipation and fear build. Slowly, almost gently, I place one hand under his chin, the other on the opposite side of his head. He tried to shake me off, but I just gripped him tighter. "Think carefully before you speak. Submit to my rule, and you can keep your pack and, for now, your life." I didn't need to spell out the alternative.

There was a small nod of his head.

"Say it."

He swallowed, fighting his instincts to tell me to go to hell. I inhaled deeply and tightened my grip just as his sense of survival prevailed.

"Fine. I submit."

I let him go and circled until I stood in front of him. "Tell me your name."

He held his chest and scowled up at me. "Father fucking Christmas, what's yours?"

My punch knocked him to the ground. Spitting blood from a gash in his lip, he glared up at me through his blonde mop.

"As I said, I'm your alpha, and I am Prime of this whole fucking prison. No one will question it if I decide you are too much trouble to keep alive. So drop the attitude. My tolerance is hanging on by a thread. What's your name?"

"Hudson." He spat out a mouthful of blood and saliva.

"Where are you from?"

"Does it matter?"

A kick in the belly made him grunt. I shook my head. "Are you learning yet?" I dropped to my haunches, but stayed out of his reach. Raising my brows, I waited.

His lip curled. "Santa Cruz."

I smirked. "Well then, father fucking Christmas from Santa Cruz. I'm giving you responsibility for this wing of the prison. Unless one of these tossers wants to kill you while you're down...?" I stood up and stepped back while I waited to see if any of the other males would end Santa. No movement. I shrugged. Fine by me.

"You'll work with my beta to get up to speed on what goes on here. We don't have many rules, but if you break the few we have, I will end you. No questions, no explanation, and no fucking warning. Understand?"

Santa nodded, looking to be in a lot of pain as he sat up. I couldn't give a shit. He glared at his other pack members, who watched him with narrowed eyes. Yeah, one of them would challenge him once I left.

"Rule one: don't challenge me or any of my pack: you will die. Rule two: you follow my commands when I make them, or you die. My pack is housed in the west wing—all people in the west wing bear my mark and are under my protection. Feel me?"

Owen sauntered to my side and tilted his jaw up. A single scar about two centimeters long marked his skin.

"All those who have that mark are under my protection, you hurt them, try and rape them or enslave them in any way, you are issuing a challenge to me. The only caveat is if they challenge you first. No alpha is allowed more than one wing. If you challenge another alpha and win, I will snap your neck. Those in gen pop are fair game for entertainment, but bare in mind, we all belong to the warden and we are here to earn him money. So if your kill count gets out of control, either the guards will deal with you or they'll get me to do it."

Santa nodded. "So you're their bitch?"

I held his gaze, totally unmoved by his statement. What I was to the running of this place didn't matter. Someone had to do it and right now it was me. Once Santa saw what we were all up against, he'd either try and take my position for its illusion of power, or he would defer to my rule without question. I had a feeling it was the former.

I left Owen with the new alpha of the north wing and walked away. It was Santa's choice now, conform or die. I smirked at the name he now had. He couldn't be taken seriously with that nickname, but I'd use it just to annoy the shit out of him.

I spent the next hour parading my strength around each pack's territory. I'd show my face in gen pop tomorrow. Right now, my wolf was feeling unsettled. Too much threat of violence without releasing it always made us dangerous.

"I'm going to hit the gym." My words informed no one in particular. I didn't need guards, I was more than capable of protecting myself, but I accepted that even I could die from a well placed blade in my back.

Stone, my third in command stepped closer. "You want some company?"

I grunted. His question was irrelevant, he'd come anyway. His muscles and jaw strained with as much tension as mine. Suppressed power was thick in the air around us, sending people scuttling out of our way as we prowled the prison corridors. There were very few ways for predators like us to release tension. Fuck or fight. No way could I face the first right now. I didn't want anyone that close to me, so fighting it was.

Stone grinned, baring his teeth and slapped my back. "Come on, my friend. Let's go bruise some minions."

I chuckled. "You mean Myles."

"No, not just Myles. Reed too. It'll wind them both up." The tension between those two males was something that never ceased to amaze me— truly a fuck or fight situation. They'd chosen fight—for now—though I had no idea what held them back from the other option. Rolling my head on my shoulders, I grunted in answer to Stone. It had nothing to do with me.

As we sauntered past the males guarding the entrance to the training area, they lowered their eyes in respect.

At the far end of the huge hall, past the ten boxing rings and the free weights area, was a whole wall of punching bags. I headed towards it. In the far corner, a single male pummeled a bag. From the free weights area, Reed watched Myles. Muscle rippled under Myles's dark skin as he punched, dipped and struck with his elbows and knees.

Stone grinned, ready to begin his plan, until a blonde woman with a killer figure strode towards us. His grey gaze filled with ice as he fixed it on Shannon, who ignored him and sashayed up to me. Not bothering to hide my irritation, I nodded at him to continue. With a scowl he did, heading over to Myles.

"Hey, boss." As always Shannon tried to sound sultry. And she did, I suppose, but I held in a growl. I was not interested in dealing with Shannon Doherty right now. I didn't want to fuck her tonight, and she wasn't part of my pack, so I didn't need to listen to her bitch about someone else. I allowed her in the training hall and kept an eye on her purely because of my past with her sister. Most of the time, like now, she was a pain in my arse. I grunted in her general direction, side stepped, and prowled after Stone. She shuffled sideways, and her hand landed in the middle of my pecs. I allowed her to stop me, but my voice was ice cold.

"What do you want?"

She pouted, which only irritated me more. "I haven't seen you in a while." She pushed right up to my side, one foot between my legs, the other flanking my thigh which left the heat of her pussy resting on my leg. I didn't even feel myself stir.

"And?" I glanced down at her. I put my hands on her waist and pushed her back so that the heat receded.

Her eyes narrowed. "And how about we spend the night together, lover boy?"

I stepped away and fixed her with an icy glare. "No. You already know I don't spend the night with anyone. And call me lover boy again, and you'll lose your privileges to come in here. If I want what's between your legs, I'll let you know. Until then, feel free to go fuck someone else."

I walked away without another thought. The punching bag was looking more and more appealing. My muscles were wound so tight, I really wanted to break something, and if I didn't get to that bag soon, it would be the next person in my way.

"Alpha," greeted Myles as I prowled closer. My dark glower never put him off being pleasant. He smiled, his perfect teeth and bone structure still intact even after so long in this shit hole. His eerie green eyes sparkled, bright against his dark skin. I suppose his ability to move like the wind might have something to do with his undamaged nose and his perfect smile. Myles had a lighter build than most of my brothers, but he was still strong, and with no fat obscuring his eight pack, he was made for agility. He stood a few inches shorter than Stone, and at least six inches shorter than me. Adversaries often underestimated his good looks and slim build at their peril.

I nodded. "Myles. You joining us, Reed?" I yelled across to my other brother.

Reed jogged over. "Where's Kawan?" Sweat glistened on his face and he panted, his eyes flicking to Myles's chest. I pretended not to notice, as did Myles.

"He's with some piece of ass in our cell, the inconsiderate shit." D stomped over, his heavy brows dipped and his scar twisted. Dagnar was Russian and his accent was heavy, and it only got worse when he was pissed off, like now. Kawan, his cellmate, and my sixth brother, was from Korea, and always busy with the females.

"No need for jealousy, D. I'm sure we can bribe a woman to be with you. There must be one desperate enough somewhere in this place," said Myles, in his upper class English accent.

D stuck his middle finger up, his heavy brows lowering into an impressive scowl. "Fuck off."

Myles smirked, and went back to pummeling the bag.

Stone looked at Reed. "Come on, chicken shit. Let's spar. I need to see blood."

"Really? Chicken shit?" Reed's brows rose, and he crossed his arms over his chest. "You don't need to resort to name calling, you miserable, uptight, sexually frustrated, grey-haired prick. You only have to ask, and I'm happy to spill your blood."

Myles laughed out loud at Stone's growl. He winked and held Reed's gaze as Stone ripped his shirt off and bounced over the ropes into the nearest ring. "Give him hell, man."

Reed smirked, and pulled off his own shirt, revealing a torso of cut muscle and smooth skin. Myles swallowed hard as Reed joined Stone. I shook my head in exasperation at the pair of them, but right now I needed to relieve my own pent up anger and need for blood.

I walked to the bag next to Myles. Not bothering with gloves, I contemplated my target. The bag was filled with sand and would be like hitting a brick wall. Good. It would hurt like a son of a bitch, but I craved the pain and exhaustion. It would force back my wolf just long enough that I could sleep for a few hours. My nostrils flared as I took a deep breath and bunched my fists. Without bothering to correct my stance, I swung. The force reverberated up my arm and into my shoulder as pain flooded my knuckles, grounding me and giving me focus. This was exactly what I needed. I yelled and hit the bag again and again.

I didn't stop punching and kicking, or using my knees and elbows, until blood flowed freely from my lacerated skin, smearing all over the bag. Drops splattered the floor, but that was nothing new. Breathing hard, I stopped and looked around. A few others were still sparring in the rings, but Stone and Reed had disappeared. Sweat dripped into my eyes, so I wiped it away and checked the clock. Seven. My stomach growled loudly. I needed to eat before Rawson's visit.

Myles lifted a brow. "You done, boss?"

"Yup." I blew drops of sweat off my nose and wiped my knuckles down my jeans. "I need food."

"Let's go, then." Myles stood up and balled his tee in his hands.

I took a breath and pulled my shoulders back. Part of me still welcomed seeing Rawson, the man I owed so much, but most of me dreaded it these days. He was so different now, more broken each time I saw him. His eyes were shadowed by the dark deeds he'd been forced to commit. Sometimes, he recounted them in detail; sometimes, he just talked about the nightmares that plagued him. The pain he was forced to inflict on innocents and criminals alike made my stomach sour, but it wasn't his fault, and I refused to judge him. He didn't deserve the existence that had been thrust upon him; none of us did. But unlike the rest of us, Rawson judged himself. If he could end his life, I'm sure he would do so, without any hesitation.

Myles walked back to the west block with me, and I returned to my cell. I walked in through the solid cell door and into the first of the two small rooms I'd been given. The outer cell I used as a meeting room or office, the inner one, I slept in. It contained a single metal-framed bed, a table, a chair, and a couple of shelves fitted to the wall. On those shelves were two more pairs of jeans, three white tank tops, three black tee shirts, three pairs of training bottoms, and some undershorts and socks. A private toilet with a hand basin finished my *suite*. I scoffed as I looked at my meagre possessions. I'd once had a big modern house with state of the art security, a wide screen T.V. computers, a fast car, and a gym.

I grunted and closed my eyes as memories assaulted me. I'd once kissed my soulmate inside that fast, expensive car. The memory of her lips under mine, the softness of her skin as I'd touched her never left me. I dropped my chin to my chest and sighed. When her wolf tried to bond with mine, I'd run away. Like a coward, I'd left her standing in the driveway of Rawson's home and driven away. I hadn't wanted to rush her into the way I would have dominated or possessed her; not without being damned certain she understood what a soul bond between a Prime and his mate meant. Only that conversation never happened. Instead, Doherty had taken everything from me; my home, my family, my job...my mate—everything.

I swallowed hard, taking some deep breaths. Sinking into the past did no good.

I stripped off my sweaty clothes and dropped them down the laundry shoot. I needed a shower, so I donned some gym bottoms, grabbed a full change of clothes and marched down to the shower block. Women ogled my bare chest and abs, but I wasn't the least bit interested. I was too busy thinking about Rawson and what he might be like at our meet tonight. I took a quick shower, hissing at the sting of the water on my broken skin. My muscles shook, but at least that meant it would be me, and not my wolf in control when I spoke to Rawson tonight. My wolf would be too busy using his power to heal my body, now that he sensed I was injured. After all, if I died because I was weakened, so would he.

I dried quickly and tossed the towel. My knuckles smeared blood over the white cotton vest top I slipped on, but I doubted Rawson would be bothered. After buttoning my jeans, I shoved my feet into a pair of socks and boots, and made my way back to my cell and into the office. I huffed a laugh. Calling it an office was a joke; it was just a room with a table and two chairs. There was no computer, no filing cabinet, no stapler, but there was a desk light, plain paper and pencils. I picked up a pencil and rolled it between my fingers. Four fucking years I'd endured this prison, and this was the only place private enough to meet with the people who knew why I was really here. My so-called employers were too chicken shit to reveal themselves, so they spoke to me through one of the guards. I couldn't figure out why they'd hatched such an elaborate plan to get me in here, but, one thing was certain; that kind of power came from being seriously connected. Hell, they'd managed to infiltrate the SBI and 'interview' me for a top secret job, which turned out to be imprisonment. Even Doherty had no idea of the extremes they'd gone to just to get me in here. The interview process had ended up with me being bespelled by some magical motherfucker, who'd come in through a portal, taken control of my body and forced me to shoot the woman who'd interviewed me, then disappeared. Believing I'd done it, Doherty had arrested me and sent me here, along with Owen.

I studied the pencil I clasped between my thumb and forefinger and tried not to snap it. I'd still no idea who'd stolen four years of my life, but they were powerful enough to infiltrate the SBI top management tiers, arrange an interview in the name of the SBI Overseer, and get me in here, right where they wanted me. I was fairly certain they'd had a hand in murdering Lyss, too.

My stomach growled noisily, as I sat down. My body needed sustenance after my hard workout, but I would not risk missing Rawson. He was one of the reasons I conformed to what the warden and Doherty required. Until I figured a way to get him out of this mess, I'd behave.

I began to sketch. I found creating the lines and curves of my drawings the most therapeutic thing I could do. Even sex and fighting didn't compare to the mental quiet I found while drawing. Needing an outlet for the images of Ember that haunted me, I'd picked up the pencil one day—and hours later found her staring back at me.

Twenty minutes passed, and a set of accusatory eyes peered out from the paper. Ember's expression as I left her standing on her driveway never left me. But I smiled. She was my beautiful weakness, my guilty pleasure to dream about when I was alone. The pain she evoked in my heart was almost an addiction, but it meant I would never forget her, that she would never truly be gone.

Carefully, I placed the pencil down, and traced the edge of the paper where her jaw and full mouth would be when I got around to finishing the sketch.

Hate for Doherty burned in my gut. Everytime I had to suffer looking in his face, I wanted to rip his throat out for killing her. I still had no idea if I was working for the good guys, but if this time served meant I got to kill Doherty, in the end it would all be worth it. Ember had died alone in the woods because of him. Grinding my jaw, I almost screwed the drawing up, but a knock distracted me. The door opened, and Rawson's familiar silhouette filled the door frame.

I remained seated until my six brothers followed him in. D was about to shut the door when Zander strode up to it. D gave him a dead eyed stare and didn't budge, his foot wedged behind the door to stop it opening.

Zander raised his dark brows, his dangerous eyes flashing crimson.

D slanted his dead-eyed look to me. "Prime?" It didn't matter if Zander could cause him immense pain, D was loyal to me.

I nodded. "It's okay, D."

"So be it," he said, with his heavy Russian accent. D never bothered to hide his origins within our pack of brothers, but he made it more pronounced out in the main pack. His rationale was it gave him a more menacing air. Not that he needed one. He was six feet of solid, ripped muscle with a square jaw and hard grey eyes. A scar cut through his shaved head, down the right-hand side of his neck to finish his *couldn't give a shit about my life or yours* look.

Zander inclined his head as he passed by D.

"No guards?" I kept my inquiry neutral and pleasant.

Zander just unfolded his arms and stared directly into Rawson's eyes, pointed at the chair opposite mine and said, "Sit."

I ground my teeth as Rawson sat, obedient as a domesticated dog, and stared blankly at the wall over my shoulder.

"Free him." I clenched my teeth.

Zander tilted his chin and remained silent. I hated it, but there was no denying he was the one in control here.

"Please."

"All in good time. First, our mutual friend, and your employer, wants you to know there is a time limit on acquiring the information he needs."

"Why? He's waited this long."

Zander grinned menacingly. "Time's up, *brother*. You need to get someone in the lab. He doesn't care how you do it. I've informed him the one person you've managed to get in so far has disappeared. You weren't careful enough —or they weren't." He sounded pissed off. As well he should. He'd had to work with me, and put his own position at risk, to get our spy in.

I was also under no illusions that if I didn't play my part, I was disposable. Not even my arrangement with the warden and Doherty would protect me. I'd had four years to get myself in place and my people under cover in the labs and I'd failed.

Zander leaned forward, studying my face. I kept it utterly blank.

"We need evidence of what's happening behind that door. Find some, or our mutual employer isn't above using any incentive at his disposal." Zander leaned forward more.

I contemplated him, my tongue running over my sharp canines, and I wondered what his blood would feel like running down my chin, how hard he would scream when I crushed his bones in my jaws.

Zander smiled coldly. "Don't even think about it."

D hit the deck, his body spasming hard against the floor. Every instinct I possessed told me to attack, to fight for my brother, but it would just make this situation worse. I narrowed my eyes, deliberately not watching D convulse.

"You are in a position of power. Why haven't you found any evidence?" I hadn't yet figured out Zander's role in all this. It seemed to me that he was a glorified hunter for the warden; someone who brought in new recruits and inmates, but who wasn't a prison guard.

His eyes glinted. "Stick to your part in this. Don't worry about mine. Do what's necessary or Rawson and your other *brothers* will suffer."

It always made me wonder why he sneered at the word brother. It almost sounded as though he was jealous of my pack. I looked into Rawson's oddly blank eyes. His body was stuck in a place of half-shift. I inhaled sharply, hating to see him manipulated like this. My fists curled and my wolf fixated on Zander's throat. I forced myself to inhale a deep breath. I didn't want to cause Rawson or my other brothers any further pain. The cocksucker had me and he knew it. It's why he came here without guards.

I nodded once.

Zander glanced down, wrinkling his nose at D who was lying unconscious in a pool of his own urine. Fury lit my chest at the degradation he had inflicted upon my friend, but it wasn't the first time and I doubted it would be the last. The others stood by stoically. They were ready for their turn.

Zander smirked at them one at a time.

They all restrained their snarls and didn't react.

He shrugged and lifted his hand. Whispering under his breath, he studied his fingernails. They grew into long black claws. I hid my distaste. They weren't the claws of any animal I recognised. Zander sliced his thumb nail into his wrist and blood welled. He squeezed the deep red droplets against Rawson's mouth and whispered in the strange language only he used.

My nostrils flared. Something dark stirred inside me every time I heard those words. It was a presence I had never acknowledged and I wouldn't begin to now. Zander flicked his attention my way as if he sensed it, too. Without reacting, I turned my unblinking gaze to Rawson and hid my anger as Rawson licked Zander's blood off his lips.

His milky gaze turned to a deep brown, and he blinked twice. His lungs heaved as if he'd just run a marathon and his huge hands clawed at the silver table.

I jumped up as soon as Zander left the room. "Hey man, it's okay. You're okay. I've got you." I held his shoulders, trying to reassure him.

"Gods damn it!" Rawson shook his head and as his eyes cleared, he pushed himself up, his bones cracking back into place as he changed back into his full human form. "Fucking cocksucking bastards!" His eyes flickered down to D. "See to him. I'm fine." His attention flicked on the clock on the wall. We had an hour, one measly hour together, then Zander would return and take him away again.

I nodded and kneeled next to Reed, who had lowered himself down next to our brother. Giving my attention to D gave Rawson time to get his mind back in the game and his body together.

D moaned and shuffled into a sitting position. "Jesus, he's one sick fuck."

"He is." Reed grabbed one arm, and I grabbed the other. Together we helped our brother up. "Use my bathroom, D."

His cheeks flushed, but it wasn't with embarrassment. His wolf flashed through his eyes, its anger a scent I totally understood. He nodded. "Thanks, man."

"There's clean jeans and stuff on the shelf that'll fit, too." I turned to face the others. "You guys, relax." My wolf was growling in my head. For once I pushed him away, which he didn't like. "I'm okay here with Rawson. Owen, you can stay, the rest of you, go and get some food, or find someone to fuck, or something."

"I'll be outside," Stone said. "Kawan you're with me." Kawan nodded.

I didn't argue; they sorted my guard detail out between themselves, even when I didn't want them near.

"D!" yelled Reed into the other room.

"Yeah, man?"

"I'll wait for you outside."

"Sure. Thanks."

Rawson watched the others disappear, then sat down. Normally I let them stay a while. They liked to know Rawson was okay and to let him know they were there for him, too. But he looked so shitty today, even more unnerved than usual, that I didn't think it was a good idea.

"Owen? Would you make sure D's okay."

"Sure, boss. D'you want me to wait outside with Stone and Kawan when D's sorted?"

I smiled at him and nodded, glad I didn't have to spell that shit out. "Thanks, man."

Rawson scrubbed his face with his hands. Giving him a bit longer to gather himself, I lowered my bulk to the chair opposite and waited. It was hard, starting a conversation with someone when you knew their life was hell, and there was nothing you could do about it.

Zander had told me the warden had taken Rawson because he was the only one I cared about. Turns out he was useful for other things too, like catching the poor buggers who tried to run from Doherty and the warden. I had no idea how, but Zander had placed some kind of voodoo shit on

Rawson, turning him into the most monstrous form of our kind. A Were. In half-shift, he was strong and vicious, neither man nor beast, and with the hold Zander had on his mind, they used him as an efficient hunter and killer.

Rawson sat back, interlaced his fingers over his chest, and tipped his head back. He stared at the ceiling, a frown creasing the skin between his brows.

"You okay?" It was a stupid question, but one I really wanted him to answer.

Rawson huffed a chuckle, though there was little humour in it. "Yeah, just give me a minute. I have…something…" He frowned. "I wanted to tell you something."

I waited patiently. Rawson's memory was shot. He sometimes struggled to be lucid when we met like this. I hated it, but there was nothing I could do to change it, or perhaps there was. If I got the information Zander and my employer wanted, maybe I could do a deal to get him out of this place.

"A woman. They made me catch a woman…"

"Yeah?" I didn't pay much attention. Rawson's recounts and sudden flash-backs were not new. Women were frequently on Rawson's hit list, and not just those that lived on the street, though I'd long since given up trying to understand how Doherty and the warden chose their victims.

Rawson nodded. "She was…familiar…" His attention shifted to the table top and onto the drawing I'd done. "Like her…" He jabbed a finger on Ember's eyes, the ones I drew from memory nearly every day. "These are her eyes. Do you know her? Did I hurt her?" His voice shook, his breathing ragged.

Rawson hated himself for being used as a hunter. Perhaps he hated me, too, for allowing it. He'd once been a powerful alpha—a huge Kodiak bear. But now, when I looked in his eyes, I only saw the spirit of a broken man. Pain rolled through my chest as he brushed his fingers over Ember's image, and it took me a while to rein in my anger. He was confused between the present and the past, he had to be, and it wasn't his fault. I needed to remember that.

"It's not her," I said, forcing patience into my words, when all I wanted to do was scream the words. I tapped the paper. "This is Ember, the girl you took in and gave a home. Don't you remember her? You loved her very much. So did I. And it can't be her because she's dead." I scrunched up the drawing and tossed it on the floor. "You must be getting a bit mixed up, my man." I swallowed against my aching throat.

Rawson shook his head. "No. No. This girl. She's not dead, I remember her. She had blonde hair and her eyes…" He met my gaze. "Her eyes burned, like those on that drawing, but with fire. Yes, that's it, fire."

Pain shot through my heart and I struggled to breathe. It was impossible to form a reply.

"Ember, you say?" he asked, filling the silence. He looked down and his brow furrowed. After a moment, his throat bobbed and he spoke softly. "I remember Ember." His face crumpled again and my chest tightened even more. "Lyss loved Ember, too." Tears formed in his eyes, and he lost focus.

My fists curled. I wanted to punch the wall and scream, but life was hard enough on him. I didn't need to make him feel worse for getting the present and the past mixed up. None of this was his fault.

"This girl had blonde hair, not red." His eyes met mine, now crystal clear and brown. "Ember was part of our family, but she was yours, your mate. She did die, I know that, but beneath her wolf, this girl smelled so like her, and scents can't be faked."

I shoved down my pain at his words. "No, Rawson," I said as gently as I could. "Ember died years ago. Whoever this girl is, she isn't my Firecracker. The girl you saved from the streets all those years ago is long gone. Don't worry, you didn't hurt her, she was beyond our reach the day they brought us here."

Rawson's jaw clenched and he fisted his shaking hands. It was hard to know if I was doing the right thing by insisting he was brought here.

He nodded. "Yeah, sorry man. Of course. I must have imagined it." He shook his head. "How about I just forget about it, and you tell me what's been happening with you. Any good fighters that stand out?"

I happily went with the change of subject. It was easier to talk with Rawson about the new alpha of the north wing than it was about Ember. I filled him in on what my brothers were doing to train the new recruits. He nodded and listened, clear eyed and switched on, thankfully. He asked sensible questions and understood my answers. It was always the same; his mind became clearer the longer he was out of Zander's thrall. Perhaps if Zander would agree to leave him here for a while, Rawson might actually function well enough to regain some of his alpha power.

I told him everything I could, or at least what I didn't mind Zander, or Doherty and the warden knowing. I had no idea how much they could glean from his thoughts and memories, so I told Rawson only what I wanted them to know about the fighters and packs on this level of the prison.

As the hour passed, Rawson became more twitchy. We both knew there was no point in fighting Zander or begging for more time—he wouldn't give it. We weren't ready when Zander quietly entered the room. Rawson stiffened, his eyes darkening, though he tried to hide his fear. My gaze met his, and I let my wolf shine through as I grasped his hand and tried to give him some measure of support. "I'll see you again soon," I whispered as Zander chanted his strange words and simply snapped his fingers.

Rawson's eyes lost focus, and my hand slipped from his grip as he roared and shifted into the hideous Were animal they forced him to be.

CHAPTER 4

*E*mber

I STARED into the dark watching for any threat. Shifting my position didn't relieve the ache in my back, or the numbness in my backside. Concrete was concrete no matter how many times you moved. Still, at least I was as far into the corner as I could be. No one could stab me in the back or attack from behind. I'd fought hard for my spot here tonight, just like I had for the past seven nights. It didn't take long after we arrived for me to realise this part of the prison was the most dangerous, and having a concrete wall at your back as you rested was a good idea.

My eyelids drooped. No matter the danger, I still had to sleep. I cocked my head and listened to the soft sounds of breathing and snoring while I measured the heartbeats of those around me. There were no signs these women were faking sleep. Even the bitch I'd fought for the corner spot was snoozing like a baby. After another few minutes, my eyes closed and I let myself relax.

The metal door clanged open, and the horn blared right over my head. I groaned, forcing myself to wake up. "Jesus." I already hated the wake up call. It signalled six am, and the guards wanted us all up and out of the cells and sleeping rooms. Why they insisted on it, I had no clue. I mean, it wasn't as if we had anything to do. Or at least I didn't. I'd worked out that some of the inmates from gen pop were forced to work in the laundry rooms, kitchens and as general dogsbodies to clean the toilets and shower blocks, but the packs all maintained their own wings, they wouldn't tolerate gen pop being in their territory.

My stomach growled loudly, but I stayed where I was. Breakfast was served in the massive food hall of gen pop and though I was hungry, waiting until the throng of women had dwindled from here and the corridors, was safer. I wasn't in the mood for another altercation, and neither were my bruised knuckles. I yanked at the damn silver collar around my neck, cursing it for holding back my healing capabilities.

Keeping my head tilted back against the wall, I watched the other women move about. Blankets were a commodity, and those who had them wrapped them around their bodies or waists, clearly not willing to lose them. There were no bunks in the sleeping hall, and the cells along the corridors were all full. It seemed this whole place was overpopulated.

"Don't worry," said the woman I'd thumped last night. Her keen hazel eyes rested on me, but they were clear of malice. "They'll take some of the women away soon, and free up some room. If we're lucky and don't get chosen, we can fight for a cell then."

"What d'you mean? Taken where?"

She shrugged her slim shoulders. "No idea. But it happens every month."

"Damn. You mean they never come back?"

"Nope."

I shuddered at the terrifying possibilities. The woman, who looked a bit younger than me, pressed her lips into a thin line. Her hair had clearly been cut spikey and short at one point but there were no salons inside, so I guessed it had just grown out. Utterly wild, it stuck from the sides of her head in a macabre Edward Scissorhands way. She thrust her hand forward. "I'm Charlie. Where'd you learn to fight like you do?" The inmates of this prison were from all over the world. I'd heard all sorts of accents and languages in the last week. Charlie's was American, east coast, I thought. But what the hell did I know? I grinned. "School of motherfucking life."

She grinned back, not seeming to mind the bruised cheekbone I'd given her. "Me too, on the streets of Detroit."

"London."

She grinned. "Kinda figured, with that weird accent. You coming for food before it's all gone and we have to fight for everyone else's scraps?"

I nodded and pushed myself up, keeping a close eye on my new friend as she did her boots up. I'd spent the last week sitting back and watching the interactions and powerplays in gen pop, and I wasn't stupid enough to think this girl was my new bestie.

This place was a hotbed of betrayal, power plays, gangs, and violence of every conceivable sort. There seemed to be four other wings, in addition to the large gen pop area, that were run by packs. I'd even heard of a Prime who ran the prison on behalf of the guards and kept the primal and vicious nature of the shifters under some kind of control. Except he didn't seem all that concerned with gen pop. There were hundreds of people here, and many were the kind you did not turn your back on—ever. They would crush you at the first sign of weakness.

The guards watched from above on their network of metal platforms, but obviously didn't give a shit what happened. I wasn't even sure why they were up there. Groups of males often dragged the weak off for entertainment, whether they wanted it or not; male or female, it didn't matter. Even males from the packs came to gen pop to hunt females for fun. Some of the women had formed small packs of their own to try and protect each other, but it seemed women who were caught on their own were fair game. I'd been in five fights so far, freeing women from the unwanted attention of some tosser who thought her body was his for the taking. He didn't think that so much when his nose was leaking blood or his junk was somewhere in his lower abdomen after my boot had repositioned it.

I smirked and cracked my knuckles as I pictured the male whose face I'd smashed my fist into yesterday. The down side was, I was making enemies, which was not a good idea. Me against a bunch of them would not likely end well, but I didn't really care much. I hadn't since Connor, Rawson and Lyss had been taken from me. No, all I had left was a shit load of resentment towards the universe, which I'd happily turn on every shit for brains rapist in here. Did I have a death wish? Probably, but I'd go out fighting.

Fire stirred and I smiled. Yeah, for me death wasn't quite the deterrent it should be.

When the hall was empty, I uncoiled my body, groaning at the stiffness in my limbs. I winced, blinking back tears at the burning pain around my neck. Like most newbies, I had blisters. The silver collar burned like a bitch, especially if my wolf pushed against it. I'd noticed those who'd been here a while had tough skin around their necks. I really didn't want a necklace of scaly skin as an accessory when I eventually got out of here, but it had to be better than this agony.

Ignoring the stinging pain, I stretched my arms high and then touched my toes, loosening my body. Contemplating my tank top, I shrugged, dropped my leather jacket on the floor and pulled it off. Standing in my bra, I grabbed the hem of my top and ripped the material until I had several thin strips. It didn't leave me much to cover my stomach with but it would still cover my breasts so I didn't worry.

Charlie watched with interest, her eyes bright and a smirk on her lips.

Carefully, I wrapped the material around my collar so it couldn't touch my skin, then secured the strips with small knots. Satisfied with my makeshift barrier, I straightened. Charlie had hold of my jacket, inspecting it with a look of awe. I shrugged. "Keep it." It was bloody hot in these cells, and I didn't think my leather jacket was going to last long anyway before someone targeted me for it. Better for Charlie to deal with that inconvenience.

"Whoa, really?" Her eyes darted from me to the jacket.

I nodded, not meeting her gaze as I turned away.

We headed out to the corridors that led down to the mess hall. Above us, guards watched our progress with disinterest. Tasers and guns were trained on the crowds milling below. I searched the walls, stairwells and rooms for any weakness in their security that I might have missed. There was nothing.

I dismissed the idea of running, for now. Even if I found a weakness I could exploit, it would take weeks, maybe even months to plan anything. First, I needed to find out more about the prison and what went on here.

Grabbing the tray an inmate held out to me, I collected my metal bowl of slop, otherwise known as porridge, and a plastic cup of water. I followed Charlie through the crowds of people who loitered in the food hall. The hairs on my neck kept rising as I felt people watch us, but I kept my head high and my swagger intact. I clutched the blunt cardboard spoon in my hand, even knowing it was useless as a weapon, but hey, I'd find a way if needed.

We found a spare table and I sat sideways, one leg on either side of the bench so I could keep an eye out for any threats, and quickly get up to fight if needed. I grunted as the cardboard spoon became soggy and fell apart before I'd finished eating. Not caring about table manners, I resorted to using my fingers to scoop the sticky, tasteless glop into my mouth. I wouldn't waste a single morsel of food; fighting took energy.

"How long have you been here?" I asked Charlie whilst keeping an eye on the crowd.

"Lost track. A year, maybe?"

"A year? Why the hell don't you have a permanent bunk then?"

Her lips thinned, her eyes searching the crowd for a moment. "I did." Her eyes rested on an older woman with beady eyes who looked as hard as nails. "I was part of a female pack for a while."

I raised my brows. "What happened?"

"Resta is a pack madame. She decides who we fuck to receive privileges, like a cell and a bed, or protection. If we disagree with her, she throws us to the wolves."

"Oh." I didn't ask any more questions. It was obvious Charlie hadn't wanted to spread her legs on Resta's orders.

"Yeah, she wanted me to be with a male that was a real weasel. I refused, and I lost my bed." She shrugged and pouted. "It was a real nice one, too."

I grinned. "Don't worry, we'll get us one each. Better than the last. You just tell me what I need to know."

She gave me a weighing stare, then nodded. "Yeah, ok."

I listened to Charlie very closely as she informed me about the east, north and south alphas and their packs. The alphas had their pick of the strongest prisoners. Becoming a member of a pack was the same as in the outside world, except it was no holds barred for challenges. The Prime didn't stop challenges, and if they were to the death, no one seemed to care. But his word was law. If he said roll over, you did. If he said jump, you asked how high.

I snarled. Dominance from an alpha male, or any male had never worked well on me, probably because I hadn't been born a pure shifter. I saw no reason to change my attitude and allow it now. Even Connor, who I'd suspected was powerful enough to become a Prime someday, hadn't been able to force his will on me. Perhaps that knowledge made me reckless with my safety, but I would not be dominated by any male—human, shifter or anything else. Being kidnapped and shoved in here was bad enough.

We ditched our trays and bowls and sauntered into one of the gen pop halls.

"What's the deal with power in here?" I asked as we found a wall to lean against. "Who does deals? Gets things?" I finger brushed my hair, not giving a shit that it looked the most bizarre it had in years. The top few inches were a shade of fiery red that looked totally dyed and the bottom was still dyed a bright blonde. Even Som's glamour had needed a little help every now and then.

Charlie chuckled. "Oh, there are plenty of people who can deal in flesh, but if you're thinking of anything else...don't. The guards come down hard on anyone in gen pop trying to trade with them for goods from the outside, and the Prime stomps on anyone from the packs who try it. There is no outside world for us now. This is it."

"Yeah, but why? I don't get it. I'm here without a trial and I'm guessing most other people are, too. What's the deal with this place? Why are we here?"

Charlie chewed her bottom lip. "Not sure, but it has something to do with the packs and the females that disappear every month."

"Hmm, sex trade?" It seemed a long shot though. Dealing people for sex was done outside prisons everywhere in the world. This would be a bloody expensive set up just for that.

"Can't see the point in locking us up for that." Charlie echoed my thoughts.

Too wound up to stand in one place, I wandered away. Exploring the wings, or at least the entrance to the pack wings, was on my agenda for the day.

Charlie followed me. "The women in gen pop can belong to a pack. If a pack agrees to accept their request, they get a pack mark, and even if the pack doesn't claim them as a full member they can enjoy its protection, they just can't go with anyone from another pack, or live in the pack's wing."

"Why not?"

Charlie shrugged. "Don't know. Too many people? Who knows?"

I gave her the side eye. "Why don't you do that then? It seems like a safer way to live."

"Nah, I don't do men. I'm strictly a women only gal."

"And? Don't the packs have gay women?"

Charlie shrugged. "Not that many, and the males in the packs generally don't want to see women together."

I rolled my eyes at their misogynistic bullshit, but kept my mouth shut. I didn't know enough about this place to understand or openly judge.

At the far end of the hall was a large doorway. Four large, hardass males stood guard. I slowed and leaned against the wall, intrigued. They let people in, checking the backs of their hands or their necks for what I presumed were pack marks.

"What's in there?"

Charlie shrugged. "Some sort of training gym. It's not for us gen pop trash. I tried to get in a few times and was thrown out on my ass. It's not worth the hassle."

I wasn't sure about that. Flashing her a grin and a wink, I prowled closer, inhaling the stink of sweat and blood that drifted out of the doorway. I stopped and leaned against the wall nearby.

Charlie's eyes were wide as she joined me. "Whatcha doin'? You have to be in a pack to get in there. That's the Prime's territory."

"Is it now? All the more reason to get in there, then."

It was hard to see much, but I eyed the room beyond the guards. I could see boxing rings and males fighting viciously, but not much more. Time to get closer. I winked at Charlie who gaped at me as I stepped away. Ignoring her, I fluffed my hair, pulled my shoulders back and stuck my tits out. I was slim and petite, but where I'd once been flat, I was now nicely endowed, and I wasn't beyond using my assets to get me what I wanted; and I wanted to see inside that hall.

The guards watched me with curiosity. One, who looked to be Korean, gave me a hard eyed stare. *Okay, no joy there, then.* I turned a pouty smile on the one in the middle, who couldn't seem to pull his gaze off my cleavage. I swerved my attention to the man next to him and swayed my hips, gliding forwards. Both of them shifted their stances, lifting their chins and puffing out their broad, heavy chests. I smiled inwardly. Males, whether shifters or fae, were so damn predictable. I couldn't even remember how many people Blue and I had caught off guard with our sexy vixen approach.

The guy on the right was another story. His brown hair was long, true there were no hairdressers in this shit hole, but he was clean shaven, so clearly the men were allowed razors. I frowned. He looked familiar, but I couldn't place why. He leaned against the wall, his large arms folded over his chest, watching me with a smirk and a twinkle in his grey eyes. Shit, he had my number. Still, no need to give up yet. I kept the sultry smile on my face despite his gaze, which was far too astute for my liking.

"Hi boys, I'm just going in to see the Prime." I lied right to their faces, and pulled my weird coloured hair over my right shoulder. I looked up provocatively through my lashes at the two guards in the middle, ignoring the other two.

There was a huff of laughter. Hiding my irritation at the familiar guy on the right, I glanced at Korea. He just watched me with a dark, steady gaze.

Yeah, a barrel of laughs, you are, I silently told him, but shifted my weight, just in case either of them decided to get handsy. My gaze shifted to the training going on beyond the door. From this position I could see to the far end of the hall. It was totally dedicated to fighting and training. A real hardcore gym. What the hell was such a grand scale place doing in a prison? I mean, sure I'd have thought every prison had a gym of some kind, but this one was huge. Not only that, it was well equipped, and every part of it was being used. Fighting inmate boredom was one thing, but hell, this was insane.

"You're here for the Prime?" The titty man asked.

I preened as he continued to peruse my body. His lust filled gaze rested on my bare stomach and the curve of my waist. I kept a sultry smile on my lips when it fixed back on my breasts again.

Bingo! I walked up to him, ignoring grey eyes whose expression had dipped into a frown, as if he was trying to place me, too. "Sure, honey. I'm his for the day." I dared to lay a hand against his chest. His throat bobbed, and his eyes widened. Resisting the urge to roll my eyes, I added a seductive smile and dragged my teeth over my bottom lip the way men seemed to like. I needed to get in that place and see what was in there—maybe there was something that I could use as a weapon.

Close enough now, I could see the bank of punching bags that lined the far end of the room. A huge male pounded the bag in front of him, punching and kicking until I was sure he was going to rip it from the brackets that held it up. My eyes narrowed and I blinked several times. He had to be at least six feet six, though it was hard to tell from where I stood. His back was a breathtaking array of hard, cut muscles which rippled and glistened with sweat. And there was something dreadfully familiar about the way the male moved. Something stirred inside me; a memory that I didn't want, one that woke my Fire. I ripped my gaze from his impressive body, not liking where the sight of it took my mind, and turned my attention fully on grey eyes. He inhaled sharply. His eyes widened, and his generous mouth dropped open before he seemed to recover, and his mouth curled into a smirk.

I didn't have time to wonder about his reaction, not when the fucker was going to make me work for what I wanted.

He looked over his shoulder at the big male then back at me before he cocked a brow. "You got a pack mark, sweetheart?"

Shit, I didn't think of that. Swallowing my nerves, I forced a smile and mirrored his raised brow. "New meat, *sweetheart*. Why? You want to keep me?"

"Not bloody likely. I'd like to keep my head." His muttered words confused me, but before I could make sense of them he continued, his voice louder. "So you're the Prime's entertainment for the day? A bit early even for him, isn't it?"

I pouted and jutted my hip sideways, my hands on my hips. "Nah, he took one look and wanted to play."

"Is that so?" He looked over his shoulder into the hall, and pressed his lips into a thin line. "Okay, well it's your choice. This should be an interesting date."

I shrugged like it was no big deal. It was pretty obvious he didn't believe a word of my lie, but he sauntered forward and brushed his fingers over my hand. I tensed, my fight or flight instinct flaring. Surely, if I had to run, I'd be able to lose myself in the hundreds of people in gen pop?

Grey eyes met Korea's gaze and some kind of communication took place. Korea walked into the hall, his face stoney, his path taking him directly towards the huge male.

Shit! Shit! Shit! I hadn't planned on that big motherfucker beating the hell out of the bag being the bloody Prime, or being escorted right to him! I'd just wanted to get into the hall. Dammit! I needed to get away. I stepped back just as grey eyes grabbed my wrist.

"Aw, now, hold on there, treasure. You've got a date with my boss, haven't you?" He smiled pleasantly, but his eyes were suddenly hard. "How about I take you to him, and you can explain who you really are? 'Cause I doubt he'll be too happy about seeing a ghost."

I couldn't think straight, not when he pulled me along so quickly behind him. The bugger was nearly a foot taller than me, and I had to run to keep up with his long strides. My instincts screamed something was wrong here. I wanted to change my mind, to run as quickly as I could back out of that door, but I curbed my desire to drop him on his arse and tried instead to take in everything about the hall.

I noted two different entrances; the one we'd used from gen pop and another one across the far side. That one was also guarded by males who were big enough to keep people from trying to sneak in. But perhaps it would be a way out for me if the Prime got too angry with my lies. I surreptitiously eyed the pairs fighting in the rings. Their interactions did not appear fun or gentle, so maybe I was the only one stupid enough to actually want to get in here.

I stumbled over one of the dumbbells that had been chucked haphazardly on the floor. I cursed, but grey eyes ignored me. My sense of dread got worse, my skin prickling. We marched past a metal lock-up cupboard. The doors were open and I could see an array of weapons; training swords, knives, stakes, poles and shields. *Shields? Seriously?* What the hell were weapons out of some medieval fantasy film doing in a prison? They were wooden, but talk about temptation! I'd still be able to inflict serious damage, maybe even kill with them. I hid my relief and pretended I hadn't seen the cupboard.

Instead, I fixed my attention on Korea, who was talking to the big guy. The Prime was so tall, just like Connor had been. Korea had to look up to talk to him. Thinking of Connor caused pain to squeeze my heart, and I briefly closed my eyes and inhaled. Suddenly my legs went heavy, refusing to work, just as the Prime's scent hit me full on.

No! Fire flared to life inside my soul.

I stumbled again, and fell to my knees, which forced grey eyes to stop and turn around.

"Shit." He squatted down next to me and looked into my eyes. "It is you. Dammit it, the shit's about to hit the fan. Well, come on, it's too late to back out now." He pulled me to my feet, but my mind wasn't working right. That was Connor's scent! I could recognise Connor's scent anywhere, I had always been able to, but how could this be him—he was dead...?

My stomach clenched, and I wobbled as grey eyes pulled me forward. I imagined Connor's face, and the pain I'd lived with for the last four years tried to surface. I wouldn't let it. Instead, I squeezed my burning eyes shut and forced them not to water. This wasn't Connor...it couldn't be.

Grey eyes halted our progress. "Hey." He shook my wrist to get my attention. "You might want to open your eyes now."

I did, and didn't bother holding back my cry. Connor's scent overwhelmed me. I was staring right at his defined chest. Sweat trickled down between his impressive pecs. My throat closed up as I slowly raised my eyes, trailing my gaze up his thick, corded neck and past his square jaw, over his nose and to the eyes that haunted me night and day. The past hit me like a freight train, my breath left me in a rush, a half-sob escaping my throat. All I could do was stare, my mouth open, gasping for air though my lungs refused to work as my legs gave out beneath me and I almost went to my knees.

His beautiful cerulean eyes narrowed on me. I swallowed as his Prime power rolled over my skin; so much more potent than it had been when I had last seen him.

"Connor?" I whispered, my voice breaking, forcing myself to straighten.

For a moment he just stared, his heavy brows almost meeting above the bridge of his nose. He inhaled deeply, scenting me. Hope lifted the vice-like feeling on my chest. He'd recognise me now...

"Who the fuck are you?" A snarl curled Connor's lips. His wolf surfaced, inky blackness swirling through the sea of blue, turning his eyes to cold chips of obsidian.

I'd never felt threatened by Connor in the past. We'd always had a connection, ever since we'd been young. I trusted him like I trusted no one else. But this version of Connor was nothing like the arrogant and playful boy I'd grown up with. But, then, why would he be? He'd been locked up for the past four and a half years. Now, he was so cold. He didn't seem to believe it was me, and the coiled violence I sensed in him had my survival instincts roaring. I twisted free of grey eyes and staggered back, putting space between Connor and me. It gave me the illusion of safety. One I'd take right now. I couldn't speak, not when his gaze ensnared me, reducing me to the eighteen year old he'd kissed and left standing alone on a deserted driveway...

His predatory gaze narrowed on me, and he inhaled deeply again. A low growl rumbled up from his chest, and pressing his lips into a flat line, he shook his head, his eyes utterly black now. Connor's wolf had always been dominant. As a teenager, he'd fought to tame it, but it looked like he'd lost that contest and wolfie was running the show now. Cursing, I realised why Connor and his wolf didn't recognise me. They were conflicted. I might be the same, but my wolf was not the one who had been his potential mate. I needed to get through to Connor, I needed to talk to him. I had to at least try.

"Connor? It's me, Ember." Fighting a wave of dizziness, and curling my fingers into fists to hide their shaking, I looked him right in the eye. *Shit!* A bad, bad idea. Don't look a Prime in the eye...

He cracked his neck and curled and uncurled his fingers, he jutted his jaw forward, growling louder, as if he might end my existence right then and there. I immediately dropped my gaze to the floor, my heart banging in my chest. I knew I was on shaky ground. I might have defied Connor when we were younger. But he didn't trust who I was now.

Godsdamn it, I needed to get myself together. Exhaling, I tried to calm my panic. Doherty would have found my dead wolf, maybe he brought it back here to torture Connor.

This is what grey eyes meant about a ghost. He recognised me.

I had to convince Connor I really was me, and what better way than to refuse to capitulate to him, no matter how scary this version of Connor was.

While I took several deep breaths, Connor snarled and leaned in. Goosebumps rose on my skin and I didn't know what I wanted to do more, throw myself on him and weep with relief that he was alive, or run. Realising neither would help right now, I stood utterly still. He inhaled deeply again then straightened, his heavy brow dipping further. I sucked in a breath, steadying myself now that the shock of seeing him was wearing off.

"No. You can't be. My mate died, *I saw her head!* I don't know what you are, but you can't be her."

Damn! His wolf was even speaking through him, and there was no way he'd listen to reason. I needed to get Connor back in control so I could tell him the truth about what had happened. Or at least see if I could trust him enough to tell him. No matter how much I wanted the Connor I knew back, he'd been in this place for four years. And I had no idea what kind of person that had made him, so no matter how much I wanted to trust him, I bit my tongue. Grey eyes and Korea watched our exchange closely. In fact, grey eyes seemed really tense. His attention flicked from me to Connor and back, his mouth opening like he wanted to say something. I wondered if he'd been there the day we'd escaped from Doherty's first prison. Was that why I recognised him? It had been so long ago, and so many things had happened since then, that it was hard for me to place faces and scents.

"Connor, it really *is* me. I'm here. I survived." I tried again, my eyes burning with unshed tears.

"Stop!" His breathing was deep and erratic. Waves of power rolled off him, making even the large males that surrounded us shift their feet and roll their shoulders.

"I-I know it's confusing, but I can explain."

His throat bobbed and he shook his head again. "Explain? How the fuck can you explain being here after all this time?"

I watched, wide eyed as Connor's body grew and his wolf tried to push through. The collar stopped him, but the thick scarred skin that ringed Connor's neck burned and blistered. Korea cursed and grey eyes inhaled sharply. I guessed Connor and his wolf didn't often lose control. His arms dropped to his sides and he took several long, slow breaths. Closing his eyes, he forced his wolf to recede. Opening them, familiar blue eyes regarded me. I shuddered, swallowing the ache in my throat. They were colder than I'd ever seen.

"I know my Ember is dead because her wolf's head was given to me as a welcome gift when I got here four years ago." His big hand shot out and grasped my neck, his thumb hooking over my jaw, and though I had dreamed of feeling his touch again, I froze. He could easily snap my neck.

My limbs trembled, my palms sweated, and I gulped reflexively.

He inhaled and bared his teeth. "Do I scare you, creature?"

"Yes." There was no point in lying. He'd know.

"Good, you should be. You carry the scent of her killer. I can smell it." He yanked me closer and lifted me until only my toes dangled on the floor. "That face is hers, no one else's. If you're a doppelganger—change it, or the next time I see you, I will kill you."

The pressure on my throat increased, making me cough and choke as my heart pounded and my eyes watered. His nails drew blood. He was going to kill me! After all this time, I'd finally found Connor, and he would be the one to end my life—and reveal my biggest secret. Fire stirred, sensing the danger to my life. I couldn't summon her at will, but I could sense when she was close to flying free. I closed my eyes. *He won't hurt me. He won't. It's Connor.*

"Hey, man..."

I opened my eyes.

Grey eyes ventured forward, his voice steady, though his face was tight. "You sure you wanna do this? Whether she's a doppelganger or a changeling or something else, she might know what really happened to your Ember."

I swallowed against Connor's grip as heat blazed through my blood and across my skin. Even in the past, when she'd escaped my hold, Fire had never burned him. Maybe her presence was the only way to convince him I was real, that I wasn't an imposter. I lifted my gaze.

Connor's eyes met mine. He drew in a sharp breath and his power rippled over me. Still I held his gaze. Seconds passed and I willed him to believe me. No one else could see the flames in my eyes, he held me too close. He flinched away, shaking his head.

"Connor?" I could barely get enough air past my vocal chords to whisper his name.

He loosened his grip and my feet touched the ground.

I panted, gasping air into my deprived lungs.

"Stay away from me. I don't know what you are but you have taken her face and her gift. Fuck knows how you've done it, but you carry the stink of her killer, so if you come near me again, I'll kill you." He didn't look away from me as he addressed grey eyes. "Owen, get this thing out of my face before I kill it."

My legs were weak, but I forced my knees to stay strong. He didn't believe me, and why would he? I'd deliberately sacrificed my last wolf to convince Doherty I was dead. I hadn't known he'd use her corpse to wound Connor so deeply, I'd thought he was dead. Now his wolf had taken control and grief wouldn't allow either of them to consider I was telling the truth.

Ensnared by his icy stare, I knew pleading my case would be a mistake. The veins in Connor's neck bulged, and the waves of fury coming off him made me want to cower away. Those around us dropped their heads and moved back, all except Korea and Owen, who seemed less affected by his anger. I kept utterly still and swallowed, trying to ease my throat, which was still in his grasp. There was no doubt, Connor was now a more powerful predator than he had ever been. Maybe he would never accept me. The thought made my heart hurt, but at least he was alive.

He curled his top lip and thrust me away. I stumbled but recovered quickly, balanced and ready to fight. Not willing to be treated like that, even by Connor, I snarled back. His eyes narrowed and he growled a low warning, but I didn't listen. I understood his grief, gods, I'd grieved for this man for years and my heart couldn't repair itself in a matter of moments, so I certainly didn't expect his to, especially when this wasn't the Connor I'd grown up with. No, this was someone entirely different. A cold and distant man who allowed his wolf far too much power. He saw me as an imposter because he scented my wolf, and she had once belonged to the woman who had killed me in those woods. My stupid heart squeezed painfully. I wanted him to believe me, but I knew I'd have to work hard to gain his trust enough to get a chance to explain.

His attention moved to something over my shoulder, and his frown deepened.

A blonde haired woman prowled forward and wrapped herself around him, resting her hand in a proprietary gesture on his chest.

I lifted a brow, hiding the pain at seeing another woman touch Connor. "Well, doesn't this day just keep getting better and better?" My voice was hoarse, and I had to force my words out, shocked to see my old enemy in front of me, let alone making like a second skin to the man I loved. He might hate me right now, but that didn't change the way I felt about him, it only made me more determined to prove who I was.

Shannon smiled and cocked her head, rubbing her generous breasts against Connor's impressive upper arm. He kept his gaze on me and wrapped that arm around her waist.

"It is you." Shannon smiled, her eyes calculating as they rested on me. Her gaze perused my body, weighing up the challenge to what was obviously her territory.

I didn't react. What the hell had she done to be chucked in a prison that her father ran? Finding out was going to be a challenge, but I added it to my ever growing list of difficult tasks. Maybe Charlie knew something.

I smiled sweetly. "Queen bitch. How are you?"

She cocked her head, indicating the healing bruises on my arms and ribs. "Better than you. Still a troublemaker, and a runt that no one wants, I see."

"Hmm, these bruises didn't come because no one wants me, Shannon, quite the opposite. But, unlike you, I don't need a big, strong man to take care of me—I never have. I can protect myself better than most alphas can, and I'm certainly never submitting to one." I allowed my cold gaze to meet Connor's for a second before continuing my conversation with the woman he'd promised he'd never fuck. *Bastard.* My chest ached at the thought of them together, and my hands fisted as I tried to deal with an utterly ridiculous sense of jealousy and betrayal. *Ah, shit, pull yourself together, Ember. You're not a child, and you've had your own fair share of lovers since you last saw him. Besides, what did you expect? That he would be celibate just in case you ever saw each other again? For heaven's sake! We both thought the other was dead!* I gave myself an imaginary slap after that stern talking to. I had to keep things in perspective, even if all this *was* sending my brain into a meltdown. "What are you doing here, anyway? Are you on a day trip to Daddy's work, or did you do something really naughty to piss him off?"

She inhaled sharply, her gaze darting around. "Shut up!"

I smirked. *Interesting.* I guessed the other inmates didn't realise she was the daughter of their kidnapper. "So..." I fixed my attention on Connor. How much did his fuck buddy mean to him? I was either in a position to bargain, or he wouldn't let me out of this room alive to tell anyone. I hoped it was the former. "You want to keep her dirty secret from the others, hmm?"

His eyes narrowed, and his wolf seeped into his gaze.

I judged the distance back to the weapons cupboard. Wooden or not, I could inflict life threatening injuries with them. I'd only have to get past Korea, Owen was on my other side and the others had backed off when Connor's power got too much for them.

"What's your real name?" Connor cocked his head, clearly weighing up his options.

I rolled my eyes. "Ember."

His nostrils flared. "No, it's not."

"Yes, it really is."

He growled. "Fine. I'll humor you for now."

I tried not to show my relief. Even that small concession was a step in the right direction.

"Shannon is here because, like the rest of us, she was thrown in here to rot by the director. She has no special privileges, and no one else will find out who she is." He pushed her away from him and stepped closer to me. "At least they won't find out from you."

My heart rate spiked, but fear was an emotion I refused to acknowledge, so I smirked, batting my eyelashes at him. "Ah, but what will you give me in return for keeping yours, or rather her, dirty little secret. I deserve something, don't you think?"

He leaned in, invading my space. His familiar spicy and warm scent made my heart squeeze. I'd forgotten how much I loved that scent. Gods, I'd missed him so much. I fought not to show how flustered his nearness made me.

"How about your life? Now keep your mouth shut and leave before I change my mind." He stood back and glared at the door.

But I didn't want to leave, not now that I'd found him again. I cursed myself for not wanting to walk away, so I deliberately ignored his threat and glanced around the gym. All activity had ceased again. Oh crap, now I was outright challenging the Prime by not leaving straight away. Well, in for a penny, in for a pound, as the old saying went.

"Of course, but how about you let me come use this gym whenever I want and I'll keep *queen bitch's* secret."

Shannon sneered. "You? What the hell do you need access to a gym for? You never could fight. You were always the weakest of our class, always the runt. Rawson should have put you down when my…"

"Shannon! Enough!" Connor snapped a warning.

The flush over Shannon's cheeks told me she'd let her anger loosen her tongue without even noticing. *As volatile as ever.* I banked that little snippet of information.

My small smile slipped when Connor turned to me. His wolf shone through again. Okay, maybe I was pushing my luck. Then I saw blue seep back into his gaze and though his face remained cold, he studied me closely, his eyes bouncing between mine. The muscles of his jaw tensed as his gaze moved down my body and back up again.

"You will leave now. Do not discuss Shannon with anyone. If you do, I will snap your neck before you know I'm near you. Are we clear, *Ember?*" He sneered my name, but his eyes were even more blue now, his wolf was losing its hold on him.

I'd lost my bargaining point and I needed into this gym, it's possibilities were too much to ignore, but at least I'd got through to Connor a bit. Surely he realised no imposter would know about my name for Shannon. I'd only ever used it when I was with him.

"Come on, time to leave, while you still can," said Owen. He went to grab my wrist, but I'd had enough of being manhandled. I spun and jabbed my elbow into his face. His jaw snapped shut, his teeth banging together. Out of the corner of my eye, I saw Korea move. He launched through the air with a perfectly executed sidekick, but I was from the school of cheat to win, so, although I could appreciate his technique, I also knew how to stop him. I dropped and slid along the mats under his flying body and jabbed a fist up into his balls. He howled and landed heavily in a crouch. His eyes flashed with fury as he fell to his knees, clutching his junk.

"No need for such tactics, boys. I can find my own way out." I addressed my comment directly to Connor who watched me with vivid blue eyes.

His face was blank. "Remember what I said."

I dipped my head in acknowledgement as I stepped around a furious Owen and Korea. I walked quickly and efficiently, not stupid enough to linger. I'd done some damage to two males who definitely wouldn't appreciate me showing my skills at their expense. Particularly in front of a room full of others. Hell, it probably meant a whole shit load of challenges coming their way. *Tough,* I decided, trying to take control of my rattled nerves.

Charlie's eyes widened as I stepped out of the training area unharmed.

And that's what it was, a training area. I'd no idea what for, but I was going to find out.

I glanced back over my shoulder. Connor stared right at me. The weight of his scrutiny sent a wave of awareness through me. My heart skipped a beat. He looked like an unattainable god; stunning, powerful and dangerous. It was impossible to hide my relief at him being alive, even if he despised my existence. I gave him a small smile, unable to stop it from forming on my lips. I had so much I wanted to ask him, but as he stood there, cold and removed, it was obvious that I wouldn't get the chance—yet. I'd just have to work on it. I was sure I'd planted a question in his mind, and I had Shannon to thank for that. I had promised to go back and save Blue, and I wouldn't give up trying to find a way out of here, but I'd be damned if I'd lose Connor now that I'd found him again.

CHAPTER 5

mber

"So what did you do before you were locked in this place?"

Charlie and I sat on the floor of one of the big halls with our backs up against the wall, as always.

Charlie smiled and tipped her head back, staring at the ceiling. "I worked from home."

I raised my brows. "Really? Doing what?"

"Oh, this and that with computers." She winked at me.

I grinned. Som had employed an IT geek on his team too. "Right. You hacked systems."

"Me?" Charlie affected an innocent look, placing her hand on her chest.

"Yeah, you, Miss Innocent."

"Okay, you got me. I did. Sometimes, I did it for money, which is how I got caught, and sometimes, for the challenge it gave me."

"Wow, how long had you been doing it before you got caught?" Charlie didn't look to be much more than eighteen or perhaps nineteen, years old.

"I've been working for myself since I was eleven. I only got caught because I hacked into a system I thought was a bank, but ended up being a subsidiary company of the SBI. There was some seriously shady stuff and transactions in there. I logged out real quick, but I guess not quick enough. I ended up here three days later."

"That sucks."

"Yeah." She eyed the drones that floated high up near the ceiling, their camera eyes flashing red. "I'd love to get my hands on one of those fuckers just to pull it apart to see how it functions."

I grinned. "I'll bet you would, but getting one down would be damned near impossible, let alone doing it without being seen."

"True." She sighed and pushed to her feet. "Maybe one day. Right now, I'm off to break hearts and have some fun. Watch your back, newbie." She winked down at me and picked her way through the crowd.

I smiled. In the last week I'd seen Charlie work her vibes on both men and women. Yeah, she physically liked women, but it seemed she'd come to an agreement with Resta. I didn't judge my new friend for using her body to get herself back into Resta's pack of females. She had a bunk again, and a relative amount of safety. Being dragged off into a corner as an unclaimed female was not fun. It had happened to me twice more so far, and I was under no illusions, it would happen again soon. I just thanked my lucky stars that I could fight my way out and that the female sleep halls were locked at night.

I'd gone back to the gym to see if I could speak to Connor, but had been blocked by the door guards each time. If I could make him see I really was me, then maybe he'd let me in that gym. I could train and keep out of the way of the gangs in gen pop. I'd tried getting Owen's attention, too, and though he'd looked a bit uncomfortable, he'd told me to let it go. Even when Connor walked down the corridors, his six bodyguards prevented anyone from getting close, and that included me.

I watched a thin dude in baggy jeans and a blood stained vest saunter over to a group of heavy set males. The group had swaggered in and were appraising the people nearby. I grimaced and shuffled back into the shadows. I was still sore and aching from the fight I'd had yesterday. Two males had decided that as I didn't have a pack mark, I was fair game for a bit of after dinner entertainment. I'd soon disillusioned them. I blew out a small breath as the group strutted through the far doorway into the hallways that led to the training hall.

Gen pop itself was a hotbed of trading if you knew where to look. There wasn't much scope for variety, but Charlie had been right, there was an abundance of flesh. It could just be taken, but it seemed even the new and callous version of Connor had some rules. If you chose to force a person who belonged to a pack, you'd pay dearly. I'd seen two of his guards enter a busy hall in gen pop and corner a beady eyed man and accuse him of just that. They'd easily overpowered him then snapped his neck with no hesitation.

I glanced up. The guards hadn't done a damn thing. Connor really was in charge down here, though it seemed he thought rape of those not in a pack *was* acceptable. I rubbed my hand over my mouth, wondering what had happened to his moral code. I'd not seen a woman killed—yet. But I guessed it was only a matter of time. My brow dipped. Like Charlie had said, females weren't protected, but they were needed for something. I watched as a few disgusting prison biscuits exchanged hands for a blanket. Extra food and commodities like blankets, a sleeping space, or a bed were all bargaining chips.

Charlie gave me a wink from across the hall. I grinned back and shook my head. She'd hunt me down when she wanted some company outside Resta's group. I didn't mind. She was a good source of information and decent company, herself. Flicking up the collar on my old leather jacket, she disappeared along the corridor into the mess hall with five other women.

I was about to follow and see if I could grab some food when I spied Shannon flounce in from the corridor that led to the west wing and head towards the food hall. If I wanted to avoid her, I needed to stay where I was. Damn! And I was hungry...

Sighing, I pushed myself up from the floor. Avoiding her forever was an unlikely possibility, and I wasn't an uncontrolled teenager anymore. I'd dealt with worse than Shannon Doherty over the past few years. If she thought she was a bad-assed bitch, she needed to visit some of the female faeries I'd had dealings with. Her being with Connor just increased my intense dislike of her. I'd not seen a pack mark on her when she'd draped herself over him, but then again, a week ago I hadn't known what I was looking for.

The most powerful pack next to the west pack, which was Connor's, seemed to be the north pack, but since the alpha had been challenged and killed just after I'd arrived, the power struggle between the packs had ramped up. Now it was uncertain who was the next most powerful alpha after Connor. My bet was on the south wing alpha. I'd only heard about Drake Alexander, but the stories painted him as big enough to make you think twice before taking him on.

My stomach rumbled. Avoiding food was silly. I needed to keep my body strong. I was not a member of any pack, and I had no intention of whoring myself out for safety. That meant until my reputation for being difficult got around, I was fair game for anyone.

Just as I straightened, the guy who had fought for the top spot on the plane came sauntering in with four other males. His long blonde hair hung over his shoulders and his keen blue eyes coldly surveyed the hall. I shuddered. His lack of remorse at dismembering those that had challenged him on the plane had stuck with me.

My eyes narrowed. Alpha power rolled off him. It dawned on me; this was the new north wing alpha. His head turned my way, so I shrank down behind the backs of two males who were in front of me. I didn't want the attention of anyone, let alone a psycho like him. I might be able to fight, but beating five males who were as physically powerful as them wasn't a smart way to push my luck.

I waited until they'd disappeared down the same corridor as Shannon, then headed that way. Food seemed even less appealing now. I sighed and rolled my head to loosen my tense neck muscles. Keeping my senses alert and letting my wolf a little nearer the surface, I headed towards the food hall.

The noise was intense. Food was served for two hours, morning, noon, and night. There were hundreds of inmates to feed and it took an army to do it.

Aware of the people moving around me, I grabbed a tray and took my bowl of slop. It was the same as every other day. A bowl of some kind of soup with nondescript meat in it and a few vegetables. I didn't care, I was starving. I grabbed a piece of bread, and, surprise! For a change it was fresh. I sought out a space at a table near the door. It wasn't my preferred spot to sit, but it was free, and these tables didn't seem run by gangs or heavy handed individuals.

I washed my bread down with the soup and watched as Shannon walked by and headed out. She had a vest top on, and crappy though it was, it enhanced her curvaceous figure. She drew eyes from every lascivious male and even some females. She clearly knew the attention she commanded and didn't care. Someone banged my shoulder as they pushed by. I cursed. I'd been licking my dish of every last drop and now I had a cut lip. There was a flash of long blonde hair as the guy from the plane stalked after Shannon, his menagerie of males following him.

I stared at my tray for a moment hoping she could still fight as well as she could in the agency programme. She wouldn't suffer any abuse from them….or would she? I still didn't know if she had the protection of a pack, and five males, crazy ones at that, could easily overpower her. I shrugged. Then again, she wasn't my problem. She'd been here a damn sight longer than me and had survived so far.

I took my tray to the stack and chucked my plastic bowl in the empties tub. My cardboard spoon was mush, so I dropped that in the bin.

I glanced around wondering if we ever got to exercise outside. I doubted it. But, I needed to exercise. I hated it if I went even a few days without working up a decent sweat. The hall was full of males with an abundance of testosterone. They had to train somewhere other than that one training hall. I tilted my head and studied some of the males. I suppose I could just get laid, it might get rid of some of my tension… I sighed and dismissed the idea. I liked sex as much as the next girl, but I also liked a bit of privacy when I played, and there was no chance of that here. Besides after seeing Connor again, none of these males did it for me.

I'd go and find some space in gen pop and do some running and push ups or something. I sauntered back down the corridor, pushing by groups of people who were making their way from one area to another. Corridors with metal doors headed off at intervals. The guards wandered around on their platforms above, or leaned on the rails, their weapons loose in their hands. I heard Shannon's voice before I saw her. She was pressed up against the wall of the laundry corridor with an arm against her throat. I wrinkled my nose, the heat and smell of cleaning detergent was overpowering.

I slowed. I had no love for Shannon, she'd always been a bitch, but I did have issues with the way males in this place took a female as if she were nothing; like she didn't count or matter.

I tipped my head back and looked at the ceiling, deciding.

"Hey, bitch, move on. This ain't your business," said a male voice with a heavy east London accent. "Unless you wanna join in?"

I slammed my hands on my hips, shook my head slightly and grimaced. *Here we go.*

He moved closer. I kept one eye on him, but watched the surfer dude. He leaned closer to Shannon and licked up the side of her face as his other hand grabbed her breast. She screeched, anger clear in her eyes as she tried to cringe away. Her face fell as her predicament became clear. She was pinned and no one gave a shit what happened to her.

I smiled inwardly, the East End guy had taken my bait. To make it more realistic, I curled my shoulders down. A submissive posture would incite his interest even more. The guy next to him looked my way and grinned, his eyes lighting up. They saw me as another toy. I put my hands up and shook my head again. "No, please. I don't...It's none of my business...Please...I just want to go..."

"Oh, no, honey, don't run away." The second guy moved behind me. "You get to play, too—or rather we do." He ran a finger down my bare shoulder and arm.

I made myself tremble. A growl rippled through one of them, his body shaking, the bulge in the front of his jeans obvious. I hid my snarl and allowed East End to step in front of me. I shifted my weight and angled my position slightly to keep Shannon in view. As if feeling my attention, she lifted her gaze. Her eyes narrowed and met mine even as the north wing alpha grabbed the button of her jeans.

I nodded a little. She smirked, a little colour coming back into her cheeks as she realised she wasn't going to suffer a gang rape without some kind of fight.

The male behind me grabbed my wrist, pulling hard to spin me into his grasp.

I went with the movement—and slammed my fist into the side of his temple. His grip fell away. I kept spinning and swung my leg in a back kick. My boot heel slammed into the jaw of East End and he toppled backwards.

When I faced Shannon again she'd managed to reduce the north alpha to his knees and was fighting the other male. My first attacker regained his balance, so I kicked him square in the chest and followed up with a barrage of punches until he lay unconscious. I was grabbed from behind by my hair and thrown across the floor. My head bounced on the concrete floor. Pain slammed through my skull, but I rolled and got to my feet, already blocking the next attack. The north alpha's fist slammed into Shannon's stomach, and she hit the deck. He stalked up to her and yanked her to her feet by her throat.

I spun behind my own attacker, smashed my foot into his knee and wrapped my arm around his neck as he went down. I swiftly placed my other hand behind his neck and squeezed hard enough to make him choke and claw at my arm as he went purple.

"Hey!" I yelled as loudly as I could. "You want your man to die!?"

The north alpha looked at me and growled, his eyes flashing dangerously.

"Let her go, or I'll kill one of your own." I tightened the headlock. The male in my grasp clawed harder at my forearm. I held the alpha's potent gaze, and though his compulsion sizzled over my skin, I didn't drop my own. His gaze narrowed.

Yeah, that's right, dickhead, that alpha shit doesn't work on me.

I sneered while the man in my death grip coughed, and thrashed, turning an even darker shade of purple.

The north alpha gripped Shannon's neck harder and she started to choke. I reciprocated. His man turned blue and started to lose his strength.

"Let her go, or he dies." I meant it, too. I had no qualms about killing such a slimy bastard.

The north alpha snorted. "Ha, you're a woman. You will not kill him. Besides if he dies at your hands, he is not worthy of being by my side." He shrugged and slammed Shannon into the wall, squeezing her neck as he undid his jeans with his other hand. She began to claw weakly at his face as her eyes rolled in her head.

Oh, hell, no, I was not going to stand and watch this. My heart hammered in my chest. "What? You think because I am a woman I have a moral compass?" I laughed loudly. "That I won't kill to make a point?"

He glanced over his shoulder at me. "I don't care."

I was aware we had drawn a crowd. The large lone shifter who had been on the plane, was at the front of the crowd, his tawny eyes fixed on the north wing alpha. A cold calculated look consumed them.

I squeezed my victim's neck harder. I needed him unconscious, but if he didn't fade in the next few seconds, I'd end him. He'd chosen to attack a woman. That had been his choice, and he had to deal with the consequences.

The moment his body became lax, I let him go and pounced. Out of the corner of my eye, I saw the big guy move. My first victim had crawled to his feet and was about to grab me. The big guy yanked him sideways, and I slammed a back fist into another male coming from my right.

My attacker's nose exploded and he screamed, so I smashed my knuckles into his throat causing his knees to buckle. Taking the opportunity, I swung an axe kick down on the back of his neck and smashed him face first into the floor.

The north alpha roared his displeasure and threw Shannon to the ground. I vaguely registered her coughing and spluttering. At least she was breathing. North alpha guy spun more quickly than I expected, and his fist caught my ribs as I darted sideways. My ribs cracked and agony blasted through my chest. I screeched and stumbled but managed to block his second punch and counter with one of my own.

The big guy was easily holding his own against the other two males, leaving me the alpha to deal with.

The alpha staggered as I slammed my foot into the side of his knee. Quickly, I followed that strike with a punch to his jaw. At the same time, his fist slammed into my belly and another against my already broken ribs. I was a good fighter and used to taking hits, but he was strong and pushing his wolf behind his strikes. I fell to my knees, winded. Beating an alpha was nearly impossible for anyone who wasn't an alpha themselves.

Shannon yelled and launched herself, wrapping her arms around his neck, trying to gain a stranglehold. She fixed her legs around his waist, but he was much bigger than her and with the collar around his neck, she couldn't get a solid purchase.

I jumped back away from the alpha, taking the time to look up. Surely the guards would step in? Nope. They looked on, their weapons trained downwards but apparently not intending to intervene.

The alpha roared and slammed Shannon into the wall. The impact loosened her grip and he threw her off.

Around us the crowd yelled, egging on the fight, riled by the sight and scent of blood and violence.

The big guy threw one of his opponents down and knocked him out with one punch.

I spat blood from my mouth and snarled at the guards. Fine. This alpha arsehole wasn't getting the better of me. I launched myself at him. He charged at me with a bellow that was a definite war cry. I darted sideways, pressed my foot to one of the walls and launched myself up and over him. As I landed, I thrust a kick into his kidneys and he sailed forward, hit the wall and fell to the floor.

A massive roar vibrated through the air, and an almighty blast of power hit us all. Everyone stilled, most dropping to their knees, others bowing their heads and shoulders as if unable to keep them up. The north alpha's body was plucked from the floor.

I forced myself to fight the oppressive power that demanded I drop to my knees. Instead, I set my jaw defiantly and lifted my gaze.

Connor's black eyes held mine. His gaze narrowed but remained on me as he spoke to the alpha who he held around the throat with one large hand. "This stops, right now." There was no explanation. It was not a request. The message was clear. Connor squeezed to make a point. Slowly, he looked at the north alpha, his fingers gripping until the male's face turned bright red. He watched the man struggle for a moment then set him back on his feet. "Owen." It was a command.

"Everyone, get out!" Owen, instructed. They did. Some even ran. I didn't blame them. Being faced with seven alpha's, one of whom was their Prime, was not something to relish.

"Not you lot." A new face growled at the north alpha's males.

"Or you," Korea said to the large guy from the plane.

Connor eyed me and then Shannon, who was just pushing herself up into a sitting position. I suspected I looked as rough as she did. And my ribs hurt like a bitch.

I snorted as Connor released the alpha's neck. "You're going to let him go after attacking your girlfriend?" Derision dripped from my words. Connor's brows knitted at my tone. I didn't care. Allowing these kinds of attacks was not acceptable. I strode over to Shannon and helped her up. "You okay?"

She swallowed, her eyelids fluttering and her fingers feeling her skin. It was clearly painful, but she nodded. I stood in front of her, blocking the others and looked down at her open jeans meaningfully. She flushed and fumbled to do them up.

"Females are fair game in gen pop, Prime." The north alpha puffed his chest out and scowled at me and Shannon.

My wolf stirred, but I merely stood in front of Shannon as she straightened her clothes.

"Neither of them are marked. They are mine to use."

Okay, now he was pissing me off! My eyes drifted to Shannon's neck. She might be Connor's latest piece of ass, but he still hadn't marked her to keep her safe. She looked me in the eye.

"No one owns me," she said quietly.

I nodded. I understood her sentiments, if not her reasons. She shouldn't need to belong to a pack in order to be safe.

Her eyes widened as someone walked up to my back. I met Shannon's gaze and smirked. I'd been waiting. It seemed Connor wasn't going to refute the alpha's right to 'use' us. I rolled my shoulders and tried to ignore the pain in my ribs. Now we were surrounded by more dangerous and egotistical males, this was a fight we wouldn't win. I huffed out a small breath of acceptance. Well, I'd inflict enough pain on this entitled prick that he wouldn't be able to get it up even if we lost this fight. I spun and drove a ridge hand strike into his junk. The north alpha squealed and dropped to his knees. Without hesitation, I slammed my fist into his jaw—twice. He went down. Out cold.

Silence fell.

"Feel better?" Connor's voice was raspy and deep. Blue bled into his obsidian eyes giving them a hypnotic marble effect.

I ignored the question. Was he serious? "If you're the Prime, why do you allow this to happen?" I didn't unclench my fists.

His face didn't change, but his wolf's anger prickled against my skin. "You are still new here, so this will be a warning..."

My patience snapped. "What!? *Warning?* Are you fucking kidding me? Four males, and an alpha, can attack a woman and that's okay? But if she, or anyone else defends her, they are the ones in the wrong? Are you for real, Connor?" I stepped closer to him, not bothered that his wolf was staring right back at me. Connor was always an arrogant prick, but never cruel or uncaring. It was clear his wolf was in charge and didn't care in the slightest about the atrocities happening under his nose.

A blast of his power hit me, and just as I'd always done when we were younger, I ignored it. His dominance had never worked on me, and it wouldn't now. The others staggered back, and Shannon cowered against the wall.

I stepped closer to him and stared up into his eyes, my hands on my hips. "What happened to you? You were always arrogant, but never cruel, not like this. You can't honestly believe gang rape, under any circumstances is acceptable! Lyss would be ashamed of you, as would Rawson. How can you even hold your head up when you allow this kind of thing to happen? And yeah, I'm talking to Connor, wolfie, so back off."

His jaw muscles twitched as he held my gaze. Within seconds blue consumed his irises. He took a deep breath and straightened, looking away from me to Shannon and the unconscious male on the floor. He shook his head and fixed his heavy gaze back on me. I swallowed hard, that gaze had more of an effect on me than any amount of his power. He stepped closer. "I'm not who I used to be. Neither are you."

I stood my ground though my heart rate stepped up a notch at his closeness.

He inhaled and his throat bobbed. "I still scent her killer on you. But..." His brow creased, his voice dropping to a whisper. "...you are too like my Firecracker not to be her."

His voice sent shivers over my skin, and though the intensity of his gaze burned me, I resisted the urge to step back. "I *am* your Firecracker...I mean Ember." I quickly corrected my verbal stumble, a flush burning my cheeks when his lips quirked. "Connor, you have to stop this. You can't allow this kind of cruelty or forced sex slavery of people, male or female, to continue."

His dark brow dipped. "I can do as I wish."

"Then change it! Because if you don't, I will. I'll work with every victim in here, and together we'll rip the dicks off anyone who forces themselves on another, whether you agree or not." His scent drifted up my nostrils and I couldn't stop my pulse rate from spiking. I wanted to reach out and take his hand, to touch him and convince myself he was real.

He tilted his head, and his beautiful eyes narrowed. Tears stung my eyes when he reached out and tenderly brushed the back of his index finger down my cheek. His whole face softened. It was such a change in demeanor that my mouth dropped open. He gently closed it with his finger.

"Okay, Firecracker, you're right. But I *am* a cruel bastard and I'm not going to start protecting everyone in gen pop. However, I won't let this type of behaviour continue." He turned away and addressed the north alpha's men. "Go back to the north wing and take him with you. If you want to challenge for his position or kill him while he's down, I don't care, but from now on, no one will be forced into sex, by him or anyone else." He looked up at the guards and frowned. They looked back, implacable in their full face masks and body armour. Black glazed his eyes again, but he forced his wolf to back down.

"Reed, Myles, go to gen pop and spread the word there. Find some people to pass on the new rule, and be very clear that those who choose to break it will be dealt with swiftly and without mercy." The two males nodded and headed away. "D. You and Kawan take the east wing. Find Shane and tell him to inform his pack. Stone?" He addressed a tall and stoic looking male with silver grey hair. I blinked. He'd definitely been at the prison we'd escaped from four years ago. The man headed forward, his cold gaze fixed on me.

"Yes, boss?"

"Go and find Drake and tell him what I've decided; not that the south pack indulge in gen pop often, but he needs to know."

"Sure, boss." Though Stone remained where he was and watched as the north pack alpha was dragged away. Only the big guy, along with Owen and Shannon remained with us.

Connor raised his brows, clearly wondering why Stone didn't comply with his order.

Stone inclined his head at me. "You've never given a damn about the shit that goes down in gen pop. What hold has she got over you that you'd change the rules at one word from her?" He tilted his head, and studied me closely. I had no doubts that I was being weighed up by a predator, who, if he found me weak or wanting, would rip my throat out.

Connor gave Stone his attention. "Are you questioning my decision?" His voice was cold and devoid of emotion. His fingers twitched and his wolf surfaced, turning his blue eyes to obsidian.

Stone kept his gaze on me. "Not you, Connor. Her. I remember her from the other prison, and she has a hold over you. That makes her dangerous."

I smiled sweetly at him. "I am dangerous."

He leaned in, close enough to whisper in my ear. He didn't smell entirely like a shifter, there was something else in his scent. Fae. It was a strange, sweet scent; one that I was very familiar with. "So am I." He held my gaze as he pulled back.

"Stone! Go and find Drake. Now."

Stone pulled back, his face cold, but he turned and walked away without further comment.

Ignoring me, Connor walked over to Shannon.

I, too, wanted to ask why he'd changed his rules, though I didn't believe it was purely because I'd made a request. Perhaps reminding him of his past, of the fact that he'd been a person with a family who had loved him and taught him values, had swayed him to control his wolf, not the other way around.

He loomed in front of Shannon, who was leaning against the wall for support. For a moment he just stood and stared at the red and bruised skin around her neck. "Will you admit you need help and join my pack?"

"No." Shannon set her jaw at a stubborn angle.

Connor's fingers tentatively touched her neck and his face softened. "I can't protect you out here, you know that."

My stomach clenched, my chest tightening to the point of pain. I looked away. I wanted to shove Shannon away from Connor. It was true, I'd thought him dead until two weeks ago, but my heart had always belonged to him. Clearly he had moved on—with Shannon, and probably many other lovers.

Shannon's attention drifted to me. "You know what I want, Connor. That's the only way I'll join your pack."

"And you know I won't offer you that."

I didn't even pretend I wasn't listening.

"Well, things will be better now—if you mean what you say about enforcing those rules." Shannon's voice was raspy and she held her throat, but she managed a shrug.

Connor sighed, then stepped back. "I do."

Unable to process the feelings in my chest, I didn't want to watch their exchange anymore so I walked past Owen and over to the big man. I held out my hand. "Thanks for helping me. It could've gotten messy. I'm Ember."

"Lionel," he answered, shaking my hand. His amber eyes twinkled as I huffed a chuckle.

"Lionel? Really? What's your animal?"

He grinned. "Lion."

I laughed louder.

"Yep, my parents had a warped sense of humour. So who's the *Prime* to you?"

Connor and Shannon were continuing their discussion, and by the glower on Connor's face, I guessed she was standing up to him.

I shrugged, trying to appear nonchalant. "An old friend—at least he was. Now, I'm not sure."

"Well, I'm guessing his new rule is going to paint a target on your back, if not mine, too."

"It is." Owen stood about six feet away with his arms crossed and feet planted firmly apart.

I rolled my eyes. "This is a private conversation."

He grinned. "Not when you're within ten feet of any other shifter." He gestured between us. "And you are."

The guards above moved back to their patrolling as Shannon and Connor walked over to us, obviously deciding the drama was over.

Connor stared at me, and the weight of that blue gaze was hard to ignore. There were so many things I wanted to ask him. I really wanted to know why he'd listened to me, but I didn't want to have such a conversation in front of everyone else. I looked away. "Glad you're okay," I said to Shannon. She'd always been a bitch to me, but no one deserved what had just nearly happened to her.

"Yeah, umm, thanks." She slid her arm around Connor's waist.

I deliberately ignored her proprietary gesture and kept my face neutral, not sure why she resisted bearing his pack mark when she clearly wanted me to know they were together.

Connor frowned and pulled her hand off him, stepping sideways a little. Her eyes flicked to him but he was busy staring at me, which had heat flushing my neck.

"So how are you here? Where've you been hiding all these years?" she asked. "I know everyone at the academy thought you were dead after what happened to Lyss, and Rawson disappeared."

Connor's mouth tightened and his throat bobbed. My stomach tightened. Did he know something about what happened to Rawson? I hadn't seen him in this prison despite searching gen pop and watching all the entrances to the other packs. True, I'd grieved for him over the past four years, but I had for Connor, too, so if Connor was alive, maybe Rawson was alive as well. That hope had started to dwindle, but maybe...

I glanced down at my tattoo, then shrugged and forced a smile. No way was I revealing what my life had become since I'd lost Connor, Lyss and Rawson. The life of a drug dealer in Faerie was nothing to be proud of and was dangerous to boot, but it had been a way to search for the elusive Walker and keep myself hidden from the SBI—until, of course, it wasn't. It certainly wasn't something I cared to share with Shannon. "I guess I got good at hiding, so your...I mean, so no one could find me, until someone ratted my boss out, that is."

Connor's spine straightened and his eyes became even more intense. "You should join a pack. It's safer that way. Even my orders won't protect everyone, and there will be a period of—readjustment for those who believe it their right to just take what they want."

I tilted my head, my voice hard. "And whose fault is that? If you'd stopped this behaviour before, it wouldn't be such an issue now." I stepped closer and poked my index finger into his hard chest. Owen growled from behind me, but I wasn't bothered by Connor's beta. I'd already figured out he was an honorable man who wouldn't hurt me unless I hurt Connor. Which I wasn't going to do.

Shannon smirked and stepped further away from Connor as his wolf bled back into his eyes. I didn't care. I was incensed that the boy I'd grown up with had turned into such a cold and callous being; one with no remorse for what he allowed to happen to people weaker than himself. "This situation is your fault as Prime. You should have controlled all the shifters in this place, not just those in your own pack. I get that life hasn't been easy since you were imprisoned here; that you gave your wolf more power and control out of necessity. But my life hasn't been a bed of roses since I lost Lyss and Rawson, either. Or you." I jabbed my fingers into his hard chest again, wanting to touch him even if it was just that small contact. My eyes burned, but I blinked rapidly, refusing to let him see my tears. "I heard them *shoot you*, for the Mother's sake! I believed you'd died, Connor, how do you think that felt? That day was the worst of my life, I lost you, Lyss *and* Rawson. Gods, I've seen enough death and depraved behaviours since that day, to last me a lifetime. But allowing the strong to overpower the weak for power and sex, is a low I never imagined you, of all people, would sink to."

A snarl curled his top lip and he leaned forward until heat rolled from him across my skin. I swallowed hard, remembering the power I'd once felt in that body when I'd touched him, how sweet and warm his tongue had been as it traced my lips. His taste... I bit back a groan as memories assailed me.

"Oh, I've stooped to far worse than letting others fight their own battles, Firecracker. You have no idea what I'm capable of now." His voice was a low growl, one that dripped with dominance and warning. His hot breath fanned my cheek and I shivered, my reaction to his closeness was something instinctive that I had no hope of stopping. My wolf surged forward and she peeked curiously out at this unfamiliar commanding presence. Connor had always affected me, but now he had this edge of danger to him, which lit my insides, stirring her lust, too. I pulled my hand away from where my palm now rested against his chest and clenched my fists as I resisted my need to grab him, and wrap myself around his powerful body. I shoved back at my wolf until she receded, grumbling discontentedly. When the rough bristle on his jaw brushed my soft cheek, I inhaled sharply, my reaction impossible to hide.

He straightened, and I watched as Connor won the battle of wills with his wolf. Blue soon consumed that obsidian gaze again, which dropped slowly over my body, lingering on the curve of my breasts and the bare skin of my flat stomach. I tried not to react, but I couldn't hide the goosebumps that shivered across my skin. It was like he'd touched me, trailing his fingers over my flesh.

"The weak die in this place. Only the strong survive—and even then they must repeatedly battle to win, and keep winning if they want to live." I opened my mouth to ask what he meant, but he interrupted me. "You need to stay out of trouble, Firecracker."

My brow creased. He'd used my nickname again, the one he'd given me as a teenager. My temper had been fiery then, too. Did that mean he accepted me as, well, as me? I offered him a shaky smile, trying to infuse some sass in my voice. "I always stay out of trouble, Prime."

He cocked a brow, and a smirk curled the corner of his generous mouth. "Really? Then trouble just finds you, does it?"

I shrugged. "I guess so."

His smile widened. "I seem to remember it always did." He stepped closer again, so I stepped back, trying to keep in control of this situation. "You've got quite a reputation already, you know. That means you've become a challenge to the males in here. Join my pack. It will offer you protection. If you belong to me, no one will dare hurt you again."

"That's a generous offer, Connor, but, just like Shannon, I prefer to have choices, and I don't fancy being at the beck and call of any male in your pack—even you." I turned to walk away.

"Ember, wait." Demand infused Connor's voice. Of course, I ignored it. I didn't respond well to demands, not even from him. Beside, I was quickly losing control of my urge to give in to anything he said, and no matter how much I loved him, I didn't know him anymore, or what he was capable of now.

"See ya later, Connor." I wiggled my fingers in farewell and kept walking. I released the breath I'd been holding when he just let me go.

CHAPTER 6

onnor

Owen barged into my cell. "She's in trouble again."

"Jesus! Doesn't she ever stop?" My heart pounded against my ribs as I curled my hands into fists. Ember had become the bane of my life. I still hadn't worked out why I'd given in so easily to her demands to protect the submissive shifters in gen pop. Ever since that day, almost a week ago now, she'd fought off gangs of males determined to prove that they didn't plan to respect my new rule and that, as the catalyst, Ember would pay for it. The body count was going up by the day, from her and my brothers, who were now bound to uphold my rule. Owen had also taken to protecting her even though I hadn't asked him to. Part of me was jealous, and hated that he wanted to, and part of me was grateful.

"Let her deal with it herself. She managed well enough last time, and you're showing too much interest in her. It's making things worse by painting a target on her back." Stone's eyes were hard.

"No." I flashed a dark look his way. True, Ember had managed so far. The last time I'd seen her, she'd had cuts and bruises but no broken bones, but that wouldn't last, and we all knew it. Her ending up abused, and likely dead was only a matter of time. My gut clenched at that thought. I had been so conflicted since she'd shown back up in my world and I wasn't handling it well, I knew it, and so did my brothers.

"Why not just mark her, then?"

I ignored Stone's question and stormed after Owen. I didn't know how I felt about branding Ember with my pack mark. I inhaled deeply through my nose and curled my top lip at myself. Gods, I was pathetic. I didn't want her out in gen pop unmarked and vulnerable, but neither did I want her carrying my pack mark which meant any male in my pack could claim her. I curled my fists, trying to control the urge to hit something. Deep down, I knew what I wanted, but I wasn't ready to admit it, not even to myself.

We strode along the corridors and into the food hall. The guards had their weapons pointed at a group of fighting people. My brows shot up. It looked like a riot. I couldn't tell what the hell was going on. There was food and trays scattered over the benches and floor. Lionel was fighting two males, easily holding them back, and a girl with spiky short hair and five other women, were pummeling the hell out of two males and a female on the ground.

My stomach clenched, tensing almost as hard as my fists. Ember was fighting three males, who looked to be taking turns attacking her. Just like the wolves they were, they were working together and wearing her down until she was so exhausted they could move in for the kill.

My wolf stirred as Ember took a kick to the ribs. She screeched, the sound full of pain, but still kept fighting. She'd always had an indomitable spirit, and four years later, she was more stubborn than ever. Her determination to win reached me even from where I stood across the hall. My wolf growled, confusion clouding our connection. He wanted to protect Ember, yet the wolf he had claimed as his mate was dead.

I had no doubts anymore that this was Ember. Her soul called to mine just as it always had, pulling at the darkness that I hid away from the world. And that glorious red hair she had tried to hide was too visible to me now. Every time I saw her, I made an effort not to grimace at the strange mix of fiery red next to the bright blonde dye. It was a bizarre combination of colours. I wanted to ask why she'd dyed it, but I hadn't plucked up the courage to actually have a normal conversation with her. She was the only person in the world who terrified me—for so many reasons.

I inhaled deeply and was hit with the metallic scent of her blood. I'd know it anywhere. I'd grown up knowing it. My wolf might be confused over her wolf spirit, but his cold predatory attention fixed on the males fighting Ember. He remembered her blood scent, too. I snarled. It was a sound born of both wolf and man. Pulling from my wolf, I gathered my power, ready to blast every single person hard enough to force them to their knees.

"Don't." Stone stood in front of me, his grey eyes glinting. "You'll make this worse for her, and you know it."

I swallowed hard, knowing he was right. If I did this; if I protected her and made it obvious I cared for her, I'd put a bigger target on her back. She had to deal with this herself, or I had to leave and let my brothers step in. My fists clenched and my body tensed, rivulets of sweat running down my spine as I wrestled control back from my wolf.

Stone's eyes narrowed on my struggle. "Dammit! I knew she'd fuck with your head." His shoulders slumped. Sighing, he squared them again.

I frowned. He was right, she *was* fucking with my head—and my heart, and everything else. Not sure what to say, I ignored him and fixed my gaze on Ember. She twisted and jammed her shoulder into one opponent and threw him to the ground. Not giving him time to recover, she slammed an axe kick down onto his chest. I heard his sternum crack, from where I stood. She had always been a good fighter. Her life on the streets had instilled an unbreakable survival instinct in her, and whatever her life had entailed since I'd last seen her had cemented it. Now, fighting viciously and without mercy, she was a sight to see.

I tried to keep my cool facade when really, seeing her dispense her brand of justice was the hottest thing I'd ever witnessed. I wanted to give in to my urge to bring every single person in the hall to their knees and storm over there, grab her and plant a kiss on that smart mouth right in front of all these males. And I'd do far more than just kiss her, if she let me. My wolf snarled. *Fine. But you'll admit she's ours eventually.* He receded, sulking at my words.

I didn't take my eyes off Ember. If it looked like she might lose, no amount of common sense was going to stop me from ending her attackers. I needn't have worried, within two minutes the fight was over. Ember spun, and her boot heel connected with her last attacker's jaw. He dropped to the ground like a stone, out cold. Lionel threw his opponent across the room, the body slamming into the wall and landing in a heap. And the women, their wolves obviously riding high, had ripped the throats out of their attackers with what looked like their teeth and fingernails. They all straightened and moved to stand in front of Ember, blood staining their faces and hands.

I hid my smirk at the defiant look on Ember's face, aware that all eyes were on me as I prowled forward. She rolled her eyes but kept her burning emerald gaze on me as she kicked one of the men under the chin when he tried to get up. He fell back unconscious.

"Hey, they started it!" Her chin tilted up and she folded her arms across her breasts, which only succeeded in pushing them up and making her cleavage even more mouth watering. My dick stirred, and my fingers twitched. Gods, I wanted to touch her so bad.

I forced a dark scowl on my face, hiding a grin at her sass. My attention rolled over the dead and the injured. I indicated the group of women. "It seems you've made friends."

My wolf still refused to acknowledge Ember. I didn't force him to, it would only make him more resistant next time. Instead, I used my own dominance to stare down those who had helped her. Adrenaline and the thrill of a kill made them brave enough to hold my gaze. I patiently forced each one to lower their eyes—even Lionel, who I could tell didn't have a submissive bone in his body. I wondered why he submitted so quickly, but that was a question for another time.

Blood welled at the corner of Ember's mouth. I fisted my hands, fighting an overwhelming urge to wipe it away and lave her split lip. My saliva alone wouldn't heal her, but my wolf's could. With a grumble, he lifted his head, watching from behind my eyes. For once he was willing to let me take the reins. "Are you injured, other than that lip?" My voice was tight, sharper than I would like, but the scent of her blood made me want to rip out her enemies' hearts.

Her green eyes flashed. "I'm fine!" But I saw the way her posture hunched and her breath came in quick, short pants.

I stepped on the man at our feet, not caring that he groaned as my weight pushed him into the floor. It was his choice to attack Ember. He deserved worse than a beating. I leaned in close to her ear, resisting the urge to wrap my fingers around that toned waist and pull her against me. "No, Firecracker, you're not. Now, do you want every single enemy you've made in this place to see how injured you are and come for you while you're vulnerable, or do you want to take a moment to recover in private?" She bit her bottom lip, and I ground my teeth as I waited. She'd always been stubborn, but maybe foolhardiness was another trait she'd picked up these last years. "Come with me." I turned my back on her, intending to take her to my cell.

Behind me, Stone exhaled sharply. "For fuck's sake!"

I turned back. Ember had disregarded my order. She stood in front of the short haired woman checking her friend for injuries.

"Ember!" I released a growl. Didn't she realise she was undermining my authority by ignoring me? I really didn't want to have to punish her in front of everyone.

"You'd better go," said the girl, unable to hold my gaze.

Ember's attention flicked to me. "No, Charlie. Not until I make sure you're all okay." She left Charlie and walked to Lionel. As soon she touched the other male, she sealed her fate.

I stormed towards her, my wolf rising as her fingers rested on his skin.

Lionel's gaze narrowed. "Ember..."

Her eyes widened as she caught sight of me, and he caught her as she stumbled back over a fallen body.

I snarled viciously, my wolf in full view in my eyes. I hit Lionel with a blast of dominance. He staggered and raised his hands but didn't lower his eyes. Instead, he straightened his spine, and his eyes flashed with the amber gaze of his lion. "Hurt her and I'll find a way to kill you."

"I have no intention of hurting her. Now get your hands off her." I resisted the urge to force him to his knees, or punch his lights out, and shifted my attention to Ember. "You'll come with me right now, or I don't care who's watching. I'll throw you over my shoulder and carry you out."

She swallowed hard, but her nostrils flared.

I grinned evilly, knowing that my words were a challenge to her independent side. She wouldn't ignore me now.

"You can't do that!"

I took another step closer. "Yes, Em, I can. You're injured, and you won't best me in a fight, you know that. If you disobey me again, and make me look weak in front of these people, I will absolutely throw you over my shoulder."

Her teeth worried her lower lip. That reaction was her tell. She wasn't totally sure of me yet, and I had no intention of letting her work me out. That bit of fear about who I was and what I was capable of gave me an advantage. Her eyes darted to Lionel as if looking to him for support. He shook his head and sighed, his mouth in a flat line.

"Too long!" She needed to be away from the lion shifter.

"What? No!"

I covered the two steps between us. I had over a foot on her in height and weighed far more. No matter how hard her punch landed on my jaw, it wasn't going to stop me. I rolled with it, then grabbed her wrist and pushed my shoulder into her stomach hoisting her up. I wouldn't hurt her—ever—but neither she, nor the rest of this scum needed to know that. I kept her weight adjusted so my shoulder rested in her stomach not the broken ribs she'd tried so hard to hide from me.

Santa Cruz stood close by with his chest puffed out and a smirk on his stupid face.

I walked right by him. The north alpha hadn't been challenged since Ember had knocked him out cold, but he'd sent people to bring her down this week, that meant he was now on my shit list, and I'd make his life as difficult and painful as possible.

I ignored Ember's furious screams and the discomfort as she gouged strips of skin off my back. I really didn't want to cause her more pain, but she had to realise she couldn't ignore me without consequences. "If I put you down, are you going to behave?" I grated between my clenched teeth once we'd left the hall. Bloody Hell, she was as fiery as a hellcat!

"Yes!"

I grinned, and lowered her gently to her feet but didn't let go of her wrist. The fingers of her other hand curled into a fist. I raised my brows, ignoring Owen, D and Stone who had flanked me, watching my back like always.

"You said you'd behave." I let go of her wrist, but carefully touched her clenched fists with my fingers.

She yanked her hands away and wrapped them around her torso. "You're a total dick! What the hell did you do that for?" She panted, holding her ribs.

"Come with me, Ember, and I'll explain."

Owen and my brothers slowly stepped behind her, obviously worried she might run.

Ignoring them, she glared at me and didn't move. I swallowed my growl at her challenge. "Please," I said, softening my voice.

Owen raised his brows at me. Stone shook his head. And D grinned. I ignored their censure.

"Fine. But do that to me again, and I'll find a way to remove your balls."

I didn't bother to hide my grin. "I'd expect no less from you, Firecracker."

Still seething, she followed me to my cell.

I opened the metal door and gestured for her to enter. When Owen and Stone made as if to come in, I barred the door with my body. "No, wait out here."

Both of them gave me an incredulous stare, but Stone's eyes turned icy as his attention fell on Ember. I didn't care about his suspicion, I owed him no explanation. As soon as the door clicked shut, Ember launched herself at me. Her open palm stung on my cheek.

"Hey! Stop that!" I growled and grabbed her wrist when she aimed another slap at me. My wolf stirred as hers surfaced in her eyes. Not amber like the wolf spirit she had housed when we were young, but a deep sapphire blue. My heart pounded, my blood heating as I spun her against the wall and held her wrists over her head. She screeched with anger as I overpowered her with my body, leaning my weight against her and stopping her struggles for freedom.

"Get off me!" She twisted and bucked, turning the friction between us into something I couldn't ignore. Heat surged through my blood.

I half-growled, half-laughed, and twisted my hips sideways as she tried to knee me in the balls. "Gods damn it, Firecracker, stop attacking me and I'll let you go." Still she fought. "Ember! Stop it, please!"

Surprisingly, she did. Her chest rose and fell rapidly and there was a sheen of sweat over her brow. I cursed myself, I'd brought her here to heal her, not cause her more pain. Without hesitation, I licked her bottom lip where it was split and bruised. The sweetness of her blood exploded across my tongue, and I clenched my jaw to hold back my groan. I wanted to do it again and again. I shifted my hips away so that the evidence of her effect on me wasn't so obvious.

Her body stiffened at the touch of my tongue. "Whoa, what are you doing?" Despite her question, there was a breathy quality to her voice.

I ensnared her wide green gaze with mine. "Healing you." *Come on, man, step up,* I beseeched my wolf. He grumbled, and though he hadn't really settled down since we'd scented Ember's blood, he still refused to help.

Ember shook her head. "No, you can't do that."

I dropped my forehead against hers. "I can, Ember. I'm the Alpha Prime. I've taken the power of all the alpha's I've killed in this place; and I have killed many. That means I can use my wolf's power to at least partially heal you." It wasn't a complete lie.

She shook her head again, confirming that she had no idea of the real reason I could heal her. "No one I've ever met, except that bastard Walker, has had the ability to heal injuries like that."

I cocked a brow, my stomach tensing at the mention of that faerie bastard. It still pissed me off that he had healed her, when as far as I knew, only mates could heal each other. "How many wolf shifters, or should I say, alphas, have you been around these last four years?"

She blew a breath out and stared at the ceiling.

I smiled when she shrugged, and a flush stained her cheeks.

"I'll take that as none, then?" Her silence confirmed it—no shifters, and definitely no alphas. My muscles unwound a little, her lack of experience with our own kind made my lie more believable. We might have a long history, but we had only kissed once and though it had turned my world upside down, we'd never discussed being mated. I'd stayed away from her because she'd been young and I'd stupidly believed I should give her time to experience life without me getting all possessive and protective of her. I trailed my nose up her neck and jaw to the soft skin below her earlobe, inhaling her warmth and smokey scent. Lust slammed through me, my heart racing.

"I can heal you, Ember." My voice was low and gravelly, but I didn't try and hide it, instead I smiled as her breathing hitched. "I've been here for four years. Doherty wants a prison full of strong alphas and shifters who can earn him money, and he needed an alpha strong enough to keep the inmates in line. I've done that, and I'm stronger than I've ever been. Let me help you." I released her wrists and cupped her cheek, revelling in the warmth and softness of her skin beneath my hand. "I can't believe you're actually here. Doherty really did give me the head of your wolf, that's why I thought you were dead."

Her brow furrowed and her eyes shone wetly as they searched mine. Holding my breath, I waited, hoping she would explain how that could happen. She swallowed hard, then tentatively reached out and mirrored my hold. Her skin was calloused, but her touch was warm and a thousand times more potent than I expected. For so long, I'd dreamed about her silky skin against mine, trying not to let those dreams destroy me in the darkness of the night. I'd wanted to touch her, to kiss her, to be inside her; but wanting something so impossible had sent both me and my wolf into a dark tailspin of anger and cruelty; one that I'd had no reason to break—until now.

"How did you survive without your wolf?" I inhaled deeply, my mind reeling at the other spirit I sensed inside her. "I can scent another wolf inside you, the one that killed you, that's why I didn't know it was you when I first saw you." I rubbed my thumb gently across the corner of her mouth. "How the hell did it kill your wolf and then end up as yours?" My voice shook, so many emotions swirling inside me, it was hard to think straight.

Ember's face darkened and she tried to push me away. I could resist but I didn't want to force her into being near me. Gritting my teeth, and hiding my disappointment, I dropped my hand and stepped away, giving her some room.

She took a steadying breath, her eyes becoming unfocused. "That day in the woods, I ran like you told me to, but there were too many of Doherty's men and I didn't stand a chance of escape, so I stayed in my wolf form and hid inside a rotten tree trunk. I was there for two days with nothing to eat or drink..." Her voice broke and she squeezed her eyes shut. "I thought you and Rawson were dead. I heard gunshots and was sure they'd killed you."

My jaw ached as I ground my teeth together. I hated that I hadn't been able to save her that day. "I'm sorry I failed you, Em." What else was there to say? No words could change what had happened to us all back then, or since.

A weak smile curled her lips. "None of it was your fault." For a moment she was silent, and I didn't push. "Doherty played games. He wanted me to think he'd pulled his men back. Twice they tried to lure me out before they actually left. I hid for hours, but it made no difference, he'd sent a lone wolf after me. It laid in wait for nearly two days in that wood. When I eventually left my hiding place, it attacked. I was in my wolf form." She blinked, the skin between her brows creasing. "I don't know what happened. There was excruciating pain in my neck as she clamped her jaws on my neck. And blood, so much blood."

I swallowed hard as her face paled and she fisted her trembling hands. I really wanted to comfort her, hating that she was so upset. I wrapped my fingers around her hand, gently but insistently pushing at her fingers, uncurling her fist until I could hold her hand. She released a shuddering breath. "And then I was standing in a kind of in between world watching my wolf die." She avoided my eyes, staring at the wall over my shoulder.

There was something else, something she wasn't telling me. I could hear the elevation in her heart rate—and she had never been able to look me in the eye and lie.

"What happened then?"

She shrugged. "I have no idea..."

I raised my brows. "Yes, you do, Em, but it's okay. I understand you don't trust me yet. Four years is a long time." I let go of her hand and she sighed, shaking her head.

"No, really I don't know. It's happened before, but it's like I'm falling, and then I die."

My brows dipped, my stomach tensing to rock. "What do you mean, *you die?*"

She rubbed her palms over her face, and then looked me in the eye. "I mean just that. Your wolf is right, my wolf, the one I have now, did kill my first wolf. I knew she was bleeding out and that it was fatal and just like when Perversion slit my throat, Fire came to life. She saved me, but she couldn't save my wolf. Somehow, Fire pulled the wolf spirit from my killer and gifted it to me as my first wolf was called back to the Mother Wolf."

Now it was my turn to shake my head. "This makes no sense. How? How can any of this happen?"

She sighed heavily and began to pace the room. I watched her, knowing I never would have believed her story at all, except her wolf spirit was totally different.

"What happened to its human counterpart? Our wolves can't live without us, and vice versa."

"I killed her human host."

I frowned, my lips pressed together in a tight line.

"Listen, Connor, I'm not lying. I've no idea how it happened. Magic, maybe? Fire's always been part of me, you know that. I just...I have no idea how she works, or what she really is." She inhaled, wincing as her chest expanded. Her gaze shot to the door, the skin on the bridge of her nose creasing, even as her arm came up protectively to hold her ribs. Stone was on the other side, and he was not a pure shifter. Had Ember figured out his heritage? There were other supernatural forces and creatures in this world, which was why the SBI existed, but Ember had seen very few of them at the academy. And only fae had even more powerful hearing than shifters. What had she been through since I'd last seen her, that she recognised a fae and immediately mistrusted him?

Perhaps changing the subject from the death of her past wolf was best. Neither of us knew what her Fire was, we never had. And demanding she reveal her secrets about the last four years would only drive us apart again—or would it? Oh, fuck it...I needed to know.

"Where have you been, Em? Who did you hide with that Doherty never got wind that you were alive?"

She limped up to the wall and leaned back against it before tipping her head backwards, a bead of sweat running down her temple. "It doesn't matter," she said on an exhale. Her face dropped, her eyes closing, but they shot open when she coughed, her brows pulled tight.

"You're wrong. If it concerns you, it matters." I stepped closer, trying to ignore the way heat from her body bathed mine. I wiped away the bead of sweat from her temple with my forefinger. "Let me help you. You're in pain."

Her eyes narrowed, and her jaw clenched as she seemed to battle her need to heal against her need to be independent. Her heartbeat was erratic and fast. I wanted it to be from being so near me, but I guessed it was more from her pain.

"Okay, but don't think this means I'm joining your pack."

"We'll see, Firecracker." I smiled and placed my hands gently on her ribs. Using my fingers, I carefully explored her chest wall to figure out where the worst breaks were. The more bruised skin and crunchy, loose bones I found, the harder it was to control my fury. I wanted to hunt down the fuckers that had survived that fight and rip them limb from limb. I tried hard to bury my instincts, but my wolf raised its head and peered out at the girl we'd always tried to protect. He was unsettled at being so close to Ember again, and he didn't understand what had happened to her wolf. Neither did I, but we both wanted her to be safe. I sighed with relief when he gifted me a gentle wave of power. Holding her green gaze, I placed my palms over the breaks.

She inhaled sharply, but whether that was from my touch or from pain, I didn't know.

"Sorry," I murmured.

"You didn't hurt me," she whispered.

My heart missed a beat. My touch, then.

Closing my eyes, I pushed a little of my wolf's power into her body, searching out the breaks and bruising, and gently coaxing her body to heal. I'd used my power to dominate and destroy for so long, it was hard to focus on such a delicate task, especially with her petite body under my hands. My fingers wrapped right around her stomach and ribs, she was so slim. I swallowed against my dry mouth; touching her was messing with my self-control.

She didn't seem to realise it, but I wasn't able to heal just anyone with my 'alpha vibes' as she called it—I was only able to heal her, only my soul mate. Gods, I'd loved her for so long. I'd never even wanted anyone else. No one else could ever come close to my Firecracker; I'd walk into the fires of Hell for her if she needed me to. And she was here. Alive.

After I discovered each break and healed it, I stayed where I was, not willing to relinquish my hold on her warm skin.

Her breathing remained elevated, her heart beating under my right palm, even as the soft swell of her breast brushed against my thumb. She shuffled a little, and the weight of that swell rested even more against my hand. I groaned quietly. I really didn't want to let go, far from it.

"Connor?" she whispered, resting her hands on my biceps, making my blood burn hotter.

I slowly opened my eyes to find myself staring directly into her emerald gaze. My gut twisted at the emotion that I saw there; the same grief that had looked back at me for the last four years. I'd missed her so much, and now she was here, right in front of me, tears in her eyes too. Silence stretched between us, the air heavy with emotion. Since I'd admitted she was alive, my heart had started to repair itself, but my mind feared she could be taken away again any second. My grip tightened, my big hands dwarfing her tiny waist. My eyes stung. I wouldn't survive losing her again.

Her hand left my arm and cupped my jaw. I clenched my teeth, trying not to groan. Gods, I wanted to kiss her, to prove to myself she really was here.

"I missed you so much. I'm so sorry Doherty used my wolf against you. I had no idea..." Her whispered words brushed my lips, making it harder to hold back from her.

I lifted one hand from her waist and cupped her jaw, mirroring her touch. My thumb brushed her soft skin, my nail growing. "Ember, join my pack. Please. It's not safe for you in gen pop, no matter how good a fighter you are. Let me protect you." I wanted more than just a pack mark on her skin. I wanted my claiming mark on her neck. But this was all too new, too raw for us both. I didn't know what she wanted, or how she felt about me. It was obvious she had grieved for me, as I had for her, but she didn't trust me yet, and I didn't blame her; not after what she'd seen happen, or possibly been subjected to, in the prison I was supposed to rule. I swallowed a growl at the thought of what could have happened to her. She was right, Lyss would have been ashamed of me.

Her face flushed and she shuffled back up against the wall, putting a little space between us, though she didn't remove her hands from my arm or my jaw. That tell-tale flush to her skin almost destroyed my self-control. I let my hand slide higher on to the gentle curve of her breast, inhaling sharply as a bolt of lust shook me. Her pupils dilated, and her breathing hitched. Holding her gaze, I moved my thumb, brushing it lightly over her nipple. It's peak hardened through the cup of her bra under that light touch, so I did it again, growling low in my throat. Gods, this woman could destroy me, she just didn't know it yet.

She swallowed hard. "Connor, don't."

"Why not?" Like hers, my voice was husky, and I did nothing to hide the erection that I was now sporting. I wanted her to know what she did to me.

Her gaze dropped to the bulge in my jeans.

I smiled, though her attention only made it more difficult to resist her. I brushed her jaw with my fingers and unable to hold back any longer, leaned in, following the trail of my fingers with my lips. "Gods, I missed you, Ember, I thought you were dead."

"Connor..."

The sound of my name whispered from her lips undid me almost as much as the taste of her. My cock throbbed, but I pulled away from her a little. "Damn, Em, I'm finding it hard to even understand how you are here, but you are, and all I want is to show you how much you mean to me."

I placed small, gentle kisses along her jaw.

Her head fell back, but I could feel her tense when I pushed closer. "Stop." Her voice held a breathless note that made it difficult to believe that was what she really wanted. "I'm not ready for this; not yet. And I'm not a belonging. I won't be owned by anyone—even you."

Her words sent a shot of ice through me. "No?" I growled, looking intently into her eyes, the shifter in me not happy with her words. "Why not belong to my pack—or me?" I couldn't keep the hurt from my voice. Prime or not, being rejected by my mate ripped at my heart all over again. "I would never try and control you. Or treat you badly."

"Because my life hasn't exactly been straightforward. And I want to be free to make my own choices."

"Em, joining my pack is not about me owning you, it's a simple matter of survival." I lightly scraped my clawed thumb nail under her jaw, tempted to mark her anyway.

She jerked back, her voice a harsh whisper. "Don't!"

I tilted my head, trying not to let her see how much her continued rejection hurt. "I don't want you in such danger out there, not when I can protect you as one of my own."

She sighed, but her eyes softened. "Connor, I missed you so much, and I'm having problems just believing you're actually here in front of me. Give me some time to process all this. Right now, I can't be just one of your pack, and risk one of your alphas coming for me."

My body tensed. This situation was totally my fault. I'd let pack males claim females, and I'd not given a shit if it was consensual or not—until now. None of my brothers would ever consider claiming her for himself, not now that they knew what she meant to me; and any other bastard stupid enough to try would end up dead.

"They wouldn't do that. You'd be mine to protect, Em..."

She sighed and briefly closed her eyes. "I don't need your protection, I haven't for years. I can take care of myself."

"No, you can't! That's why you just ended up with five broken ribs!" Snapping wouldn't help, but I couldn't help the surge of frustration at her unwillingness to admit any vulnerability.

Her mouth flattened into a tight line. I was right, and she knew it too, but as always I'd pressed her stubborn button.

"What about Shannon?" Her mouth flattened into a straight line.

I softened my voice in an attempt to reason with her. "Em, Shannon means nothing to me. And fighting for your life is okay for a while, but eventually someone will get you on your own..."

She snarled, interrupting me. "Then I'll kill them."

"Maybe, but you can't kill everyone in here, nor can you fight off an organised group. Those males were attacking you like they would prey; they were weakening you and biding their time until you were too exhausted to fight any more; then they would have gone for the kill."

"I know that!" Flames sparked in her eyes.

My muscles tensed. *Shit! I'm handling this all wrong!*

I let her go and stepped back, giving her some breathing room. Those flames only showed up when she was emotionally at her limit. And I think we were both hitting that mark. "Fine, I'll drop it for now. But you must know that I won't let any other male touch you. I can give you twenty four hours to consider my offer." I forced out my next words, knowing I couldn't leave her vulnerable even if she hated me for it. "But if you don't make a sensible decision, you'll be marked whether you like it or not." I made myself walk away from her and flung the door open.

Stone stared at me from the hallway.

"Fetch Reed and Myles."

Stone's jaw clenched and his eyes flashed.

He was right, I'd tell me to go fuck myself, too, but I held his gaze. With a growl, he spun on his heel and stormed away towards our brothers' cell. Owen sauntered into the room. He smiled at Ember, studying the way she moved, the way she paced the room, her posture upright with no sign of her broken ribs. His eyes widened and he flicked his gaze back and forth from her to me several times. I glared at him in warning. He nodded his understanding, but looked at Ember in awe, as well he might. She was the one thing we all spent our lives looking for—my soulmate.

Ember stopped pacing and glowered at me. "You can't just mark me against my will. If you do, I'll never forgive you."

My gut twisted at that thought, but her safety came first. "Oh, yes, I can, and will if I have to. I can do anything I want in this place, and as good as you are at fighting, I'm better." I prowled closer to her. Unsurprisingly, she didn't concede or let me push her back. My blood stirred at her defiance, shooting straight to my groin, but I didn't push my luck, knowing she'd retaliate if I touched her now. I smirked as her pupils dilated at my closeness. Seeing that, I dared to lift a hand and gently brush a lock of her half blonde, half vibrant red hair from her cheek. "But I don't want to fight you. I want you to come to me because you want to. I will do what I have to, though, to keep you safe. Besides, you'll forgive me eventually; you always do." I smiled. "It will be worth your anger just to know you'll be safer as part of a pack."

Ember seemed at a loss for words, looking at me like she had no idea how to respond to my remarks or my touch. I kept my gaze on her and wrapped my big hands around her ribs. Again, she let me, her eyes held captive by mine, or was it the other way around? I hid how much it meant to me that she let me touch her and kept my attention on her face as I carefully increased the pressure. She didn't wince, so I let my hands slide slowly away, immediately missing the warmth of her skin. At least her pain seemed to have eased. I hadn't fully remedied her lip, not wanting it to appear too obvious to others that I'd healed her. Any shifter who knew about life bonds and alpha matings would know what it meant, even if Ember didn't.

Shaking her head, she began pacing again.

"Is there something else you wanted, Firecracker?" I infused enough amused arrogance in my voice that she did a double take. I pointed at the door, and raised my brows, knowing it would bring out her feistiness. "You can go now. Come and find me when you're ready to be marked. Then we can fight whenever you like. It'll be fun getting to know you again." Unable to help myself, I dropped my gaze down to the enticing dip between her breasts. Heat shot straight to my groin, and I deliberately raised my eyes back to hers, trying not to let her see the effect she had on me.

Her hands fisted, her chin lifting defiantly. "What makes you think I want to get to know you again, you arrogant arse!?"

I grinned. "Yep, I am arrogant, because I can be." Despite the fact that she looked like she wanted to slap me, I stepped forward and leaned closer, lowering my voice. "And your body tells me you want to get to know me again. As do these flushed cheeks and the most beautiful eyes I've ever seen." Her face heated and her mouth gaped open. Damn, part of me wanted her to slap me, just so I could have the pleasure of subduing her by catching her wrist and kissing the hell out of her.

"W-what?"

I smirked at her stuttering response. It wasn't often Ember was at a loss for words. I decided to push her buttons a little more. "I'm telling you that you can leave, unless you'd like me to mark that lovely neck right now?"

"No!" And she stumbled back, past Stone, Reed and Myles. Her shoulder caught Stone hard in the chest as she turned her back on me.

"Hey! You wanna watch where you're going, she wolf?" he yelled after her.

She stuck her middle finger in the air, but didn't look back.

I laughed. *Firecracker* fit her perfectly. She'd always been feisty, and I loved it when she challenged me, but it was as if she really didn't give a shit about her own safety. My stomach sank and my grin faded. Well, I cared about her safety, more than she or anyone knew, and there was no way I was going to let her get herself killed out of stubbornness.

"Tomorrow, Firecracker!" I yelled. "You know you need help to stay safe!"

She just kept walking away, not deigning to answer me. I happily watched her, enjoying the sight of her fine arse swaying until she disappeared. But it took everything in me to let her go, even though I knew I'd see her again soon.

CHAPTER 7

onnor

"WHAT HOLD DOES that woman have over you, Connor? You suddenly changed the rules after just one request from her; rules that have never bothered you before. Who gives a shit about the weakest of this place? Doherty's only going to use them for his weird-assed programme anyway, and we all know they aren't walking out of here. What difference does their honour make to us? We need to keep training the strongest; that's where our attention should be."

"Shut up, Stone. I have changed the rules, so get over it. Your job is to enforce them, not question my judgement."

"Yeah? Well, what if I don't agree with your judgement? Gen pop isn't our fight. We need to concentrate on getting the next batch of fighters ready for the ring. It's only twelve weeks until the next games. And if we're not ready, or Doherty doesn't like our standard of fighter, it isn't you who suffers is it, Connor? No, it's us…"

I tensed at the accusation and resentment in his voice. Was Stone blaming me for this fucked up situation we found ourselves in? Jesus, I had always tried to protect my brothers from the suffering Doherty and the warden could inflict on them. Didn't they know that?

I glanced at the others, all of whom were now in the room with us. They dropped their attention to the floor. Did they resent me, too? I pulled myself up to my full height and towered over Stone who looked unrepentant, accusation in every line of his face. Deep down, I didn't blame him for his anger, but enough was enough. If my brothers fell apart, my dominion over the other shifters would fall with them, and this place would turn into a bloodbath. The inmates would rebel, and I'd have to kill over and over to gain any kind of order back, just like I had in the beginning. And I wasn't stupid enough to think Rawson or the men in this room, would be allowed to survive unscathed through my loss of control. Didn't Stone realise I was as loyal to them as they were to me? That I killed and sacrificed others to keep them as safe as I could from the warden and Doherty? "Do you think the fact that you haven't been shoved in that ring for the last three years is a coincidence, Stone?"

"I don't know, Connor. But maybe I'd rather fight than have the threat of pissing my pants hang over me when that red-eyed bastard presses his little button, or than having my free will taken while I'm shoved in a room with females who pay to fuck me."

I pulled back my wolf. The things the warden made us do as punishment for what he saw as my offences were totally wrong, and no better than what happened in gen pop. It was one of the reasons it had seemed pointless to stop that kind of thing. The people in gen pop would eventually be rented out to the upstanding members of the world's rich and famous, no matter what. The wealthy paid exorbitant amounts to do whatever they wanted to a shifter at the warden's *games*. Male or female, anyone not fighting in the rings was at risk. And if the females survived the entertainment rooms, they would ultimately end up in the warden's science wing.

I understood Stone's anger, I really did, but I couldn't allow his challenge to go unanswered. I'd tolerated enough attitude from him and couldn't afford to let his bitterness poison my relationship with my other brothers.

I spun so quickly, Stone had no hope of avoiding me. My hand gripped his throat, and I slammed him into the wall, quickly pinning him in place with my forearm across his neck and his feet dangling off the floor. "I do what I do to keep you out of the death rings." I snarled into his face. "Because you are my brother. But if you want to die, I can easily arrange it, right here, right now." I shoved harder, my wolf agreeing our brother needed to be reminded who was more powerful.

Despite Stone's attempts to punch my belly and face or to kick me, he could not free himself. Lack of oxygen got to him quickly, and his attempts became lethargic and weak.

"Right now, Stone, tell me, do you want to die?" His eyes grew dull, but he managed to shake his head. I loosened my hold very slightly, enough to let him breathe. "Then don't *ever* question my loyalty to you and our brothers, and don't question me about Ember. She gets my protection, that means *your* protection, whether she wants it or not."

His eyes focused over my shoulder, at least he had the presence of mind not to meet my gaze. I loosened my hold a little more, seeing he wanted to speak and willing to explain myself a little to him to get him back on my side.

"This kind of reaction is why you need to distance yourself from her, Prime. Every male in this place can see how you run to her every time she gets in a fight. You're protecting her and she's not even a member of this pack. She's the girl from the prison before, isn't she?"

I grunted an acknowledgment.

"Then tell us the real reason why you want to protect her; maybe I'll be more likely to comply."

I pushed on his throat again. "You'll comply because I tell you to." But at a look from Owen, I tried to temper my response and took a breath. "She's my friend…"

"Friend? Cut the bullshit!" He panted against my hold on his neck. "You've never fought your wolf back for anyone else."

I couldn't just let that pass. "Before we go any farther, you watch your fucking mouth before I shut it for you. Are we clear?" Once he nodded, I relented—a little. "Now, what do you mean?" Stone might be an arsehole, but at least he wasn't frightened to tell me what was on his mind, even now when I'd just threatened to end his life. The thing was, he was usually right.

"Your wolf's been dominant for years, but now you've suddenly taken control again. You might think you're fooling the others with the excuse of doing your rounds, or seeing the other alphas, or whatever bullshit excuse you come up with, but what you're doing is going to find her to make sure she's still breathing. And if I can see that, so can others. She makes you appear weak."

His words hit me in the gut. "She does not make me weak." I could feel fury building as I pushed harder onto his neck.

He began to struggle again. My wolf took over as I watched with a detached interest.

"Connor! Hey, he's not challenging you." Owen tried to get through to me.

I snarled at him, and he lifted his hands placatingly. "Honestly, he isn't, and he's not threatening Ember." He looked at Stone. "Are you, man?"

Stone couldn't answer; his face had turned purple. Bright yellow rolled across his eyes as his wolf pushed into the mix. He met my gaze. My own wolf responded to the eye contact, and shoved harder. We wouldn't tolerate a challenge like that, not even from our brother. I tilted my head watching dispassionately as he turned a deeper shade of purple. His wolf stared out at me, furious and defiant.

"Connor!" Owen's voice was tight. All my brothers watched silently, but their worry was a bitter scent in the air.

Pushing my wolf aside was hard, but I didn't back off. I snarled in Stone's face. "Drop your challenge."

He did. Grey rolled back over his eyes just before his body slumped. I loosened my hold, dropping my arm from his neck to his chest to keep him on his feet while he got his breath back.

"You idiot! Why did you challenge me like that?" My own breath came in hard pants.

"Jesus, Connor, I understand why she's important to you. Even if you're too chicken shit to admit it. But that means you now have a weakness. You've got to see that." Stone gasped for breath, grasping his throat.

I swallowed and met Owen's gaze. He'd worked it out, but vocalising it to the others would mean me admitting to myself how much of a hold she had on me. Stone was right, she *was* a weakness—but one I'd never give up. "You're right, she's my mate. And I need her to be safe, so that I can concentrate on running this place; even if she doesn't want my help right now. Fuck! I've spent the last four years thinking she was dead. Now that I know she's not, I intend to keep her alive until we can figure a way out of this place."

"What about Shannon? She won't be set aside easily."

I shook my head. "Shannon is a non issue. I can't worry about her now. I've made it clear to her from day one that she'd never be my mate, and that we are done now that Ember is here. She's just too stubborn to listen." I didn't know how Shannon had ended up here, since being Doherty's daughter apparently wasn't enough to save her. But I didn't really care, either, since I didn't trust her, never had. Stone was welcome to her and her spoilt behaviour.

"As far as I'm concerned, Shannon owes both Ember and me. She'll behave," I told them all and left it at that.

"And if she doesn't?" A curious glint entered Stone's eyes, causing me to pause.

"Then feel free to handle the situation for me as you see fit."

Stone's jaw clenched and his nostrils flared making me wonder why he was so interested in Shannon.

"Connor?" Reed asked. "Did you heal Ember's ribs?"

My nostrils flared. It was hard to admit any kind of vulnerability, but I didn't want to hide what Ember was to me from my pack. If I wanted their support, I needed to be honest with them. "Yes."

"Shit, man." Myles ran his hand through his hair. "She's not just a potential mate, she's your soulmate."

We all stood in silence.

"Your wolf's claimed her?" asked Reed.

"No, not entirely—yet. He's being a stubborn bugger."

Stone's mouth flattened into a straight line. "But she's your soulmate? That's why you've been so focused on her. If your wolf accepts hers and Ember feels the same about you, then it's going to be difficult to hide."

"True, but Ember doesn't know that only soulmates can heal each other."

"Damn, man, if she tells anyone what you did, it'll put you both at risk."

I swallowed hard, and nodded once. There was no point in pretending it wasn't. "I know."

Stone was right, anyone who saw my protective behaviour of Ember, or noticed she wasn't injured anymore, would suspect she was more to me than another member of our pack. I rubbed my face with my hands. But at least if she had my pack mark, I'd have a reason to protect her.

Stone paced across the small room. "Damn. You realise if you can't hold back from her, it's gonna make her a target for everyone in this place who wants your position? They'll try and use her to get to you. To end you."

"I know that, man. But if she finds out about our connection too soon, she'll just rebel against it—against me, because she doesn't fully trust me yet." I smiled a little. "She thinks I'm going to try and control her."

"You are." Reed smirked and wiggled his brows.

I huffed a smile, not disagreeing, and tried not to dwell on how much I wanted to dominate her, or how much I wanted her to fight me, only to give in. I swallowed hard and shook my head. The thing was, I didn't want to repress Ember, even if the thought of dominating her sent heat surging through my blood. If she gave in to me, it had to be because she wanted me as much as I wanted her.

"So what now? How are you going to keep Ember, and even Shannon, out of the entertainment rooms at the next games?" D asked.

I scowled. Beside me Stone growled. He really did like Shannon. Stupid bugger. If I'd known how he felt about her, I'd have stopped any physical relationship between me and Shannon well before now. There was only one woman I wanted to be skin to skin with from now on. I patted his shoulder, trying to reassure him, but it was an empty gesture and we both knew it. The time was coming when women would be picked and taken to the 'science wing' and even if they avoided that, the next games were looming, and with them the entertainment rooms. Both were a one way ticket to hell.

I sighed. Right now, I had a different problem to deal with.

"You guys are going to help me keep Ember safe. She's a fighter, and there's no way I'm letting them take her into that science wing. I'll kill everyone in this place before that happens." I eyed Owen and Stone. "We bring her and Shannon into the rings."

Stone swore. "Boss, if you do that, you need to stay away from her. You can't afford for all the bastards out there to know what she means to you."

"What? Like you're gonna stay away from Shannon? Would you prefer I leave them at risk of being put in that programme?"

Stone's nostrils flared, his eyes clouding with confusion.

"Yeah, thought as much. Ember's here and she's mine. You want me to stay clear headed and focused on our goal, then you need to keep her safe." I looked at them all individually, finishing with Stone. "And that includes you. In return we will help keep Shannon safe, too."

Stone let rip with a whole run of colourful expletives about *pains in the ass.*

"D, Kawan. You're on duty to keep Ember out of trouble."

"How d' we do that, boss? She'll probably try and kick our asses when she figures out what we're doing. And we can't go into the women's hall at night or the showers when she uses them—she'll castrate us."

"No, but other people can. Use whoever you need. Including Shannon. Like I said she owes Ember." I ignored Stone's glare.

❧

FURY KNOTTED IN MY BELLY, my muscles tense enough they were painful. It was two hours since Ember had stormed out and I wanted to go and find her.

Zander shrugged, but held my gaze. My anger and dominance levels never appeared to affect him at all, which pissed me off. He was an enigma. He wasn't a shifter, the power rolling off him was different and it left me unsure. He'd never used it against me, but he wasn't beyond hurting my brothers with that damn internal taser to get what he wanted.

"Connor, I believe him," Rawson said, his voice a deep rumble, his eyes clearer than I'd seen for a long time.

"Why? He's the one that brought Ember here, how can I believe Doherty doesn't know she's right under his nose?"

"I took her as part of the deal Doherty struck with the fae to take down a Digitalis dealer."

"A Digitalis dealer?" Damn, what had she been up to? If she'd bargained with the fae and they'd compelled her, she'd never want to be in that position of slavery again. That might be why she didn't want to be tied to a pack—or me. "So Doherty wasn't going after her specifically?"

"No, but I'd already been informed she was there. I made sure I got to her before Doherty recognised who he had."

Anger speared my gut, but I held it back. "So instead of Doherty using her to coerce me—you and our mysterious boss are going to instead?"

Zander shrugged. "It's been four years, Connor. He wants action. If you don't push forward with your investigation, our boss will ensure she is right in the middle of Doherty's radar. I don't know what she's done to him, but our boss has no love for her, and he wants to know what's happening in that science wing."

I pushed off the wall and stood almost nose to nose with the enigmatic guard. "I don't understand your role in all of this. You got us that fake ID, why can't you get your own people in there and find out what you need to know?"

Zander's head tilted very slightly, his lips pressing into a thin line before he gave a tight smile. "My role is complicated. For the warden I am the one who hunts down people to bring to this place. For our mutual boss, I'm the one who keeps you in line and that's it. My access to other areas of the prison is non-existent. I've told you this before, so why are we going over old ground?"

It was true we'd covered this regularly over the years and nothing had changed. But now Ember was involved, I wanted this crazy assignment I'd unknowingly signed up for to be over.

"Why Ember?"

Zander raised a brow. "Our boss agreed you need a little incentive to move things along a bit."

"Dammit, man! We've been in here four fucking years and only found a way into that science wing once and that was with your help. If you can't risk appropriating another pass, how do you think we're going to do it now?"

Zander shrugged his big shoulders. It was strange, in many ways we were alike. We stood at the same height, our noses were slightly too long for our faces, our jaws square, and we both had a cleft in our chin. The similarities ended there though; for a start, shadows swirled in his eyes before the darkness was swallowed by fire.

Zander put his fingers on my shoulder and shoved me back a step. "Too close. And how you get in isn't my problem, but if you don't, I will make sure Ember is in the next female round up. Do you understand me? Putting her in the training programme will not save her. She's here as an incentive for you to get a move on. Whatever is going on in that science wing is coming to a head, and once the warden and Doherty complete whatever they are ultimately doing here, I've a feeling this place will be buried in the snow and ice and you will all be buried with it."

My gut twisted, and not just out of worry. An idea hit me, a crazy and dangerous one. I stepped away and began to pace. Could it work? "If he gets rid of this place, his income will dry up," I pointed out.

Zander shrugged again. "I expect he will keep using the other prisons—or move on to whatever project is really the purpose of this place."

"What's on your mind?" Rawson asked, his gaze following me.

I shook my head, not wanting to share yet. "Nothing, just thinking." I turned to Zander. "Fine. I'll figure it out, but while I'm doing that, I want more time with Rawson. He deserves to see Ember."

Zander rolled his eyes. "He doesn't deserve anything. None of you do. You're all criminals, or have you forgotten he killed his mate?"

"Don't be a prick. We're here because your boss set us all up, and you bloody well know it. There are criminals in this place, but we aren't them."

Zander raised a brow. "You sure about that? How many have you killed in this place to amass all that power you have under your skin?"

I remained quiet, shoving some of that power against him, until he snarled back. I shouldn't antagonise him, but he really could be a dick at times.

"I did *not* kill Lyss," Rawson denied, his voice tight.

Zander turned his attention to Rawson and shrugged. "It looked that way when I got there. You were kneeling right beside her."

Rawson held Zander's glare. His own eyes flashed and alpha power seeped from him, something I'd not felt in a long time. I quickly stepped in front of him, but looked over my shoulder at Zander. I raised a brow in question. He shrugged as if he had no idea what I was asking. I turned my attention back to Rawson. "Hey man, tone it back. It doesn't matter what he thinks. I know you didn't do it and so does Ember."

Rawson looked at me, his brows dipping. "Will she be scared of me? She saw me as a Were-beast."

No idea. "Nah, man, she's a tough cookie. Seeing you as a Were wouldn't scare her."

"He's right. She quickly figured out you were just a puppet," said Zander.

Rawson eyed Zander with such hatred, I thought he might lunge. A growl rippled up his chest. "You could stop using me as one."

For a moment Zander's expression softened. "I can't, not entirely. The warden wants immediate access to any vassals he has enslaved. And you are too useful, he'd notice that you were gone."

"How long?" I asked.

"What for?" Zander's dark brows dipped.

"How long could Rawson stay here in the pack before he was missed?"

Zander remained silent—thinking. "My next pick up is not for a few weeks." He studied Rawson. "You'll have to be there for that or my men will notice your absence and question it. It'll get back to the warden and he'll come and investigate." Zander began to pace. "The last thing you want is that bastard singling you out."

I empathised with the fear I heard under those words. I'd learned first hand how good the warden was at inflicting both physical and mental anguish. Perhaps Zander was as much a puppet as Rawson was.

Zander stopped pacing and crossed his arms. "I suppose you could stay here until that extraction," he said to Rawson then turned his garnet eyes on me. "Why do you need him? Is it worth the risk that the warden may find out?"

"Yes. He's trained Ember before. She respects him and will toe the line better if he's around."

Rawson raised a brow at me and grinned. "Has she been giving you a hard time, Prime?"

I shook my head and grimaced. "You have no idea. If you thought she was stubborn and rebellious as a teenager, she's ten times worse now."

Rawson cocked his head and studied me, his eyes narrowing astutely. "You're different. Your wolf isn't as close to the surface."

I took a deep breath and expelled it steadily. Was it that obvious? "Yeah, she pushed him back. He's not sure about her yet and he's sulking because he doesn't recognise her wolf as his mate, but he knows Ember is mine. She gave me a kick up the arse to take back the reins from him."

I paced around the small cell. Both men watched me closely, Rawson with a slight smirk on his lips, Zander with intense focus. "She kind of got me to issue a new rule about non-consensual sex. It's outlawed now, even in gen pop."

Rawson stared at me incredulously. "What? After all these years of being a total shit and ignoring it, you've finally done something about that kind of behaviour—because of Ember?"

I grimaced, my chest feeling tight. I'd allowed some terrible and cruel abuse to happen under my watch. I shook my head, self-loathing making it hard to meet my mentor's gaze. "Yeah, she called me out on it."

"Wow, good for her. What did she say?"

I shuffled my feet, grimacing. I'd reverted to being a teenage boy in front of the man who had saved my life. It was obvious I'd disappointed him, that what I'd done—or ignored over these past years had hurt him deeply. I took a deep breath and exhaled slowly. "She reminded me that Lyss and you would be disgusted with my lack of action. That I was a bastard for allowing attacks of any kind to happen to those too weak to defend themselves, and that I had the power to stop it—if I wanted."

"And you wanted to, now that you know she's alive and the darkness isn't so heavy on your soul?" Rawson asked quietly, holding my gaze with his. I expected condemnation, but saw only understanding. He reached out and squeezed my shoulder, and I had to blink the burning sensation from my eyes.

I was aware of Zander listening in, but I didn't care. For some inexplicable reason, I trusted him with my feelings for Ember, even if I didn't trust him with everything else. I rubbed my palms over my face. Gods this was a fucked up mess of a situation. I held Rawson's gaze. "Yes, for the first time in four years I actually care about the consequences of my actions." I leaned on the wall next to him. "I've been dead inside, and my wolf has dragged me through this hell. But he only cares about the survival of his pack, he hasn't cared about anyone else—and neither have I. Ember has changed that. She's forced me to wake up, and I care a great deal about what she thinks of me, even if I don't really care about those people in gen pop." I stopped talking, having already shared too much.

Rawson dropped his chin to his chest, then lifted his gaze to Zander who studied us silently. "A few weeks you say?"

"Yep, I can manage that if you stay out of trouble and away from the guards. And I promise to bring you back after we are done."

Rawson was silent for a moment and his throat bobbed, but he didn't look away from Zander. "Thank you." He forced the words out.

I winced at how painful that must have been for him to say, but he shook it off and turned his head to smile at me. "Take me to Ember."

I grinned. "Sure. I need to find her anyway."

"Why?" asked Zander.

"I gave her twenty four hours to willingly become a member of my pack. No doubt she's going to fight me and not agree. She doesn't trust me yet, and I don't blame her after what she's seen of me so far. Maybe Rawson here can persuade her it's in her best interests before I have to make a decision for her."

Rawson's features twisted. "You said you weren't going to allow force anymore. That includes Ember, doesn't it?"

My stomach soured at his expression. "Of course. I would never force myself on her. But if she doesn't agree to become part of my pack for her own protection, then I'll do whatever it takes to keep her safe. If that means marking her against her will, I'll do it in a heartbeat."

Rawson's brows dipped and he shook his head.

I slapped his shoulder. "Don't worry, brother. I'll use my powers of persuasion, and she'll come willingly." I smirked, hoping that was true.

CHAPTER 8

Ember

I woke up and lay utterly still, keeping my eyes tightly shut. I wanted to ignore the hell my life had become for just a little longer. So much for getting out of here and finding a way back to Faerie to rescue Blue. I sighed then winced. My lip stung and probing it with my tongue only made it worse. I probed my ribs with my fingertips and felt heat fill my cheeks as I remembered Connor's warm, yet gentle touch against my skin.

The morning siren blared, rattling my ear drums. I groaned and flung my right forearm over my eyes. All I wanted was some peace and quiet. I had to make a decision about joining Connor's pack today. I was so relieved to see him alive, but at the same time what he had allowed to go on here worried me. Though I knew his wolf had been running the show, mainly. My stomach churned. I didn't want to agree to become a member of his pack just for him to make me watch him with Shannon—or any other female, for that matter. I swallowed the bile that burned my throat. Gods, dammit! I needed to know where I stood. But even if we managed to work things out, I had a promise I made to Blue to keep. I groaned. *This is such a mess!*

Around me the women's hall exploded with movement and chatter.

Someone kicked me gently. "You coming for food?" Charlie asked, sounding far too cheery.

I didn't look at her. "Urgh! What are you doing slumming it in here? And no thanks, got too much on my mind."

"Please yourself, but I'll save you a spot just in case you change your mind. You're guards are waiting outside by the way."

I sighed as she walked away. The last person I wanted to bump into was Connor. He confused me too much. I was used to being in control, and he made me feel very very *out* of control.

I understood being marked and in a pack was safer, but I didn't like to be pushed, and if I let Connor force my decision about pack membership, what other things would he try to control for me? I looked at the vines and rose tattoo on my wrist. Since I'd been freed from Som's faerie contract, I'd been my own master. I grimaced, knowing deep down the reason for resisting Connor's demands went far deeper than my stubbornness. I wanted to trust him, but just like in the past, I was convinced something would happen to take him from me, again. The bottom line was, I didn't know him like I used to, nor did I understand this place. And even though he had been a potential mate to my last wolf, there was nothing to say his wolf would feel the same about the wolf I housed now. As for me and Connor... I squeezed my fists tight, my nails digging into my palms. Well, I had always loved him, but now he was a Prime; a powerful and dominant male, and he could have any woman he wanted. I wasn't under-confident, not by a long shot, but this Connor...I swallowed hard remembering the way he'd brushed his lips against my skin. And he did say he'd never let another male touch me. Did that mean he really still cared for me, too? He had healed me, and his touch had been so gentle. Leaning my head back against the wall, I closed my eyes. His body had felt so good against mine. It had been obvious he wanted me, but my feelings for him went far deeper than just his body. I smiled. Though I had to admit, his body was a glorious fucking bargaining chip to persuade me to join his pack.

Enough! I'll get some food then I'll find somewhere to train and burn Connor out of my head for a bit.

Tentatively, I shuffled into a sitting position. I didn't know how he'd done it, but he'd healed my ribs just by touching me yesterday. I lifted my top and prodded the slightly bruised skin with my fingers. It was a little tender but nothing else; my bones were healed.

I frowned. I didn't know much about shifters. I had, after all, been living with fae and humans for the past four years, but I doubted healing power was a common occurrence in the shifter community. I'd never heard of it when I'd lived with Rawson and Lyss, and the academy hadn't taught us anything about it.

The heavy smell of porridge drifted in through the open doors. My stomach rebelled, but I needed food. Going out into the fray again, without energy, was stupid. I shuffled my back to the wall, tipped my head back and bent my knees up to my chest. Connor was right. No matter how confused I was about him, I couldn't spend the foreseeable future fighting everyone in this prison. I didn't regret asking him to change his rules, but it had gotten around that it was my fault the bastards who loved rape and violence had to keep their dicks in their pants. That meant a lot of fighting and defending myself. And Connor was right again; I was a good fighter, but I wasn't invincible. Eventually I'd end up gang raped or dead.

I sighed and pushed myself up, rubbing some warmth back into my arms. I still had no blankets and although it was hot and stuffy most of the time, my arms and bare stomach got cold enough at night, I regretted giving Charlie my leather jacket.

I groaned as Shannon sashayed towards me. I might have helped her, but she was Connor's fuck buddy—or she had been, and I hated her for it. No matter how much he pissed me off with his overbearing attitude, I still didn't want to think about her wrapped around him. I sighed. "What do you want?"

She stopped and planted a hand firmly on one hip. Her vest top was white and clean and she had on a pair of tight jeans and trainers. "Now, now, runt, I've been asked to babysit you until you go to Connor to be marked."

I rolled my eyes. "He's such a dick, sometimes."

Shannon smirked. "He is. But you could do worse than joining his pack."

I raised my brows. "If that's the case, why aren't you marked by him? "

She studied her nails and shrugged her toned shoulders. "I don't want just his pack mark on my skin. Join the pack if you want, but Connor is mine, so back the fuck off, then you and me will get along just fine." She leaned in a little, but I was too tired to find her attitude intimidating. Instead, I slowly smirked, remembering the time I'd smashed my fist into her face on our last day of school. I'd never found out why she'd not shown any signs of that attack, though I'd still ended up with some geeky teacher sending me to the headmistress's office. I shook off that distant memory and stared at Shannon. Surely, she hadn't got herself chucked in here so she could be near him? Had she? That would be really desperate. And insane. I opened my mouth to ask, but she spoke first.

"I want the ultimate mark of power and that's his claiming mark. He's a Prime. Do you have any idea how rare that is? If I have his mark, I can't be forced to become some pack whore. Any other pack mark means I could be available to anyone who fancies a fuck."

I quirked a brow at her. "Hey, I get it. It's why I don't want to be forced into a pack, but I don't know, it might be easier to defend against a pack member than the crazies in gen pop." I frowned. "But you're Connor's..." I struggled to find a less crass term than I wanted to use. "...friend." *Or you were,* I added silently to myself. "Surely he wouldn't allow anything like that to happen to you in his pack?" The same was probably true for me.

She sucked her bottom lip between her teeth. "Well, you sure think it might happen to you."

"Yeah, well, not really, but I don't really know him anymore, not like you do." It was a justification of my confused thoughts, but really I was scared to give Connor any more power over my heart than he already had. It didn't even seem real that he was alive. Overwhelming relief made me blink hard and fast to clear my vision, and breathe slowly to relieve the tightness in my chest. It had been hitting me in waves since yesterday.

"How long have you been here?"

"Jeez, I'm not sure, every day blurs into one beautiful dream here." Sarcasm dripped from Shannon's words.

I huffed a chuckle. "It does, so how long are you willing to wait for Connor to mark you as his?" I kept my voice curious.

She shrugged. "It doesn't matter now."

"Sure, it does." And it did, at least to me. I hated that she had gotten to be with him, even though I hadn't decided quite what to do with my own feelings about him. Even if he was true to his word and it was over between them, seeing them together wasn't going to help me sort out my head, or my heart.

"No, runt, it doesn't matter, because now you're here, no matter what I threaten, he only has eyes for you." She curled her lips into a pouty smile and fluffed her hair. "Unless I can persuade him the view is still sweeter this way. Now come on, your bodyguard is waiting for you." She flounced back to the door then turned and raised her brows meaningfully. "Well?"

Resigned, I followed her out.

"Morning, she wolf." Stone's grey eyes narrowed on me before his attention drifted to Shannon as if he couldn't help himself.

"Morning," Korea said.

I shoved my hands on my hips and scowled. "You have to be kidding me."

Korea smiled. "Nope. The boss wants you safe, so we're on babysitting duty until you run to him and get your mark."

Fury heated my cheeks and my wolf stirred. She was not opposed to being marked by the Prime which only pissed me off more. *I* would make the decision whether or not I joined his pack, not Connor, not my wolf, and not his brothers would bully me into it. "Well, I guess you're stuck with me since I don't run to anyone."

Despite my less than jovial greeting, Korea smiled pleasantly and held out his hand. "I'm Kawan. And can I suggest you just go with his demand? No offense, but we don't want to be here following your beautiful behind any more than you want us to be." He shrugged. "So let's make the best of it."

"Unless you wanna go and get your mark right now?" Stone's face was a dark glower.

"Oh, hush now, Stoney. A girl's gotta eat first," Shannon said, not bothering to hide the irritation in her eyes at his interference. "Shall we?"

She held out her arm like she wanted me to link mine with hers or some shit. I gave her a *'what the fuck?'* look and ignored it. She snorted a laugh and walked beside me.

I disregarded Stone and Kawan, but I was well aware of the attention our little group got from the gen pop crowd. I grabbed my bowl of thick slop and shoved three spoons of sugar in it. I gave Stone a defiant smile and dumped a fourth in for good measure just because he looked so disgusted.

Shannon laughed. "Oh, lighten up, Stoney. Girls love something sweet between their lips." She gave him a teasing smile and scooped some of my porridge up with her forefingers and sucked it between her generous lips. Yellow rolled across Stone's eyes, and a muscle twitched in his jaw as he watched her. Shannon grinned at him before turning back to me to scoop out some more.

I grabbed her wrist. "Get your own to tease him with."

Across the hall, I spied Lionel sitting on his own so I made my way over. "Hi, big guy." I swung my leg over the bench seat and took a seat opposite the lion shifter. We'd become firm allies, and I was eternally grateful to him for having my back whenever he could.

Lionel eyed my guards and raised his brows. "Well, you're not going to be in gen pop with me for much longer are you?" He smiled and leaned his thick forearms on the table, giving me a knowing look.

"Don't know what you mean," I said between mouthfuls of sweet porridge. Damn! I grimaced at how sweet I'd made it.

He laughed, his eyes twinkling. "You're kidding, right? The Prime has body guards on you, Ember. I think that sends a loud and clear message to every male in this place. Your fine ass is well and truly off limits." He reached back and interlocked his big hands behind his head, stretching out. His bulging arms and impressive pecs were really quite distracting. For a moment I forgot my porridge and just enjoyed the view—until he grinned and raised a brow. "Off limits, sugar," he drawled.

I grinned, but couldn't help looking at Shannon, who was also in the process of ogling Lionel. She met my gaze and raised her brows, then winked. Yep, it was confirmed, Lionel was hot and drool worthy. I laughed when Stone gave a low growl.

Lionel chuckled and lowered his arms, but his smile disappeared when the north pack alpha walked in and eyed me. "These guys might be here to keep you safe, and you know I will always fight for you, but it also means everyone knows you mean something to Connor, which conversely paints a target on your back—a big one."

I swallowed and glanced around. It was true, some people shot me respectful glances, but there was also malice on some faces. Stone and Kawan gave the north pack males a dead eyed stare, not in the least bit bothered by them. I didn't have their confidence, the surfer dude I'd discovered was from Santa Cruz, had brought more men with him today. I swallowed the sweetness of my porridge down with a mouthful of water.

Lionel was right. Connor might think he was protecting me, but he'd just made my life even more dangerous by advertising his protection. I needed to distance myself from that kind of attention...

I shoved my bench back and stood up.

"Where are you off to?" Lionel shoved his chair back, too, and watched me walk behind him.

"To try and get the target off my back. And make a new friend." I leaned down and slid my hands around his neck, caressing his chest. Gently, I kissed his cheek.

"As much as I'm enjoying your attention, are you trying to get me killed?" His smile was predatory, despite his words, and his amber eyes turned vivid. His skin burned under his collar as the beast beneath stirred. I smiled against his ear. Like every shifter male, primal needs were hard to control.

I eyed Kawan and Stone, who watched me closely. "Hm, I think it will take more than two wolves to bring down a big, bad lion. Am I right?" I smirked, and brushed another kiss on his jaw.

He chuckled. "Maybe not with those two, but it'll buy you some time for whatever you have planned, sugar."

My heart pounded as adrenaline surged through my system. "Thanks, big guy. I owe you one."

He grunted. "More than one. I just hope it's worth the ass-kicking I'm about to get."

I slid my hands off him as he stood too, smiling down at me, but it was clear his attention was on Stone who stalked towards us, suspicion pouring from him. I smiled innocently and his eyes narrowed. Kawan headed around the other side of the table, passing by Shannon who had moved back from the table and watched us with keen interest. I winked at her and her eyes widened.

"Now!" I yelled at Lionel.

With his foot, he shoved the table into Kawan's legs with enough force my bodyguard doubled over it in pain.

"Oh, fuck no." Stone growled as I launched into a sprint to the doors.

I didn't take the time to look over my shoulder. My feet slipped, and I skidded out of the door and bolted down the corridor. People yelled, and footsteps pounded. Santa Cruz was close on my heels. I could hear him shouting to his men so I darted between people, not willing to deal with his kind of crazy. Someone called my name, but I didn't stop to figure out who. This was the only way I could think of to get the target off my back.

I charged up the metal staircase to the next level, my feet pounding on the metal walkway, echoing loudly. Breath rasped in my lungs as I kept up my speed. My objective was clear in my head, I just hoped he was there.

"Hey! You can't go in there!" A male bystander caught my arm trying to stop me from reaching my goal. I grabbed his wrist and hand, twisted and flipped him to the ground. He landed with a slam, but I didn't falter. I jumped over him and carried on running.

"You can't get away from me this time!" yelled Santa Cruz from the bottom of some stairs. "If I mark you first, even the Prime can't claim you without my permission. You're mine."

"Shit!" I panted. He was right, but that was the whole point of this mad dash. I'd reevaluated my options and decided this was a better way for me to go. It would piss Connor off, but this way I'd have a chance to find out how I felt about him without him pressuring me to submit to his demands. I wasn't bothered about anyone in this place, so not upholding my loyalty to another pack meant nothing to me, and I knew another alpha couldn't compel my wolf, I only struggled to defy Connor. I didn't know Drake Alexander, but I'd found out he was an honourable guy, or as honourable as anyone in here was; and being marked by Santa Cruz wasn't happening. I could imagine how shitty my life would become with him. I renewed my efforts, pumping my arms and legs faster and dragging air into my burning lungs.

Three big males, and a woman with muscles almost as big as Stone's, glared at me as I sprinted up to them.

"Hey! Where's Drake?" I skidded to a halt just as Santa Cruz and his six brown-nosed buddies rounded the corner and pounded towards us.

"Don't you let her in there! She's mine!" Santa Cruz yelled.

A brown haired man with a muscled physique and glittering green eyes in a gorgeous face, studied me and then Santa Cruz. He bared his teeth at me in a wide grin. "Well, seeing as he put it like that," he drawled in a southern accent. "Please, little lady, won't ya come in?" He stood back and gestured with his hand for me to enter.

My heart pounded as I ran past the guard just as Santa Cruz skidded to a halt, or rather, was halted by the guard's hand slamming into his chest. To my delight, the contact sent Santa staggering back. I doubled over with my hands on my knees, breathing hard, but I managed to gather enough energy to give him the finger. The sexy southerner grinned at me, and then crossed his arms over his chest and barred the door, as did the woman and the other man.

"Seems like she doesn't want you. So turn your evil ass right around and head back to your own territory, Surfer Boy."

Santa snarled, his wolf shining out of his eyes. He growled viciously. "Fuck you! How about you step out here, I break your neck, and then take her back anyway? Or you can choose to live and just give her to me."

The brown haired guard rolled his shoulders and cracked his neck. He snarled, and a blast of power rolled off him. I stepped back. He was definite alpha material. Would he accept Santa's challenge or hand me back? I readied myself to fight while eyeing the people who were in the hall behind me. The south wing pack studied me with a mixture of suspicion and interest. Fuck, how would I find Drake Alexander amongst all those people? I had no idea what he looked like.

The south wing guard glanced back at me, clearly contemplating his choices. I stepped back, fists at the ready. He smirked at my stance and clear intent to fight. "No need for that, missy." He glowered at Santa. "She stays. You leave. I won't fight you, north alpha." He addressed the other two guards. "Jo! Vinny! He doesn't get in. Yo!" He beckoned over another squad of six males. "Y'all go back to your own territory now. You ain't getting in here. This is south wing ground."

I took a step away from the door and the others closed ranks in front of me.

"You gotta come out some time! And I'll be waiting, sweetheart!" Santa called out.

"Fuck you!" I yelled between the heads of the south pack guards.

"That's just what I'm gonna do! Come on out and you'll see just how I'm gonna fuck you, bitch!"

The stunning green eyed guard contemplated me with a smile. "So? I take it you're the little lady who's causing so much trouble out in gen pop? You here to talk to Drake?"

I nodded, still getting my breath back. I decided now wasn't the time to address the sickly sweet endearments, particularly since I didn't think he was using them to be insulting.

"Can I ask why?" His eyes were still doing that gorgeous twinkling.

I shook my head. "I'd rather talk to him first."

He smiled and shrugged. "I understand. Follow me then, and let's go see him."

I didn't mind complying with that command, not one bit. The view of his broad shoulders and tight arse as he walked along was fine indeed. People milled around, watching our progress across the hall with curious looks. I ignored them, but kept my senses alert for any kind of attack. I trusted no one.

He glanced back over his shoulder. "You know, they won't attack you here, not unless Drake commands it."

"Right." I kept my tone neutral.

He smirked. "You have real trust issues, don't you?"

I raised my brows and shrugged in response.

He chuckled. We climbed the stairs, and once again I enjoyed the view of his powerful body eating up the steps in front of us.

"Y'know if you keep staring at my ass like that, my pants will burn clean off."

I grinned. "Now that would be such a damn shame," I declared as he stopped in front of a cell with a solid door, much like Connor's.

Grinning widely, he pushed open the metal door and gestured inside. A frisson of sexual energy zipped between us. I held his gaze and inhaled. A mix of musk and body heat teased me making my core clench. *Damn, it's been too long since I got laid.*

He kept up that sexy grin as his gaze travelled down my body and back up again. His attention didn't rile me the same way Connor's did, in fact it was just an enjoyable jolt of lust, not a roaring need to defy him, punch his lights out, or kiss the hell out of him. It was nice, refreshing even. I walked into the room looking for the alpha of the south wing pack.

The room was empty.

"So where is he?"

The guard smiled. "Why don't you take a seat?" He shut the door.

"No thanks." I looked at the clock. I had very little time left to do what I needed before Connor came for me. "Listen. I need to speak to Drake. If he can't help, I need to know so I can move onto plan B"

He raised his brows. "Plan B?"

"Yeah, plan B," I said, already weighing up my next move.

"So, Drake's plan A?" He gave me that charming grin again and gestured to the chair. There was no doubt he could charm the pants off just about any woman he wanted. Despite my time critical situation, I chuckled and plonked my backside into the nearest chair. "Yes, he is, so is he going to come out and play?"

"He'll be here soon. While we wait, why don't you tell me why you need a plan A?" His green eyes were so intense, my skin heated. Power pulsed against my skin, not the same intensity as Connor's, but enough that it irritated me. I shuffled in my chair and glared at him. "Dial it back a bit," I said, my brows dipping.

He merely grinned, his expression assessing. "Interesting that you don't succumb to an alpha's power." There was a moment of silence. "So, since you've arrived in our shitty little world, you've fought off groups of males and defended victims too weak to defend themselves. Not only has our Prime changed the rules for you, now the psycho north alpha has his sights set on you; I'm guessing for revenge and the pleasure of breaking you. Connor has clearly riled you, so what do you want from Drake?"

A smirk curled my mouth as I stood and prowled forward. When there was barely even a hand's width of space between us, I stopped. The air between us sizzled with heat. An alpha's power might not subdue me, but I wasn't immune to its seductive and animalistic touch. I cocked my head and inhaled his scent. Lust ignited my core, forcing me to swallow a groan. He smirked knowingly and I leaned in closer, my lips brushing his cheek. "How about Drake comes and says 'hi' and I'll tell him?"

He grinned. Then curled his hand around my waist. Heat from his touch warmed my bare waist. "Oh, he's already listening, little lady, so keep talking. Tell me why I should give a shit about you, other than ripping these jeans off and fucking you up against this door, before I send you on your way back to our Prime?"

"Because if you help me, it means you have some power over the Prime," I whispered against the shell of his ear. I'd worked out who he was while we walked across the hall and no one would meet his gaze. This powerful, charming man was the alpha of the south wing pack, and I needed to persuade him to help me. I brushed his ear with my lips. He tensed and curled the fingers of his other hand around my waist too.

"And why would I want that? I have enough power. And unlike many others, I don't want more."

"Really?" I leaned my hips into his, trying hard to tempt him, but Drake tightened his hold and held me away from his body.

"It's alright, sweetness, as much as I want to fuck you, I don't need that kind of payment for my help. I've never needed to bribe anyone for sex, and I don't take a woman who isn't willing."

I ran my nose up his strong warm neck and smiled. "What makes you think I'm not willing?"

"Oh, I think your body is." He caught my gaze with his. "But I'm not so sure about your soul. You want me to mark you and make you one of my pack. So sit down and tell me why I should."

"You're right, I haven't got laid in an age and my body knows it, but yeah, sex isn't why I'm here." I chuckled, and allowed myself to run my gaze over his fine form. I didn't doubt he'd never need to force any woman to enjoy that stunning body. Placing my hands against his firm chest, I pushed away. Drake let me go and moved to lean against the wall. I walked back over to the chair and sat down, rubbing my face with my hands. "I've known Connor for a very long time, since we were kids. He's always been self-confident and most of the time, an arrogant arse. But we aren't kids anymore, and he has no right to decide my path. I'm a grown woman who can make her own choices and I want to choose my own pack, on my terms, not be forced to join one, and have no say in my path." I held his gaze though guilt swamped me for the lie. I wasn't willing to tell Drake about Connor wanting to protect me, it raised too many questions.

Drake's eyes narrowed, his brows dipping. "He's forcing you to join another pack?"

I nodded.

He shook his head. "What? Santa's? That jackass doesn't deserve a woman as strong as you."

"No, he doesn't." I smiled, seeing a way to persuade Drake to my side without necessarily lying. Just like the fae, I'd twist the truth a little… I felt a stab of guilt. But if Connor had given me enough time to get to know him again, and not painted a bloody great target on my back, then I wouldn't be in this room with Drake. "I think the north wing alpha gets excited about breaking those who oppose him, especially women."

Drake nodded, his face serious, his eyes no longer twinkling. "I understand." Drake pushed off the wall and prowled forward. His gaze held mine as he gently touched my face, his eyes tinged by something fierce, yet he was reverent. "You are too wild to be broken by the likes of Santa Cruz. And if Connor wants you, he needs to earn you. I won't stand in your way if you decide you want him, either. I get the feeling you need a safe haven for a while. And I'm happy to oblige, sugar." He cupped my face and leaned down, holding my gaze as his lips gently brushed mine. His kiss was soft and though he was hot enough to ignite my lust, he was right, that lust didn't touch my soul.

My chest squeezed at being here with Drake, and though Connor had pushed me too quickly, he was right, belonging to a pack would keep me safer, and it was the only way to take the focus off Connor and me.

Drake pulled away slightly, a small smile twisting his lips.

My troubled gaze met his. "I don't belong to anyone, not even you…are we clear? My body is my own." Nerves about what it meant to belong to a pack were unsettling my wolf and me. When I'd agreed to a deal with Som, it had had an endpoint, this wouldn't end unless another wolf claimed me as his mate, and Drake agreed to it. I placed my hand on his waist, swallowing as hard muscle rippled under my touch. My wolf snarled, not happy we were near another alpha and not Connor. I ignored her. If Connor wanted me, he'd have to work for me, I'd never be his just because he demanded it. He'd dealt with so much since we'd been parted, he'd forgotten what happened when he pushed me. Throwing his weight around just made me rebel. And having guards follow me just advertised I meant something to him. Didn't he realise it put me at more risk?

Drake perched on the table in front of me, then pulled me to my feet and between his legs. My flat palms landed on his chest. A roar vibrated the air in the south wing. "Honey, I don't wanna own you and the choice is yours, but you'd better make it quick because the Prime is on his way here, and he sounds pissed that you're with me, so if I'm going to risk my neck for yours, do I get anything in return?"

I smiled and shrugged. "You get one hell of a fighter and maybe even a way out of here."

For a moment he stared at me, his expression softening. "Oh, sugar, I can see you totally believe that, but you haven't been here long enough to accept there is no way out. Don't worry, you'll realise it soon enough." He slipped his big hands around to cup my behind, pulling me closer to him. It wasn't unpleasant to have my hips pressed against this powerful male's. His eyes zoned in on my neck. "Just for the record, I think ya got some lies mixed in with the truth, but I am willing to give you some time to work through your shit without any other males trying to wreck such a fiery spirit." He took my chin between the fingers of his right hand and tilted my head, exposing the left side of my neck. "You sure this is what you want?" he asked, his voice a low growl.

Feet pounded on the metal walkway, getting closer. Connor would stop this, and the moment he touched me, the soul deep connection between us would burn so intensely it would be useless to try and resist it. Adrenaline surged through my blood, my heart beating fast. Drake was right, I needed space to think and to decide on my path. Connor was a different man than he used to be, and I still had a promise to keep to Blue.

Another roar came, closer this time.

"Are you sure that he was going to make you join the north pack? Because it sure seems like he wants you himself," Drake said, his eyes narrowing and his mouth curling in a dry smile. "Almost like an alpha who's possessive over his mate." His green gaze pierced mine.

"I need time. Please, do it," I whispered, my voice shaking.

"Fine." Drake pulled his teeth back, exposing his sharper than normal canines.

My heart lurched, and I stared at his teeth. "What are you doing?"

He wrapped his other arm so tightly around me I couldn't move, then his legs wrapped around both of mine, effectively preventing me from moving.

I stared at his mouth wide eyed, my breathing erratic. A full on bite on my neck was a mating mark. I didn't know much about a mating bond, but I did know he'd be able to control me, that I'd be at his beck and call, for whatever he wanted. I struggled. "Don't you fucking dare! I'm not yours. I belong to someone else!"

He smiled knowingly, his voice gentle and reassuring. "I know, but I'm just helping *you* realise it too." There was sudden pain in the left side of my neck.

I winced.

"Done," Drake said and released his hold, dropping his hands to my hips just as the door flew open and Connor barrelled in.

Drake pushed me away, not to save himself, but to propel me to safety.

Before I could yell at Connor to stop, he launched himself at Drake and they fell over the table, tipping it up and slamming into the floor.

CHAPTER 9

onnor

A RED MIST distorted my vision. She'd run away from my brothers and deliberately put herself at risk just to prove a point! *Bloody stubborn woman!* I zeroed in on Drake, on his hands holding her hips. The fucker even had his canines down! I bellowed as he pushed her away from him. *Too fucking late!* I charged. My body barrelled into his, the table he leaned against toppling backwards and we crashed onto the floor and rolled.

I punched him on his jaw with everything I had. Anyone else, it would have smashed his face to pieces, but Drake was a powerful male, and his wolf had risen to my challenge. I snarled as he slammed his fist into my ribs, his wolf staring back at me.

"Yeah? Let's play, you fuck!" I snarled and let mine out. My body filled with power, and though he wanted to burst past the prison of the silver collar, he held back, so my body didn't suffer.

Drake yelled and smashed his fist into my jaw. I shook it off, grabbed him by the throat and slammed him up against the wall. My wolf snarled inside my head, blood pounding in my ears.

Kill him. Kill this male who dared touch your mate... My wolf's sentiments registered. Not our mate, but mine, he still hadn't claimed her wolf. That realisation hit me harder than any punch. She wasn't ours, and this behaviour only put her at more risk.

"Shut that fucking door!" Drake's men needed to stay outside. I didn't want their blood on my hands, but I was ready to kill this womanising Texan wanker.

Owen shut the door with a soft click and stood in front of it. My brothers watched me closely, all except Stone who monitored Ember. I took a breath and forced my wolf away, he went easily. In his mind Ember was mostly my problem, not his. My attention fixed back on Drake. He'd marked her, but if I took him out and another alpha claimed Drake's place, she would be at risk again. I eyed Ember, trying to contain my need to smash my fist into something, like Drake's face. She had refused my protection and my mark, so either she was just pushing back at me, which was likely given her temperament, or... I kicked myself, I should have known better than to push. Dammit! Maybe she didn't recognise me as her mate? My stomach tightened and I snarled into Drake's face, my throat aching and my heart squeezing painfully. Or she did and didn't want me.

"I didn't...do...anything...she...didn't ask...for! " Drake's throat moved under my grip.

A kick slammed into my kidneys, followed by another. I snarled at Ember over my shoulder, still not letting up on Drake's neck.

"Let him go, you idiot!"

"Why? He marked you! He had his fucking teeth out ready to claim you!"

"But he didn't bloody well claim me, Connor! So let him go!" she yelled right back. "I did this! It was my choice because you painted a bloody target on my back, sending them to follow me everywhere!" She gestured at Stone.

I panted, fire raging in my blood and my heart.

She stepped right up to the side of us and taking a deep breath, put her hand on my forearm.

Drake's eyes went to her face. I snarled. "Don't you fucking look at her." His nostrils flared, and he shifted his gaze from Ember to me. *Fucker...* I squeezed harder. He ground his jaw and his wolf surfaced again.

"Hey, you told me I needed to join a pack for protection, and I have—his. So by your own rules, I am now protected. If I came to your pack, it would make me even more of a target, Connor, you know that." Ember's fingers trembled against my skin, but her touch calmed some of my instinct to kill.

I tried to clear my mind and think back to the words I'd used. But she was right, and I knew it. I glanced at Owen. He shrugged and nodded his head in agreement.

"Fuck!" I cursed and let Drake go. I couldn't force myself to step away, though. I held his gaze. "Look away, right now."

He did but I leaned in, my mouth right next to his ear. "Any harm comes to her on your watch, you're dead. We clear?"

Drake dipped his chin.

I stepped back and took a deep breath. I was glad I'd told Rawson to wait behind for me. He knew what I was, what I'd done, but knowing it and seeing me rip the other alpha's throat out was different.

"Connor?" Ember ventured, her voice shaking.

Yeah, I'd pretty much made a siren call about my feelings through the whole godsdamn prison! Too late now; she'd joined another pack for nothing!

I pivoted on the ball of my foot. I could smell her blood where Drake had marked her. The need to turn around and slam my fist into his gut was visceral. It might not be a mating mark, but she was still part of his pack and beholden to him, like any pack female… I growled low in my chest, finding it hard to breathe. My fists curled, my muscles shaking. I needed some kind of release before I saw that mark on her creamy skin, or I would end Drake. I walked right past Ember and was almost to the door when she grabbed my arm.

"Connor! You can't almost kill someone because I joined their pack, and then just walk away! We need to talk about this."

I kept my gaze ahead and shook her off, roughly. Her touch burned my skin. "You made your choice, Ember, and it wasn't me. There's nothing to talk about. Drake! Have her in the gym first thing tomorrow. She's a fighter, and not around to entertain you and your pack." I looked back over my shoulder at him. He had his head tipped back against the wall and was rubbing his neck. "You remember that."

He met my gaze and nodded.

I walked out.

"Hey!" Ember yelled, clearly intending to follow me.

Stone stepped up to protect my back, as did D.

"Leave him be, Ember. You can't deliberately drive a knife into his gut like this and then just expect him to forgive you," Owen said, coldly.

I kept walking. She wouldn't get anywhere near me now unless I ordered them to let her. I couldn't do it, not yet. I needed time to work off my need to rip something apart.

"Ember! Come here," ordered Drake.

I clenched my jaw so hard, my teeth cracked. Fuck me! She'd let another male order her around, but not me! I marched out of the south wing, down the connecting corridors and to the gym.

I headed straight to the bags. Without pausing my step, I launched a brutal attack on the nearest one. My men watched me with stoic, hard faces. They knew what Ember was to me, so it was no surprise to see their tight faces and the empathy in their eyes. I'd fucked up trying to force her hand and giving her obvious protection, they knew it as much as I did. I slammed my fists into the solid punching bag over and over until blood splattered across the mats and the leather with each hit.

"Hey!" Owen rumbled when I eventually missed the bag and my arms shook so much I could barely lift them. "Enough."

I glared at him—and punched him in the gut.

"Yeah?" He growled and straightened up. "You wanna throw down, boss?" He cracked his neck and rolled his shoulders. "Let's go, fucker."

I did. I launched an attack that left us bruised and beaten and exhausted enough we both collapsed on our backs on the mats, heaving deep breaths. Owen slammed his elbow into my abs.

"Ouch! You chicken shit, we're done." I panted and coughed, wheezing a breath.

"Yeah, I know." He rasped a laugh. "But that's for being an arse, and letting a woman rule your head and actions. Stone's right. She makes you weak."

I rubbed my face with my hands. "Yeah, she does," I whispered. "Talking of bodies—D?" I said in a louder voice.

"Yeah, boss?"

"Go find me Shannon would ya?"

"Are you kidding me? You want those women to start a war over you? Or do you want Stone to kick your arse, too?"

I gave a bitter laugh despite the guilt in my belly. I didn't want Shannon or anyone else, but rejection was a bitter pill to swallow. "Ember's made it perfectly clear she prefers that Texan bastard over me, so she won't be bothered if I fuck someone else, whether it's Shannon or some other woman, now will she?"

"If you say so. But someone else will." Owen lifted his head and looked at Stone. "And just for the record, I think you'll regret fucking anyone while you're so pissed off."

"Scrap that order!" Stone loomed over me, purple fire shining in his eyes as his fae side peaked out. "You are not fucking Shannon just to get back at your mate. This is your mess, you deal with it. You don't get to use her like that ever again, Prime or not. You feel me?"

I rolled back onto my shoulders, arched my spine and flicked myself to my feet in one smooth move. I glared at Stone ready to tell him to go fuck himself when I recognised the tightness around his mouth, his curled fists and the storm in his eyes.

I cocked my head. I'd promised myself I wouldn't hurt him like that. Owen was right, I was being a total dick—again. "Okay, Stone. I feel you, brother. I'll find someone else. But..." I leaned into his space. "If you want her that bad, you need to go claim her, because she likes to play the power field; she always has. And if I'm not available, she'll go after someone else who can give her what she wants."

Stone rubbed his face. "And what's that?"

"Other than power? Fuck knows.You'll have to ask her." With that I walked off, though Kawan, Myles and Stone all followed me. I clenched my teeth, but instead of telling them to get lost, I ignored them. I'd had enough of fighting them for one night.

Despite all the hard physical training I'd just done, the tension in my body remained, buzzing underneath my skin, until I couldn't think straight. All I saw was Drake's hands on my Firecracker. I snarled as I stalked into the female section of my pack. I only ever visited here for one reason, and there were more than enough women all too willing to accommodate me. I prowled over to a tall, dark haired and curvy woman. She couldn't be any more different to my petite, red-haired Firecracker.

"You want some company, Prime?" she purred as I boxed her in with my arms and body.

"Sure do. You willing?"

"Of course." She smiled and I led her away. I didn't ask her name, I didn't need to know it. Just as we were heading down the corridor to my cell, Shannon rounded a corner. Her gaze fell to my hand on the brunette's back and her eyes flashed.

"What the hell?" She blocked our way, hands on hips.

I glanced at Stone, brows raised. He scowled, but his wolf flashed in his eyes. That made my mind up. There was no love lost between Shannon and me, but my third sure as shit had feelings for her and I wouldn't stand in his way, or lose him fighting over her.

"Sorry, Shannon, I told you before, we're through," I said, as Stone stepped around me and blocked her way.

I switched my hearing off, leaving them to argue it out. Instead, I guided the woman into my cell. Leaving the others outside, I closed the door and walked her backwards until she was up against the wall. I didn't want her in my bed. That was too intimate, and intimacy wasn't what I wanted. What I wanted was a release, and that was all. I peered down at her. "You sure you're up for this?"

She tilted her head back and smiled. "Oh, honey, if all you want is quick and dirty, then I'm your gal." She pushed her hips forwards rubbing against me.

"Good. So long as you understand. This is a one time only deal."

She grinned and lifted her face, trying to push her lips against mine. I put my fingers against her lips. "Ah, ah, no kissing."

She shrugged and smirked, grabbing my dick through my jeans. "How about this, is touching allowed?"

I swallowed, almost recoiling from her touch. There was really only one woman I wanted to touch my body. I curled my top lip ready to pull away but the mental picture of Ember doing this to Drake had my fists curled and blood roaring in my ears. Shaking my head, I forced away my wolf, and peered into a pair of dark brown eyes. "Remember my rules."

"Got it, no kissing, and no repeats."

I pulled her hands up above her head. "Good, keep your hands there, for now. No moving until I say so." And I popped the button on her jeans sliding them down her legs along with her prison issue underwear. I didn't stop to appreciate the view, I didn't care. I just needed a release for this tension, so I stood up and kept my eyes on her face. For once I didn't care about my partner's enjoyment or satisfaction, only the release her body promised. I offered zero foreplay.

"Undo my jeans," I commanded, swallowing the bitter taste in my mouth. I didn't really want this woman, I wanted Ember. But Ember wasn't mine; she'd chosen to reject me and give herself to fucking Drake.

Once my cock was free, I grabbed her thigh, lifted it up and leaned her against the wall. She groaned as I pushed inside her. But I couldn't even look at her as the heat and softness of her body surrounded me. Instead, I pounded into her, ignoring her moans of pleasure. Ember's eyes stared at me accusingly from the depths of my mind. I finished quickly, but my release wasn't satisfying; it was the exact opposite. I pulled out and straightened my clothes, not looking at the woman again.

"Go." Jesus, I was being a bastard, but I couldn't deal with what I'd just done or the guilt that swamped me. We might not be together, but my mate was alive and in the same fucking building! I sagged into a chair and hung my head, running my hands through my hair.

The door clicked and I looked up. The woman had gone.

"How did things go with Shannon?" I asked Stone.

He snarled, keeping his eyes on Reed and the other male in the ring with him. "About as well as your interactions with Ember."

I huffed a chuckle. "That good?"

"Yeah, that good."

"Reed! Push him harder," I yelled at the tall, sinewy man, who was my sixth. The male in the ring with Reed tensed. Myles grinned. He loved seeing Reed kick ass, almost as much as Reed liked to watch Myles do the same. I rolled my eyes at the pair of them. Still, we'd been here four years, I guessed neither of them would act on their feelings, unless someone else wanted to get their claws into the other man and jealousy rose its ugly head. Myles enjoyed attention from men and women, but no matter who it was, Reed was like a bear with a sore head for days when Myles got laid, and Myles was worse; so much so, I almost wanted to out him, just so the rest of us didn't have to suffer.

I surveyed the rings. All of them were full today. The hall stank of sweat and blood, and grunts and shouts of pain drowned out any nearby conversations. Kawan, D and Owen were all training the new batch of males that had arrived on the same plane as Ember and had been claimed by a pack. Santa was with Owen where my beta could keep an eye on the volatile north wing alpha. Santa took his opponent, a west wing male, down to the mat, but instead of stopping there, he stomped on the male's leg. The male howled in agony. Santa grinned widely and strutted around the ring like a fucking peacock...or just a cock.

My eyes narrowed. I might have kept Hudson's ridiculous nickname, but he was a vicious fighter whose shoulder length blond hair and surfer good looks hid the psycho beneath. I called Owen over. "Put him back with his own pack. There'll be less major injuries that way. He won't feel as threatened by them. I need these males in good enough condition to fight in the next games, and he's going to make them useless. Just warn him to tone it back."

"He's a reckless shit, so what do you want me to do if he doesn't listen?" Owen flexed his fists, his eyes flashing yellow.

I patted his back. "Not yet, my friend. But alpha or not, I'll let you kick his arse if he doesn't settle down."

"You're giving him a chance to play by your rules, huh?"

"Yeah, he doesn't know what's really going on yet, but he will soon. And I don't have the time to deal with filling an alpha spot if you take him out. We'll see what happens at the games," I said and left him to deal with Santa.

Rawson hadn't yet emerged from the cell he now shared with Owen. I didn't blame him. It must be liberating to know he wouldn't be forced to partially change and do Doherty's dirty work, even for a little while.

I tried not to watch the door for Ember. The notion of her with Drake made me want to break something, and I wanted to see her so badly it was hard not to go and rip her away from the clutches of the other male. Being with that other woman last night hadn't calmed my urge to be with Ember, but it had made me realise I didn't want any other female in my bed—or against the wall, or anywhere else, for that matter. I'd finished with the brunette so quickly it was almost embarrassing, but I'd needed her away from me, her scent and her touch had left me needing a shower. Thankfully, she'd left without any fuss, and I'd done just that.

I clenched and unclenched my fists, then rolled my head, trying to loosen up my neck and back muscles. My fists were sore from yesterday and would take at least the morning to heal. I'd had time to think on the way I tried to bulldoze Ember into doing as I wanted. I was still angry and disappointed, but more at myself than her. How could she understand how much she meant to me, when I didn't bloody tell her, or give her a chance to get to know me again? Fuck, I'd never actually spoken to her about our bond, not even after I'd kissed her and run from her years ago. That had been right before I'd gotten myself in this shitty situation. And after I knew she was alive and accepted she was in fact, *my* Firecracker, I'd just gone all alpha-prime possessive on her and tried to make her do what I wanted, without giving her a chance to even think; let alone for me to prove I wasn't as coldhearted as it looked from her point of view.

I prowled between the rings, advising and teaching both defensive and offensive moves, trying not to look like a teenager waiting for his first crush to walk in the room. Ember had always been stubborn and stood up to me, even when we were kids. If I'd tried to make her do anything, she'd always told me to go to hell. Lyss was able to manage Ember's temper by persuading or manipulating her into doing what she wanted, rather than demanding it. I stared down at the mats, my hands resting on my hips. I missed Lyss and her calm and sweet nature. I sighed heavily, she hadn't deserved to die, violently or otherwise. Someone had killed her and I'd find them eventually—or Rawson would.

My heart stopped, my breath getting stuck in my lungs when Ember walked in at Drake's side. His choice of new recruits followed—and Shannon. Shannon glared at me before her attention moved to where Stone had his shirt off and was instructing a young male shifter in the ring nearest to her. I ignored her; my attention fixed on the woman who held my heart in a vice.

Ember's gaze lifted and she looked right at me. She was too far away for me to see the green of her eyes, but I forced myself to release the breath I'd been holding. I couldn't take my attention off her, absorbing the sight of her lithe yet strong body. I'd teased her once, not only about being skinny, but that she'd become a handful for any lover to deal with. Well, I was right. Ember was a stunning woman. Her torn vest top was knotted just under the generous swell of her breasts, baring a toned, flat stomach that flared into the gentle curve of her hips. She was perfection in a petite package. I allowed myself to study her closely, which wasn't something I'd done so far. There was enough muscle on her arms and shoulders to tell me she'd not been working behind a desk for the past four years, even if I hadn't already observed her skills as a fighter; and that tattoo on her right arm and hand was like nothing I'd seen before. It wasn't especially pretty, but the vines were intricate and the thorns and blood vivid enough to look real from this distance. The thought that she might have been forced into serving a fae made me want to crush something. I doubted such a vibrant and detailed tattoo was done by any human.

Drake tapped her on the shoulder and pointed to an empty ring on the other side of the hall before he gestured to where two females fought each other. She shook her head and pointed to the women. Drake frowned, but nodded in agreement and glanced at me before walking off.

Ember's gaze met mine and her smile slipped.

I cursed. In my haste to protect her, I'd ignored everything I knew about Ember. After what had happened to her as a little girl, fighting—even killing, to survive on the streets of London, she needed to feel like she was in control of her life, that she had a choice, even in this prison environment, and I'd not given her one. I inhaled deeply through my nostrils. Drake had been her choice. I swallowed hard and held her emerald stare as I prowled towards her, trying to keep all the shit that was bouncing around in my head, off my face as her brows drew together.

A Choice. Fine. If that's what she wanted, that's what I'd give her, but I was determined she'd eventually come to me. I'd use every asset in my arsenal to ensure she'd *want* to belong to me and my wolf, just as we'd always belonged to her.

mber

CONNOR STOOD RIGHT next to me. Heat from his body bathed my skin, and this close, his musky scent was too hard to ignore. Unable to help myself, I inhaled deeply. Controlling my heart rate was as impossible as dousing the lust that had my core clenching. My wolf pricked up her ears and stretched languidly even as my stomach flipped, and I tried to hide my reaction to his nearness.

"Do you know why you're here?" His deep voice vibrated into my chest, touching all the right places.

I still didn't look at him, instead I concentrated on the woman who fought a male in the ring next to me. "Other than you told Drake to have me here for training, no." And I'd come willingly because I wanted to see if there was anything here I could use in my escape attempt. There was a moment of silence. I looked up at Connor. His brows were dipped, and he twisted his head to contemplate me. The impact of his stare hit me right in my gut. Gods damn, he'd always been handsome, but now he was all rough edges and hard angles, which only made him hotter. It took everything in me to hold that powerful sky blue gaze, but hold it I did.

Connor's lips quirked into a smile, his amazing eyes heating.

Jeez, if he was hot when he scowled, that smile could make me orgasm on the spot, no matter who was around us, and I'd do it screaming and not care.

He inhaled, and his mouth stretched into a grin as I did my best not to react. I held his gaze, and swallowed hard. *Holy fuck, I was so stupid!* That's why he went supernova on Drake yesterday. Only a potential mate could scent another's arousal. My wolf had tried to bond with Connor's four years ago when he'd kissed me, but we'd never truly discussed how either of us felt. The thought that he might want me as badly as I wanted him, made my whole body weak. I curled my fingers around the ropes to make their trembling less obvious, trying to concentrate on what he was saying.

"Okay, let me explain what's really happening in this prison, and then you can make a choice about what you do next." Connor's eyes darkened when he glanced over at Drake, who kept peering at us.

I swallowed hard. Drake was a nice guy, and gorgeous to boot, but I'd made it clear I wasn't going to sleep with him, even if he was my alpha. He'd seemed to respect that, and I'd been given my own cell, but it was clear as part of his pack, I was expected to follow his lead. It wouldn't be long before he realised I didn't do what was expected of me—that I have my own mind, and plans.

"How about I tell you what I think, and then you correct me where I'm wrong?" I said, impressed I managed to sound relatively in control when Connor's scent was doing strange things to my mind as well as my body.

"Okay, go ahead," He cocked his head expectantly.

"Fine. Ok, obviously this isn't a normal prison. From what I've learned, the unfortunate inmates are a mix of criminals and innocents, but they are all shifters of some kind. You have the power to keep them in line because you're a Prime, and Doherty needs you to prevent anarchy. At a guess, Doherty wants to use us all for something; to make money, I assume; that's usually what evil bastards like him want." I faced Connor and tilted my head. "How am I doing so far?"

He gave me that gorgeous smile again, not taking his eyes off me. "Good, keep going."

I narrowed my eyes remembering Charlie's words. "They need the women in here for something special, don't they?"

"They do, but I'll explain soon."

I grunted, not pushing for answers. Instead, I decided to trust that he would do as he said. Mother wolf, I wanted to trust him, but more to the point, I wanted him to trust me, too. And after yesterday, I had to earn it, just like he did. I continued with my assessment of the hell hole I'd been locked in. "There are four alpha's: one for each wing. Each controls their own pack of hundreds of shifters, both men and women. Pack marked females seem to be protected and left alone by males from other packs or gen pop, but any unmarked female seems to be fair game..." My voice tightened at that.

"Seemed." Connor pulled his gaze off me and leaned on the ropes, looking at his clasped hands as he quietly corrected me.

"Okay, seemed, but I still don't understand you allowing the weak to suffer for so long. That was so wrong."

He sighed. "I know. "

I gaped, raising my brows at his unexpected agreement.

Connor grinned, revealing a broken tooth, one of his canines. That smile again. I flushed, unable to drag my attention from the curve of his lips. My gut clenched. That tiny break might stop him claiming me... I blinked rapidly, pressing my thighs together as the thought of him sinking those canines into me as he claimed my body and soul, almost pushed me over the edge. It was damn hard to swallow my groan. Ok, nope, I definitely shouldn't be going there.

Slowly, he placed his forefinger under my chin and pushed my mouth closed. "Like I said, I was wrong." He cocked his head and inhaled, and his smile widened even as his eyes darkened. "And, no, this sure as shit wouldn't stop me." With his forefinger he touched his broken tooth. "Nothing would." His voice was nothing but a low resonant rumble, making the situation between my legs even harder to bear. Gods, I'd never ached for anyone else like this.

I swallowed hard and gazed into his beautiful, predatory eyes. "W-what are you talking about?" Now there was nothing I could do to stop the tremor in my voice.

"You were wondering if this would stop me from claiming you," he said, his voice a low rumble in my ear. I shuffled away a step, heat rushing through me even as my mouth dried out.

He inhaled, his dark eyes gleaming, but he let me move back, a smirk curling his lips. "I can still scent you, Firecracker. And your thoughts definitely went to me claiming you—or doing something equally as sexy."

I huffed, unwilling to acknowledge the effect he had on me. Drake may have incited my lust, but Connor took my emotions to a whole new level, even my mind betrayed me when he was near. And I didn't know how to handle what was building between us.

The fighters left the ring. Connor jumped up and stepped through the ropes into the ring. "Join me?"

Was he actually asking me?

He gave me that sexy smile of his, and I hesitated. My eyes narrowed and I bit my lower lip. "Why are you being so nice to me, after yesterday? You have every right to still be angry with me. I..."

Shannon sauntered close. "That's easy, runt." She interrupted my apology. "He got laid last night. He was so upset by you joining another pack, he forgot *all* about you and fucked a brunette, who was, oh, so willing. Careful, once he's done with what's between your legs, he'll leave you hanging without a second thought."

I froze, watching as she winked at Connor and walked off, sashaying around the rings towards where Santa the jerk was fighting with Reed.

Connor's fury was like a blast of hot air against my skin, but I was too busy trying to sort through my own emotions. I knew he could have whoever he wanted, whenever he wanted. He was hot, fit, and had power in this enclosed world of badass shifters and violence. I tried to tell myself it didn't matter, that I'd made my choice to join another pack. After all, why would he wait around for me when I'd thrown his protection, and our bond, back in his face? I bit back a groan. Gods, I *knew* alphas were dominating and protective of their mates. And instead of considering the real reason for his ultimatum, and the protection he'd given me from his brothers, I'd gone right back to being that snarky teenager, and rebelled against him. Damn, I'd been away from shifters too long; Connor didn't want to control me, he wanted to keep me safe, because I was his mate. My blood boiled and I wanted to kick my own arse for running to Drake. Fuck, it hurt like a bitch to know Connor had been with someone else last night. Even knowing I probably pushed him there.

Determined not to let him see how upset I was, I got into the ring.

Connor's face was blank, but his eyes were fixed intently on my face. I forced a smile and shrugged. Taking a steadying breath, I continued with my assessment of the prison. "So where were we? Oh yes..." I prowled to the middle of the ring and peered up at Connor's face. "So the weak are no longer fodder for the psychotic molesters in this place, but there is something else going on that I don't know much about." I began to warm up, then looked up from where I'd leaned forward over my straight legs to stretch them.

Connor's attention was riveted to my movements. I hid my smile. Yeah, he was a man, and just like any other, loved to watch a woman's body as she moved. And I wasn't quite the skinny teenager I'd been when he'd last seen me. I spread my legs a bit wider and stretched again, placing my chin on my knee, grinning into my leg when a low growl resounded behind me. He might have gotten a pissed off fuck from some other female, but that just made me want to show him what he was missing.

"Charlie told me women disappear once a month." I straightened up and twisted side to side, before leaning over to the side and stretching my oblique muscles while studying the gym. "And this hall isn't set up like this just for fun, so something else is going on." I turned back to face Connor, who had an intense look on his face as he studied me. "That's right." His expression darkened, and he gently took hold of both of my wrists to halt my stretching. "Wait. Stop for a second."

I didn't miss his throat bob, or the tightness in his jaw as his mouth pressed into a thin line. I twisted my wrists and wrapped my fingers around his muscled forearms, trying to ignore how good it felt to touch him. "What's wrong?" I whispered. He didn't speak for a moment. "Connor?"

"It's better if we discuss it somewhere private. Will you come to my cell after we're done here?"

"Wait." I smiled up at him. "Are you asking, or telling me?"

"Asking."

"Wow, that's a first." I smirked.

His broken tooth made another appearance. "Well, will you?"

"Maybe." I was being deliberately obtuse, but sue me for wanting to push, just a little.

"Ember. This is important." His smile slipped, and his voice held a note of urgency as his grip on my wrists tightened.

This close, I couldn't deny my attraction to him. Black bled into his blue irises until there was a startling mix of both. Stepping closer was instinctive. I peered up at him, my body screaming for his. I wanted to jump up and wrap my legs around his waist and kiss the hell out of his beautiful mouth. I didn't care about all the people around us in the hall, just that he was alive, even if he wasn't the same person he used to be. "Say please," I whispered.

He brought my hands between us and pulled me closer, effectively trapping them between our chests. He gave a growl that vibrated through me, but his eyes turned wholly blue again. "Please."

I swallowed hard. I hadn't expected him to give in so easily. I was at a loss now. Connor was used to ordering everyone around—including me—he always had, and I had always defied him, but now I didn't know how to behave in the face of a request from him. I had no reason not to go; besides whatever he wanted to tell me was enough to make worry darken his expression, and I didn't like it. I nodded and stepped back a bit. He released me and did the same.

"I'll explain why later, but you need to be in this gym everyday honing those fighting skills you seem to have at your fingertips." He cocked his head and studied me. It was like being pinned to the spot by a predator who was assessing your strengths and weaknesses before attacking.

I shifted back further, aware we were being watched by a large number of people, including Drake, not that I was worried. I now had Connor's alpha pack and Drake to protect me. "Who am I fighting?" I stepped even further away. Of course, I didn't need to ask, the light in Connor's eyes said it all. I shifted my weight and began to circle him, watching for any sign he might move. Blue eyes twinkled back at me as he tracked my movements, but his body remained relaxed, or as relaxed as I imagined Connor ever was. The next moment he grabbed the hem of his muscle tee and lifted it off.

My footsteps faltered and my eyes feasted on the sight of Connor with no shirt on. And what a sight it was—hard muscle met my hungry gaze, and the dips and planes of his washboard abs had me drooling. I forced my gaze away from the line of dark hair that ran from his navel down below the waistband of his jeans. Just as my eyes were landing on pecs made in heaven, an arm grabbed my throat and yanked me back. I grunted and found myself pinned against a hard, tall body with a training dagger against my neck.

Connor grinned, and leaned back against the ropes opposite me. "Distraction can be a powerful tool, Ember."

I rolled my eyes and instead of struggling, sagged into my attacker. It was strange, but the male behind me felt familiar, his scent pulling at the chords of my memory. I pushed them away and smiled sweetly. "Piss off."

Connor chuckled. "Admit it, even though you ran from me yesterday, you still thought you were going to get to spar with me, didn't you, Firecracker?" Straightening from the ropes, he began an indolent approach.

In turn, I went even more languid, like I couldn't take my eyes off him. A subtle change in stance and hold from my attacker was all I needed to realise he'd fallen for my ploy. My wolf's power flooded me, lending me strength. I growled, and despite the ropes being between me and the man at my back, I shifted my weight and drove my elbow into his breast bone. There was a satisfying crack and a muffled expletive. The big arm around my neck loosened enough to give me room to maneuver. I ignored the wooden blade and slammed my ridge hand into the man's groin. Not letting up, and determined not to be bested by anyone, I smashed a backfist into his face, grabbing the arm now loose around my neck. *Connor thinks he's so clever having this guy sneak up on me. Fine, I'll break the fucker's arm!*

"Ember! Stop..."

I froze. That voice.

"Rawson?" Taking one step out of his embrace, I pivoted on the canvas. Deep brown eyes, familiar, yet wary, looked back at me. "But you were a..." My words dried up. I wasn't sure what he'd been when I'd been abducted by red eyes.

He grimaced. "A Were. I, err, I haven't been entirely myself since we were captured and sent here."

I stepped closer to the man who'd been my saviour, who'd taken me in and cared for me, aware Connor was watching closely. Why? Did he think I'd hurt Rawson, that I'd blame him for my capture? Or was he worried about Rawson's behaviour? I didn't care, not as I looked at Rawson's beloved face. My heart cracked. His chocolate brown eyes were clouded with suffering. I had no idea what had been done to break him so badly, I'm not sure I wanted to know, but at that moment, more than my own incarceration, more than Blue's abduction and even losing Connor, I wanted to rip Doherty and this place apart for everything they'd done to him.

Without holding back I launched myself at Rawson, nearly knocking him off the side of the training ring as I flung my arms around him. I didn't cry often, especially in front of others. It was a sign of weakness I wouldn't show, but right now I couldn't help but choke out a sob into Rawson's chest. I barely remembered my birth parents, but I could recall everything Rawson and Lyss had done for me. I sniffled, and held him tighter.

His arms came around me, not as big and heavily muscled as they had been, but it was so nice to feel the warmth and safety of his hug. I relaxed into his embrace, the weight of our circumstance lifting from me. Tears burned my eyes, and this time I let them fall.

He patted my back. "It's good to see you, too," he said thickly. "Even though I think you cracked my breastbone."

I squeezed him even harder, unwilling to stop as a whole four years of emotions got tangled up in my chest. I needed a minute, or several, before I could face everyone else in the hall. My emotions were so raw I couldn't form words.

He released a shuddering breath. "I missed you, too. Connor and me...we saw your wolf's head. Gods, Ember, it looked and smelt like her, we truly believed you were dead."

I just shook my head. "I'm so sorry. I can explain..."

"Ember, we can talk about that later," Connor's voice was firm and had an undertone of warning.

Rawson dipped his head, and his shoulders curled forward. "Yes, you can tell Connor what happened—" He paused and sighed. "It's probably best you don't tell me." He breathed into my hair. "I don't know what happened, but that clearly wasn't you. That's enough for me."

I shook my head again, my face still buried in his broad chest. I sniffed and hugged him even tighter, unwilling to let him go. I could find out what Connor's warning was for later.

"Hey, loosen up a bit, I can't breathe." A chuckle rippled through him.

"Sorry." But my emotions still tumbled like a storm inside me.

"Hey." The weight of Connor's hand rested on my shoulder, squeezing gently and reassuringly. "You can let him go, Em, he's not going anywhere."

I still couldn't bring myself to release him. If I did he might disappear; he'd leave again...

"Em?" Connor leaned down and peered into my eyes where I rested my cheek against Rawson's chest. "It's okay, Rawson's staying. You really can let go." His nearness and voice soothed me, and my heart rate and breathing slowed enough that my rational brain kicked in. I was making a fool of myself. Not only that, we might as well be standing on a stage.

I broke eye contact with Connor and straightened up. Giving the hand on my shoulder a squeeze, I took a deep breath and turned to Rawson. "Hi," I said and leaned up on my tip toes and kissed his cheek.

"Hi." He smiled back, though it wasn't his usual vibrant smile.

"He's here to help you settle in—and train you."

Despite the warmth of Connor's touch on my shoulder, my spine snapped straight. "What do you mean *train me*? For what?"

Connor grinned, his hand dropping away. He shrugged, his neck muscles bunching. Gods, he made even that simple move look powerful.

"Well, you have moves, but they need to be sharper, more precise and more powerful."

"Why?" I spun to face him.

He walked further into the ring, a smirk on his lips.

Rawson dipped in through the ropes and stood a few feet away, watching us with a smile.

"There's nothing wrong with my *moves*." They didn't need to know I'd deliberately held back. It didn't make sense to showcase all my talents in front of the potential enemies in the hall—not even to prove Connor wrong.

Connor twisted his lips, and nonchalantly shrugged one shoulder. "No, except you would be dead now if that dagger had been real."

"You cheated!" I conceded that I sounded childish right now, but Connor always made me defensive. I took a deep breath and exhaled slowly. We weren't kids now, I needed to react differently around him.

"Cheated?" He raised his brows, arrogance returning to his movements and stance in spades. "Firecracker, you might not belong to my pack—or me...yet." He scowled at Drake. "But this body drew your attention enough you didn't see anything else around you. Your *moves* might be good, but you need to learn to read your opponent's mind, and anticipate underhanded actions, as well as being able to kick them in the balls. Once you can fight without being distracted, you might stand a chance of survival."

My fists curled and my nostrils flared, but I remained quiet. He had a point.

Rawson stepped between us. "Ember, if you let me train with you, you'd be doing me a big favour. I get very little opportunity to practise my fighting skills these days. It'll give us a chance to catch up, and you can tell me what you've been doing for the past four years."

I pressed my lips together, not sure that was such a good idea.

"Hmm, I, too, would love to know what you've been doing for the past four years while I believed you and your wolf were dead."

I thanked the Mother Wolf that Connor put his shirt back on. His mouth spread in a smile at the relief I showed. "I thought you said I'd be training with Rawson." I sidestepped the implied question. I'd given Connor some shit for his actions since being in this prison, and I'd been dealing drugs. Gods, how do I own up to that now?

"Oh, you are…and me—and everyone else we think are good opponents for you. Okay, I'll leave you to your secrets, for now. But tonight, in roughly eight hours, you are coming back to my cell—not going to his. We have things to discuss." He glared at Drake, then looked at the ground and shook his head.

I rubbed my forearms with my hands while shaking my head, suddenly nervous about being alone with Connor.

"You already agreed, Em," Connor pointed out tightly.

I swallowed hard. "I know, but I can change my mind."

"Not this time, Firecracker. I told you. It's too important. You need to know why I'm going to train you so hard and what really happens here." He towered over me, his jaw clenched tightly.

I scowled, but bit my tongue, trying to understand why I was nervous of him. His alpha power thickened the air. I swallowed, knowing I'd made him angry again, but I didn't lower my gaze.

"Both of you need to cool off. Now!"

We looked at Rawson and the surprise on Connor's face was priceless. I began to laugh. His smile grew, too. I exchanged a look with him. It was surreal to have Rawson snap at us, but nice to remember all the times in the past he had done just that.

"Sorry." I smiled sheepishly at Rawson.

He rolled his eyes. "Don't give me that doe eyed look, missy. There's a lot going on here that you don't know about. This isn't just a prison, it's much much more, and Connor is only trying to keep you safe. Do him and me a favour, and let him." His attention drifted to Drake. "Like Connor said, don't get distracted, or be too stubborn to accept his help, both could get you killed. Bad things happen in this place…" His voice drifted off and his eyes darkened.

"Okay." Stepping closer, I slipped my arms around him again. I hated that lost and broken look in his eyes. A moment later, he shook himself and patted my back.

"Come on, Em, people will start to talk if you keep throwing yourself at me like this."

I huffed a laugh. "Not bothered." Rawson was a few years shy of forty and a handsome man, not as muscular as he had been, but still fit and good looking. He was clever and kind and deserved far better from his life than to be stuck in here through no fault of his own. I frowned. If I wasn't bothered by what people thought of me, why had I run from Connor and joined Drake's pack? What was I thinking?

I looked at Connor, then dropped my gaze to the floor as my head started to pound. In Faerie, when I lost my temper, or fucked up, I usually didn't have to deal with the consequences. In essence, I'd just run away. It hadn't mattered to me if I treated someone badly because I never saw them again. That was a bad way to be. I hadn't meant to hurt Connor by joining Drake's pack, I'd just reacted to his ultimatum, and the situation the way I wanted to. I hadn't considered his feelings. But I wasn't a child anymore; I didn't have the luxury of just reacting. And Connor, as a strong alpha, was used to issuing commands and being obeyed; so was that sense of authority his fault or even a fault at all? He was Prime. He *had* to be in charge here or the place would descend into anarchy. The guards couldn't control hundreds of angry shifters all vying for the top spot. They'd have to kill too many if such violence broke out, and even I could see that Doherty, or whoever ran this place, wouldn't want the majority of his captives dead.

"When you two are done with manhandling each other, perhaps we can get some training in." Connor's lips were pressed tightly together, his face dark.

Rawson glanced at him, and slowly lifted his hands off me, raising them placatingly. "Sure, Connor, no more manhandling." His voice was deliberately calming. My heart did a stupid flip flop at the thought that Connor was getting all *mate* possessive again.

Rawson smiled at me, then cocked his head and assessed me. "You look strong, and it's clear you remember how to fight. I take it you found somewhere totally under the SBI radar to hide?"

I nodded. "Yes, I did." I deliberately didn't elaborate.

"Okay…" he said slowly. "Why aren't you telling me where?"

I shrugged. "Because my life hasn't been all unicorns and roses, and I've done bad things that I don't want you to know about." My eyes unintentionally flicked to Connor.

Rawson huffed a chuckle. "Sweet girl…" He used the endearment Lyss had always used for me, even though he knew I was far from sweet. "… your life has never been easy, and I don't expect unicorns and flowers. I'm certainly in no position to judge you for what you've done to survive. My life's been shit since I lost Lyss, and I've done some despicable things. And Connor does what needs to be done inside these walls. None of us are angels."

I gave a small smile, but bit my bottom lip, not able to look at Connor.

There was a pause.

I just couldn't admit to them where I'd been or what I'd been doing. I looked around a bit. Maybe when we were alone and not surrounded by all these strangers I'd feel more inclined to share.

Connor sighed. "Okay, Firecracker, keep your secrets. You can tell me when you're ready."

I flashed him a small smile of thanks, flushing as his eyes softened. Then he coughed and squared his shoulders.

"Right now, we need to see what you've got. Rawson." It was a command,

and whereas when we were young Rawson had always held the position of power, he nodded at Connor. The dynamics of their relationship had definitely changed.

Seeing the muscles of Rawson's body tense as he shifted his weight, I jumped back, only just missing the kick that he aimed my way. I adjusted the angle of my body, making myself a smaller target. Rawson was stronger than me, and quick, but he didn't know the ways I'd learned to fight in Faerie. I dropped my body weight, and on the ball of one foot, spun with one leg stretched straight and took out his leading foot. It gave me a split second to lift myself up and smash my fist into his kidneys while he was off balance. I hoped his healing abilities were still working. I bounced out of the way as he followed me, unleashing a combination of super fast punches. Within a moment, I was face down on the mat with my arm twisted painfully up my back.

"Concede."

I tried to twist out of his hold and get enough freedom to attack.

He tried again. "Ember, tap out."

"Ember, you need to know when to give in. Rawson won't break your arm —unless I tell him to, but your future opponents will. Tap out."

I glared at Connor, not willing to give in.

Rawson put the arm lock on harder.

Connor raised his brows at me, but his face was tight, his jaw muscles clenched. His eyes flickered to Rawson before his dark gaze fixed on me.

Pain blazed in my shoulder, and I couldn't hold back a screech.

"Ember..." Connor growled, his hands fisted. "Gods dammit all, concede!" He looked at me, his nostrils flared and his eyes turned wholly black. Power thickened the air.

I clenched my teeth. I had to concede. Being stubborn was putting Rawson in danger, if Connor's face was anything to go by. I slapped the palm of my free hand on the mat, twice.

Rawson released me and stood, holding his hand out. I scowled, and reluctantly took it. Once on my feet, I shook out my arm and shoulder until the pain receded.

Rawson watched me with a slight frown dipping his brows. "You're still so stubborn."

"Yeah, well, what can I say, surviving on your own will do that to a person. And I hate to lose. If you lose, you die." And that had always been true, whether I'd been in Faerie when the royal guards hunted me and Blue down, or in the shadowed streets of London.

Connor closed the distance between us until his shoulder brushed mine. Almost as if he was trying to get as close as possible without actually touching me. "We didn't leave you on purpose," he said quietly, his eyes cerulean.

Rawson stepped closer too, his fingers brushing mine. "We didn't, neither did Lyss."

Of course they hadn't, I knew that, but it didn't change the fact that life was unpredictable, and something evil was happening in this place that instinct told me could take them from me in an instant.

"And you're right, giving in or losing will result in you dying in here. So we are going to retrain you to never end up in that kind of vulnerable position again," Connor said firmly.

I nodded and blew out a steadying breath. I didn't know what was going on, or why all these people were training so hard, but it was clear both Connor and Rawson wanted me to be as strong as I could be. I wasn't so wrapped up in myself I'd turn that down.

"Okay."

They both looked at me then each other, their brows raised.

"What?" My eyes narrowed.

"Nothing."

"Nothing."

They both said at the same time.

Connor grinned. "I'm impressed, Firecracker."

"At what?" What was there about my last words that would be impressive?

"That you can be reasonable, and make a sensible decision about something I suggested, without arguing with me."

Before I had a chance to give a suitably snarky response, Stone jumped into the ring. Whilst glaring at me, he indicated with his head that he needed to talk to Connor.

I had no idea why Stone detested me so much, but I didn't care. I smiled back sweetly.

Stone curled his lip before he whispered something in Connor's ear. I strained my ears trying to use my wolf's senses to help me, but, of course they knew the right volume to use. Stone glanced at me again, and scowled—again. With no shirt on, and covered in a sheen of sweat, which only served to define the cut of muscle over his powerful body, I conceded he looked almost as jaw-droppingly hot, as Connor. Still, he did nothing for me, not like the male who stood right next to him.

I clocked Shannon scowling at me from across the hall where Stone had come from. Santa, the crazy surfer dude, eyed me from the ring she stood next to. Smirking, he turned away and vaulted out of the ring coming to a stop near Shannon. I couldn't care less about the two of them. I dropped my attention back on Connor. Stone gave me one last dark look before he stalked away. Noticing Santa hitting on Shannon, he sped up, his eyes fixed on them.

Connor crossed the mat and stood in front of us. "Rawson, I'm leaving Ember with you. Take care of her, brother."

Rawson nodded. "Of course."

Then Connor looked down at me and touched my face gently with his forefinger. It was a featherlight touch, almost reverent.

I swallowed and blinked when his hand fell away.

"Rawson will take care of you until I get back. Don't leave with Drake, we have a date later. Don't forget." He grinned roguishly, knowing his words would wind me up. "I don't need *taking care of*," I muttered. Somehow, I didn't want to argue with the rest of his sentence.

"Yeah, you do." I heard the amusement in his voice. Turning away, he strode across the mat and vaulted over the ropes.

I opened my mouth to yell something back.

"Ember!" Rawson barked my name before I could think of anything. He chuckled. "You don't always have to have the last word. Remember your defiance will have repercussions, for you and for Connor. He cannot allow public defiance to go unpunished, or it will open the floodgates for more unrest and challenges." He looked meaningfully at the people around us, some of whom had stopped their fights and were eyeing me with curiosity, others with cold calculation.

I grunted an acknowledgement. He was right. And I was supposed to be working on my attitude with Connor. "So what are we doing?"

"Fighting."

I raised my brows. "Is that it? Doesn't sound very technical."

Rawson grinned. "Oh, it is. This will be fun! Just like old times."

I laughed. "Not quite, old man, I have some moves, too."

"Show me," he commanded and threw the first punch.

CHAPTER 11

onnor

STONE AND OWEN were hard faced as I followed Zander and walked away from them. It was for the best. Doherty might be a self-serving fuck, but the warden was evil to his core. I'd been on the receiving end of his 'abilities' more than once and no matter how much power I held, it didn't work on the warden. Tension stiffened my shoulders. Somehow, I needed to find out what he was doing in this prison.

As we walked, the tension in my body only became worse. He'd broken my right hand, one bone at a time without even touching me the last time we'd had one of these meetings.

I hoped to gods this wasn't in some way connected to Ember. I needed to keep her under the warden's radar, not to mention Doherty's. The SBI director had always been obsessed with her; always quizzing me on her when we were teenagers. When I'd left Rawson's home and joined the bureau he'd still asked me about her, and I'd never managed to find out why.

I eyed the two mamma bots that hovered up near the ceiling of the sterile corridor, their weapons aimed at me. Knowing they could spew out mini bots with enough firepower to cull a riot didn't help my tension.

Zander didn't use any ID to get through the next set of security doors; it seemed they still had the same technology as four years ago. Keeping his all new weapon trained on me, he placed one hand on the pad beside the door and waited until several tiny needles had sampled his blood. As we continued on through the maze of corridors, two of the armoured bots hovered above each doorway. There was no way out of the underground facility without getting past those buggers in each and every corridor.

I hadn't seen the outside world for four years, and I yearned to see a full moon and let my wolf free to run in the wilderness that was up there. From what I'd seen that snowy night I'd arrived, and how long we'd been on the plane, I thought we were in the wilds of Canada somewhere, but I didn't know for sure. The inmates came from different parts of the world and the guards had voice changing technology in their masks. I didn't know what any of them looked like other than Zander. Shifters worked with them, but Zander wasn't a shifter. I wouldn't ask what he was, just as he'd never tell me.

Zander urged me down yet another corridor with no identifying features. I was once again utterly lost. We hadn't gone upwards toward the surface, but downwards, further into the earth.

"What does he want with me?" I asked tightly.

"No idea, but I doubt it's to pat you on the back." Zander urged me to keep walking by shoving the metal of his weapon into the back of my head.

"Maybe he knows you're betraying…"

He jabbed me in the back with his weapon. "Shut it!"

I grinned, and eyed the drones. So they had a microphone too. Wasn't surprising, but I'd needed confirmation.

"Stay quiet, or I'll make sure your friends, including your *newest* one, take a little trip down agony lane."

I remained quiet, knowing he was threatening Ember and my brothers. The corridor came to an end in front of a lift. A bot hovered above it, threatening in its silence. "Really, you trust me in a lift?"

"I don't trust you anywhere. Hands behind your back."

Darkness swamped me as he shoved a bag over my head. I hesitated to comply, my instincts urging me to fight for my freedom.

"Connor, do it, or I'll taser you."

I slid my hands behind my back, the thought of pissing myself before I saw the warden swaying my decision.

"Thank you," Zander said.

Was that relief I heard in his voice?

"What are you, that the warden gives you privileges to wander these halls, and entrusts you alone with prisoners?" I asked.

"I'm the stuff of nightmares." He lowered his voice so that the bot wouldn't pick up his next words. "And I think we can agree that there is no privilege in serving the warden."

"We can. And there's absolutely no doubt you're part of my ongoing nightmare, not to mention Rawson's."

"I know." His voice was tight as he guided me into the lift. I didn't resist, there was no point. There were a few seconds of weightlessness. Up or down, I had no idea. It was even hard to discern when the lift stopped. The doors opened smoothly, hardly any noise at all, and air breezed over my bare arms.

"Come on." Zander pushed me along by my cuffed wrists

I hesitated when my trainers sank into a soft carpet. The lack of noise from our footsteps was odd when I'd spent so much time in the echoey halls of the prison.

"Hang on." Zander stopped us again. I waited, my body wound tight, unsure what was going on. There was the almost silent slide of a door. "In." He urged me forwards with a push between my shoulder blades. "Stop," he said.

The bag over my head was removed. I blinked at the brightness, and gaped at my surroundings. Opposite me was a huge garish fireplace. Its centre was big enough for me to stand in, at least twice over. Writhing stone monsters, or perhaps they were demons, made up the massive surround. I narrowed my eyes to get a better look. Yes, demons—and angels...I swallowed hard at the other mythical creatures, werewolves were one of them. Interwoven with the supernatural beings, women were depicted in various states of sexual inter-course with them all. It was the weirdest, most garish and disturbing fireplace I'd ever seen.

In the fire grate, unnaturally red and yellow flames burned. The heat was tremendous and beads of perspiration ran down my chest and back. Despite the heat, chills skittered down my spine. Wiping my palms on my jeans, I glanced around the room as we waited for the warden. The carpet was thick, and the room was sparsely furnished, though decadent in the items that were there. Bottles of whiskey and other liquors sat on a table. I frowned, staring at an unlabelled bottle that was half full of viscous ruby liquid. I inhaled and scented blood. Why in hell would he want bottled blood? I averted my gaze and continued to study the room. A large couch sat right in front of the fire-place, so close anyone sitting on it would surely cook. There was a whole wall of black curtains but no hint of daylight, only lamps and the vivid flames gave any illumination. We must still be underground, so I had no idea what might be behind those curtains.

"Thank you, Zander." That crooning tone sent shivers down my spine.

I blinked, and the warden seemed to appear right next to the fireplace. I stiffened and glanced at Zander. As always his face was tight, his eyes burning red as he watched the warden. Zander turned to leave, as he often did during these meetings.

Dark eyes flickered to him. "No, you will stay this time, Zander. This won't take long."

Zander stiffened but nodded, and remained in his position.

The warden walked over to the sideboard and poured himself a generous helping of amber liquid from one of the bottles, then settled himself on the expensive leather couch in front of the fireplace. "Come closer, Prime." He gestured for me to approach and stand where he could easily see me.

My skin burned and sweat ran down my neck from my hairline. I didn't understand how he could tolerate that amount of heat.

"I like it cosy." He grinned, showing me his perfectly white and straight teeth. His dark eyes gleamed, the flames reflecting in them as he regarded me. There was little point in encouraging him to get on with the point of this meeting. He'd do as he pleased and that usually included making me wait for either punishment or information. Either way nothing good ever came from these meetings.

"I am bringing forward the entertainment for my clients. The fun will begin in fourteen days from now. I want twice as many candidates identified for this one, and I want more women fighting, as well as more in the entertainment rooms. They bring in as much money fighting as the alpha males do when I use them in the entertainment wings."

I froze, swallowing the choking sensation in my throat. Double the people meant almost a week's worth of fighting and hundreds of lives ruined or sacrificed to line his and Doherty's pockets, all to feed the sick satisfaction of the rich bastards who liked to degrade us or see us kill each other.

The warden took a generous swallow of his drink. "And this time I'm going to make it more interesting. I'm going to allow the people chosen to partially change." He grinned.

Bile hit my throat. I was still trying to process the hundreds of people I would identify to be slaughtered.

The warden stood and took another large swallow of his drink. How I wished for the burn and oblivion of alcohol right now. He stepped right up to the fire and I hoped he'd set himself on fire. He tapped one of the Weres on the carving. "Did you know your kind used to be under the control of Satan himself? Before you escaped through the gates of hell, into this world and developed into no more than wild dogs, you were the minions of hell. You were vicious attack hounds, nothing more, and that's all I expect from your kind now. In two weeks, you will all fight in Were form and show those who have paid to watch just what monsters you really are."

I ground my teeth, but managed to stay silent, though it took all my self control. Many of the shifters in here had not changed for years, and to be allowed a partial shift but not full, would be agony, enough to drive some of them insane.

The warden smiled at me, his dark hair gleaming in the firelight. "I can see my generosity bothers you, but make no mistake, it will happen. You are monsters, not worthy of having free will or receiving compassion of any kind.

I am only informing you of my plans so that you can prepare more fighters. They will need to be strong, and capable of surviving long enough to satisfy my guests."

Guests? That was different. He never referred to those that paid for an invitation, bet on the fights, or used us for entertainment, as guests. He fixed me with an unnerving onyx stare that was as powerful as it was cold. Like Zander, he wasn't a shifter, but something else, something that had my wolf wanting to run. And that scared the shit out of me—my wolf was scared of nothing.

"I want the best fighters you have in the rings and that means the males who follow you around like pathetic lap dogs. They will please my guests with their will to survive, and the blood they will shed." He licked his lips, anticipation shining in his eyes.

My face remained expressionless and I kept my mouth shut. No matter how much I raged inside, I'd learned the hard way not to give any response to his threats. He'd go from calm to utterly insane within a matter of moments if I even looked at him wrong. My claws lengthened just a little and my skin burned under the constriction of the silver collar. I had to work hard at studying the fireplace to keep from challenging him head on, what with my wolf's almost overwhelming need to rip his throat out for threatening our pack.

The warden rolled the glass in his fingers as he studied me thoughtfully. "Who is that beautiful creature with the red hair who you've shown such an interest in?"

I swallowed hard using every bit of my self-control not to launch myself at him. "Just another female to fuck."

His obsidian gaze seared my soul. My wolf stirred in disquiet, digging his claws into my insides. Pain shot along my nerves and I ground my teeth, trying not to cry out.

The warden grinned widely, though his eyes remained dead. "Really?" Reaching out, he traced his forefinger over the bare breast of one of the human women on the fireplace. "Then I'll have her as my companion and you can find another to empty your seed in."

"No!" I growled, my fists clenching in the cuffs behind my back, the silver burning my skin.

"No?" His voice was deceptively quiet.

I waited for the pain of broken bones to strike.

"She's a good fighter, not just a female for entertainment. If you want female fighters who can give a show for your guests, she would be better left with me." I was clutching at straws, frantic to keep Ember away from this monster.

He cocked his head and smirked. "Even better. Then she fights in two weeks, and if she survives, I'll enjoy celebrating with her." Promise laced his words. He sipped from his glass, savouring the liquid in his mouth before he met my eyes. "And if she doesn't survive, I will enjoy her anyway."

Ice wound around my heart, shadows and darkness shrouding it as my emotions tumbled around inside me. What the hell did that mean? I fought back my wolf's need to shred this creature, unsure why evil dicks like Doherty, Santa and this prick, were so drawn to Ember. Sure, she was unusually beautiful, her bright fiery red hair and green eyes catching the attention of men and women alike, but there was something else...something unusual in her aura that drew people to her, and not always in a healthy way.

The warden's attention drifted to where Zander waited. "I visited your mother last night, Zander. Once we'd—caught up..." He smirked at his own words. "She begged to see you, to ensure you are alive and well."

I sensed Zander tense and his breathing and heart rate increased. A slight burning smell filled the air, tinged with the sharp scent of fear.

"I told her you'd be down to see her as soon as I could spare you from your duties."

Zander didn't speak, but an enormous amount of heat blasted over me from behind. I tensed. Zander was always in control, except when he was near the warden, and though I hated him for his part in all of this, I couldn't help but wonder what threat the warden held over him and his mother.

The warden smirked and looking from Zander to me, downed the rest of his drink. "You can get this filth out of here now." His gaze honed in on me and for a moment I saw something predatory and cold in his eyes staring out at me.

With great effort, I dropped my eyes and studied his shiny black shoes. Lowering my gaze as an Alpha Prime was so damned hard, but not as hard as knowing I couldn't protect Ember now that she'd come to the attention of the warden—and if he knew she was here, it wouldn't be long before Doherty did.

"Don't forget the redhead, Prime. Train her and enjoy her while you can. After the games, she's mine. And I want your best fighters—your brothers. Mark them on the list and don't try to fool me; Zander will confirm who they are. Out of your best, let's see who will fall and who will rise again."

My heart skipped into an erratic rhythm, my wolf pacing and snarling. *Don't react, don't react,* but the wall that held back the darkness inside me, crumbled. Hate seeped into my soul, inciting my wolf and infecting my ability to think. My fists curled and blood pounded in my ears. Without warning Zander shoved the bag over my head from behind and grabbed my cuffed wrists. The canvas confined and blinded me, stopping me from doing something stupid. Surrounded by darkness, the need to kill faded, leaving me shaky. I panted through my nostrils, grunting when he grabbed my wrists and shoved me forward.

"Zander!"

We halted.

"What does that fucker want now?" Zander muttered under his breath. "Yes, Sir?" His voice carried across the large room.

"Don't forget your promise to your mother."

"I won't," Zander replied tightly.

One day, I'd ask what leverage the warden had over Zander. And who, exactly, his mother was.

CHAPTER 12

I WALKED BACK into the hall, my attention drawn to Ember. Rawson walked her through some combinations. A smile stretched across my face; he looked happier than I'd seen him in years, and the smile on her face was like having the sunlight filter into all the dark corners of this awful place. My chest tightened at the genuine joy on her face, and I wished I could see it more often. The big loner guy, Lionel, was in the ring with them. My hackles rose and power leaked from me as he came up behind her and put on a loose choke hold; and though I cracked my neck and forced myself to relax, a wave of jealousy rolled off me. Owen flinched as he stalked closer.

I kicked myself. I couldn't be a possessive shit every time another man went near her. My enemies would figure out far too quickly why I was so protective and territorial over her, and that would just put her in more danger. Hell, it already had. The deliberate, slow breath I took didn't help. I still wanted to yank Lionel away from her.

Ember turned, her emerald gaze searching the hall until she found me. I held her stare until she slammed her hands on her hips and her head cocked belligerently. I smirked before I turned away. Gods above, I adored her fire, it made my body burn with a need only she could extinguish. "Come with me."

Owen nodded at my instruction as I walked towards Drake.

The southern alpha had been an IT developer in the outside world. Drake had told me that Doherty had set his sights on Drake's company and when Drake had refused to work with him, he'd found himself in prison on embezzlement charges. It had all been a crock of shit of course, but somehow Doherty had made the charges stick and Drake had lost everything, including his freedom.

Right now, I was glad of his techno brain. I had an idea, and he was the only one who could help. Now Ember had hit the warden's radar, it wasn't just my faceless employer, or Zander, or even Doherty, who were a threat to her. Ember didn't know it, but if she survived the fight rings, she would be hauled out of the prison and into the warden's clutches. I wouldn't allow that to happen.

I cracked my knuckles as I approached the south wing alpha. "We need to talk. Your cell." It was a command. Drake merely nodded.

We walked in silence, Owen at my back. Drake's beta behind him.

"You can wait outside," Owen instructed the beta and shut the cell door in the woman's face.

Drake sighed. "I didn't force Ember to join my pack, Connor."

"No, you didn't." I'd already come to that conclusion myself. "I did."

His brow dipped, his face twisting almost comically. "Er, riiight."

I slapped his shoulder and grinned. "Don't worry about it. I had forgotten how fiercely independent Ember is. She does what she wants, not what you, me or anyone else tells her to do."

Drake huffed and smiled. "Yeah, I got that from her. She likes to have a choice." His eyes narrowed, and he crossed his arms over his broad chest, quirking an eyebrow at me.

I ignored the comment, irritated that he'd figured Ember out in that respect.

"So what can I help you with, Prime, if this isn't to do with Ember?"

I glanced at Owen, glad he was here. Not only was he the most objective and calm of my brothers, I one hundred percent trusted him and valued his opinion. I smirked. "How good are you with technology?"

Drake's spine straightened as he grinned. "What kind?"

"Robotics."

He studied me for a few seconds. "I'm considered one of the best designers in that field, hence why my company was so successful. Did you have a certain type of robot in mind?"

"Well, perhaps the hovering kind that can give birth to mini-bots." I kept my voice low as I dropped a little more information.

Drake raised his brows, his interest definitely piqued. "Y'all must know that's my favourite kind. And what I don't know, I can learn real quick." He smirked and his eyes twinkled. "But what learning material d' y'all have for me?"

Oh yeah, he was definitely on this. A spark of hope flickered in my chest, and I smiled. "Leave that to me. When I have some learning material for you, can you study in private?"

Drake nodded, his mouth twisting. "I can, though it would be useful to have an assistant."

"Know anyone?" I enquired, thinking through all the people in the prison and coming up empty.

Drake unfolded his arms and leaned back on his hands on the table, eyebrows drawn, obviously thinking. "Not in my pack, no."

"Okay. I'll find you someone." Though from where I had no idea. But there had to be an IT geek somewhere among all the people in this prison.

"Is there a time frame on this robotics learning curve?" Drake enquired, his green eyes narrowed.

"Yes, two weeks."

"Am I allowed to know what's going on after two weeks?"

"Yes, you are, but not yet."

"Hmm, and what's my part after your two weeks are up?"

I smiled, not being deliberately obtuse, but I really didn't know what Drake's part would be. The plan in my head was only just forming. He didn't need to know that though, and neither did Owen. "Like I said, I'll let you know as soon as I have your learning materials and an assistant."

Inclining my head to the door, I gestured to Owen that we should leave, but before we stepped out, I turned back around. My heart and soul had already claimed Ember as my mate, but Drake didn't know that. That lack of clarity couldn't continue, not when she was part of his pack. "Don't expect Ember back in her cell after training is done. She's spending her evening with me."

Drake gave me a long hard look as he crossed his arms over his thick chest, then gave a cursory nod. I didn't like the warning in his eyes, so I turned away before my wolf could see it as a challenge. My boot squeaked as I pivoted on the concrete floor and stepped out of the door.

"Choices, Prime, remember that." His voice was quiet, but full of warning.

I didn't bother to answer him. Ember could have all the choices she liked, as long as they didn't put her at more risk, and as long as she chose me.

CHAPTER 13

mber

KAWAN HELD OUT HIS HAND, and I helped him up from the mat. His handsome face was covered in a sheen of sweat, and his dark hair gleamed. He'd been training with Lionel and me under Rawson's tough tuition for the last two hours. Lionel had dipped into the next ring with D and although Kawan wasn't as heavily muscled or as tall as the lion shifter, he was fast and lethal.

"You still okay to keep doing this?" I asked Kawan, glaring at Rawson who'd enlisted the alpha's help. Kawan had been a patient and cheerful training partner. His attitude with me didn't change even when I'd thrown him to the ground dozens of times.

"Sure am." He flashed his white teeth, his canines making an appearance.

I grinned back. It took a special kind of male to be slammed into the mat over and over and not mind, especially after Lionel had bowed out, the pussy.

"I haven't had so much fun being thrown around by a beautiful woman in ages." Kawan waggled his brows and smirked.

"Cut the smooth talk, brother. You've never been thrown around by any woman as beautiful as my Firecracker."

That drawl sent my stomach into a mess of butterflies.

"Yep, totally agree, Prime." Kawan winked down at me, all charm and handsomeness. If I didn't already know that he was a killer, that smile and the amused twinkle in his dark eyes would sure fool me.

In one powerful move that left me drooling, Connor vaulted into the ring. Of course, I pretended not to notice and bent to pick up an old towel instead of ogling him.

"That's enough for today." Connor addressed Rawson then narrowed his gaze on me, his sky blue eyes studying me from head to toe and sending my heart into flutters worthy of a teenage girl. I scowled at my reaction and busied myself, retying my hair and wiping the sweat off my face and exposed skin. Out of the corner of my eye, I saw Drake walk back into the hall. He glanced at me and raised his hand. I returned the greeting, closing my eyes for a moment. At least he was unharmed after being summoned by Connor.

Connor cocked a brow at me.

"Thanks, Kawan," I said, ignoring Connor, whose nearness was prickling against my skin and unsettling my wolf.

Kawan took my hand and kissed the back of it gallantly whilst bowing low. "I am yours to command anytime you wish, Ember."

His dark eyes were so sincere, I actually believed he would come if or when I called him.

Connor watched him with one brow raised and his hands resting on his hips. "Smooth," he muttered as Kawan sauntered past him.

Kawan grinned. "Well, I *have* to answer to your commands, but for your...I mean her, I will answer with pleasure." His eyes met Connor's and they exchanged a meaningful look. Connor swallowed and nodded.

I had no idea what that was all about so I pretended I hadn't heard them and stepped up to Rawson. I went to hug him, but he jumped back holding up his hands to fend me off.

"Urgh! No, No, No. No hugs until you've had a shower. You've been training all day and you stink." He grimaced and laughed, his brown eyes twinkling though his face looked drawn. My brows dipped. I should have insisted we take more breaks, or made him sit down, or something. He took my hands and gave me an understanding smile.

"I'm fine, Em, but I'm going to take my own advice and shower. Then I'm going to get some clean clothes on and join my..." He hesitated, lines furrowing his brow as he looked to Connor.

"Your brothers?" Connor supplied gruffly.

Rawson swallowed and gave a small smile. "Yeah, my brothers, for some food."

Connor returned his smile. "You do that."

It was then I realised even if I showered, I had nothing to change into. My *date* with Connor wasn't a date, but I still had some pride. My face flushed at my predicament. I supposed I could go and see if there were any unclaimed jeans and vest tops in the laundry, but it was a first come first served basis in gen pop so I doubted there'd be any left by now.

"Don't worry, my pack has its own laundry room. We can swing by there first and you can grab some clean clothes."

Had he read my mind or maybe my face? "I need a shower, too." I scrunched my nose as my own stink wafted up my nostrils.

"Yeah, Rawson's right, you stink." He laughed as he leaned closer and I huffed at him. "But believe it or not, we have showers in my pack wing, too. And you aren't getting out of our date, you promised me your time."

I rolled my eyes, but couldn't help my smile. "Okay. Okay."

"I'll see you kids tomorrow." Rawson grinned and stepped out of the ring.

"Hey!" I yelled at him. "You're not that much older than us."

"I guess not." He grinned and waved. "See you tomorrow, Ember."

"Bye," I whispered, watching him go and having to stop myself from chasing him down. An invisible hand gripped my heart until I couldn't breathe and my palms pressed against my chest. I still didn't believe I'd see him tomorrow.

"Hey," Connor said gently. The weight of his attention held me captive, just as it always did. "He'll still be here tomorrow." His voice soothed me, releasing that vice like feeling on my chest.

"Will he?" I hated the vulnerability in my voice.

Connor tucked an errant lock of my weird half dyed hair behind my ear, letting his fingertips trail down my neck and over my shoulder. Goosebumps erupted on my skin. He exhaled, noting my response, but he didn't stop his touch, he merely continued down my arm to my fingers where he entwined them with his. His rough skin grazed mine and I swallowed, gripping him tighter rather than shaking away his touch.

"Yes, Firecracker, he will."

I looked up and willingly fell into his intense cerulean gaze. "Promise?" I pushed, wanting him to reassure me Rawson's presence wasn't a lie.

The strong column of his throat bobbed and he squeezed my hand. "Yes."

My body was shaking from the day's exertions, but I managed a nod and a weak smile. Before I'd been brought here, I'd trained every few days with Blue, and occasionally with some of Som's workers. I never asked what they did, and they never asked me, we just fought for as long as it took to work off some energy, thanked each other and left—well, except for the occasions it progressed to a naked roll on the mats.

"Come on, let's find you clothes, a shower and some food." Connor bent down to peer into my eyes. His beautiful gaze searched mine, his mouth in a firm line as he tried to work out if I believed him about Rawson.

"In that order I hope?" I smiled and made it reach my eyes. My worry that Rawson would disappear from my life again was real, and it was almost impossible to hide that anxiety from Connor. He knew me too well. My heart flipped at the thought that I could lose Connor again, too. I had never stopped missing him. Now my heart squeezed every time I saw him and when he wasn't near, I constantly watched for his return. I blinked and looked at our joined hands, a strange sensation of warmth settling in my chest.

A seductive grin curved his lips. "Okay, or we could drop the clothes altogether …" His other hand curved around my waist.

I gasped. Mother Wolf, I loved the feel of his palm curled around my cooling skin. My teeth worried my bottom lip as I itched to reach out and wrap my arms around him. "I'm sure you *would* like that." Damn, but I'd like that too. I looked down at the mat, hiding my smile at the thought of eating a meal with him naked. He could be my personal dinner plate...

Connor chuckled and let go of me, jumping out of the ring and waiting expectantly.

I followed at a much less spritely pace, my body screaming with fatigue and my wolf grumbling at how hungry she was.

"You'll get used to the aching muscles—eventually. It'll get worse in the next few days."

"Yeah, thanks for that. You sure know how to encourage a girl. Are you going to provide a daily massage for making me do this?"

As soon as the words were out, I flushed. Gods, it sounded like I was flirting with him.

"As I'll be the one who makes that body ache everyday, I think it only fair that I'm the one...the *only* one, who gets to massage away that...ache." His eyes melted into that enticing mix of bright blue and black.

My knees actually went a bit weak at the growl of possession in those words. I swallowed hard and gave him a small smile, not sure what to say to that, other than- *Hell, yeah!*

"This way." I jumped as his breath fanned my ear and he placed his hand in the small of my back, not to urge me forward, but in a way that was comforting and more than a little possessive. I really didn't mind at all. Connor remained quiet as he led me out of the training hall, even when D and Reed fell in behind us at the door.

I smiled at them, trying to muster some energy. "Hi guys." I did a double take when they smiled back. They weren't all as dark and moody as Stone, then.

Connor guided me through the west wing with his hand touching me in some way until we reached some stairs, and he had to step in front to ascend first. There was no conversation, which was fine, he seemed distracted and it was too much effort to keep up my usual snark with him. I hoped it wasn't much farther to the showers; my body was shaking, and I didn't want to make a fool of myself by tripping. Of course, as those thoughts zipped through my head, I tripped up a step.

Connor turned around and looked down at me from a few steps above. His face softened. "You okay?"

I hesitated. "Yeah, I'm just tired."

"Want me to carry you?" He grinned cockily.

I scowled. "Don't you bloody dare, not if you value your balls."

"There she is." He laughed. "You had me worried there for a moment. I thought Rawson had overdone it."

"He did."

Connor chuckled and started walking up again. At the top, he turned left, and the sound of people talking and crockery banging echoed down the corridor.

"I thought we were doing clothes and shower first."

He lifted an eyebrow, giving me his sexy smirk. "You're hangry. And I won't get anything out of you except a punch to the face if I try and have a conversation with you when you're hungry." He explained it to me as if it was the most obvious thing in the world while he picked up a tray and handed it to me. "Now come and eat."

"Gee, thanks for the concern, Mr Prime, Sir."

That sexy grin stretched his mouth further, making my wobbly legs even worse. "Call me Sir again," he purred, his pupils large and dark in those vivid eyes.

"Oh, piss off!" I barged him out of the way, though the thought of a bondage session where he made me call him *sir* had heat surging all through me causing my palms to sweat, and other areas to tingle.

The server eyed my neck looking for a pack mark. Seeing the wrong one, he looked at Connor who moved his tray alongside mine still chuckling at my response. He nodded at the man. "You can serve her."

I gave Connor the evil eye before taking my plate of rice and meat stew from the server. I thanked him and waited for Connor, unsure where we were supposed to sit. It was hard to ignore the attention we were getting. Some people tried to watch us surreptitiously, others did so openly, and there was such a varying degree of emotions it was unnerving. I kept a wary eye out even as I picked up my spoon and shovelled rice into my mouth whilst balancing my tray. My stomach cramped up at the sudden food dump, and I groaned. Connor was right, my stomach was completely empty and I was starving. D and Reed hadn't picked up any food which bothered me.

"Aren't you hungry?" I glanced at Reed, still balancing my tray with one hand while I took another spoonful of rice.

"No, we'll eat when our shift babysitting his arse is done," Reed said in his best public school accent, though he smiled and winked at me.

"What are you complaining about? It's a fine arse to babysit." Connor had an arrogant smile on his face, and a huge plateful of food on his tray. I was about to complain about the unfairness in the amount when he continued, "Don't you think, Ember?" And winked at me.

I swallowed the mouthful of rice before I could choke on it and rolled my eyes. "Jesus, you're so annoying."

All three of them laughed.

Connor led me to an empty table at the back of the pack's food hall. Connor sat with his back to the wall and D and Reed positioned themselves where they could see who approached.

I didn't talk much while I ate. Connor was right, I *needed* this food, so my attention was mostly on my meal. True, I had my back to the room but I trusted D and Reed, not to mention Connor, to watch it for me.

"Here, Prime," said a sultry voice. Two cups of water were placed on the table, both near Connor.

I looked up, and was met by a pair of large breasts almost bursting out of a low cut top. I took a moment, and studied the tall brunette who had her attention fixed wholly on Connor, but even she wasn't going to distract me from my food. I was nearly done, and I never took my time with my food, even when I wasn't ready to eat a horse, or perhaps an elephant. I shoved the last spoonful in. Damn, I was still hungry.

Connor continued to eat, but raised his brows at the woman who had more or less climbed on to the table to block me from Connor's view.

I leaned to the side and raised my brows, keeping my expression amused, though I was trying my best not to shove her away from him. "A fuck buddy of yours?" I hid my clenched fists under the table.

Connor choked on his rice. Taking the water the woman had brought, he chugged it down quickly, banging his chest.

D and Reed grinned widely, watching with avid interest.

Connor eyed the woman, then looked back at me, his grin widening, until I was sure he was going to laugh in her face. Her eyes flashed from a warm brown to slate grey as her wolf peered out, first at him and then me.

I ignored her and raised my brows at Connor.

"No, not a buddy, just a one time fuck." He held my gaze as he leaned towards me.

"Oh," I said, elongating the sound of the word. "Well, honey..." I unclenched my fists before reaching around her and across the table to grab the other drink, which was clearly meant for him. Personally, I wouldn't bring him water, or anything else. He was more than capable of getting it himself. I snorted at her actions. Some people would do anything for attention, especially from a male like Connor. I met her eyes. "...thanks for the drink, but you heard him—a one time fuck—that's all." I infused my tone with warning, allowing my wolf to the surface.

She tossed her hair and ignored me, leaning towards Connor to give him a full on view of her perfect tits.

I rolled my eyes again. *Really?* I mouthed at him.

His eyes sparkled and he leaned back in his chair and crossed his arms over his chest. "You still hungry, Firecracker?" His attention dropped to my empty plate.

I shrugged. I was famished, but I wasn't going to admit that to him and leave him here with a pair of breasts in his face so he could arrange his next tryst.

He looked up at the woman. "It was a one time deal, you know that. Thanks for the drink, but you don't come near me again. Now, go and get my Firecracker another tray of food. My brother will accompany you and make sure it arrives here clean."

Her nostrils flared, but she didn't argue, and without another word slid off the table and walked back to the serving hatch. She went down another notch in my estimation; I'd have told him to piss off, but I guess that was just me. I mirrored his posture. "I'm surprised you're still alive if that's how you treat the women you fuck. I wouldn't stand for it."

He shrugged, but his gaze was heated. "You wouldn't need to."

My stupid heart jumped wildly.

"Make no mistake, Em, I've not been a good person for the last four years. Using a woman for sex and never going there again was nothing. She was willing, and she knew what she was getting from me. I made sure of it."

"Oh? And what was that?" The words were out before I could stop them. My cheeks heated and my food threatened to make another appearance. Did I really want to know what the man I lusted over, did with his other women?

Connor cocked his head, but leaned forward and crooked his index finger at me. He lowered his voice. "She got my dick, hard and fast, and that's it. I needed release after you got me all riled up by joining another alpha's pack. You rejected me, Ember. I wanted you in my pack so I can take care of you and you ran. How did you think I'd feel? Yeah, I was so pissed off, I wanted to kill that bastard you chose over me. But I decided fucking out my anger was probably better than going back to that wing and breaking Drake's neck. It should be me who protects you, Ember, not Drake."

I swallowed, holding his stormy gaze. He was so close and it only made me want him closer. A tray banged on the table, bouncing little bits of food off the plate. I didn't even break eye contact with Connor, nor him with me.

There was huff as the brunette walked away.

"So, is that what I have to look forward to whenever you decide you're pissed at me? You running to another woman to fuck the anger out of your system? Tell me, does the same privilege go for me when you piss me off? Can I go off and fuck the anger out of my system? Seems only fair, right?" I knew I was asking for trouble, but how did he think I'd react to him telling me how he just fucked out his anger, like cheating is completely acceptable? I stared right into those eyes that were starting to show more and more black flecks.

But I couldn't hold that marbled black and blue gaze, not when I was already wondering why I'd joined Drake's pack, knowing full well Connor would lose his shit when he found out. And for what? I wanted Connor, just as much as I always had. I stared down at the plate of food, trying to sort out my churning thoughts.

"It's alright, I made sure she didn't spit in it," said Reed.

I chuckled, hiding my confusion as my emotions blew up a storm in my chest. Unable to speak, I began to eat again, glad of the distraction. "Come on, help me finish this." I tried to break the weight of Connor's stare on me. "Surely you need to eat some more, even though you got twice as much as me in the first place."

"I'm the Prime, it comes with privileges."

"Yes, so you've pointed out." I couldn't help glancing at the brunette who glared daggers at me from across the hall.

Connor smiled and picked up his spoon, but he just used it to push food on to mine every time I went to scoop up some more. At first I tried to smack his spoon out of the way with mine, but he just laughed and kept doing it.

"Stop that. I've eaten enough, and you aren't leaving here hungry," he said, his voice guttural. "And the answer to your question is no. I'll never touch another woman like that again."

My heart jumped, then raced at the implication of his words. I swallowed and briefly glanced up at him. His intent look soon had me dropping my gaze again. "Fine." And I let him push the food onto my spoon. Males always made sure their mates were provided for. He didn't let up until I'd consumed every morsel, then he led me from the food hall, back down the stairs and along a corridor. We clattered down another flight of metal steps and strode into the laundry. The heat, steam and stink of laundry detergent hit me.

"Each wing has their own laundry. We have to staff each one with people from our own pack. Detergent is in limited supply but stuff mostly comes back cleaner than when it was sent down the chutes; but not always, so it's wise to check before you take something from the shelves." He indicated the opposite wall. Shelves lined the wall and on them were piles of vest tops, jeans, boxers, white (or rather grey) panties and cheap basic bras.

He gave me a gentle push towards the shelves. "Go on, help yourself."

I found the nearest size jeans and top to my own but turned my nose up at the nasty looking 'laundered' panties. My nose wrinkled. "I'd rather go commando," I muttered, forgetting Connor was waiting at the door.

"Jesus, Firecracker, that's so not happening. I'll never get anything done if I have to think about you walking around bare."

I gaped at him, unsure what to say to that. Did I really affect him that much? I studied his profile as he yelled at the nearest inmate working in the laundry.

"What size panties and bra are you?" He perused my body, looking more pissed off at my suggestion of going commando than turned on at that moment.

I told him and he turned back to the laundry man, barking orders. I watched him, unable to drag my gaze away. I'd always been drawn to Connor in a way I couldn't explain. I'd been so happy growing up with him, then he'd left Rawson's and I'd missed the hell out of him, especially once he'd started seeing Ava. I scowled, still cross that his promise not to fuck Shannon had been total bullshit. But he'd been locked up in here for four years, and it wasn't an easy existence, not to mention Shannon had always thrown herself at him. Besides, he was a fit and gorgeous alpha who supposedly needed to fuck—regularly. Maybe Shannon really had just been a convenience. After all, he'd soon dropped her for the brunette...

I shook my head. Who was I to judge? My own sex life had been just like Connor's—no strings, no emotions, just fulfilling a physical need. I let my gaze drift over the defined muscles of his shoulders and arms. I enjoyed the rear view almost as much as the front, especially where his wide back tapered to a trim waist, the dip of his lower spine ending in the most gorgeous arse I'd seen in a long time. Yep, he was hotness personified. Then again, he always had been for me...

I swallowed against the tightness in my throat. If he threw me away like his other lovers, it would break me, thoroughly and completely.

He turned just as my gaze lowered to that delectable rear again.

My gaze shot up to his and I flushed.

He smiled. "You checking me out, Firecracker?" He stalked towards me in that fluid, powerful way of his.

I blinked, unable to find a suitably quick and acerbic response. He handed me a cellophane wrapped pile of white panties and bras. "Wow, thanks." There wasn't a chance of getting the right size undies, nevermind new ones in gen pop. I hadn't managed more than a change of washed out, grey panties so far, not since I'd been here.

He smiled down at me. Heat bloomed over my cheeks.

"Anytime. And I mean that. Right, shower." Firmly, he guided me out of the laundry.

I followed him to the communal showers. In gen pop the women got the showers in the evening and the men in the mornings, though very few paid attention to those rules, which only led to even more danger and abuse. Hence I'd avoided the showers, and Rawson was right, I stank. Connor indicated an open doorway. I peered into the showers, sighing when they were empty.

"Don't worry, we'll wait here. No one else is getting in." There was a hard edge to those words that told me he meant it.

I nodded and gave him a small smile. Being accosted in the shower wasn't my idea of fun. I grabbed a towel and a bar of soap off the shelf near the entrance and headed in. I didn't mess about, I was washed, dried and dressed in a few minutes. My hair was a mess. Using soap on it was killing its condition, and I had no hairbrush. I sighed, I'd never been particularly vain, but I couldn't even cut the damn stuff off. I finger brushed it as best I could. At least there were no mirrors in this place to see how bad I looked.

The water had eased the tension from my body and it had been tempting to linger, but the thought of Connor coming in to see if I was alright had spurred me on. I wasn't sure I could stop my treacherous body from reacting if he got too close, especially if I was already naked. I coughed and tried to take a deep breath at the image of Connor naked, his body wet from the shower, holding mine up against the wall...

"Everything alright?" said the subject of my dirty thoughts, as I walked out.

"Err, yep, f-fine," I stuttered with a quick glance at him.

Connor gave me a weird look.

Right, I never stuttered.

"Listen, I'm really quite tired." I so needed to get out of this meeting with him; otherwise I was likely to jump his bones. "Perhaps I should go back to my pack and we can talk tomorrow."

"No, Ember, you agreed. We go to my cell and talk before you go back to that other pack. In fact, you can just sit and listen to what I have to say if you are too tired to talk, which would be a miracle by the way." He smiled and placed a finger on my lips.

I wanted to both bite that finger off and suck it between my lips before running my tongue around it. To stop myself, I stared at him and pressed my lips together.

Chuckling, he dropped his finger and walked away. "If you don't follow, I'll fling you over my shoulder and carry you there."

"I just bet you would. You're a persistent bastard," I muttered, knowing he'd carry through on what seemed to be his favourite threat. So much for having a choice.

D coughed, his scar twisting as he smiled, and Reed pressed his lips together, his eyes crinkling at the corners.

Dragging my feet, I followed Connor back through a maze of corridors. We reached Connor's cell, which was right at the end of a corridor. "Come on in." Connor gestured to the door, nodding to D and Reed, who took up a sentinel pose on either side of the door.

Connor pulled the chair out. "Sit."

I raised my brows.

He sighed and blinked slowly. "Please have a seat?" This time, his voice was softer, making it a question instead of a demand.

"There, that wasn't so hard, was it?" I settled myself on the chair and smiled sweetly. That tiny difference between command and choice meant a lot, even if I had practically been forced to be here. Or had I? He'd given me a choice earlier in the day, and I'd agreed to come. I really need to stop fighting him over every little thing. The metal desk creaked as Connor settled his bulk against it. He was like a mountain rising right in front of me. I peered up. Jeez, he was so big...

He gave that gorgeous smile, baring his chipped canine.

A wave of heat washed through me. I'd never tire of it. Even so, I narrowed my eyes. He was up to something.

"No, but you're too far away." He grabbed the arms of the metal chair and yanked it towards him.

I screeched, instinctively grabbing for the chair arms. My legs flailed off the floor for a moment, just enough time for him to nudge my knees apart. When the chair stopped moving, I ended up with my knees outside his, so close to him, his body heat washed over me. His eyes widened as he took in my position, his throat bobbing as if me ending up so close was not what he intended.

"Oh, my god!" My face burned. "You can't expect me to sit with my face opposite your crotch and have a serious conversation?" I expected an arrogant remark, but he remained quiet, his face intense and a dark glimmer in his eyes. His nostrils flared and his muscles bunched along his forearms right up to his shoulders and neck. His jaw clenched, and he took a deep breath through his nose before exhaling steadily.

"I don't want to shout. And I need you to hear every word I have to say."

Um, okay. With an effort I stayed where I was, despite this position being so intimate and submissive, my cheeks flared. *Gods*, I bit my bottom lip. There was no chance of squeezing my legs together to ease the ache in my core. This close to Connor heat slammed through my body, making every nerve ending tingle. It was so hard to look him in the eye with such waves of lust ripping through me. I moved my attention to the wall behind him, instead of his stunning face, or more importantly, his body, which I itched to touch.

The room was bare, apart from some paper and pencils which were stacked neatly on the shelf. I wondered if he still sketched. Connor had often drawn me beautiful pictures of wolves when we were young. It had seemed the only thing he loved doing that wasn't fighting or weapons training. When he'd left home, I'd never seen another of his drawings. "Do you still sketch?"

"Yes."

Silence stretched, the space around us heating with energy.

I jumped when he gently took my chin between his forefinger and thumb and turned my face, tilting up to look at him. His expression was soft, no arrogance, no cruelty, no wolf, just Connor. My heart flipped. He was always so damn gorgeous to look at, but right now, with that softness warming his expression, my heart stopped before it began beating again, faster the longer he touched me.

"I really thought you were dead," he said, his voice thick, his gaze boring into mine.

My eyes widened when he pushed the chair back a little and dropped to his knees in front of me. This powerful shifter, Alpha Prime, essentially the King of thousands of shifters, was on his knees, looking at me with such a mix of emotions on his face, speech was impossible.

"I grieved for you—so much. I was so devastated when I thought Doherty had killed you, I couldn't think straight. It didn't matter how much time passed, I missed you every fucking day." His hand moved until his calloused palm and fingers cupped my jaw. His thumb brushed lightly over my lips making me shiver.

I wanted to tell him how much I'd missed him too, how my heart had broken into tiny pieces when I'd left him in that wood, and that it was only just repairing itself now that he was near me. But my chest was so tight, I couldn't speak. If I let him glue my heart back together, would he smash it to pieces again? Maybe he wouldn't mean to, just like before, but, if he actually died, there would be no repairing it. Ever...

Kneeling between my legs, his face was right in front of mine. He moved closer and raised his other hand. He brushed a fingertip over my cheek, a featherlight touch that had my eyes fluttering closed. With gentle, deliberate movements, he trailed a path down the curve of my neck, over my shoulder and along my arm. Goosebumps erupted over my skin wherever he touched, and I shivered. Opening my eyes I was drowning in a marbled sea of blue and black, so intense I couldn't draw breath. I held back a groan at the bolt of desire that made me want to grab him and yank his head to mine. I had never wanted to kiss anyone so much. To stop myself, I broke his gaze and looked at where our hands now rested together.

"When I saw the wolf's head Doherty lifted from that sack... Gods, Em, seeing, *scenting* your wolf like that? It broke me. I failed to protect you. I'm so sorry." His voice broke.

"Hey." Now it was my turn to squeeze his hands. "It wasn't your fault. None of this was."

"You're wrong," he whispered, so quietly I wondered if he'd actually spoken. He leaned his forehead down against mine. "My soul died that day, and something dark infected my heart. I didn't want to face a world without you in it, so I let my wolf take control of me. He ruled most of the time, and I took a back seat. He's a killer, a powerful one, and he killed anyone in his way to take the position of Prime in this place. Just as Doherty wanted, I killed my way to the top. I have done my best to protect those I vowed to—my brothers. I've done what I can for others in my pack, but in this place..." He sucked in a breath. "It's impossible to protect everyone from harm." He swallowed hard and closed his eyes. "You brought me back, Firecracker. I only have control of my body and my wolf again because you made me want it." He squeezed my hand harder.

His eyes opened, so intense I was convinced he could see into my soul. I didn't look away. I didn't want to. I wanted to be closer to him, even if I had to protect my heart from what I would inevitably have to do—leave him. I gave into my need. Using my free hand, I speared his hair and gripped the back of his head. With a groan, I pressed my lips to his. My wolf awoke and pushed, the silver collar preventing her from breaking free, and even though she resisted, I thrust her away. Connor was...*mine*, and not even my wolf was stealing this moment from me.

"Wait." His breath warmed my lips, which sent pure lust slamming through my body. For a moment he resisted, pulling back enough so there was merely a millimetre of space between us. His grip on my other hand was hard enough to be painful. I didn't care, it only heightened my response to him. I gave a sultry smile and flicked my tongue out against his lips, tracing the curve of them. His low moan only fired my blood more. Heat flared in my chest. Connor would never allow another female to take control like this. He was the Prime; being in control was inherent in every-thing he did.

I gripped his hair, twisting the strands through my fingers and yanked him closer, at the same time as I bit his bottom lip—hard enough my sharp canine drew blood. A low pitched growl rumbled from his chest. His hand had slipped into my hair, his other now curling around my back, pulling me closer. He'd let me take the lead, but now he was back in control. And for once, I had no desire to argue or wrestle that control back.

His mouth pushed mine open, a deep sigh escaping me as his taste and scent flooded my senses. His tongue slid into my mouth, brushing against mine, stroking and tasting. I kissed him back greedily, gripping his hair tightly, unwilling to let him pull away—like he had before.

Needing more, far more, I slid my free hand under his shirt and grazed my palm along the hard ridge and dips of the muscles along his spine. Gods, his skin was hot, burning under my touch, his powerful body trembling with a restraint I wanted to break through. His hand found its way under my own top. He encircled my waist, holding me in place. I writhed, fighting his fingers. A growl of frustration escaped me. I needed his hands, his mouth everywhere, and not gently. A firestorm of need was burning through my body and only he could quench it.

He gripped my waist and hair and held me in place as he broke our kiss and pulled away far enough to search my face.

I snarled, clutched his hair and tried to pull him back, but he was far too strong for that to work. A small smile curled his lips, and eyes dark with hunger leisurely studied the rapid rise and fall of my breasts before he looked me in the eye. Every muscle in his body was rock hard and tense.

"Tell me you want this, that you want me." His voice was deep and rough.

I inhaled deeply, the spicy scent of his arousal filling me. "I always have."

Heat flared in his eyes. "This isn't a one time deal, Ember. I know this is a shitty place for us to find each other again, but I don't want anyone else—only you." He tugged gently on my hair, so that I had no choice but to look him in the eyes. I saw something there that had my heart flipping in my chest, something he would never show anyone else. Vulnerability. His other hand left my waist and gently traced the contours of my face.

I studied him, unsure what to say. Was he asking for me to mate him? His touch was so tender, my chest tightened painfully, but I couldn't promise him anything. I wanted him, he was the only one I'd ever wanted, but our lives weren't our own, and I had a promise to keep.

"No promises, Connor, then neither of us can break them."

For a moment he froze and his face went blank. We held each other's gazes and my heart squeezed. I wanted to give myself to him fully, but there were so many unknowns, I couldn't make a promise I couldn't keep. What if I had to leave him? If we were mated that would rip my heart out, his too. Maybe he would agree to come with me? But I couldn't ask him. I couldn't afford for him to say no, or to stop me. His alpha compulsion was already hard for me to defy. If he claimed me, it would be almost impossible. Seconds passed and my stomach knotted up, then he nodded.

"Agreed, no promises between us—for now. But we'll talk more about it, and you can tell me who you have made a promise to. Maybe I can help."

I smiled and exhaled with relief. "Okay. It's a deal." I took my time and slowly perused his body. "So I get to enjoy this body more than once?"

Slowly, he grinned, the heat returning to his gaze. "You get to enjoy me as many times as you like, Firecracker."

"Hmm." I bit my bottom lip suggestively. "So you'll be at my beck and call, Prime?"

He pulled my hair until my head was tilted, giving him access to my neck. He peppered tiny kisses along my skin, nipping my ear lobe with his teeth. "Never." But I felt him smile against my skin.

"We'll see." And I let go of his hair to peel off my top. His hands gripped my hips, his fingers digging into my soft flesh, his gaze intense as I unclipped the cheap white bra he'd given me. I swallowed hard, holding the scrap of material against my skin, not because I was embarrassed by my body, I hadn't been for a long time, but this was Connor, the guy I'd crushed on since I was twelve years old.

He cocked his head, watching me, his grip loosening, though his hands remained where they were. He was giving me a choice.

I dropped my arms and let the material slide away.

His gaze devoured me, and he swallowed repeatedly. "Mother Wolf," he breathed, his voice shaking. "You're breathtaking." His hands slid up my back urging me towards him. His lips brushed my skin, dropping small kisses down my throat and across the soft swell of my breast, branding me. I moaned as he took my nipple in his mouth, sucking and biting down firmly. Desire shot to my core making my thighs quiver. His hooded eyes met mine as he slowly moved his way across to my other breast, his tongue tasting me along the way.

My hands found the hem of his tee, and he stopped long enough to let me lift it off him. I wanted to kiss my way across that beautiful, sculptured chest. I growled and pushed him back when he tried to keep kissing me.

"My turn."

His blue eyes glittered, his lips swollen from our kisses. I shoved the chair back and kneeled with him. With his chest right in front of me, I went to town. The sensation of putting my tongue to his skin, tasting what I had scented for so long, that salty yet spicy flavor that was Connor, was nearly overwhelming. I used my tongue to tease his nipples before biting down—hard. He hissed, stretching his neck as his head fell back like he was lost in complete ecstasy.

I scratched my nails down his back making him shudder before using one hand to palm the hard length of his cock that strained against his jeans. His head snapped forward and he watched with hooded eyes as my hands found the button of his jeans. Smiling, I flicked it open, and he helped me push his jeans down. His cock sprung free and I leaned back enough to peer down at his perfect erection.

He gave a mumbled, *"Fuck,"* as I took him in my hand, sliding my fist slowly up and down. Feeling the pulses as he thickened under my touch made the silken steel of him irresistible.

Gods, I needed him inside me, more than I'd ever needed anyone before. Dampness seeped from my core at the sight of him in my hand.

"Stand up." It was a breathless order.

"No, I want to be inside you."

"You will, but I want to taste you first." I stroked him a few more times and, just to torture him, leaned forward and ran my tongue, then my teeth across his nipple, never stopping the slow, yet firm motion of my hand on his cock.

The long column of his throat bobbed, and his nostrils flared, his breathing laboured—but he gently stilled my hand, and stood, taking the remainder of his clothes off. His whole body was a coiled mass of power as he stood in front of me, utterly naked, and breathtakingly beautiful.

I smiled up at him, my heart pounding. Being with Connor was nothing like the other lovers I'd had. This was the first time I'd ever knelt in front of a man like this. I'd never been willing to be in this vulnerable a position with anyone else. But right, now, with Connor, I wasn't vulnerable, I was powerful. There was a look of raw need on his face that handed all the power to me. I curled my fingers back around his huge erection and squeezed his length, and he pulsed in my hand. I held his hooded gaze as I flicked out my tongue, teasing the tip of his cock, tasting the drop of salty pre-cum that leaked out. Moaning, I tasted him again, keeping my eyes locked with his lust filled eyes. Gods, his taste, his scent were flooding my senses—and I needed more. Already I was addicted. Unwilling to wait, I slid my lips around him and sucked him slowly into my mouth until his tip hit my throat.

His groan was long and tortured, an erotic sound that sent shivers across my skin and moisture pooling between my legs. I settled into a steady rhythm, sucking, and teasing with my tongue, allowing my teeth to graze his sensitive skin. Faster and harder I moved, until above me, his body trembled. His hands wound themselves in my hair, his hips finding a rhythm with my mouth, and still he let me lead…

He groaned. "Ember…Stop…" And he tightened his grip on my hair and pulled me away. His face was flushed as he looked down, his eyes dark with a raw need that I mirrored. His rock-hard muscles were clenched so tightly his body looked like it was carved from granite.

In a move quicker than I could process, he lifted me from the ground and deposited me on the metal table. He yanked off my shoes, not bothering with the laces before he pulled my jeans and panties from my body, desperation in his movements. I leaned back on my elbows, watching him, the metal cold and hard under my legs and buttocks.

He devoured me with his eyes, his wolf seeping into his gaze. My own stirred and looked right back at him, weighing him up. Connor pushed his wolf away, his eyes blue and intense and burning into my soul. "My turn to taste." I shuddered as he dropped to his knees.

At the first touch of his tongue, I thought I might combust. My head rolled back and I arched into him, my hips tilting up into his ministrations. He laid one arm across my hips keeping me anchored, holding me still. "Gods, you're so wet for me, Em." He flattened his tongue and took another long slow lick.

"I've never tasted anything so good. I want more, and you're going to give it to me." He slowly circled the bundle of nerves that was my clit. *Mother Wolf!* I groaned as need ignited in me. *I was going to explode!* "Again." Sinfully, he flicked and circled. I cried out. "And again." He was so back in control, playing my body like he already knew every inch of me, and I was helpless to stop him. I reached out and grabbed the sides of the table, holding on for dear life. I was lost to anything but Connor's touch. I fell into the sensations of his mouth and tongue on me. A long moan escaped me when he slid one, then two fingers into the wetness between my legs, and began moving them slowly in and out. I wanted to move with him, to fuck his fingers. "Connor! Please!" I cried out and bucked against his hold. His low, dark chuckle only turned me on more.

"What do you want, Firecracker?" His movements stilled.

Gods that voice… I squeezed around his fingers, so near climax I wanted to scream.

"I-please, make me come. *Please…*" I didn't care that I was begging, I'd never needed anything this much, I was lost to reason, to anything other than Connor's command of my body. I couldn't move, despite my efforts to writhe against his fingers that curled, finding a spot that sent my vision black.

"Soon." His head dipped back down, his tongue going to work on me, his fingers pumping in an alternate fast and slow rhythm.

It didn't take long before my inner muscles tightened under his relentless actions. Looking down at his head between my legs, I released my hold on the table and grabbed his hair, urging him on as tension coiled in my body. "Oh, gods," I whispered, pulling at the silken strands, fighting to move against him. But every time I reached the precipice of pleasure, he stopped and pulled his mouth away.

"Bastard. Let me come." I panted hard, yanking his hair, beyond reason now.

Ignoring my grip, he pulled back, his mouth and chin glistening. His grin was all male satisfaction, his eyes hooded and dark. "Not yet." And he returned to his task, dropping light kisses against my hot, slick skin. "No, no, please…you have to…" I couldn't form words and tried to force his head forward. He merely pulled away completely, which pulled a loud whine from me.

"Connor…"

"Gods, Ember, say my name again." He kissed me, then bit my lip gently before he pulled back. "Fucking scream it when I make you come."

Then he wrapped his arms around me and stood, pulling me off the table and lifting me. I wrapped my legs around his hips and he spun us around so that my back hit the wall.

He cupped my face with both of his hands. "You're the best thing I've ever tasted. But I need to be inside you…so much." He sounded as desperate as me now, his breathing harsh, his voice no more than a deep growl. "I want you to come around my cock, to feel you squeeze me, and hear you scream my name as I take you over the edge."

I gripped his shoulders and looked him in the eye. "Then do it." It was supposed to be a command, but I wasn't fooling anyone, it was a breathless plea.

He pushed inside me just a little and I gasped. It had been months for me, but I didn't care about the discomfort, I needed him. Holding my gaze, he withdrew, then steadily pushed again, stopping when I moaned.

"Fuck me, Em, you're so tight." We were both panting and gasping for air. "More?" he grated out. I nodded digging my fingernails into his skin. I had never felt anything this good. He slowly thrust, not stopping until he was completely sheathed. My eyes fluttered shut at the sensation of him stretching me, of him filling me until there was nothing but him, his scent, his hot skin, his breath. He undulated his hips just once. We both groaned at the same time.

"Christ, Ember, you feel so good, gripping me so hard." His forehead rested on mine, his eyes squeezed shut.

I couldn't speak; instead I grabbed his face in my hands. "Kiss me." And I devoured his mouth with mine. He tried to hold me steady, but I couldn't keep still and my hips rocked down onto him. He groaned and began moving with me, steadily at first but no matter how long I wanted this to last, I couldn't help myself. He'd wound me up so tight I was more than desperate for release, so I urged him faster and harder, undulating my hips and digging my fingernails into his shoulders.

"Harder, Connor. Fuck me harder." I was almost crying with the need gripping my whole body.

A dark, lust filled look filled his face. "Whatever. You. Want." He growled each word punctuating them with a hard thrust of his hips.

All I could do was hold on for dear life as he dominated my body, and pushed me higher and higher. His face leaned against my cheek, and he kissed my ear, panting my name over and over as his body slammed into mine in a hard rhythm. Pain hit my spine with every thrust against the wall, but that line between pleasure and pain blurred and only made every sensation more intense.

A growl rumbled up through his chest. He pulled back and looked at me, his gaze captivating, his hips never ceasing their rhythm. "Fuck me...this...is... so much...more...than I ever...imagined."

I drowned in his heated gaze, the pleasure consuming me, stealing my speech.

"You. Are. Beautiful." He kissed me, just a brush of his lips on mine. Then his tone changed and that dark, intense look consumed his face. His hips slammed into mine, his laboured breaths rasping into the air around us, his movements urgent as he pushed harder and deeper, sending shockwaves of sensation through me. "Gods, dammit, I can't...Come for me, Ember. Now!"

It was a demand.

As if my body were his to command, waves of sensation exploded from my center and rocketed through my body, shaking me apart. My muscles clamped down on him, milking him. I couldn't stop myself. A scream bubbled up my throat as my vision turned black and my senses stopped working. His name erupted from my lungs. Connor roared and convulsed, warmth spilling into me.

As we both came down from the best experience of my life, we held onto each other as if we both might fall apart if we didn't.

CHAPTER 14

onnor

I WAS STILL in a state of disbelief. I hadn't brought Ember here with the intention of seducing her. I smiled inside, I hadn't done anything *to* her, she'd given back as good as she got—and then some. I shuddered, aftershocks of pleasure rippling through every muscle and bone in my body. I smiled. Besides, she'd initiated what had happened. Fucking wasn't the right way to describe what had just happened between us. No, it was so much more—at least it was to me. That thought should scare me, but it didn't—*she* didn't, even though I was more terrified than ever of losing her.

I dropped my face into Ember's neck and inhaled. Mixed with sex, her smokey scent was heady. The subtleties of it, of *her*, were different than I remembered, but it was a scent I wanted to stay wrapped in forever, that I wanted permeated into my skin. My wolf stirred, growling at me, reluctant to agree to that need. I reassured him and he settled. Both of us knew it was too soon to claim Ember and her wolf, but that didn't mean I couldn't work on it.

"Stay with me tonight." My breath fanned her ear and she shivered. I didn't want to let her go to another alpha's pack, and I was more than aware I hadn't done what I'd brought her here for. But the kiss we had shared all those years ago had been my last. I'd never wanted another woman's lips on mine, not after that, so when she'd kissed me, I'd been done for; utterly lost in the woman I had always loved.

Ember glanced at the door and wriggled against me. I groaned, my body super sensitive from my orgasm. The slickness from our bodies only increased the sensation.

"Don't worry, they won't let anyone in." I kissed her gently on the lips. "But we should get dressed." Her crazy coloured hair stuck to her face. Gently, I brushed it back. She was flushed and her eyes were as bright as polished emeralds. I smiled. She looked well and truly fucked, and utterly beautiful. I tried to ignore the ache in my chest, and the pull to stay exactly where I was, surrounded by her warmth. Forcing myself to move, I gently pulled out of her body and let her feet slide to the ground. She leaned back against the wall as if she needed the support. I just smiled and ran the back of my fingers down her cheek, not commenting, since I couldn't remember ever being this shaky after sex. My cock jumped as I took in her nakedness. Gods, she was stunning.

With a sigh, I turned away and grabbed our clothes off the floor. We needed to talk, which wasn't going to happen if she didn't get some clothes on.

"Would you like to freshen up?"

She nodded but didn't speak, just kept her eyes on my face.

My stomach dropped, I took her hand and led her into my cell at the back. I had a sink and towels in there. "Are you okay?" I hoped to the Mother she wasn't regretting what we'd just done. I know I didn't.

"I'm fine." Coughing she cleared the croakiness from her throat and turned to face me. "I'm more than fine," she said, her voice stronger. Her hand cupped my cheek. "Are you?" Her eyes searched mine. For what, I wasn't sure.

I hoped my smile was reassuring and I pulled her to me holding her softness against my body. She was so warm, so right in my arms. I eyed the bed longingly. Sighing, I kissed the top of her head, breathing her in. "I'm more than fine, too. Being with you was incredible, Em." Gently, I put her away from me. "But we need to talk. And if we stay naked, talking is the last thing I'll want to do."

She smiled, a mischievous twinkle entering her eyes as she dragged her gaze over me.

I growled low in my throat. "Ember..." And swallowed hard as my cock jumped under her perusal. "The sink, now." I walked out before she could be defiant and touch me again. I'd be utterly at her mercy, now that I'd had a taste of my mate. My wolf whined and I hissed as his confusion flooded me. He wanted Ember as much as I did, but he was still unsure about the wolf she housed.

It's alright, my friend, give it time. I know you're not sure. I'll wait for you.

But a heaviness dragged me down until I couldn't catch my breath. Unless our wolves were mates too, we couldn't fully bond. I could mark her, but it would destroy my wolf if her wolf wasn't his mate. I would be bound to

Ember while he would want a different female. I thrust that thought from my mind, not willing to deal with that possibility. Until the silver collars were removed there was no way we could know. Our wolf spirits were locked inside us and unable to fully bond with each other. Water splashed in the other room. Ember had explained the craziness that had happened with her wolf, but it didn't explain the hows or whys. I didn't think she even knew how her fire, or just Fire, as she had named her, worked. Fire always appeared when Em was in mortal danger. Gods, it was times like now I wished I had access to the internet or even an old fashioned fucking library would be good. Looking up what else besides a wolf lived inside my Firecracker, was something I should have done years ago.

I shoved my feet in my jeans and pulled them up my legs. I needed a shower but that could wait, I wasn't wasting any time with my Firecracker.

A few minutes later Ember emerged looking fresh, though her skin was still flushed, her eyes bright and her hair mussed by my hands. I loved that just fucked look on her, but I remained quiet. There were things she needed to know…

I found it hard not to stare at the movement of her hips as she swayed over towards me. My mouth dried out, and it was on the tip of my tongue to ask when her last fertile time had passed. I pressed my lips in a tight line deciding that was a question for another time. Females, when reaching their one fertile time every six months had a certain scent, one which drove all the unmated males nearby insane. Any female about to go into heat sequestered themselves in a cell, and only the alpha of their pack held the key. Even with the locked cell, guards were put on the door, mainly to stop those wanting to get in from damaging themselves by trying to get through the metal door. It was a system that worked.

I scrunched my eyebrows together, thinking back. It dawned on me that very few women went into heat in gen pop. Neither had there been any pregnancies in the prison. If there had been, I would have known. I rubbed my face. How had I missed that before? Because I'd let my wolf take charge and he didn't give a shit about that kind of thing. Dominance, keeping his brothers and pack safe, and the fighting rings were his only concerns.

"What's wrong?" Ember's brows drew close together.

"Nothing." How could I have been so stupid? "When are you fertile again?"

Her eyes widened. "What? It's a bit late to worry about getting me pregnant, Connor." She flicked her hair over her shoulders.

I kicked myself for bringing it up. Shifters couldn't catch or pass on sexually transmitted infections, but there was a small chance she could conceive before her heat fully hit.

"I, er, what? No, that's not why I'm asking." Or was it? I glanced down at her flat stomach. I'd never wanted kids, and would never even consider bringing a child into this awful place, but the thought of seeing Ember's stomach swell with my child sent a bolt of desire through me so strong I had to grab the table top to steady myself.

I wouldn't let the warden take her, or let Zander put her in the round up for the science wing. No, we'd be out of here by the time she was capable of conceiving. No other male was getting within ten feet of her when her hormones began to party. I'd make sure of it. Four years in this place had been long enough. It was time to up my game. I'd find the information Zander and our faceless boss needed, and get those I cared about out of here.

"Why are you asking then?" The fire was back in her eyes.

I took a deep breath. This conversation was going off track quickly, and would be over if I couldn't keep my thoughts and worries about her in check.

"Nevermind, forget it. There are other things we need to talk about."

She crossed her arms over her chest and waited. I decided to dive in, no holds barred. "This prison is a front for a lucrative fight ring."

She nodded. "The gym."

"Yeah, Doherty has Rawson and Zander…"

"Who's Zander?"

"The guy that brought you here, he has red eyes sometimes."

Her lips flattened into a tight line. "Oh, him."

"Yeah, him." I chuckled at her expression. "I can see he's not your favourite person."

"No, he's not, but then again I seem to have quite a few *unfavourite* people here."

I chuckled. "You do. Zander works for the warden. He and Rawson are tasked with bringing in shifters who Doherty has marked as candidates for the fight rings. Those who survive the plane flights are shoved into gen pop. Sometimes they are invited to join a pack by one of the alphas—or if they are strong enough, they get to choose which pack to join." I looked her in the eye and cocked a brow.

She unfolded her arms. "Yeah, well, you weren't going to give me a choice."

I let it go, though she didn't sound as convinced about that as she had, and we had other things to talk about. Arguing over the same ground was a waste of time. "The fight rings are not gentle or fun, they are fights to the death."

Her gaze shot up to mine, her body stiffening. "Death?"

I took a deep breath and blew it out between pursed lips. "I am tasked every four months with ensuring fighters from all the packs are registered on a database. I don't know how they choose who will take part in the fight ring, but it's announced over a PA, and there is no option to refuse." I balked at revealing the depths of my depraved situation, but there was no hiding from it, and Ember would find out soon enough that having morals in here was useless and likely to get her killed.

"And if they do refuse, or don't turn up to fight?" she prompted, her voice carefully neutral.

"I kill them." I got up and paced across the room, my large strides eating up the space quickly, but sitting still while I revealed the extent to which I had fallen wasn't an option. "I am the Prime for a reason, which is to keep the shifters compliant. The only way to ensure that compliance is by violence and death. That's what I do, I deal out punishment and where necessary, death." I rubbed my face, sighing. "Even if the chosen don't refuse, I send them to die in the fight rings."

"Gods, Connor, how many people have died in Doherty's sick games? How many have you had to kill?"

I looked at her, steeling myself for her judgement and accusation. Her face was utterly blank, giving me no way to tell what she was thinking.

"Hundreds, thousands, I have no idea. Put it this way, I'll be spending an eternity in Hell for being the one to kill those whose only crime was to be terrified. There will be no redemption for me." I rubbed my face. It was true, most of those that I'd ended were just scared people who had been forced into the entertainment rooms of the arena fights. They weren't fighters. Perhaps I deserved an eternity in Hell for my crimes. Damn, I needed to continue before I lost my nerve. "The unlucky fuckers who are chosen are allocated fight groups and every fight is to the death. The winner from each fight makes it to the next round, until there is a victor of that group. The victors are then pitted against one another, until there are ultimately only two survivors."

Her face blanched as the implication of my words hit her. "You mean all those people who lose, die?" She swallowed over and over as if holding back a wave of nausea.

I nodded. "The warden and Doherty bring in high fliers; the richest people in the world, who can bet obscene amounts of cash on the fights. It's how he and the warden earn money and fund this place."

"Who picks or pairs up the fighters?" She coughed, clearing the thickness from her voice, and rubbed her arms.

Curbing my instinct to pace, I perched on the desk next to her and crossed my arms over my chest. A whole new level of self-loathing hit me, not because of the amount of people I'd sent to their deaths, or for the ones I'd killed, but because there was not enough guilt in my heart for the lives I'd ended. "I've no idea, not really. Probably a computer programme."

"What happens if you refuse to kill those who don't want to fight?"

I curled my hands into fists. "They torture Rawson and my brothers, or me, until I do as they demand."

She swallowed, her eyes widening. "What do they do to Rawson? Is that why he looks so broken?"

"I don't know exactly what they do, but yeah. The first time I refused, the

275

warden broke my fingers one by one, then held me paralysed as he made Rawson scream…" I closed my eyes, Rawson's cries of terror and pain were forever etched in my mind. "Somehow, the warden can control Rawson's mind. He takes him into a living nightmare; one that leaves injuries and marks all over his body; the warden doesn't even have to touch his victims." I snapped my fingers. "He just wills it and it happens."

"What?" Her eyes widened even more, her voice merely a whisper.

"He is—something, I don't know—otherworldly. He can cause damage to a person and inflict pain without even lifting a finger."

"Bloody hell." Ember rubbed her upper arms with her hands.

"Yeah, but that isn't all they do to get me to toe the line. I am Prime, but I'm also the alpha of this pack and they know how much I value my brothers." I closed my eyes, searching for the bond with each one of my brothers as they moved through the prison. "Though they are more than brothers to me; I would die for any one of them, without regret."

When I opened my eyes she tilted her head and studied my profile.

"I have bonded with them."

Her mouth dropped open. "Oh." Her face flushed and twisted adorably. "So you, er, like men, too?" Her gaze flicked away from mine.

A chuckle escaped me. She really hadn't been around other shifters. Despite her toughness she was still naive in the ways of her own kind. "No, Firecracker, I am not attracted to males—of any kind." I gave into my need to touch her, slipping my hand through her folded arms and entwining my fingers with hers. "As Prime, bonding is something that I can choose to offer to those I completely trust. If they take a little of my blood, and I theirs, it means I can track their shifter spirit. I can even feel their energy, their life force; but if they die, their loss tears at my soul, and weakens me for a time."

"So why do it? What do you get out of it?"

"If they are lost or I need them, it can help me find them—a tracker of sorts, I suppose. If I tap into their spirit, I can even sense their emotions, but that is a huge invasion of their privacy, so I don't do that lightly."

"I see." She gave me a sheepish smile. "I thought I was going to have to compete with your men, as well as all the women in this prison, for your attention."

My throat tightened. "You will never have to compete with anyone for my attention." I kissed her gently and briefly, just a touch of my lips on hers.

She smiled, her green eyes glittering like emeralds. "Thank the Mother Wolf for that. I don't want to have to start upping my body count."

My body stirred and I dropped my hands to her hips holding her close to me. "You jealous of my brothers?"

"Not if I have no reason to be."

I grinned. "You don't. But I might have to give you some kind of reason to be jealous, just to see you fired up. Knowing you're possessive of me is a huge turn on."

She yanked her arm away and smacked my bicep. "That's a ridiculously egotistical thing to say."

I put my hands up in surrender. "Sorry. I didn't mean it."

"Yeah, you did." She smirked, calling me out.

"You got me. I'd love to see you jealous, and then show you just how much you have no reason to be." Her palm slid into mine. I curled my fingers around hers. It was nice to touch her in such an innocent way. I'd never held hands with anyone before, not even with Ava. Gods, if Ember knew how much power she had over my life, over me, I'd be totally screwed.

"Carry on telling me about the fight rings," Ember prompted as our moment of levity passed.

"My brothers were all injected with tasers. Little internal devices that can't be removed without a code. If you try and cut through the flesh around them they activate at a high enough level to kill."

Ember nodded, a frown marring her brow. "I've used similar devices before."

"Really? Where?" I was getting more and more curious about her life.

She shrugged, but bit her top lip. "Let's just say, I think we'll be going to hell together."

I smiled and bumped her shoulder gently with my own. "Hell couldn't contain you. I'll eventually get you to trust me enough to tell me what you've done that's so bad. I'm a persistent bastard."

She bumped me back harder, but avoided my stare. "I know you are." She sighed. "It's not about trusting you. It's just… the guilt you have? Well, I have it too and…" She coughed. "Well, I don't want you to think less of me…"

My stomach tightened. She thought I'd judge her, even after all she knew about me? "Sweetheart, whatever you have done won't change the way I feel about you. We all do what we have to in order to survive."

She squeezed her eyes shut and nodded, giving me a small smile. A moment of silence passed between us, and I held my breath. *Please trust me…*

She met my eyes, her teeth worrying her lush upper lip. That unconsciously sexy move made my cock twitch, but I pushed away my need to pull her into my body. This sign of trust was far more important.

Her voice was quiet when she started talking. "After my wolf died in that wood, I ran to a…an associate of mine. He is, or rather was, a fae drug dealer. I've known him since I was a little girl. He used to give me small mule jobs, you know? Deliveries where a child wouldn't be suspected."

"He used you, as a child?" My voice was a low pitched growl from thinking of at all that could mean.

"Yeah, I guess he did, but he also protected me from some of the low-lifes and dangers on the streets. He always paid me with food or money, it depended on what I needed most. When I got there that night, I had to negotiate a deal with him."

I hissed. Faerie deals could be for a lifetime.

Her fingers rested lightly on my forearm. She squeezed gently. "It's okay. Don't forget I've been around the fae most of my life and not the nice ones. I was careful and my deal with him expired over a year ago but I err..well, I chose to stay."

"Why, Em? Why stay with a lowlife like that? You know you can't trust a fae. Especially after what Walker did."

Her eyes met mine. "Where else would I go, Connor? I thought you and Rawson were dead. Som was definitely under the SBI's radar. Besides, there was nowhere else to go, so I had no choice." She took a breath and shook her a head a little. "It was a good deal for me, he could have negotiated for more." Her emerald eyes turned as dark and as stormy as a raging sea. "Being a drug dealer had its benefits. It gave me a chance to search for that bastard, Walker. I never did find him, but I was getting close when someone ratted on me and my partner, Blue." There was another pause and she said quietly, her throat moving as she swallowed. "The Fae royal guard came for us. When we got back through the portal to Som's lock up, someone had killed him. Red—I mean Zander, or whatever his bloody name is, was waiting for me. Doherty had done some bullshit deal with the fae. They got her. And Doherty got me, but he didn't recognise me thanks to Som's glamour spell. "

My chest tightened. Doherty was rounding up females, I knew that; but it looked like it was just dumb luck he didn't recognise Ember. What the hell he was doing making deals with the fae I had no idea. Then again, what did it matter? Right now, I had bigger problems to worry about. Like my mate's safety and getting us out of here. "I'm sorry." I put an arm around her shoulders and pulled her into my side, trying to give her some measure of comfort as a strange warmth filled my heart settling in deep.

This trust, her sharing her life with me was as intimate as the honour of sharing her body, maybe more.

"I'm going to get Blue back. Somehow, I'll find a way back to Faerie and I'll find her. I promised I would."

I squeezed her tighter and ground my teeth. Thankfully she wasn't watching my face. *Not if I can help it; at least not alone. Promise or no. You're mine to keep safe even if you can't admit it yet.* But that was a conversation for another day so I remained quiet. She shuffled under my hold, then sighed, turning her body into my hold. My chest squeezed as my wolf rumbled a satisfied growl. Godsdammit, I was utterly fucked. There was no way I could let her go, not now, not ever. She turned her head, kissing my bare chest and I swallowed hard. Her lips were soft and warm, the sight of her gorgeous mouth touching my skin went straight to my cock. Fuck me, I needed some space or there would be no more talking tonight. I dropped a kiss on her head, inhaling her scent like it was sustenance for my soul then reluctantly stepped away. Unable to make myself go far, I kept hold of her hand like some teenage school boy.

"So this warden and Doherty? They can inflict pain and injury on the people you and your wolf have taken a vow to protect."

I let her change the subject. She'd trusted me with some of her life, she'd share more when she was ready. "Yeah."

Her fingers squeezed mine. "And you hate to see them suffer. Connor, you are not as cold-hearted as you make out, not even your wolf is." Her eyes softened. "You have tried to protect the ones you love, the only way you can."

I swallowed hard as my wolf whined at her assessment of us.

"I have. And because if there is no Prime, anarchy would spread. There would be countless challenges and countless atrocities. Not everyone here is innocent, and violence would rain down on the weak. I keep control, and in return my alpha brothers and I are kept out of the fight rings—usually." I ground my teeth together as the warden's demands for my brothers to fight filled my head.

Ember fell silent, staring at my chest as I continued to hold her hand, giving her time to process that.

"What else is going on here? Charlie said something about the females from gen pop being taken? And Doherty seemed hell bent on getting me, even though he didn't know who I was."

I rolled my head and neck trying to loosen my tense muscles. "It's true. But what I'm about to tell you can't go any further. Do you understand? If you breathe a word of this, and it gets back to Doherty or the warden, you will disappear." I clicked my fingers. "Like that."

Her face dropped into a blank mask. I'd worked out that expression meant she was not committing to any answer. Worry twisted my belly. "Ember. This is important. I need you to know what's going on here, so that you can stay as safe as possible, but I can't tell you unless I have your word you will keep it quiet."

She threw her hands up in the air, her blank mask totally gone. "Of course, I'll keep quiet! Who would I tell? Besides I've just shared my life with you." She smiled. "I don't do that with just anybody, you know."

I gave her a small smile, knowing that was totally true, but let go of her hand, my bare feet squeaking on the floor as I paced. "Before I was taken to that holding prison where you and Rawson found me four years ago, I had an interview for a job."

Her expression turned incredulous. "What the hell's that got to do with any of this?"

"Just sit down and listen."

Her brows rose and her arms crossed over her chest.

Shit. I need to curb my goddamn bossy tongue around her. "Please."

Her brows twitched again, but she sat on the table, swinging her legs.

"It was with a woman who called herself Miss X..." Ember opened her mouth, no doubt to add some sarcastic response to that. I held up my hand and quickly continued. "I know, corny, but true. If I got the assignment, I was supposed to go deep undercover, answering only to the Overseer of the SBI."

"The Overseer? Jeez, Connor, no one even knows what he looks like. What were you supposed to do?"

I met her astonished gaze. "At the time I had no idea. Something weird happened in my last interview. A portal opened behind me and I found myself paralysed. I never saw the person who came through that portal, but they put a gun in my hand and forced me to pull the trigger. I shot Miss X."

"Oh my god! Is that how you ended up here?"

"Yeah, pretty much. All hell broke loose after that gunshot. Owen barged in, followed by Doherty and his men. Both Owen and I were accused of murder. But the weirdest part of all is that Miss X's body just disintegrated in front of us. Her ashes rose from the ground and disappeared into an air vent. I've never seen anything like it." I shook my head. I still had no idea what had happened back then. I'd never heard of the dead, not even the supernatural dead, being able to just float away.

"What about cameras?"

I shook my head again. "Whoever came through that portal knew where they were. The only thing caught on camera was me shooting Miss X with a gun that I didn't even own. Doherty arrested Brady, I mean Owen, saying I couldn't have smuggled the gun in there without help. We never saw a court-room and never went to trial."

Her eyes darkened to that deep green again. "Christ, Rawson went mad after you went missing. They told us you were dead, but he never believed it. He searched so hard to find out what had happened to you."

My throat ached for the pain Doherty had caused my family. "Rawson told me. He called in favours and managed to get into the back up feeds from the headquarters cameras. Someone had tried to erase them. But he saw the whole thing. Me shooting Miss X and her disappearing, Doherty coming in and him arresting both me and Owen. He went to see Lyss to tell her what he'd found out." I ground my teeth together hating that Lyss had got caught up in all this. "They had already killed her."

"I was there." Her voice shook and I stopped pacing. "Not when they killed her, but after. That bastard... Zander you call him? He tranquilised Rawson while he was trying to crawl to her body..." Her voice broke, her eyes bright and shining with unshed tears. "He was crawling, Connor, an alpha as strong as him. They broke him that day. They took his reason for living and ripped her apart. There was...there was just...so much blood." Her last words came out on a sob.

My fists tightened, my fingernails piercing my skin. Zander had kept that fucking nugget of information from me. He'd better hope he hadn't been the one to end Lyss's life, or I was going to rip him limb from limb, and no amount of threats would stop me. I crossed the space between us and wrapped her up in my arms. "I'm sorry," I whispered into her hair, my heart breaking for her.

Had she ever cried over Lyss's death? Hell, she never cried over anything, so I doubted it. The only time she'd ever shed proper tears was the first time she'd had a nightmare about the fire that had killed her parents. She'd been twelve years old then and had cried in my arms. I'd been scared shitless when her skin had heated so much that I'd thought she was going to self combust. And she had… sort of. Flames had erupted from her hands. She hadn't burned me, but her bed clothes had been ruined. I'd only seen her fire once since then, when we'd escaped Doherty's clutches—or rather she had, I'd been betrayed by Walker, and then ended up here.

Her sobs became sniffles, but it seemed she didn't want to move. Can't say I minded when her arms slipped around my waist.

"I'm so sorry you had to see Lyss like that." I wished I could absorb that pain and those horrible images from her.

"It's not your fault."

Her words were muffled by my chest, but I was happy to let her stay there. She pulled back in her own time, tears streaking her cheeks.

"Sorry." She gave a watery smile and wiped roughly at her wet cheeks, sniffling.

"Hey," I said, leaning my forehead against hers, my chest still tight. "You're allowed to cry for Lyss, she was a beautiful person who didn't deserve to die."

"Yes, she was." A sigh escaped her, her shoulders drooping.

I cursed myself for not thinking about her more. She must be exhausted. Brushing soft strands of hair back from her damp face, I pulled her back against my chest, letting her lean on me.

"Let me finish, and then we can get some rest." There was no argument, and a little tension fell from my shoulders. I held her closer, my stomach tightening at the thought of her going back to Drake's pack. Asshole! But if that's what she wanted, I wouldn't stop her. Keeping my voice even and devoid of the anger that burned through me every time I remembered she *belonged* to another alpha was almost impossible.

"After I'd been here a few weeks, Zander came to see me. It seems I was here not just because of Doherty, but because I'd been successful at the interview that day. The person who made me shoot Miss X, is now my employer. They knew Doherty wouldn't pass up the opportunity to get me in here; he'd figured out I was a Prime, and he needed one. That motherfucker, Zander, and my new *boss*, set me up."

"Bastards." Warm breath fanned my chest, as she held me tightly.

I smiled, deciding I really, really liked it. "My current employer won't let me out of this prison unless I find out what the warden and Doherty are really doing here."

"What do you mean?" She pulled back enough to look into my face. "The fight rings aren't it?"

"No, 'fraid not. Every month females and the weaker males are rounded up from gen pop and taken into what we've named *the science wing*. With Zander's help, I managed to get someone on the inside. That poor bugger took a great risk to get back out of there and tell us what he saw." I went quiet, unsure how to phrase my next words.

"Well? What did he see?"

"He found out they use the money from the fights to fund some kind of research, a breeding programme. I don't know what exactly, but my inside man heard babies crying, and all he did, all day, every day, was mop up blood from empty cells. He never saw what they did in those cells, but he heard the women screaming and babies crying...."

"Oh, my gods, what are they doing with the babies?"

I shook my head. "I have no idea."

"Wait, I don't understand. Why did Zander help you get a man inside? And why can't he do it again?"

"He works for both my employer and the warden."

She frowned. "He's a double agent?"

"Yeah, I suppose he is. And it was a one off. He ensured the guy got chosen for the round up, but it was a pass to get out that Zander organised. It's too risky to do again. He had to call in a favour and someone would ask questions if he did it again, or so he says. I don't know, but I don't trust him, so it could all be bullshit." I released a heavy breath from my nostrils. "He brought you here to coerce me. He and whoever my boss is knows how much I care about you. Zander saw how devastated I was when I saw your wolf, and once they both knew you were alive, Zander was ordered to bring you here to force me to find a way into that science wing."

She pulled her top lip between her teeth, tilting her head. "I actually think he tried to help me."

"How?" I couldn't help my instant suspicion. Zander was an enigma to me; not just what he was, but why he played both sides.

"He helped me hold back the fire in my veins when Doherty raided our place. I'd just escaped from Fae..." She stopped and swallowed, her eyes searching mine.

"It's okay." I prompted, my heart squeezing as she swallowed and looked away. "From Faerie."

A horrible thought entered my head, anger pulsing through me, filling the room. "If you were forced to become one of their human pets, I'll hunt down those responsible and rip them apart piece by piece…" Blood coursed through my veins awakening the beast inside me, my wolf wary of its blood thirsty appearance.

"No, no, I wasn't coerced. I wasn't a pet, either."

"So Zander helped you?" I said, keeping the focus on our current situation.

She nodded, releasing a deep breath and looking up at me again. "Yeah, he told me to control my fire before Doherty realised who I was."

"Listen, I have no idea whether we can trust Zander or not, but he has threatened to make sure you are chosen for the round up if I can't somehow find a way into the science wing to see what they're doing. It seems my boss is on a time limit and so is the warden. He's brought the next fight ring closer. It's in two weeks." I took a deep breath. "And he wants you to fight in it."

"Why me?" Her eyes widened further.

"Probably because it's got back to him that you can fight and people will pay alot of money to watch you." I held in a growl even though the need to smash something festered in my gut. "If you don't go in the fight rings, he'll either use you himself, or put you in the entertainment rooms. I don't need to explain what he'll do to you, or how the entertainment rooms work, and it doesn't matter if you are male, female or an alpha, you can be chosen for those. You're a female warrior, Em, and you'll bring in more money in the fights than any of the males, unless the males are alphas." I glanced at the door. "He wants my brothers to fight, too."

Her fingers dug into my flesh. "But they'll have to fight each other."

She'd worked it out. I swallowed the bile that rushed up my gullet, burning my insides. The vultures who bet on the fights wanted to see blood and death, and the inherent instinct to survive in the alphas would deliver that. They would rip each other apart. Eventually my brothers or Ember would die. I swallowed hard and didn't answer. I couldn't.

"So there you have it, that's what's really going on here. You are a good fighter, Firecracker, so let's concentrate on those skills for the next couple of weeks. Somehow, I'll get you and my brothers out. I promise."

But the promise sounded hollow even to my own ears. Somehow I'd do it. I'd get us out, I just hoped I could come up with something before I lost the love of my life or my brothers to the death rings.

Ember's voice broke through my inner thoughts. "Maybe we can find a way together."

Silence fell between us and at that moment I knew I couldn't let her go, not to another pack, and for damn sure, not back to another alpha. *Mine. She is mine...* From deep in my soul my wolf rumbled his agreement. Relief and desire slammed through me in equal measure.

An enigmatic smile curled her lips. "You want something, Prime?"

Her skin was warm and smooth as I slid one hand under her top and curled my fingers around the curve of her waist into the small of her back. The other I slid up over her flat stomach. Making an impatient noise, I pushed the material of her bra aside until the softness of her breast was cradled in my palm and I could brush my thumb over her erect nipple.

"Hmmm." The moan of pleasure that came from between her beautiful soft lips had my cock jumping. "Gods, but I love your touch." Her head dropped back, her eyes fluttering closed.

My heart jumped painfully in my chest at her choice of words, my voice gruff when I answered. "Do you?" Softness greeted my lips as I dropped small kisses on her exposed neck. "Then stay with me tonight. I want to touch all of you." More kisses, alternated with small grazing nips as I squeezed that hard bud between my finger and thumb, making her groan.

That sound, so full of lust, snapped my restraint. *Oh, fuck this!* Sliding my hand from her lower back to cup her gorgeous ass, I pulled her forward, pushing my hips between her legs, pressing myself into her sweet spot. Moaning at the shockwaves of pleasure that slammed through me, I kissed up her neck, taking her mouth in a hard and demanding kiss, one she returned with fire.

"Damn, Firecracker, I need to be in you."

She bit my lower lip, her eyes burning with a desire. "Yes. I need you, too. Hard, and fast."

A devilish grin spread my lips. "You want hard and fast, then that's what you're gonna get. And if you want to stop, love, you'll need to scream it."

And she was my love. I knew that now.

I squeezed her nipple one more time and pulled back my hand, then used it to unfasten my jeans, and shove them down my legs. Palming my dick, I stroked it as I undid her jeans. I didn't need to say anything, she helped me push them down.

"Gods, you're so wet for me again." Her eyes locked with mine as I trailed my fingers up her slick slit, before sliding my fingers into her moisture and warmth. Godsdammit, I was gonna come just from the feel of her.

Biting her upper lip didn't stop her whimper as I touched, and gently rubbed.

With hooded eyes she watched me stroke myself, making me hard enough I ached. Her knuckles were white where she gripped the table, as if holding back from touching me. I squeezed my hard length. "Is this what you want?"

She nodded, her panting breaths loud.

"Where? Here?" Unapologetically, I slid two fingers inside her. We groaned in unison, me cursing under my breath at the sheer perfection of her.

"Gods, yes..."

I began moving my fingers in a demanding rhythm, something dark and possessive riding me. I needed to take her now. "Say it. Beg me for it, Firecracker."

Her irises darkened more, little flashes of flame igniting in them. "I want your cock. Now. Give it to me! You promised. Hard and fast." And though she was riding my fingers, the alpha in me wanted more. I circled her clit with my thumb.

"Not good enough. You ran from me, Em. Make me believe you want it. That you want me."

Her gaze snapped up to mine, her face tight and flushed, her lips swollen from my kisses. Her juices slicked my hand, her inner muscles squeezing down on my fingers as if she liked this dark side to me. I smiled. "Prove it. Make me believe." And I pinched her clit.

Her nostrils flared and her hips bucked. "Please," she cried, "please. I want you. I'm yours, and I *need* you inside me. You promised, Connor."

I exhaled on a growl at her words. *Mine.* "Good girl." Her moan was loud as I pulled away my touch and yanked her jeans off then pulled off her top and bra. I lifted her in my arms and deposited her on the bed. "Hard and fast, baby." I looked her directly in the eye, flipped her over, pulled her up on her hands and knees, and slid my cock through her slickness. I wrapped an arm around her hips, pulled her tight to me and angled myself, lining up with her entrance—then slammed home. Her moan was loud, but was drowned out by my curse as she squeezed me so tightly it was almost painful. The sensation as I pulled back and pushed home again was incredible. I moved my hands onto her waist as I rolled my hips, but it wasn't enough, I needed to touch more of her. So I laid across her back, forced her to lower her weight to her elbows and wrapped one arm around her waist, my other hand locked onto her breast squeezing hard enough to cause her a little pain. Her groan was the guidance I needed, enough to ride that line between pleasure and pain while I pumped into her. "More." I growled and let go of her breast, flipping her back over so I looked into her lust filled eyes as I rammed into her, harder and harder. No apologies. My need to claim her overwhelmed me, and I couldn't stop. "This pussy is mine. You are mine. You always have been." I growled in her ear. "If you run from me, I will find you—always."

"Gods, Connor, why...would I run...oh gods...from this?" Her words were interspersed with pants and groans. "I've always been yours. By the Mother's grace, all of this—all of me has always been all yours."

Satisfaction slammed through me, my wolf pacing and growling, reacting to my lust and far, far deeper feelings. Possessiveness burned in my heart. She wasn't leaving me, ever. And I meant that in a far deeper sense than just physical. I gripped her harder and tilted her pelvis until I knew exactly how much friction I was giving with each thrust. Sweat trickled down my spine, my muscles like rock as I felt her pussy tightening. "Look at me." Her pupils were huge, her face flushed and her fingernails digging into my skin, drawing blood. The pain only spurred me on. "Scream my name when you come." It was a demand.

"Oh gods, Connor, you feel so good."

"Mother Wolf, so do you, my Firecracker. Now come for me."

And she did. Screaming my fucking name. The feel of her squeezing me so tightly undid me. Electricity jolted down my spine, hot jets of cum exploding from me and filling her.

We panted as I held her closely and gave both of us time to come down, me slowly moving in her until we'd recovered enough to breathe. Gently, I pulled out then immediately rolled to my side, pulling her tightly to me.

Her smile was pure satisfaction, coloured by a look I could only describe as love. My heart squeezed as she tilted her chin, leaned back and kissed me. "That was amazing. *You* are amazing," she whispered before she dropped her head against my shoulder and closed her eyes.

I wrapped my leg over hers, encompassing but not crushing her, so I could feel the heat coming from her luscious body. We could clean up tomorrow. I might need to recover, but I had every intention of getting hot and dirty again tonight. I'd discovered my new drug of choice, and I wasn't letting her out of my arms any time soon.

Ember turned into me. "Hm, this is nice." She dropped small kisses on my chest, one of her arms curling across my stomach and gripping my waist. But before long her breathing settled into a steady deep rhythm.

Filled with utter disbelief that the woman I loved was in my arms and had agreed she was mine, I watched the door and listened to the sounds around us, my wolf on high alert. In the end, though, exhaustion won out over my need to protect her, and my eyes dropped closed. Nuzzling into my Firecracker's hair, I let myself drift off to sleep, knowing my brothers would be watching my back.

CHAPTER 15

mber

"Hey." Drake's eyes narrowed as I approached his table. The south wing food hall was noisy, busy and stank of that vile slop they called porridge. A heavy buzz hung in the air, an energy that made my wolf tense. I glanced around at the tight faces and dark gazes, wincing as I sat down opposite Drake.

Drake looked up from his gourmet faire and smirked. "You look like shit."

I had to agree. I was sleep deprived and walking like an old lady, stiff and in pain. Then again, I'd spent eight hours training my arse off yesterday, and sex with Connor had worked muscles that had not been used in a long time. I rolled my eyes. "Thanks. So I guess everyone knows the fights are coming early?" It was in the dark looks of those around us and the tension simmering in the air.

Drake huffed. "You know 'bout that shit, then?"

I shrugged. "I do, now that someone's filled me in."

"That someone Connor?" Drake cocked his head and studied me.

"Yeah. I think he decided he'd like me to survive."

"I can tell. His scent is all over you." Drake carefully placed his spoon down on the table and inhaled. "You had sex with him. Was that your choice or his?"

I patted his hand and smiled, touched that he genuinely seemed to care. "Mine. Or rather, it was a joint decision." I grinned and winked.

The tension eased from his shoulders and face and he smiled. "Good. So are you staying with my pack or moving to his?"

"Erm, I didn't know I could shift packs. I haven't been around many shifters since I was a teenager and I've never been in a pack." I took a breath. "Would you do that? Let me go to Connor's?"

Drake studied me like I was mad. "Y'all are kidding me, right?" His drawling southern accent was more pronounced, and his brows disappeared under his hair. "You're sleeping with the Prime, and you think he's going to let ya come back to another alpha's pack and protection every night? Of course I'd let you go, honey. No offence, but I don't know you well enough to die for you."

I raised my brows, irritation stirring my blood. "Connor doesn't *let* me do anything. Besides, there wasn't much sleeping involved," I confessed grinning from ear to ear.

"Good lord above, so y'all spent the night together? He never does that. And now you're here—with me? D'you want him to break my legs?"

"Oh now, now, he's fine with it. He asked me if I wanted to stay with him or come back here. See? He gave me a choice and I made it. There was no issue."

Drake's mouth dropped open and he swallowed hard, looking at me like I had a second head. "Godsdamn. The Prime allowed his female to leave his bed to go to another alpha's territory?"

I just grinned at him. It was true that I'd expected at least some show of alpha-hole possessiveness. When I'd told him I wanted to go, Connor's wolf had surfaced and both man and beast had growled. It had been a kind of test. Seeing if he'd respect my decisions was important to me. He had kissed me deeply until I was panting for more and questioning why I wanted to leave his side, but despite his obvious reluctance, he'd walked me back to my cell. Myles and Kawan had flanked us wearing such big stupid grins on their faces, I'd wanted to smack them, but Connor had distracted me by thrusting his hand into my hair and kissing me thoroughly again. "Remember, you're mine," he growled, leaving me panting at the door of my cell.

"Anyway, darlin'," Drake drawled, his eyes twinkling now that his shock had abated a bit. "Glad he's treating you with some respect now. Everyone deserves that, 'specially a strong and gorgeous female like yourself. So? I guess you know how important your training is? The fight rings are no joke, and that's why you're being pushed so hard. Every one of those males wants you to survive. Because if y'all gets chosen and you die, they know their Prime will lose his shit and this place will fall apart."

"Yeah, I know." Though we hadn't openly discussed it, my heart flipped now I knew Connor had such deep feelings for me. My love for him had been with me for so long and was so deeply seated inside my soul, it had become an indelible part of me. With difficulty, I swallowed a mouthful of gloopy oats. Despite all the sugar I'd dumped in it, it got stuck in my throat, but I needed to force it down if I wanted enough energy to train. I shoved in another spoonful, and another, until I'd emptied my bowl, then swallowed down a cup of water. Only then did I look up. People came and went, some eating, some just loitering. "Do you think they have more prisons? There are only shifters here..." I mused.

Drake glanced at the people nearby. "I've no idea. But I doubt we're the only supernaturals they know about in this world."

"Hmm." I gave a neutral response thinking about the fae. Was the warden a fae? Maybe that would account for his abilities.

"Come on. Let's get to the gym." Drake stood up, then laughed as I swung my leg over the bench seat and moaned loudly.

I glared at him. "Shut up." His big shoulders shook as I followed him stiffly out of the hall.

Rawson was already waiting for me in the training hall. I glanced around searching for Connor. He wasn't there.

"Morning." Rawson grinned, inhaling and assessing the stiff way I walked. "Sore?"

I flushed, not fooled by the innocent look on his face. And yeah, I was, and not just my muscles.The shit-head chuckled at my response and held open the ropes for me to climb through. I did. Slowly.

"Everyone you go anywhere near can tell, Ember."

"Tell what?" I said, scowling at the smirk on his face.

"That you and Connor finally ..."

"Ah!" I yelled putting my hands over my ears. "Nope. Just no. You can't say that to me."

Rawson roared with laughter. "Say what? I was just going to say that you finally got together. And why not? It's true. His scent is all over you."

"It's just wrong. You're my...er...I don't know what you are any more." I flung my hands in the air. He wasn't my father, but close enough since he had brought me up and given me a home. Even if he was only eleven years older than me.

"Sweetness." He used Lyss's endearment and I didn't stop him. I didn't mind him using it, it was a nice way to remember the kind and gentle woman who had loved me alongside this male. "You're an adult who has survived some nasty shit and I'll talk about anything you want with you. But if it makes it easier, you can think of me as an older brother—or a father if that's what you want. I'm honoured either way and I'll always look out for you, just as I would anyone I love." A shadow crossed his eyes but he shook it off. "I want you to be as happy as you can be in this shit hole. Know that I saw you and Connor were made for each other when you were only kids—so did Lyss.

Connor kept himself back from you when you were young at my request. You both deserved time to grow and live." His big shoulder rose and fell in a shrug. "But now—well, now you have found each other again and it's as it should be. Be with your mate while you can, Em. Life is too unpredictable to waste such a gift."

I stared at his rugged, handsome face, so full of sadness, my heart broke. Although my eyes burned, I managed a nod and a weak smile.

"Good. Now, we need to get on with training. I'm only going to be here for a short while." He glanced up to the walkway above.

Reflexively, I did too. Zander watched us, his face impassive. Rawson, flexed his hand, the movement drawing my gaze down to it. He was trembling slightly. He gripped it with his other hand as if trying to still the involuntary movements. Nausea rolled through my belly, churning the porridge that lay heavily in my stomach, but I didn't say anything. There was nothing to say. I wasn't sure Rawson would like me knowing that he was the warden's bitch and I wouldn't take his dignity by pushing him to talk about it.

"Let's warm up slowly today. I imagine you're a bit stiff after..."

I glared at him.

He put his hands up, a full on grin stretching his lips. "Okay, I won't mention you *finally* having sex with Connor. Took you long enough by the way," he murmured through the side of his mouth.

"You're an arse, Rawson." But I smirked. "Come on then, let's do this."

"Right, but I'll need you to train with one of my brothers. My body is not what it used to be and I need rest today...And Connor will allow only them and me, to be near you."

"What?" My eyes narrowed, my irritation immediate.

Rawson sighed, and jammed his hands on his hips. "Ember, don't argue with him on this. You are his soulmate—even if you haven't gone through a claiming yet."

My breath caught in my throat. I'd wanted Connor since I was a young girl only I'd never allowed myself to believe he felt the same. But... "Soulmate?" Damn, that was enough to make my knees wobbly.

"Of course. You were always the most important thing in the world to him." He cocked his head, his expression softening. "Ember, every decision he ever made was based around what he thought was best for you. He loves you, he always has. He lost you once already. He won't trust anyone but his brothers to train with you."

"Trust? How about he trusts me? I'm not going to go and jump another man..."

"Trust has to be earned, you know that. It's not about sex, and it goes both ways. Arguing with every decision he makes isn't a way to gain his trust, or show your trust in him. He's Prime, and anyone who sees him look at you will know how much you mean to him. That puts a huge target on your back for those who want his power and his position here. If anyone managed to injure or kill you, he'd lose his shit and slaughter anyone in his path. That grief would leave him vulnerable and if anyone managed to kill him, the amount of power they could absorb would be virtually insurmountable. If it didn't kill them, they would become unstoppable."

Uneasily, I looked around at all the people in the hall. Males, big enough and mean enough to challenge most alphas, pummelled each other, their bodies hitting the ground with heavy thuds, while false weapons were being used to simulate kills.

Drake met my gaze from across the hall. *You okay?* he mouthed, a frown creasing his brow.

I nodded, queasiness rolling through me. Would someone really try and kill Connor? It hadn't crossed my mind that they would, not with his brothers watching his back all the time. Then again, they didn't follow him for show.

"Okay." I nodded. Rawson was right. Fighting Connor on this would be irresponsible. I coughed, clearing the ache from my throat. "Who am I fighting today then?"

"Me."

I spun around.

Stone's cold glare was on me.

I groaned. "Really?"

Rawson slapped my back. "Suck it up, buttercup. He's one of the best fighters in here—and next to Connor and Owen, the most powerful. Right, you two warm up while I go and get us some weapons." And he left me there with Mr Personality.

Stone's top lip curled as he glowered down at me. "So, is it clear now why I don't think you should be anywhere near my brother? You are a weakness for him; one that could wreck him, and I can't allow that."

I straightened my spine and glared at the miserable son of a bitch that was Connor's third. "Yeah, well, that must be damn awkward for you, seeing as you have to keep me safe."

"Believe me, it is. But, no matter what Rawson thinks, you aren't Connor's mate. He hasn't claimed you." He leaned in. "*And, no one* needs a mate to survive, plenty of males in here survive without one, and so will Connor. Mates leave only heartbreak behind when they go, so I'll do everything I can to stop you from hurting him like that. If I end you now, Connor might go dark again, but he'd get over it. And he'll be far less vulnerable without you."

Cold grey eyes glared at me. The hairs on my neck stood on end. He really meant it. So much for trusting Connor's brothers.

I shuffled away, not willing to turn my back on him. How would he do it? A training accident maybe?

"Right," said Rawson, climbing back into the ring. His gaze flicked from one of us to the other, a frown creasing his brow. "Everything alright? Ember?"

I kept my eyes on Stone. "Sure. Just fine and dandy." My nostrils flared. I didn't like being threatened, but I wouldn't ask Rawson—or Connor, to fight my battles.

"It will be," Stone said, his words a promise that sent my blood cold.

"Fine, but remember this is light training for now—no injuries." He aimed the warning at Stone before turning to me.

We both nodded. I met the gaze of the half-fae and curled my lip. I wouldn't look away. He snarled back, an alpha unwilling to back down.

Fine. Bring it on, faerie boy.

"Hey, Ember!" A deep familiar voice rumbled.

I allowed myself to glance sideways at Lionel. "Hi." I gave him a tight smile, and slid my attention back to Stone, who had clearly taken my glance away as capitulation, fear, or maybe even subservience. He'd stepped away and was warming up.

Yeah? Well, fuck you, I told him silently, determined that he'd soon realise I was neither caving nor scared of him.

"D'you need a training partner?" Lionel asked as he leaned into the ring and smiled, his amber eyes bright with the promise of a fight.

I turned sideways so that I could see Lionel while keeping Stone in my peripheral vision. "Yeah, I do, preferably not one who's promising to kill me."

"What was that?" Rawson walked over, his eyes narrowed. Had he heard me? I'd no idea. I wouldn't run from Stone, but I didn't want to cause tension between him and Connor either. And throwing down with Stone would definitely cause tension. But, oh, how I'd love to slam my fist into that arrogant shit's face. Still, I supposed I couldn't fault his loyalty to Connor. Stone thought I made Connor weak. I thought it was none of his damn business.

"Nothing. I think it's better if Stone goes and does whatever important things he has to do. I'll train with Lionel today."

Lionel glanced at Stone, then back at me, meeting my eyes with his amber ones. He understood. I didn't know how, instincts, maybe? But he had Stone's measure. "Yeah, I'm up for that." Grinning, he vaulted into the ring. He was extremely agile for such a large man. His long, sandy hair fell around his head like a halo, hiding most of the silver collar. He prowled straight over to Stone. They stood nose to nose but Lionel kept his gaze fixed over Stone's shoulder, never making eye contact as he told the faerie wolf what was happening.

Stone flashed me a derisory glare.

Whatever... I rolled my eyes, not caring what he thought.

"Connor doesn't want you fighting anyone other than his brothers," Rawson pointed out.

"Yeah, well, it's not up to him. It's my choice. I trust Lionel. He's had my back since we got here, whereas Stone would happily stab me in it if he got the chance."

Rawson grunted, but didn't refute my claim. "Well, you can deal with Connor later, then."

Stone prowled over. He looked down at me with his superior expression. "I agree with the lion. I am an alpha, and I deserve better than to spend time babysitting my Prime's latest piece of ass." After his declaration, he strutted away.

"Jeez, that guy has one hell of a superiority complex." But I couldn't help the rush of relief in my limbs now he'd left. He truly believed I was a weakness for Connor, an indirect threat.

Rawson watched him speculatively. "Hmm, well, forget about him now, we have work to do."

"So? Are you ready for me to kick your ass?" Lionel quipped, grinning from ear to ear.

I put my hands on my hips and contemplated him. "Well, who knew you could grin like that?"

"'Course I can, just don't often get the urge. But I'm looking forward to this." His eyes gleamed with challenge as he bounced around on the balls of his feet like a prize fighter.

I couldn't help but laugh at him. I'd not seen him so animated since we'd been here, not even when we'd trained yesterday. Then again he was a lion, he lived to hunt, fight, and take down his prey, and he wouldn't go down in the fight ring, he'd kill anyone in his way. I was glad I happened to be his friend and not an enemy, especially when he fixed his gaze on Santa Cruz, before zoning in on Stone again, who looked to be arguing with Shannon.

I snorted a laugh. Queen bitch looked like she wanted to punch the half-fae, too.

By mid-day I was beginning to shake. Rawson had pushed us both, demanding we repeat locks, throws and break falls. I was tired. I hadn't seen Connor. And I'd had about enough of Stone giving me the evil eye from across the hall.

"Come on, one more." Rawson flexed his right hand, which I could see trembling again. I eyed it uneasily, hoping it was nothing serious.

"Come on, wolfie, you got this," Lionel said, his chest rising and falling in a quick rhythm.

I scowled. Was I collecting nicknames now? If it wasn't Drake with his easy terms of endearment, it was Lionel.

Lionel grinned at my dark look, then schooled his features into his fighting face and circled me, his penetrating, amber gaze disconcerting. It was like he was eyeing up his dinner—me. I watched him carefully, the only tell he had was his chin, he dipped it minutely before he attacked. I moved swiftly, blocking his punch, and stepped sideways to miss his other hand. I just wasn't quick enough, and his knuckles made contact with my ribs. I grunted in pain but didn't let it stop me. My momentum kept me going and I gripped his wrist, twisted under his arm and punched his ribs. I pivoted until my back rested against his front and shoved my foot between his legs. Thrusting my hip into his and tilting my body, I yelled with effort. Just as I tipped Lionel's massive body over my shoulder, the energy in the hall changed. Power rippled through the air. *Connor.* I ignored it, even though my heart beat faster knowing he was near. Lionel landed with a thud and I stamped my foot down on his neck, twisting the arm lock upwards at the same time. His shoulder would be dislocated and his neck would be broken right now, if this were a real fight. I let go, and Lionel jumped to his feet. We clasped hands and hugged briefly, patting each other on the back. It was—nice. Our camaraderie had solidified into friendship. I'd fallen into a rhythm with him and we worked well together. It was strange to be so at ease with him, the only person I'd been this close to before was Blue.

"Thanks, for letting me kick your arse, pussy cat."

He flashed me a warning look.

I winked and gave him a bright smile. "What? Why should I get all the nicknames?"

All I got was a grunt. Rawson and Lionel wandered off for food and Reed sauntered over. I greeted him with a smile. Stone might be happy to take me out, or to let someone else do it, but the other brothers weren't.

"Hi, Reed."

"Hey. Would you like to go and get some lunch?' he asked, in that perfect upper class accent of his.

I blew out a shaky breath. "Sure, though I'm not convinced we can really call it lunch. In fact, I'm not sure what we are forced to eat is actually classified as food out in the real world."

He laughed, his eyes twinkling. He wasn't as muscular as the others, but he was attractive in that geeky kind of way some men had. His hair flopped onto his forehead making him look younger, and his body was sinewy and strong. Fluidly, he jumped up on the ring side and held the ropes apart for me.

I scrambled out, trying not to look too obvious as I searched the room for Connor, though the energy that accompanied him had disappeared.

"He's gone for a meeting with Drake, I believe," said Reed.

I nodded, hiding my disappointment and followed Reed to the west wing food hall. It wasn't until I'd sat down with Reed at my side, at the same table as I'd sat with Connor the day before, that I realised I hadn't even considered going to the south wing food hall. I ate what was supposed to be beef and potato pie then quickly peeled an orange. I needed my vitamins just like everyone else. Despite our limited ability to heal with the collars holding back our shifter traits, if we kept ourselves well fed and healthy, it helped—and it seemed the warden knew that too. I chugged down a cup of milk and wiped my forearm over my mouth. Reed looked at me like I was crazy.

"You can slow down, you know, no one's going to whip it away before you have finished."

"No, but they might decide to pick a fight before I'm done eating, and that would be a waste."

"You aren't in gen pop anymore." A slight frown creased his brow.

"No, but old habits die hard. And they started way before I came to this place."

He shook his head, but didn't say anything else.

Finished with our food, we made our way back to the training hall. Stone stood at the entrance to the main corridor. I ignored him though Reed nodded. Stone waited until Reed had passed him, then shoved his arm out anchoring it on the wall opposite. "You can't go through yet."

I resisted the urge to head butt him. "Why not?"

"The Prime wants the corridor kept clear until he says otherwise. That includes you—she-wolf."

"What's with all the godsdamn nicknames today?" I rolled my eyes and looked to Reed for help.

He frowned, but didn't argue with Stone. "How long?' he asked instead.

Stone frowned, still staring down at me. "He didn't say."

My attention was captured by movement in the corridor. One of the laundry guys pushed a cart of stinking garments along, his face blank, his eyes dull. At least he wasn't likely to have to fight to the death in two weeks. My nerve endings ignited as a familiar wave of energy washed over me. Connor was near. I strained to see what he was up to. Above us the guards were doing their normal pacing, not really paying attention to what was happening in the corridors below. They were mostly gathered on the walkways above the food hall, talking. A group of them peeled away and without any interest in what was happening below their boots, one pulled off a glove. I watched from under my lashes as the guard placed a smallish hand on a glass pad and was locked in position. It was the same blood and DNA recognition they'd used for years. Part of me rejoiced, the information wasn't much, but I'd learned something. The guard pulled off her helmet and waited while one of those floating robots scanned her profile and matched up the blood, DNA and bone structure.

Another movement caught my attention. I inhaled and Connor's spicy scent hit me. I waited to see him, my stomach doing weird jumps, but he didn't turn our way at all, he just strode by with purpose on his face. I did a double take when Zander walked by behind Connor.

"I need to see Connor." I didn't, but I wanted to know what he was up to.

"No. He knew you were there." Stone inhaled. "After all, your stink is mixed with his. If he wanted you with him, he would have called you to heel." He half-smirked, half-snarled, keeping his arm in my way.

My hands fisted. In this position, his chest was open to an attack. Was he that stupid he didn't realise? Or just so arrogant he didn't think a mere female would attack him? Then I saw the expectant glitter in his eyes. He was goading me, leaving himself vulnerable. I wasn't that stupid. Nonchalantly, I shrugged, and with my back against the wall, slid to the floor. "I might as well have a seat then."

Reed lifted one big shoulder. "Of course. Would you like me to find you a chair?" He frowned at my position on the floor.

My eyes widened, and I opened my mouth ready to snap at him for that sarcastic remark—until I realised he was absolutely serious. "I...er...no, I'm good, thank you." Bloody hell, he really was a gentleman. How on earth had he gotten mixed up in all this shit?

Stone snorted, flashing Reed a *what the fuck?* look.

I ignored them both and leaned my head back against the wall, closing my eyes just enough so that I could still see Stone. I didn't trust that fucker at all.

Reed frowned down at me, but I couldn't care less about my position. It was nice to just sit for a moment. My body was aching, and I was far more weary than I'd admit. When Reed sat on the other side of me, keeping his vigil as my guard, I actually let myself relax. Stone took his hand off the wall and leaned against the door frame, watching.

His gaze didn't bother me as much as I think he hoped it would. I tried peering into the corridor beyond him a couple of times, but it was quiet and empty. It was at least ten minutes before people started moving around again. When the first people came from the direction we were going, I went to stand. Reed jumped to his feet before I could get to mine.

"Here, let me help you up," he said, holding his hand out for me.

I didn't need help to get up, but I didn't want to be rude. Besides, Reed was just being nice. Stone rolled his eyes as I accepted.

"Thank you." I smiled at Reed. When the nice guy turned his back, I gave Stone the finger. He snarled, his eyes flashing purple as he took a stride towards me.

I quickly stepped up to Reed's side and through the door into the now busy corridor.

"Hey," greeted Myles.

Reed actually flushed a little. "Hey, man, what are you doing here? Did the boss put you on Ember watch?" He winked at me.

Ember watch? Not only did I get silly nicknames, so did anything related to me it seemed.

"Nah," Myles said, his gaze running down Reed's body and back up to his face like he couldn't help it. "I need you." His voice and eyes held such heat, the meaning was clear.

"Me?" replied Reed, though he swallowed hard, not missing the suggestive tone in Myles's voice. "I, erm, I can't. I need to get Ember back to the training hall."

"I'll be fine, Reed." I smiled widely. Well, wasn't this interesting? Reed's heart rate and breathing had kicked up a pace and his face had flushed more. "You go and, err, see what Myles needs you for." But it was pretty bloody obvious to me.

"No." Reed took a step back from Myles, whose eyes narrowed. "I was given a job by my Prime and I'm not abandoning it." He glared at Stone accusingly.

I almost laughed at Stone's pissed expression. He glared at me like him leaving the training ring this morning was my fault. I just put an innocent look on my face, knowing that he shouldn't have left my side, but still glad he had.

Myles flinched at Reed's refusal. He covered his reaction quickly and smiled tightly. "Okay, I'll see you later."

Reed gave an equally tight smile in response.

What the hell is going on between these two?

Myles walked off without another word, his hands fisted at his sides.

Stone followed him.

Reed glanced over his shoulder at them, a spectrum of emotion crossing his face before he began walking again. We walked in silence for a few minutes. I glanced up at his tight face, not missing that his movements were stiffer than normal.

"Hey." I bumped his shoulder with mine. "You okay?"

He sighed, not looking at me. "Yeah."

"What do you think Myles wanted?" There were obviously some major unresolved issues between them, and knowing what was coming up in two weeks, I thought that was a sad way to be. People you loved could be ripped away so quickly.

"I have no idea." He avoided looking at me.

"Yeah, you do. Is that why you wouldn't go with him? Don't you want him as a lover? Because it was obvious to me he wants you—badly."

Reed's footsteps faltered, and he pulled me to one side. His face fell. "It's not that. I do want him, but I don't show it, or try not to, for the same reason Stone would harm you."

I frowned. "What on earth are you on about?"

"Myles is my brother, we can't become lovers, it would compromise our position as protectors of the Prime. People would know we are a weakness to each other and use that to get to Connor."

I snorted and placed a hand on his arm. He looked so crestfallen that I just wanted to cheer him up. "But you wouldn't allow that to happen, would you? Besides, Connor is a big boy..." I wiggled my eyebrows suggestively. "I should know."

He grinned. "Yeah, you should."

"He's the most powerful shifter in this prison, and he can take care of himself. I've also known him for a long time and he would not want either of you to be unhappy because of him."

Reed blew a breath from his nose and leaned against the wall watching the guards pace above. "Yeah, you're right, I know you are. I guess if we both agree we won't allow our feelings for each other to be used against us, it wouldn't matter..."

I chewed on the inside of my lower lip sensing his reticence. He wouldn't meet my gaze. "But...?"

Silence.

"Reed, it's okay. I won't break your confidence." But I stayed quiet, letting him make up his own mind if he could trust me or not. Alphas were like just about every other man on the planet. Feelings were something women talked about, not tough men whose sole purpose in this place was to dole out pain and punishment when needed. Alphas, even one as polite as Reed, had to be in control and deemed powerful at all times or risk a challenge.

His gaze slid to mine. My stomach tightened at the turmoil in his eyes. Whatever was going on in his head was something that had been stewing in there for a long time. I didn't know Reed all that well, but he seemed like a nice guy and he deserved to be happy.

"I'm not saying I can do anything about it. But it might help just to tell someone, and I'm not in the business of judging." I shrugged one shoulder and gave him an encouraging smile.

"I'm scared," he said quietly, looking away.

"Of what?"

He huffed a quiet laugh. "Have you seen Myles? He's like a force of nature. He's full on alpha."

"So are you."

"Not like him and Stone—or Owen. They all have enough power to take on Connor if they want."

I gave a sharp intake of breath.

He shook his head. "Not that they would. They all worship him, and he has their undying loyalty, just as he has mine."

I gave him a reassuring smile, though I wasn't so sure about Stone. "What's that got to do with having a relationship with Myles?"

"Nothing...except, I don't think Myles wants a relationship. He just does what most males do in here. He uses his lovers until he's bored with them and then moves on." He took a deep breath, exhaling slowly. "I don't just like him, Ember, I feel far more than like, or lust, I have for years; and every time I see him with another lover, male or female, it cuts me up inside. If I let him in and he discards me, it would break me. And that kind of distraction in a place like this would put Connor—and my brothers—at risk. The predators in here would sense my weakness and attack."

I took his hand and gave it a squeeze. He gave me a watery smile in return. "Who says it would end badly? Maybe Myles does want more with you. I mean, come on, you've both been here a long time; he knows the stakes as well as you do." I bumped him with my shoulder again, but the smile fell from my face. "You know what's happening in two weeks. What if he has to fight— or you do, and one of you loses? Neither of you will have had a chance to say how you feel. Don't you think that's sad after loving him from afar for so long?" Slipping the 'L' word in was deliberate. Reed was right, what he felt for Myles was far more than lust. Reed didn't deny he loved Myles, just released a heartfelt half-sigh, half-growl.

"Yeah, I suppose it is, but so would opening my heart to him, only to see him die." The column of his throat bobbed, his eyes briefly closing. "Or for us to have to kill each other."

"But at least he'd know how much you love him." The thought of anyone in this place being forced to kill someone they cared about sent a wave of horror rolling through me. At least Connor wouldn't have to fight, Doherty and the warden needed him.

Reed closed his eyes briefly. "Yeah, he would."

"And something tells me he feels the same." I blew a breath out, hating myself for the relief washing through me that Connor would be safe when so many others wouldn't. I dropped his hand and swung my fist to the side and into the wall. "This place, this whole situation is so godsdamn shitty."

"Yeah, it is. And if you're going to have to fight in a fortnight, you need to get back to training. You have to survive to keep our Prime's head in the game. Come on." He took my hand and dragged me towards the Gym. "You would do well to watch others fight, too. Knowing your enemy is half the battle..."

Just before I got back in the ring with Rawson and Lionel, Reed pulled me to a halt. He kissed my forehead, earning some incredulous stares from the two waiting men. "Thank you."

I smiled up at him, not sure I'd done anything to warrant his thanks, but I'd take it. It was nice to talk, to have a meaningful and peaceful exchange of words, rather than having to fight my way through every hour of every day. For some reason an image of Lyss handing me that great big fluffy pink bunny she'd bought me when I first set foot in her home, came to me. Sometimes it was nice to just be offered friendship, no strings attached.

The rest of the day was round after round of punches, throws and fighting techniques. Reed commented and made suggestions from the side, and he didn't leave us, even when Kawan came to take over his watch. It was nice to think he stayed because he wanted to and not because Connor had ordered him to.

CHAPTER 16

onnor.

IMPATIENCE BUZZED through me as I waited for Drake. Steam and heat bathed my skin and caused drops of sweat to bead up on my forehead and neck until it trickled down the groove of my spine. The stink of acrid industrial detergent stung my nose and made my eyes water. I growled. I hated enclosed spaces, especially this one. It was so dark even I struggled to see and my wolf balked at being so closed in. I beckoned Kawan. He had his hair mussed and his posture was curled forward along with his shoulders. He kept his gaze on the ground and to those above would look like any other laundry worker—weary and submissive.

Zander had disappeared as soon as we had our cargo in the laundry room. He hadn't explained how he'd managed to get hold of it, and I didn't ask. "I don't know how the hell you're going to get it to work in here." He'd gestured to the prison with a sweep of his arm. I just smiled and kept my mouth shut. Just as he wouldn't tell me his secrets, I had no intention of telling him mine. "Just remember if you're in the system too long, it will flag up unauthorised activity to the security hub." With that parting comment, he'd left.

Dipping my head down, I pretended to root through the clothes in the dirty laundry basket as a guard walked overhead. As their footsteps disappeared, I ducked into the shadows, letting them cloak my bulk and keep me out of sight of the guards. A small part of me rejoiced at the darkness, just as it always had.

I'd discovered this small corner years ago. It was near the huge industrial washing machines and dryers and couldn't be seen from the platforms above. Besides, it was so dark and steamy in the laundry room, I didn't think the guards ever saw much of it from above. The atmosphere probably steamed up their visors. I grinned at the thought. They never paid much attention to the space, not unless there were the sounds of a fight...which I'd forbidden in here; I liked to keep their attention away from this hidden corner.

I peered at the wall hoping to find the power outlet to the huge machines. It was my guide. I'd only seen what I was looking for once before, and that had been years ago, dismissing it then as being of no use.

Kawan dipped in beside me and regarded the industrial powerpoint skeptically.

"That amount of power will blow it up. And the socket's sealed anyway. How are we going to wire this laptop into that power source without killing ourselves?"

"We're not." I ran my fingers down the wall right to floor level and reached into the small space behind the washers until my fingers hit the metal of the other power socket I sought. My heart banged against my ribs and I grinned widely. "Pass me that power cable." I peered up, making sure no guards were near.

Kawan quickly did as I asked.

Fumbling with the plug, I cursed. My hand was twisted at an awkward angle, and I had no hope in hell of seeing what I was aiming for. All I could do was move the metal prongs over the socket until it slid into place. Finally it slid right in. "There." I sat back, panting, and gave Kawan a wide grin.

His eyes widened. "What? You're shitting me? There's a socket down there?"

I chuckled. "Yeah. I found it years ago, but ignored it. It served no purpose until now. The other laundry rooms have one, too. They must be a throwback to some old machines they had that weren't wired into a sealed unit, or perhaps from when they built this place. Who knows? The thing is, it wouldn't help us with anything...normally." I grinned and out of sight of the guards, rummaged in the laundry cart. My fingers gripped the smooth metal of the laptop and I pulled it out, careful not to let it slip from my grip. "But now it will."

"You hope," said Kawan, eying the computer with doubt. "What are you hoping to do with that anyway?"

I shook my head. "You know better than to ask questions like that."

"I suppose." But his smooth brow furrowed.

"Don't worry, brother. You'll know everything you need to, when you need to. But, you also know the drill; the fewer people who know what's happening the better. The warden is very persuasive when he wants to be."

Kawan rubbed his face. "Yeah, he is. Right, well, I'm on Ember watch now, so I'm off. Hey, didn't you ask Stone to watch Ember this morning?"

I frowned. "I did, why?"

Kawan frowned too. "No reason. I just wondered."

My stomach flipped. He was covering for Stone.

"Why? Was she on her own?"

"No, boss, the lion was with her, and Rawson. Stone must have been called away to deal with something."

I grunted. "Yeah, probably." I'd find out later exactly why Stone had ignored my orders and left my mate's side. The half-fae had always been difficult to control, but I didn't question his loyalty to me, not at all. It was just that his thought processes were definitely arse about face sometimes, probably because he was more than a little bit fae in his outlook on right and wrong. He'd do something morally questionable and be able to justify it convincingly, a classic wrong thing for the right reasons, guy. Then again, I scoffed at myself, isn't that what we all did in here? I was the last person to judge anyone's morals. I'd left mine in the outside world until Ember had reappeared. She was a burning light in the darkness of my current life.

I fought the urge to go with Kawan and find Ember—not for any other reason than I wanted to be with her. I had scented her in the corridor, but had fought my need to stop and pull her into my arms. This plan had to work, or in two weeks she might die—hell, she might still die in the fight rings before I could save her, but I could at least try.

I rubbed my face, not sure how to deal with the need she had ignited in my soul, especially after last night. Letting her return to her cell in Drake's wing had made me want to rip his throat out, but if I wanted her to trust me, I needed to show my trust in her and give her some independence. I was very aware the more people who saw us together, the bigger target I would paint on her back, and having Drake on her side made me worry less. I'd talk to him later about releasing Ember from his pack. Not that I'd accept no for an answer.

Kawan waited until the guards were at the other end of the suspended walkway and shot out, heading back towards Ember.

I watched him go. Knowing he'd be closer to Ember than me in the next few minutes just made me want to follow him. Grumbling, I shoved the cart into a position that would hide the light from the laptop screen and powered it up. I wasn't a techno whizz by any stretch of the imagination but I knew someone who was. I only hoped Drake was as clever as I needed him to be.

DRAKE LOOKED like a kid in a sweet shop. His eyes were alight and his southern drawl more pronounced than ever.

"This thing is amazin', man." Leaning forward, he studied the outside case of the computer which was still in my lap.

I quirked a brow. "I'll take your word for it. Can you get into it?"

Drake shot me a dry look. "I'm gonna pretend you didn't ask me that."

He took the computer from me and sat on the floor, his back up against the wall. I watched him press keys and peer at the screen. His face tightened and his gaze flicked to me, irritation in his eyes. "I'll give you an update later, Prime. Don't you have somewhere else to be?"

I chuckled, and let myself be dismissed. Drake wouldn't bring anyone else in on this unless he asked my permission. And I believed he would update me as soon as he had something to say.

The guard above walked across the platform towards our position. I waited for him to reach the walkway above our heads then twisted out of our hiding place, matching his strides and staying a little way behind him where I could watch him until I slipped out of the laundry room unseen.

The corridors of the west wing were fairly quiet as I made my way to the gym. No one made eye contact with me and no one was stupid enough to challenge their Prime. It didn't mean I wasn't listening for a possible attack from behind. As soon as I walked into the training hall, eyes flicked my way, heads dipped forward, and a whole mix of emotions ripened the air making it fetid enough to burn my nostrils. Used to that kind of reaction, I ignored it and leaned against the wall.

Ember was fighting the lion with Reed and Kawan shouting encouragement from the ringside. I grinned as my Firecracker leaped, wrapped her legs around Lionel's neck and flung herself down onto the mat with enough momentum to take the big male down with her. I held in a growl at seeing her thighs wrapped around another male's neck. My wolf surged forward. There was nothing sexual about this fight, but that didn't matter to me. Ember's pussy was far too close to the male's face and my possessive instincts roared to life, a wave of energy escaping me. My whole body tensed, ready to fight, but I fisted my hands and forced myself to remain where I was.

I heard a loud thud as Lionel landed heavily. Even from as far away as I was, I saw his slack jaw and the whites of his eyes. Kawan and Reed gaped. I chuckled. Apparently none of them had taught her that move. I puffed my chest out, proud my Firecracker could take down one of the strongest males outside of my brothers that I'd met in years.

Rawson tensed as he sensed my presence and glanced over, a wary look on his face. I understood why, he was expecting me to run over there and break that male's legs.

Lionel's gaze swung towards me and despite his dominant nature, the blood drained from his face.

Reed and Kawan shuffled their stances both watching me through narrowed eyes.

I lifted a hand in greeting, and forced my wolf to back down. He urged me to show the lion who Ember belonged to. *Not today, my friend. I trust my mate, even if you don't. She will not forsake us.* He snarled, but reluctantly settled.

Rawson cocked his head, then nodded and raised his hand in return.

Ember climbed to her feet and looked directly at me. Her bright smile warmed my soul. Panting, with sweat running down her face, she looked like a warrior; so strong and beautiful. And so mine. My heart flipped. It was all I could do not to go to her, drag her against me and kiss the hell out of her in front of everyone. I smirked at the thought, but I didn't want to scare her away by smothering her. She was too wild and too determined to forge her own path through this shit hole of a prison, and although I wanted to make sure every male in here knew she was mine, I had to agree with Owen and Stone, it would only make her more of a target to those who coveted my power.

Instead, I contented myself with running my gaze over her curves. My wolf peered at her through my eyes. He growled at the red marks on her skin and the small cut on her lip. I inhaled, scenting her blood even from this distance. It was a unique smell that was ingrained in my mind, one I'd memorised years ago when I'd first seen Rawson draw blood in one of their training sessions.

I grappled with my need to go to her, and instead, I forced myself to walk to the other side of the hall where Stone was training Santa Cruz, or rather kicking his arse. Owen worked nearby with a group of newbies. I'd get the low down on which were the best fighters later. Shannon's eyes flashed as I strode up to Owen's ring. She stood at the ringside, her blonde hair tied over one shoulder and her plump lips in a thin line.

I held in my irritation and smiled tightly.

She raised her brows.

"Oh, get over yourself Shannon. You aren't upset about me moving on, only that you didn't end up with my claiming mark on your neck. You aren't my mate, you are a power seeker nothing more," I said, calling her out.

"And? What's wrong with that? That runt is only after the same thing as me." She indicated Ember with her chin. "And I've been here longer. I deserve to stand next to you and wield the power you hold."

I stared down at her, not understanding her pissed off, or entitled attitude. I was never going to mark her as my mate and I'd never pretended otherwise. I lowered my voice. "Your father threw you in here because you tried to blackmail him. That power play didn't end well. Don't make the same mistake with me, Shannon. If you mess up my relationship with Ember, your ending will be far worse and extremely painful. Are we clear? Not even the fact you are Ava's sister will save you."

Her gaze dropped. She nodded, but despite her lowered eyes, her chin remained high. "You'll regret falling for her, Connor. She was never right for you. She's unpredictable and will do whatever she needs to do to get out of here, that includes betraying you if she has to."

"What? And you think you know her better than me because…?" I shook my head. "She was special to me long before I even knew you existed. She's always been passionate, loyal and fiercely protective of the people she cares about. Completely the opposite of you. You, Shannon, care only about your-self. You go after what you want with no thought about who you hurt in the process. You have no loyalty to anyone, including your family, despicable though your father is. So yeah, *you* were never right for me. You were nothing more than a way to release some sexual tension. Now I don't need you." I kept my voice utterly cold. But it was me alone who had decided I had a responsibility to keep Shannon safe because of Ava, and she was still in a dangerous position as an unmarked female. No matter what I'd done with the rules, lone women were still vulnerable. So, despite my threats, I needed her to be marked—if not for the relationship with, and then the way I'd unknowingly betrayed her sister, then because my brother felt something for her.

"You need to choose, Shannon. Pick a pack or be rounded up with the spare females from gen pop and end up the Mother only knows where."

She tossed her blonde hair over her shoulder. "I will not be owned by anyone, not unless I get something out of the deal. And although I enjoyed your body, Connor, I will not give myself up to be used by any male who sees fit. This is mine, no one else's." She gestured to her body.

I rolled my eyes. "I've told you that isn't the way it works in my pack—or Drake's. The north and east wings are the ones you want to avoid. Their rules are not much better than gen pop's. Especially since Santa Cruz took over."

"So fix it."

I bristled at her demand. "I have other, more pressing issues to deal with." A war with the alpha males in those packs was not high on my list of things to do. Besides, Shane, the east wing alpha, was new enough to be working on his pack's behaviour and I hoped Santa would end up neutralised in the games.

She rolled her eyes. "Don't you always."

"Stone! Come with me." I was tired of my spat with Shannon. I was tired of Shannon, period.

Stone's face became unreadable. I zoned in on his heart rate and his breathing, trying to pick up on any changes. I noted a slight hitch in his heart rate, but he was already breathing hard. He rolled his head on his shoulders, his bare torso gleaming with sweat and rippling with power as he jumped out of the ring, landing right next to Shannon.

She scowled at me and then him. He merely stared right back at her, holding her gaze until she looked away. I hid my smile. Stone was a force to be reckoned with, one not even Shannon could defy for long.

I strode back through the halls and up the metal stairs, not bothering to speak to Stone. I led him into my cell and rounded on him in a burst of speed he had no hope of escaping. My hand clenched around his throat. I kicked the door shut and slammed him up against it, my muscles screaming under his weight. His eyes misted into a deep shade of violet, but his fae magic couldn't push past the wall of his more dominant side—his wolf, and that was trapped by the silver collar.

"You left Ember this morning." It was a statement not a question. My wolf surfaced, his fury fusing with mine. I squeezed Stone's throat, almost crushing his trachea. "You put my mate at risk after I ordered you to protect her!" I jerked him in my grasp and he flew across the room, hitting the opposite wall with enough force to crack the plaster. He crawled to his feet—and charged.

I expected no less from him. If he didn't fight back right now, I would kill him for putting my mate at risk and leaving her vulnerable.

"She makes you weak!" he yelled, barrelling into me.

I grunted, forced back by his momentum. Calling on my wolf's superior power, I slammed my fists into his kidneys, then pulled back and hit his rock hard abs several times.

"You call this weak, you stupid bastard!" I picked him up, slamming his bulk into the concrete floor.

Breath exploded from him. "Not physically weak—emotionally! If she suffers, then so do you! If you let yourself love her, it will ruin you when she dies. All mates are a weakness. She will destroy your soul! You'd be better off if she died now!" His chest heaved, such raw emotion in his voice it brought me up short.

"What the fuck are you talking about?" I stared in horror at the pain in his eyes.

His throat bobbed over and over. "Nothing." But his voice broke.

I stood above my third, and he just lay there not meeting my gaze at all. This was not Stone at my feet. This was a broken man, someone who was hurting so bad, so lost in his own pain, he had lost his fight with rationality.

"Who did you lose?" I asked, my voice still rough and deep.

"No one."

"Stone, you tell me what the fuck you're talking about or I will snap your neck right now for threatening Ember's life."

He swallowed and stared at the ceiling.

My stomach lurched. He was actually considering letting me end his life. It dawned on me how close to insanity Stone had existed these last years. I hadn't seen his pain, mainly because I had been drowning in my own. He actually thought ending Ember's life was better for me than dealing with a broken heart—like his. What he couldn't see was how broken I'd been all this time, and that Ember had put me back together. I watched him closely. If he didn't talk, no matter how much I cared about him, I'd end him. I couldn't afford to be challenged by him, not now, and I needed to be able to trust him with Ember.

"I'd do anything for you, Stone, you know that, but I can't let you take Ember away from me in some fucked up belief it will keep me from harm."

I flipped him onto his stomach and yanked him up to his knees. I placed one hand on his head and one under his chin. He didn't even fight. I swallowed hard.

"They will always be our biggest weakness," he whispered.

"Who?" I steeled myself to do one of the worst things I'd ever done. But Ember came first.

"The ones we love with every fibre of our being."

"Tell me who she was, you stubborn bastard." My grip tightened, I was ready to jerk my grip and break his neck, no matter how much I didn't want to do it. I'd killed so many, it frightened me how easily I justified my intentions.

He swallowed against my hold. "My mate." Those words almost choked him, but still he remained compliant in my hold.

I loosened my grip a little, releasing a whoosh of breath.

"She was the most beautiful thing in my universe, the little bit of light I had in my life. I was always nothing. I existed between this world and Faerie. A child of both, but I belonged in neither. Both worlds saw me as an abomination, something that should be killed. But she saw me as someone worthy of her love. She gave me purpose and a reason to live. And then Doherty took her away. When he came for me, he killed her."

I swallowed and let go of his head. Life was just shit at times, it really fucking was.

Silence fell between us, only the sound of our heavy breathing audible.

"Stand up."

He did, his eyes downcast.

"Her death was not your fault, Stone. I can't make you believe that, only you can, but taking Ember away from me isn't going to be something you ever contemplate again." I forced my will on him, using the power of compulsion I had as his Prime. It might not work, he was an alpha in his own right, but I was willing to use anything in my armory to keep Ember from harm. Fuck, if I couldn't trust my brother, who could I trust?

He nodded, still not looking at me.

I sighed, suddenly weary. "You can go now," I said.

He looked up at me, the devastation clear on his face. "I am still loyal to you, Connor, I would never challenge you."

I rubbed my face not sure how to make him understand. "I know you are loyal, but taking Ember from me when I ask you to keep her safe… It would devastate me. I'd lose you both." I looked him in the eye. "If you ever hurt her, directly or by omission, know that I will not hesitate to end you."

Stone nodded, and with his head lowered he opened the door. Before he stepped through, he hesitated. "I'm sorry," he whispered, not turning to face me.

"I know," I replied to his receding back. "But I will still kill you if she is harmed on your watch."

CHAPTER 17

Connor

After my 'talk' with Stone, desire to go and find Ember nearly consumed me, but I held back. She needed to come to me. As much as I wanted to bury myself inside her warm body, I also didn't want to crowd her and send her running. I'd wait.

I grabbed some food, not caring what it was and sat with Owen. Disappointment laid like a led weight in my belly when she didn't come to the food hall. After we'd eaten, mainly in silence, we went back to my cell.

"We have some good fighters." Owen twisted the register he had in front of him so that I could see the names. They blurred into one mass of letters.

I grunted, a wave of anger sweeping through me. I shoved the chair back with my legs and stood.

Owen sat back, his gaze steady as he watched me pace. "You okay, Con?"

"No, I'm not fucking okay! None of this is okay! I'm about to send hundreds of people to their deaths—again! Either their own or someone else's. I'm sick of it!" I ran a hand through my hair, my fists clenching. *Maybe smashing them into the wall would feel good...*

Owen's lips tightened into a straight line, and he exhaled heavily through his nostrils. "I know. So am I. But we have no choice. And we all need you to keep your shit together. What's happening with Drake?"

I carried on pacing, my wolf's snarls ringing in my ears. I wanted to break

310

this fucking prison down with my bare hands and pull Ember to safety, but that was impossible. I cracked my neck, trying to get back with the programme. I appreciated my beta trying to refocus me on the only thing that might help us. "He got in the laptop, but he needs someone who can hack into their system. I don't know anyone with those skills, let alone someone we could trust."

The door clicked open and Ember's sultry scent hit me. I wanted to rush across the room and yank her to me. My cock instantly hardened, ready for her. I ground my teeth, resisting my primal urge to take her right there, right now, in front of my beta.

Owen raised a brow. "You alright there, boss?" He smirked, clearly sensing my need.

"Fine!" But I was unable to drag my gaze off Ember. She was so fucking gorgeous, her curves, her emerald eyes and that fiery hair. My nostrils flared. I wanted to twist it around my fist while I fucked her over and over.

Her eyes dropped briefly to the obvious bulge in my jeans. "What do you need a hacker for?" Her gaze lifted and narrowed on my face, even though she had a little smirk curling her lips.

"Close the door."

For once she didn't argue.

"I have an idea I'm working on, and for it to succeed, I need someone who's good with computer systems, or more specifically, hacking them."

"My friend Charlie's a hacker." She shrugged a shoulder like it was no big deal. "I'm sure she'd help."

I met Owen's gaze. He raised his brows slightly. "Worth a try."

"What do you need her to hack?" Ember asked.

"I can't tell you."

That didn't go down so well.

"Why not?"

"Because you don't need to know. It will just put you at more risk."

She crossed her arms over her chest which only served to make her cleavage even more distracting. I curled my hands into fists at my sides.

"Don't you dare decide what I do or don't need to know, you arrogant shit!"

Gods, the way her fire lit my body up...

"Tell you what." Owen straightened from the table where he perched. "I'll catch up with you tomorrow." Grinning widely, he picked up the register and sauntered out, after nodding to Ember. I made a mental note to thank him later. It was painful being in the same room as my mate and not touching her. It suddenly crossed my mind that perhaps she didn't feel the same.

"Why did he run off like that?" A frown marred her perfect face.

I covered the space between us so quickly she couldn't escape my touch. I pulled her into my arms. "Because he knows how desperate I am to kiss you."

She smiled and wrapped her arms around my waist, tilting her chin up. "Well, what are you waiting for then?"

I didn't need another invitation. My lips came down on hers, groaning with pleasure at the softness of her mouth. Her sweet taste was intoxicating. I pushed my tongue between the warmth of her lips, exploring her luscious mouth. Lust fogged my thoughts so thoroughly it caused my cock to strain against my jeans to the point where it became painful. Heat shot straight through my blood. Gods, I wanted her. Unwilling to let her mouth go, I deepened the kiss, unapologetically dominating her. Her groan when I nipped at her lower lip sent a wave of desire barreling through my body strong enough that when she bit me back, I swayed.

"Fuck, Ember, you taste so good," I murmured against her soft flesh.

I wrapped her crazy coloured hair around my fist, kissing her harder. The heat of her pussy soaked into my leg as she rubbed against my thigh, pleasuring herself. I made a mental note to ask about her hacker friend, later. Right now, I couldn't think past her taste or the sensation of her rolling her hips over my leg. I thrust any thoughts of my responsibilities away. Panting hard, I released her hair and grabbed the perfect globes of her arse, lifting her. She wrapped her legs around my waist and I carried her into my bedroom with her biting and sucking on my neck the whole way. That pain, mixed with the pleasure of her lips and tongue, sent shivers down my spine. I couldn't think as she nipped along my jaw, her arms resting on my shoulders and her fingers twisted in my hair.

I lowered her to the bed and went to pull away, but she grabbed my t-shirt, ripping it over my head.

"Hmm," she purred, running her hands over my pecs and abs. "So pretty." A smirk curled her lips as she popped open the buttons of my jeans until they were loose enough for her to reach in. Her small hand lowered and we both groaned as her fingers slid down my rock hard length. Goosebumps erupted over my hot skin. It was incredibly erotic watching her touch me, knowing that she wanted me as much as I wanted her. I watched her play and pump and tease me with those deft, clever fingers, but as much as I enjoyed it, I yearned to touch her, too. I gripped her wrist and stilled her touch.

"My turn." Urging her to sit forward, I pulled off her top and unclasped her bra, while her hot lips kissed my chest.

"Lay down," I instructed, my voice downright guttural, as my wolf joined in.

She swallowed, and my heart hitched at her compliance. Without a word, she laid back, her vivid eyes watching me closely as I undid her jeans and pulled them off.

She stretched and arched her back, pushing her perfect breasts towards me. Her pink nipples were hard, begging to be kissed. I licked my lips and feasted my eyes on every glorious dip and curve of her naked body.

"You are so fucking beautiful." I ran my fingertips over her smooth skin, trying to ignore the marks and bruises left from her training session. I thanked fate, destiny, the Mother Wolf, and whatever gods existed out there that she was here and alive, and mine... I clamped my mouth shut, fighting my primal need to sink my canines into her neck, to take her blood and mark her.

Mine...

I swallowed hard, trying to fight the dark voice in my head that urged me to mark what was mine. It snarled and fought as I pushed it away.

"Keep your eyes open. Watch me as I pleasure this beautiful body. Don't close them." My demand was low and gravelly. My wolf rumbled his approval, enjoying Ember as much as me.

"What will you do if I don't?" She purred, her eyes hooded.

I let my wolf surface in my eyes and grinned. He growled as the amber eyes of her wolf swallowed Ember's jade, and she stared right back at us. A challenge. His attention narrowed in on her, his interest piqued. A female who would challenge him... just like my Ember challenged me...

"You want to come tonight?" I ran a fingertip from her kiss swollen lips right down her body to the apex of her thighs. I stroked her, teasing her sensitive folds before slipping my finger through her slick entrance.

She arched, thrusting her breasts towards me. "Connor..."

My name was a plea from that beautiful mouth. I smiled, my heart hammering in my chest. Working my finger along her inner walls, I brushed my lips against hers, revelling in her panting and her whimpers of need. "Then do what I say," I whispered against her lips. "I want you to watch me touch you before you beg me to let you come."

Keeping my hand in the heat and nectar between her legs, I trailed teasing kisses down across her jaw and neck. With my tongue and lips, I kissed the soft skin of her breasts, teasing her nipples, squeezing one between my finger and thumb while I grazed the other with my teeth. She showed her appreciation by arching her back, her fingers twisting into the sheets above her head. Gods, she was the picture of sensuality, laid out before me like this, and she deserved to be worshipped. I devoted slow and languorous attention to every bit of her beautiful, strong body with my mouth and my hand until she trembled, her inner muscles clamping harder on my finger. I grinned against her damp flesh.

Her eyes closed and she grabbed my shoulders, digging her nails into my flesh. I growled. It damn near drove me to the edge of my self-control. "Eyes on me, Em."

Her mewles of pleasure were so sweet to my ears, all I wanted was to see her fly apart. I slipped two fingers inside her and her muscles clamped down even harder on me as she arched her pelvis forward.

"Connor…" she half-moaned, half-whispered, her fingers entwining in my hair, and her eyes flickering closed. I loved that look of ecstasy on her face, but I was in charge. I stopped.

"No, don't stop! Please."

"Eyes, Ember." An evil smile curled my lips, though my restraint almost snapped at the need in her voice. But I wanted to push her self-control even more. "Let's make this more difficult." I gently took her wrists. One at a time I tucked her hands flat under her lower back. Having them there tilted her pelvis up, as if she were presenting herself as my own personal feast.

"No. Please. I want to touch you." Her amber and green eyes were hooded, her voice husky.

"I know. But what do you want more?" I blew on her swollen clit. "To touch me…" Another breath, "or to come?"

She gritted her teeth and tried to push herself against my fingers. A bead of sweat ran down my temple as I pulled far enough away so that she couldn't reach. She groaned, her stomach muscles tensing as she twisted. "Both."

"Not tonight."

With a little whine, she moved her hands under her back, getting comfortable while she cursed under her breath.

I grabbed her hip with one hand and held her against the bed as I drove my fingers back into her heat. Her hips began moving in time to the thrust of my fingers. She arched her back and threw her head back, her eyes fluttering closed.

"Open them." My demand was full of dominance.

She did.

I couldn't take my gaze off her flushed face or dark eyes as she chanted my name like a mantra, her body undulating to the rhythm of my touch. The sight of her was too much, my cock throbbed painfully, and my wolf was practically frenzied. I pressed my thumb lightly against her swollen clit. She screamed my name as waves of pleasure rocked her and her internal muscles clamped down, pulsing around my fingers. Fire flared in her irises. *There it was.*

Fuck me, but my body was on fire, too. I stroked her back down from her climax until I couldn't hold back any longer. I stood and gently pulled my fingers from her tight flesh. She stared at me from under her dark lashes. I slowly licked one finger, groaning at the taste of her.

"Your turn," I said, pushing my fingers to her lips. And damn if I'd ever seen anything quite so hot as Ember arching her spine, lifting her head, taking my hand, then sucking her juices off my finger, her long hair hanging down and brushing the bed. Her soft tongue swirled around my finger and my imagination ran wild at erotic images of her with my cock in her mouth.

"I need to be inside you, right now."

She gave a sultry smile and bent her knee. Shaking, I settled myself between her creamy thighs. With one slow and steady thrust, I sheathed myself fully inside her. We moaned in unison and for a moment I stilled, just absorbing the sensation of being surrounded by her heat. My heart squeezed hard. I wasn't capable of living without her again. I squeezed my eyes shut at that thought.

I moved my hips slowly, placing gentle kisses across her face and neck, showing her how much she meant to me. Gods, I was being a pansy, but I needed her to know. Keeping my eyes closed, I fell into the sensations of my Firecracker as I made love to her. I rocked against her, angling her hips to reach deeper into the heaven of her body.

"You were made for me, Firecracker..." I whispered against her ear.

Her hands caught my hair and pulled me back until she could cup my face. Our bodies stilled. Holding me, she leaned up and kissed me gently, sweetly. "And you for me," she murmured.

In that moment of sincerity, I was lost. She had my heart and soul, and I would sacrifice everything to keep her safe.

I lifted my weight to look down at where we were joined and the sight took my breath away. She grabbed my hips, urging me to move harder and faster, gasping my name over and over. I felt her core grip me, her body undulating against mine until I was helpless to control my own response.

"Come with me?" It came out as a plea. The muscles of my lower back tightened and goosebumps erupted over my skin as my balls spasmed. I shuddered, moaning her name as I lost myself in her.

Languor seeped through my limbs. I would happily have stayed in the haven of her body forever, but I didn't want to crush her. Gently, I kissed her forehead and slipped free of her warmth.

Her jade green eyes were glassy, her cheeks and neck flushed, and her mouth swollen from my kisses. I rolled onto the tiny space left on the single bed and tucked Ember into my side. She made a contented sound and snuggled in.

"Hm, that was..." She smiled, her eyelids drooping.

"What? Amazing? Mind blowing?"

"Arrogant asshole..." she mumbled, then leaned up and kissed me gently on my lips, looking me right in the eye like only she could. "But yeah, that was the most amazing, mind blowing sex of my life."

I kissed her back. "Good, because it was all that and more for me. You are all I could ever want." My voice shook a bit.

"Really?" There was a vulnerable edge to her voice that had me pulling her closer.

"Yes."

Her arms snaked around me pulling me closer, like she wanted to get inside my skin. She smiled, her eyes closing. "Good. Because I'm not sharing you."

Warmth kindled in my heart, pushing at the shadows that had protected it, chasing them away. I swallowed hard. Monsters threatened us at every turn, but I would give my life for hers if it meant she'd be safe. I angled myself so that I could see the door and rubbed small circles on her back. Ember might not know it, but she'd given me back my humanity. I had not killed Stone because I understood how broken I would be if she was taken from me again. I peered down at her peaceful expression and my heart squeezed. I had only ever loved her, no one else, and I'd protect her with everything I had.

CHAPTER 18

Ember

I AWOKE SURROUNDED by heat and Connor's heady, spicy scent. I inhaled deeply and murmured in contentment. Noise and movements echoed outside Connor's room. I held in a groan as it dawned on me, we'd have to move soon, and I didn't want to, not at all, not when I was so close to Connor. I opened my eyes, and smiled. His gorgeous chest was right in front of me. I couldn't resist running my fingers over the hard planes of muscle. I enjoyed the view, lowering my gaze and taking my time as I admired the dips and ridges of his stomach, right down to where the happy trail of dark hair disappeared below the sheet.

He's mine...

The thought rocked me, the need to show him a savage thing inside me. I latched on to his nipple and bit down.

"Fuuuuck." He groaned and arched his spine, throwing his head back.

I smiled and pushed him onto his back, throwing my leg over his hips. I continued to wake him with kisses, rubbing my slick folds along the hard ridge of his erection. Lifting my weight on my knees, I held his length and guided him deep inside me, not even giving him a chance to moan before moving on him. His eyes flew open when I bit down hard on his neck, suckling his skin. Marking him. It was near impossible not to sink my canines deep into his flesh and claim him utterly.

"Ember?" he whispered as I twisted my head to peer into his wide eyes which swirled with the black and bright blue I loved so much.

I swallowed hard and hid my canines. "Not yet." I kissed him as I began moving my hips. I wouldn't claim him, not until we were both ready, and we knew if our wolves were mates, too. I pushed away the thought that we might never get these damn collars off and find out, and sat up, arcing my spine and undulating my hips in a more urgent rhythm.

His thumb brushed my clit, distracting me from my dark thoughts. Tension built in my core—hotter and hotter...

"Oh gods." My insides were coiling tighter. The feel of our bodies joining, and the sound of our groans filling the room, urged me on. I cried out, the orgasm taking hold of my body. Connor grabbed my hips, thrusting upwards in a desperate rhythm. With a deep groan he came, thrusting hard and emptying himself inside me.

I collapsed on top of him breathing erratically. Warmth filled my heart when he wrapped his large arms around me and held me like he wasn't letting me go anytime soon.

"That has to be the best wake up call I've ever had." His breath tickled my neck.

I giggled and rolled my eyes. I'm not stupid when it comes to Connor; he was hot and had always been a player. He was also a Prime and needed sex like he needed to breathe.

"Oh, please, you cannot expect me to believe you've never had an early morning booty call?"

He lifted me up, his face far more serious than I was prepared for.

"Not since before this place. And none that made me feel like you do."

"And how's that?" I swallowed hard and held my breath.

"Like I want to lose myself in you, like there is nothing else important in this world but you..." he paused and squeezed me more firmly, his gaze intense. "Ember, I haven't kissed anyone since I kissed you all those years ago; and I sure as hell haven't let anyone stay with me. So no, morning booty calls are not a thing for me."

"Really?" I whispered, my eyes wide. An ache started in my throat as I looked down at his stunning face. His eyes glittered with a soft look that I'd never seen in them before, and it both elated and scared me.

"I think we should get dressed," I said, climbing off Connor's beautiful body. I tried my best not to stare at him laid out in full view before me. I frowned accusingly at his pile of clothes. Gods, it really was a shame to cover that amazing body up...

"I heard you say something about needing a hacker?" I asked, changing the subject.

My feet slapped against the concrete floor as I headed to the sink. I leaned on the rim for a moment trying to stop the floor from tilting under me. He'd left me standing on a driveway after that kiss. Gods, four years? Four years and he'd never kissed anyone else? Not *slept* with anyone? I shook my head and took a deep breath. Sex, yes, but actual intimacy... With shaky fingers I turned on the tap and used the cold water to wash away the evidence of our early morning *booty call*. No, it had been much more than just that... Swallowing hard, I glanced at Connor. He watched me from under heavy lids, his mouth tight.

The air between us was heavy with unspoken words, but the sickening fear that he would be taken from me, or that our wolves would not be mates, lingered in my heart. The uncertainty was killing me, even though I did my best not to show it.

Connor sat up and rubbed his face with his hands, then ran his fingers through his already messy hair. I blinked, lost for words for another reason, now. How could one person be so godsdamn hot?

"Yes, I need a hacker, and no I haven't changed my mind about telling you why."

Oh right, my question. I opened my mouth to argue then snapped it shut. Rawson was right. Connor was a clever and devious leader, who would not put his pack at risk. I swallowed my disappointment when I remembered I wasn't part of his pack. That wasn't his fault, it was entirely mine.

I turned away and picked up Connor's toothbrush, brushing my teeth like I was trying to punish myself for that reckless decision. Maybe I should just broach changing packs with him now...

"You know," he purred, slipping his arms around my waist and looking at me in the plastic mirror that distorted our image. "Even though you've joined Drake's pack, if we mated, you would become part of mine. You would become mine and I would be yours."

His voice shook and I gulped. "Really?" *Oh my gods...* The thought of him sinking those canines into my skin made me break out in a whole body flush. My wolf whined, her worry filtering to me. She was right, even though I wanted it badly, there was no way of truly knowing if our wolves were mates; not until we got these godsdamn collars off and they could touch.

"Tell me what you're thinking, Firecracker." His voice was a whisper.

I turned in his arms and placed a chaste kiss on his lips. "I want to—so much."

He stiffened and pulled away. "But our wolves?"

The only way to block out his dark expression was to close my eyes. My heart ached, but I didn't want to lie to him. "Yes. You know it would be cruel..." I took a deep breath and exhaled slowly. Godsdammit, I hated this! "If we weren't stuck in here, I would do it now; without a moment's hesitation. But this whole place, this situation..." I sighed and cupped his face in my hands. "We can't do that to our wolves. I want you so badly, but it would break us all if they aren't compatible. I don't know if I could survive that pain."

He leaned down and kissed my forehead.

Bile flooded my mouth. Gods, I was such a coward!

"You're right. It would kill me, too." He leaned in and brushed a kiss against my skin before he pulled back. A smile curled his beautiful mouth, though his eyes remained dark, his wolf in the mix. "So we need to get out of this place and go somewhere safe where we can shift and they can be together."

⁂

THE BLOOD DRAINED from Charlie's face, and she slowly placed her spoon down, looking like she wanted to bolt when she saw me enter the food hall of gen pop with Connor at my back. Then again Connor did have that effect on most people in this area of the prison. He let out a low pitched rumbling growl—a warning, his alpha vibes bringing those he decided were too close to their knees. We didn't have any of his brothers with us which made me nervous. Connor had sent them away, whether that was to keep me to himself or because he didn't want them involved in his scheme, I wasn't sure.

I cocked my head and rolled my eyes at him as another male sank to his knees and lowered his gaze.

"Don't look at me like that. It makes it safer if no one gets near you—I mean us," he corrected, glaring at me defiantly.

"I don't need protecting, Connor," I reminded him gently, though I couldn't help but secretly love that he wanted to take care of me.

He scowled. "Maybe not, but I'm still keeping the crazy shits in here away from you."

I rolled my eyes, but smiled a little. "So much for not making it obvious that we're together."

He shrugged one massive shoulder, his expression unrepentant. "It's my job to keep you safe."

I threw my hands in the air despite my smile and marched to Charlie, who seemed frozen in her seat.

"Hey, girl."

She gulped, her eyes sliding warily to the big, wolf shifter at my side who was throwing off all sorts of dominant waves and glaring at any one nearby who so much as twitched.

"Jesus, Connor, rein it in. You'll have them shitting their pants soon. Come on." I yanked Charlie to her feet. "We need to talk to you."

"What about?" She gulped.

"Don't worry, he's with me. I dragged him here." The lie came easily. After all, it was only to put her at ease. Connor had wanted to charge down here by himself, telling me he was going to train, like I wouldn't see through his ruse. I'd disillusioned him of that. Charlie would bolt into the female halls if he scared her, and getting her help after he chased her down would be hard, even if he compelled her. Everyone worked better when they weren't terrified of their boss. "We need a favour." I lowered my voice and whispered in her ear, not wanting my words to carry through the near silent food hall.

Charlie nodded, and let me lead her away, keeping her gaze off Connor, who glared at the room like he expected a mass attack.

"Where to?" I asked Connor.

"The gym."

At the doors to the gym Connor stopped. "Wait. You need to come with me," he said to Charlie. She swallowed, her gaze flitting from me to Connor.

I narrowed my gaze at him in warning. His alpha vibes had settled to a tolerable level, and Charlie didn't look as though she were ready to bolt. She gave me a weak smile and nodded.

"She'll be fine. Now go and train. Owen! Stone! With me!"

His beta and his third stopped what they were doing and moved our way. "Well, go on." He smiled and gently kissed my forehead before giving me a little push towards Rawson and Lionel who were sparring on the mats.

Charlie gaped, her brows damn near reaching her hairline. *You and him?* she mouthed.

I shrugged and winked before sauntering away, very aware of the work I needed to do to survive the death fights that loomed ever closer. I was a good fighter, better than I'd revealed, but I was willing to learn from anyone in order to survive with my wolf intact.

Stone walked by me. I stared at the bruises covering his face and neck. He didn't meet my gaze as he passed. It was so unlike him, my heart skipped a beat. I deliberately didn't look back. No way was I going to make a big deal of his injuries, but I doubted that anyone other than Connor, or perhaps Owen, could leave Stone looking such a mess. Either way, it was obvious he'd had his arse kicked. Connor didn't need to defend me, but at the same time a weight lifted off my shoulders knowing I wouldn't have to watch my back with Stone. I smiled, my heart warming at the thought that Connor's protective instincts had reared up and he'd seen through his brother's intentions.

CHAPTER 19

onnor

THE CORRIDOR outside the laundry room was busy, but I still needed a reason to linger. "Lean against the wall." The guard at the far end of the walkway turned and sauntered back towards us just as the bitter scent of fear hit my nostrils. "I'm not going to hurt you, girl. I need your help. Just don't run from me, or my wolf will be compelled to hunt you down." It was a necessary warning and very true. I was a predator through and through, and if someone ran from me, I would chase them down to get what I wanted.

Her gulp was audible, but she did as I instructed. I leaned against her, dropping my head like I was nuzzling her ear, trying my best to ignore her anxiety at being this close to me. "Keep your eyes on that guard and tell me when his back is to us."

"Okay," she whispered. A few seconds of silence passed. "Now."

Checking that the other guards weren't paying too much attention, I ushered her into the blind spot.

"Who's this?" Drake looked Charlie over from her short, messy hair to her standard issue sneakers.

I had to admit, Charlie appeared very young. I inhaled and Ember's smokey scent wafted up my nostrils, stirring my blood. I narrowed my eyes. The leather jacket Charlie had on had been Ember's.

322

"This is Charlie, she's your hacker."

Drake eyed her skeptically. "Her? She can get into a top level security system?"

"No idea." I looked right at her, and she seemed to shrink in on herself. "Can you?"

Her spine straightened as if insulted we'd questioned her abilities. She briefly met my eyes and nodded.

"You trust her with this?" Drake asked carefully, inhaling the scent of her fear. He was as much a predator as I was, and his eyes zoned in on her, sensing her need to run.

I shrugged. "Sure. Because if she breathes a word of this to anyone, she'll only do it once." I let my threat hang in the air, but hit her with a wave of power, enough to make her stagger—just to make my point.

She leaned a gloved palm on the wall, her breathing quick and heavy as she fought to stay on her feet. "Hey, don't judge a book by it's cover. I hacked the SBI databases once." But her voice trembled. She'd understood me. Good. I couldn't afford for my plans to leak out.

"Really? That why you're locked in here?" Drake asked.

She attempted a cocky grin clearly proud of the achievement despite the outcome. "Yep."

I had to admit, it was an achievement, but also pretty stupid; she was lucky not to be dead.

"Okay, it's all yours, sunshine. I've got into the laptop but can't break through to the maintenance and repairs system."

Charlie asked no questions about what they needed to get into the systems for. She just sat down next to Drake and cracked her knuckles.

"Maintenance?" She blew out a breath, her face scrunched in concentration.

"That's right. As quickly as possible."

"Which part? It'll probably be sectioned."

"I'll let you know when we're in." Drake caught my eye and I nodded giving him permission to tell her what she needed to know.

"Watch a master at work." Finding her courage again, she winked at Drake.

Drake gave me a *where did you find her?* look.

I smiled and shrugged. "Find me when you have something to report."

Drake nodded, distracted by watching Charlie's fingers fly over the keyboard.

I shook my head at their focus. Computers really weren't my thing.

Outside the laundry, Myles peered up from the neck of the female who was his cover. He kept a careful eye on who went into the laundry. Those working in the sweat shop wouldn't get curious, but I needed to keep Drake and that computer safe and hidden. Myles's green eyes gleamed against his dark skin. I nodded at him as I walked by and he got back to nuzzling the female's neck, making a show of hitting on her. It was all for the guards, at least, that was the plan, though who knew? Myles was a powerful shifter who needed sex often. So long as he didn't get distracted, I couldn't care less.

I strode back to my cell, doing my best to ignore the anxiety churning in my belly at my next job. Two prison guards, garbed from head to toe in black armoured jumpsuits, heavy boots, helmets and visors, watched my approach. They stood on either side of my cell door and trained their weapons on me. I was aware that above me more guards followed my progress with the barrels of their weapons. I kept the snarl off my lips and ignored them.

My cell door was propped open and Owen sat in the chair, a familiar computer in front of him.

Zander leaned against the wall, a small device in his hand. There was no love lost between Zander and Owen. Owen saw Zander as a threat despite us all working for our mutual unnamed boss. He also blamed Zander by proxy for this situation and the pain inflicted on us all. He thought Zander was Doherty's lackey, his henchman, and no matter what spin Zander put on it, it was true. Zander went out and caught innocents and criminals alike, bringing them here for a life of torture, and, eventually, death. Whichever way you looked at it, he was a cold hearted bastard, no matter his reasons. Then again, weren't we all?

As I looked at them both, I didn't know who I'd put my money on to win a fight. Zander clearly had supernatural power in his body, but I had never seen the full force of it, only ever the burning fire in his eyes. Owen on the other hand, was a vicious and powerful alpha wolf who would never concede defeat.

Doherty had made it clear that he wanted Owen here to act as my beta. He'd wanted me to survive the first bloodthirsty challenges and take the mantle of Prime. I couldn't help but wonder if that scheming bastard had marked me for this since Cain Rawson had saved my skinny arse as a young boy. At the shifter academy I had been put in the top groups, and when I'd started my SBI training it had become even more apparent that I was a powerful alpha. Doherty had observed my wolf could be more powerful, stronger, and far more vicious than any other shifter's and he'd trained me hard, using all the resources at his disposal.

I'd learned to dominate my wolf in my early teens, never allowing him to control me. Until we'd been imprisoned in this place, and Ember's loss had consumed me, we had worked as a team. Now our predatory coldness was difficult to control, our souls shrouded in shadow. Ember had become an anchor; the light to balance my darkness.

"Hey, man, I've divided the fighters into pack groups and I've marked the newbies," Owen said.

I nodded and leaned my elbows on the table, peering at the screen. The newbies were those who had arrived with Ember's cohort. The other fighters were already in the system. I might not pick each fighter who would go into the ring, but with Owen's help, I identified the best fighters and any potential alphas or betas among the packs. Those that were left were fodder for the entertainment rooms.

The day before the fight, names would be announced—hundreds of them. On that day, if a fighter didn't show, another was sent into the arena. But there was no escape. I was sent to hunt and kill the no shows. And down here it didn't take me long to find them.

My heart rate rose, my fists clenching at the thought of Ember fighting for her life in the rings while crowds of the corrupt and depraved wealthy looked on.

Owen glanced at me, his brows drawn. I took a long slow breath and controlled myself. The last thing I needed was for my brothers to sense anxiety in me. If they did, then others would, too, and that would start all sorts of complications and challenges.

"I'm fine," I reassured him before I glanced at Zander. "Are other prisoners being brought in before this fight?"

"No idea." Zander purposefully looked at the door.

He was right. It was stupid to ask questions when the guards were only feet away and able to hear. Appearing interested in the screen, he prowled closer. "Whose this one?" he asked loudly then lowered his voice and leaned into my ear. "I've not been asked to retrieve anyone else."

I nodded. That meant Rawson could potentially be around. I briefly closed my eyes, hoping they wouldn't take him away. I'd need him to keep me grounded when, no if, anything happened to my brothers, or Mother Wolf forbid, Ember.

"Any ideas about getting into the science wing yet?" Zander asked, keeping his voice low.

My plan was as secret as it could be, and it was staying that way. I wasn't about to spill it to Zander. I had no idea whose side he was really on. I'd only tell him when I needed something from him. "No, I'm working on it though."

"Sort it. For Ember's sake." Zander resumed his position against the wall, where he could see the computer screen, but his attention stayed on me.

My hands fisted and my heart hammered. It would be easy to end the bastard right now...My wolf agreed, surging forward.

Owen rumbled in his chest. A low pitched warning growl.

I pulled my focus from Zander.

Owen's attention was fixed on the door where the guards watched us. I swallowed my anger at Zander and pushed back my wolf. "Thanks, man." I hadn't had too many interactions with the guards over the years, but they were never pretty and usually ended up with me shot full of sedatives and beaten badly.

Owen deliberately went back to identifying which of the newest inmates were fighters and which were not. I kept my attention on the screen, not looking at Zander or the guards again, though I listened intently to the beat of their hearts. I doubted they would attack just for the hell of it, but it was a habit to constantly assess those around me.

Zander prowled around the table, standing with his back to the door. "Hurry up, the warden wants this information today!" he snapped.

I growled up at him, blinking when his eyes burned with flame.

"All my assignments have been cancelled. For now, Rawson will stay here and train with the rest of you." His voice was quiet enough the guard near the door wouldn't hear.

"Will you make him fight?" I asked quietly.

"You know it's not up to me. The arena will be needed for longer than usual this time though." He paused and blew out a soft breath. "To get whatever he needs, the warden is willing to sacrifice hundreds of lives. Get as many of your people ready as you can for the arena but..." He met my gaze. "...time is running out—for all of us. The warden wants a high death count more than he wants money, and we need to know why."

I'd never sensed fear in Zander before, not even a hint of it, but I did now. My throat tightened. Finding out what was happening in that science wing was vital, and instinct told me it was far more dangerous than the fight rings.

Once the system was up to date, Owen shut the laptop with a snap. "Here." He held it out to Zander, who took it, tucked it under his arm, and left without another word.

I paced, thinking hard, something niggling at my mind.

Owen let me be, remaining silent and watching me patiently.

Think. Think. I pushed two fingers against my forehead, trying to remember the procedures of the arena guards, the warden, Doherty, anything that could jog my memory.

"There has to be a chink in their procedures, a way to get out of the arena and into the prison beyond."

"How? The warden himself has to open the doors from the arena to the prison. Even the dead bodies can't be moved without him—and he has a squad of guards for protection. There are no other exits and it's impossible to reach the upper level and take out those sick fucks who bet on us, even in our Were forms. If those damn spikes that are fixed around the arena don't stop us, then the guards will. And you'll be forced to watch, just as you always are. You won't even be in the arena."

I halted and stared at Owen.

"What?" His eyes narrowed.

I shook myself. "I need to see Drake." Without any further explanation, I walked out of my cell.

CHAPTER 20

"WE HAVE to fight inside cages? They really do think of us as animals, don't they?" I hit the focus pad Reed held up for me. The impact of my gloved fist against the pad barely released any of my fury at this abhorrent situation.

"Yeah, though we mean less to them than animals would. We are expendable."

Reed had been getting steadily quieter and more introspective over the last few days. I didn't blame him, the death rings were only five days from now, and it was likely all the brothers would have to fight. I swallowed hard and began a concerted effort to pummel the pads as Reed moved around and changed their position. I was as fit as I'd ever been, training hard all day, every day. Connor and Rawson were determined I wouldn't die in this fight, but part of me hated that if I didn't, I'd have to fight one of their brothers. And that would destroy Connor. Either he would see his brother die or think he'd lost me.

"Concentrate, Ember. Worrying about what might happen isn't going to help any of you." Rawson's interjection was stern when I missed a pad.

"Damn it, Rawson!" Using my teeth, I ripped open the velcro to my gloves and yanked them off, chucking them forcefully to the ground. "None of this is going to help any of us! Gods! How have you stood this for so long?" I looked from Rawson to Reed and over at Stone who was watching us stoically from the sideline. "How can you know that some of you will die, and still function?" I rubbed my face with my hands, pacing across the soft mats.

"Because some of us believe death is not the end. And as cliche as it sounds, it can be the chance for a new beginning with those we've lost, or perhaps to be reborn and live a different life," Stone said quietly.

"Bullshit! Most people just die, Stone. There are no do overs or second chances for their souls. They are just dead. The end." And I hated that because if one of the brothers killed me, my wolf would go to the Mother to be reborn, and I would take their wolf spirit as payment for mine. I would even be reborn. If they died—that was it; they would lose their wolves and their souls. And if I killed one of Connor's brothers to protect my secret and save my wolf, he'd have to endure the pain of their severed bond.

Sweat from my palms stung my eyes as I rubbed my face. The injustice of it all tore me apart.

"Maybe it is, maybe it isn't." Stone shrugged and turned his attention to Shannon who was fighting Santa Cruz in another ring. The atmosphere between queen bitch and the half-fae was always heated and strained, but no matter how vile they were to each other, Stone always had one eye on where she was.

Reed's hand was warm on my forearm preventing me from pacing further. "Em, there is nothing you can do but survive. Connor needs you, not only to keep his wolf in check, but to hold onto his humanity. He almost lost that part of himself once, and if he loses it again I don't think he will ever come back; his wolf will consume him. Shadows linger in his soul from all he has done here. Being an SBI agent with honour and standing is a far cry from being the king of prison shifters. He's had to kill, threaten and coerce just to try and protect those he cares about. And it wasn't just his wolf; Connor, the man, has had to make hard decisions too—he still does."

I slammed my hands on my hips and tilted my head back, blinking away tears. I wouldn't cry. I never cried. Crying didn't solve anything. It just made me look splotchy and gave me red eyes.

"Will there be weapons?" I asked, changing the subject.

"Yeah, but it depends on what the clients want to see. The highest bidders can request which ones we use," said Reed.

I rolled my head, my brain buzzing at the implications. "Great."

"Don't get too excited. There are no weapons that could be launched out of the arena at the audience."

"No, of course not. That would be far too easy."

Rawson smiled. "Yeah, it would. I've fought with knives, daggers, staffs, whips, an axe; all that kind of thing. I even had a halberd at one fight."

"Right." A scowl creased my face. Oh, this just got better and better. Another thought occurred to me. "Are the fights always one on one?"

Reed inhaled, his nostrils flaring and his wolf showing. "No. If the clients want a full on massacre and pay enough, our people are literally thrown to each other's wolves."

"Gods, that must be carnage, especially in Were form." Connor had told me and his brothers that Were form would be forced on us all. I wasn't worried, I trusted my wolf, but for some who had been stuck in here for years and not shifted, it would be torture. The pain of half-shifted bones, the stench of blood and the need to fully release their animal would most likely drive them mad.

I sighed not wanting to think about it any more. If I exhausted myself, maybe I would just sleep without thinking. "Weapons, then?" The storage cupboard was wide open, a vast array of training weapons stacked up. I wasn't strong enough to wield an axe with any skill or speed—so I picked up the heaviest wooden axe I could see. That's right. Meet your demons head on. I grinned and turned to Lionel. "Ready for a two on one?"

He winked, his smile feral. "Oh, yeah. You up for it pretty boy?" he asked Reed.

Reed rolled his eyes, but there was definitely a challenge shining in them.

I smirked. There was the alpha who was strong enough to fight by Connor's side.

Myles, who was watching Shannon fight, turned our way when we all stepped in the ring.

"Do you know how to use that?" Rawson asked skeptically. He pulled the axe from my hand and swung it a few times, studying it like he was eying up a potential enemy.

I shrugged. "Not so much, but I can't think of a better time to learn."

Rawson grinned and handed it back, looking more like his old self today, less pale, less tired and way more alpha. He wasn't shaking and his eyes were a clear steel grey that had an astute gleam in them. Not being Zander's, or the warden's, bitch agreed with him. I stretched up and kissed his cheek.

He raised his brows. "What was that for?"

I stepped back and swung the axe. Fire would help me survive, but she couldn't stop my family and new friends from dying. "Because I wanted to. And sometimes life is too short not to tell people how much you love them and that you appreciate everything they've done for you. So, thanks." I smiled and shrugged, but my voice was thick.

His throat bobbed and he inhaled deeply through his nose, his eyes darkening to a slate grey. "Yeah, that it is. And it was mine and Lyss's pleasure," he said hoarsely.

I looked down, my heart aching for them. How he had survived without her, I couldn't even imagine. I rubbed at my chest, unable to comprehend that loss. Connor's face came to mind. My belly tightened and I bit my lip. I would not lose him. Lionel and Reed seemed to sense my mood. Both lowered their stances, and attacked.

AFTER TRAINING WAS DONE for the day, I hung out with Reed and the others in the west pack's communal area, playing cards and talking strategies for the rings. It seemed D had been in the fight ring the most. I swallowed realising he'd beaten hundreds to still be alive and sitting with us. My respect swelled for all of these males. They had all been chosen at some point and had ultimately triumphed over their opponents. They all had blood on their hands, but it wasn't by choice.

"The final is not in a cage," D informed me as we played cards. "Or at least it wasn't last time. It was just in a plain old boxing ring."

"They don't see us as a threat when we are injured and exhausted," Stone said, his face dark, his wolf surfacing in his eyes.

"They don't," Reed agreed.

"Why? Are the sick bastards who watch too far away for us to leap up and reach them, or to throw a weapon and kill one of them? You said that's why we had to fight in cages for most of the rounds." I looked at Reed.

"Twist," said Lionel, tapping his finger quickly on the table top.

The others scowled at him.

"What?" His face was a picture of innocence.

I hid my smile. He obviously had a good hand.

Reed slipped him a card. "It's true. When the winners of each group fight each other, the warden brings in his personal protection detail. So we have even less chance of escaping."

I scowled. "Is that why he brings them?"

"I expect so, but no one really knows. Connor's been trying to figure out what the warden does with all of the bodies from the fights. Each day, they get piled near the door to the science wing," Kawan said quietly, running his fingers through his black hair.

"And then once the final bout is done, he opens the doors to the prison and his men take the bodies away." Myles's attention flickered between his cards and Reed, who sat opposite him. Reed flushed every time he caught Myles's gaze.

"Hmm," I said, trying to picture the arena in my mind. I shuddered at the thought of being caged in. "So where are the bastard spectators in comparison to the rings?"

Stone's cold gaze drifted towards me. He was standing guard with Owen. Owen sighed, and kept his focus on the room as he talked. "They're on a balcony a level above the rings. It's where those who cannot fight are sent to entertain the perverted, cruel fucks who not only pay for blood, but for flesh, too."

My eyes widened and my mouth dropped open as I absorbed what he was saying. Connor had said something about that, but I hadn't really processed what it meant. "They sell our bodies as well as our lives?"

"They do." Owen's expression was one I didn't often see in his eyes—pure killer. He was a patient and astute person, but there was also a reason he was Connor's beta. His voice turned hard. "Many of those poor buggers never come back, and some who do are just shells, their spirits completely broken."

I swallowed the bile in my throat, thanking Connor for forcing my hand into being a fighter.

No more was said about the fights, and I had lost any desire to know more. The whole thing sickened me. To think Connor and some of these poor people who were here for no other reason than being shifters, had suffered this for so long... No wonder their humanity had been virtually erased.

We finished up our card game. I hugged Rawson and gave him a goodnight kiss, earning myself some raised brows.

"Not sure the boss would like that," grumbled Stone.

"Oh, lighten up buddy," Owen said, slapping his shoulder. "They've known each other a long time, and Rawson's the only one he'd not deck for touching his girl."

"For gods sakes, I can touch who I like and I don't need Connor's permission to do so," I said, and to make a point I went around to all of them, including that miserable arse Stone, and kissed them all on the cheek. "There." I beamed.

Owen was laughing out loud by the time I was done, and the others smirked. I'd saved Stone until last and he looked like he wanted to throttle me. I felt someone's attention burning into my back, and turned to see Shannon glaring at me. If looks could kill... I blew her a kiss too, just for good measure.

"Oh, you're really cruisin' for a bruisin' tonight aren't you, sweetness?" drawled Rawson.

I shrugged and left them all, hooking my arm through Stone's just to piss him and Shannon off. He shook me free with a growl. "Okay, okay." I raised my hands and took Owen's instead, who just grinned widely as they escorted me back to my room in Drake's wing.

The next day was much of the same. I chose to fight with wooden daggers this time, that were basically just blunt lumps of wood, but it was better than nothing. Rawson decided to fight, too, and we paired up. His alpha vibes were getting stronger, so I allowed myself to move faster, winning as many fights as I lost. After a while, with so much alpha energy buzzing around me, I decided a lay down would be good. I was hot, breathing hard, and my wolf was clamouring to burst free and play with these hot men, so I let Rawson sweep my leg and landed on the mats on my back, using my free hand and legs to break my fall properly.

I closed my eyes, trying to get my breath back and calm my wolf, happy to stay right where I was when Rawson and Lionel didn't yell at me to get right up. A little disconcerted at the quiet, I opened my eyes.

"Hey, Firecracker." Connor smirked, letting his power brush my skin. I inhaled his scent as he leaned over the ropes, peering down at me. I narrowed my eyes. Though his eyes were sparkling with laughter, dark circles shadowed the skin underneath. My gut twisted. What he was doing with Charlie and Drake, was anyone's guess, he'd even met with Zander a few times, but it was enough to take all of his time, leaving him tense and quiet.

"Hey, asshole," I whispered, and smiled up at him. Lying flat on my back, gazing up, Connor looked good enough to eat. I didn't know how to deal with the gratitude that bubbled in my belly every time I saw him. Such emotion left me vulnerable, and I hadn't been vulnerable in a long time. I flipped up onto my feet and spun to face him.

Stone was at his back today, and he watched me blankly before giving his attention to the room, his eyes resting on Shannon. Shannon glanced over and glared at him, tossing her hair over her shoulder before she got back to training. Shannon had always been a good fighter, but she allowed her temper to get the better of her much of the time. She still hadn't picked a pack, and though I held no love for her, I could understand Connor's concern. I almost laughed when she stubbornly refused to look at Stone again who glowered at her like he hated her, but couldn't look away. I had to wonder if he even knew he was doing it.

Warm fingers wound in my hair. "Do I get any of your attention?" Connor murmured in my ear. Shivers skittered through my body and my wolf surfaced, whining at the restrictive effects of the collar that held her back from Connor's. Calming her was hard when all she wanted was to see if he was her mate.

I bit my lip and exhaled through my nose. If I mated with Connor and our wolves were not compatible, it would mean them being alone forever. I couldn't do that to them. I pushed those worries away. Being with Connor right now was all I needed, the future was too precarious.

Past caring who knew about my relationship with their Prime, I slipped my arms around his waist and tilted my head up. I grinned at the disgruntled look on his face, revelling in the fact that he didn't like my attention on anyone but him. "Of course, but if I remember rightly, aren't you supposed to be at my beck and call, not the other way around?"

"When we get out of here, I'll be your willing slave anytime you want." He gave me a small, sexy smile.

I smirked back and tightened my grip on him. Oh, the possibilities! Just to make a point to everyone watching, especially any female who had their eyes on him, I reached up on my tip toes and kissed him before I gently bit his bottom lip. I delighted in the goosebumps that erupted all over his skin and the soft growl that rumbled in his throat.

I glanced at Stone, who stood behind Connor, and winked. Stone shook his head, and with a grim face looked away to watch the room again. Owen, who stood at Connor's side, grinned at me before he positioned himself where he could watch the room, too. Myles, D, Kawan and Reed all headed from their own positions around the hall to surround us, remaining casual but alert.

Connor stiffened, his hands tightening in my hair. "As much as I'm really enjoying your undivided attention now, do you really want a target on your back?"

I grinned and met his eyes in a sultry fashion. I shrugged and cupped his sexy behind with my hands. "I'm used to being a target. Besides, you're mine now and everyone in here, especially all those females eyeing this up, need to know that." I dug my fingers into his flesh. He grinned, his eyes melting into a dark and sparkling sapphire blue as his wolf joined in.

I was so past giving a shit about challenges just because I was his lover. And I sure didn't give a rat's ass about what anyone else thought. I'd had to fight for everything in my life and if I had to fight for Connor, to be with him, then bring it on. Life was too short. And Fate was a fickle bitch that tended to take those I loved away from me.

Connor stared down into my face, and though he didn't take his attention off me I knew he sensed the mood and position of each person, not to mention every move they made in that massive hall.

He smirked. "You really are a bad girl."

I cocked my head, my life in Faerie hitting me right between the eyes. "You have no idea how bad." My gut twisted when I thought about Blue and what that faerie warrior was doing to her. One way or another, I had to get out of here and help her.

Connor's eyes narrowed. "You're worried."

"Yeah, but not just about the fights. I have to get out and get to Blue. I can't just leave her." My tattoo glimmered in the bright lights of the hall, mocking me. I sighed heavily and tightened my hold on Connor, not caring who watched. Right now, I needed the strength and reassurance he offered.

"I won't let you die, Firecracker," he murmured into my hair, pulling me even closer.

That hadn't been my main concern, Fire had my back. But I wasn't sure how he was going to stop everyone else from dying, or get us out of here so that we had a chance of finding a way back to Faerie. "I'm not worried about me. It's like it was in the woods. If Fire senses I'm about to die—or I do die, she will bring me back. But I'll lose my wolf and the problem is, Fire wants a life for a life. She'll take the shifter spirit from whoever kills me and gift it to me. I'm also scared shitless I'll lose Rawson, again—that they'll put him in the ring. And I kind of like your brothers. I'm worried what will happen to them all—" My warm breath fanned his chest where I rested my head.

"I know. Welcome to my world." And there was no reassurance he could give me. Because if I revealed Fire to the warden, or Doherty, we both knew I was as good as dead.

CHAPTER 21

mber

I PLONKED myself on the mats right under the punching bag and pulled off my gloves. I might be able to heal more quickly than a human, but Rawson had upped the speed and viciousness of our fights. Against Connor's wishes, he'd pitted me against other shifters. It was logical and I agreed with his rationale. I wouldn't only be fighting his brothers, I'd be fighting someone whose moves and fighting style I didn't know.

I had bruises and a broken rib. My lip stung like a bitch from a kick to the face, and though I was exhausted, I was unsettled. I yanked at the collar around my neck. For the most part I could ignore it, though I was always aware of its presence. Today though, it burned my skin, its weight strangling me. Perhaps it was a full moon in the outside world.

My wolf paced and snarled in my soul, wanting to be free. She needed to run and she needed to find a release for her power. I flipped myself up and began to prowl away from Reed and Myles.

Reed frowned. "You feeling alright? You've been antsy all day."

"Yeah, I'm fine." Right. I was anything but fine. The fights were closing in, my friends were at risk, and I had no idea what Connor was planning. Not only that, I'd not seen him for three days now.

They both scrambled to their feet.

"No!" I held out a hand. "Just...stop." I closed my eyes and took a deep breath, releasing it slowly. "I need to be on my own for a bit," I said softly.

They both looked at each other.

"No."

"No."

It was impossible to hold back my screech. I turned on my heel and headed back to my room. I marched down corridors and up stairs then I spotted the showers. I smirked and ignoring their protests, I grabbed a towel and soap and headed in.

"Ember!" Myles's deep voice resonated through the space as he followed me in.

I smirked as I began to undress. "You staying to watch, Myles? Perhaps you should bring Reed in here and have a little fun together while I shower?"

He rolled his eyes, but couldn't hide his grin. "You're really something, you know that?"

I shrugged and grinned back. "Yeah, that's why Connor finds me irresistible."

"He does. But please, keep those undies on for a moment while I see who else is in here. If Connor catches me ogling that gorgeous body, he's going to break my spine."

I put my hands on my hips and waited while he checked out the other women in the showers. None of them were bothered, they just smiled at him, and carried on. I shook my head. Yeah, Myles's ebony skin and fine bone structure, paired with his stunning green eyes made him irresistible to both sexes.

"I meant it about Reed, you know." I held his eyes. "The fights start in two days. Time is short. Do you want to lose him without ever resolving what's between you?"

Myles's full lips tightened, and he dropped his chin to his chest, sighing before he looked at me again. "No, I don't. But Reed knows how I feel and wants to deny what's between us, so..." He shrugged heavily.

As he turned around we both saw Reed standing in the doorway, his gaze anchored on Myles's face. Myles ran a hand over his shaved head which gleamed with moisture from the showers, his t-shirt clinging to his defined body. Reed's gaze travelled slowly over the other male's torso and back up to his eyes, hunger plain on his face.

"Right, well, we'll leave you to it," Myles said gruffly.

"Myles," I said quietly. "Do something about this thing between you before it's too late. He loves you."

He nodded once and prowled up to Reed, who watched him intently. The tension between them filled the room and I couldn't look away.

"When D and Kawan come and take over, we're going to talk. And you aren't running away this time," Myles said, his face tight and intense.

Reed's throat bobbed and he flushed a little, but he nodded. He met my eyes and smiled almost shyly as they left.

I released a breath, I didn't realise I'd been holding. I rolled my neck trying to relieve the ache across my shoulders. It didn't do anything. I dropped my bra and panties and stepped under the hot water. Facing the wall, I closed my eyes, resting my forehead on the wet, cool tiles. I let the hot jet of water hit my upper back, emptying my mind from thoughts other than Connor; the way his hands moved on my skin, the way he filled me so completely, not just my body but my heart. God, I wanted him, but it was more than that, I missed him, every moment of the day.

A few minutes later a deep spicy scent filled my nostrils. The tension in my body ramped up, my heart rate spiking and my wolf growled long and low. A smile curled my lips, but I didn't move. I didn't bother to hold back my moan when large hands smoothed up either side of my spine, curling over my shoulders and then my neck. I groaned as Connor kneaded out the knots in my muscles. When his hands stilled, I shifted my weight to push back against him, unprepared for the stab of pain in my broken rib. I gasped and tensed. Instantly, his hands found the bruised skin above the break and warmth reached into my flesh and bones, tingling in the unique way only his power did.

"Does that feel better, Firecracker?" he murmured in my ear, sending a delightful shudder through my wet body as his erection pressed into my lower back.

"Hmm." Nope, I couldn't speak, not when his hands were against my wet skin and his naked, hard body pushed against mine. Then a thought occurred to me. My eyelids snapped open. *No way!* I turned to face him, slipping my arms around his waist and looked around his muscled arm. Yep, we had an audience and there was no way I was sharing Connor with the women who were eyeing his bare arse like it was dinner and they were starving.

"Get out!" I growled. "He's mine." I let all of my wolf's dominance and power push through my eyes and into my voice, even Fire jumped to my assistance. Flame burned in my eyes, changing my vision into hues of red and orange.

For a split second the two women stared at me wide eyed, frozen to the spot. "Fuck. Off." I snarled viciously. No way was I letting them ogle Connor's glorious body, and he sure as shit wasn't looking at any other naked woman. "Now!" I yelled.

A chuckle resonated from Connor, but he didn't move from my embrace. He just waited, his gaze branding me as they gathered their shit and left.

As soon as we were alone I loosened my grip on him.

"Wow, that was so hot. But you don't need to worry, I'm yours and only yours, I always have been."

Possessiveness still rode me. "Prove it." And I cupped his balls with one hand, running my other hand up over his wet body to cup his head and pull him down into a kiss.

There was no softness in our touches. The underlying awareness of the upcoming fights lay between us, driving me as I kissed and kissed him, only coming up for air when I needed to.

He rested his forehead against mine, peering into my eyes. I had learned that was something he liked to do. "Will they make you fight?" I asked the question I'd been frightened to ask before.

"I don't know." His voice was heavy. "I haven't been in the ring for three years, but something's changed and I don't know what. Something tells me the warden doesn't care about keeping any of us alive anymore..." His voice petered off, and he nibbled at my ear and neck as if he couldn't help himself. "Like Zander said, we are running out of time."

There was nothing else to say. My heart pounded painfully in my chest. I would ultimately survive, yet Connor could be ripped away from me in an instant. If he died it would shatter me. I grabbed him tighter, unwilling to lose contact with him.

"I can't lose you," I whispered against his lips, baring my soul and my heart to him.

He stilled and with his large hands he cupped my face, holding me gently. His vivid eyes held my attention, so intense I wanted to fall inside them and lose myself in that sea of blue. "And I will not lose you. No matter what happens I will always come back to you. Even if it's in the next life, Ember. I love you. I always have." And he kissed me sweetly, like he was giving me his heart and soul. This was pure Connor, no wolf. I kissed him back, trying to give him all of my heart too, the words I really wanted to say stuck in my throat. I did love him, so much. But fear stopped me; if I told him I loved him, it might jinx him; and then he would be taken from me just like before.

He pulled back and searched my eyes. I dropped my gaze to his chest. He leaned in and kissed my forehead tenderly. "It's alright, Em, I understand," he whispered against my skin. "When you trust that I will always be with you, that I will always find a way back to you, no matter what happens, then you'll give me your heart."

"Connor, you have my heart already, you always have."

"Then that's enough," he said and kissed me as his fingers curled around my thighs and he lifted me. With my back against the wall he slipped his hard length inside me and made love to me slowly and thoroughly until we were both shaking and spent, our breath mingling as we came down from the cloud of pleasure. Unwilling to move, we stayed wrapped around each other under the warm jets of water until Kawan coughed loudly and yelled in, "You okay in there, boss?"

We both laughed. "I guess it's time we moved," Connor murmured, kissing me.

I agreed, and slowly unwrapped my legs from around him, biting his neck gently before we moved apart and got dried and dressed.

CHAPTER 22

onnor

THE HUNDREDS of speakers that were fixed to the rafters up above the guards' platforms crackled into life and all noise in the gym ceased. I met Owen's steady gaze and despite my stomach doing somersaults, I straightened my spine and lifted my chin. This announcement would be bad—for so many people. The warden wasn't just bringing up the fight for money. Both Zander and I had come to that conclusion. There was something bigger happening here, and my gut instinct told me to be very afraid; not for myself, but for every other soul in this place. We were cattle to slaughter, all of us.

I nodded subtly at my brothers. Without hesitation they came to me. Rawson and Lionel brought Ember closer. I met her eyes, before dipping my chin at the two males, who nodded back.

The shit was about to hit the fan. I had no idea how many people would turn on me, but it usually happened soon after the announcements. People were angry and scared at being chosen and they thought I was responsible.

The warden said he believed us descended from the Weres who had guarded the gates of hell. My nostrils flared, a familiar darkness rushing through my blood. *Well, he'd better hope he's not right, 'cause if Em doesn't survive, I'll find my way back there and rip that fucking realm apart.*

"You ready, boss?" Owen's voice was quiet and cold as ice, but his attention didn't waver from those around us.

Across the gym, Drake met my eyes. He strode over. "I'm going to find Charlie," he stated, his voice tight.

"No," I said, glancing at Ember. "Firecracker?"

Her face quickly closed down into a stubborn mask as she worked out what I was about to say. As much as I loved her defiance, I prayed silently for her not to challenge me. My anxiety was heading through the roof at the thought she'd be caught in the riots about to happen, but I'd give in to whatever she wanted. "Drake, you stay here, we might need you. Ember, go and find Charlie. We need to know she's safe."

The weight of my lover's defiant gaze was enough to have my gut tightening with desire. Despite my worry, I smirked, my brothers would laugh their asses off if they knew how pussy whipped I was.

"Why do you want me to leave? What's happening?" Her eyes narrowed on the people around us.

"They're about to announce the fighters for each day. Only there will be more fighters, and more days in the arena than usual, that means more death, and some of these shifters won't like that. If their mates are called, some will be looking to punish the one they hold responsible. Me." I held her beautiful gaze. She bit her lip and swallowed before scanning those around us, hesitating. I stepped up to her and kissed her temple. "I need to know you're safe, Ember."

Her mouth opened like she wanted to argue, then she nodded and stepped back, cracking her neck and rolling her shoulders.

"But right now, I need you to do something for me. Charlie has to stay safe and be here for Drake. He needs her, we all do. And she'll not run from you." It turned my stomach that I couldn't share my plans with Ember and my nerves jangled with fear for her. I swallowed rapidly at the thought of what I was going to do. I hoped to the gods, and any other deity listening, that Zander and Ember were right, and ultimately my Firecracker would survive my plan. My hands shook, so I quickly crossed my arms to hide them. She had to. I wouldn't consider otherwise.

"Lionel. Rawson. Stone. Go with Ember and find Charlie. Be ready for anything." I glared right at Stone. "And make sure they get back here—even if you don't."

Stone's face remained stoic, but his eyes flickered with remorse. He nodded. "They'll get here. But I'm asking permission to get Shannon, too."

I almost smiled. He looked so pissed off by vocalising that request, clearly refusing to acknowledge how deep his feelings ran for that woman. I nodded and a little of the tension ebbed from his jaw.

I brushed a light kiss over Ember's lips. "You make sure you get back to me, even if you have to kill to do it."

She smirked though there was no levity in her eyes. "You know I'd end anyone who tried to stop me from reaching you." And she walked away with the others.

I dragged my attention from her and rolled my head, loosening my neck before cracking my knuckles. I growled. "Ready, brothers?"

"Hell, yeah." Without exception they all agreed and, as was their right, pulled on the power of our bond. I gladly lent them some of my wolf's strength.

An unemotional disembodied voice crackled through the speakers.

"There will be four pools of fighters for this arena spectacle. Refusal is not an option and will result in death. Your Prime will hunt down any cowards and end their lives. Once the fighters have been announced, those of you chosen to entertain our guests will be identified. Again, there are to be no refusals."

I didn't react, but the depravity of this whole thing had my blood boiling. The volatile atmosphere fed my wolf, who growled, urging me to kill anyone who dared threaten us. The shadow in my soul fed on the danger, and no matter how I tried to hold it back, it infected my wolf. He bayed for the blood of our enemies, pushing my conscience and morals aside. Despite Ember's influence, I let him. We were more likely to survive that way.

"Day one: pool one..."

We all stood and I waited, my body tense and ready. It took fifteen minutes for the first attack to happen. A wolf shifter from the north pack launched himself at me. Santa Cruz merely watched his pack member from the sidelines, clearly sacrificing him to weigh us up. I let Owen deal with it. The fight didn't last long. Once the attacker was pinned to the ground, writhing and swearing under Owen's grip, my beta looked at me.

"You can't make him go! I'll kill you..." the attacker screeched, his eyes wild.

Pinching my eyebrows lower, I released a slow breath. This had to happen. If I let one live, the damned flood gates would open. I nodded, once.

Owen exhaled heavily and hung his head. But it was only for a moment. The snap of the male's neck was loud even among the chorus of angry voices. Owen met my eyes and despite the ice in his gaze, he shook his head. Yeah, this whole situation was fucked up.

The guards looked down from above. Those bastards knew what would happen, that this always happened and they never lifted a finger to stop it. They just waited.

"Boss." Owen nodded to the door.

Ember strode into the hall with Charlie by her side and I released a deep breath. Both Rawson and Stone had blood on their knuckles and looked pissed off, but otherwise okay. I nodded to Shannon, who walked on Ember's other side. Her eyes flashed, her mouth was tight and her nostrils flared as they halted near me and she stood beside Stone, ready to unleash her vicious nature.

The voice through the speakers continued. One after the other names were announced.

A scream resounded through the hall and a woman fell to her knees as a man put his arm around her shoulders. One after the other yells and cries filled the corridors and halls of the prison. My wolf watched, not immune to their pain, no matter his strength, but he willed them not to be weak, to fight for their survival even if the odds were against them.

When Ember's name was read out in group two Reed closed his eyes. His name had been announced only moments before. One of them would die. No matter the pain in my chest, I kept my face blank.

Hours passed as hundreds of names were announced. My men dealt with the attacks as they happened, then a whole group of distraught shifters ran into the gym. Shane, the alpha of the east wing ran in after them. He halted at the entrance and searched me out. I snarled at him. His expression dropped and his shoulders stooped, but he nodded at me. After a quick word with someone behind him, more shifters piled in. The bunch of distraught men and women had no idea they were surrounded.

Ember glanced at me, narrow-eyed. Without instruction, my brothers dropped into their fighting stances. I briefly closed my eyes, my soul ached at what we were about to do.

I pushed in front of my men, hoping to spare them this task. With a roar that shook the walls and even the platforms above us, I sent a wave of power strong enough to knock the distraught group down. Some fell to their knees, groaning as my power floored them.

Stay down. I narrowed my eyes on the attacking shifters. Some did, some crawled away, but some didn't. They staggered to their feet and ran, yelling loudly, their fury palpable, their eyes wide and wild. There was no saving them now.

In moments we were breaking bones and necks.

I picked up the male who reached me first. Without hesitation, I rammed him down onto my thigh, snapping his spine. I threw him aside, even as his wolf's power entered me, replenishing what I'd gifted to my brothers. Shane brought his own men into the fight. After that it was over in seconds. Bodies soon littered the ground around us.

Panting and huffing through my nose, I stretched my arms wide, took a huge breath, tipped back my head and in unison with my wolf, released a war cry; a roar that rattled the air and shook the walls of the prison.

My brothers did the same.

The roar escalated until it was followed by hundreds of voices, all bellowing in unison. Death may wait for us, but the spirits of my brothers would not be broken by this arena of death and depravity.

Ember's lips curled, her chin rose and her eyes flashed. Warmth expanded in my chest as I looked upon the resolve on my mate's face, but still my wolf hungered for blood. I tilted my head back, opened my arms and bellowed up at the guards. "Is that it? Have you got your fill of our deaths for today, you sick fucks?" I staggered as the power from all those I'd killed hit me.

Energy buzzed through my veins, my heart pounding. I eyed the distance between me and them. It no longer appeared too far. I bent my knees and before anyone could stop me, I leaped.

The nearest guard pointed their tranq gun at me. The female tiger, I could scent her.

I snarled. It didn't matter. I'd be on them all before they could kill me.

The first dart hit my bicep, then another embedded in my side. I didn't care. Vengeance burned in my blood for the last four years of genocide I'd been forced to commit.

My fingers hit the metal base of the walkway and I curled them, grasping it and hanging by one arm. I blocked out the yells from those below and swung my other arm, latching on. Another sting, this time a dart in my chest.

Another. And another.

"Shit! How many is it gonna take to bring this bastard down!?" a guard from my right yelled.

There was no answer. The first guard just stepped forward and shot again —and again. Each one stung like hell; still my wolf clambered to get to her, to every single one of those fuckers. The collar around my neck burned into my skin as my wolf pushed for freedom. But even that pain didn't dim my resolve to kill. We were both livid that these people had put Ember at risk, that they were throwing her into the ring with my brothers. That they demanded my brothers kill, that they expected me to kill, for no good reason.

My vision blurred, but was totally focused on the guards. With one massive effort, I shoved power through my burning muscles and heaved my bulk up. I peered down, weaving slightly. A sea of faces gaped up at me. My brothers looked on with grim expressions. Ember's face was ashen, her eyes bright and wide. She shook her head, her lips forming a plea.

"*No.*"

I shook my head and fisted my hands. *These evil bastards had to pay...*

Another dart hit me from the right. I plucked it from my skin and dropped it to the ground below, then plucked out another and another, throwing them over the edge of the platform. I zeroed in on my prey while my fingers worked and was on the guard before he could fire the lethal weapon again.

A feral grin stretched my mouth and I ignored the shouts and the stampeding feet as other guards ran for us. This fucker was dead! He was nearest. I snapped his neck then faced the next guard. That grin on my face turned to a snarl as I stared down the barrel of a gun. "You think a silver bullet, or even a whole fucking clip, is going to stop me?" I growled, grinning as the female's heart rate spiked and the stench of fear hit me. "Yeah, you better fucking shoot me, because if you don't kill me, I will rip your heart out for all you have done here."

"Don't you shoot him!" bellowed a voice from behind.

I kept my attention on the guard, ready to do just as I'd promised. Armour or not I'd rip the bitch to shreds.

"Connor!" Zander's eyes were that eerie mix of red flame and shadow as he stepped between us. "You have to stop. If you lose your shit, they'll put you down—permanently, and that puts Ember at risk. Is that what you want when you've just got her back by your side?"

I snarled, even with all the tranquiliser and power humming through my system, I realised he was right. Darkness fogged the edge of my vision, a metallic taste flooding my mouth as the tranq drugs hit me. I stumbled against the rail, unable to do anything as the guard ran.

Fucking coward.

A metallic click from the door told me she was beyond my reach. I peered down at Ember and my wolf huffed his understanding, allowing me to retake full control and see my woman. "No. But either she's going to die or my brothers are." My chest was tight, my voice nothing but a whisper.

"She won't die—trust me. She's even told you that herself."

Zander walked forward, halting about four feet away. His head tilted, and he studied me. "Are you going to try and rip my head off?"

A low chuckle rumbled up from my chest, but the room was tilting. "Nah, man. I think I'm more likely to pass out on you."

Zander huffed and smiled, his eyes fading to russet brown. He marched up to me and hauled me upright. Pulling my arm over his shoulder, he grunted and lowered his voice. "You need to go back to your people, brother. They all need you; your strength and your leadership. This is a fucked up situation and none of them deserve to die, but many will and your job is to keep them as calm as you can until it's their time—or you can get them out. You understand? You owe your brothers and your mate more than to die in this piece of shit prison."

"Can't. Walk." I shook my head, struggling to process his words, but my legs felt like I'd had a skin full, in other words like I'd downed a bottle of whiskey with a couple of beer chasers, and they wouldn't hold me up.

"Sure you can, brother. I'll get us back down there, but you're going to walk your ass back to your cell. You are their leader, their king, their Prime, so yeah, you owe it to them all to be that for as long as you can."

My head lolled forward, my muddled brain agreeing with him.

"Hey!" He slapped my face with his free hand. "Your Firecracker's waiting on you. Come on you big assed pansy. You gonna let a few darts stop you from getting back to her?"

"Don't you...all...her. Firrr...cracker. Thaas my name, fer...her." Fuck, I couldn't even talk sensibly anymore.

"Course it is. And pansy ass is mine for you," Zander replied, hauling me back to the railing. "Now hold on."

"Whaa?" I managed to say as my pansy ass was lifted and this red eyed demon or whatever he was, held me draped over his shoulders and hauled us both up onto the top rail. Air fanned my face followed by a thud. His body tensed. The sudden stop rattled my ribs and forced air from my lungs. I was tilted again and my feet hit the ground. I staggered. "Strong, fucker, aren't...er?"

He grinned. "You have no idea."

"Connor?" Ember's voice was balm to my soul.

I lifted my head and gave her a drunk smile, my eyelids heavy. "Hey, Fer cracker."

The sound of a slap reached me right before a sting burned across my cheek. "Don't you *Firecracker* me, you idiot! What the hell were you thinking!?"

I grinned, unable to take my eyes from my fucking amazing woman.

"Let's take this elsewhere, Ember." Zander's voice was firm, but I didn't miss the amusement in his tone.

"Fine!" Ember bent down and whispered something to Charlie, who sat on the floor. Charlie nodded, but stayed where she was.

My eyes didn't stray from Ember once, not even to my brothers who glared at me. Their fury prickled against my skin, but I didn't care. I'd killed at least one guard. Bonus, as far as I was concerned. Besides, all I wanted was to kiss my Firecracker and drag her glorious body under mine.

Zander must have read my mind because he leaned into my ear. "Like I said, pansy ass."

"Fuck off."

He chuckled at my response.

Zander and Rawson half-dragged me over the dead bodies. Drake and Shane joined their own betas and seconds to our group, ensuring we had enough men for protection. I silently thanked all of them for their loyalty, noting Santa Cruz was nowhere in sight.

Once back in my cell, Zander let go and Rawson dumped me on my bed.

"Fucking hell, Connor, that's was some crazy-assed move you pulled there," Rawson grumbled, peering into my face.

"Sorry, bro,'" I mumbled and my eyelids drooped, the hard on I'd been sporting for Ember, nowhere in sight.

"It's okay, I'll stay with him."

I smiled drunkenly at the sound of her voice.

"Good luck. He looks like he's been on a major bender." Rawson smiled, clearly not going to argue with my Firecracker.

"I'll be back when he's awake." Zander's bass voice resonated through the small room.

Knowing Ember was safe for now, I allowed myself to drift off. I'd have the mother of all headaches when I awoke. I had no idea how much tranq was in my system, but I couldn't even lift my head to look at Ember when she sat next to me. Her fingers entwined in my hair and her lips were gloriously soft against my cheek.

"Sleep it off, you idiot. Then when you wake up I can kick your selfish arse."

I managed a smile, but that was it before I was out.

❦

I DOWNED my fourth cup of water in a row and sighed, smacking my lips. Ember raised her brows. "Damn, do you want some more?"

I grinned, and shook my head, then swore under my breath. That was a dumb move. My head thumped until I had to hold it in my hands. "How about some painkillers?" I asked, leaning my elbows on the table.

She huffed and rolled her eyes. "Yeah, right."

We both turned as the door opened. Zander strode in, his eyes bright, but not burning with flame. His presence pushed against me. He might not be a shifter, but his power pushed against mine. He'd done something to boost it and it's weight pulsed against mine. Did he have to kill one of his own to get such a boost—like I did? My fingers curled into my palms, but I kept the self-disgust off my face.

"We need to talk," Zander said, staring meaningfully at Ember.

Her spine snapped straight and she cocked her head, a sly smile curling her lips. She had her vest top tied up to expose her flat stomach and her toned arms pushed her breasts into a sexy cleavage when she crossed them. "Then talk."

"Not to you, to him." Zander's attention flicked to me.

He might have saved me, but I still didn't completely trust him around Ember and I was in no fit state to help her if he decided to hurt her. Gingerly, I pushed myself up from the chair and walked over to her. She eyed me disapprovingly.

"You should stay sitting down before you fall down," she advised sternly.

I grinned, albeit more like a grimace. "Listen, it's okay. Zander isn't after harming me. He wouldn't have brought my jacked up arse back here, now would he, if that was the case?"

Her eyes narrowed on him and then me. "Yeah, he would. Bringing you through the prison and back here proved a point to the inmates; that you could be stopped and therefore so can they, and that he is strong enough to haul your arse on his back and jump from a platform twenty odd feet in the air. It showed them all he is as strong as you and should be feared."

I took her chin between my fingers and thumb and peered down into her narrowed eyes. "You're right, but Zander doesn't do anything without a plan. I respect what he did, and he got me back here before they could kill me. If he wants to talk to me, it's for a reason."

"I'm not leaving," she said, her jaw muscles tensing under my touch.

I leaned in and brushed my lips against hers. I loved her stubborn streak and defiance and normally I'd rise to the challenge, but I needed to talk to Zander. I could see the tension in his body as he paced, his gaze flicking back and forth between me and Ember.

"How about a deal?" I asked gently against her lips. "You send in Owen, so I'm not alone."

She pulled her bottom lip between her teeth and glanced at Zander again. "I'll leave if Owen comes in. I'm not leaving you alone with him."

Zander stopped pacing. His eyes flashed red. "If I wanted to hurt him none of you could stop me, but if it makes you feel better, the beta can come in. No one else." His boots clicked on the floor as he resumed pacing.

Ember nodded. "I need to make sure Charlie's okay, anyway. She's been chosen for the entertainment rooms."

"I'm sorry." I sighed, knowing I could do nothing for her friend.

"So am I," she whispered, her face falling. "But she's strong, she'll survive it." She blinked slowly and her huff of warm breath hit my lips. "I just have to convince her of that."

I hated to see such emptiness in her eyes. Ignoring Zander's low growl, I kissed her, my tongue gently tangling with hers before I pulled back. She smiled at me, then snarled at Zander before she left. A moment later, Owen came in. He leaned back against the door to keep it shut, one knee bent and his foot flat against it, waiting patiently.

I turned to Zander. "So what's so important? You're taking a risk coming back to me today."

"I know how to get in the science wing."

That got my attention. "Go on."

Zander's gaze met mine and he rubbed his hands through his dark hair. He exhaled heavily. "You aren't going to like this, but it's our best shot."

CHAPTER 23

mber

THE MECHANICAL VOICE called my name. Despite the sudden nausea, I was almost glad. Watching Connor pace across the gym and cast me worried looks when he thought no one else was paying attention, had wound me up to a breaking point.

I nodded and took a deep breath, slowly exhaling. It did no good, my gut churned worse than ever and a rush of saliva filled my mouth.

Connor marched over and pulled me into his chest, his hold so tight it was hard to breathe. I inhaled his scent deeply, enough so that it was ingrained in my mind. Digging my fingers into his skin through his tee, I gripped his back.

"No mercy, no matter who your opponent is," he whispered and pulled back. I gulped. His wolf peered down at me before Connor took control again.

Reed had gone down to the arena this morning. Connor hadn't told any of us what he'd sensed and none of us asked. We'd find out soon enough who had died. Part of me wanted to know Reed had survived, part of me dreaded it. I wanted him to live, but at the same time, I didn't want to have to fight my friend. I swallowed hard. I'd die for him, even if it blew the existence of my other self wide open.

"Here, take this," Myles said, passing me an apple. He rubbed the back of his neck when I accepted it. "Um, there's no food down there and it could be hours…you know?" His voice petered out and his face fell. He wouldn't meet my gaze.

Myles and Reed had been inseparable recently, and my heart ached for both of them. I took his hand. "I'm sure he's fine," I said, but my voice sounded hollow.

With a tight smile, he nodded and pulled away. "Yeah, 'course he is."

I watched him go, my eyes burning. I wanted to reassure him Reed would live—but nothing was certain in this place, though I'd already decided to help my friends any way I could; even if it meant losing my wolf.

My wolf whined. *I know, sweetie, I don't want you to leave me, either. My back up plan is in place though, so fingers crossed you won't have to.*

It was true, my back up plan was already in motion. I swallowed hard, hoping Zander was true to his word. The day he'd asked to speak to me and not Connor, he'd come up with a way to ensure we all got into the science wing. And I'd agreed. I had no idea what we'd find in there, but I wouldn't leave without Connor. Zander had told me about Connor's plan to get in— but it was one that he would never be able to follow through on—both Zander and I knew it, even if he didn't.

I stepped away from Connor and my heart fractured at the devastation on his face. Neither of us spoke, no words of undying love or false platitudes.

I turned and nodded at the remaining brothers. Owen's face was bruised and his knuckles were still healing, but he'd triumphed over group one. "Good luck," he said, giving me a nod and a small smile. I shook my head, he was always so composed, even in the face of such a shitty situation.

D and Kawan both watched me with blank faces, but nodded their farewells.

Drake watched me. "Ember?"

"Yeah?"

"Be ready for anything," he said quietly. "At any time. In the ring and out of it."

His breathing hitched and his pulse rose, but there was no point in asking what he meant. Neither he, Connor, nor Charlie would tell me what they had planned.

I kissed Rawson's cheek. My throat tightened. I had no words.

He gave me a brief hard hug and cleared his throat. "Go on, now."

"No mercy, Ember." Stone echoed Connor's sentiments as my gaze rested briefly on him.

I lifted my chin, regressing to the drug dealer I'd been before seeing Connor again. "I have no mercy," I told him coldly and walked away from my new family, hiding my heavy heart.

Under the direction of the guards, a group of about twenty-five shifters gathered. All the guards' hardware was set to kill. I studied the tight faces of those around me. The prisoners watched the guards with cold eyes and tight faces. Santa Cruz smirked at me from across the line of heads. I dropped my gaze, keeping my head low and spine bowed. He gave a huff of laughter, and I hid my smile.

Yeah, you believe me submissive and weak, you arrogant fucker.

It was the way I wanted all these potential enemies to view me. I'd fought hard in the training ring these past weeks, but I wasn't stupid, showing all my tricks in front of any possible opponents would have been a mistake. I wasn't worried about losing, nor was I worried about ending any of these people. I didn't care about any of them, except Reed; and I'd do what was necessary to survive, protect my wolf—and get back to Connor.

The guards yelled, pulling me from my thoughts. We were forced to walk down a wide stairwell which exited into a massive caged area. Once we were corralled, the guards closed and locked the door to the stairs.

The noise from the arena rattled my ear drums. With no escape from the reality of our situation, the others began to fan out. I found a seat on a bench in a corner where I could observe everyone and tried not to think about what was happening to Charlie. She'd taken some of the darts that Connor had thrown to the ground. I hoped like hell they would at least give her a chance to save her life when she needed it.

A large, naked male limped back into the cage from the arena entrance. I noted the way he leaned heavily on his right leg and flexed his right hand like it hurt. Blood trickled from his broken nose and the multiple lacerations on his back and shoulders. Automatically, I assessed and clocked his weaknesses and planned how I'd end him.

I ignored Santa Cruz, who spent more time staring at me than he did anyone else. I shrugged it off, and instead spent my time observing and sizing up my potential enemies; those who survived their fights and returned to the cage.

A water dispenser had been placed in one corner and there was access to a toilet block. That was it; no food and no hope of escape. After a couple of hours of just sitting, I got up and began to stretch and loosen my muscles. Some people watched me, others didn't care, their shoulders slumped and their eyes pinned to the ground.

Once my body was limber again, I paced to the front of the cage, right next to Santa Cruz. We observed the small amount of the arena we could see.

"You're gonna to die, cute ass," he drawled, looking down sideways at me.

I shrugged, observing a large male who fought a smaller woman. Both had been forced by those silver collars into Were-form. A Were-wolf fighting a Were-panther. With their forms caught in a half-shift, they were clumsy, their movements haphazard, though vicious. Out of my line of sight, animalistic noises from other cages filled the air, along with the roar of the crowd.

The fight between the man and the woman didn't last long. The Were-panther didn't stand a chance. She wasn't a bad fighter and was quicker than the Were-wolf, but his strength far outmatched hers. I didn't look away when he snapped both of her arms, sliced her throat open with his claws and then broke her neck. When it was done, and his collar had been set back to full power, he reverted to his human form. Panting and falling to his knees, he growled at those cheering from above. The uproar of clapping and jeering made my ears ring.

The guards used cattle prods to force the man to his feet. His torn clothes fell from his damaged body, leaving him naked. Uncaring, he snarled and spat as they drove him from the ring, down the caged passageway and back into the corral.

"Not even you can beat someone twice your size," Santa Cruz said, such a cocky smile on his face, I wanted to smash my fist into it, right then.

I looked away and swallowed hard, my fingers curling around the bars of the metal cage. "Maybe not, but I will try." I made sure my voice trembled.

He huffed, his lip curling at me. "You're pathetic. Why the Prime is so taken with you, I'll never understand."

I remained silent, my gaze avoiding his and my posture curled in on itself. With wide eyes I observed the next fight. Santa Cruz eventually grunted, then paced to the back of the cage, sitting down again.

I lifted the apple Myles had given me and bit down. My stomach churned and tried to reject the sweet flesh, but any amount of energy was better than none. I forced myself to swallow it, core and all, then stood in line to grab a drink of water. My stomach grumbled. I should have forced myself to stomach some breakfast this morning, but food had been the last thing on my mind.

I spent another hour moving between prowling, sitting and then stretching before the dreaded voice called my name. Santa Cruz was called too. He glared at his opponent. A male about his own height and build. The male growled and stared right back. Out of the corner of my eye, I observed my own opponent. I didn't engage in eye contact or verbal sparring or growling, I merely shrank in on myself and shuffled forward.

I saw the male, who was almost a foot taller than me straighten his spine and crack his knuckles. I remained small and meek even as we were forced down the metal covered walkway to a ring in the far corner. There was a manic roar from the crowd, and a glance at the spectator balcony showed me the betting taking place.

"The axe!" yelled a voice.

"No! The swords," yelled several others.

I fought to keep the electric atmosphere from getting to me. *Focus. Focus.*

"I'll make it quick," muttered my opponent.

I didn't look at him.

From a small opening at the top of the cage, an axe and a small, six inch knife were dropped in front of us. My opponent bent down and swooped up the axe. I stared at the knife, hesitating to pick it up. There was a sizzling sound and pain shot down my spine, my muscles spasming until I fell to my knees. *Motherfucker!*

"Pick it up," ordered the guard who'd zapped me.

My opponent's gaze followed me as I curled my shaking fingers around the handle and picked it up. I weighed the balance of it even as my hand obviously trembled.

"Now get in the ring."

I followed my opponent, the stench of perfume, blood, alcohol and urine, nauseating. My jaw dropped, and I stumbled in a circle as I lifted my gaze and took in the sheer scale of the arena. All the time, I watched my enemy through the corner of my eye as I scoped for exits and possible escape routes. The entrance to the corral was furthest away from me. There was one other door which obviously led up to the balcony, and a double metal door on the far side of the arena that was heavily guarded. The science wing. It had to be.

The door to the balcony was my best bet. I peered up. A familiar face stared down at me and my stomach lurched. Doherty stilled, his champagne flute halfway to his mouth. Peering from the window of what must be a private viewing room, he stared, and blinked, then blinked again. A sour taste flooded my mouth as he smiled. He was once again a predator watching his prey, getting ready to pounce when the mood took him. He raised his drink to me, then took a big swig and swallowed. I looked away keeping my face utterly blank, as if I hadn't recognised him.

I slid the knife into my left hand. Another misdirection. I was right handed, but my opponent didn't need to know that was my strongest side.

Yelling and bellows hit me from the direction of the other rings. My collar hummed, burning the skin around my neck. I couldn't hold back a scream as the frequency changed and my wolf howled in agony. Nearby, my enemy released equally pained cries. Raising my gaze, I forced myself to concentrate on him. His eyes took on a crazed look. His face elongated and hair sprouted from his skin, but I couldn't maintain that contact when my own bones broke, reforming into a distortion of my wolf. My vest top stretched tight over my deformed chest and breasts. No matter, I would not hide my deformed body. Instead, I remained in a crouch and urged my wolf to fight with me, not against me. She settled, remaining alert, but allowing me to take the lead. Her power and strength hummed through my misshapen bones, easing the pain. I respected and loved her, and we'd always worked together, never fighting over dominance, and we wouldn't now.

The Were-wolf stretched to his full seven foot height and bellowed, sending a shower of saliva over me. I stayed on my haunches, submissive, frightened—and waited. When he leaped, swinging the axe above his head, I was ready. I launched myself. Staying low, I darted around him and in swift and precise strokes, I slashed my knife across his ankle tendons. He howled in agony and fell to his knees. The axe thudded to the mat. Without hesitation, I leaped forward, yanked his head back and slit his throat, not caring that the sickos above wanted a longer fight.

"No," he gurgled, clutching at the gaping wound with clawed fingers as if he could stop the deluge of blood.

I took a step backwards as he swayed on his knees. The crowd let loose, some cheering, some yelling obscenities. I watched as the man fell face first to the mats, his blood pooling under him. My collar vibrated and my wolf gracefully receded, allowing me to change back with relatively little pain. My vest top was torn around my back and hung loosely from my shoulders. It still covered me, but my bra had snapped open and hung uselessly under my top. My jeans were shredded, the waistband ripped wide open leaving them hanging low around my hips. There was no point trying to keep them up, I let them fall down and kicked them off. I'd long since lost any shyness about my body. That done, I pulled off my vest and dropped the bra to the ground. I ignored the jeering and catcalls from above. I put the baggy vest back on and tied a knot in my prison issue underwear to keep them up. They wouldn't survive my next change, but it was better than sitting naked for the next few hours like some of the victors in the cage had been forced to do.

A glass was thrown from above and smashed into pieces on the metal cage. Shards flew through the air, lacerating my exposed skin. I winced, but paid no attention to the blood rolling down my body.

Another cheer went up. I glanced over to see Santa Cruz rip out his opponent's throat with his claws, before punching him in the stomach and kicking him down. He plucked a hunting knife from the mats and opened his arms wide as he strutted a victory lap around the mat. The crowd went wild, demanding more blood. With a roar, Santa Cruz leaped and drove the blade into the male's belly, slicing him open.

Forcing myself to ignore the gruesome sight, I watched the way he moved, and tried like hell to cower when he stared at me, triumph burning in his eyes. Moments later, I was prodded and electricity sent my muscles into spasm.

"Move!" The guard wielding the prod yelled.

I didn't look back at my kill. If I did, the blood on my hands would destroy me. I may have killed before and I would do it again without hesitation, but each time I did, I could feel myself losing a piece of my soul.

It was impossible to miss the glass, and I winced when small pieces stuck into the soles of my feet. The other rings were also covered in glass and blood, but half-starved shifters with drooped shoulders and vacant expressions were already coming to sweep the debris aside, while others tossed the dead to the pile at the side of the arena. The sight of that pile of dead Were bodies was enough to make me vomit. In death they kept their form. I heaved what remained of the apple up onto the mat, praying that Reed wasn't in there somewhere.

"Get a move on!" yelled the guard.

I raised my hands, unable to hold back a cry as each step pushed glass further into my feet. I had to balance, and yank the shards out while still trying to move. Lingering wasn't an option. The other survivors were forced off their mats and back into the cage, too, some of them with feet as bad as mine.

"You survived, did you?"

I glanced up from beneath my eyelids at the sound of that smarmy voice. A naked Santa Cruz stood directly in front of me. I blinked and looked away from his athletic body. My adrenaline was ebbing and I was beginning to shake. The last thing I needed right now was this arrogant arse buzzing in my ear and his stink invading my mind.

"Didn't think you'd have it in you to kill. Shows that cute ass was made for me to kick right before I fuck it. I'll bet that crowd will enjoy watching me take you as you die, don't you think, *Firecracker?*"

Not caring enough to answer, I leaned against the cage, closed my eyes and tilted my head back. Moments later, his horrid stench receded. After I'd recovered my breath, I moved through the thinning crowd and grabbed a drink of water. It was then I saw a familiar face. Reed sat butt naked in a dark corner, studying those returning to the cage. His eyes were hard and his jaw tight. Had he studied me as I returned? I limped over and lowered myself next to him.

"Hey."

"Hey," he responded, flatly.

"I know you won't, but don't pull your punches with me."

He looked at me and for a moment his eyes softened. "You're right. I won't."

"Good." I coughed. Godsdamn, a break from the stench of blood, fear and death would be nice. He was naked and I was half-dressed but we were just two bodies in a sea of others. "So you and Myles, hm?"

He smiled a little, losing some of his alpha personality. "Yeah, me and Myles—after all this time." He closed his eyes. "Ember, he told me he loves me." He twisted in his seat and tilted his head.

A gasp escaped me. Tentatively, I reached out and traced my fingers over the deep red claiming marks, vivid on his neck.

"You mated?" I expelled a soft breath, elated, yet horrified at the thought of them losing each other so soon.

He nodded. "I can feel him, deep in here." He tapped lightly over his heart. "It's amazing to be so connected." His throat bobbed and he looked me right in the eyes. "Ember, if I don't make it out of here, promise me you and Connor will always look out for him."

I swallowed hard, the anxiety in his eyes almost too much to bear, especially when it wasn't there for himself but for the man he loved. "Of course, but you'll make it out."

Reed nodded, and entwining our fingers lifted my hand to place a kiss on the back of it. "'Course I will." But his words were hollow.

We settled back, but I couldn't relax. I disentangled myself, kissed his cheek and left him. Trying to ignore the pain in my feet, I hobbled across the cage. Even with the help of my wolf they wouldn't be fully healed before my next fight. Keeping an eye on the survivors, I stretched my body as my wolf concentrated on healing my damaged feet.

My next fight came. I couldn't look at Reed as I walked out, it would ruin the carefully constructed walls protecting my heart from what I had to do. The fox-like creature narrowed its yellow gaze, studying me. In half-shift the male wasn't much taller than me, but that didn't mean he wasn't a vicious and cunning fighter. His attention zoned in on my feet and the shards of glass that once again littered the arena. Biting my lip and trembling, I didn't meet his gaze. Instead, I glanced up at Doherty who watched me intently. Ice coated my insides. The warden stood by his side, dressed in a perfect dark suit and wine-red shirt, his dark hair slicked back and his dark eyes vivid against his pale skin. A slow smirk graced his mouth. Zander stood by his side, his eyes burning red, but his face utterly blank; indifference? Or hiding his own fury? Like mine, those eyes of his only burned when his emotions or power were raised.

I drew my attention back down to the Were-fox. He paced on his own side of the ring, pushing the glass into a line as he moved.

I'd been given an old sword, one that was hard to grip, but not as tricky in my clawed hand as the small knife had been. I lowered the tip to the mat and stepped up to the line of glass, ignoring the jeers for us to start fighting, and the stream of urine that hit the mat, splashing onto my legs. With a precise jerk of my hand, I flicked a large shard of glass towards the fox. He moved exactly as I expected, trying to duck from it, and the next shard impaled him directly under his right eye. He gave a high pitched screech. Again and again, I used my blade to launch the glass. Shards jabbed into his face, and where he tried to protect himself, his hands. Judging the right moment, I flicked a piece into first one eye, then the other. He screamed and dropped the length of heavy chain he'd been given as a weapon. Clawing at his eyes, he yanked out the glass. Blinded by blood, he began flailing his fists, stepping on the remaining slithers of glass, ripping his feet to shreds. He screamed and cried, smearing blood over the mats as he fell against the cage before staggering over more glass, utterly blind.

It took everything in me to remain detached, but there was no room for weakness. I walked around the edge of the mat, prowling behind him. When he had exhausted himself and fallen to his knees, I looked Doherty straight in the eyes and swung at my opponent's neck. The blade sliced through his flesh, vibrating through my deformed hands and arms as it crunched through his spine. Tensing my muscles, I yanked the sword out. Warm blood shot over me, it's coppery tang filling my mouth and nose. His corpse fell sideways, his head attached by only a slither of skin and tendons.

"Lose the weapon!" the nearest guard yelled.

I did. This time when the collar burned my skin and I was forced to change back, my clothes were gone. My hair spilled over my shoulders, the ends still blonde. Not willing to cower from those above, I stood with my spine straight and my shoulders back. I tilted my head and glared at the warden, and then Doherty. Doherty lowered his eyes, taking me in, but his eyes remained cold, even when a small satisfied smirk curled his mouth. My wolf snarled, but I merely turned my back on them.

Back in the cage, even Santa Cruz's lecherous gaze didn't affect me—because I wasn't really there. My wolf had yanked my conscience out of her way after I'd questioned whether I should let myself die to save at least one life. She eventually reminded me that all these people would die anyway, whether by my hand or another's. That my only achievement would be to become a lab rat for the warden and Doherty—and to lose her. My stomach lurched. Her spirit and my life were linked. I could be reborn, but she couldn't. So I let her killer instincts take over. Otherwise, I wouldn't survive this bloody nightmare with my mind intact.

I lost count of the amount of fights I had. Even the passage of time escaped me. I limped back to the cage, my adrenaline reserve gone and my whole body shaking. I left a trail of blood behind me from my lacerated feet, my body black and blue and my ribs cracked.

My gut clenched, and I had to stop to lean against the metal cage as I retched up blood, bile and spittle. My throat burned and my eyes watered. Pain assaulted me with each heave, but I wouldn't crawl for these motherfuckers. My wolf snarled in agreement, urging me to the water fountain. We both needed fluid. I only looked around the cage when I'd drunk my fill, forcing my stomach to accept it.

Santa Cruz stood in front of me. "Looking for your harem buddy?"

His gaze on my blood-soaked body left me utterly cold, and I couldn't summon the energy to answer.

"He's fighting. Maybe he's dead." He grinned, baring his blood stained teeth.

I lifted my gaze to his, grinding my teeth. I clenched my fists. *What would it be like to smash those pearly whites right out of his mouth?*

"Damn girl, you get me hard, all covered in blood and guts. Pity I'm going to have to kill you before I can fuck you."

"Assuming she doesn't kill you first." Reed stood right behind Santa Cruz.

With my blood coated fingers, I wiped away the water that dripped down my chin.

Reed prowled away from us. Across the cage he sat on a bench seat and leaned his elbows on his knees, refusing to look at me. Cuts and bruises peppered his skin, but he wasn't badly injured, or at least he was hiding it well.

"You think she's strong enough to end me?" Santa Cruz raised his voice to be heard above the noise from the arena.

Reed lifted his head, his wolf flashing through his eyes. "I think she's strong enough, and devious enough, to kill anyone she pleases."

My eyes burned at the respect I saw in the gaze, first of his wolf then the man. My heart melted just a little and I gave him a small smile. He merely looked back down at the ground. Before I had a chance to speak, me and Santa Cruz were called. My wolf urged me to straighten my spine and walk with my head up. I thanked her for being my rock. We were both exhausted, but she would not let either of us go down without a fight.

Reed never looked at me. My nostrils flared and I lifted my chin. It didn't matter. I would survive this fight and I'd see him again.

I waited as the sick bastards above yelled out the weapons they wanted us to use. My skin tingled as a familiar energy caressed me. My heart missed a beat and my breath hitched. I looked up at the warden's private viewing room, and Connor stared down at me, his jaw tight, his eyes dark.

I swallowed the ache in my throat, lowering my gaze. Pushing the burn from my eyes, I clenched my jaw and reinforced the wall around my heart. Emotion was useless and would get me killed. My goal was my enemy—dead at my feet.

Santa Cruz picked up the staff a guard shoved through the hole. The lethal blades on each end were already covered in blood. Keeping my eyes on my opponent, I leaned down and picked up the heavy axe they'd dropped at my feet. I limped after Santa Cruz, biting my cheek at the stab of pain from my ribs and the agony in my feet.

My gaze took in Santa's chest lacerations and the deep cut behind his knee. The axe hung heavy in my grip, my arms too tired to swing it for effect. Posturing wouldn't affect him anyway. His swagger remained even after so many fights, and he obviously didn't see me as a threat.

Misogynistic prick.

The audience yelled and jeered. I'd made the mistake of looking up into the balcony once before. I wasn't doing it again. The lewd acts being performed out in the open, or aimed down at the fight rings were enough to make me vomit again. I inhaled and let the stench of piss, blood and semen fill my nostrils. My wolf snarled, her power pickling across my skin.

I set my jaw, calling upon every little bit of fighting experience I'd ever had.

Santa's lustful gaze lingered on my tits. I tipped my hip out in response, and hid my smirk. Santa had a huge weakness, one that he didn't even know about, and I was about to exploit it. I'd get out of here one way or another.

The skin around my neck burned and my wolf surfaced. White fur sprouted from most of my body, but she hit a wall and my bones no longer broke and reformed. I'd done this enough now that the pain of a half-shift was merely a discomfort.

Santa loomed in front of me, all alpha; huge, dominant, and a total predator. Standing over seven feet tall, he'd just helped me with my strategy.

I allowed my body to become fluid, my arms and legs relaxing to the verge of being unsteady.

Santa's eyes narrowed, then he looked up at Connor and roared. Connor snarled right back, his wolf raging in his eyes. The warden whispered something in Connor's ear. Connor froze, his eyes darting to me. The warden smiled, his dark eyes feasting on my skin. Doherty on the other hand whispered something to the warden, gesturing wildly to me. Connor's jaw tightened, though he didn't move. The warden shrugged and with a flick of his wrist, he sent Santa flying towards me.

Using the techniques Som and my other Fae...acquaintances...had taught me, I glided sideways and snapped a kick into Santa's throat when he stumbled. The impact stung my foot but didn't slow him much. He staggered into the cage, but was back on his feet in a second, stretching his throat. With his eyes fixed on me, he twirled the staff, his skill obvious. It was then I realised the cage was slowly getting smaller, pushing us closer together. I needed to act quickly or he'd rip me apart with that weapon. The axe needed more room to swing and use it effectively. The staff could be used to stab and jab.

Santa leaped at me, wielding the staff in a sweeping motion. I bent my spine back, and it grazed over my chest, but I didn't stay in the limbo position, I ducked and twirled behind him and sliced the axe blade across his recent wound, opening it more. He roared but didn't go down. I spun back upright, but let the axe blade rest on the mat. It was too damn heavy to hold higher.

Santa moved quickly. Back on his feet, he snapped the staff across his enormous thigh. Damn, now he had a weapon in each hand. Thrusting his head forward, he snarled, his eyes following my movements as I stepped on a shard of glass and screeched.

The crowd roared, and even though I was quick at blocking his attack, when he changed direction, the blade caught me in the gut, slicing my flesh open.

My wolf roared, and together we tried to block the pain and ignore the coppery stink of our blood. Another shard of glass jabbed right through my foot, and I cried out, stumbling. I couldn't reach down and pull it from my flesh; he would end me.

Santa grinned, his elongated mouth and teeth bared.

I prepared myself for his onslaught, my muscles shaking, but I had to lean against the axe to keep myself upright. All I could do was gape at him with wide open eyes as my chest heaved and the cage shrunk further. There was no way I could out manoeuvre him with glass embedded in my feet. My heart raced and sweat mixed with blood ran down my torso, my vision fading. I'd already lost too much blood and used every bit of energy in my body.

Santa snarled. He couldn't stand upright any longer, either, but he sensed my defeat.

His pupils flared and his gaze narrowed on me as he began slowly spinning his weapons. I tensed as he moved faster and faster and tightened my grip on the axe handle, not moving my wide-eyed stare from him. He roared and moved fast for such a large, deformed creature.

Just before his blade slashed my throat, I pulled on every bit of remaining strength. I snapped my spine straight and jumped back. At the precise moment I'd timed, I brought my weapon up, a battle cry bellowing from my lungs. The axe sliced up through his groin and his muscled abdomen before lodging in his sternum. I roared and yanked it free, in time to step away from the guts that slithered from him and onto the floor. He looked at me and then down at his insides. His brow furrowed.

"Bitch." He fell to his knees.

The two blades fell from his weak fingers. Unsteadily, I bent down and picked one up. I leaned forward and looked him directly in the eye. "You have no idea." And I stabbed it right through his heart.

Santa sank back on his haunches, his grotesque head lolling forward as his eyes dimmed.

The crowd roared wildly. Their blood lust was sickening. The cage roof was so low now I was forced to my knees and it snagged on Santa's head stopping his corpse from falling over. The collar sent a tingle against the skin around my neck, but Santa didn't revert to human form, he would stay a Were.

My heart thundered, my attention shooting to Connor. Gods, dying as a Were meant his soul and his wolf would be unable to separate. I kicked myself for not thinking about it before, looking at the bodies piled against the arena wall.

Connor's throat bobbed, his eyes riveted on me, but the relief on his face was something I'd never forget. Even crawling naked on my hands and knees from the cage until I tumbled into the caged corridor, did not bother me. I just pictured his face, his eyes, and fell into that image. With shaking fingers, I pulled the glass from my feet, nearly breaking my teeth, I clenched my jaw so hard. No way was I screaming for this crowd's enjoyment. Doubled over and holding my stomach, I shuffled back into the corral, leaving a trail of blood behind me.

Reed watched me intently. "I knew it would be you," he whispered as his arms came around me. "That bastard needed to die."

Despite my injury and the blood that covered us both, I huffed a laugh into his naked chest. "This isn't awkward, much."

He pulled back and chuckled too, some of the darkness leaving his gaze. "Nah, I'm not in the least bit turned on by you; you don't have the right junk for me." But his smile didn't reach his eyes.

I collapsed on the bench. "So what happens now?"

He exhaled a heavy breath, seeing the full extent of my laceration. "Shit you need healing. You need Connor."

I didn't look, but there probably wasn't much holding my insides in place. The bench beneath me tilted and turned like I was on a boat in the midst of a storm. "Why?"

Reed looked at me like I was mad. "Because only your soulmate can heal your body. Even without fully mating, a kindred soul can heal another."

I gripped onto the sides of the bench, waves of nausea washing over me. Closing my eyes didn't help. "Why don't I know that?" I whispered more to myself than Reed. Which was a good thing because when I managed to crack open my heavy eyelids, he wasn't near me.

"Hey!" He banged the cage to get the attention of the guards, swearing viciously when they ignored him. It didn't matter, the next moment the stairwell doors were flung open. Connor, Myles and Stone ran in.

"Ember!" Connor's eyes widened when he saw the state of me, his gaze fixing on my stomach. I looked down and groaned. Now my wolf had faded and her power was gone, pain stormed through the layers of skin and tissue that were laid open.

"Hey." I tried for a smile, but it came out as a sob.

He dropped to his knees by my side and placed his hands against my stomach. Warmth and power tingled through me, easing the pain. Tears burned my eyes. It was over, for today at least. I began to shake uncontrollably. I squeezed my eyes tightly shut. I wouldn't think about the people I'd killed, and possibly condemned to an eternity of unrest. I wouldn't...

"Don't you shed any tears for them, Firecracker. You did what you had to do to survive and keep your wolf alive. Never forget that."

Stone stood at Connor's shoulder, looking down at me. "No mercy." He dipped his chin before his gaze shifted to where Connor's hands healed me. For a moment, his expression softened. He was ridiculously handsome when the hardness left his features. But it soon returned. "If you are still here, you fought well," he said stiffly before moving away.

Connor met my gaze, his eyes shining damply. "You fought more than fucking well. You're fucking amazing."

"Hey." I tried to give him a reassuring smile, even as my heart squeezed. I don't think I'd ever seen Connor look like he might cry. "I'll be fine. I'm here and tomorrow's another day."

I looked over at Myles who had his big hands around the back of Reed's head and was kissing him desperately, before he peppered small kisses over his face and neck, not looking in the least bit bothered by who was watching. Reed looked stunned.

The pain began to ease in my stomach and heaviness blanketed me, dragging my eyelids closed. "Connor, I need to sleep."

"I know." He took his tee-shirt off and helped me sit up and put it on. He pulled back and grinned apologetically. "Don't junk-punch me, but I'm carrying you back to my cell. Okay?"

I couldn't think of anything I wanted more than to be in the arms of the man I loved. I reached up. In a moment, I was cradled against his chest. I turned my face into him and inhaled deeply, his scent a balm to my frayed soul. I wanted to purr at the softness of his skin against my cheek.

"If you try that with me, I will definitely junk-punch you." Reed's pissed off declaration made me smile.

"Then walk," demanded Myles.

Still smiling, I kissed Connor's chest, then let myself drift into oblivion where no pain existed and blood didn't cover my hands or my soul.

CHAPTER 24

onnor.

THE NEXT DAY Stone and D waited to be summoned. Stone refused to even look at D. He sat off to one side. The worst of it was, none of us knew if they'd meet in the heats, or if they'd both survive to the finals, like Reed and Ember.

Ember's eyes glistened as she glanced at them and then me. Now she understood the shadows in my soul, the darkness into which I'd fallen, and brought my brothers down with me. Yes, death was a part of our lives here, but with every one of these fights more of my soul was consumed. Flashbacks of the dead being piled at the edge of the arena hit me. I squeezed my eyes shut and swallowed repeatedly. I'd even seen dead bodies being carted down from the entertainment rooms, praying to the Mother that none of them was Charlie. I curled my lip. The way those poor souls had met their end was likely worse than fighting for your life in the ring.

I rubbed my arms and studied my soulmate. My jaw tightened at her too pale face and her stiff movements. Even though the wound to her abdomen had been a straight and clean cut, there was only so much I could do. Her body had to do the rest.

Reed and Myles hadn't joined us yet and I'd be damned if I would disturb them. I only wished they had longer together. My mind recoiled, and I rubbed the ache from my chest, but I knew who needed to win tomorrow.

I'd held Ember close to me all night last night and I wouldn't leave her side this morning. I couldn't. She flatly refused to let me stay in my cell with her when my brothers needed me. When I'd refused to leave, she'd dressed in the clean clothes I'd found for her and walked out of the cell, knowing that I would follow. Hell, I'd follow her anywhere, even to the gates of hell itself if it meant I could be by her side.

Seeing her naked in that ring, bared to everyone and ready to fight for her life, I'd wanted to kill the warden and Doherty so badly I could taste it. But it had been the look on Santa's face that had enraged me. Yeah, the sick bastard had wanted her, but it had been his lust for pain and suffering that had terrified me more. The warden had sensed my wolf surface and frozen me to the spot. I'd been unable to look away from their fight and gods damn it, if her cunning hadn't just made me love her more. She'd been clever enough to hide her fighting talents from all of us, including me. I recognised that method of combat had been learned from the fae. I'd seen them fight, and fought them myself, in the shadows of London. It was clear my Firecracker had held back in the training rings.

I held her distraught gaze, but shook my head, unable to muster even the semblance of a reassuring smile. And no matter how much I wished it was otherwise, I couldn't reassure my brothers. One of them would die, if not today then tomorrow. Owen and Lionel had survived their kill rounds and would fight in the final. Drake would fight tomorrow in the same group as Shannon. Myles, Kawan and I were not fighting, but the only wing alpha not picked to fight was Shane. He had proved solid, and had joined me everyday to help control the prison and watch my back while my brothers fought. We hadn't spoken much, mainly because it was impossible to find anything civil in me to say. I dealt with any discontent or violence with crushing power. While my brothers and my mate killed people in the ring, I ended lives or doled out punishment outside it. I glanced at the few shifters who congregated in the hall, aware that I needed to do a round through the prison. "You up for a patrol with me?" I asked Ember, sliding my hand over her clenched fist which lay on the table in front of us. Her uneaten porridge sat congealing in front of her. My brow furrowed. She needed to eat or she wouldn't heal and be strong enough to survive tomorrow.

Sighing, I stood and walked over to the counter. Picking up a bowl, I got her some more porridge and dumped plenty of sugar in it.

"Wow. You've developed a sweet tooth, big boy." Shannon patted my flat stomach, earning a scowl from Stone who watched her every move. "This won't stay so sexy if you keep that up."

I huffed, trying not to growl at her; this fucked up situation wasn't Shannon's fault, despite her father being at the top of the food chain. I stared down at the melting sugar in the bowl, pressing my lips together. Then again, maybe he wasn't top of the food chain. When Doherty had demanded to talk to

Ember yesterday, the warden had cut him off. Doherty's eyes had narrowed, a muscle twitching in his jaw as he had argued she *had something that belonged to him*, but the warden had refused point blank. There was no point wondering what, Doherty wasn't likely to share that information.

"You okay about tomorrow?" I asked Shannon instead.

Shannon's face dropped for a second before she did what she always did and painted on a tough mask.

"I'm fine."

"Talk to Ember..."

"Why? I don't want to know what sick shit I'm going to face out there, courtesy of my ever loving father. I'll either survive or I won't, but I'm not spending today cowering away from everyone. I'll fight as hard as I can, but if I die then I guess that's my fate and I'll be reunited with Ava again."

I stirred in the sugar to Ember's porridge. "I never said sorry for Ava," I said quietly, unable to meet Shannon's eyes.

Shannon turned to me, her eyes hard and cold, her mouth tight. She flicked her blonde hair over her shoulder until it cascaded down her back. "No, you didn't, because until you were shat on by my father, you believed the sun shone out of the SBI's arse, even if you didn't like him." She paused and took a breath. "You never really loved Ava, did you? She was just a distraction from the person you really wanted." Her chin dipped towards Ember. "Her. After Ava, I thought if I tried hard enough I'd get you to notice me, but it took me being thrown in here by my father to get you to even look my way. Ember's a lucky girl. Even when we were young, I saw the way you looked at her, and I wanted that."

"What? You wanted me to look at you like I look at her?"

She smiled and rolled her eyes. "You always were hot Connor, but no, not just you. I wanted someone, *anyone* to look at me like I meant something. No one ever has."

I stopped walking. She halted and looked back at me. Her cheeks were tinged with pink and a rare vulnerability shone in her eyes.

"You wouldn't have to look far, Shannon." And I looked with meaning at Stone.

She laughed out loud, causing even Ember to turn and look at us. "Now you really are taking the piss. Him? He hates my guts."

I smiled back, but if she couldn't see it yet, maybe Stone wasn't ready to let his feelings for her show. I just shrugged. "You sure about that? I agree, he's a shit to everyone, but think about how much time and attitude he's expended recently, just on you."

She watched me place the bowl of food in front of Ember before she walked away with a frown creasing her brow.

I sat down.

Ember's eyes followed my movements. "What did *she* want?"

I smiled, and ignored the question knowing it would wind her up and ignite a spark of fight in her, one that had been lacking so far that day. "Eat."

She glared at me, her green eyes flashing like emeralds in her ashen face. Resting her forearms on the table, her fists curled.

"Ember." I growled a warning, loving these little moments of challenge she threw my way; they gave me something to live for. "Eat, or I will feed it to you, even if I have to tie you to that chair to do it."

She held my gaze a bit longer, but I was more practiced. I gave her a few more seconds, then shrugged and reached my hand towards the bowl, ready to carry out my threat.

"Fine!" Her hand shot out and grabbed the bowl and the crappy, cardboard spoon.

It was almost painful watching her force food down that she clearly didn't want, but it was necessary. I didn't pay attention to anyone else, just kept my unwavering gaze on Ember. Every now and then she glared at me, but otherwise kept her eyes down and ate.

"There, done." She pushed her dish away.

The speakers crackled and everyone stilled. All noise ceased as the next batch of names were announced. I met Stone's hard gaze before looking at D. My brothers eyed each other coldly. There would be no quarter given by either of them. Stone stood. Slowly and deliberately, he turned to Shannon. He didn't touch her, but leaned close and murmured something in her ear. She nodded but didn't look at him. He hesitated, and I was sure his fingers lightly brushed the tip of hers before he walked away without a backward glance.

THE DAY PASSED SLOWLY and even with Ember's presence, my wolf prowled inside me, his anxiety filtering into my emotions, and vice versa. In turn, I stalked around the prison. Even those with their wolves near the surface gave me a wide berth. It was wise since I was spoiling for a fight, something to release the tension in my body.

I began what must have been my fourth round of the halls and corridors.

"Enough." Ember's voice was sharp enough to get my attention.

Kawan and Shane sighed. We hadn't eaten and it was late in the day, but I wasn't hungry. My body was wound to a breaking point as I waited for the inevitable.

Ember placed a hand on my arm and glanced at the two alphas. "Give us a minute, would you?"

They stepped back and she leaned her shoulder against the wall. Her jaw was tight, but she patiently stared at me, giving me the time to think that I wouldn't give myself. She was right; wearing us all into the ground wasn't going to help. I dropped my chin to my chest and took a deep breath before releasing it slowly. I raised my gaze, but couldn't look her in the eye. Instead I studied strands of her bright red hair. My heavy sighs lifted them, until they danced and sparkled like tiny threads of fire in front of my eyes. I blinked, clearing my fanciful thoughts. "I know I'm supposed to have no feelings." I thumped a clenched fist over my heart. "I have killed so many and have a river of blood on my hands, so it's assumed I don't feel. But I can't stand waiting for one of my brothers to die." I swallowed against the painful ache in my throat. Briefly, I closed my eyes. "I would rather it was me."

Her fingers were cool against my hot face as she urged me to look at her. "I wouldn't. This is not your fault. Do you hear me?"

I dropped my gaze and she hissed. "Don't you do that. Lift your eyes. You are the Prime. Connor, you may not be able to stop any of this, but your brothers will need you no matter who ultimately survives."

I touched her cheek, her skin soft under my finger tips. "I know. But losing them, any of them is unthinkable. I've failed them. I've failed Rawson, too. He might not be fighting, but I've no idea where he is, or if he's even alive."

I hated the way her face dropped at the mention of Rawson, who had just disappeared. No one had seen him since the night before the start of the fights.

"Rawson's a survivor, he'll be fine." Her gaze pierced me. "Tell me what you have planned to get us out."

I swallowed hard and took her hand in mine. "I can't, I'm sorry. If the warden gets in your head, he will make you spill every piece of info you have."

Her face tightened, but she nodded and didn't push. "Okay. Fine. But once we've got the information you and Zander need, we get out. If anything happens to me, you don't try and save me—not at the cost of your own life. Do you understand me? Because I will always survive."

I didn't respond. I already knew that ultimately she would survive, but knowing it didn't make what I had planned any easier.

"Connor!" she snapped.

I nodded, but a deep, gut wrenching fear coated my insides with ice and I hoped with everything I had that her Fire would step up when it really mattered.

✦

IT TOOK another hour before the agony hit me. I roared and fell to my knees clutching at my chest. A piece of my heart fractured as the tiny part of my brother's soul that I held was wrenched away.

"Boss?" Kawan yelled, his voice breaking.

Tears burned my eyes. I held my hand out to keep him away. Leaning forward, I bellowed, panting as those tears ran down my cheeks. "You fuckers!" I yelled up at the guards, my wolf raging and trying to break free. He wanted revenge, on them, on me, on the world for allowing his brother to die!

Ember stepped close. Her scent surrounded me, her fingers delving into my hair, the only thing keeping me grounded. She pulled my head against the rough denim covering her thighs. And gods dammit if I didn't let her. "Shh." Her voice was thick and shaking as she tried to soothe me.

No one asked who it was that had died, and I couldn't speak to tell them.

I closed my eyes and concentrated solely on my breathing and Ember's touch as I promised my brother vengeance. My heart rate slowed a little and my mind settled enough for rational thought. I unlocked my arms from around her thighs and pulled back.

"You okay?" she asked, her eyes large and dark, sparkling with unshed tears.

"No, but..." I pushed myself to my feet, took a deep fortifying breath, and exhaled through the tightness in my chest.

"Who was it, boss?" asked Kawan, his whole body tense.

"D."

Kawan nodded once before he turned and walked away. I let him go. He and my Russian brother had always been close. I watched, but he only made it as far as the door before he stopped. His shoulders slowly straightened before he turned and stalked back towards us. "It will be over soon. Stone will need us."

I exchanged a look with Ember, swallowing at that show of solidarity and strength. Even if Stone had ended D, his loss wasn't Stone's fault any more than those deaths yesterday were Ember's. Silently we sat on either side of Kawan. Ember tentatively slid a hand over one of his clenched fists.

I swallowed back the ache in my throat. For all her toughness, my Firecracker was a kind and empathetic person to those she cared for.

Shane sat opposite, there for us all. I nodded my thanks, trying to express how much his support meant, too.

Half an hour later, the doors to the arena stairwell clicked open, and we were allowed down to retrieve the survivors. My fists clenched. Two survivors—out of so many. Saliva rushed my mouth as the stench of death hit me. Pain punched me in the gut and I fought not to crumble. I'd lost one of my brothers today, and D wouldn't be the last—tomorrow would bring more tragedy. Gritting my teeth, I threw my shoulders back. No way would I give in now. My men and Ember needed me, they needed my guidance and strength, though fuck knew, I didn't feel strong. I inhaled the subtle essence of the woman at my back, thanking the gods for giving her back to me. Ember probably didn't even realise how much strength she gave me just being by my side.

I took the lead down the stairs, my long legs allowing me to descend two, sometimes three at a time. The guards had opened the doors at the bottom, directly into the cage. They pointed their weapons directly at me, but I didn't care. I barely registered their presence. My focus was honed in on my brother.

The others ran in directly behind me. There was an audible gasp from Ember.

Stone sat naked and as still as his name's sake. He said nothing to us, merely got up and went to walk straight past me. Ember tried to mask her horror at the state of his face and body, but it was hard. Even I swallowed hard. Deep gashes marked his flesh. It had to have been him and D who had fought. No one else could do this amount of damage to Stone. And D had got in some vicious strikes. Stone's face was bruised, his eye socket deformed, and his nose was so swollen it was bent out of shape. Blood trickled from his head, staining his silver grey hair that hung loose around his shoulders, and just like Ember's had been, his feet were torn to ribbons. He stank of piss and alcohol and blood.

But it was his eyes that scared me the most. They were utterly devoid of any kind of emotion. Dead.

I opened my mouth...

"Don't!" His ravaged lips dripped blood, and something dangerous flashed in his empty gaze.

I nodded, carefully watching my other brothers as they approached him.

Kawan eyed Stone dully. Unblinking, they stared at each other. Ember moved towards them, but I held her back and shook my head. Their emotions hit me in a wave just as Stone's shoulders caved forward, his devastation surging through me.

Owen ran in, followed closely by Reed and Myles. They all halted. Understanding and forgiveness joined the sorrow that thrummed through our bond. I loosed a long low rumble which was joined by theirs, our bond flaring in my chest before my wolf took over and howled mournfully for our lost brother. My heart cracked for what Stone had been forced to do. And as broken as he already was, I wasn't sure how to help him come back from this.

The guards watched on impassively, their weapons directed at us. Ember's eyes glistened as I howled a lament to D. I hoped his soul and his wolf spirit could hear us from the beyond; that the Mother would find and welcome D's wolf and bless it to be reborn to a worthy soul. But that hope was an empty one, and I knew it. Staying in Were form wasn't something any of my kind did by choice, it was too painful. But Ember had reminded me that according to Were legends, our soul and animal spirit were trapped, twisted together within the shell of our body if we died in Were form. That had to have something to do with what the warden was doing. Why else have us in half-Were form when we fought?

I reined in my grief. Just as Ember was a warrior and would not shed tears for the fallen in front of our enemies, neither would I. Tears were a luxury I couldn't afford right now. *I will find a way to set you free—to set all of them free. I promise, brother.*

Stone limped up the stairs independently. No matter the state of him, he wouldn't accept help of any kind. I tasked Shane to take care of the other wolf who had survived, a woman from Shane's own pack. Ember eyed her surreptitiously as Shane covered her with his own tee and then helped her up the stairs.

I didn't blame Ember. There would be one more day where Drake and Shannon both would fight in this barbaric arena, and then it was Judgement Day. All the winners would fight each other and I would be expected to watch. I refused to consider what that would do to us all. We had time—*I* had time to change the outcome…I had to believe that.

"Come on, Em." I kissed the top of her head, inhaling her scent as I urged her up the steps and through the door to the hall. Maybe it was my heightened emotions, but whereas normally her scent calmed me, oddly, now it only served to make me more tense. My body responded and a wave of protectiveness hit me, driving the breath from my lungs. I bit my bottom lip hard, my nostrils flaring as I squeezed my fists shut to keep from grabbing her.

"Are you okay?" she asked, a small furrow between her brows.

My voice was gravelly, but I managed a tight smile. "I'm sorry, I've not looked after you properly today. You need food and rest."

I glanced at the others who were half way across the hall, Stone and the woman leaving bloody footprints. Drake waited by the entrance, his arms folded over his chest, and he looked directly at me. His face was tight, his gaze too intent for me to ignore.

Ember saw the line of my gaze and took my hand. "Lead the way. If you need time alone with Drake, I'll go and eat while you catch up with him. But tonight perhaps you'll let me care for you, instead of you caring for me." She squeezed my hand hard then raised on her tip toes and kissed my cheek.

I snarled, irritation and irrational anger tightening my gut. I didn't want to let her leave my side, but she hadn't eaten all day and she deserved better than my dark mood and selfishness.

We got near Drake and I didn't bother to hide my frustration. "Come with us. My Firecracker needs feeding."

Drake raised his brows and peered down at Ember. She gave a mischievous smile and shrugged. "I'm important, alpha, you should know that."

"Don't call him alpha, he's not your fucking alpha. I am." My temper was as volatile as my emotions right now. I spun towards Drake ready to slam him up against the wall by his throat. My heart raced and my wolf saw red; no one was taking Ember from us. And she wouldn't belong to anyone else. She was mine to take care of. *Mine!*

"Hey, whoa!" Ember jumped between us, facing me, and placed her hands on my chest.

Drake narrowed his eyes and stepped back, his hands raised placatingly. "It's okay, brother, I know that. No one, certainly not me, is going to try and take her away."

I breathed heavily, trying to get a handle on my wolf and my reactions. I didn't own Ember and she didn't wear my mark—yet. I needed to curb this possessive streak before I did something stupid and pushed her away...

Ember took my face in her hands. "Hey," she whispered. "Look at me, not Drake."

I did. My wolf thrashed against the restraint of the collar, trying to reach our mate. Did that mean he'd accepted her wolf as his own? That we could be a fully mated pair? Our humans and wolves bonded together?

She leaned in and kissed me gently, her lips slanting across mine before nipping at my bottom lip. I couldn't stop the rumble of desire that came from my chest.

"I'm sorry," I whispered against her lips.

"It's okay, I know who I want and need, and it isn't Drake, or anyone else." She kissed me again. "It's you—only you. Right now. And it's what you need too." She gave me an assessing look and cocked her head. Her gaze was intense as it travelled over my chest and abs, down to my groin where it lingered before resting back on my face.

I blinked slowly, my blood heating. She was right. I needed an outlet for my tension. Fuck or fight, and I wasn't fighting anyone tonight.

She jumped and wrapped her legs around my waist, threading her fingers through my hair and kissing me with abandon, not bothered by our audience.

"Fuck, that's hot," Drake muttered. He ran his hand through his hair, and stretched his neck, taking a deep breath.

"Go find your own woman." But my anger had dissipated into unbridled lust. Though I hesitated as Ember's stomach gave a loud rumble. "What about food?" I growled.

Her groan shot straight to my cock. "I don't want food, I want you."

I couldn't think straight any longer. My body trembled, I wanted her right here, right now. I didn't care if it was in front of all my brothers, let them see what they could never have... The shadow of two guards moving closer to us along the overhead walkway brought back some semblance of sense. I wouldn't let my enemies see my mate and me together....

"I'll see you in the food hall in an hour," I said, striding past Drake. I held Ember easily with one arm and marched up to my cell, muttering curses as she peppered kisses everywhere on my face and neck as I got us there. Fuck, I needed to be inside her. Right now! I wasn't going to last much longer.

I flung the door wide then kicked it shut with a slam. Ember's hair fell about our faces as I hitched her higher. I cradled the back of her head and kissed her with everything I had, baring myself to her.

Not one to be outdone, she kissed me back until my own mouth was bruised and swollen and we were gasping for breath.

"Fuck, Ember, I need you..."

She grabbed my hair and yanked my head away, a sexy, devious grin curling her lips. Her stunning eyes flashed with flames.

I inhaled, scenting her arousal.

"So what's stopping you?" Using her thighs she lifted herself before pushing her heat down against my straining cock.

With shaking hands, I unbuttoned her jeans. "Drop your legs."

She pouted.

I grinned, hoping she could see the feral lust in my face. "Not for long."

She did. I kneeled in front of her and a fresh wave of her scent hit me. I inched her jeans and her panties down her legs, dropping teasing little kisses against her flesh. "You want this, don't you, right...here." I flicked my tongue against her clit. She groaned and tilted her pelvis toward me. I relented and pushed my tongue into the heat between her legs. I inhaled, growling as a fresh wave of desire made my cock pulse.

"Yes." Her fingers curled into my shoulders for support, her legs shaking.

I threaded my arms under her thighs and lifted her, straightening my legs. She squealed, then smirked as I stood us and leaned her back against the wall with her legs over my shoulders. "Good, because I'm hungry." I swiped my tongue along her sweet flesh. Now it was my turn to groan. "You taste like heaven." I couldn't get enough, and I was relentless. Her writhing only turned me on more. I held her tightly, but there was no escape for her, six feet in the air with my face between her legs. She screamed through her first orgasm and moaned through her next. I wasn't going to stop, I needed her begging, begging for me to stop or to fuck her, I didn't care, either was good for me...

She panted, her fingers digging into my scalp. "Connor...please..."

"Please what?" I hummed against her slick heat, not willing to break contact.

"I need you inside me, now."

I glanced up. Her face was flushed, her eyes no longer bright but dark and hooded. I dropped another kiss on her swollen flesh, then groaned. I was addicted, I didn't want to stop...

"Connor..." She squirmed and pushed against my forehead.

I growled, but lowered her to the floor, not giving her a second to recover before I was devouring her mouth with mine. "I can't get enough of you." I ground my aching cock against her. "I can't be gentle."

"Good." Her fingers went to my jeans and unbuttoned them. She shoved them down far enough to free my cock. I closed my eyes, lost in the sensation of her fingers encircling me. I rolled my hips as she moved her small hand, squeezing me hard.

"Damn, I can't wait..."

Her mouth slanted across mine, kissing me deeply as she released me and lifted herself easily on me, clutching her legs around my waist. I groaned against her lips as she impaled herself hard down my entire length. Clutched in her tight heat, my mind went off line and my instincts took over. I grabbed her hips and slammed into her, over and over, letting the tension in my body be used to pleasure both of us. The noises coming from her throat, the look of ecstasy on her face as I rammed into her faster and faster were like nothing else I'd ever seen. Warmth flooded me, reaching right into the recesses of my heart.

Her eyes flew open, her pupils black and huge in a sea of green. "Don't stop." And she flung her head back. "Fuck, Connor, don't...you...stop..." and she screamed, her pussy clamping down on me mercilessly, her nails raking my back and shoulders. That bit of pain tipped me over the edge even as her internal muscles gripped me, milking me dry. I roared, black spots filling my vision, but I wouldn't look away from the rapt look on her face. My canine's dropped. "Mine!" I growled the word from deep in my chest, but I didn't move to mark the sweet flesh of her neck. I wouldn't do it without consent—ever.

Her eyelids fluttered open, her stunning green eyes holding my gaze. "Mine." But she made no move to mark me either.

My throat ached, my heart heavy as we both hesitated, but now was not the time to bind ourselves. The future was an unknown, and if I died...I couldn't stand the thought of breaking Ember's heart like that again.

She dropped her gaze, her breathing ragged. "I-I can't. I'm sorry...not yet, not just yet."

Still inside her, I kissed her slowly. I pushed in further making sure we stayed joined, then raised her chin with my forefinger. "Don't ever apologise to me, not for that." I swallowed the ache in my throat. "We will bond when the time is right."

She nodded and we held onto each other. I kissed her gently, taking my time and savoring her swollen lips against mine, even as my cock stirred again. She pulled back a little and smiled mischievously, undulating her hips in a sensual rhythm. "More..."

"Witch," I whispered, unable to deny her what she wanted. I moved my hips slowly, her soft moans sending shivers over my skin. I leaned back slightly so I could rub my fingers against her swollen clit. Her moans sped up with the movement of my hips. A flush spread up her neck and over her cheeks, her eyes glassy but locked on mine. Then with a sudden arch of her back she came. "Gods, you're so fucking beautiful." There was no chance of me holding back, not as she pulsed around me. Heat flashed over my skin as my balls squeezed, making my whole body shudder while I let out a roar and joined her.

My high slowly faded and my muscles shook, a heavy lethargy invading my limbs. Not willing to drop her, I walked her back and leaned my palms against the wall to support us both. I nuzzled the soft, warm skin of her neck, pushing into her body. "I want to stay here forever."

Ember giggled. "Wow, I think we might kill each other if you do."

I huffed a chuckle, and though thoughts of my brothers lay heavy on my heart, my mind had settled enough to think. "I told you before, not even death could take you from me. I'd find your soul in heaven or hell, or anywhere in between."

She kissed me hard, her gaze piercing and intense. "Likewise."

I slowly withdrew from her warmth and let her down. It was hard not to complain at the loss. She raised a brow and kissed the corner of my mouth before she ducked under my arm and padded into my bedroom. Water soon ran so I took a moment to recover. I leaned my forehead against the wall and considered what I needed to do next. Being with Ember might have seemed selfish, but all the fucked up things that had happened, D dying… I released a controlled breath. I'd needed that release, and close contact with my soulmate. It had given me a clear mind.

Ember padded back in and picked up her clothes, so I pushed off the wall and took my turn at the sink. I could feel her gaze on me, and gods damn it was tempting to go for round three, but I had many things to achieve tonight.

We both dressed, our movements interspersed with touches and brief kisses. I found I couldn't keep my hands to myself, I needed contact with her. As soon as I let her go, my wolf began pacing and anxiety started to seep into my mind again. I tried to reassure him that she would be fine, but it didn't work for long. "Come on, let's go and find food and the others. I want to make sure Stone is okay."

"I'm not sure he will be okay for a very long time…let's face it…he wasn't okay even before this." Ember's words were not vindictive, merely frank.

"I know." I sighed, and ran my fingers through my hair. There was nothing else to say really.

I took her hand, and we walked quickly down to the food hall. The others were still there. Reed smiled at Ember and wiggled his brows. Reed was her friend and now my emotions were on a more even keel, I was able to process the attention Ember got in a rational way.

Kawan had opted to stay with Stone, and no amount of cold threats or protests from Stone deterred him from being by his brother's side. I silently welcomed that loyal show of support, glad there would be no blame. The other's stayed close to Stone, too. In turn, my half-fae brother seemed to settle a little; his clenched jaw muscles relaxed though his eyes remained empty. We ate together as a group, and Drake soon joined us. I just missed Rawson's calm presence. Nope, I wasn't going there. I hated that I didn't know what had happened to him. I couldn't ask Zander and I had no idea if I'd be able to find Rawson and get him out with the rest of us.

"We need to talk," I said to Drake once I'd quieted my mind enough to force some food into my stomach. "Em, we all have another long day tomorrow. Why don't you go back to my cell?" It was half a request, half an order. I wanted her in my arms, and if she declined and went to her own cell, I'd just go there. After what we'd shared, I didn't want to fight with her and I didn't think she'd want to fight just for the sake of it, either. She nodded. "Of course, see you soon." And a knot of anxiety unfurled inside my chest.

"Thank you," I whispered before I slanted my lips over hers. Despite everything, my body instantly reacted to that contact. I pulled away, wondering if I should get Shane to escort her back to my cell. The mood was one of dark acceptance in the prison, but it didn't mean those shifters left wouldn't take revenge on my lover, if they got a chance.

"Owen would you stay? The rest of you go and get some rest."

Reed and Myles said their goodnights and left, their arms wound tightly around each other. D was...gone. Stone and Kawan stood. Stone met my gaze, but his face remained implacable. I nodded at him and together they made their way out. Owen watched them go, gazing at the door like he wanted to follow them, but I needed him with me and Drake. Drake's fights were tomorrow and as painful as it was to think about it, there was a possibility he would die. All our plans needed to be finalised tonight.

A large imposing figure strode into the hall. All conversation ceased and the guards above watched with interest.

Zander approached, his face tight. I leaned back in my chair and crossed my arms over my chest. Animosity rippled off the shifters nearby who tracked his progress. His eyes flashed red, and he glared at them before unleashing enough power to make them stagger. He'd never bring them to their knees like I could, he wasn't their Prime, but he definitely had the ability to incapacitate them and they knew it. Most turned and left the hall.

"Zander. Isn't coming here a bit risky, right now?" Carefully, I watched the guards, who were taking too much interest in Zander.

His eyes flitted from me to Ember. "No offence, brother, but I haven't come to talk to you, I've come to talk to Ember."

Instantly my spine stiffened, my instincts kicking in. "No. You stay away from her."

Ember raised a brow, but put a hand over my clenched fist. "I'll be fine. Zander will look after me. Won't you?" She looked at Zander expectantly.

I scowled at her, my instinct to forbid her to go with him, hard to control.

She pretended not to notice. "Connor's busy, anyway. How about you escort me back to his cell?"

Zander raised his brows at me and smirked. I glowered back, trying to curb my need to punch that amused look off his face. I trusted Ember, though neither one of us could do a thing if he had an ulterior plan. His drugs and weapons meant we were helpless to stop him. I tried to control my anxiety, shoving my palms against my thighs and grabbing my own flesh to resist hauling her against me where I could at least try and protect her from whatever he was doing.

Owen's eyes narrowed on me and even Ember shifted her stance and rubbed her arms. Zander's face softened minutely. "It's alright, brother, I'll not harm her. I'll make sure she gets to your cell safely. I only want to talk to her."

I nodded. For some reason I believed him. I stood, needing to leave before I was unable to make myself walk away from her.

She laid a hand on my arm. "I'll be fine."

"Okay. I'll see you soon." She opened her mouth to speak again, but I turned and walked away, Drake and Owen flanking me. My Firecracker was an independent, strong soul who could take care of herself. Besides, I needed to ensure our plans would be as foolproof as possible.

Two hours later we were as prepared as we could be. Before she had been dragged away, Charlie had done her best to educate Drake on what he needed to do. I clenched my fists. I'd not been able to get Charlie out of the debauched entertainment rooms, but I would not leave her there.

Owen escorted me back to my cell, his brow furrowed. "What do you think Zander wanted with Ember?"

I glanced at my beta and best friend. "No idea, and I doubt she'll tell me."

He smirked. "Probably not. What about his plan to get into the science wing? Do you think it will work?"

I released a heavy sigh, foreboding shuddering through me. "It has to. We're all out of options. Our faceless boss is clamouring for information and the warden seems to have lost his shit. Whatever he's doing, he's moving it to the next level. It's like he doesn't need us or this place anymore. And that scares the fuck out of me. We have to get out." I turned to him. "That means no matter what happens to me or Zander, you get our brothers out and as many of these other poor buggers as possible. Don't stop, don't surrender and don't give up. Wherever you go, I'll find you."

Owen nodded, his jaw tight. "I'll do my best."

"I know you will, but until I find you, you'll take on the role of alpha. You're strong enough to do it."

"I don't want that position." He growled, his wolf surfacing.

I shoved my face into his. "I don't care. I'm telling you to take it and to care for our brothers and people. Do you understand me?" I snarled back and pushed enough power against his mind, he staggered. "I don't have time for a debate, Brady. And I trust you. You're level headed and powerful enough to quell any challenge to your authority."

"Yeah? What if they start to believe you aren't coming back and one of our brothers challenges me? What then?"

"I will tell them my wishes, but if they're stupid enough to challenge you, then you end them," I said before I walked on.

I stopped in front of my cell door. I couldn't sense Zander, though I was pleased to see Shane standing by my door with two of his pack males.

He shrugged. "Thought you'd like her looked after. She doesn't know we followed her back here. I thought she might kick my Irish arse if she did." He grinned.

I slapped his shoulder. "Thanks, man. And yeah, you're right, she would."

Owen and Shane exchanged a few words before the east alpha wandered away.

I turned to Owen. "Are we agreed?"

He met my gaze. "Of course, but you will survive, you're too gods damned stubborn to die. What about her?" His chin dipped towards my cell.

I chuckled, hoping it disguised the heavy weight that lingered in my heart. Ember had a part to play in my plan that even Owen couldn't know about. "I think Ember has her own plans. But that's Ember, she'll always be an unpredictable force that no one, not even me, can fully tame."

Owen smiled, but he tilted his head. "Is that why you haven't marked her?" He lowered his voice, clearly aware Ember might hear us.

I rubbed my open palm over my face, before yanking on my collar. "No, not at all. We both agreed to wait. Our wolves...You know?"

"Yeah, I get it. But your wolf rises to protect her, and I've seen hers watching you through Ember's eyes. Your bond is strong enough that I think those fears are unfounded," Owen said.

"Maybe. But we all have to survive tomorrow before I will even consider claiming her."

"We will." He leaned against the wall, clearly intending to watch my back until Myles came to take over.

I swallowed the ball of emotion clogging my throat at his loyalty. "Night, brother," I said, clapping him gently on the shoulder before I opened the door and made my way inside to the woman I loved.

CHAPTER 25

DESPAIR AND DEATH permeated the air. I lifted my chin, my nostrils flared. Well, death could go fuck itself! And no way would I give him my despair. He could go to the deepest reaches of hell and burn!

I peered at my fellow competitors, trying to keep the contents of my stomach down. Was this the beginning of the end of my new family? My secret would be revealed today—but I'd rather that, than I have to live with killing them. My wolf's resolve to do what she could for them only made me love her more.

Drake and Shannon had survived their rounds. Shannon's indomitable will to live, despite her volatile temper, had served her well. Stone hadn't let anyone touch her after we'd gone down to retrieve them from the cage yesterday. She'd been in as bad a state as I had been, maybe worse. More of her ribs had been broken, but today she'd looked almost healed. No one had commented this morning when she'd limped into the food hall beside the silver haired half-blood, though even I now knew only a soulmate could heal another so quickly. It was Drake I was most worried about. He had not healed fully and was still weaker than he needed to be to survive. Connor had pushed some alpha vibes into him, but without the touch of a soulmate his healing would take far longer than the eighteen hours he'd had to recover.

We were lined up in the caged walkway. Stone glanced back at Shannon who stoically refused to look back at him. The guards banged against the walkway, ordering us onto the four rings that had been left standing, their cages now dismantled.

I glanced up, taking in the distance and obstacles between us and the observation balcony where the crowd jeered and made lewd gestures. My hands itched to hold a weapon, if only so that I could launch it right at them. But today was going to be fists and claws; they wanted us to rip each other apart.

Reed walked ahead of me, his powerful body moving fluidly though his shoulders were tense. A wave of weakness came over me and saliva filled my mouth. The concept of *him or me* was unthinkable. I couldn't kill him, not even to protect my wolf. She whined, but her agreement filtered through me. I wouldn't kill any of my friends.

Each pair of finalists veered off into their own rings and faced each other. Drake and Shannon. Stone and the woman from the east pack, Owen and Lionel, and Reed and me. I couldn't look at any of them. Whatever happened here today would change all of our lives.

I looked away, searching the glass-fronted viewing room for Connor.

His gaze was fixed on me, his eyes so blue and full of power, they seemed to glow. Zander stood on his other side, and next to him, Doherty glared down at me. I froze as he mouthed one word. *Fire.*

He knew!

My stomach flipped, my heart pounding harder and harder.

You're mine, he mouthed.

Swallowing against my dry throat, I forced myself not to react. Deep breaths didn't help. I wiped a bead of sweat from my temple. He couldn't have told the warden, or I was certain I'd have been hauled into that science wing quicker than I could blink. Or maybe he was waiting for proof and he hoped this fight would give it. I just hoped Zander would come through on our agreement before Doherty got to me, and that Reed would do what he needed to do—kill me.

The warden smirked and flicked his wrist.

A horn sounded. We all stiffened—and did nothing.

The crowd howled, their anger a living thing. Bottles, knives, plates, even chairs were thrown down at us to a chorus of: "Fight! Fight! Fight!"

We all straightened our spines and chins and remained still.

"Fight, or I will kill you all." The warden's disembodied voice filled the arena, though his lips remained utterly still.

Ice creeped through my flesh and bones. Nothing human or shifter could do such a thing. Fire cringed at the sound of his voice, and my wolf whimpered.

Still, none of us moved.

My heart pounded as I willed Reed to move. I met his eyes and he shook his head, a determined look on his face.

The warden's voice growled around the arena. "So be it."

Before I could process what was happening, my collar buzzed and my wolf was forced forward, the skin of my neck blistering. Reed was forced to partially shift, it wasn't even a half-shift, but he didn't move. He just stood there, a grotesque statue, as if he was frozen. My claws grew as an outer force, something dark that echoed around my mind, commanded my half-shift. No matter how much I screamed at my wolf to hold back, she couldn't; harsh, strange words controlled her actions. Trapped inside her, a scream ripped from me as my wolf leaped and slammed her claws into Reed's chest, tearing at his flesh and bone.

Roars and shouts of disbelief erupted from the other rings. Horror rushed through my body as Reed collapsed against me. I screamed and screamed, the coppery scent of his blood invading my senses as my wolf receded, whimpering and shaking.

The crowd roared in a frenzy of sick glee as blood gushed from Reed's chest and he collapsed to the mat.

I fell to my knees. "No. No. No. It was meant to be me. I was meant to die," I said, my voice no more than a broken whisper. Blood gushed between my fingers, my hands slipping as I tried to stop my friend from dying.

His eyes met mine. "It's okay." Blood bubbled between his lips, his voice distorted by his wolf. "Not...your fault..Tell Myles...I love...him...."

"No. No. No. You have to tell him yourself. You can't go...I didn't mean this...you..."

Reed's elongated face became lax, his eyes fixed on nothing.

Tears rolled down my cheeks and for once in my life I didn't care. I had just killed my friend and my heart was breaking. I leaned down and kissed his cooling cheek. "I'm so, so very sorry." My words fanned his cheek, though he could no longer hear me.

"Bring the girl to me." Doherty's voice boomed from the speaker of the viewing room.

Connor's face was grey as he stared down at Reed's body. *I'm sorry*, I mouthed to him, my heart tearing apart at the devastation in his eyes. Tears fell down my cheeks, but he wasn't looking at me, his gaze was fixed on Reed.

"The rest of you will fight, right now, or I will make you, and I will choose the victor." The warden's voice was full of promise, but I couldn't tear my gaze from Reed's pale face to look at the others.

I didn't struggle as rough hands grabbed me and hauled me from the ring.

They dragged me unceremoniously up some stairs and threw me onto the floor near Doherty's feet. Closing the door, the guards took up position on either side of it.

Doherty grabbed my chin and peered into my face. "Remember me?"

His proximity made me recoil. "Of course I remember you. You were the perverted bastard always staring at me and watching me. Is that what this is about, you're finally going to get what you want?" But I couldn't bring myself to care. *Reed... oh gods what did I do?* Tears dripped off my chin.

He laughed softly. "Oh no, I couldn't care less about you. But the warden has agreed you can entertain me until those sorry bastards down there kill each other off. He thinks you will still be around to fight the winner." He leaned closer, his eyes bright, his teeth bared. "He was wrong. Tell me, do you remember the fire that killed your parents?"

I gulped, hating the goosebumps that erupted across my skin at the mention of that night.

He smirked knowingly. "I see you do."

I could barely breathe as my gaze lifted to Connor. His marbled black and blue eyes stared at me, full of sorrow. My eyes burned at the pain I'd caused him. I'd killed his brother. He would never forgive me. Tears tipped down my cheeks. With a shaking hand, I swiped them away. "No. I don't," I said, my voice weak and my whole body shaking.

Doherty shrugged and stood up. "You're lying, but it doesn't matter."

I swallowed down the desire to fold in on myself and, grabbing onto the strength of my wolf, glared up at him.

A smile curled his lips, and he scooped up a splash of Reed's blood off my arm, wiping it on my cheek. "When I was a boy, I read a book on ancient mythology, and I knew then that I was meant for more than this mortal life, that immortality wasn't just a dream, but was attainable. I devoted my life to looking for your kind—for your mother. She was going to be my salvation, until the selfish bitch ended her life. Now you are going to take her place."

I spat in his face. "I'll die before I give you what you want."

He laughed loudly. "Will you? I don't think you can. Tell me, Ember, how did you survive the knife I stuck in your gut that night?"

Connor's eyes flew to Doherty's face.

Zander looked at me, his irises burning as he palmed a knife. I dipped my chin and held his gaze for a fraction of a second.

"You ruined my life, you bitch. You didn't die before your mother, like you were supposed to. Instead you lived. *You* took my wolf and sent him back to the Mother, and disappeared with my chance to live forever." Doherty's face twisted. "I don't know how you did it, but since that night, I've been nothing but a human because of you; fragile and easy to kill. But no more." He took a flat circle of metal from his jacket pocket. It gleamed with an unearthly glow.

"This will rip your soul apart and take the gift that should be mine. I *will* be immortal."

My mind spun and my arms collapsed, unable to support my weight as I became lost in the past. Gods. The night my parents died came rushing back. I gasped for air, my eyes fogging over as the nightmare played out. I was a little girl, safe in my bed, surrounded by warmth and softness.

My eyes fly open as fire tears through my tummy. There's a man standing next to my bed and I scream, my heart beating really hard. I don't understand why my tummy hurts, but I know this man is bad, that he's here to hurt all of us. I cry out for mummy, my tummy hurting so bad I can't move. No one comes, no matter how much I cry and cry. Smoke fills my room, burning my eyes and my throat. Still no one comes. Tears run down my cheeks and I look at the knife sticking in my tummy. There are flames dancing on the bed clothes and up the curtains of my pretty pink bedroom. But it doesn't matter how bad I want to find mummy and daddy, I can't move. I know I'm going to go to heaven soon. I feel very cold even though there is a fire in my room. My eyes get bigger as the weirdest thing happens; the fire jumps right inside me, but it doesn't hurt. Instead it makes the pain go away and whispers for me to let my life go. So I do. I just let myself float away, my wolf friend whining sadly as I let her go. The fire spirit stops her, holding onto her, and I know in my heart, my wolf's spirit is a gift she can only give me once.

Fire settles in my soul and she demands a life for a life. Looking around from this strange land of in-between, I find the energy of the evil man who took my life. Fire seems pleased. I watch, but I am not scared as she rips the wolf spirit from him, and bids him return to the Mother Wolf.

That night, Fire and I made Doherty human...

I lifted my gaze to Doherty's, I'd never realised it was him.

"You didn't die as you should have. But now you will, and I will take that fire from your soul and wield it as my own. You, dear girl, are going to make me immortal."

"No. I'm not."

He sneered as I struggled to my feet. "Ah, but you have no choi..."

"Ember!" Zander yelled. A blur of movement and I snapped my hand out catching the blade he threw in my direction. "Connor!" he shouted, his arm blurring with movement.

I couldn't see what he had thrown Connor; I was already moving. The guards weren't ready for the speed of our attack. In unison, Zander and I shoved our blades in through the weak section of their armour beneath their right ear. I grunted and twisted the knife, going down with my victim as he struggled and his knees collapsed.

This hadn't exactly been the plan Zander and I had come up with, but it would still work. I glanced at Connor, hoping he would forgive me for hatching my own plan with Zander, but most of all for killing Reed...

CHAPTER 26

onnor

I CAUGHT the handle of the blade Zander threw my way. His body moved fluidly alongside Ember's. It was hard to concentrate on my task as worry for her surfaced, but they had the guards covered; all I had to do was end Doherty and we had a chance of getting out of this room.

Reed's death was a vicious pain in my chest. I bellowed as my heart was torn apart, my brother—gone. My breath exploded in ragged pants. And Ember... I could see she believed it was her fault, but I knew better. The warden had killed him, not Ember, no matter what she believed.

The knife weighed a ton in my grasp. Ember was our way into the science wing. But first... I spun on my heel...this fucker had ruined so many lives.

"No!" yelled Doherty, his eyes wide. He didn't stand a chance against me. He'd revealed his weakness. He was human. I didn't know how Ember had done it, how her gift, her fire, worked, but he blamed her for losing his wolf. Not only that, he truly believed killing Ember would make him immortal, which explained his obsession. A pained grunt left his mouth as I thrust the knife right through his perfect fucking designer suit and between his ribs. I pulled it out and gave freedom to all my pent up rage, stabbing the bastard's chest over and over until his bloodied corpse finally sagged. I stepped back, letting it fall in a heap to the floor. That yellow metal disk he had threatened Ember with glowed as it rolled away across the floor and under a chair.

Ignoring the blood coating my hands and arms, I searched for my soul-mate. I had hoped my escape plan would be in motion before the start of the final, but I couldn't get to Drake to ask what had gone wrong...not yet. Zander and I had planned on getting to Ember before they needed to fight. I glanced down at my brother's body. I'd failed them both.

Gunshots reverberated through the air and screams echoed in the balcony. I snarled with satisfaction. Thank the Mother! The escape was in motion, and unless security figured out where the new programming for the bots was coming from, there was no stopping it.

Outside the viewing room a bot hovered. It fired into the balcony while shedding its mini bots. In turn, those mini bots zeroed in on the people who screamed and ran in a panicked crowd, trying to escape the flying bullets.

I snarled as I watched a man fall to his knees, bullet holes riddling his back. "Die you motherfuckers."

There was a metallic click. The collar fell from around my neck. I gasped as power flooded me, my wolf clamouring to break free. "Jesus!" I staggered under the weight of his power, fighting him for control as I somehow righted myself.

I inhaled and growled. "Ember..." My voice was deeper than ever. I turned to find Zander staring intently at Ember. She met his gaze and something passed between them.

Zander moved.

I couldn't stop him. No matter how quick or powerful I was.

"No!" My heart stopped as time slowed. The sight of his serrated-edged knife entering her chest just below her heart was something I'd never forget. And something I could never have done, no matter what I'd agreed to do.

His face morphed into something dark and otherworldly. Horns flashed into existence on the side of his head. His red eyes burned, shadow obscuring his features, and wings appeared on his back. Those hellish eyes met mine before that demonic appearance flickered out of existence.

Ember fell to the ground, her face turning as white as porcelain. She met my gaze, her eyes so green and bright they seared my soul... and she smiled. "So you didn't have to," she whispered.

Red filled my vision and I charged, slamming into Zander and sending us both sprawling. The shadow that I had contained all these years erupted, swirling through my blood. It merged with my wolf creating a being full of darkness and fury. No matter what I'd agreed to with Zander, it wanted revenge.

So did I.

I jumped to my feet as my wolf roared and punched through my skin. He had been contained for four long years, but finally he was free—only now the darkness attached itself to him.

"Connor! Don't!" Zander's eyes burned.

Kill him, I ordered both my wolf, and the dark being in my soul. My senses were scrambled by the scent and sight of her blood, even though my logical mind knew this was what we'd planned, only it should have been me who killed her.

Baring his large teeth, my wolf launched at Zander's neck.

"Connor!" Zander yelled again, twisting away in a blur of speed. "Stop! We need to work together now! It's what she wanted! This was her plan! She wants us to get in that science wing and stop whatever is happening there, but she didn't want you to have to kill her. She knew it would destroy you—especially if something goes wrong and she doesn't come back."

Zander lashed out with a knife. It wasn't a kill attack, but one meant to warn, or at the most, wound, and slow me down.

Infected with the darkness from my soul that I'd always kept at bay, my wolf didn't care, all it wanted was to kill. The monster that I'd become landed to one side and circled Zander, looking for a weakness.

Zander stepped closer to Ember. Holding my gaze, he placed his fingers against her neck.

My growl reverberated through my chest and into the air, shattering the windows. His swallow was audible. My eyes narrowed, my fangs grew longer, my vision changed and I could hear the heartbeats of everyone in that arena. It was like a storm of thunder in my soul, insistent and demanding. The screams of agony were like music to my ears, a balm to the creature of destruction that I had become. I inhaled the stench of terror and blood and revelled in it, that darkness inside me growing. Such chaos was the most seductive scent I'd ever inhaled; it eclipsed Ember's existence to the point I no longer cared about her. The blood leaking from her body called to me, the flesh on her bones merely a feast for my soul.

I peered out from my clouded mind, horror coiling around my heart. What the fuck was this monster that had awakened inside me?

It, no *I*, took a step towards Ember, hunger striking at my belly. Not just for her flesh but for her soul...For the first time in my life, true fear hit me.

Zander's image morphed into the demon I'd seen before, horns, wings and long talons flickering in and out of existence. His wings rippled before disappearing. It was as if he couldn't keep that image or part of himself there for long.

Cold satisfaction swirled through the monster that controlled my wolf and me. *Together we are stronger than him,* it thought.

"Don't do it, Connor. You can control the darkness just like you did your wolf. It wants to dominate and use you. Don't let it." Zander's voice was guttural and like nothing I'd heard before. The darkness thrashed and urged me to ignore him. I snarled, recognising a kinship with Zander's other form—and a rival strong enough to destroy us.

Without pause, I lurched, trying to clamp my jaws around his throat.

With inhuman speed, he moved. Talons thrust into my belly and pain seared through me. I let loose a howl, except the sound wasn't my wolf. It was something—other. Wrong, it was utterly wrong. Zander threw me across the room. I slammed into the wall and landed on top of Doherty's corpse. Saliva hit my mouth and hunger consumed me. Ignoring Zander, I tore chunks of flesh from the director's bones.

"Connor! Stop! Fuck! Use your wolf! Dominate the darkness. Push it back! Ember's still alive! Do you hear me!? She's alive, but we don't have much time!"

I glanced up at him as bone crunched between my teeth. Doherty's flesh was bitter. My lips curled back from my teeth. Evil made it taste that way, but it didn't matter, this creature that I'd become loved it.

What the hell is happening to me?

My wolf growled, and helped me force the darkness away long enough to meet Zander's eyes. He lifted Ember and, holding my gaze, bravely moved closer.

"Listen to her heart."

A dull thud reached my ears, a faint and slow heartbeat. It wasn't much, but it was enough. Ember wasn't dead. Using all my strength, I slammed my will into the monster. It roared and fought, but it was newly born, and there was no way it could permanently take over my human body or my wolf.

"Connor! Shift back. We need to get into their clothes and use her body to get into the science wing. She'll heal, Connor, she will."

Pushing my wolf back, I was soon naked in front of Zander. He wasn't taking Ember anywhere, not without me. He pointed a weapon at my gut, and a snarl curled my lips, but he was absolutely right, he shouldn't trust me.

"Get those clothes on." Zander gestured to the fallen guard.

Riding my wolf's dominance, I hesitated.

"Now, Connor, or I'll shoot you and finish this without you. I need her, not you." His face hardened, his jaw setting. "It's what she wanted, to help us get inside and see what's really happening in there."

"I know that, but seeing her like...this." I gestured to the red stain spreading across her chest and swallowed hard. "What if she dies and doesn't come back? What if that fire in her soul doesn't work?" My voice was still gravelly and deep.

Zander glanced through the broken glass and down into the arena. "Like I said, we just have to believe that she will. Come on. Hurry up!"

There was a war going on down there. Thankfully, I hadn't sensed any more of my brothers die, and I prayed to the Mother to spare them.

"Please, brother," Zander entreatied, looking closely at my face.

"I'm not your brother!" I snapped. "My brothers are either dead or fighting for their fucking lives!" I breathed hard and fought the urge to shift again, if only to rip the world apart.

Zander's face hardened. "Stick to the plan, Prime. We need a body to get out of this balcony and down into that wing, and she knew it. She didn't want you to have to kill her. This knife? I slid it into her to save you the guilt of doing it. Now get those clothes on and come and take her." He glanced out of the window again. "The warden's come out to take the bodies. Quickly! The arena guards are fighting against the bots and the shifters, this is our only chance!"

Fuck! I should have known Ember would figure out our plan—that or Zander had told her because he knew I could never sink that knife into her. I tried not to look at her deathly pale face or the blood dripping through her clothes and hitting the floor. My heart missed a beat as I detected a faint sign of life. There was still hope. Maybe she could regenerate or be reborn or whatever the fuck she did, but part of me couldn't just let her die. No matter what Zander said, if her gift didn't work, she'd be gone forever.

My hands made quick work of the dead guard's clothes, though while I dressed my stomach roiled. Doherty's remains surged up my throat and I heaved, spewing them from me. I had to pause dressing to vomit twice more. Damn, he was nasty, though I didn't want to think too much about the monster that had relished eating his remains.

The clothes and bullet proof armour were tight and the boots too small, but I gritted my teeth and forced my body into them. In the dark and chaos of the attack, no one would notice.

Outside the window, an attack drone hovered, laser bright light exploding from it in short bursts, taking down more of the prison guards who retaliated until bullets ricocheted off the walls.

I spat the vile taste of Doherty from my mouth and grabbed Ember from Zander's arms, hating that his scent permeated her clothing. Unable to look at her waxen features, I watched the battle unfolding below the window.

Zander stripped and donned the uniform of the other guard. The grimace he gave as he shoved his large feet in the boots gave me a small amount of satisfaction. Sliding daggers into the sheaths on his thighs, Zander picked up the discarded weapons. "Let's go."

I followed him out, letting him take point. I couldn't shoot, not with Ember in my arms.

Zander led us down the flight of steps, slowing as we approached the bottom of the stairwell. A bot hovered in the entrance. I gripped Ember more tightly, ready to protect her with my own body. Dressed as we were, that machine would see us as the enemy, but before it could spin, Zander shot it. A precise strike right where Drake had advised. The thing went down with a clatter that was absorbed by the battle raging around us.

Lupines, felines, bears and other shifters ripped guards apart with teeth and claws. It was carnage.

"Fuck! We have to get across there." Zander gestured to where the warden's guards kneeled in a perfect formation. When one fell another filled its place. As a wall of weapons and force, they fired on the swell of shifters, all the while moving forward and pushing the shifters back.

Despite being out weaponed, my own kind fought hard, but they blocked our way across the hall. Some clearly didn't care about getting out, they were seeking revenge. The sight of them dying sickened me, but Zander was right, Ember had agreed to this. She had refused to leave with the others, telling me she wouldn't leave me behind.

Right now, she was barely hanging onto life. If I could get in that science wing, maybe I could find a way to save her and keep her wolf with her, as well as discover what the warden was truly doing with the bodies of my people.

"Here, take her."

Zander put his weapon in its holster and took her without question. I pulled my own, but it was for show—I hoped. I sent a wave of alpha power out, enough to disorientate those shifters in our way and clear a path to the warden's guards.

"Now!" I yelled through the mask.

We sprinted across the mats. Even Ember's weight didn't slow Zander. A huge wolf lunged at me and I had no choice but to fire. I aimed to injure, taking it down to the mat. I kept running, my heart pounding. I glanced back and saw the wolf's yellow eyes flicker to a familiar grey.

Owen! Fuck!

Owen's huge wolf slammed into the floor and he shifted back. His gaze met mine, his eyes wide. My gut flipped as I held his stare. I hadn't shared my whole plan with him because I didn't want him risking his life by trying to help. I had no idea what we would find in the science wing, but instinct told me it would be powerful and far darker than anything we'd seen before. I pushed a wave of compulsion against him, urging him to leave.

Another group of shifters bounded between him and me, and I saw someone drag him out of the arena. I swallowed hard and hoped he didn't think me a traitor to him and our brothers.

We ran through the front line of the guards and they closed the gap behind us. Another team of guards grabbed the fallen bodies and dragged them into the prison. At least half of the arena belonged to the guards now, even though fighting continued around the fight rings and in the balcony.

I looked across the hall to where more drones flew in, and grinned behind my mask. Drake had escaped the arena and had taken control of them. A drone hovered above, its huge eye twisting as if looking for someone. It rested on me and I allowed my wolf to rise to my eyes, hoping Drake could tell it was me. Then I raised my weapon and released a blast into the drone. Hopefully, he'd get the message; *run!* The drones loosed a barrage that had the guards ducking behind their shields, giving the shifters a chance to retreat.

Zander nudged my arm. I gave him my attention. He was right, he carried Ember, but I needed a reason to get in that wing. I tried not to gape as the guards reached down and picked up a body in each hand. Those bodies were shifters, some still in Were form, some in full shifted animal and some in human form, either way they would be heavy. These guards picked them up as easily as lifting a shopping bag. It was insane. Zander looked out of place carrying Ember so carefully with one hand under her thighs and one around her back, her head lolling against his chest.

These guards were not remotely careful.

I caught up with Zander and kicked his ankle, gesturing to the dead. He understood and lowered Ember gently to the ground. I was ready to lend him some power to do what the other guards were doing, but he merely leaned down and scooped a body up in each arm. I blinked. He was a strong mother-fucker, as strong as the guards surrounding us.

Gratitude filled me. He was handing Ember back to me. My stomach churned and my legs shook as I studied the stab wound in her chest. My mind couldn't process what I needed to do. It was all I could do not to turn us around and run at the thought of taking my beautiful mate into the warden's lair, but neither could I go in and leave her behind. I couldn't deal, so I called upon my wolf. He growled in understanding, and I allowed him to take control. The symbiont shadow inside me surfaced, but I held it back, allowing it just enough freedom to temper my human emotions. I scooped up the limp body of the woman I loved in one arm and grabbed another body by its ankle, dragging it behind me.

We joined the guards who were ferrying the dead into the corridor beyond the doors. The warden stood just inside, watching the bodies pass him by with a gleaming hunger on his face.

"Wait," the warden ordered as I came level with him. My heart rate sped up and my body tensed, ready to strike.

He stroked his fingers through Ember's hair, such a ravenous expression on his face, I readied to drop the other body I held and bolt with her.

"This way," he ordered, then murmured something to the guard by the door.

I followed him down the corridor. Zander was one guard back when the warden strode into a small room with a metal table, a sink and little else. It stank of old blood, with an underlying aroma of faeces and fear. I swallowed down my panic, searching for an escape route. This wasn't supposed to happen. But, then again, I was just winging this whole situation; there was no plan between Zander and me now that we were in this place.

"Put her on here." The warden seemed unable to tear his hungry gaze from Ember's face.

I let go of the other body. Large slash wounds gaped open on its neck. I ignored it, and using a huge amount of self-control, relinquished my mate, placing her on that hateful metal table. I couldn't move away as the warden approached. With every fibre of my being, I wanted to break his neck and stop him getting close enough to infect her with his evil. But, despite my power, he was capable of feats far greater than my brute strength. No matter how much I wanted to rid the world of this evil creature, I wasn't strong enough, not alone. He was pure evil, something way beyond my comprehension.

The newly risen creature in my soul cowered away from the warden. That in itself was enough to prevent me from even trying to end him. I ground my teeth and held myself and my spirits in check, knowing no matter his strength, I would sacrifice everything I was to save her.

The warden inhaled deeply and leaned down. "It's true. She's the one. No wonder Doherty wanted her." He placed his face millimetres above Ember's and whispered something in a language I didn't understand.

Claws pushed through my fingers and I fisted my hands, stepping closer.

"Out of my way, imbecile," he barked, and with a flick of his fingers sent me crashing into the far wall. "She still has life and soul, and she has no heir. I can suck her soul and her fire spirit from her body and open the gate," he whispered, his attention solely on Ember.

My blood ran cold. I wouldn't let him take anything from her. Whatever power he harboured, I'd stop him. She deserved that from me. I stared at Ember's soft features. I loved her so much that my heart ached. I could at least save her from him, even if I couldn't save her wolf. Maybe, she would still come back to me...

"Get that other body and get out!" the warden dismissed me with a twist of his shoulders, looming like a dark spectre over my soulmate.

I got to my feet and slid a knife from the sheath on my thigh. The metal whispered against the leather. Forcing my claws to recede, I gripped the handle with a shaking hand.

Chanting emanated from the warden, and Ember's body bucked. Blood no longer flowed from her wound, her face now a deathly, beautiful mask devoid of emotion and surrounded by a halo of soft fiery hair. Pain ripped at my chest, and all I wanted was to reach out and touch her.

Prowling quietly, my footsteps no more than a whisper against the tiled floor, I approached them. Not even my wolf could dampen the devastation tearing me apart. Ember and I were matched souls, perfect for each other, yet constantly being torn apart. The thought of her being enslaved sickened me. Even if she did die, her soul should be free, not belong to this piece of shit. Before I could think about the consequences, I called my wolf and leaped. The warden's head snapped up and his eyes widened, his hands lifting. He was too slow. I sunk the knife between Ember's ribs and into her heart with all my strength.

Flesh tore and my fist thudded against her chest wall, the knife embedded to its hilt. Now she was free and this monster could not enslave her soul or her magic.

I left the blade embedded in her chest and ripped off my mask, gasping for breath. My heart shattered into tiny pieces, so painful I could barely think. I howled and roared, my voice amplified by my power. *Please come back to me. Please come back...*

The warden snapped his attention to me. He snarled, a deep eerie sound that sent ice skittering through my blood and along my bones. Hell stared back at me from his eyes, veins of fire running through the obsidian orbs. He gave a sinister chuckle. "You can never save her, wolf. Her soul is eternal and belongs to us."

I blocked my ears to his lies. She didn't belong to him. She was mine! Something tugged deep inside me and agony tore through my whole body. My wolf howled and my knees buckled even though I fought to remain standing.

The warden's demonic eyes followed my movements. He lifted his chin and inhaled deeply. A malicious grin bared his too perfect teeth. "You must know you were never going to leave my little prison, Prime. You and your kind were made to serve my lord, and now you have expedited your end. You will serve in my legions and become one of my best soldiers—but not yet, first I will cause you great pain."

I tensed as he lost all pretence of civility. Razor sharp teeth grew from his gums, his whole body distorting and enlarging until his twisted horns reached the ceiling.

Breathing hard to control the pain that still racked me, I summoned my wolf. It fought so hard to explode from my skin, only nothing happened. Sweat slicked my spine and palms and dripped down my forehead. The strong and beautiful spirit clawed at my insides, trying to hold on to me, only something much stronger pulled at him. He howled even as his presence faded from my body. A scream ripped from my lungs and I clawed at my belly, doubling over as hollowness, vast and unending, gaped inside me. My knees sagged and I hit the ground with a thud.

My wolf!

The demonic creature chuckled. "Killing her gave you such pain. I can taste it." He licked his lips with a black tongue.

I couldn't speak, unable to comprehend what had happened. The darkness in me clamoured to fill the void left by my wolf. Nausea slammed through me and I retched, sending a stream of bile to mix with the old blood stains on the tiled floor. I shivered violently. My mate was dead, my pack was gone, and my wolf had been taken from me. I didn't know how, only that he was gone.

I had nothing.

Slowly, I raised my head. I had no power, I was utterly human.

The demon bared its rows of fangs at me.

I launched forward, sprinting as fast as I could. I ripped the blade from Ember's chest and skidded between the demon's legs. It spun, its clawed feet screeching on the tiled floor. Swiping a muscled grey arm down, it tried to take me out with a vicious swing of its taloned hand, but I darted away and slashed the knife across the back of its heels. Nothing happened. Its hide was leathery and impossible to slash open with such a small blade. My heart pounded and breath exploded from me in big heaves as I tried to stand. It was impossible, a wave of dizziness washed through me and my legs trembled too much to support me.

The demon stomped, twisting its huge ugly form until it faced me again.

This was my end.

I fixed my attention on Ember and my vision blurred. I'd never really cried, but for her, for everything we could have been, I did. Pain exploded through my neck and I screamed, agony swamping my back. The demon hoisted me up and the blade fell from my fingers. I couldn't think past the pain that saturated me. The demon launched me towards the wall. The room spun, the momentum smashing me through the plaster and I exploded into the corridor among a cloud of dust and debris.

No matter how much I tried, I couldn't get my legs and arms to respond. My arm was twisted at an odd angle, but strangely there was no pain.

The creature smashed its way through the wall to get at me.

I looked past it, my gaze drawn back to my mate.

Ember's body was burning, the most beautiful, red, gold and blue flames licking over her porcelain skin.

"No," I cried. She should be gone—her soul safe. But it had been a fool's hope that I could save her from him.

Once again, the creature grabbed me by the neck and lifted me. My wrecked body hung limp in its grasp.

It glanced back at Ember.

"You think you saved her?" He pulled me up to his face. "You didn't. I will wait for her to return, and your sacrifice will have been in vain."

"Fuck you," I mumbled and closed my eyes. I was done. I couldn't move my fingers, or cough away the stink of his sulphurous breath. Even breathing seemed difficult.

A pulse of energy filled the air. It pounded against my ruined body making it sway in the demon's grasp. I was dropped to the ground, landing with a thud in a crumpled heap. The creature twisted towards the wrecked room just as a bluish white light flared.

A portal flashed into existence.

I'd seen one once before when that betraying bastard Walker had run. My heart lurched and tears rolled down my cheeks. "Impossible," I whispered. Ember now stood, wholly flesh and blood. Sobs burst from my lungs, my heart squeezing in my chest. I didn't understand how her gift worked, but I would take the sight of her to my grave. Flames swathed her body and her red hair glowed with stunning hues of red, her irises illuminated with emerald fire. Her hands curled into fists, ready to take on the world.

Those burning eyes flicked from the beast to me, a broken heap of flesh and bone on the ground.

Her fire flared around her body and she sent a column of flames blasting into the demon. It merely laughed. Naked and glorious, Ember lurched forward. "I'll kill you!" she yelled at the beast, her voice shaking.

Her fury, her need to protect me, pulsed against my blood. I cried out as an echo of my wolf brushed my soul, as if it were reaching for me.

The demon snarled and leaped.

Before Ember could move, a man stepped from the portal. Metal armour glowed almost as brightly as his white hair. Walker narrowed his gaze on me.

I blinked. Perhaps I was hallucinating.

Fast as lightning, Walker wrapped one arm around Ember's stomach and fired some kind of weapon with the other. The strike hit the creature in the chest. The impact slowed it, but didn't stop it.

Ember screamed my name, her voice echoing as the portal collapsed in on itself.

What had just happened?

Recovering from its forward momentum, the demon spun and stomped back to me. It smiled, a hideous and frightful sight. I didn't care. Ember was alive. I didn't know how or why, but she was out of this hell hole. It didn't matter what happened to me now.

The demon licked its lips. "The chamber," it growled.

Several pairs of heavy combat boots came to a stop in front of me. Rough hands moved me. Pain shot from my injured neck and down my spine, my nerve endings on fire. I bit down a scream as I was yanked up and over someone's broad shoulder. The warden had always revelled in pain and fear. I would not give him mine.

"You are working with someone who has great power."

I could see nothing, just someone's back, yet I knew he was talking to me. He must have shifted back into his human form.

"They have taken my key and I need it. You are going to tell me where she is."

I chuckled, blood bubbling from my nose and dripping from my mouth. Darkness was taking my vision and I could barely breathe, which meant my injury was far worse than I'd hoped. "I'm...not telling...you...jack shit." And that was the truth. I had no idea where Walker or Ember were. And what the hell was the key? A key to what?

The warden grabbed my hair and yanked my head up. "You think you won't, but you will. I will heal you and break you. I will cause you such agony you will beg for death, only I won't give it to you. You, *Prime,* are mine now, and even the strongest souls break under my persuasion." He let go of my head.

Pressure filled my skull. My head was going to burst. Unable to hold back, I screamed.

The pain ebbed enough that I could think. I found myself back in the alleyway where Rawson had found me. I was skinny and young, just a boy, and my lower half was naked. My jeans had been ripped from my body by the dark haired fae who tried to coerce my mind with his magic and glamour. But the darkness in me sensed its presence and uncovered it. I freed my dark side, welcoming it as shadow licked along my bones. Dark and vile, the shadow consumed me and I happily used it to slam the fae into the ground.

He screamed as I took his knife, and even though my too thin limbs ached and shook, I stabbed the tall supernatural being, over and over, until blood covered me and him, dripping from my hair and chin, staining my bare thighs and hands.

A laugh echoed around me.

Breathless, I pulled back and stared at the fae. My heart stuttered, horror filling me. "No!" I yelled, dropping the knife and falling off the body.

Ember's bloodied remains lay at my feet. Her emerald green eyes stared at me accusingly and she reached out a shaking hand. Her mouth opened, but no sound came out, she just coughed and coughed. Blood spurted from between her bloodless lips and fell from the wounds on her chest. I lurched forward. I had to stop the bleeding. I hadn't killed her. I hadn't... But my hands were too small and no matter how hard I tried, blood pumped between my fingers.

I'd failed again.

I always failed her...

Coldness enveloped me and a cruel laugh echoed in my head, right before pain exploded through my skull once again...

CHAPTER 27

mber

In Faerie...

The world tilted. Energy burned against my skin. I screamed when pain pulled at my chest, horrified as I watched the large ethereal form of an obsidian wolf float in front of me. Connor's wolf. My heart lurched, he looked frightened...and lost. Beside him, my own wolf spirit floated. She had lingered close when I died and when Walker pulled me into the portal, she had been pulled in with me. Relieved she hadn't left me, I quickly tethered both wolf spirits. If they were let loose into the void of the portal I would lose them forever.

Keeping two spirits anchored to me was hard when all I could see was that creature holding Connor by his neck. My mate had been so broken, he was near death. But it wasn't his broken body that had shattered my heart, it was the utter desolation in his eyes. He'd given up. I closed my eyes, my heart breaking. I'd done that to him. Connor hadn't deserved to have his wolf ripped away, not when he'd been trying to save my soul.

Hot tears stung my eyes.

Taking his wolf was the payment Fire required. A life for a life. She would bring me back no matter the consequences and I'd never hated her more for

396

it. I'd rather end my existence than leave Connor to die alone and empty. But Fire wouldn't allow it, nor would she allow my own wolf to leave me. The proximity of that demon had made it impossible for her spirit to return to the Mother Wolf.

The need to get back to Connor, to save him from that monster and explain why I took his wolf, tore at my insides. A single tear ran down my face. Angrily I swiped it away. Connor wasn't dead, he wasn't!

I clenched my jaw and looked Connor's wolf in the eye. His dark eyes narrowed, a snarl baring his teeth. *We will go back, and we will find him,* I vowed. Pain pulsed against my own maelstrom of emotions, although, amongst all those feelings, I sensed the slightest flicker of hope. My own wolf, pure white and vivid next to his darkness, whimpered, trying to reassure us both.

I would find a way to keep both of these beautiful wolves with me, to house and protect them. And I'd find a way to get Connor's wolf back to him, no matter what it took.

A muscled arm, covered in shining armour held me tightly against a hard body. Power rippled from whoever it was, brushing against me. I didn't fight, there was no point. The portal would take us to its end point, no matter how much I wanted to escape.

Within seconds my feet hit solid ground. The arm released me and a firm hand pushed me away. I heaved in a breath, fighting a wave of vertigo as both wolves slammed back inside me.

Connor's wolf whined, his emotions too confused to ignore. My own tried to soothe him until he snapped at her. She snapped back, snarling viciously before turning her back on him, ready to come to my aid.

The portal had been far more powerful than any other I'd ever been in and my senses were reeling. Instead of falling to my knees, I forced my body upright. Being reborn always made me weak for a time, but no matter—I fell into a fighting stance ready to take on the unknown. I didn't allow the fact that I was utterly naked to distract me.

"Damn." My vision was blurry. I blinked furiously, trying to clear my eyes, honing my other senses and relaxing my body, getting ready to defend myself.

Slowly the world came into view. I was in a large room that looked like something out of a fairy tale castle. Stone arches curved high overhead and large lead lined windows framed with thick, luxurious sky blue and silver drapes let sunlight flood the room. The rattan flooring underfoot was rough and creaked a little, releasing a smell like cut grass when I moved.

Around the edge of the room, warriors in fae armour watched me carefully. Their hair was pulled back and lay in one long plait down their backs. Without exception, they were all tall and had the kind of focus that made goosebumps rise over my skin. They were powerful, as in magical power, the sort I couldn't fight without a weapon. They held their own weapons loosely, though there was no question they were ready to take on any attack from me.

I studied them, my palms sweating. Running would be pointless. I was somehow in Faerie but had no idea where. Besides, I didn't fancy running naked through a foreign land with no goal in mind. My attention settled on the fae who had pulled me away from Connor. He was as intimidating and aloof as I remembered.

"Walker."

His long white hair was pulled back into a tight braid, his white eyebrows dipped and his lips tightened into a thin line. He was severe looking, yet beautiful with his fine bone structure and angular jaw. Silently, he watched me. A smile twitched my mouth. Connor had named him after the white walkers in the Game of Thrones stories because of his silence, his ice blue eyes and his white hair.

Walker cocked his head and his eyes glowed. "I never did understand that name." He looked so perplexed I wanted to laugh, until I remembered it was him who had betrayed us and left us at Doherty's mercy four years ago.

Anger flared inside me; even Fire stirred. I closed my eyes as her power rushed through my veins. When I opened them again, Walker eyed me warily. As well he might; he'd left Connor behind a second time. He swirled his fingers and a blanket appeared around my shoulders.

I tilted my head, my fingers curling into the soft wool as I grasped the edges closed. "Why did you pull me out of there and not Connor?" My voice was cold, despite the fire in my soul.

"Because he isn't as important as you. We had to get you out of there."

"He isn't as important? What the hell are you talking about? Of course he is!" I yelled.

"No, he isn't. Connor was sent to that prison to get into the science wing and uncover what was causing the surge in dark energy coming from there." Walker folded his arms, his face inscrutable. "He has completed that part of his assignment, but he still has a job to do, as does the other half-breed."

"A job?" I asked incredulously. "He could be dead by now!" I took a step forward. I'd rip Walker a new one if he couldn't come up with a better reason for why he left Connor behind. There was a clatter as the fae warriors lifted their weapons and pointed them at me. I halted, but didn't lose my focus on Walker. He held his hand up and they lowered them again.

He inclined his chin. "Yes, he could."

"You could have saved him."

"No, I couldn't. Your rebirth triggered an energy pulse. That's how I traced you. At our last encounter, your power and fire told me what you are. I had to leave you then because getting Connor into the prison was a priority. I also needed to come back here and research more about what you are."

"What do you mean? What am I?"

"Walk with me." He gestured to the door at the far end of the room.

I stiffened, but there really was no choice. I needed to find out what the bigger picture was here. Connor hadn't known he was working for the fae. He'd always been confused by who had wielded enough power to manipulate the SBI, but it seemed so obvious now. The fae were a powerful race, and the most powerful among them even had the ability to manipulate human minds if they wished. My eyes narrowed on Walker, perhaps he could tell me why both the warden and the fae wanted me.

Walker led me into what appeared to be a private library. I'd never been anywhere like it. Books lined the shelves right up to the ceiling. But it wasn't the size of the room that had my jaw dropping, it was the *feel* of it. Magic seemed to pulse from the words between the pages. In my view, books *were* magical. They had the ability to transport readers to other worlds and rip them away on a tide of emotions, but this was something more, something tangible.

"These books are ancient. They contain the history and magic of my people, hence there are guards at all of the doors. The room and my quarters are warded and no one gets in—or out, without my permission."

I didn't bother to comment. Above us, beautiful effigies looked down—fae fighting on the backs of strange creatures, their weapons drawn, their foes demonic and ugly. I glanced out of the nearest window as we marched past— and gasped. Stunning, manicured grounds dropped away across terraced gardens. Frost dusted the grass, the sunlight catching it so that it sparkled as though covered with diamonds, and the clearest water I'd ever seen flowed from extravagant fountains. Below us, people with blue or white hair meandered around the carefully designed walkways.

"Where are we?" I asked, my heart beating faster. The last time we'd met, I'd worked out Walker was high fae, but this place wasn't just for the high fae, this was a freaking palace! I was in the lair of one of the four fae kings. My mouth dried out as I considered the frost on the grounds and the armour Walker and the guards wore. It wasn't like any I'd seen before, and instinct told me that wasn't a good thing. I was wanted in Faerie. The Winter Kingdom's royal family had issued a warrant for my head years ago when one of its fae princes had overdosed on digitalis. I'd heard about his death of course, but I was always good at ignoring my guilt and pretending that the people who bought from me had a choice…

I swallowed hard, realising how shallow I sounded, even to myself.

"In the Winter Kingdom's palace," Walker confirmed, not slowing down.

My stomach churned. "Where are we going?" I wished my voice didn't sound so shaky. Not only had I been forced to leave Connor behind, now I had to find a way to get out of here before they discovered who I was and killed me. My heart gave a sudden lurch. Perhaps Blue was imprisoned somewhere in this place, unless they had killed her for her crimes.

Walker halted so suddenly, I almost walked straight into him. He spun and faced me, his eyes harder than diamonds.

I stepped back, calling on my wolf, though I doubted I would be powerful enough to fight Walker alone. Connor's wolf snarled and I swallowed hard. I wasn't alone.

"I know who you are. You killed my son," said Walker.

I opened my mouth to protest, only nothing came out. "You're the Winter Court King?"

"I am, and along with that other human, you murdered my son. Oh, I know you didn't force him to become an addict, my son was always looking for a way to escape his responsibilities, the life destiny chose for him. He was a troubled young soul who sought oblivion from his anxieties and failures, and you handed it to him. If you hadn't been dealing that foul shit, he would have at least lived."

I looked at the stone floor. I doubted his son would have accepted his lot in life if he'd truly been that unhappy, but Walker was right, I had been in some way responsible for his death. Indirectly maybe, but that didn't absolve me. I'd chosen to work for Som. Som's had been the only place I could go to escape the SBI radar. Working for him had given me a reason to exist after the people I loved had died, but in the end, I'd known what I was doing was wrong. But leaving Som would have meant leaving Blue—and she had been my only friend.

I had no words. Nothing I could say or do would change what had occurred. Losing a child must be beyond painful and to stand in front of the person you held responsible without ripping out their throat? "I'm sorry for your loss," I said, raising my gaze to his. And I was, to lose a child must be utterly devastating.

His hard eyes narrowed, his top lip curling. "Don't worry, I'm not going to kill you. You are too important to the safety of my world."

He turned back around and walked down the length of the room, halting near an old tapestry. I followed with more than a little trepidation. His guards pulled the heavy cloth aside. Walker put a gloved finger on a small book with gold writing on its spine and pulled it forward.

"Really? Very Harry Potter. All you need now is a wand."

Walker scowled. "Who is this Harry Potter? And what is a wand?"

Despite his animosity towards me, I grinned. "A fictional character...like a white walker, your name sake." I didn't try and explain it any further, the dip of his brows into a fierce frown, the tip off to stop.

There was a grating sound as the books and shelving swung outward. One of the guards grabbed the door and swung it wider. Walker hurried inside, disappearing into a dark stairwell. Lights flickered on as the sound of his footsteps receded. I hesitated. If he wasn't going to kill me, what was he going to do? A swift shove in my back told me I had no choice but to follow. I trotted down the winding stairs after Walker. Down and down we went, my bare feet making no sound against the cold stone.

Far from being old and dusty, the stairwell was well used and clean, though the air became frigid the further into the earth we went. My breath came out in large puffs of mist, and I shivered under the blanket. My feet were freezing, but I wasn't going to complain. I still didn't know what was going on or why I was here.

"You cannot escape from me in my kingdom. Even if you try, I will hunt you down and bring you back. For now, you will stay in the palace."

"Thanks, I think." How in the hell was I supposed to escape, naked and weaponless?

He glanced over his shoulder at me. "I'll provide you appropriate clothes and anything else you need."

We reached the base of the stairwell and I padded after him. He waved his hand and a metal door at the end of the corridor opened. We stepped inside and it shut, sealing us in. Walker faced me and waved his hand again. The blanket disappeared and a black dress covered me, its soft folds enveloping me from my neck to my feet.

I frowned, but decided it would be rude to point out it wasn't my style.

Inside the room which looked to be cut into the stone, it was warm and light. Two people leaned against a large round table which dominated the space.

A stocky man with short brown hair and brown eyes regarded me steadily, his corded forearms crossed over his chest, his smile friendly enough. "Hi."

My attention flitted to the woman at his side. Blonde hair hung to the centre of her back and her face was pretty with full lips and large, blue eyes. "Hi, Ember. Remember me?" Her lips curled into a smile and her eyes sparkled.

I wasn't easily stunned, but my mouth gaped open. I was staring at a ghost.

The guy chuckled. "I think you shocked her."

"Yeah, I think so, too."

Walker huffed, impatience pouring off him. "Ember, meet Lance and Ava."

I swallowed hard, trying to wrap my head around what was happening. Ava was Shannon's older sister. But she was dead…

A squeal from another doorway pierced my ears. I twisted to face the sound, and was nearly bowled over by a body hitting mine.

"Ember! It's me!"

A woman with rich chestnut hair that gleamed with gorgeous tones of red, grinned at me.

My heart flipped. "Blue?" Unable to stop a sob of relief, I wrapped my arms around her, hugging her tightly. "I thought you'd be dead, or at least enslaved."

"We are not murderers," said a cold voice.

My attention focused on the tall, regal looking fae who stood behind her. He was almost too beautiful to be real. His hair shone like turquoise silk, his facial features perfectly in proportion. But I stiffened. He was the fae who had glamoured Blue and taken her prisoner, leaving me behind to my fate.

Blue rolled her eyes at his words. "Oh, don't mind him. He's always a miserable bugger." She leaned in, her lips near the shell of my ear. "He doesn't know how to have fun."

Walker took up a position near the other fae, looking down his nose at Blue. Standing shoulder to shoulder, the likeness between the two fae was obvious. Both shared the same height and bearing, and similar beautiful bone structure, only their eyes and hair were different. Walker's ice blue irises were lined with an emerald ring, the younger fae's eyes were wholly filled with a stunning pale green.

"This is my oldest son, Prince B'nar, and you know *her.*" Walker's tone was derisory, as if Blue were nothing but a necessary irritation. "My son's human *project.*"

What he meant by those words, I had no idea, but I could find out later. My mind was whirling at a hundred miles an hour, yet I still noticed the use of names, real names. Then I remembered, the high fae had power over humans and other fae whose names they knew—but shifters were harder to control.

"Like father, like son." Blue smiled and shrugged nonchalantly, but her nostrils flared and she swallowed hard. My friend wasn't nearly as good at hiding her feelings as she thought. Blue slipped her arm around my waist, and I placed mine around her shoulders in a gesture of support—except it was really me who needed her support. I was totally lost and out of my depth. I needed to get back to Connor and whatever this shit show was, it was stopping me.

"Why am I here, if it's not revenge for your son?" I asked Walker.

Walker flinched, as though mentioning his son was a blow. B'nar eyed me with undisguised hatred, and although he looked at Blue with the same expression on his face, I saw his eyes soften.

"We have been looking for you, or rather your kind, for years." Walker crossed his arms over his chest, his gaze boring into me.

My heart banged against my ribs, my wolves ready to spring to my defence. I swallowed, my nerves calling up the fire in my soul. "Why? What am I?"

Walker held my gaze, his arms folded over his broad chest. "A phoenix. An immortal being. And you are the key to opening the gates of Hell and reigning destruction down on every world in existence."

I made a strangled noise in my throat. "The phoenix does not exist." I'd always refused to look more deeply into the fire that lived in my soul. I didn't know why, not really, only that its origins had always scared me. Especially after my parents had died.

Ava smiled gently. "It does exist. *You* exist. It's who you are. We've been looking for you for years. Lots of people have. Or, rather, they searched for your mother and found her home in ashes. We knew she had passed her phoenix to her heir, or she would not have died. But it wasn't until King L'nar Voltair returned here after having been imprisoned and told us of a young woman named Ember who could command fire, that I suspected it was you."

I swallowed, not wanting to think of the fire that had killed my mother. I blinked. Doherty had wanted the phoenix that lived inside me, and he had been willing to kill me for it. The image of a glowing gold circle, etched in symbols that I didn't understand, flashed into my memory. I had no idea what Doherty had found that could separate me from my phoenix, but I wasn't about to mention it to anyone here, not when I had no idea who I could trust.

Walker cocked his head. "All we can assume is your mother sacrificed herself and gifted you her phoenix so that you could live."

I stared at Walker's cold face and blood pounded through my ears.

"Ember?" Ava's enquiry was soft as she reached out a hand.

Blue shook her head and squeezed me tighter.

I tried to stop shaking, but even deep breaths, and focusing on the power of Connor's wolf, didn't help.

"It's alright, I've got you. That's enough for now, majesty. Ember's had a shit time of it. She's lost her mate for the Mother's sake, and been reborn. Damn, I've no idea what else has happened to her, but I doubt it's been a walk in the park..." Blue guided me away from Walker with the arm around my waist.

"It's enough when I say it's enough! She stays!" His fist smashed into the table.

Blue stiffened, her mouth flattening into a tight line, but she turned us back around.

Walker strode up to me, towering over me. I fought not to cringe away as his ire sent frost prickling over my skin. Connor's wolf snarled and pushed in front of mine, ready to burst free and rip his throat out.

"My world is at risk, and so is yours. I don't need the two half-breeds anymore to discover what's in that prison."

My spine snapped straight, and I couldn't keep the snarl off my face. But Walker continued regardless.

"I saw that demon's reaction with my own eyes when your magic lit up like a siren call. Hell wants us all, and you are the key to freeing the demon army. When you are sacrificed upon the gates of Hell, the fire of your rebirth will burn them to ash and they will then be wide open. There will be nothing left to hold the armies of Hell back. Your phoenix will be ensnared by the gates forever, and the generals of Hell, maybe even Satan himself, will have a portal to Earth. You have no heir, so you cannot choose to die and pass the phoenix to another. If I could kill you and make you stay dead, I'd do it right now. You had a part in killing my son and you could mean the end of my people, if Satan sets his sights on my world after he destroys yours. Believe me, I would take solace in your pain, but I do not have the means to end your life—yet, and, unfortunately, I need you to help us fight this war."

I stared into his cold eyes. It was one thing to know what you chose to do with your life was wrong, it was another to face the consequences of your actions. I swallowed. I hadn't killed his son, and I wouldn't accept all the responsibility for it. The prince had clearly had other issues, one's that Walker himself wasn't facing, but maybe I'd played a part in his death. At his side, Prince B'nar watched me carefully. No matter the reason I was here, Walker, or perhaps B'nar, was my only way back to Connor, so for now I would play their game.

"How? I can't do any more than any other shifter. Sure, I can be reborn, but that's all. Save Connor and Zander, both of them are far more powerful than me."

"They aren't, but we will get to that." Walker crossed his arms over his chest.

I ground my teeth together, trying to be patient. I needed to know what he thought I could do, but my soul cried out to get back to Connor. "Fine. What was that demon thing in the prison?"

"Berith." Walker's tone was sharp.

Ava gasped.

Lance tipped his head back and exhaled. "Shit."

My patience snapped.

"Enough! Who the fuck is Berith and what the hell is he doing with my mate?" Fury surged through me. I'd been forced to abandon him before, but this time I would not leave him to his fate. I glared at Walker. "You'd better give me a good fucking answer, *Majesty*. Or I'll burn more than the gates of hell to get him back, I'll incinerate your whole fucking world."

"Whoa, calm down, Ems." Blue dropped her arm from my waist and shook out her hand. "You're getting a bit heated. And I don't mean figuratively." She raised her brows.

"I don't care. I have no idea what a phoenix really is, or what I can do, but I'm pretty sure I wasn't some weird assed version of big bird when I got up and looked in the mirror this morning."

From his position by the table, Lance laughed. I ignored him and glared at Walker. "I'm not asking for your help. All I need is a portal back to that prison, then I will return and help you however you wish."

Walker ignored my request and chose to answer my question instead. "Berith is a general of Hell. A powerful demon whose sole purpose is to incite chaos and murder. He somehow entered this world and has used the prison as a means to make himself stronger. Forcing shifters to kill each other has fed that strength. He consumes negative emotion; hate, fear, self-loathing, all of it. But he thrives best on death itself. Like many demons, he can consume the souls of those who die, but he can also keep them as his slaves, particularly Weres. Their shifter-spirits and souls cannot leave their body in Were form, the half-shift binds them to their body."

"If he can control their souls and the animal they house, what happens to their bodies?"

"He will use them as vessels for his demons. Shifters in Were form are the only species strong enough to house hell-spawn. The most powerful shifters will become what Werewolves were originally created for; to be the sentinels of the Hell gate and protectors of the key—the phoenix, and that is you."

I shook my head and blew out a heavy breath. "Damn, anything else?"

Walker continued, his icy gaze not moving from my face. "Once a general of Hell finds a way into a world, he can use a rift between that realm and Hell to bring a hell-spawn through. But the rifts are always fleeting and although they re-occur they are not permanent; he can only bring one or two demons through each time. That's why he needs you. Satan and every one of his generals will hunt you down now that they know you exist." His gaze was piercing, sending goosebumps over my skin. "If Berith ever lays his hands on you and drags you back to Hell, he will use you to release the might of Hell's army. He will destroy Earth and then move onto our world—and he won't stop there."

I blinked, trying to process his words. If Hell was real, did that mean Heaven was, too? Then where were the angels when you needed them? So many people had suffered and died because Hell wanted out onto Earth. I cracked my neck, my nostrils flaring. And it needed me to do it. Well, Satan could go fuck himself! I had other plans for my life.

"Really? Well, like I said, I want out of here. I'm going back to get Connor and you'd better hope he's still alive." I eyed the Winter King, baring all the rage in my soul. "You left him there with a fucking demon prince!" Fire pushed my wolves back, clamouring for freedom. I indulged her, allowing my fury to burn. Flames lit my arms, not harming me, but plenty lethal to everyone else. "I meant what I said. If he dies, then the gates of Hell will be the least of your worries, because it won't be that demon army who destroys your world, it will be me. Connor is mine. My mate. And I protect what is mine." I walked right up to the Winter King. "I might be the key to destroying this world, but that means I am also the key to saving it. If you want my cooperation then you will promise to help me get Connor and my friends back. If you do that, I will help you stop Berith and every other monster who dares threaten your world and mine."

Walker's eyes gleamed and my heart jumped as magic sizzled into my soul. His hand grabbed my wrist through the flames and steam rose as my skin burned. But it didn't burn with fire; it burned with ice.

I looked down. A stunning ice white and blue dragon had been tattooed into my skin.

"I promise, so it's a bargain." Walker's mouth curled in a tight smile, though there was no humour in his eyes and he flexed his burned fingers.

Blue puffed out a breath and raised her hands, dropping them with a slap to her thighs. "When will you learn not to make a bargain with a fae without thinking about it first? You know you need to negotiate the finer points."

Fire settled as I crossed my arms over my chest, unwilling to admit Blue was right. But right now I would do whatever it took to get Connor back. "If it gets me Connor back I'd bargain with the devil himself."

"That's the problem," Blue said, glancing at B'nar, who watched me, his face nothing but a blank mask. "If you want them to trust you, they need to know you won't do that. Not even for Connor."

I turned to face my best friend, unable to remember how many times I'd worried about her over the past months, but here she was, free and well; not dead, not being tortured, not a prisoner. "What happened to you, Blue? I thought about you everyday since he took you away." I nodded to B'nar. "I promised I'd find a way back to you. What have you been doing while I was imprisoned and fighting for my life? Did you strike your own bargain to save your life?" That question by itself, despite the look on her face, made me hold back some of the trust we had once shared.

"I'm as much a prisoner here as you are." Her voice was quiet and her gaze dropped to the ground.

My brows dipped. "Well, trust goes both ways, Blue, you know that. And even when it is earned, it has to be nurtured."

Blue frowned a little, but I faced Walker, rolling my head on my shoulders and loosening up my neck. He had walked to the opposite side of the room, stopping near Lance. He reached out and pressed the side of a metal panelled door. Silently, it slid open.

It was my kind of storage unit. Inside was all manner of weapons; blades of all sizes and designs gleamed, guns and bows were displayed, all made with modern faerie technology. Walker picked up a bow and chucked it at me. It slapped against my waiting hand. I curled my fingers around the cold silver and blue metal and studied the weapon, weighing its balance in my grip. It was perfect.

The others watched me with interest as I studied the other weapons and then the room. The round table was covered in some kind of glass with fae symbols etched on it. I read a little fae, but these were beyond my knowledge. The metal doors of the storage units continued across the entire wall space, also etched with symbols, and I could only assume more weapons were stored there.There were no windows and the main doors had some kind of fae glyphs glowing on them.

Curiosity got the better of me. "What is this place? And why is the High King and his son working with those he considers no better than bugs to be crushed?" I gestured with my free hand at the others. "One human, two shifters and a 'half-breed' like me. It's true I can be reborn, maybe I am a phoenix, I don't know, but why trust me and them in this room with you?"

"His majesty isn't just working with humans," interjected a voice.

I turned to see a man of average height stride into the room. He was handsome in a geeky kind of way, and strangely familiar.

I blinked, trying to place him, my struggle obvious.

"Miss Rawson." The man nodded a greeting, his smile easy and charming.

It hit me. "Mr Blaze?" I tried not to gape and forced my mouth to close. This geeky teacher had been there the day Shannon had gone into full queen bitch mode on my last day of high school.

He gave a disarming smile, his eyes sparkling. "That's me. Though I think it's appropriate for you to call me Alex now."

"I see you've already met," Walker said.

"Er, yeah." I couldn't pull my gaze from this hot version of the man I'd always thought was a geeky teacher.

"We met a few years ago," Alex explained. "I helped Miss Rawson out with a slight problem she had on her last day of school." He shrugged shoulders that were toned and bigger than they used to be.

My brows dipped. Was he a fae who could glamour? If so, which had been the glamour, the skinny, hard faced geek, or this confident, charming version with buff shoulders and a tight ass?

His brows lifted and he grinned. "Are you checking me out, Miss Rawson?"

I flushed, anger running through me from both me and Connor's wolf. "No! I'm not interested in you other than to know what you are and what you're doing here."

"Oh, you were so checking out my fine ass."

His arrogance sparked Fire, and along with Connor's wolf, she rose again. I didn't have time for this idiot. Connor needed help. "Yeah, so I can kick it right back out of this room." I snarled and took a step toward my ex-school teacher.

"Enough! He is part of the team I assembled to battle the evil that is trying to gain access to your world, mine, and every other that I know of. There are other team members that you will meet as time goes on, but for now, these are the people you will work with. Lance and Ava look after the weapons training. B'nar, which, by the way, means 'heir', heads any physical combat training, and Blue looks after all of our technology and research along with Alex."

"What about Connor and Zander, the half-breeds as you so nicely call them? Where do they fit into this operation you've got going on here?"

"They are undercover, and only Zander knows who he works for. Connor has never been told," he confirmed, his arms crossed over his chest. That posture accentuated his toned chest and arms and made him seem even more imposing.

I got the feeling that was one of his favourite poses. My brow lifted and I tried to keep my anger in check, forcing Connor's wolf back again. "You've kept Connor in that shit hole for *four* years working for you? Without telling him?"

He shrugged elegantly and fixed me with a hard stare. "He didn't need to know. We both know he may very well have refused to do anything to help, especially when he believed you were dead. And Zander has worked under-cover for far longer than Connor. This whole situation is bigger than either of them, whether Connor is your mate, or not. You work for me now, Ember, and you don't need to know everything about this operation. As you said, trust is a two way street. For now, you will get to know your new colleagues and new weapons. And while B'nar works to ensure you are proficient with our weapons and your fighting skills, I will tell you more about your phoenix."

"Why, what more can she do?"

"Far more than just die and be reborn. Keep her in check for now. When my son says you're ready, I'll show you."

I wanted to punch his stoic face in and force him to take me back to Connor, but I knew that approach would be useless on someone as powerful as Walker. Instead, I called upon my wolf, vaulted over the table and grabbed a round of arrows. I knocked the clip into the chamber and fired it in the space of seconds. I'd used this kind of weapon before. Blue had designed one just like it. The short, deadly arrow thudded into the wall behind Alex. His eyes widened, and he stared over his shoulder at where the arrow protruded from the wall. I tried not to freak out that the arrow had penetrated the stone with complete ease.

"I'll be fine using the weapons." I pointed the bow at Walker. "Take me back to get Connor, right now."

Walker flicked his fingers and the bow was yanked from my grip and into his. "No."

My heart thumped as my chance for rescuing Connor disappeared. "We have an agreement. You help me, I help you." I tried negotiating in my most reasonable voice, though even to me it held a note of desperation.

"True." Walker passed the bow to B'nar. "Enlighten her," he said and walked out leaving me staring after him.

B'nar settled his attention on me. "You didn't specify a timeline. Blue was right. It's always about the finer points in a deal with the fae. So when I say you're ready and we have made a plan for extraction, then we'll go and get your wolf." He spoke to me patiently as if talking to a child.

My gaze met Blue's. She shrugged, her face soft.

My hands fisted, my skin heating. "Fine! But perhaps if you fae were more honest in your dealings you'd find trust easier to come by! Well, let's get started then."

"Not right now, Firecracker."

A surge of anger and pain burst through me.

Connor's wolf roared in my head.

I had Alex pinned against the wall in the blink of an eye. My anger matched the wolf's. "Don't you dare call me that—ever. Only one person calls me that and it sure as shit isn't you, not if you want to keep your head on your shoulders."

Connor's wolf pushed to escape. His power was immense and I struggled to hold him in check as he tried to force his will on me. My wolf jumped forward. Snapping and snarling, she bolstered my strength and together we demanded he release his hold on my body. When he resisted, we forced him to retreat. He growled and snarled, but begrudgingly relented to my wolf. She continued to snap until he fully receded. The warmth of his respect for the she-wolf that was both strong enough to defy him and brave enough to protect her host, filtered into me. I sighed as his dominance lessened. It was hard to imagine how strong Connor was to control this beast all day, everyday.

Alex held his hands up in supplication. "Sorry, it's just Connor always called you that when he talked about you. What else should I call you? Is Ember okay?" He dragged his fingers through his hair giving it a sexy, mussed vibe, his mouth twisting.

My anger didn't dissipate at that *little lost boy* look, but it was clear if I wanted to get Connor back, I required Walker's portal, and with no idea how to open one or get it to the correct place, I needed these people. I had to have back up, too. My knowledge about demons, or generals of Hell, was sorely lacking and I sure as shit didn't know anything about being the key to the gates of Hell. The thought sent a full body shudder through me.

Well, I had to start somewhere. I blew out a deep breath and tried to curb my anxiety for Connor. Patience and planning... A tight smile curled my lips when Alex warily shook the hand I held out.

"Ember is fine, or Em."

"Not Yellow?" Blue raised a brow as she smirked.

I forced another smile onto my lips. "Nope. Yellow disappeared the day *he* took you from our world and I ended up in that prison." I glanced at B'nar and dipped my chin in his direction.

"I'm sorry for what happened to you, Ember, but you're right, I had to strike my own deal. It was die, or become B'nar's human project, as Walker calls me. Basically, the prince holds my life now. I belong to him."

I cocked my head and at the look in her eyes, I knew her life wasn't as ideal as it seemed on the surface. I nodded and held her gaze. It was a look we'd shared many times in the past; one that said we'd talk more later, when we were alone. I turned to B'nar. "Fine. When do we start?"

"Right now," he said, and the heat of fae magic warmed me. When I glanced down at myself, I was covered in similar clothes to his, as were the others.

"Wow. You look good, girl." Blue gestured to the figure hugging suit.

I smiled at her. "So do you. Is that why he chose these uniforms? Does he get a kick out of seeing your curves?"

She snorted a laugh. "Damn girl," she said, her eyes darkening as she pulled me into a hug. "It's good to see you here. I knew you'd be an awesome addition to our little group. And I do trust you—completely." Her face morphed into a mischievous grin and she winked. "And I don't think the prince notices what I wear." She tapped her nose as though telling me a secret, but we all knew a fae's hearing was way better than even a shifter's. "I don't think B'Nar, or should I say the *prince heir*, knows how to have a good time. Man or woman, I'll bet he even screws with a scowl on his face. Maybe it's the frost. Maybe things just get frozen in one position." Her eyes widened comically. "Do you think that's why they scowl so much? Are their cocks frozen too...?"

Despite my messed up circumstances, I bit my top lip trying not to laugh as she goaded the obviously serious prince. He scowled at her, not deigning to answer. "If you wish to become a valuable and effective member of our team, you need to be good at everything, not just fighting and weapons."

I stared and crossed my arms over my chest, because what else was there?

"You will become proficient in tactics, the culture of our kind and your own; you will learn demon and angel law, and you will master how to have a refined conversation whilst mingling with the higher classes of both of our worlds. But first you will learn to control the additional wolf inside you."

I shuffled from foot to foot. "I won't have to wear a dress and shit like that will I?" I asked, twisting my fingers together.

Ava grinned. "Don't worry, honey, that's my department."

"Great." Connor would laugh his arse off at seeing me in a dress. Pain squeezed my heart at the thought of how I'd last seen him. "How long will this all take?" I asked quietly, addressing B'nar.

He shrugged. "That all depends on you. So let's begin." He gestured to a stack of practice weapons. "Choose your weapon. Blue. On the mats with her."

Blue grinned and grabbed her favourite weapon of choice, a bo staff. She sauntered to the centre of the mat twirling the six foot long wooden staff with a cocky swagger. She whispered two fae words. A frown creased my brow. I didn't recognise them, but whatever they were, runes appeared on the staff, and it turned from a harmless wooden bo into an armour covered staff with daggers at both ends. I cocked my head, studying the energy that crackled around the blades.

"Ready to get your arse kicked, *Ember*?" Blue sneered playfully.

I huffed and narrowed my eyes. Walking to the nearest weapons shelf, I chose two training daggers. Palming them, I swaggered to stand opposite her, rolling my head and shoulders, the fae suit clinging like a second skin. "You first."

Despite my circumstances, I smiled. My friend was safe and well, so I made another promise—to Connor.

And attacked.

HOPE YOU ENJOYED THE RIDE! Please leave a review HERE and join my newsletter to be informed when RUIN (next in series) is up for release! Or follow me on AMAZON HERE

ACKNOWLEDGMENTS

I wanted to say a huge 'thank you' to all the readers who have supported me by reading my books. This author journey of mine wouldn't be possible without you, neither would it mean as much. There is nothing like receiving a review or an email from someone who has really enjoyed one of my books!

Being an indie author is a multi-faceted career of being a small business manager, cover designer, formatter, marketer, editor, writer, accountant, social media manager, mailing list manager, graphic designer, and all round multi-tasker! All my love to all other indie authors out there! You are awesome. Don't give up! This is a crazy thing we do but it's so worth it when someone enjoys all the words!

Because I want to provide more ways to obtain my books and make it financially viable for me to continue to produce them, including audiobooks, I have started a Patreon. To my new Patreon supporters, I thank you from the bottom of my heart. My platform is very new and I have only two supporters, but hopefully more will join us for exclusive content and early access to ebooks, and signed paperbacks. You definitely get a mention here as you are the first to sign up to support me. I appreciate it so much.

Supporters:

J Soderberg

Rhianne Roynon.

A special mention to Nic Page who has done a fabulous job of copy editing Wrecked. I appreciate your time and eagle eyed attention to detail!

RUIN

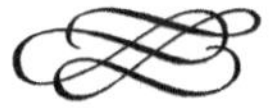

KAREN TOMLINSON

RUIN

SHADOW SENTINELS

CHAPTER 1

MUSIC CARESSED MY SENSES, drifting up the wide, curved staircase from the far end of the plush ballroom where the string quartet played. Goosebumps erupted over my exposed shoulders and arms as tears pricked my eyes. The notes were strung together in a hauntingly beautiful melody, calling to me, making me want to glide down the glittering marble steps and into the arms of the violinist. I grunted and shook off the grip of the music. I'd been in Faerie long enough to know the music was as beautiful as it was dangerous and alluring. It could lull and hypnotise a person who had human blood in their veins. And thanks to my father being a shifter, I had plenty of human DNA zipping around my body. Shifters are essentially human hosts with a symbiont spirit. In other words, shifters without their animal spirits are utterly human.

Blinking rapidly, I cleared the burn of tears from my eyes as the music released its grip on my emotions. My mind was stronger now. It had been a case of sink or swim in this strange world without my mate. I lifted my chin and inhaled deeply. I'd promised myself and Connor that I would be strong. Walker had developed a challenging new training regimen for me. But with the help of my new friends...or team...or whatever the hell they were, I'd become physically and mentally stronger. Carrying two wolf spirits was a huge battle for my body and my mind every damn day, but I'd learned to cope.

It was better than the alternative, and being without either was unthinkable. The ebony wolf that challenged me every day was Connor's, the most powerful Prime alpha I'd ever heard of, and, coincidentally, my lost mate's animal spirit. The growl inside my head told me Connor's wolf knew I was thinking about the man we both had lost. My own wolf stirred, sending a soothing wave of comfort through me, reaching out to him. She was my saviour, the only reason I had been able to get a handle at all on his power and aggression.

His growl settled to a grumble, the need to let him burst through my skin and shift, to give him freedom, receded. I exhaled and fisted my shaking hands. Controlling him would be impossible without her. They had connected in a way that I had never thought possible, even though I'd hoped for it.

My first wolf spirit had always seen Connor's wolf as her mate. But she had been killed when I was barely eighteen and had returned to the Mother Wolf to be reborn. So much had happened since her loss. I had lost Connor; I'd even thought him dead until I had been arrested and sent to a prison where, unbeknownst to me, he'd become the powerful alpha Prime—the King of Shifters in that fucked up and violent place. Even when Connor and I had found each other again after so many years, we hadn't been able to tell if the new wolf spirit I housed could be a potential mate for his Prime. My fingers ran gently over the scarred skin around my neck; a cruel reminder of the silver collars that had been locked around our necks in the prison. It had held back our wolves, preventing a shift, and by imprisoning their spirits, kept them from knowing if they were mates.

Rolling my shoulders, I uncurled my fists. I'd only been in that shithole of a prison for a matter of weeks, Connor and his pack had been there for over four years. Running my fingers through the frost that covered the carved bannister in front of me, I hoped the shifters, who had become as much my family as they were Connor's, had managed to escape. According to Walker, the prison was located in the wilds of Canada. All the prisoners there had been shifters, mainly wolf shifters, but surviving in the wilderness, hunted by the demon guards that worked for the prison warden, or rather the demon, Berith, would be near impossible.

This time it was Connor's wolf, Prime, who sent a wave of reassurance through me. I could feel his belief in his pack, that they were alive; that Owen would lead them as he had promised Connor he would, and that Stone would stand by his side.

My throat ached and I tried to swallow away the lump of emotion. I missed them all, but I missed Connor so much it hurt. Connor had been connected to his brothers; he'd been able to *feel* them. Maybe his wolf could still feel that connection.

Below me in the elegant ballroom of Walker's palace, a sea of well dressed fae mingled. I tried not to scowl. I'd been brought here to Faerie to train and to prove myself trustworthy. I wasn't sure what Walker, a.k.a. The High King of Faerie, would do with me if he thought I wasn't. After all, I couldn't be killed, but that didn't mean I couldn't spend an eternity in a cage somewhere. I scanned the crowd below looking for anything suspicious. Not only was Walker here tonight, but his heir, B'nar, the tall, stoic fae who was my babysitter, or gaoler, depending on how you looked at my situation, was by his side.

Part of my *training* was to work an undercover security detail with my new 'colleagues'. It had been weeks since I was brought here, and holding back the other spirit that inhabited my body had taken every ounce of my self-control. I'd already proved to Walker that I could control my phoenix; that I could summon her and send her away at will, yet he still wouldn't commit to finding Connor.

Prime rumbled inside me, his discontent affecting me just as it always did, by feeding my own worry and anger for my mate. Taking a slow, deep breath, I let go of the heat that burned through my veins. The beautiful ice crystals that coated the bannister in front of me melted away. I swallowed and concentrated on my breathing. Losing my shit now would not help my cause.

Taking another long slow breath, I calmed my phoenix. Reluctantly she settled, curling into that place in my soul where she slumbered. Prime huffed when my own wolf, who I'd named Mea, moved to stand guard over my phoenix. He seemed to find it amusing that I needed her to keep the fire in my soul calm, though I could sense his respect for both of those spirits.

My chest ached as I pictured Connor's beautiful face, his burning blue eyes staring down at me. When we had broken the shifters free of the warden's prison, Berith had captured me intending to steal my phoenix. Connor had tried to save my human soul by killing me first. What he hadn't realised was that by killing me, he would lose his wolf. I hid my bitterness from the spirits inside me. My phoenix always demanded a life for a life when my physical self was killed. Without exception, she took the life of my killer—or their shifter spirit—before gifting me back my body. My phoenix had taken Connor's wolf in payment. My stomach clenched as a wave of guilt hit me. *I* had taken Prime, leaving Connor human—and broken. Before I could save Connor from Berith's wrath, Walker had grabbed me and pulled me into a portal, bringing me here—to Faerie.

I lingered at the top of the curving white marble staircase, just watching the crowd of flamboyantly dressed guests below. I was reluctant to join their frivolous party despite my purpose. My heart ached so much, I wasn't sure I could be Walker's spy among his own kind tonight. Connor's wolf grumbled in agreement. He was a part of me now, but he missed his true human vessel as much as I did.

King L'nar, or Walker as I knew him, had organised this ball to officially acknowledge his eldest son as his heir. All the royal fae castes from each of the Faerie kingdoms were here, along with selected families of the high fae. All were dressed in their finery, ready to suck up to the Winter King and the prince heir himself. I pressed my lips into a thin line, my brow furrowed at the sight of all the pomp and circumstance. It was a dark expression I'd adopted almost permanently these past eight weeks. Part of me knew Connor was likely dead. I'd only gotten a brief look at him before Walker had dragged me into the portal. He'd been bloodied and battered, and looked so broken. I swallowed hard. Gods, so broken. I resisted the urge to rub my face with my hands, my heart beating hard and fast against my chest wall. This was all such a mess! I just wanted, no I *needed*, to know if he was alive, or if his soul had been taken to Hell instead of mine.

This whole *'training until Prince B'nar thought I was ready'* was now irrelevant. I'd made sure I was in control of Fire, and become a good enough fighter to take on even the strongest of opponents. I'd learned how to use fae weaponry and fight like them. I had no way back to Connor without the compliance of my phoenix, or Fire as I'd named her when I was a little girl, so I'd beseeched her to help me, to work with me. Together, we'd worked day in and day out to gain control. Walker had shown me the ways he used to summon his magic and together with B'nar and Blue, my human best friend, we'd figured out which ways worked best for me and Fire. Now, I could call her at will. I hadn't fully shifted into the fiery version of big bird yet, at least that's what I presumed would happen. To be honest, the thought of giving myself over wholly to a creature of fire and destruction, frightened me. I squeezed my eyes shut, remembering the fire that had consumed my parents. No matter Walker's intention in bringing me here, there was no way I would risk setting fire to this beautiful place. Gods, this was the winter kingdom and this palace was made mainly from ice and wood with a bit of metal and stone thrown in. I didn't think it would fare well against my phoenix.

Prime huffed, his thoughts making me smile. *Yeah, always good to know I could cause some damage if I needed to,* I agreed.

Now that I had better control of Fire, I needed to find a way back to Earth to begin the search for Connor. I swallowed hard, my fists curling so tightly my newly polished nails scored my palms. The problem was that Walker held the key to forming a portal—a ring that he never took off. I'd asked around, but it seemed that it was one of a kind. There were obviously other ways to summon a portal. Som, the drug dealer that I'd worked with for years, could open them. Granted, he hadn't been able to open and close them instantly, he'd had to keep them open, and closed them only when Blue and I had returned home. I knew he was from Orth, the dark faerie realm, where the shadow fae and the monsters of Faerie lived. Maybe if tonight's plan went to shit, I could get there and find out from the shadow fae how to summon a portal. Shadow fae were dangerous, unpredictable creatures, prone to betrayal. They didn't make bargains because they, too, couldn't lie, but they did twist words and circumstances to serve themselves. No matter, I'd risk anything right now to get back to Connor.

My stomach clenched as I tried, unsuccessfully, to dampen my fear for him. I took a deep breath and exhaled slowly, determined to control my anxiety and keep a clear head; my current plan relied on it.

Walker lifted his attention to my face. The High King of Faerie, narrowed his blue green eyes. He stoically studied me, then in a minute movement only I would see, cocked his head expectantly. That tiny gesture spoke volumes. He wanted me down there, just where I promised I would be. I was to mingle and listen for any rumblings of dissension or treasonous acts. I stared right back at the icy cold fucker. Little did he know that the biggest treasonous act tonight was going to come from me and my small band of friends.

Frigid air fanned my cheeks, rising from the open doors to the palace's frost covered grounds. The air in the world of Faerie was the purest I'd ever breathed, but here in Walker's kingdom it was amazing, as if it cleansed your soul. I huffed and looked away from him.

Yeah, the streets of London don't really compare.

An abundance of brightly coloured outfits and beautiful fae faces merged in the ballroom below. The last thing I wanted to do was mingle with these arrogant, entitled faeries. Opening my fingers, I deliberately stretched them, trying to get some of my tension to evaporate, then wiped my palms down the skirt of my stunning black gown. No matter my reluctance to join the guests below, I had no choice. Part of my training was to be able to socialise in high society and this was at least the fourth royal gala I'd attended. I conceded I could control my facial features better now and curb my tongue where I needed to. It didn't mean I wasn't envisaging how to break someone's neck if they pissed me off, though. And that happened frequently, seeing as I looked human and human flesh was sought after by the high fae...

Warm fingers curled around my own, giving them a squeeze. "You still with me?"

I turned to Blue and nodded, giving her a weak smile. "Yeah, sorry."

"Hey, we'll get him back."

My friend had never met Connor, but she knew how much he meant to me. She was already willing to dive into danger for him based just on that. And I loved her for it.

"Come on, we've been noticed." Blue tugged on my hand urging me to follow her as she turned to the stairs. My friend looked amazing. Her cheeks were flushed, her eyes glittering and her smile bright enough to give the crystal chandeliers a run for their money, even if much of that outward sparkle was an act.

I smiled and dipped my chin towards Prince B'nar. It hadn't escaped my notice that the prince's pale green gaze hadn't left Blue since we'd walked through the gold gilt doors and stopped at the top of the staircase to survey the room below. "Well, *you've* been noticed. In fact, I don't think B'nar has eyes for anyone or anything other than you."

Blue swung back to me, the floating sea green material of her dress shimmering with hundreds of tiny crystals. She swallowed hard and inhaled deeply. The skin between her brows creased and her eyes lost some of their shine. "B'nar is a twatwaffle of the highest degree. He can look all he wants but I will never give him my name so I can become his human plaything."

I burst out laughing, though I understood her concern. According to the laws of Faerie, if a fae discovered your name they could keep you as their property. Hence the prince that watched Blue now was known simply as *Prince Heir* or B'nar. Only his father knew his name, his mother having gone to the Beyond when he was a boy. But with his kind of magic, B'nar could command my friend's body to do as he wished. She was his prisoner, she was also fully human, which made her susceptible to faerie magic. I didn't bring up that sore subject though. B'nar had never hurt Blue like many believed he should, for being one of the people who had helped kill his youngest brother, but it didn't mean he wouldn't. The fae were vicious and uncompromising when they needed to be. "A twatwaffle?" I said instead, laughing out loud. "What the hell is a twatwaffle?"

My best friend humphed and crossed her arms over her chest. "An idiot, an arse, an arrogant, miserable fuck who won't ever treat me with anything other than disdain and coldness..."

"Whoa!" I put my hands up and shook my head.

B'nar had been given Blue as his property after he vowed to his father he could change Blue's outlook on life, and pointed out that she would be useful to the unit of specialists Walker had put together to investigate the corruption of the SBI back on Earth. According to Blue, she was to atone for working with Som, the disavowed fae I had considered a friend, and me for dealing the drugs that killed B'nar's brother. That meant Blue had been sentenced to a lifetime of belonging to B'nar—her only alternative being death. I wondered if my own incarceration here was much different. I was under Walker's thumb, my existence dependent on his favour, and my ability to get back to my own world resting, literally, on his hand.

"I get it." I stepped up and prised her arms from across her chest. Taking her hands in mine, I kissed her cheek. "Just don't let him ruin your night, my lovely friend. Ignore him, but don't get yourself into hot water with any of those other beautiful males down there just to get your own back, either.

They will flock to you like flies to honey, but they are likely far more dangerous than even the 'twatwaffle'. Lesser fae can become addicted to human pheromones and you know as well as I do that if they get a chance to take you, they will cage you to keep you as theirs alone. And you don't deserve to be caged, not by him or anyone else, you are a beautiful butterfly who needs the freedom to fly." I dramatically opened my arms, keeping the grin on my face.

Blue giggled. "So very poetic of you."

"I have my moments." I looked down at the crowd again. "But, just be careful...please? B'nar gives you a lot of freedom when he doesn't have to. Don't throw that in his face too much or he just might revoke it, and then where would you be?"

Blue's eyes hardened. "I know. Don't worry, I'll do my job for these royal pains. If only so I can stay with you."

"I know you will. Besides, we need Walker to be exhausted and able to sleep soundly by the end of the night. That's your main job."

Blue kissed my cheek and winked. "He will be."

We both looked at the King. Walker was in deep conversation with a petite fae who had hair like the sun and delicate wings fluttering at her back. Summer fae, I guessed.

"Are you coming, Yell?" Blue had her foot on the top step and was looking back at me, wisps of rich auburn curls framing her face. I could see why B'nar wouldn't want her flirting with other males. Prisoner my arse. My friend was stunning, and something told me B'nar thought so too, or she'd be dead by now.

"No, not yet. You go and have a good time. Find a nice summer fae lord to dance you around the room and make B'nar just a little bit jealous."

Blue rolled her eyes. "Yeah, that's not gonna happen. At least, not for the right reasons. I'm just his little human pet." Lifting her chin, she elegantly descended the curved steps into the ballroom. B'nar didn't take his eyes off her, but Blue ignored him and was soon surrounded by fae admirers. Humans in the world of fae were a novelty. I just hoped none were stupid enough to steal a possession of the royal family. Fae *did* covet human flesh, and some would do anything for it. Hopefully these High Fae were not so foolish and just wanted the pleasure of Blue's company and unique looks.

I glanced up. Far above my head, hanging from the vaulted ceiling, chandeliers of ice glinted, reflecting the light from the magical faerie candles that illuminated the royal ballroom. Frost lined the walls and prettily adorned the edges of the huge mirrors, the tables and the curtains. It was all done with Walker's power and was beautiful enough to steal my breath, but no matter the beauty of my surroundings, all the sparkle in the world couldn't erase the heartache and loneliness from me. The emptiness in my chest threatened to consume me every day that I lingered here in Faerie.

"You look beautiful."

I turned to the voice.

Alex looked ridiculously handsome in his formal attire, the fae silks shimmering in a way no earthly material ever could.

"Thanks." I peered at his eyes and raised a brow. "Really?" Today, one was coloured a deep burnt orange and one a deep forest green. Yesterday they'd been grey.

He shrugged and smirked. "What? I couldn't decide which colour complimented my outfit best, so I went with one of each."

I shook my head and chuckled. Alex's ability to change his appearance was really disconcerting to say the least. "You are so weird."

He grinned and winked. "You have no idea, but I'm having great fun playing while you find out."

Alex Blaze was a doppelganger, part of an ancient race of immortal shapeshifters who could take on another's form, right down to their mannerisms and voice. He didn't carry a spirit inside himself like me or other animal shifters, but he could assume the appearance of other humanoid forms. In between shape shifts, Alex liked to play with things like his hair and eye colour. I was sure he did it just to screw with my head.

He held out his arm and I took it. "Wanna come and dance with me? You know Walker wants you to be able to dance with the grace of a swan. Most of the time though, you just look like an elephant, but I'm sure I can change that." He winked down at me.

I rolled my eyes. "Yeah, well, Walker is nuts. Maybe when I'm fighting I can be graceful, but dancing? Not a chance in Hell. I'm more likely to break your toes. Even though I'm not anywhere near as heavy as an elephant, you cheeky arse."

Alex chuckled. "True. But yeah, your calling is definitely not grace and poise on the dance floor."

"Well, don't you two look cozy? What are you going to do when you see Connor again? Strike up a threesome?"

Me and Alex looked at Lance who had just arrived with Ava on his arm. Ava looked amazing as always; slim, tall and blonde. It wasn't difficult to understand what Connor had seen in Ava. I gritted my teeth at the stab of jealousy and pushed that useless thought away. She was with Lance now.

Lance's ice blue shirt set off the deep brown of his hair and eyes. Tall and muscular, he looked amazing too—the bastard. He grinned when he saw me looking.

My eyes narrowed. "Fuck off." I didn't bother with names. Even when my fellow shifters were being utter dicks, we didn't use names in the open. Prince

B'nar and King L'nar Voltair, which I'd discovered meant *son of Voltair*, knew all of our names, except Blue's. But unlike Blue, none of us were totally human, so fae compulsions and mind trick games didn't work as easily on us.

Lance gave a smug smile and pulled Ava closer. "Already done that. I just need to refuel before going again."

Ava rolled her eyes. "Mother Wolf, lover boy, stick a sock in it." She gave me a smile. "Sorry, Yellow, he's still learning how to play nice with the other children. Besides a threesome with this stud..." She lowered her gaze down Alex's body and back up again. "...and Connor sounds off the charts. Daayum, girl..." She fanned her face while winking at me. "I'd totally hit that."

Lance's brows dipped comically, his jaw muscles popping and his eyes darkening. "What does that mean...?"

Ava patted his cheek and smiled sweetly. Yeah, Lance knew her and Connor had been lovers once, and he looked furious that his words had backfired.

I smirked, knowing she wasn't trying to hurt me, only wind Lance up.

Ava smiled placatingly. "Nothing at all, lover. They might be hot, but you're more than enough for me. Besides one of them shot me before, so, yeah, that could be awkward." She winked at me again, letting me know there was no venom in her words. "Now come along, we need to mingle and pick up the juicy goss on who's shagging who, who's planning to overthrow Walker, and who's going to attempt to kill B'nar..." Their voices faded as she pulled him towards the stairs.

I gave her a small smile. Ava had our backs. Her past relationship with Connor was just that—past, though I had no idea why she had forgiven Connor so readily.

"Come on, we need to do the same: mingle and all that. I know Lance is an ass, but we're all a team now." Alex pursed his lips as he glanced at my face.

I tried to smile, but being reminded by Lance that I was here, living it up while Connor was likely being tortured or might even be dead, did not help my mood. Just like Ava, Lance had a reason to hate Connor. Connor had shot both him and Ava after Doherty had accused them of being traitors; only Walker's magic had saved them. But Lance, the bastard, knew how much I missed Connor, so suggesting that Alex and I were a thing was cruel.

"Are we a team?" I supposed we were, though at times like this I wasn't so sure.

Walker had brought us all together. He'd been training the others for years, along with Zander. Together they'd been spying on the upper levels of authority in the SBI. That was how Walker had found the prison. Even Connor and Owen had worked for him, albeit unknowingly. We all had different skills that he deemed useful not only to infiltrate the SBI, but to fight Berith, a general of Hell who seemed determined to unleash Hell's army on the unsuspecting people of Earth. Walker was also a ruler who planned for the future. He knew the demon of murder and chaos would not stop at one world, and he was honest enough to admit he didn't want Faerie to be next. By putting us in position to fight Berith on Earth, he was protecting Faerie.

"Yes, we are. It's new and a little fraught, I know that. But I have always been a loner, and finding a tribe to belong to is a novelty for me; one that I hope won't wear off. Besides, we all have a common purpose, don't we? Stopping Berith..." He led me to the stairs and we began a slow descent, smiling politely and dipping our heads with our right hand palm down and flat over our chests as was the custom formal greeting in this society. "And finding Connor. You're not alone in that, Yell." He glanced sideways at me. "I was alone when I met Connor; surviving hand to mouth and trying to stay under the SBI's radar. He should have killed me, but he didn't. Instead he gave me purpose in my life. I really do believe we can all work together to find him. He's alive, I know it."

I swallowed the ache in my throat, hoping he was right. "How did you meet him?" Connor had been my closest friend when we were growing up together, but then he'd moved out of our home, the one we'd shared with Cain and Lyss Rawson, two shifters who had become like parents to us. When Connor had graduated at eighteen from the SBI academy, he'd become an agent for the Supernatural Bureau of Investigation, often going undercover for weeks at a time. The higher up the SBI ranks he went, the more we'd grown apart. It was as if he'd deliberately put distance between us.

Alex glanced down at me. I was only five foot four to his six foot frame. "Connor discovered my rare skill set when he was undercover. We came to a mutual agreement about my need to continue breathing. If I wanted to, then it was in exchange for my help. I didn't mind, I actually liked the guy, even though he was a tough son-of-a-bitch. I helped him, and in turn he kept my skill set hidden from the SBI."

I smiled. "Sounds like Connor. He always gets what he wants. Which was what with you?"

Alex patted my hand. "You. Safe. He convinced the school board he needed an undercover agent in the school, telling them it was classified agency business. No one ever questioned it, not when he was a top agent. For me, it was a win win. I stayed alive and got a regular job, money and a home. All I had to do in return was keep you safe and out of trouble at school."

My footsteps faltered as his words registered. "Me?"

"Of course. He always knew you were his mate, and after that boy attacked you when you were only a young girl, he didn't trust the school to keep you safe."

"Mother Wolf, is that why no one ever bothered me after that?"

Alex's generous lips curved upward. "I think it had more to do with how hard you worked to stay under the radar. It was only that last day that I needed to save your skinny arse."

"I never did thank you for that. I always wondered why Shannon and the others had no memory of me punching her."

"It wasn't just the punch, it was the burn you left on her skin. Explaining that would have been difficult, so I got rid of it, wiped everyone's minds, and then called Connor."

"You called Connor?" My eyes widened at this newest revelation.

"Sure did, sugar."

To his surprise, I reached up and kissed his cheek. Alex had gotten me out of a lot of trouble with Doherty, the director of the SBI, that day. Shannon was his daughter. Heat churned in my belly, my nostrils flaring. That bastard had gone after my foster family. Remembering Lyss's beautiful smile, I felt heat roll over my skin. Mea growled, the sound echoing in my mind. Prime sent a soothing wash of alpha power through us and she settled, but Fire didn't listen to him. Lyss had been cruelly dismembered and it had utterly destroyed Rawson. The air around me began to shimmer.

"Hey, hey, settle down, it's okay." Alex squeezed my arm in a reassuring fashion. "Now's not the time to become a flaming candle. You'll melt Walker's decorations and he'll be well pissed at you."

I glanced at the high fae king. His pale blue face was as stoic as ever and his silky white hair was starkly beautiful next to the turquoise blue of his son's. "Fucker deserves it." And he did. Apparently, I was the key to Hell's gates, so Satan needed the phoenix that resided inside me to open them. How they would pull Fire, my phoenix, from me, I didn't know, but once she was released they could chain her to the gates and turn them to ash. Earth would become a buffet of flesh and souls for Satan and his army.

I glanced away from Walker and B'nar, and studied some of the other angular, almost androgenous faces of the high fae. They were all beautiful and all deadly in their own way.

"Hey, come on. Let's get through this night and then, if Blue plays her part well, we'll find Connor. After all, I owe him. He's been a prisoner for four years because of Walker. Poor bugger didn't even know who he was working for. He did what Walker wanted and found out who the warden really is, and what Doherty was up to. It's time to get him out of there."

I kept my mouth shut but gripped Alex's arm tighter. It was nice to know we were on the same page, even if we both knew Connor might already be dead.

CHAPTER 2

onnor

SHIVERS RACKED MY BODY. I hugged my knees tighter as tears burned behind my eyes. Having the ability to tense my muscles was both a miracle and a curse. Berith was one sick motherfucker. He'd give me the use of my body, only to rip it from me whenever he felt like it. He'd broken my neck three times since I'd become his prisoner. The last time was a haze. Whether my brain, or the dark creature that clung to my soul had blocked it out, or I'd genuinely been too out of it to comprehend what was happening, was debatable. The pain though? That stayed with me.

A rocking motion began to make me feel nauseous. Yeah, I found I did this a lot lately. Rocking back and forth, sitting on my boney arse while praying for this nightmare to end.

I had no idea how long I'd been stuck in this cycle of depraved living and dying. That moment when Ember had been ripped away from me was vivid, the shit storm of pain since then, not so much. I blocked it out, not willing to give my brain the chance to reduce me to useless tears and hopelessness. Berith had said he would make me suffer for an eternity. I swallowed, not sure if he meant here or in Hell, but I did know he meant it.

My heart pounded at the sound of a door slamming in the distance and I gripped my lower legs tighter, laying my cheek on my knees and straining my ears as I shuddered uncontrollably. I was no longer a Prime, no longer even a shifter. I was completely and utterly human…and very breakable. My emaciated body started to tremble harder, and I had no say in it. Stopping it was impossible when I was so weak. Food was provided, usually a husk of bread or dry crackers, or something disgusting and unidentifiable, along with water to drink. It was enough to keep me alive, but slowly starving. And may the Mother Wolf damn me for accepting it, but I didn't want to die. I wanted to find a way back to my Firecracker. So I took whatever was offered and forced it down my throat, no matter how disgusting or rotten it was. My large frame was nothing but skin and bone, now, but I'd be damned if I'd give up. My Firecracker, *my mate*, was out there, somewhere, and I'd find a way back to her. Somehow.

I listened to the screams and roars that were muffled by the metal door and the thick stone walls of my prison. Those terrible sounds were constant and a sign that I wasn't the only one being kept here. I wondered who else was unfortunate enough to have Berith as their new cell buddy. I looked down at my bloodied hands and thin legs. My gaolers didn't even bother with shackles any more. I was too human and too weak to escape, and that was the horribly pathetic truth. Outside this prison was miles of forest. Even if a miracle happened and I got out, I'd die in that wilderness. I could only hope Owen had gotten the rest of my brothers away from here, that they weren't the ones being tortured. I searched for any connection to them, but my wolf was gone. And the piece of me that could connect with the alpha wolves, the ones who had pledged their allegiance, had gone with him.

I suspected Ember had taken Prime from me. She'd told me how she had taken the wolf of her previous murderer. It was why she still housed a wolf spirit when Doherty had sent his team to kill her. When he'd slammed the head of her first wolf in front of me, I'd thought she was dead.

The loss of Prime left an empty hole in my chest, but that would never change the way I felt about her. I lifted my head and straightened my spine. Maybe Zander would find a way to help me out of this personal fucking hell and back to her before Berith's darkness consumed me. If not, I would do it myself. I hadn't seen anything of Zander, though, and wondered if he was dead, or if he'd just run. It didn't matter. My body might be ruined, but my soul still belonged to her. I'd find a way back to her—somehow.

I unwound my hands from my knees and slowly rubbed my eyes. They didn't bother with lights in the cell. Unless, of course, they wanted to torture me by leaving them on, night after night, to burn my eyes while Berith commanded my eyelids to stay open. I blinked and forced away thoughts of what my next session of torture would hold. Sometimes it was twisted nightmares of my past, others it was physical torture and pain, until I couldn't take any more and I shut down and passed out; only for that demon fucker to bring me back. Yeah, and in the torturous virtual reality that Berith created in my head, my bastard father always played a starring role. Just like my real life had been with him, these nightmares were full of beatings and verbal lashings of never being strong enough, or fast enough, or vicious enough; only in Berith's version, my father always found new and interesting ways of hurting me, which is saying something; my father was one sick son-of-a-bitch. When Berith decided he'd tortured me enough, he'd put the pieces of my mortal flesh and bones back together, leaving me some injuries as a present. Sometimes I was still paralysed when I woke up, not able to eat or drink. The only thing my body was capable of was blinking, shitting and pissing all over myself. Even if I died in the aftermath, that fucker would resurrect me.

I shuddered and rocked, my feet numb with cold. Berith had taken great pleasure in telling me how he'd resurrected my brothers. Reed's and Dagnar's souls were stuck inside the monstrous werewolves Berith had commanded them to become before they were killed in the fight rings. There had been no gentle passing of their wolf spirits to the Mother Wolf to be reborn. Instead, every shifter that had died in Berith's vicious games had had their human and shifter souls imprisoned, their bodies stuck as Werewolves ready to host a demon and become a soldier in Satan's army.

I swallowed the bile in my throat, hoping that once I found my brothers, I could find a way to bring them back. Hugging my knees again, I dug my filthy, jagged fingernails into the skin of my forearms. Pain zipped down to my elbows. At least that told me this wasn't a dream. Not this time.

I heard another scream. A moment later, a faint tingle of power brushed my skin. This time a single tear slipped from my right eye. I wasn't a pussy, my tears weren't for my broken and starved body or my empty heart, they were for the part of my soul that had belonged to my wolf. That mild brush of power meant Berith was still torturing my kind. I had been their Prime, the top of the power tree and the one who was supposed to have protected them —and I failed. I missed my wolf every waking moment. In the darkness, as I lay waiting for my turn to scream, I searched for his spirit. My only comfort was that my Firecracker would take care of him; at least of that I was certain.

I released my legs, tipped back my head and let out a roar, emptying my grief into the darkness. Or it would have been a roar if I hadn't been so weak. Now it sounded more like a pathetic cry for help. I dropped my forehead back down on my knees, my body shaking from that one sad action. I'd rest for a moment, then I'd check the door for weaknesses—again.

"Shh, it's alright, Connor. I'm going to get you out of here."

"Ember?" I swallowed against my painfully dry throat and tried to turn my head. Thankfully it moved, which was a fucking miracle. I'd been convinced

Berith was going to break my spine again. He usually started with the lower part of my body and broke me in segments as his minions cheered him on. This time, I'd been dragged to that ridiculously out of place plush room he used and thrown at his feet in front of the ugly assed fireplace that dominated the room.

Nothing else had been different, though. He'd gone into a place in my mind that he seemed to be obsessed with. The first time I'd comforted Ember after she'd lost control of her fire. Her flames hadn't burned me and even as a teenager I'd known then that we were potential mates.

The room was dark apart from the fire which burned beside me, sending shadows dancing around the walls. I blinked. Each shadow took form as a grotesque werewolf.

Cool hands brushed my sweat soaked hair back from my face. Slowly, with my heart pounding, I peered up into the face of my beloved Firecracker. Uncontrollable shivering racked my body. I wanted to reach out, to touch her, but I'd fallen into that trap too many times to count. I jerked away from her touch.

"Connor? It's me, your Firecracker. Let us help you."

Another figure stepped from the shadows, his eyes glowing brighter than the fire. "Zander? You came back for me?" I squeezed my eyes shut. Berith had never used Zander before. Hope sparked in my chest. Fuck, maybe this *was* real. My gaze flew back to Ember's beautiful green eyes. My heart flipped and tears came unbidden, falling down my cheeks. I forced my weak arm to lift so that I could touch her face. "Firecracker? Oh, Mother Wolf, I—how?"

"Hush now. Zander, come on. Help me get him up." She beckoned the big guard who had become my partner in the fucked up world of Berith's prison.

Zander strode over, his shoulders as wide as ever. Together they heaved me up and leaned me against the soft cushions of the huge sofa.

Ember kneeled next to me and leaned in placing a gentle kiss against my lips. I frowned, her lips were cold, they'd always been so warm. My gaze flicked to the fire. Why wasn't she warm when the flames scorched my skin? Worry for her had me trying to push myself up.

"Just lay still, Connor." She smiled and turned to Zander. "And watch."

Watch? Watch what? Zander stepped up to her and slipped his arm around her waist, yanking her up and in close enough to him that her hips were moulded against his.

"What are you doing?" My voice was no more than a whisper, but the nausea that overtook me was intense.

"Saving you. I'm letting you go, Connor. You are just a weak shell of what you once were. You cannot protect me." Ember laughed coldly. "Damn, look at you. You can't even protect *yourself*. So I think it best if you stay here and I will fight this war without you." Her hand lifted and brushed Zander's square jaw. I honestly didn't think I had any heart left to shatter, but the pain I felt as she leaned in and took Zander's mouth told me otherwise. It destroyed me. *Zander and my Firecracker?* I stared on in horror as she unbuttoned his shirt and trailed that beautiful mouth down his torso, shaking my head as her slender fingers unbuckled his belt. "No. No. We were becoming *friends*, Zander! This is all wrong! I won't watch this." But there was no choice. My eyelids were forced open.

"But you must, my love. It's time for us to say goodbye. You are useless, a dead man, and I am the key. I want better, I *deserve* better." Her strong shoulders shrugged as she turned back to Zander. "Besides, you have given me what I need to know." And she pulled Zander's head down. His eyes met mine just before he gripped her and their mouths and bodies met.

Not real. Not real. It is not real... But telling myself that as I was forced to watch the love of my life fuck my frenemie, just wasn't working. With each touch, each kiss and each thrust I died a little more inside until there was nothing left. I didn't care about my life anymore, not even when I was left staring at an empty room, my eyeballs dry and scorched from the heat of the fire.

Berith's perfect features filled my vision. He smiled smoothly. "Did you enjoy the show? I thought you'd appreciate one last night with your lover, even if it was only to watch her leave you. Now? You're done. But you have at least given me something useful. And just so you know, *Prime.* There will be no coming back from this one." His head cocked and I froze, waiting. The crack of my neck was loud in my ears. All I could do was watch Berith smile as I gasped for breath, my mouth opening and closing like a fish out of water. Yet even as I suffocated, unable to move my chest to drag air into my lungs, I could only think of Ember. Real or not, that scene with Zander had finally broken me. Tears began to fall in earnest onto my hot cheeks, turning to steam from the heat of those infernal flames. Ember was my everything. That stupid organ in my chest that slowly ceased to beat actually healed a little at the realisation that, although once again Berith had used her to hurt me, she wasn't anywhere near him. I could only hope that she stayed away and didn't try to find me.

Berith smiled, his eyes consumed with the burning forms of lost souls. "That's it, die for me, human. Die."

I screamed as those tortured souls dragged me into the darkness.

CHAPTER 3

mber

I sat on the edge of my bed, my restless legs bouncing. The ridiculously ornate gold clock ticked away patiently. I peered at it where it sat on the mantelpiece. *Three am. Time to go...*

Nerves bubbled in my belly. I hoped I was strong enough to do this, not just getting the portal, but dealing with what I might find on the other side. Briefly, I closed my eyes, it was worth the risk, *Connor* was worth the risk. Prime rumbled in agreement though I could feel Mea's anxiety. Prime, sensing her worry, turned his big head, nudging her gently and sending waves of reassurance through us both. As a Prime alpha, he was powerful enough to control other alpha shifters, and such softness and sympathy from such a mighty and bloodthirsty creature had tears burning my eyes.

An ache developed in my throat. Mine and Connor's wolves were becoming close. I could feel the bond between them strengthening. They were potential mates. I swiped a tear from beneath my eye. I had been scared to tell Connor how I truly felt, worried that our wolves would reject each other. It was ironic that they'd found each other and become close, when we were forced to be apart. Prime had made no move to mate with Mea and I wondered if he wanted to wait until Connor had returned—or we knew he had gone to the afterlife. A pain jabbed at my chest and I rubbed my right palm over my heart. It was too painful to think about what would happen to us all if that had happened. Swallowing hard, I hoped Connor heard my whispered plea, the one I sent to him every damned night. *Hold on, my love. Please. I'm coming for you.*

Fire flared, her heat burning through my belly, her soul just waiting to burst free at my command. I jumped up and paced across the room and back again, chewing on the soft skin of my bottom lip. Three-o-five... My soft leather boots made no sound on the woven rug. I rubbed my sweaty palms down the material of my faerie armour-coated thighs. Besides this one, I had three more suits of faerie armour hanging in my closet, along with boots, and many other every day and frivolous items that Walker had deemed necessary for me.

I grabbed my hair tie and quickly plaited my bright red hair, letting it hang down my back. My mouth was dry and my heart beating hard against my ribs. Was I really doing this? I hoped Walker and B'nar would understand and not come after us before I'd found Connor. Blue and Alex were part of my plan and were meeting me outside the King's quarters, but Lance and Ava? Well, I couldn't risk them destroying the only chance I had at getting back to the prison by snitching on me to B'nar or Walker. I had no idea where their loyalties really laid but I doubted very much they were to me, or to the man who had tried to kill them.

I swallowed down a glass of water, then dead on a quarter past three, carefully opened my bedroom door and crept down the dark, shadowy corridors of the vast palace towards King L'nar's personal space.

My warm breath formed small clouds as I moved through the darkness. The palace was viciously cold, as the home of the Winter King should be. Only certain rooms were kept warm for mortals like us. The Winter King and the Prince Heir had no need for warmth, their blood ran as cold as the ice that coated their kingdom.

The corridors were quiet, no guards. Walker preferred all of his soldiers on guard outside of his home—all except his Ice Sentinels. When I'd asked why, he had laughed and told me if his enemy got past the army who guarded his home then they deserved the chance of a one on one battle with him before they died.

Silently, I slipped in behind the large statue of a past king who fought an ugly beast that seemed caught between a bug with multiple spindly legs and an obese woman. The plaque said it was the Bogwart queen. Urgh, she was one ugly-assed fae, even uglier than Somnelaire.

Blue and Alex both jumped at my soundless arrival.

"Jeez!" Blue placed a hand on her heart. "You bloody scared me."

"Me too," Alex grumbled.

I grinned briefly. "Sorry. Right, the Digitalis should have worked by now and he should be sleeping like a baby. How about the handsome prince? Did he get his dose too?"

Blue grimaced. "Dick prince, more like."

I just raised my brows, there was no time for Blue's snark, no matter how justified it might be.

"Fine, yes, he's out. I checked just now. Though that summer fae he was shagging asked me for double to keep her mouth shut."

I rolled my eyes. "Who cares? So long as he's out of our way, it doesn't matter how much you gave her." I peered at Alex through the dark. "You ready, princey?"

"As I'll ever be. Give me a moment."

I gritted my teeth, trying my best to be patient. Now my plan was in motion, my heart was hammering in my chest. I had to swallow down my fear at the thought of being caught. I doubted Walker would be very forgiving of me drugging him and his son and stealing his prized portal ring. I blew out a steadying breath from between my teeth. *It will be fine,* I told myself as Alex's face morphed into B'nar's and his body lengthened and became broader.

Blue gaped up at him. "Wow."

"Yeah, wow. You sure about this?" Cementing myself onto Walker's hit list was one thing, but putting Blue and Alex there too didn't sit well. Alex peered down at me from a familiar icy visage; one that made me swallow hard. Blue poked his cheek, something she would never dare do to B'nar. "That's one hell of a party trick, mister."

Alex squared his shoulders, taking on the air of one born into power and privilege. Arrogance and entitlement dripped from him. "Get off me, human. You are my pet, nothing more." The disdain in his voice was believable even if the pitch was a little high. "Now move from my path. I have work to do."

Blue swallowed hard, and even shuffled back a step. "Here." She passed him a taser. "It's set to stun. Killing the High King of the fae, and starting a war with Faerie would be too much to deal with on top of a demon invasion, so try to get out without doing that."

Alex lifted his chin and huffed. "Out of my way, before I turn you into a human popsicle."

Blue quirked her brows. "Really? B'nar would never use a word like *popsicle.* I doubt he even knows what one is, it's beneath him."

Alex shrugged and stepped out into the dark corridor mimicking B'nar's elegant, prowling gait to a tee. The Ice Sentinels, nine foot tall warriors made only of ice, that lined either side of the moonlit corridor, creepily all turned their heads and watched his progress towards them.

One stepped directly in his path.

Alex crossed his arms, but we couldn't see his face. "I will speak with my father. Move from my path, sentinel."

I held my breath as the Ice Sentinel studied Alex, releasing it only when the giant walking ice sculpture stood back at his post.

"He did it," whispered Blue, her eyes wide and catching the moonlight.

We watched Alex walk straight in through a set of gleaming double doors without bothering to knock. "Father!" He yelled before closing the door.

Not normally given to superstition or prayers, I crossed my fingers, hoping the digitalis Blue had slipped into Walker's faerie wine had done the trick and the High King was sleeping like a baby—I gulped—alone, or we'd all be up shit's creek without a paddle.

The corridor was silent as the minutes ticked by. I tried not to bite the skin off the edge of my nails, which was a bad habit I'd started again whenever my thoughts were consumed by Connor and the impossible task of finding him.

Prime growled, his grief filtering into my own damaged heart. I curled my fists at the surge of power he released into me. Fire hissed and it was all I could do to hold her back, let alone soothe the Prime alpha wolf inside me. Sensing my struggles with both of the strong spirits, Mea enveloped Prime's spirit with her own, calming him. I uncurled my fists and panted gently. It was getting harder and harder to contain three powerful shifter spirits in my mortal body. Through no fault of their own, I felt like they were slowly consuming me. I hadn't dared shift into my wolf while in Faerie as I wasn't sure if Prime would push Mea aside. There was no hope of me controlling an alpha Prime. Even Fire and my own wolf together wouldn't be able to help me if he refused to let me change back.

Blue's fingers were cold as she grabbed my hand and squeezed. I pulled my attention to the heavy gilt doors that opened once again. Alex strolled out purposefully and pulled the doors closed behind him. He didn't address the sentinels, it wasn't necessary. B'nar wouldn't bother.

Alex turned the corner where we were still crouched down behind the statue but he didn't stop, merely continued on without looking at us. I frowned but let him go, we were to meet down in the training cave, anyway. Maybe he just didn't want to bring attention down on us.

I grabbed Blue's wrist and we moved through the shadows, following Alex.

Alex led us to the training facility entrance in the king's library. There was one other entrance from B'nar's wing of the castle where we had all been given rooms, but this entrance was nearer to Walker's rooms. Alex opened it up with a touch of his hand and some whispered words that we had all learned. I darted across the library, Blue close on my heels, and we ran down the cold spiral stairs trying to catch him up.

"Hey, Alex...slow down!" I breathed heavily as I caught him up and clutched at his arm.

He peered down at where I touched his forearm and cocked a brow just like B'nar would. I giggled. "Bloody hell, you look so like B'nar it's creepy."

"Of course I look like him."

"Yeah, well, I didn't know you could do it so well. Anyway, you can change back now. Did you get it?"

Alex held up Walker's ring in a pincer grip between his thumb and forefinger. The milky blue stone glowed gently in the darkness of the cave. "I did. So how do you plan on getting it to work? Don't you need raw magic?"

I grinned. "Yeah." The snap of my fingers was sharp, and immediately I summoned enough flame to crackle along my forearm and hand, surrounding my limb in a soft cloak.

"Ember!" A deep voice yelled from the corridor.

My heart lurched and my head swung towards the door.

B'nar came barrelling in, breathless and dishevelled with blood trickling from his nose and mouth. "Don't tell him anything! That isn't me! It's the prince." Alex morphed back into himself. Well, almost. To keep his clothes fitting him, he had to remain B'nar's height.

"Fuck!" My curse only seemed to amuse what was clearly the real prince.

B'nar shrugged. "You didn't really think you could drug my father without me noticing, did you?"

Blue cursed and slapped her hand on the weapons cabinet. B'nar flicked his attention Blue's way and spoke with authority. "Stop." She did.

"Don't you fucking do it!" She screamed at him, her body frozen with her hand raised.

The snarl on his lips was vicious and my stomach clenched. He might not know her name to control her mind, but he could still use magic to control her body. Just like he had before.

"Then don't try running from me, human. You are mine, and I will never let you go." He growled, his nostrils flaring. "Now, kneel."

Tears lined my friends eyes as she had no choice but to do his bidding.

"Hey! Stop punishing her! This was my idea, not hers!" The wolves in my soul both growled, straining to push through at my need to protect my friend. Sweat beaded on my brow as my body grew, claws bursting from my fingers.

"It matters not. I will punish her—and you—as I see fit. You are as much to blame for my brother's death as she is. But your life is not mine, hers is, and she will learn that she cannot run from me. Do you think I will just allow her to leave when she pleases? Especially when she just helped you to drug and steal from my father!" B'nar's normal icy calm was nowhere to be seen as he bellowed those words. "It is clear you planned to escape, and I could end you all, without trial, for treason against the crown!" He blinked slowly and took a deep breath, releasing it steadily. "Which I won't, but what if someone else had discovered your plot? There are many that would love to get their hands on two mortal women." His eyes flicked to Blue. "Especially a full human!" He strode nearer to me, his magic crackling against my own. He lowered his voice so only I could hear him, his green gaze holding mine. "Godsdamn it, Ember! I know how much you want to find Connor, but don't put her at risk again. Do you understand me?"

I nodded, but I didn't really. His obsession with Blue was beyond anything I could relate to. Or was it? I was just as obsessed with getting back to Connor.

B'nar raked a hand through his beautiful blue hair, which, for once, was loose, and shone like liquid silk. He looked pointedly at the claws protruding from my fingers and held up a palm. "There is no need for your beasts to come forth. I am not here to stop you, I merely wish to help you..." He glanced back at Blue whose furious gaze was fixed on him. "...and keep that stubborn headed female from getting hurt. We have tarried here in Faerie too long while Berith builds his army. You hold enough control over your phoenix to summon her fire, but my father is right, we cannot risk you being captured. I will help you get back to your world, but you will not be left alone." He looked at Alex. "Alex, you will come with us. We may need your talents to get into Berith's stronghold. You will stay by Ember's side and watch out for her. Keep her safe. I will be by my human's side. Together we will find Connor, then return here to formulate a plan to infiltrate Berith's world and send him back to Hell where he belongs. Lance and Ava will remain here and deal with the fall out from my father when he wakes and finds his ring gone."

"What?" I was wholly confused. "You're helping us? Why would you do that?"

"Because I do not wish to feel your pain every moment of the day."

I quirked a brow at him. "What's that supposed to mean?"

B'nar shook his head and waved his hand like it was nothing. "I'm empathic, I feel the emotions of others." His brow furrowed, and he narrowed his gaze on Blue. "Except hers. Somehow, she can block her feelings from me. But I know you cannot embrace your phoenix until your anxieties over Connor are put to rest, and therefore your mind and emotions are more controlled. That means before we can go on the offensive with Berith, we need to retrieve your mate. His loss is stopping you freeing your phoenix fully and calling her on demand. You may be a danger to your world and by default mine, but only if Berith can tether you to the gates of Hell. Once you can free Fire at will, I believe we should go on the offensive, not be on the defensive, waiting for an army from Hell to consume our worlds." His strange ice blue and green eyes softened as they rested briefly on Blue despite the frown that creased the bridge of his nose. "And I need to be with you to protect her."

Despite the wrath in Blue's eyes, it was obvious B'nar felt far more for Blue than he would admit. "Of course you do. She's your prisoner, after all. Just like me."

"No. No, she's not like you. Not at all. I believe my human is unique." B'nar murmured almost to himself, a lost look on his face before he blinked.

My heart lurched and I couldn't stop myself putting a hand on his arm. "She is, so why don't you release her? She's so mad at you now, you'll need to sleep with one eye open, if only so you can see the knife coming as she stabs you."

B'nar huffed, silently commanding Blue to stand. Magic shone in his eyes, turning them an eerie green. "I release you."

Blue shook her head as if clearing her thoughts and ran right for him.

"Blue! Stop! We don't have time for this!" I jumped in front of her.

She glared at me, and though her eyes burned with fury, she skidded to a halt and dropped her fists. Her gaze went to him. "You'd better hope I never find a way to break your magic, you evil fuck, because I will rip you to pieces." And on that note, she gave him her back.

I marched up to B'nar and took the ring from his fingers as he watched Blue. The silver settings of the ring were plain and sturdy, the stone gently glowing. After giving it some thought, I held it back out and B'nar took it, a question on his face. "You'd better use it. I don't really have a clue what to do with it."

He smirked. "Then why did you try and steal it to begin with?"

"Because I'm desperate enough to try anything."

"I'm beginning to see that. But what were you going to do? Just blast it with magic and hope for the best?"

I shrugged. "Yeah, something like that."

He muttered a soft faerie curse and shook his head.

"Can you pinpoint a specific part in the prison?" I asked. I had no idea whether to believe B'nar's reasons for defying his father by helping us, but I wasn't going to question it too much. His feelings for Blue were a tornado of hot and cold, and the Mother knew *I* was confused by them, so he must be an utter mess. The only one who seemed definite in her feelings was Blue, whose hatred was palpable as she glared at the prince. The muscles in his jaw popped as he ground his teeth.

"No, but the ring will remember where it has been before. We just have to hope it recognises my magic and blood as being similar to my father's. It's his ring, and as such is bound to his blood. If it accepts me, I will ask it to show us where it has been. You must watch carefully and tell me when you see something you remember, then I can connect the ring to my magic and open a portal we can go through. My father is much more experienced with the ring. He can pinpoint people or magic, like he did with you. Unfortunately, he has not shown me how to do that."

I detected a slight bitterness in his tone but didn't ask. His relationship with his father was none of my business and he wouldn't tell me anyway, so I just nodded.

"Let's at least get enough firepower to protect ourselves while we're there."

Blue stalked up beside him as he opened the weapons store doors. "Yes, let's."

B'nar studied Blue's tight face. "I will allow you a weapon, but if you try and use it against me, I will take it away and leave you with nothing. Do you understand?"

Blue just glared at him as she grabbed a multifunction gun, ammo, several knives, and turned away. "Not if you're dead, you won't." She muttered and smiled sweetly at him. "Do *you* understand?"

I could have sworn B'nar's lips twitched up at her words.

"Hey! You two play nice. We don't have time for anymore shit between the two of you."

Blue just rolled her eyes, but B'nar nodded. "I'm willing to play nice if she doesn't try to run or to kill me."

My friend looked at me, and her eyes softened. "Fine! I'll save it until we've got Connor back."

I squeezed Blue's fingers. "Thanks. I need you both. Please don't kill the prince heir, or we'll have the Faerie army to fight as well as Hell's."

When I'd commandeered my choice of weapons—a multifunction gun like Blue's, more ammo, two knives, which I strapped to my thighs; and the bow infused with faerie technology that made it super accurate and its arrows deadly, I nodded at B'nar.

The prince stood next to Blue. "Ready?" His green eyes began to glow.

The wolves inside me rumbled their agreement as I nodded my head.

B'nar nicked his thumb with a blade.

Blue grunted. "I'd have cut you, if you'd asked."

B'nar gave a feral grin but didn't reply, which I was thankful for. More angst between them would only delay things, and now we were so close to getting back to Connor, I wanted to *move*. B'nar smeared his blood over the blue stone, and it flared to life. He chanted over and over, his voice gaining power and momentum. Power prickled over my skin and the portal burst into life beside the glass topped table.

Images flickered through the space between the edges of the portal like the trailers to a movie. Wind eddied around us. I was glad Lance and Ava weren't coming with us. I doubted that the first meeting with Connor would go all that well, and I needed this to go as smoothly as possible. I wiped a bead of sweat from my temple. Who knew what state Connor might be in, if he was even still alive.

"There! That's it!" The metal table that I had died on flickered into the image. The room was empty, the only light coming from the open door which hung from its hinges, the rubble from the wall in a pile.

"Jump in. Now."

I didn't need telling twice.

CHAPTER 4

mber

GRABBING the two wolf spirits which had been yanked from my body by the energy of the portal, I leapt out. Landing solidly, rubble crunched under my feet. The wolves slammed back into me, and I staggered under the agony and power that flooded my body.

"Mother...fucker!" I dropped to one knee, slamming the palm of one hand against the wall, breathing hard as I regained my equilibrium. "I hate it when that happens."

Blue jumped from the portal, B'nar right behind her. "Yeah, must be a bitch." Blue had her weapon out and set to kill as she ran to the hole in the wall and peered carefully into the corridor beyond. B'nar took up a position opposite her on the other side of the ragged hole. Alex vaulted from the portal and closed the distance between us. "You okay?" he asked gently. None of them carried shifter spirits so they didn't suffer like I did when they travelled through a portal.

"Yeah, just give me a mo'." The wolves inside me were settling, but I was still shaky.

"Sure." He held a weapon loosely by his side, his soles crunching through the rubble no matter how hard he tried to stay quiet. "Hey, B'nar? Think we could shut this down before it tells every demon in the vicinity we've arrived?"

B'nar whispered in fae and the portal collapsed in on itself. I swallowed, hoping we hadn't just made the biggest mistake ever, leaving Walker behind and in the dark. No doubt he'd have another portal ring somewhere and follow us as soon as he figured out what we'd done. I glanced at B'nar's strong profile and wondered just how much trouble he'd jumped into with us. Walker would not go easy on him, in fact he would probably be punished more severely for his betrayal. I looked away. That wasn't my problem, B'nar had made his own choices.

Without the portal, it was dark and eerie. The prison seemed quiet, deserted. Overhead lights flickered dimly, giving just enough light to make out the blood stains on the floor near the wall, but there were no voices, only the sound of stones falling and rubble shifting.

I moved up to Blue's side and stared at the ground. Mother Wolf, that was where Connor had collapsed. His blood stained the ground, dried into a dark stain. Exhaling through my nose, I stood tall and pulled my own weapon.

"Where to?" asked B'nar.

I carefully stuck my head out of the hole and peered into the corridor beyond. It was deserted. I don't know what I'd expected, but it wasn't for this block to be completely empty. My stomach sank. If Connor wasn't here, where in the hell would they take him? I refused to acknowledge the fact that he might already be dead and gone. "I'm not sure." I eyed the corridor, twisting my head to look up and down. One way led out into the arena which had contained the fighting rings and the room where we'd killed Doherty, the other led deeper into the maze of the prison and the science wing.

The stench of rotting corpses wafted through that open doorway. "That way," I said, nodding deeper into the science wing. Berith hadn't planned on keeping any prisoners in the arena, so he'd just left the dead that were of no use to him.

Using measured, careful steps, I crept down the corridor, weapon at the ready. Blue and Alex flanked me and B'nar brought up the rear, watching our backs.

My skin prickled beneath my suit, the hairs on my neck rising. Evil contaminated the air in this place, every shadow, every patch of darkness was a hideous thing that seemed infected with it.

Each cell we passed was ruined, their doors hanging off their hinges, the metal tables stained with blood. But there were no bodies. The silence was broken only by the crunch of grit and stone under our boots. I paused just before rounding the corner of another corridor. A soft grunting sound, like the breathing of a large animal, reached my ears. Goosebumps rose on my skin. I signaled for the others to halt then lowered to my haunches and peered around the corner.

No matter if I thought I was prepared for seeing the werewolf, I wasn't.

The creature stood malformed and naked next to a set of double doors that led to what looked like a stairwell. It looked back and forth, never once faltering in its duty. I swallowed the nasty taste that coated my mouth. This had been one of my kind, a shifter forced into a half change by the warden, right before it had been killed. I peered at it again. There didn't seem to be any injuries. Whatever magic Berith used to reanimate the dead Weres and shove his demon spawn inside, healed their bodies, too. I deliberately shut down any thoughts of D and Reed. I needed to find out what had happened to Connor before I worried about our pack brothers.

The werewolf, lifted his elongated nose and inhaled. Then snarled.

"Shit! Incoming," I whispered harshly.

Blue lifted her gun. Quickly, I shook my head and holstered my weapon, pulling a hunting knife. It wasn't huge, but it had a vicious serrated edge. Closing my eyes, I summoned Fire. She responded immediately, filling my veins and my flesh with power and warmth.

Counting the thing's footsteps, I judged when it was no more than two feet away and spun out to meet it. The clash of weapons, and even the pop of silenced bullets would be heard by its creepy-assed friends; hand to hand, not so much. Before the Were could even growl, I moved, slashing its throat. Warm blood splashed down my arm, splattering my face. Darting sideways, I slammed a fist into its chest, Connor's wolf lending me the strength I needed. With my hand in the monster's chest cavity, I pushed Fire forwards and sent a wave of heat and flame through its organs. When its eyeballs started to burn, I let it drop to the ground.

"Damn! Remind me not to piss you off," mumbled Alex as he jogged forward, followed by Blue and B'nar.

Through the doors, the staircase went downwards, further into the earth. I gulped, trying not to equate this with the feeling of descending into Hell. "It's just a staircase." My whisper echoed off the dark walls.

"Shh," Blue answered, and tapped my back to indicate she'd go first. We'd worked well together tag teaming like this in the past. B'nar's scowl was easy to see even in the darkness. He strode by me easily before gently but firmly grabbing Blue's shoulder and pulling her back so he could take point. Blue rolled her eyes and flashed him a pissed look, but didn't argue. Now wasn't the time.

We crept down another flight of dark and silent steps. The deeper we went the colder it became, until we reached another set of double doors. These had no glass, so we had no idea what was on the other side.

"Are you ready for this?" I asked Alex quietly.

"Of course." The shape shifter grinned. "I could change into a werewolf, you know?"

"Yeah, but you'd lose your clothes and I'm not sure my brain can handle that right now, and definitely not when you have to change back."

He chuckled. "Fair enough. We'll save that for emergencies then, yeah?"

"Absolutely." I tapped B'nar on the arm to indicate I was ready. His eyes were glowing eerily and he moved his hand and his fingers indicating which direction we should cover, then counted down. *Three. Two. One...*

We burst out into the corridor beyond.

Never, for as long as I live, would I forget the sight that greeted us. Weres carried tiny babies, and not with care. They were held in any manner that was convenient for the monster—with teeth, claws, hands—it didn't matter. The doors had blocked off the sound of desperation, the cries of pain and hunger, but now we were in the thick of it. The pitiful wailing of these poor babies froze my soul. Connor's warning about the women being rounded up and sent to the science wing slammed back into my head.

"What the Hell?" I uttered.

For a moment we were all frozen in place, even the ice prince watched wide-eyed as a werewolf threw a naked woman to the ground, followed by the baby he grasped in one clawed hand. The naked woman hit the ground, crying out. But it wasn't that sign of pain that galvanised me into action, it was the way she desperately tried to catch her child. But the Were had thrown it further. It would slam to ground with nothing to save it.

Gripping my bow, I yanked on the power of my wolves and threw myself forward, my arms outstretched, determined to catch the baby. The werewolf narrowed its wholly-black eyes on me—and charged. Wailing at the top of its little lungs, the falling baby landed in my left arm and I instinctively curled it around its tiny form. This left me with nothing but my shoulder and hip to break my fall. Pain slammed into me, but before I'd even finished sliding over the floor, with my other arm, my finger on the automatic trigger, I raised my bow. My tattoos burned as magic lit the weapon. It flowed into the arrows that released as I fired three shots; two into the Were's heart and one right between those horridly unnatural eyes. At the same time, the others began firing at the Weres that filled the corridor.

What these monsters were doing with so many prisoners outside their cells was anyone's guess, but it looked like they were transporting them somewhere.

Pushing myself up after setting down the screaming baby, I kept firing, aiming at the tall werewolves' heads. At least their prisoners were smaller and were mostly shoved sideways, until the Weres got smart, dropped the babies, and lifted the women as shields.

"Take him!" I yelled at the woman, who snatched up her child and, before I could stop her, ran for the stairwell. The doors slammed behind her and I hoped to the Mother that she would make it. Gods knew the outside world would be harsh to them both with no clothes and food but I guessed it was worth the risk when this place was a den of monsters and death.

"Ember! Shoot the bloody things! They're regenerating!" Blue's gun popped in quick succession.

"I am!" And to prove a point I pulled my gun in my other hand and squeezed the trigger, sending a volley of silver bullets into the attacking monsters. That was the only way I could think of them. They *were* monsters. These poor buggers had been forced to fight and die in the warden's fight rings, only death wasn't the end for them. Dying in Were form meant both their human soul and their animal spirit remained trapped within their body. Werewolves in particular were physically big and strong. Just like Walker had warned, Berith was using the Weres as vessels for his demon army. What they were doing with the babies I didn't know.

"Not that kind of shooting!" Blue yelled as we all loosed another volley of bullets into the Were's. "That!" She gestured wildly to the bow as each of her kills fell to the ground bleeding black blood, not red.

"Shit." Letting them get in front of me, I sheathed my gun. She was right, we'd waste too many bullets if we continued like this. I loaded an explosive arrow and raised the bow. Magic zipped from me into the weapon, igniting the magic in the arrow.

"Shoot!" B'nar's roar almost made me drop the damn weapon. He blasted the oncoming rush of Weres with a wave of icy magic. The first three froze, the ones at their backs pushing them out of the way. As they hit the ground they exploded, sending their demons screaming into the air, their misty forms being dragged back to Hell. Okaaay, that was also a good way of sending these demons back to Hell.

I targeted a huge chest right at the center of the oncoming surge.

"Ember!"

I didn't allow Alex's bellow to distract me. Exhaling steadily, I let the magic infused arrow fly. It flew in a streak of light, faster than even my shifter gaze could follow, and thudded right into that chest. The werewolf shot backwards from the force, taking out a few others before he slammed onto his back.

"Down!" I bellowed, hoping the innocent women would listen and protect their babies, though I knew some of those closer to the blast would die. I squeezed my eyes shut and covered my ears. The blast wave was not hot as you would expect with an explosion, but startling in being just the opposite. Ice crystals scored my skin, the pressure of the explosion throwing me to the ground. Even though I covered my ears, they still rang. Screams were the only sounds I could hear.

I pushed myself up, straightening my elbows. About six feet away, B'nar was covering Blue. Literally. He'd engulfed her with his large body until I could barely see her.

"Get off me, you idiot!" She shoved him backwards.

He allowed it, but didn't drop his hold on her. He merely looked her over then grunted as if satisfied she was unharmed before letting his hands drop away. His icy green glare rested on me and then Alex before he stood. Pulling another gun, he prowled forward ending the still moving Weres with a magic infused bullet in the brain. They didn't move again. Apparently decapitation, burning them, and shattering their frozen bodies apart weren't the only ways to end them.

Dead bodies surrounded us, but some of the women were still alive, their babies clutched to their chests.

"Come on, Em, up you get." Alex helped me to my feet. I shook the ringing from my ears and started helping the women. They looked emaciated, barely strong enough to stand, their babies scrawny and wasting away. I had no idea what horrors they'd been through, but they really needed to get out of here before more of the demon horde descended on us. As if on cue, roars resonated down the corridors, coming from every direction. I sent a quick prayer to the Mother Wolf, hoping she could guide the spirit animals of the women and babies back to her. "Please take them, help them find a way home," I whispered under my breath looking at a dead Were. His eyes were a clear deep brown, Unfocused in death, but devoid of that consuming blackness.

I bent and swooped up the bow. Pulling another clip of arrows from the quiver on my back and clipping it into place. I jogged down to B'nar who was peering around another corner. Immediately, he began to fire. His eyes started to glow with magic and he slammed one of his weapons into its holster.

"We aren't going to be able get to Connor right now, if he's down here. There's too many of them."

My heart sank. Carefully, I peered around the corner. A sea of deformed bodies rushed down the corridor towards us. Oddly, with no sound except their claws scratching on the tiled floor. Frustration tied my belly in knots. My mate could be behind one of the nearby doors, and I couldn't get to him. I kept my hold light but steady as I levelled up the bow and homed in on my target. I squeezed the trigger. "Down!" I yelled, but Blue and Alex were already ushering the survivors back through the doors and up the stairs. They were right, those women and babies needed to get outside. We'd help them survive—somehow. Or rather Blue and Alex would, I wasn't going anywhere.

"Yeah, you're right," I said, firing another arrow. "You go and catch up with Blue, I'll be right behind you."

I pretended not to notice B'nar's icy gaze resting on me before he loosed another volley of bullets into the oncoming wave of crazed Were's. Some dropped to the ground, others ran on.

"Forget it, Ember." His large hand grabbed my shoulder and hauled me back towards the stairwell. "You aren't staying behind to risk getting caught. My world relies on you remaining out of Berith's hands, so you will come with me." And he shoved me through the doors.

I tripped up the first step but soon got my balance. "You bastard! I have to find him!"

"You can't do that if you're chained to the gates of Hell."

I hated that he was right, but instead of admitting it, I welcomed the anger that burned in my chest. Fire stirred and Prime howled, wanting out to go and search for his other half. Claws pushed through the nail beds of my left hand. Ignoring the desperate need I had to shift, I slipped my free hand under a naked woman's arm and hauled her at a run up the stairs just as the door at the bottom crashed against the wall.

"They're coming! Run!" bellowed B'nar, turning and shooting ice at the floor and walls.

"That won't stop them! Here! Take her! I'll stop it, but you all need to be gone!"

At my warning, a determined look crossed his face. He grabbed the woman and hauled her over his shoulder taking the steps three at a time. I heard Blue's gun popping from a distance and hoped to the gods there weren't as many monsters up above us.

Come on, lovely, I need you. Help me save those poor women and babies. Don't let me down, I beseeched my phoenix. My fingers stretched wide though my hands remained down by my sides. Tension made my body rigid but I wasn't scared of my gift like I had been. It did take an enormous amount of concentration, though, to summon the power buried deep inside me. My wolves roared as fire flooded my body; even Prime was pushed down by her. My whole body lit on fire, until I was swathed in flames. She didn't harm me or my clothes, merely waited to be told what to do.

Kill the monsters, was my only instruction. And though my feet remained where they were, I felt her stir to life. She grew and grew until heat and flames engulfed the air of the stairwell. As the first wave of monsters rounded the corner of the steps, I let her fly. She shot forward and engulfed our enemy. The demons inside these suits of flesh didn't even have time to screech before the Were bodies they inhabited burned to ash. Scorched by the bright burning light, the demons were sucked away. Calmly, I walked forward, burning each one as I went. But though my phoenix was powerful, I had not learned how to make her burn for long periods of time and already I was weakening.

"Ember!" roared B'nar as he rushed back down the steps followed closely by Alex.

Alex's eyes widened at the sight of my burning body. He'd seen me train and summon flames to burn objects, but he'd never seen my whole body on fire. I turned more of my kind to ash, but my body began to quiver, my flames stuttering.

B'nar's eyes narrowed on me. "Let her go! We need to get out! Now!"

I let Fire recede and leaned against the wall at the bottom of the stairs. B'nar blew out a deep breath and sprinted down the steps. He'd sensed my weakness. *Empathic*, I remembered him saying.

Alex ran past me and stuck his gun out of the door, firing into the corridor where the demon possessed Weres hid. Light bathed my face. B'nar's magic glowed, engulfing him much as Fire did me. His skin became covered in ice, his blue hair turning white and crystalised. Then he let his magic fly, commanding that power to build a wall of ice between us and our enemy. As soon as the door was sealed, he turned to me. "That won't hold them forever," he said, and just as he had done to the other woman, he threw me over his broad shoulder, running up the stairs with an ease that made me jealous. I swallowed my frustration at being so weak, but Prime and Mea soon stepped up, feeding me gentle waves of energy to keep me conscious. By the time B'nar and Alex barged through the doors into the arena, I fought to be let down.

B'nar lifted me and unceremoniously lowered me to my feet. But there was nothing I could do to prevent the shift Prime and Mea forced on me. They would not let me put myself at unnecessary risk, not when they could sense my weakness. Together they burst through my skin, the shift so quick very little pain registered. I marvelled at the way they were joined and could only wonder what they looked like merged together.

I bounded past both men into what had been the fighting arena. My wolves snarled as the stench of old blood and death flooded our senses. My kind had died by the hundreds in here. I had been forced to kill a friend here, and nothing could change the hate I had for this place—that we all had.

Blue was pinned nearby. With her were six naked women. Five cowered against the wall holding their babies, but one, the woman whose baby I'd caught, stood proud by Blue's side, utterly naked, skinny and bleeding, her body was covered in scars and I didn't want to imagine the horrors she'd suffered at the hands of the demons. She had one of Blue's guns and was firing into the on-slaught of Were animals piling in through the far doors of the arena. I looked up to the destroyed balcony. Prime weighed leaping up there to make an escape.

We could do it, but that would mean leaving all the others behind, and I won't do that. I felt his confusion, these people were not his pack, he didn't owe them anything. He wanted to get me, and Mea, his chosen mate, out of here and to safety, and then return to find Connor.

Mea snarled, not happy with his decision to remove us from the fight.

We stay, I agreed with her.

Prime snarled right back but bowed his head. I smiled to myself, he was as cold hearted as they came, except to those he loved, and his pack. In this form I could feel his respect for his mate, and his utter belief his other pack members and Connor were alive. I couldn't feel the connection Connor and he had with each other, or with our brothers; I just hoped they were away from this place and safe.

B'nar blasted over our heads with shards of green ice that stabbed the Weres. His focus was on Blue and getting to her.

Prime pushed his power through me and Mea, and took us both over. He bounded towards Blue and the women, leaped onto a Were's back, clamped his massive jaws around the monstrous neck and bit down. The Were's neck snapped like a twig. Blood hit Prime's mouth and I cringed as blood lust flowed through him. Prime was the most powerful wolf spirit I'd ever met and my own had lost the battle for any kind of dominance. He trotted over to Blue and nudged her hand. Warmth spread through my chest. He knew I was worried for her, and was making sure she was okay for me.

"Yeah, I'm fine. But we need to find a way out of here." She popped more bullets into the oncoming Weres.

"You aren't fine." B'nar's voice was hard, but there was an edge of worry in it too.

Blue glanced at the two deep claw lacerations on her hand that dripped blood onto the floor and slicked the handle of her weapon. It looked like her fae armour had protected her from further injury, but the cuts were deep and must have hurt like a bitch. "It's a scratch."

B'nar narrowed his eyes but kept his mouth shut. "You know any way out?" He addressed the question to me, though he walked closer to Blue.

Prime snarled and shook his great head.

"I do," said the woman. "My name's Selina. I was walked up into the guards quarters above as their fuck toy more than once. If you want out, I can take you, on the understanding you get us out of here. All of us," she said, aiming her gun on a Were that ran into the room. With accuracy, she pulled the trigger, hitting him in the middle of his forehead.

"Of course," answered Blue, her tone soft. Yeah, it had registered with all of us what the women had been used for. "If we can get through that door, where do we go?"

Selina didn't take her eyes from the doorway. "Up the stairs and left down the corridor. The bots don't function anymore, so we won't have to deal with them, but there's an army of those motherfuckers up on the cell levels. They've still got some of our kind locked up in them."

"Shit. So not everyone got out?"

"No."

The baby which lay on the ground at Selina's feet began to wail. Prime sniffed at it and growled. Selina immediately pointed the gun at us. "Don't even think about it, wolfie. That's my son. If you try and hurt him, no matter who or what his sire is, I'll stick the rest of these bullets right between your eyes."

I agreed with her, so did my wolf. These were pure newborn souls. No matter if they were sired by demons they were not inherently evil. Together Mea and I made Prime take a step away. He grumbled at us, but didn't push back against our warning.

Selina moved her gun to the entrance and delivered another volley of shots at the same time as Blue and Alex.

"Shit, we need to go," Alex said, sweat running down his forehead.

"Yeah, we do. Selina? If I can get us through those doors, can you lead us out?" B'nar turned his icy eyes on the naked woman.

"Yep."

"Come on. Get up." Blue gently encouraged the other women to get to their feet. "You go in the middle. We'll protect you. Okay?" But I heard the worry in her voice, so did Prime. He huffed and stood behind the group of naked women.

"Alex! Stay with Blue." B'nar's tone was enough to make Alex comply.

Prime glanced around and behind him, looking for an attack from the rear and above as B'nar began thrusting ice laced magic at the doorway. Prime's gaze landed on the room where I'd last seen Connor alive. The events of that moment flashed through my mind. Zander and I had stabbed the guards; Connor ending that mean bastard-Doherty. Zander had then stabbed me right through my gut, just as we planned. I'd needed to appear dead to give Connor and Zander a chance to get past the warden's guards and into the science wing; only that plan had backfired. Berith, a.k.a the warden, had spotted me in Connor's arms and he'd sensed my human soul lingering. If he had taken my soul, he could have imprisoned my phoenix; chained it to the gates of Hell, and burned them to the ground. I tried not to think about what could have happened, like me being responsible for unleashing Hell's army on Earth.

Something about that time niggled at my mind. Urgency surged through Prime and then me. *We go. Now.* And he took off.

"Ember!"

Prime spun back to Alex and snarled viciously. I prayed Alex would take the hint and go back to the others, they needed the protection far more than I did right now.

"Dammit, Ember! That icy bastard's gonna have my hide, immortal or not." But Alex sprinted back to the women and herded them along behind B'nar and Blue.

Prime quickly leapt over the fallen bot, which blocked the entrance up to the viewing room. He bounded up the steps and into the room, a growl ripping from him at the sweet stench of rotting flesh. I gasped at a memory of something dark taking hold of him and Connor. It was a memory he hated. He'd been out of control, lost to the darkness of another creature. I gasped; one that lived inside Connor just like Prime did. It had become consumed by the need to kill and devour the flesh of its victim... Prime huffed and lowered his head. He and Connor had lost themselves to this shadowy presence; they had lost sight of protecting me before Connor had wrestled back control.

It's alright. We can think about what that was when we find Connor again. Don't worry about it now. Whatever it was, it's with Connor not you.

His relief at my thoughts was almost palpable. I guided him to where Doherty had once stood. The remains of his bloated corpse lay face down on the ground. *Not so smart now, are you?* I hoped his soul was lost in the Hell he well and truly deserved. What I was looking for wasn't in the mess that was Doherty or even near him. Prime got down on his haunches and we searched under every piece of furniture.

Damn! It's not here.

Shouts came from below followed by gun fire. Prime's hackles rose, adrenaline and power surging through him. A frisson of fear shivered through me. Like this, Prime was so dominant and powerful, I worried about getting him back inside me. I desperately needed Connor; he was the only one strong enough to contain him. If I didn't have Fire and my wolf to help me, Prime's spirit would have drowned me by now.

Prime charged back into the arena, the stink of fear and determination raising his blood lust. But it was the other scents that sent joy surging through us both. Other shifters! At least one of them was one of his blood bonded—his pack. Connor's brothers had come for him! Bullets ricocheted from the walls as Prime skidded, his claws scratching for purchase on the concrete floor. Gaining his balance, he quickly retreated behind the cover of the door frame.

My heart sank as Prime peered around the door frame. Guards were moving forwards. They were dressed in black armour that looked to have been taken from the prison guards, and they were surrounded by Werewolves —bloody big ones.

They were blocking all the exits. *Godsdammit!* Prime growled in agreement with me before he snarled, ready to rip his enemy apart. He was strong but not strong enough to stop the bullets from four guns.

Shit. Shit. Shit. How the hell do we get out of this one?

I supposed I could try and change back and use Fire again. She stirred, willing to try but Prime blocked my shift back to my human body. I reluctantly agreed. If I got caught, it would spell annihilation for the human race.

Prime growled long and low, pulsing power through our—no, his body, and charged out into the middle of our enemy without giving me or Mea time to object.

Blood flew through the air. His claws ripped the throat out of the nearest werewolf before I could even blink. I knew there was no stopping him now. He was free from my control, and he was looking for vengeance for Connor. Quick as lightning, he dodged a bullet and leapt, his teeth clamping around the head of a guard. No matter the blade that sliced his flesh, he grabbed the guard's body and ripped his head clean off his shoulders.

Loud gun fire rattled through Prime's ears but there was no sting of being shot. He snapped his head around to fully see the movement that he had caught in the corner of his eye. A large man ran into the arena, followed by three more figures, all had weapons and with efficiency, shot the Were's in the back of the head.

I felt Prime's joy right before he launched his big body to the side and knocked down a large Were who had greasy blonde hair mixed in with his wolf pelt. The Were roared and stabbed his long claws into Prime's side. Pain flooded Prime, but it didn't faze him, it only made him angrier. Power exploded from him. The Were thrashed, his demon black eyes glittering, a familiar snarl baring his long black fangs.

Mother Wolf! Santa!

Prime clamped his jaws over the thing's face and neck. I quickly closed off my senses, not wanting to see this level of violence, no matter what possessed the creature that had once been Santa Cruz.

When I felt Prime charging forward again, I opened my eyes. He bounded over to the gun toting people who had helped us. A large man with close cropped brown hair, a beard and clear grey eyes watched us, his face full of disbelief.

Oh my gods! Owen! I wanted to shriek, but could only do it in my head. He'd made it!

Prime launched himself with a roar and knocked Owen to the ground.

Owen laughed. "Get off me, you great lummox." And he shoved at Prime pushing the huge wolf away. Prime allowed it, but I felt his surprise at how powerful Owen had become. Owen stood. "That you in there Con?" he asked.

It was then I realised Owen and Connor's brothers had no idea what had happened to him.

Prime snarled as I tried to push through. He didn't want to leave his brothers yet. No matter if I was desperate to get back to my human form and tell Owen what had happened, Prime wanted to greet his third as well as his beta. Or is that what they were, now? The dynamics had changed.

Stone was as stoic as ever. He remained still, his gun held across his broad chest, though his face softened and his throat bobbed as he looked at Prime. He stood in front of a blond haired woman, who also had a gun at the ready.

"That's not Connor," Stone said, immediately pointing the gun at us. Prime snarled, but my wolf intervened this time, blocking his need to get to Stone and put his brother right.

Owen casually lifted his gun, too.

Prime! Let me back out, I can tell them what happened. They can help us find Connor...

Prime reluctantly agreed. Within seconds he was pulling back inside me, along with my wolf who wanted to console him. He didn't understand why his brothers didn't recognise him as their alpha, let alone their Prime. I swallowed the ache in my throat. He was upset. The great alpha Prime was hurt that his brothers didn't recognise him. I left my wolf to pacify him and forced my way through the shift. Moving my bones and skin to the surface.

"You've gotta be shitting me," Stone uttered, when I stood in front of him. "You?'

"Jeez runt. How d'you do that?" Shannon gestured to my fully clothed body. Yeah, I'd learned a few new tricks with my *Fire* power. Manipulating molecules was one of them. It wasn't that hard. It wasn't that much different than shifting body molecules. I had to laugh though, trust Shannon to comment on my clothes before anything else!

"Ember? What the fuck? How are you hosting Connor's wolf?" Owen's face was full of suspicion.

More gunshots came from the stairwell and my stomach clenched. "The others?"

Owen nodded, his expression falling into one of stern leadership. "You're right, we can talk about this later. Let's go."

I pulled the high tech bow from my back which earned me a narrow eyed stare from Stone. "Jealous?" I asked, jogging past him.

"No, but I'd like to know where you got that."

"I'll explain when we aren't about to get ripped to pieces."

He grunted, and pushed past me. I let him, settling in beside Shannon.

"Still Mr Personality, huh?"

She rolled her eyes. "You have no idea."

I grinned and followed her.

Owen led us up stairs and down corridors. It was obvious he knew the prison layout like the back of his hands. I wondered just how many times they'd been back here, fighting the Weres—or maybe looking for Connor? We burst through some double doors on another floor and began running towards the louder gunfire.

"Myles!"

My heart clenched as I saw Reed's mate firing into a dark corridor where shadows moved. He was flanked by an organised group of five men.

"Pull out!" Owen yelled. Myles glanced at us, then pulled back, yelling his own commands. The corridor in front of him heaved with movement. I skidded up next to the handsome, dark skinned shifter.

"Ember?" Myles's eyes gleamed like emeralds in the darkness of his skin. His face was thinner and he had lost the glimmer of health he'd once had, but that didn't stop him being beautiful.

I grinned, my heart aching at the grief I saw in his eyes. "Yeah." Lifting the bow, I let an arrow fly. Magic made it glow as it shot forward. I grabbed Myles's wrist. "We need to get out of here!"

He nodded and followed me as I sprinted up the next set of stairs after Owen and Stone. My lungs burned, still not fully recovered from using Fire. I let Myles go past me, getting my breath back as I waited for B'nar, Blue and Alex, who were helping some of the women up the stairs, to pass me. Prime grumbled, but pushed a bit of power my way so that I could keep up with them. I really needed to figure out how to replenish my energy after using the power of my phoenix, or I was going to be useless not only in finding Connor, but in this war against Berith.

Once again, I burst out into another corridor, but this time frigid, snow laced wind rushed by my sweaty face.

Bloody hell! The outside!

The others were already running through the old door, which hung off its hinges letting flurries of snow into the corridor. I rushed after them, my boots slipping on the wet floor. The fresh smell of forest and snow hit me. Gods, I'd missed the smell of the outside world—*my* world. Faerie was a beautiful place, but it wasn't home.

Stone and Owen were crouched behind some storage crates, firing at the tower near the perimeter of a broken metal fence. I took a moment to peer at the compound. No planes graced the runway, but plenty of dead bodies covered the ground. Some were surrounded in fresh blood, others were just mounds of snow with a limb poking through the surface to tell me what it was. I wondered how often Owen attacked the prison. Berith certainly didn't appear short of werewolves, that was for sure.

I saw my friends with the women. They were sheltering behind a large metal storage crate a few feet from the doorway.

"I'm going to them," I mouth to Shannon who was with Stone and Owen. She nodded and gave me cover fire, darting out alongside as I ran for them.

When I skidded on my arse beside Alex, Shannon landed right beside me. I looked back. Stone glared at Shannon from his position. She scowled and stuck her middle finger up.

I chuckled, peering around the edge of the container. A guard stood in a tall watchtower picking off Owen's men. We were isolated from the hole in the broken fence where Owen's men had clearly got in. "Can you cover me?" I asked Shannon. She nodded.

"We'll do the same," B'nar said. "About time you showed up with that bow. My magic can't reach that far."

"Wow, that must grate on your ego," I muttered, rolling my eyes. Blue snorted a laugh and B'nar shot her a death glare.

"On three," I said, holding in my own laugh. I loaded an explosive arrow and held the bow ready. "One. Two. Three…" I stood tall trusting the others to have my back—and let the arrow fly. Seconds later the tower exploded, sending a plume of smoke into the air.

Owen was already moving even as the debris fell. "Let's go! Round them up!"

Stone and Myles did. I was pleased to see Kawan amongst the soldiers that ran out from the building, bloodied and dirty, but alive.

He nodded at me, but now wasn't the time for reunions. I nodded back and fixed my bow away, pulling my weapon instead. We ran through knee deep snow and out through the metal fence, into the forest. I was very aware we were leaving a trail of footprints for our enemy to follow, but there was nothing to be done about it.

"This way!" yelled Owen from the front. I followed his lead, B'nar, Blue and Alex staying close by my side as we helped the poor naked women through the snow. We were soon faced with a raging river of ice cold water.

"You've got to be kidding me? We can't shift, none of us can, and we'll freeze if we get in there. My baby will die," said Selina, shaking her head violently.

"Yeah, well, no choice if you don't want an army of those demon fuckers breathing down your neck," Stone said.

B'nar walked forward and put his hand into the water. "No need to risk anymore lives."

Stone's suspicious gaze followed his movements, but those same narrowed eyes soon widened as B'nar's magic turned the raging river to ice.

"This won't last long, so you'd better run! Now!" urged the fae prince, grabbing Blue's hand. "With me, human," he said and sprinted down river, freezing the flow as he went. Blue looked as white as a sheet at that display of his power, but had the sense not to argue with his demands this time. We needed to get away from the prison. Part of me didn't want to abandon my search for my mate, and Prime was all kinds of angry at leaving Connor behind, again, but it would be suicide to stay.

My feet slipped on the ice and I fell more than once, but at least I had boots on. Without shoes, the poor women were falling behind. They had no energy to shift. Dammit, they'd soon die out here with no protection—so would their babies. That was if they still lived. My heart pounding at our stupidity, I turned back to help them. Myles and Kawan saw where I was headed, so did Owen. Watching us approach, Selina gripped her son to her chest, attempting to shield him from the cold. My heart squeezed, the babies were utterly silent. Too silent, after all that screaming I'd heard earlier. I didn't know much about babies, but I knew that was bad news.

We all got to the small group of women at the same time. All three men ripped their coats and shirts off immediately. Owen beckoned another two men over. "Get your clothes off. Give your coats and trousers to the women and wrap the babies in the shirts."

Selina eyed him suspiciously and shuffled away from him, inhaling deeply, scenting him. In a sudden move she snatched the shirt from his hands. "Thanks. Pity you all didn't think of that before our babies were nearly dead with cold."

Owen's wolf rolled across his eyes, even though his voice remained steady, so tightly controlled, I thought he might snap. He was always calm, so it showed how badly he wanted away from this place.

"Yeah? Lady, my priority is the lives of my soldiers. If you want something, you have to speak up, or go without. Now cover that child before you put this fucking coat on. Or don't. Either way, we're moving out." And he dropped the coat as he stripped, his boots, trousers and boxers quickly coming off, totally unbothered by his nakedness. "You! Shift! Now!" he ordered the shifters who had stripped off their clothes to give to the women. He looked around and every other shifter had run after B'nar. The ice below our feet began to crack and a couple of the women squealed in fright. "Shift! Now!" he bellowed at Kawan, Myles and I, and he did the same.

I let my wolf slam through my flesh. She was quicker to my aid than Prime. Owen's wolf snarled at the naked woman who had just managed to wrap her baby in his shirt. It was clear he wanted her to get on his back. She scowled, but looked down at the ice beneath. More cracks appeared, water covering our feet. Owen growled. Selina quickly shoved her arms through the thick coat. In one arm she gripped her child, with her other hand she grabbed Owen's fur and pulled herself onto his broad back. The others did the same and took off after him. I ran behind the slowest, to make sure they all made it. I'd use every bit of Prime's power to make sure these shifters saved these poor women.

We made it to the bank down river just as B'nar's magic faded and the river sent huge chunks of ice tumbling away.

"Bloody hell, that was close," muttered Blue.

"Yes, it would have been worse if we'd had to swim, though. It would have ruined your armour," B'nar said, and Blue looked at him as if she wasn't sure if he was being funny or not.

Owen howled, a loud haunting sound that carried through the snow laced forest, calling the rest of the pack to him.

I stayed in wolf form, content to let Mea keep me warm, sorry that Blue, Alex and the women didn't have the option to shift to protect them from the cold. Most of them had only managed to get a coat on their bodies before we'd had to run.

Owen led us on, and we were joined by more shifters as we went. I was utterly exhausted and completely lost. The forest was coated in a white blanket and the scents my wolf picked up were all unknown, except the brothers'. There was nothing I would be able to follow back to the prison.

CHAPTER 5

mber

I LOST track of time as Owen led us on, Selina clutching to him with her boney fingers, the baby caught under her chest. The warmth from Owen's fur must have been keeping the little thing from freezing to death. We travelled through thick snow until a rugged cliff face came into view.

The closer we got, the more scents I picked up as the cliff face disappeared behind the trees. Around us I could sense shifters watching. Owen had this place locked down. No demons or Weres were getting close to this camp without his knowledge.

Through the trees, a fissure in the rocks became visible. I gave my wolf a nudge. Within moments, I stood fully clothed, armed and walking beside Owen's wolf. All of those who had shifted had left their clothes behind. Shifting was only used as a last resort, or when planned to allow our animal spirits to run free. Unlike me, most shifters couldn't make their clothes disappear and return at will. The tension in Owen's wolf seemed to ebb a little the closer we got to the cave. Stone strode over, not having shifted. Even his face had lightened a little.

"Welcome to camp," Shannon said, eyeing Selina who was sliding semiconscious from Owen's back. "Whoa!" Shannon's hands were outstretched as she made a move to grab the emaciated woman. Stone moved quicker and caught Selina. Shannon ran around and grabbed the baby that was bundled in Owen's shirt. "Mother Wolf, he's so pale." Her worried eyes caught Stone's.

"Shit! Get these women inside right now!" bellowed Stone. "And get something to feed these babies with."

"Like what?" said Shannon

Stone's brows dipped. "How the hell do I know what babies need? I've never been this close to one before." And he peered down at the child looking so perplexed even Shannon had to smile. "Don't worry, Stoney, I'll sort something. Let's get them inside first."

The wolves shifted back, still not in the least bit self-conscious about their nakedness. I guessed in a camp like this, full of shifters, where clothes were in short supply, there was no place for bashfulness. Owen shifted and frowned at Selina and then the baby.

"I'll take her," he said to Stone whose expression remained stoic as he handed over the half naked woman.

"I'll bring the baby. Where are we going, boss?" Shannon's expression tightened, and when I looked around, I saw that anxiety mirrored on the faces of the other shifters, who now carried a woman, or a silent baby.

Myles strode up with a tiny bundle in his arms. "We need to get them warm quickly, or they're going to die. This one's blue. The women have been outside too long, and they have no reserve, they've been starved, and if they die, their babies will die, too."

I poked at Fire. She stirred agreeing with my request. "What's it like in there? I can warm a small area for them if you have one. Do you have any blankets or extra clothes for them?"

Kawan passed a baby to me. I took the child, trying not to freak out when it was pale and still. Gods, the poor thing looked dead already...

"Yeah, I'll find them something. Shannon, you go with our alpha, I'll find some kind of food for the women." And he jogged into the cave.

"Come on!" Owen began running. I followed close behind, keeping my eyes off his beautiful, naked form. I could really appreciate all the male beauty around me just like the next woman, but now wasn't the time for ogling such things.

Unsure what I'd find in that cave, I kept close to Owen. It wasn't that I mistrusted him, or even Stone, I was more nervous that I'd see starving and injured people. But I couldn't have been more wrong. He led me through the small opening and down a tight narrow fissure which opened into a large cave. The people inside were fully clothed, it was mainly prison issue clothes, and clothing clearly taken from the guards they'd killed, but it was better than I'd expected. There was the smell of cooking, and in general people looked clean and reasonably well fed. I stopped looking around and concentrated on keeping up with Owen.

He walked, long legged and purposeful, right across the cave and to where a small fire cast a shallow light. Beyond was another entrance, just big enough for me to walk through, but Owen and Stone had to duck down. We stepped into a small cave which was dimly lit with another small fire. Owen jogged across the floor and leaped onto some rocks on the far side which were placed, or had fallen, just like a ladder or steps which led us up onto another level of tunnels. A short way down this one, he hung a right into a medium sized cave with a small roof. This one would be big enough for all of the women. It was cold but dry, and the floor was smooth as if millions of years of water flow had smoothed it before it had disappeared.

Kawan ran in followed by a face I recognised. "Lionel!" I ran back to him and he met me halfway, pulling me into his huge arms and lifting my feet off the floor. I shuffled the baby sideways to keep the little thing from getting crushed.

"Hey, trouble. Gods, it's good to see you. I thought you were dead."

"No," I said into his broad chest, my voice muffled. "You should know my life is more complicated than simply dying."

He huffed a laugh. "Well, you better be ready to tell me everything, cause I wanna know what happened to you. But right now I'm here to help." He walked over to Owen who had taken a blanket from Kawan and laid it on the floor. "What do you need, alpha?" he asked.

Owen glanced at the lion shifter. "This floor isn't going to be warm enough. Go see if there's anything we can put on the floor for them to lie on. Get whatever you can. Blankets, towels, clothes—anything."

"Sure boss, I'll spread the word and see if we have anyone who can help them with the babies. I've no idea what they need to eat."

I huffed a laugh. "They don't eat anything, you plonker! They need their mother's milk, so you need to find food and something to drink for the women."

"All right, smartass." Lionel grinned. "And what are you gonna do to help? Or are you here just to pretty up the place, sugar?"

I smirked, and placed the baby I carried on Shannon's other arm. Stone watched her struggle to balance them, his face tight, though I didn't miss his throat bob as he watched her. He approached her warily. "Here." And he held his arms out looking uncertain about what to do, but utterly determined to do it anyway. Shannon gave him a small smile of thanks, and I could have sworn Stone looked almost embarrassed. "Don't get used to me taking one of these rugrats," he said. "I'm only doing it 'cause you might drop one."

"I know, but still. Thanks, faerie."

Stone huffed and settled the child in his large arms, watching its pale little face.

I gave Fire a nudge, wanting to get these poor souls warm. She gladly awoke, ready to help me. My skin began to glow and I knew my hair was catching fire, along with my eyes.

"Er, okay..." Lionel put his hands up and stepped back.

I walked to the center of the cave and pushed more power out. Not enough to ignite the oxygen in the air, but enough to keep steady waves of heat pulsing out to warm everyone.

Blue walked as close as she could without going up in flames herself. "You gonna be okay doing this? You used too much energy back in that prison."

"Yeah, don't worry, Prime's been a good boy, and given me his power. I'm not tired now."

"Okay, well, if you get tired, you stop. We'll find another way to save them."

"There isn't one, Blue, and you know it. Getting a fire started and warmed will take too long. They need heat and food, now."

B'nar shuffled back near the entrance. Yeah, I knew we were polar opposites and he'd hate being this close to such heat.

"Kawan. Take our new guests to find food, and to rest somewhere. If you can find anyone willing to help to look after the babies, that would be great." Then Owen addressed B'nar, clearly understanding that B'nar's power and dominant attitude was the product of more than a regular fae. "Ember will be safe here. She is my Prime's mate. And we are all sworn to protect her, no harm will come to her at all in this camp."

B'nar and Alex nodded. "You okay with that, Em?" asked Alex.

I nodded, concentrating on keeping the temperature warm but not blazing. My friends walked away, Blue with a smile in my direction before B'nar took hold of her wrist and pulled her along with him. I knew they'd all be alright with Kawan.

Owen laid down and pulled Selina in closer to him, curling his big body around her, spooning her. Covering them both with a blanket, he tucked it around the sleeping woman, foregoing most of it from himself.

"All of you, use your body heat to warm them until help comes."

Shannon sat as close to me as she could and cuddled the tiny baby close. I blinked. Shannon being caring with a baby wasn't something I'd ever considered seeing. Neither had Stone by the look of him. He split his attention between watching Shannon, and the tiny being in his arms. More than once their eyes met and each time the tension between them was almost painful. I had no idea what had happened between them, but now wasn't the time to ask.

The cave warmed quickly. Tired, I sat cross legged in the centre and kept the ambient temperature nice and toasty. My wolves seemed content and at peace for now. Prime was curled up with my wolf, allowing Fire to take the dominant place in my soul. Fire happily burned, finding this level of power expenditure an easy role. I smiled and closed my eyes. After a while, the women stopped shivering and the cave was silent other than the breaths of the sleeping babies and women. I worried about the babies being fed, but guessed Kawan would bring food as soon as he could to feed their mothers. Then they could, hopefully, feed, too. I eyed Selina's emaciated body. Her bones stuck out sharply under the blanket and she looked tiny wrapped in Owen's big arms. I remembered reading somewhere that if a woman was starved, or unwell, their milk could dry up, and I doubted we had canned baby food out here in the wilderness.

Owen carefully shifted, lifting his head so he could see me and still keep Selina protected and warm. "So? Do you want to tell me what happened? If Connor isn't with you, and you are here, what makes you think he's still in that place—or that he's even still alive?"

I blinked, slowly. Fire studied him, weighing up his threat to me. After a moment she went back to keeping the women warm, caressing them with licks of heat that she would not allow to burn or injure them. Owen watched her curling tendrils of red and orange magic, his gaze steady and unafraid as she brushed over his shoulder.

He quirked a brow at me.

"Oh, no, no, no. That's not me feeling you up, you perv. That's the phoenix that inhabits my soul, along with Connor's wolf and my own, keeping you warm."

"Bloody hell, Ember. You hold three shifter spirits? Two wolves, *and* a phoenix? Damn, girl, I knew you were special if you could bring Connor to his knees, but that's some heavy power you're controlling."

"Yeah, it can be a bit overwhelming."

"I'll bet." He looked down at Selina as she moaned and snuggled in closer to him. His brows dipped and his biceps tensed as he pulled her closer before he looked back at me. "So, we've got time. Why don't you tell me what happened after we started that escape?"

I nodded and gave him a small smile. "Sure."

While I spilled about Faerie and being the key to the Hell gates, Lionel returned with more blankets and clothes to use as makeshift pallets. Kawan came back with another male. Between them they carried a massive industrial size saucepan full of stew. The smell of wild garlic and meat wafted up my nose and my stomach let out a loud rumble. Even Selina stirred, her eyelids fluttering.

Although pale, all the women looked better, and the babies were stirring and beginning to whimper. No full on caterwauling yet, but I think that was more because they just didn't have the energy for it. I knew I'd have to discuss with Owen what we were going to do with the poor little things. I mean, was there any knowledge at all of how half-shifter, half-demon babies could be integrated into society? Gods, I hated to think about what the options, other than bringing them up as shifters, would be.

"Don't worry, I'll not let any harm come to them because of who they are," Owen rumbled. He must have seen my gaze land on Stone, who still watched the baby in his arms carefully, though his main focus was Shannon. Yeah, these weren't the first half-breeds in existence.

Selina's eyes flickered open. The bridge of her nose creased when she saw me sitting in the middle of the floor like a human torch, yet I wasn't screaming or flapping my arms around trying to put myself out. Then her face flooded with colour and she shuffled away from Owen. But that only succeeded in dragging the blanket from his body which flustered her even more.

"Oh my gods! Where are your clothes? Get away from me!" she said, her voice both breathless, and if I wasn't mistaken, full of a mix of fear and disgust. She looked away and her eyes fell immediately on her baby. Shannon got up, walked over, and sat down, placing Selina's baby back in her arms.

I smiled. I might not have Connor back, but we had done something good here today. These women, and their babies, would have died in that place.

CHAPTER 6

mber

"So what you're saying is, you refuse to take us back there?" Keeping my voice level and calm was proving a challenge. We'd all eaten, and Owen and the others were once again clad in jeans and prison issue t-shirts. We sat at the back of the main cave near a fire that illuminated the darkness and provided a decent amount of warmth.

"Yeah, pretty much. But it's not a case of refusing just for the sake of it, Ember. Even if Connor is in there, he'll be in the lower levels where the cells are nearer to the warden's rooms. We just don't have enough manpower or weapons to take on a whole army of demon possessed Weres."

Pushing to my feet, I began to pace. I could feel Prime's hunger to go back and find Connor, no matter where he was. "Tell me more about the prison break and what's been happening in that place, since."

Owen shifted on the log he had perched his big body on and leaned his elbows on his knees. Steepling his fingers together, he rested his finger tips against his lips. "We got out of there, but it was a bloodbath. Drake managed to turn the bots against the guards and killed loads of them; that gave us extra weapons that we picked up as we ran. The guards on the surface didn't stand a chance; our numbers overwhelmed them. I think we only made it because some crazy fuckers stayed behind to get revenge. Mother knows how many of them actually made it. We know the demons are using those that did survive as fodder for entertainment. They rip them apart for blood, flesh and fun."

I closed my eyes briefly. Such evil had to be stopped, somehow. But Owen was right. Going back into a general of Hell's lair without backup was insane. Then again, no one had ever accused me of being sane.

"So what about all your supplies? Today can't be the only time you've been back there; this food and the blankets and stuff you use, had to come from there."

"You're right. We've done six raids so far. The first few were mainly to get supplies and weapons. We didn't have shelter and we were starving in those first few days. The Weres didn't come out into the snow, probably because Berith was still using the dead to stick his demon spawn in, so we pushed further into the prison and found the kitchens. We took food, clothes and bedding, and ran further into the woods." He met my eyes. "This was the first place I found that was big enough to shelter most of us. We still have to have a significant amount of our people on guard in the forest, and I have people watching the prison for activity. If the demons send out a search force..." He pulled a radio from his waistband. "Then we have these. The batteries are getting low, so how long this will last I don't know. Just bear with me, Ember, help will be here soon, it really will; then we can go in and find Connor."

I cocked my head and stared at him, then studied the faces of his brothers —Connor's brothers. None of them would meet my gaze.

"You think he's dead already, don't you?"

Stone pulled his gaze off B'nar and eyed me in his cold way. "Yes. I have always been able to feel his connection to me and I haven't since the day we escaped."

"That's because I took his wolf. It's what my phoenix does, she demands a life for a life. Connor ended my human body to stop Berith from getting my human soul, but he didn't know it meant he'd lose his wolf; that she'd take him. That's why your Prime is in me and not Connor. That's why he's still a prisoner, and that's why I'm going to get him out. He needs help and you all owe him that."

Stone kept his eyes on me. "We do—if he's alive. But even if he is, Connor is human without his wolf, and that's why Owen won't risk more lives to go and get him." Stone looked me in the eye, his silver gaze as cold as B'nar's. "Ember, he could not survive being tortured—not by a general of Hell."

"No!" I yelled. "He is *not* dead! How can you sit here and not even consider getting him back? Gods, he'd burn the world down to find you! Any of you! How can you just abandon him like this?"

"Ember, try and see it from our point of view. Ever since he took our bond, we have all felt him. I haven't felt a godsdamned thing from him since we left that place. Don't you think that kills me?" Owen took a deep breath, his muscles rippling under the tight t-shirt. "Until you showed up, we believed him and our Prime, dead. Gods, I hope I'm wrong and he isn't, but I can't risk the lives of this pack. They are not all warriors and if we went to the lower levels, we'd be overwhelmed and likely never get out. We need to wait for back up. Drake will be here soon and he is bringing tech—loads of it, and reinforcements." Owen's voice was irritatingly reasonable. Gods, how I hated it when people spoke to me like that. It made me beyond furious, and I just wanted to punch them for being so reasonable rather than seeing things my way! I rubbed my face realising my hands were hot.

Blue watched me as she sharpened one of her knives. I met her gaze and then Alex's. B'nar watched Blue before he met my eyes. He might agree with Owen from a strategy point of view, but he knew Blue wanted to help me, and whether she knew it or not, that made him willing to help me too. My heart jumped. I understood my friends as clearly as they understood me. I sat back down. "Fine." I sighed. "What's your plan?"

Owen leaned back. "Drake and Charlie went for help. We kept in touch via these." He pulled a phone from his pocket. I gaped at the thing. I'd seen hide nor hair of technology like that in Faerie. "When we got into the IT room, Drake hacked the system and found a town about three hundred miles south. He also found a phone on one of the guards. He made a few calls and he rings this at seven o'clock every night to keep me updated on his progress. He's coming back tomorrow night, the day after at the latest. We should wait for his back up before we send anymore people into that prison to die."

I clamped my mouth shut until my jaw ached, trying to wrangle Prime's need to reassert his dominance over these other wolves. Connor wouldn't leave *them* to die—or would he? I rubbed my eyes which were stinging with tiredness. Connor was a strategic player, a top agent; maybe he would do exactly what Owen was suggesting. And did I really want to put more lives at risk?

"I understand. Right, so do you have somewhere we can grab some shut eye? It's been a really long day."

Owen smiled sympathetically. "Of course. One of the smaller back caves near the women, will be free. It's cold back there but I guess that isn't a problem for you."

I smiled and stood, along with my little entourage.

Shannon hopped up too. "I'll take you." Stone openly watched her but remained quiet.

We followed her through the main cave where people bedded down, some with a blanket, but most without. The main cave was far warmer than the small tunnel she led us down. I couldn't believe how big this network of caves was, or how lucky Owen had been to stumble across it. They'd all be dead from exposure by now if he hadn't found it.

"Here." Shannon shoved a large black torch at me. "It's from the stash of equipment we took off the dead guards."

I clicked it on, but passed it to Blue, who grinned.

"Thanks, bitch."

B'nar just shook his head. It was almost funny seeing his disapproval at the way we spoke to each other. He clearly had no idea about our quirky interactions and it really amused Blue to wind him up.

"Welcome. I don't need it." I grinned and lit up a ball of fire in my left hand, holding it out to light our way. Not to be outdone, B'nar didn't even leave it a second before he did exactly the same with his magic, lighting the cave easily. Blue rolled her eyes. "Always the showoff."

"What's the matter, human? Jealous? Now, put your puny torch away."

"I like my new torch. So, no."

B'nar shrugged and lit the cave further.

"So, runt? What's your plan?" asked Shannon as she led us to a small dark cave which was cold enough our breath made clouds of mist.

"Yeah, what's your plan?" Alex stepped right up to my flank.

"Yeah, sweet thing, what's your plan? 'Cause if you're stupid enough to put yourself in danger, which you definitely are, then the big man would want me to help watch your back." Lionel stepped in front of me and winked. I hadn't heard him prowl along behind us, which was very disconcerting. "You didn't think you'd be able to get away without me, did you? Besides, Owen knows you'll try and leave, so he sent me here to make sure you don't."

I quirked a brow. "So you're going to defy your alpha?"

Lionel crossed his massive arms across his equally massive chest. "Haven't you worked it out yet? I have no alpha. I respected Connor's power, and I respect Owen, but I will not answer to them or ask their permission for anything. I am my own master."

Smirking, I let Fire settle back down seeing as B'nar seemed content to use his magic to light the cave. "That makes perfect sense." I cocked my head and studied B'nar. The prince wasn't tired like the rest of us, or at least, he didn't look it. In fact, he appeared more powerful. I guessed the cold environment suited him.

I studied the rock floor, most of it was smooth, and there was no ice or dirt on the floor so I sat myself down. I knew exactly what I needed to do. Blue sat near me and I could feel her curious gaze. Peering at my friend, even in the slightly blue tinged light that B'nar emitted, she looked cold and couldn't hide her shivers. "You okay?" I asked as she shivered some more.

"Yeah, it's just cold enough to freeze the rivers of Hell in here."

B'nar immediately strode over to her, eyeing her with what looked like concern. Alex's lips twitched into a smile. Lionel watched them curiously, weighing them up as he did everyone. It was obvious to me that B'nar was conflicted over Blue, even if he wouldn't admit it. He looked at me and then at Blue, his jaw muscles clenching. I took pity on him. Making him ask was petty, and I wasn't going to let my friend freeze to death. Fire happily gave me access to her magic, so I shuffled away from Blue and became a gentle full body torch in the middle of the cave.

"B'nar? Can you get us back into the prison with the ring?"

The prince didn't look surprised by my request. "Yes."

"Then that's my plan, folks. I'm going back to look for Connor. He's my mate, and I will not rest until I know if he is alive—" I swallowed rapidly, panic trying to set in. "I need to know, one way or another." Glancing at the faces of my friends, even Shannon, I sighed. "Listen, I need B'nar to get me there, but none of you have to…"

"Yes, we do," Lionel interrupted.

"He's right we do," agreed Alex.

"Yeah, you needn't think you're ditching me, either," said Blue, with a small smile. She looked better now but there were dark shadows under her eyes. My friend was totally human, and I kicked myself for not thinking about her more. The rest of us could keep going on much less rest than Blue.

I smirked. "I wouldn't dare."

"You're such a liar." But she smiled and blew me a kiss.

"Well, I'm coming too, runt."

I leaned back on my elbows and stretched my legs out in front. It didn't feel right just leaving Owen and the others, but I couldn't wait for Drake and his back up. Something inside me urged me to return to the prison. I'd go immediately, if I thought we all had enough energy to fight.

"Fine. We all go together. We're a team now." I glanced at B'nar. "All of us." And I meant it. B'nar didn't have to help me, nor did he have to let Blue be by my side. After all, by faerie law she was his. The Prince inhaled and his spine straightened a bit. It made me wonder if he'd ever been part of a team, or always on the outside looking in. It struck me then that his life might not be all pretty icicles and snowflakes. His father was the High King and he was the heir to all that responsibility. That must be hard on him. I gave him a small smile, surprised when he returned it. I glanced at Blue, but she didn't notice, she was too busy staring at B'nar's uptilted mouth.

I hid my grin. "Let's get a few hours rest, then we'll sneak out."

"Fine. Can we leave from here?" Shannon's gaze met mine, her mouth in a tight line. "Owen, and definitely Stone, will have my ass if I defy them."

"You don't need to come, Shannon, not if it will get you into trouble with them…"

"I'm coming," she interrupted, making a dismissive gesture. "Stone will forgive me…eventually. So that means Owen will too. Besides, I owe Connor. He helped me in that prison, even when I was a bitch to him. And we both know he didn't need to." She got up and brushed off her jeans. "I'll be back soon with food. We'll eat before we go. Who knows when our next meal will be."

I inhaled through my nose, trying not to think about the ways she paid him back for his help.

Her eyes narrowed. "Don't go there, runt. It meant nothing to him, and you know it."

I closed my eyes. Knowing she was right didn't make it easier to stomach.

"See you soon," she said quietly before leaving us.

B'nar stared at Blue who had laid down as close to me as she could get without cooking. Two lines appeared on the bridge of his nose. "Human, come here."

Blue's mouth flattened into a stubborn line. "Not bloody likely."

"It is not your choice. Come." He hooked his finger at her and beckoned her.

Blue's nostrils flared and she met my gaze, fury burning in her eyes before she sighed heavily. "Fine." She pushed herself onto her knees. "What?"

B'nar ignored her and shucked his heavy armoured jacket off, followed by his shirt. Even I had to admire his naked chest. He was a beautiful male specimen, leaner than Connor, but the dips and ridges of muscle did not sport any extra fat. His skin was pale and almost translucent, not blue like his father's. Blue swallowed, hard. I couldn't help but feel sorry for my poor friend. Being attracted to her captor must be a special kind of Hell.

"Lay down here." B'nar patted the thin mattress of his clothes. Blue kept her face devoid of expression as she did as he said. B'nar looked almost surprised by her compliance. When my friend had settled stiffly right next to him, B'nar touched the edge of his jacket. It sparkled. Magic covering it.

Blue gasped. "It's warm."

I blinked. So B'nar could do fancy things with his magic.

"It's supposed to be. My magic will keep my body heat, such as it is, sealed in my clothes and stop the cold seeping into you. Now sleep. You need to rest." Blue watched his face for a moment. He held her gaze. I swallowed hard, the energy between them was off the charts. B'nar raised his brows. "Sleep, human. You will not get cold." Blue closed her eyes, squeezing them shut when B'nar laid down next her and pulled her into his big body. She gasped, but he didn't let her go. "I will keep you warm." And he closed his eyes, keeping her locked in his arms.

I swallowed a lump in my throat. I had a feeling my friend had no idea how deep the prince's feelings for her ran. At least, it looked like they did. I sighed, hoping they would both realise it soon. It was easier to close my burning eyes than watch them locked so closely together. I missed Connor so much. After that first time I'd thought him dead, I didn't think my heart could hurt or break ever again. Then he put the pieces of me back together, only now he was gone again. I had to hold onto the hope that he was still alive, or I would shatter. He was the glue that held me together and without him I would always be broken. It had been too long since I had felt his warmth seep into me, or the touch of his lips on mine… My wolves both whined, the tear that escaped my eye, turning to steam on my cheek.

Shannon returned a few hours later. I hadn't really slept, too impatient to get back to the prison, but at least Blue looked more rested—and really confused by waking in B'nars arms. She seemed too shocked to move for a while, and just stared at his face. As if feeling her attention, his eyelids opened, his pale green eyes glowing as he registered her attention. Blue flushed, and shuffled away from him, not meeting his eyes again.

I looked away, their feelings for each other were none of my business, and I needed to save my energy for finding my own soulmate; not worry about them working things out. Could a human even be a match for the second most powerful fae in Faerie?

"Here." Shannon passed out some energy bars and cans of diet cola.

Alex took a huge swallow. "Gods, that's so good."

Shannon grinned. "Yeah, thank the guards' kitchen for that. It was one of the first places we found when we raided the prison."

Lionel stretched out his big body, unfurling in a smooth, predatory move. "Yep, it was worth the battle to get in there—and the laundry; that was important. Got all sorts of clothes and blankets from there before we couldn't carry anymore between us."

Hearing Lionel explain more about the raids helped me understand how much Owen had done to save the people in the camp. I was sure Connor would be proud of his friend's determination and fortitude.

Gulping down the last of my coke, I quickly finished my meagre meal.

"So Owen's already left with most of the others to sweep the forest. Apparently, Drake is arriving later today and they want the forest clear of Weres." Shannon's face was tight. "Stone didn't even bother to tell me he was leaving —that bastard. He wants me to stay here, out of the way; well, he can piss off if he thinks that's happening."

My stomach lurched. "I didn't realise Owen meant Drake was coming so quickly."

Shannon shrugged. "He didn't know. Drake contacted him after you left the cave last night. They'll be here by this afternoon, I would imagine."

"Will they attack the prison straight away?"

She raised her brows. "No. Owen's too much of a planner, and far too careful for that kind of rash behaviour. And if we wait around until they get back, they will stop us from leaving."

"Why?"

"I don't mean all of us. He'll accept help from them." She pointed at B'nar, Alex and Lionel, and even included Blue. "Maybe even you—but not from me. Look, no matter how much I respect Owen—and Stone, even though he's an arse most of the time—they can't help but be alphas. They would stop us both going to fight, and you know it. Protection is an alphas greatest strength and their most bullshit weakness—especially with...well..." Her eyes met mine. "You know what I mean."

I cocked a brow. "You mean Stone wants you where he can control what happens to you, and you are defying him, so he gets pissed at you—and Owen will support him. Is that why you're still not together?"

Shannon scowled. "No one gets to control my life but me. Look, I want to help you, like you once helped me, and I owe Connor. Not even Stoney will stop me from doing what I think is right."

I raised my brows. "*Stoney?* Surely calling him pet names is one sure fire way to piss him off?"

She grinned and shrugged, crossing her arms over her chest. "Exactly. He deserves to be annoyed; he annoys me enough. Besides, it amuses me that I'm the only one he lets call him names."

I huffed a chuckle, but didn't ask more. Just like Blue and B'nar, I wished them well, but I was more invested in my own love life, which I would never have if Connor was gone. I swallowed the knot of fear in my throat and listened to the urging of Prime.

"Ready?" I asked.

B'nar nodded. I didn't bother to hide my impatience, not now that Connor's wolf was growling in my head, his impatience infecting me. "Let's go then."

We all secured our weapons and B'nar fed his magic to the ring. Within seconds the portal appeared. He found the corridor where we'd discovered Selina. It looked deserted. The rest of the prisoners, even the dead bodies were gone. Taking a deep breath, I leaped. Gritting my teeth, I stubbornly held onto my two wolf spirits; Fire helping me keep them inside my flesh and bone body. I burst from the energy surge, landing firmly on the other side. Not slowing my momentum, I ran a few steps and skidded into a crouch against the wall, not moving until the others were out of the portal.

Alex grabbed Shannon's arm. Yeah, I'd warned her to keep her wolf spirit close and told her going through the portal would hurt like a bitch, but nothing could really prepare her.

She swallowed and nodded. "Yep. I'll be fine. Let's go."

Lionel swore, breathing deeply. "Shit, that's a horrible experience."

"Yeah. You good, big man?"

He nodded, pushing aside his discomfort. His lion rolled across his eyes in a flash of amber. "Let's go."

Slowly, we crept forward. Overhead, the lights only flickered on and off and it was eerily quiet. We needed to find where they were keeping the rest of the prisoners. Hadn't Owen said something about the lower levels, near the warden's quarters?

I gasped as something tugged at my chest. It was a pull that urged me onward. The further into the prison we went, the more urgency I felt. My heart banged against my ribs, beating faster with each step I took.

"Where are we going?" Blue whispered when I took the left fork instead of one to the right. I didn't answer, mainly because I couldn't, my breath caught in my throat. It was a feeling; a painful one, urging me on. Another turn, then another.

Damn, this place is huge!

In the distance, I heard footsteps. Running, desperate footsteps. The distant growls of Weres filtered into the quiet. Something yanked at my chest and Connor's wolf howled, pushing against my skin. Before I could even think about the stupidity of it, I was sprinting down the corridor as if my life depended on it.

A set of double doors at the bottom of the dim corridor burst open and three people stumbled through.

"Oh, my gods!" My words were nothing but a whisper of disbelief. My heart pounded and I sheathed my weapon. "Connor!" I yelled, tears burning my eyes.

Zander's red eyes widened as he recognised who was barrelling down the corridor towards him and the emaciated figure he was half dragging, half carrying.

I skidded to a halt in front of them and fell to my knees so that I could stare up into Connor's face. Tears fell unchecked down my cheeks. He was starved and beaten, covered in scars and bruises. I took his face in my hands and lifted it. His eyes fluttered open but they didn't look vibrant, they were dull and full of darkness. My heart stuttered. "Oh, Mother Wolf, what did he do to you?" Though I wasn't sure I wanted to know.

"Ember?" Zander uttered, his voice shaking, his eyes glowing a deep red. A cacophony of howls resounded from the other side of the double doors he had barged through.

I gently let go of Connor's face and jumped up from my knees, ignoring how much they were shaking. I needed to be strong. "We need to get out of here. Now!"

Zander nodded, so did the dark haired woman by his side. Right at that moment, I didn't care who she was, I only wanted to get Connor away from this place and help him heal. Gods, I had never seen him look so weak.

Zander's eyes glowed brighter. "Can you take him?" He asked B'nar, who stood silently behind me. I felt his power crackling in the air. It was ready if we needed it.

"I am stronger than you." It wasn't an arrogant statement from the prince; he was merely stating a fact. "You are weak. I sense it. I will deal with them. You will run," the prince informed Zander.

Zander didn't argue. He must have agreed because he glanced at Alex. "Help me."

Alex immediately put his weapon in his other hand and pulled Connor's arm over his shoulder. Together they moved Connor away from the doors just as they burst open.

B'nar cracked his neck, his eyes glowing that eerie green, magic whirling around his hands. Blue lifted her weapon, Shannon mirroring her.

I snarled and grabbed B'nar's arm. "No. They're mine." These were the ones who had kept my mate from me. They were no longer shifters, but vessels for demons who would destroy those I loved. Prime's anger amplified my own, his blood lust as strong as my own. I would find Berith—maybe not right now, but once Connor was healed, I would hunt him down and send him back to the fiery pits of Hell. "Protect them from me." My instruction was for B'nar.

B'nar didn't speak. He merely turned around, his footsteps crunching through the debris behind me. I grinned at the monsters sprinting towards me—and unleashed Fire. I burned and burned. Even when my enemy had been incinerated, I burned. I melted the rooms and everything in them, burning hotter and hotter as my anger at what they'd done fed my power.

Only the desperate urging of my wolf penetrated my rage. She urged me to stop, or I would end up killing my friends and my very human mate. Slowly, I brought Fire back under control and we turned to check on them. Prime's need for release, to kill and feel blood run down his throat, to rip and destroy, was consuming. Behind the wall of ice B'nar had erected, Connor's dull eyes watched me. His image was distorted, but I saw the shadow that swirled around him, trying its best to escape. Connor's face tightened and it disappeared back inside his body as if he worked hard to control it. My eyes narrowed. I'd seen that shadow around his body before, but it had never looked as if it was trying to escape him. I met that pain filled stare and my heart skipped a beat. He was alive.

My wolf rumbled low. She was right. Vengeance would be mine, eventually. Right now, Connor needed my help.

CHAPTER 7

*E*mber

SHANNON'S EYES WERE WIDE. I glanced at her, my fury burning hot, but I had no inclination to explain my power or how it worked. I waved my hand in front of the ice and it fell away.

"Hey man, you look done. Let me take him for a while." Lionel shoved his weapon in its holster and went to take Connor from Zander.

"No!" growled Zander, pulling Connor closer, his eyes burning, and his skin splitting showing what looked like small veins of lava.

"Okaaay, whoa!" Lionel said, raising his hands.

Zander glared, heat emanating from him. The dark haired woman placed a hand on his arm. His eyes flickered to her. "It's alright, Zander. No one's going to hurt him anymore. You got him this far. And they are here to help."

"I know." His voice was gravelly and animalistic. Still he didn't release his hold, and shadows similar to the ones I saw dance around Connor, swirled around him forming what looked like wings at his back. "But I can manage." He set his jaw. "Ready?" His question was directed at Alex.

Alex nodded. "Lead the way."

"Zander, do you know the quickest way out?" As I asked this question an unholy chorus of roars shook the walls.

The thin dark haired woman trembled. "We must go." Her voice was barely a whisper. "He has sent them for us."

"No, not the stairs. I can hear them coming. Down there." Zander directed us to a corridor off to the right.

Lionel and Shannon ran ahead. B'nar and Blue followed behind me. I stayed close to Connor, wondering why Prime wasn't clamouring to break free of me and back to Connor. I had no idea how to get him back in my mate's body, but I'd find a way. Maybe Walker would know. Mother knew, I'd grovel on my knees for forgiveness from the King of Faerie if it meant Connor could be fully healed.

This corridor was in shadow, the overhead lights broken and hanging down from the ceiling. Not wanting to advertise our direction, I kept Fire locked down. That meant we all had to use our enhanced sight. Blue was at a disadvantage, but B'nar held on tightly to one of her arms, guiding her as she trained her gun into the shadows we left behind. Even the woman with Zander seemed to revel in the darkness. Behind us the sound of crashing came, howls ripping through the air.

"In there." Zander said. "There's a back exit into the service tunnels."

We pushed through the door and locked it for all the good it would do. B'nar stopped and speared me with his gaze, his face hard. "They cannot be allowed to take you. Without fighting, I have enough magic for one more portal, and that's enough to get us out."

I nodded, impatient to get Connor out of this place. "Let's do it. Back to the caves?"

B'nar nodded, his eyes gleaming like twin green orbs of ice.

"Move over there."

Blue did as B'nar asked, her gun trained on the door, but her eyes flicked to him. Beyond, was the unmistakable sound of stamping feet as the Weres approached. Zander shifted himself as B'nar began to chant, the ring illuminating the room.

Zander's eyes glowed brighter. "What's going on?"

"We have another way out."

He looked at me suspiciously, but hitched Connor up as he sagged, unconscious, between him and Alex. The woman stood in the shadow at Zander's side.

The ring reacted to B'nar's fae words and pulled my attention back to him. The air in front of him collapsed in on itself and then expanded outward, pulling in a breeze. The shadows at B'nar's back erupted, the door burst in and a Were with burning eyes lifted some kind of weapon and launched it at his back.

"No!" Blue screamed and leapt into the path of the demon possessed werewolf. The weapon struck her in the shoulder with such force it thrust her into B'nar's back knocking him forward, before she crashed to the ground.

"Jump! Now!" he yelled, looking at me. Holding the hand with the portal ring on out in front and keeping it steady, he turned sideways and blasted the demonic creature backwards with ice. The creature ducked but I was waiting. With my bow, I released an arrow, followed closely by another. The werewolf crashed back against the door, forcing it closed, again. My heart hammered against my ribs. This werewolf was possessed by a demon but I would know it anywhere. It had been me who had looked into its eyes as I killed it; and I couldn't do that again, I had to see if there was a way to get this demon out of my friend; because that's what Reed had become while I'd been a prisoner here—my friend.

"Zander! Get Connor out of here now!"

His demonic eyes widened. "Mother!" he yelled over his shoulder, indicating with his head for the woman to jump. Without hesitation she did, and I had to wonder if this wasn't the first time she'd seen a portal.

"Lionel! Help me!" I wanted to get Blue out first, but I also needed Reed. Even if I couldn't save him, I could find a way to send that demon back to Hell and free his souls. I bent down at Blue's side. Her face was so pale, fear speared my heart. "No…"

"I will take her!" B'nar roared. "Get out now! They are coming!"

I shot bolts of flame towards our enemy, giving Lionel a chance to grab Reed's huge body. The descending Were army pulled back as the first through the door burst into flame. Lionel roared and his shirt and jacket split as he half changed, pulling on the power of his lion. He lifted Reed and flung him over his shoulder before running into the portal. I prayed to the Mother that it wouldn't kill him. Going through a portal always tried to pull a shifter's animal spirit out, in Were form, I had no idea what would happen.

B'nar swooped down, his face utterly icy. "In the portal. Now. I have her. She is mine."

No way was I arguing with that. B'nar was as powerful as his father, if not as experienced, and his voice held that possessive, growling quality I'd heard too many times to wonder what it meant. I ran into the portal, the power of the vortex tugging at me, but I held onto my wolves. Prime snarled as Connor and Zander fell out of the portal and into the caves that I could see getting closer. B'nar chanted as I was pulled along to the end of the portal. I looked back and the portal behind B'nar collapsed, preventing any of the swarm of Weres from pursuing us. He must have wanted to run with Blue but I knew he wouldn't leave me behind, if only so that no Were, or Berith himself, could pull me from the portal.

As soon as we sprinted from the portal, B'nar lowered Blue to the ground and the portal collapsed. Running across the cave, my focus was on my mate. Zander lowered Connor to the ground and I fell to my knees beside the man who held my heart and soul.

"Connor? Please wake up." I tenderly cupped his face in my hands, tears filling my eyes and rolling down my cheeks. His eyes fluttered open. "Fire-cracker?"

A sob broke free from me. My chest hurt. I had honestly thought I'd never hear him call me that again.

"Hey, Shannon's gone for help." Lionel told me, his hand squeezing my shoulder. That gesture of support helped me be strong. I nodded and looked at Zander. His body crumpled and he sank down next to the woman on the cave floor. Both of them leaned their backs against the cave wall, looking exhausted.

"What the hell happened to him? The last time I saw him, Berith had broken his back. He's weak, but I saw him take some weight through his legs..."

Zander swallowed, his strong throat bobbing. When he opened his eyelids again, his irises were burning with red fire. His jaw muscles tensed and his lips flattened into a tight line. "He did break Connor—and not just his back, Em." Zander ran a hand through his dark hair leaving the rich dark strands messy.

My heart flipped, an ache tightening my chest. "What do you mean?" But my skin was already cold. Part of me knew his imprisonment would have been crueler than anything I could comprehend.

"Berith is a special kind of depraved bastard; a demon with such power that he will stop at nothing to get what he wants. He broke Connor over and over. Every day, Berith tortured him with visions of you, while breaking all of the bones in his body. Sometimes he would heal him and then torture him again; sometimes he'd leave Connor in his own filth with a broken back and not heal him for days. He..." Zander swallowed, his eyes burning and shadows flickering around him. His head and shoulders bowed.

My hands curled into fists. I never thought I'd see the day that Zander looked broken.

"He tortured my brother—so much." His voice cracked with emotion, and my heart stopped and started again.

Brother?

Connor stirred at his words, his eyes widening a bit before swirling with a light I'd never seen before.

"Berith is pure evil, born in the depths of Hell." The thin woman said. "He is a high calibre demon, who, I'm sure you know, becomes more powerful by feeding on the chaos of men: on murder, on dissension, and on pain."

I turned to the woman who had a strange kind of energy emanating from her. It wasn't the same as Walker's or B'nar's or even Stone's, but it was simi-lar. Again, shadows swirled around Zander and the woman as I stared at her.

"Who are you?"

The woman lifted her chin. "I am Tyen."

"Um, hello Tyen." In a lightning quick move, I pulled a faerie dagger and pointed it directly at her heart. "And who are you, *exactly?*"

"No," bellowed Zander, shifting his bulk to push in front of Tyen, his eyes wide and panicked.

Tyen rested her fingers on his arm and he allowed her to push him aside, though his jaw remained tight and his eyes watchful as shadow and smoke swirled around him.

"It's alright." Tyen's obsidian eyes met mine and she took a deep breath. "I am Zander's mother."

I shot Zander a look, my eyes wide. "Really?"

He sighed and nodded, looking suddenly weary. "Yes."

Things started to click into place, and I lowered my weapon. "Who is your father, Zander?"

He lifted his chin, looking as defiant and stubborn as Connor ever had. "Berith." Whether he knew it or not, the shadow that seemed to cling to him, enveloped Connor as well. And it hit me. I shuffled sideways, brushing my palm over Connor's jaw. "Why have you always tried to protect Connor? Why Zander? Why have you risked your life getting him out of that place, and away from your father?"

Zander clenched his jaw and looked at Tyen. She nodded. "It's okay, we can tell her. He's safe, now that he's away from that bastard. We all are."

Connor's top lip curled a little.

Zander sat forward, his eyes flickering between me and Connor. He was clearly reluctant, but took a deep breath. "Because Connor is my brother. Tyen is his mother, too."

My mouth gaped open, my attention shooting to the woman. "You're his mother?"

The woman seemed to grow taller. Her eyes took on a dark glint and her chin tilted up. "That is the truth. His father was a wolf shifter, a bastard of a man who bought me from a supernatural slave market. When I didn't provide him with more children, he sold me to the warden for the promise of more power and wealth."

"Oh, Mother Wolf. Does Connor know? That you're his mother? That you're his brother?" I couldn't get my head around this new information.

"Well, if he didn't, he does now," muttered Alex. He was right, Connor was looking at Zander with eyes so dark they were black. I couldn't see anything of the Connor I knew in those eyes. They were utterly cold. A spike of fear made me shuffle away from him. I wasn't sure why, he was human after all, but I couldn't help my reaction to the hate in his eyes as he looked at Zander.

Zander sat forward and held Connor's gaze. "Didn't you ever wonder why I tried so hard to help you?"

Connor huffed, his top lip curled. "Why would I? You were the one who helped imprison me, weren't you? Then you brought Ember into the mix. You blackmailed me with her safety." He took a deep breath as if talking was too much for his weak body. "You led me right into Berith's lair. You used me to get in there—and then left me there to be tortured."

Zander's face fell. He shook his head. "No, you're wrong, I didn't leave you, or use you. Gods, I came back for you as soon as I could. Berith was always there until those last few days. I had to wait until it was safer, to get you out. If he had suspected I was going to help you escape, he'd have locked me up with my mother. And I needed to free her, too…"

"Save it. I don't need to hear your fucking excuses." Connor's voice was so weak, yet so full of hate and pain my anxiety spiked. I'd never heard Connor sound so cold. But then, I supposed it was to be expected.

"Zander, please. Let's leave it for now. He needs to rest. You can explain things better when you're both stronger."

"Yeah, you're right. Now isn't the time." Zander just sounded weary now, and I wondered how much he'd suffered, too, because of Berith.

A thought struck me. "What did Berith do with Rawson? Have you seen him, Zander?"

Zander stared at Connor, a deep furrow appearing on his forehead. Connor had lost interest in Zander, and was staring at Tyen. The brow furrow got deeper. After a moment, Zander looked at me and then held my gaze. "No. I haven't seen him since you were first brought to the prison."

That was a lie and we both knew it. We'd all been together many times. I blinked slowly. He just held my gaze before he slowly shifted his attention back to Connor. "Oh, okay." But it wasn't. Why was he lying? He had a reason, I could see that much, but one he didn't want Connor to know?

CHAPTER 8

SHANNON RETURNED with Owen and Stone. Behind them Myles and Kawan loitered, staring at Connor as if they didn't know what to do. I tensed. Owen was their alpha now. I moved in front of Connor. Owen could easily kill Connor, after all, Connor was human without his wolf spirit, and Berith had abused him so badly his body was emaciated and broken. I couldn't feel any power around him. I inhaled, searching for his scent, my stomach sinking when it was so faint I could barely find it.

Myles froze when his attention was pulled to the massive werewolf Lionel guarded. Reed was unconscious and still. Pain flared in Myles's eyes at the sight of his mate brought back from the dead, only to realise he was possessed by evil. The Mother only knew what kind of creature Reed was inside. My heart and mind had enough to deal with so I blinked my burning eyes and watched Owen approach Connor, flanked by Kawan and Stone. My hand began to burn and though I didn't look down, I was sure I heard a chuckle from Connor.

Owen's face betrayed his horror. Not caring about appearances, he dropped to his knees and pulled Connor into a fierce embrace. Connor might have lost his bulk, but even as skin and bone, he wasn't small. It didn't faze Owen, and I lost my battle with my emotions, tears falling down my cheeks. Owen and Connor had been together since they were new SBI recruits, right up to the point Doherty had betrayed them both. They had been through hell together. For a moment, Owen just hugged Connor. "Gods, brother, I thought you were dead. It's so fucking good to see you."

Connor huffed and pushed away.

I relaxed a bit, pulling Fire back. If Owen wasn't going to challenge Connor, or try and kill him, then the others wouldn't either.

Connor looked away from Owen, basically dismissing his brother. His face remained blank and his eyes studied who else was around him before his attention fell on me again. My skin prickled, but not in a good way. I don't know why. Perhaps it was the coldness in his eyes, or the way his scent had changed—he was different. But then, guilt spiked me. Of course he was different, he'd been a victim of torture for weeks.

"Hey, I know you all want to see him again, but maybe reunions would be best left until he is stronger." Thankfully, Owen agreed with my gentle suggestion.

Connor wasn't the only one who needed some time. Being around him again wasn't what I had expected, or hoped for. I wanted to be close to him, yet I also didn't know how to act, or what to do. It seemed like there was a chasm between us. I stood, confused about my feelings. When I'd first seen Connor in that prison after believing him dead for four years, it hadn't been anything like this. I'd felt an instant connection to him. Why am I not feeling that now? Had Walker done something to me to separate my bond from Connor? I tried not to let my fear show, aware his gaze followed me as I greeted Drake. "Hey, you. I didn't see you sneak in at the back."

The handsome southerner shrugged and smiled before he pulled me into his arms, hugging me tightly. "Hey, it's good to see you, too, sugar. I'm so glad you're okay." His eyes drifted to Connor. "How's he doin'?"

My eyes burned, but I wouldn't cry, not yet. "I-I don't really know."

Drake nodded, his handsome face serious. "Yeah, it's gonna be hard on you both for a while. But you leave that prison and the bastard who runs it to us. We'll stop him. I've got some better living quarters outside. We'll get Connor in one of those, and then you can spend some time together while we set up the rest of the camp." He took my jaw in his fingers and thumb and tilted my head. His thumb grazed the mark he'd left under my jaw. "Remember, I'm still your alpha, if you need me, I'm here for you."

Drake's words were genuine, his green eyes dark and sincere. It was hard holding in the emotion that threatened to overwhelm me. I wasn't convinced I really had my mate back, but I had my friends, and my alpha was safe and well. There were others I wanted to check on and I had to talk to Zander about Rawson. Clearly something had happened that he didn't want to discuss in front of Connor. That thought by itself had my pulse rate rising. And regardless of Drake's confidence, we still had a war with a demon lord and his army to fight if we wanted to keep our world safe from becoming Hell's playground.

"I just need to check on Blue first, then we'll talk again. Okay?" I took his hand and stood on my tiptoes to kiss his cheek. "It's really good to see you, Drake. I'm glad you're here."

"Sure thing, sugar. I'll get you to somewhere you can rest, and then you can find me when you're ready."

Taking a fortifying breath, I turned to where my friend laid pale and unmoving in the fae prince's arms. Blood oozed down B'nar's jacket and pooled under her. Shannon passed him a wad of gauze from a small first-aid kit.

Connor moaned as Stone and Owen hoisted him up between them. "It's okay, Em," Owen said. "You see to your friend. We'll take Connor to a cabin..."

A cabin? I wondered exactly what equipment Drake had brought with him. But my whole body tensed as they stepped away with Connor. I growled, both Mea and Prime unhappy about being parted from Connor so soon. "No! Hold up. Wait for a moment; I'm coming with you. He's my mate and I won't leave him."

"It's okay, Em, we'll wait," Owen agreed calmly, lowering Connor back down.

Reluctantly, I left Connor to be cared for by his brothers. Zander sat back, watching carefully as Kawan, Myles and Stone all lingered near Connor. It seemed Zander didn't know what to say to Connor now, but the others had all accepted him back as their friend and brother if not their alpha–yet. Prime rumbled inside me, inhaling the air deeply before a menacing growl resounded in my head. Goosebumps shivered over my skin as foreboding invaded me. Prime wasn't clamouring to reach Connor, quite the opposite, in fact.

Trying not to panic about Prime's, or my feelings for Connor, I dropped to my knees by Blue. Her hand was so cold when I took it in mine, I gasped, dread dragging at my heart. B'nar looked up from where he tried to stop the blood oozing around the entry site of the weapon in Blue's shoulder. He snarled when Alex approached, even though he'd not reacted when Shannon or I had come closer. My heart went out to the fae prince, and my friend. "Blue? Come on, girl. You need to hold on. Fight to stay with us, I need you..." My eyes went to B'nar's tight, yet beautiful face. "B'nar needs you. Come on, who's going to give him sass if you're not around?"

B'nar snarled again as Alex dared to come a bit closer.

"Hey, it's alright, I'm not going to touch her," Alex said, stopping so that B'nar didn't get any more aggressive. "How's she doing?"

"She's dying. I can't stop the bleeding." B'nar's voice actually shook. He looked at me, his eyes a darker emerald than I'd ever seen, lines furrowing his brow. "I need to take her home. My magic is stronger there, and our healers can help her. I can take this thing from her shoulder, but if I do it here, she'll bleed to death."

I nodded, but I knew it didn't matter if I disagreed. B'nar had already bitten into his finger so his blood dripped down onto the ring. He lifted his hand and chanted. Even Connor raised his head, his eyes focusing on the portal as it appeared. Once again, a strange sense of dread filled me, and Prime snarled. I pushed my worry aside and leaned forward, giving Blue a kiss on her cold cheek. "Fight, Blue. You get better, you hear me, bitch? You're tougher than this," I whispered into her ear as the portal energy whipped the air into a frenzy.

B'nar scooped Blue into his arms and held her close to his chest. "Come with us?"

I shook my head, my gaze landing on Connor and the others.

He nodded, his blue hair gleaming in the light of the energy which zipped across the portal. "I didn't think you would, but I have a feeling my punishment for defying my father and taking that ring, will be worse because I have left you behind. I doubt he will allow me to return here, unless it is to bring you back to Faerie. Take care, phoenix. Remember our world, as well as your own, is depending on you not getting caught."

"I know, B'nar." I rested my hand on his arm and squeezed. I'd have kissed him, I was so grateful for what he'd done for me and Connor, but I couldn't reach him with Blue in his arms and his height. I doubted he would appreciate such touchy, feely sentiments, anyway. "I know you've risked a lot to help me, and I'll do everything I can to stop Berith. I'll not let him catch me or use me to set his army free."

B'nar nodded, but didn't say anything. I think we both knew such a powerful demon was going to be hard to stop, let alone stay away from. He peered at Alex, cocking his head in question.

"No, Prince, I'm staying for now. I owe Connor, and I promised you I'd watch out for our phoenix...so, later man."

B'nar didn't bother with a goodbye, merely stepped into the portal, Blue cradled close to his chest, and disappeared. I pushed aside my worry for Blue and tried to concentrate on what was happening around me. If anyone could save my friend it was B'nar—and Walker. All assuming the High King didn't lock Blue, or even his son away as punishment for taking the portal ring.

I turned around to see everyone staring between me and the air beside me where the portal had been.

"Damn, those things are real then?" asked Owen, his wolf flashing in his eyes.

Stone turned a hard expression on him. "Of course they are, how do you think me, or any other fae got into this world? I have lived in both worlds. But illegal portals are hard to find and are never kept in the same place for long, or they are hunted down by the SBI and destroyed. It's harder in Faerie to stop them from being used, as the High King's forces are spread thinly across the whole of Faerie, and politics and borders stop him getting to those in realms other than his own."

"Oh, right. 'Course." Owen looked like he wanted to ask Stone more questions, but turned to me instead. "So who was that?"

Owen's question was directed at me, but I remained quiet, watching the way Connor stared at where the portal had been. I noticed Zander's narrowed gaze rested on him, too. Connor had seen a portal before, at least twice, so why did he look like a starving man in a bakery, right now? Zander's creased brows dipped further. Ignoring the unease prickling the back of my neck, I fixed a little smile on my face and looked at Owen, even though my heart was racing and my palms were suddenly sweaty as thoughts whirled through my mind in a storm. I didn't know what to do with that sense of dread, so I answered Owen's question.

"That was B'nar, the Prince Heir to the High King. So if you ever see him again, I suggest you play nice. He's powerful in magic and political position, and he makes a better friend than an enemy."

Owen cocked a brow, and Stone stared unblinkingly at me.

"Damn."

"Shit." They muttered at the same time.

"Exactly," I said, then glanced around the cave. "Can we get Connor settled somewhere a bit more comfortable than this, now? You mentioned cabins…?" I looked at Drake. His bright eyes were full of compassion as they held mine.

"Sure did. Come on. Let's get our Prime settled somewhere." It dawned on me Drake didn't know about me holding Connor's wolf. I glanced at Owen. It seemed the wrong time to divulge that little piece of information. Maybe only his brothers could sense he was different?

Zander grunted, and with what looked like a great effort, stood, pushing himself up with a hand on the wall. "I'm coming too." Reaching down he offered his hand to his mother.

I shook my head. Connor's mother. Except Connor wasn't looking at Tyen with awe or even the resentment he might have for the woman who had abandoned him; there was a predatory gleam in his eyes that made me shudder. That gleam was one of a hunter, it was almost lustful. I rubbed the prickling from the skin on my arms and shook my head. I was tired and emotionally strung out; I was just seeing things. I blinked, and when I peered at Connor again that hungry gleam had gone. Instead, Connor shifted his intense gaze, and glowered at Zander.

I didn't understand that look, but I was beginning to suspect why it was there; I just didn't know what to do about it. I laid a hand gently on Zander's arm. So many questions burned on the tip of my tongue, but now wasn't the time to indulge my impatience and just blurt them out. "Umm, perhaps it's best if you leave him be tonight, Zander. I'll find you as soon as I can and we'll talk. Okay?"

Zander looked from me to Connor, his jaw clenched. Tyen placed a hand on his cheek and made him look at her. "He will be safe with his mate. No one here will harm him."

"It isn't him I'm worried about." His muttered answer was cryptic enough my body tensed. With three shifters inside me, one of whom was in large part the alpha of all shifters, my hearing was astute. I heard his mumbled words as if he had yelled them. Who else *was* he worried about? I tried to catch his attention with my gaze, but he wouldn't look at me.

Tyen's dark brow furrowed, but before she could ask what he meant, Zander spoke. "Fine." His face was drawn and it struck me again how exhausted he looked.

I looked at Owen, pleading with my eyes.

"Stone, when we get to the cabins, find Zander and his mother somewhere to rest, then ensure they get food brought to them." Owen pushed a little power against Stone, making his point. Stone's nostrils flared and his chin lifted, but he didn't argue. He clearly respected Owen as much as he did Connor. With emotions already running high, Connor's brothers were going to need the extra push to willingly help Zander. Considering the brutalities and humiliation they suffered at his hand in the prison, forgiveness was going to be a long process. Owen's compulsion, though not as strong as Connor's had been, was enough to make sure the pack did nothing to harm Zander—or Tyen. Though I seriously doubted Tyen was in danger. She had never harmed them.

I observed Tyen, wondering why she had been in that prison in the first place. She didn't look mistreated. As a matter of fact, she looked well cared for and her clothes were expensive. The silk dress she wore fell down below her knees, the material brushing against the soft leather of her black boots. But there was something in her eyes that spoke of great suffering. Shadows danced around her features, but not in a bad way. Almost as if they were trying to protect her and hide that suffering from the gaze of others. She gave me a small smile. I smiled back and hoped she didn't take offense at my staring.

I shook my head. Connor's mother. Gods, he hadn't even spoken to her yet. How that must hurt, to have her child reject her so completely. Though after so many years, I couldn't help but wonder what she expected?

"Come on," Stone said coldly, eyeing Zander with glacial silver eyes, his wolf tinting his irises with vivid yellow before he brought it back under control. "I'll find you both somewhere to sleep. So long as you don't have that fucking button on you, you'll be left alone. If it looks like you do, nothing any other alpha can do will stop me from ripping your throat out, followed by hers." His eyes flashed purple this time, his vicious fae side peeking through.

Tyen tensed, but didn't step away despite her already pale face becoming even more devoid of colour. The shadowed area she stood in seemed to darken.

I heard Connor chuckle, but when I looked at him his eyes were shut.

Zander nodded, his expression closed. "I understand, but please believe I have no desire to harm any of you. My purpose in that prison was to protect my mother and brother, as best I could. I might not have done a great job of that, but harming anyone else was not something I enjoyed—ever. My actions were unavoidable, given the situation with my father, if I wanted to protect the ones I love."

Tyen squeezed his hand, her eyes almost fully black, that strange shadow wrapping her in a fine mist.

"I'll come and find you once I've had some time with Connor. I need some answers." My eyes held Zander's as I walked closer to him and stared up into his handsome, drawn face. "About many things."

"I know." His shoulders slumped a little and he looked almost defeated. I couldn't comprehend what his life had been like all this time, working for Walker and living a lie to save his mother and brother from his evil father. On instinct, I stood on my tip toes and kissed his cheek. "Thank you for bringing him back to me."

He blinked, glanced at Connor, and swallowed. Then, he nodded. "Find me as soon as you can, Ember. It's important we talk."

Owen stepped closer to Reed, studying the big Were. "Lionel, Myles, Reed needs restraining with the silver chains we took from the raid." He narrowed his eyes on Myles. "You good with that order?"

Myles growled, a low rumble in his chest, his wolf in his eyes. My heart ached for my friends. They had mated amongst the stress and violence of the fight rings, and then had their love ripped apart when Reed died at my hands. I had no idea if I could do anything for Reed, but I was going to damn well try. I left Zander and walked over to Myles. I didn't really know what to say to him. If he struck me down, I wouldn't blame him. Nervously, I took his hand and squeezed it. He squeezed back, but directed his comment to his current alpha. "He's a Were with a demon squatting in his body. I have absolutely no problem chaining him down until we figure out how to save him."

Connor snorted. "You can't save him."

I frowned, that sense of dread back with Connor's cold words "Why not? We have him now. There has to be a way."

"Oh, there is. But ripping a demon from a Were's body isn't something any of you can do. You need an angel, or at least a part of one..." He snapped his mouth shut as if he'd said too much, his brows dipping as that shadow swirled through his intense eyes. He frowned and growled.

My stomach lurched as the metal disc came to mind. "The disc? The one Doherty had? Do you know where it is? Or even what it is?" I narrowed my gaze on his. "Does Berith have it?"

Connor's eyes widened, and for a moment he looked surprised before he snorted another dry laugh. "What? You're kidding, right? Me and that demon piece of shit weren't exactly buddies, you know. We didn't exchange small talk, *Firecracker*, he tortured me, for Christ's sake."

The way he sneered my name hurt. I clenched my jaw but didn't bite back. I couldn't. The dread in my belly solidified into a heaviness that began to drag at me. I didn't know if my suspicions were founded or not. That's why I needed to talk to Zander. Something was keeping me from connecting with him, and the feeling that this wasn't my Connor was getting stronger by the minute. And Zander knew something.

I carried a terrible guilt, knowing I'd capitulated to Walker's ridiculous demands. Connor was my soulmate, and I'd abandoned him. He had every right to be angry with me. Only this didn't feel like anger. This felt like hate.

I waited patiently while the others walked across the cave, then lowered myself beside him, my heart hammering in my chest. "I'm so sorry, Connor. I should have come for you earlier."

Alex stood quietly at my back. It hadn't escaped my notice he hadn't spoken to Connor yet. Didn't Connor recognise him?

Connor closed his eyes and inhaled deeply, his fingers curling into tight fists as if he was fighting the urge to smash them into something. I hoped that something wasn't me. He'd never hurt me before, but this wasn't the Connor that I knew. Unexpected fear clawed at my belly. Prime snarled. Mea stepped up to calm him and Prime reluctantly settled, but not until he'd pushed me to inhale Connor's scent deeply. It definitely wasn't the same, almost as if all those weeks in a prison of demons had infiltrated his skin—or something else had.

"Yeah, you should've. But hey, you're here now, right?" His gaze scanned over his brothers who were helping Myles get Reed onto some kind of stretcher. More people had arrived to help move him. I forced a little smile to my lips, determined not to let my suspicions, or my emotions get the better of me. This had been one hell of a day, and it wasn't over yet. I dared to reach out and put my hand on his forearm. "I am, and I can help you get through this. You're strong enough, Connor. We can do it together."

The sneer that curled his lips and his snide tone of voice had me flinching before I could catch myself. Thankfully he didn't notice. He grabbed the back of my neck and his fingers tightened in the hair at the base of my skull. I winced. He lowered his voice to a whisper, pulling me forward until my forehead rested against his. "You know the one thing I didn't get in that prison?" I shook my head, not sure how to react to this version of my mate. He sneered. "Fucked. Yeah, I got everything else, but that." His hold tightened further and I gritted my teeth against the pain and the dominance in that grip. Prime growled, but didn't step up; if anything he seemed very confused about what to do, which scared me. I was used to Prime's aggression and determination to find Connor. It matched my own. But seeing Prime so unbalanced stole all of my self-confidence, and I froze. "I'm hungry for it, *Firecracker*. And you're gonna give me that booty call when I'm ready for it."

Heat from his hand seeped into me, even Fire stirred at the feel of his too tight grip. I wanted to pull away, but I endured it, if for no other reason than I didn't want him to get suspicious about my uncertainty. I couldn't hold his gaze, not unless I wanted him to see my confusion—and fear... So, I just nodded.

A grin stretched his lips. "Good girl. Go and get cleaned up for me, I'll be back to full strength and ready to fuck this gorgeous body, in no time at all. Tell me, has anyone else enjoyed it while you left me to rot?"

Before I could pull away, he yanked me forward and kissed me so hard, my bottom teeth cut into my lip. I was stunned, not just by his actions, but by his words. This was not my loving mate. All I could do when he pulled away was stare. He chuckled. Lust and something far darker burned in his eyes. I opened my mouth to...to I don't know what...I could feel my brain literally stutter.

"Uh, uh," he said. Slowly, he scooped a little of my blood onto his forefinger and sucked it into his mouth. "Mm, yum." His gaze dragged down my body, making me cringe at the look of raw hunger in his eyes. "Can't wait."

A tall shadow fell across us before I could pull myself together enough to react.

"Hey, how 'bout we get you somewhere comfy to sit your ass for a while, Prime. Then you can talk with Ember again." Drake's harsh tone made me jump. My face flushed as I realised all of these men had witnessed the way Connor had just spoken to me. Tears burned my eyes; but not from humiliation. From what had just become painfully obvious to me. Connor hadn't escaped that awful place after all. Drake turned to me. His wolf eyes shone in the light of the torches the others held, but his face was impassive. I appreciated him hiding his reaction. I was reacting enough for us both. I was at a complete loss as to what to do. I needed to talk to Owen, and to Zander, about my suspicions but Connor watched me so closely, I couldn't move without him knowing. I felt so boxed in, I couldn't breathe. My chest tightened until I couldn't pull air into my lungs. I couldn't deal with this! I swallowed the ache in my throat and turned away, but not before Drake saw the tears in my eyes.

Fuck! No one needed to see me cry right now. I needed to get myself together and find a way to deal with all...this.

"Ember? Why don't you follow behind us, you look beat. We'll find Connor a room. He can take a shower and rest while we catch up," Owen said.

I swallowed and nodded, keeping my eyes down.

"Nah, you know what, man? How about she does what I said? Gets cleaned up and comes when I call her pretty ass?" Connor's growled words sent ice into my heart.

Standing next to Owen, Drake stiffened, and I swallowed as he snarled, but at my pleading look, he let the matter drop. My legs shook so much, I couldn't even follow when Owen and Alex helped Connor to his feet and he walked painfully slowly into the dark tunnels. Connor looked over his shoulder, grinned and winked before he disappeared into the shadows.

Drake stared at me for a moment, before he cocked his head. "Get some rest, Em. We can sort this mess out later." He peered at the tunnel, then back at me. "He's not going anywhere. You'll be safe."

I rubbed my face and nodded. Mea whined, so I shut her and Prime down. These emotions, this pain, fear and guilt, they were mine, they didn't belong to either of my other souls...just mine.

Using Fire had almost wiped me out, and seeing Connor so changed, fearing maybe we hadn't brought Connor back at all, was more frightening than anything I'd experienced before. My legs trembled and I slapped a hand against the cold wall ignoring the cut of the stone into my palm.

"Hey, girl, you okay?"

Closing my eyes didn't erase the fact that I wasn't alone, so I opened them again and pushed away from the cave wall, determined not to crumble in front of Shannon, or Drake, who watched me carefully. I felt a pulse of reassurance from him and he gave my hand a squeeze. "I'm going to make sure he rests," he said darkly and marched out when he saw Shannon would stay with me. I wished he'd stayed. I needed to tell someone, I knew I did...but I just...I didn't want to admit what I knew in my soul to be true, because that could mean I'd lost Connor forever.

"Hey. Yeah." My voice was tight and the astute look in Shannon's eyes told me she wasn't fooled for a second. "Yeah, just peachy." I decided sarcasm was better than bursting into tears.

"Yeah, sure you are. Come on. Looks like Drake's brought a fucking army with him." She lifted an automatic weapon, it's black metal gleaming in the torch light. A wide grin stretched her lips. "And he brought new toys to play with. Not to mention, we now have decent cabins. There are even proper beds and hot fucking water! Oh, and you're bunking with me."

My eyes widened. "Really? What about Stone?"

Shannon laughed. "He's still a miserable bastard, and I want girl company."

I was glad of the excuse not to dwell on Connor. "But I thought you two were soul mates?"

She hooked her arm through mine and, whereas once I might have pushed her away, right now, with my best friend gone, my mate here—yet not, and my friends all busy trying to imprison the monster that had once been Reed, I was glad of Shannon's company. She shrugged and tossed her thick blonde hair, cocking her hip as she flung the gun over her shoulder. "Maybe, I haven't decided yet. Either way, it doesn't mean I'm joined to his hip. This war we have with demons and werewolves is real, and you know as well as I do that being close to someone who can be ripped away, isn't a good idea."

I stiffened.

"Ah shit, sorry, runt, I didn't mean that...ah, damn... sorry."

I swallowed. Gods, I must look broken if queen bitch was apologising to me and stammering over her words. "It's fine." I gave her a watery smile. "It's fine."

"Nah, it really isn't. Nothing about this shitty situation is fine. But it will be."

"Yeah, maybe. Eventually." I couldn't help the sigh that escaped me.

Shannon glanced sideways as she led me out of the cave. "Come on...hot showers...doesn't that do it for you, runt? And then we can get proper food. Mother, I knew Drake was loaded but, damn, he's come with everything. In fact, I'm considering dumping Stone and getting my claws into Drake."

I allowed myself a small laugh. It seemed my once biggest enemy was now a friend. I appreciated her efforts to make me feel better, though. Gods, how things changed. "You don't mean that." It was in her voice.

She smiled and winked. "Course not, but Stoney doesn't know that. He's gonna have to work for it if he wants to tap this gorgeous ass. I wouldn't want him to take me for granted, now would I?"

I shook my head and smiled. "No, you certainly would not."

CHAPTER 9

mber

I PULLED my fingers through my wet hair before picking up the bendy hose that was attached to some kind of automatic hair drier. It was slow and steady, but I took my time, enjoying the feel of the warm air buffeting my hair and scalp.

It had been getting dark when Shannon had brought me to our room. I hadn't realised how long we'd been in the prison and caves, but I'd crashed. Even with no food in my belly, my brain had short circuited and I'd slept, not well and my mind was full of doubts, and guilt and pain, but I *had* slept.

Shannon had been summoned from the room by Stone, who looked less than happy with Shannon's current sleeping arrangements. I smiled. Maybe she was right, he'd never take her for granted if she was always this unpredictable.

I brushed my hair until it shone. Its strands were all bright red now, the blond long since cut from its ends. I dressed in a pair of jeans and a tee, all clothes courtesy of Drake, and pulled on my boots. My faerie armour was hung in the small wardrobe of the cabin. I'd cleaned it as best I could and decided to leave it there until we next went on a raid.

I steadied myself against the wall of the cabin as wind buffeted it from the whirling of a helicopter overhead. I'd occasionally seen and heard them land at the SBI headquarters when I'd been at school, but I'd never been so close before. They couldn't land in the forest, but had been able to lower the cabins in this clearing in front of the cliff face. An amazing amount of supplies were still incoming. Drake had no intention of letting us lose this battle with Berith from a lack of equipment.

I waited for the walls to stop shaking and took a breath. I wasn't scared one of the bloody great things would drop on me, not really. Huffing at my own lie, I picked up my bow and flung it across my shoulder, fixed my knife to my thigh and stuck the fae equivalent of a gun that B'nar had left me into a holster on my hip. Satisfied I was armed enough, I pulled the door open—and squeaked in surprise.

"Godsdammit, Alex! Give a girl a heart attack why don't you?"

He smirked. "Aw, come on. You're a badass, surely my beautiful face doesn't scare you."

I snorted, and gave Alex a playful push away. Zander's scent drifted up my nostrils. I turned around just as his broad frame disappeared out of the cabin doors. I narrowed my eyes on Alex. "Where's he going? I need to talk to him."

Alex scratched his nose and raised his brows. "What? Him? Ah, I think he's going to see Connor."

"Oh, okay." I had no intention of following him to Connor. My heart stuttered and my palms went clammy. I needed to talk to Owen and the others. Even if they listened and agreed with me that this was not truly Connor who had returned from the prison, I still had no idea how to banish the demon that I believed currently inhabited his body. I blinked my burning eyes. I didn't let the horrible thought that Connor may be lost to me forever, take root. Instead, I shook it off and started down the short corridor. We passed four other doors. If Tyen and Zander had one room, who was in the others? Maybe…?

"He's not in here. He, um, well…" Alex raked a hand through his hair and looked at the floor.

I swallowed, my stomach like lead. Even though I didn't want to be near the creature that had stolen Connor's body, it was still hard to look at him and not see my mate. So it still stung. "He didn't want to be near me, did he? Only wanted me to be ready to run to him when he calls."

Alex exhaled. "No, he didn't." His eyes narrowed, his gaze sharpening, and he cocked his head. "But something tells me you have an idea why he's being such a dick."

I swallowed the ache in my throat. "I do. Do you?" Alex ran a hand through his hair again before meeting my gaze. "That isn't Connor. I'm sorry, Em."

It was painful to hear my suspicions confirmed by someone else—but also reassuring in a way. "It's fine. I'm fine. I needed you to say that." I marched from the cabin. "Let's go and find Owen and the others. We'll talk to them about how to handle this because I'm damned if I know."

"Me either." Alex's face was dark.

"So what have you found out about this camp and all this expense, my many-faced friend? Anything useful?"

"Nah, not really. Drake's not saying where all this equipment came from. I mean, I know he has the money, but this stuff…" He gestured with a dip of his chin to where more weapons were being unloaded from the crates that had just been dropped. "It's insane."

"Hmm." I had to agree. Now that it was light, I could see the extent of the camp. Not only that, I saw the live electrical wires that ran around the edge of what was now a military style camp. A generator hummed in the distance and cables ran along the ground taking electricity into the caves. I was glad the people here, particularly the women and their babies, at least had decent light and food. "So who's in charge?"

Alex's brows dipped. "It looks like Owen is. Drake hasn't challenged his role as alpha and no one else has, either; not that many men came with Drake. Maybe a force of about thirty. But one squad of ten look military to me. They've kept to themselves while the others have all been setting up the camp."

"Do they wear a uniform?"

"No, not really, well nothing that would identify them or their allegiance."

I remained silent and watched people moving around. There seemed to be teams, all led by people I didn't know. Each team was doing a different job either moving equipment, food, or other supplies.

"Where are Drake and Owen, now?"

"That cabin." He pointed to one which stood apart from the others. "It's the ops centre. Just watch your ears as we get close."

My brows dipped and I turned my head to look at him. "Why?"

Alex grimaced. "It won't bother me but you're not gonna like it."

I gripped his arm and raised my brows, my nerves already stretched. "Alex."

He stopped walking at my growled warning. "It's okay,. It's nothing dangerous, just uncomfortable to shifters. They've set up radio frequency and acoustic disturbance equipment. I guess they don't want anyone listening in on the conversations going on in there. It doesn't hurt me like it will you, but I still can't hear through the noise it makes."

I raised a brow. I shouldn't expect any less from Drake, the clever bastard. "So this will hurt?"

"Yep, like a bitch. But according to Stone it gets better. When you've done it enough times, it stops feeling uncomfortable."

"Oh great, encouragement from the most miserable and unfeeling of us."

Alex grinned. "Yeah, sweet, isn't it?"

"Come on. Let's get this over with. We need to deal with *that...that issue.*" I wouldn't use Connor's name again unless I had to. It wasn't him.

Two soldiers, that's all I could describe them as, watched us approach, their attention unnerving. One narrowed his eyes at me. I met his gaze, my hackles immediately rising. Prime jumped into the mix. I snarled. *Shit, shit, shit.* I needed Prime to back down from this male if I was going to keep his presence in me a secret.

"Ember, now's not a good time to let that wolf play alpha," Alex mumbled.

"I bloody know that. But he doesn't know these wolves and he wants to kick some arse."

"Jeez, now really isn't the time. These guys don't mess about."

"Yeah, well, neither do I, and he's a Prime."

"Damn, Ember, have you ever met another Prime?"

I slowed my steps, not relinquishing the soldier's gaze. His brow dipped and his top lip curled into a challenging snarl. "What's your damn point," I snapped at Alex.

"Together, he and Connor are *the* Prime. Don't take this guy on, please, Em. It will give away the power that you're carrying, and I don't just mean Prime; they will wonder how a female shifter is carrying the only alpha Prime known to be in existence, to people who we can't trust."

I could feel my need to take this guy on being fuelled by Prime. He was trying to burst from my skin and take this guy's throat out if he didn't submit...

"Pull me away! Now, Alex!"

Alex grabbed my arm just as another presence registered in my head. I fought Prime, not willing to let him burst through my skin. Prime snapped and growled, his claws pushing through my nail beds.

"Hey, princess." A hip nudged me to the side, away from my path to the soldier. I inhaled sharply and Prime growled, but not as aggressively. He recognised that scent.

Mea pulled on Prime, helping me force him back. He still rode me high and I panted, my heart racing as I paced and forced my attention to the sky and the great fir trees that towered above our heads. I inhaled; the scent of the forest grounded me, and I just focused on taking back control as Mea snapped and growled at Prime.

"It's perhaps best if you don't challenge the soldiers with guns, Ember."

I stopped pacing and lowered my eyes from the grey sky to Kawan. A grin curled his beautiful mouth, making him stunning to look at. But that smile, gorgeous though it was, didn't reach his eyes. His expression was dark and intense. He knew I was fighting with Prime. I paced again, aware the two soldiers were watching me intently, almost as closely as Kawan and Alex.

Kawan didn't say anything more, merely watched silently. Slowly, Prime's aggression ebbed completely. I stopped pacing and inhaled a deep, pine filled breath, then exhaled, allowing the cold air to take my tension. When I stopped, Kawan cocked his head and gave me a small smile, his chocolate brown eyes a little lighter. "Hey, princess, you seem a little more...feisty, than usual. You okay?"

His eyes locked with mine. I swallowed hard. Prime loved his brother, but he wouldn't stand any challenge, to me, or his own authority.

"Hey man, why don't you just look at me for a moment?" Alex gently encouraged Kawan.

Grey flashed across Kawan's eyes, his wolf pushing into the mix, and Prime started to push against my control again.

"Please," I whispered, desperately trying to control this situation. Kawan's brow furrowed, and I knew Prime was visible in my eyes.

Kawan's nostrils flared and his fists curled. "Ah, shit, sorry, Ember. I saw you shift into Prime in the forest; I'm not trying to challenge him but my wolf's a little riled himself with these new males being around." He dragged his attention to the ground, his jaw muscles tense as he forced his wolf to obey.

Prime's push lessened again and I leaned over my knees. Breathing deeply helped, the forest's energy calming both Prime and me. "I get it, really I do, but please, just keep your eyes down from mine, and get me in that cabin. We can talk more then." No way was I telling him about my suspicions in front of two hard-faced males who I didn't know or trust.

Kawan's face was grim. "Just walk behind me and stare at my back. Don't make eye contact with anyone, not until we get you inside. The pain from the acoustic pulse is a bitch the first few times you go through it, but it will get less once you get used to it."

"Yeah, Alex warned me."

Alex stepped closer and gave me an encouraging smile. "Don't worry, Em, I'll watch your back. Just don't let Prime out to play and turn and bite my head off."

Fixing my gaze on Kawan's black jacket, I followed behind him, ignoring the soldiers, and deliberately holding my breath so that their scent didn't rile Prime up further. Mea huffed then snarled at Prime who was pushing to get past her.

We approached the cabin and at first there was just a prickle against my senses, one that quickly became an assault of vibration in my ears. Mea howled and Prime snarled.

"Ah!" I stumbled forward into Kawan. Prime leapt forward and fur broke through my skin, claws pushing from my fingernails. My head was going to explode!

"Keep moving, Ember!" Alex hissed. "Dammit, man, get her inside."

The urgency in his voice did nothing to calm Prime. I felt myself propelled through a door and skidded to my knees. I forced my head to turn.

Owen's eyes were wide, as were those of the three other males at the table. "What the fuck!?"

At that moment I lost the fight for control. Prime burst through my skin, landing on his paws, his hackles raised and his teeth bared. He snarled. I could feel him searching for the bond with his pack, and his confusion when only a whisper of it was there. I tried my best to reassure him. Even though he was the Prime, it was Connor's blood that had bound him to his brothers.

"Lower your eyes and heads. Now." Owen's words were controlled and calm, but an order, nonetheless.

Mea whined, trying to help me reach Prime, but he refused to let me take control back yet.

Stone's eyes glinted a beautiful amber, ringed with purple before he dropped his gaze. Myles, Kawan, Drake and Owen all kept their eyes down. Prime growled, long and low. He wanted submission from his brothers—to keep me safe. My heart squeezed. He'd pushed through to make sure his brother's were not a threat to me.

"More," said Owen. "On your knees—slowly, and do not look at him."

The others complied, even Alex.

Prime padded up to Owen, towering above him. Owen tilted his head allowing Prime access to his neck. I saw his clenched fists and realised how hard it must be for an alpha like him to be this submissive. Prime knew it, too. It was the ultimate sign of loyalty and trust to expose your throat to another alpha wolf. Prime huffed and moved on to Stone, then Myles, sniffing at Drake, and finally Kawan. Slowly, he walked back across the room and, satisfied that his current vessel wouldn't be challenged, allowed me to shift.

My bones cracked as I dragged my human self back.

Damn it! Don't do that again!

Prime merely huffed and plonked himself down near Mea, who studied him steadily before turning her back, clearly pissed at him for ignoring both of our pleas. I panted and thrust them both from my thoughts before I pushed myself onto my knees. I was more than aware I was now naked in front of the males that had become my family. My clothes were in a ragged mess on the floor, and I hadn't had the control to disband the molecules and bring them back to me, not with that forced shift.

"Fuck me, I've not had to deal with Prime like that in a long time. You okay, Ember?" Owen ran his hand through his hair and got to his feet. "That bastard's still as powerful as ever. I'd kinda hoped you'd be able to control him, like your other wolf, but I guess he's not letting you have control? At least not of him?"

I swallowed and resisted the urge to cover my breasts and lady bits. "He's not pushed before, not until we came back here. He never forced a shift on me in Faerie."

"Yeah? Well, it would have been a *really* good idea to tell us he can do that." Stone snarled as he stood and began to pace. He looked pale and a little shaky despite the irritation in his tone.

Prime pricked his ears up and inhaled. I tensed. The last thing I needed right now was him wanting to discipline one of his brothers for his bad attitude. But he sent me a ripple of reassurance. He sensed his brother's shock and respect and that was what he'd wanted—for them to realise he was still there, and still as powerful, and to not challenge me—and by default- him.

"Stone, if you don't want him to come tearing out of my body to rip you a new one, then I suggest you shut up, and listen to what I have to say."

"There she is." Drake leaned back in his chair, crossed his arms over his chest and smiled, his vivid green eyes sparkling. He winked, and I couldn't help but smile at him, relieved he was there, and in my corner.

Stone turned and glared at me before scowling at Drake.

"Hey, scowling isn't a good idea, either," Alex pointed out unhelpfully.

"Nope, he's right, it isn't. Play nice." Drake smirked at Stone who gave him an even darker scowl, a snarl curling his lip.

"Stone, it's okay. I have him back under control for now. But if he wants out, no matter how hard I try, I can't keep him contained. He just wanted you to know he's here and he's as strong as ever."

"So are you our Prime now?" asked Myles, his beautiful face marred by deep lines across his forehead. "How is that even possible?"

My stomach clenched. Everytime I looked at him I was reminded that I had killed his mate; had just driven my fist into Reed's chest and ripped his life away.

I thanked Owen as he pulled off his t-shirt and handed it to me. I slipped my arms through the sleeves and let the cotton fall to my mid thighs, covering my nakedness.

Prime relaxed further, so I took a deep breath and steadied my nerves. It had been easier to contain him in Faerie because he hadn't wanted out; other than on the turn of the two Faerie moons when the pull to run and hunt had been too much for him to ignore. Here and now, he had his own agenda, one which I couldn't control unless he let me.

"No, Myles, I'm not your Prime. Like I said before, I've been carrying him since the prison breakout, and it's possible because I am not just a shifter, I am a phoenix. My body can hold more than one spirit because of her."

"A phoenix? But they're just legends and fables…"

I snapped my attention towards Kawan. "What? Like humans always believed werewolves and vampires were? Yeah, that turned out well for them, especially when supernaturals were revealed and they began breaking human laws. That's why we have the SBI...or had you forgotten?" I called upon Fire and ignited the air over my palm. "Why do you think I can turn into a living torch and not turn to ash?"

"Hot dayum, sugar, I knew you were special; all that gorgeous red hair and green eyes." Drake grinned.

I shook my head and rolled my eyes at him. He just winked. I pulled Fire back inside and walked over to Owen, looking up into his handsome face. "We need to keep this just between us, or at least our pack, Lionel and Shannon included."

"Why?" Owen's stare was intent.

Prime grumbled.

Owen's eyes moved to my clenched jaw, and he cracked his neck, reluctantly looking up at the ceiling. It was a wise move.

I dragged my bottom lip between my teeth, biting on it, trying to hide the pain that lanced my heart at admitting out loud that Connor had never really returned to me. "I don't..." My voice was thick, my throat tight. I swallowed hard and tried again. "Connor isn't...Connor. That thing out there is not my mate. It's why I can't feel our connection, and why Prime has made no move to try and get back to him..." I hesitated and took some big gulping breaths. There I'd said it. My worst fears were out in the open.

Owen's big shoulders rose and fell, his jaw tightening. He rubbed his face with his hands. "I know. I sensed it, too." His eyes met mine. "I'm so sorry, Ember. I can't imagine how hard this is for you. I honestly thought he was dead. I had no idea he was still in the prison all this time, or I would have smashed that place to the ground to get him out."

"I know you would." I placed my hand on his arm, trying to reassure him that I held no one to blame but myself. If I hadn't waited so long to get back, we might have stood a chance of saving him. Now it was probably too late. The floor creaked under my feet as I walked towards the table at the centre of the room. I couldn't stand still any longer, my body was coiled tighter than any spring.

"So does being a phoenix help you be a vessel for more than one supernatural spirit?" Myles asked curiously, perching on the edge of the table.

Blueprints of the prison adorned the center of it.

"It must. Fire, my phoenix, gifts me immortality, but if someone takes my life, she demands their soul in payment. So, if it was a human they would die. If a shifter kills me, she takes their spirit animal in payment." My legs were wobbling so I sat on the edge of a chair and pulled the tee down to ensure my lady bits were covered.

Drake smirked at me, his gaze lingering on my legs. Gods, he was such a flirt, but then again he was a wolf, and a very hot alpha. "Damn, Ember, that's some power to hold in that small, and perfectly formed body." He grinned and waggled his brows.

I rolled my eyes at him, but was thankful for his lightheartedness and harmless flirting. It lessened the weight of the situation just a little. "I think having two spirit animals, one of which is immortal, is the only reason I can hold Prime at all without him ripping me apart. How Connor contained and controlled him, I'll never know."

"Yeah, Connor has to be a powerful soul to manage it alone," agreed Kawan.

"I can still sense power in Connor," Stone said steadily, watching me as if he was testing how I would react to his words "Evil power, more than in the Weres we have killed." He was leaning against the wall, his arms crossed over his chest, his brows drawn.

My shoulders shifted the light material of Owen's t-shirt as I squirmed, and scowled. "Don't call that thing Connor. It isn't him, not anymore."

Stone's eyes glowed with purple. I studied him, *really* looked at him. Out here in this forest, away from the silver collars, his fae side was riding him high, almost as strong, if not stronger, than his wolf.

"That's what I thought," he said.

"So does anyone have any idea how to get a fucking demon out of Connor's body?" asked Owen. "Do you, Em?"

"I do. It's an artifact. Doherty was going to use it to steal my phoenix and my wolf spirit from me. He told me that he'd killed my parents. My mother carried the phoenix. She knew she was being hunted and she passed it to me right before she died, to save my life." I released a deep breath and met Owen's gaze. "He murdered me that same night. My phoenix brought me back, but took Doherty's wolf in payment. He'd been searching for me ever since. It was Connor who stopped him from ending me again; he ripped him to shreds."

"Bastard deserved it," muttered Drake.

Owen glanced at him. "Sure did. So what does this artifact look like?"

I frowned, trying to recall the details. "I can't remember much, all I know is it was a gold disc with some kind of runes on it."

Alex's face paled. I glanced at him questioningly, but he pressed his lips into a tight line. Okay, whatever was bothering him wasn't something he wanted to share right then.

"Right, so we need to go back and hunt for it."

"What about Zander?" asked Drake. "He helped break that demon out of the prison. Might he have seen it? Should we even trust him with any of this? He could be working with Berith, and using Connor as their excuse to get out into this world and hunt for either that artifact—or Ember, herself."

Tipping my head back, I considered his question. I'd thought about this all night. Instinct told me we could trust Zander, if only because I really did believe he was Connor's half-brother. "I don't know for sure. Berith didn't need Connor to get into this world. He'd been here as the warden for a while. However, he does need me to unlock the gates of Hell and unleash Satan's army into the world." I met Owen's gaze. "He's using Connor to get to me."

All of them stared at me, their eyes wide, their mouths pressed together.

"A phoenix can burn away the gates of Hell. That's why Berith has come after me, and he's using Connor to get close to me." I ran a hand through my hair, before I blew out a steady breath. "Zander looked as if he realised something was wrong with Connor..." I nearly choked on his name. "When we were in the cave yesterday." I paused and considered all that Zander had told us. I thought about Tyen and her story, and everything Zander had done for Connor and me in that prison. "I think we can trust him."

"Hmm, I'm not so sure," said Owen, a small crease on the bridge of his nose. "But I'm willing to give him the benefit of the doubt until we can talk to him and find out what he knows."

"I'll do that," offered Alex, a little too quickly.

My gaze shot to him, but he wouldn't look at me; he kept his attention on Owen. My eyes narrowed. He definitely knew something...

"Fine. You go and find Zander and feel out his thoughts about the demon. In the meantime, one of us needs to be with you, Ember, at all times." Owen paced across the small room and back again in a controlled and fluid gait. He stopped directly in front of Stone, whose face dropped into a deep glower.

"So, Ember-watch again, then?" Drake chuckled at Stone's frustrated growl. "Suck it up, Faerie. We'll get our Prime back; there has to be a way. Until then, Em has the pleasure of our company."

"Can't wait, honey buns," I fired at him, rolling my eyes. I stood and eyed the remnants of my clothes and boots. "I'd better go and find some new clothes."

"Yeah, go back to your cabin, sugar, and I'll get someone to bring you some more things to wear. I brought plenty of supplies—even girly undies." Drake was already standing.

I forced a smile. "Of course you did. And that was just for yourself!"

A wide grin transformed his face from handsome to stunning. "Ha! Don't tell these guys! I'll never hear the end of it," he joked. Then he cocked his head and looked a bit more serious. "But, of course I brought plenty. A community of shifters with short fuses and a serious need for revenge? Yeah, I thought a supply of undies, amongst other things, might be a good idea."

I stood, and then holding the t-shirt in place, dropped carefully to my knees to pick up the remnants of my clothes. I wasn't leaving my ripped underwear on the floor for any of these assholes to pick up.

"Ember, Stone will go with you back to your room and stay with you for now." I felt the weight of Owen's alpha gaze on me, and knew what was coming next. It didn't make it any easier to hear. "Once you are changed, we will find the demon and restrain him in the same cave as Reed until we can find a way to banish it without killing Connor."

I couldn't look at Owen—or any of them. We all knew that Connor was likely already dead. He was human not Were.

My gaze remained on the floor. All strength leaving my body, my mind sluggishly trying to accept what he was saying.

"Ember? Come on, up you get. I'll take you," said Stone, stepping close enough I could see the creases in his shit kickers. I swallowed, unable to pull myself out of the spiral of grief that was slowly drowning me.

Squatting in front of me, Stone lifted my chin and forced me to meet his eyes. With his thumb, he gently wiped away a tear from my cheek. His eyes turned wholly purple, his expression telling me to be strong.

Owen's hand rested on my shoulder for a moment, but he addressed Stone. "Stay with her, brother. I'll send word when we're ready." Owen's wolf rolled over his eyes. "We'll deal with this together. You are not alone, Ember. We are your brothers as much as we are Connor's."

With a warm strong hand under my upper arm, Stone urged me up. "Come on, she-wolf, let's go. The sooner you are prepared, the sooner we can call out that slimy fucker that has possessed your mate."

I looked to Drake who gave me a supportive smile and pulsed some comforting vibes against me. I grabbed them gratefully, along with the reassurance Owen was throwing my way. I didn't know how to express my gratitude to them, so I lifted my damp eyes and smiled as best I could. There was still hope that Connor's soul had survived.

Back at the cabin, Stone pushed open my door, and I strode past him. I perched on the edge of the bed and stared at my bare knees, both wanting the demon in Connor restrained, and hating what I knew we'd have to do. I gripped the bed cover, my fingers digging into the soft cotton. Stone's energy and the weight of his gaze drilled into me.

"I won't let that demon hurt you, Ember," he said quietly. "This will be hard—for all of us, but Connor would want us to do this, he'd want to be restrained so that he can't hurt you."

I swallowed. Another enemy that had become a protector and friend—no, Stone was more than a friend, so were the rest of Connor's brothers, we were a pack now, and that meant family. I couldn't look up as tears dripped off my nose and onto Owen's tee shirt, staining the material.

"Stop your tears. That thing out there sure as fuck isn't the alpha I know, but that doesn't mean he's dead. Don't lose hope, she-wolf. You are Connor's Firecracker. He would fight Satan himself to get back to you. So you fight for him, don't give up on saving his ass, not yet."

My weapons hit the bed next to me. I hadn't realised he'd picked them up after my shift. I felt the weight of his stare before the door clicked shut behind him. I sat and stared at nothing, listening to the sounds of the camp that echoed outside the prefabricated walls of the cabin. Footsteps thudded in the other rooms as people moved about. Doors clicked shut, and voices that I didn't recognise, filtered through the plywood and plastic.

The skin of my face was tight where my tears had dried. I rubbed at them before I slapped my hands back on the bed, tilting my head back and staring at the aluminium strips in the ceiling.

I'd carried the guilt of abandoning Connor for months, and now I would carry the pain of seeing him chained in a prison of our making. But Stone was right, I needed to fight for Connor. I'd find that disc, if it was the last thing I ever did. I huffed. Blue would kick my arse if she thought I'd given up after all of our planning and scheming, and risking the wrath of the High King to get back here.

I sent a silent prayer to the Mother Wolf that my friend was alive and healing. "Hope Walker hasn't kicked your arse too viciously, either, B'nar," I muttered into the air.

Giving myself a mental slap, I stood and pulled off Owen's t-shirt. His scent still clung to it, and it really wasn't the male scent I wanted flooding my senses. I stepped into the shower for the second time that day. With scalding hot water and soap, I scrubbed away my guilt, replacing it with determination. Rawson had brought me up to be strong, and I would do this for him and for Connor. An ache bloomed through my chest at the thought of my guardian. I placed my hands on the shower wall and leaned my head down under the hot spray, letting it take some of my tension away.

"Where are you, Rawson?"

I wished he was here. He'd know what to do about this, I was sure of it. I'd find out what had happened to him, but even I knew the possibility of him being alive was small. Rawson would have found this camp weeks ago. He was as highly trained as Connor and Owen.

I switched off the shower and dried myself with a rough towel, before pulling on the clothes I found at the bottom of my bed. Combat boots, black cargo trousers, a black tee and a warm jacket that was a little small, but still welcome for its warmth.

"Thanks, Stone!" I called through the door knowing he'd hear me. Maybe the guy wasn't all bad.

Ember

STONE'S rugged features were set in his customary hard mask as I stepped out of my door with new clothes and a new sense of resolve.

"Took you long enough."

Despite the dread in my soul, I grinned at him and winked. "A girl's gotta look good to kick demon arse."

His heavy silver brows twitched upward, and his lips curled in a smirk. He cocked his head, his silver hair gleaming as it shifted around his shoulders. "Not alone, remember?" he rumbled gruffly.

Yeah, Stone was not comfortable with conveying emotion, but I appreciated his effort to support me. I nodded and shrugged my shoulders. "Yeah, some moody bastard with purple eyes reminded me of that a little while ago; so I guess it's time to step up and kick a big bad demon back to Hell. Then search for my mate, before Mr Moody kick's *my* arse for being a pathetic sap."

Stone peered down at me. "You're welcome, she-wolf. And I'll happily kick your irritating, English *arse*, anytime. Now, let's go and see if we can find the demon spawn. Owen said he'll meet us at the room he gave Connor. Zander is coming and so is Alex."

I took a deep breath to steady my nerves, but couldn't stop my palms from sweating as we left the cabin and walked out into the cold night air.

"How are we going to do this?"

"Careful she-wolf, I can smell your fear. You need to hide it better, or that demon will use Connor's face and body to tear right into your heart, and then Prime will tear into him, no matter who Connor once was to him. And if it is possible to save Connor, he needs his body to be in one piece."

I just grunted. Confronting a demon wearing Connor's face wasn't something I was looking forward to, but I needed to be level headed. I couldn't contain Prime, even with his brothers around, if things got violent; he'd just force his way out.

I cracked my neck, the weight of the knife strapped to my thigh, and the bow I clung to with my sweaty hand, giving me a small amount of confidence. We crossed the compound, Stone leading me through the buzz of people who were still unpacking big crates and setting up cables and water pipes.

"Bloody hell, this isn't a temporary camp, then?"

"No. Drake and Owen are in charge of the camp and are working with an a-hole military guy. He's some kind of special forces prick who doesn't like anyone else being in charge. They think there is a rift into Hell in that prison, which is how Berith and some of his demons made it into this world. It also explains why he is reluctant to leave this place."

I smiled, trying to imagine a complete stranger trying to control the blood brothers who had fought side by side together for the past four years. "Now I really want to see mister military a-hole trying to push his dominance on you guys. I'll bet it's really fucking entertaining." I laughed, imagining all the growls and posturing around that small table in Owen's ops center.

Stone glowered at me, but his lips twitched.

"Oh, come on, Stone, it must have been funny, him trying to control just you, never mind Owen and the others, too."

Stone smoothed his features out and stared forward, though his eyes sparkled in the moonlight. "I don't know what you mean, she-wolf. I respect everyone, just so long as they are one of my pack."

"Thought so."

Soldiers dressed similarly to me but with baseball caps and combat vests on, caught my attention. They were all fit, the muscles of their big arms, backs and chests straining under their jackets. I slowed my steps. Stone matched my pace. They patrolled the electrified perimeter fence in pairs, automatic weapons held relaxed, but ready to use. A group of them sat outside a two story cabin, clearly this was their quarters. I kept my feet moving when one of them raised his head as if sensing my attention. I casually let my gaze drift away from him, not willing to allow Prime to sense his attention on me. Happy with the presence of his brother by my side, Prime took no notice.

A tall, muscular guy with a buzz cut and bad attitude strode deliberately into our path. Stone growled, ending up almost nose to nose with the big male.

"Move." Stone's voice was utterly devoid of emotion. His eyes glowed purple before yellow rolled over them.

The newcomer snarled. "Don't fucking think so, half-breed."

Oh, shit! This guy might be a soldier, but Stone had spent the last four years killing anyone who got in his way. Stone moved so quickly, I didn't even see him. His forehead smashed into the guy's face. There was a loud crack and blood exploded across buzz cut's face and splattered over Stone's mouth.

There was a chorus of: "Oh, Shit!" "Whoa!" "Fuck!" And many other curse words as Stone's fist made contact with the guys jaw, knocking him flat on his back.

Prime perked up at the sound of bone breaking and the scent of blood. I braced myself for his fury, but it seemed he found his brother's actions justified. Satisfied, he settled back down to watch, happy his third was nearby to protect me. When Stone took a stride towards the fallen male, I jerked into action. "Stone! No!"

His head whipped towards me. I inhaled sharply. His eyes were a stunning mix of purple and yellow and claws gleamed at his fingertips. He inhaled and snarled, so I snarled right back. "Leave him. You've proved your strength, and we aren't in that prison any more. It stops here. No killing."

Stone held my gaze, his big shoulders rising and falling hard as he struggled with his wolf, trying to contain his dominance in the face of all the soldiers who now pointed weapons at us. Stone dropped his gaze from me, but raised it again, his teeth lengthening as a weapon safety was clicked off.

"Lower your weapons. Now," said a calm authoritative voice. Without hesitation all the soldiers did as commanded. I ran the few steps needed to reach Stone. "Hey. Look at me, not them." An encouraging touch on his arm and he did. Prime raised his eyes and melded his gaze with mine. Stone's nostrils flared, but he lowered his gaze, the pulse of his alpha power lessening.

"Thank you," I said quietly to him as Prime turned his attention to the man on the floor, considering whether or not to burst through and rip his throat out. He decided it was his third's fight and settled down. Stone nodded his head, his irises now the silver grey ringed with purple I was getting used to seeing. Neither his fae side nor his wolf were dampened by that fucking collar anymore and I could now see how strong he really was. He might be a half-breed, but that didn't make him less dangerous, it made him *more*. A predator with the viciousness and magic of a fae. Damn, these soldiers might not be as good as I was hoping if they couldn't figure that out.

"No, *thank you*, she-wolf," Stone said, cracking his neck. His eyes narrowed, and his gaze fixed on the guy who pushed himself from the floor.

"Well, this place is full of surprises," said the calm voice from behind me. "A female who can tame an alpha who isn't her mate. Interesting indeed."

I turned my attention from Stone to the tall, ruggedly attractive male. The skin tight top he wore molded to the cut of his defined and generous muscles. My focus grazed over his flat, washboard stomach, right down to his shit-kickers. I smirked. Ok yeah, he was scorching hot. I could appreciate that as a woman, especially one who hadn't had sex in months, but getting some bump and grind wasn't the purpose of my lustful stare; nope, not at all.

His spine straightened and a small, confident smile curled the corner of his generous mouth. His eyes sparkled with amusement and interest when I met his heavy gaze and held it. I didn't need to look again to know he had three knives on him and a hand gun that had the ability to taser. His knuckles and the back of his hands were scarred, and his forearms were thick with muscles and veins. This man was a fighter, a leader who got his hands dirty, just like Connor. He was measured, his voice told me so, but he was pure alpha; a man who exuded authority and presence, so I doubted that measured attitude would last. I wondered what his shifter spirit was.

Prime growled long and low, sensing a threat. Gritting my teeth against his rising aggression, I forced him back. Mea stepped up, distracting him while I dealt with the newcomer. It was a fight not to roll my eyes as the male's smirk widened.

Stone growled low in his chest. I patted his defined pecs, not taking my attention from the huge newcomer. "It's fine, I got this."

The male raised one brow, his derision at Stone for allowing me to take control, obvious. Clear hazel eyes narrowed as I took a step closer. Like most male shifters, especially alphas, he didn't step back; after all, I was just a petite female shifter, I wasn't a threat. I gave him a smile and looked up through my lashes. If I hadn't had Connor to compare him to, I might have drooled at the sight of his sexy smirk. His confidence and power were off the charts, and the long dark lashes that framed his eyes were to die for. Yep, he was a hot bastard, but I didn't bother dropping my gaze from his intense stare, even when he pushed some strong alpha vibes on me.

His heavy brows dipped.

I smiled wider. "That's right, your alpha mojo doesn't work on me." I snapped my thumb and middle finger together and a flame ignited. I didn't need to snap my fingers, but it was more showy. I twisted my palm and held up the pretty blue and green flame, playing with it by passing it along my fingers like a coin. "So back off." I growled, letting Prime use me to warn the male off. But this guy saw only the short red headed woman in front of him. That was probably a good thing or we'd have ended up in a full-on alpha challenge. He grinned, but still didn't step back. "I like my women with fire, makes life more interesting."

"Yeah, well, I'm not your woman. Come too close and you'll get that pretty face burned right off."

He chuckled. "Wow, feisty. I like you. So what's your name, honey?"

Honey? Oh, he did *not* just say that.

"You first, *darlin'.*" I raised my brows a little.

He smiled, his eyes sparkling with laughter; then surprised me by answering. "Jedediah Hawk."

"And what are you doing here, Jedi?"

"A-ah, nope, no nicknames. Besides, it's your turn. What's your name?"

"Well, it sure as shit ain't honey, *Jedi.*"

He just raised his brows higher and chuckled, crossing his arms over his large chest. "So, what is it? Because I'd love to get to know a little spitfire like you." He cocked his head and contemplated the flame dancing along my knuckles. "You aren't just a shifter, that's for sure."

"No shit, Sherlock." I rolled my eyes and pulled the flame into my palm before lowering my hand. "Same as you sure as shit aren't here for the scenery."

His eyes flicked to Owen, who approached from behind me. Prime rumbled, sensing his brother, too. Jedediah's gaze moved back to me, and though his body gave off the appearance of being relaxed, I could see he was anything but.

"What's going on, Hawk?" Owen's voice was as cold as I'd ever heard it.

He didn't like this guy, and alpha shit aside, I had to wonder why. Owen was usually even-tempered and easy going with just about everyone, even Zander had been shown some respect from the alpha of this camp. This guy, not so much.

Hawk shrugged, his handsome smirk still in place. "Just getting acquainted with your pack members, Brady. Calm your tits."

Owen glanced at me and then Stone, whose wolf was right near the surface and ready to launch at Hawk. Owen stopped by my side and I was grateful he didn't look me in the eye. Prime was stirring and pushing against Mea and Fire. He was getting pissed at this guy, and he'd break through eventually.

Owen spared me a quick glance, his wolf staring down at me. "You okay, Ember?"

"Ember, is it?" Hawk jumped straight on Owen's words, his eyes narrowing on me until Prime snarled at the predatory look in his eyes. "Well, now, *Ember,* to answer your question, I'm here on a very special mission, and it just got a whole lot more interesting. Next time we meet, we'll find a nice quiet spot, just you and me, and I'll explain all about it."

"No, you fucking won't, shithead. You're here because I'm allowing it—for now. Don't push your luck. Stay away from our Prime's mate, or I don't care who the fuck you work for, I'll end you—if he doesn't get to you first. You good with that, Ember?"

"Sure." I shrugged one shoulder and affected a couldn't give a shit expression, which wasn't true, at all. It hit me right in the gut that Connor might never be around to kick anyone's arse ever again. But this soldier didn't need to know that.

I really, really wanted to know who this male was, and why Owen thought it was necessary to warn him away from me, but keeping Prime contained was my priority right now; as was dealing with the demon that wore Connor. I turned away and took Stone's arm. Hawk would find me eventually; he wanted something, I saw it in his eyes. Under that predatory gleam, there was another emotion; one I'd seen many times before in Faerie—greed. I'd find out, one way or another, why he was here; it wasn't just to fight the soldiers of Hell. With all the firepower Drake had brought to this forest, the shifters in this camp, with Owen leading them, could manage to contain the werewolves in the prison. Whoever had paid to get Hawk and his men here, was after something. My senses tingled in warning, but I flashed Hawk a smile and wiggled my fingers before giving him a cheeky wink. "See ya later, Jedi. Tell your men to leave everyone in this camp alone, and that includes me. If they, or you, become a problem, I'll incinerate you all." The bolt of fire I sent from my fingertips hit the ground at his feet.

"Fuck!" He jumped back. The damp ground went up in flames—because I'd told Fire to burn it. "Godsdammit! Get something to put this out!" he yelled.

I just kept walking with Stone while I killed the flame. "Well, I think that went well. Don't you?"

Stone chuckled. "I think you made a friend."

"He's not your fucking friend, Ember. Stay away from him unless one of us is with you. He's dangerous." Owen's face was deadly serious.

"What are you talking about, Owen? What's really going on?"

"Shit." He ran a hand through his hair, his whole body tense and power rolling off him. It wasn't like Owen to lose his cool like this. "Just...don't trust him. Okay?"

"Why not?" I pushed, not happy to leave it at that. Owen knew something, yet he didn't want to share. "You have to give me something here, Owen."

"No, I don't." He growled, then ran another hand through his already mussed hair. "Look, as far as I know, he's here to help put Berith down. But he's a snake, someone who is being paid by one of the most wealthy supernaturals in this world. Drake wouldn't tell us who his current partner is, all he told us was that Hawk came as part of the deal."

"So we don't know Hawk's real agenda?"

Owen released a heavy breath, his face dark. "No, but I've met Hawk before. He works for money, lots of money, nothing else. He's good at what he does, but honour and loyalty are foreign to him, and I don't for a moment believe he's here just to help us. Neither should you."

Nodding, I accepted his words. There were other things to think about right now. "Where's Zander? I wanted to talk to him before we put Connor in chains."

"He'll meet us at Connor's room."

We walked the rest of the way to Connor's cabin in silence. The closer we got, the more my stomach hurt. I was on edge and Stone must have felt it.

"Just remember this isn't Connor. Whatever filth comes out of his mouth is not your mate."

I nodded, took a fortifying breath, and unhooked my arm from Stone's before jogging up the steps, Stone and Owen behind me. Pulling open the door, I stepped inside. Warmth hit me along with the scent of other male wolves. Under it all I could scent the demon; a burning, slightly sulfurous scent that had clung to Connor's body in the cave. I walked towards Connor's door.

Determined not to chicken out, I raised my hand to knock when I noticed it was slightly ajar—and was that *Shannon's* voice? I choked back a snarl, my heart rate rocketing. *No fucking way!*

"Come on, baby. You know you still want me."

Using every bit of self-control not to react to that deep bass voice, I slowly pushed open the door. And blinked. And blinked again. My brain tried to process what I saw. Shannon was utterly naked and straddling Connor's, or rather, the demon's lap. All he had on was a towel around his waist.

Connor's torso was covered in new scars; his skin pallid and missing the muscle he'd once had. With his large hands he grasped her hips as he ground up into her, only the towel separating them. Fury rushed my throat even as pain ripped at my heart. I knew this wasn't really him, but the sight of my mate with another woman sent me to my knees.

"No..." My voice was nothing but a pained whisper, but it was enough. Connor turned his head. His eyes glinted, a dark smile curling his lips. Shannon looked at me. Her face paled and she froze. "Ember?" she whispered.

The demon smirked, chuckling, and his towel seemed to just melt into nothing.

"Oh, fuck no!" Shannon muttered, and before it could grab her hips and slam Connor's hard cock into her while looking right at me, Shannon yelled: "Now!"

Shadow erupted on the other side of the bed and a huge horned demon with wings and burning red eyes materialised. There was a flash of yellow. Something slapped into Shannon's outstretched hand and she yelled, a deep sound that was more male than female, as she shoved the circle of glowing yellow metal against Connor's skin, right over his heart.

Connor roared and bucked his hips, punching Shannon in the jaw.

"Shannon!" Stone came barrelling through the door. He skidded to a halt taking in the scene. I turned my tear filled eyes up to the half-fae, so sorry he had to see Shannon naked on the floor of another male's bedroom.

"Oh gods, Stone, I'm sorry," I whispered.

Stone's wolf emerged in a second. It leaped towards Connor, only to be tackled to the ground by another wolf—an identical one.

What the hell was happening? Shannon had disappeared, and Connor was rolling around the bed in agony.

"You fucking traitor! You will not beat me, Zander. You think being my son will save you? I'll destroy you, and everything you love. There will be nowhere you can go; I will hunt you and your mother down!"

Zander calmly walked around the bed, ignoring Connor's ranting. Except…that voice. It wasn't Connor's voice anymore, just the same as that burning, and now overpowering sulphurous smell wasn't his. Zander stopped in front of me and reached down a hand, his eyes burning. "I will not hurt you. Take my hand."

I swallowed against my dry throat. "Zander?"

"Yes. Now stand. That thing on the bed is not Connor—but you already knew that didn't you?" For a moment pain flickered in his eyes before being swallowed once again by fire. I took his clawed hand and got to my feet.

"Enough!" Zander waved his hand and uttered some words in a language I'd never heard. Both wolves froze mid-fight. "Alex, turn back before Stone rips you apart. You are no killer, my friend."

In front of my eyes, the wolf morphed back into my friend, clad in jeans and a t-shirt and boots. "Oh, my god, Alex? But you…you…" I motioned with my hand to Connor's writhing form.

He cringed. "Yeah, well, needs must. Please don't mention it again."

Stone changed back. Totally naked, eyes wholly purple and so full of fury, I almost stepped between him and Alex, but the demon that was Connor let out an almighty bellow. I whipped my head around to watch as the metal disc began to spin in his chest wall, searing away his skin.

"Oh Mother, you found the disc?"

Zander carefully wrapped his huge arms around me. They were covered in thick black leathery skin with bone spurs sticking through his forearms and triceps. "I did. And no matter what he says, or how much he screams, you can't help him, Ember. That disc is an angel's Halo, an ancient one; Lucifer's to be exact. When he fell, God took away his Halo. It is the only way known to our world of extracting an unwanted spirit from another's body. That isn't Connor. *That* is Berith."

Unable to tear my gaze from Connor, I gaped as light engulfed him.

"Ember? Ember? Stop it, stop *him*. He's lying to you. He's a demon! He's trying to kill me and take me from you again!"

I shook my head, my lip curled into a snarl. Prime growled and together we spoke. "Go to Hell, you mother fucker!"

The demon reached out, and with a sudden roar launched himself up off the bed, charging towards me, utter hatred and fury blazing in a set of black eyes that were nothing like Connor's. Zander thrust me towards Stone, who caught me and slammed down some kind of shield between us and them.

Zander twisted, and with his wings, knocked Berith back. Berith slammed into the wall, his body contorting. Shadow danced around his body, mixing with the burning white light from the Halo. Connor's spine arched as Berith forced himself from his flesh causing Connor to fall back on the bed. Berith wasn't whole, though. His form was flickering in and out of translucence, but the longer he was out of Connor's body, the more solid he became.

"Shit, he's getting stronger," Alex said, standing next to me and Stone, who seemed ready to jump in front of me if Berith escaped. Owen stepped up to my other side but I couldn't look at any of them; my whole being was centred on Berith and my mate.

Zander looked at me, and for a moment his face morphed back into the strong-jawed and handsome guard that I knew. "Tell my brother I love him, and not to blame our mother; none of this is her fault."

"No." I shouted, dread filling my heart. "Don't, Zander! *Please.* Don't do it!"

His smile was small and sad, his own body flickering between human and demon. "I have no choice. There is always payment for using a gift of God. It is sending me to Hell." His eyes met mine. "Destroy the rift before Berith can get more soldiers through. Tell Connor it's the fireplace."

And before I could shift and use Prime to stop him, Zander opened his wings and propelled himself at Berith. The Halo fell from Connor's chest, its light fading even as it reached for Zander. Berith lowered his huge horned head, ready to stand his ground, but Zander's momentum was too great. He hit Berith in the stomach with his horns and sent them both into the Halo's fading light. The Halo flared, and an explosion of power knocked us all from our feet. Stone roared, throwing his shield towards Connor. It deflected the power of the blast outwards blowing out the side of the cabin.

My head smacked on the floor and for a moment I couldn't think past the pain and the ringing in my ears. Ignoring my body's need to lay still, I forced Prime and Mea to lend me some of their power and stumbled to my feet. On instinct I pushed Fire against Stone's shield and burned straight through it. Alex and Stone were still scrambling up off the floor when I reached Connor's side. Noise erupted around us, voices yelling and shouting. I ignored them all. Connor was deathly still, his chest not moving, a circular burn in the center of it. With shaking hands, I cupped his face. "Please, baby, wake up." Was he gone? "Alex? Alex? Tell me he's going to wake up..."

Alex knelt next to me, tucking the Halo into his shirt out of sight. "I...I'm sorry, Ember. I don't know how it works. Zander...he knew. He told me it would get rid of the demon in Connor's body, and that he would be taken in payment, but nothing more."

A sob broke from my chest. "No. No. He has to come back to me...he has to..." My heart squeezed as tears dripped off my chin. I stared down at Connor's waxen skin. My worst nightmare had come true. Connor was really gone. Feeling my heart shatter, I fell across Connor's damaged chest and sobbed; even Mea and Prime couldn't reach me.

I GRITTED MY TEETH. I would *not* fucking scream. Not here, not now, not ever. I staggered under the weight of my chains, chains that burned my skin, over and over again. Bracing myself, I forced my knees straight. There was no end in sight for me. This was it. My soul was stuck here in this strange existence. This must be the outer reaches of Hell. I stared at the wall of bones and rotting flesh that disappeared into the distance; a never ending barrier between here and the land of the living. The gates opposite me were made of some kind of black wood, carved with the agonised faces of men and monsters. The gates didn't open so much as shimmer when a soul was cast into Hell.

There was an anguished scream as one fell through the huge gate, landing at the feet of the Were who stood opposite me. He snarled, his once amber eyes swallowed whole by the demon that now controlled his body. Dagnar, my brother, had been turned into a Hellhound. Berith had healed D's half-shifted flesh and bone, only to house a demon in his half-shifted form. My brother was my guard, a cruel twist of Berith's meant to hurt me even more. I looked up. I knew Berith had ordered his hounds to chain me here, staring at this gate for a reason. I didn't know what that reason was but I did know it had something to do with Ember.

I snarled. *The gates of Hell.* They were so huge there was no top to them, they disappeared into the swirling darkness of the sky above. On either side of the gates, huge waterfalls of blood rained down, falling into deep pools that ran into the burning river that surrounded the island of bones I was chained upon. More Hellhounds guarded the gates, and they were merciless. Souls were given form here; a flesh and blood body that could be broken over and over. They had one chance to get on the ferry boat which would take them across the burning river to their destination in Hell—if they refused, or tried to get back to the gates, these soldiers of Hell would rip their limbs off one by one until they begged to be allowed on the boat. The few who never begged had their heads ripped from their bodies before being cast into the burning river of fire that flowed around us. Moments later their bones fused with those under my feet. There was no escape from this fucking awful slice of Hell—except through those gates.

Thirst raged in my body and it never abated, neither did the hunger, or the lust that burned low in my belly. It was as if the screams and agony of the souls here were trying to take me to whatever realm of Hell they'd been assigned.

I studied the Were who had once been my friend...my blood brother. A scar still marred his face, and the hole in his chest that Stone had inflicted had healed raggedly. I knew Dagnar's soul was stuck inside his Were body alongside that damned demon, but I had no idea how to reach him.

My knees sagged under the weight of my chains, the silver links scoring my skin, again. A low growl of pain escaped my clenched jaw. Yeah, guilt was a bitch, but I deserved all that pain, and more. So many souls had died at my hands, or because of me; I deserved to be here.

I forced myself to stay on my feet. If I bowed under the weight of my sins, I would be dragged down into the fiery flow of the river. I pressed my lips into a straight line, and my nostrils flared as I sucked in a sulphurous breath. I would not break, and *she* was my reason. Somehow, I'd find a way back to her; to my salvation. I didn't know why, but I did know that Berith wanted Ember, and he had taken my body, using me as a suit of flesh, blood and bones to get to her. Deliberately I exhaled, trying to calm my fury and fear, hoping that Ember wouldn't be fooled by him. The thought of him using her, of him touching her in any way, made me want to claw my way through those gates —except...my wolf was gone, lost to me. I couldn't claw my way through anything now.

My eyes burned, but I blinked against the hot wind, snarling in disgust at the stench of rot that was carried on it. I swallowed against my dry throat, wondering how long I'd been here. Time was non-existent in this place.

A gust of wind rocked me and I stumbled and fell to my knees. The chains rattled as link by link they slithered into the molten river, hissing as each one disappeared under the surface. I had to get up. I couldn't let Berith win. He'd taken everything from me, but that burning desire in my gut to fight for Ember. The need to take my life back had only flared hotter in this world of suffering. Yelling under the weight of the chain, I pulled one knee up and put my foot flat on the white dust that covered the island of bones. Snaking my arms around the thick links, I tensed my muscles and pulled. Beads of sweat ran down my forehead and temples, dripping from my chin. Using my thighs and my back, I roared and pushed up against the weight of my sins and stood tall.

Grey and amber flashed through the eyes of the Were who had been my brother. I grinned. "That's right D, you fight that fucker! Don't you let him win. Ever. I'll find a way out for us."

The demon chuckled as D lost his fight and disappeared, but that little sign my brother was still in there, somewhere, only made me more determined to find a way back, to get us both out of here, even if it was just to free his wolf and human souls. He didn't deserve this for an eternity, none of my kind did.

I snarled at the demon. "Come on, you ugly bastard. Come and get me..." If I could goad him into coming closer maybe I could grab his weapon and somehow get out of the chains. Just as the demon took one step towards me the gates began to vibrate and shimmer.

"Damn." My chance had just disappeared. Two bodies came hurtling through the gates and thudded to the ground, sending dust into the air as they rolled across the bones. One was huge, and as ugly as sin.

Berith!

He rolled to his feet, huge wings exploding from his back. Without so much as a pause, he launched himself at the other guy. The other demon spun away and landed near me. Black horns curled around the side of his head, and his red eyes bored into mine right before his wings snapped out and he launched upwards, away from Berith.

"Zander?"

Shadow danced around him, hiding him the closer to the dark clouds he got. Berith followed, his furious roar rattling the bones under my feet. Moments later a figure came hurtling down. Zander's face came into view, his jaw set and his eyes focused on me. No, not me...the chains. He yelled as the wind flayed his skin until his cheekbones and jaw were visible.

Berith swooped down, closing in on Zander.

"Come on, Zander! Do it!" My voice was hoarse, my throat too dry to shout loudly, but Zander heard me. Just before Berith could reach him, Zander roared and dove. He slammed his fists against the chain and it snapped. I struggled from under its weight just as I felt a force tugging at me, dragging me towards the gate.

Zander rolled to a halt, his clawed hands and wrists broken beyond comprehension, shattered bones sticking through the torn and bleeding flesh.

"Zander?"

His eyes widened and I was sure he mouthed one word: *brother...* and smiled. That crazy mofo, actually, smiled... I tried to take a step towards him, but the power of the gate dragged at me. My feet scraped through the thick bone dust, leaving trails.

Berith landed, his hate filled gaze fixed on Zander. "That was stupid, Son. You think that will save him, or his whore? They are both mine! And I will make them suffer, just for you, every single day for a fucking eternity..." And with the talons at the apex of his leathery bat like wings, he stabbed Zander through the chest.

"No!" I fought. Mother, how I fought to reach the guard who had become my friend. I bellowed as Berith ripped those vicious spikes from Zander's chest and grabbed him by the throat. Zander's eyes widened as I slammed one foot back into the ground towards him.

"No...Go...Ember..." He gurgled, black demon blood spraying from his lips and covering his burnt charcoal skin.

I shook my head, but had no choice but to leave my friend when a horrid, ear piercing screech came from the gate and I was dragged into a vortex. My whole body started to tingle. I peered down at my fingers, panic gripping me when they were translucent and my cells disassembled, floating away like grains of sand...

CHAPTER 12

onnor

"Please, Connor, please, come back to me!" Quiet, despairing sobs pulled me from that place of screaming wind and searing heat. It was the voice that had haunted my dreams and nightmares. But this time I felt her touch. Her scent filled my nostrils and seeped into my blood and bones, settling in my soul. My heart missed several beats, its rhythm erratic and painful, as if it was learning how to beat again.

"Ember?" I forced my eyes open, and found myself looking right into her stunning, tear filled, emerald eyes.

"Oh, Mother Wolf. Connor?" Her hands rested on my chest, bringing my attention to the searing pain there.

"Ember? Yes...it's me," I managed to say, my voice scratchy, my mouth dry. "Is that really you?" Please don't let this be another dream.

Another broken sob wrenched from her chest and she wrapped her arms around my shoulders, burying her face in my neck. With that contact something in my soul clicked into place. Inhaling deeply, I ignored the agony in my chest and lifted my arms, wrapping them around her. Slowly, my eyes focused on the white faced people who stood gaping at us. Owen and Stone were covered in dust and had small scratches on their faces and necks.

"Brothers?" My voice was loosening up. "Mother Wolf, it's good to see you." And it really was, but I wasn't about to release my hold on my mate to get up and greet them.

"Yeah, you too, man." Owen grinned, relief obvious on his face.

"Prime," Stone said, his eyes a curious mix of silver and purple.

My eyes rested on the man who stood shoulder to shoulder with my brothers; my *free* brothers. This wasn't the prison that was obvious. I had no idea where I was right now, other than noticing that the walls behind me had been blown out and frigid, snow-laced air was blowing in.

"Alex? Wow! Alex Blaze? What the fuck are you doing here?" I stared at the man I hadn't seen for years. The last time I'd seen the doppelganger, he'd been posing as a teacher at Ember's school.

Alex came and knelt next to Ember. "Hey, Commander. Good to see you, too. I came here to help your Firecracker get you back. But it looks like we brought the wrong you back. Zander saw it. He saved you, Connor. Your brother saved your ass and forced it back out of Hell."

Oh, shit, Zander...

He was in Hell, and by the looks of it, about to become Berith's new toy. Berith wouldn't end him, I was sure of it, but he would make his existence one of agony. I squeezed my eyes shut. He'd saved me—at the cost of his own freedom.

I hugged Ember closer to me, my soul pulsing against hers. Even without my wolf, I could sense hers lingering just below the surface. A dark growl, followed by a keening sound, echoed in my head.

Prime!

My heart ached and that empty void in my soul gaped wide. My head suddenly seemed too busy, my heart too full of emotion. I had my mate back and she was alive and safe in my arms, but my wolf was hers now. I rested my head back against the floor and closed my eyes, a tear running from the corner of one eye. "Godsdammit, this better not be another dream." It would utterly break me this time... "No more," I begged. "Please."

Ember lifted her head and she took hold of my face in both of her hands. "No, this really isn't a dream, Connor, I promise. You really are here with me and your brothers. Oh gods, I'm so sorry for leaving you in that Hellhole for so long."

I opened my eyes and looked at the devastation in hers. "What? No, don't you do that. None of what happened to me was your fault." I gently clasped her chin between my thumb and forefinger. "Do you hear me? None of it." I brushed my thumb over her lower lip, wanting to reassure her, but I was a starving man, and that small contact snapped something inside of me. I pulled her towards me desperate to taste her, to know without a doubt that she was real. The second her lips touched mine, a deep groan left me. Her taste erupted across my tongue and I devoured it, absorbing everything about her into my shattered soul.

A loud cough registered. "Hey, you two! Knock it off would ya? There's rooms for that kind of thing."

I pulled away from Ember enough to look up into Shannon's shining eyes. "Good to see you too, Shannon."

"Hey, Ember, why don't you let Connor sit up? Hm? He needs checking over by a medic," Alex suggested.

My beautiful Firecracker glared at him, but didn't speak, instead, her fingers curled over my shoulders, holding on as if she would never let go, let alone let me up for medical help. I glanced down and wrinkled my nose in distaste. I could scent the stink of that Demon piece of shit on every part of me. I needed to get rid of it. I buried my nose in Ember's neck and inhaled her scent again. At least he hadn't fooled my Firecracker into getting into his bed. "Hey, sweetheart, it's okay, I'm not going anywhere. And Alex is right. This burn really does sting."

"Oh, damn, I'm sorry. Of course, I just…" She sat back on her heels staring at me wide eyed and pale. "I can't believe this is really you; that you're really here." She swallowed hard. "I'm afraid to let go," she whispered.

I squeezed her hand, giving her the reassurance that I knew she needed—because I needed it, too.

Owen strode closer as I struggled up into a sitting position trying to ignore the roar of agony in my chest, and the weakness in my body. Once upright, I blinked away my dizziness. Owen helped Ember to stand, then Alex and Owen helped me to my feet. My legs wobbled and I growled, looking down at myself. I was a shadow of my former self, my muscles wasted and weak. Granted, I didn't feel as weak as I had as Berith's prisoner, but still, not good.

Now that I was upright, I immediately reached out for Ember and pulled her into me, hissing when her head brushed against the burned skin of my chest. Frigid air brushed my naked skin, though I couldn't give a shit that I was standing in my birthday suit. Hell, everyone in this room had seen me naked before; but I did care about the guilt I could see in every part of my mate's face. Carefully, I put her a little distance from me. "Listen to me. You do not need to feel guilt for anything that happened to me."

Her shoulders rose and fell in a shrug. "I'm sorry it took me so long to find you. It was really Zander who saved you, Connor. Not me. He and Alex figured out how to send Berith back to Hell." Her throat bobbed as she swallowed, pain in her eyes as she glanced at Shannon and then Alex.

Alex shook his head. "Don't you even go there. Riding him was not my finest moment."

"Yeah, and taking my female's form to do it, was something I will never forgive you for, you perverted shit." Stone stepped forward, his fists clenched.

Alex jumped back almost behind me, his hands raised. "Hey, Zander said it was the only way to throw him off guard."

Stone snarled. "Yeah? And how do you know what she looks like naked?" He glared accusingly at Shannon, whose mouth dropped open.

"Are you kidding me? You think I slept with him?"

"How else does he know what you look like naked, Shannon? After all, it wouldn't be the first male in this camp you've fucked, now would it? Seems you're happy to be with anyone *but* me."

"Oh, my gods, are you for real?" Before anyone could react, Shannon slapped Stone's face. His head jerked to the side. "Fuck you, you faerie bastard." And she turned on her heel and stormed out.

Stone's eyes flashed bright yellow, purple burning in their depths. He made a move to go after her.

"No!" I snapped out the order on instinct. "Leave her to cool down. You need to, as well. And just for the record, that was a low blow, Stone."

Stone dropped his head and took a deep breath, but surprisingly did as I ordered and stayed where he was, his gaze on Alex like he wanted to rip him to pieces.

"Explain." I glared at Alex.

Alex's wary eyes stayed on Stone. "Zander told me he had just broken you and your mother out of the prison when he became suspicious you weren't your normal self..."

"What did you just say?" I growled low, not sure I'd heard him right.

Alex swallowed and Ember's hold on me tightened. She took up his explanation.

"Connor, it seems Zander really is your brother—by blood—and he was forced to work for Berith because his mother, your mother, was also a prisoner there. Berith coveted her, she was his prisoner as much as you were, but Zander somehow managed to get you both out. I can only assume that Berith *let* Zander and Tyen escape with him." She blinked, a frown furrowing her brow. "I mean you, because he knew I'd come for you; that I'd find you eventually. And it's me he wants."

I shook my head. "Zander is my brother—by birth? And I have a mother? That can't be true, Berith is not my father. He called Zander his son."

"I know. You have the same mother, not the same father. Tyen is a fae, you are half-fae, half-shifter, Connor; like Stone."

Darkness swirled around my mind, infiltrating my thoughts and telling me what it had done for me. The monster of shadow that had burst forth and ripped Doherty to shreds, had also protected my thoughts; it had shielded my memories of Ember and my brothers, and it protected my mind from Berith's tortures as much as it could, absorbing the evil realities that he'd tried to force on me. I closed my eyes and thanked it, knowing I'd be nothing but a broken shell without its help, glad to finally be able to acknowledge and understand it. The darkness pulsed, letting me know it was happy to have my human soul back, even if my shifter spirit was still inside Ember.

I blinked slowly. My mother was alive? And Zander? Mother Wolf, I had a brother who had sacrificed his freedom for me! I needed time to absorb all this new information, but I *would* deal with it. I swallowed the ache in my throat. My mother. I remembered very little of her. When I was young, I had deliberately shoved her from my mind so that my father couldn't use her memory to hurt me. That evil fucker had told me she had left us for another shifter. I snarled. *Lying bastard.*

I took a deep breath and nodded. "I would like to meet her—very soon. But right now I need to rest." I met Owen's steady gaze and felt that connection with my beta. No, he was now an alpha in his own right. "You up for filling me in? As soon as I can stand on my own two feet without help, of course." I gave him a rueful grin.

Owen returned it. "Sure, but you always were a pussy, so that might take a while."

I huffed and raised my middle finger. "Piss off."

Even Stone smirked, though his attention kept drifting to the door.

I glanced back at Alex. "So you pretended to be Shannon because Berith knew from my memory we had history?"

Alex flinched and nodded looking at Stone. "Hey, man. I'm sorry, but it was the only way. And you should go apologise to that woman, because we sure as shit didn't do the horizontal tango."

Stone snarled, and I noticed Ember's small smile as she looked at the doppelganger. They seemed to have become friends in my absence. I growled at Alex who was a good few inches shorter than me. "Did you grind on me, you perverted shit?"

Ember bit her lip and giggled, her shoulders shaking.

Alex's cheekbones tinged with pink and he stepped back. "I had to..." he sputtered.

I grinned and smacked his back. "S'all right, man, I'm messing with you." My grin stretched as his shoulders relaxed, such a look of relief on his face it was hard not to mess with him even more. But I took pity on him. "So what did Zander do to bring me back from Hell?" I already knew I wouldn't leave my brother to suffer at the hands of his merciless father. He'd found a way to get me out, and I'd do the same for him. He'd put on a front of working for both sides, when in truth he'd had no choice but to work for Berith. I didn't know, but I suspected working for the fae was his back-up plan to get us all out.

"He used this." Alex pulled his shirt to one side and a stunning yellow metal disc glinted. I'd seen it before. Doherty had planned to use it on Ember to take both her wolf and her phoenix. Alex quickly covered it back up, his gaze flitting across the crowd that had gathered outside the ruined cabin. "It's a fallen angel's Halo; Lucifer's Halo, to be exact, and the only one known to exist outside Heaven. It is the only known way to pull a spirit from its host. But it opens the doors to Lucifer's realm when it is used. The user can prevent themselves and the spirit from being propelled through the gates of Hell, but they must use angelic words to do it. Zander didn't use the words because he couldn't. He told me he doesn't know how to speak angelic. He knew using the Halo would send Berith back to Hell; but that he'd be sucked in with him..."

"Mother Wolf, Zander knew what would happen. He sacrificed himself for me. To get me back here..." I met Ember's gaze. "To you."

She closed her eyes and nodded. "It seems that way."

I had no words. My brother, my flesh and blood was suffering in Hell—for me. Gods, I'd never considered anyone doing anything like that for me, and now I didn't know what to think, how to feel in the face of that sacrifice.

"Come on, man, let's get you to Ember's cabin. I'll get a healer to see you, and then you can rest. When you feel stronger, we can talk more and I'll explain what's happening here," Owen said.

I nodded, suddenly exhausted. My knees buckled and dizziness overwhelmed me. I was aware Stone took my weight on one side, while Owen held me up on the other. I didn't have Prime with me, but I could feel him close by, and when I looked at Ember, he was staring right back at me, his power pulsing against my soul. I smiled and nodded. I didn't know how, but I knew that there would be a way for us to rejoin—I just had to find it.

"Don't worry, we'll find a way together." Ember's voice soothed my frayed soul. I blinked as I looked at my beautiful mate. I couldn't remember everything Berith had tortured me with, but I knew times like this, when I was full of hope and joy at seeing my mate, were when he broke me.

Her hand on my cheek felt warm. "It's real, Connor." Her smile was reassuring, but I didn't miss the darkness in her eyes. I hated the thought that she blamed herself for any of this.

"Good. Then take me to bed, Firecracker. I've been without you for too long." And I winked.

She rolled her eyes and smiled. Yeah, we both knew I wasn't strong enough to even walk, let alone do much else. I grinned. But that was only temporary.

CHAPTER 13

mber

Cold hit me as I stepped out of the cabin and jogged down the steps.

"Hey, slow down."

I looked back over my shoulder at Myles. I hadn't left Connor's side since he'd truly come back to us two days ago. Alex had explained Zander hadn't wanted Berith to have any chance to pull me into Hell, so he hadn't waited for me or the others to arrive. Instead, he'd got Alex on board and they'd formed a plan.

Myles jumped off the top step and landed agilely beside me. "He's safe, Ember."

"I know, but he needs feeding."

Myles smiled. Owen had sent food for us, but Connor hadn't really woken to eat. I'd laid next to him listening to his stomach rumble as he slept. I wanted to get him something so that it was there when he woke up. "I know Stone's on Connor-watch, but I want to get back before he wakes up."

Myles cocked his head. "I know you do."

I took Myles's arm, hating the shadows under his beautiful green eyes. I leaned my head on his bicep, and he kissed the top of my head.

"He loved you, you know," he said as we walked.

I swallowed the pain in my throat, my eyes burning. I didn't need to ask who he was talking about. Once I could talk past the guilt that choked my throat, I pulled him to a stop. "Myles, I'm so sorry for what I did to him. I...I...didn't ever... I didn't think..." No matter how much I tried, I couldn't get my words out. How could I apologise for killing his mate? For sending him to Hell. "Gods, how can you stand to be near me?"

Myles pulled away. He placed his large hands on his hips and lowered his head to stare at his boots. His shoulders rose and fell as if he needed time to get himself under control.

Right, he really *couldn't* stand to be near me... Clenching my fists, I turned away.

"Hey, where are you going?" His voice was thick but strong.

I kept my eyes down, unable to face the condemnation that would surely be in his. "It's okay, Myles, you don't need to babysit me. Prime's much calmer now that he knows Connor is near. I'll be fine alone."

"Ember, look at me."

I turned my back on him and squeezed my eyes shut. I'd never forget the moment my hand clawed through Reed's chest, my werewolf utterly out of my control. I shook my head. "I can't."

Gently, he turned me to face him and lifted my chin with his fingers until I had to look at him. "I know it wasn't your fault. Do you really think I'd ever believe you would hurt him willingly?"

I just stared up into his face. His features softened. "Well do you? Because Reed would seriously kick my arse, if he thought I did. We mated because you gave him the push towards me that he needed. I won't forget that, Ember, no matter what happens to him in the end."

I blinked, and before I could overthink it, I threw myself into his body, wrapping my arms around him.

"Hey, come on, I'd rather deal with your smart-mouthed attitude than your tears. We have to be strong for him, Em. Just like he would for us. And there's still hope we can bring him back."

I sniffed and nodded before I pulled away and wiped my snotty nose. "Yeah."

"Will you come and see him soon? It might...well, help him. You know? He might be in there somewhere behind that thing that has taken him. Maybe he can hear us."

"Of course." And I would, as soon as I knew Connor was really okay.

❧

I walked past Stone, who lifted a brow at the amount of food I'd brought my mate. "Oh, shut up," I said, but smiled as Myles opened the door for me.

"See you later." Myles grinned, and I flushed as he winked at me. "Much later, if I know Connor."

I walked into my room carrying a tray piled high with bacon, eggs, tomatoes and toast, plus two huge thermos mugs of coffee. I'd kiss Drake when I saw him again. How he'd pulled off this amount of luxury in the middle of the Canadian wilds, I had no clue.

"Hey, Firecracker, where've you been?" Connor's voice was little more than a growl as he stepped out of the shower cubicle, only a towel around his hips while he rubbed water from his shoulder length hair with another. His blue eyes fixed on me, but I couldn't stop my gaze grazing down his chest and over his stomach, amazingly the circular burn was already healing. He'd lost a lot of muscle and his body was a criss cross of scars that hadn't been there before. I swallowed hard. It didn't matter to me what he looked like, he still affected me the way he always had. My heart raced ridiculously fast in my chest and my face heated as he stopped rubbing his hair and threw the towel on the bed. "Come here." It was a gentle command, one I was more than happy to comply with.

I'd laid on the bed with him all day yesterday and he hadn't wanted to let me go. Everytime I'd moved, he'd pulled me closer and nuzzled his nose into my hair, breathing me in. He'd been naked apart from a towel that Owen had fixed around his waist, but I'd remained fully dressed. Exhausted, he hadn't said much except to ask me to stay with him and let him hold me.

Swallowing hard, I stepped close enough that his body heat bathed me. We were silent as we studied each other. Words seemed hard to form, so many emotions slamming through me that my legs wobbled. His eyes were bright, his jaw clenched and his whole body tense.

"Hey," I said, my voice barely more than a whisper. I just wished I could take away some of the fear I saw in his eyes.

He lifted his hand and slowly trailed the back of his forefinger down my cheek, before wrapping a lock of my hair around it. I shivered at his touch. Connor leaned in and inhaled. "You're real," he whispered, almost to himself. The next second I was wrapped in his arms and crushed against his chest. With his spine bowed, he buried his nose in my neck. "You're really here." His voice broke, and his arms crushed me. Tears burned my eyes at his shuddering breaths. Ignoring the discomfort of his overly tight embrace, I held him as close as I could, trying to reassure him that I was with him, even as Prime and Mea whined, reacting to our distress.

"I really am. Gods, I'm sorry for what you've been through. Walker—he took me to Faerie and I couldn't get back to you."

Connor pulled back and searched my face, his own darkening. "Yeah, I saw that prick take you."

A huge breath left me. I'd forgotten he had no idea who had been pulling his strings all this time. "He did. But he didn't hurt me. Connor, he's far more than you think he is..."

Connor didn't let go of me, instead he pulled me to him again. "Tell me in a bit. Right now, I just need to hold you. I need to know that you aren't going to disappear."

I wrapped my arms back around him. "Oh, gods, I need to hold you, too. You're not alone, I promise. I'm scared that this, that *you*, will disappear. But we really are here, together." And it was true, something in my soul calmed when I had contact with Connor. It was different from the spirits that inhabited my body, as if the pieces of our souls clicked into place, fusing together as they were meant to be.

He dropped his hold to my backside and lifted me. Without hesitation, I wrapped my legs around his waist and he walked us to the bed where he laid us down, rolling onto his side so that he could hold me close.

"Well this is unfair. You're dressed and I'm not."

I smiled against his chest, inhaling deeply. This warmth, this deep spicy scent, it was all Connor. "Well, I'm not going anywhere. So you can rectify that if and when you're ready."

He squeezed me closer. "I just want to hold you." His stomach rumbled loudly.

I chuckled. "I think your stomach has other ideas."

He huffed. "Yeah? Well, my stomach can wait."

His hips pushed into me and I inhaled sharply at the contact. Gods, I'd missed him. But… "No. Food first. Like I said, I'm not going anywhere, and you need your body to be strong. *I* need your body to be strong. First, for me." I tilted my head up and back so he could see the heat in my eyes. "But, then, we have to stop him, Connor. Berith, I mean. Owen has a small army, now that Drake has pulled in all of this equipment, and more men. And you are still Prime of this pack."

He sighed and pushed himself up. "Okay, you win; food, then I want time with just you. Keep explaining while we eat."

"Okay, well, I suppose the most important thing for you to know is, Berith wants me because I can free Hell's army."

His brows dipped and a dark look crossed his face. "Why does he need you to do that?"

"Well, you know about my fire." It wasn't a question, but he nodded anyway. "It turns out I'm a phoenix, the only being who can burn through the gates of Hell. Satan needs my phoenix to keep them open, so he can invade our world." I lifted my hand, raising a small flame in my palm. It flickered, reflecting in his eyes. "If he pulls Fire, my phoenix, from my body with the Halo, he can chain her to Hell's gates and keep them open forever. As long as my body and human soul remain together, she will live, but if I die, and I have no blood heir for her to connect to, so will she."

Connor raised his hand and placed his palm over the flame. It didn't burn him. "Then at least we know Berith won't kill you."

"No, he won't, but he can take me and torture me—like he did you; and there will be no end to it."

His throat bobbed. "Then we won't let him get you."

I nodded. But I had no intention of hiding away in a secluded fortress somewhere. No, I would still fight alongside my mate and my friends to stop these demons and soldiers of Hell from destroying my world. There was another loud growl from his stomach. I patted his chest. "Come on, let's eat."

Reluctantly, he let me go, but his gaze didn't leave me. "Fine. But you're coming right back into my arms when we've eaten." His towel had fallen open, and I couldn't help but stare at his glorious body. He growled. "If you keep looking at me like that, neither of us will be eating any time soon."

My breath caught in my throat, and heat flooded my body. I allowed a small smile to curl my lips and let my gaze sweep over the full length of his body. His dick twitched under my attention. "*Ember...*"

The smile stayed on my face as I turned away and piled a plate high with food for him. "Here." When I turned back to face him, he'd covered himself with the towel again and propped his back up against the headboard. Without any further words, he fixed his gaze on the plate of food and began devouring it. The groans that came from his mouth with each new flavour were almost sinful. "Mother Wolf, it's been so long since I've tasted anything this good."

I laughed, happy to see him demolish his food. He'd been starved, and clearly hadn't had a proper meal for months. I passed him some coffee and again he groaned when he tasted it. "Gods, it's amazing how much you can miss something that you've always taken for granted. Stale water just isn't quite the same."

While he drank, I swapped his plate for mine.

"Oh, no you don't. Eat." And he shoved the plate back at me.

"Connor." I rolled my eyes. "You need it."

"So do you. Now eat—or maybe you'd like me to feed it to you?"

My scowl was hard to maintain when he was right, I really was hungry. Besides, I didn't want to fight with him. "Bossy bugger," I muttered. Who said I had to give in gracefully, though?

He grinned, and raised his brows.

"Fine." I sat down next to him and ate the food. As soon as I was done, Connor took our plates and cups, pushed his big frame off the bed and deposited them on the table. His ice blue gaze rested on me, sending my stomach into all kinds of flutters. His nostrils flared. Shadow swirled through his eyes and around his face before it disappeared.

"What is that?"

His face remained intense. "It must be my fae half. I have another...spirit in my soul, as well as Prime. My mother's a fae. Did you know that?"

I nodded my head. "Yes, I sensed she was, but not what kind."

"Do you think she can tell me about it? Help me control it? It controlled me once before..." His throat bobbed. "And it's a vicious creature."

I contemplated the floor. "Probably. We should go and talk to her soon."

Connor nodded.

"Do you think someone has told her what Zander did? Gods, Connor, what if she doesn't know what's happened to her son?" I rubbed my face. "What if she does?" I couldn't imagine how awful it would be to know your son had chosen to launch himself into Hell with his demonic father, to save his brother...

"Hey, I'm sure Owen has spoken to her, but we'll go and see her...together." He stalked to the bottom of the bed, his vivid eyes darkening as he studied me leaning against the pillows. "I want you to tell me everything that happened to all of you since those bastards ripped us apart. But right now, I don't give a shit about anyone else but you."

He unfastened the towel and let it drop from his hips. Blood roared through my ears, my heart beating hard against my chest wall. Holding my gaze, he kneeled and lowered his body forward over mine supporting his weight with his hands flat against the wall to either side of my head.

"I want to kiss you, Ember." His words were heavy with lust...but I didn't miss the slight tremble in his voice. He needed this reconnection, just as much as I did. My voice deserted me, so I nodded my head. A tiny, and damn sexy, smirk curled the side of his mouth. "Words, sweetheart."

"Yes." Was all I could manage. I'd done nothing but dream about being back in his arms with his mouth on mine. Now we had a second chance with each other and his scent and warmth and godsdamned sexy body were over-whelming my heightened senses. Prime's rumble filled my head and I let him meet Connor's gaze.

"Hello, my old friend. We'll be together as one again, soon. I'll find a way." Prime blinked and receded, Mea's desire drawing him back.

"They are mates." Connor leaned further forward. "I can feel their connec-tion. I can feel *him*, in here." And he lifted a hand to touch his chest right over his heart.

"You can?" My voice was hoarse and quiet.

He nodded. "I can. Now I just need you to be complete again."

His lips descended onto mine in such a sweet, gentle kiss it stole my breath. His whole body was tense as he held himself just above me, his naked-ness not touching me. He pulled his head away just enough so that he could kiss each corner of my mouth, then leaned up. Automatically I closed my eyelids and he kissed each one. "Gods, I missed you so much."

I swallowed the ache in my throat. His voice sounded so broken. But he didn't need sympathy, he needed to realise how strong he was for surviving that fucking prison, for surviving *Hell*, and he needed to know that I loved him. I wrapped my fingers in his hair and pulled his head back so that I could look at him. "And I missed you." I thrust my hips up and pushed against his erection, grinding against him. "I need you, Connor. I need to feel you inside me." I dropped my hands to his hips and thrust again against his hard length. "There are no collars between us now, and Mea and Prime are mates..."

His throat bobbed, that shadow he carried seeping into his eyes, mixing with the blue like Prime's often did. A groan erupted from him as I yanked his head down and devoured his warm lips with my own. I couldn't wait, I was like a woman possessed. The need to have him, to take him as mine burned through my blood and bones. Prime roared and grabbed Mea with his teeth. I blocked them out, sinking my own teeth into Connor's bottom lip enough to draw blood.

"Ember?" His lust filled groan only fuelled my desire.

I didn't let up, kissing him, needy and passionate. A growl left me, an animalistic need driving me to be with my mate; to claim him.

Connor's hands left the wall and his weight sank onto me, pushing me into the mattress as he yanked my hands from him and pushed my wrists flat against the pillows. His chest rose and fell, his defined muscles expanding and contracting under his skin. "I can't claim you, not without Prime."

"I know, but I can claim you. You're mine, Connor, and I don't want to lose you ever again."

His nostrils flared. "But I'm not a shifter. Not until Prime can be returned to me. I'm half-fae, half-human..."

I leaned up and nipped his lip. "It doesn't matter to me what you are. You are mine, my mate."

His eyes darkened to midnight blue. "Then claim me. But I get to unwrap this beautiful body first."

He released my wrists and grabbed my hips pulling me flat underneath him. "Keep those hands up there. And don't test me, Ember. I'm not feeling in the mood to be defied. This shadow in my body has no mercy and it will take what it wants, how it wants; claiming or not."

I stared up into his dark face and instinctively knew he was right. Without Prime, his fae side was riding him high. Yes, it had protected his mind from Berith, but its darkness was not one even I would antagonise. Straddling me, he slowly unbuttoned my shirt, kissing each inch of skin he revealed. Unable to help myself, I arched my spine pushing myself against his featherlite lips, needing more contact. My nipples contracted. He bent his head, teasing one with his tongue, before sucking it in. I groaned, clutching at the bedding as he gently bit down, and sucked, increasing the pressure to exquisite pain before he laved the sting away with his tongue. It was pure sin when his tongue circled my navel before licking a trail down to the waistband of my jeans.

"Connor, please." I lifted my hips, begging for him to take this further.

He shuffled back, sat me forwards and slipped my shirt off, before unclipping my bra and pulling it from my arms. He blinked slowly, the shadow consuming his features. A frisson of fear shivered through me, but that edge of danger from Connor had always excited me, even now it sent a rush of warmth between my legs, not fear to my heart.

His big body shimmied down until he kneeled between my parted legs. Deftly, he unbuckled my belt and popped open the button on my jeans. Gods, I could barely breathe, I wanted him so much.

There were no words exchanged between us, but his intense gaze flickered between my eyes and the juncture of my legs. In answer to his silent question, I lifted my pelvis again. Swiftly, he pulled down my clothes, then leaned back to slide them from my body. He stood at the bottom of the bed and I couldn't help but stretch seductively under his lust filled gaze.

His pained look made me want to break something. It was horribly obvious Berith had used me to torture my mate.

"Firecracker," he whispered. "Am I really here with you?"

"Oh, Connor. It's ok. Trust me. I'm real." I sat up and grabbed his hands.

"I didn't think I'd ever get to touch or taste you again, that all I would ever get were beautiful images of you that turned into my worst nightmares when you were ripped away."

My heart stuttered. "Hey, I swear it, I'm here. Really here." I could feel tears threatening, he was breaking my heart so bad.

With his big hands on my thighs he pushed my legs apart and dropped to his knees. Nostrils flared, he inhaled deeply. "Yes, you are. That's one thing he could never do, replicate your scent." His face lowered near my core and he inhaled again. "Especially *this* scent. I'd always figure out it wasn't really you. That's when he would end me or take hold of my body and make me hurt or kill you."

I blinked slowly. No fucking way. What Berith had done was beyond words. I lifted my head. "Connor, you know this is me. You can feel it's me. Breathe in my scent if that helps. Believe I am yours. Use that. Erase those nightmares and make *me* your reality."

He nodded and lowered his mouth to my skin, placing tantalising kisses and nips along my inner thighs, holding my hips still when I tried to push myself against his teasing lips. Painfully slowly, he kissed and licked his way up to my folds, then slowly dragged his tongue through my wetness, tasting me, over and over. The soft touch of his tongue drove me wild.

"More," I begged.

He growled and his stokes became firmer and more punishing. I gasped as two fingers pushed inside me.

"*Yes, Connor...*"

He lifted his head, his eyes once again bright and cerulean blue. Lust poured from him, and I squirmed beneath his gaze as he continued to work his fingers. There were no words and I got it, I really did. He needed this, needed *us*; without barriers or fear. His expression darkened and his features sharpened, becoming more fae than human. Without mercy he dove back in, sucking on my clit until I exploded around him.

I was still coming down from my high when he removed his fingers and moved his big body to hover above me. "Ember, look at me."

I did.

"I can't be soft, love. I'm sorry. I need this. I need you..."

In answer, I let my legs fall open and lifted my pelvis. He swallowed hard, his eyes closing as I reached down and held his hard length, running it through my wetness. I positioned him at my entrance. "I'm here. Now take what you need. Erase those nightmares."

With a roar he thrust forward, unapologetic and hard. I threw my head back and groaned. I'd adjusted to his size before, but I hadn't let anyone or anything inside me since I'd last had Connor, not even my own fingers. I hadn't wanted it. Now, sensation overwhelmed me, I was stretched to the point of pain.

"Fuck, Ember...I can't... Gods, you feel so good. I need...to move..."

I gripped his behind and let my claws grow a little, digging them in. "Then move."

And boy, did he. He swung his pelvis back and slammed forward. His eyes rolled shut.

"Look at me," I growled, not wanting him to go back to his nightmares.

His eyes were feverish and bright, but the more I commanded him to go harder and faster, the darker they became until they were swallowed by his fae side.

"Don't want...to...hurt ...you."

I grinned wickedly. "You won't hurt me." I let Fire shine through my eyes. I stretched my arms above my head and pushed against the headboard, meeting each thrust of his hips with one of my own. "Now fuck me like you mean it."

He did, he stopped only to lift my legs over his shoulders before he pounded into me, making me scream with the glorious pain and intense pleasure. Sweat rolled down us both, our bodies slamming together. My canines lowered. I could feel them digging in my lower lip.

Connor's eyes darkened. "I...can't...hold...back."

"Good. Neither can I." My body was coiled as tight as a spring.

My eyes widened as his own fangs grew and he snarled, his face wreathed in shadow, his eyes black. Fae. Connor was fae, too. They bonded just as shifters did—by blood. My whole body erupted in goosebumps. We could still claim each other. "Do it, Connor."

"Fuck, Ember. Make me yours first."

I placed my mouth against the strong column of his neck, feeling the blood rush beneath my lips. Then sank my teeth in. Hot and salty, his blood ran across my tongue. The moment I swallowed, heat rushed through me, but nothing could prepare me for the way our souls snapped together. Connor's whole body spasmed and he roared, filling me with warmth over and over, until he was shuddering uncontrollably. There was a sharp sting in my neck, offset by the pleasure as he continued to work me. I shivered, pleasure assaulting my body and soul. Prime and Mea howled and Fire roared through my veins as he took long drags on my vein. An orgasm ripped through me, tearing through my body with each swallow he took.

Prime snarled and released Mea. They had mated too. I could feel their bond, just as surely as I could feel mine with Connor slip into place. Prime howled, his call echoing inside my head. Mea called back, but I couldn't concentrate on what was happening with them. My senses were consumed by Connor, by the blood roaring in my ears, by the pull on my chest towards him, by his body heat, his scent...everything about him consumed me.

My senses didn't return to me until Connor released my neck. We both panted hard, and I could feel him shaking as he held some of his weight off me. Blood dripped from the puncture wounds on his neck. Sluggishly, I tried to lift my heavy head to lap at them and stop the steady stream of blood.

"Shh, lay still let me heal you first." His tongue was soft against my neck. The puncture wounds stung at first but soon settled as he lapped at them.

"Hmm, you can heal me like that?" I was struggling to keep my eyes open now. I had never bothered learning much about claimings, but Connor had told me only mates can heal each other.

"Yes, sweetheart, I can. And you can heal me."

I squeezed my eyes shut, my chest tight. "But I thought only shifters can heal their mates. I took him from you."

He held my face between both of his hands as he leaned on his elbows. "Ember? Look at me."

I forced my eyes open—and gasped. Prime stared out at me from Connor's eyes. "He's back with me."

"Oh, dearest gods. How?" I searched inside myself. Mea whined. *I'm sorry.* But she sent a wave of love my way. *He is where he should be. We will join every-time you and your mate do. We are all one now.*

Connor dropped his head to mine, blood still trickling down his neck and dripping onto me. I didn't wait to hear his answer, I just lapped at the puncture wounds until they started to heal.

"Leave them to heal a little so that I am left with your mark."

"Oh, so that's how it works?"

"It is." He pulled back, his blue eyes fixed on my neck, darkening until Prime was looking out at me, mixed with the shadow that seemed to be part of Connor now. "I claimed you as a fae would." He searched my face, so I gave him a reassuring smile. "It was instinctive. But as soon as I swallowed the first mouthful of your blood, it was as if it opened a way back for him. Our connection is soul deep, Em, so he came back to me."

"Oh gods, I'm so happy for you both." My eyes burned and a tear ran down my cheek. He kissed it away.

"I don't know how it happened and I don't care. He's here with me now. Thank you for taking care of him." Connor lifted himself and looked down to where we were still joined. A low rumble came from his chest. "He claimed your wolf...Mea...you have named her?"

I nodded.

"It's a beautiful name for her. Prime likes it." An intense look flashed over his face, and he rolled his hips again. I moaned as he grew inside me. "Now he wants her again and he wants me to claim you as a shifter, not a fae."

And there was nothing I could do this time but hang on. Connor's power overwhelmed me. Prime had merged with his dark fae spirit and there was so much power rolling from him, and into my blood it was hard to think.

"Then don't think, Firecracker, just feel."

"You...heard my thoughts...ohh." The pleasure he unleashed on me left me helpless.

He grinned. "We are one. All of us." Prime's voice growled through with Connor's, mixed with something dangerous that sent goosebumps of excitement rising on my skin. "Your mind is as open to me as your soul. And now I will truly claim your body." And he angled my hips to push himself deeper and harder. I raked my nails down his hard back, staking my claim on him, but before I could sink my canines into him again, he plunged his teeth into my neck, keeping them there, sucking with each powerful stroke of his hips. Release barrelled up my spine and through every cell in my body as his power exploded outwards. He didn't let go even as his body shuddered through his release. My mind went offline, consumed by sensation. I was aware of soft words being spoken in my ear and against my lips. I whimpered as Connor moved his weight and pulled out of my body, but I couldn't force my eyes to open. My whole body was both sated and exhausted.

"*Connor? Don't leave...?*"

His voice brushed against my mind. "*Never. I'm only going to the bathroom.*"

A few moments later a warm cloth pressed against me, soothing and caring for me. "Mmm, thank you."

Before I'd finished my mumbled words, I was wrapped in his arms. His leg wrapped over my thighs, holding me close, one big hand in my hair, holding my head into his neck. This was where I was supposed to be. And I wouldn't let Berith or anyone else take him from me again. My heart swelled. "I love you." I should have said those words before, but I was scared of what could happen between our wolves, that they might reject each other. There was no chance of that now. He was right, we were all one soul, merged until death found us.

His arms tightened around me, and I felt his shoulders shake. "And I love you more than you can ever know," he whispered into my hair. "I will do everything in my power to never be parted from you again."

CHAPTER 14

onnor

I FOLLOWED on the heels of my Firecracker like a lost puppy as we stepped out of our room after another whole day of claimings—from both of us.

"Prime. You're both still alive then? It went so quiet, I was getting worried you'd killed each other." Stone quirked a brow at me, but I didn't care, not that he needed to know that, so I stopped and snarled at him, Prime showing through my eyes.

"Whoa, he's back with you." He immediately dropped his peculiar purple gaze. It was funny, now that I'd connected with my own fae side, I could sense Stone's power. He pushed his wolf forward, but even that didn't dim his other power.

"He is. We are one with our shadow beast, too."

Stone's eyes widened. "Shit. That's a lot of power, Connor."

"It is. As is yours."

Stone nodded once. He could challenge Owen now that none of us were confined by those silver collars, that much was obvious to me; and I was no longer sure who would win. Stone's viciousness, like mine, was inherent. Owen's alpha power and predatory instincts were powerful, but still...

Stone met my gaze. "I have no interest in a challenge."

I grunted and nodded, glad to hear it.

Ember had reached the door, but she turned. "You coming?"

Of course I was. "You aren't going anywhere without me." I didn't hide the possessive growl in my voice. She smirked and stepped out of the door before I got to her.

I sped up and leaped from the top step landing right behind her. My arms went around her waist and I pulled her back up against my front. She tipped her head back and smiled coyly.

"Don't test me, not now, Em." And I slanted my mouth over hers, taking her lips in a hard kiss. I didn't care who was around us. They all needed to know she was mine and I was hers. I had never felt this strong, or this possessive of anyone or anything in my life, and I was trying my damnedest to control my urge to drag her, caveman style, back into that tiny little bedroom. Prime and my fae rumbled as one. I took a slow breath trying to contain the power in me. Now that they had merged I had to learn how to master them both again.

Ember bit my lip, and pushed me away. The sting from that warning bite shot straight to my cock. I knew, after a claiming, it was hard for mates to calm their responses to each other, but controlling myself as she patted my cheek and walked away was almost impossible. I was shaking with need.

"Damn, Prime, you have it bad." Stone's arms were crossed over his chest, his eyes narrowed.

"Fuck off."

His mouth tilted up at one side, and he huffed a laugh. For a moment, I stared at him. He never laughed.

"Umm, she's getting away." He dipped his chin and raised his brows.

"Shit!" I ran after Ember, not caring about the big alpha fae following behind. I felt the eyes of a group of soldiers bore into me as I chased Ember into a cabin. Prime growled. I'd get him to show me his memories of them later, right now, Ember was too far away from me.

All noise ceased as I charged into what had to be a canteen of some kind. I snarled and walked up behind Ember in the queue.

"Hey, what kept you? You want bacon?"

I scowled at her and she laughed, raising her brows. "Come on, you know you want some." A coy look crossed her face. "After all, you did use a lot of energy yesterday...oh, and last night. And this morning." My lips twitched as she waggled her eyebrows, and my chest tightened at the bright sparkle of happiness in the jade of her eyes. Had I done that? Made my mate happy? Gods, she made my heart swell, and my stomach do all sorts of stupid somersaults when she looked at me like that, even as my blood ran hot at the memory of all we had done. "Yes. I want all of it—again. And some bacon."

She swallowed as she met my lust filled gaze. Now it was my turn to grin. Her gaze dropped to my lips as I leaned in close enough my breath fanned her lips...and picked a piece of bacon from the serving plate. The poor woman behind the counter paled as I turned my attention to her. "Pile me a plate high. I'm ravenous. My mate used me up and I'll need all my energy to keep her happy."

Ember rolled her eyes, but her cheeks flushed, giving her away. A grin plastered across my face. I loved seeing her blush.

"He meant to say please."

I looked at the woman who immediately began to shake. I tried not to snarl. Such weakness always irritated me. Lower shifters should submit to me, but having no backbone around a powerful predator was asking for trouble. It made me want to hunt them down. Prime snarled, so did I.

"Connor!" Ember's sharp words snapped me out of my predatory intent. "Go and sit down. I'll get our food. Stone? Would you go with him, please? He's a little—er, riled up today."

"She's right. Not so sure it's a good idea for you to be out in the compound with her today."

"Yeah? Well, fuck you, Stone. Where she goes, I go. And I need to talk to Owen to find out what's going on here. So you're going to keep me out of trouble. Aren't you, brother?"

Stone grinned. "Depends on who's stupid enough to antagonise you."

I plonked myself on a bench seat, noticing everyone nearby kept their eyes averted. Good.

Ember went to sit next to me on the bench. No way was that close enough. Before she could sense my intention, I grabbed her small waist and lifted her easily into my lap.

"Hey!"

"Not close enough."

Her eyes narrowed on mine. I had sensed her thoughts each time she had totally succumbed to me last night, even felt her pleasure as my own, but now she had gathered her strength again, and it pissed me off that I couldn't sense her thoughts anymore, only her emotions. Fire flashed in her eyes. I just pulled her closer. "Sit here and eat."

"What? No way. I'm not going anywhere, Connor. Now be sensible and let me sit down."

I clenched my teeth. "No."

Fire flared in her palm. "Let me down, now."

I shrugged. "Nope. You know you can't burn me."

Her lips thinned. "No, but I can withhold sex."

My balls tightened. Not because of her threat but because of the challenge her words meant.

"That was the wrong threat, Ember." Stone supplied helpfully, watching us with interest.

"Really? Well, I mean it, and I might not be able to burn *you*, Connor, but I can hurt your brother."

"Hey!" Stone didn't look too thrilled by that idea.

Prime growled, and one look in Ember's eyes, at her stubborn face, and we knew she meant it. Prime wanted to protect his fae brother, shadow filled my vision and I could feel the beast's agreement.

"Fine. But you sit close."

My mate smirked and kissed me on the cheek. I reluctantly let her slide back onto the bench.

"Gods, this is going to be a pain in the ass," Stone muttered, stuffing a piece of toast in his mouth.

"Stop mumbling, Stone. Guarding your Prime is better than working guard duty with those soldiers, out there," Ember said.

He nodded in agreement. As we ate Stone explained much of what Prime had shown me through his memories. I knew everything Walker had done for Ember through Prime's memories and what she'd been doing since I was taken. I leaned in and nuzzled her neck, unable to stay away from her. She kissed me back, a big smile on her face. "You done?"

"Nowhere near." And I curled my fingers over her upper thigh

She smirked. "Hmm, good. But I meant with your food."

Keeping my eyes on her face, I nodded.

"Good. Come on then, let's go and find Owen."

"He was going to see Selina and the baby," said Stone.

"She's one of the women you rescued?" I asked.

"Yes. Owen seems to spend much of his spare time making sure they are all cared for. I think he has a soft spot for Selina, but I don't think either of them will admit it yet. A bit like this one and Shannon."

Stone snarled, his purple and silver eyes flashing yellow. "Hey, my relationship with Shannon is none of your gods damned business."

I had him slammed up against the wall in a second. "Respect my mate."

Stone wisely dropped his eyes and nodded.

Ember grinned and patted my chest, but her eyes were burning with green flame. "It's nice to have a bodyguard, but you can't go slamming every male that's got a mouth on him up against the wall. I can still fight my own battles, Connor. Very well, in fact. How about you let your brother go?"

I ground my teeth, but let Stone go.

He stretched his neck. "This is going to be a long day," he muttered.

I glared at him but stayed quiet. He was right.

We walked into the cave and found Owen sitting on a protruding rock by himself staring broodingly at Selina who appeared to be ignoring his presence.

"Hey, man."

Owen's gaze shot to me and widened. "Shit. You're—you. How did you get Prime back again?" He noticed our ravaged necks, then he chuckled, his face suddenly lighter. "Ah, that." He grinned. "You sure you should be out here with her already, Prime? Isn't that a little dangerous for everyone?"

Ember slipped her arm around my waist. "Hey, it's fine. Connor has control."

I pulled her in close to my side, loving that she squeezed me tighter. "I do." I glanced at Stone. "Mostly. And we need to talk about the pack, my brother, you know that." Owen met my gaze and nodded, his face serious. Yeah, I was Prime, but I needed him to know he was still alpha of this pack.

"My priority, right now, is to stop Berith. He's after Ember and he isn't going to get her—ever."

Owen met my gaze, his eyes flicking to Selina. "I get that," he said quietly, and smiled at Ember.

"Knew you would."

He laughed, and I released my mate to embrace my brother. "It's good to see you, man."

"Yeah, you too; now that it's really you. Berith, as you, was a real dickhead."

"How did you know it wasn't me?"

He shrugged. "He spoke to Ember like a piece of shit. You'd never do that, no matter what had happened to you. Zander figured it out as soon as you were back here. I spoke to him about it and he said he had a plan."

"Alex?" asked Ember.

Owen ignored Stone's low growl. "Yeah, Alex said Zander didn't want us there when he sent Berith back to Hell. He knew the Halo would do something to him, but he didn't want to risk our lives too."

I swallowed my regret for Zander and my anger at how Berith had treated my mate. My fists curled at the memories Prime supplied. "Yeah, I'd never treat Ember like that," I murmured under my breath, glad Zander and Owen knew me so well.

Ember wandered across the cave to Selina and took the baby for a cuddle. Half demons. I could only wonder how Berith hoped to control them. He couldn't control Zander; but maybe he had found a way. The baby let out a little wail and my stomach clenched, my heart jumping at the sight of my mate with a baby in her arms. She cooed and rocked the little thing until it stopped crying. I swallowed the ache in my throat. I'd never even considered having a family of my own, but the thought of having a little one with my Firecracker burrowed into my soul, and I already knew that thought wouldn't let me go.

She smiled at me, and I smiled back.

"We've got a lot of catching up to do." Owen distracted me from staring at Ember.

"Yeah. You got an ops room?"

"Sure do. This way, boss."

"Ember! We need to go."

She nodded and placed a kiss on the baby's forehead, passing it back before coming and taking my hand. It seemed so natural, so I accepted her offering, surprised and pleased she'd do such a thing. Ember had always wanted to prove her independence and strength. Holding hands wasn't something either of us would have done with anyone else. But this was different, *we* were different.

I followed Owen across the compound, taking in the people, the way they were organised, the equipment, and the firepower of the guards that patrolled the perimeter. It was an expensive operation.

I winced as we passed through some kind of acoustic barrier, squeezing Ember's hand when she winced, but the discomfort soon passed. Owen opened the door of a large, ground level cabin and we stepped inside.

"Connor!" Drake's face lit up as he strode towards me. His palm slapped against my forearm, his fingers gripping me, and I gripped him just as hard. He pulled me in for a bro' hug, but laughed out loud when he saw I hadn't let go of Ember. "Hey, Em. You a bit happier now you've got him back?"

Ember smiled. "I am." She twisted her hand from my grip. "Now I get to say a proper hello and thank you." And she wrapped her arms around him, hugging him. He kept a wary eye on me, and it didn't last long, even so, claws pushed through my nail beds.

Drake carefully put Ember away from him and took a step away, his hands raised.

Ember turned and smiled reassuringly, before raising on her tiptoes and kissing my cheek. "Connor, you're the only one that I'm interested in, you know that."

"I do." I released a long slow breath. Maybe being out with her so soon wasn't such a good idea. I'd waited so long for Ember that I was having problems controlling my need and possessiveness. "Just—please, don't push me, love." I couldn't help my voice being a low growl. Grinding my teeth, I made myself turn away from her, instead of pulling her into me. "How did you fund this camp, Drake?"

Drake smiled, but a shadow crossed his eyes. I didn't comment. Getting all of this had come with a high cost for my brother.

"I pulled in a lot of favours—and had to agree to some terms which means we have the company of a group of asshole mercs to deal with."

"Why? What are they doing here?"

"They're here on the request of my business partner."

"Your business partner? I didn't think you had a partner."

"I didn't, but this guy bought my company from the SBI. In order to get any rights back to it, even though it was taken illegally, I had to agree to certains terms from him. It was that or not get back here with all the equipment and manpower we need to end Berith."

"What are the terms, Drake?"

Drake leaned on the table, his hands flat, and hung his head. "It doesn't matter. My lawyers are working on a way to get them nullified. My company was seized illegally."

"Brother? Tell me." I infused my voice with command and even as powerful as Drake was, he couldn't ignore it.

"Gods damn it, Prime..." He fought it for a few seconds, but I pushed harder. "Fine! To get access to all of this." He moved his hand in a sweeping gesture. "I had to sign a contract to marry his daughter, at which point a controlling share in my company is handed back over to me. Part of the agreement was the mercs who returned with me are to be allowed access to all of our meetings and planning, in return they will help us fight the Weres and destroy that Hell rift Berith has been using to bring in his demons."

For a moment we all stared at Drake.

"You mean you would marry an utter stranger, a woman not your mate? To help us?" If this didn't show his devotion to us all, nothing would. He would have stood a chance of getting his company back without strings if he had waited, but he'd chosen to accept a term that no shifter would ever want to tie themselves to. Committing to a female who would never be able to bond with your wolf was something a shifter never did. It was what had held me and Ember back from claiming each other in the prison. It was an unspoken rule—shifters just didn't do it. It could drive you mad if you met your mate and couldn't claim them.

Drake glanced at Ember, then Stone and Owen, before he looked at Myles who had just walked in with Kawan and Lionel. I'd always been a little suspicious of the lone feline shifter, but the guy had stuck around; that meant something. I inhaled Ember's scent and sensed her happiness at seeing her friend. Stamping on my jealousy, I nodded a greeting at him. If he made her happy in any way, I couldn't deny her his company. I hid a smile, not that she'd let me.

Drake straightened, his chin jutting out, his arms folded over his broad chest. "Of course I would. You are more family than any I have ever had. I would never abandon you; any of you. Certainly, not for a person that I've never met, and probably never will."

Ember squeezed my arm. I pulled from her grasp and held out my hand. "Drake, you are my brother also." I let Prime shine through my eyes. "You honour us all with your loyalty. Will you pledge yourself to our alpha pack, and be blood bound to me as your Prime? You will remain an alpha, but if you accept my rule, you will always have my protection, and my loyalty. If you ever need us, we will always come."

Drake glanced at Ember, and pain flitted over his face. Did he really believe he would never have a chance to find his own soul mate? I hoped that wasn't true. I was amazed by what he'd given up for us, and I'd do my best to help him get his company and freedom back once we'd won this war with Berith. He nodded.

"At the next full moon we will seal our bond, my brother."

Drake nodded. "It will be my honour, Prime."

"Good. Now these soldiers, who do they belong to?"

"I can't tell you. He doesn't want anyone knowing his identity. All of our agreements were done through the company lawyers, and they won't talk."

"Well, that's not dodgy." Ember raised her brows and shoved her hands on her hips.

Lionel huffed a laugh.

"Yeah, well, unfortunately I can't investigate. If I do, he'll whip this equipment and my company from under our noses in the blink of any eye, and, according to his lawyers, have me back inside a jail."

"What? He really has that much influence?" My stomach twisted. There was only one person I knew in the supernatural world with that much power.

"Yes. He really does; and more. I get the feeling he's a dangerous man to cross."

Ember frowned. "Damn, that's a lot of power."

"Yeah, it is. He's given us this equipment and shipped it all in, but don't for one moment think he doesn't want something out of it."

"But what? Access to the rift? The Weres? He can't know about me; not even any fae beyond B'nar and Walker know what I am." Ember's brow crinkled.

I wanted to kiss away those lines…

"He's into weapons isn't he? How about the babies?" she asked, her wide eyes finding Owen's.

A vicious growl escaped Owen, who looked at Myles and Kawan. "Those tossers get nowhere near the women and the babies." Myles nodded, and after he and Kawan dipped their head respectfully my way, they disappeared out of the door, just as Alex came in.

The doppelganger clasped an envelope in one hand.

"Doppelganger."

Ember hit my bicep. "Use his name and don't be an arse."

Alex smirked at Ember, then raised a brow at me. Yeah, I hadn't seen Alex in four years, but before that he had become more than a useful acquaintance to me, he had been my friend. Through Prime, I knew he had been working with

Walker. There were other things Prime had shown me that I couldn't deal with right now. I knew I'd have to, but it could come later. I curled my mouth into a smile and nodded. "Alex. It's good to see you, man. It seems I owe you thanks for looking out for my Firecracker while she was in Faerie, and beyond."

"My pleasure, Connor."

My eyes dropped to the envelope in his hand. "What have you got there, my friend?"

Alex glanced at Ember, then me. He sighed and ran a hand through his hair. "It's for you, from Zander." He held it out.

For a moment I stared at it. Zander had protected me as best he could. My fae spirit let me see memories of him smuggling me food and fresh water. He had even tried to heal me as best he could; but we had both known only a mate could fully heal another. He was my brother and a fae, and I had discovered from him how to communicate with the darkness inside me and channel that spirit to protect my mind. I swallowed the ache in my throat. He had made the ultimate sacrifice. His life for mine. My gaze flicked to Ember, and I sucked in a shuddering breath. He had given me back my life with my mate. Mother Wolf, I even had a chance to see my mother again because of him. He was a true fucking hero...

I blinked, determined not to let anyone see the devastation in my eyes. All these years he had tried to tell me, to hint at what he was to me, and all I had done each time he had called me *brother* was shoot him down and insult him. I rubbed my face with my hands, then before I lost my nerve, I snapped out a hand and pulled the letter from Alex's fingers.

CONNOR, I guess by now you know the truth. You really are my brother, but it's okay, I forgive you for being such a bastard about that word. I deserved your hate and disgust. Don't be angry with our mother. She was always his prisoner. It wasn't until Berith was distracted by using you to find Ember that I could break the wards holding her to him. Find it in your heart to get to know her. You are her first born and for a dark fae that means a lot. There is much you should talk to her about, not least about the fae side of your nature.

*The Halo will send me to Hell, but as I sit here writing this to you, know that I am fucking smiling, because it means my bastard of a father will be there, too. No matter what happens to me, it will always be worth it, **you** are worth it. I'm sorry I couldn't tell you who I was, but it was necessary, not only to keep our mother safe, but to get the information Walker needs to fight the generals of Hell. They are looking for Ember, of course, her phoenix is one of a kind and they will never let up. She will need you, always.*

Use the Halo to bring your brothers back. You will need angelic help to use it safely, but other than another more powerful supernatural being ripping the spirit out, it is the only way to rid a person of a demon possession without killing them. Guard it with your lives. I read in an ancient text that it can be used to free whole armies, but I have no idea how; that, my brother, I leave to you to discover.

Now I must tell you about Rawson. I am ashamed of all I forced him to do at my father's bidding, and I could not allow him to be tortured any further. I convinced my father he was killed in the break out, and set him free from my father's wards. I got him out of the prison and back to civilization. I'm afraid I don't know what happened to him after that. I hope you can forgive me for all I had to put him through. It was either do my father's bidding or watch our mother suffer; that was always part of Berith's sick games.

I fear we will never get the chance to speak as I once hoped we would, but know that I will always be your brother.

Zander.

I LOWERED my bulk into a chair and read the letter again before it dropped from my fingers.

"Are you okay?" Ember whispered.

"Not really." Admitting that didn't seem like a weakness in the face of what Zander, my mother and I had been cheated out of. I looked up, my shoulders rising and falling as I tried to control my devastation. My brother had been with me all these years and I had never known. Now I had lost him to the fiery pits of Hell.

Ember came closer. I pulled her between my legs to let her in closer and she slipped her arms around my neck. I rested my forehead against her, letting the warmth of our connection seep into me and calm me.

"Rawson is alive." My voice was raw.

"Fucking hell! He's alive?" Owen exclaimed. "Is he still in that prison? Have we missed him like we missed you being there?"

My brother sounded so distressed, Prime rumbled.

"Owen, my brother, you didn't miss me. You couldn't sense just my fae side. Why should you? And no, Rawson isn't there. Zander broke him free, so yeah…" I peered into Ember's tear filled eyes. "He's alive. He got away." Gently, I wiped a tear away with my thumb. "Shh, don't cry. He's strong. He'll be eating a burger and fries somewhere he's safe, while we fight this war."

Her watery smile broke my heart. "Yeah, 'course he will. I just…I miss him."

Standing, I pulled her back into my arms and kissed the top of her head, inhaling the scent of her hair. "So do I." I met my brother's gaze. "Start talking. Tell me everything that has happened since I shot you. Sorry about that by the way, but you needed to get out of that prison, not stay and fight. You made me a promise, and you had to keep it."

"Yeah, well next time just yell it at me. It took me bloody weeks to heal properly from that wound." His eyes landed on Ember who was still wrapped in my arms. His gaze softened. "We don't all have a mate to heal us."

"I know. I'm a lucky bastard."

Drake poured some coffee out into five mugs, filling them to the brim. The smell made my mouth water. "Thanks, man." I took the mug he offered as Ember and I took a seat, listening carefully to everything Owen had to tell us.

<h1 style="text-align:center">CHAPTER 15</h1>

mber

I SAT QUIETLY and listened to Owen tell Connor about his war with Berith's demons. All the while I looked down at Zander's letter that I clutched in my hand. Hundreds of Weres had died in the fight rings at that fucking prison. Even with the Halo that Alex had just passed to Connor, we needed an angel to make sure when we used it that we weren't sucked down into hell. I swallowed hard. Reed was lying chained to a rock because of me, his mate's heart breaking. I had to do something to help.

Connor frowned at the Halo before he tucked it inside the waistband of his jeans and covered it with his t-shirt.

"How many fighters do we have?" Connor frowned down at the old prison plans that had been spread out flat on the table, the empty coffee cups used to hold it still.

Owen blew out a breath and ran a hand through his hair. "We have around two hundred people here. I got Shane to start making a record of their names, but he's finding it hard. Some of the people in that prison were there because they really are criminals, and they don't want to be found. If they don't agree to be registered then they're thrown out in the wilds on their own. I mean, I don't care if it's a false bloody name, I just need to know how many people are here. But now we have the women and the babies from the prison, we have dependents to care for. We'll have to leave guards here."

Connor stared down at the map, his brow furrowed. "Do you have a core force you take into the prison?"

"Yeah…"

"Good. And now we have proper weapons." He glanced at me and eyed the bow I had slung across my back. "Is there any way to contact Walker for help?"

I shook my head. "I don't have a way. He did say he could track me when I called on Fire. So I guess we could do that, and hope he's pissed off enough at me to come running."

His mouth twisted in thought. "Hmm, not yet. I want to think through all angles of this first, and he's one sneaky bastard. He's orchestrated this whole thing and manipulated Zander and me for years. He says it's for the benefit of both our worlds, but I have to wonder at his motives. Why is he bothered about our world when he is the ruler of his own?"

"He said it's because if the gates between here and Hell are opened, his world would be next."

"Hmm, makes sense, I suppose…"

The door swung open and a wave of dominance hit me. Connor growled and his spine snapped straight, his eyes narrowing on the intruder.

"Well, now, Drakey boy. What's this? A meeting happening without yours truly?" Jedi tilted his head, and tutted.

"Who the fuck are you?" Connor growled, Prime pushing into his gaze. All the alphas in the room tensed and power filtered into the air. I shuddered as Mea whined.

Prime already knew who this guy was, so that meant Connor did too. He was deliberately hiding that knowledge.

Jedi shook his head at Drake. "Tsk, tsk. Did my new bitch forget to tell you I'm part of his new friendship group?"

Drake snarled, his eyes flickered and before any of us could respond to Jedi's comment, a huge sandy and grey wolf launched at him. Drake landed on Jedi's chest and knocked him to the ground. Jedi roared and held Drake's jaws from his throat, but couldn't stop him from ripping into his shoulder. With another roar Jedi shifted, and a huge gorilla threw Drake across the room.

Connor snarled and grabbed me, spinning me away from the fight between the two powerful weres. Jedi was all muscle and raw power, but Drake was a huge wolf, powerful and quick, maneuvering around his enemy with blood dripping from his jaws.

"Stay away from them." The beast shining through Connor's eyes was a mixture of shadow and wolf. I cocked an eyebrow at his order, but the sight of Drake with his teeth embedded in a gorilla's neck stopped me from arguing. Besides, it gave me the warm and fuzzies to hear the protective growl in his voice.

Connor spun around to face the room—and shifted. Prime burst through his skin, his black fur wreathed in shadow. I gasped. Prime was huge; far bigger than he had ever been when he pushed a shift from inside me. His power pulsed, and I knew if Prime called upon the darkness of Connor's fae side, the merging of those two powerful spirits would make Prime unstoppable. But I felt Connor's reluctance to show that dark side of his power to this stranger—yet.

Connor dipped his head and shoulders, and snarled at the two warring shifters. The blast of power that hit them was enough to make Stone and Owen stagger. It just washed over me, prickling against my skin.

I watched, fascinated, as Drake immediately released the back of Jedi's neck. Jedi snarled, taking his advantage, and grabbed Drake, flinging him over his head and across the room. Drake flew through the air and slammed into the wall cracking the flimsy construction. Without missing a beat, he rolled to his feet and bent his legs to attack again.

Connor roared.

Drake immediately stopped. Jedi didn't. He had no idea how powerful Connor really was and blasted out a bellow of challenge.

Prime was quicker and far more agile than the gorilla. He sent a blast of power out against Jedi before he launched himself over the table and clamped his massive jaws around the gorilla's neck. Jedi roared and tried to grab Connor, but it made no difference. Connor sank his teeth in further. He could rip Jedi's throat out and kill him instantly, but he was waiting. He wanted to give this powerful shifter a chance, and he knew Drake's future was on the line, so he held back.

I sauntered over and squatted next to Jedi. It was risky and he did what I thought he would; he grabbed me around the neck and snarled. Fire erupted from my skin, and he howled, pulling his hand away, staring wide-eyed at me and then Connor.

I tilted my head and peered down at him, my brows raised. "Well, I guess you've worked out you aren't the biggest bad here. That must dent your big ego. But Connor doesn't want to kill you."

Jedi, or I supposed I should call him Jed, snorted and snarled again, staring up at Connor.

"Uh, probably best to keep your eyes lowered. Believe me if he wanted you dead, you'd be minus your throat and most of your blood by now. And I could have burnt you to a crisp. So how about you drop the shitty attitude and work with us, not against us. Disrespect my friends again and it doesn't matter if Connor wants you to live, I'll burn you, your men, and that fucker who sent you here, into a cloud of ash to protect them. We clear?"

Within seconds Jed was back, fully clothed. Hmm, he knew that neat trick, too. I guessed it was time to teach my friend's how to do that, if they were going to work alongside these males.

Connor released Jed's neck and leaned over his face. He bared his teeth. Jed had the sense to keep his eyes down.

Connor changed back, completely naked, but didn't pull away from Jed. He straddled his body, his hands either side of the other man's head, hovering close to his face. I wondered what he was doing. Humiliating him? Before I'd even finished that thought, Connor's head slammed into Jed's nose. Bone cracked and blood spurted.

"You ever fucking touch her again, and I'll crush you one bone at a time before I let my fae side feast on your marrow." He grabbed Jed's jaw and made the soldier look at him. "You feel me, motherfucker?" And his head morphed into a beast that made even me gasp. It wasn't a wolf, not this time, it was something otherworldly. Darkness oozed from its pores, its eyes flickering between red and black while it wrapped Jed in shadow.

Jed yelled, writhing under Connor's hold. Connor stared down at him, his body beginning to shift fully into the dark fae that lurked beneath his skin.

"Connor! Stop." I wouldn't be scared of him; no matter how dangerous I sensed this beast to be. I reached out and placed a hand on his ridged back. His head whipped towards me. And then a surprising thing happened, those unfeeling black eyes softened. "Enough," I whispered. "There is no threat to me."

"*Mine!*" He growled, his voice like nothing I'd heard before.

"Yes. I am. Now come back to me." It was a gentle demand, but a demand nonetheless. His eyes turned blue and with one last snap at Jed's wide eyed form, he came back to me and climbed off his victim. He stared at me while Jed climbed up and went to lean against the wall, visibly shaken, though trying to hide it. Lionel took his shirt off and handed it to him.

"Here use this. You're making a mess."

Drake walked back towards the table and sat while Lionel and Stone silently straightened the room, both keeping an eye on Jed.

Connor didn't remove his attention from me. Stormy and the colour of the deepest sea, his eyes focused purely on me. I waited, not lowering my gaze even though my cheeks heated at the obvious lust pouring from him. He was still trying to wrangle in all the power that fought to escape his body, and with the claiming riding us both high, it was taking all of my self control not to climb his stunning body and start riding him in front of everyone.

Owen coughed, his brows raised and a smirk on his face, though all of the males in the room had moved far away from us, or rather me. "Hey, you two need a minute?" he said.

I swallowed hard, my throat dry as Connor raked his gaze down my body and back up, standing totally naked, with a raging hard on and not a bit of embarrassment. "No, we need more than a fucking minute." Clothes shimmered across his body. "So let's get this meeting done." His voice was still a low growl. "Come here."

My nostrils flared. I wanted so much to smile and step back, to push his buttons, but that kind of challenge was dangerous for us both right now. A bead of sweat ran down his temple and his jaw muscles tensed. A wave of power rolled over me and I knew he was close to losing control. I wouldn't drop my gaze, but I did walk into his body, then slid my arm around his waist. His body was like rock; he was so tense. He pulled me in and faced the others.

Jed stood at the other side of the room with the shirt shoved under his nose, his face swollen.

"So you're the Prime?" Jed mumbled.

Connor didn't bother answering, just stared.

Jed slid his gaze from Connor—right to me. Connor growled. Jed quickly looked away.

"So where have you been, Prime? Your pack thought you were dead."

Connor's predatory gaze bored into Jed. After a pause that got uncomfortable, he decided to answer. "I was a prisoner of Berith's. I escaped a couple of days ago."

Jed's eyes narrowed, but he wisely didn't ask anything more.

"No more questions about me or my mate. You can be here for operational meetings; as I believe that was the agreement between Drake and whoever sent you. Anything else to do with this pack—which is now under my protection—is off limits. Keep your men away from my shifters. If they harm any of them, male or female, I will not ask questions, they will die."

Jed raised his brows, but nodded once.

"Wise move, man," muttered Lionel.

"Owen, you remain alpha here, but I am Prime. You will keep me informed of any issues you think I need to know. You, and every member of this pack get my protection and loyalty, and in return I expect yours."

Owen nodded and smirked at Connor. "Always, Prime."

Connor nodded back, and the respect these two had for each other was clear. Jed watched them silently, and I wondered what kind of loyalty his band of mercenaries had for him.

Connor spoke to the remaining men. "I am your Prime. Any questions about our attack on the prison come to me. Anything to do with pack life goes to Owen. Are we clear?"

Lionel, Alex and Stone nodded their agreement. Connor turned to Jed and met his stare. I willed Jed to move his gaze, and not test Connor's word. Jed might operate outside a pack, but he was dealing with a cold-blooded killer.

One who it seemed was willing to give him a chance—for now. *Don't push your luck...*

Jed dropped his gaze and nodded.

"Good. Let's go through the fire power and warriors." Connor turned the plans to better see them. "We need a game plan."

It took the rest of that day to agree on assault tactics for the prison. Connor and Owen were both experienced former SBI operatives, as it turned out, so was Jed, who settled into professional mode quickly. The small army of shifters they had was split into squads. One to deal with security at the camp, one to take the science wing and rescue any more prisoners, one to hold the prison compound, one to defend the way out from ground to science wing level, and another larger force to destroy Berith's rooms.

"The rift is a huge fireplace in this room." Connor jabbed his forefinger on the plans. "I always thought it was evil. The fire that burned in it was constant and viciously hot. The fireplace itself is also big enough to walk through." He tensed, his top lip curling. "It was in my nightmares and torture sessions more than once." I placed my hand over his. He twisted his head and smiled tightly at me. "Berith once told me hellhounds and Weres are the same thing. Weres were the guardians of Hell's gate—until we grew a backbone and left through it. It was Zander who told me that the King of the Weres revolted and pulled his kind through those gates right before they were sealed shut by an army of angels, leaving Satan to guard his own gates."

"Damn, really?" breathed Lionel, his eyes wide.

"Yep. Apparently an angel, the deity we know as the Mother Wolf, guided them as spirits into newborn humans whose souls were pure enough to host a Were's."

"I never knew that. Why isn't that in our history books?"

Connor shrugged at Owen's question. It was Alex who answered. Doppelgangers were immortals just like high fae, so I guessed he had a whole load of accumulated knowledge rattling around in his head.

"Some hellhounds were gifted forms other than lupines by the Mother, but all of them cycle back to a human who is strong enough and pure enough to carry them. Sometimes, that is the newborn of a shifter, sometimes it is of a fully human couple. Weres age; albeit very slowly, but their human side is not immortal. When humans pass on to the afterlife, their animal-spirit returns to the Mother Wolf to be reborn. And as with many things, over time, fact gets twisted into legend or it gets forgotten."

I bit my lip, wondering how old Alex really was. "So does that mean that Prime is the actual Were that was the original King of the Hellhounds?" I looked up at Connor. "That *you* are now one with the Were King? The one who led them to freedom?"

All eyes turned to Connor, waiting for his answer. Prime surfaced in his eyes, but my skin prickled when I felt something more inside him. Connor's body stretched and changed shape. It wasn't a quick change, but a slow morphing of his body, one that would have taken immense control. He only stopped when a huge Were stared down at me, his head and shoulders bent down under the roof, he was so tall. Fangs elongated and his eyes darkened to endless pools of black. The others all took a step back from his huge form. His voice rumbled in my mind and he lowered his head, bending a knee until he was in front of my short frame, staring into my eyes. *Yes, I am—yet, I am now—more. Fae magic is an addition I have never had before. It is...interesting.*

I smiled. "I'll just bet it is."

"What? You can talk to him in your mind? In Were form?" asked Alex, as the others gaped at us.

The King huffed a gravelly chuckle.

"Yes, I can." I shrugged like it was no big deal, but I knew it really was. Weres could sometimes communicate, but it was rare, or like Reed had done with me right before I'd ended his life, using short growled words. Connor, or rather Prime, was in my head. This wasn't just the powerful wolf that Connor's strength and fae side made more powerful, it was the ancient spirit of the King of Hellhounds.

I thank you for taking in my wolf spirit and caring for him. Without our human host, the soul we are bound to, we were lost.

Being fearful of this creature was not an option so I rested my hand on his thickly muscled arm. "It was my pleasure. But I'd really like Connor to remain in control and come back to me. Will you let him?"

The King of Weres cocked his head. *Of course. I allow him control all of the time, but will come when he calls. He is powerful, but together as Prime, hellhound, fae and man, we will command enough strength to fight even the armies of Hell.*

I swallowed, realising how much power Connor now commanded. "Thank you."

He nodded and faded away leaving Connor staring down at me. "Fuck me, that was insane," he muttered, cracking his neck and rolling his shoulders.

"Damn, Prime, how many beasts you got in there?" asked Stone.

Connor ran a hand through his hair. "Three that I know of."

"Fuck me," muttered Jed.

"Not even if Hell freezes over." Connor's heavy gaze stayed on me. "But we're done here. Owen, I trust you to complete the tasks we set out to make sure our plan goes smoothly. I'll be with Ember if you need me." His gaze shot to Owen's.

Owen smirked. "Yeah, I think I'll manage. I'd rather keep my head on my shoulders."

"Good. We'll be back out—later."

"Sure, Prime. You, er, want food brought to you?"

I opened my mouth to protest, but Connor beat me to it. "Yes." His look made even my cheeks heat, and I wasn't one for blushing. "We'll be busy—until morning."

"What? Connor, you can't ask people to wait on us...that's not..."

Before I finished speaking I was upside down over his shoulder. "Are you kidding me?" I screeched. "Connor! Put me down."

"No. We haven't finished our claiming time yet, and I've stood seeing you near other males enough today. You're mine, all mine, for the next twenty four hours, so get ready to be ravaged."

Hanging upside down and being unable to do anything about it was not my finest hour, but the tingle through my body at his cavemannish treatment told me I didn't really care. It was pointless threatening him with Fire, she couldn't harm him and I would never want to. He'd blocked Mea, so I couldn't shift. Besides, all that hussy was interested in was getting to her mate, so there was no help there. So instead of fighting it, I rested my hands on his fine arse and squeezed—hard.

Connor growled and strode to the door.

"Later, Ember." Lionel held the door open and winked as Connor strode past him. I grinned, totally on board with another heavy sex session with this powerful hunk of a male who had his mind set on ruining me.

Stone rolled his eyes and walked after us. I could see Shannon training with a group of males on the far side of the courtyard. She was kicking ass and looking gorgeous while she did it. "Hey, Stone? Prime is the King of the Weres, his power is riding high right now, I think we'll be safe. Why don't you go and stamp your territory—before Shannon gets distracted with one of those other males."

Stone's head whipped around to look where I pointed. He growled. "Prime?"

"Go."

Stone didn't need telling twice. He strode in Shannon's direction with a look of utter determination and fury on his face. I wasn't sure quite how that would go down with Shannon, but, hey, I had other more pressing things to occupy me.

Connor's long legs covered the ground between our cabin and the ops centre so quickly I couldn't be sure he wasn't running. No one stood in our way, not after Connor let loose a roar and hit them all with a blast of his power. Most fell to their knees, the rest staggered and quickly moved.

All I could think about was the way his hands and mouth had felt on my skin, how his body had stretched mine... My blood started to hum as I absorbed his power and it zipped like a jolt of lust right between my legs. I bit my lip trying not to groan.

Connor flung open the door to our room and kicked it shut with his foot.

He flung me down on the bed, falling on top of me before I'd even stopped bouncing. Warm and wet lips descended on mine, and I couldn't help the moan that escaped me when his tongue tangled with mine. My fingernails raked over his t-shirt and down his back feeling the muscles shifting under my touch, tensing as I pushed my hands under the material.

"Need to touch you," I muttered against his lips.

"Me too." And he pulled away, smirking when I whined. Quickly, he removed his clothes. A wave of desire hit me so hard, all I could do was stare and pant. My fingers went to the waistband of my jeans. "Here, let me." He hooked both hands into my jeans and ripped them apart, followed by my t-shirt. I stopped him at my bra, though. "Hey, not the bra. This one is comfy and it fits. Don't ruin it."

He grinned. "Okay, I'll take it off, carefully—so long as I get to ruin *you* afterwards. I haven't finished claiming you yet." His face dropped into a serious mask, his thumb brushing over the scars on my neck. "I'm thinking these marks should never be allowed to fade. I want everyone to know you're claimed by the King of the Weres."

It was a beautiful thing to witness, his pride in his new knowledge of who Prime really was. I tilted my head and offered up my neck. Only for Connor would I bare my neck like this. Submission to anyone other than him was unthinkable.

Inky black bled into his blue irises as he lowered his head, kissing slowly along my neck until he pulled in a mouthful of skin sucking harder and harder. The nip of pain sent warmth through me and a fresh wave of desire to my core.

"Gods, Ember, I love your scent. He rubbed his hard cock, over and over, through the slickness between my legs, teasing me until I was arching my spine and lifting my pelvis to get closer to him.

"I need you inside me…ahh."

Before I'd even finished begging, he thrust into my willing body, not giving me a moment to adjust.

"You can take me. You are mine." He reared back and thrust harder, making me moan. "And this body was made for me." Again he thrust, picking up the pace, hitting that spot inside me that sent my mind offline. I was mumbling incoherently, flying on waves of pleasure until his pumping hips and the slide of our bodies were too much. I wrapped my legs around his thighs, gripped his backside and with a thrust and a scream, I exploded around him.

"Oh, shit, Firecracker…" And Connor groaned, a sound so full of utter pleasure it was enough to make me clench around him again.

We lay in each other's arms panting and coming down off our high—or so I thought until Connor rolled his hips again, groaning. "I need more…"

I swallowed, but my body had its own ideas. Heat was building low in my belly and I didn't fight the urge to move with him. "Then take it," I whispered against his hot skin before I sank my canines into his neck, drawing his taste and power into me as if my own life depended on it.

So he did. He took, and took...

CHAPTER 16

onnor

THE SMUG SMILE that curled my lips was growing all on its own. The king inside me was feeling pure pride. Prime lifted his head, happy, tongue lolling, and even the fae shadow that was becoming an active spirit inside me, swirled in a satisfied way. Gods, I'd had no idea I was part fae. After the day I'd lost my mind to the darkness in my soul and viciously killed my would be rapist, I'd locked it down, unconsciously using Prime's power to suppress it.

My father had been an utter bastard. One who loved both the sound of his belt hitting my back, and my cries of pain—until I learned to grit my teeth and not give him that satisfaction. That bastard had told me my mother had left because of me, because I was weak and she couldn't stand the sight of me. I rubbed my hands over my face. And Mother Wolf forgive me, I'd believed every word, feeling as worthless as the dirt on my shoe; so I'd blocked her from my mind. It had been easier to pretend I didn't have a mother.

I exhaled slowly. I knew I couldn't put off meeting my mother any longer; she must be going mad with worry over the son she had actually raised being in the hands of his father. I needed to see her, even if it was going to be hard. It was wrong, but I couldn't just forgive her for leaving me. Childhood wounds were just too hard to heal, no matter the reasons they were inflicted.

Ember winced as she sat opposite me on the bench seat in the dining cabin.

I chuckled, my smile stretching.

"What are you smiling at?"

I tried to school my features into a blank mask, but I missed by a mile. "Nothing. You okay there, Firecracker?" The look on her face was priceless as she thumped my arm.

"You smug bastard, I'm as sore as hell, and you know it. Sitting there all cocky and shit…"

I tried to look innocent. "Who me?"

She just raised her brows, but I didn't miss the tiny smile she was trying to hide. I leaned into her ear. "You loved every minute, every position and every earth shattering orgasm."

The goosebumps on her skin and flush on her cheeks had my cock twitching in response. "Is it too soon to say I already want you again?"

She swallowed hard and her eyes shot to mine. "You're not serious right now, 'cause you know how sexy I find you, but damn it, I can hardly bloody walk…"

I burst out laughing even though it was cruel. "I'm teasing you, Firecracker. I'll give you at least a few hours to heal that gorgeous pussy before I fill it again."

Her eyes narrowed on mine before she grinned too. "Give me an hour at most…"

I kissed her nose. "Really?" Now I sounded hopeful. There was shit that needed sorting out today for our raid in three days, but damn, I wasn't joking when I said I needed her again already. I was going to have to find a way of dampening down my need…or at least controlling it. Because every time I saw her curves sway or inhaled her scent I was a goner.

"Hey, boss." Myles sat down next to me. Gods, I'd been so caught up in claiming my mate I'd neglected my brothers. Myles had dark circles under his eyes and had lost weight. His ebony skin had lost that natural healthy lustre he'd always had, and his shoulders were bowed forward as if carrying a heavy burden.

"Hey, man." I clasped his outstretched hand before pulling him in for a hug. We clapped our hands on each other's backs. "It's good to see you, brother," I said. "I'm so sorry about Reed."

Ember looked down at the table, her face dropping.

"Yeah, so am I. Hey?" He leaned forward so he could see my mate's face, and despite him being my brother, I tensed. He was an alpha who had lost his mate, because of mine. No matter that it hadn't been her fault, she'd still ripped a hole in Reed's chest. I'd only seen Myles briefly since that day, so I trusted him as far as I trusted any shifter who faced the one who had killed his mate.

"I already told you, you hold no blame for what happened to him. He's still in there somewhere, I feel it," Myles said, his face grave.

"So, how is he?" Ember asked, though her voice was small, and she bit her top lip. I reached over and squeezed her hand. She blamed herself for what had happened. For all her physical toughness, Ember had a soft and loyal heart; she loved as fiercely as she fought, and of all my brothers, she had connected with Reed the most.

Myles shrugged and took a big swallow of coffee. "He's possessed by a demon, so pretty shit I would imagine. His body is fading away because I won't let anyone near him. His demon needs blood or innocent souls to feed from. And I am starving it." He gulped more coffee, but even that action couldn't stop his wolf from peeking out. I felt its distress and fear at hurting their mate. It was destroying them both. I sent a wave of reassurance to my brother, who squeezed his eyes closed, and inhaled, accepting my gift with a nod.

"Innocent souls?" Ember paled, her eyes wide as she stared at his face.

"Yeah. That's what the demon bastard demands of me, everyday. And we're a little short on innocent souls and spare blood, here."

My attention shot to Ember when she started to hyperventilate. "Em? You okay? You look like you're gonna throw up."

"I...oh, shit..." And she twisted her legs over the bench seat and put her head down.

Anxiety spiked through me. "Ember? What's wrong?"

"I, err..." She took another few deep breaths. Gently, I rubbed circles on her back, giving her time. After a few minutes, she sat upright again, still looking pasty.

"The women and babies," she said, grabbing my hand and squeezing it.

I looked at her blankly. "What women and babies?"

Her brows dipped. "The ones from the prison; the ones we rescued. That's what Berith needed, or still needs, them for. He is feeding them to the demon Weres as they come through the rift; or more to the point, he's piling up a fucking larder for Hell's army for when they are freed. The women supply the blood, and the babies supply the innocent souls."

"Shit." Suddenly, seeing her so nauseous made sense. Prime growled. Neither of us had given much thought as to why Berith had needed to take those women from the prison, but suddenly it all made complete sense. It had never been just a breeding programme as we'd suspected.

At least Owen had managed to save some of those innocent souls from being consumed. I rubbed my face, shuddering at the thought of how many more were locked away in those other cells. My shadow fae rumbled as I tried to sort through my memories. My hands began to tremble, but I pushed through. He hid my most painful memories from me. I didn't want those nightmares back, but he agreed he would return them if I asked. *How many other voices could we hear from our cell?*

Suddenly, a chorus of high pitched screams and crying hit me, echoing through my mind. My chest tightened to the point of pain. Not all of that crying was from adults, some were pitiful little cries from babies.

I shoved my chair back and pulled Ember to her feet. Parting from her was gonna hurt, but I needed to rethink our plan for an assault on the science wing. There were far more cells than that old plan had shown. All those years of women being taken and babies being born. Those babies may be half-demon but they were still innocent. And my brother was evidence of the goodness that they could carry. I would not let them die. I held Ember's shoulders. "I need to speak with Owen and Drake, and even that arsehole Jed. Our plan for the science wing needs to be rethought. We need a back up plan to care for the women and children that we get out of there."

Ember nodded at me and slipped her arms around my waist. I held her tightly for a moment before I pulled away. "I have to go." I hated that I did, and that I knew she needed to do something else. I glanced at Myles. "Myles needs you, sweetheart, so does Reed. See if you can get through to him. The demon in him will be getting weak, but Reed's soul and his wolf spirit are still there. Tell him to fight and that I will find a way to help him very soon."

She nodded, her beautiful bright red hair brushing against my chest, releasing her heady scent. I pulled away before I could do what I really wanted, which was kiss her until she couldn't breathe. Instead, I leaned my head down until my lips brushed her ear. "I love you," I whispered and contented myself with the way she shuddered before I pulled back and brushed my lips softly on hers. "Take care of her."

Myles nodded, but Ember tutted and rolled her eyes.

"I don't need 'taking care of'. But…" She linked her arm with Myles's. "I do want to spend some time with my friend, and see Reed."

"I know you do, sweetheart, that's why I'm letting you leave my side. Even though it goes against everything I feel right now."

She raised a brow this time. "You're letting me?"

"That's right." Despite the fact that I needed to go and find Owen, I grinned.

She jammed her hands on her hips, her scowl only making her look cute to me. "Why, you sexist son-of-a-bitch."

I laughed. "Yep. And I'll think you'll find most alphas are. Aw, sweetheart, you know I just don't like it when you're not by my side where I can protect you from harm."

"Yes, well, I don't need protection, and you know *that*."

I brushed a finger down her cheek. "Humour me, love. I can't help wanting to keep you safe, even though I know you don't *need* me to."

She sighed, her shoulders relaxing and her eyes softening from a deep stormy green to a soft jade. "Fine." She grabbed my hand and kissed it. "But I just might start tying you to the bed to keep *you* safe."

I chuckled. "Is that supposed to be a threat or a promise?"

She grinned. "A promise, if you want it to be."

"Oh, I do," I purred in her ear.

Now I could scent that gorgeous smell of her arousal. I took a step forward.

"Ah, ah. Nope. Off you go. Still recovering here, remember?"

Myles chuckled at the same time as a satisfied grin stretched my mouth. "Okay, Firecracker. You go your way and I'll go mine. But you'd better be ready for me later. Staying away from you isn't going to happen—ever."

CHAPTER 17

mber

Walking into the dimly lit cave where Reed was being kept was one of the worst things I'd ever experienced. Yeah, Berith had controlled me. But it had been my fist that he had rammed through Reed's chest wall. There wasn't a day that went by where I didn't feel what I'd done, or think of it in some way. My feet ground to a halt, my attention resting on the figure strapped down by heavy silver chains to a pallet of some kind. Big bolts had been driven though the chain into the ground.

My hand covered my mouth. I thought of myself as a strong person, I mean, I'd been through some shit in my life, but seeing one of my best friends like this hit me like a boot upside my head.

"Oh Mother." I turned to Myles. "I…I'm so sorry…"

"Stop. I stand by what I said before. This is not your fault. Ember, he needs to know his friends are still here for him."

Another large male entered the room, his shoulder length sandy blonde hair gleaming in the dull light. "He's right, Em." Lionel's voice was deep and rumbled around the cave.

For a moment, I closed my eyes. This guilt I felt wasn't going to go away any time soon, but they were right; I didn't kill my friend on purpose. My change into Were form had been driven by that silver collar, and even my attack had been forced by Berith.

"Come on. Where's my tough, kick-ass, friend?" Lionel crooned.

"Oh, piss off." I mumbled. "I'm still here."

"Good. Then go and give your friend, who's stuck in his own personal hell, some hope that we can help him. We don't know if he's in there, but what if he is? Hmm? Don't you think he would need to know he hadn't been abandoned?"

I nodded and turned, the sole of my boot grinding on the rock. Cautiously, I walked up to Reed. Mea snarled, so I blocked her from my mind. Dark eyes followed my movements, and a shudder rippled down my spine.

"Reed? I don't know if you're in there—if you can hear me or not, but I really want you to know how sorry I am for what's happened to you…"

The Were's huge deformed chest began to shake with laughter. The creature clearly couldn't form words or speak like Reed had done, but its mocking laughter told me plenty. It soon stopped laughing when I called upon Fire and she wrapped me in flames, my hair floating around my face and my eyes alight. I lowered my head right next to his, so that I could speak directly into his ear. "That's right, you ugly piece of shit, I could burn you to dust and send you right back to Hell. The only thing keeping you alive, is the fact that I want my friend back. So let me see him, because if you don't make me believe that he's still in this shell, then I'll just end you."

I straightened and stared down into those coal-black eyes. He snarled and held my gaze.

I shrugged. "Fine. You think I won't burn you because I want my friend back?"

"Ember?"

My heart pounded at the fear in Myles's voice. But I ignored him and looked into those dark, cruel eyes. "Let him through or I *will* burn you and send you right back to Hell."

The chains clanked as he fought against them, snarling, and huffing through his snout. I placed a hand on the chains that ran across his torso. They heated, and he bucked against them.

"Ember!"

"Steady, man. She knows what she's doing," said Lionel.

Come on… The stench of burning fur and skin filled my nostrils.

The demon's roar hurt my eardrums. I pulled my flames away and peered into those dark eyes. Slowly they changed to a deep chocolate brown.

"Reed?" It was so damn hard to stop my voice from shaking.

The Were huffed, but gently this time.

"Oh, my gods." Myles ran over and dropped to his knees by Reed's head.

Again Reed huffed, his eyes full of pain and love as he looked on his mate's distraught face. I knew we wouldn't have long, and even though Reed was showing through, he couldn't speak. His Were wasn't really under his control.

I stood behind Myles and peered down at my friend. "Reed? Listen to me." He tore his eyes from his mate. "We'll find a way to bring you back. Don't you give up...ever," I told him, my voice thick.

He dipped his head once, and his eyes started to flicker between the demon's and his. He snarled but I had no idea if that was Reed or the demon. Either way, Reed came back and held Myle's gaze. Even though it was only for a moment, that look spoke such volumes. I curled my fists as black seeped across his irises until there was nothing but demon left. I wanted to punch something—or someone. Without waiting for Myles or Lionel, I spun on my heel and marched away from the damning sight of my chained friend.

Connor had that Halo, and the only thing we needed to use it without us being catapulted into Hell, was an angel. I pressed my lips together. Where the fuck would I find an angel? Before I knew where I was heading, I'd stomped through the caves and out into the compound. I noticed Stone leaning casually against the rock face. His attention moved from Shannon who was helping Selina by holding her baby, to me.

Shannon glanced over as I stomped past Stone. "Take it she hasn't forgiven you yet?" I don't know why I asked as I had no intention of stopping. I was headed to the far side of the camp, where there was a training area.

"Where are you going?" Stone asked, ignoring my question. I turned my head. He was scowling as usual.

"Gods, no wonder Shannon doesn't want to be around you. You're a miserable bastard." Yeah, I was spoiling for a fight, so I kept walking, knowing he wouldn't take that kind of shit from me. In fact, I was counting on it.

"Hey! What's eating you?" He stalked behind me, closing the distance between us.

"Nothing. Why don't you go back to perving over the woman you want to fuck, but don't have the balls to?"

Stone's footsteps halted. My nostrils flared as I heard his mumbled curse. Footsteps caught me up. An iron grip wrapped around my arm. "You're right, I don't, but that isn't what this is about."

"Let go." I snarled and narrowed my eyes, Mea rolling across my gaze.

His wolf glinted in his eyes, coming out to play just like I wanted. I'd issued a challenge, an order. One he wouldn't comply with.

"I don't think I will."

Holding his gaze, I smiled and let Mea through a little more, just enough to enhance my senses. I inhaled deeply. The scent of determination and adrenaline hit me. Stone wanted this as much as me. I hadn't given Mea freedom for weeks now and she was itching to be let loose, to fight and run. Stone's pupils dilated.

"Oh, I think you will," I said.

Stone grunted. "You want to fight." It was a statement not a question.

"Yes, I fucking do."

Stone let his hand fall away and looked at the cave mouth where he knew Reed was. His eyes softened.

"Don't you do that. I will not take your damned pity."

He snarled. "I don't fucking pity you, girl." He leaned closer. "But I do know what you need. And if it's punishment you need, I'm happy to oblige."

"Good."

"And Connor?"

I shrugged and curled my top lip, but we both knew Stone was putting himself at risk by fighting me. "You can walk away, if you're too chicken-shit to fight me."

A slow animalistic grin stretched his full lips. "I never walk away from a challenge." And in the blink of an eye, he shifted. So did I. Mea burst through my skin and leapt sideways to avoid Stone who launched himself at me, his jaws snapping. His wolf was stunning, a deep silver with a strange aura of purple mist around him. He stood far taller than Mea, possibly even as tall as Prime.

He bounded forward, changing direction at the last moment and nipping at my hind leg, ripping some fur and skin from my limb. It stung, but wouldn't incapacitate me. Mea snarled and flicked her body around. Despite challenging a more powerful wolf, her excitement for the fight rolled through me. She jumped up intending to leap over his back, grab his neck and body roll him to the ground. The move totally backfired. Stone dropped to the ground and Mea missed her mark. She fell awkwardly. Stone immediately snapped his jaws and grabbed her around the back of her own neck. He could easily rip out our spine.

I snarled, pissed off with how quickly he'd beaten us.

He flicked his head and threw me across the ground. The back of my neck stung and I could smell blood. He prowled towards me his wolf's predatory gaze fixed right on my face. He bared his teeth. I couldn't submit. It wasn't in my nature, even though I was beaten and I knew it. Fire stirred, but I locked her away; I wanted to fight with just me and Mea. Yes, I could turn this situation around easily with my phoenix's power, but that wasn't the purpose of this. My attention flicked to the trees beyond the compound. It was drawing me in, the smell, the promise of freedom, the solitude, all of it. Stone was almost where I wanted him. I kept up my pretense of being weak, drawing him in until I could leap up and grab his throat, when a huge roar rocked the air and a blast of power knocked Stone sideways.

Connor! Shit, he's going to be pissed at me for doing this.

Mea whined her agreement, and ignoring Connor's battering of power, got to her feet. Stone watched his Prime, no, his *king*, bound across the compound towards him. There was no understanding in Prime's eyes, none.

Damn! I met Stone's gaze and took off over the compound, heading for the guarded entrance. A furious howl told me Connor wasn't far behind.

Come on Mea, faster. Let's get him away from Stone.

Mea's muscles tensed, pushing more power into her stride, leading Connor away from the wolf who had drawn blood on his mate.

No way would I allow Stone to take a serious beating because of my own emotional meltdown, and I knew Connor would hunt me down. Like any predator, he couldn't resist the chase, and he would never let his mate run from him, especially if she was injured. He'd scent my blood and pursue me, no matter how far I got, or where in this forest wilderness I went.

He was so close, anger, determination—and fear seeping through our link. My heart raced and I forced Mea to go faster. I darted between the trees and jumped small jutting rocks. The pine needles stirred under my paws, that damp earthy smell invading my senses. Mea panted hard, her reserves of energy fading.

You can't outrun me, little wolf.

Connor?

A growl sounded behind me. I made Mea look behind. He was so close, he could stop me whenever he chose. Prime was even bigger now that the King had revealed himself and merged with them. My heart pounded hard at the realisation. One leap and Mea would be under his body. He was letting me run, letting me exhaust myself.

Who else were you expecting?

No matter the danger he exuded, Connor's jealous tone also excited me. I wanted to push him before I collapsed from exhaustion...

Hmm, there are plenty of males in that compound, so let me think...

Before I knew it I was under Prime. Mea's legs collapsed under the sheer weight of his huge body. Prime rumbled in his chest as he flattened her to the ground, the air heating between them. Despite the desire that rippled through me from her, I didn't fancy being party to their coupling.

Nope. No you don't missy...

Mea snarled, but all I could concentrate on was Connor's deep rumbling chuckle in my head. His power pushed on Mea, compelling her to retreat. And soon I was lying on a carpet of pine needles, naked, with Prime sprawled on top of me. He chuffed a laugh as I tried to move him—and couldn't. So naturally I kept trying.

"Urgh, get off me, you great oaf!"

He just licked my face. Once I'd exhausted myself trying to shift him, I fell back panting against the ground.

"Connor! Move!" Demanding that of a Prime alpha was not the smartest thing to do. In a second Prime was gone and Connor lay butt naked across my body. The feel of his skin against mine took my mind offline. I couldn't think about anything other than his scent and his weight bearing down on me. I was too tired to fight, and when he lifted his weight, grabbed my hips and flipped me onto my belly, I squealed.

He grabbed my wrists and held them above my head, laying his body down on me, his thighs eitherside of mine, his hard body imprisoning me, and the steel of his sex rubbing along the crack of my ass. My heart hammered against my ribs. My whole body was tense, desperate for more.

"What was that back there?" he growled in my ear, his voice tight and low and dripping with fury, but I could feel his fear as he inhaled.

I twisted my head so that my cheek was flat against the pine needles. They poked in my naked breasts and stomach lending jabs of pain to his dominant treatment. He bit gently on my right shoulder, then laved the stinging pain away with his tongue. I moaned, secretly enjoying that primal treatment when I didn't respond to his question.

"Tell me." He bit me a little harder on my other shoulder when I remained quiet, unwilling to tell him about my guilt and need for punishment. I shuddered as he ran his tongue, slowly this time, over that sting. He pushed his manhood against me, rolling his hips against the softness of my behind. I groaned, sweat breaking out on my body, as I pushed against him. He pulled away so that I couldn't reach him. I mewled in frustration. He, of course, gave a deep and gravelly chuckle.

Oh gods, my escape, that little reprieve from his ire, had been to let me get further away from the camp. He could have caught me at any point.

"That's right, my Firecracker. So that you can scream to your heart's content...and you *will* scream. You are about to be punished for allowing another male close enough to harm you." He licked the back of my neck and the stinging pain reminded me that Stone had drawn blood. Connor was healing me. It was so erotic, the sensation of his soft tongue along with his firm hold of my wrists and the way he ground his pelvis into me, only to retreat when I tried to entice him to enter me. It sent me both to Heaven and Hell. My desire to move to get up on my hands and knees and let him take me from behind was something I couldn't deny, but no matter how hard I tried, he held me captive. Once done healing me, his weight lifted and he lowered his body to the pine needle carpet at the side of me, keeping hold of my wrists and trapping my lower half with a heavy leg over my thighs. A slap echoed around us, followed a split second later by a stinging hot pain that bloomed through my right ass cheek.

"Hey!" I wriggled as the burn hit me.

"Tell me why you let my brother harm you."

"No," I ground out between my clenched teeth, guilt at what I'd done to Reed riding me high.

His sinful tongue licked up the side of my neck circling my outer ear. I shuddered as a tingle of power washed over me and through me, tugging on my heart and mind. Mea whined, wanting to give into his compulsion to talk. I squeezed my eyes shut and ground my teeth to keep from admitting my reasons.

His voice softened. "It's okay, Firecracker, I know why. I just wanted to see if you'd tell me. You should trust me enough to tell me anything."

I squeezed my eyes shut at the disappointment I felt from him.

"But if punishment is what you desire, then you come to me. No one else." His tone hardened. Another crack. I squealed in surprise, though the burn sent a rush of desire through my flesh, even if I would never admit to being turned on by this rough treatment. "You don't ask my brothers to punish you —ever again. Do you hear me?" He nipped my ear lobe before soothing his actions with his tongue. Before I could get my thoughts together enough to speak, he lifted himself until his body covered mine and rolled his hips against me again. "Do you want me?" his voice was heavy and dripping with lust.

I nodded, unable to find my voice.

He pulled back and laid beside me. I whined at the loss of his weight and heat, not even satisfied when one heavy leg was slung over my thighs, again. I tried to wiggle closer to him, but he still held my wrists. "Good. Then tell me you understand, or..." His fingers slipped through the wetness of my pussy and he pushed them inside me, unapologetically hard. I gasped, trying to grind back down onto them. He groaned and dropped his forehead onto my back. "Damn, you do want me. Tell me, promise me you won't ever hurt your-self on purpose again."

I tried, but I couldn't think when he moved his fingers, slowly adding another. "I...I..." Oh, jeez what was the question?

Suddenly, his fingers were gone. "Promise me, right now. Or I will not take you again until you do."

I nodded my head, desperately trying to raise my hips to entice him, I needed him so badly it was consuming me.

"Words, Ember, I need words."

"Yes...Mother Wolf, Connor! Yes. I promise. I promise."

Now his fingers were back, sliding forward across my clit before moving back inside me. "What do you promise?" His voice was filled with lust and sin, brushing over me as he teased me mercilessly. My brain struggled to form coherent thoughts. "I promise..." His fingers pulled out completely. I cried out.

"What, Firecracker?" He slid his fingers back inside me stretching my already sensitive inner walls.

"Um, I...mmm."

He pulled out again and I gave a frustrated moan, bucking and twisting to try and escape his hold on my wrists so that I could touch him. Fire stirred in my blood, my lust becoming hers. "Ipromisetoneverhurtmyselfagain."

His fingers slid forward again. "And?"

I cried. "Oh gods…I'll never…use your brothers…to punish me….again."

"Good girl." He circled my clit until I was sobbing with need.

"Connor! Please!"

"Now you can have me, Firecracker," he whispered in my ear. And I cried out as he released my hands and his weight was soon on me, his scent surrounding me. With an arm around my stomach, he pulled me to my knees and held my hips with his large hands. We both groaned as he slipped home and my inner muscles gripped him, not wanting to let him go.

"Damn, Ember, you feel so good." He panted, driving into me again and again.

"Harder." My demand was met with a dark chuckle.

"Whatever my queen demands." Conner gripped my hair and pulled me up until I was arching my back. I swallowed as his hand gently encircled my throat while he pushed power into me, the overwhelming rush making breathing hard. With his thumb he moved my chin until I could just see him. The blue of his eyes was mixed with the darkness and shadow of Prime. A king looking at his prize. "Mine…" he growled.

I swallowed, not sure how much of him was beast, and how much was man. "Connor?"

He stilled, those amazing eyes focused on mine. "Yes, it's still me, Firecracker. We are all me." He pulsed that combined power into my core. A moan escaped me at the rush of pleasure it gave me.

He growled, his eyes narrowed, watching my reaction to his combined spirits and the surge of power they sent me.

His hand remained lightly around my throat, possessive, but not pushing further. "Is this okay?"

I blinked at his question, deciding I really liked, no I loved this primal side to Connor.

I smiled, knowing Fire showed in my eyes under my lowered lids. Lust burned through my body. "Yes." I thrust my sex backwards, rolling my hips as best I could. His grin was pure hunger, right before he kissed me, consuming me with his taste and the softness of his lips. He took back control, holding my hip with one hand and my neck with the other. I whined at the loss of his mouth, but was soon crying out for a different reason. His hand moved from my hip to my clit, stroking as his angle changed, hitting the most sensitive part of my inner walls. Just as I was struggling to breathe past his power, consumed by everything that was my mate, he pinched that sensitive bundle of nerves, sending me hurtling into the most powerful orgasm I'd ever experienced. Finally he reined in his power and that rush of sensation only tipped me over again. I thrust myself back against him, desperately rolling my hips as best I could. He kissed me again, deep and hungry, then released his hold on my neck and that rush of oxygen only tipped me over again.

"Connor!" I screamed his name over and over, as my climax kept going, milking his own from him. He roared, a mixture of beast and man, and sunk his canines into my shoulder, releasing another wave of pleasure that sank right through my flesh and bones and into my very soul. Fire erupted, surrounding us both. Connor released my skin and bellowed my name, his thrusts erratic as the sound of his pleasure echoed out into the forest. We collapsed to the ground, both of us panting.

My whole body tingled and my ears rang. I couldn't move even if I wanted to, and I really didn't.

After a few minutes, when we were both breathing normally again, a featherlite kiss brushed my cheek. "No..." I reached around trying to grab Connor when his weight lifted off me.

"Shh, it's alright, I'm not leaving you."

My arm flopped back. I was relieved to hear that but still hated the loss of his skin, of his warmth against mine. "Come on, sweetheart." Strong hands rolled me over, before I was lifted.

I let my head rest against his broad chest and wrapped my arms around his neck, my eyes dropping closed, too tired to keep them open. Fighting Berith, finding Connor; the claiming, seeing my friends again—Reed, my guilt...it had all caught up with me. And not just physically, but my mind wanted to shut down for a while. "Where are we going?" I mumbled.

"Back to the compound."

"Not...mmm...naked..." He chuckled at my half-hearted protest. If we waited, I was sure I'd have enough energy to shift and walk back in as Mea.

"Not any more, beautiful." His power rolled over my skin and despite my exhaustion, I managed to peek. "I have enough power for us both," he said by way of explanation. Before I could ask what he meant, he'd dressed us both in jeans, shirts, coats and boots.

I smiled up at his gorgeous face before levering myself higher so that I could kiss the corner of his mouth. "Thank you."

He gave me a sexy smirk. "Well, it was a chore to cover this beautiful body. But it's okay, I forgot the underwear." He winked down at me, his eyes gleaming with mischief. "Makes it easier when we get back, and I feel the need for what is mine—again."

I knew he was teasing me, but... "Again?"

Now he lifted me up and didn't miss a stride as he kissed me, thoroughly. "I'll always want more. I will never have enough of you, *my mate.*"

I swallowed hard and burrowed my nose into his neck, inhaling deeply, whispering the words I knew were etched into my very soul. "I love you."

In answer he pulled me closer and kissed my forehead. "And I love you. I have since the moment I laid eyes on you. You were always mine, and you always will be."

I smiled against his skin, nipping it between my teeth. "I am, but that means you're mine, too."

"I really am, my Firecracker."

CHAPTER 18

onnor

MY FIST CRACKED into Stone's jaw. That tough bastard's head twisted sideways, but he was soon glaring right back at me.

He snarled, but kept his purple eyes just shy of making eye contact. My fae side growled at the feel of Stone's magic escaping his control. I had no idea what his fae powers were, and mixed with his shifter side, I couldn't help but wonder how much longer he would submit to my dominance over him. The thought was a sobering one. Yes, I could overpower him...or so I believed, but I didn't want to lose my brother.

"She was asking for a fight, Boss. You know that."

"Yes, I do. Which is why you are currently still alive, but you should have refused. She knows your wolf is stronger and more dominant than hers, but you just *had* to jump at the chance to release your own anger, didn't you?"

Stone's jaw clenched. "You don't know that."

"I know you, you arrogant prick. And she had just seen Reed. She wanted to be hurt, to be punished for what she was forced to do to him."

Stone sank down onto a nearby rock and rubbed his face with his hands. "She did. But you're right, I'm a cold bastard. I wanted to accept her challenge...so I did."

I raised my brows trying to contain my anger. "Yeah, you're a bastard indeed. You did it hoping I'd come and kick your arse, didn't you? You wanted the same fucking thing as she did. Damn it, Stone, you have to get your shit together." I glanced away.

Stone released a heavy sigh and with his face a grim mask, nodded in agreement. Silence settled between us. "Is she okay?"

I could feel his genuine concern, and his remorse. It echoed through my blood.

I sat down next to him. "Yeah, she's fine. I let her run herself out, then forced her wolf to back off and let me near her."

"You healed her?"

"I did." I growled my words. "Tell me why you accepted her challenge." Stone was hot-headed and didn't trust anyone easily, but I knew he had grown to respect Ember, not only because she was my soul mate, but because she had earned his respect. I knew without a doubt that this had something to do with Shannon. He'd been messed up about his last mate, and finding another possible match in Shannon must be blowing his mind. I could imagine all that guilt he carried was warring with his need. Stone took a deep breath and dropped his head back, exhaling heavily as he stared up at the snow filled sky. "Shannon."

I huffed. "Guessed as much. So what did she do this time? Refuse to speak with you?"

"No, she spoke alright. She asked why I want to be with a whore like her, then told me to go to Hell...before she started fighting other males."

"Ah." I didn't know what to say. I'd known Shannon a long time, and she was as stubborn and hotheaded as they came. "Just don't give in. She'll never respect you if you let her win."

Stone turned his face and stared at me, looking more confused than I'd ever seen him. "She pisses me off, but it only makes me want her more."

I laughed out loud. "Yeah? Well, I know that feeling, brother. These females who are chosen by the Mother to become our heart and soul will always make us work for it."

He grunted, staring into the forest longingly, his emotions and need for solitude and nature tumbling into my mind.

"How long is it since you shifted?"

He looked at me, his silver eyes glinting as snow started to fall softly around us. "Except the short shift to fight Ember? Not since we brought her and the others back from the prison with the women and babies."

"Too long then."

He nodded. "Yeah."

"Go, I'll get Kawan and Lionel to guard Ember and me tonight."

He swallowed, expelling a heavy breath. "Thanks, brother."

I nodded. Stone's temper and emotions were dark enough that I knew we'd have a problem if he couldn't rein it in around Shannon and keep a clear head for our mission. He stood up, shaking the snow flakes from his silver hair. "Listen, I'm sorry...for Ember. You're right, I let Shannon cloud my judgement. It won't happen again."

I nodded, not sure I was happy to hear the cold way he ended his words. It seemed he was about to totally shut down his heart again. I wondered if Shannon knew what a shit storm she was stirring up in his soul. He'd lost one mate, and allowing himself to feel anything for another woman was a huge deal. She'd shut him out and now he was shutting down his feelings again. He'd fucked up and lost his judgement because of his anger and frustration with her. Stone hated being out of control and the only way to get it back, was to shut her out completely. I saw it in his eyes as surely as I felt that barrier come down, rippling through my connection to him. But none of this was my business. I was their Prime not their relationship counsellor.

"Be careful out there, Stone. I'll let Owen know you're running alone. If you're not back by dark, he'll come looking for you. Understood?" I let Prime, the King of the Weres, show through, mixing my power with that of my fae side. I would allow my brother the space he needed, but our enemy still prowled through this forest, and alone, he would be vulnerable, no matter how powerful he was.

Stone swallowed, and dipped his head, his silver eyes gleaming with respect. "Yes...my King."

Now it was me that swallowed and tried not to react to his words. I played it cool and nodded my head. "Go."

Stone undressed, then leaped and changed before his paws hit the ground. His stunning wolf dipped its head and shoulders before meeting my eyes. He howled up into the snowy sky and took off, bounding across the compound and around the corner of the nearest cabin.

Quiet settled around me and I listened to the whisper of snow falling around my body. Ember was asleep and safe. I smiled, warmth filling my chest. It was true, I had allowed her to exhaust herself before halting her escape. The powerful wolf inside me wanted to rip Stone apart for injuring our mate, but the sensible human part of me knew that the reasons for both of them to give into a fight in their wolf forms was so deep, it would have not have achieved anything other than Ember hating me, and me losing my brother; one I had been through too much with to cast aside, no matter how hard my instincts were riding me after claiming her.

I lifted my face to the sky and let the soft flakes brush my skin. I smiled as a haunting howl filled the air. "You're welcome, my friend," I whispered, feeling through our blood bond where he was located. Off to my right and moving fast. *Watch your back out there, brother...* The calm of the forest filled my soul as snowflakes covered me. After a while the sound of a baby crying roused me from my introspective thoughts. I'd find Owen and then return to my Firecracker.

Inside the cave, Owen sat with his back to me. Opposite him was Selina. A scowl graced her strong features, her dark hair falling in a plait over her shoulder. In her arms, her baby squealed at the top of its lungs.

"Just let me try, Selina."

"No. I can do it!" And she pulled the baby closer, rocking him up and down.

"For gods sakes, woman. I *know* you can. The point is that you don't have to."

For a moment her face fell and she bit her bottom lip, then she swallowed and straightened her spine. "Yes, I do. Who knows when we'll have to leave here. Then I'll be alone again. No, it's better that I manage alone."

I sighed. I understood that uncertain look. It didn't take a genius to know there was no future set out for these women. Yet another thing I needed to sort out with the alpha of this pack. Prime growled. He agreed we had to make sure they were all provided for. My own brother was a demon half-breed, and he had shown himself to be someone I could trust with both my heart and my soul. I would not let these little ones down because of their sires.

"Selina." Her face paled a little at the demand in my voice, but she lifted her eyes to mine. There was no challenge in that look, merely a kind of desperation that pulled at my protective side. "Listen to your alpha. Let him take the child for a few minutes. You can trust him."

She swallowed and met Owen's eyes. His muscles remained stiff, his jaw tight, but he managed a small smile.

"I know," she whispered, then unable to defy me, she passed the bundle of flailing arms and legs to my brother.

I remained silent as Owen took the baby.

"Thank you."

Owen visibly relaxed at her words, and he wrapped the baby tighter in its blanket and held it up near his big shoulder, rubbing a big hand against its back before patting it reassuringly. The baby immediately stopped crying. Selina's mouth dropped open as it gurgled happily.

"See?" I said and sat down next to my brother.

The baby promptly let out an almighty belch.

"Mother Wolf, how did that come out that little thing?" I was genuinely amazed. I'd never had much to do with babies.

Owen grinned. "Oh, that's nothing compared to what comes out of the other end sometimes."

My grimace was real.

"Hey, that's my son you're talking about." Selina jumped in defensively.

Owen grinned before turning to kiss the baby's head. I blinked. My brother was more than a little taken with this child. I glanced at Selina's face. Her eyes softened, and I had to admit the sight of my huge, tough friend with this tiny soul in his grasp was something I'd never expected to see.

"Yes, I know." Owen's gaze met Selina's and she flushed. "Look, he's fine with me. Nothing will happen to him. Now, go and get some food."

"I...er..."

"Go." Owen pushed his compulsion against her. I felt it, watching to see what happened.

"Don't do that," she hissed, her brows dipping and her fists curling.

Owen grinned and leaned forward. "Then do as I said, and go and eat."

Her nostrils flared and she stood up, clearly intending to take her baby back. "Don't order me around. And you can give him back now."

Owen merely leaned back and smiled at her. "No. I'm keeping him until you have eaten a decent meal and had a few hours rest."

I almost laughed at the indignation on her face, but she didn't know Owen like I did. He was kind and diplomatic, but a stubborn fucker when he wanted to be. And if I wasn't mistaken Selina had just defied his compulsion, that meant she was a possible mate for him and there was no way he'd let her continue to exhaust herself and deny her need for food.

"You can't do that!"

He sighed at her anger. "Yes, I can." He leaned the baby down supporting the back of his head with one big palm. "We'll be fine, won't we?" The baby cooed and his little mouth stretched up in a smile as if he were agreeing.

Serena hovered. "But..."

"No buts, Selina. He can sense you're tired and upset. That's why he was crying." Owen stood up cradling the child securely. Something tugged at my heart as I looked at that tiny baby, and I swallowed. "Look, please, just go and eat. He will be safe with me, I promise. I will never let anything harm him. When you've eaten, you can come back and check on him and then go and get some rest. He won't need feeding for another couple of hours at least." He reached forward and squeezed her hand. "When you are rested and more settled, he will be, too."

Selina looked close to tears but nodded her head. She leaned forward and kissed her baby's head, stroking his cheek with the back of her finger.

"Okay." She whispered before looking into my friend's face. He smiled down at her. "Go on. He'll be fine. If I'm not here, I'll be in my cabin. Okay?"

She nodded and walked off, looking back no less than three times before she left the cave. Each time Owen gave her a reassuring smile. Once she was gone, his shoulders caved on the huge breath he released. "Jeez, that woman will be the end of me."

I had to laugh. "Met your match, hmm?"

"I think maybe I have." His eyes met mine. "My wolf is getting possessive of her."

"Damn. You okay with that?"

His eyes drifted to where Selina had disappeared, before he looked down at the sleeping baby. "Yeah, I think I am. Or at least I will be if she ever lets me in."

I slapped his back, happy he had a chance at finding a mate. "Gods, both of us, hmm? Even Stone is having a hard time with Shannon. What the hell is it with our women not accepting us?"

He chuckled. "Well, that's not the case for you, anymore. Me and Stone might be having issues with stubborn females; but the whole godsdamned compound heard Ember screaming your name earlier, even from such a distance." He grinned at me and I grinned right back, not hiding my smugness. "Good, then they all know she's mine."

"True. So what can I do for you?"

"Keep an eye on our brother. Shannon keeps pushing him away, and he's shutting down again. Just like before." I leaned forward peering down at the sleeping baby that was making strange sucking noises and whimpers. "Is that normal?"

Owen shrugged. "Well, he always does it, so I expect so. I don't know much more than you about babies."

"Yeah, well, you look like a natural father," I said, meaning it. My friend looked more than comfortable cradling this little being in the crook of one arm. "Did you know Stone had a mate before?" Owen's eyes widened. "Yeah, exactly. She was killed by Doherty. I don't know what happened between him and Shannon, but they are drawn together. He's a lucky fucker to have met another match." I shrugged. "Maybe she is his soul match and his other mate was not; who knows? But she is ripping his heart apart right now by rejecting him, even though he's an intense, moody bastard, and would never tell her that."

"Right, so what do you want me to do about it, boss? I can hardly order her to accept him."

I huffed a laugh at the thought. "Nope, you can't order Shannon to do anything. She has to want to do it. No, I just want you to watch out for Stone. His head is not in the right place for this attack, and I need him to be functioning properly. He needed to let his wolf run free and find his calm again. Right now, he's in the woods, but so are our enemies. Just make sure he comes back safely when night falls. I'm going to my mate, but tomorrow we finalise our plans. Tell that wanker Jedi or whatever his bloody name is, to be there too. We'll keep him close until we know what he's really after."

Owen snorted and grinned, raising one brow. "Jedi? He's hardly as smooth as a Jedi. He's a bloody great gorilla."

I shrugged and smirked. Owen's smile dropped as he watched the other people who used the large cave as a warm communal area. "I've met Hawk before. He has a look in his eyes that I don't like...at all. He's a shifter, but no matter how many men he commands, he's a loner. He has no pack and no loyalty to anything but money."

"True. So we keep him close. Especially with Ember being what she is. From what she's told me, Walker didn't want her back here, not until she was able to shift into her true form. There has to be a reason for that. And that immortal fae arsehole knows far more about the demons and portals of Hell than we do. No matter if he's a lying and betraying piece of shit. If he thought her at risk here, then there was a reason." The fact that Walker had lied to me; stolen four years of my life, and then kept my mate imprisoned in his own lands didn't help my feelings about him, either.

Owen stood with me. I wanted to get back to Ember now that I knew he'd watch for Stone's return.

"I'll walk with you. I want to talk to Drake before I go back to my cabin with this little one."

I smiled, and nodded down at the still sleeping baby. "It suits you, you know?"

Owen smirked back. "Yeah? Who knew? This little dude deserves a shot at life. And if Selina will allow it, when all this mess is cleared up, I'd like to be around for him."

I smacked him on the back. "I hope it works out. So what's his name, you can't keep calling him 'it' or 'little dude' forever."

Owen chuckled as we walked. "Nah, his name is Devon."

"Devon?"

"Yeah, it's where I was born, right before my parents moved to London and sent me to that school where I met wankers like you."

"Selina let you name her child?" I stopped walking unable to contain my shock.

Owen even flushed a little, and ran his spare hand through his hair. "Well, I...er... I didn't really. I just came up with some ideas when she was talking about it a few days ago." He shrugged uncomfortably. "She said she liked it."

I just shook my head. "That's amazing. Naming a child? Damn." I couldn't help but feel a stab of jealousy that he had been given that kind of honour. I frowned, thinking back to my distant conversation with Ember about her season. She had been vague about when it was. My dick twitched, my fingers curled into fists and the hair on the back of my neck rose at the thought of being around her when that happened. I'd not let another male anywhere near her...

"You okay there boss?" Owen glanced at me, and I realised I had been staring at Devon.

"Yeah. Yeah, I'm good." I cleared my throat. "I'm going back to Ember now. I'll see you in the morning. Kawan and Lionel are guarding my door tonight, so they won't be there for the morning meeting, you'll have to update them after they've slept. I want all my brothers alert and rested for the attack." I glanced around the compound. "We'll address the others tomorrow, and make sure they all know their part."

"Sure thing. And don't worry about Stone, I'll send Myles to shadow him."

I nodded and left him, crunching through the fresh snow. I sped up at the thought of sliding into bed and pulling Ember's soft, warm body into mine.

"Hey, boss," Kawan greeted from outside my bedroom door.

"Hey, man." I exchanged a few words with Kawan and Lionel, who, as usual, looked highly amused when I edged towards the door, impatient to be with my mate again. I'd showered with her as soon as I'd got her back in our room, taking her gently again before I dried her exhausted body and helped her to the bed. She'd fallen asleep in my arms and I'd slid away not wanting to wake her. She needed to rest and recover. Yes, she had more power than most females, human or shifter, but now I was more, too. Prime was inhabited by the king of the Hell-beasts. That meant that I was now fae, wolf, Hell-beast and human, and since the king had been set free, I didn't feel tired, or cold, all I felt was an insatiable need to be with my mate. When she was near I felt whole, away from her there was a piece of me missing, and I hated it. I wondered if she felt the same.

"She's not woken," Lionel said.

I immediately stiffened and growled. He lifted his hands. "Sorry, Prime. All I meant was, I haven't heard her moving around. I haven't been in there," he said quickly, turning his gaze to the ground.

My fingers curled around the door handle and I tried not to rip it off its hinges at the thought of another male watching her sleep. I snarled at Lionel and opened the door, making sure I closed it behind me with a click rather than slamming it. I didn't want to wake Ember. Her scent hit me, and I was suddenly desperate to be near her. Within seconds, my clothes were gone. Naked, I slipped under the covers. Her warmth hit me, and I sighed, my tense muscles relaxing; even Prime relaxed. Ember murmured and backed straight into my body, sliding her hand down my hip to pull at my thighs as I wrapped a leg around her and drew her in close; close enough that we were touching everywhere. I inhaled deeply and kissed her head, enjoying the silky feel of her hair against my lips. I smiled as strands tickled my nose.

"You left me," she whispered into my arm, her breath warm against my skin. Her fingers reached down and curled possessively against my thigh as she pulled me closer. My heart squeezed.

"I did. You were tired, and needed to rest...I had to see Stone."

Her body tensed and she released a shaking breath against my skin. "Did you hurt him?"

I sighed, but couldn't help but smile at her worry for Stone. "No, not much."

The silence that followed left me wondering what she was thinking, until she moved her body into mine. "Good. He didn't deserve to be."

I kissed the back of her neck and tightened my hold on her, enjoying her closeness. I'd never wanted to hold a woman so close, now I couldn't imagine sleeping without her beside me. "I know. He has...issues with Shannon, and his past isn't helping."

She turned her head just a little to look at me through sleepy eyes. "His past?"

"Yes, he had a mate before and Doherty killed her. He's confused, or at least that's the only word I can use to describe what Prime feels from him. But it goes far deeper than that."

She kissed my arm. "I guessed he was messed up, but not why. Poor bugger. I hope they can work it out."

"Me too."

She tilted her head back again and I kissed her, thoroughly and gently. "Sleep, love. We both need it."

She snuggled deeper into my hold and soon her breathing was even and regular.

I closed my eyes and slid my hand around her body, resting my palm flat across her lower belly. I drifted off with my mate in my arms, thinking about what it would be like to feel her belly swell with my baby.

CHAPTER 19

onnor

ON MY ORDER, Owen had not attacked the prison since I had arrived, instead, I wanted intel. I'd sent small squads to observe. I would not put my people at risk until we were ready to annihilate the demon army squatting there.

Weak dawn light filtered into the communal cave. Even at this early hour there were people milling around.

Males loitered around in fighting gear. Other males sat waiting, chests naked, ready to shift to practice fighting in wolf form. The large cave was used for downtime, but some of the smaller back caves had been turned into inside training areas to avoid the harsh weather. The compound's on duty guards kept the peace. With an abundance of shifter males in a confined space, fights inevitably broke out.

Two women with babes in arms sat talking, another couple of women reading books from the small collection Drake had supplied. He'd thought of everything a community could need. He'd even brought enough necessities for the women and babies; they didn't want for anything. I felt a swell of pride that such a good male was fighting by my side. I had gained men I could trust in Lionel, Alex and Drake; even Shane, the leader of the old East pack from the prison, had proved a trustworthy male to have around.

I tried to ignore it most of the time, but there was a permanent ache inside my soul where Dagnar's and Reed's bonds had been. Reed was so close, yet I couldn't reach him, and every time I saw him, I was reminded of my impotence. The beast inside me growled, and a sudden memory consumed me. I stopped walking and clutched my head, closing my eyes.

"Hey, you okay?"

I nodded at Ember's question, sensing Lionel and Kawan move closer.

"I'm fine." My voice came out a deep growl, and I forced myself to stand tall, unwilling to show any kind of weakness to those around me. I looked at Lionel and Kawan, who still looked alert even after a night on guard duty. "Who's taking over for you?" I'd accepted long ago that, as Prime, I was a target, and even though I was more powerful than I'd ever been before, having someone watch my back and protect my mate was only sensible.

"Me." Alex sauntered up to Kawan's side—and morphed into a huge and mean looking Were. I smirked, trying to hide how much being hit with the memory of my brother, Dagnar, guarding the gates of Hell, had hurt. My beast only returned my more painful memories when he felt they were necessary. Hiding them helped me function, and I had no desire to fully remember the physical and emotional agony of the torture Berith had inflicted on me. I kept my voice strong. None of my brothers needed to know I'd seen D in Hell. But Alex's little show had given me an idea for our upcoming battle. "Fine. You're both dismissed. Go and get some sleep."

They nodded and said their farewells.

"Change back, you idiot, before someone shoots you." Ember smacked Alex's bicep.

His eyes grew comically wide, and he peered around as if someone might have a gun trained on him already. In seconds he was back.

"You really don't think sometimes, do you." I raised my brows and grinned at him.

"Well, at least it made you both smile. Besides, immortal. Remember?"

"True. Alex you're with me. I want to see my mother, but then I have something to discuss with you."

Stone's scent hit my nostrils. He walked up to Ember and my muscles tensed. "Ember? You want to train with me and Shannon?" His eyes met mine. His wolf was more settled today, and I sensed his genuine intentions. Relaxing, I gave him a nod that told him I was happy with that. Ember kissed my cheek oblivious to our silent exchange. She just looked relieved Stone wasn't a mass of bruised flesh and broken bones.

"Sure. I can teach you how to shift with clothes on."

Stone raised a brow. "You can teach us that?"

"Yep. So where's queen bitch?"

Stone raised his silver brows as they turned away. "Why do you call her that?" he asked.

Ember giggled, and in a move she did just to piss him off, she took Stone's arm in hers. He frowned down at her, but didn't pull away. "I'll tell you before she comes…"

Their voices faded and I turned back, spotting a dark haired woman sitting in the shadows at the back of the cave. *Shadow fae…* I took a deep breath and walked towards my mother.

Her shadowed face lifted as I approached, her dark eyes softening, though I didn't miss the way she clasped her hands nervously in her lap. A pang of remorse hit me. I had been so angry with this tall, elegant woman my whole life. When I was a baby up until the time she had left, she had never been there when my father beat me, and she had only rarely been around to hold me and comfort me. Then she had left and the beatings, or discipline as he'd called it, had only gotten worse. Now I understood how shit her life had always been. My father had likely locked her away, keeping us apart. All these years, I had blamed my mother for leaving when it was *he* who had lied to me.

Mother Wolf, he had *sold* her to a fucking demon general. I breathed in to calm my anger. She tensed as if sensing my emotion. But it wasn't directed at her, it was directed at the man who had given me life, and then destroyed it. As I'd gotten older, I'd worked out that the bastard who was my father wanted a successor, one who in his mind was strong enough to stand beside him. I hadn't planned my escape from him, but when he'd taken me on a business trip to London from our mountain home in France, I'd run. It had been a spur of the moment decision, an opportunity where the fates aligned to give me a few seconds freedom. He had just left the room and was talking to my guard, and the guard had left the door slightly ajar. Without thinking about it, I'd darted into the hall and jumped down the laundry shoot. I'd hit the bottom and broken an ankle, but the pain didn't stop me. I'd known I needed to get away before my father broke me completely.

There had been no way I could get out before his guards found me, and even if I did, he'd hunt me down by scent. I'd hobbled to the detergent store and poured the perfumed powder over my head, rubbing it in my skin and hair, and then chucked a load of sheets over the evidence on the floor before I shimmied back into the laundry shoot. It had only been minutes before they came searching. I hid in the darkness praying to the Mother that they would be fooled and think my faint scent in the shoot was from where I'd slid down it. They did. Even my father had told them to leave it, that I would have run. Yeah, he really hadn't known me, at all.

Everyday, I climbed out and poured that disgusting powder over my skin. Then ignoring the pain in my ankle and the burning on my skin and in my eyes, I climbed back in and used my good foot and my back to jam myself back in the shoot. At night when the staff had left and I was thirsty, I sneaked to the nearest tap to drink, but I didn't dare try and find food. I pushed the memory of my escape from my father away and concentrated on my mother.

"Hi," I said gently. She gave me a weak smile. "May I sit?" I indicated the chair opposite her.

She nodded, her attention not wavering from me.

Alex mumbled something about privacy and moved a respectable distance from us.

"How are you?" I asked, a little unsure where to start. I understood now why she had left, but I still had questions—about so many things.

"I am...fine."

I nodded, my fingers gripping the chair arms tight enough to make them creak. "I'm sorry about Zander. I know how much he loved you, and I know how much he sacrificed for me. I, umm, I don't know what to say about him." I couldn't help my next question. I couldn't stop it tumbling from my lips; it had been rattling around in my thoughts for so long. "Why did you leave me? Why did you go?"

She sighed, and looked down at her hands. "I had no choice. And my life may have been full of pain and abuse but I have two beautiful sons because of it. I love you, Connor, I always have, just as Zander loved you. From the moment I told him about you when he was a young boy, he loved you, he vowed to find you. When he found out from King L'nar that you had been recruited by him, too, Zander did everything in his power to keep you safe, while trying to protect me from Berith."

Regret dragged on my heart because of my treatment of Zander, but it seemed we had both done things we regretted. "I can see that now. I treated him badly."

"Yes, and he treated you and yours badly. Connor, none of this is your fault, or his. He never wanted to hurt you or your friends; but life is never simple."

I swallowed hard. "I know. I just wish he was here now. I had genuinely started to like him, and I would have loved to get to know him as my brother."

A small smile curved her mouth. "I'm glad. He always wanted to meet his big brother. Then when you arrived, King L'nar warned him not to tell you who he was."

My brows dipped. "Why?"

Her slim shoulders rose and fell. "So that you wouldn't lose your focus. Or that's what Zander thought. Walker, as you call him, even let Zander know where Ember was living. Somehow, Walker knew how much that girl meant to you. He made Zander leak the information of a powerful female shifter working for a banished fae, to Doherty. Walker even sent his son to make a deal with Doherty for the human girl who worked with your mate, to get her out of the way."

"Wait, so Doherty genuinely thought Ember was a killer? He didn't know who she really was?"

"No. Zander made sure she didn't reveal herself with her fire to that bastard. Zander loved you, and he wanted you to be happy. That's why he really brought Ember to you, it wasn't to threaten you, though that's why Walker wanted her there."

I rubbed my face. "Dammit, I thought Zander had brought her to the prison to use her against me; to make me work quicker."

She blinked slowly. "No. Zander kept her safe, and when he realised how much she meant to you, that she was your soul mate, he planned to get you both out as soon as he could."

Now it was my turn to close my eyes briefly. "Gods, his life was more of a prison than mine. He was trapped by Berith *and* Walker."

"He was, but he knew that the High King would give us a way out eventually, all of us. That's why he did what he did. Don't be angry with him. He had no choice."

"I'm not angry, not anymore. I just wish I'd known." I blew out a deep breath. "He sacrificed his life for me. I'm so sorry, Mother."

She gave me a watery smile. "It's not your fault. Zander is strong willed and powerful, you couldn't have stopped him, no one could, even if he'd told anyone his plans, which he didn't. But I do miss him. He was always my rock, my reason for living after I lost you. He took so much abuse from his father...as much as you did from yours." Her voice broke and she coughed, raising her eyes to mine.

She squeezed her eyes shut. "I owe you an explanation for disappearing from your life." She opened them, her face tight. "I am shadow fae, but I have no powers to speak of. Here in this human world, my magic is smothered, a wisp of shadow that is of no use to me." She blew out a long breath. "In Faerie, I was a princess, an heir to Orth's throne. As the eldest daughter, I was to take the crown when my parents were killed in battle with the Bogwart queen. My sister challenged me—and she won. I never was a good fighter." She peered down at her clasped hands, remorse clear in her voice.

"Not everyone can be," I said, trying to reassure her, my heart banging as I heard the first bit of information I ever had about my own mother and her past.

She gave me a weak smile. "My sister sold me to a trafficker who had a portal to this world. Your father bought me. He wanted to breed me, thinking his heir would be stronger and faster, even meaner, than any pure shifter offspring. That's why he pushed you so hard. And I couldn't stop him. When I tried..." Her breath hitched as she looked away from my face, the shadows slithering across her body as if trying to provide comfort. I had a feeling I didn't want to hear her next words, but I knew I needed to know the whole story. "Please, tell me what he did to you?"

"Whenever he was displeased with you, he would punish me for what he saw as your weaknesses. He would rape me at every opportunity, always trying to get me pregnant, believing more children with supernatural blood would give him the empire he needed to rule the world." She grimaced. "He kept other women in his house, all supernatural to some degree. When it became clear I would not conceive again, he beat me to unconsciousness. Once my bruises had faded, he sold me."

Pain squeezed my chest. It never occurred to me she had suffered at his hands as much as I had, but hearing it now definitely explained a lot. Leaning forward, I placed my large hand over both of hers. "I'm sorry, for everything you have been through. I vow, once this is over, wherever he is, I will hunt him down and make him pay for what he did to you."

"I don't care about him." A tear trailed down her cheek and she sniffed. "I'm sorry. Gods, those two words. They're so inadequate. I wanted to say them to you for so long, but I never could because it didn't matter if I was sorry, I could do nothing to help you. Your father, he was a violent, sadistic man."

I swallowed the ache in my throat. *I'm sorry.* I always thought those words were what I wanted to hear, only now I wasn't so sure. As a child, I'd had no awareness of what my mother had suffered. Now I did.

"I really do love you, as much as I love Zander. It killed me to never know what had happened to you. Zander loves you, too, Connor. He sacrificed his life to save yours, so he could give you a chance at a life with your mate. Please, promise me you will try and bring him back to us."

I knelt in front of my mother, looking straight into her eyes as I spoke. "Zander has saved my life so many times without ever telling me who he really is. He isn't innocent in his treatment of my brothers, or even me, but he protected the woman I love, and he helped us all to fight back against his father. So rest assured, I will never stop trying to get him back."

Tears filled her eyes and her bottom lip trembled. I opened my arms, but didn't move. This poor woman had been through so much abuse in her lifetime, I had no idea how she wasn't broken. So any physical contact, from this moment forward, would always be her choice, if I had any say in it. A sob broke from her chest and she leaned forward into my embrace. My eyes burned as I held her fragile frame close, giving what strength and comfort I could. "I will always take care of you, Mother. You will be safe." I whispered soft promises into her dark hair. "No one will ever hurt you again. Whatever you want to do, wherever you want to go, I will make it happen."

She took some hiccoughing deep breaths, and I wondered when the last time was that she had cried. "I want to stay with you. You are my son and I have missed out on so much of your life." Her breath hitched again. "I want to know everything about you and how you came to be who you are…"

I smiled and wiped away the tear that trailed down my cheek. I didn't care how it appeared, here in the shadows where we were alone, and I had a feeling that my mother would never judge me, or think me weak. "Then you'll stay with me." I pulled back and beckoned Alex closer. He looked from me to my mother, his brow furrowed in concern at her damp cheeks. I didn't try to cover the evidence of my emotion; I was more worried about my mother. "Alex would you fetch us both a warm drink, please, and some food for my mother?" With Zander gone for now, it was my responsibility to make sure she was cared for and brought back to health. I'm certain Alex understood that.

She wiped her eyes and smiled. "I could eat, yes, but not too much."

Alex smiled at her. "Sure, any requests? The bacon sandwiches are pretty good."

She smiled and nodded.

"Okay then, anything for you, boss?"

"Bacon sandwich sounds good. Thanks, man."

"No worries."

As he walked off to do my bidding, I returned to my chair and turned my body so that I could watch the room, but I kept hold of my mother's hand. She raised her brows a little. I shrugged. "Force of habit to watch for trouble. Now, where should we start getting to know each other?"

She smiled happily and squeezed my hand tighter. Warmth spread through my chest. I had an opportunity to purge my anger about the past, and I wasn't going to waste it.

"How about what your father told you when I left..."

I nodded and began to talk about my past, with the one person I thought I'd never see again.

CHAPTER 20

mber

SNOW FELL in quiet whispers around us. Despite my heavy boots and thick socks my feet were frozen. I hadn't wanted to call on Fire yet. She could easily warm me, but calling on her burned through my energy as if she used it for fuel. The snowsuit I had on over my fae armour kept my body warm though, for which I was more than grateful. I glanced around. Not everyone had as good equipment and clothing as me, but I guess that was a perk of knowing the guys that held all the power. Connor wouldn't let me freeze, and neither would Drake.

Connor laid beside me, his huge body hidden by the white and grey snowsuit he wore as well as the layer of snow that had settled on both of us. I knew he didn't need it for warmth, but more for camouflage—until he decided to change into Prime.

We were keeping watch on the main gate and compound from the tree line. Behind us the majority of our armed force hid in the snow, those who were in wolf form blending into the trees. The prison was not reachable by any roads and according to the data bases Drake and Charlie, who was working from Drake's offices in Texas, was totally off the SBI radar.

The Were patrols we'd hunted down on our way here had been quickly and quietly dispatched by our advance squad; taking prisoners wasn't possible.

Connor narrowed his eyes not needing any equipment to help him see the enemy that guarded the entrance to the prison. I swallowed hard, squashing my emotional link to him, just a little. Being party to all of his feelings was taking its toll on me. Yesterday I'd tried not to cry when I saw him walking hand in hand with his mother. It broke my heart that they'd lost so much time together.

A lone werewolf stalked into the prison gates carrying a weapon similar to all the other Were guards. He stalked across the empty runway and towards the main doors, not acknowledging any other Weres. No guards challenged him. It was enough that his imposing presence was covered in shifter blood and his eyes were consumed by the black of a demon. I held my breath as he disappeared in through the door.

"Easy," breathed Connor, a wave of reassurance filtering into me.

We had stayed far enough away that our scents wouldn't reach the mix of Weres and demon guards who were dressed in the armoured jumpsuits Zander had worn in the past.

Connor's brows dipped, and his gaze followed the line of the cleared runway.

"What is it?"

"The runway. There's no snow and very little ice. They've had, or are expecting, a plane to land."

He was right. "What does that mean?"

"Nothing. We carry on as planned."

Time ticked by. I shuffled in the snow. Damn, my whole body was a block of ice. Connor glanced at me and his gaze softened. "Call her. You have to be warm enough to fight."

"I'm fine," I said before he could say anything more. Him seeing me as weak was the last thing I wanted. He raised his brows, his mouth twitching before he turned his attention back to our enemy. "I would never think you weak," he murmured from the side of his mouth. My heart banged in my chest as we waited in the ever increasing shadows for Alex's signal.

Around us the forest was silent, the wolves looked more like mounds of snow than animals but none of them moved, neither did our 'soldiers'.

Our whole force had split well before we reached the prison. Two squads would cut the fences and enter the compound at the side and rear, and our main force would break through the main gates as soon as we got Connor's go ahead. The element of surprise would only help if Alex succeeded. If he didn't, then Drake would use his tech to block the camera feeds, but that would take far longer.

Until three days ago, the prison's cameras had been offline. That meant somebody in there knew how to fix stuff like that. I bit my lip, hoping the clear runway didn't mean Berith had received supernatural reinforcements.

My gaze drifted to the grey, snow filled sky before lowering back to the runway. Or that demons had been sent out in the world.

Connor's eyes narrowed, his vision honing in on the nearest camera. "The camera's are off, Alex has done it."

I tensed and called upon Mea and Fire. Both of my girls responded and warmth invaded my body, loosening my tight and cold muscles.

"First squads—go," Connor commanded, the tiny microphone fitted to his throat picking up his voice vibration. Within seconds the metal gates were blown wide and the first two squads rushed into the compound from where they'd cut the fencing. The Weres guarding the compound quickly turned their attention to them, leaving the bare minimum of guards near the main gates. I cringed as bullets from the remaining watchtower rained down on our forces. A lone demon fired indiscriminately. Answering gun fire echoed, but no matter how many bullets hit this demon, he wouldn't go down. We pretty much needed to annihilate their vessel to send a demon back to Hell.

Groaning at the stiffness in my joints, I swung my bow off my back, tuned out the noise of the attack and knocked an explosive arrow. I steadied my body and using Mea's help, honed my vision through the thick falling snow and in on the demon. Gripping the bow string lightly, I lifted my elbow a fraction more, judged the light wind, released a steady breath...and let the arrow fly. Under my coat, my tattoos burned, but they always did when I used the faerie bow. I shook the snow off my shoulders and held the bow loosely in my grip as the tower shattered in an explosion of metal and wood.

There was another almighty explosion from the back of the building that was the entrance to the underground prison. Flames and smoke billowed from a hole in the roof. I ran towards it, hoping Alex was safe. He'd blown the security centre to shit, as per Connor's plan. No bots or cameras would be working now.

Weres poured out of the entrance, sprinting over the snow towards the squads that fought their way across the prison compound.

"Move!" Connor's voice boomed out. His pupils sparked with deep red flames that I had never seen before, his voice full of power and authority. Not a single shifter or wolf hesitated. It was as if Connor had been keeping them all still, but now they were compelled to move. "Show no mercy!"

Connor launched himself into a run. I spinted after him as fast as my shorter legs would take me, not wanting him to leave me behind.

Wouldn't dream of leaving you, Firecracker. Come on, your cute little arse can run faster than that.

He must have tapped into his Hell-beast to talk to me as he was still running. I scowled at his back. I could hear him laughing at the finger I mentally gave him.

Now, now. Is that any way to behave towards your King? He huffed a chuckle, turned and waited for me to catch up, his eyes glowing.

King, my arse, I answered while flinging my bow up into my grip. The silver and blue dragon tattoo Walker had given me tingled again and a flash of blue energy lit the bow. I silently thanked the Winter King. The tattoo had always gifted me enough fae magic to increase the power of the fae weapons I used. I fired towards a Were who leapt from the top of a pile of storage boxes. An arrow thudded into the centre of his chest and he slammed onto his back in the snow. One arrow in the chest wouldn't normally stop a demon-fuelled monster but these weren't ordinary arrows, they were fae. He roared up at the snow filled sky, thrashing in what looked like agony as we ran past. I didn't stop, I just ducked when the arrow exploded. I had no arrows left.

Connor fired silver bullets into the chests of two black clad guards. They didn't go down.

"Ember!" He shouted a warning, but I was already moving. He hit his attacker straight in the visor with a fist that caved it in as if it was paper, then yanked his clawed hand out. From the corner of my eye I saw the guard collapse, but didn't stop to gawk at my mate's strength. The other guy was on me. I lunged sideways, ducked under his first punch, straightened and slammed my bow down on the back of his neck then caught him right at the vulnerable spot under his helmet. The solid blow made him stagger. I pulled a blade from my thigh sheath and drove it into the same spot. It had been a long time since I'd killed, but these were not people, not anymore, they were demons, and they deserved to go right back to Hell.

Moving swiftly, I severed the demon's spinal cord, then sprinted across the snowy ground until I stood beside Connor, our backs up against the wall of the small building. A group of wolves bounded up, their jaws bloodied and their eyes bright with the thrill of battle. The lead wolf snarled, but dipped his head at Connor.

"Brother," Connor greeted Kawan.

The wolves stood back. One man nodded at Connor, then kicked open the door, throwing in a grenade. "Down!"

Instinctively, I covered my ears to the blast. Before we could run in, the doors burst outwards and more Weres staggered out, shaking their heads and roaring. Bullets only slowed them down, but having their throats ripped out by a wolf stopped them; for now at least.

Connor placed a hand over my stomach, holding me back. "Let them go in first." He nodded to the waiting men and wolves. I snarled at him, but before I'd even completed my sound of defiance, he was standing over me, his palms planted firmly against the wall on either side of my head. His eyes flashed dangerously. "You are *mine* to keep safe. And it has taken all my willpower to allow you to be by my side, knowing you are hunted by Satan himself. Listen to me, so that I can keep you safe, or I will drag you kicking and screaming from this place if I have to."

My indignation left me, and my whole body leaned towards him. I kissed him softly, hoping he could feel my understanding. Despite his power and strength, I felt just the same way about his safety. But an alpha like him, a king of his kind, wouldn't accept that protection from me. "I will." I nodded to the door and gave him a crooked smile and a cheeky wink. "But let's go kill us some demons, huh? You can make me kick and scream later."

He gave me his bad boy grin, grabbed my hand and pushed me behind his bulk as we entered. The men were waiting for us. Kawan's eyes glowed in the flickering lights; lights that soon went out. Alex had reached the generator room. I prayed to the Mother to keep him safe.

Kawan padded ahead, leading the men through the dark corridors of the prison. We were all shifters, so seeing in the dark was possible as we crept over debris and stepped around dead and decaying bodies. The stench was horrendous, and my stomach heaved.

I squealed as something crashed down through the ceiling tiles. Eight big Weres landed among us, blocking escape from any direction. One landed behind me. I grinned over my shoulder, hung my bow in its holder and cracked my neck. Calling fire to my arms and hands, I stepped forward.

Connor roared and leapt in front of me.

"Hey!" I yelled, pissed that he'd stolen my kill.

He just turned his huge head back towards me and snarled, baring the biggest fangs I'd ever seen. *Okaaay...* It seemed Connor and Prime had embraced his Hell-beast and fae side, and rolled them into one terrifying creature. And I was *not* going to argue with him. His reflective red eyes flashed with bright blue and remained narrowed on me. He added a deeper growl. I rolled my eyes. "Fine!" I stepped back and let him take on the Were, though I kept my fire swirling around my hands.

Behind me snarls, growls and the pop of silenced weapons sounded. I glanced over my shoulder. Kawan and the others had overpowered the Were-wolves, one of the men with a sword decapitating them. Grimacing, I turned away from the gruesome sight and back to Connor. He stalked forward one step at a time. My brows dipped. The Were just stood frozen, ensnared in Connor's predatory, burning gaze, not even trying to move. The Were's eyes widened, and he dropped his gaze just as a sharp pungent scent hit me.

Fear.

Mea growled and Fire surged through me. Everyone behind us stilled and watched this formidable and dangerous creature approach the demon possessed werewolf. Connor had subdued it with nothing more than a look. He emitted a deep snarl and bared his fangs, drool dripping from his jaws. Goosebumps shivered over my skin. Connor would never hurt me, neither would Prime, but I wasn't sure how much of Connor's humanity was in the King of Weres right now.

I am still here...

I gasped at the voice in my head. It was Connor, with the deep growling quality of the King. *But this demon does not deserve my humanity or mercy. The only way to free these trapped souls without the Halo is to kill the demon and send it back to its master in Hell while I compel the shifter and human souls to find their afterlife.*

Connor slowly straightened his muscular and frightening body. Darkness swirled around him, following his every move.

The werewolf trembled as Connor loomed over him. At least eight feet tall, his head brushed the ceiling, his body swollen with unyielding muscle under a fine covering of ebony fur. Ensnaring his prey with his gaze, he growled and leaned forward. The Were dropped to its knees. It didn't take a genius to know Connor controlled the Were's movements. The demon might have taken control after the Were had died, but the shifter inside still responded without question to the superior power of its king.

Connor grabbed either side of the Were's head. *"I set you free. Go back to the Mother..."* He growled out, his voice demonic and low. I could hear the shock in the gasps from the others. No other shifter could speak that clearly in a half-shift, but I think we were all realising Connor was no longer just Prime, but far, far more. The sickening snap of bone made me flinch, but he was right, there was no choice. Even if we had the man-power to take prisoners, we couldn't use the Halo, not without ending up in Hell, and there was no way I'd lose Connor to that place ever again.

After lowering the body gently to the ground, Connor changed back, clothes and weapons intact. He stalked over to me and I was as ensnared by his beautiful sunset spangled blue eyes as that damned Were had been. I gulped at the raw power I felt caressing my skin. He looked down at the fire still burning around me and took hold of my hand in his before lifting his other and running his finger down my cheek. Without a word he took my mouth in a swift and hungry kiss. A low growl rumbled up through his chest. "Don't put yourself at risk when I'm here to protect you."

My mouth dropped open at his soft yet demanding words. Without giving me a chance to utter a suitably snippy response, he turned me around and pushed me gently towards the others. To a man, they all had a look of awe on their faces as their king strode past them and towards his brother. He glared at three male shifters. "You three bring up the rear. Nothing gets near her. Do you understand?" His eyes flared red, and they dropped their gazes, quick to respond.

"Yes, Sir," they all barked simultaneously.

I rolled my eyes, but my gaze went straight back to my lover's impressive behind as he stalked forward, strength in every movement of his body. Heat flashed through my body and I threw off my thick, goose down coat. A waste, but I couldn't fight in it. I blew air over my hot cheeks. Surely, it had never been this hot in this place before?

"You're here to shut that rift to Hell, Firecracker," Connor threw over his shoulder, waiting for me to catch up to him, like he couldn't stand to be too far away from me. "That doesn't mean putting yourself at risk beforehand, not if you don't need to." It was hard to be angry with him when he engulfed my small hand in his, and brought it to his lips, kissing it. I just nodded my head mutely. He was going to be so angry with me when I executed my plan, but there was no way I was going to stand back and let everyone fight for me.

"Good. Move out." At his order the others moved forward through the dark.

Connor released my hand but murmured, "Stay close to me, love. I'll destroy anything that seeks to harm you."

Swallowing hard, I met Kawan's wolf eyes. My brother, because that's what he was now that Connor had claimed me as his mate, shook his head and huffed before turning and trotting away in front. Yeah, he was right, there was no point in trying to argue with this hyper protective version of Connor. I was his mate as much as he was mine. Opening my mind to my mate I sensed his determination and focus to succeed, but also the underlying fear and love he carried for me. He glanced back again, and his gentle smile, which was so in contrast to his hard outer demeanor, knocked the breath from my lungs. He was stunning, especially in the midst of a damn battle, with his clothes moulded to his muscles and that defined ass…

A huge explosion rocked the reinforced concrete building and I slammed my hand against the wall to keep my balance as dust fell from the ceiling. I shook my head. Where in the hell did my head just go? Damn it, this was not the time to get distracted by my sexy-as-fuck mate.

The rumble stopped. I breathed a sigh of relief, thankful the building hadn't collapsed on our heads. Stone and the small force he had with him, including Jed and his men, were supposed to hunt down the other prisoners, as well as the women and babies. Connor didn't trust Jed and refused to have him with us.

After I fell over yet another rotting corpse, I swore under my breath. "Bugger this!" The ball of flame I pulled up lit the corridor with a kaleido-scope of coloured flames.

Connor glanced back at me.

I shrugged. "What? They know we're here. No point in tripping and breaking an ankle, now is there?"

Connor smirked. "None whatsoever."

Damn, maybe I should walk in front of him so I quit getting distracted by that yummy view... and I tripped again. Of course, he laughed. My cheeks flushed. Yeah, he was distracting. I wiped my sweaty palms on my thighs, refusing to look up as I felt amusement mixed with lust filter through our bond.

The walls vibrated again and there was another dull explosion. I met Connor's eyes and moved quickly to get closer to him. I knew I could fight, but that didn't mean I was comfortable with this kind of situation. Berith had been sent back to Hell, but none of us had any idea if he could get back through that rift. After all, he controlled it. Our biggest enemy could be waiting in the shadows for us, ready to pounce. I'd done a few months of my agent training programme, but I'd never completed it or done any fieldwork, and I'd freely admit, despite all my time dealing in Faerie, I was scared. My mate was as tough as they came, and there was no place I'd rather be than right beside him when the shit hit the fan.

Together we crept down dimly lit corridors. Even knowing we had a small army at our backs didn't help to calm my fear. Coming in here to rescue Connor was one thing; he had been my goal and my focus. My own safety had come second to saving his life, but this saving the world shit? I was walking towards a rift to Hell, for goodness sake! That thought had my gut twisting, so instead, I worried about my friends. "Is Stone still alive?"

"Yeah."

I sent a silent thanks to the Mother that Stone was unharmed. He was a pain in the arse, but he was also my friend and utterly loyal to Connor. I even sneaked in a little prayer for Shannon; yes, she had been my nemesis at school, but I kinda liked her now.

We turned a corner and the sight that greeted us coated my insides with ice.

CHAPTER 21

onnor

EMBER GULPED. I immediately moved closer to her, already assessing the heaving mass of Werewolves which blocked the corridor and our progress to the Hell rift. That rift needed closing, and Ember was the only way to do it. Berith knew that and had positioned his biggest Weres here to protect it. I wasn't stupid enough to think that these Weres were it, either. No, he'd have his squad of demon guards protecting the rift, right before he stepped from it to try and grab my mate. I growled and placed a hand gently on her arm, trying to get her to move behind me. I glanced down sideways at her, not surprised when she went to push my hand away.

"Connor, I can't hide behind you while you all fight." Her mouth set in a stubborn line before she gestured to the approaching Weres. "They need to be stopped. You know that as well as I do and we can't set their souls free, not even you can do that in a battle, there's no time, so we have to kill them."

My nostrils flared and I felt the agreement of the Hell-beast. "I know." There was also no way I was fighting anywhere but by my mate's side. Losing her simply was not an option. If she were to fall in battle, I would raze Hell itself to get her back. My beast growled, the sound echoing in my head in resounding agreement.

The others ran past me, all except the three who now protected Ember's back. The roars and clash of claws and teeth vibrated in my bones. I speared her hair with my hand, feeling the aggression and the scent of blood tug at my beast. Holding her gaze, I kissed her deeply, pushing my love against her to be sure she *knew*, grateful to feel it echoed in her. I refused to acknowledge the pain in my chest. We both knew this was it. We needed to fight to protect the whole Earth. It was imperative the rift be closed before Berith could send any more demons into our world.

Using every bit of my self-control I pulled away, nipping her bottom lip between mine as I uncurled my fingers from her shoulder. I didn't want to let her go. But I had to, and we both knew it.

Her lids opened, her gaze consumed with flames of indigo, violet, orange, yellow and jade. I swallowed hard, finding it almost impossible not to be consumed by the beauty of the immortal being that stared back at me.

"I'll see you on the other side, handsome." Her grin was full of sass. And before I could bend to the will of my wild side and grab her to me again, she winked and turned, sprinting into the mass of fighting bodies. I roared and shifted into my beast. He darted among the fighting bodies, trying to keep up with Ember. When she was opposite Kawan, who had his teeth embedded in the throat of a huge Were, Ember's whole body lit up with that same beautiful flame. She swirled the fire around her arms creating a fire bomb that heated the whole corridor.

The Weres saw us and ran.

Her light had only made the darkness deeper, so I sucked in the shadows and sent a thick cloud of darkness to engulf them. The nearest Were didn't stand a chance. I tore at his flesh before I thrust my clawed hand into his chest and ripped out his heart, commanding his wolf to leave and return to the Mother. His human soul floated into the ether, quickly taking its escape from the demon that screamed before being sucked back into Hell. Ember was right, I couldn't save all of their souls, but I could save some.

Ember unleashed her own brand of death upon the Weres. I wanted to dash towards her, but I had faith in her skill and power, so I forced myself to remain, and with a heavy heart killed my own kind, setting as many imprisoned souls free as I could. Too far away from me, my mate burned our enemy to dust. By the time I had killed each and every Were in the shadows, Ember had gone.

Shit! I howled an order, my heart pounding in my chest. *I can't lose her.* Twisting on my clawed hind foot, I lowered my head, dipped my shoulders forward, and ran.

The other wolves, Kawan included, bounded down the corridor by my side, leaping over the fallen and the chunks of debris that were littered everywhere. Doors hung off their hinges, the floating bots smashed to smithereens and scattered. Only the cameras remained intact, and now they were offline.

Barrelling through a set of half-closed doors, I knocked them clean off their hinges along with most of the wall. I skidded to a halt, breathing hard and strained my supernatural hearing, trying to *feel* Ember's position with the bond we shared. I roared. She was already below us—and moving fast.

I growled and tugged on Kawan's blood bond. He immediately halted his big body and peered over his shoulder at me. My eyes met his, and I told him what I wanted. He nodded. He'd sensed the army that waited for my mate, just the same as I did. *No mercy, brother,* I confirmed after our silent conversation. Kawan dipped his head.

"Go with him. All of you." None questioned my growled order, they couldn't fight the wave of compulsion their king sent their way. My men followed Ember down into the battle she was raging below, but I knew my Firecracker. Determination and fear continued to filter through from her. There would be no way for them to reach her that way. She would not allow it.

Once they had all left, I moved in the opposite direction. This corridor was one Zander had marched me down many times over the past four years. Loss squeezed my heart, but I thrust it away. I couldn't help my brother right now.

I prowled along, revelling in the cloak of shadows that clung to me like armour. As I approached the next corner, I shifted. In human form I could carry out my plan, as the King of Weres, it would not work. Pulling my gun from the holster on my thigh, I crept forward, trying to ignore the echo of Ember's emotions.

The scent of Weres hit my nostrils. I snarled but kept the aggression of my beast locked down. I stepped around the corner, and growled, loudly. The approaching group of seven Weres snarled right back. My lip curled away from my teeth, and I cocked my head. "Santa." The huge Were at the head of the group was even uglier than the day Ember had killed him. His injuries were gone but I would recognise him anywhere. And unlike the demon possessed Weres, whose souls were trapped in the Hell of their half-shifted bodies, his eyes were totally clear and not engulfed by a demon. No, Santa had sold his soul to the devil and become a beast of Hell willingly. He was now a servant of Satan; his human and shifter souls had been given willingly to his new master.

He gave a dark chuckle. I grinned right back, fighting my instincts to shift and kill.

Fallen concrete crunched behind me. I didn't turn, sensing the three Weres that now stalked me. Santa hesitated when I shot the Weres on either side of him in the forehead. Their heads jerked back and they fell, thudding heavily to the floor.

Santa Cruz snarled, his lip curling back to reveal yellowed fangs, his eyes glowing with a ring of fire.

"You sold out, Santa. Not a surprise from a piece of shit like you."

I turned and shot the Weres behind me, but my bullets missed. My eyes widened at the speed these Weres moved. And then it dawned on me. They were all servants of Satan—by choice. Some in this shit hole of a prison really had deserved to be there, and it seemed they were the ones who had jumped at the chance of an eternity creating chaos and pain.

I heard the unmistakable sound of a blade being drawn. I spun and dipped sideways, but it was too late. The blade hit me in the shoulder.

"Fuck!" I roared as they attacked from both sides. I shot my weapon over and over, but they moved too quickly. My silver bullets hit them in their torso, which didn't even slow them down.

My beast thrashed to burst free and rip our enemy apart but I held him back. Ember had run from me. I knew her well enough to realise she had done it to try and keep me and our shifters away from the rift—to protect us; and the only way to reach her was in my human form, so I hid my true power and fought as a man, kicking my nearest attacker in the chest before slamming my fist into another, followed by my elbow. Over and over I used my body to inflict damage, pulling on enough power to grow my claws and rip into their chests. I staggered when a blow came to the back of my head. Shaking off the pain and fogginess, I turned and let loose a barrage of punches, but each move I made only made me bleed more. I wanted to rip the blade from my shoulder but I had no time. Another blow to my head sent me to my knees. I roared as my attacker slammed something into my skull. Pain exploded and bright lights flashed across my vision. My beast clawed at my insides, trying his best to escape, but still I held him back. I didn't let him out even when my head was whacked again and a rivulet of warm sticky blood dripped down my neck, soaking into my t-shirt.

I swayed on my knees, following Santa's progress as he prowled closer. With a snarl he lifted his foot and slammed his heel into the knife blade. Agony exploded through my chest and arm. I roared and it took everything in me not to shift. I landed on my back, heaving breaths that became harder and harder to take. I swallowed down the pain as my body tried to heal around the knife blade. Prime snarled and pushed his will against mine, but I was the alpha, the one in command of our band of souls; no matter how powerful he, or the Hell-beast was, it was my body and my mind that controlled them all.

Santa loomed over me. I snarled up at his burning eyes, fighting my need to rip his head off. He huffed a laugh and in a swift and vicious move, kicked me in the head. This time I didn't fight the wave of darkness that washed over me.

mber

MY HEART BEAT painfully under my ribs. Oh, gods! I'd left my mate to come and fight a small army of demons—alone. My hands trembled, but there was no way I'd put Connor or anyone else in danger if I could help it. Carefully, I pushed my shoulder into the swing doors at the bottom of the stairwell. It swung open with a creak. I cursed. No way they didn't hear that. The corridor beyond was dark. I stepped through and shut the doors. The breath I blew out didn't do much to calm my nerves. Light flared around me as I sealed the doors with a blast of heat.

I tilted my head. People and wolves rushed down the stairs. *Sorry, guys...* I jumped back when Kawan leapt at the doors, rattling them with his big body.

"Please stop." I lifted my eyes and met Kawan's as he howled at me. "I don't want you hurt," I whispered. He cocked his head, narrowed his eyes and launched himself at the door again. "I'm sorry," I said, and turned away. They'd leave when they realised there was no getting through those doors.

Connor wasn't with them. My belly squeezed as I pictured my mate's stunning face—and how angry he'd be with me right now. Well, I made a vow to protect what was mine too, especially those I loved. And, gods, I loved him so much it hurt. Doherty had taken my parents from me. He had taken Lyss. He'd ruined Rawson. And then, because that wasn't enough, he'd taken Connor from me. Four fucking years I believed my mate dead. And just when

I thought I finally had Connor back, Berith took him from me. Never again—I'd make sure of that.

I curled my fingers into fists before stretching them out, claws pushing through my nails. Yeah, I was out for blood and no one would stop me from burning this evil place and everything in it to ash.

Taking a breath, I turned to face my enemies. The Weres stood eerily still and silent. Behind them were the guards. Fire pushed against my control, and beads of sweat ran from under my flaming hair. I cracked my neck, certain now that no matter his power, I had been right to keep Connor away from here. I could feel the evil permeating the air. Connor was trapped here before. I couldn't chance it. He was my world. He had been from the moment I stared into his nordic blue eyes when I was a girl. I wouldn't survive losing him again.

Berith's voice echoed in the dark hallway. "So nice to see you again, *Firecracker*. I knew you'd come. It's like trying to keep a bee away from the nectar it craves. You think you've come here to destroy my little doorway to Hell, but in truth Hell calls to you, to your phoenix. The power from my world, where you belong, feeds your own. That beautiful creature made of the sun's hottest rays and Hell's most savage flames, craves to be freed, and you cannot deny her forever."

"Bullshit," I snapped, my voice steady despite the growing fear that he was right. Fire was thrashing against me and I was beginning to think I might lose control of her. "My phoenix does not belong to Hell, or to you; she's mine. And yeah, I am here to destroy *you*, not just your doorway."

"We shall see." His tone was smug and full of a knowledge that sent goosebumps across my skin. "But even if you succeed, it will not stop the demons who are now free in this world, nor will it seal the other rifts on this mortal plane. You are too late to prevent the war that is coming. My master will bring it to its knees, and rain destruction down upon these pathetic mortals who believe their race invincible. This world, and all of its souls will be his before he moves onto the next. All we need is your firebird back in her rightful place, chained to the gates of Hell so that once again my lord can bring Hell to Earth; then you, little wolf, will belong to me. Are you ready to be fucked by a true beast? One who hasn't been weakened by his dependence on a mortal for his existence?"

My heart missed a few beats at his demonic chuckle before racing along at a hundred miles an hour. No way was I going to become his fuck toy while my phoenix opened the gates of Hell. But destroying the rift was my goal. I wouldn't run from him, no matter how powerful he was. Not willing to show him my fear, I smirked and without hesitation sent a wall of flames hurtling into the first wave of Weres that launched themselves towards me.

My chest ached. The poor souls trapped inside the Weres screamed as they were sent back to Hell. They'd been condemned—by me.

Berith chuckled. "I can taste your pain, she-wolf. Satan's balls, I'm looking forward to drinking your anguish and fear, girl. Bring her to me," he barked out in a voice no longer remotely human. It was all demon. "So long as her heart still beats when she kneels at my feet, you can do as much damage to that mortal body as you wish." The eyes of his guards flashed a deep, hungry red. I swallowed hard and watched them fan out in a precise, coordinated fashion.

These were not only demons, but highly trained soldiers, and with the strength and healing capabilities of a demon, stopping them would be damn hard. "Shit!" My whispered curse was heard by no one else. Without wasting any more time, my enemy shot a barrage of silver bullets towards me. I threw out a shield and winced everytime one of them slammed into my flaming wall of protection. It was like being stung by a swarm of bees.

Behind me the doors rattled. The seal I'd burned on the doors still kept my friends out and away from danger. I wouldn't let them get hurt trying to protect me, not even if it meant me ending up as Satan's prisoner.

Taking a breath and hoping that my energy held out, I pushed more energy into my flames. The stunning tattoo that Walker had marked me with heated beneath my fae armour, even Som's roses seemed to burn. With a mere thought, I directed that fae power to merge with Fire's.

I burned a hole in the chests of the first three. Their bodies fell to the ground but they started to regenerate immediately. Holy Mother Wolf, they had to be powerful to regenerate so quickly! I kicked one in the face on the way past and jumped over another before landing and ducking underneath the next Were's attack. I grinned and shot fire into the closest guard's face, incinerating his head. His body thudded to the ground, his gun clattering to the floor.

Regenerate from that, sucker!

Again and again, I attacked, holding my shield against their bullets. My limbs started to shake, but I ignored my tired body, and kept fighting, trying to conserve my energy. My heart clenched as I realised this was a coordinated attack. They were deliberately weakening me. Damn, I should have known better!

I attacked a guard on my left, but stupidly left myself vulnerable. A fist smashed into my jaw from the right. It rocked me, but I didn't stop, merely lit my body on fire and spun, slamming my heel into one guard's chest before I drove the fae dagger I held through his chest plate. It was almost ridiculous how easily that fae weapon penetrated their body armour.

I fought, kicking, punching, stabbing and incinerating my way down the corridor until the door to the warden's office came into view through the darkness. Ash and blood covered me; my own and my enemies. My breath came in heavy pants and my limbs shook, but I couldn't stop. I had to get into that room. No more demons would be released into this world from this evil place. To conserve my energy, I let my shield go and concentrated on fighting.

My fist slammed into another guard. His grunt was loud as I followed that strike with an elbow to his abdomen, right below his armour plate. His knees buckled—but before I could get in another strike, agony sliced along my upper back. I screamed, but didn't stop fighting. Twisting on my knees, I drove an uppercut into my attacker's groin. He cried out but swung the knife blade back cutting me across the top on my chest.

Motherfucker!

I screamed, but neither were fatal wounds. I silently thanked Walker for his fae armour. If I'd been wearing normal clothes I'd have been sliced and diced by now. I shrugged, death wouldn't stop me, but it would slow me down, and I didn't want Fire taking any of these poisonous demon souls as payment. A shudder rippled through me. That was one reason not to die here. Despite my immortality and kickass suit, my wounds were debilitating enough to slow me down and make Fire's power, and my wolf's strength, falter.

There were only three demon guards left now, but I had to achieve my goal before I passed out and—I swallowed hard—they dragged me to Hell. Fear gripped my chest. It hadn't really occurred to me before that I would fail —mainly because I hadn't let it. Jeez, I'm such a fool. I had left my friends, and even my mate behind thinking, in my arrogance, that I could just incinerate my enemy and destroy the rift with no help at all. Now I wasn't so sure. My shifter abilities were enhanced by Fire, but I was fading fast. Blood soaked into my clothes, saturating the fae armour.

I reached out trying to find my bond with Connor but all I found was darkness. It killed me that I couldn't feel him, but it had been my choice to leave him behind. Ice coated my stomach. He couldn't be hurt—or worse. No. He was too strong...

I squashed that useless worry, staggered up off my knees and leaned against the wall for support. Ignoring the burning pain from Walker's tattoo, I slammed my foot backwards into the chest of a guard. I couldn't see what happened to him; the one in front had a vicious looking blade in his gloved hand that made my blood run cold. Gritting my teeth, I dodged sideways, spun, whipped my empty bow off my shoulder and slammed it into his helmet. It caved in and he staggered sideways. I grinned. "Yeah, take that you pissant demon!" Panting hard, I thrust a small tendril of flame forward. It engulfed his gloved hand and he yelled, dropping his weapon. In a move I practiced over and over with B'nar, I flicked the empty bow into my grip and rammed the weapon up through his throat. I threw it aside and its fae magic ebbed away.

A quick glance up showed me there was one guard left, but there was no way I could destroy a portal to Hell with no energy left, so I pulled Fire back. I swooped down and picked up the knife I had dropped and sprinted towards my remaining enemy. Thanking Walker, B'nar and Lance for their arse-kickings and relentless training regimen, I built up speed and drove myself a few steps up and along the wall before I pushed off and somersaulted over the demon's head, grabbing his chin. Landing, I yanked his head to the side and drove the knife into his throat, slicing sideways.

"Go back to Hell, you evil bastard," I muttered and let his corpse fall to the floor.

My legs shook as I skidded to a halt in front of the door to the warden's lair. Breathing heavily, I reached out and pushed the door open. A blast of heat hit me. Fire flared to life, once again pushing against the confines of my body.

Ignoring her fight to burn me from the inside out, I inched forward, keeping an eye on the shadows, my heart racing.

The carved fireplace was as beautiful as it was hideous. Huge Weres snarled out from its carved surrounding. Some of them had their muscled arms wrapped around beautiful women, their mouths and bodies locked in sexual acts, others dragged screaming souls back into the flames that awaited them.

Heat from the flames reached my fae suit. Despite its technology and ability to deflect blades and bullets, it began to burn. I cocked my head and looked down. Even as my skin was revealed by the burning material, I felt no pain. Because I didn't burn, I never had, not since Fire had chosen me.

"Beautiful. Isn't it?" said a smooth, unnervingly hypnotic voice behind me.

I spun, my speed hampered by the thick pile carpet.

Berith stepped out of the shadows. My jaw dropped. This wasn't just the warden standing in front of me. This was a stunning demon general, one made for the first hierarchy of Hell, a being dedicated to stirring up murder and unrest. His dark eyes flickered, reflecting the flames of the underworld that burned in the rift. His mouth tilted into a smirk when I stood naked in front of him. I didn't bother summoning clothes, it would take too much energy.

"Hmm, stunning. I will enjoy playing with you…"

My nostrils flared in anger. "I'm not here to play."

He raised a dark brow, his smile growing, evil oozing from his every pore. "Oh, but you will agree to play with me." The snap of his fingers echoed through the room and out into the corridor. I tensed. It was a signal. There was a commotion coming from the corridor and a group of Weres entered the room dragging a slack body. His scent hit me right in my chest and my heart stopped beating. Pain lanced me and I couldn't look away from Connor's broken body. "Oh, Mother, what did you do? You bastard!" I panted, so shocked at seeing my mate, the King of his kind, broken and bleeding, that I couldn't tear my gaze off him.

Berith chuckled. "It seems he wasn't as strong as he—or you—thought. Trying to protect you only made it easier for us to catch him. You see, my soldiers were given the chance to be reborn stronger and faster, and they took it. He couldn't beat them because he has that sliver of humanity in his soul. No matter that he used to be King of the Hell-beasts. He is now king of nothing! He will die here today. You will become mine, and when you have burned the gates of Hell to the ground, we are going to have an eternity to play..."

I didn't wait for any more of his fucking noise. I called Fire to me and let her burst from my skin. She no longer wanted to reach for that powerful flame, no, she wanted to become it. She felt my anger and my grief, and she fed upon it. My gaze landed on Connor's swollen face. He'd been beaten until his eyes had disappeared in their sockets, his nose broken and his lips split. I glared at the Were who stood over him.

"You..." My voice was little more than a growl.

Santa smiled, his elongated mouth stretching to reveal his fangs. He might be a Were now, but his eyes were the same, full of evil.

He pulled his foot back and slammed it into Connor's stomach. I screeched in anger and instinctively reached for the flames behind me. As I called them, they flickered over my skin feeding my power. Fire engulfed me and my vision changed. The world became a beautiful aura of purples, greens, blues, reds and golds. My vision narrowed. Santa Cruz pulled his leg back to kick my mate again.

But Connor snarled and caught his foot. Jumping to his feet, Connor flicked Santa backwards. "Don't change, Ember! Fight as you are!"

A sob lodged in my throat at the sight of my mate jumping to his feet. I didn't understand what had happened, but he was on his feet and fighting, despite his injuries. In an unbelievably swift move he leapt in the air. A huge roar escaped his lungs causing the walls to rattle. By the time he landed, he had shifted into the King. He slammed his weight down into the floor, and even Santa had the brains to look scared of what Connor had become.

Power rolled off my mate as he glared at the Weres.

"End him! I will take the girl." The warden grinned at me. "You might want to ignore your lover and shift, my dear." He cracked his neck—and shifted.

"Shit!" I sucked the flames from the fire into my body and sent them barrelling at Berith. The tough skinned demon just shook it off and roared.

Damn, of course Hellfire can't hurt him.

I turned and leapt over the couch. Near the door Connor was ploughing through the Weres. He had Santa by the neck and with one move separated his head from his body. I ignored the gruesome sight, Santa was a bastard of the highest order and he deserved an eternity in Hell. Connor certainly would never save his soul.

I screamed as a huge hand grabbed my leg mid jump. I slammed down into the couch face first, trying to kick Berith's hold off my ankle. He merely laughed at my pathetic efforts. "Connor!" I screamed as Berith dragged me towards the fireplace. "Noooo!" On my stomach and being dragged backwards I couldn't see to attack him with fire. I couldn't reach him. Damn it! I wouldn't lose this easily.

I had no other way out of this. I called on Fire. Closing my eyes, I went limp and allowed Berith to drag me into the rift. I opened my eyes and stared at my mate. His burning eyes widened as the flames engulfed me. His roar of pain tore at my soul, but there was nothing I could do as Berith pulled me closer to my destiny.

"Ember!" Connor's bellow faded as a hot vortex of air swallowed me.

I closed my eyes and smiled.

Now.

And I let my phoenix fly.

CHAPTER 23

onnor

PAIN TORE at my soul as my mate was dragged from this world into the depths
of Hell.

"Ember!"

A clawed hand thrust into my back. I barely felt the pain, the agony of
losing my soulmate was far worse. I twisted and grabbed the Were's arm,
yanking his claws from my flesh. Before I could kill the evil fucker, a wolf
snarled and landed on his back ripping his neck out.

Shannon snarled at me before she changed back, standing naked as the day
she was born in front of me.

Stone made quick work of the remaining Were and changed too. "What
the Motherfucking Hell happened?" he snapped. "Why did Ember lock Kawan
and the others out? I had to unbind the doors with magic to get in here."

"She wanted to stop the others from getting hurt. I should have known
she'd never let them, or me, near Berith! Dammit, Ember!" I bellowed. I didn't
need my mate to keep me safe, I was the godsdamned King of Shifters, a beast
born in the fires of Hell, and I would not leave her there...

I looked between Stone and Shannon. "Where are the others?"

"I sent them to help Owen. The warden isn't planning on letting any of us
out of here. He had an army of Weres and demons waiting deeper in the
forest. They attacked while we were down here. Owen was nearly overrun."

He ran a big hand through his mussed silver hair, his eyes glowing. "We were played, Connor. He knew we'd come…"

"Yeah? Well, get back up there and help our pack. They need you more than I do." I pulled on my inner beast, feeding from his fury. I grew even taller, even more monstrous. I stomped over to the fire, peering into the flames before throwing my head back. I released a howl that echoed down through the rift into Hell itself. An answering roar echoed back at me.

That's right, you fucker. I'm coming for my girl…

"Hey! Where are you going?"

I looked back at Stone's grim face. My voice was nothing but a low growl, my words distorted by my long jaw and teeth. "I'm going to get my mate. Leave. Now. Or you'll die, because when I've destroyed Berith, I'm going to destroy this place."

Stone nodded once and looked down at Shannon. "Shift. Now."

For once Shannon didn't argue. She shifted and bounded from the room with Stone close behind her. There was a stuttering sound. Slowly, I twisted back to the fireplace and for the first time ever I saw the flames die. I huffed out a breath, peering into the dark abyss beyond. I ducked my head and shoulders and stepped over the grate. I had no idea what the flames going out meant, but it didn't matter, all that mattered was finding Ember. Berith would never get her soul, she was mine!

"Mine!" I roared down into the rift.

One step in and I saw the flicker of flames in the distant darkness. Before I could process what the light was, it was almost on me. A rush of hot stinking air hit me, making me stagger backwards.

Run!

Ember's voice was in my head. I didn't question it. I turned and ran. I leapt over the couch and sprinted for the door, skidding out into the hallway. The explosion of heat and flames knocked me off my feet. Bricks and rubble fell, pinning me to the floor as the breath was crushed from my lungs. My ears rang, but there was one thing for sure, Ember needed me. I shoved the heavy debris from my back and pushed to my feet. The corridor was alight with the most stunning flames I'd ever seen, and right in its centre, as if she was protecting me, was Ember. A deep and ominous rumble came from inside the warden's room.

Shit…

"Ember! Let's go…"

She looked back over her shoulder at me, and shook her head. "No, not this time. You have to go. The pack needs you. They are losing. Please, go and save our friends, our brothers." She smiled sadly. "This is my time to fight for you. Please…go…" Her pleading hurt my chest, but I shook my head.

"Connor! Leave! Now!" It was pretty much the order I'd given Stone and

Shannon, which by the growl I heard behind me, knew they hadn't followed either. I looked at my brother, who shifted.

"She's right, brother, we need to leave. I can feel him coming…and with the army already up there on the surface, we are going to lose if you get yourself killed now."

Stone was right, something was coming. "Oh shit, Ember destroyed the rift, but Berith has followed her back…"

I launched into a run towards my mate, but before I could reach her, the biggest demon I'd ever seen barrelled through the walls and grabbed her. Unfurling red leathery wings it propelled them upwards. On instinct, I leapt and grabbed onto its tail. I knew from past experience that Berith's skin was too hard for me to dig my claws in, so I gripped on with my claws and my teeth as he blasted through the floors of the prison like they were paper. Up he went, taking my soulmate with him. Berith howled and tried to fling me off, but I wouldn't let go.

My roar, as he launched up through the concrete and into the snow filled air, was loud enough my brothers all roared back. Below us, the ground swarmed with Weres and guards. It was hard to tell who was one of my pack and who was the enemy. No matter Drake's new firepower, we were outnumbered.

Grunting with effort, I clawed my way up Berith's back. He tried twisting and diving, but could not shake me loose.

Clutched in his claws, Ember glowed like a sun, except no matter how much fire she blasted out, it didn't harm him. I snarled. No, it would take a beast to end a beast.

Ember, set her free…Fly, my heart. Go and help Owen…Get those women and babies to safety.

Her stunning eyes found mine, and she blinked.

You can do it. You can control her. I know you can.

The smile she gave me, coupled with the warmth of her love, infused me with strength.

Berith roared as my Firecracker shifted into the most beautiful creature I'd ever seen. A large bird of fire, her flames glowing, slipped from his grasp, and soared away. I swallowed down the lump in my throat and watched her swoop through the air, turn an elegant loop and drop towards the battle below. Like the magical creature she was, Ember left a trail of shimmering flames in her wake.

With my mate safely out of Berith's grasp, I let loose a bellow and speared my claws into the softer skin I'd felt near Berith's wings. Hellfire couldn't end this creature, but beheading it would send it right back to Hell where it belonged. First, I needed it on the ground. I yanked on the bond to my brothers, and their answering howls echoed through the air.

Berith bellowed, rolling in the air, but he couldn't dislodge me. Over and over, I speared his skin. Dripping with his blood, I reached into the hole I'd made and curled my fist around the ligaments of his wings, ripping them from his flesh. He screamed and rolled, no longer able to use that wing.

We fell fast. Before he could land on me and end my life, I jumped. Branches tore at my skin as I fell to the forest floor, landing in the snow with a thud. By the time Berith crashed into the ground about twenty feet away, I was on my feet and running with my brothers by my side. Kawan was there first. He launched himself onto Berith's neck tearing at the skin, but he left only scratches. Stone shifted, becoming fae just before he got to the demon. His eyes glowed purple and glowing shackles encircled Berith's wrists. Stone grunted as he yanked the demon's arms above his head. "Go! I don't know how long I can hold him."

Owen and I ran forward. Together we ripped at the skin on Berith's neck as he twisted and fought. His tremendous strength was too much for Stone's magic. He broke free and tossed Owen sideways, sending my brother crashing through the trees.

Around us, the wind picked up, sending snow into the air. Before Berith could get up, I thrust my claws into the shallow cuts we'd made on his skin. Kawan joined me, but once again Berith threw us aside. Stone yelled and thrust more magic around Berith's wrists.

From out of the swirling snow, a cord of ice blue appeared and wrapped around Berith's neck. The whoosh of arrows sounded at the same time the scent of a new army hit me. I didn't pause to look, but launched myself at Berith once again. Stone yanked at Berith's arms at the same time as slivers of ice wound up and around Berith's legs.

I grinned at the white haired fae who stood at my side.

"Walker."

"Hell-beast."

"King Hell-beast to you."

Walker raised a brow. "Then it's King L'nar Voltair, to you."

"Hmm? Son of Voltair."

"That's right. Not Walker..." His white brows dipped to the bridge of his nose. "I never did understand that name you gave me."

My lips pulled back from my large teeth. In this monstrous form, my smile looked like anything but. "Nevermind, you can't be perfect."

"Debatable, Son. Now let's send this creature back to Hell where it belongs."

Walker lifted a hand and ice shards appeared from the air. They speared the thick skin of Berith's chest as easily as stabbing a knife through butter. Berith's yell was laced with agony and the Hell-beast in me loved it. The ground vibrated as he collapsed back. I held my hand up for my brothers to stand fast. This was my kill.

"Where's your son?" I asked, wondering about the fae who had helped my mate become the fighter she was, because no matter how hard I had trained her, her fighting technique and control of Fire was better than it had ever been.

"B'nar is with Ember. She can win alone, but without some help, she may kill those she doesn't wish to harm. She doesn't yet know how to control that which fate gave her."

I grunted. "Then let's finish this. I want to be by her side again."

Walker met my gaze. "I know. So let your beast take control. Let go of your humanity, then you end this creature."

My nostrils flared. Walker was right. My human side was scared that if I let myself be consumed by the power of my beasts, I would be lost to violence and bloodlust.

"She will always call you back. You cannot be lost with your mate to guide you home."

For a moment I saw sadness in his eyes, but it was soon replaced with that ice blue, remorseless stare.

Giving in to the surge of anger and hatred inside me, I drove my teeth into the thick hide of Berith's neck. The demon howled, the sound gurgling until he fell silent. Blood coated my tongue feeding the primal side of my beasts. I roared in triumph as I ripped at his flesh until his head fell from his shoulders.

Walker stood and watched silently. When I turned, blood dripping from my jaws and body, he raised a pristine silver sword covered in fae runes. The carvings were so intricate my eyes couldn't take them all in. "Stand back, Son. Time to send this demon back to Hell." He lithely jumped up on Berith's chest, avoiding the gore and mess I'd created, and drove that blade down through Berith's heart. Keeping both of his hands wrapped around the handle he chanted in fae. I didn't understand the words, but I did understand what he was doing. Berith was immune to fire, but he wasn't immune to ice. Walker's magic began to spread. He yanked the sword from Berith's chest and jumped down. Ice consumed Berith's massive body. I stood to my greatest height, curled my massive claws into fists and bellowed as I slammed them down on Berith's frozen chest. The demon exploded into smithereens.

I sensed my brothers standing by my side, there to back me up, as always. I sent them a wave of gratitude, but my attention was ripped from Berith's remains as an explosion ripped through the air. Above the treeline, I saw Ember blaze across the snow laden sky in a trail of fire. Even from this distance I sensed her exhaustion as I saw her spiral from the sky towards the ground. Without another word, I ran.

CHAPTER 24

mber

LETTING Connor go was the hardest thing I'd ever done. But he was right. I couldn't help end Berith. I'd been wrong, so wrong. I'd destroyed the portal, but Berith had shifted into his true form and flown ahead of my destructive wave, following me out of the rift before it was sealed.

I let Fire free. She consumed me and I dropped from Berith's grasp, soaring away from my mate.

Spying Owen below, cornered near the fence by a group of four Weres, I gathered my energy, spread my wings and flew towards him. It was the weirdest feeling, to spiral towards the ground and not be afraid. I might not know how to fly, but my phoenix—who was older than time—did. I let her take control, telling her what we needed to do.

She landed, bigger than the Weres themselves. They turned to face us. As they growled Fire cocked her head—and incinerated them.

Owen shifted back. "Ember! Connor needs me."

I peered at the metal, razor-topped fence. Spreading my wings, Fire guided me closer. Swiping my wing across it melted the metal to nothing. Owen shifted mid-leap and raced into the forest as Connor fell from Berith's back, crashing down into the trees. I let loose a screech, but Mea grounded me. She let me feel our bond with him, he was still alive. I launched upwards and spun in the air. All around, Weres attacked my pack.

616

Huddled near the prison door was a group of naked women, holding their babies close. Jed and his men fought alongside Drake to protect the women, but even as I twisted in the air to get a better line of sight, two fell, leaving only three men fighting five guards. Drake's gun stopped firing. He changed mid leap and landed on a guard. I sent out a screech.

Drake looked up. Understanding, he leaped, knocking Jed sideways, out of reach of my fire, as I burned their enemy then launched skyward, leaving a trail in my wake. I swept my wings harder, rising in the sky. It was so cold up here. I sensed Fire's strength ebbing, but there were still so many more of the enemy below. I circled to the back of the prison where small pockets of shifters tried to hold their own against the Weres.

Again and again I burned them.

I pushed against the sudden wind. Below me a portal glowed and even as I watched, an army of blue and silver clad fae ran forward.

Walker!

As if hearing me, Walker raised his face. He merely nodded, and ran with a small force into the forest—to Connor. I felt a tear fall from my eye. It evaporated in Fire's heat...

B'nar stepped from the portal. He raised his hand to me before he dropped his attention to the guards who ran towards him and his men. He lifted his weapon, and they rapid-fired into the demons. I knew silver bullets couldn't kill the demons or Weres, but as the demons fell, one after the other, it became clear that fae magic could end them.

I sagged, feeling exhaustion hit me like a freight train. I glanced down, my fire flickering. Below me, the tide had turned, and with the help of the fae, we were winning. I smiled.

It's okay, my beauty, you can rest now, I told Fire. Mea whined. I chuckled, agreeing with my wolf that it would have been better to say that when I was on the ground.

Icy air fanned my cheeks as I fell. In the distance I heard my name called.

Connor. He was alive...

I smiled and let my mind close down.

CHAPTER 25

*E*mber

WARMTH—AND beeping, surrounded me. I shook my head to get rid of the noise...and groaned. Shit, who put a hammer inside my skull?

"Hey, hey, lie still, sweetness. You're okay."

"Connor?" My throat was so dry my voice was nothing more than a croak.

"Of course." His voice rumbled into my chest, settling into my heart. The mattress dipped as his weight settled on it, and my head moved a little as his hands landed on either side of me, resting on my pillow.

I smiled.

"Yeah, he wouldn't let any other male in here, don't be ridiculous."

I opened my eyes, but didn't turn my head towards Shannon. No, I wanted the first thing I saw to be Connor's gorgeous face. I forced my eyes open and blinked the dryness away. "Hey," I whispered. His mouth stretched into a relieved smile, his eyes softening.

"Hey, beautiful." His breath ghosted over my lips.

Ignoring the pounding in my head, I inched forward and brushed my lips over his...then cringed and lifted my hand to my mouth.

He raised a brow. "What are you doing?"

I just shook my head. "Mmm."

His face scrunched up, confusion echoing through our bond. "What?"

618

Shannon giggled. "I think she's trying to tell you she has morning breath and to back off, stud."

"Oh, right." He grinned and moved away. "Yeah, I guess you do stink a bit, but you have been sleeping for like...four days."

"Four days!" I screeched and sat up, managing to pull my I.V out and make my head pound again.

Connor calmly stood and grabbed a piece of gauze off the table. "Yes, four days." He returned and pressed the folded gauze to my now bleeding vein. "Press," he ordered. I did.

"But...wow...four days." I fell back against my pillows. "But what about everyone else? Are they okay? How are the women, and the babies? Oh, gods, what about Kawan? And I saw Drake and Jed fighting too. Are they all okay?" I gingerly turned my head towards Shannon, who looked gorgeous as usual in her tight jeans and cream sweater, her blonde hair falling down her chest. "You're okay too? And what about Stone? Oh gods, did I burn anyone? I tried so hard not to, but I got so tired..."

Large hands framed my face forcing my attention away from Shannon. Connor smiled as he kissed my forehead. "Hey, stop. We suffered losses, yes, but that's battle. All of our brothers are alive. We are healed and well, we have the women and babies, and they are being cared for." He kissed my nose. "You are what's important now. You need to eat and drink and get your strength back."

"Yes, but Walker...and B'nar...is Blue here?"

Connor sighed, and I could feel his resignation through our bond. I smiled sheepishly. He smiled back. "No, Blue isn't here. She's still unconscious..." He lifted a hand as I went to interrupt. I bit my lip as worry for my friend flooded me.

"Blue is being cared for," said a deep voice from the doorway.

Connor growled, but I slapped his solid bicep. "Hush. He's allowed in."

"Says who?" snapped Connor.

"Me." And I pushed him back, sitting higher so that I could see B'nar who sensibly stayed near the door. Connor leaned in and snarled gently. His eyes flashed with his beast. He wanted to protect me, and was ready to defend me from anyone, especially other males while I was vulnerable. It occurred to me his attitude was a bit extreme, even for an alpha Prime, but I didn't complain, not when a blast of jealousy hit me and lust rolled straight to my core. Yeah, this was so not the time to get turned on by his possessiveness.

B'nar smirked and raised his brows.

A flush crept across my cheeks, but I managed to ignore the fact that his fae nose could pick up my need for my mate as much as Connor's could. "Is Blue going to be okay?"

B'nar's mouth tightened into a thin line, and he lost any sign of amusement. "I cannot lie, so when I say I do not know, it is the truth. But she is not getting worse. I am doing everything I can for her, and I will not give up looking for a way to cure her. The spear was tipped with some strange kind of poison that came from Hell. None of our healers know what it is, or what the antidote is."

I swallowed at the pain I saw in his eyes. Their interactions had always given me cause to wonder about B'nar's feelings towards my friend, but it was obvious he cared for her deeply. Probably far more than the heir to the fae world should, considering royal matings were not about soulmates or love, merely about power and stability. I blinked and forced a smile to my lips.

"Promise me."

Demanding a promise from a fae was a dangerous thing to do, and Connor shifted to stand almost in front of me. If B'nar decided not to give me that promise, he could take my demand as a challenge. But there was not a moment of hesitation.

"I promise I will never stop looking for a cure. I will never abandon her, and I will care for her until her dying day."

Tears sprang to my eyes, a wave of gratitude and relief coursing through me. "Thank you."

B'nar nodded, his face stoic. "When you feel able, my father would like to talk with you both."

I nodded. "We'll be there soon." But all I really wanted was to be with Connor, to touch him and convince myself we were both okay.

B'nar nodded and left.

Connor turned and brushed my face with his calloused fingers. "We are fine, love." He inhaled and a tingly feeling washed over my skin as his eyes travelled over my body, hidden only by a thin hospital gown and cotton sheet. His deep scent thickened. "And I want you just as much…"

Shannon huffed a husky laugh. "Gods, you two are enough to make me want to play as a threesome."

Connor whipped his head towards her and growled. She grinned and winked. "Chill, boss man, I'm going. But you might want to give her some time to recover and eat before you pin her to the mattress. Besides, I think the pack would appreciate seeing their king."

Connor grunted and squeezed his eyes shut, but Shannon was right and we both knew it. Four days… And I doubted Connor had left my side. Owen would have cleaned up after the attack and organised the camp in Connor's absence, but the shifters needed to see their king, to know what the future held…

"Good to see you awake again," Shannon said and she smiled. I returned that smile. For once there was no sarcasm in her words.

"Glad you're okay too, Shannon."

She nodded and left.

"Come on, get me up. I need a shower, and I need to brush my teeth. My mouth is disgusting."

Connor's deep chuckle resonated through my body, causing my nerve endings to twitch. Damn, hearing his voice, or feeling his touch was like lighting a match to my skin. I had always been turned on by Connor, but this wasn't that. This was...

I stilled. Damn, it couldn't be, could it? I racked my brain, trying to remember when my last season had been. I couldn't think. It didn't matter, I couldn't be with Connor if it was, I had no contraception.

Still, once this meeting with Walker was done I should discuss it with him. I shifted uncomfortably, I wasn't sure either of us were at the point in our relationship where we wanted children. I mean, there were still demons out there, for Mother's sake. They needed hunting down. And we still had to figure out who had been supporting the warden and Doherty. Someone was, both financially with the prison and with gaining voyeurs for the fight rings, because those people sure as shit hadn't all been humans...which meant supernaturals of one form or another were a part of that sick practice.

If I got pregnant, Connor would never let me continue to fight. I frowned. Would I even let myself? My nostrils flared as I placed a hand on my lower belly, the thought of Connor using that stunning, powerful body to help me through my season, made my legs weak. Though repeated sex with my mate was one reason not to be sedated through my season this time, or lock myself away for my safety. I bit back a groan as a wave of need hit me.

Connor raised a brow, only making himself look sexier. "You okay?"

I swallowed hard, only able to nod. Now wasn't the time for lust. I needed to see Walker before he left again.

"Yeah, well, stop going where that dirty mind is taking you, or I am not letting you out of this bed," he growled.

Swallowing hard and wishing I could take him up on that threat, I held out a hand. "Fine. But you are so keeping me and my dirty mind in bed after this meeting is over. Now, give us a hand up, would you? I feel a bit shaky. And if I don't get to that toilet in the next five seconds there's going to be one hell of a mess on the floor."

Connor grinned. I yelped as he bent down and lifted me. "Can't have that, now can we?"

"Nope." I smiled, but more words wouldn't come. A ball of emotion tightened my throat and I nuzzled into his neck, blinking back the burning in my eyes. The fear in my chest eased as I breathed him in. He was alive and unharmed. "Did we do it? Is the rift closed?"

"It is. You did it."

"We did it," I corrected.

Connor kicked open the shower room door and let my feet slide to the ground. Not caring if he watched, I planted myself on the toilet and sighed as I released my full bladder. "Damn, it's amazing how good that feels." Then heat swamped my cheeks as he leaned on the door frame, watching me—and grinned. "Hey, turn around. You can't watch me pee!"

He laughed out loud. "It's a bit late for that." But he took pity on me and turned away to flick the shower on, rifling through the cupboards of the hospital cabin's bathroom for shampoo and shower gel.

Gods, it was hot in the shower and my skin felt so sensitive that I only grazed over my nipples and nether regions. Maybe it was the drugs, or perhaps the remnants of letting Fire soar free, but I couldn't ever remember the build up to a season being like this. It was usually slower and less brutal. I only hoped I made it through the meeting and had some time to talk to Connor about it before it hit me fully. I was sure Drake would have something to dampen the effects—or at least some protection if Connor didn't want to risk a pregnancy. Goosebumps peppered my skin, despite the hot flush swamping my body. I moaned as I inadvertently grazed my sensitive lady bits with a finger.

"You okay in there?"

I closed my eyes and gritted my teeth, trying to smother my lust. Gods, just the sound of his voice had a burst of arousal slicking the skin between my legs. I gasped, my hand slapping against the shower wall as my stomach cramped and my legs shook.

"Yeah, sure...nearly done," I yelled, hoping the glass shower cubicle would keep back the scent of my need for him. A heavy sex session was not appropriate right now.

Connor's shadow loomed on the other side of the shower door, hesitating as if contemplating getting in with me. I fisted my hands, half-praying he would yank it open and take me no matter how many people were waiting on us. A few seconds more and he turned away. I released a breath and quickly rinsed away all evidence of my desire, not sure if I was disappointed or relieved.

Thirty minutes later, I was showered and dressed in clean clothes, and my hair was dry. Connor had made sure I had food and a steaming hot cup of tea waiting for me when I stepped out. It had been months since I'd tasted a decent cup of tea. Being English, coffee didn't always hit the spot. I smiled up at Connor. "Thanks."

He leaned down. "You're welcome," he breathed in my ear, making me shiver. "I can sense your need, Firecracker." He gently bit my ear lobe.

"Yes, but we have to go to a meeting," I squeaked out, my cheeks flushing.

Connor just chuckled and folded his bulk fluidly down onto a chair. I gulped at the bulge I could clearly see in his crotch. He grinned. "Listen to you, all responsible and everything."

I just rolled my eyes at him. I didn't want to be responsible, but the 'baby' talk needed more time than we had right now.

After I'd finished eating. Connor's hand found mine, holding firmly as he led me to the cave where he knew Walker and Owen waited.

"Where's the Halo?"

Connor peered down at me. "In Drake's safe. Only my brothers know that we have it."

I frowned.

"Don't worry. It's safer there than anywhere else in this camp."

I relaxed. He was right.

"So is there a way we could use it to bring Reed back?" My voice had a pleading quality that I didn't like, but I'd do anything I could to bring my friend back.

Connor sighed and put his muscled arm around my shoulders, pulling me close. He kissed the top of my head, the warmth from his body seeping into me, and my own responded immediately. I gently pulled away so that he wouldn't feel the wave of heat washing over me. Goosebumps broke out across my skin and I wanted to climb him and devour him so badly my hands trembled. I crossed my arms over my aching breasts and stepped further away, unsure what was happening to me. This reaction to him was off the charts...and I didn't know how to handle it.

"You know I can't, Ember." His head cocked minutely, a small crease appearing between his brows as I let go of his hand. "We don't have anyone who can speak angelic. But we'll find someone soon, I promise."

I nodded, biting my bottom lip. I didn't like to push, but... "But can't you resist the pull of Hell without the chant? You're a Hell-beast?"

Connor gave me a small smile. "I don't know. Maybe...I'll talk to Walker about it after this meeting. Maybe he'll know a way."

I swallowed my pain for Reed and nodded. "Yeah. Okay."

I didn't reach for his hand again, worried the contact would cause another burst of need in me. I desperately tried to remember exactly when my last season had been, but with everything that had happened it was impossible.

"Hey, I'm sorry about Reed. Don't be angry with me, love, I would bring him back if I could."

"Oh, I know you would! And I'm not mad..." I shook my head, feeling guilty.

"You sure?"

"Yes. I'm just tired."

Connor narrowed his gaze on me. I felt a pulse of suspicion and worry, so

I quickly closed my mind. He opened his mouth, but I spoke before he could comment on me closing down our emotional link.

"Come on, everyone's waiting. I can hear them." I grabbed his hand, ignoring another rush of heat across my skin, and marched into the large cave.

Owen, as attuned to Connor's presence as always, noticed us first. He grinned. "Acknowledge your King and Queen!" he bellowed and leaned his head back howling loudly.

My mouth dropped open as one by one the shifters followed his lead. *Queen? Holy shit!*

Connor's eyes flashed red and I was sure my cheeks were now that same glowing colour. "What are they doing?" I hissed up at him. I was not prepared for this.

He grinned. "Honouring their leaders." He shrugged his massive shoulders as if it was the most natural thing in the world. I couldn't tear my eyes from his body. Damn...when he moved like that...I licked my suddenly dry lips, glad I'd muffled our link, but I couldn't muffle my scent.

"Stand." His voice was full of command. I flushed as Connor glanced at me, and smirked. "You're distracting me, Firecracker."

I gulped and looked away. Maybe I should just drag him aside and tell him. If my body kept moving along at this rate, I could hit the height of my season right here. I glanced around noting the amount of males around me... unmated males. Shit, it would be a bloodbath!

Walker and B'nar smirked at my face, misreading my frown. I blinked, sure I'd never seen either of them smile like that before. They just shrugged as if I should accept my role as Queen at Connor's side. I guessed they were right. He was my mate and there was no way I was relinquishing my claim on him. I blew air over my hot cheeks, which didn't seem to be cooling at all, and pulled at my sweater with my other hand, blowing down the neck and across my skin as heat seemed to radiate out from me.

"You okay?" Connor asked, his hand squeezing mine harder. Heat sizzled all the way through my body again.

"Yeah, fine," I lied, trying to remain calm as some of the nearby males inhaled, their faces dropping into confused frowns as my pheromones hit them.

I tugged on Connor's hand, my feet grinding to a halt. "But maybe we could leave..."

He leaned down and peered into my eyes. "You look a bit flushed...and your scent...Damn, Ember..." His eyes flickered to the nearest male who took a step forward, his eyes fixed on me. Connor cracked his neck and angled his body in front of mine. "Turn the fuck around, before I break your neck." His voice held a deep warning growl.

He was so close, his scent so strong that I couldn't stop myself. I stepped in front of him, speared his hair with my hands and slammed my mouth against his, devouring his lips. Lust shot through me, heating my core. I was dimly aware of dozens of eyes on us, but I couldn't stop. I didn't want to stop.

Connor grabbed my face between his hands. But I didn't want to stop kissing him. "Shit," he mumbled against my lips. More kisses. "Em, stop...what the..." I pulled back, my face hot and sweat beading on my brow.

Connor inhaled again and his eyes widened. Moving swiftly, he lifted me up as though I weighed nothing. "Out of my way!" he bellowed, and I willingly wrapped my legs around his waist rubbing the apex of my sex against his rock hard erection which seemed to have sprung to life in a matter of seconds. I groaned. "Connor...I need you so bad." My skin was burning, need twisting my insides. "Ah, it hurts," I cried in his ear.

"I know, love. I'll make it better. I promise. Owen! Make sure no other males get near us. If they get through. I'll rip them apart."

"Sure, thing, boss. Kawan, Stone, Myles, Drake. With me."

Then Connor was running. Howls resounded across the compound. I was only dimly aware. Crying out as another twist of desire ended in pain. "Connor..." I sobbed, trying to find some kind of release as I moved against him but it wouldn't happen. "Mother Wolf, what's happening to me?" I'd never felt anything like this before... "Oh shit...Oh gods...Connor. I'm..."

"It's okay, I know," he growled. "And your mine. I'll kill anyone who tries to get to you."

I glanced over his shoulder to Owen, whose wolf was riding him high, his eyes reflected the light of the compound. Shit, I hoped his brothers could withstand the need to mate. It shouldn't be like this, I thought. Not when I'm mated. "Why are there so many howls?" Fear coursed through me.

"Fuck. You're scent...It's off the charts." Connor panted, beads of sweat rolling from his hairline and down his temples. A female in heat was a calling card to all unmated wolves, but it should lessen with me being Connor's. My body hadn't gotten the memo though. Powerful pheromones were leaking from me and into the air.

"Shannon...the females... They'll be better protection for us. Don't put your brothers at risk. Please, Connor..." I almost wept when he nodded. None of his brothers except Myles were mated.

"Myles, stay with us...Owen! Leave with the others. Send Shannon..."

"It's alright, I'm here," said a female voice.

I almost cried at the sound of my friend's voice. No matter what had happened between us in the past, I trusted her. "Thank you," I mouthed at her. She smirked. "No worries. Maybe you can do the same for me in the next few months." I saw Stone stare at her before Owen pulled him away.

Walker and B'nar appeared from the mouth of the cave and sprinted towards us.

"We'll watch your room," Walker said. "It's her phoenix. Now that she's been released, it's sent her body into overdrive."

Connor grunted, his own face flushed. Without a word he ran up the steps and into our cabin. The others stayed outside. I had no time for embarrassment at my effect on the camp, not when another wave of desire rode me and wetness seeped from between my legs, soaking my panties.

"Fuck. Me. You smell good." Connor's chest heaved as he placed me on the bed—and stepped away.

I stared up at him, confused as lust clouded my mind. I reached out to him, but he stepped back more. "What are you doing?" I managed to ask.

His throat bobbed. "Is this what you want?" He ran a shaking hand through his hair. "I...er... can get Drake to..." His eyes dropped to the floor before coming back to me. His eyes were bright and his face flushed. He inhaled then groaned, blinking slowly as he blew out a breath. "*Fuck*...Some drugs. Okay? If this isn't what you want..."

I watched his throat bob, my stomach squeezing. "We're mated. I would always want this with you."

"Em, we have no protection..."

My heart lurched. I pulled my hand back and closed my eyes. "Oh...right. You don't want a baby." It was a dull statement. He was right. This wasn't the time. My body chose that moment to release another wave of heat. I groaned, inhaling that deep heady scent of his. It filled me, making me want him more.

"Mother Wolf, tell me you want this, Em. Tell me if you end up pregnant that you want my child—if you aren't one hundred percent sure, I will leave this room and hunt down Drake. He has to have brought some kind of drugs or protection with him. I could find them..." He ran a shaking hand over his face.

The thought of him leaving me filled me with horror. I speared his gaze with my own, my heart doing a flip in my chest. He wanted this? "I one hundred percent want this. But only if you do." And suddenly I realised the total truth of that statement.

His strong throat bobbed and the air thickened with his scent, making me squirm under his heated gaze. His spine straightened and his chest rose and fell rapidly, his own arousal clearly reaching a point where he was losing control. With just a thought his clothes disappeared and he stood utterly naked, a feast for my greedy gaze. "Gods, you're so gorgeous, Connor." His eyes flickered with surprise. Hadn't I told him how stunning he was before? Right then, standing in front of me, with his thick erection standing proud he looked like a *god*, nevermind a king...

A low rumble came from his chest, his eyes glowing the deep red they did when his beast was right beneath the surface. He grinned and snapped his fingers. Mea and Fire both watched our mate through my eyes as my clothes fell away from my skin, disintegrating into nothing.

Connor blinked as another wave of lust hit me, twisting my insides. His self-control snapped and he fell on me claiming my mouth. He overwhelmed me, pushing me into the mattress as he kissed me senseless. I bent my knees to the side to accommodate him, and with one hand he grabbed his cock, dragging the tip through my wetness. Kissing me desperately, he thrust into my body with an explosive roar, digging in as deep as he could go. I cried out and my nails sank into the skin of his shoulders trying to bring him closer to me. The pain of being stretched turned to pleasure as I lifted my knees and opened not just my body but mind to him, offering him everything that I was. Without releasing my mouth, his tongue duelling with my own, our moans merged as he pumped into me harder and faster.

"More, Connor." And I slammed my hips up to meet his, gripping hard to his sides.

Sweat slicked our bodies, my canines fell at the same time as his. I wanted him to take my blood, to mark me again, make me his. I twisted my head, giving him access to my throat.

"Mine." His voice was deep and gravelly, his hips still pumping a hard and desperate rhythm. His canines scraped my skin before clamping down. I sucked in a breath at the sharp pain and wrapped my legs around his thighs as he thrust into me, his body slapping against mine. I couldn't think beyond the pleasure in my body as he drew deeply on my vein. Pleasure welled up, until I mindlessly whispered his name, totally consumed by him. My insides fluttered and he took another deep draw on my vein, his pelvis striking against mine as I grabbed onto him. He hooked an arm under one leg and lifted, changing his angle. "Oh..." I moaned as he hit a sensitive spot inside me. One more hard pull on my neck and I was gone. I fell apart around him, coloured lights flashing behind my eyelids.

"Connor!" I cried out, my nails digging in his skin as the fiercest orgasm I'd ever had careened through my body sending it into spasms. Pleasure rocketed through me and I screamed.

His canines left my neck and his mouth released my skin with a gentle pop, but he wasn't done, nor was my body and we both knew it.

He kissed me deeply, still moving his hips, but in gentle, sensuous circles, giving me time to recover. Holding my gaze, he dragged me to the edge of the bed and put his feet on the floor then hooked both of my legs over his shoulders. I gulped. He gave me a primal grin, his eyes hooded. "You ready for me?" This time, gripping my legs tightly, he thrust in hard and fast. I groaned as intense pleasure took my breath away. "That's it, Ember, you can take me...all of me." And he ground his hips faster and deeper until I was begging him.

"Harder, Connor. *Harder.* Make me feel you." Sweat ran down our bodies as he worked me again, hitting my g-spot with every thrust. Everytime I began to squeeze around him, he stopped until my climax receded. I groaned, totally lost in a fog of lust.

"Beg me, Firecracker. Tell me what you need." The demand in his raw voice had me mindlessly obeying.

"I need you to come inside me. Please, Connor. Don't stop. Please...please let me come with you." Tears leaked from my eyes as I stared up at this adonis above me. "By the gods, I love you."

He leaned down and kissed me thoroughly, never ceasing his hip movements. My chest burned at the blast of love that poured into me from him. "And I'll *never* stop loving you." He pumped his hips harder and harder, his breathing erratic and his blue eyes tinged with fire.

"Harder...Oh, Connor...harder..." I breathed as sensation coiled tighter and tighter inside me until it was almost unbearable. He held my gaze as my canines fell and I grabbed his head.

He didn't resist as I pulled him down and sank my teeth into his neck, claiming him again, knowing he would be a part of my soul forever.

He roared as his release barrelled through him. I held him in place against my lips, letting his essence and power fill up all the dark corners of my soul. "Come with me!" he half-demanded, half-pleaded.

"Oh!" My orgasm, mixed with the taste of his blood and the rush of power that hit me almost made me black out. I moved around his neck, kissing his skin as I held onto his shoulders for all I was worth. Slowly the room began to come back into focus.

He kissed me again so tenderly, and I pulled him closer, unwilling to let him go. When we had both recovered our breath, Connor shifted his weight to the side so that he didn't squash me. Still embedded in my body, he kissed me again. "So, umm, yeah, that was the best orgasm of my life so far." He grinned and gently brushed some hair back from my sweaty brow.

I leaned up and kissed his chin. "Really?" I shrugged. "It was just okay for me."

He snorted a laugh and stroked his fingers down my cheek. "So how long before you need me again?"

I swallowed. "I, uh, I don't know. I've never felt like this before."

His nostrils flared and anger pulsed from him, his voice deep and growling as he spoke. "What happened during your past seasons? Who were you with?"

I reached up and cupped his face, inhaling the combined scent of our lust, sex, and a scent that was all Connor. "I never needed anyone. I always made sure I was in Faerie as it seemed to dampen the effects. It was always a shadow of this..."

Before I'd finished speaking he'd rolled back on top of me. "Good. Because you're mine. That also means I don't need to hunt down and kill any past lovers..."

My body immediately reacted to his possessive tone and the weight of his muscled body dominating mine. I rocked my pelvis. "No, you need all your energy for me, lover boy." I grinned up cheekily. "You ready to go again, stud...because I am." I groaned as his hips rocked forward.

"I'll always be ready for you, Firecracker. I'm yours to command..."

CHAPTER 26

onnor

GROANING, I lowered myself down onto a chair in the ops center. Owen grinned. Even Stone raised a brow at my slow movements.

"Don't you fucking dare say a word." My warning fell on deaf ears.

"Mother fucking Wolf, Con, what did she do to you?" Myles's eyes were wide. "You're the King of Weres! Jeez, I'm glad I like men."

Alex laughed as Lionel clapped Myles on the back. "Looks like a safer option. Daayum, Prime, looks like she used you all up."

I grinned and slumped against the chair back. I felt stronger than ever inside, but, yeah, my body was used and still recovering from the best five days of my life. I couldn't keep the stupid grin off my face, and I didn't need to, not with my brothers, or Walker and B'nar who watched with identical smirks curling their lips. And yeah, Alex, Lionel and Drake were counted amongst those I trusted now. They were my brothers and my pack.

"Bloody hell, Connor. I've never seen you looking so exhausted...or happy." Owen's joking words were full of happiness for me.

"Thanks, man." I folded my arms over my chest, and grinned wider. "It's been the best and most exhausting experience of my life, but hey..." I cracked my neck, happy to bear the scars of Ember's claimings.

"Damn, Connor, it looks like she tried to eat you. You sure she's not part vampire? Those fuckers pop up everywhere, especially that cold bastard, Balt-

630

hazar. He'd know if she was his kind," said Kawan, his eyes sparkling with laughter.

"Piss off." I threw my coffee mug at him. Which he duly caught and placed on the table in front of him. "She's no more vampire than you are, you shit."

"No, she's an immortal spirit who needs protection from our foes," said Walker gravely, bringing us back from our light hearted banter. "We sent Berith back to Hell, we didn't kill him."

I pulled my chair in and fixed the faerie king with a serious stare. He was right. My mate was out of danger from any unmated males in the compound, and her hormones had settled again; but she needed to be kept hidden from any of Berith's spies. That runway had been clear for a reason and I was sure he had sent demons out into the world. We needed to go somewhere he couldn't find her. Another smile stretched my lips at the thought of a lifetime with her by my side. But we both needed to recover from the physicality of her season before we could make plans. My stomach tightened. My mate... fuck, she could be pregnant right now. That thought had everything inside me twisting, including my heart and soul. It was hard to stop myself from marching right out of this room and to her side so that I knew she was safe and protected.

"Yeah, every victory comes with a price. And now all the shifters in this camp know what she is. We can't lock everyone up, or prevent them from sending out word to the bastards who'd pay to have her." I peered at Walker. "She'll be a target for every supernatural who wants to do a deal with the devil."

"She will." Walker leaned forward and held my gaze. I forced myself to disregard it as a challenge. Walker's face was grave, his body language stiff. Whatever he was about to say was important to him. The green ring around his blue irises deepened. "I have a proposition for you, King of the Shifters."

I sat up straight, wondering what he was up to this time. Walker was a clever and devious ruler. I glanced at Owen who understood. He moved closer to me, standing behind my shoulder, protecting my back and showing his support. Walker had orchestrated not only my capture, but Owen's as well; and Owen still held that grudge even if he wouldn't act on it without my say so. I had yet to find out how Walker had managed to manipulate the hierarchy of the SBI—but I would.

I rested my elbows on the table, forcing myself to appear relaxed. Walker and B'nar had watched my back while I'd been with Ember, so I trusted them...to a point, but doing a deal with the fae wasn't always wise.

"Keep talking, High King of the fae."

A smile ghosted over Walker's features before he once again became the Ice King. B'nar stood at his back as Owen stood at mine. But the prince heir's posture, although ready to fight at a moment's notice, was not aggressive, he merely watched the door.

"You are aware that I went to great lengths to get you both into my employment?"

"I am."

Walker waited as if expecting me to say more. I held his gaze and remained silent. The hows were not important to me, right now, and I already knew the whys.

Again the ghost of a smile. "I did not expect you to become the King of Shifters, or be as powerful as you are. Nor did I expect that you would be powerful enough to house a dark fae beast; but it matters not, I have a feeling all that power will prove to be essential to help you with what's to come."

"And what would that be?"

Walker leaned his elbows on the table and clasped his hands together in front of himself. "Together with my son, and a few others I believe Ember has told you about, I have put together a task force to hunt down the Hell rifts and any demons who are in this world. Now that we know where Ember is, she must be kept out of Hell's grasp." His disturbing eyes met mine. "I'd like you to head that task force, and keep her in the shadows."

I raised my brows. "And how do I do that when I have a species to rule over? We have to find a home for our kind..."

"What about here, boss? We could make this settlement more permanent..." Owen suggested.

Walker shrugged. "It is possible. Though as far as Ember's safety is concerned, I have a facility back in Faerie with weapons and training space..."

"Faerie? Nope, sorry, Walker, I'm not leaving my world and people to go to Faerie."

"Not even for your mate? She will be safer there, Connor."

"Safer? For how long? Besides, she wouldn't agree to leave this world. It's her home..."

"Is it? She lived in Faerie happily while you weren't there..."

Behind Walker, B'nar's face darkened. I kept my face impassive. It seemed the son did not agree with the father.

"How do Lance and Ava feel about me leading this little group of assassins you have put together? I can't imagine they are all that happy considering I shot them both."

Walker inclined his head. "They weren't. But their lives belong to me; they do as I say. And once they realised you'd be in that prison, they jumped at the chance to set up the dominoes that got you there. Besides, your ex-lover developed a friendship with your current one while they worked together in Faerie. They were friends, and Ava wants to help keep Ember secure and safe."

I let a small growl escape me. "Ember will be safer by my side than she would be in Faerie."

Walker sat back and mirrored my posture, crossing his arms over his broad chest. "In that case, let me search out a facility on Earth. Somewhere secure. You have shifters who are loyal to you. They will protect her from harm. Once I find somewhere I will bring your new team to this world and you can begin hunting demons, and with Ember's help destroying the rifts." He paused. "But it has to be done under the radar of the SBI. There is still corruption in the higher echelons of that organisation and I am working with others to uncover how high up that deceit goes."

"Why? Clearly you have powerful friends, to arrange getting me and Owen framed for murder, but what does SBI corruption have to do with you?"

The corners of his mouth lifted. "Let me worry about why I'm involved, you just need to work under their radar, stick to the shadows."

I sat quietly, my elbows on the table, my fingers steepled. Walker let me think. I could run a search and destroy squad. It's what I'd been trained for, and now, with all my extra strength, enhanced senses, and lack of company rules to hold me back, I would be better than ever...But would it be best for Ember?

Walker pushed his chair back. "I'll give you time to think it over. I can help you keep Ember safe. I have the technology and the wealth. Work with me and you will be in a better position to make sure nothing happens to her."

"Yeah, I know. Just give me a while to discuss your proposition with my brothers, and my mate."

Walker nodded. "The rest of the team will be here at your go ahead. They are ready and waiting for word from me. And Connor?"

"Yeah?"

"Both Ava and Lance hold no blame against you. Doherty tricked and manipulated you into doing as he wished. They know that."

I smiled tightly. "Hmm, and now I have to make sure no one else uses me the same way, don't I, High King? After all, you manipulated me and my beta, not to mention Zander, into doing as you wished. Your plans ultimately destroyed Rawson and got his mate killed."

"True. But there is a difference this time, Shifter King." Walker's eyes and expression were as cold as the ice he controlled. My beast reared up, peering at the threat it sensed in that powerful gaze. "This time you know what the deal is. Work with me; if you don't and the key becomes a liability, then I will do what is necessary to neutralise the threat it poses to both of our worlds."

My beast sprang free and I reached for his neck—only to find a wall of ice blocking my way and a fae prince with a sword to my neck.

I snarled. I could break through the ice and we all knew it. Aggression burned in the air. My brothers blocked the door.

"If you fail her, nothing you do will stop me from taking Ember. I control armies in my world and this one. No matter how angry you are at my words, you know I am right. She is a danger to us all—unless you both stay hidden in the shadows, and away from the attention of Satan's spies. I can give you that anonymity."

I pulled away, my beast settling back at my instruction, but I did not drop Walker's cold glare.

Drake inched closer to me. "You can still be our king, Prime. Rulers are rarely physically visible to all of their subjects. Ruling from the shadows would be easily done. Technology will help with that. And if His Majesty here can come through with his promises to provide a technologically sound building and grounds for us to train your new squad in, it's something we can set up together."

Owen looked at me and cocked his head. "Up to you, boss. I'm in whatever you decide."

I dipped my brows. "What about your responsibilities here...this pack?"

He huffed a laugh. "Oh, c'mon, Connor. I *can* be an alpha, but I only ever took the role because you made me vow to do it until you returned."

"But we can't abandon these people."

"You won't have to," Walker chimed in. "I will fund making this compound permanent."

I stared out of the window to where Shannon and Ember walked out of the dining room and back towards our cabin. I smiled. Walker's *offer* was the sensible route to take. I had not really thought about my future with Ember, but he was right, she was a target if we stayed out in the open. Working from the shadows was the safest option. My fingers curled into fists, my gut churning, especially as she might now be carrying my child. I rubbed my face and turned to peer at Owen.

"Fine. Do you have anyone in mind to take the alpha position here?"

"Yep, Shane. He's always been loyal to you and has never faltered in whatever we've asked him to do. He will ensure everyone who chooses to remain here is cared for."

I nodded, Shane was a good choice. "So be it." I straightened and watched Ember and Shannon disappear into the cabin. I was glad they were friends. Ember needed friends, especially since Blue was still so ill. I hoped Ember would get some rest now. I was bone deep tired and my elation at being with my mate for so many days undisturbed was being scrubbed away by the heavy dose of reality Walker had given me. I turned back to Walker and B'nar, who had sheathed his sword. "Do what you have to do. Give me a couple of hours to talk Ember around. I know she is desperate to go in search of Rawson. I'm not sure she'll want to go straight into hiding."

Alex grinned. "Just tell her we'll be hunting bad guys. She'll agree to it without even knowing she is being protected."

"Yeah, until I refuse to let her come with us on missions."

"You just spent five days shagging like bunnies. Tell her you're concerned she might be knocked up. That's your excuse for keeping her under lock and key," supplied Lionel with a wink.

I snarled. The thought of my precious mate fighting bad guys while carrying my child lit rage in my belly. "I don't need an excuse to keep her out of harm's way."

Stone scoffed. "You're kidding, right? You'll never keep her locked down. She'll kick your ass six ways from Sunday if she thinks you're protecting her or keeping her a prisoner of any kind, even to keep her safe."

I couldn't help my grin. "Yeah, she will."

"So do you need more time or are we agreed? You will remain king of the shifters and pull your race into some form of order. You, your brothers..." He waved his hand at Owen. "...or your council or whatever you wish to call them, and Ember, will be provided with a secure place to live and train, and I will bring Lance, Ava and the rest of the team to you in the next twenty four hours." He walked towards the door then stopped with his hand on the handle. "Hmm, I have an idea where you can go until I have somewhere more secure for you. Begin sorting out your people Shifter King. You will be moving on very soon. B'nar? With me. We have things to discuss."

The quiet prince gave me a respectful nod, despite having a blade at my throat only a few minutes ago. Once father and son had left, I sat back down.

"Brothers? Please sit. We have much to discuss..."

Four cups of coffee, two bacon sandwiches and a steak burger later, I sighed and rubbed my face. "Mother Wolf, who knew there was so much to sort out here?"

Shane, who I'd sent for, laughed. "And this is only the beginning."

I stood and stretched. It was late, but there was something else I wanted to do, or at least try and do before I made my way back to Ember. I hadn't seen her or Shannon come back out of our cabin, and I couldn't feel any emotion through our bond. I was glad. She needed to sleep. I wondered if she'd eaten since I'd seen her earlier. After this last task, I'd bring her something. The thought of sliding into bed next to her warm, soft body had me adjusting myself in my jeans. Godsdammit, but I couldn't stop wanting her, even now after we'd enjoyed each other so many times, in so many different ways. I inhaled, imagining her body and scent wrapped around me and the taste of her on my tongue.

A cough had me opening my eyes and a frustrated growl erupting from my throat.

"Hey boss, you alright there? You zoned out again." Owen chuckled and slapped me on the back. Only he would get away with that, and he knew it. "C'mon. Let's go. The sooner we try this, the quicker you can go back to being totally pussy whipped."

"Laugh it up, Owen. One day you'll all find your mate, and then I'll take great pleasure in taking the piss out of each and every one of you."

He just laughed, along with the rest of my brothers. Even Stone cracked a smile.

"We should all be so lucky," Drake muttered, his green eyes glittering.

"Yeah? Well, I hope you all are one day. Come on, I don't want Ember to come looking for me. If this doesn't work, then I don't want her to be disappointed."

Myles stood and blew out a breath. I could sense his nervousness and stepped up to him, giving his shoulder a squeeze. "I can't promise anything, you know that, right?"

"Yeah, boss, I know. But it's worth a try. His body is wasting away, but he can't die. That evil leech won't let him."

"Come on, let's go."

Together with my new council, Owen, Stone, Alex, Kawan, Lionel, Myles, Drake, and the newly named alpha of the Western Canadian shifter pack, Shane Dower, we marched across the compound and into the cave.

From where she helped some of the newer mothers with their babies, Selina's attention fixed right onto my beta. I hid my smile, their dynamic wasn't lost on me, and I hoped for Owen's sake he would find with Selina what I had found with Ember. I would talk to him about taking her and her son with us when we left. Owen's attention snagged on her before he pulled his gaze back to where we were going. "You alright there, beta?" I asked in the same tone as he had used on me not long ago. He gave me a scowl, his easy-going manner lost.

"Trouble?" I asked.

"You have no idea," he murmured.

We marched through the cave system to where my brother was still chained to a pallet. Reed stank, not just unwashed and animalistic, but that sulphurous stink of Hell lingered around him. I took a deep breath as the demon opened his eyes and began to chuckle, a cold sound that set Prime snarling. I didn't fight him, I let him out. We merged, all the spirits in me becoming one monstrous creature. The demon soon stopped laughing. Instead, he screamed as I stalked towards him.

I cracked my spine and stretched my jaws, drawing on the power in my veins. I'd ingested enough of Ember's blood to make her fire simmer with mine, augmenting my own strength. Ember's power was to open and close the doorways to Hell; my own was to control shifters of any kind.

I glared down at the emaciated and chained body of my friend, praying to the Mother that this would work.

"Connor, what are you going to do?" asked Myles, his voice tight. I sensed his worry but knew I couldn't alleviate it. This was going to be hard on both Reed and me.

"My human side is going to join with Prime, the King of the Hell-beasts, and along with my fae side, Prime and I are going to rip away this mother fucker's hold on Reed. I'm going to keep his shifter and human souls tethered to me, then give Reed the satisfaction of pushing that evil bastard out of his body."

I heard Myles gulp.

"Don't worry, I know this will work. The King has done it before, and he will guide me. If Reed isn't strong enough to throw that demon out, I'll happily toss what's left of that putrid fucker back to its master. But it isn't taking Reed's human or wolf soul with it. Not while I still have breath in my body."

Without another word, I placed my huge clawed hand on Reed's chest and thrust my consciousness into his mind. I ignored the demon's enraged yells and worthless threats, and slowly pushed my claws into Reed's skin, piercing his flesh as I used my strength to pin his weakened body to the pallet. My spirits and I merged and became one, snarling as we searched through the fear and darkness that filled Reed's mind. There it was, a disgusting inky stain, slithering through my friend's thoughts and memories. I hunted it, pushing it to where I wanted it to be, to where it could no longer run, right up against the wall behind which it had trapped Reed's souls. I snarled and fixed my gaze on it. It froze, knowing its time was at an end. The predator in me savoured the power I held. I prowled closer, my claws flexed, ready to shred it into pieces. The demon screeched as my gaze burned into it. I cocked my head, a thrill running through me. He was...lesser, no match for me at all, a mere leech, hitching a ride in my friend's body. But this wasn't about me. Reed needed to kick this parasitic evil out of his body himself. I knew my friend, and he would gain at least some self-respect and power back by being the one to expel it.

I pushed my way towards the demon. It screeched and flailed, twisting itself all around me, trying to deter me from my purpose. I roared and shoved it backwards, pinning it against the wall. The king lent me extra power as he showed me what I needed to do. Thrusting that power forward, I shoved the demon sideways. Fervently, I beat my fists against the wall the demon had erected, and within moments it cracked and exploded. I didn't hesitate and pushed into Reed's mind.

Reed? Brother? I'm here for you. Come on out of this fucking darkness and fight this piece of shit! You are better than him, stronger than him. It's time to kick his arse out! Take back your body, my friend. Come back to your mate, and stand by my side once again.

A small answering pulse of hope pushed against my mind. *That's it, brother...I'm not going to leave you. If you don't want to do it, I will. Either way, you are coming back to us. You feel me?*

The demon slithered forward. I could feel it trying to rebuild the wall and trap my brother again. I growled, and instead of throwing its touch off me, I grasped it with my mind, burning it just enough to weaken it, fully prepared to tear it out of my friend. But first, I wanted to give Reed the chance to expel this demon himself. My goal wasn't to kill Reed and set his souls free. It was to save him. And to do that, Reed had to be strong. I felt the air heat outside my physical body as my power surrounded us all. Holding the demon still, I fed Reed more and more of my energy. I wanted to throw that slimy demon fucker back to Hell, but Reed deserved that honour. I sought out Reed's wolf and human souls and held on to them with everything I had. I strained to keep them anchored in his body as the demon fought me.

A blast of hatred and determination hit me and, despite my shaking limbs, I grinned and released my grip on Reed's wolf. *You strong enough, brother?*

There was an answering growl and a pulse of alpha power.

Then, by all means, have at it.

Reed's wolf spirit tore past me and swiped the demon from my hold. I let it go. His wolf ripped and tore at the screeching demon until it gave a final squeal and released its hold on Reed's body, hightailing it back to Hell. I felt it. A wave of belonging as Reed's wolf and human souls settled back in place within his body.

As soon as I felt that connection, I sighed and pulled out of Reed's head, panting and shaking.

"Oh, Mother Wolf..." breathed Myles as Reed's Were body shrank into an emaciated man.

I fell to my knees by my brother's side, my bulk dwarfing his starved form. Carefully, I pulled my claws from his flesh, but pushed more and more of my energy into him, not stopping until he moaned. His eyes fluttered open, his gaze going straight to his sobbing mate. Reed's smile was one of such utter love and relief, that even in beast form it left a tight feeling in my chest.

I urged Prime to recede. He did and I sank back, panting, beads of sweat running down my face.

"Fuck me, Connor, you did it. You pushed that demon out and kept hold of Reed's souls. That's amazing. You didn't even need the Halo," Owen breathed, his voice shaking.

I blew out a relieved breath and stood. "Reed got rid of the demon himself. I just helped free our brother and gave him enough energy to fight." My knees wobbled from the effort it took to hold my weight up. The others all looked on in awe. Yeah, I hadn't actually allowed myself to believe I could do this without the Halo—but damn, it had worked, and I couldn't be happier. I patted Myles on the back as he whispered encouraging and calming words to his mate while healing his wounds. My throat ached at the sight of them together. I swallowed, hoping Ember could feel my relief. I should go now and tell her... I pushed against our bond searching for her...still nothing.

I sighed. She was probably still asleep. And that was exactly where I wanted to be, asleep, with her warm soft body in my arms. Protected and safe.

"Stone, Alex, stay with Myles while he heals Reed. Drake would you help move Reed to somewhere better than this pallet? He deserves better. And get them what they need, and I mean anything; medicine, food, drink...whatever." Drake was already talking into his phone. Alex and Stone moved up to stand beside Myles and Reed. Man, even Stone's eyes looked a little misty. I turned away, knowing they would all take care of their own; our own. "Owen? You and Shane have some organising to do, the rest of you help Owen get us ready to move. I'm going back to Ember. She deserves to know about Reed."

"Yeah, she'll be made up," Owen agreed. Then his shrewd gaze rested on me. "I'll get some food sent over to you in a couple of hours, boss. You look beat to shit. Go back to your woman and get some sleep. We'll look after everything."

I slapped his shoulder and gave my best friend a smile of thanks. He knew how much pushing that demon out of Reed had taxed me. There was no way I could free every Were who became possessed by a demon, not like that. It would be too exhausting and time consuming. I still needed to track down an angel. And I still had to find Rawson, and somehow set Zander free from Hell. I sighed as I made my way back to Ember. All I wanted was to slip into Ember's warmth and hold her to me.

As I hurried across the compound, my heart beat faster, a sense of foreboding settling into my soul when I still couldn't feel her. The cabin was pitch black. No lights. *She could just be asleep...* Bursting into a run, I crossed the compound and leapt up the steps into the dark corridor. I inhaled and frowned. Shannon's scent hit me, but it was faint. Ember's was even harder to smell.

"Ember!" I strode down the short corridor and pushed open the door, slamming my hand against the light switch.

The bed was empty.

I ran back out, trying to find her sweet scent. Nothing. I tipped back my head and released a howl. It rocked the night air and males began running out from the cave.

I inhaled, my chest heaving as fear and fury flooded me in equal measure.

Stone and Owen skidded to a halt. "What's wrong?" Owen barked.

"Ember is gone."

"What do you mean? Shannon was with her. Perhaps they've gone for a walk, or shifted..." Stone tried to reason.

"No! Ember was exhausted, she had no energy to shift. Using her phoenix depleted her, and then with the past five days...Fuck! She'd never leave without telling me. We have a bond and I can't feel her." I swallowed my fear. "At all. I thought it was because she was asleep."

Stone inhaled...and growled. "Shannon is over here." He began jogging around the back of the cabin towards the fence. Then he began sprinting, right when the coppery smell of blood hit us. Shannon's blood...and Ember's.

Stone headed to a cluster of storage boxes. He ripped the lid off the top one. Shannon was a jumble of arms, legs and blonde hair. Blood seeped from a hole in her chest. Stone roared, his fury a living thing that matched my own. A purple haze drifted from his body into the air, charging it with energy before he pulled it back inside himself. As carefully as he could, he lifted Shannon's body from the basket. Her face was bruised, her fists and arms cut as if she'd fought hard against multiple blades, and there was a huge swelling and blood on the back of her head.

Prime burst from me. I released a roar, a battle cry that promised pain and death to whoever had taken my mate. I stomped up to Shannon, my monstrous form casting a shadow across her and Stone. He snarled at me, a male protecting his mate. I didn't care, I roared in his face. He'd back off or I'd end him. He roared right back, his eyes a mix of wolf and violet magic. I lifted my arm to swipe away his challenge when ice wrapped over my fist, holding back my strike.

I panted, inhaling the scent of my mate's kidnappers.

Jedediah Hawk.

Glaring with fire filled eyes at Walker, I snapped his ice magic and took off after her kidnapper.

I charged through the forest, the tracks through the snow and the scent of her blood leading me. It went for miles, right back to the prison. The scent was already faint and the tracks were icing over.

The prison was deserted but I could smell fresh aviation fuel. I bounded down the runway and found what I was looking for. My world crumbled. A helicopter had landed; a big one, the indent of its landing wheels almost covered now with snow. I bellowed, desperation and anger tearing at my soul. She was gone, that was why I'd felt so little from her. I'd stupidly thought her safe and asleep when that fucker Jed had taken her from under my nose! I'd failed her. The one person in this world I'd vowed to keep safe and I'd failed...

The sound of wolves howling reached my ears. I sank to my knees in the snow and stared up at the sparkling stars above. My claws dug into my flesh as I grasped my thickly muscled thighs. I had killed before, many many times, and my soul was as black as the night sky above me. But when I caught up with Jed, and the bastard who had paid for this extraction…and I would…their deaths would be as long and as painful as I could possibly make them—and if they had harmed her in any way, they would find themselves in a Hell purely of their own making; one that would never end. I'd make sure of it.

As the Mother was my witness, I vowed that I would bring the other half of my soul back to me.

The wolf pack that approached carefully, lowered their bodies in submission, but I sensed their sorrow for me. I stood and without a word struck out back towards the compound.

Walker waited for me in the ops center. I could scent him. Anger rode me high, and I didn't try to temper it. Thankfully Stone had hidden Shannon out of sight. My rational brain knew she had fought hard for my mate, but my mated soul told me she had still failed, that she was at fault. So for now, until I could think clearly again, I would stay away from her.

Drake shifted and ran to my side. "They stole the Halo, too."

My stomach lurched. They wanted a deal with the devil.

"As soon as Shannon is awake, bring her to me. If she isn't awake before we leave, then she comes with us."

"Where are we going, boss?" asked Drake.

"I'll tell you soon. You have connections. Get me a helicopter or a plane out of here. As soon as I've spoken to Walker I'll tell you the flight plan. And Drake?"

"Yeah?"

"Do not tell that fucker you're working for, or anyone who works for you, a godsdamned thing."

His eyes narrowed, but he heard the warning in my voice. And Drake was my brother, so no matter the cost to him, he merely nodded.

"Sure thing. I've got friends I can go through instead. I'm on it."

I nodded. Owen shifted and followed me in to see Walker.

Walker watched us with a level and cold stare. To the side of him were faces I hadn't seen in years. I should have been elated to see them, even if they had every right to hate my guts, but right then I didn't give a shit about Ava or Lance, or even the beautiful woman who stood behind Walker. Who by all accounts should be a ghost.

"I need your help."

Walker gave an accepting nod. His eyes narrowed on my dark face. "You know who took her." It was a statement not a question.

An evil smile curled my mouth. "I do. And our reunion has been long overdue. The only thing I don't know is where he is."

Walker folded his arms over his chest. "Do you know where to start looking?"

"I do. Europe. He will avoid America, too many powerful enemies here."

Again Walker nodded. "Do you want to tell me who you are looking for?"

I sneered. "No. You want me to work in the shadows, then that's exactly what I am going to do to bring Ember back. I don't trust you Walker. You have threatened Ember too many times, but I do need your resources. So, if you want me to secure the key to the Hell gates, you are going to give me everything I need to get her back."

"Fine, but my son works with you. He has trained this team, and they have access to Fae weaponry that far surpasses anything you have in this world. They will train you and your brothers to use it." He uncrossed his arms. "Bring her back, Connor."

"You…" My gaze slid sideways. "Or your son, harm a hair on her head, and Faerie will be looking to elect a new king and heir."

Walker lifted a brow but said nothing, the epitome of cold self-control. Instead, he turned to his son. "You will do everything in your power to find the key. In return, I will care for your human. Once this mission is complete, we will discuss your futures."

B'nar nodded, another male of few words.

"Drake is organising transport. Gather the equipment you need, we leave as soon as possible," I commanded to the people in the room.

Walker held my gaze. "You will not need a plane. Ready your men and be in the training yard in thirty minutes."

"Why?" I growled in no mood for vagueness.

Walker smiled tightly. "A portal is far quicker. There is a place in London, under the SBI radar where you can work from. You will need no supplies. And your new crew have all the weapons you will need. Just gather your brothers, and any personal belongings you need."

Thirty minutes later, Stone stood with Shannon cradled in his arms. I had nothing but the clothes and weapons I wore. My brothers stood around waiting, all armed to the teeth, even Reed, who leaned heavily on Myles. Selina watched from the shadows. I wondered if Owen would ask her and the little boy to join us, but we were walking into a shit storm and he knew it as well as I did. He didn't know who our enemy truly was, none of my brothers did… but I did. So did my mother…

I looked down at her. I had asked her to come with me and she had agreed. There was nothing for her here, not since Zander had been taken. I was her son, too, and she wanted to be with me, or so she said, and although I didn't know how to feel about this strangely quiet woman who was my mother, I did know I could learn about the darkness that attached itself to my Hell-beast. That fae part of me was an enigma; it made me stronger but maybe I could harness it to help find Ember.

Walker breathed words onto the ring he wore, and motioned in a circle with his hand. The air shimmered and a portal appeared. The sound of water and wind rushed through, and a scent so familiar it brought tears to my eyes. I hadn't thought I'd ever return. In the distance car horns blared, and the stale stink of sea water and rubbish drifted through. A yard of some kind came into view and on the other side of the portal waited a squat and ugly being.

"You need to go now. London awaits, Shifter King."

I took my mother's hand. "You ready for this?"

"As ready as I've been for all the changes in my life so far…"

I nodded, and gripping her hand, stepped through. The power of the portal pulled at all the spirits in my soul, and I roared but kept them locked inside me. Damn, had Ember suffered like this every time she'd used a portal?

The short fat dwarf-like creature that awaited us, stepped back in alarm as the anger that permeated the air around me reached him.

Behind me my brothers and our new squad of shadow sentinels stepped through the portal. My brothers staggered a little, all except Stone who had used a portal before and knew what to expect.

Walker followed. Purposefully, he strode to the dwarf and glared down at him with a look that promised death. "Meet, Somnelaire. This used to be his property, it's now mine. He works for you, but his life is mine. If you wish to end it, you will ask me first."

My eyes narrowed. "You're the Bogwart fae?" I stepped closer. "The drug dealing toad, that used my mate?"

He put his slimy hands placatingly in the air. "Er, now now, she always had a choice. She didn't have to stay."

"You marked her…" My cold glare drifted to Walker. "You both did. Why?"

"Oh, that. Purely a tracking device. I can find her anywhere in Faerie with it." Somnelaire shrugged as if it was nothing. But my attention was mainly fixed on Walker. I'd never asked him before now about the tattoo he'd placed on Ember.

He remained cold and unemotional. "As the Bogwart said, it is a tracking device. When Ember uses her Fire, it reacts against my ice magic and tells me where she is, that's how I knew where you were, and that she was fighting with her phoenix."

I frowned. "But you can't track her without her using her magic?"

"No, I'm afraid not."

"Well, let's hope she uses her magic then," I said darkly, though I actually hoped for the opposite. If Walker found her before me I had no doubt she would end up lost to me forever.

"Come, come, Prime. There is much to show you. My King has done much to improve my humble home, and it is now yours to use as you wish."

I grunted and narrowed my attention on the Bogwart. "I thought you were dead? Ember thought you were."

It was Walker who answered. "He was never dead. I had another enemy of mine brought here, and killed him myself. This...criminal is too useful to me to kill. It was just window dressing for Doherty."

I grunted again and with my pack at my back, I followed Som up the steps and into the rickety old building. This was where Zander had first found Ember...

I glanced behind. Walker was saying goodbye to his son. I didn't care about him, not really, other than what he could give me to find Ember. I'd never let him get to her before I did...and I had the advantage—I knew who had my mate. All I had to do was track him down. He had all the money in the world, but no amount of wealth or technology, or even his own private army, would stop me getting her back.

I looked down at my mother. She lifted her dark eyes and nodded. She knew it too. With determination in my soul, I stowed my fury, banking it for the moment I would unleash it—on the man who had stolen my soul mate, the queen of my people and the keeper of my heart.

Hold on, Firecracker, I'm coming for you.

THE END (For now.)

Join Connor in his search for Ember in the final instalment of their epic love story! Coming summer 2021

ACKNOWLEDGMENTS

As always my main thanks go to all of you who read my books. I'm still a baby author but there would be little point in spending time, effort and money producing books if you didn't read and enjoy the worlds and new characters I create—so thank you!

To Judi Soderberg who edits my books, I can't thank you enough for what you do to support me, and to her very generous daughter Stephanie, who stepped in to copy edit, I'm really grateful and appreciate your help.

My last acknowledgement is to my very small amount of, but terribly important Patreon supporters. I'm grateful beyond words for your support towards audiobook production.

Judi Soderberg

Justine Blaber

Michelle Chantler

If you'd like to listen to my books in audio, then you can support my writing career by becoming a patron on

https://www.patreon/karentomlinsonauthor

REIGN

USA TODAY BESTSELLING AUTHOR

KAREN TOMLINSON

REIGN

SHADOW SENTINELS

Kick back, grab your reading poison of choice, and enjoy the escape and the wild ride Ember and Connor are gonna take you on! xx

CHAPTER 1

mber

FIRE BURST ACROSS THE SKY, the setting sun painting the horizon with shades of citrine, coral, and red as it dipped down behind the expanse of the turquoise ocean. It was mesmerising. Every night I felt it sink, its final flare calling to my soul before the darkness arrived. I bent my legs and jammed my heels on the smooth concrete bench, squeezing my arms around my knees and hugging them to my chest as I watched the blazing orb of the sun shimmer and flash before it disappeared beyond the horizon. Tears burned my eyes, my nails digging into my forearms. What the fuck was wrong with me? I was alive. I had survived. With jerky movements, I swiped at the dampness on my cheeks. But surviving wasn't living, was it? Yet another day had ended, and nothing had changed, except I didn't know what it was that I wanted to change. Since my accident, there was a hollowness inside my soul, one that never eased no matter what I did.

The air temperature dipped, but on the Amalfi Coast, the breeze remained warm and was infused with the scent of citrus. I pushed a few strands of my red hair from my eyes and inhaled deeply. All the scents from this beautiful part of the world seemed heightened at night, especially around the time leading up to a full moon. I shuddered, my fingernails scoring deeper into my skin. My headaches and nightmares had been worse than ever since the last full moon. For three nights, as it waned, my head pounded, and my nights were filled with visions of wild animals, monsters and fire.

Pushing those dark images from my mind, I glanced up. Above me, the semi-darkness was a staggering canvas of twinkling lights, as if the gods themselves had taken a brush and showered the heavens with starlight and then added a sprinkle of magic. It was beautiful.

"Hey," said a deep voice.

It was a rich and sexy sound that had grown on me and was one of the only things familiar to me now. I smiled up at my fiance. His hazel eyes sharpened, honing in on the blood that welled from my self-inflicted nail marks. A soft crease appeared at the bridge of his nose, his brows drawing down.

"Hi," I replied, doing my best to smile. I was trying so hard to be happy with my life, but this hollowness in me had become much worse lately, more so with the lead up to the full moon. It was strange, almost as if my happiness was trapped inside. Was I depressed? Was that normal after a head injury? I had no idea.

Jed sat down next to me on the small stone bench, grabbed me around my waist and pulled me into his lap. He didn't usually push the intimacy side of things, but his focus was on my scratched skin. A low growl came from his chest. "What's this?" His grip on my forearm was gentle but firm.

Yanking away from his grasp and off his lap, I mumbled, "Nothing." Crossing my arms over my chest, I leaned on the low wall that overlooked the terraced gardens of my father's luxurious and well-guarded home.

It seemed I was engaged to the powerful and handsome man behind me, yet I still wasn't comfortable with such closeness. I hadn't been since I'd awoken from my head injury. I'd had no idea who I was then, and I still didn't —not really. My father and my boyfriend, if I could call the tall and ridiculously well-built man behind me a boy, had told me who I was.

During my wakeful moments in the hospital, they had shared my past; photos of me as a little girl, stories of my time growing up here, of our engagement party—of my life, and I couldn't remember a damn thing. My throat ached as tears pricked my eyes, and one rolled down my cheek. If my life was here, and I had been so happy and privileged, why did I feel so empty —so sad?

Jed placed his big hands on my shoulders. "You'll remember eventually, Sarah. It's okay."

"No, it's not okay. None of this is okay." I sighed and rubbed my hand on the back of my head, where the pounding always started when I got upset or stressed.

"Maybe not right now, but it will be. Look, I know you don't trust me yet, but just know that I'm here for you. Whenever you want me."

I swallowed that ache in my throat and gripped the stone balustrade.

"Really? Are you going to spend tomorrow with me then?" My voice was stilted and needy, and I hated it. I didn't want to need anyone. Did I?

Jed tensed, silence seeping into the air around us. It was a common theme between us since I'd come home from the hospital six weeks ago, or rather I'd woken up in a room in this house. I had no memory of how I got here from the private hospital I'd been in. Jed worked for my father and spent very little time at home during the day. Or at least he spent very little time with me, as he was always with my father, and I got it, I really did. He worked as my father's security advisor and was always busy, but I was supposed to marry him next year. A pain stabbed through my head and I grabbed onto the wall for support, wincing. I wanted to get to know him. At least, I thought I should try. I was supposed to love him, after all. Mostly, though, I was just so lonely.

The only visitors to the house were my father's business acquaintances. They were not interested in a young woman with amnesia, who could barely hold a conversation without getting a headache, or who got so muddled in her mind she couldn't talk properly. After the first few times of trying to be interactive, I'd given up.

My father's house rested in the cliffs above the ocean. It was a plot of land difficult to reach from any direction other than the single track road that led from the mountainous main road above. The house was a huge place with tiled floors and a minimalist look. Secretly, I hated it. Not the house itself; that was stunning, with lots of glass to appreciate the sea views. But it was so cold—and empty. Oh, there were security people surrounding the property and patrolling around the house, but inside it was hollow. I rattled around by myself, constantly feeling like some huge part of me was missing.

Dad was a rich businessman; property and *other interests*, he told me. God only knew what they were. He'd promised to show me the business, in time, when he and Jed felt I was ready, but both of them wanted me to rest for now. It was hard to argue when I had no idea what I could even do to help with such a global company. So I spent most of my days walking around the stunning gardens alone or reading books about werewolves and vampires that Jed had bought for me. I wasn't sure why he'd picked those types of books, but they were fun. There were also beautiful swimming pools, both indoors and out. I used one daily, sometimes twice a day, but I still wished I could get to the clear blue ocean and dive into its cool depths. Unfortunately, there was no way of reaching the ocean, not alone. The cliffs were sheer, and the base of them was rocky and dangerous. There was definitely no jumping. I shuddered. That would lead to more than a head injury.

Jed brushed his lips over my ear, sending a shiver down my neck. I almost pulled away. It wasn't that I hated his closeness, but I didn't feel one hundred percent comfortable with it either. Perhaps I never would. That thought alone had ice coating my insides. I had no idea what I would do if that happened. He seemed like a nice guy under his tough exterior, and he'd been nothing but patient with me, but...

"Let me talk to Rex. I'll do everything in my power to be here for you tomorrow," he said, his voice quiet. "You come first."

I huffed a little. "Yeah,' course I do," I muttered, hating that I was almost begging him for some attention, but loneliness was a bitch. It didn't matter how many times they told me my past or how many photos I looked at. I remembered nothing of who I was. And this, all of it—me, this house, my fiance, my father—felt so alien.

I twisted to look into his beautiful hazel eyes. His full lips tilted into a soft smile. "You do. Hey, it's my job to keep you safe and happy."

I returned his smile with a small one of my own. What the hell was wrong with me? My gorgeous fiance had just said I was the most important thing in the world to him, that he was going to spend a whole day entertaining me tomorrow, so why did I still feel so empty? Something tugged on my heart, and my chest tightened at the same time as a sharp pain hit the back of my head, making me cringe.

Jed pulled me gently back into his arms, and I tried to relax, to accept his support. "Is your head hurting?"

"Yeah, it's getting worse, not better," I confided.

He kissed my head. "I'm sorry. Let's go in. I'll get your painkillers. Your father will be home soon, and then we can eat. I'm starving. I've not eaten since breakfast."

I smiled. And this time, it was genuine. I'd never seen anyone eat like Jed. He could pack away the equivalent of two of my meals, sometimes three when he'd been training in the gym below the house with his men. I'd never seen the gym. Dad had instructed it was absolutely off-limits to me until I was not getting headaches anymore. The doctors had informed me that I was unlikely to have a brain haemorrhage again, but I should be careful. Apparently I'd been in a car accident on the road outside our home. I couldn't remember any of it...for which I'm told I should be thankful. But I suspected that's where my nightmares of fire came from.

Jed took my hand in his big paw and gently pulled me along. I couldn't help but smile at his eagerness to get to the dinner table.

"Buenas noches, señor y señorita," said Valentina, my father's spanish maid.

I smiled at the slim, dark-haired woman. "Evening, Valentina."

"I hope you're hungry," she said in her husky voice. She wasn't looking at me, though; she was staring right at my fiance. I hid a frown, certain she was talking about something other than food. Even though I was unsure of Jed's and my relationship, he was my fiance. Surely, flirting with him was wrong?

Jed grinned and winked at her, dropping his hold on my hand. "Always, Tina. You've been here long enough to know that."

"Si, is true. I know you *very* well, Señor Hawk. Where is Señor Manivera? Will he be joining you?"

I tried not to react to that little inflection in her voice. So she knew my fiance *very* well; it didn't mean anything.

It wasn't worth me answering her question. I never knew what my father's commitments were. Not wanting to listen to Tina chatting up my fiance, I poured myself a glass of red wine and left them to it. The terrace was cool and inviting, the scent of jasmine drifting on the air. When I'd commented on how acutely I smelled things, my father had explained my sense of smell had heightened due to my head injury. I smiled and inhaled again, enjoying the gentle perfume as I watched a cruise ship sail slowly across the horizon, its lights twinkling.

Jed's musky aftershave drifted into the mix with the perfume. It was a little like sandalwood, only deeper. I smiled despite my reservations about him. Such beauty and prettiness mixed with his deep allure was a heady thing indeed.

"Here." He held his hand in front of me while stepping close enough his chest brushed my arm and shoulder. Heat bloomed between us as I inhaled again. I pushed away the horrible hollow feeling that haunted me and gave myself a chance to enjoy some contact with his powerful body. Tension zipped between us, but he didn't move, and for once, neither did I. I swallowed and looked at the two small white tablets that sat in his calloused palm.

"Thanks," I said, keeping my voice steady.

"You're welcome."

I took the tablets from his palm, and, finding my courage, I lifted my gaze to his as I popped them between my lips. He looked at me, his eyes glinting and his jaw clenched. He swallowed hard, the thick column of his throat bobbing. Slowly, as if giving me a chance to pull away, his hand curved around the small of my back, pulling me closer into the steel of his embrace. My insides tightened. I didn't drop my gaze. Instead, I pushed against him. Time to start trying...

He exhaled sharply and rested his forehead against mine. "Sarah...what are you...?"

"You shouldn't be drinking that with those painkillers."

I jumped, my cheeks flaring hot. I turned my head to greet my father, but Jed didn't let me go. He gave me enough room to twist a little, but that was it.

"Rex." Jed's greeting was stilted, his face dark.

Ignoring the irrational guilt at being caught in Jed's arms, I smiled and pulled back a little, patting Jed's pecs as a signal to loosen up his hold. "I'm pretty sure I can decide what I drink, Dad. And if I can't, I guess my fiance will suggest an alternative." I shrugged like his words were no big deal, while all I really wanted was to down the whole glass in defiance. Surely no adult woman allowed her father to dictate what she drank?

Rex raised his brows and crossed his arms over his broad chest. He was tall and well built, with muscles that he worked out regularly despite being a successful businessman. He was in his early fifties yet looked ridiculously young, with a full head of brown hair and smooth tanned skin that belied his true age. With his eyes narrowed on Jed, he shrugged. "If you trust him to do the right thing by you."

I leaned up and kissed Jed's cheek, determined to try and capture some of the feelings I must have had for him at some point. "I do." *Well, mostly...I think. Or, I want to.*

Had I loved him? I hid my sigh behind another sip of my wine. I had no idea, but if he was spending the day with me tomorrow, maybe I could start to figure it out. First, I had to persuade my workaholic father he didn't need my fiance.

"But I have seen so little of him since I came home, Papa." I pushed away from Jed and walked up to my dad, giving him a hug and a kiss on his cheek. Again it was alien closeness. He was my father but, at the same time, a complete stranger. It didn't mean I couldn't try and twist him to my will, though. I peered up at him and widened my eyes, changing my tone. "Please, can he stay here with me tomorrow?"

Silence.

My father narrowed his eyes at my pout. "Why? You have every luxury you need to keep you entertained. You can read, paint, swim, you have a cinema room, the sun, and an army to keep you, my precious daughter, safe. What more can you possibly want?"

I sighed, trying not to grind my teeth. *My life. My memories. Me.* "Company, Papa. Besides, how can I get to know either of you again if you are both working so hard all of the time?"

My father's mouth twisted up at one side, but it didn't look much like a smile, more like he was thinking about something. I slipped my hand into his and squeezed. "Can't you at least let him go a bit early tomorrow?" I hated that I was practically begging.

There was a moment of silence, and I held my breath, praying for my father to release Jed for at least a little while. God, it was pathetic how desperate I was for some company.

"Fine. I can see keeping you alone all these weeks has made you crave companionship, and who better than your intended? You can spend as much time together from now on as you would like. Jed, you will fit your work in when you can and keep me apprised of your progress with our current project." My father's face was hard as he held Jed's steady glare.

As soon as he realised I was looking at him it was replaced with a softer smile. But I hadn't missed the warning in that gaze. A distant alarm bell rang in my head. Why would my father be giving my fiance a warning look? I plastered a false smile to my face, something I was good at these days.

"Thanks, Papa." I flashed Jed another look, but he didn't return it. With cold, hard eyes, he watched my father walk back into the house where Valentina was serving dinner. Keeping my smile in place, I took his hand and pulled him towards the room. He didn't budge. Instead, he pulled me towards him. One of his hands speared in my hair, cradling the back of my head. With the other, he held my hip in a firm grip. He tilted my head up, and I had no choice but to meet his gaze. My heart went crazy at the dominance in that hold. I wasn't sure if I liked it or if it made me want to knee him in the nuts. *No, you're trying...*

"Be careful of your papa, beautiful. He is relentless when he wants something."

My brows dipped. "But what can he possibly want from me?"

"Not just from you. From us both."

I swallowed at the intensity in his gaze, my libido stirring for the first time in months at being held so close to him. In my head a voice screamed to step away, but it was dampened by the pleasant buzz from the painkillers and the wine, so I slipped my arms around his waist.

"Yes, but what is that?"

"A baby."

CHAPTER 2

onnor

"ANYTHING?" I strode into the large room that doubled as an IT and meeting room. My wet top stuck to me as I peeled it off and flung it into the corner. My body was so tense, frustration riding me so hard, it took every bit of self-control I had not to punch the wall.

The poised blonde woman who stood in front of the nearest flat-screen monitor turned and appraised me. Her greedy eyes travelled from my wet hair down to my chest, past my stomach, and headed in the inevitable direction she always went whenever she did this, straight to what she could only imagine was below my belt buckle. My jeans were wet, but I drew the line at dropping them in front of this woman. She'd just have to keep imagining. She was as much a predator as any of my brothers, and I'd spent the last two months trying not to get caught in her snare.

"Xania? Any new information?"

Xania raised her brows at the demand in my voice. Yeah, she was still as cold as she had been as Miss X. It was away from this room and the professional responsibilities that Walker had assigned her, that she'd become a huge pain in my arse. She was as tight-lipped as ever about her boss, not to mention her ability to regenerate, and it was obvious that, although she was here working *with* me, she still, without a doubt, worked *for* Walker. She might want to get in my pants, but her life revolved around Walker, and she was utterly loyal to him.

Alex wandered in from the opposite door and kissed Xania on her cheek. She huffed at him, her platinum blonde brows dipping. Alex grinned, always ready to wind up his unemotional sister. "Hey, how you doin', sis? You find anything with that clever brain and cool tech yet?"

I rolled my eyes at Alex's attempt to appease his sister. Both were Doppelgangers, and both could be an asset in this war, not only to save Ember but in fighting the demons that were trickling through the nearest Hell Rift. But X, as the rest of our team called her, wasn't much of a team player.

"I'm fine, *brother.* Or at least I was until *you two* disturbed my thinking space." She peered over to where Lance and Ava worked side by side. "At least they're quiet. And no, I haven't found the girl yet. I can't see what the rush is. She's immortal. They can't kill her any more than they can kill me—or you, brother. Not unless they have a succubus demon or some kind of Faerie spell we haven't heard of yet."

I cocked my head, hearing the bitterness in her words.

"X." Alex sounded exasperated. "You know they can unleash Hell on Earth with her phoenix."

X shrugged. "Then we persuade Walker to let us go back to Faerie. That's my home now, not this shitty planet with men that are too frigid to fuck. At least the fae embrace their baser needs."

I ignored her snark and the way her eyes slid to my groin. Instead, I began to peer at the day's images that graced the large bank of screens. There were hundreds of pictures from all around the world. Walker's spy network was vast, but no matter how many spies worked with us, they still hadn't helped uncover where that fucker Jed had taken my mate. Every sighting we got of a woman matching Ember's appearance, I sent one of my brother's to check it out. It had been nearly two months now, and each sighting had been a dead end. Neither had there been any demands from Jed or the man he worked for. There had been no rumblings from the supernatural community about the Halo, either, which in itself made me worry about what they were waiting for. The Halo had been stolen by Jed when he'd kidnapped Ember. And it was as dangerous as my mate if used by the wrong hands. Zander, my brother by blood, had sacrificed himself using that damned thing. He had left me a letter explaining it all. A letter I had kept and reread every night. I wouldn't forget my brother or leave him in Hell. *"It's a fallen angel's Halo, Lucifer's Halo, to be exact, and the only one known to exist outside Heaven. It is the only known way to pull a spirit from its host. But it opens the doors to Lucifer's realm when it is used. The user can prevent themselves and the spirit from being propelled through the gates of Hell, but they must use angelic words to do it."* Zander hadn't used the angelic words because he couldn't.

I flexed my neck and rolled my head on my shoulders, stretching my fingers out from the fists they'd rolled into. The tension in my muscles was almost unbearable. I needed to fuck or fight—or both. And as I wasn't going near another female, my need to fight was always there, smouldering in my gut.

"Hey, boss, you find anything?" Kawan asked as he prowled into the room as wet as I'd been. It hadn't stopped raining for weeks; even London's streets were waterlogged, the drains overflowing. I just grunted at him. That was answer enough. He came and stood next to me, dripping all over the floor. I could feel his need to speak as surely as I could sense his hesitation to incur my wrath.

"Don't fucking say it," I growled.

"He doesn't need to. You know as well as everyone else that the demons are overrunning this city. This Rift is now bigger than the one in the prison ever was. Something or someone powerful is feeding it. We need to pool our resources into hunting demons, not expend them searching for Ember. She's gone, Connor. For now, at least."

My nostrils flared, my stomach knotting with anger. Everyone stopped talking. Slowly, I turned to face Stone. He was dressed in grey leathers etched with fae runes. *Brotherhood. Strength. Loyalty. Bravery. Wrath.* Those same runes were now tattooed down the strong column of his neck and across both of his pecs. Beside him, B'nar assessed me with his strange, pale green fae eyes. Side by side, it was clear they were from the same race, and it wasn't human, not by any stretch of the imagination. Together they looked a formidable pair—because they were. Myles and Reed walked in, their hands unclasping as they entered the room. I sensed Drake and Lionel behind me but didn't bother to turn and greet them. As my brothers entered the room and power seeped heavily into the air, Lance and Ava looked up from their workstation.

Lance crossed his arms over his chest and smirked. "Oh, this should be a good fight."

Ava slapped the back of his head. "Don't be a dick, love."

He rubbed it. "What? I can't help it if I wanna see blood. It's in my nature."

I ignored them both, my focus on my brother.

"Fuck you, Stone. We could hunt and kill every demon in this city, and it would make no difference in the end, as you well know, because, if they sell her to the Devil, he will invade this world and kill everything in it."

Stone cocked his head. A minute movement that meant he was angry. If I didn't know him, I might have missed it. But I did know him very well. His gaze narrowed on me and his top lip curled up, revealing the permanently sharp canines that hinted at his fae heritage. "Then why don't you tell us who's really got her? And I don't mean Jedediah Hawk." He stepped forward, his large body relaxed but ready to defend himself. "Why aren't you sharing that little piece of information? Hm? Because I know you well, brother. You know who it is; you have from the moment they took her. Yet you're sending our brothers and me chasing damned ghosts all around the world." His purple flecked, grey eyes narrowed. "Why?"

Prime's anger flared along with mine. "Ember is not a ghost!" I bellowed.

Stone closed his eyes and pinched the bridge of his nose. "That isn't what I meant, and you know it! But you have no idea where she is! And sending us far afield on this search is leaving you vulnerable *and* allowing those demon pricks to get more and more of a hold on this city!"

I didn't know how to answer that. He was right, of course. I was wasting precious resources and time on following up leads that always led to nothing. He was right to question me, and I hated that. So, of course, I went on the attack. I snarled. "I am your king. You'll do what I tell you."

"Don't you pull that fucking card on me! You are more than my king; you are my brother...*our* brother." He covered the ground between us, squaring up nose to nose with me, but he kept his eyes focused just past my head. "And you are holding back from us. You've known all along who has Ember. Now, dammit, talk!"

Challenge rang loud above the frustration in his voice. Claws instantly pushed through my nail beds, and the spirits I held became one with me. I could put my brother down, kill him for challenging my decisions...I wrangled with my anger and my need to destroy even as Prime balked at the thought of killing our brother. My dark fae side was becoming stronger, feeding off my disheartened emotions, ones that had plagued me since Ember had been taken.

Another level of power filled the room. All alpha and not happy.

"Hey." Owen stepped up close to us, closer than the others would dare get when I was like this, which was often lately; my self-control was on a knife-edge, and they all knew it. "Stone. Back off a little, you've made your point."

Stone slowly turned his head and stared right at Owen, a snarl curling his lips. Before anyone could process it, Owen had head-butted Stone, punched him in the face, brought him to his knees and had him in a headlock.

"Whoa!" Lance chuckled. "So the beta does still have what it takes."

I flicked my gaze to Lance and growled. Lance grinned and raised his hands. But he was right. It wouldn't hurt for our newest members, or for our brothers, for that matter, to be reminded why Owen was Beta. He was even-tempered and reasonable, a good leader who should be the alpha of his own pack. He wasn't because he didn't want to be, not because he couldn't be. There was a huge difference. Owen was as well trained as me and could be equally cold and vicious when required. He chose not to be—most of the time.

"You wanna die today, half-breed? Because if you piss *me* off, as well as your Prime, who I shouldn't have to remind you is your *king*, then that will happen quicker than you can pull your fancy fucking magic into the air."

Stone managed to grind out a strangled, "No."

"Fucking A. Now, I'm going to let you go. Think carefully about your next move," Owen advised.

I stood back, allowing Prime to stay close to the surface, though I would not interfere if my brothers fought for the place of my beta. Wolf packs survived on hierarchy, and though we were a different kind of pack, to say the least, that hierarchy was there for a reason. To intervene would be the biggest insult I could give to them both. They were evenly matched physically, and even with Stone's magic, I was unsure who would win a throwdown. Both were vicious and coldblooded when they were in full-blown predator mode. As far as being my right hand was concerned, both had their strengths. Owen's calm and logical mind was his biggest strength, and Stone's honesty and willingness to call me on my bullshit was his. I simply cocked my head and waited for this to play out.

Owen released Stone's neck and stood back. He rolled his shoulders and cracked his knuckles, the cold look in his eyes one I had seen many times before—as had Stone. It was a chilling sight when someone as amenable as Owen turned into a stone-cold killer.

Stone stayed on his knees, breathing hard, clearly trying to rein in his temper. The tension in the room was palpable. Everyone knew these two were evenly matched. Reed glanced at me, and I felt his distress through our link. I knew how hard it had been for him to recover from being demon-possessed, and he was always unhappy when I separated our brothers or sent one away...I could feel it all the time. But I wouldn't step in here, not even to save him the anxiety of seeing our brothers fight. Owen needed to reassert his strength. Since being out of the prison, he'd had no cause to show his more dominant side to our pack, and even Stone was forgetting why Owen was my beta.

Stone kept his head down, his big shoulders rising and falling as he made his decision. Owen didn't take his eyes off him for a second, neither did I. I would let them fight, but I wasn't prepared for one to kill the other. Not when we had already lost so much. I tried not to think about D and Zander; every damned day I tried, almost as much as I tried not to think about Ember, and every damned day I failed.

Stone pushed his big body up, cracked his neck—and held out his hand. "No, I don't want to challenge you. I never have, brother."

Owen nodded. "Good. Then next time you have a question like this, you come to me first." He stepped back and glanced at everyone in the room individually. "Connor is our brother, but he is also your Prime and your king." He fixed Lance with a dark look. "Remember that—all of you."

Stone's silver brows dipped, but he nodded.

"Let's talk. Now." I glanced at Lance and Ava. "That means everyone." It was time to tell them the truth. My palms began to sweat. I might be powerful now, but I'd been a helpless boy once, one who'd been not just physically but mentally beaten, and that meant Rex Manivera would always have an emotional hold over me. I walked across the room, my boots thudding on the wooden floor, echoing in the now silent room until I stood at the head of the large table that was positioned at one end of the space.

Som inched forward, giving B'nar a wide berth, and stood to the side, his shifty dark eyes flitting between the fae prince and the others. He was always nervous around B'nar. I guessed breaking the laws of your own kind enough that the High King of Faerie hunted you down and then gave the privilege of your life or death to his son made a fae, even an ugly, squat criminal like Som, a little nervous. B'nar ignored the Bogwart fae and took a seat next to Stone. The stoic fae prince seemed most comfortable with my fae brother, so I often paired them together to go demon hunting. The prince was a quiet presence, though I hadn't decided if that was arrogance, perhaps a belief he was too good to be here, or if he was simply the quiet and observant type—like Myles.Walker had assigned B'nar to us to acquaint us with fae technology and train us in their weapons. B'nar had done the training so well I'd made him our chief combat trainer. It was during that training that he had gained the respect of my brothers with his obvious strength and prowess. That he refrained from using the abundance of fae magic at his disposal is what earned *my* respect.

He had taught Stone more about his magic, and when the others weren't around, we explored the dark fae spirit that was a part of me. I had at least mastered how to control its need to kill. My mother had helped by telling me what she could of her home. But even in Orth, the dark fae realm, where life itself revolved around war and death, it seemed spirit carriers were rare and always male. That meant she couldn't help me understand that part of myself much more than B'nar could.

The others came and settled themselves in chairs. Only Drake was missing. He'd taken a trip back to his office in Texas to see if he could uncover any information on where Rex Manivera lived now.

Owen sat to my right, Stone to my left. Myles and Reed sat together, and Kawan took his seat next to Owen. Lionel, Alex, and the others grabbed a chair wherever there was one.

I glanced at Som. "I need a drink. A strong one."

His chins wobbled as he smiled his toothy grin and nodded his head. "What is it you wish for, Shifter King?"

"Whisky. Neat. And don't be shy with it." I might not be able to get drunk easily, but I needed the burn.

"Of course, of course."

"And, Som?" The fae turned back around. "Ask my mother to join us, please."

He inclined his head, his chins wobbling, again. "Of course."

B'nar watched the fae as he waddled from the room. His gaze rested back on me, but he didn't speak, merely waited. Yeah, he'd learnt patience sitting in his father's court. I had no idea how old B'nar actually was, but I knew he was far older than he looked. And his experience and maturity showed.

I took a deep breath. I had hoped never to have to address this part of my past. But it was time. Time to come clean both to myself and my pack. I'd wanted to have current info or at least a plan before I had to fill everyone in on the painful details of my childhood.

I rested my elbows on the table and clasped my fingers together, resting my thumbs against my lips and feeling off-kilter.

"Connor?"

My gaze met Owen's. He deserved to know. They all did. I exhaled from my nose and sat upright. "The bastard we are looking for is Rex Manivera. He's the one who took Ember from me."

"What? The 'property' billionaire? The shifter who's an arms and super-natural artifact dealer? Fuck. I wondered who Hawk had sold out to. I didn't realise he was stupid enough to get sucked into that fucker's world." Owen's face darkened. "How do you know for sure it's him?"

"Because I scented him near the place the helicopter took off from with Ember. My guess is he was the pilot."

"Shit," breathed several voices. Everyone in the room knew who Rex Manivera was.

"So why didn't you tell us this before? And how did you know his scent?" asked Stone.

The chair creaked as I leaned back and crossed my arms over my chest. I held Stone's gaze before I looked at my beta. "Because he's my father. And I hate that fucker enough to have not wanted any of you to know he sired me. I wanted to hunt him down and get Ember out of his clutches without ever having to admit to you who he was to me. But he's a clever bastard. I honestly didn't think it would take this long to track him down."

Silence.

Owen pursed his lips, letting out a low whistle. "But I thought Rawson brought you up?"

"He did, kinda. I was already fourteen when Rawson and his mate, Lyss, offered me a home. I'd been living on the streets for four, nearly five years before that. Rawson was the one who taught me how to control my temper and my shifts, how to handle the power I had. My father only taught me how to fight and kill. "

"Did he throw you out, or did you run from him?" Lionel's amber eyes were narrowed. I held his gaze for a moment. His amber irises darkened. Yeah, he knew where I was coming from. We all had a past, and very few of us had a happy one.

"I ran." I looked back at Stone, hoping he wouldn't push for more. I didn't want to talk about how badly Rex had broken me, nor how rough my time on the streets had been before Rawson had taken me into his home. "I checked on the house he used to own when I was a kid, but he'd moved on soon after I ran away according to the real-estate dealer who sold it. Drake's trying to trace him for me. That's why I sent him back to Texas. He has access to people who can help."

"Damn, was it Rex that Drake had to get into bed with for that equipment we used back at the prison?" Myles asked.

"It's likely, yes. Rex is rich enough to fund that kind of operation, but Drake doesn't know for sure. It was all done through Hawk—and that fucker will work for whoever offers the most money." I met Myles's gaze. "All Drake knew was a wealthy businessman, with a shitload of power purchased his company from the SBI, and that whoever it was, wasn't willing to sell it back without a deal. Drake sold his future to get what we needed to fight Berith. I knew Jedediah Hawk was there for something more than keeping an eye on Drake or being a merc. Turns out he was there for Ember. So either Hawk was sent to get her by that same businessman, or he sold her to the highest bidder—my father."

"Do you think Rex knew about you? Who you are to him?" asked Owen, "Could that be why he helped fund the camp and fight against Berith?"

I contemplated the amber liquid in the glass that Som placed in front of me. Pleased when he placed the bottle next door to it. I grunted my thanks.

"My lady Tyen will be here in a moment," Som informed me. My eyes flicked to his face. Som was a Bogwart fae, and that meant he was a dark fae from the depths of Orth. To him, my mother was a full-blooded royal fae, one who should have taken the throne before her brother sold her into slavery to my father.

"No." I looked at Owen. "My father never gave a shit about my welfare when I was a boy, other than what I could become for him—a strong heir. When I was too weak, too slow, not vicious enough, he would beat me sense-less, or beat my mother for giving him a weak son..."

"Enough, Connor, please," my mother said, her words tight. "My life is not one I can change, but it is also not one I wish to be aired publicly. Especially not with the Prince Heir of my world sitting at the table." Her reprimand wasn't harsh but quiet and ashamed.

"My lady, Tyen, you have no cause for embarrassment or shame, not on my account," B'nar said sincerely.

"No, you don't. Not on anyone's account," I added, getting up to take her hand and guide her to a chair next to Lionel, who greeted her with a warm smile.

My mother sat with her shoulders curved forward. Shadow curled around her arms and body, embracing her like a living thing. My own shadow fae pricked up its ears, sensing its kin close by.

"I'd still rather keep the details of my life private, my son."

I swallowed. "Of course." I leaned down and kissed her cheek. "Sorry, I didn't mean to cause you any embarrassment."

She smiled and rested her palm on my cheek. "You haven't, but I'd still rather keep the details of my inadequacy to protect you between us."

I nodded, my throat thick. Is that how she viewed her years with me? As being inadequate? I thought back to all the beatings, and the times I'd wished she'd been around when my father had 'disciplined' me or ordered his men to do it; to how many times I'd prayed to the Mother Wolf to ask her to come back and catch him at it so that she would realise how evil he was and take us both away. I hadn't realised then that he had locked her in a room and only let her out once a day to see me. Or that he used her every night to see if he could get her pregnant again, beating her for giving him a son who he believed was too weak to be of use. Rex's whole existence sickened me.

The only light in my dark childhood had been my time with her, the times she'd held me as I cried, telling me how brave I was. Then she'd disappeared, and I'd been beaten for the tears on my cheeks—until I'd no longer cried at all.

I squatted down by her chair, not caring about the attention focused on us. I loved my mother and didn't care who knew. She'd not left me by choice, and now that I knew that, I was overwhelmed with my love for her everyday that she was here with me. "You were never inadequate. You were my light in his darkness." I kissed her forehead and prowled back to my seat. Tyen sniffed, but when I looked at her again, her back was straighter, her chin lifted.

"As I was saying, Rex is an all-round bastard who was never happy with his heir...me. I doubt he'd even know who I was, let alone believe that his son survived and is now Prime and King of Shifters." I chuckled bitterly. "He'd have come for me long ago if he'd known his son was so powerful. If only to try and kill me."

"Does he have more children?" Reed asked.

"I've no idea." I glanced at our bank of computers and then at Xania. She stared right back at me before studying her nails. My nostrils flared, my jaw clenched. I wouldn't ask her to investigate that, even though I was kicking myself for not doing it earlier. I'd just assumed I was his only child, but that had been stupid. Shifters aged slowly. He could have sired a small army by now.

"Oh, for Mother's sake," muttered Ava, rolling her eyes and shaking her head. "I'm on it, Connor. I'll see if I can find anything. Do you know when Drake's returning here?"

I shook my head. "No, he's due to video call me in three days."

"Hmm, I'll give him a call later and see if he's found anything out about darling Rex. C'mon, Lance, you can help me. "

I smiled warmly at her, a little of the tension easing from me. Ava was tenacious when she was assigned a task. "Thanks, Ava."

"Welcome. Right, come on, Lancy. Let's get on it."

He gave her a quizzical look and crossed his arms over his chest. Ava cocked a brow at his stance. "Stop being an ass."

Lance just mirrored her raised brow.

"Mother Wolf." She rolled her eyes. "*Please.*"

"That's better, baby." He grinned and stood. "Anything else you need me for, boss?" he asked me.

I shook my head, suppressing a smirk. Ava had him under her thumb even if he wouldn't admit it, though it was plain he loved his mate as much as I loved Ember.

"So, what's the plan?" asked Stone.

"While Ava does some homework on Rex, we start clearing this city. We need to be careful we don't catch the SBI's attention, though. Walker's still working on the corruption there. But tonight we go hunting..." Som's frown caught my eye. "What's up, Som?"

"Rex Manivera, you say?" The Bogwart fingered his whiskery chins.

"That's right." I fixed the Bogwart with a predatory look, calling Prime to my eyes. "Why, what's on your mind? What do you know?" The fae was, after all, a criminal, and that meant he knew more about London's underworld than any of us.

"Nothing much, other than he's a powerful shifter whose enemies turn up dead more often than not."

"But?" I prompted sensing there was more.

"But the Count might know something. I've heard rumblings in the past about a fighter who may be associated with Manivera. She earns the Count a pretty penny or two, but no one knows who she is except him. He keeps her identity secret."

I sat back and tilted my head, a small smile curling my top lip. "But you know who she is?"

"No. All I've heard is that she is some kind of associate of Manivera's. No idea what that means, but mayhap the Count's club is a good place to hunt down more info' about Yellow."

I growled, hating that Som had influenced Ember's life enough that he'd given her a name. "Her name is Ember."

"Of course, of course, Prime," he simpered.

"Bogwart, leave us," B'nar ordered, correctly interpreting my brewing resentment with the creature.

"Connor, that fae is not your enemy," my mother said quietly.

"Nor is he your friend," pointed out B'nar. He looked steadily at my mother, who lifted her chin and held his gaze. "Nor should you trust him, Lady Tyen. Somnelaire may be dark fae, but he only ever looks out for himself."

My mother nodded. "I will bear your warning in mind, Prince B'nar." She looked at me. "But wasn't he the one who gave Ember a safe place to live after you and Rawson were arrested, and Lyss was killed?"

I held her gaze, then exhaled, letting my grudge go with it. Instead, I smiled. Tyen was becoming more confident now that she understood she had no oppressor, that she could speak her mind with no painful consequences, that she could go where she wished, and see who she liked. And she was right. Som had given Ember a life; whether it was safe or not was debatable, he had used her to deal drugs in Faerie for him, but it *had* been under the SBI's and Doherty's radar.

"Trust Balthazar to be the one we need to ask for help," muttered Owen, guiding the subject away from Som.

I met his gaze. "Indeed. That bloodsucker has to be the one person I don't want to owe anything to."

"Yeah."

"Although…" I stood up. I could maybe swing this situation so that he also owed me. "Get cleaned up, brothers. The demons can wait. Tonight we're going clubbing."

"What club?" asked Stone.

Owen chuckled. "The Gambit. It's the most popular underground club for supernaturals in London. Count Balthazar Rossi owns it, along with other top-notch nightclubs worldwide, but the Gambit is his most successful—and oldest club. It's dark, sexy, violent and bloodthirsty. And only for those tough enough to not get eaten alive. You play by his rules and survive your night, or you end up at the very least broken, if not dead. Whether or not you agree with what goes on there, you don't interfere."

Stone crossed his arms over his chest, the leather of his jacket creaking. "Can we fight?"

Owen grinned at the same time I did. "Oh yeah. Fight, fuck, kill, whatever you like."

"Good. Ready when you are then."

Shannon wandered in, shaking out her wet hair, and stopped short at the sight of us all gathered around the meeting table. She inhaled and cocked a brow. "What's going on? You all stink of excitement."

"Shannon." I'd gotten over my anger at her being with my mate when she'd been kidnapped. Apparently, Jed had distracted them both. His men had attacked from behind with an injection into Ember's neck before she could call Fire or Mea to her aid. Shannon had fought for Ember against all of Jed's men, but in the end, she had been one against five big male shifters. Ember had regained some consciousness as Shannon fought, but one of Jed's men had hit my Firecracker over the head with a gun butt. According to Shannon, Ember had not woken after that, even when Jed had flung her over his shoulder and carried her off. I curled my fingers into fists, resisting the urge to let my claws push through. My anger surfaced every time I saw Shannon, but she had fought hard, even with all of her injuries, and it had taken a bullet to bring her down.

"Yeah, it's me. Now tell me what's going on. Why does the air stink of male hormones and anticipation?" Her eyes flicked to Stone. "Are you going hunting?"

I smirked, slapping my hands together. "If I have anything to do with it, we are, but not demons. Right now, I need to get showered. Stone, fill Shannon in." I looked at the others. "Be ready in an hour." I grinned and cracked my neck, actually looking forward to a night out with my brothers in such a violent atmosphere. We all needed to let our wild sides out to play.

CHAPTER 3

onnor

MY BROTHERS and I prowled towards the doors to the Gambit. They were open, music and fluorescent purple light oozing out into the night. To either side of the doors stood a tall, heavily muscled man. Each wore a long, dark jacket and had a yellow security identification armband visible. Yeah, they were human. They didn't have a hope in Hell of stopping a supernatural being of any kind, but that wasn't why they were there. No supernatural who wanted to live would mess with Balthazar or his club. No, these guys were there to take care of any human problems. Humans knew the supernatural community existed, but most trusted the SBI to protect them from its ever-present threat—like the bloody fools they were.

To humans, the Gambit was an upper class, gothic nightclub, a plush place that was reached by a curved glass stairway lined with mirrors. Dark glass chandeliers hung from the ceilings, casting a soft glow which mixed with the purple neon light that oozed from the edge of each step. Inside, the nightclub was decorated in purple and black velvets and silks, which adorned the false grand windows, giving the appearance of being inside of a huge mansion-like space. We'd cased out the Count's club a few weeks ago while I was still trying to get a feel for the London I used to know so well. Balthazar had definitely upped his game. The club had been redecorated, and for those rich enough, it now offered private booths that could have their glass walls darkened with the flip of a switch. It was pretty damned obvious what went on in those booths. I smirked. Those rich humans might think they were being so dirty, fucking in a private room, but they had no idea what really went on in the other parts of this club. Dance music filtered down the stairs to the entrance —but we weren't headed up there. Nope, we were going to the Count's 'real' club.

The doormen watched with blank faces as we headed in through the doorway and walked right past them, then headed down another set of stairs and into the darkness. They didn't bother stopping us. It was obvious we weren't human, none of us. All males, all huge, and all-powerful. I smiled. No doubt they were already letting the staff and the club owner know we were heading their way. Good. I wanted an audience with Balthazar. And I wanted the word to get out that there was now a shifter king. I was in the mood for taking down threats to my power and rule and hoped there would be many, both tonight and in the weeks to come. I flexed my fingers. Violence was in my blood, my killer instinct only amplified by the loss of my mate. And Prime's anger and grief only intensified mine.

I led my pack down the dark stairwell, leaving the neon lights of the entrance behind. Cameras followed our progress. Four large males stepped from the shadows when we reached the bottom of the stairs.

Vampires.

I grinned and cracked my neck, reining in my power.

"Who are you?" said one, stepping close but not so close I could reach him. He studied me coldly. He wasn't the biggest bloodsucker there, but he was definitely the most dangerous. I could see it in his eyes, hear it in his voice.

"King of the Shifters. I'm here to see your boss."

The vampire chuckled showing his fangs. "There is no King of Shifters; not even a Prime has been seen in years."

"Really?" I kept the wild grin on my face and shifted enough I was taller than the vampire by a foot, then let Prime's presence surface. Yeah, he saw me now. Part human, wolf, Hell-beast and fae, all wrapped up in one bad-tempered and muscled body. No one was fucking with me tonight, especially not this vampire. My vision was swamped with red, and I knew my eyes glowed as I looked at the vampire. "I am the King. And you test my patience."

To his credit, the vampire appeared only a little surprised. "Indeed, it seems you are," he said, lifting a brow.

Let him and his pack enter.

I heard the voice crackle in his ear, my hearing as acute as a vampire's, but they didn't need to know that. With an elegant gesture, he indicated that we should follow him. Two vampires walked with him in front of us, two at the back. I didn't bother tracking the ones behind me. My brothers would deal with them if necessary.

We walked towards a thick metal door that swung open as we approached. More vampires and two demons guarded the entrance to the true Gambit.

We were led down more stairs. Booming music and the sound of the club filled my ears. Energy and the scent of supernaturals, blood and sex hit my nostrils. I inhaled and grinned; I couldn't help it. Tonight I would release some of the anger and anxiety for my mate that churned in my belly.

"All weapons go here," the vampire informed us. A scantily clad female smiled from behind the counter of a small enclosed room. She held out her hand. Her blonde hair fell over her shoulders, her breasts almost falling out of her bra top.

Owen grinned and raked his eyes over her, winking as he dropped a dagger hilt first into her palm before handing over a gun.

"Nice," she drawled as she studied his weapon.

"It is, and I'll be back for it." He gave her a savage grin, watching her intently as the others handed over their weapons.

"Counting on it. Now strip those shirts, boys, and show me what you got under there."

B'nar raised his brows. "Is she serious?"

"Oh honey, you're not shy, are ya?" She appraised him top to toe, a smirk on her full mouth and a gleam of lust in her eyes. "You fae are always so pretty to look at and usually generous in the dick department. But, don't worry, either way, I won't judge."

B'nar shook his head and scowled. I laughed. I'd been here many times before, in my past life, and I knew the drill. Trousers on, shirts off, and a body search. But it was worth the look on B'nar's stoic face not to have warned him this would happen. He didn't need weapons; he was one, we all were, but even so, it was amusing to see him at a loss as he was forced to remove his fine clothing and bare his tattooed body to the female's appraising gaze.

The female, some kind of demon from what I could tell by her scent, sauntered out from behind her counter and eyed us all up like we were dinner, which had Reed snarling when she fixed her dark gaze on Myles.

"Oh, for fuck's sake, stop flirting and get on with it. The boss is waiting," the vampire barked, crossing his arms over his chest.

The female pouted. "But this could be such fun."

"Yeah, well, the boss wants to see them, right now, so hurry it along. You can fuck them, or at least fuck with them, later."

"Fine," she snapped back.

Before I could process it, she'd grown multiple arms and was rubbing her hands along our legs and into our crotches. Then it was Myles's turn to snarl when she lingered on Reed's thighs, brushing his junk with her fingers. She giggled and pulled in her tentacles. "Chill, Wolfie, I'm just messin' with ya." And she sashayed around to the other side of her desk before handing Owen a tag. "For your weapons. Come see me to get them back—anytime tonight." Her voice was low, her meaning utterly clear.

Owen leaned in. "Sure. Those extra hands might be fun."

"Oh, honey, they really are."

Owen groaned, a slow, wide grin stretching his mouth as he looked down at his crotch where she'd wrapped an extra hand around his erect dick.

I laughed. "Jeez, brother, that's quick work, but it'll have to wait. Information first then fun."

Owen smirked at the demon and pulled her hands off him. "You heard my king, but I'll be back to play later."

"I'll be waiting. Been a while since I got me some alpha wolf."

Owen walked to my side, fastened his shirt and shook his head. I looked sideways at him. "You going to tap that?"

He shrugged. "Might as well, not like I've got anyone waiting at the compound for me."

No, Selina was still in Canada. She'd wanted to stay with the newly freed women and babies. Owen missed her and little Devon, but he'd never admit it. He was right; he had nothing to get back to the compound for. My gut tightened. Neither had I, and that thought hurt like a bitch.

"Remember, no shifting or use of supernatural powers, not unless you're in the ring and the curtain has been dropped." The vampire looked over his shoulder to make sure we'd heard.

I smirked. Yeah, we'd all behave and not use our power unless I told my brothers to. B'nar knew the rules, I'd told him, but he was a law unto himself; he did what he wanted. And I doubted even Balthazar could stop him if he decided to use his fae magic. But we would respect the Count's rules and stay human. Shifts only took place in the fighting ring once Balthazar's witch had dropped a containment spell. I didn't think the spell was to protect the club's clientele, more for self-preservation on the Count's part. If the clubgoers had to remain in human form, he was less likely to be attacked by any power he was unprepared for. Around us, vampires stood at the edge of the club, watching everyone closely. Balthazar hadn't lived for so long by being sloppy. He had his own army of loyal men and had plenty of technology placed around the walls and ceilings to dissuade anyone of the notion they could plan and execute an attack on him on his own turf.

The vampire led us through a crowd of supernaturals who jeered and cheered at the male and female dancers who flung their bodies around the poles they were chained to. Yeah, they were slaves, there to entertain the crowd. If they weren't already being fucked by someone, they would be soon. Loud music thumped in my ears, and I was aware of the gazes that followed us. It was true. There were no wolf packs in London now. The SBI had stopped that practice. Lone wolves were the only ones living outside the influence of the supernatural bureau. I cracked my neck. Every lone wolf would be offered a pack, or at least access to an alpha and a community if they wanted one. I'd make sure they knew it. Stone was right. I'd been neglecting my duty to this city and my kind. I'd bring in the strongest alphas, and they could fight it out for who would ultimately run London, under my rule, of course. Word would get around about me after tonight. I was here to see Balthazar, but I was going to make a big fucking statement too. So were my brothers. We were led through the club and down a corridor that was guarded by still more vampires.

"In here. He's expecting you."

"I know," I said as the vampires took up a stance on either side of a thick metal door.

"Only you," the vampire stated.

I grinned. "Only me and my beta. You know how we work."

He cocked his head, listening to a reply from his boss, who I knew would hear my words. "Fine."

I turned to the others. "Go have some fun, but not too much—" I grinned and looked at Reed and then Lance. Reed was from London and knew this place as well as my ex-SBI partner and me. "—yet. Go and educate the others. When I'm done, we find every shifter in here. They submit, or they bleed."

Lance grinned and cracked his neck, rolling his shoulders. "Gods, I'm going to enjoy this."

"Too fucking right," agreed Reed, whose eyes were shining, his wolf sensing a place to release his wild side. Myles didn't take his eyes off Reed, clearly turned on by his mate's excitement and not in the least bit bothered about it showing. The others were all reacting to the noise and electric atmosphere too. Stone's eyes glowed, and even B'nar seemed tense and rolled his shoulders, his canines more pronounced. We were inherently wild, all of us, and a place like this was like drugs were to humans. A total rush. "Have at it, brothers. Fucking and fighting only, until I'm back, then we kick-arse. Watch each other's backs."

"Sure thing, Prime," growled Kawan.

Lance grinned at me. "Glad I left my woman at home. I wanna get bloodied tonight." And he cracked his knuckles, setting off after the others. Yeah, Shannon and Ava were at the compound. Whether that was their choice or not, I had no idea.

I stepped into Balthazar's office, followed closely by Owen. Cigar smoke hit my nostrils, but it wasn't the acrid smoke I'd normally associate with a cigar. It was different, smoother, almost soothing.

Balthazar sat with his feet up on his antique desk, the cigar between his teeth. His ridiculously long black hair fell to his waist, and his oddly pale blue eyes were fixed on my movements. He flicked the fingers of his right hand,

and the door slammed shut behind us. Silence settled. I observed him, and he studied me. We'd met before. Many times. I'd been a pain in his arse in the past when I'd been hunting down a mark, but we had an agreement, he stayed out of my way and let me hunt in his club, and I didn't bring any of the SBI down on his head.

Things were different now.

"Connor Rawson."

"Count Balthazar Rossi."

In one lithe move, he pulled his feet off the desk and sat upright. His cold eyes had my beast growling and ready to burst from my skin. I heard a low pitched snarl from Owen. Balthazar was, without a doubt, the most powerful vampire in Britain, maybe even Europe, bar the King of the Vampires. I wasn't just talking about his personal power, but his political power, too. He was born of original vampires and had been the vampire king's protege until about two hundred years ago when the king had sent him to rule the vampires in Britain. Europe was now plagued with a vampire war between the original bloodlines and the new 'made' bloodlines. Balthazar could make or break that war by taking a side; especially now the vampire king was dying. As far as I knew, he was loyal to his king despite the threats and bribes of the European sects who wanted him with them.

"Please." He gestured at the two chairs in front of his desk. "Take a seat and tell me who you seek."

I grinned, though it didn't reach my eyes. "You know me well."

He returned a smile, but, like mine, his eyes remained cold and calculating. "Not as much as I used to, it seems." He cocked his head. "You are...different. I'm not sure how; your scent is giving me mixed signals."

I just smiled and remained quiet. Balthazar knew I was a Prime, but he had no idea what else lurked under my skin. It paid to keep one's enemies and friends—and whatever Balthazar might be, guessing about that extra power he could feel. For now.

He shrugged and turned his attention to Owen. "But your second is as he has always been, albeit more powerful." His eyes narrowed. "Interesting indeed. How does a shifter increase his strength and power...?"

Owen just looked at the vampire and remained quiet.

"I'll cut to the chase, Count. I'm looking for a woman. A fighter. She frequents your club and earns you a lot of money."

The Count smiled tightly and steepled his fingers in front of him, his manicured fingernails sharp and dangerous. "I have many females of many different races fighting for me. You'll need to be more specific."

"Fine. I need the woman who works for Rex Manivera."

Silence fell. "I see."

"I don't think you do." I let Prime show himself in my eyes, and my voice deepened, my power filling the room.

Balthazar just watched with curiosity, no fear apparent anywhere in his scent or his features. No, he was too old and too powerful himself to be intimidated by my shifter spirit.

"And what makes you think I know details like that about any of the women who fight or fuck in my club?"

"Let's cut the bullshit. You know more than anyone in this club wants you to. That's why you have sex slaves chained to the poles out there. You are more than willing to use any information you have to bribe, manipulate or force people to work for you."

He smiled and gave an elegant shrug. "They all know what they are risking when they try to harm me or mine. Do not feel sorry for any of them, Shifter King; you will soon see making an example out of the worst of your subjects is a necessity. Order and loyalty, whether by fear, or respect, is a must, or you will lose control, and that's when things become tediously messy." He released a long slow breath and studied me steadily. "I also believe a good working relationship between those in power helps to keep the status quo, and if our supernatural world is settled, so too is the human world. Unfortunately, we are symbiont with the weakest species on this planet. It is for that reason I am willing to give you my time. What do you want with Rex Manivera?"

"He has taken something that belongs to me. Two things, in fact. I want them back."

Balthazar held my gaze to the point that I was ready to accept his challenge, then he calmly stood and went to a liquor cabinet. He pulled out a bottle of Jonnie Walker blue. "Whisky?"

"Sure." He was thinking. I'd give him that time by drinking with him. Perhaps he was considering how many of his men would die tonight if he didn't help me.

He poured a generous measure of the amber liquid and placed the glass on the table in front of me, and then repeated the methodical process for Owen. He walked back to his old leather chair and sat down in a controlled, fluid movement. "So, they took a woman, then?" He gave a brief smile. "You would never ask me for help for something insignificant. And to us supernaturals the most important thing another could take is their woman. Either she is your mate, or you want her to be."

I took a decent swallow and let the whisky burn smoothly down my gullet. "That's right. My queen."

His brows flicked up a little higher. "Your mate and your queen?" he steepled his fingers. "So if I help you find this fighter you seek, what's in it for me? You no longer work for the SBI, Connor, so you cannot keep me out of the public eye if things get violent and bodies start turning up in your wake."

I shrugged. "That's true. But I will keep any higher profile killings away from you and your precious club."

Balthazar contemplated the whisky in his glass before he took a swallow. "I'm not worried about the dead racking up. The amount of bodies turning up in this city is keeping the SBI and the police looking elsewhere for now."

"You have full blooded demons here every night," pointed out Owen. "It won't be long before the SBI comes knocking on your door. I know I would."

Balthazar inclined his head in acknowledgment. "Indeed. But the demons who are a part of this community, by and large, keep to themselves. They are the ones who have gotten out of Hell, or been called here by some human idiot playing with forces they don't understand, and then can't return. They have no desire to be found by human demon hunters or the SBI, and they generally keep a low profile. If they cause problems in this city or bring undue attention to my club, they know I will end them." He took a large swallow of whisky. "No, they are not the ones causing havoc in this city." His pale gaze fixed and narrowed on me. I glared right back. His gaze deepened until hues of dark ruby shadowed his irises. "But you know that, don't you, Shifter King?"

I smiled. Balthazar Rossi was anything but stupid. He'd worked out there was a connection to my arrival and the influx of demons. He was also a better ally than enemy. "I want an oath of silence, and your support when the time comes."

He raised a dark brow and we studied each other more. I waited. He knew whatever was happening was dangerous to all of us and he would protect his kind, not to mention his interests, with the same loyalty and viciousness I would protect mine. I had the answers he wanted, and he had to give something in return. And it wasn't as if asking for an oath would cost him anything.

A muscle in his jaw ticked as he considered my offer. "I don't give out oaths or promises lightly." His voice was tight and low, his brows pulling together.

I blinked. Perhaps there actually *was* a cost to him for taking an oath of silence. "Understood. But the cause of this influx of Demons will affect us all —and soon. Don't you want to be prepared for the war that is coming, Count?"

The small curl of his top lip was chilling. "I am always prepared for war, because in one way or another, I am always fighting one."

"Not this one. This one is coming from a direction you can't prepare for. It needs prevention, or we could all die. And the status quo that you keep amongst the supernatural underworld? *That* is going right out of the window, *very* soon."

Another silence. I raised my glass and tipped some of the glorious whisky into my mouth. I could happily sit here and drink his whisky while I waited for his response. I didn't technically *need* his support, but it would help things move quicker. I *would* find Ember, and I *would* get that Halo back, even if both ended up in Lucifer's hands first. It just remained to be seen whether it would be before or after Lucifer destroyed this world.

Balthazar sat upright and lowered his arms, folding them in front of him on the desk. The silk of his purple shirt shone where it creased over his upper arms and shoulders. "You have my oath of silence, Shifter King. And my support." He winced as if something had caused him pain.

I nodded, hoping the cost for his oath wasn't too great, but not all that concerned if it was. "The woman who he took *is* special; not just because she's my mate and queen, but because she has the ability to open the gates of Hell."

Balthazar's eyebrows twitched up very slightly, but otherwise, his face remained blank. "A phoenix?"

Of course, the ancient bastard would know what I was talking about. "Yes. But that isn't all Manivera took from me. He has Lucifer's Halo." I *was* surprised by the sound of the Count's nails digging into the desktop, scoring the wood, even though his face remained coolly controlled.

"Do you realise what he could do if he gets that piece of himself back?"

There was no point in pretending. "No. All I know is that demons squatting in other creatures can be exorcised with it by using an angel's power." I didn't volunteer that I could do this for my kind without the Halo. There were only so many secrets I was willing to reveal in one night.

"That is true, but if Lucifer gets his hands on that piece of himself, he will not only be able to destroy this world, but he will be able to re-enter Heaven. Halos are like a key to the different levels of Heaven. Only the most powerful angels have one. He will not only destroy the fabric of this world but have access to all other higher powers in existence. The deities of every world will be at war with him, not through choice but because he will kill them if they don't fight back."

"Damn," breathed Owen.

I downed my whisky and smiled tightly. "Then you need to help me find the woman I'm after and hope to whatever deity you worship that she can help me find Manivera—or we're all dead.

CHAPTER 4

mber

A WARM BREEZE fanned my body, and I stretched like a cat. My towel ruffled underneath me, but my bikini had dried ages ago. A shadow fell over me, and I smiled though I kept my eyes closed.

"Hmm, I'll never get tired of seeing that beautiful view when I come home."

I opened one eye and raised a brow, though my heart didn't beat much faster at the deep timbre to Jed's voice. "Really?" And though I sounded sarcastic, my cheeks warmed at the heated way he looked at me. Butterflies fluttered in my stomach. It had been the same for the past couple of weeks. My desire for him had been slowly building, not to any great heights, but it was hard to know if my need was really for him or if my body just needed a release from the tension coiled inside. Did I even *want* to want him? I'd tried to push myself to connect with him, but it hadn't gotten me anywhere. He'd just pulled away whenever I tried to get closer. I didn't understand it, not after he'd told me my father's goal.

Perhaps his relationship with Tina had surpassed meaningless sex. Maybe it was beginning to mean something else to him...

I kept the smile on my face, determined to keep trying the relationship thing. I owed him and my father. Besides, the past week or so had been better, I wasn't as lonely, and I actually felt, if not content, then at least more settled.

He'd taken me down to the beach several times and often sat next to me on the patio while we read, not saying anything but just enjoying each other's company. We'd dined together every day, and I'd even fallen asleep in his arms on my bed a few times, though he hadn't pushed for more. If anything, he'd backed off when I'd tried to touch him.

I'd slept a little better, if not soundly, and I'd started to put some weight on, my breasts were fuller, and my hip bones weren't sticking out so sharply anymore.

My father had been true to his word and had let Jed spend time with me every day. I knew why he was pushing Jed and me together, but I couldn't really blame him. He hadn't had a son, and he had no one to leave his company to. Jed told me everything would go to me, but I knew as well as they did that I couldn't run a global corporation, and Jed said he had no desire to run Rex's business interests; he was happy with being head of security.

Jed grinned and gestured to the panoramic view of the ocean. "Sure, this view's the best thing in the world."

I laughed and dipped my hand in the pool, flicking water on him. "So, do I have you all day, again?"

He smiled, his eyes sparkling as he cocked his head and studied me. Damn, he was a good looking son of a bitch. I could appreciate that even if I didn't feel anything deep for him. "You sure do."

I smiled back. We had enjoyed each other's company recently, but I still didn't know him, not really. Every time I steered our conversation deeper, he'd deflect it back to me and how we were going to fill our days or how my memories and headaches were improving. It made me suspicious and made me question why he didn't want to share himself with me.

"That's great. Let's go and get some lunch at that little cafe on the quay, and then you can take me shopping. And while you drive us down into the town, you can tell me why you, an American, work for my father. You can tell me about what you do as his head of security, and you can tell me again how we met." I stood up, deliberately holding the towel around me. I don't know why I felt suddenly self-conscious under his intense gaze. After all, he was my fiance, but his continued rejection of my need to get to know him bothered me more every day.

He grinned at my obvious attempt to cover myself and stalked closer. Instinctively, I lifted my chin. I wouldn't back away. Instead, I faced him and placed my palm flat against his t-shirt covered chest. Heat seeped into me, stirring a warmth low in my belly. "And you can also tell me why every time I try to touch you, you pull away."

He sighed, his eyes He sighed, his eyes turning deep and stormy, the hazel flecked with deep brown. He gripped my fingers but didn't retreat. "Because I know how much it hurts you when you have contact with me."

I lifted my chin. "It doesn't hurt," I lied.

"Em—I mean Sarah, yes, it does. I see you wince, and I know you well enough that I can tell when you are hurting." He ran his other hand through his hair. "Do you think I like causing you pain?" he asked quietly, his shoulders tense, his muscles rock under my touch.

Damn, I was a selfish bitch. I'd never considered that it was my pain that stopped him, or rather us, being together. I still wasn't one hundred percent sure about having sex with him, but unless we kissed and touched, I'd never know how I felt about that kind of intimacy. Maybe once we started, my headache would settle. Perhaps it was just the tension of being turned on that was the problem. Or perhaps...

I slid my hand up his chest and cupped his defined jaw. "No. I don't think you want to hurt me. But I need to understand your feelings if we are going to try and work things out between us. Don't you find me attractive anymore? Is that the problem? Obviously, you and Tina have a...thing going on, so if you don't want me, I totally understand. I mean, you are definitely fit and have needs, and I am not really ready and...."

A deep chuckle made me raise my eyes to his and halt my sudden babbling. He was grinning from ear to ear, his eyes back to a glittering hazel. "Oh, honey, you are adorable." His big hands cupped my face, gentle in a way that seemed impossible for such a big man. My gaze snagged on his as if he compelled it to be there, and I couldn't look away. My heart raced, thudding against my chest wall. It was confusing not to know if my reaction was desire or fear of the headache that would follow his touch.

"Listen to me. You are without a doubt the most beautiful woman I've ever met, or probably ever will meet. Tina is nothing to me. We shared a bed once, well before I met you, but not again. Before you, I only ever slept with a woman once and then never saw her again. I didn't have time for entanglements or commitment." He brushed his thumb lightly over my mouth. "Getting to know you all over again is consuming my thoughts." He swallowed hard, and a line appeared between his brows. "And it's...confusing."

"Confusing?"

His face relaxed, and he smirked a little. "Yes, confusing. You confuse me with this beautiful face." He released his hold on me only to brush his fingertips over my forehead and cheeks, and mouth. "These beautiful eyes and this kissable mouth."

Well, if I wasn't turned on before, his husky voice and those godsdamned words certainly stirred something inside me. I'd have to be made of stone for them not to. He inhaled, and his gaze darkened, his hands caressing my neck.

"But most of all, I'm enjoying all the time I get to spend with you just having fun. It's not something I've done before." He shrugged a little, resting his hold loosely around the base of my neck, his fingers curling over my shoulders.

"Oh, so it's not me then?" It was an awful sensation to have such a lack of self-confidence but I was so unsure of everything in my life.

A growling sound came from deep in his chest. "No, it's not you, not in the way you believe, anyway."

Was that even an answer? The pain started as a dull throb at the back of my head, but I ignored it, fed up with it dictating my life. I needed to find out if I felt anything real for this man. "So why don't you kiss me, then?"

His grip tightened, and he leaned in. "Be careful what you offer...Sarah." Warning rang in his words, but set on my course of action, I stepped closer, slipped my other hand around his toned waist and gently kissed the base of his neck. He stiffened but didn't pull away this time. With the next brush of my lips, I moved a little higher. His taste wasn't unpleasant. I licked my lips. Salt, and a deep scent of...wildness...My head pounded with a vengeance as something angry stirred in my blood. I gritted my teeth and pushed it away, kissing the underside of his jaw.

I slid my hand into his hair and gripped onto the silky strands. My lips continued to trail a path up his neck and jaw. Standing on my tiptoes, I reached the corner of his mouth and kissed him tentatively. He was inflexible under my touch, my lips. My heart sank at his lack of reaction—and mine, but I wouldn't give in completely. "Kiss me," I whispered against the softness of his lips.

With a loud groan, he gave in. He grabbed my hair and angled my head so our mouths could fuse together. And boy did he kiss me. He kissed me until I was gasping for air, and my head was spinning, but then I heard it. A distant mournful howl. The pounding in my head changed to a sharp, vicious pain as Jed's hand found my breast, gently pinching my nipple between his thumb and forefinger. I arched into his touch, but the howling in my head became so loud I couldn't concentrate on anything else.

"Sarah?"

Jed's voice came from too far away. All I could hear was that mournful howl. Damn, there was a bloody wolf stuck in my brain! Or that's what it sounded like. I groaned and held my head. My skull was going to explode... *"Ah! Shit!"* I hissed. The pain was too much... I cried out and gripped my hair, wanting to yank the damned noise from my skull. "Please, Jed....Please. Make. It. *Stop!*" I screamed my last word.

Jed picked me up and ran. I didn't know where we were going, and I didn't care. He lowered me to a soft mattress. The howling in my head persisted as if whatever made the noise was getting stronger.

"Here! Open your mouth."

Jed's barked command was the only thing that seeped through the pain.

"Drink."

He placed a tablet on my tongue, followed by the coolness of a glass against my lips. I gulped down his offering. Those tiny tablets were the only thing that could stop the pain and the noise in my head. The wolf's howl became desolate as she faded. My heart ached, and I felt my chest hollow out all over again. I curled into a ball and wrapped my arms around my stomach. Tears seeped from my eyes, but for some reason, I didn't want Jed to see them. I turned my head into the pillow. "I'm sorry," I whispered.

"It's okay. Just sleep now, you'll feel better again soon."

I closed my eyes, but it wasn't Jed I'd been apologising to; it was the beautiful wolf I could see in my mind, the one who became nothing but mist.

CHAPTER 5

onnor

THE CROWD ROARED as Owen slammed the demon into the hard floor of the fight ring. A shiver of anticipation rolled over my skin, causing Prime to pace and snarl. He wanted out again. I'd fought to keep him contained as I'd taken on more shifters who wanted to challenge me. The Count had messaged me and suggested we visit the club again tonight and that I challenge the previous night's winner. So I had. I didn't know his agenda with that fight, but I was willing to run with it. The fight hadn't happened as yet, though we had warmed up with some shifters who had banded together to attack me; they apparently didn't agree with my having power over them. Subsequently, the bodies of those stupid enough to refuse to submit were gone while the rest were now my subjects and giving me a wide berth. I huffed a laugh as Owen smashed his fist into the demon's face, breaking his nose and sending blood flying through the air.

Prime snarled at me. He wanted to release his wrath, his blood boiling with the need to destroy. As well as the shifters who we'd fought near the bar, I'd fought twelve rounds in the ring. Sweat rolled down my naked chest and back, but I hadn't met a fighter yet who could truly challenge me. Killing all of them wasn't an option. Balthazar would be pissed at me if I did, though I was certain that he had bet on me tonight and was happy to rake in more money at my expense. I glanced over at him and lifted my beer before chugging it down. He smirked and nodded, his eyes alight with an odd ruby glint.

The atmosphere of the club was electric. The bloodshed and tension my pack and I had provoked was off the charts, even for this place, and now word was out that the Count was condoning it, more shifters piled into the club. Whether it was to see their new king or to try and prove themselves against my brothers and me, I had no idea, but Balthazar knew it needed to happen. It had been the same for nearly two weeks. He'd agreed to let me establish my rule without intervention while he sought out Manivera's woman. He'd given me his oath, and it seemed he took that very seriously. He'd also seen the human body count in the city rising as more demons appeared. I'd meant it when I told him I'd give him all the information I had once I knew where Ember was. In the meantime, my brothers and I fought those demon fuckers every night and sent them back to Hell. We were fit, mean and far more experienced than the shifters who challenged us and more than happy to flaunt it. I cracked my neck and grinned as I saw two more shifters approach from my right.

Stone and Lionel snarled. I slammed my pint glass down and grinned. "Let them through, brothers."

They returned my grin and stepped back. "Sure thing, boss."

B'nar huffed and stepped back.

"You running away, Prince?" Stone smirked at his friend. Yeah, that's what they were now; friends. Good ones.

B'nar snarled. "No, I just don't want blood on my clothes. This kind of violence is messy and requires far too much effort."

I'd have laughed in his face if I hadn't needed to dart sideways to avoid a barrage of punches. I grabbed each of my attackers by their throats and squeezed, holding them still. Urgh, it was too easy. I eyed B'nar. "Prince, you need to loosen up. Swear once in a while, go and fuck someone, fight. You are no better than us when it comes to hankering after some good old fashioned violence. I see it in your eyes." And I threw both of my attackers down. Not far enough away that they'd give up. I was enjoying myself too much and wanted to continue.

Stone laughed at B'nar's bunched brows and disgruntled expression. "Come on, man, let loose. No one here's judging you. Fuck, they don't even know who you are. You're not a prince here. Just one of us."

B'nar stared at Stone; his head cocked as he contemplated those words. Then a smile stretched his mouth. "You're right." He watched as the two shifters got back on their feet and rushed me, the crowd around us baying for blood. Excitement and adrenaline pumped through me, and I roared. This made them hesitate, and a waft of fear hit me.

"Oh, no, you fucking don't." And I grabbed them as they turned to run.

"Fight, you cowards! You wanted me; now you've got me." My fists connected with each of their faces until they were groaning on the ground. Myles and Reed grinned as they pulled the males by the scruff of their necks to their feet. They swayed but managed to remain standing, just. Neither of them looked at me. "That's right; you are mine now. Swear your life to me, submit to my rule, and I will let you get on with your lives." I glanced at the Count, who watched closely. The vamp really deserved something for letting me trash his precious club every night. "Refuse, and I'll give you to the Count. He might kill you or put you to use in others ways. I don't know, and I don't care."

There was no hesitation.

"I submit."

Reed kicked the back of one of the males' knees, Myles the other one's. "Add, my king or Prime on that, you piece of shit."

"I submit, my King." They both growled out.

I grinned. "Good, now go and spread the word. I'm here to stay. If you or any other shifters want to fight for the Alpha position of London, then be ready when I send the word out for the trials."

"Yes, Prime."

"Much better. Now get out of my face."

They left. B'nar watched them go, then fixed his gaze on the ring. "My turn." He grinned at Stone and me. I laughed out loud at the excitement on his face.

"Fucking-A!" Stone smacked his friend on the back. "But don't you want to protect your finery, Prince? Might wanna strip." He tipped his chin to the women who had been trying hard to get our attention all night. "The females love seeing some naked chest."

B'nar glanced at them, and his lip curled back. I wasn't sure if it was a snarl or a smile, probably both, but he unfastened his leather jacket, shrugged it off, and ripped off his shirt. He threw them at Stone and, grinning, vaulted into the ring, his tattooed body and blue hair gleaming in the club lights.

Catcalls and whistles rang through the air. Owen grinned and slapped B'nar on the shoulder as he leapt out of the ring. On the far side, a huge vampire jumped in; clearly, he didn't like the fae. His face was a picture of hatred. B'nar bared his sharp teeth and let his famous control go—a little. He prowled in a circle, fluid and ready when the vampire used his super-speed to attack. B'nar spun, caught him with a hard punch to his solar plexus and dropped the vamp to the floor.

I chuckled. It was good to see him loosen up. Stone and the others yelled encouragement, though we all knew he didn't need it. B'nar could have broken the vamp's neck in that first attack if he'd wanted. He let the vamp land a punch on his jaw, and we all hollered.

We all fought in human form, no shifting, no magic, not for any supernatural inside the Gambit, unless it was one of the Count's wagered fights, and a containment spell had been conjured around the ring by his witch. There were no exceptions; it was considered cheating and punishable by the laws of the club—which, depending on his mood, was subjugation or death by the Count's hand.

The Count sat on his throne, a strange-looking yet beautiful woman kneeling at his feet. She was nearly naked and covered in runes from the top of her shaved head to her toes. He had the leather straps that attached to her collar wrapped loosely around his hand. She tilted her head up and said something. He stared at her for a moment, his face utterly devoid of emotion before he leaned forward and whispered in her ear. She pulled back and frowned; her nostrils flared as she looked over at a fair-haired girl at the bar. With a look of determination, she leaned in and kissed Balthazar roughly, biting his lip when she got no reaction. The Count yanked her head down, and she had no choice but to back off. His eyes flared and his lip curled back from his fangs. He snarled more words, and she turned around and kneeled with her back to him, her face a mask of fury. He ignored her and met my eyes before looking at the curtains at the back of the club where the regular club fighters congregated. A nod was all I needed to know the fighter he wanted me to meet was up next.

The ringmaster, a flamboyant Asian vampire, had dressed half of his body drag queen style, and the other half as you would expect a perfectly coiffed and tailored vampire to be, in a black, long-tailed jacket, complete with half a top hat and a cane. He vaulted into the ring as soon as B'nar knocked his opponent down. B'nar jumped over the ropes, landed smoothly, and accepted his shirt back from Stone, who was grinning as if it had been him fighting. It was a revelation to see both of these stoic males finally relax in this place. B'nar used his fine shirt to wipe the blood and sweat off his skin. I raised my brows and exchanged a look and a smirk with Owen, who grinned.

The ringmaster's antics were as bizarre as they were entertaining. He changed his or her voice and style depending on which side of the club he addressed. The side with the most females got the vampire, the side with the most males, the drag queen. My stomach tightened, and Prime growled as the ringmaster looked right at me. This was it.

"And now ladies and gentle supernaturals, you need to show me just how excited you are for our main event. Let me hear you roar!"

The crowd went wild, roaring and yelling and banging their feet and their glasses on the tables.

"Ha! Not good enough. You know the sexy Velvet will not come out unless you give her some encouragement! AGAIN!"

More roars until my ears were ringing, and Prime was scratching at my insides to get out. I fought him back. The rules still applied even to me. No shifting until the Count gave us his blessing.

"Better! Now give it up for the battle for the new King of the Ring!" The drag queen was talking now. "Let's hear it for that sexy thang Velvet, and the one you've been waiting for...King of the Shifters! Get in here, you luscious supernatural beasts!"

The crowd went wild. I vaulted the ropes into the ring. Prime snarled and then howled, his dominance and power rolling from me...

They are all ours. They should kneel.

I rolled my shoulders, gritting my teeth against the need to release my power and do as Prime wanted; make all these creatures bow at my feet.

Air brushed my skin...

Balthazar stood behind me. I tensed. "Careful King," he whispered in my ear. "This is my domain. Follow through on that need to crush all, my kind as well as your own, and you will die by my hand, oath or not. Control your power."

Then he was gone.

I turned. He leaned forward slightly, his elbow propped on the armrest of his 'throne' and his chin resting on his fingers. His look told me that I hadn't just imagined his voice in my ear, but it had happened before I could even blink. It was hard not to respect power like that. My acknowledgement was a brief dip of my chin and a smirk. He returned the gesture without the smirk.

We had an understanding.

I pulled in Prime, along with my need to crush the supernaturals in this club to my will. Instead, I turned my attention to the female who climbed fluidly into the ring.

Her severe cut, jet black bob swung a little with the dip and turn of her body. She was lithe and slim, but with enough defined muscle, it was clear that she was strong and trained hard. She straightened, and I couldn't help but compare her to my Firecracker. Ember was petite where this woman was tall. Ember's eyes were a bright jade green, where this woman's were a vivid blue. My heart squeezed as the loss of my soulmate hit me in the gut once again, but I pushed that pain away. There was no room for weakness.

The woman was at least six feet tall or just under, and she had a confident arrogance that raised my hackles. Perhaps it was for show—perhaps it wasn't.

Prime snarled. *One of our own.*

Not just a shifter.

He huffed in agreement.

Another power lingered around her; only I didn't recognise it. That made me more wary. Most supernaturals could shift their appearance to seem human. As humans, they kept their particular species traits, but their true power was hidden until they took their true form.

I assessed my enemy. Starting at her feet, I studied her body as she prowled around me. She favoured her right side. My eyes narrowed, or did she? The boot heel on her left foot was more worn. Interesting—and clever. I hid my smile. A good misdirection tactic. Her stomach was flat and covered in tattoos. Beautiful, inked wings peaked out from under her cropped top, curling around her ribs and the curve of her waist. Her arms were generously muscled, except it wasn't that which caused me to pause; it was the face that stared out at me from her upper arm. His features were as clear as day.

Drake.

My gaze flicked up to her face. Why the Hell had she gotten a tattoo of my brother on her arm? Things got even weirder when I stared into her face. I knew her. But I couldn't, for the life of me, place from where. She was a stranger.

"You have an issue fighting a female, Prime?" Her smirk was tinged with underlying irritation as if she'd had that very issue before.

"No. Just admiring your ink. It's very well done. Who's the guy? Someone here I should worry about when I beat your arse?"

Her laugh was bitter. "No. He's not real, just some man I drew from my imagination." She sighed dramatically. "*Real live* men, whether supernatural or not, are just soooo disappointing."

I moved around the edge of the ring, mirroring her speed and movements. The crowd grew loud and impatient. "Is that so? Well, I happen to know your imaginary guy. Very well, in fact, so I'll do you a deal. When you lose this fight, and you will lose, you'll owe me a huge favour for not killing you. Agree to help me solve a problem, and I'll even agree to tell you who your fantasy man is."

She snarled. "Bullshit! He's not real. And even if he is, what makes you think I want to meet him? Reality is often a bitch of disappointment."

I grinned. She had a weakness. Her connection to Drake. It didn't matter that she'd only met him in her dreams; for her, the connection was real. And once a supernatural dream-shared with another, they were connected forever. Had Drake ever dream-shared with this woman? He'd never mentioned it, but then again, it wasn't as if we ever got to such personal shit like discussing dreams.

"Oh, believe me, he's very real and definitely not a bitch." I cocked my head and grinned. "And those dreams you've been having about him? Has anyone ever told you what they mean?"

She stopped prowling, her face hard though colour leached from her cheeks. "They mean nothing; none of it means anything."

So, yes, then. I chuckled and jabbed out, deliberately going slow. The crowd roared and she ducked, slamming her fist into my abs. She winced. Chuckling, I danced a few steps away. "Is your fist alright, there?"

She shook it out and scowled. "Yeah, I'm good. What're you made of, though? Iron?"

"No, that's one thing I'm not made of, but part of me thinks that metal is like poison to my beast, so let's not mention it again, hm?"

She grinned. "Ah, the great new King of Shifters has a weakness. Interesting."

I shrugged, letting her believe she had one over on me. "We all have weaknesses. Yours is Drake. And dream-sharing is your supernatural soul searching for his." Light-footed, I darted away from her back kick and caught the punch she threw, drowning her smaller fist with my grasp. "And it will only get worse until finally those thoughts and dreams of him consume you."

She swallowed. Without giving her time to process that piece of information, I swept her front foot out. She was ready, as I suspected she would be, and went with the sweep before landing to snap a punch to my face. I jumped back, blocked her next punch to my ribs and kicked her to the ground. She landed with a thud.

"Having a weakness doesn't make me weak, same as *he* won't make *you* weak. Say you'll help me, and I'll introduce you to Drake."

Her blue eyes narrowed, but she swallowed hard. "Drake? Is that really his name?"

Got you!

I cocked my head. "Maybe. You haven't agreed to my deal yet. So unless you agree to help me with my problem, I'm not helping you with yours."

She flipped to her feet and grinned, unleashing a barrage of kicks. Each one connected with my body and face in some way. She was relentless. I could easily have stopped her, but I didn't want to, not yet. I wanted to learn her moves. I could tell a lot about her by her fighting style. She was confident, calculating, and well trained, but she was arrogant. She believed she'd beat me, no matter who or what I was. She believed herself powerful enough to take me down. Maybe she was, but not until she could use her supernatural power. I allowed her to push me back, but my satisfaction was hard to hide when I turned the tables and pushed back. Not enough to end the fight, just enough to dim that arrogance a little. The crowd wanted a show, after all.

She was good, really good. She held her own against me, catching me a couple of good hits on my jaw and a swift kick in the kidneys that hurt like a bitch.

Too soon, the Count stood and banged his cane on the ground. Immediately, the whole club went silent. Excitement charged the air. He pulled the tattooed woman to her feet. She glared up at him with glittering eyes and a snarl on her lips. His cold gaze lifted from her to me. His eyes flared with ruby, and he tilted his head to whisper in her ear, yanking her collar up tight under her jaw. She rose on her tiptoes, but her mouth moved, her fingers worked as her tattoos swirled over her slim body.

I braced myself. Soon everyone would meet Prime. He roared and paced, ready to be freed. "Time's up, Velvet. We aren't playing now. I have a point to prove here. Either submit to me and live, or I will kill you as a warning to the rest of the people in this club, including the Count, who at the moment thinks you are safe. He believes I need you. I don't. It would make my goal quicker to reach, but don't for one moment think I won't kill you."

"Ha, you shifters are always so fucking sure of yourselves. It's sickening. You deserve your arse handed to you, *King*. Why would I help you?" She slapped Drake's image. "Him? I don't know him except in my nightmares, and I sure as fuck am not submitting to a shifter's rule or agreeing to a deal with some arrogant prick who thinks himself a king. All you fuckers ever do is lie and bully your way through life…."

I cocked my head. Balthazar's witch was kneeling once again at his feet. She had let her spell free, and it had encased the fighting ring. Prime knew it. He snarled and pushed. Even if this female wasn't a full shifter, he wanted her baring her neck to him. I pushed him back, my top lip curling at her continued vitriol. My words had served their purpose. She was angry and off guard. I shifted, letting Prime free. He was no longer just a wolf but a monstrous Hell-beast, one that stood on two clawed hind feet, with the viciousness of my fae side at his beck and call. Or rather, mine. I controlled Prime, not the other way around unless I allowed it.

I leaped across the ring, my jaws wide and ready to clamp down on her neck. Pain blasted through my body, and I flew back. I hit the spell wall at the edge of the ring and bounced, landing flat on my face. The crowd went wild, my brothers snarling and standing as close as they could without touching the spell that encased the ring.

Balthazar's mouth twitched at one corner. His version of a grin. That snide fucker knew what this woman was capable of and wanted to see what I could do. I fixed my gaze on my quarry. Wings flapped behind her. Not physical. The crowd that bayed for our blood couldn't see them, but the Hell-beast in me recognised the light of those wings. Her nostrils flared.

"Yeah, that's right, *King*. I'm not just a shifter, and I'm never submitting to your kind. Just as I said, an arrogant prick."

I slowly uncurled my huge body off the floor and cocked my head, calling forward more of my power. This time when I stalked closer, I felt out where Velvet's power made a wall between us. I lifted a clawed hand and grinned at her, baring my fangs. With one sharp nail, I drew a line from above my head right down to the floor.

She didn't take her white, glowing eyes off me, but her throat bobbed.

There was no way she was getting away. She didn't realise it, but she had just sealed her fate. "Now we play, angel."

Her eyes widened, colour leaving her flushed skin. "How do you know what I am?"

"I see your true form, just like you see part of mine. As I said, I am the King of Shifters, and in my wolf lives the spirit of the King of Hell-beasts." I stretched my neck forward. "I see the aura of my timeless enemy."

She cocked her head. "I'm not your enemy, but nonetheless, I'm not submitting to you—or anyone else." And before I could step closer, she snapped those stunning wings together in front of her and sent a wave of light and power my way as she bolted for the far side of the ring.

Head down and teeth bared, I charged forward through that force, yanking on the bond with my brothers. Had they seen her run? The crowd had. They were baying for blood. She reached the far side of the ring and blasted a hole outwards. Diving through it headfirst, she shoulder-rolled and was on her feet in seconds, running for the back of the club.

"Stop her!" I yelled at Owen as I ripped a hole in the spell wall large enough for me to fit through. He bolted past me. The others followed, all except Lionel and Stone, who waited, ready to protect my back.

Once through the curtain, the scent of fear hit my nostrils. I skidded to a halt. Balthazar held the girl by her throat. Her feet dangled off the floor, and she thrashed weakly, hitting his arms and face. Her wings, still not fully visible, hung limply, brushing the dirty floor. I cringed. It was obscene to see such beauty dragging in the filth of this place, even if they were more of an apparition than anything.

"What do you want an angel for, Shifter King?" Balthazar's almost colourless eyes rested on me, seemingly unaffected by Velvet's choking and weak efforts to escape.

My brows dipped. I did not want her dead before I could use her. "I didn't know she was an angel. You know I need her to help me find Manivera. He has my mate."

The woman stopped struggling at my words, but, if anything, her scent went from angry and scared to downright fearful at the mention of my father. I growled. She wasn't the first female he'd hurt, and I doubted she'd be the last, but my priority was to get to Ember.

"Ah, but now your Hell-power has unveiled her to the darkness in me. And an angel is worth a lot of money to some of my kind."

I didn't have time for more negotiation. If that was the case, he wasn't going to kill her—but I needed her. And he'd taken an oath...

"You took an oath, Count."

He held my gaze. "I did. To help you find this female. I have done that."

"She cannot help you or your kind," said B'nar, stepping forward. "You want her to reverse your oaths. She cannot. Only a full-blooded angel can do that." He glanced at Velvet, his eyes narrowed, his brows dipping. "She is terrified."

The Count snarled. "Of course she is. She hid her true self from me, and she ran from a fight. Both are rules that, when broken, leave her at my mercy."

B'nar cocked his head. "No, not of you...of Rex Manivera."

The Count's ruby gaze slid to Velvet. "Interesting."

"She has wings, but she is only a half-angel, which is why she cannot manifest her wings physically. Her angelic power is not strong enough to help your kind."

Balthazar snarled at B'nar, but the prince was back to his stoic self and just stared back coldly.

"I could still sell her. My kind would not know that if I did not."

I growled and shifted back, pulling the molecules of my clothes to me. Balthazar's brows twitched at my neat trick. "Fine. What do you want for her?" He commanded the British vampire nation, not to mention he was close to the prince of vampires, now that the vampire king was almost dead. If the London Rift grew stronger, he could bring in reinforcements from Europe. I needed him on my side.

Velvet squealed, the sound trapped in her throat by his hand. She kicked him in the knee cap—hard. It earned her an irritated look and a shake. "Be still. You broke your contract and ran before the fight was over. Your life is now forfeit. You know the rules." He looked at me, his head tilted, his gaze shrewd. "Five hundred grand—and your blood."

"Fuck off! You don't get his blood! He is our king." Owen's words were followed by his shift.

Balthazar didn't even acknowledge Owen's wolf. But Owen stood, hackles raised and ready to pounce. My other brothers shifted. The biggest Lion I'd ever seen prowled behind the Count. I'd never seen Lionel's shifter form, but now wasn't the time to admire him. Stone's wolf shimmered with purple magic, ready to slam a shield down to keep the Count contained.

Balthazar lifted a brow.

I shrugged. "They are loyal; what can I say?"

"You can say yes."

"Why the money?"

He shrugged. "Why not?"

I had to smile. He didn't need money, and we both knew it. He was old and had billions locked away. "Fair enough. Why my blood?"

"Because you are powerful, and your beast is like nothing I have ever met or seen before. What is it exactly?"

"Not it—them."

Velvet shrieked and clawed at Balthazar's face, leaving scratch marks on his skin that instantly began to heal. He shook her roughly. "Cease your wriggling, or I'll throw you in my blood bin for others to use while I decide what to do with you."

"Velvet." She might not be a full shifter, but she was still part shifter, and I was her Prime, whether she wanted to acknowledge that part of herself or not. "Stop struggling. Now." I sent a wave of command to the wolf buried in her soul.

Her gaze slid sideways, and she scowled through her red and swollen face. But she stilled.

I glanced at B'nar. There was no way I'd give the Count any power over me. "Prince, what can he do with my blood? Is it the same as me taking my brothers'? Does it connect me to him in any way?"

B'nar didn't take his eyes off the Count. "No. He is not a shifter. He can only compel his own kind or those who have weak minds, like humans. It will, however, give him a taste of your power. He will know your strength."

"Hm." I cocked my head and pretended to consider it. Really I was compelling my fae side to pull from our connection. It did, disengaging from Prime and his Hell-beast. Prime hated that part of us was forced to let go, even for a short time. I sent some comfort to him, prepared to let the Count have a little of my blood if that was the price of getting to Ember, but he wasn't learning all of my secrets.

"Fine." My pack all snarled. "Quiet, brothers." I directed a little reassurance their way. "Let Velvet go. You'll have your money tonight, and you may take one draw of my blood. That is all." I scented his excitement before I'd finished speaking, as did my brothers. They growled, Owen and Stone snapping their teeth.

Balthazar licked his lips. I smirked. The Count was known to play with males and females, but this wasn't about sex; this was about power. He wanted to know the extent of mine, and he knew I would never tell him. I wasn't about to show him, either, but he didn't know that.

He released Velvet's neck, and she dropped to the ground. Before she could bolt, B'nar encased her in a wall of ice. I nodded my thanks. He blinked once.

I held out my wrist. Balthazar raised a brow, and I huffed a chuckle. "No, Count, the only one who gets to sink their fangs into my neck is my mate."

He actually smiled and let his gaze travel the length of my body. "Shame, but I understand. I feel the same. Wrist, then?"

I nodded and turned my wrist with the soft, pulsatile side up. In a blur, Balthazar was on me, his fangs embedded in my wrist. After one long draw, he pulled away. His eyes flared that disturbing ruby red as he straightened, standing almost nose to nose with me, not touching, but very nearly. He held my gaze, and with a deliberate, sensual movement, he licked drops of my blood from his lips. "Mm, a shame indeed that only your mate gets to taste more of you. You taste...of power and sin."

I grinned. "I am both. But I thank you for respecting my wishes. You could have taken more, but you didn't." He nodded, it was true, and we both knew it. "Now we are even as far as Velvet is concerned. Our other deal still stands. When I have my mate, I will return and tell you where those demons are coming from. But if I am too late, be prepared to fight because Hell *will* come, and I doubt Lucifer will be forgiving towards those who have given his demons sanctuary rather than sending them back to their master."

"Then I wish you luck, Shifter King." Balthazar glanced at the cage of ice that Velvet tried to kick her way out of. "Take her with you. I trust you to drop the rest of her payment off before dawn." And with that, the Count walked back into his club.

CHAPTER 6

My stomach clenched, and saliva rushed my mouth.

"Oh shit."

I stumbled out of bed and just managed to make it to the bathroom before I promptly fell to my knees in front of the toilet and retched up my insides. I spent the next ten minutes with my head stuck down the bowl and my guts trying to find their way out of my mouth.

Once my stomach had settled, I gingerly got to my feet and stuck my mouth under the running tap. It was heaven to rinse the bile away and brush my teeth. Straightening up, I tilted my head. The two red marks that had always been there on my neck seemed more pronounced than ever today. I ran my fingers over them, hating the hollowness in my chest every time I looked at them. Perhaps I could see them more today because my skin was paler than usual. I'd not spent time in the sun with Jed the past few days. Instead, I'd preferred to sit quietly in the shade, reading, or just resting. I'd been utterly exhausted. And even though I wasn't eating, I was putting on weight—it was so irritating. Maybe I should force myself to do some exercise? Ugh! That thought just made me even more exhausted.

Jed had been nothing but attentive, making sure I was eating and resting. I'd thrown up every morning for the last few days, and though there were no questions, his concern was obvious. I didn't understand the soft, worried look in his eyes. He'd even taken to staying in my room, never touching me, other than to hold me when I had a nightmare. It was a relief even though I hadn't felt any desire for him, not since my head had nearly exploded six days ago.

The dark circles under my eyes were a testament to my lack of sleep. I leaned towards the bathroom mirror, my breath leaving puffs of steam on it. Blinking did nothing to alleviate the scratchiness in my eyes, either. I sighed, leaning against the cool marble of the sink. Perhaps, I should see a doctor about some sleeping tablets… My dreams were more vivid than ever. Wolves. Always wolves—and fire, and a huge werewolf-like creature with eyes of the brightest blue I'd ever seen. I'd awoken screaming last night as fire consumed me, the monstrous creature howling plaintively in the distance. I could feel him searching for me, always searching…

I swallowed and tried to shake away the trembling in my hands. I didn't feel scared by that creature, so much as unsettled, as if he was important to me in some way.

My head throbbed. I reached for my painkillers only to knock them on the floor. "Dammit!"

I felt Jed's attention boring into my back before I straightened and met his gaze in the mirror. He frowned, his jaw muscles tense as he looked at the brown pill bottle on the floor.

"I'm fine. Just a stomach bug."

"Is it?" He almost growled.

I huffed a laugh. "Well, I'm not pregnant, am I? I have no idea when we last had sex, but it sure hasn't been recently, and you told me you were away when I had my accident. So, unless I was having an affair…" I gave him a weak smile and raised my brows, but he didn't laugh. I'd never seen him more serious, and that was saying something. It was unnerving, and his dark look sent a shiver through me.

He scowled and leaned down, picking the bottle off the floor and pocketing them. "Sarah, this is important. No more painkillers. And, please, don't have dinner with your father tonight."

"What? Why not? To both of those statements. I need something for my head. And dad's coming home from Paris tonight and wants us both to eat with him." My stomach tensed at the scent of…something…I wasn't sure what, in the air. Whatever it was, it made my palms sweat and made me want to run from Jed. Something was very wrong; he was tense. I inhaled and almost gagged again at the vivid scents around me. Anger and worry. It should be impossible to tell his mood from the smell in the air…but I could.

"I know. I'll tell him you're not feeling well. You can't see him tonight."

I gripped the edge of the sink, not sure why he was suddenly against me spending time with my own father. "No, honestly. I'll be fine."

A growl rumbled from his chest. I froze, something inside me going on alert, a distant howling making my head throb more viciously.

"No! You won't!" He strode forward, and grabbing my shoulders, spun me around. To keep from stumbling sideways, I grabbed his hips. I needn't have worried, though. He steadied me immediately. I liked the feel of his solid strength under my hands, so I didn't remove my grip. My heart flipped as his pupils dilated, his gaze darkening. He slowly raised his hand and brushed my messy red hair back from my face.

"Sweetheart, your father...he's a dangerous man."

I frowned. "What do you mean? He'd never hurt me."

"I know you think he has your best interests at heart, but he honestly doesn't. He is the kind of man who looks after himself, and only himself."

My brows dipped. Why was he suddenly warning me off my own father, the man he worked for? "Jed, stop. What are you talking about?"

His wide shoulders rose and fell as he expelled a deep and slightly shaky breath. "I'll tell you everything soon. I promise." His gaze landed on my lips, and a pained look crossed his face.

My stomach twisted. I shook my head, my throat so tight my words were almost whispered. "Jed, you're scaring me. What's wrong?"

He huffed a bitter laugh. "Everything. But I'm about to put it right." He swallowed hard and cupped my face with his hands, his stern face softening. Something tightened in my chest. Holding my gaze, he leaned in and brushed my lips with his, then pulled back. "Gods, I wish you were mine. But it's too late for that. And I won't let any harm come to you, not now."

"What do you mean?" I whispered, holding him tighter. I didn't understand, but I could hear the pain and regret in his voice.

"I mean, this is all a lie. This house, our life, even you, but the one thing that is real is that I wish you really were mine."

I wanted to reassure him, to tell him that I was his, but the words wouldn't come. They weren't true, and we both knew it.

"It's okay, sweetheart, I get it, and, I swear, soon you will too. Listen, I have to go out for a while. Please, if your father comes home early, stay away from him."

I nodded, not understanding but willing to trust him. After all, what did I really know about my father? Or even Jed? Nothing. But of the two, I trusted Jed more.

Jed's mouth curled into a soft smile, and he rested his forehead on mine. "Good girl. Don't worry, I'll be back soon, and I'll tell you everything." But he made no move to pull away. Our breath mingled, electricity zipped between us, and I saw the moment his eyes flared. "Oh, fuck it. Just one more time." His lips pushed against mine, warm, soft and consuming. For once, as he touched me, my head didn't hurt. This wasn't a kiss full of passion or need; it didn't set me on fire. But as his lips moved over mine, his tongue stroking gently against mine, as his taste filled my senses, it felt more like a sensual goodbye kiss, one full of longing. I felt tears prick my eyes though I couldn't say why. This time instead of a wolf howling, all I heard was a sad kind of whimper, as if that imaginary being inside me sensed Jed's mood.

He pulled away and smiled, but it looked forced. "I'll be back soon, and I'll explain everything." He brushed my cheek with his fingers. "I only hope that you will forgive me."

"Why would I need to forgive you? What have you done?" My fingers gripped his shirt.

He tipped his head back and blew out a breath between his pursed lips. When he looked back at me, his eyes were dark and shining. I swallowed hard, knowing I was the cause of the devastation I saw there but unsure what I'd done.

"I've betrayed you, Em, I've lied to you, I've kept secrets from you, I've taken you away from the people who love you, but most of all...." The column of his throat bobbed, his face twisted. "I've fallen in love with you, and I can't let Rex destroy you any more than I can be a part of your destruction or unhappiness any longer."

With that, he turned and walked away. I stood frozen, my mouth agape, staring after him. What the fuck? He loved me? Why was that so terrible? We were engaged. Weren't we? I released a shaky breath, his words suddenly registering. Not caring that I was dressed in my short nightie, I bolted after him. I needed to know what was going on.

"Jed! Jed! Wait!" My feet slapped against the marble floor, my heart racing. But I was too late. By the time I ran out of the front door and onto the court-yard, his bike was disappearing down the driveway.

Dread dragged at my chest. I hoped he'd return soon, I needed to know what the hell was going on, but instinct told me I wasn't going to like it.

CHAPTER 7

onnor

THE TANTALISING AROMA of strong coffee filled my nose. I inhaled deeply, glad of its soothing fragrance as I watched people meander by with their designer and boutique shopping bags. My seat was in the coffee shop's window, just as the message on my phone had instructed.

"Sophie, stop fidgeting."

"I can't. He'll know I'm here. I know he will." Sophie's gaze darted over the people outside before studying the faces of those in the cafe.

"How? You can glamour your appearance as well as any fae or doppel-ganger I've ever met. And whoever sent me this message did it after we booked into our hotel. They don't know you are part of my team. Unless you used the same name at the Gambit as you did when you worked for him?" I narrowed my eyes on the woman who had once only been known as Velvet to me. She was nervous, and the alpha in me hated that I could sense her anxiety and her underlying fear, especially when she was normally ultra controlled and, if anything, cold towards others. Her hair was jet black and bobbed, her face covered in piercings, and her makeup was thick and brash. The goth look suited her, but I wasn't sure if she liked it or if it was just a way to hide what she really looked like.

"I, err, changed my name."

I took a deep breath, wishing she'd been as sensible as I'd hoped. "Never-mind. So Sophia…"

"Sophie."

"So, *Sophie* is your real name?"

"Yes."

"And your last name?"

"It's not Archer."

I couldn't help but raise my brows at her avoidance. Still, perhaps I shouldn't push. "Okay. But you are now Sophie Archer and you look completely different from the way you looked in your angel form, and I presume when you worked for Rex?" She nodded. "Then he won't know who you are even if you come face to face with him."

She huffed. "You have no fucking idea what he's capable of." She peered down at her espresso, her fingers pulling at her sleeve.

I put my hand on hers, trying to set her at ease. "Believe me, Sophia, I do."

"It's Sophie," she snapped as I knew she would. I smirked, and she rolled her eyes. "You can't distract me that easily. Unless you've lived and worked with him, you can't possibly know what he's like. He's got a godsdamned army in that house. And they all know me. If you lose this fight, I'm not hanging around. I can't let him catch me. He'll never let me out of his sight again."

I held her gaze, keeping my voice even and my face serious. She needed to know she could trust me. She hadn't told me exactly what she had been forced to do for Rex. Whatever it was, she was scared of him, and she wasn't the type to be scared of anyone, me included, but long term scars ran deep—I should know. "I do know. Better than you think."

"Hm, we'll see." She took a sip of her coffee, as did I. "You know, that text can't mean anything good. He's probably playing you already."

I shrugged one shoulder, already suspicious. "Maybe, but what it does mean is that someone who works for him knows we're here, probably from the hotel staff, and one of two things is about to happen; either Rex will attack us, or that person is truly willing to betray him. If that's the case, they also know who I am and probably why I'm here, and they are still willing to help me."

"Porca!" she muttered under her breath. "You mean you want to sit here and wait to be attacked—or not."

I grinned. "Sì, è giusto. Aspettiamo, e poi sappiamo."

"We wait, and then we know? Are you kidding me? And when did you learn to speak Italian?"

"No, I'm not kidding you. Now relax. And I was an agent for the SBI, we had to speak other languages, but I don't speak Neapolitan. Don't worry; that fae armour you're wearing will protect you, as will Stone's and B'nar's magic.

How about you distract yourself and tell me why you are so scared of Rex Manivera?"

Her gaze followed the waitress as she walked by our table. However, the waitress was more interested in making doe eyes at Stone and B'nar than watching us.

I laughed. "Believe me; the waitress has far more interesting things to look at than you. And these people only work for Manivera because he threatens them. They hold no loyalty to him. They need a new master to serve, and who knows? Maybe they'll have one soon."

"What? You?"

I shrugged and leaned forward. "I could easily take this town from him. But the only thing I'm interested in is getting my mate back. Right now, I'm stopping myself from ripping into that house in the hills and getting her out. I'm giving this person…" I flicked the note. "…the benefit of the doubt because I'd rather not get my pack, or you killed, if I can rescue Ember without loss of life. So, while we wait, tell me why you hate him so much."

She sighed, and perhaps unconsciously, placed her palm over Drake's image on her upper arm, hugging it to her chest. "When I was a little girl, Rex put me to work for him. He taught me how to observe people, how to learn the weaknesses of others, how to manipulate, how to kill. You know? All the things a little girl wants to know. And I wanted him to be proud of me, so I did everything he asked to the best of my ability—always." She looked out of the window, her black lacquered nails digging into the soft skin of her upper arms. "Once he thought I was sufficiently talented at those skills, he put me to work learning about his business interests. I was basically an assassin. But all others saw was an innocent girl that went on business trips with her daddy, someone the authorities would never suspect."

My heart lurched as I gripped the edge of the table. "You're his daughter?" My question was remarkably calm considering that bombshell.

A bitter laugh escaped her, but her eyes were dark and full of pain. "Yeah, and he destroyed me and my life. I never had a childhood because of him, and I have done things that I can never atone for or take back." She tapped her chest, right over her heart. "This is empty because of him. I will never allow myself to love or to be loved because of all the lives I've destroyed for him. I don't deserve it."

I swallowed the ache in my throat, but it wasn't enough; it closed up on me anyway. And I couldn't pull my gaze from her face. *Her eyes…* That's why she looked so familiar. Her eyes were my eyes…our *father's* eyes.

"Are you okay? You've gone a bit pale."

Prime whined, sensing my shock. I shook myself and forced my attention over to Owen. His brows dipped. He knew me well and sensed something had happened to rattle me. And holy shit, I *was* completely rattled. A sister! I had a sister, and she had no idea who I was to her.

"Connor? Are you okay?" Her mouth tightened into a thin line. "I know, I'm disgusting...all the things I've done."

"No." I coughed to clear my throat. "Sophie, that's not what's wrong, not at all."

Her chuckle was full of disbelief. "Yeah, right. That's why you look like you're going to throw up."

Ok, that was enough! "Sophie. Look at me." I didn't force her; I couldn't, not now. I was too thrown, completely blown away by the fact that I had a sister, as well as a half-brother. I may not have been able to save Zander, but I could make damned sure nothing happened to my sister. I rubbed my forehead and sighed. "Sophie, you cannot take any blame for what that man did to you."

"Yes, I can. I did it. I hurt people; I destroyed families. I ruined them..." Tears shimmered in her eyes.

I wasn't one for soft gestures, but fuck me; I couldn't let this go. As a child, Rex had almost destroyed me, but I'd gotten out. He'd definitely destroyed my mother's life, and he'd manipulated, abused and used my sister, or rather half-sister, too. I reached over the table and took her hand in mine. Her eyes widened, and she stared at my hand holding hers. I felt a pulse of concern from Owen. Under the table, I raised my hand to let him know we were okay. "I know it isn't your fault, Sophie, because he tried to do the same to me. I got out, and yet I'm still a killer. While I was in prison, I killed because I had to and because of who I am. Part of that is Prime; part of it is me. You have suffered years of his manipulation, and you were still strong enough to get away...."

"But I wasn't. I'm back here now."

"I won't let him hurt you. Ever again."

Her attention bounced from where I held her hand up to my eyes. "Why? Why are you so bothered about the life of a stranger? And how do you know so much about him?"

"Because I know what it's like to be hurt by him. I know because I'm also his son. I'm your brother, Sophie, or at least your half-brother."

"What?" Her question was no more than a whisper.

"I ran away when I was a young boy. He might have searched for me, or maybe not. He always thought I was too weak to be his son. He beat me regularly, trying to make me stronger...."

"You, you're...my brother? That son-of-a-bitch! He never told me I had a brother!"

I huffed. "Why would he? I stopped existing for him the moment I ran."

"Oh, my gods, Connor. Does he know that Ember is your mate? Is that why he's got her and hasn't sold her yet?"

I glanced out of the window, watching as a large male on a motorbike pulled up across the square. "I hope not. I don't think he knows it was me in Canada when he funded our fight against Berith. I think he knew about Ember from someone who escaped that prison, and he wanted her. It was an easy in for him when Drake wanted his company back. Rex did what he always does; he manipulated Drake to get what he wanted—a chance to kidnap the key to the gates of Hell."

Sophie tensed at the mention of Drake, but she didn't ask any questions about him. She knew we had a deal. Shit! Life really was full of strange surprises.

My phone beeped, letting me know I had a text. *Damn, speak of the Devil.* Drake had just landed and was meeting us at the hotel in an hour. Mother Wolf, could this day get any more crazy?

"So Rex isn't hunting you? Or setting a trap for you, then?" Sophie's gaze searched my face.

"I doubt it. I think he quickly gave up on me once I escaped. I was too much trouble, too defiant, and according to him, too weak."

She sighed. "Connor, I'm ..."

"No," I growled. "Don't you dare apologise; for him *or* yourself. He's a bastard. And if I have anything to do with it, he's gonna die for his sins."

The door tinkled, and a familiar scent drifted up my nose, one that had me half-shifting and out of my seat and across the room in a second. My claws dug into Jed's throat. I had to fight to keep control, not just snap Jed's neck then and there. Only Jed didn't fight, didn't even try to defend himself. Instead, he lowered his eyes, and even though I was cutting his air supply off, he went utterly limp and compliant in my grip.

What the ever-loving fuck?

He was the one who'd betrayed me, taken my girl and hurt one of my pack. This bastard worked for my father, yet he was the one who was betraying him now? It made no sense.

"Speak!" I demanded, releasing my grip enough for him to suck air into his lungs.

Stone snarled from behind me. I didn't reprimand him. Jed and his men had hurt Shannon, and although they weren't mated, it was obvious to everyone but them they belonged together. I would let Stone take this kill if I decided Jed needed to die. He'd taken Ember, and that was enough to sign his death warrant.

"I know where she is."

His words made my heart stutter. I pushed Prime back and snarled in the fucker's face. "I know you do. Now tell me."

His gaze rested on the table. "Sit?"

"Fuck off! Speak, and speak quickly, or I'll rip you to shreds and let Stone finish you off."

His attention didn't waver from the table. "She's at Rex's house right now."

"Tell me something I don't know, and you'd better hope it's good enough to warrant me keeping you alive."

"I can get you in."

"Stone."

Stone complied with my order. He wound purple twines of magic around Jed's arms and hands.

"That should hold him, boss."

"Good. If you try anything, that fae prince over there is going to pin you to the ground with shards of ice while I feast on your insides. We clear?"

He nodded.

I stalked back over to the table. Sophie had moved to the back of the coffee shop, and it didn't escape my notice how she stayed out of Jed's line of sight. "Sit." I pointed at the chair I'd been sitting in. I didn't give him the opportunity to inhale Sophie's scent, just in case he knew her.

He lowered himself heavily and looked at me. There was no challenge in his gaze. If anything, he couldn't hold my stare. His gaze slid past me, and he looked around the coffee shop. "Keep your attention on me. No one here will hurt you unless I will it. And no one who works here will hear you speak. They are currently on their break, and the coffee shop will remain shut until we are done."

Lionel and Myles stood outside the doors. It was obvious to anyone who looked at them that the cafe was off-limits. I leaned forward, the wood on the chair arms splintering under my grip. I wanted to rip this bastard apart. "Is she alive...and unharmed?"

"She is."

I didn't hide my relief. My body slumped, and for a moment, emotion filled my chest, but I wouldn't give Jed the satisfaction of seeing my weakness. I straightened and eyed him coldly, deciding whether or not to kill him anyway. But the rational part of me knew I needed to hear his information first.

"I don't know how you found out where he lives, but you won't get in, not even with the men you've brought with you. I can help you."

"Why? Why help me? You're the one who took her from me. And if you dare mention money, we are done. Or rather you are. I'll rip your heart out."

He huffed a bitter laugh, his shoulders caving forward. "You don't need to. She already has."

I cocked my head and studied him. He was...different, still tough and physically strong, but his eyes were shadowed. I stiffened. I knew that look. He was worried, anxious for someone he loved. My nostrils flared. What the fuck did I do with that knowledge? My top lip curled. "How the mighty and cold-hearted have fallen. Who is she?"

He met my gaze, then looked away. It took me a second. Then my fist connected with his jaw, and he tipped out of his chair, smacking his head on the floor. "You fucking bastard! It wasn't enough that you took her from me! You had to try and make her yours, too?" I leaped on him and punched him again. "Did you fuck her, you raping, kidnapping son of a bitch?" I roared.

I felt hands under my arms yanking me back. I shook them off and raised my fists to hit him again, and this time there'd be no holding back; I'd kill him!

Heat surrounded my fist. No matter how hard I tried to land that killing blow, my arm wouldn't move.

"Connor, that's enough. Ember is alive, and this male, no matter what he's done before, has come here to help you. I can sense the truth of his words; he has fallen in love with Ember, and he wants to help her." I didn't want to hear Sophie's words, not at all, but then B'nar backed her up.

"It's true, Prime. I can also feel his emotions. He is as confused by his love for her as you are angry at him for it. His hope that you can help her is real."

I nodded to Sophie, who released her hold on me, and I lowered my fist. But I didn't move my weight off him. My capitulation didn't mean I was done with him.

He spat a mouthful of blood on the floor. "She is alive and physically well."

"What does that mean?"

He closed his eyes. "She has no memory—of you, of who she is, that she is mated, or that she is even a shifter. She has no memory of the supernatural world at all and believes herself to be utterly human."

Behind me, Stone and Owen swore. I climbed off the gorilla shifter and plonked myself in my chair, my whole body heavy. After all this time, I'd finally found my mate only to discover she had no idea she was mine, or even who, or what, she really was. "Get him up."

Stone kept the magical bindings in place and roughly pulled the male to his feet before pushing him into the chair opposite me.

"What did you do to her?" I forced myself to look at Jed.

"I didn't do anything to her. Rex has been searching for her kind for years. He knew what she was when he saw her in the fight rings in the prison."

"He was there? With you?"

Jed nodded. "I went once." It was the look of disgust on his face that saved his life at that moment. "Rex tried to buy her that night from the Warden, but he wouldn't sell her."

"Did he ever see me there?" Maybe there was something to Sophie's idea that this was more about me than Ember...maybe...

Jed met my gaze. "I honestly don't know. He never mentioned looking for an alpha Prime. Why? What would he want with you?"

I grinned evilly. "None of your fucking business. Now keep talking. Tell me why my mate can't remember anything about me or her pack." I leaned back and let Prime stare at him too. "And I suggest you convince me that you haven't used her in any way, fast."

That elicited a snarl from him as his eyes darkened. Good. He was as off-kilter as me. Gods, I wanted to destroy this motherfucker. For stealing Ember from me, but even more for stealing her entire life from her. I couldn't even comprehend how scared and confused she must be.

"Rex has labs, cells for test subjects, in a facility under his house. He had developed a substance that can suppress a shifter's animal spirit long before I took a job with him. In tablet form, it releases a chemical slowly, and when taken regularly, it can induce amnesia, too. It also gives the user severe headaches if their animal spirit fights the substance and needs to be suppressed further."

"You've been *drugging* her? The woman you profess to have fallen in love with?" My teeth cracked, I ground them so hard.

His chin dropped to his chest, and he sighed heavily. "Look, I took a job as a security consultant with Manivera just over a year ago. I normally don't work more than one job with a single employer. That way, I don't get sucked into their shit. But Rex made it clear I could stay in his employ and be paid a shitload of money or disappear without a trace. I'm good at my job, but I can't watch my back twenty-four seven without sleep. So I continued my employment with him. He had me work with Drake and you so I could determine if Ember was at the camp. Together we planned to get Ember away from you." He paused. I just stared at him, my anger boiling, my breathing deep and quick. A growl began in my chest. He swallowed and carried on.

"Ember needs to get away from Manivera. Her wolf is fighting the drugs, and it's taking more and more tablets to suppress it—but she can't take them anymore."

"Why?"

Jed slumped against the chair back, his breath leaving him in a whoosh. He lifted his gaze to mine. "Because she's pregnant."

I heard several sharp intakes of breath but had no idea who they came from. Blood was roaring in my ears; Prime was howling and scraping at my insides. I stood so fast my chair flew back. I needed to get away from Jed, or I was going to kill him. He'd kept my pregnant mate from me...

I shot out of the back of the cafe and into a small courtyard. The stink of stale rubbish and rotting food hit me, but I didn't care. My Firecracker was pregnant. She was carrying my child. And they'd been kidnapped, *from right under my nose!* I'd let them both down...

"Hey, you okay, Con?" Owen's question was careful and soft.

"I can't...I can't..." I blinked hard. I didn't know what to say. I couldn't breathe.

"I know, it's okay. Let loose all you like, man. No one else is here or watching."

At Owen's words, I leaned forward, supporting myself with my hands on my thighs, gulping down air into my lungs and feeling as if I was drowning in guilt. I took some deep breaths, closing my eyes and picturing the greenest, most stunning eyes I'd ever seen until my heart rate calmed a little, and Prime backed off. I straightened and released one long deep breath. "Shiiiiiit."

"You good?"

"No, not one bit." I shook out my trembling hands. "But I will be when I get Ember back, and to do that, I need to talk to that kidnapping mother-fucker in there." I knew the child was mine, not his. It had to be. Ember had finished her season when they took her from me. I swallowed hard, knowing the two most important souls in this world were in danger because I'd taken too long to find them.

"Yeah, you do. And don't kill him. At least, not yet. He's here because he's fallen under Ember's spell. It's in every line of his body. He genuinely does care for her, and he's here for her, not you, so let him help her by giving you the information you need."

I nodded, fortified my resolve, and, leashing my wrath, I headed back in. Jed's gaze followed me warily. I stood over him. Yeah, I wanted him to feel small and powerless, just like I had for weeks, unable to find Ember, not knowing for sure if she was alive or dead. "When did you find out she was pregnant?"

"Only a few days ago. Her scent has slowly changed over the time she's been with me...."

I growled. "That better not mean what I think it does."

He gritted his teeth before he spoke. "We haven't had sex; let's get that on the table. But I have slept in the same bed as her. I've held her..." His eyes went to where my nails scored into my palms, blood dripping onto the floor. Stone and B'nar came and stood behind me, knowing as much as Owen did that if I killed this shifter, we'd have a harder time getting Ember out. They wouldn't be able to stop me if I chose to rip his head off, but they could slow me down, perhaps even enough for Owen and Sophie to get Jed out of my grasp alive, if not in one piece.

"She has been having nightmares more and more recently. I stayed with her to make sure she was okay."

"That's it? You didn't touch her or try and fuck her?"

He looked me in the eye. "I didn't say I didn't touch her. But you wanna keep torturing yourself? Or shall we get to the point of my visit? This isn't about you or me; she's in danger, you asshole." He froze when he heard the rumbling around him from the mounting growls.

"Yeah, watch your tone. You're walking a knife-edge right now. And I sure as shit won't stop them if they decide it's time for you to die."

"Sorry, but Rex is returning from a business trip tonight, and once he catches the scent that she's pregnant, he'll lock her down so tight you'll never find her. He knows what a pregnant female smells like. He's had women locked up, trying to get them pregnant, for years; even succeeded a few times from what I hear, though according to him, many of his offspring died when they weren't strong enough for his training regimens."

My eyes met Sophie's. My sister, one who'd been groomed and suffered at the hands of that man for years. How many others had there been? Whatever I did to Rex would never be enough.

"How do we get to her?"

Jed smiled, though there was little humour in it. "Right through the front door. I'll give you the security codes for the front gate. There are always two guards in the gatehouse, and all of the guards carry weapons. They are all shifters of one kind or another, and they are all party to what happens in that house; the experiments, the imprisonments, the beatings and rapes." His nostrils flared.

Yeah, my father was despicable, but Jed should have walked or gotten Ember out when he learned what Rex was doing. A little voice nagged that he was doing just that now, helping get Ember out.

"There are cameras on the driveway, but I can disable them before you attack. Come at one am when Rex is more likely to be alone in his room. I'll do my best to keep Ember away from him this evening. Make sure you have access to silenced weapons."

I nodded that we did.

"Good. I'll keep Ember in her room. When the fighting starts, I'll stop her from running out and getting hurt." He looked me in the eye, and I saw his silverback glare out. "But remember, when she does see you, that she'll not know you or trust you, not at first."

"Don't tell me what *my mate* will, or won't, do. No matter what you think, she is mine! And if it takes me the rest of my life, I'll make her see that."

He scowled, but his mouth ticked up very slightly. "I doubt even you'll be able to *make* her do anything, Prime. Even with her wolf and phoenix trapped, she's as stubborn as a mule."

I grunted, not willing to acknowledge he knew her that well. "Do you have a map of the house?"

"Yes. If you give me your email and unbind me, I'll send it to you now."

I indicated to Stone. The binds around Jed's body dissolved into nothing. Jed stretched out his limbs and reached into his back pocket to pull out his phone. He placed it on the table. I watched the screen as he pulled up some plans of the house, typed in my email and pressed send.

"In all seriousness, Prime, she's suffered a total loss of memory, not just from the drugs but from a head injury too. Her identity is lost. She knows that her headaches and dreams mean something. She just doesn't know what. If you come in all guns blazing and try to force her to remember, she'll just run. She isn't the same woman you knew. She's different…more fragile. She'll need time to get to know you again, to learn to trust you, and to recover from the suppression of her wolf."

I smashed my fist into the table, breaking it in two and sending his phone skittering over the floor. "And whose fault is that!?"

Jed stiffened, his shoulders heaving with shallow, frantic breaths. "Alright! It's mine. Fucking hell, Prime! I'm sorry for all the hurt I've caused her, not for you or your band of merry men, but because she deserves better than being kept in the dark about who she is. Shit, she doesn't even know she's pregnant! She thinks she's throwing up because of some stomach bug and that her headaches are purely the result of a head injury she got in a car accident. And yeah, it's partly my fault she thinks I'm her fiance; and because of that, she trusts me. But I'm trying to put this right. I can't watch her keep getting more depressed and confused about what's going on in her head, not for Rex Manivera. He *wants* her pregnant. That's why he didn't sell her to the Devil himself. He wants to keep her child to study it, dissect it, see what it can do, and see if it will benefit him if the Devil does unleash Hell on Earth. As soon as Rex scents that she's pregnant, he'll have her in those labs under his home; definitely long before she has any idea what the fuck he's doing or why."

He lifted his gaze to mine, and my fists clenched. So, he fell in love with my mate. But that wasn't enough to exonerate him from stealing her away from me. I was grateful he'd decided to return her to me, but he'd get no sympathy from me. None. He was lucky I didn't rip his heart out, and the only thing stopping me was his knowledge of where she was.

"Ember has to stop those meds," he rushed on, his brow furrowed. "I have no idea if they could hurt a baby, and I might be a cold-hearted bastard, but even I draw the line at hurting or imprisoning innocent babies. That's why I'm here, I want you to get her out of there, and as much as I don't want to let her go, especially to you, it's where she belongs. It's your child she's carrying, and I will never come between a male and his child, no matter how much I don't want to let her go."

I snarled, Prime pushing through my skin. My bones shifted in the blink of an eye, and I towered over the man who, along with my father, had taken my soulmate from me. Warmth covered my body. It was an instant soothing blanket that quelled my anger, not extinguishing it, more tempering it so that

I could think clearly. Prime shook his head, as did I, feeling almost drunk, or drugged, or something. I shifted back.

"Connor, walk with me." Sophie's words were not a request. "Owen? Why don't you get more details from Jed. Our Prime needs to process all the information he has so he can decide what's best for his mate and how to get her out safely."

I heard my beta growl. "Yeah, I'm sure his mind's blown to shit by this wanker's confessions."

I didn't look at Jed again, not sure I'd be able to contain my fury a moment longer. No matter if he was trying to do right by her now, he'd touched my mate, slept with her when he knew she was mine! *Mine.* And pregnant with my child! He'd taken advantage of her when she was vulnerable, manipulated and lied to her about who and what she was. I snarled, my fury heating up all over again.

"Out. Now." Sophie gave me a shove towards the door with her magic, so did B'nar and Stone. Together their force was enough to move me. Outside Sophie linked her arm with mine and pulled me across the square and along the road. She didn't speak, and I was grateful. My head was a mess. What was I going to do when I saw Ember? How the hell did I convince her who I was? That I was her mate. Would she feel our bond? Mother Wolf, she'd spent months believing Jed was the one she loved. What if her memories never came back?

I wanted to smash my fists into the wall of the nearest building, but there were humans everywhere, kids and their parents just spending time together. Me tearing down a building with my bare hands would pretty much bring the authorities down on my head, as well as inform my father someone powerful was sniffing around his turf.

"Connor, she's your mate. She might not recognise you, but she will know you mean something important to her."

Sophie held my hand, guiding me through the small streets until I found myself standing outside the hotel doors.

"Come on, let's get a stiff drink. It'll give you something to do until Owen gets back, and you can plan the attack. I can check the floor plan Jed sent and tell you if anything is missing or any additions that weren't there last time I was. While you drink, I'll tell you more about my life with Rex, what I know about his men, the security systems, and the way his set-up works. It will help you beat him. And you have to now because if you don't, he'll never stop hunting you—or me, down."

"Oh, he's definitely gonna die. But first he'll tell me everything about his operation, his set-up, his other prisoners, and any other siblings we might have."

Sophie ordered us two whiskeys, and we sat in a quiet corner of the bar. I was intently listening to her tales of Rex when I sensed someone watching us. I met my brother's gaze, too strung out over the attack and too impatient to get to Ember to worry about this meeting. Still, I knew this would be a big thing for my sister, so I shoved my own anxieties down and tried to ease this for her. Drake had no idea what the next few minutes would mean to Sophie —not unless he had been dream-sharing with her too. And he had no idea who she was to me, not yet.

"My angel powers aren't fully-fledged, of course, but I can pretty much control them. I hide them mostly because, just like Rex and the Count, there are supernaturals who want angels for one reason or another, and not one of them is pleasant..." Her words dried up when she saw my attention was on a spot over her shoulder somewhere.

"Hey, man! Sorry to barge in on your meeting, but I need to talk to you." Drake's deep voice resonated through the air and before she even saw his face, the colour drained from Sophie's face. I smirked, though I was a little worried at how sick she looked. Yeah, she'd been dreaming about my brother for years. She even had his face tattooed on her arm. He was her mate. I wondered if he'd realise it immediately or fight it.

I stood up and clasped Drake's hand, pulling him in for a quick bro hug. "Hey, Drake. Thanks for coming."

"Don't sweat it, Prime. Ember's worth it. Besides, you and those other miserable sons 'a bitches are my pack now. Where else would I be?"

I forced a laugh. I was pleased to see Drake, but I couldn't get past the heavy feeling in my chest. I pulled back and looked directly at my sister, whose cheeks had gone from pale to bright red. She'd pulled the sleeve of her thin sweater further down one arm to cover his image. I grinned, unable to help it. "Drake, I'd like you to meet Sophie. She worked for Manivera in the past and showed me where his home was located."

Drake glanced at Sophie. "Hey." He smiled politely, nodded and looked back at me. It was a cursory greeting, and it was clear he had no idea who my sister was to him. Was that normal? She'd dreamed of him since she was young, but did it work the other way around? I honestly had no idea. I'd recognised Ember as my soulmate the moment Rawson had introduced us, but I'd been a hormonal teenager. Was it different with a grown male? Did it take time? I brushed it off. I had other things to think about. My sister's love life was way down my list.

"You've found him then?" Drake's face fell into a serious mask.

"Yeah, I know where he's going to be tonight. And we have inside help."

Drake ordered a beer from the waitress and folded his bulk down into a comfy chair. His gaze briefly flicked to Sophie again, who sipped her whisky quietly, pretending to watch the news on the wall-mounted T.V. Small lines appeared at the bridge of my brother's nose, but ever polite, he smiled before he looked away again.

"Great. When we get him and Ember's safe, it means I can fight to get my business back. I can get my lawyers to go after that agreement made under duress and ensure I don't have to marry his spoilt, ugly-assed daughter. That contract can be torn up. Man, I thought there was no way out of that for me. I'd resigned myself to a shitty marriage of convenience, but if I can prove he's done underhanded deals, kidnapping and other illegal activities, it'll work in my favour to get my company separated from his other assets."

Shit! I'd forgotten about that contract. Stupid!

Sophie's brows drew together, and before I could speak, she did. We had already decided not to tell anyone who she was to me, but before Drake could dig himself a bigger hole, I wanted to set him straight. It was Sophie that Rex had meant when he'd forced marriage to his daughter onto Drake; unless we had another sister, which wasn't impossible.

"What makes you think once Rex is out of the picture that his legal assets won't still go to his daughter? Maybe she will fight to keep her income from his legitimate businesses."

Drake's attention shot to Sophie, his expression dark. "It will take years to separate his legal from his illegal assets. The SBI will seize everything. She won't get a thing for years unless she does a deal with whoever takes down her father. Either way, my company isn't his. He paid Doherty to have me arrested for false embezzlement charges, then paid that bastard again to get his hands on my life's work. But this isn't just about that. He didn't only steal my company; he stole four fucking years of my life. So no offence, but I'll use every cent I have to make sure she doesn't get my company or benefit from her father's evil."

"Maybe she'll have no choice. Maybe his businesses will be her only income."

Drake's attention narrowed on Sophie and she glared right back. He appraised her. I gritted my teeth at the spark of interest I saw there. Damn! This was my sister. I should stand up for her, except... My gaze bounced from one to the other. No, this was their fight...I kept my mouth shut and sat back. Sophie could tell him who she was or not. I'd back her either way.

Drake chuckled a deep and resonant sound. "It doesn't matter anyway. Rex is too much of a dick to allow his businesses to go to a female, daughter or not. He'll have someone else lined up to take over, so my focus is on getting out of that contract before I have to take that male down, too."

Sophie's face dropped. That meant whoever took over Rex's business interests would have a say in both Sophie's and Drake's future. My nostrils flared. It didn't matter who was named in his will. If I took the fucker out, I'd claim everything.

"You think she's just some spoiled rich bitch who couldn't possibly have a mind of her own or the intelligence to run a business?" Sophie's words were bitter and almost resigned, which I didn't like.

Drake cocked his head and studied Sophie. She looked away. His glower changed and softened, and his eyes narrowed. I waited. Had he worked out who she was to him?

"I didn't say she wouldn't be capable, but I do think Rex is a misogynistic prick who would happily use his daughter as an asset, one he can manipulate, which is why he wanted me bound to him and his empire legitimately. He didn't get my company by any above-board means, and I want it back. He knew it would take me years and shitloads of money that I don't have to take him through the court system. He gave me a choice: sign a marriage contract with his daughter, and get a stake in running Drake Industries, or fight for it and not get the money and resources I needed at the time to help Connor and Ember."

Sophie didn't look at him, her words soft. "So you sold out for money?"

Drake's expression darkened once again. "Yes, to help my Prime, and I'd do it again in a heartbeat." He didn't take his gaze from her face. "I do know you have no fucking right to judge me or why I do things, so no offence, but this is none of your business." He dismissed her by looking back at me. Drake was never outright rude to a woman, I didn't think it was in his DNA, but he could certainly be dismissive, as could any alpha with his amount of power. I glanced at her, and my brows raised a bit. My meaning was clear. Did she want me to intervene? She shook her head, her brows furrowed, and her mouth pressed into a tight line.

"No, you're right. It isn't my business. But if Rex's daughter knows about your contract, maybe she'll think you're a shallow, money-grabbing prick, just like her father is, and she won't want to marry you, either."

Holding her sleeve over Drake's image to make sure he didn't see it, she stood. "Connor, just let me know when Owen is back, and you need me. I'll leave you to catch up with Mr...."

Her glance at Drake was icy. Shit, maybe I should just tell him who she was. This hadn't gone the way I'd wanted it to at all.

"Alexander." Drake's hard gaze wasn't an expression I was used to seeing on his face.

"Right. Mr Alexander."

"Yeah, see you later." I caught her hand. "Get some rest, okay? It's going to be a long night."

She nodded. "It always is where Rex is concerned."

I watched her walk away, as did Drake before he downed his beer in one long drink. "How the hell did you meet that cold-hearted she-devil?"

I couldn't help it. I smiled. "Oh, man, she's as far from a she-devil as you can get."

He glowered. "Didn't seem like it to me."

I kicked his foot with mine and smiled. "That's just because she called you a prick. Give her a chance. You don't know her yet. Maybe she'll grow on you."

He flashed me a sceptical look. "Really?"

"Yes."

"Well, you seem to trust her. Who is she to you? Ex-lover? Friend? What?"

I smirked, ignoring his question. "It's not important. Now tell me about what you found."

CHAPTER 8

JED LEAVING SO SUDDENLY HAD unsettled me even more than my constant headache or the waves of nausea that had me kneeling on the hard floor with my head shoved down the toilet bowl. The things he'd said… I spat bile from my mouth. He'd lied to me? About what? Was that why he hadn't pushed to sleep with me? Had we been arguing when I had my accident? Were we breaking up and that's why he wouldn't sleep with me? Why I don't feel drawn to him?

Godammit, this was impossible! I needed to stop worrying over his words before it drove me mad.

When I was sure my stomach had settled, I pushed to my feet, groaning as blood flowed back into my numb knees. I took a fortifying breath and grabbed a bottle of peppermint mouthwash, rinsing the bitter taste of bile from my mouth.

I honestly didn't know what to think or feel. Had my father done something to make Jed mistrust him all of a sudden? But Rex was my father, wasn't he? Damn, I was so confused. My head started to pound. I massaged my temples, swallowing repeatedly so that I didn't succumb to another wave of nausea.

Jed had taken my painkillers with him, so I couldn't take any. It was probably for the best. Having headaches like this for so long after my accident meant there was something more going on, and I needed to seek help. I wasn't an expert, but even I knew these headaches were unusual, especially when they were making me feel so sick.

The sun was high in the sky and despite the air conditioning, it was hot in the confined bathroom. A bead of sweat rolled down the groove of my spine, and it was difficult to stay standing on my shaky legs. I hadn't eaten anything since yesterday, and it looked to be well after noon. I needed some food. I wrinkled my nose. But first I needed to clean myself up. I stunk of vomit and sweat.

Taking a shower took far longer than it should. My limbs were heavy and I had to keep stopping to get my breath. I chose to dress in a pair of shorts and a light, floaty white shirt. The material set off my golden tan, but nothing could hide the shadows under my eyes or my hollow cheeks, not even a light brush of concealer. A pulse of what felt like solace throbbed through my chest as I looked in the mirror. Instead of ignoring it, or pushing it away like I usually did, I smiled and embraced it. I had no idea where that feeling came from, but it had been warming me more and more lately as if my subconscious was trying to comfort me. Pinching my cheeks made no difference to my exhausted appearance, but I'd be damned if I'd let Valentina see me looking so tired. She would gloat and think it had something to do with the problems between Jed and me.

Thankfully, I didn't bump into Valentina and managed to make it to the kitchen unseen. Quickly, I grabbed some cold chicken, fresh bread, olive oil and some olives which I suddenly had a craving for. I stuffed one in my mouth, and then another, while I rushed back to my room. Jed had said to stay out of everyone's way so that's what I would do, until I could talk with him again.

I sat out on my bedroom balcony and tried the internet on my tablet again while I ate. The salty taste of the olives was heavenly. The pleasure, however, was short-lived. I grunted when I realized that once again, the internet didn't work. But then, it never had. The signal was so poor out here in the hills. I had no choice but to wait for Jed and get answers to my questions directly from him. What I'd really wanted was to Google my father. I'd tried to find an internet connection on his office computer once when I'd snooped around a bit, but my father had caught me before I succeeded. I frowned, realizing he had locked his office door ever since. It had never seemed like a big thing—until now. I shook off a stab of guilt at trying the internet again. I'd wanted to see some photos of dad, mum and me all together as a family, not just to search for him or Jed, or so I told myself. I couldn't help the seed of suspicion that was growing in my mind. They had told me that my mother had died when I was a baby, and my father didn't keep any photos of her. It never occurred to me to ask why not, but it should have.

Enjoying the warm breeze that caressed my skin, I tried to concentrate on my e-reader, only by late afternoon I was exhausted, and my eyes stung as I tried to keep reading. Across the room, my bed looked too inviting to resist. I kicked off my sandals and padded over, groaning as I laid down and relaxed. I'd just close my eyes for a moment, then Jed would be back.

❖

A SCREECH LODGED in my throat, my heart pounding. But the warm hand that cupped my mouth felt familiar, *smelled* familiar. I blinked and blinked again, but it was dark, I couldn't see a damned thing.

"Shh, it's okay. It's me," Jed said in a low gravelly voice.

On a whoosh of breath, I relaxed. My right hand reached out and felt his jaw line. Stubble scraped my skin. He was tense, his jaw muscles bulging. "What's wrong?"

His eyes gleamed in the moonlight as he searched my gaze. "We need to get..."

Gun fire echoed from outside. I shot up from the bed, my heart pounding. An explosion rocked the house and glass shattered in the next room as if a window had been broken. "Oh my god! What's going on? Are we being attacked? Where's dad?" My words were quick and breathless.

He grabbed my hand, his free one curling around the back of my head. "It's okay. I promise. Please trust me. We just need to stay in here. We'll be fine, I swear, and when all the noise has died down, we're going to go out there, and I'll tell you everything I promised you earlier."

I stilled. My brain fired a hundred questions, but I felt the sincerity in his words. "Ok, but, that's *gun* fire, Jed," I stopped speaking. Tilting my head, I listened through the pounding of my heart and all of the noise. "What's all that growling?" Ice curled around my heart. "Are there *animals* out there?" I pulled away from him. "Why are you in here, instead of out there fighting whoever this is? Where's your gun?" My voice was shaking.

"Ember, it's okay. Look..." Slowly he lifted his jacket. His gun was holstered against his ribs where it always was. "It's here."

I pulled my hand from his and ran to the door, looking back over my shoulder at him. "Then what are you doing? Shouldn't you be out there protecting my father? Or helping your men? Why are you still in here?"

"Because they're not my men, Ember."

My breath caught. "Why are you calling me that? My name is Sarah." Confused, I shook my head.

His face dropped into a twisted mask of regret and pity. "No. I'm so sorry, sweetheart, but your name is really Ember."

I had a flash of...something, memory maybe? Something that made that name seem familiar. And that frightened me more than anything because if it was true, it meant I knew nothing about my life, or even myself. That thought froze my lungs. I couldn't breathe! I had to get out!

As I turned to run, Jed stepped in front of me, stopping me cold. In the moonlight his face looked harsh, his body bigger than ever. He swallowed. "Please don't run. I need to keep you in here for your own safety." His voice was deep and, although soft, laced with a level of command that made me shiver. I sucked air into my lungs, but it wasn't enough. *I'd trusted this man.* Who was Jed? Or Rex? *Who the hell was I?* Shit! I needed to get out! Yanking it open, I bolted out of the door.

"Stop!" His bellowed command kicked me into top gear.

Ducking down, I sprinted through the shadows towards the sound of voices. Men rushed through the house, holding guns and firing them at my father's men. I bit down on my panic and hid behind some long curtains. When the corridor cleared, I dashed into the open plan living area where I could hear my father yelling. I had no idea what I was going to do, just that I needed to get out of there.

The roar of a huge animal behind me spurred me on. *This is just a nightmare. It's not real. It's not real...*

The glare blinded me as the overhead lights were switched on. Totally unprepared for that, I skidded on unsteady legs, twisting my ankle. Screeching in pain, I fell to the floor, sliding on my arse and coming to a halt right where a huge man stood over my father.

For all of his power, Rex Manivera now kneeled at the feet of the invading conqueror, beaten and bloody. His eyes fell on me and widened.

"Sarah! My sweet Sarah, don't listen to what these people tell you. You are my daughter. Mine! They can never take you from me if you don't..."

The man punched him, and he fell sideways. "Shut up! You don't speak to her!"

I whimpered, and even though the pain in my ankle sent waves of nausea through me, I skidded backwards, horror filling me. An odd warmth pulsed inside my chest, warring with my fear. Some strange part of me wanted me to run towards this...victor. *What the everloving fuck?* I couldn't breathe as he turned towards me, his face full of fury and wildness. *Oh gods! I'd seen this man before. He'd haunted my dreams as much as the monster I'd felt searching for me.* My breaths were huge and panting, my heart rate spiking. The room began to spin, my fingertips going numb. I knew I was panicking, but I didn't seem able to stop it.

I couldn't breathe. I couldn't run. No matter how scared I was, an equal part of me wanted to stay near this man. I simply couldn't make my body obey me.

He prowled closer, stopped a few feet away—and squatted down. His hard face softened. His eyes were so blue they completely ensnared mine. He was every bit a predator, and he'd finally caught his prey—me.

"It's okay. No one's going to hurt you."

I snarled and backed up some more, until the wall was behind me. "I don't believe you." I managed to squeak between my panting breaths.

He pointed over his shoulder at my father. "I know you don't understand all this right now, but that man there is not who you think he is. He is not your father."

I swallowed, Jed's words coming back to me. My head throbbed, a loud whining sound in my ears. "He...I'm..." My thoughts were slow, my brain muddled. I looked back into the man's eyes. He watched me carefully, his brow wrinkling as he saw me clutching at my t-shirt. "Listen, how about we get you off the floor and look at your ankle?"

I just blinked, not sure I could actually get up. I was shaking too much, and my ankle was throbbing worse than my head ever had.

"My name's Connor." He touched his chest over his heart. "And I promise you on my life that I will never hurt you, Ember." There was that name again. "Will you let me help you up?"

I met his gaze again. He didn't rush me, didn't look impatient, he merely waited. His gaze darkened, and a warm wave of...something washed over me and through me. I swallowed, and the knot of fear in my chest unwound a little. A small smile curved his lips. God, he was hot. The kind of hot that made everything in me tingle just being this close to him. He shuffled closer, his strong thighs taking his weight and pushing against the material of his combats. His black fitted top molded to his defined muscles as if it was painted on. I swallowed hard, my already racing heart ramping up a notch, I inhaled as he reached out. A glorious spicy scent hit my nostrils and the whining in my head calmed. My whole body relaxed. I could feel the panic in my chest unwinding enough I could breathe easier.

What the hell was happening to me? Jed never had this effect on me. Before I had time to think about it more, Connor's voice rumbled right into my bones.

"I'm going to put one arm around your waist and another under your legs and lift you. Is that okay?"

My voice had all but disappeared, so I nodded. I didn't really have a choice, and he knew it. I couldn't stand, or walk, I was in too much pain. I watched him warily as he did just that and then stood up, lifting me like I was a child.

"Put your arms around my neck."

Without conscious thought, I followed his order. It was as if he had some kind of hold over me. But it wasn't bad, it felt really really good. Before I could stop myself, I sighed and relaxed against him. It felt like I belonged in his arms; more than I ever had in Jed's. I couldn't tear my gaze from his face.

His jaw was strong and square, his hair a deep brown, and his eyes? They were like getting lost in the bluest ocean and clearest sky all at the same time. They seemed to see right into my soul. I shivered and made myself look away, my cheeks flushing.

"Let's sit you here." He lowered me onto the sofa. His attention kept coming back to my face as he plumped cushions behind my back and made sure I was sitting comfortably. "There. Is that comfy?"

"Yes. Thank you," I added.

I glanced at my father who was semi-conscious and moaning. What the hell was I doing? This man had just killed my father's men and invaded our home. Except I didn't feel scared of him.

Connor didn't stand over me like I expected but knelt beside me, blocking my view of my father. His face was carefully controlled again, but his eyes were stormy with emotions I could only guess at as he studied my face like he couldn't look away. I had no idea why, but I didn't want to look away from him either. Suddenly I had an irrational need to cry. My chest ached. I wanted to reach for him. Something inside me screamed that this man could fix me … fix the emptiness in my soul…

"Gods, I don't know where to begin…" He rubbed his hands over his face, his jaw clenched. He searched my eyes. "Mother Wolf, I can't believe you're here…" His voice cracked, and he reached out and stroked my cheek with such gentleness I had no hope of holding back the tears that had been burning in my eyes since I'd first seen him. It made no sense, I had no idea who this was, I'd never met him in my life, yet I felt as though I knew everything about him, and that somehow he was my whole life. Tears ran down my cheeks and he wiped them away, his own eyes shining. "It's okay, Firecracker. Everything will be alright now."

My heart lurched. What had he just called me? Why did that word make me want to sob harder? "Who are you?" I whispered. Wiping away my tears I tried to pull myself together.

Connor took a deep breath and exhaled. "Okay, I know this will be hard to understand but it is the truth. My name is Connor Rawson. And I'm your real…fiance."

"What? But I don't even know you…"

"Ember?" My attention whipped towards Jed, who stood about eight feet away, his face drawn and wary. He moved closer.

Connor curled his top lip back and growled. Even I knew it was a warning. I didn't know what to think about that, so I ignored it.

Jed, however, paled and stopped right where he was. "It's okay, Prime. I'm not coming any closer. Ember, think about what he tells you. Everything I said earlier, it was all true. Your real name is Ember, not Sarah. Your father isn't really your father, he's a dangerous man who wants you for your…"

Connor growled again. Jed closed his eyes and nodded. "Fine, you can tell her about that…" Another growl. "Okay, about everything." He looked back at me, his face almost sad. "Listen to him, Ember. I am not, nor have I ever been your true fiance. Connor is more than that to you." Jed looked at my father, his eyes cold. "Please believe that I betrayed *him* to help and protect you. I have done many bad things in my life for money, and it was no different with you. Rex paid me to play a part. To be your fiance in a world that was just a sham."

I shook my head, but didn't speak. I couldn't. I had trusted him. I had listened to him, even tried to get him to touch me… I shuddered. Gods, what the hell was happening? Part of me believed him, but the other, more rational part of me, didn't. I had photos. I'd had an accident. What about my headaches and injury? Not even him or my father could make me lose my memory or give me headaches, could they?

"Please…" He took another step forward.

"Don't you dare come anywhere near her." Connor's anger hit me in a wave. I shrank back from him even though his anger was directed at Jed.

Jed's eyes darkened, a snarl on his lip. Another man with short hair and a confidence in his stride similar to Connor's placed a hand on Jed's shoulder. "Don't. He'll kill you where you stand."

My heart lurched, my eyes darting to Connor. On instinct, I grabbed his arm. His gaze shot to my fingers and his throat bobbed. "Don't hurt him...please."

Jed swallowed. His attention flicked to me before he dropped his gaze to the ground. "I'm sorry, Ember. For all of this. I hope one day, when you've remembered who you are, and everything about your life, that you can forgive me."

No words would come, so I just nodded, my chest hurting as he turned away, his shoulders stooped.

"Owen! Lock him up. He doesn't leave. We need all the strong fighters we can get, and he owes me...and Ember, big time." Connor curled his lip and nodded at my father. "And get that piece of shit from my sight. I'll deal with Rex when I've made sure my mate is safe and well."

Owen cracked his neck and flexed his fists. "Yes, Prime. Lionel!"

Another huge and good looking man with a shock of shoulder length blonde hair, stepped forward. He smiled at me and for some reason I felt compelled to smile back.

"Take B'nar and get that gorilla locked up," Owen commanded.

"Yes, Beta." Lionel gave me another encouraging smile and waited for a tall, elegant man with bright blue hair and strange pale green eyes to join him.

Connor turned his attention back on me. "Everyone else out!"

There was a general chorus of: "Yes, Prime." I hadn't looked at the other people, I'd felt the weight of their gazes since Connor had approached me, but his eyes had snagged mine and refused to let go.

I swallowed against my dry throat. "What does prime mean?"

He smiled and my heart squeezed. "Leader, I suppose. Though in our world it's more than that."

I pulled away a bit. "What are you? Some kind of cult or something?"

He chuckled, a deep rich sound that did strange things to me. "No. But I think that's an explanation for another day. You have learnt some painful truths tonight. Let's leave it there and concentrate on healing your ankle."

My brain might be mush, but even I knew that wasn't possible. "You can't heal a sprained ankle," I scoffed.

He grinned, his eyes flashing. He leaned in. I pressed back against the cushions until I couldn't go any further. His breath brushed my lips. My heart skittered and goosebumps rose on my exposed skin. "What will you give me if I prove you wrong?" His gaze fell to my mouth, his thumb brushing over the plump skin of my lower lip.

"What do you want?" I asked, my pulse suddenly racing even though part of me knew it was wrong to be turned on by a man who had invaded my home and captured my father. Yet, he hadn't hurt me, and I was pretty certain he wouldn't. It was my father I wasn't sure about.

He smirked. "A kiss." His eyes darkened again, and I gasped, sure they had flashed red and hot. He turned away and when he looked back at me they were that hypnotising mix of blue and intense darkness; the colours so at odds with each other they captivated me. That flash of red must have been my imagination. On his knees, he shuffled down the length of the couch to my feet. I stiffened when his big hands wrapped around my injured ankle. "Relax," he said softly. "Remember my promise. I will never hurt you."

I gulped and did as he said, relaxing into the cushions. Warmth tingled into my throbbing joint. It got more intense, travelling from my ankle up to my thigh. When it reached the juncture between my thighs, I shuffled, not sure what to do. I bit back a moan. The wave of warmth left me tingling in places that hadn't been touched by anyone but me in months. God, it felt so good. I stifled another groan, trying to hide what he was doing to me. In fact, what *was* he doing to me? My ankle was forgotten. All I could think about was the pleasurable sensation between my legs. My head fell back against the soft cushions, and, consumed by desire, I couldn't stop the groan that worked its way up my throat.

"That's it, Firecracker. Let me heal you...all of you." His voice was ragged, his breathing as erratic as mine. One hand stayed on my ankle, pushing heat into it, and I was aware his other caressed up my calf, over my knee and up my thigh to the hem of my shorts.

"Oh. My. God." My hooded gaze met his. His face was tight, his eyes dark and lustful. His throat bobbed, and his gaze dropped to the juncture between my legs. As if he had lit a match, my body exploded in the most intense orgasm I'd ever had. It was so fast and violent, and the pleasure hit me with such force I couldn't stop my guttural scream.

Panting, I threw an arm over my eyes, my body taking a while to come down. His fingers trailed down my thigh, the lightest touch that made me shiver. Oh shit, what had just happened? I'd orgasmed from him just touching my leg and looking at me! What the fuck? Shame heated my cheeks, and I dropped my arm, pulling myself away from him.

He let me put a little distance between us. His face was flushed, his eyes dark, emotions I didn't understand warring across the angular planes of his face. His body was an unyielding mass of muscle and gorgeousness, his jaw clenched so tightly, he looked as if he might break his teeth. My breathing didn't settle, if anything his nearness only made me worse. I wanted to climb him, to feel the erection that was pressing against the front of his combats, sliding into my body. *What. The. Hell?* The aftermath of my world shattering climax had left me confused and dazed. I had to get away from this god-like man who had taken command of my body like it belonged to him.

"You owe me a kiss," he whispered when I didn't speak. But he didn't lean in, and I knew right then, I had a choice.

"Do I?" I managed to croak. My gaze dropped to his full and totally kiss-able mouth. I should refuse...

Holding my gaze with his, he leaned in. Still I didn't move away. If anything I tilted towards him. His lips brushed mine, and electricity hummed through my veins. He repeated that gentle kiss again, then his hand was in my hair, holding me close as his mouth pressed harder, his lips warm and soft. I groaned as my whole world was reduced to the *feel* of his mouth against mine. He tasted devine. My tongue brushed his, a desperate moan bubbling up my throat. My fingers twitched, and I raised my hands to grab him, but just as I touched him with my eager fingers, he moaned and pulled away.

I had no idea what to say. Any attraction I'd felt to Jed was utterly obliterated by the draw I felt towards this man.

Our breathing was heavy, and he seemed at as much of a loss as me. His gaze snagged on mine.

"*Fuck,*" he muttered on a long exhale of breath. Jerkily, he pushed to his feet, his gaze dropping from mine as he lowered his head and took some deep breaths, his hands on his hips.

My mind was swirling with confusion, my body tingling from the after effects of his touch. I couldn't think straight. I had to get away from him, if only to process everything that had happened. While his attention was on the floor, I took my chance. I sprung up from the couch and bolted for my room. No one stopped me. They just watched me curiously as I ran down the corridor before I darted inside and slammed the door, locking it behind me. I laughed at my own ridiculousness. If Connor wanted in this room, then that flimsy door and lock wasn't going to stop him; he was built like a brick shit house, a solid wall, a human battering ram—a...what *was* he? I mean, he *growled!*

With my back against the door, I sank to the floor, hyperventilating. I rubbed my temples. My headache had returned with a vengeance. It had the moment I'd run from Connor. No, wait, that wasn't why my headache had come back. That made no sense.

A gentle knock at the door made me jump. "Ember?"

"Go away." I pulled my knees up, hugging them. Oddly, my headache receded again.

I heard his sigh.

"It's normal for that to happen between mates, sweetness."

God above, he was talking about that orgasm! My cheeks heated, and I dropped my forehead to my knees. Jesus, he'd barely even touched me and I'd gone off like a fucking firework! And *sweetness?* That sounds familiar, too.

"And I swear to you, I'm not lying. Jed is not now and never has been your fiance. *I* am your mate. And I am not leaving you, not until you have your memories of me—of us, back again."

I had no words. Mate? A strangely primal term to use, even if it was him I was with before my accident. I swallowed hard. Then again, I was already questioning his humanity.

"I know you don't understand, and I know that all of this is terrifying for you, but I promise you I am telling you the truth."

Silence from me. Yeah, I had no idea what to say. I eyed the window. *Maybe I should try and get out through the gardens...*Though my heart wasn't really in that thought.

"Okay, we can talk about it tomorrow. Get some sleep." Another pause. "And you'll be completely safe. I'm not leaving this spot, and I'll have men outside your window so no one can get at you from there, either."

Damn. No escape that way, then. I didn't know what was wrong with me, but I was almost glad he'd taken that choice away.

"We'll eat breakfast together in a few hours. Okay?"

Silence.

"All right. Get some sleep. I'll be right here if you need me."

There was a sliding sound, and I could *feel* him on the other side of the door. I could imagine him mirroring my own position, but with his long legs stretched out in front of him. Unable to understand my actions. I shuffled my knees underneath me and leaned my head against the door with my ear flat against it. His breaths were slow and deep. After a minute he added. "By the way, I'm glad your ankle feels better." I could hear the smile in his voice.

I gasped. Oh, my god! I'd run back to my room. He was right! He'd healed my ankle. Experimentally, I twisted it in a circle, and smiled. Damn, whatever he'd used to fix me sure was some potent shit. Especially if he could heal me *and* give me a world-shattering orgasm at the same time. I huffed a laugh. He should bottle and sell it.

He must have heard me because his own soft chuckle reached right into my chest and settled in that deep and empty place that had been there since my injury, filling it with that missing warmth.

"Sleep, Ember. And on the bed, not on the floor. You'll be completely safe, I promise. I'm not going anywhere."

Exhausted and mind blown as I was, I still didn't want to move away from the door. His presence had soothed my headache again, and even though I was confused, I trusted that he wouldn't hurt me. Reluctantly, I took his advice and laid on my bed, sure I wouldn't sleep. But I did. There was no howling in my head, no nightmares and no headache. For the first time in months I slept soundly all night.

onnor

THE SUN ROSE SLOWLY, filling the corridor with light. I'd not even tried to sleep. There was no way I could close my eyes and switch off when my pregnant soulmate was in the next room. I knew she was still asleep. I could hear her deep, regular breaths through the flimsy door.

Gods, I hadn't meant to bring her so much pleasure last night, but being so close to her, touching her, after thinking she was dead, had sent both Prime and me into a storm of emotions. I'd tried to control us both, but the lure of her had been too much. Prime had found his mate, but Ember's mind had her locked down tight. It had been a harsh reminder. My mate was confused and vulnerable, and I had taken advantage...Gods, what must she think of me? I rubbed my face, exhaustion and no small amount of guilt weighing me down.

I sensed Sophie before I saw her.

"Hey." She sat down beside me. "How are you doing?"

I blew out a long breath. "Honestly? I've no idea. I know I need to sort out Manivera—and deal with Jed, but I don't want to leave her. Not for a second." I didn't look at Sophie. Sharing my feelings was a weakness I never allowed, but I needed to tell someone. My gut twisted, my palms sweating as I spilled my greatest fear. "I've been without her for so long; both of our lives have been ripped apart by the actions of others. What if she never remembers who I am, what we are? What if she runs, or someone takes her again? Gods, I don't know if I'll survive it, Sophie. She's my world. I didn't think I could feel more for her, but her carrying our child…" I clenched my shaking fingers. "I'll kill anyone who tries to harm them."

Sophie took my hand. It was funny. I'd never let anyone but Ember comfort me physically, but it seemed right to allow my sister, my blood, to do this. We didn't know each other well, except we did. We had both survived a childhood at Rex Manivera's hands. I met her gaze, and she smiled, no judgment in her eyes. "Rex will still be there when you're ready to deal with him. So will Jed; however long it takes."

She let her glamour fall away and let me really see her. Her golden hair shone, falling down over her shoulders. Her facial piercings disappeared, her eyes as vivid and blue as mine had ever been, just more almond-shaped. Not for the first time, I wondered about her mother; who she'd been, if she was still alive, or if she'd been sold off by my father. Sophie smiled, and my whole being relaxed as light and warmth flooded me, easing my fears. I knew this was my sister's influence. Just like I could use Prime's power to influence the mood of others, so, it seemed, could Sophie.

"And she will come back to you. Have faith in her. But, yeah, maybe use a bit more patience than you did last night." She grinned and winked.

I smirked but couldn't hide my guilt. "You heard that?"

"Ha, I think the whole compound heard her scream, brother."

Someone coughed quietly. I'd heard Drake approach, even though one ear was trained on Ember's steady breaths as she slept, but part of me wanted him to see Sophie, really see her, not just the version she put out to the rest of the world.

She scowled at me. I grinned and shrugged.

Drake blinked and shook his head as Sophie put her glamour back in place.

"Everything alright here, brother?" He asked, his brow furrowed as he watched Sophie clamber up off the floor without her usual grace.

"Yeah, as good as it can be."

He nodded and held out a cup of coffee for me. "Here, thought you might need this."

"Thanks, man. Could you sort out some food for Ember and me? Jed said she's been sick a lot in the mornings, though, so nothing greasy."

"Probably some dry toast and ginger tea would be best," Sophie chimed in. "But what she really needs to keep her settled and comfortable is her mate by her side."

We both looked at her in surprise. "Oh, for goodness sake. I may be an assassin, but I'm not heartless or clueless. Ginger is supposed to help with morning sickness, though I've no idea if it works. And one of the females who worked for my…" She inhaled sharply at her verbal slip up. She glanced at me, then back at Drake. "*With* me once, years ago, told me when a female is suffering, the bond with her mate can soothe her."

"Of course," rumbled Drake and me together. But I was convinced he hadn't known that any more than I had. We exchanged a look and a shrug. Neither of us had been near a pregnant female who'd had a mate.

"Sophie, would you send Owen and my brothers to me? I need to sort out a plan for Manivera."

"I will." Sophie walked quickly away, her black leather trousers and fae armoured top hugging her trim figure, which I noticed Drake was having a hard time pulling his gaze from.

Drake coughed, clearing his throat. "I'll go and sort you both some food," he managed to say before he strode after my sister.

Silence settled. My mate still slept. Her breathing remained steady and deep on the other side of the door, and I let it soothe me as much as I hoped I could soothe her.

CHAPTER 10

mber

I AWOKE SLOWLY, my whole body relaxed and at ease. I hadn't slept so well for as long as I could remember. Granted, that was only a few weeks, but even so... I bit my bottom lip. Was it the earth-shattering, no-touch orgasm that I'd had the night before? Or the man that I sensed outside my door who'd eased my mind enough to sleep? Something about him settled me, took away my headaches, and filled that empty ache in my chest. Turning my head, I stared at the door. I could still *feel* him on the other side. Deep voices resonated in the hallway. If I strained my ears, I could even pick up the occasional word or phrase.

...Take the Halo... Manivera will pay but... The count will ....vampires on our side... You are the King...

I swallowed hard. Why were they talking about vampires? A count? A king? What the hell? I mean I'd heard the news, well, I'd read the subtitles, I couldn't speak more than a few words of Italian. I knew that supernaturals lived in our world; that they existed. What I didn't get was why they were discussing them like they were part of that supernatural world. I'd gathered that the supernaturals were bound by a different set of rules than humans, that they were ruled over by a powerful organisation called the Supernatural Bureau of Investigation. I'd even asked Jed about it before, but he'd not told me anything that I hadn't heard on the news, so I'd let it go. But if the SBI

732

ruled the supernatural community, then who was this *king*? Had Rex done something to anger a supernatural king? I frowned, thinking about both Jed's and Connor's words from yesterday. If Rex Manivera was not my father, why the fuck had he kept me in his house pretending I was his daughter?

My bladder didn't give me any time to contemplate all my questions. Rushing to the bathroom, I shut the door and relieved myself. My body felt stronger than it had since the accident. I didn't want to think too deeply about why I felt this way, but I knew I didn't want to look like a hot mess when I saw my drop-dead gorgeous captor for breakfast. Besides, a shower was a good way to start what was sure to be a very strange day. I reached in and switched it on. My mind was clearer, my heart not as heavy, but the memory of 'my father' unconscious on the floor made my stomach twist. He'd seemed so powerful, with his army and his money, and his business, but not just that, he'd always maintained distance, which gave him an air of authority. I huffed. *There is always someone more powerful and more ruthless than the most powerful and the most ruthless.*

Water cascaded over my red hair and down my back. I still didn't know what to believe about Connor and Jed. Jed had lied to me, and explosive orgasms and tingly warm feelings aside, I didn't know Connor. I switched off the flow of hot water and stepped out. I was drying myself when there was a knock at the bedroom door. My heart rate spiked, and I took a deep breath. I could do this; I could face the stranger who told me I was everything to him, the one I remembered nothing about; the man I had totally lost control with the night before. It occurred to me he hadn't needed to knock; he could easily force his way in and put me at an instant disadvantage. But he hadn't.

"Hang on!" I threw on a robe and squared my shoulders. Before I reached it, the bedroom door opened.

I was struck dumb. Connor had not shaved, stubble covered his jaw, and he was in the same clothes as last night. But whereas last night my brain had been muddled, today I was well rested. Holy cow! He was stunning! Like, seriously hot. His body was To. Die. For. A dark, fitted shirt in some strange shimmery material covered his large arms, his impressive pecs and hugged his washboard abs. *Dayum...* I openly gaped, drinking in the sight of his powerful and controlled movements as he walked to the balcony, balanced the tray, opened the glass doors with one hand, and put the tray down on the small table.

I shook my head. So he was gorgeous, that didn't mean I should blindly trust him.

He sat down and eyed me, his piercing blue eyes sparkling, a small smile curling his mouth. My pulse spiked, and warmth hit me between my legs, making my center feel alive just like the night before. My nipples pebbled, and I flushed, hyper-aware I was naked beneath my robe. His gaze heated. He inhaled, his smirk turning predatory. My fingers curled into my soft robe, pulling it closer around me.

Tension filled the silence. He took a big breath and exhaled, pulling his gaze from where my fingers grabbed at my robe. Instead, he turned his attention to the breakfast tray.

"Proper tea or ginger tea?" he asked as if the tension between us didn't exist, and eating breakfast with his captive was a perfectly normal thing to do.

Maybe it was.

Come on, be brave. He hasn't hurt you yet, and if you want answers, you need to play nice. And ginger tea? What the fuck? I wrinkled my nose. "No. Who drinks that shit? Proper tea, please." I frowned. Since when do I speak with such snark? Was that more like who I really was?

He grinned, clearly pleased with my response. Chuckling, he poured some tea into a cup. His big fingers grabbed the milk jug, and he put a bit in with the tea. "Milk, no sugar. Just as you like it." Still grinning, he held out the steaming mug and winked at me.

My stomach did a stupid flip. Not feeling in the least bit in danger, I walked forward taking the cup and lowered myself into the chair opposite him. The skin on my arms tickled as if being brushed by static. I rubbed at them. Connor tracked my movements but didn't comment.

"Did you sleep okay?" he asked, sounding genuinely concerned.

I thought about lying, but what was the point? "Yes." I leaned forward, staring at his handsome profile. "I want to see my father, I mean Rex." Maybe it was stupid to antagonise my captor, but for some reason, he made me want to challenge him.

"He's not your father. He's...someone else's." He paused and cocked his head, studying me. "So, no sickness this morning?"

My eyes widened, and I almost choked on the sip of tea I'd just taken. "How did you know I've had a stomach bug?"

He shrugged those impressive shoulders and smirked. "I know lots about you. So have you? Been feeling ill this morning?"

I shook my head, realising with a jolt that I hadn't. "Umm, actually, no." I had to concentrate hard to stop my cheeks from heating. Had that been his orgasmic magic too, or was my stomach just recovered? In answer, my stomach rumbled loudly. I grasped at it through my robe, groaning in pure embarrassment.

He chuckled. "Good. That means you can eat. Come on. We'll eat together."

I glanced at the huge amount of scrambled eggs and bacon he had brought. I was ravenous, but should I eat with him?

"It's okay; eating with me doesn't mean you are siding with the enemy or that you believe me over Rex. You can shelve your guilt for a while and just eat. You need your strength."

He piled two plates high and leaned forward, setting one in front of me. I looked up from the plate and found him still leaning in, his attention on me. That enticing spicy scent that seemed to be uniquely his filled my head. I inhaled deeply, unable to help myself. He smiled, all relaxed and friendly, the sort of smile you'd give someone close to you. And gods damn, it was beautiful. The chip I noticed in his canine only made him more devastating. Butterflies took flight in my stomach, and my skin downright buzzed. Heat washed through me, settling between my thighs, causing me to shiver. I took another gulp of tea to cover my reaction, but when I sneaked a peek at him, that smile had turned into a satisfied smirk.

"Toast?" he asked innocently, but I got the feeling he knew exactly what effect he had on me. He smiled and held out the toast rack.

"Thank you." I picked a piece, determined not to let him throw me so much. "In fact, thank you for all of this." He didn't have to look after me so well. This was really confusing. My reaction to him was completely off the charts. I'd never even really wanted to be touched by Jed until I'd decided I should at least try to be his fiance. And even then, even though I'd grown to like him, even when I'd felt a little attraction to him, it had been nothing like this. Jed had never sent my senses reeling or my heart rate sky high just by being near me.

"Anytime. And I mean that," Connor said softly.

It was strangely comfortable eating with him. Every now and then, he snuck a look at me, almost as if he were checking to see if I was eating enough. He seemed satisfied when I'd finished my plate of food, eaten two slices of toast and had another fresh mug of tea in front of me.

He smiled again, his eyes soft. "Better?"

I nodded. Surprisingly, I was. I'd been throwing up for days. No matter what I ate, it hadn't stayed in my stomach long, and now I seemed utterly settled.

"That's good." He rested his elbows on the table and clasped his fingers together in front of his mouth. "I'll give you some time to dress, then we'll talk again."

I swallowed but nodded. Why did I feel so comfortable with him? He was a killer. "Alright, but I want to see my father...I mean Rex before we talk."

His face hardened, and he stood. Damn, he was tall. Much taller than me. My body went fluid. What would it be like to be his? To have his hands on my waist, to be thoroughly wrapped up by that powerful body?

"No. You aren't going near that man. Ever again." His jaw was tight, his eyes almost black.

I clamped my mouth shut, my nostrils flaring. Answering him back probably wasn't the best way to go—but...fuck it! I jumped up, shoving my own chair back, and glared at him. "If you want me to believe a single word you say," I hissed as I gathered my courage and stalked right up to him, "then you will let me talk to him and make up my *own* mind about who's telling the truth!"

"I am!" He snarled, his fists clenched.

Anger radiated off him, and I fought the urge to step back. Instead, I took a step forward, slammed my hands on my hips and glowered up at him, my heart hammering. I was too angry to step away, despite the warning howls that echoed in my skull. I shut the noise down. No matter how gorgeous this dangerous man is, he could not just invade my home and take over my life and not expect me to fight. "How the hell do I know that? All I know is you broke in, killed most of our men, somehow got the man I thought to be my fiance to betray the man who I believed was my father, knocked my father out in front of me, used some kind of supernatural power to heal my ankle, and then gave me the best fucking orgasm I can remember without even touching me!" My chest was heaving as I let my anger have free reign.

His eyes flared with red flame. *Oh shit! Supernatural, then!* I had no chance of escape, and I knew it. He moved so quickly I couldn't even flinch away. His hand speared my hair, and his mouth descended on mine. Lust washed through me like a tidal wave. His mouth moved over mine, demanding I submit. And, goddammit, I did. I kissed him back frantically, sliding my tongue along his, my hands clutching at his top like I was trying to climb inside his skin. He devoured me. Taking everything I offered. There was nothing else, only him, his taste, his scent, the feel of his rigid body against mine, his steel arms encasing me in warmth and strength. He filled me, completely eradicating that empty space in my chest. And I knew. I knew this was where I was supposed to be. This man, this total stranger, somehow, he was my world. It was that shattering realisation that filled me with utter terror. I was at his mercy, and I had no idea what to do about it.

Connor pulled away first. Our gazes locked, and we both panted heavily. His hands dropped from my waist, and I shivered at that loss of contact, but at least my brain could work. I uncurled my grip from him and stepped back. Not to get away, just so that I didn't grab him again. God, what was wrong with me? Was he using his supernatural voodoo on me again?

His eyes flared, and he raked his gaze slowly from my face down my body, setting my skin on fire as he trailed his gaze back up, lingering on my breasts as if he could see straight through my robe to my skin beneath. My nipples tightened instantly. *Traitors!* I crossed my arms over my chest.

His throat bobbed, his jaw tightened, and he abruptly stepped away, banging into his chair and sending it skidding across the balcony with a clatter. "Don't for one second think that I am letting you go again. You are mine,

Ember, just as I am yours. Rex Manivera is not your father. He is a supernatural crime lord. He was going to sell you to the highest bidder. He has fucked with your mind, taken your memories of the people who love you, of your mate—me! And for that alone, I will rip his fucking heart out!"

I swallowed at his words, and he took another breath blowing it out steadily, clearly trying to get a hold of his emotions.

"I'll be patient, Firecracker. I'll wait as long as I can, give you the space you need to remember, but I won't wait forever. I need you under me. I need to be inside you. I need to mark you as mine again—especially now." His voice was raw, not much louder than a gravelly whisper. His attention settled on my stomach. Desire darkened his face again, and his fingers curled into fists. My gaze dropped to where an impressive bulge strained at the zipper of his cargo pants. My whole body went limp. I wanted to encourage him, to drop my robe and offer myself up as a willing sacrifice. But I didn't. He was right. I needed to remember him, to remember us.

He raked a hand through his hair, mussing it. "I should let you be for a while. Come to the living area where we were last night when you are dressed."

I swallowed and nodded. As soon as the door closed behind him, I rushed into my clothes. Jeans, a fitted tee, and trainers. I pressed my ear to the door and listened—hard. No heavy breathing and I couldn't sense him on the other side. Maybe he needed a moment away from me, too.

CHAPTER 11

 mber

I QUICKLY CROSSED MY ROOM, grabbed the knife off the breakfast tray and dropped to my hands and knees. I looked at the knife. Did I know how to use a weapon? I had no idea, but it felt natural to pick it up, so maybe I did. Connor didn't seem the type to have a weak girlfriend, either. I grinned. And if that was the case, he'd understand my next move. If Connor wouldn't take me to Rex, I'd find Rex myself. If that asshole wasn't my father, that meant he'd kidnapped me, lied, and kept me prisoner for months. He'd stolen my life and my mind, and, godsdammit, I wanted it back!

Carefully, I edged out onto the balcony. Stone balustrades that had gaps between them made it easy to peer across the gardens without being seen. The tall, elegant man with the bright blue hair stood with his back to me. He inhaled and his eyes honed in on the balcony, then he shrugged and turned fully away to talk with another big male. This one had silver hair and seemed to have the weirdest purple mist hanging around him. A whimper in my skull had me shaking my head. I had no painkillers with me, and my headache was coming back. My stomach churned too. Damn it! Maybe I'd eaten too much. Too late now. I just hoped I wouldn't throw up before I got to Manivera.

Another ridiculously handsome man with midnight skin and a shaved head called out as he strode down the path. "B'nar! Stone! Boss wants you ready inside! Reed and I will take over guarding this part of the gardens."

I took my chance while they were all concentrating on each other. Staying low, I ran across the balcony and then vaulted over the balustrades onto the next part of the terrace. This one was outside a guest room. The doors were smashed, and glass littered the floor. I crouched low and ran through the empty room to the door. Holding my breath, I slowly twisted the door handle. The door clicked open. Breathing a sigh of relief, I peered out. At the far end of the corridor, a woman with long blonde hair faced away from me. I darted from the room and ran in the opposite direction, hoping she wouldn't turn around before I got to the end of the corridor. There were no shouts, so I kept going. No guards stopped me. It was oddly disconcerting that there weren't any when I'd expected to have to fight my way out. I ducked into a store cupboard when I heard Connor's deep voice inside Rex's office.

"Yep, got it. I'm out." His footsteps approached my hiding place. "Dammit, Shannon, I'm being as quick as I can. Tell them to go to where we arranged. We'll wait there for her." His voice wasn't much more than a growl. Through the horizontal slats of the door, I saw him stride closer, holding a phone to his ear. My breath caught in my throat at the sight of him, and for a moment, I thought he'd heard my gasp. He seemed to hesitate outside my hiding place. He swallowed, and his nostrils flared. "Yeah, almost. No, don't! Give her some time. She'll be where we expected in a few minutes."

If he was waiting for me to come out of my room, I wondered how long he'd give me before he came looking. I relaxed when he continued walking and disappeared. Cautiously, I peered through the slats. I was about to dart out of my hiding place when Valentina crept down the corridor towards the office door. She was covered in dust and blood. I narrowed my eyes. It didn't look like hers. In her hand she held a gun, and on her right thigh she had a knife strapped. Had she managed to hide from Connor all this time? I almost called out to her when I remembered my distrust of this woman. *Housekeeper, my arse.*

She stealthily approached the office door and pushed it open with her foot, her gun held in a steady grip. After a couple of seconds she disappeared. Swallowing down my disquiet, I stepped out of my hiding place. Valentina with a gun was bad news. It only confirmed that Rex had been lying to me.

Cautiously, I tiptoed to the open office door. I strained my ears. It was silent. The only sounds were the birds twittering outside, and the deep murmur of male voices further in the house. I stepped in, relieved when the room was empty. My gaze flitted to the safe. The reinforced door that hid it from view was still closed. It looked like a floor to ceiling mirror. It was a good hiding place, unless you happened to notice the tiled floor near the very edge of the mirror was scraped slightly—for no apparent reason. Either Connor hadn't found it, or he wasn't interested in what was in the safe and hadn't bothered trying to get in. Valentina had disappeared. There had to be a way out down through the gym. My stomach twisted. If she came back, I was fucked. My butter knife wasn't going to stop a bullet.

In the far corner of the room a set of steps curved down to the floor below where the gym was located. There was an ornate floor to ceiling gate covering the entrance to the steps. I swallowed hard, my heart pounding. It was open. Valentina had to be down there.

Clutching my pathetic weapon, I slowly descended into the gym. It had to be where Connor was keeping Rex. It was the only 'down' Connor could have referred to the night before. I shook my head, trying to erase the headache that had returned with a vengeance, and swallowed down a wave of nausea. Fear skittered down my spine when I realised most of the lights were off. I'd never been down to the lower floor, but it was clear it was more than just a gym. There *was* a gym to my left and it was shrouded in shadow, but it was the long corridor that disappeared into the darkness that hooked my attention. A sliding glass door separated it from the training area. One that was open. I darted into the shadows at the edge, trying to calm my breathing enough to listen. Where was Valentina?

Dread tightened my belly, but I'd come this far, and if I didn't find Rex now, I knew Connor would never let me near him again. A quick glance over my shoulder told me no one was there.

"This is a bad idea," I muttered, but crept forward anyway.

Along the corridor, glass rooms that looked more like cells were illuminated. The walls between them were brick, but the whole front was glass. The first two were empty, but the next one wasn't. My heart lurched. Jed had his eyes closed and his head tilted back against the wall. His knees were bent up, and his forearms rested loosely on them.

"Jed?"

His eyes snapped open. "Ember? What the fuck are you doing down here? Where's Connor?" He darted a look behind me.

"Not here. Why are you locked in here?"

"Oh, come on, Ember," his face twisted. "You think your mate is going to let me near you?"

I scowled. "Why wouldn't he? You brought him into this, didn't you? You got him in here."

"That he did, my dear," said a dark, rough voice from behind me. I jumped and spun. Rex was staring at me from his cell. His eyes turned murderous as he glared at Jed.

"Oh, fuck off, you evil bastard. She deserves far better than to be used and damaged by you."

"Him?" I scoffed. "You participated too, Jed. What role exactly did you play in taking my life away?"

"Yeah, tell her, Hawk. Tell her how you sold her to me. How you were just going to rip her away from her mate and dump her with me until I stopped you leaving."

I swallowed down the ache in my throat at Rex's sneered explanation.

Jed jumped up and stormed over to the glass putting his palms against it. "Ember, please, don't listen to him. It wasn't like that…" He shook his head. "I mean, it was to start with, but then it wasn't." He lowered his voice. "I love you, Ember. I couldn't let him keep doing this to you."

"Oh, cut your bullshit, Hawk! She doesn't trust you anymore, and she sure as shit doesn't love you. I can see it in her face. Ember? Ember! Look at me! I can save you from that asshole up there. I can get us out. All you need to do is go to that panel on the side. There. Look…" He pointed to a silver and black keypad with a flashing red light. "That's right. Key in 560173, and we can get out of here."

Jed met my eyes and shook his head. "Don't. He'll hurt you, Ember. Go back to Connor. Trust him. He will keep you safe."

My stomach lurched at the utter conviction in Jed's voice. He professed his love for me, yet he would send me to another man. "Why? Why do all of this? Erase my memory? Take me from my family? Pretend to be my fiance? Then give me away? Why do any of it only to end up like this, in a prison?"

He leaned his forehead on the glass, his dark eyes holding mine. "Because I really have fallen for you, and returning you to the strongest of our kind, an alpha who can keep you safe from people like Rex, is the best thing I can do." His face fell. "And because you can never love me back, Ember. You have a soulmate, and it isn't me, no matter how much I want it to be."

Tears pricked my eyes. I couldn't question his feelings when he'd done such a selfless thing as to give me up to make sure I was safe. But he had answers, and I knew he would tell me what I needed to know.

"Who am I, Jed?"

He swallowed hard. "Your name is Ember, Ember Rawson. Connor is your mate. And you are so, so special. But because you are, it means you are in danger from people like him." He nodded at Rex. "You are rare, even among our kind."

"What kind?"

His gaze never left mine, no matter how hard Rex banged on the glass or how loud he shouted. "You are both a wolf-shifter…and a phoenix."

"A *wolf-shifter*?" My legs gave way, and I slid to the floor. The howling in my head was real.

"That is bullshit!" Rex bellowed. "I am your father! Let me out!"

I ignored Rex. The gravity in Jed's gaze told me he wasn't lying. A shifter? I had no idea what that meant. And I couldn't even begin to think about a phoenix. My hands shook so much I dropped the knife. It fell to the tiled floor with a clatter.

"It's okay. Look at me." Jed's voice dropped an octave and became more commanding. "Ember!" My attention snapped to him. "Leave. Go and find Connor. Stay with him. He will tell you whatever you want to know. And he will always keep you safe. You are his. And as much as I want you to be mine, you aren't. Now leave!"

My throat was dry, my head pounding, and nausea churned in my belly. I nodded. My thoughts were foggy, just like they always were when my headache started. I wasn't sure anymore why I had needed to see Rex so badly. Getting to my feet, I turned from Jed.

"Let me out! We can escape from here. Those people up there are your enemies, not me. I love you. You are my daughter. I know a way out…"

"Ember! Behind you!" hollered Jed.

Air fanned my hair, lifting enough strands to tickle my face. An arm encircled my throat, and the cold bite of a blade stung my skin. The coppery scent of blood hit my nose. My belly squeezed, and my breathing hitched, shallow and fast.

"Don't you fucking hurt her!" roared Jed.

I couldn't see him, but I could hear his fist slamming against the thick glass.

"Hello, Rex," purred Valentina.

He smiled, animalistic and cold, and it only just occurred to me that his face wasn't as bruised as I had expected. Damn it! Was he supernatural too?

"Valentina. I'm so glad you are alive. Did you bring it?"

Keeping me anchored with the blade at my throat, she lifted a circle of gold with her other hand. "I did, Papa."

"Good girl, now get me out of here."

"Move," she whispered in my ear and urged me towards the keypad. I didn't fight. A flick of her wrist is all it would take for her to slice open my throat.

Behind us, Jed bellowed a guttural, ferocious sound. He pounded the glass, and I felt the vibrations through my body.

Rex grinned as Valentina let him out. She handed him the circle of gold. I couldn't see it clearly but did get a quick flash of metal with runes of some kind on it. Rex grabbed it and tucked it in his waistband under his shirt. The hateful look he gave Jed turned my blood to ice.

Jed snarled, and though I couldn't see him, that animalistic sound told me he was a shifter too. Another barrage of thuds hit the glass, and there was a huge crack.

Rex grinned. "Give me your gun."

Valentina did, and then she spun me around. "You have to watch this." Her breath fanned my ear. "Let's see my papa kill my lover." She giggled, an insane sound, and I shuddered. Protruding from under her top lip were elongated fangs. Long and sharp. *Don't scream. Don't scream.* "You're a *vampire?*" I managed to whisper, my eyes wide.

She giggled again. "I am." Looking at Jed, she licked up the column of my throat. "Mm, your heart is racing. All that blood ready for the taking." She lifted her chin at Jed. "So, puta, what do you think now? Still think him sexy?" she asked.

I gasped.

From behind the panel of thick glass, a huge silverback gorilla stared at us, snarling and looking really, really pissed.

Rex raised his gun.

"Don't!' I shrieked, earning myself a deeper cut on my neck. I froze at the stinging pain.

Rex still had his gun aimed at Jed when a shard of glass suddenly penetrated his shoulder, right through from one side to the other. "Fuck!" Rex yelled.

From out of the shadows, a huge and terrifying creature charged. Rex yelled and raised his gun, shooting it over and over. Valentina shoved me away, and in one swift move, threw the blade. It slammed into the creature's shoulder, but that didn't stop it. It didn't even flinch. It barrelled towards Rex, who backed up against the glass of Jed's cell. Another shard of glass—no, not glass, ice, speared Rex's forearm. He dropped the gun, and it clattered to the floor.

Seeing his prey was cornered, the creature's fiery eyes fixed on Valentina. Her eyes widened, and she suddenly disappeared. But she didn't stand a chance. The creature vanished into shadows as if it were made of them, reappearing on the far side of me, clutching Valentina's throat. If vampires were fast, this creature of shadow and fire was quicker.

I blinked, unable to tear my gaze from it. Lava like veins flowed across its skin and under its fur. It was huge, its head brushing the ceiling. Razor like claws tipped its fingers, and its huge elongated jaws were rammed full of sharp teeth. It was terrifying. I scrambled away until my back was up against the glass of Rex's cell. This was the demon that had haunted my dreams. I yelped as the cut on my neck opened further. The creature inhaled, and its burning gaze locked on me, its eyes narrowing on my wound.

"You cut her!" It roared and snapped Valentina's neck like it was snapping a twig, then dropped her body to the ground.

Jesus fucking Christ!

My eyes widened further as the huge demon werewolf twisted, his eyes searching the floor in front of Jed's cell. "Where's Manivera!" he bellowed. My hand shaking, I pointed at the open panel in the wall between Jed's cell and the next. From the darkness, a pack of wolves appeared, followed by the man with blue hair. I gulped. He definitely wasn't human either. He was too beautiful and exuded power just like the others.

"Go!" the creature ordered. The wolves howled and charged down the narrow passageway.

"What about him?" the blue-haired man calmly asked as if it was perfectly normal to have a raging gorilla nearby.

"Leave him. I'll deal with him." The creature growled, and suddenly I was scared for Jed. He wasn't who I'd thought he was, but he had still tried to help me. I wouldn't let anyone hurt him. I let go of my neck, ignoring the fresh blood that trickled down my skin. Diving across the floor, I grabbed the gun and lifted it, staring the huge creature in the eye. I gulped, but instinct told me he wouldn't hurt me...I hoped.

"Don't you hurt him!" My voice hurt, but I held the gun out even though my hand trembled, and a wave of dizziness hit me. I shook myself, aware that my headache had settled again. Jed stopped pounding the glass, instead just huffing air through a crack behind me. His warm breath fanned my neck. Was I stupid getting this close to a pissed off gorilla? Probably. But no matter if he was a shifter and I didn't understand what the fuck was happening, he was my friend, and I'd fight for him, even if I would lose.

The creature cocked its head and stared at me, then slowly moved its gaze to Jed.

Silent seconds passed by. Then it changed. One moment the terrifying creature studied me; the next, Connor was staring at me, his blue eyes burning. Somehow, that change didn't surprise me. My heart had known it was him and that he would never hurt me.

His nostrils flared. "You're bleeding. Let me heal you."

"No. Not until you promise me Jed will be safe."

He stalked closer. There was no way I could do anything when he pulled the gun from my weak grip. I couldn't shoot him. The thought of hurting him made my chest ache.

Jed snarled.

"Quiet!" Connor snapped. His attention moved over my shoulder. "Move away from her."

Jed huffed. Then I felt him move away. His heat disappeared from my back.

Connor reached out. I flinched away.

"No," I whispered.

"Yes."

"Not here....please." I might not be in love with Jed, but I wasn't going to rub his nose in it by letting my 'mate' heal me and make me climax in front of him.

Connor's gaze darkened, and he glanced at Jed.

A woman walked closer. Her long dark hair swung over her shoulder in a braid. She was dressed very similarly to the way Connor's men had been, combats, heavy boots, and that same kind of shimmering, metallic top. "Perhaps you should take her back to her room, Prime. Where you can heal her in private."

"I don't want to fucking wait until we're in private. Let him watch; then he'll know she's mine. Not his."

"Fucking hell, man. I know that, anyway. Why do you think I got you in here? Just please, take her away." Jed's voice was thick and caught on his last words.

I couldn't even look at him. He had brought this situation on himself, but I still didn't want to hurt him. My legs wobbled, and I slipped sideways. "Dizzy," I said to no one in particular.

Connor swore loudly and swept me into his arms. "I'm going to be awhile. But when I'm done I want an explanation for what just happened. How did that vampire bitch get here before us? And find out if Rex has that fucking Halo!"

"He does," Jed confirmed.

"Shit! Shit! Shit!" Connor spat. He twisted to look at Jed. "You and I aren't done yet. But she comes first."

"She does." Jed looked at me, a deep furrow at the bridge of his heavy brow.

I'd suddenly had enough of all this. Shifters. Werewolves. Vampires. Two men fighting over me. Almost having my throat cut... Yeah, enough.

I turned my head into Connor's warm chest and inhaled. Immediately his scent calmed me, and I let myself drift away.

CHAPTER 12

onnor

EMBER'S FACE WAS RELAXED. Asleep, she looked peaceful and free of worry. It didn't do much to dull my fury, though. Rex had gotten away. Somehow, that slimy prick had evaded a pack of wolves. He'd had a secret passageway down through the cliff and to the water's edge. He'd been more than halfway across the bay on a speed boat by the time Owen and the others had found the exit.

Sophie looked at me. She had stayed by my side in Ember's room. I wasn't sure why, but it was kind of nice to have the company of someone who expected nothing from me. I wasn't Prime or the King of Shifters to her; I was her brother. She was my sister.

Sophie's eyes widened, and her gaze flicked to the door. Panic flitted across her face before she closed herself down into a blank mask. Her flushed cheeks gave her away, though.

"How's she doing?" asked Drake, his face worried as he peered in through the door.

"She's okay. Exhausted and overwhelmed, but she's strong. She'll process it all soon."

He eyed Sophie, who refused to look at him. He exhaled, a crease appearing between his brows before he looked back at Ember.

"Come on in, man. Sit with us for a while." I kicked out another of the chairs I brought in from the terrace. I didn't really want another male near my pregnant mate, but I had to deal with my increasingly possessive feelings towards Ember. Drake had been her alpha, the one she'd chosen to be her first protector. I knew he'd never hurt her.

"You sure?" Drake eyed me warily and then pointedly looked at Sophie. "Y' already have company."

"It's fine. I was going anyway." Sophie stood. "Let me know if you need anything." She squeezed my shoulder then was gone.

Drake raised his brows and took her seat. "What's with you two? What's the story? I know you're not cheatin' on Ember. But you treat her differently than the rest of us."

I raised my brows. "What do you mean, different?"

He leaned back in the chair and shrugged his big shoulders. "Different. What's between you? History?"

I studied my brother with a small smile on my face. "She is different from your ugly arse. But it isn't my story to tell. Ask her."

"What? Sophie? No way, man. She's more vicious than you when she's all riled up."

"Ha, I never figured you for a coward."

"Nah, I'll keep my distance. Life's complicated enough. You still mad Rex got away?"

I'd hit the gym and let my temper free once Shannon and Sophie had come to sit with Ember, but I'd calmed a bit now. And I wasn't mad at anyone else. Yeah, Rex had escaped, but it hadn't been anyone's fault but my own. Mostly I was pissed off for formulating a plan that had gotten Ember hurt. *Fuck! She could have been killed!* I took a long slow breath. Even without her memory, I'd known my Firecracker wouldn't sit and wait for permission to do what she wanted to do. I'd left her alone, knowing if I refused to let her see Rex, she'd find a way by herself. I'd hoped she'd see for herself what he really was without me forcing it on her. Not for one moment had I suspected that fucker had another daughter willing to fight for him. I rubbed my face. Not only had I killed a sister, but now both Sophie and I wondered how many other siblings we had out there. If there were any more, would they want to kill Rex or help him?

And, Mother Wolf help us; Rex had the Halo, too. Jed had told me about the safe, but even he'd no idea of the combination to get in.

Ember moaned, and I stiffened. Concentrating and keeping my power gentle, I caressed her with it, stroking her hair and face until she settled again.

"You healed her?" Drake's voice was deliberately hushed.

"Yeah." I had, without any of the pleasurable side effects I could use if I wanted. It had perhaps been wrong of me to reintroduce myself with an orgasm of epic proportions yesterday, but I'd lost control when I'd touched her. I'd wanted to pull her flat on that couch and spear her with my cock until she couldn't think of anyone or anything else but me, especially Jed. That motherfucker had stolen the last two months from us.

"Good. You know, if that was Rex's daughter you killed yesterday, I could already be free of any contracts he made."

"True. But I think there is another one."

Drake raised his brows. "Really? Well, shit. How many offspring did he produce?"

"Fuck knows, but all of this from his office holds some answers. So far, I know of one other daughter who survived." I gestured at the pile of paperwork at my feet.

"Shit." He was quiet for a moment. "If there *are* other siblings, they might know some of his passwords, or other information, that could help us get into his systems before the SBI gets wind that his operation is up for grabs. Or, it will be when he's dead." He sent a piercing stare my way. "I presume his death is your endgame, considering what he did to you as a kid, and what he's done to Ember now."

I nodded, my face grim.

"In that case, we need to ensure you get control of his legitimate businesses and assets on his death and use them to our advantage. You're his son, and I presume, his eldest child. If he has no will, you stand to inherit."

"True." I tapped my finger against my lips. "What if we find his daughter?"

He shrugged. "If she pops up, and is named in the contract with me, you know I'd still be willing to go through with it. If I married her, it would give me access to my company a lot quicker than going through the courts. And I presume you wouldn't want to kill any more of your siblings to take his assets if she is named beneficiary of his will?"

My top lip curled back. "If they're like that bitch Valentina, I would. But so far, it doesn't look like there are any others like her."

His eyes glinted. "If you took control of your father's estate, you wouldn't be so reliant on the High King. Walker's helped us, but I don't trust him. If he pulls out, I'll have enough money to keep us going, so long as I get my company back through that marriage."

I swallowed hard. He was right. But it was Sophie's choice whether to marry him. We'd found a copy of that contract in the safe. Or rather, Sophie had. She'd discovered the open safe and the bank of security cameras it held. Valentina had hidden from Ember, taken the Halo, and followed her down into the underground prison.

I'd told Sophie to go through the contents and bring anything she thought was important right to me while I sat with Ember. She had; many things that were shocking even to me. There were detailed accounts of the women he'd kept, their supernatural abilities, those he'd sold, those he'd killed, and the offspring he'd fathered. It seemed any other children he'd sired had not been strong enough to survive his violent training regimes or the demands he placed on their young bodies. Twelve children in total. It disgusted me. Only three of us had survived. And now there was only Sophie and me alive. I'd talk to her about the future soon, but both of us agreed that it was better to leave that kind of discussion until Rex had been properly dealt with, and we had closed the ever-growing rift in the centre of London. Whatever she decided to do about Drake would be her choice. The contract had come as a shock to her, but even if it solved our financial dependence on Walker, I wouldn't make her marry anyone. It would be up to her. I'd find another way to fund our operation.

"Let's deal with hunting down Rex, and the situation in London, then we can decide what direction to go in with funding."

Silence fell. It wasn't uncomfortable, but after a while, Drake got up.

"Hey, Drake? Brother?"

"Yeah?" His green gaze fixed on me, his head cocked.

"Thanks. For being willing to sacrifice your life like that...for the pack...for me."

He chuckled. "It's not completely selfless. I get my company and my money back as soon as that marriage is in place. Besides, there was no stipulation about consummating it or not getting divorced. If she's a real bitch, I'll wait until we clear her out of all her dirty money and then leave her."

I frowned, unused to Drake sounding so callous and cold, especially when I knew it was Sophie he would need to marry.

"Maybe. Or maybe you'll get lucky and fall in love."

Drake scoffed. "Yeah, not happening. If she works for him, she'll have done some shady shit and ruined lives. Not my kind of woman."

I swallowed hard but bit down on my retort. Sophie's life story wasn't mine to tell. However, if Drake thought he was going to disrespect her because of what she'd been made to do by that bastard, then he had another thing coming. "When Ember's awake, we're heading back to London. Get the plane sorted, would you? We'll have a meeting when we're in the air."

Drake nodded his head. "Sure, Prime."

"Are you sure that's the best way to play this?" Owen asked, staring at Jed.

"I'm telling you the truth. As far as I know, now that Ember's not taking the drugs, her memories stand a better chance of returning. The drugs were to suppress her wolf, which is why she got so many headaches. It's a side effect. Rex told me that when a shifter spirit tries to communicate with its host, it fires up their pain receptors and causes migraines." Jed looked directly at me, though with sincerity, not challenge, his lips pressed tightly together. I held his gaze, keeping my need to destroy him in check.

"What if her memories don't come back?" growled Reed.

I stood and stared at the faces of my council, my brothers. Reed and Myles sat together, their bodies close. Reed had improved physically, thanks to the hard training regimen B'nar had organised for us. And my brother was more than a little pissed at Jed for taking Ember away. Reed had a huge soft spot for Ember, as I knew she did for him, and she hadn't even recognised him when we'd travelled to the plane. He was hurt and ready to rip Jed a new one.

He wasn't the only one.

Stone glared at Jed, his eyes a vivid purple. He didn't even try to conceal his hatred for the man who had ordered his men to kill Shannon. Shannon herself watched Jed with cold eyes. She sat next to Sophie, who I was pretty sure was staying out of the way of Drake. Her eyes remained on the door to the flight deck where Drake had gone to talk to the pilot. Owen sat at the front, lounging by himself on the seat he'd turned to face inwards. I lowered myself into another plush leather seat and leaned my elbows on my knees. I'd vacated it to pace the plane when the conversation about Ember had begun. B'nar occupied a place next to me, watching us all silently.

Kawan reached into the fridge and passed me a beer.

"Here."

"Thanks, man."

He nodded. "No problem."

I hadn't wanted anyone but my brothers with me when we brought Ember back. Lance had been my partner in the SBI, but I didn't trust him anymore. We were both different people, and I *had* shot him, and his mate. I'd left him with Ava, demon hunting and watching for any increased demon activity on the streets, and left Alex as his back up. Alex was really there to keep an eye on them and Xania. I didn't trust his sister. And he'd confided that neither did he. I hadn't wanted to leave them alone with my mother, either. Lance and Amy worked for Walker, not me. And Xania did whatever the fuck she wanted to do. I'd given up trying to get her to work with me. She seemed determined to do her own thing, though her attitude and resistance were more of a 'fuck you' to Walker, who'd left her in this world when she wanted to be back in Faerie.

Those people weren't my priority. Ember was. I met Reed's worried look. "Ember's memories will come back," I said with conviction.

"Prime, you know she suffered a head injury too; maybe that's part of the reason for her memory loss." Jed sighed and rubbed his hands over his short hair. "Even when the drugs have worn off, she may still suffer."

"And who's fucking fault is that?" Stone growled, his canines bared.

"Oh, for fuck's sake. Mine. Okay? I *know* that. If I hadn't agreed to take her, she'd still be fine." He looked at me. "I know it's no excuse for taking your mate away, but Rex gave me no choice; it was either help him or wake up dead."

"There's still time for that to happen," Shannon sneered.

Stone glanced at her, but she was too focused on Jed to notice.

"Yeah, alright. I get it. You all want to rip my throat out for taking her from you."

"Yes. But I also want to rip your throat out for what you did to *her*," Stone said, his voice low and promising violence as he nodded at Shannon.

Jed glanced between them, but focused his attention back on Shannon. "You were with her. I remember. I'm sorry for what my men did to you. It wasn't personal. You were simply in the wrong place at the wrong time."

Stone shot out of his chair and, in the blink of an eye, had his big hand wrapped around Jed's throat.

"Stone! Sit down!" I yelled.

Stone met my gaze, his eyes glowing. He shoved Jed back in his chair. "We aren't done, motherfucker." He snarled but did as I ordered.

Shannon followed his movements. He held her gaze, and the tension between them was scorching.

I rubbed my face. I was so damned tired. I'd sat up with Ember all last night and spent the time while she slept going through the contents of Rex's safe with Sophie. Then Owen, Stone, B'nar and I went through the other documents Owen had found. We'd locked up the compound before we'd left. No locals knew what had happened, and if anyone did get in the house, there was no one there. No prisoners, no dead bodies; they'd been disintegrated into nothing by B'nar's ice magic, and their remains dumped in the sea.

"Guys, let's just be gentle with her, okay?" I said, taking a swallow of my beer. "She's been through a lot. Fuck. She doesn't even know she's pregnant."

Shannon snorted. "Gentle? With Ember? This *is* your mate we're talking about, isn't it? She doesn't need gentle. She needs a kick in the ass to remember who and what she is."

I huffed a laugh. "Maybe, but not yet. Let's give her some time to remember us all."

"Is there no other way to help her memories come back?" Reed looked at Jed.

Jed sighed and leaned his head back. "Not that I know of."

"Fine, for now, we keep her in the compound and treat her with kid gloves. No one lets her fight or go out alone. She's my mate, and she's carrying my child. And for Mother Wolf's sake, remember to keep that to yourselves."

There was a general murmur of agreement. Even Jed nodded.

"Good. When we get back, I'll get an update from Lance, Ava, and Alex, and we'll come up with a strategy for dealing with the demons and the Rift without Ember."

Their faces tightened. Yeah, I didn't know of a way to shut the Rift without Ember's phoenix either.

I walked down the aisle and towards the cabin where Ember slept.

"Hang on a mo'." Sophie stopped next to me and lowered her voice. "I might know of a way to get Ember's memories back."

I looked at her with my brows raised.

She leaned against the wall and crossed her arms. "Balthazar."

"Shit," I muttered. It didn't surprise me. As one of the most ancient vampires, he had mind tricks and magic not many supernaturals would understand. But he'd need her blood, and he was never getting his hands on that. She was mine, and I would never allow another being near enough to her to bite her. I growled.

"Connor, if you want her back, at least consider it. He might be your only option."

I ground my jaw but nodded. "We'll wait and see if she comes back to us without him first. I might need his army and his help, but I sure as shit don't want him messing around inside Ember's head."

CHAPTER 13

CONNOR and I travelled from the private airstrip in the back of a new Range Rover. Owen sat in the front passenger seat, and the guy called Drake drove us. They didn't speak much, though the silence was not uncomfortable. The radio played in the background, providing a welcome distraction. I tried to watch the rain-soaked countryside pass by, but my mind constantly went to all I'd learned in the last forty-eight hours. It was hard to understand what it meant to be a shifter. Connor had reassured me, and I trusted him when he said I shouldn't worry about it for now. Once the drugs wore off, if I felt my wolf pushing through, he would be there to help me. I swallowed, trying to control my fear of that unknown.

My attention slid to Connor. I couldn't help it. His presence overwhelmed me inside this confined space. All I wanted was to crawl into his lap and wrap my arms around him. His scent was driving me mad, and whenever I touched him, my anxiety settled. I snuck a look at his neck. Two white scars peeked over the collar of his button-down shirt, and though I had no idea what they were, they turned me on each time I saw them. I shivered and ran my tongue over the tip of my canine, sure it was longer and sharper than usual.

He glanced at me and smiled, though I could tell his thoughts were else-where. "You okay?"

I nodded. He'd been nothing but attentive since Valentina had cut me. He reached out and pulled the neck of my sweater aside to check my wound dressing. My chest tightened as his fingers brushed my skin and gently peeled the tape away. "It looks fine. You'll be healed by tonight. It's just taking a bit longer than usual."

"It is?"

"Yes. Those drugs Rex and Jed gave you have suppressed your wolf. It will take time before Mea can heal you."

"That's her name? Mea?" He nodded. "What about the phoenix part of me?" I wanted to know more. It was still a lot to get my head around, but I needed to understand.

Connor sat back and studied me. "I don't know. When you were a young girl, you used to burn, as in setting on fire, when you were really upset, or you felt threatened. But that settled as you got older. You told me recently that Fire, your phoenix, only appeared when your life was ebbing away. Or, that was the case until you were taken to Faerie where the High King and his son, B'nar...."

"The one with the blue hair, right?"

He grinned. "Yeah, that's him. They helped you learn to control your phoenix, so maybe she'll return when your wolf does, or maybe you'll have to learn how to call her all over again. Either way, we'll figure it out together."

I nodded and bit my lip, staring at the passing countryside. "Do you think I'll ever get my memories back?" My voice was quieter than I liked. I needed to be stronger about this. Yes, I'd had my life stolen from me, but I had it back now. It was up to me to learn who I was, to find my own way through this shit show.

Connor leaned forward and took my hands in his. "I really do. We are your family, your pack; we'll find a way to help you remember."

I offered him a small smile and gripped his hands back. I may not know him, but this felt right. He looked at our clasped hands and swallowed, closing his eyes like he was in pain.

My gut twisted, my eyes burning, not for me, but him. Not once had I considered how hard this must be for him. I'd been his mate, his partner, and he'd lost me. It was obvious he'd loved me enough to hunt me down, only to find out that I had no idea who he was anymore. It must be heartbreaking for him. On impulse, I scooted closer. His huge body stiffened, until I looked up and gave him a cheeky smile. "This okay?"

He grinned and pulled his hand from mine, wrapping his arm over my shoulders and pulling me closer. His whole body relaxed, and it felt good to be held against that powerful body. "Always."

I PEERED through the rain spotted windows as Drake maneuvered the four-wheel-drive through some thick metal gates and into a large compound. I frowned. It looked familiar, but I couldn't say why.

Connor hadn't moved his arm from my shoulders the whole time, and he gave me a tight reassuring squeeze. "Do you recognise it?"

"I don't know, I feel something…but I don't actually remember it."

"It'll come. Don't force it."

I turned my head into his chest and inhaled as I nodded. His scent calmed the nerves in my belly. "Yeah."

"Come on, Firecracker." But he didn't move. Instead, he looked down at me, nestled against his impressive pec. A few seconds passed as we just sat quietly and held each other. He kissed the top of my head and sighed, lifting his arm off my shoulders. Immediately, I shivered. He pushed the door open. Quickly, I grabbed his hand. "Hang on." It wasn't because I was apprehensive. I trusted him enough by now to know he wouldn't hurt me or put me in danger, and neither would the others. I just wanted to touch him. Sitting next to him, I'd been settled and had a sense of belonging that I couldn't ever remember feeling before. He watched me, a small smile on his face as I shuffled over the seat to clamber out with him.

The yard was unremarkable, just rambling buildings that looked like they could do with some tender loving care. The others got out of their vehicles and surrounded us. I had the feeling of being completely protected.

"Hey," smiled a guy who was holding the hand of the beautiful ebony-skinned man. They'd been the ones in the garden.

"Hi." I smiled at him, trying not to let my guilt at not knowing him show in my face.

"I'm Reed. This is my mate, Myles. I know you don't remember us, but that's okay. I just wanted you to know I'm really glad you're home with us now. You're gonna be fine." He lingered as if he wanted to say more.

"Hey, c'mon, man. Let's let Prime get her settled in."

Reed gave me another smile. "Yeah, 'course. See you later, Em." And they wandered off together.

"Ember?" I jumped a bit at Connor's voice. I'd been studying Reed, something tickling the back of my mind. He tightened his grip on my hand. "Come on, let's get you inside, then I'll introduce everyone properly."

"Okay." Suddenly I was nervous. Where would I stay? Would he expect me to be in the same room as him? I was learning to accept the new reality of my situation, but sleeping with him was a bigger step than I was ready to take at the moment. Trying to control my anxiety, I followed Connor, who led me up a set of rickety metal stairs.

Inside, the building was bigger than I expected, with solid walls, security doors and plenty of security cameras dotted around. The crumbling, dilapidated exterior was obviously a ruse. Keeping hold of my hand, Connor led me down a corridor and into a large room. At one side of the huge space was a bank of screens and computers. Across the other side, a large table stood surrounded by chairs.

"Owen? Would you call everyone to the table? I'd like to officially introduce Ember to everyone."

I stiffened. Oh shit, I didn't want to be on display. Keeping hold of my hand, Connor walked to the head of the table. Without causing a scene, there was no other choice but to go with him. He sat down, pulling me onto his knee. I perched awkwardly and avoided his eyes. The others sat in the chairs. Drake pulled out a chair for a dark-haired, strangely beautiful woman to sit down. She stared at me, her head cocked. Then she smiled almost shyly. I smiled back, sure I should know her, and sad that I didn't.

It took a few minutes for everyone to settle in. Two women and a man stood at the back with the ugliest man, creature, *thing* that I'd ever seen. If I hadn't already seen Jed shift into a gorilla and the strange blue-haired man throw shards of ice like weapons, I'd definitely believe in the supernatural now. He watched me with beady eyes. I swallowed hard and looked away. He grunted, and when I peeked back at him, he shook his head.

"Don't you be scared of me, young 'un. I've cared for ya since you were knee-high to a daisy. You're among friends here."

Giving him a real smile and a nod was easier after those words, and I was grateful for them.

"Quiet down, everyone. I'm really happy that Ember is back with us. That part of our mission is thankfully over. Ember?"

I looked over my shoulder at him. "Yes?"

"The people sitting at the table are our pack. I'm the alpha of this group of unlikely looking bastards." There was a general chorus of "hellos".

I let my gaze meet each one individually, weighing them up and deciding if they would be a threat to me. They all smiled, then looked down at the table. Instinctively, I knew that they were doing that to show me the same kind of respect they showed Connor. I'd noticed they would look at him for a short amount of time and then train their gaze over his shoulder before looking back again if they needed to. I'd wondered about that, but, strangely, now it made sense.

"So you're in charge of all of them?"

He gave me a slow and sexy smile, and some of the others snorted at my term. I didn't want to show my ignorance in front of all these powerful supernaturals, but if I was going to learn about my old life and forge a new one, I had to get over my embarrassment at asking.

"That's right. I guess I am."

I stared at his mouth. Ach! Now wasn't the time to remember the way those beautiful lips felt against mine, how the touch of his tongue had set me on fire. Damn! I needed to control my obvious reaction to him…I cleared my throat, my cheeks heating.

His smile stretched. "Are you okay?" His fingers brushed my hot cheek. "Did you remember something?"

"No," I croaked, quickly asking my next question, but the light in his eyes told me he knew exactly what I remembered. "So are you Prime to more than these people?"

Now he did grin. "Avoiding my question, Firecracker?" He smirked. "That's okay. Yes, I'm Prime to more than this rabble."

"Connor is more than our Prime, Ember," said Owen. He met Connor's gaze. "He is our king."

I gulped. "King?" My eyes went wide. Connor was a king? *Oh shit!*

"That's right. That makes you, as his mate, our queen."

My gaze shot to Connor's. "Queen?" I whispered.

He slipped an arm around my waist as if worried I might bolt. He was probably right. I was still coming to terms with being a shifter and a phoenix. Now I was a queen? Damn! How much more could one woman be?

"That's right, Em," said the blonde-haired woman, who seemed totally at ease amongst all these huge men, er, males. I gave her my attention. Anything to look away from the question and compassion in Connor's eyes.

"I'm Shannon, and we're besties, or at least we are now. We were enemies when we were younger, but we're not anymore. So you need to grab your memory by the balls and force it to return, 'cause I want my friend back. You get me? You don't take any shit from anyone, and this quiet, unsure version of you is confusing as fuck. So knock your head again and remember, or better still, let me do it. I was always good at knocking some sense into you." She grinned to soften her words, and I couldn't help but grin back. Her no-nonsense attitude was just what I needed.

"It's a deal. If I can't find a way." I shrugged. "I'll let you knock some sense back into me."

"No, you won't," Connor whispered in my ear, making me shiver. "No one lays a finger on you ever again." And his gentle kiss on the skin under my ear sealed that promise. I shivered but didn't miss the warning look he gave Shannon, who just rolled her eyes and muttered, "Get a room."

Even I had to giggle at her attitude towards her supposed king.

❧

AFTER THE MEET and greet was done, Connor suggested some food then some rest. We all wandered into a large dining area that had plenty of tables and chairs. The short ugly creature, Som, had made a huge pot of chilli and rice.

"Here. Have a seat, and once we've eaten, I'll finish showing you around and then show you your room."

I relaxed as he answered the question I hadn't dared ask. "I won't be sleeping with you then?"

His smile was rueful but not judgemental. "No, sweetness. You can have your own space for as long as you need it. If and when we are together physically again, it will be your choice. I'll never force you."

My heart beat so hard, I was sure everyone in a mile radius would hear it. He was giving me a choice. How hard must that be for him? I nodded and looked at my plate, considering his words. Taking a deep breath, I looked back at him. He sat opposite, patiently waiting for me to formulate my thoughts. "What if I don't ever remember us? What if I never want you that way again?" Gods, we'd been together. His hands had explored my body. He'd been inside me... *Fuck me.* That fantasy was enough to make me squirm. He clenched his jaw but leaned forward over the table and cupped my face with one big hand. Leaning into his touch was the most natural thing ever.

"Then I guess I'll have to work hard to win you all over again." He gave me a devastating smile and sat back, folding his arms over his chest, which made his biceps bulge. And again—*fuck me.* I wanted those arms around me, now. He lounged back with an air of utter confidence. "Besides, it could be fun to persuade you that you belong in my bed. And, you forget, I've had prior experience. I know what you like, what makes you squirm, what makes you moan and scream."

I gulped. *Well, shit.* Now I couldn't wait!

"And I'll win your heart." He let his heated gaze graze over my breasts and my face and smirked. "You're mine, Ember. *My* Firecracker. Just as I am yours. Even if you never remember what we had, you will not be able to deny what we are and always have been to each other."

I swallowed against my suddenly dry throat. But I lifted my chin and gave him a shaky smile. What the hell did a girl say to that? My mind and body were definitely up for it. I wasn't entirely sure about my heart, though. I had a feeling this powerful and gorgeous man could very easily break it. Tension simmered between us as I held his gaze. Som plonked a plate of food down in front of us both, breaking the spell.

The meal was tasty, and the company was actually fun. It was nice to see all these people laughing and joking with each other. I'd been so lonely in Rex's house, even with Jed. Now I understood why. I needed people around me; their energy settled my soul. Even Jed was there. He was seated as far from me as he could be, but I had a feeling that wasn't his choice, not when the looks he gave me lingered and his smiles were sad. I was still angry at him for his part in taking my life and family from me, but at the same time I got why he'd done it. Money and staying alive were strong motivators, but by helping Connor find me, perhaps there was redemption for the cold and callous person he'd been. I just hoped he didn't return to hurting anyone else as he had me. I glanced at Connor. I doubted Connor would allow that to happen. Jed needed to prove his worth, not just to Connor and his pack, but to himself, or instinct told me they wouldn't let him leave.

I stifled a yawn. I'd recovered from my injury, yet for some reason, I was utterly exhausted. I glanced at the clock on the wall. Nine PM. It wasn't even that late yet.

"Come on." Connor stood and held out his hand.

I looked at it, debating whether I wanted to go everywhere being led like a child. Before I could make up my mind about the invisible thread that made me want to reach out to him at every opportunity, he dropped his hand to his side. "It's okay."

"Where are we going?" Swallowing my guilt at the hurt in his eyes, I pushed my chair back.

"You're worn out. I'm taking you to your room. You can have a bit of peace and rest, and then tomorrow, I'll show you around the rest of the compound." He stood back and gestured for me to walk in front of him.

I smiled. He seemed to know, without me saying anything, what I needed. Peace. And a comfy bed. Once we'd left the dining room, I looked back in question.

"Down the corridor to the end, then take a right."

He moved along behind me, his power tickling my senses and awakening something in my soul. Something bright and wild. I tried to grasp it, but I couldn't.

We arrived at a set of stairs with a locked door at the bottom. Connor used the keypad at the side. "3002," he told me.

I raised my brows. "This is your part of the building?"

He smirked. "Well, I am a king. I deserve my space. And so does my queen."

He let those words sit and pulled open the door, walking up the stairs. Swallowing hard, I followed. Nerves churned in my belly, but I wouldn't shy away from this, from what this man made me feel. He was right, I didn't remember him, but my soul did. He said he belonged to me as much as I did to him. Possessiveness stirred in my chest as I watched him climb the stairs ahead of me, his body moving with restrained power. Deep down, I knew I wouldn't have to work hard at building a connection to him. It was already forming in my heart.

CHAPTER 14

mber

CONNOR'S ROOM was next to mine. He'd left me quickly after telling me he'd fetch me early the next morning. My room was sparse but functional. I dropped onto the bed without even bothering to undress or take off my shoes. That night a beautiful white wolf with amber eyes visited my dreams. At first, she sat and stared. I stared back, feeling as if I were in a cage looking out. I reached out, but invisible walls stopped my hand. Exploring, I found those walls all around me.

The wolf cocked her head and snarled, encouraging me to push at the walls that kept me away from her. I did. I flattened my hands and pushed. And pushed some more, so sure I could get out. And I did! Suddenly, I was free.

She yipped and bounced in a circle, then playfully looked back at me. Laughing, I ran after her, a feeling of freedom flooding me. I giggled and sprinted faster. We ran through what looked like a forest, but when I tried to peer more closely at the trees, they changed to brick walls—and bars. It was a prison. Men fought in rings, surrounded by a baying crowd. Horror dragged my feet to a halt, and the image disappeared. The wolf, *my* wolf, Mea, yipped again and took off. I followed. More images showed themselves, yet each time I stopped to try and look more closely, they disappeared. *Memories. My memories.*

When Connor's image hovered above me, his face dark with lust, his gaze intense, I slowed, wanting more of this memory. He reached out to touch me. My heart lurched, and I reached for him, too. As soon as I did, he disappeared, and another memory replaced that one. This time he was chasing me. I could feel him behind me... My heart beat faster, but I wasn't scared. I wanted these images and all the feelings that came with them. I'd been empty for so long. And this? This was the start of me reclaiming my life. I wanted to grab these parts of my life and keep them close, but they just kept floating away. So I kept running, watching the people who were my pack fight hard for their Prime and then for survival. I watched them laugh and shout, I watched them bleed, and I watched as I thrust my fist through Reed's chest and ended his life. My wolf howled, drawing me from that awful memory. I let her pull me away, not willing yet to hold onto that one.

I ran to where Mea sat between two large tree trunks. In the shadows, a magnificent black wolf stood and stared at her. His gaze drifted to me. Instinctively, I knew who this was.

Connor?

The wolf cocked his head, and his mouth stretched almost as if he was grinning.

Is she really my wolf?

He dipped his big head.

I stared at Mea. She was stunning, her white fur shone, and her amber eyes gleamed. She was the light to his darkness.

She is your wolf-spirit.

I jumped. Connor appeared beside his wolf, shrouded in darkness that floated around him like a mist.

Hey, Firecracker. His smile was devastating, and my heart flipped. *They are mates. Just like us.*

Prime narrowed his eyes on Mea. She stared right back as he prowled closer, brushing her head with his. He was nearly twice her size. As soon as they touched, the energy between Connor and me ignited. His piercing eyes met mine, his chest rising and falling rapidly.

They want to seal their bond again, Em. He took a deep breath.

I gulped and shook my head. *Oh, er, nope. No way am I watching them go at it.*

His eyes glinted as if he found that funny. *Then you should probably go back to your sleep. If we stay here, their reclaiming is going to make it hard for me to resist doing the same with you.* His eyes briefly closed.

But we're in a dream. It won't be real, I whispered back

Our souls are connected. The pleasure will be just as real as it is in the physical world.

I cocked my head and smirked. *So their lust transfers to us?*

His throat bobbed. *It does.*

Why haven't I dreamt about you before?

The drugs Manivera gave you have blocked your wolf. Prime couldn't find her any more than I could find you.

He groaned as Prime and Mea brushed against each other.

Ember, you need to get back to your deep sleep. I want our first time together to be with our bodies and souls, not just our souls.

So do I, I admitted.

Prime snarled and leapt on Mea.

Connor covered the ground between us. *Then leave.* But he speared my hair with his hand and held my head so that his kiss could devour me. Gods, this man knew how to kiss. I drowned in him, melting into his embrace. I tried to grab onto him—except he was too insubstantial, and my hands slipped through his shadowy form.

He pulled away, his look heated and full of longing. *Go. I'll not be far away.* And he pushed me gently backwards. I fell through the air and into sleep.

❧

BY SEVEN THE next morning I was up and dressed and excited about spending time, not just with Connor but with everyone else. Getting to know them and whatever they were doing in this strange headquarters with all their tech and security intrigued me.

I squared my shoulders and took a deep breath when there was a knock on my door. Gods, I had wanted Connor so badly last night. But I also wanted to get to know him. Would he consider that weird of me? Would the others? After all, we had clearly already had sex. Jeez! Who wouldn't want to get physical with a body like his? I wiped my sweaty palms down my jeans and took ahold of myself. He was giving me time to get used to the idea of an *us*. But truth be told, I was hoping I wouldn't need it, especially after the flashes of memory Mea had led me through last night.

I grasped the cool metal door handle and pulled open the door. Connor gave me a slow grin. My breath caught in my lungs as he reached out and touched my cheek, almost as if he couldn't help himself. "Morning, Firecracker."

And just like that, the dull headache and slight nausea that had bugged me since I'd woken up disappeared. I couldn't help but return his smile, my chest warming at the sight of him.

"Hey."

"How are you feeling?"

I considered his question. Now that I thought about it, my headaches and nausea had been damned near unbearable at Rex's house. Now they were just an irritation. "Actually, I feel surprisingly good this morning." And that was the truth.

His smile stretched enough that I saw his cute broken tooth again. "Good. Let's go and get some breakfast then, shall we?"

"Okay." I was absolutely starving now that my stomach had settled again.

He set off down the corridor, and I hurried after him. After last night, I wanted to touch him. Not jump his bones. I grinned. Well, maybe that too, but I also just wanted to be in contact with him. Reaching out, I slipped my hand into his. His eyes widened, but his smile was blinding. I smiled back, and his fingers tightened around mine. My chest warmed. I'd made him happy.

Connor spent the morning showing me around the compound. It was much bigger than I'd expected. The living quarters were near ours, just down a floor. It was all a bit old and run down in parts, but otherwise clean. There was the dining area, a gym, where B'nar and Stone trained together with Reed and Myles. Shannon sat on the sidelines watching, or rather watching Stone. I wondered if they were a pair. The tension between them was thick, but they seemed to avoid eye contact, only looking at each other when the other was busy.

Connor led me through the storerooms, the kitchen, and back to the large room lined with computers and screens.

"Hi," said a pretty blonde woman. "I'm Ava."

I smiled and greeted her and the others.

"Lance," said a thick-set man with perceptive brown eyes.

Another woman eyed me coldly. I wanted to shrink away but didn't. "So you're what all the trouble has been about." Her eyes slid over me. "You hardly seem worth the effort."

"Xania! Get back to monitoring the streets."

Xania glared at Connor but did what he said.

"Don't pay any attention to her. She's just bitter because she's in this world when she wants to be back in Faerie."

"Faerie?"

"Yeah, like I said before, you've been there too." He smiled. "But I think you have enough with this world at the moment, so let's leave that for another day."

I nodded gratefully. "Okay. Sounds good."

We shared some lunch, and I was shown the chair to Connor's left when there was a pack meeting later in the day. Connor and the others were heading out to hunt demons. I swallowed, wondering if I had the sort of skills needed to help, or at least if I used to. I stared at Connor's face as he spoke, every bit the leader.

"Right, you all have your orders for tonight. Ember is with Owen and me."

"What about Manivera? Shouldn't someone go and scope the Count's club?" asked Stone.

Shannon scoffed a little. "Yeah, and you'd just love that to be you, wouldn't you, Stone?"

He glared at her.

"I don't know about him, but I know our beta would. Eh, Owen?" said Kawan, laughing at Owen's grin.

"Oh, yeah. That octopus demon was one hell of a ride. I'd go back for more, anytime." Owen waggled his eyebrows comically.

Drake laughed, his green eyes glinting like jade chips. "Well, seeing as you're working with the Prime tonight, how about I keep her busy?"

Sophie cast him a dirty look and pushed her chair back. "Is that all, Prime?"

Connor's eyes narrowed on her and his gaze flicked between her and Drake. "Yes, Sophie. That's all." Then he hesitated before nodding almost to himself. I swear I *felt* a pulse of resolve from him. "Actually, no, that's not all. You won't be doing street surveillance tonight. Stone's right. We need eyes in the club. If Rex is going to sell the Halo somewhere, he'll take it to the one person who has contacts in this realm and access to Hell."

Sophie swallowed, and I swore she looked slightly green. "You want me to go back to the club?"

He set his jaw and gave her a steady look. "Yes. You will be safe. Balthazar will not claim or kill you, not if you are with one of my pack."

"Are you joking?"

Owen growled. "Careful, she-wolf, he is still your king."

Sophie glanced at him, then back at Connor. "Fine. But I won't be safe. He thinks I betrayed him. And he never forgives a betrayal."

Connor smiled, but it was cold, not reaching his eyes. "Maybe not. But he also wants an alliance with me, and to keep it, he will be careful not to break our laws. He will not kill, or take one of my pack as his prisoner. Besides, you will be going with Drake, and he can charm the pants off anyone. Maybe even the Count. I hear Balthazar likes men as well as women. That could be useful."

"Prime?" growled Drake, all levity gone from his face.

"Yes, brother. You will take Sophie into the Gambit and keep your eyes and ears open for anything that could help us hunt down Manivera. If you hear anything, you'll call me, and we'll be there." Connor glanced at Sophie, then Drake. "You will make sure no harm comes to Sophie. She is yours to protect…"

"I don't need his, nor any other male's protection, Connor, and you know it!" Sophie snarled.

Connor glanced at her, a smirk curling his mouth. Jealousy stabbed me right in the heart at the look that passed between them. They obviously knew each other well enough to read each other's thoughts.

"Maybe not. But perhaps he needs yours."

Sophie rolled her eyes at Connor, but her mouth curled upwards. "I guess he probably does. All those women being octopus demons and all, trying to get in his pants. He's probably not capable of fighting them off."

Drake growled, his eyebrows dipping over the bridge of his nose. "Who says I want to?"

Sophie tipped her head and smirked. "Oh, please, hot stuff, if you let more than one handsy female demon play with your junk, you'll be lost to the pack forever. They'll give you the night of your life just before they suck out your soul. And, just like every other male I've seen in that place, you'll be too high on sex hormones and pleasure to realise they're doing it."

Drake cocked his head. "Just how many times have you been to that club?"

She laughed. "More than you have."

Drake opened his mouth, but Connor chimed in first. "Drake, listen to Sophie. She knows what she's talking about. I want you both low key and watching every fucker that goes in and out of that place. You're there to back each other up. I don't want any mistakes. You both stay in one piece and safe." He glared at Drake and then Sophie. "Understood?" Connor's eyes turned black and, for a brief moment, flared with flame.

I shivered at the power emanating from him. Drake swallowed hard and met Sophie's gaze.

"Yes, Prime," they said simultaneously.

After the pack left, Connor took me back to the dining area. The ugly Faerie, Somnelaire, who I'd discovered was a shadow fae, served us. His brows dipped as he studied me. "You know the Count could help with her memory," he said to Connor. He peered into my eyes. "D'you not remember me at all, girlie?"

I thought back over my memories from my dream. There was nothing. "No, sorry."

His already thin lips thinned more. "Well, it's not your fault, I don't suppose, Yellow."

Connor frowned. "Her name is Ember."

"Yes, and in Faerie names have power, so I will always call her Yellow, just as your mother is My Lady."

Connor grunted and watched Som waddle away.

"What did he mean? That the Count could help?" I wasn't sure who the Count was, but nevertheless, I understood he was powerful—and that Connor didn't trust him.

Connor frowned. He glanced at the door to the kitchen then the door to the corridor. There were two simultaneous thuds as they shut and clicks as they locked. "Just so we're not disturbed while we...talk about this," he said and shuffled his chair closer. My skin tingled, and Mea released a low throaty greeting. Connor's eyes flashed with ebony. He twisted my chair around to face him and laid his palms flat on both of my thighs, his fingers gripping me gently but possessively. I gulped as heat from his hands seeped into my skin, making it hard to concentrate on anything else.

"I've heard that original vampires, the most powerful of their kind, can see into your mind and your memories..." His gaze lingered on my neck, right where I knew my two scars were. His voice became gravelly, sending a shiver over my skin. "...when they sink their fangs in here..." He traced the forefinger of his left hand over my neck. I gasped. His pupils dilated. "...and drink your blood while your mind is weak with pleasure."

"Really?" I whispered, unable to prevent myself from glancing at his canines, which had lengthened considerably. My heart banged against my ribs. Only it wasn't in fear. Desire flooded me, weakening my limbs. I licked my lips, my voice going raspy. "And do shifters use these to give pleasure?" shivering with anticipation as I reached out and touched his chipped canine with a finger.

His smile was darkly sensual and full of danger. "Yes. When we claim our mate." His tongue traced the sharp points of his teeth. "Though we can bring each other pleasure with our bite, too."

Heat flooded me as his hand traced in a featherlight touch down my arm to my hand, and he intertwined his fingers with mine. Gently he tilted my chin and leaned in, brushing his lips across my scars. "These are my claiming marks." He dropped more light kisses against my skin, and I grabbed onto his muscular forearms as sensation flooded me. Gods, he only had to touch me, and I was lost. "And the pleasure I will give you when I claim you again will be more than any other creature in any other world could ever give you because you are mine." He took my skin between his teeth and sucked gently until I moaned. Gripping his forearm, I tried to urge the hand that rested on my thigh higher. I needed him to touch me, but I didn't know how to ask with words. I gasped, a groan escaping me when he sucked hard, his teeth scraping my skin. That small amount of stinging pain only brought more pleasure.

Grabbing his hand, I whimpered as I tried to move it towards the juncture between my legs, unable to think of anything else but chasing the pleasure I knew only he could give me.

He released the skin of my neck with a small popping sound and grabbed my hair, tilting my head. "Tell me what you want." His voice was husky, his eyes dark and full of lust.

"I want you."

"And I want you, but you have to trust me first." He kissed me, allowing me to taste him only to pull away when my tongue brushed his. "Do you trust me enough to do this?" He pulled back enough to watch my expression as he flicked open the button on my jeans. His breathing was rapid as he slid his hand down my gently rounded stomach and his fingers grazed over my panties. I groaned, lifting my pelvis towards his touch.

"More," I demanded.

His throat bobbed, flames burning in his eyes. "Do you trust me enough?" he asked, his fingers stilling.

I looked him right in the eye. "I do." It was true, with every part of my being. "I want this."

"Then lift," he urged me. I did. He quickly pulled my jeans and underwear down enough to give him free access. I gasped as he slid a finger down between my folds. His groan was shaky. "Fuck, Ember…you're wet for me."

I bit my lip and nodded, moving forward and rocking myself against his finger. His expression turned hungry. He held my head firmly, his knees on either side of mine protecting us from the sight of anyone who might walk in, despite the locked doors. But I didn't care about being seen. I didn't care about anything but the man touching me and the aching desire burning through my sex. "Does this feel good?" he asked just as he slipped a finger inside me.

"Yes." And it did. So, so good.

"How about this?" Another finger.

"Connor! Oh, gods. Please…" I rocked my hips harder against his hand. He withdrew his fingers and thrust them in again, curling them in until pleasure mixed with a pleasurable pain that had me babbling incoherently. "That's it, Firecracker. Ride my fingers…Let me give you this pleasure."

He urged my head back with my fisted hair, and my eyes flew open. His face was dark, full of a rabid hunger, his canines down. "Do you want me to make you come, sweetness? Hmm? Is that what you want?" His fingers thrust forward. In and out with his words.

All I could do was nod and moan. "Yes. Yes."

He gave a satisfied smile and looked down, the pad of his thumb rubbing gentle circles on my sensitive bud. "Then come," he whispered hoarsely before his mouth devoured mine.

It was so easy to let go and allow the pleasure he offered to wash through my flesh and bones. It consumed me until I clutched at him, curling my fingers into his back to save me from floating away.

onnor

AT LEAST THE damned rain had stopped. It was bloody cold and damp on these streets, though. I glanced at Ember. Her hand was in mine, and it was warm. Her skin was flushed with the cold, but she looked bright-eyed and happy, not scared. If anything, hunting seemed to exhilarate her. The last two demons Owen and I had ended had worked together to try and get to Ember, as if drawn to her. There was no way I would allow them anywhere near my pregnant mate, so they had died quickly.

It was a risk bringing her out to hunt demons with me, but I couldn't bring myself to leave her, either, not yet, and I needed to work just as hard as my brothers to find the Rift. No one was exempt from helping, not even me.

Owen checked his watch. "It's nearly dawn. We'll only need to be out for another half an hour or so." He glanced at Ember and smiled, answering her question before she could ask. I smiled; Owen knew her well. Ember was always curious. "We don't hunt so much in the daylight. The demons that are newly formed and from the Rift hate the sunlight. They tend to be more active at night, so that's when we hunt. We use the shadows as effectively as they do. They are our friends when we hunt. We watch from them, and we wait in them."

Ember huffed a chuckle and cocked her head, her jade eyes gleaming. "Shadow Sentinels. There to fight the demons and evil of this world."

I smiled as widely as Owen. "That's right," he said, nodding.

"Listen, man. I'm going to take Ember back now. She's been out long enough and should get some rest. You good on your own?"

Owen nodded and checked his phone. "Yeah, I'm going to meet up with Kawan. He's been in Chinatown the last couple of hours and has a few more places to check out up there."

"Sure thing. See you for the meeting at five."

" 'Kay. See you later, Em."

Ember smiled at Owen, and he jogged in the direction of the underground station.

Squeezing Ember's hand, I turned us back to where I'd parked the SUV.

"Are you tired?" I asked as she stifled a yawn. Her hand then dropped to her stomach. Shit, I should have taken her back earlier…

"I am a bit. And I'm *starving*. I guess I'm not used to staying awake all night. But I don't want you to leave me behind." She added quickly.

I smiled and wrapped an arm over her shoulders, turning her into my kiss. Her arms wrapped around me, winding under my jacket with no hesitation as she kissed me back. Gods, I'd never get enough of this. Of her. When she pushed against me, I groaned and pulled away. Her response to me got stronger each time we touched, making it harder to restrain myself from taking her. And out in the street, up against the nearest wall, wasn't where I wanted that to happen. "Come on, sweetness, let's get you fed and to bed."

A sassy smile curled her lips, making my stomach squeeze. It looked so much like the old Ember. "Maybe I don't need food, just a bed." She came up on her tiptoes and brushed her lips against mine. "With you in it."

I swallowed hard and smiled back. "I can do that."

She stilled, looking unsure again, and that band that had loosened around my heart tightened again. My Ember was still in there, but this wasn't her, not yet. "Really?"

I held back my sadness. I loved this Ember as much as I always had, I desired her as much, but a part of me would always grieve for the missing piece of her that remembered us. She didn't need to know that, though. "Damn, Em, can't you tell how much I want us to be together?"

She smiled, and another sexy little smile curved her mouth. Her small hand rubbed my hardness through my jeans. "I've got an idea," she quipped as she gave me a squeeze, then let go and grabbed my hand, pulling me along.

I grinned, hope warming me. Oh yeah, she was still in there. Maybe she would come back to me soon.

As we approached the shiny black Range Rover, the air temperature dropped, and the stench of demons hit my nostrils. Prime burst through my skin. "Behind me."

Ember didn't argue. She knew the drill by now and shuffled away from the squad of demons that approached from the shadows in front of us.

"Connor, there's some behind us." Ember's voice shook.

Eight demons approach from the front. I glanced behind me. Eight more approached. Normally even those odds wouldn't faze me, but having my pregnant mate by my side changed things. Fear spiked through me, and for once, I let my fae side join Prime, dropping to all four of my clawed feet. My bones stretched further, and blood lust hit me.

Ember's eyes widened.

"Pull that gun, Em," I growled. "You know what to do with it. Let your instincts out to play. Stay alive. When I've dealt with these fuckers, I'll deal with what's left."

Her face paled, but she nodded. Drawing the gun with one hand, she unclipped the sheath of the long bladed hunting knife I'd strapped to her leg with the other. "Okay," she said. Without pause, she raised the gun and squeezed the trigger.

The demons moved swiftly, pulling their own weapons. Bullets didn't harm me, but Ember had to duck behind a metal dumpster.

I roared. This was an organised attack. They'd waited until we were alone. I rushed the demons nearest to me, ripping and shredding.

Behind me, Ember shrieked as the demons worked together and dragged the dumpster away from her, exposing her.

My heart thundered, all of my spirits burning with rage as we saw how vulnerable our mate was. I kicked a demon across the street and ripped another in half before I changed direction.

Within seconds, I was engulfed in fire. Stunning multi-colour flames licked around me. I could feel Ember's fury and the comfort she sent my way. She wanted me to know she was okay. I stalked closer to my mate, whose back was against the wall, her eyes full of iridescent flames.

"They tried to kill me—and you," she said, her voice full of power. "I won't let them hurt you."

I shifted back, my body naked. I reveled in the touch of her flames as much as in her words. I lifted a hand and cupped her cheek, my heart squeezing. "I know, baby. But you have to stop now. You've killed them all. We are safe. Your flames are bright enough and powerful enough to draw attention from other supernaturals."

She looked at me, and I let her see my own flames. The Hell-beast that lived in me. "You aren't burning."

I smiled. "No, you are my Firecracker. You can never hurt me."

She slowly raised her flaming hand to my cheek. "Good."

"Send Fire away again, sweetness. We have to go."

She nodded, her hands dropping to my hips, her gaze travelling down my nakedness. A smirk tilted her mouth. Dammit. She was so sexy. I swallowed as my body reacted to her touch and her sultry gaze.

"Ember, sweetness, send Fire back to rest. We are safe now. No one is going to hurt us." Swallowing hard, I clothed myself and her, placing a hand on her lower belly. She didn't know why, but I did, and I needed to reassure myself that our baby was unharmed. A small pulse of energy hit my hand, and I relaxed.

Ember rested her forehead on my chest, and the flames receded. I breathed a sigh. "Well done. Come on, let's get out of here."

She straightened and nodded. I got us in the car and drove out of there quickly. All the way back to the compound, Ember rested her hand on my thigh. She was quiet and tense. I didn't talk, just held her hand. She'd met her phoenix for the first time tonight. She'd need time to process that.

CHAPTER 16

$\mathcal{E}$mber

BACK AT THE COMPOUND, I made myself release Connor's hand. I didn't want to, and it even made me angry that I had to. Seeing him walk naked through the flames I'd somehow created had been the sexiest thing I'd ever seen. If I'd had any doubts about him being mine, I didn't now. And I wanted him. Badly. So much I'd barely been able to think about anything else on the way back.

I pulled him away from the SUV, up the steps, and inside. As soon as the door was shut, I rounded on him. Grabbing his jacket, I slammed him up against it. At least, he let me slam him up against it.

I gazed up at him, my heart thudding against my ribs. "I don't want anyone taking you away from me." My words were growled, and I knew my connection to both Mea and Fire was amplifying the protectiveness I felt. I couldn't help it. Releasing the flame that burned through my soul when I'd seen how outnumbered we were had been instinctive. Fire had swamped me, and her anger still rode me, right alongside the fear that had torn at my heart.

"No one can ever take me from you. Not even the Devil himself could do that." Connor's voice was rough and low, his eyes intense.

I jumped up and clamped my legs around his waist, slamming my lips against his. "Good," I said when I let us up for air. "Because I'll burn anyone who tries."

He smirked, and his eyes dropped to where my breasts rose and fell

772

rapidly, pushing against the material of my shirt, before he stared down at the juncture between my legs and then back at my face. He inhaled, and his eyes darkened. "Do you want me, Firecracker?"

I leaned in and kissed him again, my tongue dancing with his. We were both panting when he wound my hair around his fist and held me back. I snarled. I wanted to kiss him. He was *mine*. "Yes. Right now."

"Thank the gods, because I'm going to take you back to my room and make you come screaming my name. Then I'm going to claim you again. You're mine, Em."

He lowered me to my feet and straightened my clothes. I met his beautiful cerulean and black gaze. Slowly, to show him I wanted this as much as he did, I reached forward and ground my hand down the impressive erection that was straining against the material of his jeans.

He closed his eyes and groaned. "Fuck. It's been far too long since I felt your touch on my skin."

He swung me into his arms, and I didn't complain, not when he kissed me deeply and strode towards our rooms. The door clicked open without him even touching the keypad, and we were up the stairs without his mouth leaving mine for a second. I drank him down, his taste, his touch; I couldn't get enough of him.

He lowered my feet to the floor and pulled off my top, unclipping my bra before my shirt had even hit the ground. I fumbled with his belt, desperate to get his clothes off him and see his glorious body again. I'd only just managed to get his belt open when he shoved my jeans and panties down. He held my wrists.

"Me first," he rumbled and dropped to his knees. I balanced with my hands on his rock hard shoulders. He looked up at me, almost as if he was worshipping me. Slowly he slid my bra straps down, his gaze feasting on my full breasts. My nipples had been super sensitive lately, and as soon as the cold airbrushed them, they stood out. His gaze only made them harder and ache more than ever. I bit back a groan as his hands cupped them, squeezing gently. He rose up just enough to take a nipple in his mouth, worshipping it with his tongue, teeth and lips before he released it and gave the other the same attention.

"Connor..." My pleas were just frantic whispers. I wanted him to stop and take me. I wanted him inside me. Yet, I didn't want to stop feeling his hot mouth on my skin.

"Shh, I want to kiss you everywhere, Firecracker. I've missed you so much. I need to do this to prove to you that you belong with me. That you truly are mine."

I already knew that. I had since I'd first seen him. And connecting with the phoenix in my soul had freed another part of me that knew it too. "I know I am yours. Because you are mine, too." I swallowed hard at the thought of this powerful shifter king being mine. My mate. Mea howled her agreement. Connor snapped his head up. "Prime and Mea need each other again, too. But I need to taste you, to worship you first."

And worship he did. His mouth kissed me everywhere, his hands holding my waist, my hips and finally curling around my buttocks. He reverently kissed my lower tummy, his gaze fixed on there as if he could see inside me. "Hey," he whispered and kissed my skin again. His gaze lowered and darkened as he looked at the glistening skin between my legs. He buried his face in my heat and inhaled deeply.

"Mine," he growled.

At the first stroke of his tongue, I shuddered and groaned long and low. "Oh. My. Gods."

He did it again and again. I gripped onto his shoulders for dear life, my legs no longer able to support me. He was relentless, licking and sucking the sensitive bundles of nerves at my apex. He moaned and pushed two fingers inside me, curling them to touch my g-spot. Pleasure built like a storm inside my pelvis, and I came, squeezing his fingers and groaning his name.

Without giving me a moment to recover, he lifted me onto the bed. All I could do was stare up at him, drinking in the sight of his body as he toed off his boots and got rid of his remaining clothes. His erection bobbed free, standing proud and so fucking beautiful. I reached out and wrapped my hands around it, my body burning with desire.

"I need you," he ground out, his whole body coiled, his muscles tense.

I nodded. I understood, my craving for him just as strong. I raised my knee, baring myself to him. He wasted no time, as desperate for me as I was for him. He lowered himself over me, supporting his huge body on his elbows. Jerkily, he rocked his pelvis forward, dragging his erection through the slickness that coated my skin.

"Are you sure?" His throaty question reached into my heart. He'd still stop if I wasn't ready, no matter how much he wanted me.

In answer I reached down to grab his hard length, guiding him to my entrance. He ground his teeth, breathing hard through his nostrils.

I wrapped my heels around his thighs and thrust my pelvis up, taking him inside me in one swift move.

"Ohhh shiiit," he breathed, relaxing his weight into me. I tilted myself further, opening up for him. He was huge, and I'd had nothing inside me for months. I groaned, half in ecstasy, half in discomfort. It was painful until he pulled back and slowly thrust forward again. More of him went inside me with each steady, firm thrust until the tip of him brushed my cervix, hitting me with each rock of his hips. Pleasure flooded me, and my eyes rolled as I gripped onto him for dear life.

Panting and groans filled the air. Connor's ragged breaths hit my skin.

"Gods, Ember, I love you. I've missed you so much." He kissed me deeply, and I kissed him back, digging my fingernails in his skin as I succumbed to the pleasure he gave me. I wouldn't worry about the fact that I wasn't really his Ember, not yet... Even after meeting Fire, the fear that I might never be cooled my desire a little until he thrust into me forcefully and ground himself deep, pushing me into the mattress.

"You will always be you." He kept his weight against my pelvis but stopped moving. "Even if you don't get your memories back, you are still Ember, just the new version of you. And I love you no matter what. My soul knows you, belongs to you, and I will spend the rest of my days proving that to you."

My eyes burned, but I didn't allow a single tear to fall. Instead, I lifted my head and fused my mouth against his, telling him without words how much that meant to me. He grinned against my mouth when I fought to move against him, chasing the pleasure that was building inside me. "Are you ready for me?" He rasped.

"Yes, give me everything you have."

And, oh, he did. He made love to me furiously, reclaiming my body. Lifting my legs until my knees were bent and my feet over his shoulders, he pounded into me, sweat coating us both. Stars crossed my vision. Pleasure pain from each thrust of his hips turned my bones to liquid.

"Yes. Connor...more...*more*..."

A fierce and determined look darkened his face. He lowered my legs, hooking one arm under one thigh and changing his angle. He dropped his head to the side a little, increasing the tempo of his thrusts.

The strong column of his throat was above my face, his veins engorged, sweat coating his skin. I licked up the column of his throat, not surprised when my canines lengthened, just as Connor's had. I snarled and gripped his head, yanking his hair so it gave me better access to him.

"Mine," I growled in a voice I barely recognised.

"Yes," he groaned. "Do it. Claim me again, Firecracker." The longing, along with the command in his voice, broke me. I had no idea what to do, so I just went on instinct. I struck hard and fast and drew a mouthful of blood. It was the best thing I'd ever tasted, sweet and salty and something uniquely Connor. His spicy scent flooded me. I couldn't get enough. I swallowed hard, aware his thrusts had lost rhythm, becoming rapid and desperate. I took another big draw, and he bellowed, a roar that shook the walls as he emptied himself inside me. I pulled my teeth away, staring up at him. He was panting, staring down at me with such raw love and desire my whole body strained for him. His canines grew more. "Your turn, sweetness." And he pushed my jaw over with his nose. He licked my skin, inhaling deeply. I gasped as there was a sharp sting. He sank his teeth in deeply, the low satisfied rumble deep in his chest making a very primitive, female part of me preen with satisfaction. The first draw of his tongue and mouth had me moaning in pleasure. The second sent a rush of heat and lust as I'd never felt before, right through every part of my body. I groaned and urged him to move, rolling my pelvis against him. I knew he'd come already, but I couldn't help myself. I wanted to feel him moving in me. He growled and began to move again. I echoed him when I felt how hard he still was.

Each roll of his hips was sensual. Moving in circles, he ground against my clit, never letting his pelvis leave mine. He pushed against me as he suckled until I exploded around his length, screaming his name. Lights flashed behind my closed eyes. He sucked harder, and tears leaked down my cheeks as the pleasure continued, squeezing across my belly until I was sobbing and begging him to stop—or to keep going, I had no idea. He gently withdrew his teeth from my neck and grabbed my hands, holding them over my head. His burning blue and red gaze ensnared mine, not releasing me as he rocked into me harder and harder. I met each thrust, unable to believe the utter pleasure this man could give me.

He changed his angle, lifting one of my thighs wider and to the side while holding both of my wrists in the other hand. He hit me deeply each time, and I pulsed with each thrust, my pleasure building again.

"Come. With. Me."

"Yesss," I breathed.

He watched me closely, his gaze never leaving mine until I once again reached the edge of orgasm. "Now, Firecracker..." His face twisted in pleasure, and he groaned. Heat filled me again, my body exploding, gripping him and milking him.

Slowly, he stopped moving. Both of us were panting and gasping. He groaned my name and collapsed on top of me, but he still managed to hold some of his weight on his elbows. I was grateful. My body was boneless, utterly sated, and exhausted.

I wrapped my arms around him and held him tightly, kissing his throat. Instinctively, I licked his neck. He relaxed and sighed, resting his forehead on the pillow, his head turned to allow me access. I watched, fascinated, as his skin healed.

"Enough," he whispered, looking down at me. "I want some marks left. I want everyone to know I am yours again."

"Then do the same for me?" The thought that our pack would know he was mine, including Sophie and that cold bitch Xania, filled me with satisfaction. His pleased smile warmed my whole being. He carefully tilted my head and laved my skin.

"There," he said, once he was satisfied.

He kissed me deeply, and I welcomed it. For the first time in months, I felt whole. My chest was completely filled where before I'd only felt emptiness. He smiled and kissed my face, small, sweet kisses before he pulled away. My eyelids were too heavy to watch where he was going. I jumped when I felt a warm cloth between my thighs. "Shh, it's okay. Let me take care of you," he said softly.

I nodded, both a bit embarrassed and genuinely touched that he'd do such a basic thing for me.

"We can shower later. Right now, I want you in my arms. I need to hold you close."

From under hooded eyes, I watched him slide in next to me. "I wouldn't have pegged you for a cuddler."

He grinned. "Only ever with you." And he pulled me in close. I wrapped my arms and legs around him, holding him just as closely—and I slept deeply.

CHAPTER 17

onnor

THE PHONE in my pocket buzzed. I slid it out and unlocked it. Drake's message was short and to the point.

"We have to get to the club—quickly."

Owen grunted. "Let's get going then."

I glanced down at Ember. "Can you keep up if we run?"

She cocked a brow and glared at me, but the small smile that curled her lips was sexy enough to be distracting.

I grinned. "Okay, then. Sorry."

Since we'd reclaimed each other nearly two weeks ago, I'd not wanted to leave her side, but she was becoming more independent and more confident with each day that passed. My mother had cautioned me against not telling her she was pregnant. Since we were back together, Ember's nausea had settled, and her headaches had resolved. Her memories were coming back in sporadic dreams and flashes, which I knew was disconcerting for her, but it was a relief not to have to ask Balthazar for help. We were both certain that, given time, they would return fully.

We covered the distance to the Gambit at a steady run. I didn't want to go too fast. Ember might not know it, but *I* knew she carried our baby, and I didn't want her to trip or get too tired. Owen glanced sideways at me as I checked on her again, taking in her breathing rate and complexion. He raised

778

his brows. Yeah, I'd had the argument that was in his eyes with all of my pack, especially my mother. They argued she should stay in the compound where it was safe. But over the past fourteen days, she'd begun to remember her fighting abilities and her fierce spirit. Leaving her behind wasn't an option. One, because she'd find a way to follow me, and two, because I selfishly didn't want to be separated from her, at all, for any length of time. My anxiety spiked at the thought of losing her again, and even though she'd called Fire to her, the only way I knew she'd be safe was if I was by her side.

My mother was right, though. I needed to sit down with Ember and tell her the truth. I'd only kept it hidden because I didn't want to overwhelm her while she was still remembering who she was. Finding out she was pregnant might prevent her memories from returning if she became too stressed. And I didn't want to lose her. Not just physically, but I didn't want anything stopping the full version of *my* Ember from coming back. I wanted her to remember every touch, every part of our past together, every bit of my claiming her, everything...

We slowed as the club came into view. I cracked my neck and my knuckles. I wanted to run in and get my hands on Manivera, but the leader in me knew if I wasn't careful, he could just slip from my grasp again, no matter my allies.

"Shifter King," greeted Davlov. The vampire had been the constant in my dealings with Balthazar. I nodded at him. His gaze landed on Ember, his pupils dilating.

I snarled viciously. "She's mine. Stay away from her."

A smug grin stretched his lips, his eyes glinting, but he nodded. "Understood."

Ember cocked her head and studied him, a smirk of her own in place. "You could never give me the pleasure he does, anyway," she drawled and sashayed up to me, kissing me soundly.

Davlov chuckled but didn't comment. "He's expecting you. He has your goods in his office."

I nodded, keeping my face blank, resisting the urge to roar and charge down there to kill my prey. Instead, I walked calmly down the steps and into the club. Ember had been in with me before and was cool with surrendering her weapons, as was Owen. He didn't even flirt with the female demon tonight. He was all business.

"You up for playing tonight?' she purred at Owen as she accepted our weapons.

"Nope, sorry, doll. Not tonight. Tonight is business, not pleasure."

She didn't hide her disappointment. Neither of us acknowledged it. Ember gave her a smile and shrugged before moving on past. I hadn't actually told her why we had been called to the club, only that Drake had told us to meet him and that the Count had something for me. I wouldn't have my pregnant mate anywhere near the male who'd taken her and abused her mind so much.

I walked toward Balthazar's office. Drake and Sophie waited by the bar. Both of them looked impatient.

"Thank fuck."

I growled a low warning.

Drake stopped short, swallowing his next words.

I leaned against the bar and pulled Ember into my body until she was flush with me. The roses in her cheeks told me my distraction tactic had worked. Her reaction to me was instant; her body melted against mine. That response had only gotten more and more pronounced the longer we were together. I swallowed hard. It wasn't just her that reacted to our closeness, either.

The others inhaled and shifted uncomfortably. Yeah, it was pretty obvious to everyone around us that we needed each other pretty much all the time. It was hard to control my thoughts, but I wouldn't be distracted from my purpose.

"Ember, I've just got a bit of business to do, then I'll be back. Stay and have a drink with Sophie, okay?"

"Me? Why am I staying behind? I should be in there with you," snapped Sophie.

"No. You shouldn't." With my back to Ember, I used my compulsion to hold her eyes and force my will on her. She pursed her lips, her gaze furious. "You will stay with my mate, *and you will guard her with your life,*" I growled in her ear. "*You cannot be in there. Not if you want to keep your identity from your own mate.*"

Her eyes widened, and she paled. Silence stretched between us.

"Hey, you two okay?" asked Ember, her eyes narrowed on us.

"Yes, we're fine. Aren't we, Soph?"

She gritted her teeth and smiled overly brightly. "Yeah, sure."

Ember frowned suspiciously. "Why don't you want me, or her, in there?"

I kissed her forehead. "Because the Count doesn't trust many people. He will only have me and Owen in his office. He doesn't know either of you."

"What about him?" asked Sophie, not looking at Drake, just pointing in his general direction.

I raised my brows, but decided to give her an answer...this time. "Drake is there to protect our backs. But he will be outside the office, not in it."

Sophie grunted, still looking pissed off, but I had a feeling that was more because I'd called her out on Drake being her mate than anything else. She was somehow blocking herself from him.

Ember pouted when I released her, and it was adorable.

I grinned. "Sophie!" I made a show of shouting over the music. "Would you get Em a drink? Nothing alcoholic, though."

Ember rolled her eyes.

"You're working, Firecracker. You can't go demon hunting with alcohol in your system."

"Yeah, yeah." She smiled and leaned her back against the bar. I walked away, a grin plastered to my face when I felt her gaze burn into my arse.

Balthazar's guards surrounded the door to his office. They didn't stop me, and I didn't bother to knock. The Count greeted me with a bloodstained smile. "Shifter King."

I scowled. *Shit.* "That wasn't part of our deal." Now there was a very real possibility he knew far more than I wanted him to, especially if Rex's mind wasn't strong enough to keep him out.

He straightened, still gripping Rex's hair. Vampires were strong, and if they'd just fed, stronger than most shifters. Except, perhaps, me. And Balthazar Rossi was the strongest vampire I'd ever met. I doubted I'd win easily.

Balthazar elegantly shrugged his shoulders. "But his memories are certainly interesting." He smiled and yanked Rex's head up. Rex was pale, but his eyes still held a burning contempt, one that meant he hated where he was, at the feet of a vampire, a species he considered lesser than himself.

I cocked my head, not feeling sorry for him in the least. He'd brought this on himself. He had a whole lifetime of evil deeds and pain to atone for.

"Where's the Halo?" I asked Balthazar.

He licked the blood off his lips, then bent down and licked up the rivulets from Rex's throat. "Shall I heal him before we have our discussion?"

I shrugged. "For now. You can drain him dry very soon."

Rex struggled, but he was no match for an original vampire. Balthazar pulled Rex's head back with his hair and held his chin with his other hand, his sharp fingernails digging in his skin. Balthazar hovered his mouth over my father's, not quite touching. He exhaled, and a fine grey mist entered Rex's body. Rex's eyes rolled back, and he groaned, shuddering and trying to get closer to Balthazar. An erection grew in his jeans, and he strained forward. I curled my lip and tried to hold in my impatience and disgust. Watching Rex get off on Balthazar's Vampire voodoo wasn't on my agenda.

Rex's skin healed quickly. "Enough," I barked.

Balthazar grinned and straightened. "What? You don't want to see him humiliated that way, Shifter King?"

"You can do what you like when I have the Halo."

Balthazar looked down at Rex. "Well? Shall I give it to your son?"

Rex's face paled, his mouth dropping open. It was fleeting, but that shock was unmistakable. His face hardened at the same time as his eyes did.

"You? You're my son?" he jeered before a gleeful look crossed his face. "That woman, the phoenix. She was yours." He laughed loudly. "You always were a weak little shit. You lost your woman to me. Fuck, you might not be small anymore, but you're still that pathetic boy who couldn't do anything right. Did Hawk tell you how he fucked her? How she screamed his name right before I took her memories...."

I wouldn't show him how much fury was burning beneath my skin. Not yet. Jed had never touched her... I swallowed. He couldn't have. He'd never have been able to hide it from me. It wasn't true. I didn't answer, just stared at him.

"Connor." Owen's voice held a warning. Yeah, we needed the Halo before I killed the fucker.

Rex grinned, his eyes wide, almost crazed. "She can't tell you, can she, what he did? Because she doesn't remember. Mm...She doesn't remember my cock pounding into her either, does she? I wanted her pregnant with a child. It didn't matter whose. Can you imagine how much an offspring of a phoenix is worth?" On and on he went. I didn't say a word. I didn't flinch or move. I just stared at him. Slowly he ran out of steam and stopped, panting hard.

Balthazar watched curiously but didn't let go of Rex's hair. I moved my gaze from Rex's face to Balthazar's grip. "Do you have the Halo?"

Balthazar hesitated, then nodded once.

"Then let him go."

The Count raised his brows at my order but pulled his grip from Rex's hair.

Rex cracked his neck. I met his glee filled gaze and smiled right before Prime burst through my skin. I allowed the piece of shit to get to his feet and take two steps towards me before I sent a wave of compulsion his way. He snarled, still fighting even in the face of the monster I had become. He had no chance against me, but he was too arrogant to believe he was weaker than the son he had beaten and humiliated. I was still that feeble little boy to him. He yelled and cursed but had no choice but to drop to his knees as his wolf succumbed to my greater power. I stalked closer, letting the fire that burned in my soul blaze in my eyes. With one claw, I slowly cut him open across his throat and watched as he bled out. "Karma's a bitch, isn't it...dad? Your weak, pathetic son is the King of all shifters."

His gaze widened, panic entering his eyes as he tried to stop, his blood leaking out over the floor. And found he couldn't move.

"The woman you raped and then sold—my mother, gave me the power of a shadow beast, and my wolf gave me the strength and ancient wisdom of the King of Hell-beasts. You were never stronger than me, Rex. And you will never be as cruel as I can be." I cut a deep gash across his torso, watching as his guts slithered onto the floor. He coughed and choked on his own blood, his eyes wide and filled with pain.

"Mercy," he gurgled.

I had none.

"Know this. Sophie is alive, and she is part of my pack." I leaned in and rumbled in his ear. "I saw all of your records: how many of my siblings you pushed to break, how many women and children you tortured and killed with your struggle for more and more power. As your son, I will claim your money, and Sophie will help me fight the evil you intended to bring into this world with that Halo. And you? You will be gone. From this day on, neither of us will mention you again, nor will your name be uttered among my people. As far as anyone else is concerned, you never existed."

I stood tall. Not for one moment did I look away. Rex's death was just as he'd made life for so many people, full of pain and cruelty.

CHAPTER 18

"So? Are you going to get me a real drink now he's gone?" I grinned at Sophie, who grinned back apologetically.

"You're kidding, right? Connor'd kill me."

I cocked my head, keeping my grin in place and hiding my irritation. Wouldn't anyone stand up to him? "Aw, come on, Sophie. It's been a tough few weeks, and I'd really love the burn of some alcohol right now."

She laughed. "Gods, you're persistent, aren't you?"

"Yep!" I put my back to the bar again and swayed my hips to the music, letting the beat vibrate into my bones. I'd been here before, and each time Connor had left me with a babysitter while he'd gone to talk to the Count, who I'd yet to meet. The last time he'd left me with Shannon, which had been fun, especially when I'd noticed Connor leaning against the bar after his meeting, watching me on the dance floor with heat in his eyes as I swayed. Stone had ground his teeth hard enough it looked like he might do himself an injury. Shannon had just pretended he wasn't there, to the delight of the shifter she was flirting with.

While Connor and Stone had glared at all the other males, Shannon had pointed out some of the vampires and different supernaturals to me. All the supernaturals looked more or less human while they were in the club. She'd also explained why a few unfortunates were chained to poles, dancing as if they couldn't stop, which they couldn't, thanks to Balthazar's compulsions.

While Sophie debated buying me alcohol, I watched as customers negotiated with Balthazar's vamps for time with the bespelled prisoners. I was uncomfortable knowing they were being bought and paid for, but this wasn't my domain. I knew nothing about this world, not really. Interfering in the Count's business would piss Connor off big time and quite probably get me killed.

I'd no idea if I'd liked clubbing in my life before Rex, but no matter the weird clientele in here, I was enjoying it now. I leaned back with my elbows on the bar and moved my hips to the music. Sophie, the coward, ordered us two diet cokes. I rolled my eyes, sure the barman in a place full of demons, fae, shifters and other supernaturals didn't get asked for soft drinks often.

"Here, that's the best I can do, I'm afraid." She pushed the cold glass into my hand.

"Thanks. But it's not as if I can really get drunk," I pointed out as I accepted the drink.

She grinned. "You can on the demon juice the Count sells in here. It's some lethal shit."

I waggled my brows, my interest piqued. "You mean there's some juju juice that we supernaturals can party with? Really?"

She grinned and shook her head, making a zip over her lips.

I rolled my eyes but grinned. "Killjoy." My throat was as dry as a bone, so instead of bitching more, I took a big swallow. "Mmm." No matter how much fitter I'd gotten recently, my legs were still shaking after our run through the dark streets. I smiled, thinking about my mate's hands and mouth on me...Yeah, sex on top of the training regimen Connor insisted on me doing every day definitely had *some* benefits—fitness was only one.

Sophie nudged me with her elbow. "Hey, that guy over there's been eye-fucking you since he got to the bar."

Grinning, I peered over my shoulder at the big male. He sat on a barstool staring right at me. Jeez, did all supernatural men, males, whatever, have to be so damn hot? He had a close-cropped beard and shoulder-length hair streaked with a little grey, which only made him hotter. Lines etched the strong planes of his face, and his brow was heavy. It dipped down a little as I held his gaze. If anything, he looked confused, not lustful.

I downed my coke, for some reason uncomfortable with his regard. He *felt* familiar, though he definitely wasn't one of Connor's...I shook my head...*our* pack.

"That's not eye-fucking, Sophie." And it really wasn't. The male's jaw tensed, and his fingers turned white on his beer bottle.

"What is it then?" Sophie asked, turning and cocking her head in the male's direction. "'Cause he sure looks like he's fascinated with you."

"No idea." I turned away, discounting the male, and grinned at Sophie. "Ignore him. I'm going to pee. That coke's gone right through me. Then let's go dance!"

She giggled at my enthusiasm. "I'll come with you."

"Nope. No, you won't. I can get myself to the bathroom without supervision, even in here."

Sophie raised a brow. "What about your stalker?"

I grinned and glanced at the other end of the bar. "I wasn't that fascinating. Look. He's gone."

"Fine. Go on then. I'll wait here in case Connor comes back and freaks when he can't find you."

Thankfully the bathrooms were near our end of the bar. I could even see Drake as I walked past the entrance to the Count's offices and back rooms. He raised his hand, and I smiled back. He was a nice guy, except he sometimes seemed hard on Sophie. I wasn't sure why other than I'd discovered she hadn't been in the pack that long and already had Connor's ear. Jealousy tightened my gut, but I pushed it away. Connor was mine. I was the one he slept next to and made love to every night, and every morning, and whenever else we could fit it in.

Grinning to myself, I turned into the small corridor that led to the bathrooms, happily distracted by thoughts of Connor's naked body. I screeched when a large hand landed on my shoulder and spun me around with such force I stumbled.

"Ember?" rumbled a deep voice.

Instinctively, I let my fist fly...right into the stranger's jaw. He didn't even flinch.

Shit!

"Ember, stop! I'm not going to hurt you." He grabbed my hand like it was the most normal thing in the world and pulled me towards the dark end of the corridor.

"Come on. We need to talk."

"Oh, no, we really don't. One, I have no fucking idea who you are, and two, things are going to get messy real soon if you don't let me go and pee."

"No. We need to talk. Now!" He growled, his voice deepening. "I've only just found you. I thought you were *dead*. So no, I'm not letting you go. Zander got me out of that shithole of a prison, but it was Walker who found me and got me back to London. He ordered me to watch the new Rift."

He dragged me further down the corridor, and even calling on Mea wasn't enough to stop him.

"Look, I don't know who you are, just let me go…" And I dug my heels in the floor.

He halted and looked sideways at me. "Stop messing about, Em." He ran his other hand through his long hair, and his eyes changed colour. Power seeped into the air along with the acrid scent of frustration—and grief. "I thought you were dead, just like Lyss." His face twisted and his voice broke as he pulled me into a tight embrace.

Okay. That was enough. I kneed him in the balls and ran. There was a fire door at the end of the corridor. Was that where he'd been taking me? Was he trying to kidnap me? *Shit.* I rammed through it and burst into the alley beyond. Outside of the club, I was totally alone. *Damn! Bad idea, Ember.* Okay, all I had to do was avoid the guy until Connor came. I wasn't sure how our bond worked, but I tugged on the tight feeling in my chest that I always got when I wasn't with Connor and felt a faint pulse in reply. My chest squeezed, and my breath caught. I hadn't even thought about using this connection before. Would he realise I needed help? "Dammit, Connor. Where are you?"

Mea howled, reaching out for Prime. There was another tug. This time it was harder. Mea sent me a pulse of reassurance. *They are coming.*

Not wanting to wait around to see who found me first, I took off into the darkness.

"Stop!" roared a voice that sounded anything but human now. Power rippled over me.

I looked over my shoulder. Big mistake! A huge Kodiak bear lumbered after me, getting closer with every stride.

"Shit!"

Increasing my speed, I bolted down the alley, wishing I knew how to shift. Mea howled, her frustration seeping into me. *I know. I know. I wish I could too.* It was too late to ask Connor to teach me. Maybe what I should ask him was why he hadn't even mentioned shifting to me? Careening around a corner and not looking where I was going was mistake number two. Rubbish covered the small alleyway, and it was too late to avoid it. My sole slipped in some non-identifiable slime, and that was it. My momentum carried me forward while my body fell. My head hit the wall with a bang that sent stars flashing across my vision. The last thing I saw was the huge jaw of a bear hanging open above my face.

***

"Hey, come on, Em. Wake up."

My skull had a hammer beating against it. I groaned, wrinkling my nose at the stink of urine and rotting food. A wave of nausea hit me, and I retched, spitting diet coke onto the ground, adding to the already disgusting layer on the alley floor.

Firm pressure on my head sent a new wave of pain into my skull. I knocked away the hand that held a wad of material against my head. A pair of grey eyes watched me, full of confusion.

"Why in the Mother's name are you running from me?" the guy from the club said.

"Because I don't know you. And dragging me off into the shadows was more than stalkerish behaviour," I grumbled, more pissed off that I'd failed in my escape attempt than scared.

I swallowed back another wave of nausea and blinked against a dizzy spell. Yeah, running out of the club wasn't my best idea ever. I should have gone back towards Connor and Sophie—except this big tree of a man had been blocking the way.

"Can you stand? This ground's pretty grim."

"Really? I hadn't noticed." Yeah, sarcasm probably wasn't the best idea while I was vulnerable and alone in an alley with a bear shifter. Damn it, how did I get into these situations? My wolf whined and then huffed. *Thanks for the support* I shot back at her. *And it's not always my fault.*

It seemed churlish to refuse his help when the guy placed a firm hold under my arm and helped me up. "Sorry if I scared you." He brushed me down, and something about that act of kindness seemed...familiar.

I peered more closely at him. His face... Under the streetlight, he *looked* familiar too. "I'll survive. So, you know me?"

His smile made my heart ache. I rubbed my chest, not sure what was happening, but this man, er, male, meant something to me, I could feel it.

"Of course I do. What's going on, Ember? Why don't you remember me?"

My head was pounding, but the churning in my belly was marginally better. I heard voices, frantic voices, and felt Connor getting closer. I relaxed a bit. This guy might be almost as tall and stacked as Connor, but I didn't feel any threat coming from him. If anything, he gave me the warm and fuzzies. Gingerly, I touched my head, and winced.

"You took quite a bash there. Are you okay? Here." He held out his blood-stained shirt.

"Yeah, I'm fine. Just a bit of a headache." I accepted the offer of his shirt and pressed it against my head wound. "Listen, I'm sorry if you know me. I genuinely have no idea who you are. I lost my memory a few months ago and it isn't back yet." I felt tears prick my eyes, although I wouldn't let them fall. I buried it most of the time but losing my whole life, my memories, my feelings, all the things that made me, well, me, had affected me deeply.

"Ah, that makes sense. But you are still with Connor?" He inhaled, and a huge, daft grin stretched across his face. "No need to answer. I can scent him on you."

I eyed that ridiculously happy grin. The guy must be a little crazy. "I am. He found me..." My voice trailed off as a familiar voice roared. My attention snapped to Connor.

"Ember!" Connor stalked forward in beast form, huge and terrifying. Dark shadows swirled around him, his eyes burning. He walked on two legs, the claws on his hands longer than ever. His attention shifted to the guy who had moved to stand in front of me. I blinked. The guy was protecting me. I swallowed hard. Reaching out, I touched his shoulder. It just seemed the right thing to do.

Connor snarled, stalking closer.

"It's okay, this is Connor, my mate," I said, trying to reassure the bear shifter.

The guy's stiff spine relaxed a little, his breath leaving him on a shudder. He turned sideways, his gaze bouncing between the King of Shifters and me. In a swirl of shadow, Connor disappeared, and then reappeared in front of us. "Rawson?" His voice was low and rasping.

It was my turn for the bouncing gaze. There was a moment of shock, wide eyes—the works. Then they were hugging each other. I didn't want to interrupt, but...way to make a girl feel inconsequential. After a minute or two of letting them ignore me, I coughed, irritated at once again not having a clue what was happening.

"Umm, does one of you want to tell me what's going on? You know, 'cause memory loss girl here...and everything..." I let my words trail off. Connor glanced at me and grinned at my folded arms and flared nostrils. Yeah, I was probably acting childish, but I'd gotten used to my mate's undivided attention, and I really didn't like that this Rawson guy was someone Connor would hug, yet I couldn't remember him. It just added to the hurt I carried about the void of my past. I moved my hands to my hips and tilted my head as I studied them, pressing my lips together. With his arm still around the man's shoulders, Connor turned to me.

"Sorry, Firecracker. This is Cain Rawson. He's like our very responsible older brother. He raised you and me, well, mostly, but he's not old enough to be our dad, and I fucking refused to ever call him that anyway."

Rawson grinned and pulled from Connor's hold, playfully punching him in the stomach.

"Oomph," Connor's fake pain response didn't fool me. I'd never seen him so goddamned happy. His smile was blinding, and I wished I'd been the one to put it there, but it was so good to see him like this.

Rawson gave me a grin, his grey eyes sparkling. "Mother Wolf, I'm so happy to see you two are still together." He inhaled. "And with a fucking pup on the way." He smacked Connor on the back while my world went cold. Connor's face dropped so fast his smile could have been my imagination. The colour leached from his skin, and his gaze darted to me.

"Em?" He didn't move or say another word. His eyes widened, and that's when I felt it; the truth in those words. My stomach sank, and my legs shook.

Pregnant? Was I pregnant? I couldn't be. Connor would never lie to me like that. My eyes burned, and the nausea that had settled when he'd come near me reared its ugly head again.

"Connor?" My whole world somehow relied on that one word. His name. And a whole shit load of silent questions that I couldn't even begin to voice.

Rawson's gaze bounced between us, his face screwing into a dark frown. "What the..." He looked at my expression, and his eyes widened. I must have looked as crappy as I felt because he raked a hand through his messy hair. "Oh, shit...you didn't know? I mean, I could be wrong; maybe you're not... " He looked helplessly at Connor.

Connor's face hardened. And it was that which broke me, even more than everything that had been done to me by Rex and Jed. My mate, the one I'd given my heart, and my total trust to, had lied to me.

"Is it true?" I yelled at him, heat bathing my insides, igniting my blood.

"Calm down, Ember. Please."

My nostrils flared. "Don't you fucking dare tell me to calm down! Did you lie to me?" It was all I could do not to launch myself at him. My blood began to heat.

"Let's get back to the compound, and we can discuss this in private."

His voice was slightly shaky, his face pleading, but somehow that only made me angrier. It was an admission of guilt. "How dare you!" I screeched. "You had no right to keep such an important thing from me." And then it hit me, like a smack in the face. My heart literally hurt. "Jed knew too, didn't he? That's why he let you in Rex's home. He knew; that's why he gave me up. He knew Rex would lock me away. He gave me up because he knew I was pregnant..." Agony ripped at my heart, but I kept my chin high as I asked the question that was burning into my soul like acid. "Is it yours?"

Silence. Nothing but fucking silence. My mate's face said it all. It was a second or maybe two, but it was enough. I staggered back, my legs going weak. "Ohmygodohmygodohmygod..." I was panting. I had to get away, or I was going to faint in front of them. I couldn't let the pain in my heart break me, or I'd never survive this.

"Ember, Stop! Please...let's go home..."

"No!" I literally exploded. My phoenix stormed forward at my anger. I felt her confusion at my fury towards my mate, but she was mine to control. She had no choice. I knew it as surely as I knew Connor had kept this life-changing secret from me. My voice came out as a powerful screech and flames licked across my skin. "You fucking lied to me!" I met his gaze, my tears drying on my flame-drenched skin.

"I didn't lie!" he roared back, Prime half breaking through his skin in his temper.

"Am I pregnant? Tell me the godsdamned truth!"

"Yes!" he bellowed, his voice breaking. He swore and made to reach for me. I couldn't let him touch me; if he did, I'd be lost. His touch did something to me; it was like a drug. I needed to be alone, to think, to clear my head. What was I meant to do with the knowledge my mate and everyone I'd learned to trust over the past few weeks had lied to me? "Fuck this," I muttered under my breath.

"Firecracker, please don't do this, don't go…"

Tears blurred my eyes. "Tell me this baby is yours…."

"It is, Em. It's mine," he whispered.

I smiled sadly, despite the relief that washed through me at his confirmation, and swallowed the lump in my throat. "Then I don't understand why you kept this from me."

His face softened, Prime gone, and he rubbed a hand over his mouth and chin, exhaling deeply. "Because you had enough to cope with, love. I didn't want to make things more stressful."

I blinked, my voice catching. I felt Connor's sincerity, but it didn't make anything better, only worse. Is that what he'd always do? Lie to protect me? Make decisions on my behalf if he believed it was best for me? "I get it, I do. You think you were doing me a favour. But you can't make decisions about my life and expect me to just accept them. It's wrong, Connor, especially after what Rex and Jed did to me."

"Ah, shit, Em, I know...But…"

I lifted a hand. "No. No 'buts." I swallowed hard, fighting the pain in my head and the sense of betrayal this whole situation created in me. "I need to be alone right now." Fire reassured me she was ready, and I believed her. I could remember everything about her, including that we had become a team in the past to fight our enemy from the skies. Wings unfurled at my back, their flames iridescent and lighting the darkness of the alley.

Rawson gaped. "Holy shit," he muttered.

"No!" Connor's face twisted into a mask of fear, his hands reaching for me. But I launched into the sky, knowing that was one thing the King of Shifters could never do...fly.

CHAPTER 19

onnor

IT HAD BEEN ALMOST twenty-four hours since I'd made the biggest fucking mistake of my life. Ember had left me, and I'd been in a dark place ever since. Prime was near frantic with worry, and it was getting worse. I couldn't even track her properly because of my fear. Every time our mate had appeared on the camera feeds, or I'd managed to pinpoint her through our bond, I'd jumped in one of our SUVs and sped across London. And each time, she'd felt me approach and had run again.

"AHHH!" I yelled and smashed my fist through the wall of the most recent derelict factory where I'd sensed her.

"Hey!" Owen growled. "That isn't the way to get her back. You need to keep your cool. She's scared, brother—And pissed at you," he added.

I turned on him. "Anything else, Beta?" I snarled, getting up in his face. Owen didn't step away; he merely smirked at me. Yeah, he knew what I was after.

"You know what, Prime? Yeah, there is. We all told you that you needed to be honest with her and tell her about the baby. Even your mother did. Tyen knew this was coming, and so did we. You *should* have told her. I understand why you didn't, but you should have." His voice softened a little. "She just needs some time to think, that's all, then she'll be back. She loves you, brother, just the same as you love her."

I didn't like having my fuck ups pointed out so bluntly, despite the fact that he was right. I hadn't wanted to address the baby with Ember for fear that she would shut down completely, or panic and run away, or even tell me that she didn't want it. I'd known I'd have to tell her, and soon, but I'd hoped her memory would return first. Shit, I hadn't known how she would cope with the knowledge she was going to be a mum when she didn't even remember us surviving her heat together.

Knowing I'd fucked up didn't help my temper any, though.

I hit out, my fist smashing into Owen's face. "Anything else you wanna say, Beta?"

He spat blood on the floor and cracked his neck, rolling his shoulders. "Yeah, did you for one second believe that shit Rex spouted about him or Jed being the father?"

"No." But I *had* doubted. Mother Wolf, for that split second, when Ember asked if the baby was mine, I'd remembered Rex's words, and the image of my beloved mate naked with him or Jed rutting on her, using her body, had made me so furious that I hadn't been able to speak.

I roared and hit out again, Prime as furious with me as I was with myself. The scent of that baby was mine as much as Ember was. I should never have let my bastard of a father sow any doubt in me whatsoever.

Owen was waiting this time. He blocked my punch and smashed me back. I relished the pain. It felt good.

"More!" I roared, locking my gaze on Stone and Myles. They both grinned. Yeah, they were all strong, strong enough to be alphas in their own right, but none of them alone could best me, not even Owen. They'd give me what I needed, though, which was an outlet for my fury and frustration and a distraction from my fear of what had become of Ember. Of how she was surviving in the city on her own with no money, food or shelter.

Stone attacked first; his speed fast enough a human wouldn't have seen him move, even a shifter would struggle, but a king…? I grinned and punched him in the belly before I landed one on his jaw. Myles jumped in, but I called on my shadow, melting in and out of existence. Drake and Kawan arrived late, their howls mixing with ours. Under my command, they all shifted, and we fought as wolves. Rawson watched from the sidelines. Yeah, he knew better than to get involved in our fights. He'd avoid it. He was an alpha, and he was strong, but he'd always avoided unnecessary violence, even in the prison. And I wanted him to watch Jed. That fucker would help me find Ember, and when we did, I'd make him reassure her that he and Rex hadn't used her body.

Claws and teeth tore at me. I could stop them all with a thought, but I wanted to feel something other than my raging guilt at pushing Ember away. I'd hurt her so badly, and even though I couldn't admit it to my pack, I was lost without her by my side. And this time, she hadn't been taken. This time it was all on me.

Another deeper roar joined the wolves around me. I snarled and pushed Prime more to the fore until the King of Shifters was tall enough to stand. I homed in on Jed. His gorilla growled, showing his fangs, his eyes glinting, his heavy brow dipped. I grinned, showing my own teeth. The fury and fear that was in my eyes? I saw it reflected in his. He wanted this fight as much as I did. He was in love with my mate, and maybe I couldn't blame him for that, but he had taken her from me. He had started all of this, along with Rex. And I deeply blamed him for that.

He charged towards me, and there was no way I could stop him, so I used his momentum. Ducking my shoulders, I rammed his stomach and flipped him up and over my back. He landed with a huge crash but rolled back to his feet. He lashed out, and I let his fist connect right before I slammed mine into his ribs. He grunted and fell to his knees.

Owen shifted back. "Prime! Stop! You have to stop! If you still doubt you're the father, then ask him! He fucking loves her, Connor. He gave up everything for her, to give her what she needed—which is you! You can't let this go on. Being without her again is killing you."

I twisted my huge torso, and snarled down at Owen's half naked form. He could shift with clothes now but his chest and back were cut and bruised and bleeding. He'd heal quickly. He was too powerful not to, but I knew from experience, clothes rubbing against the wounds we'd inflicted would be a bitch.

"Dammit, Connor. Fucking listen! You know she was with you and only you during her mating season, her heat. You know the chances of a female conceiving in between heats is little to nothing. So even if they did rape her, she would already have been pregnant with your child!"

I lost my mind at hearing that word. Rape. My gut burned hot, as hot as the Hellfire in my veins. Fury roared through me, and my skin split as power boiled through my veins—Hell-beast, wolf, human and shadow fae, we all burst through as one powerful nightmarish creature.

Jed released a bellow from deep in his huge chest, his eyes focused on me. I knew that look. He wanted to kick my ass for letting my mate go. He'd wanted her safe with me, and I'd been the one to drive her away. Maybe I deserved his wrath as much as he deserved mine, but I was still King of the Shifters, and he did not get to punish me.

"Oh shit!" Owen jumped out of the way just before Jed crashed right into me. I didn't fall. I merely wrapped my arms around him and let his momentum push me backwards, my clawed feet ripping through the ground. He pushed away, swinging furiously. His punches hurt, but I refused to punch back. Instead, I grabbed his throat and used my power to help me lift him from the ground. Jed's eyes widened.

Shift back. I commanded. *I will not fight you—today*

Jed couldn't deny my compulsion. He shifted. I lowered him to his feet. He stood naked and panting, his face murderous, though he wasn't stupid enough to hold my gaze. "Where is she? What did you do that has you so fucked up and her not at the compound?"

All of my brothers shifted. All decided on combat trousers and no tops, their torsos cut up and bleeding but already healing. I shifted, fully clothed and healed. I ignored his question, countering instead with the one that had been eating away at me. "Did you or Rex rape her before you took her memories?" Around us, the sounds of the city hardly registered, but Jed's surprise did.

"Mother Wolf, Prime. I know I'm not an angel, but I have never, and would never inflict that kind of attack on anyone, least of all Ember."

Prime rumbled, pretty sure he was telling the truth.

"He speaks truly," said B'Nar, who appeared from nowhere and studied both me and Jed.

I nodded my thanks. B'nar was as good at reading emotions as he was a warrior. I wondered what he made of mine. I was a damned mess in my head and heart.

Jed crossed his big arms over his chest, his eyes narrowed and assessing. I refused to let him see the guilt that ate at me for believing anything that had spewed from Rex's mouth.

"Where the fuck has this come from, and why has Ember bolted?"

"Rex. We caught him, or rather Balthazar held him for us. I killed him."

"Good. But what did the bastard say that's driven Ember away?"

I ground my teeth together. "He told me that both he and you raped Ember repeatedly before he took her memories."

"What!?" roared Jed, his silverback pushing against his skin. He panted and fought for control. "That fucker!" he bit out as he took back control of his emotions. He raised his gaze, but kept it slightly below meeting mine. "No, Prime, no one laid a hand on her because I wouldn't let them. Not only that, the night we took her, she woke from the drugs, and she fought. Fuck me, if she wasn't the firecracker you've named her. I was flying the helicopter, and Rex and his men were in the back with her. She killed two of them before Rex managed to hit her over the head with a fire extinguisher. When she woke up in the cell under his home, he'd dressed it as a hospital. When we knew she'd live, he began giving her the drugs which locked her wolf away, just like I've told you before. I was with her most days, Connor. No one touched her."

"Except you." I couldn't help the bitterness in my voice.

Jed swallowed and looked down. "I won't apologise for that." He put his hands on his hips and tipped his head back, looking at the city stained night sky and released a heavy breath. "I started falling for her way before we took her from you. I knew she'd never return my feelings, and she never did, not even when she believed I was her fiance. She always looked so sad, as if she was missing her heart and soul. The more time I was with her, the more I fell for her, and the more I knew I'd never let Rex hurt her. I'd already begun trying to find you when my informant in the town told me of the arrival of a group of alpha shifters. I knew it was you. You'd come to take her back, and that was the best thing for her. She was already pregnant, Connor. You are the father of that baby, not me, and certainly not Rex fucking Manivera. He played you. He couldn't destroy you physically, so he sent his rotten words to eat at your soul and destroy your bond with Ember." He raised his gaze, and I let him meet my eyes. "And he succeeded. Your mate is out there, alone, confused about who she is, maybe even whose baby she is carrying."

I released a low growl. He didn't need to remind me how badly I'd fucked up. "I told her it was mine," I snapped. "But, yeah, she's fucking angry with me and everyone else, including you, because none of us told her about the baby. She's lost her trust in all of us, but mostly me. Now, I have to find her and work at earning it back."

Jed didn't look away. He had balls. I'd give him that.

"So what the fuck are you going to do about it, Prime?"

I looked at my brothers. "Owen, Jed, you're with me. Stone, get back on the monitors and search every dark corner of this fucking city. We work in the shadows; let's use them to find her. Drake?"

"Yeah?"

"Can you feel your alpha bond with her?"

"No, boss. Not since you claimed her."

I swallowed down my relief that I was the only one connected to her that way, petty as it was when she needed to be found. I was hers, and she was mine, and that was how it should be.

"Then use that clever brain to figure out another way to track her."

Drake grinned. "I have an idea."

"Good, show me. I'll meet you back at the compound."

And I walked into the shadows.

CHAPTER 20

mber

THE CAMERA MOVED SMOOTHLY as its mechanism whirred. Once it had stopped, I darted out of my hiding place behind the metal fencing and ran across the road. My stomach rumbled, and even though nausea had dogged me since I'd left Connor, I was still starving. I'd waited outside a busy MacDonald's until someone had chucked their half-eaten food in the bin and then grabbed it. My stomach both rumbled and turned at the memory of eating someone else's leftovers. But my choices were limited. I was weak and desperately needed to eat something for the sake of my baby, if nothing else.

My limbs were so heavy it had been hard to drag myself from my makeshift den in the old warehouse. Still, I'd needed some food before I could think clearly enough to decide about going back to Connor.

I grimaced as my own stink wafted up my nostrils. I also needed a bath. I'd let Connor find me soon. I'd just needed to get away for a little while. To have some space to think about what he'd done and how I felt about it. It still hurt that he'd lied to me, even if it was only by omission. It must be these damned hormones messing with me because one minute I was roaring with anger at him, and the next I missed him so badly I just wanted to curl in on myself, lay down, and let him find me.

My head pounded where I'd hit it, and I hadn't slept a damned wink last night. Every time I'd closed my eyes, flashes of disjointed memories hit me.

797

My brain was already overloaded with images and questions of my past life. I had kind of hoped my memories would fully return before I let Connor find me. I could feel his fear for me, and it was making my own anxiety about our baby worse. I had no idea about being an expectant mum, but I didn't think hanging out in an old warehouse was the best thing for either of us. I laid my palm flat on my lower belly as I walked. I really did understand why he hadn't told me. It would have been a shock. But was he questioning if this baby was his? I blinked rapidly, swallowing down a wave of disgust. Had I been raped? I shook my head. No, I didn't believe that Jed would be that depraved. He wouldn't have done that to me. Rex might have, but I didn't think he'd have given me to Jed if he believed I could be pregnant with his child. That thought sent a shudder down my spine.

I blinked, my mind fuzzy from all the flashes of the past returning and the exhaustion that rolled through me. What was I going to do now? Mea growled. *Yeah, right. Sorry. I'm going to let him find us.*

Even this upset with him, the desire to go back to my mate was a strong pull, right in my soul. Covering my head with an old hoodie I'd found, I sped up towards the warehouse. Aeroplane lights flashed, and there was the shadow of one of those drone things flying overhead, but there were no stars. The city killed them.

The thought of seeing Connor again gave me butterflies. Still, I knew I didn't want to be anywhere else but by his side.

I headed back towards the creepy abandoned warehouse, and slipped through the broken fence, jogging inside the dilapidated building. Immediately, goosebumps erupted over my skin, and a sense of evil invaded my bones. Mea bucked wildly against my skin. It was the first time I'd felt her do that. I gasped, but I knew that she couldn't push through. Since my bump on the head last night, she'd been able to communicate with me properly. She'd told me that shifts were prevented by the Mother Wolf while a female was pregnant. I hadn't shifted, or even had the urge to, because that part of me was suppressed by nature. Connor had known about that too, which was why he'd avoided talking to me about Mea. I rubbed my face and pushed my disappointment in him away. There was danger here. That was my priority.

Fire sent me a pulse of power, sensing my tension. I cocked my head, examining the shadows. Slowly, I turned on the spot, ignoring the returning thump of a headache. It was too late to run. With all my might, I yanked on my bond with Connor. The answering blast of relief and joy almost made me cry.

"Our master wants you." A sinister voice chuckled.

I whirled around. A man stepped from the shadows, except no....he wasn't a man, he was a demon. I'd felt their energy while I'd been hunting with Connor. It dawned on me how alone I really was. It had been stupid to stay out here with no mate, no pack, and no friends. That didn't mean I'd go down without a fight. My nostrils flared. I had another soul to protect now, and I'd fight the Devil himself to protect her. I squared my shoulders and flexed my fingers. "Really?" I drawled. "Well, I'm expensive, so what's he offering?"

As the demon stalked closer, more footsteps echoed at my back. There was no point in turning to look; I knew exactly where they were. I could sense their malevolence. The demon closed in enough that his ashen skin and black eyes were obvious. He chuckled darkly. "Oh, he's offering nothing in return. You belong to him, and he wants you back."

My brows twitched up. I had no idea who his master was, but I sure didn't intend to find out. "Really? Hm, well, too many men have tried to control my life recently, and you know what? I've about had enough of their bullshit. So how about you run along home and tell your *master*, whoever the fuck he is, that I'm busy doing my hair."

The grin dropped off the demon's face. He let out a weird screech, and they all ran at me at the same time. "Whoa!" Instinctively, I let the heat in my body explode outwards. Wings sprouted from my back, my body wreathed in flames, and I incinerated them on my way into the air.

Another kind of power hit me. Wind dragged all the loose debris towards its source, including the ash of what had been the demons. I stared at the portal. Where it came from was just one more thing I didn't understand, though part of me felt like I should. Unsure, I stayed in the air as a man with long white hair, a perfectly beautiful face, and impressive armour stepped onto the ground below me. He looked up and quirked one brow.

"Ember? Why are you up there?"

I peered down. Great. Another sexy, supernatural man that I should know but didn't. I sighed. When would my life get easier to understand?

I cocked a brow. "Why are you down there, Mr whoever you are?" I allowed my fire to burn hotter. A warning.

He merely raised his other brow to match. "I prefer to talk to you face to face, phoenix."

I tilted my head and studied him. This guy had pointy ears like B'nar, and his magic felt similar, just as powerful, only far more ancient. He was dangerous, but whether he was a danger to me remained to be seen. Did I trust him? Fatigue tugged at me. I decided I wasn't willing to take the chance. I needed to get out of there before Fire needed to rest. It was hard to appear nonchalant and strong when my energy levels were falling fast. "Nah, you know what, I'll just stay up here. Who are you?"

For a moment, surprise registered on his face. "You don't remember me?"

"No. Should I?"

"Yes, child, you should."

"I'm not a fucking child. Who are you?"

"I'm a friend."

My smile widened, and a bitter laugh escaped me before I could stop it. "Yeah? Well, I've had a father, a fiance, a mate, and a whole pack of friends who have lied to me recently, so why should I believe you? Come to think of it, maybe I'd be better off with whoever they were going to take me to." I pointed at the piles of ash.

He didn't like that comment. His white brows dipped, and he narrowed his eyes, considering me.

I didn't mean it, of course, but he didn't know that. He opened his mouth to answer when another voice cut him off. "Firecracker?" Connor's voice was rough, almost broken, as he tentatively murmured my name.

My wolf whined. I understood her joy at seeing him; my own heart squeezed. But I wasn't going to let him know that I'd decided to forgive him. Not yet anyway. He needed to know overriding my life wasn't going to happen again.

"Connor." I stared at the newcomer, then back to Connor, and even though Fire flickered, I stayed floating above their heads.

"Ember? Please come down. We need to talk."

Even from twenty feet away, I felt my mate's regret and pain. My whole being wanted to give in to the pull between us and the brush of reassurance he sent my way. I swallowed hard as he opened his arms.

"Firecracker, you don't have to speak to me until you're ready, but please, come back to the compound where I can keep you safe."

Gods, I wanted to, so badly. But I needed at least one answer first. My stomach churned. "Was I raped? Is that why you hesitated about who the father is?" I almost choked as the terrifying words left my mouth.

The white-haired guy turned his head to study Connor before his icy attention fell on me. I didn't look at him. Connor was the only one I was interested in.

Connor rushed forward and stared up at me. Without breaking my gaze, he changed into Prime. Fully upright on his back legs, he was not that much lower than me. As he neared, Fire stuttered, or rather my hold on her did. His clawed hand reached up and brushed my leg, his voice echoing in my mind, which was a bit disconcerting. He hadn't done that before...that I knew of.

No. You weren't. I thought you could have been. Rex. He spun me some lies. I'm sorry I let him poison my thoughts with his words.

My insides turned cold but I nodded. It was as I thought. "Rex? That evil bastard said he'd touched me?"

Connor nodded but didn't even let me take another breath before he reassured me. *He didn't, sweetness. Jed confirmed neither he nor Rex forced themselves on you. Jed wouldn't let anyone but him near you, especially Rex. He protected you as best he could.*

Connor had explained how Rex had treated him as a child. Rex must have gotten into his psyche in the Count's club. Even though Connor had escaped when he was young, I knew psychological and emotional damage had already been done. Rex had tried to manipulate his son again. And it had worked. Or almost.

Movement caught my eye. Owen and Jed stood shoulder to shoulder behind the fae. Jed met my eyes and nodded. I returned his nod, thankful that he had put any lingering doubts to rest for both Connor and me.

Please, Firecracker, come back to me. I'm so sorry I didn't tell you about our baby. I should have, but I didn't want you to have to deal with knowing you were pregnant, not until your memories returned. And then Rex sowed that seed of doubt about the baby... I let him get to me, and I shouldn't have. It was so stupid."

The white-haired fae's magic touched my skin. I easily brushed it away and focused on my mate. I hated the hurt in Connor's eyes. Even as the King of Shifters, I had the power to break him. Without thinking how it would seem to Connor, I shook my head. Connor's shoulders caved, and he shifted back to his human form, leaving his chest naked. His face hardened, and no matter the sadness in his eyes, I knew he was going to fight for me.

My heart lurched. "No, it's okay. I'm not going to run. I just... I need you to promise that you'll not do anything like this again. I'm your mate, Connor. We can't keep secrets like this from each other. And you can't make decisions for me. You might not think so, but I'm strong enough to make my own."

Howls filled the air, and B'nar stepped from the darkness to stand next to the white-haired man, the rest of the pack halting nearby.

"Father," he greeted stoically.

Connor rubbed the back of his neck. "I know. I'm truly sorry. But that is my baby you're carrying, and you are mine. That means I can't let you go. I need to keep you both safe. You are a part of me, you both are, and right now, no part of me can let you just roam around unprotected. I simply can't."

There was a loud snap of wings behind me. I whipped my head around, my eyes widening at the male who hovered nearby. His bat-like wings created a downdraft, his dark eyes glinting with a hint of ruby as the city lights reflected in them. He didn't smile, nor did he come closer, but his naked torso rippled with muscle, and I knew I'd never have outflown him. He was too powerful; his wingspan far greater than my fiery wings. And I was weak, my body shaking. I needed to rest, to sleep.

"Back off a little, Balthazar," Connor said quietly.

With my head tilted, I studied the powerful vampire. "So you're the Count. I didn't know vampires could fly."

Balthazar smirked and flapped his wings, making his muscles ripple. "Only the most powerful of our kind can."

I refrained from rolling my eyes at his arrogance and glanced back at Connor.

"I can feel your weakness, Firecracker. And I don't like it. Satan is looking for you. Do you have any idea what that means? He wants you so badly he's sending more demons through the Rift in this city every day. And the more souls they kill here and feed back to the Devil, the bigger the Rift gets." He looked at the piles of ash around him. "And this? It was just the beginning. He'll not stop looking for you. He wants this world and all the souls it offers, and you are the key to all his grand plans."

I folded my arms over my lower belly, my heart racing. "Why? What does he want me for?"

Behind Connor, the white-haired fae's lips worked as he whispered musical words. No...I shook my head...his name was Walker...and he was a king, *the* King of Faerie. I cried out as memories assaulted me, my fiery wings stuttering and then disappearing from existence. I dropped towards the ground, right into Connor's waiting arms.

"What the fuck are you doing, Walker?" he bellowed. "Em? Em? Are you okay? Please, baby, talk to me."

But I couldn't talk. Memories were flooding me, swirling around in my head like a movie that was on fast forward.

"It's not me, Connor. I'm not doing this." Walker's words were calm but tight.

Connor turned away from the two fae and his brothers and strode out of the derelict warehouse. Within moments he had me cradled in his lap in the back of the SUV as we sped through the streets of London. I glanced at who was driving. Reed's profile was dark, but I knew it was him. Emotion bubbled in my chest. I tried to call his name, but it came out as a croak. My brain was overloaded with my past. Between each memory flash of my life, I would open my eyes. And each time I did, Connor would glance down at me, pull me closer, and kiss my forehead.

"It's going to be fine, baby. I'm here. I'll take care of you."

And no matter what he'd done, I *knew* this to be true. His expression was grim, his jaw clenched, but he held me with infinite tenderness, murmuring words of comfort and reassurance in my ear. Fatigue dragged at me. Once again, my body and mind needed to process the whole fucked up mess of my life that had just slammed into me like a kick in the head. I was done. I fought it, trying to stay awake, but it was hopeless.

Connor's warmth surrounded me, and with my memories back where they belonged, all I wanted was to crawl inside his skin. Along with my memories of us, I wrapped my body so close that no part of me, not my mind or my body, was separated from him. Wrapped all cozy, my arms around his waist, I rested my cheek against his naked chest. Turning my head, I gently bit his skin then smirked sleepily at his sharp intake of breath.

"Ember?" He tried to pull back, but I just squeezed him harder and dug my nails in his back.

"Hey, asshole," I murmured. "Don't lie to me again, ever, or I'll kick your arse." I snuggled closer. "How's Rawson?" My whispered words and lips brushed his skin.

I heard his hard swallow. "I'll never lie to you again," he whispered and tightened his big arms around me. There was only a beat before he spoke again. "And Rawson is fine."

"Good, while I take a nap, tell him I'm going to kick his arse for not finding you and me sooner."

Connor's chuckle rumbled through me, and I let myself relax into my mate. "Welcome back, Firecracker."

CHAPTER 21

PATIENCE WAS NEVER one of my strong suits. I prowled around our bed, rolling my head and trying to stop myself from shaking Ember awake. Godsdammit, she remembered! The relief and excitement to see my mate whole again were driving me insane. I wanted to make sure she remembered everything, that she really knew who I was, what *we* really were.

Claiming her had sealed our bond again, but things had been different. I'd held back, and so had she. It had been odd, like we were bonded, but not really a couple; the intimacy of our souls had been muted. We'd accepted a future together but with no shared past experiences. And it hurt like a bitch. I'd shared my life with Ember since I was a boy, and the grief of that loss had made me distant from the woman who was my mate. I'd hoped that distance would disappear in time. Now, though, I didn't have to worry anymore. I had her back, wholly and completely.

I paced over to the window and leaned my forearms against it.

"Chill, Connor. If she feels your anxiety, she'll wake earlier. She needs to sleep." Rawson looked at Ember, and his whole face softened.

Time and loss had taken a terrible toll on our childhood benefactor. Rawson had always been such a strong and generous soul. It was hard seeing that powerful alpha appear so cold and empty. Then again, seeing your mate's dismembered body would ice over anyone's heart.

I stretched my neck and inhaled deeply. I couldn't even imagine the pain of that.

"Yeah, I know." I forced my backside into a chair by the window where I could watch Ember sleep. Rawson was the only one I'd allow in the room with my sleeping pregnant mate. I trusted my pack, but I was an alpha, and she was mine to protect. Rawson had protected her while we were growing up, but even he'd known I would take over that role eventually.

"Did you get more info about the Rift?"

"Yeah, it's already bigger than it was two nights ago. The Count is already calling in favours. Many of the vampire covens answer to him anyway and are already on their way."

"When will they be here?" I had a bad feeling in my gut. Demons had swamped the area around the compound last night while Ember slept. It couldn't be a coincidence. Ember had used her phoenix power, and Walker had felt it.

That meant Satan had, too.

Rawson met my eyes. "Don't worry, Balthazar already has this place surrounded. Owen's called in more shifters, too."

"Hmm," I sat back, thinking over our options. I needed to call a meeting, but I didn't want to leave Ember.

"You have a beta, the High King of Faerie and his son, both of whom are ancient and warriors through and through; you have me, and a pack of able and powerful alphas. Use us all."

I inhaled and exhaled. As usual, Rawson was right. I had capable people; I just needed to trust them.

Ember turned over onto her side, her eyelids flickering half-open. "Hey." Her smile was enough to squeeze my heart. "Go be a king, hot stuff." She smirked, her eyes glinting with mischief.

Rawson huffed a laugh. Her attention went to him. "Hey, you."

"Hi." He smiled back.

"When I'm more awake, I'm going to kick your butt. Where have you been?"

His grin couldn't get any wider. "Here and there, Em. I'll tell you when you get your arse up and out of his bed."

She yawned. "Yeah? Well, that ain't gonna be yet. Now let me rest. Both of you." Her gaze drifted back to me. "I'm fine. I just need a bit more sleep." She snuggled down and pulled the duvet right up to her ear, just peeking at me over it. "Go on, bugger off. I'll be fine while you work up a plan to kick demon arse."

I chuckled and stood up. I wanted nothing more than to strip and slide into the bed next to her, but she was right. I had shit to do. My pack deserved to have a leader who was present and level-headed. And, despite wanting to fuck my mate senseless, now that I knew she was back with me and safe, I could wait for that pleasure. Then I'd make her wait for her pleasure, wait until she was begging me... The moment her eyes widened I knew she scented my arousal.

Rawson coughed. "I'll wait outside. See ya soon, sweetness." He left the room grinning.

The door had only just clicked shut when I pounced. I gripped the blanket and yanked it back. Ember squealed. "Hey, that's mine!"

I grinned. "Nope, it's mine. And so are you." Without pause, I fell over her kissing her deeply and with total abandonment. Our teeth and tongues clashed, and her groan hit me right in my balls. "Damn, Ember. I need you."

She gave a breathless giggle. "Connor, we can't...you have men to organise...."

"Hush, woman, I'm busy." And I was. I sat back on my heels, watching her breasts rapidly rise and fall. She was breathless after our kiss. Slowly, I grazed my eyes over my t-shirt where it laid across her curves. Her nipples peaked, pushing against the material. Fuck, I wanted to feast on them. Her fingers curled into the sheets, and her pelvis squirmed on the bed. I grinned, my lower stomach tightening and my cock twitching. Sex with the Ember who didn't remember me had been good, but now she remembered who *we* were, who *I* was, wholly and completely? I inhaled. The scent of her arousal was strong in the air. Rumbling low in my chest, I slowly lifted the tee's material, exposing her beautiful thighs and that sweet pussy to my gaze. I could see her arousal as it glistened against her skin. By now, I was holding onto my self-control by a thread. But if I gave in, I wouldn't stop for hours. I lowered to my stomach and grabbed her thighs, pushing them apart, unable to tear my gaze from her swollen sex.

"Connor..."

I smiled at the need in her voice. "Yes, Firecracker?" And I blew gently on her exposed skin. Her groan had my cock twitching and straining against my zipper. I ground against it, pushing my hips into the mattress, hoping the pain would ease me. It didn't. Holding her thighs, I flattened my tongue and licked all the way up her slit, groaning at the taste of her; pure honey. I circled her clit once, and she bucked her hips. Or tried. One glance of a warning was all I gave her.

"Are you ready? I need to taste you before I leave. You're going to come hard and fast."

And with her nod, I dove in, running my tongue up and down her sweet folds, feasting on her before sucking into my mouth that tight bundle of nerves at her apex. She writhed and groaned, rolling her hips in time with the suction I gave her. I grunted and moved an arm across her hips, holding her but careful not to press on her abdomen. Without pause, I slipped a finger into her warm, silky heat. Fuck me, but she was tight, the way she squeezed, holding me in. The knowledge that we were once again in sync made this experience better than ever. I added another finger, curling them forward against her g-spot as I increased my assault on her clit. Her internal muscles tightened, and within seconds she exploded, coating my fingers, and crying out my name. I stroked her slowly down from her orgasm as I whispered, "welcome home, Firecracker," and she collapsed back against the pillows, panting hard. Pulling my fingers gently from her, I licked her clean before sucking every drop of her from my own skin.

She watched me from beneath heavy lids with a beautiful smile on her face. But I could sense her fatigue. I climbed off the bed, covered her and pulled up the blanket.

"Hey, what? No, you can't go now, not like that." She gestured at my hard-on that was straining against my zipper.

I grinned. "Sweetness, you're the one who reminded me of my responsibilities not long ago."

Her pout was the cutest thing I'd seen in months. "Yeah, but that was before you revved me up. Now I want more." And she reached for my cock.

I took hold of her wrist before she could touch me. Damn, if I didn't leave right then, she would break my self-control. "Go back to sleep for a while, baby. I'll be back soon, and then you can play until we are both exhausted. Okay?"

She nodded sleepily, but her smile was mischievous. "Okay, *baby*."

I chuckled at her sass, my lips still curved into a smile as I gently kissed her. Using every bit of determination in my soul, I walked away, the taste of her arousal thick on my tongue. I knew everyone else would scent her on me, and I couldn't give a fuck. I wanted every single unmated male in this compound to know she was mine. I grunted. Right now, that meant every male. Only two of my pack were mated. My brows dipped; hopefully, that would change. They all deserved the connection of a mate in their lives.

⁂

"Collapsing that Rift is the only way forward," Walker pointed out, his voice calm and his face as cold as always.

"I will not put Ember in harm's way again." I hadn't forgotten Walker's past words. He'd threatened to take Ember out if she became a danger to the safety of this world or his. The High King of Faerie didn't make idle threats, and that's why he was in this room. If he was here, I could keep an eye on him. Keep your friends close, your enemies closer and, whatever the hell *he* was, practically in my lap.

"You won't have to," Sophie said, touching my hand, which rested on the tabletop. Everyone's attention was on her, except Drake's, whose gaze was fixed on where her hand touched mine. "I have been studying the Halo and the angelic runes."

"Since when do you speak angelic?" Drake almost snapped. "I thought you were just a shifter assassin who sold herself to the highest bidder?"

She shot him a cold look, pulling her hand from mine. "Since all my life, asshat. And I'm far more than you could ever hope to know."

"Who says I want to know?" His gaze shifted to me, and I glimpsed a darkness there that made me tense. Drake was a good guy, but he was an alpha shifter, and he didn't get to lead one of the prison packs without being ruthless when he needed to. "Seems others know you well enough for the rest of us." Drake's eyes raised to my face, moving away just shy of a challenge. My nostrils flared, but I let it go. His words reminded me that none of my pack knew who Sophie was to me. After her capture at the Gambit, I'd sworn my brothers to secrecy about her angel side. And that's how it would stay. The element of surprise was something we needed to win this war, and there were still those in this room I didn't fully trust, but I'd talked to Sophie about telling my brothers who she was to me. They deserved to know, and she agreed.

Drake ground his jaw, his eyes narrowing dangerously on Sophie's face. I looked from him to her. Tight-lipped, she nodded.

"Drake! Treat her with the same respect you do everyone else in this room."

"Why? Who is she to you?"

Standing tall, I crossed my arms over my chest. "She's my sister, you asshole. And your betrothed."

The murmurs of everyone else paled into the background as Drake's gaze flew to mine—and his eyes darkened to the colour of a stormy sea. I remained relaxed, but I'd never seen him so obviously furious before. His fists curled, and his wolf shone through his eyes. "You knew who she was all this time? And you kept that from me?"

Ah, shit, I'd done it again, managed to lie by omission. I sighed and rubbed my eyebrows with my fingers, shaking my head. *When would I fucking learn...?*

"It wasn't his decision. It was mine." Sophie came to my defense, even though it couldn't change the decision *I'd* made not to tell Drake. He held my gaze; his nostrils flared. I forced myself to let him, for a moment.

The others all watched on, Xania with a bored look and Lance with his usual vigour for angst between us all. He smirked, waiting for someone to try and kick my arse.

Drake shook his head. My warning growl was low but enough for everyone in the room to hear. Drake's top lip curled, but he nodded once. Grinding his teeth, he dragged his gaze from mine. "Fine, no challenge here,

Prime." He looked at Sophie. "But you and me? We have shit to discuss when this is all over."

Sophie nodded and released a shaky breath. No one else heard it, but I did. "I know," she said.

Drake glared at her, and electricity crackled between them as she held his stare. It was Sophie who looked away first. Drake continued to stare at her as if his eyes were glued in her direction. His body remained tense, but his voice was calmer when he spoke. "Are you saying we can use the Halo to close the Rift?"

Sophie's dark hair swung over her shoulder as she nodded. She'd pulled it back into a tight, high ponytail that exposed the angular features of her face. I knew this wasn't her true appearance. Drake had also seen her true form when we'd been at Manivera's place, but it had only been briefly. He hadn't asked about it, but he was studying Sophie so closely, I wondered if he was questioning which one was her true appearance. The others at the table, mainly Walker, didn't need to know she was an angel. As Balthazar had said, those born of angel descent were hunted by other supernaturals. Their blood could do many things, and I wasn't willing to put my sister at risk before it was necessary.

Sophie nodded. "Yes. I won't get into how right now as it's a complicated mix of angelic chants and...other stuff."

Angel juice then, I surmised. "Okay, I trust you, Soph. But we still need troops to fight if the Rift can't be closed."

Sophie frowned but thankfully remained silent. I'd learned never to rely on one plan, no matter how foolproof it may seem.

"Owen, where are we with manpower?"

Owen grimaced. "At the moment, we're pretty much it, from a shifter point of view. I've sent out messengers to the shifters we've recruited in the past weeks, the few city packs that have pledged their allegiance to you, and those further afield who haven't yet declared their loyalty, calling them to fight by their king."

"Hm, is there any way to call in the lone wolves we recruited at the club?"

"Yeah." He glanced at the Count, who silently observed everyone in the room, looking bored. I wasn't fooled for a moment. His ears worked just fine, and he wouldn't miss a thing, including heart rates and breathing and any other sign of fear, betrayal, or discord among us. "You can send word through Balthazar's underground network," finished Owen.

I narrowed my eyes on Balthazar and waited patiently as he slowly turned his attention to me. It was a game with him. He was used to calling the shots, but he knew if we failed in this, his empire and power wouldn't mean jack shit.

The dark-haired vampire met my eyes and nodded once.

"Good. Owen, do that. Balthazar, do you have a colleague who can assist my beta?"

"I do." He shifted his disturbing gaze to Owen. "I will send Davlov, my right hand, to you this evening."

Owen nodded, holding Balthazar's gaze just long enough to show he wasn't intimidated by the Count but not long enough to cause offense. Balthazar smirked a little. So did I. Owen was a good beta.

"Good, that's settled then. We'll need every warrior we can get if the Rift doesn't close." I met Owen's gaze. "We'll deal with the alphas and lone wolves who ignore our summons after we've dealt with Satan."

I leaned back in my chair, crossed my arms and tilted my head back—thinking. "Balthazar? How many vampires have you called in?"

The Count cocked his head. It was full daylight outside, but the original vampire wasn't bothered by such trivial issues as the sun. He was far too ancient and far too powerful for that—other vampires not so much. "Two thousand warriors from the four main English covens. Their leaders are loyal to me and will be on standby where you tell them to be. I can't provide more as we are already fighting to protect our king in Europe."

I nodded my thanks, not questioning his reasons. The Vampire King lived somewhere in Europe. He was ailing, and the war to take his throne before he died and his young son was crowned was already in full force. I had no idea where Balthazar fit into that world other than the Vampire King's representative in Britain. That meant he was the ultimate vampire power in this country. One of the main reasons I kept him on my side.

"Shifter numbers?" I asked Owen.

"Five hundred confirmed for now. But like I said, more to come..." His phone rang, and he pulled it from his jeans pocket. His brows dipped. "Selina? Why are you ringing me on Shane's phone?" His expression darkened. "Why? Where is he?" A pause. "You're his what!?" A pause. His voice lowered to a growl. "Since when? Fine. When are you expecting him back? Damn it! That's two days from now! No, I can't tell you what it's about over the phone. Okay...wait." He met my eyes but then looked quickly away. "How's Devon?" Another pause. "Good. I'll be in touch later." He put his phone down, took a breath and unclamped his teeth. "Shane's on a hunt and won't be back until Friday."

"Dammit!" I had hoped to use Walker's portal to get extra men from the Canadian pack. We needed to shut the Rift down, but we also needed to eliminate the sea of demons that had gotten through it.

B'nar raised his eyes to mine. "I'll still go through the portal. Your beta can come with me and talk to Shane's beta. Maybe we can work something out even if Shane is absent."

"Fine. Owen, do that. Who is Shane's beta now?"

Owen's eyes met mine, and his nostrils flared. His shock and anger filtered into me. "Selina."

"Good on her," drawled Shannon. "It's about time a female got a position of power."

I rolled my eyes at her. "You're free to challenge my beta anytime you wish."

Owen tensed and cracked his neck as if he expected Shannon to actually do it. I grinned. She *was* unpredictable enough to fight him if she was in the mood.

Stone's eyes flared with purple as Shannon sat back and smirked at Owen, looking down his body and back up again. "Nah, maybe we can tangle another time, beta."

Now it was Stone's turn to growl.

"Enough!" We didn't have time for territorial alpha confrontations. "Owen, go with Walker and B'Nar and bring back as many fighters as they can spare. I'll square it with Shane another time..."

Ember's scent hit me the moment before she strolled into the room. "Hey, guys, did you miss me?" She smirked at everyone, her beautiful hair gleaming and hanging in waves down her back. She wore jeans and a tank that exposed her arms and moulded to her breasts and ribs. The gleam of defiance that had been missing from her eyes since Italy was back with a vengeance.

"Hey, biatch!" Shannon smirked and wiggled her fingers. "'Bout time you got your ass back to us! The other you was boring as hell."

Ember laughed. "Don't worry, I'll come find you to kick your arse soon enough. Then you might change your tune."

Shannon laughed. "We done, Prime?"

I nodded. She pushed her chair back and strutted over towards Ember, grinning. "Come find me, and I'll kick *your* ass..." She winked and lowered her voice, which was pointless. "When he's done fucking it."

Ember laughed, and they high-fived as Shannon walked out.

Stone was quick to follow Shannon but stopped beside Ember. "She-wolf." He nodded and wandered off after Shannon.

It was only when Ember's eyes landed on Reed that her attitude faltered. "Reed? REED!" She squealed loud enough to make everyone remaining wince and ran across the room, launching herself at my brother. He quickly stood up, just managing to catch her as she leapt into his embrace. My brother was mated, which was the only thing that saved him as she wrapped her arms around his neck, and he hugged her close.

"You're alive." She sobbed into his neck.

"Yeah, I am."

While my mate sobbed and clung to my brother, everyone but Myles left us.

"Ember, I'm fine. You can let me breathe now." Reed chuckled, but his brown eyes were shining, his voice gravelly.

"No. Not letting you go. Godsdammit, I *killed* you, Reed. Then I watched that bastard demon eat away at your body."

Reed lowered her to the floor, but she didn't let go and I didn't miss his wince as she gripped his upper arms so tightly her nails scored his skin. He glanced at me, clearly ready for me to rip him apart. And, normally, if she touched any other male like that, I would. But right then, I was overjoyed she remembered him properly. And she was so overcome with relief that she needed to touch him to convince herself he really was alive and well.

"Honestly, I'm fine. Ask Myles."

Ember looked at Myles, who grinned and nodded. "Honestly, he really is."

She hugged him again. "I'm so sorry," she said, her voice breaking. "I couldn't stop myself."

He held her close again. "It wasn't your fault, Em. Not in any way. Don't you ever think it was."

She turned her head, laying her cheek against his chest, and sought me out. "How?" she whispered.

I took pity on Reed, who she was still gripping too tightly. Gently, I pried my mate's grip from my brother. "Let him breathe, and I will tell you."

"Oh." She pulled back, flushing a little at the scrapes she'd left on his skin. "Sorry," she said sheepishly.

Reed glanced at his arm and then grinned widely. "I'll take it." He leaned down and tapped his cheek. "Plant one there, and we'll call it even."

She grinned, then smacked a big kiss on his cheek. He straightened up and looked at my fisted hands. "Er, I think we'll go now. Catch you later, Ember." He winked at her, and he and Myles walked out.

Before I could move, Ember launched into my arms, wrapped her legs around my waist and kissed me so hard she stole my breath. "You saved him? Without the Halo?" she breathed against my lips.

I nodded and smirked. "Obviously."

"Arrogant arse," she muttered and bit my bottom lip. That bit of pain shot straight to my cock. Fuck, I was fast losing control. I almost threw her on the table and fucked her there, only Lance was smirking from across the room, and as much as I wanted to bellow at him to get out, we had demons to find, and he needed access to the tech to do that. Holding Ember with one arm, I marched out of the room and past Owen and Walker, who were talking quietly in the corridor. Neither of them said a thing. There was no point in reminding me we were in the middle of a war against Hell, one that could devour our world; nothing would sway me from this time with Ember, and everyone knew it. She'd been present yet absent since we'd saved her in Italy. Right now, we needed this time to remember who we were.

CHAPTER 22

mber

I KEPT my arms and legs curled around Connor, holding him tight. My heart was going to explode. I was certain of it. Over the past few hours, all of my memories had hit me, the good, the bad, and the downright fucking ugly. But I was here, and I had Connor back; wholly and completely.

Pregnant! With *his* baby. My insides clenched at the memory of how that had happened.

"I can smell how much you want me," he rubbed his nose along my neck, nipping me with one of his canines. "You ready for me, Firecracker?"

"I might be. We'll see. I'm still pretty angry at you for lying to me."

"I didn't lie, I omitted, and it was to protect you from being overwhelmed with even more information when your brain was already struggling to process everything that had happened."

"I know, but you don't get to make that kind of decision by yourself. We're a couple."

Even if I kinda understood why he'd omitted to tell my amnesiac self I was pregnant, I was still pissed that he'd done it.

"Hmm, I know. But you should have trusted me, not run from me."

"Trusted you? Fuck you, Connor. You couldn't even reassure me the child was ours. You let that bastard Rex sow a seed of doubt in your head." I pulled back and looked him directly in the eye. "Have you any idea how that doubt, no matter how fleeting, made me feel?"

His footsteps halted, his expression softening. "You're right. I did let him in my head. I should have been stronger, and I should have told you about the baby, for that, I am truly sorry." Then his gaze darkened. "But you shouldn't have kept on running. If you'd stayed with me, I could have told you I'd made a mistake, but you chose to put your life in danger instead. Walker found you first. Do you have any idea how much *that* scared me? You're mine, and he has already threatened to take you from me if there is a chance you could be captured and open the Hell gates. You need to stay away from him, and don't go anywhere alone."

I nodded gravely. Walker had always been an arse, and his threats weren't new; he'd said exactly the same thing to me in Faerie. But Connor was right, we were on the verge of war, and I was the key to destroying worlds. If Walker could kill me instead of putting his precious Faerie world at risk, he'd do it.

Connor squeezed my buttocks through my jeans, hard enough to make me groan. "So, we good? What do you say? Are you ready to play, Firecracker?"

I grinned. "Yes. Are you?" And I sank my teeth into his neck.

"Fuck! Stop that!"

But I didn't. Instead, I reached down between us and rubbed his cock, hard. He stumbled and groaned. "Ember...Stop! Don't you dare..."

I growled in my throat and rubbed even harder as he tried to prise me from his neck. But I was playing dirty. After all, first come, first served. I sucked hard on his neck, swallowing down his blood as our wolves tangled their souls together. He made it as far as the door to our room, crashing it open before kicking it shut behind us and collapsing back against it. I swallowed another mouthful of his blood, feeling his power rush through me. Fumbling, I managed to pop open the top button of his jeans. Reaching down inside the denim, I rubbed his hard length between his boxers and the heel of my hand, my fingers gripping where they could. He gave up the fight when my fingers slipped inside the material of his underwear. Curling my hand around the steel of his erection, a groan escaped me. His guttural, pleasure-filled moan had my internal muscles clenching. I ached for him, but I wouldn't stop. I just gripped him harder and moved my fist faster. I grinned against his skin, loving the power this gave me over him. He swore under his breath and, seeing he had no choice, my alpha Prime mate submitted to me. I sucked firmly at his neck and worked him harder and faster.

"Damn, Ember." His breathing was ragged and erratic, one of his hands leaving my backside and moving behind my head, holding me closer to him as he rocked his pelvis into my touch. One more hard draw and, he shuddered against me, his groans of pleasure in time to the spurts of warmth that spilled over my hand.

I gently pulled my teeth from his neck and laved his skin. His head fell back, and he watched me through hooded eyes. "You're mine," I told him. "That means you don't hold back information. You don't decide alone what's best for me or us. And you never, ever lie to me." I rubbed my hand along his still hard length, then squeezed his balls hard.

He half snarled, half-smiled. His response was feral and dangerous, and I loved the frisson of fear it gave me, so I squeezed again.

He winced, but his grin remained. "Understood."

"Good." I removed my hand from his clothes and deliberately wiped my fingers on his jeans. He watched me with a dark look, and my heart rate skyrocketed, my satisfaction at overwhelming him suddenly shifting to nerves. His pupils dilated as he sensed my trepidation.

"Done?" he asked in a deceptively low and quiet voice. I swallowed hard. He grinned and grabbed my wrist before I could pull away. "Now it's your turn."

He picked me up and flung me over his shoulder before I could contemplate fighting. Not that I would, I loved this dominant and slightly dangerous side to him. He slapped my right buttock hard, the sting only somewhat muted by the denim of my jeans, before flinging me on the mattress. By the time my gasp had ended, my clothes were gone, ripped from my skin like tissue paper. His gaze raked over my body like he was seeing me for the first time. I remembered our sex sessions in the past few weeks, and the heat in his gaze had always been so controlled, his passion never burning as hot as this. He'd been grieving for me—for us. My heart hurt at that realisation. How hard had it been for him to have a shell of me by his side, unsure whether I'd ever be the person he'd fallen in love with? Or even if I'd truly love him back? And then I'd run from him. Gods, how I must have hurt him.

While he lowered his jeans, the evidence of his recent pleasure shining on his skin, I scrambled off the bed and kneeled on the floor at his feet. Just like Connor, I didn't have a submissive bone in my body, but right now, I wanted him to know I understood. And that I was sorry.

I lowered my head, feeling incredibly vulnerable like this. Connor was the *only* one I would ever do this for.

For a moment, he was silent, his shock reverberating through our bond. "Ember? What are you doing?"

I didn't raise my eyes, but I smirked a little at the gruffness of his voice, at the change in his energy as he stared down at me. He liked this. He was a dominant alpha male, Hell-beasts and fae aside, and the power this position gave him over me...? I sneaked a look up through my eyelashes, and yeah, the evidence he liked it was right in front of my face. I licked my lips, tempted to give into my willful side and suck him down into my throat. But I didn't. Instead, I lowered my gaze again. This was for him. He'd never ask this of me, so I'd give him the gift of my submission.

"I'm sorry I ran from you, my King. I know I'm yours, and I give myself to you wholly and completely."

He hissed, his gaze heavy on my bowed head. Silence fell, and he didn't move. I heard his hard swallow, then his big hand wrapped in my hair, pulling until my head tilted back. His face was dark and full of lust...and love. "Good, because I intend to possess you wholly and completely. In every way, Firecracker. Now open wide."

I hid my delighted grin and did his bidding.

"YOU CAN STILL WALK THEN?" Shannon grinned at me and waggled her brows.

I grimaced but grinned back. "Only just."

Connor smirked from across the room, puffing his chest out. I gave him a sickly sweet smile but couldn't hide the heat in my cheeks or stop him scenting my arousal as I thought about last night's marathon. When he'd said he'd possess me wholly and completely, he had meant it. His smirk turned into a full-on grin as he sensed my emotions, and for once, I was glad only he could scent me fully. I'd long since lost any embarrassment over everyone else scenting my arousal. They couldn't actually scent *me;* only Connor could. But every supernatural had super senses, and scenting arousal was just one of those things we all got used to. It was annoying at times, like in a club like the Gambit, but you learned to ignore it. I smirked; until it was your mate's. And there was no way I couldn't be turned on every time I looked at his honed body and gorgeous tight arse.

A sharp slap on my cheek brought my attention back to the blonde bombshell in front of me. "Hey! Focus. You need to get that ass back in shape, sister. And quit with the horniness. I'm gonna have to open all the windows soon."

Connor growled at Shannon from across the room, snarling at her bitch slap. I rolled my eyes. "Ignore him. Yeah, you're right. I do need to get back in shape. I couldn't remember a bloody thing about fighting, but I can now. So let's go."

Connor wasn't quite ready to let me out of his sight again. And he flatly refused to let me fight any of his brothers or the other males in the compound. The only one he'd agreed to let me train with was Rawson, and he'd gone out. Connor's possessive streak was riding him high, and I knew better than to push it. I smirked. At least, I wouldn't push him until I wanted another night like last night.

Grinning, I walked into the middle of the floor space. We'd managed to come to a compromise of sorts. My mate knew I'd not drop my need to train, not now I remembered who I was and my fighting capabilities. Agreeing to fight only the females in the pack was the only concession I was willing to give. Thankfully, he'd not argued. So they had moved the big ugly table in the ops room aside and set up a training area. I'd also managed to extract a promise that he wouldn't interfere once we started if Shannon, or Sophie, managed to land the odd punch or kick. I hadn't bothered inviting Xania. I didn't trust her. She was a cold bitch and kept to herself or followed Walker around with her face as hard as his. Damn, maybe they should be a couple. My giggle at that thought was hard to contain.

I groaned, stretching out my aching muscles. Some hard physical training was what I needed to get my body and mind back into survival mode. The training I'd done as my forgetful self had been tough enough to keep me in shape, along with the workouts Connor and I regularly got in the bedroom, but now that I remembered my skill set, I wanted to practise it. My disappointment at not seeing Rawson was gnawing at me. I'd hoped to catch up with him while we trained. Connor refused to tell me where he'd gone or why, though common sense told me it was something to do with the Rift. Apparently, Rawson had been spying on the demons for months, and Connor was going after the Rift tomorrow night. We couldn't wait any longer. Demons were flooding the streets of London, and the SBI and human police were overwhelmed by the sheer number of deaths and attacks on human citizens. People were beginning to panic.

"You keep away from her belly. Understand?" Connor yelled over at Shannon as we started to warm up.

Shannon scowled. "Of course, I will, Prime. I'm not stupid!"

Tyen watched us curiously. I'd invited her to join us. Not to fight, but mainly to spend more time with her. I wanted to get to know the quiet woman who was my mate's mother. Sophie ran in, out of breath and dressed for action. Her slim body was athletic, but the curves she did have were accentuated by the lycra yoga leggings and tight figure-hugging top.

"Hey." Her smile was bright and she was almost bouncing with energy.

I raised my hand and grinned. "Hey. You ready?"

Shannon smiled and high-fived Sophie. Everyone knew who she was to Connor now. Most of our pack had accepted her, though Drake's attitude towards her needed a bit of work. And I was more than happy to have her on our side.

"Sure am." She glanced at Tyen and her gaze softened. "Do you want to train with me for a while? I can teach you some basic fighting moves."

Tyen contemplated her. Maybe a shadow fae didn't need basic fighting skills, but her heritage hadn't saved her in the past. She seemed to come to the same conclusion. "I'd like that very much," she answered and stood up, uncoiling her tall willowy frame and squaring her shoulders.

After two hours of drills with basic blocks and punches, we moved on to weapons. We'd kept swapping partners, and I was back with Shannon. Across the room, B'nar wandered in and spoke to Connor, who grinned and nodded. The blue-haired Faerie prince approached in the fluid way he always walked. I blocked Shannon's knife attack and inclined my head at the approaching prince. She got the message, and we both stopped, placing our weapons back in the sheaths on our thighs.

B'nar nodded a greeting and held out the bow he clutched in his elegant hand. "Remember this?"

I traced my fingers over the runes and carving. "I remember the one I had. This is similar but not the same one. *This* is the one I almost shot Alex with."

B'nar actually smiled. All of us gaped, which seemed to amuse him more. "That's right. You remember. I'm glad."

"Where is Alex? Didn't he go with your father to Canada?"

"Yes, he did. They haven't yet returned."

I spun the bow in my grip and lifted it, drawing back the string. Energy zipped through me, and the tattoo on my arm ignited, sending the Faerie magic Walker had used to create it into the bow. Runes glowed across the bow. I had no arrow in it, but I grinned as I eyed Connor across the room and targeted him. He smirked, his gaze dropping down my body and back up to my face. I inhaled and smirked right back. Yeah, scenting arousal worked both ways. I lowered the bow before I was tempted to drag him off into the nearest store cupboard. My eyes landed on the table. In fact, that old flat surface was looking good right about now.

"Mother Wolf," Shannon muttered. "What's with you? Are baby hormones making you super horny or something?" She poked my ribs. "Up here, lady." She made a ring around her face with her forefinger. "Focus."

I laughed and pushed her away. "Get lost. And yes, they are if you must know." Then I remembered his mother was standing right next to me. Oops.

Tyen just shrugged, though there was a glint of playfulness in her eyes that surprised me. "He was made the same way, though I expect the way your baby got in there was far more enjoyable."

I wasn't quite sure how to answer that, so I focused back on B'nar, my eyes narrowed.

"How did you get this, anyway? I thought you were going to Canada with them?"

"I was." He shrugged. "But something more important turned up."

"What?" I wasn't sure what was more important than securing more fighters for this war.

He smirked. "Just something I needed to take care of."

"Oh. Did Walker bring this?" I studied the beautiful weapon.

"He did...and he didn't. He brought someone else, who brought it with them." The Prince smiled and nodded over my shoulder. I was a bit nonplussed. I'd never seen B'nar smile so much in such a short space of time.

"Hey bitches!"

I squealed and threw the bow down, racing into my friend's waiting arms. Her gorgeous chestnut hair covered my face as I squeezed her tightly. I blew it from my mouth, making silly noises like she was suffocating me with it. I wasn't about to let her go, though. We held each other tightly, and I didn't bother to hide my tears. Once we'd both calmed down some, we broke apart a little, but I still grabbed onto her hands. My smile was wide, but it was hard to contain my worry. Blue didn't look well; in fact, she looked like shit. "It's so good to see you."

"Yeah, you too, girl." She eyed the nearest chair. "Mind if we park it for a mo'?"

"Oh, of course." I turned to the chairs; only B'nar was already there. He pulled one out. "Here. Sit." He eyed Blue sternly, and there was no confusion about who he was talking to. I smirked at him. He ignored me. Blue rolled her eyes but didn't argue.

"Glad you didn't lie and say I look great because I know I look like shit." Her face twisted.

Lying wouldn't work with Blue since she'd see right through it, so I didn't. "Yeah, you do."

"She does not." B'nar's words made us both look at him. He glanced down at Blue, who he was hovering over with his arms crossed. "She is alive, and that looks good on her."

I gaped, as did Blue. She turned her attention back to me, her eyes comically wide and her cheeks slightly pink. "Okaaay." She missed B'nar's slight smirk at me.

I grinned and nodded enthusiastically. "It surely does."

"Thanks, but this is only temporary."

"What do you mean, temporary?" B'nar snapped before I could ask. I scowled at his interruption to our catch up.

Blue looked him in the eye. "Your father has managed to find some kind of cure for whatever Hell poison was on that arrow, but it's temporary. He tried it once before. I remained awake for a week, then went back into the land of nod."

"How long will you stay awake this time?" I asked, trying not to let my fear for my friend show.

She shrugged. "He seems to think it has something to do with the Faerie moons. When they are high in the night sky, the cure he found is activated and will work until they wane; so about a week."

"Will that count in this world? Won't you just stay awake now you are here?"

"That's not how Faerie magic works," B'nar replied gruffly. "It will still sense the magic of our world, and much is based around the cycles of the moon." He peered down at Blue, his expression grim. "The cure will still fade, human. You will fall again, and my father will return you to Faerie—where you belong."

Blue scowled up at him. "Damn, for a minute there, Prince, I thought you'd grown some feelings, you know compassion and the like."

He cocked his head, his face expressionless, but I could see the worry in his eyes. I knew him far better than Blue by now, and he wasn't immune to her plight. But for some reason, one known only to him, he was intent on hiding it from her.

"No. Why would I have compassion for the woman who helped kill my brother?"

Blue paled and swallowed hard, the hurt on her face immediate, but she rallied just as she always did. She shrugged. "Oh, I don't know, Princey, maybe because you're fighting alongside the other woman who was in cahoots with me; and living in the same building as the shadow fae, one of your own kind, I'll just point out, who sent us there to sell Digitalis for him."

B'nar's nostrils flared. "Just because I'm required by the High King of Faerie to work with them, do not for one second think that my benevolence stretches to you. You are mine. *My* prisoner, and when this curse takes you again, you will still belong to me, not my father, and definitely not anyone else. You will be at *my* mercy, not the High King's. Remember that."

Blue glared daggers at him, and for a moment, I thought she might kick him right in the balls. Her foot twitched, so I placed mine over hers to stop her. Such an attack, satisfying though it might be, would only make things between them worse.

"I'm going to get a drink," he muttered, turning away, but he hesitated and looked back at us, his eyes focused only on Blue. "I will bring you something."

"I don't want anything from you," she snapped.

A snarl curled his lip, but he remained quiet and walked away.

Silence fell between us. Blue met my gaze, her deep brown eyes, which had been dull, now glittering, and her cheekbones highlighted with colour.

"Why does he hate me so much?" she whispered. "I can't even remember selling *Digitalis* to anyone who looks remotely like him. Can you?"

I pressed my lips together and shook my head before I decided to speak my mind. Who knew when my friend would be taken from us again. Her time to listen was short. "He doesn't hate you."

"Really?" she interrupted. "He reminds me at every opportunity that I killed his precious brother and that I'm his prisoner."

I gave her a small smile. It was unlikely she'd listen to my words, and I had no idea what was going on inside the prince heir's mind, but I could see he'd never hurt my friend. He'd saved her life, and, yes, he'd been gruff and hard with her but never violent, not even when he easily could have harmed her. "Yes, that's true, but I have never seen him smile more than I have this morning, and the only thing different in this world for him today is that you are in it."

Now she did laugh loudly. "Oh, you've got to be kidding me? I made the ice prince smile with my mere presence?" She lifted her chin and affected a snobby royal voice. "Me, a mere dirty human, who even dares to breathe the same air as him?"

I grinned. "Yeah, you, you silly cow. Now forget about B'nar and tell me how you really feel because you really do look awful, and I'm worried about you."

Any levity in her face disappeared, and she sighed. "I'm so tired I could curl up on the floor and sleep right now, but I refuse. I've been doing nothing but sleeping in between these rare days of wakefulness, and I'm not wasting a moment. Don't worry. If I eat and drink and refuel my body, I'll get back to more or less my full strength." She cocked her head. "And you have some demon arse to kick by the sounds of it, so I'm going to help you."

"What? You're strong enough to fight?" I hadn't meant to sound so sceptical, but she looked like a stiff wind would blow her over.

She grinned. "Fuck off. 'Course I am. Or I will be. I only woke up yesterday, so give me a chance. And I'll be with you for at least seven days, so let's make the most of it."

"Here," said a gruff voice. We both gaped as B'nar, Prince Heir to the throne of Faerie, placed a tray piled high with sandwiches, fruit and tea on the table next to Blue. "Replenish your body, human. You need to survive to return to Faerie as my prisoner." He looked at me. "There is some for you too. You need to eat properly."

Blue opened her mouth to give some kind of snarky response until I kicked her and glared meaningfully.

"Thanks." And I meant it, touched he'd do that for me without even being asked.

"Thank you," Blue managed to say, even though it sounded like the words choked her.

B'nar looked taken aback for a moment.

"Eat," he growled out, then gave us some space, striding over to Connor, who'd watched the whole thing.

"Why have you got to eat properly? Does he bully everyone like that?" She shot him a glare, which he studiously ignored, though I was pretty certain he'd feel her wrath even from across the room. I was grinning when she looked back at me after shoving three grapes in her mouth at once. "War...oo..innin...ah?" I giggled at her garbled words. She swallowed quickly, greeting the others who all placed themselves in chairs near us. "Sorry." She swallowed again. "Now tell me what you're grinning at."

I grinned at the others too and then bounced in my chair, unable to hold in my happiness. I'd gotten used to the idea of becoming a mum, and the thought of having Connor's baby growing inside me made me so happy I could burst. "I'm pregnant," I squealed.

"Whaaat!" Then we were hugging again.

Connor smiled indulgently at us from across the room. I blew him a cheeky kiss and spent another two hours catching up with Blue before we were both too tired to continue. Tyen and Shannon came and went several times. Sophie went over to speak to Connor, and once Ava had caught up on some surveillance, she plonked herself down with us and hugged Blue. Shannon and Tyen returned, and we all ended up sitting at the table, chatting amicably. It was the happiest I could remember being in weeks when it didn't directly involve Connor. I yawned and leaned forward to hug my friend, then glanced at Connor, who seemed to understand that I was weary all of a sudden. Within moments he was right beside us.

"Blue?" He held out a hand, and she met his gaze head-on. He hadn't met my friend yet, only heard about her. Fully human, she wouldn't see meeting his gaze as a challenge, and I knew Connor wouldn't, but B'nar didn't look so sure. He frowned and edged closer to Blue. I hid my smirk in Connor's arm as I grabbed his hand and pressed a kiss to his hard forearm. B'nar might not admit it, but he had it bad for my friend.

"Yeah. You must be Connor." She cocked her head and grinned up at him before giving him the once over. "I can see why my girl's hot for you."

I playfully kicked her, knowing she was just winding me up. "Hey, he's spoken for. Get your own man."

Blue rolled her eyes and pulled a face. "No, thanks. They're more trouble than they're worth."

Connor chuckled but pulled me out of my chair and into his arms. "Is that what you think, Firecracker? Too much trouble for the reward?"

Grinning, I turn coy, shrugging a little. "Oh, not too much, not when the reward is *so* good and *so* frequent."

Blue and Shannon made a gagging sound.

"Mother Wolf, Prime, take your woman away and give her her rewards. Just the sight of you together is so sickeningly sweet it makes me want to vomit," Shannon grumbled.

Blue and Ava giggled. Even Tyen smiled widely at the disgust on Shannon's face.

For the next two hours, Connor kept me spooned against his body. His arms were tight, and he never let me go. I sensed his tension, and even Mea, who couldn't push through because of the baby, was unsettled. She whined, only calming when Connor sent a wave of reassurance her way, and Prime wrapped himself around her. Deep down, I suspected that Connor's mood was because he didn't want to leave me. Despite the powerful supernaturals coming to the compound tonight for a meeting about our assault on the Rift, ultimately, Connor was going to lead the attack.

"Connor?"

"Mm?" He nuzzled my neck, inhaling as he pushed his face into my hair.

"Will Walker bring his Fae army to Earth to help us?"

He stiffened. "I don't know. He has no reason not to help us, but he hasn't said he will."

I nodded. Walker was secretive. He had a larger plan, but none of us had any idea what that was. I doubted even his son did.

"Get some sleep, sweetness. It's going to be a long few days."

That was easier said than done, no matter how tired I was. My head and my heart were in a conflicted mess. I wanted to fight beside my mate and my pack. But I had a baby to protect, and if Satan was hunting me, the last place I needed to be was at a doorway to his fucked up world. Connor's palm flattened over my lower belly, which had become more curved recently. At least now I knew why, rather than blaming it on my lack of activity. He kissed the top of my head. "Sleep. We'll talk about it later."

It was no surprise he knew exactly where my thoughts had gone. Holding his arms tightly to me, I pushed my body flush against his, entwining my legs and feet with his. My heart squeezed. He was my world, him and the tiny little bean growing in my belly. I refused to lose them, either of them.

Eventually, Connor's warmth and the security of his embrace lulled me, and I dozed, finally falling asleep.

CHAPTER 23

THE MEETING TABLE had been dragged back into place, and I stood at the head of it surveying the hard features of those present.

Rawson had messaged me to say he was on his way back with new information. I hoped it was good news but doubted it. Walker had opened a portal in the compound yard an hour ago, which meant that my beta was back, with Shane and his beta. I watched Selina. She was tight-lipped, and though she was aloof, her gaze kept drifting to Owen, who stood to my right. My beta met her gaze and held it. I held in a sigh. I'd had hopes for them as a couple, Owen had obviously felt something for her, but now she was Shane's beta, it would be a logistical impossibility for them to begin any kind of relationship without her giving up her position—and it didn't look like that was an option, not when she was also Shane's lover. A fact the Canadian alpha had been very clear about to us all. How Owen was holding it together, I didn't know. We had bigger issues; that was probably how. I shelved my concern for my brother and studied the room.

Stone stood on my left. Reed and Myles were at my back, watching the crowd, and Lionel and Kawan flanked Ember, where she lounged against the wall to my right. They'd protect her if everything went to shit. I'd wanted her by my side. It had been Ember herself who had persuaded me otherwise. She wanted a chance to study the people in the room without them watching her

824

too closely. All these strangers in our compound weren't something I liked, but it was necessary. Trust was earned on both sides. These shifters had managed to avoid the attention of the SBI and were determined to keep it that way. But SBI aside, word had spread that I was the Shifter King, and each one had pledged his fealty. That didn't mean I trusted them.

My eyes narrowed. The amount of power in the air was making some of the weaker shifters restless and agitated. I glanced at Drake. He glowered at the nearby shifters when they shuffled too close to Sophie and him. They had the presence of mind to move away again. I'd commanded him to stay by Sophie's side. He'd let his displeasure show enough to get him a punch in the solar plexus. He'd needed a reminder who was his alpha. I *was* protective of Sophie. She was my blood, just like Zander. I hadn't protected him, but I had every intention of keeping my sister safe. And I needed to rely on my brothers to help me do that. Besides, Drake needed help recognising his soul-mate. Maybe then he'd stop being such an arse to her.

I glanced at Lance and Ava, who were hanging near the bank of computers. They nodded. They kept an eye on our tech, and B'nar guarded the entrance to our weapons stash, Blue by his side.

Around the table stood the Count and Davlov, his second, the man who often greeted me at the Gambit, Shane and Selina, and five more alphas from the bigger packs of London and the South of England, all with their betas. Walker stood opposite me. No one watched his back, but I had no doubt if anyone tried to attack him, they'd be dead before they did any real damage. I pulsed out a vibe of dominance, and the room fell silent immediately. Some even bowed under the force of it.

Ember smirked and rolled her eyes. "Show off," she mouthed.

I didn't let my amusement show, but it flared through our bond. I was *the* Shifter King; weakness was not something these supernaturals would respect. "We're all assembled here because we face the biggest threat yet to our existence on this planet. The SBI can't help, and neither can the human police. There is a Rift between the fabric of this world and Hell. And it's in London. With every day that passes, it is getting bigger."

"Why? What's happening to make it bigger?" asked a dark-haired wolf shifter. He didn't make eye contact, but he wasn't weak or frightened of me, either.

"The demons who have survived the Rift and found a body to inhabit here send more souls back to their master. A Rift is always connected to the general of Hell who summoned it. As they grow in power from the souls that are reaped, so will the Rift."

"You've seen one before." It was a statement, not a question. He had a hard look and seemed in his late forties, but all shifters aged slowly compared to humans, so he was likely far older.

"I have, and with help from our Fae allies, my pack and I destroyed it and the general who controlled it."

Many gazes drifted to Walker, who stoically ignored them.

"If you're so powerful, *my King*," sneered one of the other alphas at the table, "then why do you need us? Sounds like you and your pack can manage fine without us. Why should I risk the lives of my pack fighting a bunch of demons who exist far from where I live? Or is it that you have so few numbers you are too weak to defend your territory from invasion?"

I glanced at Owen.

He grinned.

We were prepared for this. It was expected that one or two of the alphas would try and assert their strength. And as we had in the prison, we would crush that rebellion now. Owen stalked towards the male, who had stupidly sat in the chair provided. Sitting had made him vulnerable. By the time he had realised Owen's intention, it was too late. My beta's powerful punch knocked him from his chair, and he hit the floor. Owen calmly wrapped a thickly muscled arm around the male's throat and dragged him into a chokehold. The male's beta growled. "Do not move out of that chair," Owen warned quietly. Looking conflicted, the beta sat back. "Do you want to live?" Owen's voice was resonant enough it carried to everyone in the room, and there was no doubt he meant the question.

In Owen's grasp, the shifter breathed heavily, his eyes narrowed, and his nostrils flared. He tried to drop his weight and flip Owen over his shoulder, but Owen was far too experienced a fighter for that to work.

"Answer him!" I roared, shifting and letting Prime push through, my vision changing as flames flared to life in my eyes and my body grew.

The male's eyes widened. He nodded rapidly. Owen let go and shoved him forward. The male landed on his hands and knees. "Then crawl to your King, and mean it when you pledge your fealty."

I held in my disgust as the male did it. I didn't enjoy subjugating my people, but there was no room for petty power struggles and betrayal in the next twenty-four hours. These powerful shifters needed to fear me as much as they feared Satan, or we could lose everything. I didn't glance at Ember even though I wanted to. I'd get a thousand people to crawl to me on their knees if it meant she'd stay out of the clutches of Hell.

"Get up," I growled down at the male. He stood. I leaned forward, my jaws just in front of his face. He blinked but didn't flinch away. I grunted, respecting the male's bravery. I could rip his head from his shoulders without breaking a sweat, and the scent of his fear told me he knew it, yet he didn't cower. "Do not question my strength or the strength of my pack again."

"Understood, Prime."

"I am powerful, and I am your King, but I am not arrogant enough to believe I am invincible. If we fail and the Rift remains open, the demon war will be long and brutal. Those demons are here looking for the key to the Hell gates, and they will not give up. If they find it, they will open the gates, and this world will be lost. That's why you are here. If we fail, you will be fighting not for me but for the survival of this planet and everyone on it."

Well, that got their attention. Ember's grim comment filtered into our bond.

I shifted, covering myself in combats, boots, and a fitted tee. Owen returned to my side. There was no acknowledgement between us. It wasn't necessary.

"Where's the key?" asked Balthazar, his pale eyes sharp, his gaze unrelenting. My blood went cold. I knew without a doubt if he discovered Ember's involvement, he'd end her, as would Walker if we failed to close the Rift.

"Safe."

His eyes narrowed but didn't drift towards Ember. Good. None of my pack would talk. Not even Som would give up Ember. That old goat actually cared for her. It was in his face every time he looked at her. But if Balthazar even so much as sniffed a reason to believe that Ember was involved, he was powerful enough to read any one of their minds by biting them. Pushing aside my worry, I continued with the meeting. We hashed out plans and resources until we had everything planned down to the last detail.

That night, I held Ember close, my hand resting lightly across the small swell of our baby. Anxiety coiled in my gut, and it took everything I had to keep it from our bond. No matter if we won and closed the Rift, we would always be hunted. I swallowed hard. If we had a daughter, she would always be hunted too. She would inherit Ember's phoenix when Ember was ready to go to the beyond. My eyes burned at the thought of ever losing her, either by my death or her own. Sleep didn't come that night, so instead, I contented myself with holding my family close and planning our future.

CHAPTER 24

mber

"HEY! CONCENTRATE." Rawson easily knocked my punch aside and raised his brows.

"Sorry."

"C'mon. Break time." He led me to the table where Som had placed some bottles of water. I broke one open and chugged half the bottle in one go. Wiping my mouth, I sighed.

"Em, you know he can't let you near that Rift."

I scowled and plonked myself down on the mats. "I do. Doesn't mean I have to be happy about it."

He smirked at my snark and joined me. We sat side by side, and my heart squeezed. It had been just over five years since Lyssa had been killed by Doherty. Rawson was still a handsome man, and though he was in his late thirties, as a shifter, he aged slowly, as did all shifters. I had a feeling the grey streaks in his hair were more from the stress of losing his mate.

"No, you don't. But would you really put your baby at risk by going? Even if Connor wasn't doing what every protective male would do for his pregnant mate?"

"Urgh, why do you have to be so bloody reasonable all the time?" But I smiled. He was right. I wouldn't risk our baby.

We sat in companionable silence for a while, the sounds above us in the main building loud and busy. Rawson cocked his head and listened, a slight dip to his brow. My heart warmed. I couldn't quite believe he was sitting right next to me, that we had been training just like we used to. I took his hand in mine, and he turned and smiled at me.

"I'm so glad you're okay."

He huffed and smiled. "Yeah? I'm glad you are too. And that you are with Connor." His gaze dropped to my abdomen. I wore yoga leggings and a cropped top, determined not to give up my normal wardrobe until I was forced to by my changing body. My stomach gently curved outwards, nothing to alert anyone who wasn't a shifter that I was pregnant. A brief flash of pain filled his eyes before he hid it. "Lyss would be so pleased for you both," he said, his voice thick.

I swallowed against the ache in my throat. "I know. Are you?"

He squeezed my hand. "Of course I am. I always knew you'd end up together. I saw it that first day I brought you home, and Connor wouldn't leave you. Do you know he sat outside your room every night for a fortnight after you arrived? In the end, I threatened to kick his arse if he didn't leave you to go and get some sleep."

A warm feeling spread through my chest. "He sat outside my door?"

"Yeah, he did. You're with the right person, Em. And I couldn't be happier that you are having a young one."

I peered down at our joined hands, the question I'd always wanted to ask but never got a chance to, tumbling from my mouth. "Why didn't you and Lyss have any children? Was it because of Connor and me? Were we too much for Lyss?"

"What? No, of course not." He pulled his hand away and rubbed his face. "We tried for years, but I guess it wasn't meant to be." He looked right at me and took my hands in both of his. "Don't ever think you held us back in any way. We took you in because we wanted to, both you and Connor. And nothing that has happened would ever make me regret that."

"Do you still miss her?" It was a stupid question. Of course he did, but I needed reassurance that he was okay, or that he would be okay.

His gaze dropped to the floor as his throat bobbed. "Every minute of every day, but so much has happened since she was taken from me…" He gulped, his own eyes shining and his heavy brow dipping so low it bunched together over the bridge of his nose. His voice was almost a whisper when he spoke again. "Sometimes I can't remember her face, or I can, but it's blurred, you know? Then I get scared that I'm forgetting her, so I try to remember her laugh, or the way she would stroke her fingers through my hair, or how she looked when we made love. So many things." His voice broke.

My eyes burned, and tears trailed down my cheeks. I didn't hide them. I'd loved Lyss, and I still loved Rawson. His pain was my own.

"But even though my pain is still there, I guess I mostly feel numb." He banged his heart with his fist. "In here. I don't think I'm capable of ever loving anyone that way again."

I didn't know what to say, so I moved closer to him and wound my arms around his shoulders, giving what comfort I could.

I LEANED against Connor's chest and held his massive body close. The strength of his embrace made it hard to breathe, but I wasn't going to point that out. I didn't want to let go—ever. Oh, gods, Connor was going out there without me. It didn't matter that he was stronger than all of our kind or that his wolf spirit was born in the depths of Hell. He was my mate—mine, and I couldn't let him go…

"Em? Baby? I have to go."

There it was again, that endearment. My heart squeezed. He was worried. Why was he so worried if everything was going to be okay?

He kissed the top of my head and buried his face in my hair. "Firecracker, you have to let me go."

I shook my head. "No, I don't. Mine, remember?"

His smile moved my hair. "I am. And I'll still be yours when I get back. But, unfortunately, it doesn't change the fact that I need to go and kick those demons back to Hell."

Reluctantly, I pulled away. "I know. Doesn't mean I have to like it, though."

Connor gave me a cocky smile which I knew was to reassure me. It didn't. "King, Hell-beast, shadow fae, and wolf, remember? I'll be fine."

"Yeah, 'Course you will." I crossed my arms over my chest, my gaze fixed on the strong column of his throat where my claiming marks were white against his skin.

He stepped closer, but I still couldn't look at him. I had a terrible feeling about this attack. I couldn't tell him, though, because I couldn't put my finger on what it was. He cupped my face and tilted my head back.

"Look at me."

I did.

His gaze softened, turning my insides to mush. "What's wrong? Are you mad at me for making you stay behind with Ava and Lance?"

My heart hurt as I studied his ridiculously handsome face. I grabbed his fae armoured top, the material silky beneath my fingers, and yanked him forward. Did he think that's why I was unhappy? "No, of course not. It's just, I don't know. It's…I have a bad feeling about this."

The rough skin of his fingers left a tingling trail down my cheek, then he leaned down, resting his forehead against mine. "We will win. We have to. Sophie knows how to use the Halo. We will be fine, and I'll be back before you know it."

"Yeah, okay." I kissed him lightly, still not convinced.

We headed down to the courtyard of the compound. Even Tyen was accompanying our assembled pack. She and Connor were going to shield all our people from the city cameras that would pick up our movements. That, and the spies who worked for the authorities, were a real threat.

Rawson had confirmed the Rift was in an old abandoned car lot near Greenwich Park. He'd been watching it and fighting the demons alone since getting back to London. He'd heard about the King of Shifters when he'd come to the Gambit a few weeks ago. After that, he'd been going to Balthazar's club regularly, hoping to see us.

The images Rawson had taken on his phone of the Rift were from all angles, the most useful looking down towards the ground. He must have been hiding in the rafters to get them. The gateway itself wasn't visible, but he'd snapped some images of grainy black shapes as they seeped up from the ground. He'd even got some video of the demons slithering into the bodies of the dead their brethren had collected. It was disgusting, and no matter how much I didn't want my friends, or my mate, to go near that place, I knew this had to be stopped. All of these deaths were my fault. They were searching for Satan's key...me. It made me wonder if this would ever stop, even if we managed to close the Rift.

Connor halted and pulled me close again. We held each other's gaze, so many words said yet not a single one spoken. He lifted me, and I curled my legs and arms around him before I kissed him fiercely. I didn't care if the whole world was waiting for him. No one shouted or jeered now. Tonight, some of them might not come back, Connor might be one of them, and they all knew it. He pulled away before I was ready to let him go and put me down. His face fell into a hard, inscrutable mask, but he touched my face once more before he turned away.

"Owen!" He bellowed. And that was it; my mate had become King to the people who awaited him.

"Hey, how you holding up?" Blue asked.

I gave her a weak smile, swallowing down the nausea that plagued me when Connor left my side. "Fine. You will be careful, won't you? Something doesn't feel right about this."

Blue lifted her brows. Our instincts had kept us alive in Faerie. "What do you mean?"

My sigh wafted a few strands of her hair. "No idea. Fire isn't happy. She's bubbling under my skin, and she hasn't done that since Berith tried to control us." I met her gaze. "Just watch your back, okay?"

"Oh c'mon, I'll be fine. And where's my friend? What have you done with her? She'd never ask me if I was going to be okay. I'm a kick-ass chick, and she knows it."

I laughed. "Okay. Okay. I'm blaming pregnancy hormones. But yeah, I know you'll be fine. You are kick-ass. And you also have an ancient Faerie prince by your side, who is one of the best warriors in his world. You have fae armour and fae weaponry on top of your own awesome skillset, so yeah, I know you'll be fine." But I was still worried for her. She wasn't up to full strength.

"Damn right I will." She hugged me tight. "Just make sure you're safe too."

I rolled my eyes. "Oh, come on. I'm behind these walls, and with all the Faerie magic Walker left protecting this place, we're all far safer than you."

"Cool." She glanced across the compound's yard. B'nar was easily visible, his blue hair gleaming amongst the other people milling around. "Listen, I'd better go before princey comes searching for me. It'll only piss him off."

"True, but I thought that was your mission. To piss him off while you're still awake."

She laughed. "Yes, but maybe not while he holds all the weapons. He'll have to give me one tonight, or I won't be of any use, so..." She wiggled her brows.

"Yeah, like you'd shoot him." I rolled my eyes.

She shrugged, and her face twisted comically. "I guess it would be a waste of a pretty face," she murmured.

Grinning, I gave her a hug before she wandered over to B'nar. I stood back with Ava and Lance as Connor addressed our pack to ensure they were all clear about their roles. They all had throat mics, earpieces, and fae weaponry that sent lethal doses of ice magic into the enemy, freezing, then exploding them. There were explosive devices, knives, and they all wore the tight-fitting, silky fae armour on their torsos, everything they needed, really. Walker had really come through. Except that he had disappeared this afternoon and no one could locate him. B'nar didn't know a thing but calmly pointed out that his father followed only one person's rules, and that was his own. Connor was pissed off at the High King. He'd been hoping Walker would come through with a fae army to help. He had reassured everyone we didn't need Walker's help, but I knew how much was riding on Sophie closing the Rift. If she failed, we'd need all the help we could get.

As the focus of the operation, Sophie was to be protected by five brothers. Drake, Reed, Myles, Kawan and Stone. She was where I should be. It should be me out there closing the Rift, just like I had in Canada. My hand landed over my lower abdomen. Except...

I watched as Sophie moved surely between the men, checking her weapons. At least she was a strong fighter. I could only hope that she stayed alive and that Connor wouldn't lose his sister tonight.

"Come on, we need to get set up." Ava gently pulled me towards the door.

Reluctantly, I followed her. I might be staying behind, but she was right, I still had a job to do, and I'd do it to the best of my ability.

CHAPTER 25

mber

"YOU GOOD WITH ALL THIS?" Lance asked, no sarcasm or levity in his question. He was all business. When he was acting like an arse, it was easy to forget he'd been Connor's second at the SBI before Owen.

"Yeah." I nodded and sat at the chair in front of my bank of screens. And I was. This was the kind of thing we'd all been drilled for in Faerie. All of us; Alex, Blue, Lance, Ava and me. We had been trained with weapons, fighting, Faerie tech, and how to manipulate and spy. Not that I'd used those last skills or likely ever would, but who knew? I entered my I.D and password and the computer let me into the drone programme Drake and B'nar had developed together. B'nar had given Drake the magic and weapons technology for them to integrate. But the armoured drones were Drake's creation, well, Drake's and Charlie's. I hadn't spoken to Charlie since my memories had returned, so if we all survived this, calling or even visiting, my prison bestie was on my list of things to do.

I shot Charlie a quick message to see if everything was running according to plan at her end. She had a squad of drones under her control from her office in the U.S. I was running another squad here. Lance and Ava were watching the street cameras and the feed Rawson had installed at the deserted car.

I'd never been into gaming, but right now it felt weird, like I was playing a game. I pulled back with my thumb on the controller, raising my squad of drones. The lead drone caught Charlie's squad on camera as it rose skyward. I nudged the drone around until I could see Connor and the others. He peered up at me, or rather at the drone, and smiled before he raised his hand. A signal to the others. "Move out!"

The familiar forms of my pack and friends marched from the gate, joining those who waited in the streets beyond. Tyen walked at the back and then just seemed to melt away. I blinked. *Wow, that's some neat party trick.*

Mea whined in agreement, watching through my eyes. It was the most freedom I could give her for the next six and a bit months.

Keeping the drone above and a little bit behind the small army was fairly easy. It was a calm night with barely any wind, which helped a lot. I watched for a little while, then edged the drone up nearer to where Connor walked, leading his army with his brothers and his sister by his side. My gut squeezed. Although I wanted to keep our little bean safe, I also wanted to be by my mate's side. Exhaling heavily through my nose, I put the pre-programmed software into play. It would take over the progress of the drones to automatically follow the trackers placed in Connor's shoes. Drake and his clever mind, along with B'nar and Charlie, had developed a programme that would attach each drone to a shifter. All the drones would be flown by Charlie, Lance, Ava and I, but if necessary, could be overridden and flown by that individual via their mobile phone. It was a fail-safe in case our systems crashed.

Som plopped a plate with a cheese sandwich and a steaming mug of tea down in front of me. I muttered my thanks, not taking my eyes from the screen. Som hovered behind my shoulder. "Y' know, girlie, I can help ya if ya want to eat that food I bothered to bring ya."

I glanced at him and raised my brows. "You can fly drones?"

He snorted and scowled. "I can do way more than just be a skivvy for other folks, and ya know it well."

"I do." I grinned and gave up my seat. "Go on then. I need to pee, but you'll be fine until I get back. Just don't press anything and mess it up."

Som's face darkened, and he glared at me. "Kidding!" I coughed and quickly made my escape. I really did need to pee. It was a downside to the hormones zipping around my body, as well as really achy boobs and tears that seemed to spring from nowhere. I rushed down the corridor to the nearest bathroom, did the quickest pee ever and then ran back. Connor and the others were just reaching the derelict ground.

Lance peered around his screens at me. "You ready? I've got drones one to five already armed."

I nodded. Lance would watch them and take over when the shifter on the ground needed extra backup. We could fire the weapons from here.

I took drones five to ten, and Ava worked with Charlie.

My screens showed me that Connor and the others were entering the car lot building. No one else was visible, thanks to the shadows that covered the derelict ground. Tyen was doing her job well. I swallowed hard. There was no fighting. That meant Balthazar and his kind had come through and taken out the demon guards without bloodshed on our side.

I unmuted the audio of Connor's drone. It was crackly, but his words were audible.

"Owen? This seems a little too easy so far. Thoughts?"

"Hmm. Maybe, or maybe whichever fucktard general is running the Rift for Satan this time, just isn't that good. Maybe he doesn't expect us to attack."

"Maybe." Connor's answer was clipped.

I took control of Connor's drone and let Som watch the rest. Floating it to the ceiling gave me a better view. As each shifter entered the empty warehouse, they disappeared into the ever-growing darkness. My stomach twisted as the concrete floor below the drone wavered like it was melting. My gaze was riveted to the screen. Connor signaled urgently to stop more shifters from entering the space.

A dark shape emerged, but this time it wasn't just a cloud of evil. It had form—a form I'd hoped to never see again.

"Hello, son." Rex Manivera grinned. Even with the grainy image from the drone camera, I could see his wholly dark eyes, empty of everything other than satisfaction and pure evil.

"What the fuck are you doing here?" Connor's reply was reactionary and gave away his surprise, not just to me but to his small army.

Rex shrugged and cocked his head. "Where did you think I'd go when I died? Up there?" He pointed upwards.

"No, I guess not." Connor lowered his voice. "Owen."

Owen's throat and mouth started working as if he was talking, only he was far enough from Connor and the drone for me to miss his words. My fingers squeezed into fists. This was bad—very bad. Rex was a full, soulless demon, one who would be far more powerful now that he was indoctrinated into Satan's service; not only that, he held a grudge for his son...a big one.

"Satan's willing to give you a chance, son. Give him the bitch with the key, join him back in Hell, and he'll let your brother live. Continue this useless war against him, and he'll make Zander, you, and your bitch suffer for an eternity."

"Really? You think I'd give up the key to join him in that shithole?" Connor laughed loudly.

I nudged the drone around a little. Sophie had emerged from the shadows behind Rex, the others surrounding her.

Connor nodded to her. Being out in the open would put all of our cards on the table, particularly when she revealed the Halo, but there was no choice. Sophie had to try and close the Rift before Rex called for more backup. She pulled the Halo from her jacket and put it on the floor, pulling a dagger from her thigh.

"What the fuck are you doing?" Drake's voice came from the bank of computers near Lance.

"My job," Sophie hissed and cut open her arm, aiming a stream of blood onto the Halo.

Drake swore and ordered the others to form a wall between her and Rex.

I gasped and leaned forward, trying to catch the strange words she uttered. The Halo began to glow.

Rex glanced over his shoulder at her. "Now that's not nice, princess." He held out his hand as if to grab the Halo. It shot forward between Drake's legs. None of them had a hope of stopping it.

"No!" yelled Sophie, diving to catch it, but Drake grabbed her arm and pulled her away.

A shield of purple magic slammed down between the Halo and Rex. He bellowed and sent Stone flying into the air. B'nar immediately hit the Rift with a massive blast of magic. Ice covered the ground in front of Connor, covering Rex's legs. The demon howled as the ground steamed and then exploded outwards, sending Connor skidding onto his back, across the floor.

The full scale of the Rift finally came into view. B'nar's magic had revealed it.

"Fuck!" I cursed. It was at least twelve feet wide. As if they had been waiting, more demons rushed through the hole. We'd been fooled. The Rift was far larger than Rawson had been allowed to see.

With no hesitation, I fired into the midst of the demons. The first wave fell before the world around me exploded, sending me tumbling out of my chair and across the room. I slammed into the wall. Pain shot through my left arm, and my lungs burned as a fireball sucked all the air from the room. All I could hear was a deep ringing sound. I blinked, turning my head. What had just happened? Dark, blurred shapes appeared. I tried to move, tried to see where Ava, Lance and Som were, but the air was full of smoke and dust.

"Find her!" roared a familiar voice.

"Walker?" I croaked, my throat bone dry, the moisture sucked out by the hot, dry air.

"Move! Leave the others. She's our target."

Oh, shit! Pain burst through my broken arm. Biting my lip, I forced myself to half-slither on my belly, half-crawl towards the nearest door. The fucker had double-crossed us! I peered through the dust. The approaching figures were all dressed in dark clothes, but it didn't look like fae armour. They all held guns, but none appeared to be alight with magic. One came close enough I could see the insignia on his uniform. Double-crossing mother fucker! SBI! He was working with the SBI. I snarled. He should have brought his army to take me. These guys were going down right before I took that icy bastard out. Fire simmered beneath my skin. Mea might be contained by pregnancy hormones, but Fire wasn't. My nostrils flared, and Mea growled. I hadn't really thought Walker was cold enough to kill my baby and me. My heart hammered against my chest. *My baby!* That fucker was *not* getting my child!

I slipped my knife from its sheath and, ignoring my pain, slashed the tendons at the back of my enemy's knees, both of them. He screamed and fell. I pulled his weapon off him and shot him in the back. No remorse. It was my baby and me, or him. I had no issue with saving my baby above all else.

Bullets ricocheted off the wall behind me.

"Stop firing," roared Walker. They did. "Ember, come out now, and your friends can live."

A pause.

"Fine."

Holding in my scream of pain, I darted to a nearby table and crouched down. Peering over the top, I could see Walker through the dust, illuminated by the flickering overhead lights. There was a scuffle, and another shadow appeared in front of Walker. I squinted. My chest tightened.

Ava.

"Ember? Come out now. She'll die because of you if you don't."

"She'll die if I do."

"Don't, Em! Run!" screamed Ava.

He pushed Ava away from him, aiming his gun at her chest. "What if I give you my word?"

"Too late, you backstabbing pissant of a king!"

"Fine. Get her! Dead or alive. It makes no difference now." And he aimed the gun he held at Ava. Through the darkness, a huge wolf leaped just as Walker pulled the trigger. The wolf growled and fell to the floor but rolled straight back onto its feet. Another shot.

"Lance! No!"

I heard the agony in Ava's voice, but the wolf rose again and snarled, using its strength to sink its teeth into Walker's leg.

Walker yelled, hitting the wolf.

Where was Walker's magic? He wouldn't use a human gun, either...

Bullets hit the door, and there was no more time to think. I let Fire free, sending shot after shot of flames into the shadowed shapes of the SBI agents. They disintegrated. I couldn't reach Walker, not with Lance and Ava so close.

"Run, girlie!" Som roared as another wave of agents barrelled through the broken wall.

No way was I running.

Lanced growled and leaped again, knocking Walker away.

"No! You run!" I shouted, my voice crackling with flame.

Som's eyes widened.

"Ava, Lance!" he yelled as I sent a column of flame into Walker's chest. The High King flew backwards. I pulled my flames into a wall in front of me and waited for his answering magic to attack me. But it didn't. He was on his back in the rubble, screaming as his clothes burned.

I ran to my friends. Lance was on his side, bleeding badly. I didn't go closer. Fire was still ready for battle and wasn't listening to my requests to back down.

"Som, get them out."

I ran to where Walker's body had fallen. And found nothing, no burnt clothes, no blood, no body, no sign of the High King at all.

I turned to the computers. "Damn it!" They weren't intact anymore.

"Go! Find Connor, tell him we've been double crossed," Ava ordered. Tears and blood stained her face, her hands smeared in Lance's blood. My heart broke for her, but I nodded and ran out through the destruction, forcing wings from my back. I didn't fully shift, not willing to risk depleting my power. I launched skywards and headed towards Connor as fast as my wings of fire could take me. I had to get there before Walker. Who knew what he'd do next. If he couldn't get me, were Sophie and the Halo his next target?

CHAPTER 26

I DOVE towards the Halo and plucked it from the ground. "Sophie! Here!" Flicking my wrist, I threw the Halo towards her like I was tossing a frisbee.

Drake snarled and shifted into his Were form. As shifters, we didn't like the in-between, but it gave him the ability to stand upright on his two back legs. With more height, he easily caught the Halo.

Sophie turned towards him, already chanting. I had no choice but to turn away to slay the demons running at me. I swung hard and fast, fighting in my human form. The first one fell, my fist embedded in its chest. The evil cloud of its dark soul slithered back through the Rift. It would be reborn, but not tonight. I scowled at the fiery gateway into Hell. Getting the Rift shut. That's all that mattered. And once it was, I'd hide Ember away and make sure no one could find us.

I spun back to find Sophie with her eyes fixed on the Halo. She was chanting as a soft glow came from her now pale skin and blond hair that hung in waves down her back. Her glamour was gone, replaced by her true form. Drake, Myles and Reed were fully shifted now, ripping and tearing at an influx of demons. Stone fought with his magic. Incinerating any demons that attacked my sister from her back. My brothers were working together to keep Sophie protected.

"Ember! Open fire at the Rift again."

Nothing. Dread filled my heart.

"Lance! Ava!"

Silence.

"Fuck!"

My father laughed maniacally from where his legs were stuck in a thick sheet of ice. It didn't stop the bastard using his hands though, and now Hell had gifted him with even more power. He pulled some of the weaker shifters that had entered the warehouse alongside us towards him, breaking their necks before throwing them into the consuming fire of the Rift.

"Mother fucker!"

He grinned and turned his demonic power on me. Prime pushed through in the blink of an eye. And not only could I feel my loyal wolf there, but the Hell-beast himself, mixed with the dark fae monster that inhabited my body. My grin matched my father's.

"Connor! Help us!" Sophie's wings glowed, and she floated just above the ground.

A demon jumped, trying to grab her ankle. Drake roared and leaped onto its back, snapping his jaws closed on its neck and flipping it over his head. As a man, he was big; as a wolf, he was huge and powerful.

"B'nar! Keep him still!" I roared, pointing towards Rex. B'nar did, sending wave after wave of ice to hold my father, keeping the Rift from melting it away.

More of our allies had entered the fight, and there were wolves and demons locked in battle everywhere. I barrelled through the fray towards my sister and my brothers and skidded to a halt beneath Sophie. She looked down. The wound in her arm bled freely, leaving the Halo covered in it. Drake froze and looked up at Sophie as he caught the scent of her blood. He snarled but could do nothing.

"Now!" I yelled.

She threw it in the air over the Rift, holding the glowing yellow disk aloft with the force of her angel side. Chants left her lips. The runes began to glow just as a dark, ominous vibration rocked the ground. The Rift glowed brighter.

"No!" yelled Sophie.

I looked up. *No. No. No.* Despite her wings, Sophie was being dragged into the vortex of air above the Rift, the Halo along with her.

Drake fought the demons and the storm-force funnel of wind. He ripped and tore to get to her, but there was nothing either of us could do, not when a huge, black column of evil rose from the Rift and plucked her from the air.

"Sophie!" I yelled.

Drake howled and leaped for her at the same time I leaped for him and threw him sideways. He took out three demons as he crashed through them, skidding to a halt on his side before he shot back up. "Do *not* go after her!" The wave of compulsion I sent his way knocked him down to his belly. He snarled and growled and snapped, but it made no difference. He could not defy me.

I howled. The signal to Balthazar to come running. We'd lost. Satan had the Halo, and with it, my sister. I caught Owen's eyes. He snarled, but the wave of compulsion I'd hit Drake with extended to every shifter at the battle. None would follow me. I launched forwards, Prime lending me his speed. The King of Hell-beasts flooded me with his power, turning my blood to lava and my body indestructible to the fire that raged around us. My eyes narrowed, my vision honed in on Sophie. I would not let her fall. I charged through the heat and the raging wind as if it were nothing and plucked my sister from the vortex that dragged her down. With a roar, I threw her from the clutches of the Rift.

Her scream ricocheted off the Rift walls. I looked down. The Halo was being dragged further into the Rift by the vortex. There was no choice. With one last look at my world, I dove into the fiery pit of Hell.

CHAPTER 27

*E*mber

THE BATTLE RAGED both inside and outside the beat-up old building. I surveyed the mess below me. The stone and metal structure was big, but it was still too confined. Balthazar's vamps couldn't get in quickly enough to answer Connor's call for help. My stomach twisted. I'd heard it; I'd felt his anguish. The vamps and extra shifters had been a back-up, which meant Sophie had failed.

With a gust of hot air, I cleared the roof of the vamps trying to get in through it. They landed heavily on the hard ground, but hey, they were immortal...mostly...A hard landing wouldn't kill them.

Fire answered me. Together we heated the roof and then ripped the building open like we were opening a tin can.

As I searched the area below, Sophie came flying out of the pit of fire that was the Rift. My wings grew larger, and without hesitation, I plummeted toward her as she reached the apex of her ascent and began to fall. Drake leaped for her. Shifting into a man, he caught her, burned wings and all, but his speed wasn't enough. It looked like they would both fall into the Rift if I didn't help.

Spiralling, I swooped, and with my wings, knocked them sideways. Stone threw a net of magic beneath them. They landed safely, though it was amidst the fight. No matter how many demons were slain, more kept appearing.

I looked around frantically. No Connor. Ice coated my stomach.

Connor?

Nothing. No bond...just nothing.

Keeping my panic contained, I landed next to Owen, who fought side by side with Rawson. They shifted back to males, both wearing nothing but combats and boots.

"Where's Connor?"

"He dove in there, the stupid bastard." Owen snarled towards the Rift.

"Owen, listen to me. Walker tried to kill me. Do not trust him if he comes here. Stop him before he can stop you."

Owen's face blanched, and he snapped his attention towards B'nar.

"No, I don't believe B'nar knows anything. He's a good man, Owen, you know that."

"I do." His snarl lessened, and he gave me all of his attention.

"Good. Then take care of them all. Rawson...?" My stomach twisted when he briefly closed his eyes and nodded, his lips pressed tightly together.

"I know...go."

Without even taking another breath, I ran. I ran toward the doorway to Hell, and yeah, fuck the consequences because I was not letting Satan take the man I loved or use me to destroy this world. Fire's pulse of reassurance was all I needed. She wouldn't hurt our baby if I fully shifted into her form. She couldn't. We were her salvation, and she would always keep my baby safe. A new wave of determination hit me, and I shifted.

Voices yelled. To stop or to encourage me, I had no idea. It didn't matter. I wouldn't be swayed from this course. Spiralling high, I peered through the eyes of my phoenix. Then dove, straight as an arrow, after my mate.

✦

HOT AIR TRIED to flay my fiery feathers, but nothing could harm me here. I was born of Hell, conjured from the flames of the damned, that scorched this realm, gifted with the immortality of the goddesses who had birthed me with their power and souls. I flew down faster and faster, aiming for the falling form of my mate.

He reached forward, his arms outstretched towards the vortex that clutched the glowing Halo. The runes on it burned brightly. Sophie had unlocked its power, and now Satan himself had a hold of it. My heart hammered, sulphur filling my nostrils. Fire screeched, the sound swallowed by the roaring red hot winds. Connor's dark monstrous form fell faster the closer he got to the vortex. As if he was being dragged down too.

No, Hell would not take Connor, not again. If he fell into the clutches of Hell, this time as the King of Hell-beasts, he'd never escape.

Five inches. Four. Three. Two. One. Connor's large hand gripped the circlet and yanked. It didn't budge as a horrible grating laugh boomed through the air.

I narrowed my eyes and screeched. Catching up, I snapped out my wings to slow my speed and plunged my claws into the swirling shadows, sending a wave of bright flame through it. The vortex disintegrated, and the Halo was free. Connor grabbed it and flung it upwards. "Ember! Take it. Fly! Get it to Sophie and get out. Leave me. Close the Rift!"

I screamed, my heart breaking. Because there it was. My choice. Save my mate. Or save my world and everyone in it. The Halo kept on its upward journey.

Connor looked at me. "Please! Go! Save our family."

My eyes steamed as a tear slipped free. He didn't just mean our baby, he meant everyone who was a part of our lives. They all held a piece of our hearts. "Don't let them die, Ember." And then he was gone. He slammed through the gates of Hell. I didn't know what was on the other side, but I knew if I followed, there would be no way to close this Rift.

Keening with agony, I left my soulmate and propelled myself through the air. My beak snapped closed around the Halo, and I pushed myself harder than I ever had, flashing through the air and bursting from the Rift. I threw the Halo to a shaken Sophie. Wide-eyed, she caught it. I hovered and shrieked down at her before diving back into Hell's embrace.

Yeah? Fuck you, Connor, if you think I'm ever leaving you in Hell again.

CHAPTER 28

onnor

I SLAMMED INTO THE GROUND, but there was no pain. Familiar, white dust coated my clawed hands and my body. I snarled and sprung to my feet. Satan's vortex had disappeared as soon as Ember had speared it with her flames. I grinned. She'd listened. She'd gotten out, and that was all that mattered. Before me was a sight I'd hoped never to see again. The blood still fell in raging torrents from the top of the Hell gates. The rivers of blood around the island of bones still flowed and bubbled. At least I didn't have chains this time.

I moved my attention to the Weres guarding the gates, hope squeezing my chest. And there he was. D, my brother. He surveyed me with a cold hard gaze, his grip tightening on his spear-like weapon. That little movement was enough.

"That's right, you motherfucking demon spawn. I'm coming for you."

The demon inside my brother snarled. Dust exploded under our feet as we both charged. I hit him head-on, my shoulder crushing his ribs. My arms encircled him, my claws spearing him through his back even as he tried, and failed, to do the same to me. He wasn't strong enough, and a Were's claws couldn't penetrate my tough skin. "I am your King!" I roared, trying to get through to the wolf buried in D's mind. "You will do my bidding!" And I physically forced him to his knees. This wasn't going to be gentle as it had been with Reed. I had no time for that, and I was stronger here than I'd ever been in my own realm. The spirit of the King of Hell-beasts thrived on the power of the underworld. He relished it. But I was still in control, and Prime was mine. I controlled him, not the other way around. I clenched my jaw and thrust my spirit into the mind of my brother.

The demon screamed. It had become complacent and lazy here in the confines of Hell. It believed itself safe. I chuckled darkly. How wrong it was. The wall in D's mind wasn't strong, and I smashed through it quickly.

D? We are in danger. I can't be gentle. I'm going to force that fucker from your mind, but you need to be ready to retake your body. If you don't, you will die all over again, and next time there will be no chance of redemption. These bastards will never let you go. Fight, brother. You hear me?

D's wolf answered with a deep spine-tingling growl, the spirit of the man right beside him. The wolf protected his human counterpart even now.

I took that as confirmation he was willing to try. Without hesitation, I searched through D's mind and body for the oily presence of the demon. It scrambled as I hunted it down and cornered it. I surrounded it with my shadow and dragged it kicking and screaming from my brother's Were body, keeping it locked in the grasp of my power. D fell to his knees, his shoulders slumping forward. "Fight!" I hollered at him.

The demon shrieked, trying to force itself into me. I laughed at its pathetic efforts. "I am a King of Hell!" I growled. "Now die, you oily little bastard!" And I shoved it under the boiling surface of the river of blood. It fought and screamed—until it became nothing.

"Oh, Hell-beast," crooned a smooth, sinister voice.

I turned around. My gaze slid over my brother, but it was enough to see he was already moving, trying to stand. *That's it. Get up.* I sent a wave of determination and compulsion into him. His head snapped up, and he growled, not in anger but thanks. I willed him to stay as a Were. His scarred face twisted, but he nodded. Only when I knew he was on his feet did I look at the source of the voice. My heart hammered. A tall, dark man with elegant angular features and the coldest, black eyes I'd ever seen watched me. The satisfied sneer on his upper lip was enough. I knew who this was. He should incite terror in my soul, but we'd beaten his rule before. We'd do it again. No matter his guise, he no longer scared me.

Prime growled, but it wasn't fear he felt, only a determination never to become this creature's servant ever again. I felt the heat of the red river against my back. We'd end our existence here if necessary, but we'd never bow before him again.

"Hell-beast, you disappoint me. You have returned only to kill my soldiers? Surely you know I don't tolerate such betrayals." He cocked his head, his eyes flaring with burnished ruby flames.

I didn't speak. Instead, I fortified my mind. Satan could manipulate and control minds as easily as a human could breathe. It was one of his favourite forms of torture.

"Hm? No words?" He pushed against my mind, and my shadow fae, not of this world or the human realm, blocked his probing power with a wall of its own. Satan grinned. "I'd love to play with you, Hell-beast, to break you down to nothing more than a begging mess at my feet, but I have other toys, which are vastly more important to me than your stinking hide." His face turned cruel and he reached out, his arm disappearing into a rip in the air. When he withdrew it, his limb was black and red, claws ripping into his prize.

My fury could not be contained. Flame and shadow burst from me, swirling around Prime like a firestorm.

Satan chuckled.

My howl ripped from my throat, echoed above and beyond the gates of Hell. Zander turned his head towards me, and I bellowed my fury. His face was skeletal, his naked body emaciated. It seemed all life had been sucked from his flesh and all energy from his soul. His tortured eyes met mine. No matter how he had suffered, he shook his head, and I understood. *Don't give in to him.*

"Hm, I gave your brother to my succubus demons. They can be so cruel, can't they?" He tightened that clawed hand around Zander's neck, his nails digging in deep. "Every time they sucked the life from him, I brought him back. His screams amused me." Zander's blood dripped from the wounds Satan's nails had made in a steady stream. "Now, where is my Halo?" He dangled Zander out over the boiling red river. "Tell me, and he gets to keep his flesh and bone body. Defy me, and I drop him in. His body would boil to death, but his soul, ahh, now that would be mine for eternity."

I snarled and took a step forward. Satan's grin was pure evil, his eyes flaring with delight. "Now, now. That's not how this works." He lowered Zander until his feet were in the blood lava.

Zander screamed and thrashed. Satan lifted him. "Tell me who has my Halo and I will let you all..." His eyes flicked to D, who stood at my shoulder, strong and determined. "...serve me, in my new kingdom."

He meant on Earth.

"Don't. You. Fucking. Do it," growled Zander, panting, his face like a death mask.

Satan shook him. "Hush, now." And he sealed Zander's mouth shut with a look, blocking his nostrils so he couldn't breathe. And even in Hell, flesh and blood demons needed the sulphurous air to survive. Zander thrashed weakly.

I growled and snapped my teeth. The other guard turned his head. D glanced at it, then me.

"Kill it. That river will end any living thing, flesh or spirit."

D snarled, then launched himself into a sprint. There was no compassion in him. I could feel it. Killing the Were, as well as the demon, was a mercy. His determination to end its suffering filtered into me.

Satan sighed and looked at his wrist as if he were wearing a watch. "Time's a-ticking, Hell-beast. But, no matter. Your time is up. You have served your purpose. And my army awaits." His dark gaze rose to the gates.

What the fuck did that mean? With dread in my heart. I looked up. A beautiful firebird shot through the gates of Hell and dove for us.

"My Halo is, of course, not my main objective." Satan shrugged and winked at me. "But keeping you here meant she would come for you. Love is so predictable." And he threw Zander in the air. Huge bat-like wings exploded from Satan's back, and he spiralled upward, heading right for Ember at the same time as swarms of winged demons descended upon her.

I lost my breath. I could not fly. My heart broke as my mate approached her destiny, and our world neared its apocalypse. My brother fell through the air towards his demise. No matter if we lived or died, I would not fail him. I thrust out my shadow and ensnared my brother, dragging him from the air before any more of his body could touch the bubbling blood lava.

His feet were burned and blistered up to his ankles, his body covered in scars and bruising. D helped me drag Zander away from the gates. Zander's face was blue, his eyes closed and his chest heaving in an attempt to breathe. Satan's magic was born of this realm, and I had nothing like it. With no other choice, I shoved my fingers into the burning lava, gritting my teeth against the pain. But it was nothing compared to the agony in my heart. Above us, my mate fought the army of Hell and its king, alone. Returning to Zander's side, I lifted my fingers above his sealed mouth and nose. "This is going to hurt."

Zander didn't move.

I dripped the boiling lava against his mouth and nostrils, hoping against hope that it would burn through the magic.

Above us Ember fought. She fought so hard. Fire spewed from her great beak, and she incinerated demon after demon. But her fate was sealed. She couldn't win. I felt a pulse of fear—hers. Satan changed form, becoming bigger, his reach far more than a phoenix less than half his size could evade. His red wings caught her in their snare and brought her, still fighting, into his embrace. She screeched down at me, a pulse of love hitting me so hard, it drove me to my knees. I let loose a soul-deep roar and launched myself at the gates, slamming my claws into the bone like substance, and clawed my way up to where Satan had her in his grip, only to slip and fall to the island of bone.

Satan crushed Ember's burning form against his body, his eyes burning with a glee the fire in them couldn't conceal. His laugh echoed throughout the realms of Hell, only to receive an answering clamor from his awaiting army.

"Mother Wolf," breathed D after he shifted back to his human form. "He planned this, didn't he?"

I flipped onto my feet, shifting back too, Prime simmering just beneath my skin. "Yes. He let us find the Halo. He let us bring it to the Rift, and he dragged Sophie in knowing that I'd rescue her." I eyed Zander, who still looked slightly blue. The blood had opened his mouth and nostrils, leaving them burned and blistered but free. "He also knew I'd fall in here again and try to rescue you and my brother. It's why he kept you here, near the gate. That's why he let me see you when I was here before." I shook Zander. "Wake up, brother!"

Zander groaned.

D swore. "I'm sorry, Prime."

"Don't be ridiculous. How could you know? Or do anything about it if you did? He used us, all of us, to get what he wanted. The key to the Hell gates." Anger and terror mixed in equal measure in my gut. My soul mate and my baby were in the hands of the Devil, and there was nothing I could do...

Above us, Ember shrieked. Her pain hit me straight in my soul, dropping me to my knees, both me and Prime bellowing loud enough we shook the gates of Hell.

CHAPTER 29

THE GLOWING HOT chains wound around me, tethering me to my fate. Fire's voice was loud in her rage. But beneath all that anger was fear, a fear so cold it nearly severed my connection to her.

Satan could trap us, but he wouldn't end us. None of that really mattered much, though, since, in my heart, I knew I did not want to live without my soul-mate and our family. What would be the point? How could I exist, knowing that I caused the downfall of our world and every other, including the kingdom of Heaven, if Satan found his Halo again?

It had to be destroyed—as, I feared, did I.

Below me, Connor tried to climb the gates, his desperation to reach me heartbreaking. I squawked, trying to get him to leave me. But where would he go? He fell backwards.

"Do not worry about them, little firebird. They can go nowhere. I will kill his brothers, of course. But I think an eternity of staring up at the mate he can never touch, knowing she still carries the child he can never hold, will be a delightful punishment for the King of Hell-beasts, the traitor who stole my creations and gifted them to another world."

Fire burned hotter, keeping me locked in the safety of her embrace. The one thing Satan couldn't do, even with all his power, was force our spirits to

851

part. Not now that I was pregnant. I felt the strength of my connection to Fire, now more than ever.

Chained to the side of the gates, I felt the moment they started to vibrate. Satan laughed. "This is your purpose. These gates feel your power." He touched a finger to my wings, and when he pulled it back, it was blistered. "Interesting." He cocked his head. "The goddesses who made you and these gates wanted you to be a weapon against me, too. Maybe once I have conquered your world, and my creatures are free, I will return and destroy you. Keeping these gates open will not be important to me then." And he dove elegantly backwards off the gate, spiralling down and swooping over Connor's head before he rose skyward. His winged troops gathered behind him, the stormy sky turning black from the swarm about to invade the world I loved.

Unbidden, flames spread from my wings. I fought and sobbed, but there was nothing I could do as the massive gates absorbed my power. They shuddered and burst into flames, Fire turning them to ash within what felt like seconds. Chained and captive, I was forced to watch as I unleashed Hell on Earth. Horror filled me. This was my fault. I should have let Walker end me. A rush of wind hit me as thousands upon thousands of demons flew through the gaping expanse, Satan bellowing his war cry as he watched his army invade Earth.

I sobbed. Fire couldn't cry, but her pain at what we had done tore at my soul. Mea growled at us both, but her nudge to fight for our freedom, although well-meaning, was useless. Every time we thrashed against the chains, they tightened further. I screamed my frustration and agony. Slowly, darkness and lethargy invaded me. I looked down, needing to see my mate whole.

Don't you ever give up!

His voice was in my head. I swallowed my tears. Even Hell couldn't break our bond.

Far, far below me, he began to climb.

CHAPTER Twenty nine
Owen

"Ember! Don't you fucking do it!" I bellowed. But she didn't hear me or chose not to. The stunning bird of fire somersaulted in the air and dove into the Rift with a screech that tore at my heart. "Godsdammit!"

I swooped down and picked up a fae weapon off the ground, hoping against hope that my King and Queen would be successful, but the chances were slim.

I met Sophie's gaze before searching out my brothers. All in wolf form, they howled loudly. Rawson's bear lumbered towards Jed, who was fighting a pocket of demons alone. We were winning, but if we couldn't close this Rift, they would keep coming.

The ground beneath our feet pulsed and vibrated. Loud buzzing, like a swarm of locusts, echoed from the Rift, accompanied by a roar that froze the blood in my veins.

Shit, Connor had been right. *He* was coming. "Sophie! Close it! Now!" I bellowed.

Sophie had long since shed her gothic, fighter girl look. I'd been there when Balthazar had caught her trying to run from him at the Gambit, so I knew that she was part angel. I blinked, almost blinded as she began to glow. Her wings burned brightly, and her golden hair shone, her whole body so bright it was as if she'd been injected with sunlight. She might only be half-angel, but her angel side definitely outgunned her shifter. She moved her wings with a beauty and grace that was breathtaking.

I cracked my neck, ready for our final battle. Connor, the stupid bastard, had known he was going into Hell. I had no idea why he'd just let himself fall into the Rift, but he sure as fuck could have gotten himself out if he'd wanted. He was extra powerful there, and Hell hadn't kept him contained before. I just hoped it wouldn't now. We needed him. *I* needed him.

Pushing those weak thoughts from my mind, I concentrated on Sophie.

She held the Halo above her and lifted it towards the heavens. I had no idea what she would do, but I prayed to the Mother Wolf it would work.

Her sweet, melodious voice carried through the air even above the clatter of the fight. The Halo flashed into life, the runes upon it burning brightly, sending a signal into the night. Around Sophie, the air exploded with light, the night sky so lit up I had to cringe away from it. The fight zone suddenly went quiet. The only voices were those of my brothers and allies. When I looked aloft again, an army of angels floated above us. A magnificent woman touched Sophie's cheek. I swallowed hard. Her beauty hurt my eyes. I had no idea who she was or where these beautiful supernatural beings had come from, but I wasn't going to question it. Not when the ground shook enough to knock us from our feet and send the unsupported aluminium walls of the building tumbling outwards.

Drake howled up at Sophie. A warning. He couldn't protect her when she was up there. She ignored him.

"They are here!" she yelled. "Get back!" We all heard her. Every single one of our supernatural armies as we fought side by side.

Ice covered my skin. This was it. Judgement day. For our world and all others.

"Look!" B'nar bellowed. He pointed at something behind me. I turned as the wind whipped dust into my eyes and mouth. The portal was huge, and pouring from it was an army like none I'd ever seen. Fae warriors dressed in gleaming armour and wielding weapons alight with fae magic sprinted through, Walker at their head.

He ran to his son, embracing him. Ember's words came back to me. I had no idea how Walker had been at the compound and in Faerie. But there was no time to figure it out. The ground beneath us surged upward then collapsed into the Rift.

"Fall back!" I yelled, sprinting for safety. Whatever was coming, it was immense; the Rift was no longer a Rift. We had failed. Ember had been caught, and she had opened the gates of Hell.

Heat surged from the ground, superheating the air we breathed until it burned my lungs, sulphur filling my nostrils.

Above us, helicopters whirred. I recognised the insignias on the pilot uniforms and the type of helicopters.

The fucking SBI is working with us?

A surge of relief hit me, along with a huge helping of surprise. How or why they were here could be answered if we survived. We might not have the numbers Hell had, but we weren't going down without a fight.

Walker signaled the helicopters to fire on the Rift. The angels held back as the gunships pelted shells at the first surge of winged demons.

Sophie chanted, and the Halo lit up again.

I sprinted towards Walker. "Hey! Walker! Pull the 'copters back!"

Sophie and the others needed a clear shot at this. If it didn't work, then all the helicopters and firepower in the world wouldn't stop what was coming. My nostrils flared. I glanced at Selina. Just like always, I *felt* her. I knew exactly where she was, and even if she didn't want me, I'd fight and die for her and Devon. An image of Devon flashed in my mind, fortifying my determination. As if she felt my attention, she glanced over. It was hard to drag my gaze away before she caught me looking. She already held far too much power over me, but she didn't need to know that.

Walker watched me approach, his face as cold as ever.

"Walker, pull them back. Sophie knows how to use the Halo." I pointed upwards to the army of angels with glowing wings. "They all do."

Walker met his son's gaze. B'nar nodded once. It was enough.

Walker motioned for the birds to move back. They did.

Sophie pointed the Halo down towards hell and then dove, driving herself forward. I gaped as the army of angels followed her into the underworld, driving the deluge of demons back with their light.

Drake howled and raced to the edge of the burning pit. Reed and Myles shifted and grabbed him, dragging the distraught wolf from the edge.

I shifted and bolted over towards Selina, ripping and fighting my way to her. Just like Drake, I had my reasons, whether I wanted them or not. Selina watched me approach. She hadn't shifted; instead fighting with the fae weapon she had been given. It struck me as odd that she had chosen to fight in human form, but now wasn't the time to question her decision. Blood covered and magnificent, her chest rose and fell, a fierce glint in her eyes. I drank in the sight of her, snarling at the lacerations across her arms and face. No matter her injuries, she was a survivor. Pride warmed my heart. Her soul would burn brightly enough I would always find her, in this life or the next. She may try to push me away, but no matter what, I'd protect her. Beside her, Shannon ended another foe, and in wolf form, lay on her belly, panting heavily. She had a deep gash in her hind leg that dripped blood on the floor.

"I don't need you to babysit me," Selina snapped.

I ignored her. If we were going to die, like it or not, I would be by her side.

Rawson lumbered over and shifted while he walked. Shannon was too exhausted to shift. He clothed himself only to rip off his shirt. He was about to press it against Shannon's wound when a layer of purple magic fell around Shannon. Stone snarled at Rawson, who shrugged and threw the shirt away with a shrug. "All yours, brother," he rumbled.

Lionel and Kawan joined us, as did Jed. His silverback turned away, guarding our backs. I huffed. He deserved respect for not running when he could. He'd fought hard. B'nar and Walker joined us just before Balthazar appeared in a flurry of shadow, his razor-sharp fingernails on display and his long canines and chin covered in blood. A murderous light gleamed in his eyes as he pondered the entrance to hell.

I observed him through the eyes of my wolf, scenting his desire, the lure of the darkness and flames of Hell. His jaw clenched, but he held back from jumping, fighting the pull of the underworld.

The ground continued to vibrate, but no more demons emerged. The red fire turned to white light, the fire of Hell drowned by the light of the angels.

Side by side with my brothers, both old and new, we waited.

Armageddon.

Or redemption.

Only destiny knew the answer.

CHAPTER 30

mber

THE GAPING VOID stretched out as far as my eyes could see. Hot sulphurous wind howled, dragging at my fire which burned and burned, keeping the gates from reforming.

Ember! Baby, don't you give up!

I peered down, a spark of hope kindling deep in my soul. Even from so high, I could see every contraction of his muscles, hear every determined grunt he gave. Below him, Zander lay on the ground. His head tilted back. Joy hit me. He was alive. But he didn't move. He had to be injured. Another male knelt by his side. I had no idea who it was—until he too peered up at me. Dagnar! Connor's brother had been killed in the fight rings by Stone. Dagnar must have been possessed by a demon, and Connor must have freed him the same way he did Reed. *Thank you, Mother Wolf. At least Connor won't face an eternity here alone.*

My attention fixed back on Connor, and I didn't take my eyes from him. With every jab of his long claws into the frame of the gates, he got closer. The determination on his face never faltered, his grip sure and powerful. Mea whined, willing Prime closer as I willed Connor closer. I'd always thought I'd be strong enough to free myself from any situation I found myself in. When I'd lost everyone before, when Lyss had died, and Connor and Rawson had disappeared, I'd made a promise to myself that I would never again need or rely on anyone to save me. I blinked. How wrong I'd been. I hadn't realised that strength came from the people I chose to surround myself with. My mate would fight for me no matter the outcome to himself. My friends and pack would fight for me, Mea would never let me fall into despair, and Fire would do all she could to keep me alive.

A blast of light hit my face. I looked up, and relief flowed through me.

Sophie dove down, spiralling between the falling carcasses of burning demons.

From the burning Rift, the angel army descended head-first into Hell. Together they extended their wings, and light exploded from the Halo Sophie held in front of her.

The power of its light catapulted Satan back into the deepest reaches of Hell. He roared, his bellow fading until it became nothing.

The ash of the demon army fell like a macabre rain into the boiling river of blood.

Connor reached me. He anchored his bulk with his clawed feet and grabbed the chains in his huge hands. His muscles contracted and bulged as he thundered, the veins in his neck engorging. He met my eyes and increased his efforts.

Sophie hovered nearby. "Mother! Get the others! When she's free, the gates will close. Hurry!" She pointed down to D and Zander. Four angels plummeted down. "Connor! Hurry! We don't have much time. The Halo has banished him to the lowest level of Hell, but he will fight its power to return and keep his key."

Connor's body shook with the effort, and he bellowed at the top of his lungs, the sound rattling the air. His size increased, and his muscles bulged under the strain, the chains creaking and groaning.

"That's it! It's working!" yelled Sophie.

The angels carrying Zander and D whooshed passed, propelling upwards through the hot winds. Connor looked me in the eye.

Go! Please! I whispered down our bond.

He snarled, baring his teeth. With a final "MINE!" at the top of his lungs, the chains snapped.

Free, I spiralled toward the ground before regaining control so Fire and I could swoop back up. In a move that required utter trust, Connor leaped into the air. I wrapped him in my Fire, dragging him away from the gates as they reformed behind us. A furious roar rattled the air. I grinned and stuck up a middle finger to the Devil himself.

Sophie flapped her beautiful wings, wings that were charred by the heat of Hell and covered with the burned bones of demons, but she didn't stop. Gritting her teeth and clutching the Halo, she propelled herself forward.

I slowed, allowing the angels to gain distance from us. I could feel the energy of our world merging with the winds of Hell. The fire that blazed along the edges of the cavernous Rift touched neither of us. Satan might be stuck without me to open the gates to his prison, but his minions weren't; and with a Rift this big, their numbers would soon overwhelm the British Isles.

Fire was strong after absorbing the fires of Hell. So was Connor.

We need to close it.

I know.

Together.

No, Firecracker. This is all yours. Do your thing. Destroy it. I will be waiting for you on the other side. Now put me down. I can walk.

Those were always my words to him when he carried me. Grinning, I did. Fire felt my amusement and gave a high pitched cry. His claws gently brushed my wings, his Hell-beast shining through his eyes. Then he was gone, running through the air as if he were on solid ground, his speed so fast he was a blur.

I peered into the vortex of wind and fire. The gates were no longer visible; nothing was.

Let's do this.

Mea howled in unison with Fire's cry, pulsing her own brand of power into my soul. My wings grew. Fire grew until our wingspan was just short of touching the sides of the Rift. We dove back down towards Hell, then, when we had enough speed, somersaulted and drove upwards spiralling, whipping the flames into a destructive vortex. Fire took control of them then, moulding them to her will. I glanced down through her eyes. A whirlpool of fire followed us, dragging the sides of the Rift inwards, collapsing it in on itself. Up. Up. Up.

The world became nothing but flames and wind.

We burst through the Rift into the night sky, an eruption of flame in our wake. Fire spiralled into the sky and stopped. With her, I peered down, searching for my mate.

Connor stood, panting by the edge of the collapsed and smoking Rift, surrounded by his brothers and our allies. The angels hovered nearby. The angels would not touch their feet to the earth. They couldn't if they wanted to return to their own realm. Sophie and what had to be her mother landed. I wondered how they had come back together, where Sophie's mother lived... was she half-angel? But those were questions for another day.

Fire cried out her gratitude and flapped her wings, sending sparks into the night. Together we bowed our heads low. It was the only way I had to convey my heartfelt thanks for the risk the angels had taken. Not just for Connor and me, but for our world.

Sophie's mother embraced her, and I felt a tear slip from my eyes as Connor's sister clutched the beautiful woman. A male angel lowered himself and gently tapped Sophie's mother on the shoulder. She nodded, looked at me, and then glanced at Connor before her fingers lightly brushed her daughter's cheek. She extended her stunning wings and raised upward. I didn't know where she was going, but it seemed the other angels did. In the blink of an eye, they were gone. Just streaks of light in the night.

Fire faded back a little, happy, now we were safe, to let me take back control. I lowered myself to the ground, but it wasn't relief that was tightening my belly. As soon as my boots hit the ground, I wrapped the High King of Faerie in a swathe of fire. "You fucking traitor! You tried to kill my baby and me!"

"Ember! What in the Mother's name are you doing?" Connor yelled as I did my best to burn the silver-haired bastard to death.

Walker fought me, his magic hissing as it hit my flames.

"Ember! Stop!" yelled another voice. "It wasn't him!"

Alex ran at me, his face twisted and pale.

I snarled. "Yes, it was. I saw him! He shot Lance!"

"No! No, he didn't! It was Xania! Please. Stop."

Connor shifted and stood directly in the path of my flames. B'nar leaped, pulling his father away.

"What are you doing?" My mate's blue eyes were so bright, so beautiful. All I wanted was to hold him, to rejoice at our triumph, but Walker had almost killed me, and by default, our child. He wouldn't get away with it. Not this time. "He betrayed us again. He shot your friend."

"Sweetness, no, he didn't. Look."

I turned to where Connor pointed. Alex held Xania in some fae cuffs. Her posture was upright, her face furious. My mouth fell open, and I glanced from her to Walker.

"Alex has his sister in cuffs for a reason. I think we should hear him out first." His mouth tilted up a little. "Before you incinerate our allies."

My eyes narrowed. "I'll incinerate anyone who tries to kill our child."

He reached out and touched my cheek with his fingertips. "As will I. But I get the feeling that it wasn't Walker."

Walker shook off his son's assistance and strode towards me. "Whatever you think I did, it wasn't me. I was in Faerie. Gathering this army."

For the first time, I took in the sheer amount of people that surrounded the ruined car lot. My gaze still narrowed on him. "Well, it sure looked like you."

"Ember. Shapeshifter. Remember?" He looked at Xania. His eyes were so cold I thought he might freeze her on the spot.

"That was her? But why? This makes no sense to me."

The thump thump thump of rotor blades disturbed the air. We had to wait for the helicopter to land before we could speak again. The rotors soon slowed enough to talk again.

"I know it doesn't. But it will soon." Walker crossed his arms and looked towards the group of people climbing out of the belly of the SBI gun-ship.

Balthazar quietly stood back to allow a diminutive female to enter our group.

She looked to be about thirty and stunningly beautiful. Her petite figure was curved and flawless, and there was not a single jet-black hair out of place. She was utter perfection to look at, but her grey eyes were cold and shrewd. Despite her tiny stature, there was an air of power about her that prickled against my skin like Connor's used to. I gaped as all the males nearby stared at her as if unable to tear their gazes away. All except Connor and Walker. Even Alex had relaxed his hold on his sister.

Walker's brows twitched down minutely, and he flicked the fingers of his right hand. Alex shook his head, blinking rapidly.

The woman smirked and lifted her chin. "High King L'nar Voltair. What is the meaning of this? You requested my presence. I am here. Now explain." The woman's gaze fell on Xania, and for a fraction of a second, I swore I saw panic flare in her eyes.

Walker cocked his head, his face blank. "First, let me introduce you." He looked at me and then Connor before glancing at Owen. "This, my friends, is the Overseer of the SBI."

I inhaled sharply. "The Overseer?"

I met Connor's gaze. The identity of the Overseer had always been a secret to the masses of shifters and agents of the SBI.

Walker whispered some words, and all the males who seemed to have been in a daze straightened and shook their heads as if clearing them.

"That's right. She's a succubus. A clever one. One who has manipulated the fools in management of the most powerful supernatural organisation in this world to do her bidding."

The woman smiled and shrugged. "Lust, sex and power are potent tools of persuasion."

"They are," he agreed. "This succubus is the one who started all of this. She led Doherty to follow Berith with promises of riches and power. And she has manipulated other directors within the powerful levels of the SBI to do what-ever she asked." He looked directly at the Overseer. His magic whipped out and wrapped around her like a vice. She shrieked and fought, but he made her drop to her knees. "There is no use fighting, succubus. I am more powerful than you will ever be, and now I know who and what you are, I can protect myself and all these people from your influence. You are done. It's over."

"This is really interesting, Walker, but my feet are killing me, my back hurts, and if I don't get to pee very soon, this is going to get messy. What's this got to do with nearly killing me and my baby?" I snapped.

Connor's mouth twitched, and he wound an arm around my waist, pulling me close. I melted into his side and mirrored the gesture, revelling in the warmth of his naked skin.

"Because this succubus did a deal with Xania—to betray me and kill you both." Walker's attention landed directly on Xania. The doppelganger met his gaze, her chin lifted, and her eyes burned with hatred. "You were the one who betrayed me." Walker's words weren't a question, but Xania sneered.

"Yes, and I'd do it again. I've had to put up with your self-righteous bullshit for the past three hundred years! First, my mother and father used me and then sold me. And then, you used me. For years, I have been worth nothing to you except for the usefulness of my ability to change my appearance. Not once has anyone cared who I really am or what I want in this never-ending nightmare of existence."

I gaped at her then my anger exploded. "It was you? You tried to kill me and my baby! *You* killed Lance!"

"No, I didn't try to kill you, or you'd be dead." She sneered. "The others got hurt because they were stupid enough to get in my way." She stared right at the Overseer. "*She* wanted you so that she could do a deal with the Devil. *She* thought she'd be able to manipulate the King of Hell himself if she had you and the Halo as bargaining chips."

"And what was in it for you?" Connor's voice was low and gravelly, his eyes flaring red.

If I wanted to kick her into Hell for trying to harm me and our baby, Connor wanted to rip her apart.

She smiled bitterly and met Walker's gaze. And there it was for all to see. Love. But not one that meant happy endings and joy. It was a love that had turned to bitterness and hate. "Death."

"Whose?" I asked.

"Mine..." she whispered, and met Walker's icy stare. He held her gaze. "Done," he said and shot his magic into her chest. Alex let go, his eyes closed, his face twisted, and his hands fisted. My heart went out to him. He might not have been close to her, but Xania was still his sister, his blood.

Xania fell sideways and began to wheeze a laugh as ice covered her body. "Do you know how much I hate you? All these years of serving you, of being faithful—of loving you and no one else." Her voice broke, and tears seeped from her eyes only to freeze on her cheeks. "And..." she gasped... "Not once...did you look...at me...as anything other than...your slave," her breathing turned labored." She smiled, then collapsed back. "If I can't. Have you, then no one else can either... The clock is ticking. King Ventris L'nar Voltair."

Walker's face blanched of all colour, as did B'nar's. B'nar took two strides and squatted down, grabbing her shoulders. "How do you know his name? What have you done?"

I'd never heard B'nar sound so frightened.

In Faerie, names had power...

Xania just wheezed, her gaze fixed on Walker until the ice covered her completely. Walker put his hand on B'nar's shoulder. "It's too late, son."

B'nar turned to the succubus. "What did she mean?" he growled. "What did she do?"

The succubus gave him a sultry smile. "Set me free, and I will tell you."

B'nar snarled. "Your kind doesn't affect me. Just like my father, my heart is ice. Tell me!" he roared.

She smiled, her eyes glinting. "My freedom and life for that knowledge, Prince Heir—or watch your father die...slowly."

"Fine. Father? Grant her freedom," B'nar snapped.

Walker met his gaze, his jaw set. Giving in wasn't Walker's strong suit.

Connor edged closer. He met Owen's gaze, and something passed between them.

"She could be lying." Walker's eyes never left her face. "Succubus are not like us. They lie through their teeth, just like humans."

I stiffened but didn't miss it when B'nar's gaze flicked to Blue.

The succubus smirked, her luscious full lips mesmerising. "Oh, I'm not lying, High King. Wouldn't you like to know how you're going to die? Because the wheels are in motion. Some actions will result in your death; others will not."

"Father. Please." B'nar growled the words in Walker's ear.

I'd never heard B'nar ask for anything. It was a testament to how worried he was. Blue stared at him like she was seeing him for the first time. Her gaze didn't stray from him, not even when I willed her to look at me.

Walker met Connor's gaze, his lips a thin pale line. He nodded. "I will not end your life, Succubus."

She smirked. "Oh, I am not that stupid, High King. Guarantee no other person in this gathering will either."

Walker nodded. "Guaranteed. You will be freed from my bindings as soon as you tell me the truth."

Her smile was satisfied. But she spoke to B'nar, not Walker. "Xania is old. She has spent years trying to find a way to kill not only herself but her master. She both loved him and hated him. Now that she has uttered his true name, your father is cursed. He cannot return to Faerie. As soon as he steps over the borders, he will die—slowly but surely. The curse will eat away at his body and mind until there is nothing left but a shell."

"How did she discover his true name?" B'nar asked, his face paler and his eyes colder than ever.

The succubus shrugged. "All she told me was that she had the curse made by a shadow fae in Orth many years ago when he first rejected her, and she has kept it close all these years. All she needed to activate it was to utter his name. She didn't know it until a few days ago." She studied Walker, who stood with his jaw clenched and his hands fisted. "She asked you so many times to end her life, and you'd never do it. She had nothing to live for. A soul that broken is easy to manipulate. The only thing they crave is an end to their loneliness and suffering. I offered it to her. I can suck a soul from their vessel until there is nothing left." She smiled, all darkness and cunning. "And be certain they enjoy it whilst I do it.

"How do we break the curse?" B'nar asked.

She laughed. "You can't. A deal with a fae is binding. I answered your question. You get no more. My freedom and my life. Now."

B'nar looked murderous. "No."

"Let her go, son."

B'nar turned his murderous gaze upon his father.

"Do not question me." Walker met his son's gaze—and neither backed down.

B'nar's nostrils flared, his whole body tense, ready to kill the threat to his father and his King, even if it meant defying Walker himself. Blue moved her arm. Walker couldn't see it, but I knew my friend. She had reached out, finally, to support or soothe, or perhaps both. I had no idea. B'nar's jaw remained clenched, but his shoulders relaxed minutely. Silently, he nodded.

Walker unbound the succubus. She stood and turned...directly into Owen. He smiled down at her, his large body effectively stopping her escape.

Connor snarled. It was a signal.

Owen shifted. Before the succubus could blink, he snapped his jaws closed around her neck and ripped out her throat. Walker watched dispassionately as she fell to the ground in a puddle of her own bluish blood, choking to death.

Owen met Connor's gaze, and my mate nodded. Owen shifted back and wiped his mouth. We all got used to the taste of blood in our mouths after a kill, but he spat hers from his mouth, his face contorted. "Ugh. She tastes disgusting."

Remembering what Connor had said about Xania's ability to regenerate, I unwound my arm from my mate's waist and looked down at her ice-encased body. Without any regret, I called up Fire.

"Wait," B'nar hissed. Green magic hit Xania with enough force to shatter her remains. His beautiful face didn't alter. "Will that end her?" He looked to his father.

Walker nodded. "If Ember burns her and the ash is separated—yes."

Without another word, I used my fast ebbing energy to burn her body to ash before turning and doing the same to the Overseer. "Deals with the fae are tricky things," I murmured to her glassy eyes as my flames consumed her.

"Specifics are what you need. Most of us in this room aren't just people. You were in your ivory tower for too long."

Connor eyed the grounded helicopters, then Walker. "So? The SBI, hm?"

Walker straightened his spine and nodded. "I'd suspected it was her causing problems in the SBI for a long time. Proving it was hard. She had files on us all, including me. This whole situation, from me being betrayed by Xania to the attack on Ember, was orchestrated by her. She wanted to do a deal with the Devil." He huffed. "A succubus demon who wanted to return to her master with enough power and bargaining chips to dictate the terms of her existence. If we hadn't ended her, Satan would have taken what he wanted and finished her, anyway."

Connor nodded. "Well, it's done now. Let's get this place cleaned up."

Walker took in everything as he observed the carnage. "Indeed. For now, I will be heading the SBI troops on Earth. We have helicopters. We'll use them to ferry the injured to the nearest SBI hospital. Any who don't want to be treated in a facility can be treated here. And then take their chances."

FOR HOURS, I helped treat the injured, then got them into some kind of transport to be moved. Som and Ava arrived with our SUV's. Ava's face was dull, devoid of any emotion. She functioned like a robot, doing what was asked of her. I hated that emptiness in her eyes. It reminded me so much of how Rawson had been after Lyss had died. And I got it; I really did. She'd keep her shit together...until she didn't have to anymore. And when that time came, I'd be there for her—we all would.

I forced my eyelids to stay open, my body to keep functioning, but I glanced at my battle worn and injured friends with concern. I wanted to talk with them, especially Alex, who smiled sadly at me, nodded, then disappeared into the melee. My gut twisted. Seeing your sister die, being a part of that, and hearing the lengths she'd gone to, just so that she could die? It must have destroyed him. I hoped he'd come back to us, but time had little meaning to an immortal. I swallowed hard. I might never see him again.

Blue sat with her back against a wall, watching B'nar and Walker as they talked, surrounded by royal guards and SBI agents. I wondered what would happen to the High King now.

Connor's brothers stood around him like the protective wall of muscle and power they were. Even Jed was a part of that circle. Only Shannon and Stone were missing. Som and Ava had taken Stone, Shannon, Tyen and Zander back to the compound.

Rawson worked alongside me, as did Lionel. I tried to hide a yawn as I passed a bandage to a shifter who was missing a chunk out of his upper arm.

Rawson eyed me with concern. I smiled, but his scowl only depended. Damn, I'd seen that look so many times over the years. He was about to give me a hard time.

"Ember, we have to get you to the compound. You need food and rest, in that order."

"I'm not leaving my mate," I said stubbornly, searching out Connor, who had joined Walker and B'nar.

Rawson raised a brow. "You are if he tells you to. Lionel, watch her."

Lionel grinned and winked at me. "S'alright, we know you won't run away. Rawson just wants you safe, same as we all do, you carrying a royal heir and all that."

I rolled my eyes but smiled to myself as I helped the shifter bandage his arm. When we were done, I sat down. My hands trembled. Yeah, my adrenaline was used up. Fire was used up, and Mea couldn't give me any more energy.

"Come on." I held out my hand, and Lionel heaved me up. Without waiting for Rawson to ask Connor, I walked to my mate's side.

"We still have an accord, King of Shifters?" I heard Balthazar say in his midnight smooth voice. He looked at me with amusement as I shuddered and slipped my hand into Connor's. Rude? Yeah, probably, but the Count's voice had that kind of effect on me. He was dangerous. Connor gripped my hand harder, his nostrils flaring, but he nodded calmly.

"We do, Count. If you need us, we will come."

"In that case, me and mine bid you farewell." Count Balthazar Rossi bowed his head graciously to Connor and me. Then he was gone.

I blinked at the space where he'd just been. "Um...just...wow."

Connor's mouth ticked up at the edges. "If that's all it takes to impress you, my queen." He kissed me gently. "Then I can oblige."

I scowled. "What? You would run from me that quickly? That's not impressive; that's insulting. And when I find you again, I'll kick your balls into next week for leaving me."

He laughed loudly, then his eyes narrowed on my face. "You're tired?"

Rawson lifted his brows expectantly and crossed his arms over his chest.

"I am." Exhausted and ready to collapse was a better description, but I wouldn't admit that in front of everyone.

"Then let's go. Owen? Stay until Walker is satisfied the area is secured."

"Yes, boss." Owen's face remained inscrutable. He had to be as exhausted as the rest of us, but he'd do as his Prime asked, always and without complaint.

"I'll stay too," said Selina.

"Where's Shane?" asked Connor, glancing at Owen.

"They've taken him back to the compound. He was injured," said Selina.

Then why are you here, instead of there, if he's your man? But I kept that to myself.

Owen nodded but gave no other reaction. "Lionel. Kawan. With me." He walked up to D. "Good to see you, man." He embraced his brother before patting him on the back. "We'll catch up later."

"Sure." D coughed and stepped back.

Yeah, it had to be a total mind fuck to be dead, then not be, but be stuck in Hell only to have your King set you free. Then find yourself back in the land of the living with your brother—who killed you. *And poor Stone! He's going to freak when he sees D!*

"Maybe we should get a therapist for everyone," I murmured into Connor's chest as we snuggled into the back of another SUV. "We've put our pack and friends through some crazy stressful shit recently."

He chuckled and hugged me close. "Then the therapist would need a therapist."

"Hmm, probably," I murmured. Smiling and inhaling his scent, I let the feel of his body against mine calm me. Smirking, I threw my leg over his lap and wound myself koala bear style around him. "I wanna go to bed and sleep for a whole week." His claiming scars were rough under my lips as I kissed his neck. "Well, maybe not sleep *all* week."

His deep chuckle vibrated through my whole body.

I gripped him tightly. "We won," I whispered, my whole body beginning to shake. "We won because of Sophie."

"And you," he said, pulling back to look deep into my eyes, his own full of love and pride. His gaze dropped to my stomach at the same time as his hand. "Is the little bean okay?" His voice broke.

"He or she is fine." I gripped him so hard my nails scored his skin, but I couldn't help it. "Fire cannot hurt a child of mine. She told me she can't."

"You're sure?"

I nodded.

He crushed me close, cupping the back of my head. "Thank the Mother," he murmured into my hair before kissing me until I couldn't breathe. And I didn't mind a bit.

CHAPTER 31

I FELL BACK against the pillows, utterly exhausted, my throat sore, and my mouth dry. Hands swiftly took our son away.

"Come on. One more push, baby."

I glared at Connor, ready to tell him to *"fuck off and never come near me again."* But then he had to go and call me baby. I glared at him. He knew I'd do anything for him if he called me that. Bastard.

He smoothed my damp hair back from my brow, his eyes softening. His mouth was still tilted in a sexy smile as he read my reaction—perfectly. Before I could call him out, he kissed me gently. "Come on, let's meet our little girl, Em."

Nodding, I gritted my teeth. I panted. I pushed. And I godsdamned screamed.

A tiny little cry rent the air. My head twisted to look at where the doctors and nurses checked over our son on the resuscitaire. Monitors beeped, and the lights and heater glared down on him. His little arms and legs flailed in the air, his cry getting angrier.

"Is he okay?" My voice trembled.

Even though Fire had reassured me she could never hurt our child, when I'd found out I was carrying twins, I'd been more than worried; questions swirling around my mind. A phoenix could only be passed from daughter to

867

daughter. What if we had a son in my womb, and she had only protected our daughter?

Connor grinned, his eyes shining, the blue of his irises more vivid than ever. "He's fine. He's a tough cookie. Listen to that cry."

Another contraction hit me, and that was it. Pant. Stop. Don't push. Push. Gods, I became so bloody confused—and so weary. Mea growled inside my head.

I'm not giving up. I just need a rest...

*No, you need to push...*my wolf commanded.

But I just wanted to rest.

"No. No. Come on, Firecracker, open your eyes. You've nearly done it. She's almost here."

In the distance, I heard monitors beeping and urgent shouts. I didn't care. I just wanted to sleep. Our son caterwauled at the top of his lungs. But my daughter... I concentrated all my strength into my abdomen and pelvis—and pushed.

"Got her!" shouted the midwife exultantly.

I smiled and let myself drift.

"Shit! She's haemorrhaging!" someone yelled.

"Ember! Ember! Wake up!" Connor yelled and shook me hard, except I couldn't feel it. No, I was standing looking down on the scene, my soul breaking. One of the nurses felt my pulse and then started chest compressions. Another pulled an alarm bell. Between my legs was a pool of blood, red and bright, and spreading. Even supernaturals were not immune to the dangers of childbirth.

Connor stumbled back out of the way, his face contorted and grey, as they worked on me. He flattened himself against the wall as they hung up bags of blood and gave me drugs. I'd never seen him look so lost, so shocked.

Another team ran in, but not to help me. On another resuscitaire, my daughter wasn't moving.

Beside me, Mea stood, her soul separated from mine by death, and beside her, an ethereal bird of Fire floated. She looked from me to my daughter.

I smiled sadly. "I understand. But you don't have to choose." And like any mother would, I smiled and pointed to my daughter. "Save her."

I looked back at my mate, who was staring at me. "Ember...?" he whispered. No one heard him. The noise in the room was too great.

On the other side of me, Mea growled and charged back towards my body. Connor narrowed his eyes, his mouth tight and his neck muscles bulging. Prime sprung from him. Together they pushed Mea's spirit back into my body.

"Connor, no! Our little girl needs to live; she needs a chance at life. I can give her that."

Connor shook his head, his eyes shining wetly. "I can't. I'm sorry. I love you too much…" And the King of Hell-beasts and Shifters pushed his power into my flesh and bones, giving my body the strength to heal my ruptured vessels. Fire swooped above us and stared down at my daughter. My heart broke. Without my phoenix, my baby girl could die.

Fire hovered over our tiny baby girl and looked at me. As a tear escaped my body, so did one escape her. I watched as it dripped off her beak and fell into my daughter's lax mouth before a mask was placed over it.

On the resuscitaire next to her, our son screamed, his arms and legs kicking and punching the air. His little fists opened and closed when he reached towards his sister as if he was trying to grasp her very soul.

Connor tugged, and Fire shot from above my daughter back into my flesh and bones.

"No!" I screamed. "Save her!"

I coughed and choked and pulled out the tube that had been shoved down my throat. I dragged in a huge breath, and screamed, grief consuming me. The next few minutes were a blur.

"She's stopped bleeding," the obstetrician stated. He didn't sound surprised, only relieved. In this SBI hospital, I doubted exceptional healing was rare.

As I struggled to sit up, the team continued working on our daughter. Connor helped me up, his face pale and his hands shaking. I gripped his cold fingers, but couldn't tear my gaze from the little blue body of our daughter, not even when he peppered my face and head with kisses, thanking all the gods in existence for my life. I knew the moment they decided to stop. They made eye contact, their faces sad but professional as they looked at us.

"My baby…" I sobbed, holding out my arms. I just wanted to hold her.

Connor let go of me long enough to take our daughter, who had been wrapped in a soft white blanket.

I'd never seen Connor so pale or so shell-shocked. He brought her to me, and with every step, his shoulders curled downwards even further. "I'm sorry…I couldn't let you go…"

There was no anger in me, only a great emptiness that I knew would be filled with a drowning sorrow soon enough. I took her and looked up at him. "Lyss," I whispered. "I wanted to call her Lyss, but maybe that name is a curse…"

"No…" His voice broke. "It's perfect."

He looked up as the midwife gently placed our screaming son in his arms. I cried. I didn't care who saw me. This was supposed to be the happiest day of our lives, not the one that broke our hearts.

"Hi, my beautiful son." Connor looked at me. "Ash?"

I nodded. The name we'd picked suited his explosive nature.

How could we be so blessed yet so cursed?

"I'm so sorry. This is my fault…" It had to be.

"No, it's not. Don't ever say that." A sob escaped Connor's chest as he kissed our son's downy head and then placed him next to our baby girl. Ash immediately settled, turning his head towards his sister. His little fists escaped the blanket, and his tiny hand touched his sister's face.

Connor leaned forward and kissed Lyss's head—and pulled back in shock. He sucked in a huge breath, his eyes wide.

"What? What is it?" My heart beat faster at his expression.

"She's warm," he croaked. Fumbling, he unwrapped the blanket. As he did so, our twins touched hands, their little fingers entwining, and together they let out a huge, triumphant cry.

"Mother Wolf! How!?" Connor looked at me, tears of joy on his cheeks as he took it all in.

Fire pulsed inside me.

I took a shaky breath. "The tears of a phoenix," I whispered against his cheek as he embraced us all.

mber

"Are you sure?" Connor asked, his face grave.

I nodded, my chin lifted high. It had been two months since Fire had saved Lyss. It wasn't just me who wanted this. It was Fire, too.

I turned my back to the huge audience and opened my robe, baring my naked chest to my mate. His nostrils flared, but not from passion or lust, not this time. I could feel his grief.

Ember...?

This is the right thing to do, Connor.

I blinked back my tears. The pain of this moment would last a lifetime—a shifter's lifetime, mine. Fire pulsed. She understood and even welcomed this freedom. She did not want to be a risk to our daughter and, now that every demon in this world knew what I held, Lyss would always be a target. Unless we publicly exorcised Fire and relied on word of mouth to spread the knowledge that she was gone from this world.

Connor lifted the Halo and pushed it against my skin.

Pain seared me. Sophie's chant was drowned out by the roaring in my ears. I screamed, my spine arching back.

Connor shifted. "Ember!" he bellowed and caught me, his eyes alight. The Halo tugged at Fire, pulling her from me even as Prime and Connor gripped onto Mea, keeping her inside me. Fire burst from my body and screeched. For a moment, she hovered above us before she brushed her wing lightly against my face. From there, she gracefully glided over to Rawson, who held Lyss.

Everyone gasped.

I managed to turn my head and saw Fire send sparks into Lyss's eyes before she looked back at me, gave a plaintive cry, and spiralled up towards the burning heat of the sun and was gone.

The Halo cooled and fell from my skin. I collapsed against Connor.

Connor supported me as he gently drew my robe closed. The circular burn on my chest would heal, but the emptiness of losing that part of my soul never would. I blinked and looked at Rawson, who kissed Lyss's head. Fire wasn't totally gone, she was just safe from the hands of Hell, and once word got out that neither our daughter nor I held the key to the Hell gates, it would make all of us safer.

"Let it be known, the immortal Phoenix is forever gone from this world!" bellowed Connor, and he picked me up and carried me away from the prying eyes of the crowd.

Hours later, I lay in Connor's arms, our children cradled in my embrace. Lyss watched me through eyes so like her daddy's it made my heart want to burst with love, and Ash? He gripped her hand like he was daring us to take her away from him. His fierce little frown made me smile.

"Any regrets?" Connor's voice was soft, but I didn't miss the edge of guilt in it.

I answered with absolute conviction. "Absolutely none. Living our lives together as a family is worth the sacrifice." I peered down. "*They* are worth *any* sacrifice, as are you. I love you all, and I will never regret it."

"I love you, too, Firecracker." Smiling, he kissed me.

When he pulled away, the sun fell on my face. There was a warm pulse of energy in my chest, and I knew then that Fire would never truly leave us. She would guard us from afar, always there, always watching, and ready to come to our aid if we ever needed her.

Read on for the bonus chapter....

If you loved Ember and Connor's story, why not join my mailing list? Copy and paste: https://www.karentomlinson.com/reader into your browser. K Keep an eye out for Owen's rejected mates novel, coming next in the Shadow Sentinels world. Read on for Chapter 1, now!

Don't forget extra chapters and deleted scenes are an added bonus of being a PATRON of mine. To join my Patreon please search for Karentomlinsonauthor on the Patreon site.

873

*E*mber. One year later.

"WHAT THE FUCK IS THAT!" exclaimed Shannon. "You are kidding, aren't you? You can't give that to those poor kids."

"What?" I stood back, my hands covered in chocolate icing, and studied my childrens' birthday cake. "It's a train," I pronounced, trying my best to remain poker faced.

Her eyes widened and a choked sound came from her throat. "But it looks like a giant turd."

"No, it doesn't." I defended my creation and licked the chocolate frosting off the spoon to cover my mirth. But, it really did. Baking wasn't my strong suit. Who knew?

Blue couldn't hold back any longer, she laughed loudly. "It so does."

I flicked chocolate frosting on her face. "How dare you?"

"Oh, I dare." She grinned and scooped her fingers through the bowl and flicked it at Shannon. It landed on her chin.

Shannon's face was a picture. "Right, this means war."

Screaming and laughing, we fought over the bowl of chocolate frosting, flicking it and smearing it all over each other until we were covered.

"Hey, watch the cake!" I yelled as Blue knocked the stand and it wobbled.

I felt Connor just before the door opened. He walked in, followed by B'nar and Stone, who had remained close friends. Despite B'nar's new responsibilities in Faerie, he made time to bring Blue back to see me, and to catch up with us all. The only downside was as the Prince Heir and King in waiting, he could only stay for a short amount of time, and he came with a royal guard now. Blue was in her conscious cycle and I was overjoyed that she could be here for Ash and Lyss.

Shannon mistimed her missile attack. A jelly sweet covered in chocolate frosting, sailed through the air and splattered against Stone's cheek.

Silence fell.

We all fell about laughing, tears streaming down our cheeks. I peered up to find even Stone and B'nar were smiling.

"Sorry," Shannon wheezed, wiping her eyes.

Stone wiped the mess from his cheek with his finger. He shrugged and with a predatory look, stalked towards Shannon. She stopped laughing as he stopped in front of her, his eyes dark and swirling with purple. He held up his finger. "I'll forgive you...if you clean it off."

"Whoa," whispered Blue in my ear.

"Dayum," I agreed as Shannon grabbed his wrist and sucked the chocolate from his forefinger.

I met Connor's bright blue stare, and coughed. "Er, right, um, anyway...the cake's done."

Connor's eyes widened as he took in the chocolatey mess. B'nar coughed and stared at it like it might jump off the plate and attack him. Blue giggled.

"Oh, bugger off, all of you. Lyss and Ash won't care. It'll go all over their faces anyway."

Connor grinned and carried the giant turd, a.k.a our children's first birthday cake, out into the living area of our new home. It was a huge place, big enough for our pack to live in together and still have space for a dozen or more guests. It was out in the rolling hills of the Scottish borders, down a long private road and behind huge walls, away from prying eyes. Security was a mix of Fae and human technology, and it was the safest place we could make for our family and pack.

Walker stood close by, watching us curiously. I guessed birthday parties weren't something immortal fae celebrated.

"Is she really going to make those children and us eat that?" B'nar whispered to Blue, who giggled.

"I heard that!" I couldn't help the big smile on my face though.

Our two beautiful creations were sitting in their highchairs being entertained by Owen and Devon. At nearly two years old, Devon was a handful, but he seemed to adore Lyss, our little girl. I laughed as he toddled over, handed her a rattle and she giggled and threw it on the floor for him to pick up again.

"What the Hell is that!?" exclaimed Owen, staring wide eyed at the chocolate covered monstrosity Connor placed on the big table.

Connor laughed out loud at his brother's shock. Even my lips twitched.

"Now, now. It may look like a turd. It is, however, delicious," I assured him and winked.

"Bloody Hell, Em, don't take up baking seriously, will you?" Rawson chuckled. "The sight of your cake decorating once a year will be plenty."

I threw my hands in the air. "Enough, already! We have to sing happy birthday and blow out candles. Selina? Can you grab Devon?'

But Devon wasn't having that, he screamed and kicked, holding his hands out to Owen. Selina scowled and glanced at Shane, who stood blank faced at the back of the room, staring at Owen and Devon.

"Come on, little man, let's do this together," crooned Owen.

Devon giggled happily, and Selina shook her head, deliberately not looking at her alpha. Owen did though, a look of triumph in his eyes. Yeah, that situation wasn't resolved...yet.

With a grin on my face, I watched Connor light the candles, one green and one blue. I wasn't doing pink, I never did. Ash's eyes were green, and Lyss's were blue, just like her father's, so that's what I ran with.

Reed and Myles sauntered in holding hands. I grinned at them, and they smiled back. Shannon stumbled in through the kitchen door, Stone behind her, both of them looking flushed. I rolled my eyes, wishing they'd get their shit together. They were both playing hard to get and at this point it was getting old. Lionel, Kawan and D wandered in, Jed behind them, all trying to hide their grins as they saw the cake. I stuck a middle finger up to them.

"Come on, Drake," I muttered as Connor carried the cake over to the three children. All three of them eyed the burning candles with wide, innocent eyes, as if mesmerised by the tiny flames. For a moment my heart stuttered. I missed my phoenix, but I could still feel her. And I knew if we ever needed her, if Lyss or I called, she would be there for us.

While we waited, Walker sauntered over. The High King hadn't returned to Faerie. He was now the Overseer of the SBI—and our ally. In fact, we worked for him, or rather with him. The demons that had escaped into this world needed hunting down, and with the technology of Faerie, and the power of our pack, that's what we did. With Sophie's help, any new Rifts were closed by the power of the Halo and Connor's Hell Fire. As a team we worked in the shadows; we were assassins, the sentinels that protected our planet against threats from this world and beyond.

I glanced out of the window. A pulse of warmth answered me. Fire was always watching. But we both knew I'd only ever call as a last resort. She needed to be kept safe and away from Satan, as did my daughter. All three of us were safer that way.

Sophie and Drake sprinted past the window and burst in through the door, out of breath. "We're here! Sorry. The plane was delayed by thirty minutes," Sophie yelled.

"That's cool! You're here in time to sing happy birthday!" I chimed with a wide grin. The two were due to be married soon. And though they were still at odds with each other about so many things, they seemed to have called a truce for now.

Drake rolled his eyes. "I thought you said we'd miss that bit."

Sophie ignored him and clapped her hands. "Great! Let's do it!"

We did. It was one of the funniest things I'd ever seen. All these powerful supernaturals singing to two little babies who didn't have a clue what was going on, but it was also one of the best moments of my life.

Devon helped our twins blow out the candles, and then I hid my tears of laughter as I served out some baby-spit covered cake onto paper plates.

"You're not really going to make us eat this, are you?" muttered Connor.

I just winked at him and then looked at Blue and Shannon, who disappeared into the kitchen and returned with the real cake—a half unicorn, half-dragon cake, that I'd ordered weeks ago, along with a huge bottle of champagne.

I burst out laughing at the sighs of relief. After serving it out, I slipped my arms around Connor's waist and peered up at him. "I love you." I grinned, drunk on love and happiness.

He laughed and watched our little angels smear cake all over their faces, squash it between their chubby fingers, and wipe it over their highchairs and Devon.

"I love you too, Firecracker." He glanced out at the sun, his face falling a little. "Any regrets?"

"None. I'd give up everything for them."

And my mate nodded and kissed me. There was no need for words. So would he. The kiss he gave me tasted of chocolate cake, champagne and something uniquely Connor. I pulled away and kissed my babies, chocolate covered faces and all, and thanked the Mother for the chance to live my life.

Mea sent me a pulse of love, and together we revelled in the love of our mates, and the pack that surrounded us.

The End!

PLEASE LEAVE A REVIEW ON AMAZON> IT REALLY HELPS WITH VISIBILITY. THANK YOU DEAREST READER.

ALPHA SCORNED.

CHAPTER 1

wen

I BOUNCED Devon on my knee, laughing as his chubby hand wiped cake all over my light blue shirt.

"Down. Down," he demanded, wriggling so much I had no choice. I placed him on his feet, ready to catch him as he wobbled a little before he toddled over to Lyss. A grin stretched my mouth, and for the first time in months, I allowed myself to feel a spark of joy. Seeing Devon dressed in his trendy little trainers, trousers, shirt and waistcoat was one the cutest things I'd ever seen. And all the cake he'd smeared on his face only made him cuter.

Connor, the King of Shifters, our alpha Prime, and the most powerful shifter in this world, grinned just as widely when his daughter of one year threw her rattle on the floor. "Ack. Ack," she babbled and glared at Devon, banging her hands on the highchair tray and splattering more cake everywhere.

Devon dutifully bent down and placed it back on the tray, only for Lyss to throw it again. Devon giggled and picked it up.

I chuckled. She had the poor little boy wrapped around her little finger already.

"Oh, she has so got the right idea," said Shannon, grinning ear to ear. "Get them running after you, sweetheart. Never run after them."

I rolled my eyes and glanced at Stone. My half-shifter, half-fae brother didn't react, he just watched her like a predator watches his prey.

"Might be more fun for you if you did some running towards what you wanted, instead of away from it," murmured Ember, her green eyes fixed on her friend and her brows raised.

Shannon scowled at our shifter queen. Surprisingly, she leashed her vicious tongue and with a quick glance at Stone, went to fill her champagne glass. She'd already drunk at least four glasses of the vile stuff, but she showed no ill effects. Shifter's could get drunk, but not easily. Our metabolism was too quick. Stone watched her, his face blank. I met Ember's gaze and grinned. She winked at me.

Everyone knew Stone and Shannon were a perfect match. It was just the two of them that wouldn't admit it. I guessed they both had their reasons, and those reasons were strong enough to keep them from sealing a mate bond, or even pursuing it. I wasn't in a position to judge them. I'd let life get in the way of my own mate bond, and then it had been too late. I gritted my teeth. Sometimes life threw you a curveball, and there was nothing you could do about it.

My gut tightened and my wolf rumbled. We could both feel the proximity of our mate. I'd promised myself, and Connor, that I wouldn't cause any shit over her and her lover being near me, but fuck if I didn't want to just smash his face in, throw her over my shoulder cave man style and show her she was mine. My gaze travelled to Selina, and my stomach flipped when I caught her staring. Her beautiful chocolate brown eyes met mine. I lounged back in my chair and folded my muscled arms over my chest, causing the material of my shirt to tighten over my biceps and shoulders. Her eyes drifted over my muscles, drinking me in. She might deny our bond, but her body couldn't. I could scent her desire even from across the room. I smirked. Only mates could pick up on a change in the other's scent, especially their partner's desire.

She scowled, but I didn't miss the rush of heat to her cheeks. The more I stared, the deeper that pretty flush got. My fingers curled into my chair arms and I shifted my position, leaning forward again, hiding the evidence of my lust. Unclamping my fingers from the chair before I splintered it, I fisted my hands, and took a slow deep breath. No matter how much I wanted to go over to my soul-mate and claim her, I couldn't. She had another lover, and even if they weren't mates, she had chosen him over me.

My chest tightened painfully, a sensation I was all too familiar with whenever I thought of Selina with Shane. My wolf growled, and it was all I could do not to leap across the room and challenge the fucker. But Selina and Shane had a right to make their own choices, even if it wasn't the one I wanted. Except... My wolf rose and I fixed my gaze on Shane. I could easily rip his head off. He might be an alpha, but so was I. And I was far stronger. I just chose to serve my king and brother, rather than run my own pack. Shane felt my attention and turned his head towards me. He met my gaze, and his eyes narrowed when he saw my wolf so close to the surface. My nostrils flared and I stiffened, ready to take down the alpha of the Canadian pack.

A wave of Connor's soothing alpha power hit me, forcing my attention to him. It was strong enough to force my wolf to back down, giving me time to take back some control of my emotions.

Connor raised his brows and cocked his head minutely. Others might miss his silent question, but I'd known him for too long. He wanted to know if I could handle Shane and Selina being here without losing my shit.

I flattened my lips together and rolled my head on my shoulders. Pushing back my wolf, I nodded once. The King of Shifters nodded back. It was a lie, of course. The longer I was in the same room as Selina, the more I wanted her, and the more I wanted to challenge Shane and show her he was weaker than me. I resisted the urge to shake my head. Ever since I'd found out about my Lina's relationship with Shane, my world had imploded. All the plans I'd had for us and little Devon had meant fuck all in the end.

I studied the carpet, still unable to understand why she'd chosen Shane over me, her soul-mate. Yeah, it hurt my ego, but more than that it hurt my heart and soul. I'd never met any other possible mate match, and Selina wasn't just a possible mate, she was my soul-mate, my perfect match—and she'd rejected me.

Lyss threw her rattle again, and it smacked Devon on the head. Ash, Lyss's twin brother, squawked with laughter, his giggle loud as he delightedly banged the tray of his high chair with a spoon. Devon let out a pained squeal, but didn't cry. Instead, he picked up the rattle and launched it at Ash.

Connor swiped it from the air, grinning widely. I pushed aside my own issues. I loved these kids so much, and their antics always made me laugh. I raised a brow at Connor. "Rivals in the making?" I quipped.

"Maybe, or maybe they will be brothers with a healthy rivalry."

Connor gave the rattle back to Lyss, who threw it to the floor. I shook my head as Devon picked it up, but instead of passing it back to Lyss, he lifted his little fist ready to launch it at Ash, again.

Keeping my back to Selina, I stood and scooped up Devon, carrying him back to my chair. "Nope, little man, you can't do that." I plucked the rattle from him. He scowled at me and wriggled, his little fists tightening.

"Down," he demanded.

"Not this time, Dev." I sat him firmly on my thigh and grabbed a baby-wipe, cleaning his face and hands of the sticky cake. He didn't like that one bit, and I bit my lip to keep from laughing when he started to screech angrily, twisting his head side to side to evade me. "Sorry, Dev, you have to get cleaned up." He glared at me, angry tears in his eyes—and began a full on temper tantrum. I shrugged. He was a fierce little boy and did this often when he couldn't get his way, so I'd let him wriggle and wait him out until he realised he wouldn't get his way with me and calmed down.

"Here, let me take him."

As always, Selina's voice caressed my senses. My whole body tensed, my balls tightened and my dick pulsed. Instinctively, I inhaled her sweet scent. It smelled like cherries and fresh air.

"It's fine." I gritted my teeth at the ache her nearness set off in my chest, and continued to clean her son's face, not wanting to give him up yet. And it was not just that. She knew I could calm him down far more easily than anyone else, even her, when he was like this.

"Owen, he needs to go for a nap. He's tired." Her voice was firm, though she chose to stare at her son rather than meet my gaze.

I could stare at her though. In fact, it was hard for me to look anywhere other than at her strong and stunning face. I swallowed. Lina was my everything, yet she was my nothing at all. She had been one of the women our group of shifters had rescued from a prison run by a demon general. I'd known, even back then, that she was a potential mate for me, though I hadn't realised until later that she was my soul-mate. I'd always intended to go back to the Canadian pack lands and claim her, but she hadn't waited. She'd shacked up with the alpha, Shane Dower, and become his beta and his lover. My nostrils flared, but I held my anger at bay.

Devon stilled and looked at me, then he lifted a chubby hand and placed it on my cheek, instantly stealing my anger.

"Nap, nap," he mumbled, and he curled up against my chest, eyeing his mother from under hooded eyes, as if he was daring her to take him away.

"It's okay, Lina. I'll take him." I stood and adjusted his weight. He was big for nearly two—and heavy. It would be a long way for Lina to carry him. Without giving her a chance to protest, I marched from the room, deliberately meeting Shane's gaze and giving him a glare as I passed, Lina in tow.

I felt a pulse of warning from Connor hit me, but I ignored it. Fuck being civil. If Shane wanted to throw down with me, I was more than up for it. But I knew he wouldn't, that fucker might not like having his nose pushed out of joint, but he didn't value Selina enough to risk losing his pack or Alpha status over her.

Keeping Devon cradled against my chest, I marched through the stone corridors of the huge Scottish castle, and up the stairs to the third floor.

"How do you know which room we're in?" Lina asked tightly.

I halted and turned to peer down at her. Her auburn curls shone in the sunlight that filtered in the small diamond shaped windows, highlighting the reds and golds hidden in its strands. "Because I told Ember you'd like this room for Devon. It's next to yours." *And that fucker's...* "And I got that room allocated to you…" *And that fucker you're sleeping with.* "…because I knew you'd love the view across the hills to the ocean."

"Oh, I, err…thank you… I guess." She looked down at the floor and my heart squeezed. She looked…unsure.

I might be pissed off, but I didn't like seeing her uncomfortable around me. I took pity on her, and tried to be pleasant. "You told me that you loved the ocean but had only seen it once. I thought you'd like to see it every time you look out of the window."

I heard her gasp. "You remember that?" Her words were whispered. "That was over a year ago."

Of course I do, I remember everything you ever told me, I answered silently.

I balanced Devon in one arm. The little guy had fallen asleep against my shoulder. I opened the door to the turret room, careful not to jiggle him. It was large and airy, and had been set up with a little junior bed in one corner, one with a small side to stop him rolling out. It took me four strides to cross to his bed where I placed him down, careful not to wake him.

When I was satisfied he was safe and comfortable, I leaned down and kissed his soft cheek, then straightened, turning to face my mate. I froze. The sun slanted in through the windows, glinting in Lina's gaze, and fierce want twisted my gut. I couldn't drag my gaze from hers. She must have sensed my battle with my primal side as she shuffled back a couple of steps, swallowing hard. Her unique scent and proximity sent my wolf nuts. He scratched and snarled at my insides, demanding that I claim what was ours. Dammit! I needed to get out of here before I lost it, and slammed her up against the wall with her legs spread, just like I wanted to.

Growling low in my chest, I headed to the door.

"Owen!" Her voice broke on my name. "Don't go….please? Just…stay for a while."

Anger ripped at my chest. "And what, Lina? Make polite conversation?" Grabbing the door, I yanked it open. "No." But before I could walk through it, I heard her run across the room then clamp her fingers down on my wrist. Instant lust burned through me, her touch branding me. I spun, twisted my wrist out of her hold and grabbed her instead. With my momentum, I spun us both back into the room, and didn't stop until her back hit up against the wall. I kicked the door shut with my foot and leaned in close, trapping her wrist between my body and hers.

I stared down at her, keeping her ensnared in my gaze. "Careful, Lina. I might think you actually want me."

Her eyes widened, her breathing deep and erratic, her breasts straining against the soft jersey of her dress. "I…I…"

"What?" I glared down at her, my own breathing hard. My wolf howled, pushing against my will at being this close to our mate. Her wolf didn't surface in her eyes, but I knew mine had. His power and dominance flooded me. Her pupils dilated, her breath catching on a sharp intake. I smirked, but it wasn't with amusement; it was with satisfaction that I could affect her as she did me. Shit, if she knew how much power she had over me, I'd be lost.

I'd never allowed myself to get this close to her before. I bit back a groan. Her softness felt so good trapped beneath me. Mother Wolf, the thought of her in another male's bed, not mine, filled me with white hot fury.

Her soft mouth parted, her breath panting and mingling with mine, warming my lips. "Say it, Lina." I pushed my pelvis forward, leaving her in no doubt how much I wanted her. I huffed a bitter laugh at my own thoughts. *Wanted her?* I fucking lusted after her with every fibre of my being. "Say you want me."

She moaned, fuelling my desire, and I couldn't stop myself rolling my hips.

"Owen…" She whispered my name. A plea to stop, or to keep going? I had no idea, but hearing my name fall from her lips like that broke the last bit of my self-control.

I slammed my mouth against hers, devouring her soft lips. I'd often thought about how I would kiss her for the first time, and it had never been like this. Anger, resentment, and pure lust fuelled this kiss; on my side, anyway. On hers? I hadn't a clue. Right then, I didn't even care. She was mine, and I would take what was mine…. I pushed my body up against the lushness of hers, forcing her mouth open with my tongue, and spearing her mouth. It wasn't gentle or sensual. No, I wanted her to know how fucking angry and hurt, I was. My movements were hard, almost cruel, but I couldn't stop myself. Disgust coiled around my gut. She'd suffered at the hands of her captors in the past. What the fuck was I doing, forcing my will on her? But I couldn't pull away and her long, lust filled moan only made me more desperate.

I released her arm and grabbed her other one, slamming both of her wrists above her head and holding them with one hand. She was tall for a woman, nearly six feet, but I was a good half foot taller, and far stronger, no matter if she had become Shane's beta.

I speared her mouth with my tongue, moving it like I wanted to move inside her. Hard and fast, before I swept it around the inside of her mouth, tasting her.

My wolf howled, pushing me to take more. He was right. I let my dominance wash out from me in waves. Her moan, and the compliance in her body hit me. My dick twitched, hard and aching. I rolled against her, trying to find some kind of relief.

Fuck, this was insane….I'd never lost control like this…

Her body trembled beneath me. The predator in me loved it, loved that I could bring her to this quivering state of moans and compliant flesh.

I pulled away a little, biting her bottom lip with just enough force to make her gasp. We both heaved air into our lungs, the scent of our lust filling the room. Gods, her sweet scent was infused with the musk of her lust. It was heady. The softness of her breasts against my chest, and her body under the control of mine, was enough to scramble my damn thoughts.

"Tell me you want me, Lina. Tell me, and this continues. I can give you everything. A home, security, a safe pack where you'll be loved, and so will Devon. I'll take care of you both, you'll want for nothing—ever." I paused and took a deep breath. Gods, I felt I was drowning in her eyes, her scent, her touch. But this was it. I couldn't see her with Shane and not want to kill him for taking what the Mother Wolf had made as a perfect match for both my wolf and me. I exhaled slowly, my breath ragged and shaking. "Reject me again, and we're done, Lina. I can't keep seeing you with another male. Not when you make me feel this out of control." My voice dropped to a deep growl, and I meant every godsdamned word. "If I see him touch you, I'll kill him."

She stiffened, and I heard her swallow hard. Silence fell, our heavy breathing the only sound. Seconds ticked by. Coldness invaded me, surrounding my heart in a layer of ice when that silence continued.

"Owen...please. I...I can't..."

Hurt slammed into my chest, ripping at my soul. My wolf howled, his pain at our mate's rejection making my own even harder to bear. I yanked myself from her, letting her go, pain clouding my mind. She didn't want us. Even now, when I'd offered her everything. My eyes burned, proving even an alpha could be reduced to tears. I blinked slowly, forcing my emotions to shut down. Fuck, this was gonna tear me apart, but I wouldn't give her the satisfaction of seeing just how much. There was nothing left to say. I spun away from my soul-mate and marched for the door. My wolf kept howling and scratched at my insides, but I locked him down.

"Owen! Please...!"

Her broken voice tore at me, even more than my own pain. Shit, I needed to get away from her before I begged her to let us in, to accept everything we'd offered, and made a bigger fool of myself. I slammed the door behind me and mid-stride let my wolf free. He willingly took over my body, but I was still his master and wouldn't let him turn back.

"Owen! Owen! No, please, don't go! Let me explain."

Run! Now! I told my wolf, forcing him to leave the woman who held my heart behind us. We were done. I would never see her again. Wolves couldn't cry, but he felt my utter devastation just the same. He bolted down the stairs.

Stone was at the bottom of the large staircase. His purple magic zipped towards us. "Owen! Hey! What's up, brother?" Concern etched his hard features, his eyes flashing with purple at my loud and mournful howl. "Fuck."

He understood, I could feel it, even see it in the hard lines of his face. But it was the pity in his eyes that burned the most.

Connor's howl echoed through the halls, and I knew he felt my pain through his bond to me. I couldn't deal with my Prime or my brothers. Having to explain that my soul-mate had spurned me was too much. I'd deal with my emotions, find a way to bury them deep so that I could function, and then I'd return—when Lina and her lover had left, or there would be a bloodbath. I wouldn't put Connor in the position of having to punish me for killing one of our own.

Stone tilted his head, his lips pressed together. "Take your time, brother. I'm here when you're ready." Without expecting any kind of acknowledgment, he strode to the door and opened it.

Fresh air and the scent of the sea hit me. I darted outside and bounded through the gardens and into the woods, inhaling deeply and trying to erase the taste and scent of my mate from my mind and my memory, even though deep down I knew it was useless. She'd be a part of me forever, even if I never saw her again.

ACKNOWLEDGMENTS

As always my main thanks go to all of you who read my books. There would be little point in spending time, effort and money producing books if you didn't read and enjoy the worlds and new characters that I create—so thank you!

To Judi Soderberg who edits my books, I can't thank you enough for what you continue to do to support me.

My last acknowledgement is to my very small amount of, but terribly important, Patreon supporters. I'm grateful beyond words for your support of my career, and the help towards audiobook production.

Judi Soderberg
Justine Blaber
Michelle Chantler
Cherylyn Tilley

If you'd like to listen to my books in audio in the future, then you can support my writing career and goal to have all my books in audio, by becoming a patron on:

https://www.patreon/karentomlinsonauthor

You can choose from different levels of support, and will receive exclusive benefits, chapters, and a personalised ebook/paperback of every release (before they become exclusive to any platform) dependent on your level of support.

ABOUT THE AUTHOR

Karen Tomlinson is a USA Today Bestselling author of fantasy and PNR/UF books.

Karen adores books and will read any that catch her eye. She was whisked away by fairies as a child, has been a dragon rider, and grew up learning to kick ass. (This bit's true!) She likes nothing better than an epic story full of romance, fantasy, fast-paced adventure, strong women, and beautifully imperfect characters.

She lives in Derbyshire, England, (think Mr Darcy territory) with her husband, twin girls, and her dalmatian. When she's not busy working, writing, reading (or eating cake and drinking coffee) Karen likes to keep fit by practicing karate, going to the gym, walking in the hills, or dancing around the kitchen with her earbuds in and singing badly!

Join Karen's mailing list to receive free stories, writing updates, and hear about new releases and deals. Sign up here ➜ https://www.karentomlinson.com/social

She loves to connect with her readers and you can find her on:

Follow my Mighty Network Here: Karen Tomlinson's Shadow Sentinels.

Blog-https://www.karentomlinson.com/news

Facebook page-@ktomlinson.author.

Facebook group-Karen Tomlinson's Silver Guardians.

Twitter-@kytomlinson

Instagram-@karentomlinsonauthor

Book Bub-@karentomlinsonauthor

Patreon-karentomlinsonauthor

TikTok-karentomlinsonauthor

Goodreads

Or **Join my mailing list to keep up to date** <HERE>

Web site: http://karentomlinson.com